THE AMERICAN NOVELS AND STORIES OF

Henry James

THE AMERICAN NOVELS

AND STORIES

OF

Henry James

EDITED, AND WITH AN INTRODUCTION, BY

F. O. Matthiessen

. 1 9 4 7

NEW YORK: ALFRED A. KNOPF

CONTENTS

INTRODUCTION

CONFRONTED with so voluminous a writer as Henry James, we may always gain fresh insight into his work by following a single phase of it from first to last. His most distinctive contribution, the portrayal of American characters against a European background, has overshadowed his treatment of the American scene. But the novels and stories he wrote with America as their locale form a coherent and relatively compact cross-section of his work as a whole. They span the half-century of his prolific career from his first published story to the novel that was broken off by the shock of the first World War. They thereby provide an unfolding example of the evolution of his style. They also furnish his answer to questions that always absorbed him, what were the prospects for American fiction? what particular problems and difficulties would its writer have to face and overcome? In answering those questions — if only obliquely and partially, as he would have been the first to admit — his American novels and stories possess the further interest of affording us vistas into the manners of their time. Henry James believed that the function of a major novelist like Balzac was to record the moral history of his age. James was no Balzac, and he saw only limited parts of the human comedy in America. But he saw with a remarkably trained and tenacious eye. His skills were most analogous to those of a painter, and his street-scenes and interiors, as well as his many portraits and occasional landscapes, belong to the lasting gallery of American art.

In the spring of 1865 Henry James, Senior noted: "Harry has a story in the current (March) number of the *Atlantic*. Considered good . . . 'The Story of a Year' by H. J. Jr." That story, written when its author was twenty-one, has not previously been reprinted; and looking back at it, James no doubt would have held that it was not immeasurably better than the stories by the literary ladies who then graced the *Atlantic* in the interim between Hawthorne's death and Howells' first stories a few years later. James' triangle against the background of the war is certainly conventional enough, and it would seem unwise to read into it any deep personal significance. But it is always of interest to observe where a great writer started, and notwithstanding some stilted and amateur phrases, James is here already emulating the most ambitious master, no less than Balzac himself.

Indeed, in one of his first reviews he had just pointed out to Harriet Prescott Spofford the value for any practitioner of studying *Eugénie Grandet*, since Balzac "is literally real: he present objects as they are." But in turning to the new realism rather than to Hawthorne's romance as his primary model, he also knew that accurate details were of significance "only in so far as they bear upon the action," that in Balzac "each separate part is conducive to the general effect, and this general effect has been studied, pondered, analyzed: in the end it is produced. Balzac lays his stage, sets his scene, and introduces his puppets. He describes them once for all; this done, the story marches."

"The Story of a Year" does not march. It has enough material for a novel, but none of it is really developed. Yet James had already addressed himself, through its vacillating heroine, to the analysis of complex states of mind, and of the power of evil to haunt like "an unlaid ghost." He sensed that he had gone beyond his depth when he said "I cannot describe these things"; but he had begun to possess his gift for conveying his characters' thoughts in terms of visual images, even though his opening presentation of the scattering clouds of the sunset as an "allegory" of war's end is the kind of set-piece of moralizing that he would not have allowed himself later. He hardly portrayed his New England village and its neighboring manufacturing town in more than the faintest crayon strokes.

James was to develop very slowly, and did not feel that he had produced enough good stories to make a book until a decade later. He then collected only six of the two dozen pieces he had printed in magazines, and only one of these, "The Romance of Certain Old Clothes," deals even nominally with an American background. This story is of interest chiefly in that it shows James imitating Hawthorne's methods of allegory in a way that he soon outgrew. Its passing suggestion of eighteenth-century Salem is too pale to make it worth reproducing here. The same applies to the other New England tales of his apprenticeship. They hardly go beyond his first story; and to have read one is to have seen enough of what he still had to learn.

His first attempt at a short novel, *Watch and Ward*, was serialized in the *Atlantic* in 1871, but he felt so unsure of it that he did not issue it as a volume until seven years later, and then only after he had rewritten it. It deals with a Boston bachelor who falls in love with and finally marries his young ward; and here James tried to handle a wide canvas. He sent his hero off on a trip to South America and his heroine to be educated in Rome, and finally united them, after melodramatic difficulties, in New York. But the book is not a real study of manners anywhere. It seems made-up, not observed, and even in its revised form scarcely holds the reader's attention. By the time he published it, his reputation had been established by *The American* (1877); and "Daisy Miller" was presently to bring him his moment

Introduction

of widest popularity. His first full-length novel, *Roderick Hudson* (1875), had studied the disintegration of a young American sculptor in Rome. In revising it more than thirty years later for his collected edition, he remarked that its opening chapters in Northampton, Massachusetts, had failed to meet the challenge of the intensity of Balzac's provincial towns. That challenge seems to have been ever present in James' early years, however much he may have preferred George Eliot as a moralist, and however much he may have failed to find in his rapidly changing America anything like the fixed solidity of French manners and customs to base his own work upon. He began to voice his doubts on this score in a letter to Charles Eliot Norton in 1871, after he had returned from his initial year of being abroad on his own. He was discussing *Suburban Sketches,* Howells' first volume of fiction: "Looking about for myself, I conclude that the face of nature and civilization in this our country is to a certain point a very sufficient literary field. But it will yield its secrets only to a really *grasping imagination.* This I think Howells lacks. (Of course *I* don't!) To write well and worthily of American things one need even more than elsewhere to be a *master.* But unfortunately one is less!"

Shortly before *The American* appeared James had decided to live in London, and there, during the next couple of years, he wrote two short American novels, *The Euro-* *peans* and *Washington Square.* Neither attempts to bite deeply into American society, and he quite properly sub-titled the first "A Sketch." One is laid in Boston and a neighboring village, and the other in New York, but both of them deal with the period of 1850, the period of James' childhood. In the light of that fact, a passage in his essay on Turgenieff, written a few years before these novels, assumes a particular relevance: "Turgenieff gives us a peculiar sense of being out of harmony with his time — of having what one may call a poet's quarrel with it. He loves the old, and he is unable to see where the new is drifting. American readers will peculiarly appreciate this state of mind; if they had a native novelist of a large pattern, it would probably be, in a degree, his own."

But though James' realism in its prime, in a book like *The Portrait of a Lady* (1881), is more akin, by the delicacy of its method, to Turgenieff than to Balzac or Flaubert, his two novels about the older America do not exact any such ambitious comparison. William James objected to *The Europeans* as being "thin," and though Henry was depressed by that verdict, he rejoined: "I have a constant impulse to try experiments of form, in which I wish to not run the risk of wasting or gratuitously using big situations. But to these I am coming now. It is something to have learned how to write, and when I look round me and see how few people (doing my sort of work)

Introduction

know how (to my sense), I don't regret my step-by-step evolution."

He was unquestionably right. A comparison of any page of *The Europeans* with "The Story of a Year" can demonstrate that during the intervening period he had mastered the first requisite of lasting fiction, the discipline of concrete presentation. The opening vista, from the windows of the Parker House, of the cemetery in the midst of the downtown city, and of that city under the blanket of a snow-storm in May, takes us unerringly into the milieu and its immediate moment. James had gained that skill partly through his many portraits of places, so that when he wanted to suggest a late eighteenth-century house he could do it with pictorial discrimination: "It was an ancient house – ancient in the sense of being eighty years old; it was built of wood, painted a clean, clear, faded grey, and adorned along the front, at intervals, with flat wooden pilasters, painted white. . . . A large white door, furnished with a highly-polished brass knocker, presented itself to the rural-looking road, with which it was connected by a spacious pathway, paved with worn and cracked, but very clean bricks. Behind it there were meadows and orchards, a barn and a pond. . . . All this was shining in the morning air, through which the simple details of the picture addressed themselves to the eye as distinctly as the items of a 'sum' in addition."

Such a passage makes one won-

der how much James was also thinking of Hawthorne's more diffuse and shadowy presentation of his older House of the Seven Gables, for Hawthorne's book had also dealt with the period of 1850. James' study of society is, to be sure, altogether less serious than Hawthorne's. He had projected a companion piece to *The American*, with the situation reversed: instead of Christopher Newman discovering Europe, he would bring back to this country two Europeanized Americans. None of his characters here are drawn with the living thoroughness of Newman or Madam de Cintré. James composed this study of manners around two contrasting views of life – as discipline or as enjoyment, and he sketched in very lightly his New England types: Mr. Wentworth, Harvard 1809, who has his office in Devonshire Street, and whose face looks "as if he were undergoing martyrdom, not by fire, but by freezing"; his son, who has just been "rusticated" from college for drinking; his cousin, who has engaged in the China trade; his two daughters, and the young Unitarian minister who is courting one of them. Into this subdued, largely joyless existence he introduces the Baroness Eugenia and her symbolically named brother, Felix Young, and works out the slightest of plots to show who can and who cannot find satisfaction in such a simple society.

Washington Square has frequently been James' favorite novel with readers who don't really like James. That is not to say that it has not been admired also by those who believe that he reached his summit in *The Ambassadors* or *The Wings of the Dove*. But its method is much simpler than the one he used later, since it concentrates on the single tension caused between Catherine Sloper and her father by his opposition to her marriage. Some critics have objected to the title on the ground that there is hardly enough of the city in the book to justify it. James' center of interest was unquestionably his heroine, but he made her very different from the young girls in *The Europeans*. He endowed her with none of the usual charm of his heroines, and began by describing her as "plain" and "dull." He then proceeded to develop her, through her unshakable devotion to her one deluded love, into a woman of heroic dignity. The book might more accurately have been called by her name, and he may very well have taken a backward glance at Eugénie Grandet for a model of such goodness of heart.

Here he was writing about Americans largely independent of the influence of Europe. Indeed, Catherine, in her early twenties, had "never met a foreigner." In a way unusual for him, James introduced his description of the Square with a personal reminiscence of how it looked in his infancy; and in sketching the Battery and a Seventh Avenue oyster-house, he drew on the same material that he was to use far more profusely in his autobiography. Yet he would probably have agreed that he had fallen short of his title. He wrote to Howells that he had produced "a tale purely American, the writing of which made me feel acutely the want of the 'paraphernalia.' "

His use of that last word had risen out of a controversy. Howells had just reviewed his critical biography of Hawthorne, and had taken him to task for his now notorious enumeration of "the items of high civilization, as it exists in other countries, which are absent from the texture of American life." This passage throws far more light on James than on Hawthorne; and another reason why it stands apart from its context with a rhetorical flourish is that it was originally designed for another purpose. In a hitherto unpublished notebook James had written: "In a story, some one says — 'Oh yes, the United States — a country without a sovereign, without a court, without a nobility, without an army, without a church or a clergy, without a diplomatic service, without a picturesque peasantry, without palaces or castles or country seats or ruins, without a literature, without novels, without an Oxford or a Cambridge, without cathedrals or ivied churches, without latticed cottages or village alehouses, without political society, without sport, without fox-hunting or country gentlemen, without an Epsom or an Ascot, an Eton or a Rugby. . . . !' "

Introduction

When he incorporated this speech into his study of Hawthorne, he dropped out "a picturesque peasantry," which would have made a particularly easy target for any democratic economist, but he added "no museums, no pictures." He was discussing the negative blankness of the material recorded in Hawthorne's notebooks, and introduced this passage as the kind of indictment that a European might make of it. To Howells' objection he rejoined: "It takes an old civilization to set a novelist in motion — a proposition that seems to me so true as to be a truism. It is on manners, customs, usages, habits, forms, upon all these matured and established that a novelist lives — they are the very stuff that his work is made of; and in saying that in the absence of those 'dreary and worn-out paraphernalia' which I enumerate as being wanting in American society, 'we have simply the whole of human life left,' you beg (to my sense) the question. I should say we had just so much less of it as these same 'paraphernalia' represent, and I think they represent an enormous quantity of it. I shall feel refuted only when we have produced (setting the present high company — yourself and me — for obvious reasons apart) a gentleman who strikes me as a novelist — as belonging to the company of Balzac and Thackeray." Not that he failed to admire Hawthorne greatly, even though he may have taken too much for granted his unexcelled moral depth. But James, as a practitioner, was most concerned with the future of fiction, and he then believed that future to lie with realism rather than with romance. He ended his letter with a mock-serious charge to Howells to "be the American Balzac. That's a great mission." But for the "big" novel that he had been promising William, he took Isabel Archer abroad.

Soon after *The Portrait of a Lady* was published, he came back to America for a winter, an experiment which convinced him anew that for his temperament and talents the decision to live in England had been the right one. He was not hostile to this country. He might remark in his notebook: "Boston is absolutely nothing to me — I don't even dislike it." But he wrote from New York to George du Maurier (who had illustrated *Washington Square* for its appearance in the *Cornhill*): "Though I am 'New Yorkais d'origine' I never return to this wonderful city without being entertained and impressed afresh. New York is full of types and figures and curious social idiosyncrasies, and I only wish we had some one here, to hold up the mirror, with a 15th part of your talent. It is altogether an extraordinary growing, swarming, glittering, pushing, chattering, good-natured, cosmopolitan place, and perhaps in some ways the best imitation of Paris that can be found (yet with a great originality of its own)."

He used his eyes as always, and

three stories written after he had returned to London can indicate how he went about to get fresh material wherever he was. In the slightest of these, "A New England Winter," he tried for nothing more than "a certain impression of Boston" (as he described it to Howells). But Howells was enthusiastic: "I must bear my witness to the excellence particularly of some of the bits of painting. In just such a glare of savage sunshine I made my way through Washington street in such a horse-car as you portray, the day I read your advanced sheets. Besides that, I keenly enjoyed those fine touches by which you suggest a more artistically difficult and evasive Boston than I ever get at. The fashionableness which is so unlike the fashionableness of other towns — no one touches that but you: and you contrive also to indicate its contiguity, in its most ethereal intangibility, to something that is very plain and deeply practical. . . . The study pleases me throughout: the mother with her struggles — herculean struggles — with such shadowy problems; the son with the sincere Europeanism of an inalienable, wholly uninspired American. As for the vehicle, it is delicious."

"The Point of View" is hardly a story. It uses the device of a series of letters, which James had handled a few times before, to present all the contrasting opinions about this country that had been renewed for him by his trip home. He was to speak of it in his later preface as "a small monument" to "its author's perverse and incurable disposition to interest himself less in his own (always so quickly stale) experience . . . than in that of conceivable fellow mortals, which might be mysteriously and refreshingly different." He re-introduced some of his characters from "The Pension Beaurepas," but he now brought them over here. Some of their observations are designedly superficial, but when Miss Sturdy, on her return to Newport, sees that America has plenty of vulgarity but too little coarseness, she makes a remark that was echoed by the creator of J. Alfred Prufrock. Her further remark that "Longfellow wrote a charming little poem called 'The Children's Hour,' but he ought to have called it 'The Children's Century,'" might still serve as a rubric for the continual sentimentalization of our popular culture. The visiting English M. P. deplores the growth of "an idle and luxurious class"; while the French Academician, less resilient than Tocqueville, adds to the list of items left out of American civilization, but takes an ironic sideglance at James' own fiction when he says: "They've a novelist with pretensions to literature who writes about the chase for the husband and the adventures of rich Americans in our corrupt old Europe, where their primeval candour puts the Europeans to shame. *C'est proprement écrit,* but it's terribly pale. What isn't pale is the newspapers." James' most deliberate con-

Introduction

trast is between Louis Leverett, his oversensitized Harvard aesthete (who had also figured in "A Bundle of Letters"), and Marcellus Cockerel, the young lawyer who makes a vigorous if somewhat strident justification of his country on grounds that many critics seem to have thought James incapable of even positing.

In "Pandora" James designed a companion-piece to "Daisy Miller," the account of whose adventures, in its Tauchnitz edition, an earnest young German diplomat is introduced reading, in the hope that it will prepare him for "some of the oddities" of American life. But he soon recognizes that Pandora Day is quite a different kind of girl, even though her nineteen-year-old brother is a grown-up Randolph Miller, and she also has a little Daisy of a sister. James described his subject in his notebook as the presentation of "the self-made girl," that is to say, the girl who had gotten into society by her own brightly acquired culture which had left her family as far behind her as Utica. Speculating on where he might best show her triumph, he decided that he would take this opportunity, "to *do* Washington," as he had just come to know it, to "work in my new notes, and my very lovely memories, of last winter. I might even *do* Henry Adams and his wife." The result was Alfred Bonnycastle, who "was not in politics, though politics were much in him." There was no pleasanter house in Washington than his wife's, though the com-plaint was heard that "it left out, on the whole, more people than it took in," and though Mr. Bonny-castle himself sometimes thought "that for Washington their society was really a little too good." Unmistakably in the Adams tone is his reflection at the season's end: "Hang it, there's only a month left; let us be vulgar and have some fun — let us invite the President."

Once again James had travelled with his sketch-book. He had preserved glimpses of the river-wharf and of the Capitol uplifting "its isolated dome at the end of a long vista of saloons and tobacco shops." He could remember parties where the members of Congress might easily be confused with the waiters, and where a lady from what she called "the Sooth," the relict of a commodore, looked like "the *vieux jeu* idea of the queen in *Hamlet.*"

When James decided to include "The Point of View" and "Pandora" in his collected edition — the only two of his early stories laid in America so chosen — he touched them both up a little. His analogy for his process was that of the painter's freshening sponge and varnish-bottle. He made no changes in outline or structure, but he enlivened several sentences with brighter details. The phrase, "the *vieux jeu* idea," is a characteristic example. So also, in "The Point of View," is his filling out one characterization of New York with "rich and predominant, but unprecedentedly maladministered and disillusioned," and "great desperate eternally swindled." Where he had remarked, in "Pandora," on the lobby of the House "adorned with artless prints and photographs of eminent Congressmen, which was too serious for a joke and too comical for anything else," he made the sentence more telling by tucking in "defunct" after "eminent," "all" before "too serious," and "a Valhalla" in place of its loose final phrase. The German diplomat no longer finds, in the revision, conversation in the United States "more psychological than elsewhere," but "more yearningly, not to say gropingly, psychological"; and "persons of leisure" are suited to the American climate of opinion by becoming, in one of the largest expansions, "that body which Vogelstein was to hear invoked, again and again, with the mixture of desire and deprecation that might have attended the mention of a secret vice, under the name of a leisure-class."

In looking back at a novelette like "Pandora" as the chief exhibit he had to show for his renewed observation of America, he spoke candidly in his preface of his "insuperably restricted experience," and carried further his discussion of the problems and the choices for our artists. He felt that he could not adequately portray New York, since "down-town" was "the major-key — absolutely, exclusively"; and the workings of its business world had been inexorably closed to him by every chance of his upbringing and education. This disqualification was not limited to his special case; it touched anyone who had been at all conditioned by the genteel tradition. Even though Howells, in the best of his New York novels, *A Hazard of New Fortunes* (1890), introduced a detailed account of a street-car strike, the major passions involved in our new industrial and financial tensions were to have to wait for their expression until the development of a more thorough-going naturalistic approach. The best that Howells could do towards dramatizing the central issues of post-Civil War America was to follow Edward Bellamy's lead and resolve them in a Utopian novel, *A Traveller from Altruria* (1894).

In James' view, the only alternative to "down-town" for the social observer was "up-town"; and "up-town" in the New York of the eighteen-eighties was limited as no inhabitant of a European city could imagine. In his New York childhood James had vaguely visualized, as he overheard the conversation of his elders, that all the activity of the nation must be carried on "by three classes, the busy, the tipsy, and Daniel Webster." And now, as a visitor, he had felt himself alone in the "up-town" world: "alone, I mean with the music masters and French pastry-cooks, the ladies and children — immensely present and immensely numerous these, but testifying with a collective voice to the extraordinary absence (save as pieced together through a thousand gaps and indirectnesses) of a serious male interest." Any novel constructed of such materials would inevitably fall into a minor-key, as Edith Wharton would later testify.

At the very time that James felt the strict limitations of his alternatives, *Huckleberry Finn* was being produced. To those who like to dramatize the utter cleavage between high-brow and low-brow in our culture, and who take it for granted that James must have been blind even to Twain's existence, a further passage from this same preface to "Pandora" may come as a surprise. For James said explicitly that there was an escape from his alternatives in "the vast wild garden of 'unconventional' life in no matter what part of our country." But having watched the local color movement develop — and Twain's portrayal of "old times on the Mississippi" emerged from that background — James naturally connected "the great neglected native quarry" with the use of dialect: "the key to the *whole* of the treasure of romance independently garnered was the riot of the vulgar tongue." Mencken would agree, and for those who believe that criticism consists in berating writers for not being something other than they were, James already stands convicted for not seizing upon this other key himself. But his ear had been trained to cosmopolitan speech, in Paris and London as well as in New York; and he made another distinction that could be of great use to us in our present

tendency to confuse pseudo-folksy with popular art. He believed that dialect could be a true medium only for those who use it "precedent to the invasion, to the sophistication, of schools and unconscious of the smartness of echoes." That distinction could serve to separate Twain's pure evocation of what he remembered of his earliest surroundings from all the imitations that have been fabricated by those who, in James' words, merely fall into "the bastard vernacular of communities disinherited of the felt difference between the speech of the soil and the speech of the newspaper, and capable thereby, accordingly, of taking slang for simplicity, the composite for the quaint." There could be no apter description of the weaker pages in Steinbeck or of most of Saroyan and the Hollywood scripts. James' standards for speech were too conservative and aristocratic to meet the full needs of a varied democracy, but he developed the only medium that was natural to him — a speech not rooted in the soil, as that of Thoreau and of Emerson, to a lesser degree, could be, but basing its tone on the kind of cultivated conversation that had flourished in his town-bred family circle. In finally carrying this medium to the point at which it was responsive to every nuance of his mind, he met at least the primary obligation for his style, that it should be himself.

The next large book that he undertook after *The Portrait of a Lady* was his most ambitious effort to handle an American city. Already out of the mainstream of post-Civil War development, Boston did not demand for its portrayal so much knowledge of "down-town." After outlining his plot in the spring of 1883, when he was again in this country for several months because of his father's death, he summed up his intention: "The subject is strong and good, with a large rich interest. The relation of the two girls should be a study of one of those friendships between women which are so common in New England. The whole thing as local, as American as possible, and as full of Boston: an attempt to show that I *can* write an American story . . . Daudet's *Evangeliste* has given me the idea of this thing. If I could only do something with that *pictorial* quality. At any rate, the subject is very national, very typical. I wished to write a very *American* tale, a tale very characteristic of our social conditions, and I asked myself what was the most salient and peculiar point in our social life. The answer was: the situation of women, the decline of the sentiment of sex, the agitation on their behalf."

The chief suggestion that he had received from Daudet's novel, which had just appeared that year, was in the hold that its somber dominating Madame Autheman, a fanatical proselytizing Calvinist, had gained over the emotions of a young girl. But in reviewing it James declared that in this case Daudet had "got up" his material "solely from the outside," and that Madame Autheman in particular was "quite automatic" and "psychologically . . . a blank." He thereby indicated his different hopes for his own novel.

Until a year and a half later he was still without a title, and was afraid he might "have to call it simply — *Verena*: the heroine. I should like something more descriptive — but everything that is justly descriptive won't do — *The Newness, The Reformers, The Precursors, The Revealer* — all very bad and with the additional fault that people will say that they are taken from Daudet." Then, in a letter to his brother William declaring that he felt he had a better subject than he had "ever had before," he added: "It is called *The Bostonians*. I shall be much abused for the title, but it exactly and literally fits the story, and is much the best, simplest and most dignified I could have chosen."

The first objection, not to the title but to some of the content, came, to his consternation, from William himself who, after reading the first installment in the *Century*, took Henry to task for basing Miss Birdseye too closely upon Elizabeth Peabody, Hawthorne's sister-in-law, who was still alive. Henry was outraged that his character who, although subordinate, he felt to be the best single creation in his novel, should be thought a literal copy. Furthermore, he could not see how anyone could take offense at a characterization which he had summed

Introduction

up in the sentence: "She was heroic, she was sublime, the whole
moral history of Boston was reflected in her displaced spectacles." He therefore wrote a firm
answer to William, and developed
therein one of his most illuminating accounts of how his characters
came into being: "I care not a
straw what people in general may
say about Miss Birdseye — they can
say nothing more idiotic and in-
sulting than they have already
said about all my books in which
there has been any attempt to represent things or persons in America; but . . . I absolutely had no
shadow of such an intention. I
have not seen Miss P. for twenty
years, I never had but the most
casual observation of her, I didn't
know whether she was alive or
dead, and she was not in the
smallest degree my starting-point
or example. Miss Birdseye was
evolved entirely from my moral
consciousness, like every other person I have ever drawn, and orig-
inated in my desire to make a
figure who should embody in a
sympathetic, pathetic, picturesque,
and at the same time grotesque
way, the humanitary and *ci-devant*
transcendental tendencies which I
thought it highly probable I
should be accused of treating in
a contemptuous manner in so far
as they were otherwise represented in the tale. I wished to
make this figure a woman, because so it would be more touching, and an old, weary, battered,
and simple-minded woman because that deepened the same effect. I elaborated her in my mind's
eye — and after I had got going
reminded myself that my creation
would perhaps be identified with
Miss Peabody — *that* I freely admit. . . . The one definite thing
about which I had a scruple was
some touch about Miss Birdseye's spectacles — I remembered
that Miss Peabody's were always
in the wrong place; but I didn't
see, really, why I should deprive
myself of an effect (as regards
this point) which is common to a
thousand old people. So I thought
no more about Miss P. *at all,* but
simply strove to realize my vision."

Once he had the whole book before him, William retracted his
"growling" letter, and pronounced
The Bostonians "an exquisite production." He thought the psychological description might be too
redundant for some readers, but
delighted particularly "in the way
you have touched off the bits of
American nature, Central Park,
Cape Cod, etc." He might have
enumerated many other particulars, for here Henry had included
a wide variety of scenes, ranging
from Newspaper Row to the Music Hall, and from the desolate
suburban view across the Basin to
Harvard's then new Memorial Hall
to the Civil War dead, "the ornate overtopping structure" which
was "the finest piece of architecture" that the young Southern
lawyer, Basil Ransom, had ever
seen. Some of the novel's best
touches are in its passages of social comedy, as when Olive Chancellor's cottage on the Cape is

epitomized as containing an inadequate number of chairs but "all George Eliot's writings, and two photographs of the Sistine Madonna"; or when Miss Birdseye, earnestly discussing women's rights with Ransom on a horse-car, turns to him with: "Do you regard us, then, simply as lovely baubles?" But how inept James could be when he moved out of the circle whose speech he knew is sufficiently instanced when he makes a cop say: "Yes, it's always intensely private." That's pretty steep, even for a Boston cop.

James himself, with the remarkable detachment that always characterized his attitude toward his productions in retrospect, advanced much graver strictures. He agreed with William about the psychologizing: "There is far too much of the sort of thing you animadvert upon, though there is in the public mind at the same time a truly ignoble levity and puerility and aversion to any attempt on the part of a novelist to establish his people solidly. All the same I have overdone it. . . . All the middle part is too diffuse and insistent — far too describing and explaining and expatiating. The whole thing is too long and dawdling. This came from the fact (partly) that I had the sense of knowing terribly little about the kind of life I had attempted to describe — and felt a constant pressure to make the picture substantial by thinking it out — pencilling and 'shading.' I was afraid of the reproach (having *seen* so little of the whole business treated of) of being superficial and cheap — and in short I should have been much more rapid, and had a lighter hand, with a subject concerned with people and things of a nature more near to my experience."

His subject, as he had worked it out, had involved a combination of elements from his background and reading. The aftershine of transcendentalism had come from his memories of his father's world, for Henry James, Senior, in his vivid contacts with the Fourierists as well as with Emerson and Alcott, had himself shared in the hopes of those "long-haired men and short-haired women." But his son the novelist, presenting the Boston of the eighteen-seventies, was accurate in his appraisal that New England's great age of reform was over. To be sure, exceptions like Wendell Phillips could have been found, but James' view of reform was closer to Hawthorne's than to his father's, that of the skeptical observer rather than of the participant. When he seized upon mesmerism as a means of satirizing a charlatan like his heroine's father, "a moralist without moral sense," he must certainly have remembered *The Blithedale Romance*.

In considering the new movement for women's rights, his interest was entirely in its effect upon a character like Olive Chancellor, who, as the most complex nature in his book and the one most typical of New England, enlisted the greatest share of his attention. He does not satirize her, he sees her as essentially tragic, although her possessiveness over Verena cannot help making her unattractive. But the weakest part of the novel is the denouement, the conventional love whereby Ransom rescues the heroine. Ransom, as the critic of feminism, has also dissatisfied readers who demand from a social novel an affirmative protest. For this native of Mississippi who fought for the South in the Civil War is a "reactionary" whose doctrines are described by a New York editor in the novel as being "about three hundred years behind the age." An "immense admirer" of Carlyle, he is no more a spokesman for the author than Olive is, since James, despite his political inactivity, never wavered in his devotion to Lincoln's cause, and he expressed elsewhere some of the same suspicions of Carlyle's arrogance that his father held. In his belief that the novelist's function is to dramatize objectively various points of view, he showed again the influence of Turgenieff, and the social study he produced was necessarily static.

He concluded his comment upon it to William by saying: "If I have displeased people, as I hear, by calling the book *The Bostonians* — this was done wholly without invidious intention. I hadn't a dream of generalizing but . . . meant only to designate Olive and Verena by it, as they appeared to the mind of Ransom, the Southerner and outside looking at them from New York. I didn't even *mean* it to cover Miss Birdseye and the others, though it might very well. I shall write another: *The Other Bostonians*. However, this is only by the way, for after one of my productions is finished and cast upon the waters it has, for me, quite sunk beneath the surface — I cease to care for it and transfer my interest to the one I am next trying to float."

But the criticism was even less favorable than he had foreseen. Nearly all the American journals took the most stupid line and, blind to the function of satire, solemnly attacked James for his want of local patriotism. None of his previous books had received such a poor press, and even the few critics who praised some aspects of it were doubtful of his increasingly analytic method. Mark Twain, much less appreciative of James than James was of him, wrote to Howells that he "would rather be damned to John Bunyan's heaven" than to have to read such a book. Howells, to be sure, demurred, and returning to *The Bostonians* twenty-five years later, he saw in it some of the qualities that have attracted subsequent readers: "Closely woven, deep, subtle, reaching out into worlds that I did not imagine you knew, and avouching you citizen of the American Cosmos, it is such a novel as the like of hasn't been done in our time. Every character is managed with masterly clearness and power. Verena is something absolute in her tenderness and sweetness and loveliness, and

Introduction

Olive in her truth and precision; your New Yorkers are as good as your Bostonians; and I couldn't go beyond that. Both towns are wonderfully suggested; you go to the bottom of the half frozen Cambridge mud. A dear yet terrible time comes back to me in it all."

But James felt no temptation to try another American novel. Even while *The Bostonians* was running serially, he was at work on *The Princess Casamassima.* It is significant that he had thought for a while of following his study of Hawthorne with one of Dickens, for *The Princess Casamassima,* his one attempt to grapple with the larger economic forces in English society, is his nearest approach to the Dickens kind of novel. But James' detached treatment of revolution, so different from Dickens' social sympathies, proved hardly more popular than *The Bostonians;* and he turned from these two wide canvases, in *The Tragic Muse,* to the life of the theater. Shortly thereafter he embraced his long deferred hope of writing plays, and that episode absorbed the greater share of his energy for five years. When he finally had to admit failure in meeting the demands of the current stage, he salvaged much of what he had learned from this experience by intensifying the dramatic structure of short novels like *The Spoils of Poynton* and *The Awkward Age.* These books followed along from his plays in all dealing with English society, and only after the turn of the century was he drawn

back to his older vein of Americans in Europe. Then, reinforced by the full development of his technical resources, he produced in three successive years his three major novels.

During all this time he had written only one story laid wholly in America, and as its title, " 'Europe,' " suggests, it was a resumption of one of his earliest themes, our American longing for a richer culture. He stated in his notebook that he had also wanted to recapture something of his long buried memory of the widow of the historian John Gorham Palfrey, who had lived on to an incredible age. Since the old lady was the dramatic center of his story, he kept it entirely in her New England town, instead of following the procedure of his much earlier "Four Meetings," where he had pursued his frustrated heroine abroad. Consequently, " 'Europe' " belongs in our collection, though it represents no further development of James' handling of American material. In collecting it himself for his New York edition, he did not arrange it with "Pandora" or "Julia Bride," since he quite rightly believed its chief interest to lie in its form rather than in any particular content. He singled it out fondly as one of the cases where he had proved that he could be brief: "The merit of the thing is in the feat . . . of the transfusion; the receptacle (of form) being so exiguous, the brevity imposed so great. I undertook the brevity, so undertaken on a like scale before, and again arrived at it by the innumerable chemical reductions and condensations that tend to make of the very short story . . . one of the costliest, even if, like the hard shining sonnet, one of the most indestructible, forms of composition in general use."

While he was still working on *The Golden Bowl,* he felt a keen desire, though already in his sixty-first year, for an exposure to fresh experience such as might "convert itself, through the senses, through observation, imagination and reflection now at their maturity, into vivid and solid *material,* into a general renovation of one's too monotonized grab-bag." The source of such experience he now believed could only be America which, as he went on to say to his brother, "Time, absence and change have, in a funny sort of way, made almost as romantic to me as 'Europe,' in dreams or in my earlier time . . . used to be."

He travelled from Boston to Florida and out to California, but the strongest impression was made upon him by New York. It was no longer the easy-paced city of his childhood when Fourteenth Street had formed almost the up-town limit, nor even the entertaining city that he remembered from his last visit, over twenty years before. With his first sight of the harbor he sensed something different from anything he had previously known, "in the bigness and bravery and insolence, especially, of everything that rushed and shrieked." Read-

ing the symbolical significance in the way that Trinity Church was overshadowed by the earliest skyscrapers, he discerned that here all other aspirations were dwarfed by the money-passion, "restless beyond all passions." The only way to present in fiction the immense new "human aggregation" would be to possess the crude vigorous appetite of a Zola.

James felt that his own limited knowledge restricted him even more than before to "up-town," and the four stories that were his creative response to his new American impressions all deal very obliquely with the life of the city. But their overtones separate them sharply from any American stories he had written before. The least considerable of the group is "Crapy Cornelia," wherein he contrasts old-fashioned Cornelia Rasch with glitteringly modern Mrs. Worthingham in order to repossess a vignette of history from "those spacious, sociable, Arcadian days . . . north of Washington Square."

In the interval since *The Bostonians* and particularly since he had taken advantage of the typewriter and had begun, in the mid-eighteen-nineties, to dictate his work, James had evolved his final elaborate manner, the qualifications and circumlocutions of which strike many readers as oppressively disproportionate in a story of such small content as this. But another quality that goes far to alleviate any impression of overstuffed heaviness is James' resilient

Introduction

refinement of the gift he had always possessed for visual images, so that for the attentive reader this story establishes its imaginative effect through the repetitive counterpointing of the gleam, glare, and hard dazzle that always surrounds Mrs. Worthingham against the comforting dusky restfulness of Cornelia.

His pictorial skills reached one of their summits in "The Jolly Corner," in his presentation of the interior of his hero's old house, at his moment of crisis, solely by means of the light that flickers in from the street to heighten the mystery and terror of his ghostly encounter. James' ghost-stories would make a chapter by themselves, but here the presence that Spencer Brydon stalks down is James' means of symbolizing another aspect of the past and present of New York. For Brydon, in his mid-fifties, has lived in Europe for thirty-three years, and has come back now only to attend to some questions about his "property." Once here, he begins to speculate on what he might have been if, instead of spending what he knows to be deemed a frivolous idle life, he had stayed at home and gone into business and become "one of those types who have been hammered so hard and made so keen by their conditions." He gets his answer in his horrified vision of his *alter ego*, whose mutilated hand drops to reveal his "evil, odious, blatant, vulgar" face, and thus becomes a sign of his crippled spirit.

A woman like Cornelia Rasch could maintain a fugitive refuge in her memories of the past, but any man would inevitably be more exposed to the naked force of the city which, to James' view, was brutally indifferent to anything but its immediate competitive drives. The harsh light that environs Mrs. Worthingham is also reflected from money; and when James turned once again to the American girl, in "Julia Bride," he no longer produced a heedless Daisy Miller or a high-spirited Pandora Day. For now he felt impelled to write about a girl whose freedoms have caught up with her, who as a consequence of her mother's reckless divorces and her own unsupervised foolish engagements finds herself shut out from the correct marriage that, with her lack of money, she desperately needs.

In his earlier pictures of "uptown," money had been an element, to be sure, but not the searing blight that it now appeared everywhere he turned. In "A Round of Visits," the last short story that he published, he gave embodiment to a theme that he had first recorded in his notebook as a Hawthornesque abstraction, fifteen years before: "The notion of a young man . . . who has something — some secret sorrow, trouble, fault — to *tell* and can't find the recipient." He had sketched out the possible line of development: "So he wanders, so he goes — with his burden only growing heavier — looking vainly for the ideal sympathy, the waiting expectant, responsive recipient. My little idea has been that he doesn't find it; but that he encounters instead a sudden appeal, an appeal more violent, as it were, more pitiful even than his own."

James recurred to this theme several times, but it remained unexpressed until an impression of the heartlessness of the modern metropolis, sometimes more oppressively lonely for the solitary individual than the wilderness, crystallized its setting. James intensified the city's violence by contrasting a savage blizzard with the heavy heat of the luxury hotel, so that it was only a step "from the Tropics to the Pole." One of the most brilliant of his sustained metaphors extends the startling flora and fauna of the hotel lobby into an oppressive jungle, where the plumaged women are shrill birds of prey.

Financial peculation has met Mark Monteith almost as soon as he landed from abroad, in the news that the friend to whom he had entrusted the management of his funds has just absconded as a swindler. In this way "down-town" seeped into James' "up-town," and as the situation developed, his new sense of widespread corruption could find no resolution for this story except in a suicide.

James did not write these New York stories until three or four years after he had returned to England, overwhelmed with "an immense impression of material and political power." He under-

took a searching criticism of this country in his remarkable travel-book, *The American Scene,* and spent the better part of the next two years selecting and revising his novels and stories for the New York edition. He was severe in excluding a great deal of his earlier work, and his passing over *Washington Square* has often been regretted. He was himself disappointed that Scribner's limitation to twenty-four volumes necessitated leaving out *The Bostonians,* which he now described to Howells as a "too diffuse, but . . . tolerably full and good . . . production" which had "never received any sort of justice." In the last year of his life he was still dwelling, in a letter to Gosse, on how much he would have liked to revise this novel and provide its preface: "It would have come out a much truer and more curious thing (it was meant to be curious from the first)."

In 1909 he told Howells that he had "broken ground on an American novel," but his work was soon to be interrupted by several months of nervous ill-health. Then, after William's death had left him the last survivor of his immediate family, his mind was naturally drawn to preserve his image of the past in his memoirs. Only in 1914 did he begin working out his full plan for *The Ivory Tower,* and he had composed about a third of it when the outbreak of the war made it impossible for him to concentrate his attention further.

This unfinished novel, with James' extensive passage of dictated notes, can take us into his methods of composition to a degree that we are permitted with few authors. It also rounds out the full cycle of his style, from the painstaking but amateurish "Story of a Year" to the point where, after half a century and after the most sustained production of any novelist yet to appear in America, his elaborate patterning of his characters' thoughts began to show signs of great tiredness. *The Ivory Tower* is thoroughly written up to the end of book two, with all of James' skills at their ripest amplitude; but the third book and the fragment of the fourth seem hardly more than sketched, and Graham Fielder's reflections begin to get fuzzy and rambling and are not pulled into form. But enough of this novel was completed to reveal its conception, and that conception places it among James' most important achievements.

One of the chapters in *The American Scene* was called "The Sense of Newport," and James had contrasted the eighteenth-century town, as he remembered it from living there in 1860, with the new millionaires' resort, overcrowded with its line of showy villas. He found one image for its transformation in "a little bare, white, open hand" suddenly crammed with gold. When he spoke of the old group that had centered around William Morris Hunt and had been united through their feeling for art and their sense of

Europe, and added that they had also sacrificed "openly to the ivory idol whose name is leisure," he was close to the central symbol that he developed for his novel.

James was particularly sensitive to architecture as an index to cultural history, and from his presentation, on his opening pages, of the florid "cottage," "smothered in senseless ornament," he established the kind of life we are to expect, with its wasteful idleness so different from the creative leisure of the earlier group. Years ago he had said: "Money is the most general element of Balzac's novels; other things come and go, but money is always there." No matter how much more closely akin James' talent may seem to that of other masters, he had never forgotten the lesson of Balzac, whom he had singled out as the novelist to lecture about during his American tour, and whom he then declared again to have taught him more about his craft than "any one else."

He saw at last how he could suggest the effects of "down-town" on an ample scale, since with this Newport set, as Mr. Betterman, one of his millionaires, remarks: "Money is their life." The tone of this set is much harder than any he had portrayed as being mitigated by the pressure of one of his American girls. Indeed, his sophisticated Cissy Foy says: "I loathe the American girl"; and though James shared none of that loathing, he had come to feel, in the face of the new brutalizing forces he had observed, that even an Isabel Archer or a Milly Theale would be too frail a carrier of culture. He had, therefore (in *The American Scene*), shaped a final soliloquy for the type, and had let her pour out her sense of defeat: "How can I do *all* the grace, all the interest, as I'm expected to? — yes, literally all the interest that isn't the mere interest on the money. Haven't I . . . been too long abandoned and too *much* betrayed? Isn't it too late, and am I not, don't you think, practically lost?"

He included now a new gallery of social types, the possible growth of which had made the visiting Englishman in "The Point of View" most apprehensive. The Bradhams are some of the most likely products of Veblen's kind of leisure class. Davey, like so many other specimens from Harvard or Yale, is not vicious but just "a sponge of saturation in the surrounding medium." His wife Gussy is far more aggressive: "She wants everyone for something so much more than something for everyone." She bears out Veblen's analysis most fully when James adds: "She was naturally never so the vulgar rich woman able to afford herself all luxuries as when she was most stupid about the right enjoyment of these and most brutally systematic . . . for some inferior and desecrating use of them."

The overshadowing background is constituted by the two old dying millionaires, Abel Gaw and Frank Betterman, both of whom have been "ruthless operators," though the latter has repented and sees how the very air has been poisoned by their rapacious careers. The two leading figures, Betterman's nephew and Gaw's daughter, are fuller developments of characters we have already seen something of. Graham Fielder is more serious than Felix Young in *The Europeans*, but he is another sensitive American who has been formed entirely by Europe. Rosanna Gaw, in her lack of obvious charm and her moral massiveness, is a more thoughtful reincarnation of the heroine of *Washington Square*.

Both react strongly against their wealth. To Rosanna it has long seemed that her resources "are so dishonoured and stained and blackened at their very roots" that no "'benevolence' . . . can purge them." Fielder, more hopeful at first, thinks that he may find a function in disposing of his inheritance to public services "after the fashion of Rockefellers and their like." But as James intended to work out the plot, Fielder also was to arrive at a sense "of the black and merciless things that are behind the great possessions." He was to come to this realization through discovering how his money put temptations in the path of his scheming friend, Horton Vint, and how in part, therefore — in a manner that shows James' grasp of moral complexity — he was responsible for calling out the badness in Vint's nature.

At this point Fielder was to be

glad to let his inheritance go, and to return to Europe. What James prefigured thus was not the union between wealth and culture that Mr. Betterman hoped for in willing his property to his nephew. It was rather a possibility that had hovered before James all his life, the union between form and spirit, between European culture and American idealism, between Fielder and Rosanna. The lines on which he projected this union here may not seem very convincing, and it is hard to think of any very effectual future for such an "out and out non-producer" as Graham Fielder. To be sure, many Americans were still carried to Europe with something of Fielder's hope, in the generation after James' death, the generation between wars, though few took with them James' serious moral sense. But now, with a ruined Europe in need of resuscitation, any such dream would appear to be that of the idlest dilettante. With the beginning of the first World War, indeed, James himself had been shocked into the realization that his proposed synthesis looked very flimsy. As he wrote to a friend: "The plunge of civilization into this abyss of blood and darkness . . . is a thing that so gives away the whole long age during which we have supposed the world to be, with whatever abatement, gradually bettering, that to have to take it all now for what the treacherous years were all the while really making for and *meaning* is too tragic for any words."

In the same year that the completion of *The Ivory Tower* became no longer possible for James, Dreiser produced *The Titan*. Here was the immersion in the crude facts of American existence that James had felt beyond his scope, but had recognized none the less to be necessary if an American Balzac was to exist. Dreiser is our nearest equivalent for an American Zola, and his clumsy stolid humanity brought within his grasp qualities of our ordinary life quite missing in James. Yet looking back now to *The Ivory Tower* and *The Titan*, it seems doubtful whether Dreiser, with his broader social scene and with all his ability to suggest Frank Cowperwood's ruthless vitality, penetrated any more deeply into the evils produced by finance capitalism than James managed to do. James' final chapter of our moral history now looks as permanently valuable in its way as anything that the naturalistic novel has yet produced.

F. O. Matthiessen

THE AMERICAN NOVELS AND STORIES OF

Henry James

THE STORY OF A YEAR

MY story begins as a great many stories have begun within the last three years, and indeed as a great many have ended; for, when the hero is despatched does not the romance come to a stop?

In early May, two years ago, a young couple I wot of strolled homeward from an evening walk, a long ramble among the peaceful hills which inclosed their rustic home. Into these peaceful hills the young man had brought, not the rumor, (which was an old inhabitant,) but some of the reality of war, — a little whiff of gunpowder, the clanking of a sword; for, although Mr. John Ford had his campaign still before him, he wore a certain comely air of camp-life which stamped him a very Hector to the steady-going villagers, and a very pretty fellow to Miss Elizabeth Crowe, his companion in this sentimental stroll. And was he not attired in the great brightness of blue and gold which befits a freshly made lieutenant? This was a strange sight for these happy Northern glades; for, although the first Revolution had boomed awhile in their midst,

the honest yeomen who defended them were clad in sober homespun, and it is well known that His Majesty's troops wore red.

These young people, I say, had been roaming. It was plain that they had wandered into spots where the brambles were thick and the dews heavy, — nay, into swamps and puddles where the April rains were still undried. Ford's boots and trousers had imbibed a deep foretaste of the Virginia mud; his companion's skirts were fearfully bedraggled. What great enthusiasm had made our friends so unmindful of their steps? What blinding ardor had kindled these strange phenomena: a young lieutenant scornful of his first uniform, a well-bred young lady reckless of her stockings?

Good reader, this narrative is averse to retrospect.

Elizabeth (as I shall not scruple to call her outright) was leaning upon her companion's arm, half moving in concert with him, and half allowing herself to be led, with that instinctive acknowledgment of dependence natural to a young girl who has just received the assurance of lifelong protection. Ford was lounging along with that calm, swinging stride which often bespeaks, when you can read it aright, the answering consciousness of a sudden rush of manhood. A spectator might have

The Story of a Year

thought him at this moment profoundly conceited. The young girl's blue veil was dangling from his pocket; he had shouldered her sun-umbrella after the fashion of a musket on a march: he might carry these trifles. Was there not a vague longing expressed in the strong expansion of his stalwart shoulders, in the fond accommodation of his pace to hers, — her pace so submissive and slow, that, when he tried to match it, they almost came to a delightful standstill, — a silent desire for the whole fair burden?

They made their way up a long swelling mound, whose top commanded the sunset. The dim landscape which had been brightening all day to the green of spring was now darkening to the gray of evening. The lesser hills, the farms, the brooks, the fields, orchards, and woods, made a dusky gulf before the great splendor of the west. As Ford looked at the clouds, it seemed to him that their imagery was all of war, their great uneven masses were marshalled into the semblance of a battle. There were columns charging and columns flying and standards floating, — tatters of the reflected purple; and great captains on colossal horses, and a rolling canopy of cannon-smoke and fire and blood. The background of the clouds, indeed, was like a land on fire, or a battle-ground illumined by another sunset, a country of blackened villages and crimsoned pastures. The tumult of the clouds increased; it was hard to believe them inanimate. You might have fancied them an army of gigantic souls playing at football with the sun. They seemed to sway in confused splendor; the opposing squadrons bore each other down; and then suddenly they scattered, bowling with equal velocity towards north and south, and gradually fading into the pale evening sky. The purple pennons sailed away and sank out of sight, caught, doubtless, upon the brambles of the intervening plain. Day contracted itself into a fiery ball and vanished.

Ford and Elizabeth had quietly watched this great mystery of the heavens.

"That is an allegory," said the young man, as the sun went under, looking into his companion's face, where a pink flush seemed still to linger: "it means the end of the war. The forces on both sides are withdrawn. The blood that has been shed gathers itself into a vast globule and drops into the ocean."

"I'm afraid it means a shabby compromise," said Elizabeth. "Light disappears, too, and the land is in darkness."

"Only for a season," answered the other. "We mourn our dead. Then light comes again, stronger and brighter than ever. Perhaps you'll be crying for me, Lizzie, at that distant day."

"Oh, Jack, didn't you promise not to talk about that?" says Lizzie, threatening to anticipate the performance in question.

Jack took this rebuke in silence,

gazing soberly at the empty sky. Soon the young girl's eyes stole up to his face. If he had been looking at anything in particular, I think she would have followed the direction of his glance; but as it seemed to be a very vacant one, she let her eyes rest.

"Jack," said she, after a pause, "I wonder how you'll look when you get back."

Ford's soberness gave way to a laugh.

"Uglier than ever. I shall be all incrusted with mud and gore. And then I shall be magnificently sunburnt, and I shall have a beard."

"Oh, you dreadful!" and Lizzie gave a little shout. "Really, Jack, if you have a beard, you'll not look like a gentleman."

"Shall I look like a lady, pray?" says Jack.

"Are you serious?" asked Lizzie.

"To be sure. I mean to alter my face as you do your misfitting garments, — take in on one side and let out on the other. Isn't that the process? I shall crop my head and cultivate my chin."

"You've a very nice chin, my dear, and I think it's a shame to hide it."

"Yes, I know my chin's handsome; but wait till you see my beard."

"Oh, the vanity!" cried Lizzie, "the vanity of men in their faces! Talk of women!" and the silly creature looked up at her lover with most inconsistent satisfaction.

"Oh, the pride of women in their husbands!" said Jack, who of course knew what she was about.

"You're not my husband, Sir. There's many a slip" — But the young girl stopped short.

"'Twixt the cup and the lip,'" said Jack. "Go on. I can match your proverb with another. 'There's many a true word,' and so forth. No, my darling: I'm not your husband. Perhaps I never shall be. But if anything happens to me, you'll take comfort, won't you?"

"Never!" said Lizzie, tremulously.

"Oh, but you must; otherwise, Lizzie, I should think our engagement inexcusable. Stuff! who am I that you should cry for me?"

"You are the best and wisest of men. I don't care; you *are*."

"Thank you for your great love, my dear. That's a delightful illusion. But I hope Time will kill it, in his own good way, before it hurts any one. I know so many men who are worth infinitely more than I — men wise, generous, and brave — that I shall not feel as if I were leaving you in an empty world."

"Oh, my dear friend!" said Lizzie, after a pause, "I wish you could advise me all my life."

"Take care, take care," laughed Jack; "you don't know what you are bargaining for. But will you let me say a word now? If by chance I'm taken out of the world, I want you to beware of that tawdry sentiment which enjoins you to be 'constant to my memory.' My memory be hanged! Remember me at my best, — that is, fullest of the desire of humility.

5

Don't inflict me on people. There are some widows and bereaved sweethearts who remind me of the peddler in that horrible murder-story, who carried a corpse in his pack. Really, it's their stock in trade. The only justification of a man's personality is his rights. What rights has a dead man? — Let's go down."

They turned southward and went jolting down the hill.

"Do you mind this talk, Lizzie?" asked Ford.

"No," said Lizzie, swallowing a sob, unnoticed by her companion in the sublime egotism of protection; "I like it."

"Very well," said the young man, "I want my memory to help you. When I am down in Virginia, I expect to get a vast deal of good from thinking of you, — to do my work better, and to keep straighter altogether. Like all lovers, I'm horribly selfish. I expect to see a vast deal of shabbiness and baseness and turmoil, and in the midst of it all I'm sure the inspiration of patriotism will sometimes fail. Then I'll think of you. I love you a thousand times better than my country, Liz. — Wicked? So much the worse. It's the truth. But if I find your memory makes a milksop of me, I shall thrust you out of the way, without ceremony, — I shall clap you into my box or between the leaves of my Bible, and only look at you on Sunday."

"I shall be very glad, Sir, if that makes you open your Bible frequently," says Elizabeth, rather demurely.

"I shall put one of your photographs against every page," cried Ford; "and then I think I shall not lack a text for my meditations. Don't you know how Catholics keep little pictures of their adored Lady in their prayer-books?"

"Yes, indeed," said Lizzie; "I should think it would be a very soul-stirring picture, when you are marching to the front, the night before a battle, — a poor, stupid girl, knitting stupid socks, in a stupid Yankee village."

Oh, the craft of artless tongues! Jack strode along in silence a few moments, splashing straight through a puddle; then, ere he was quite clear of it, he stretched out his arm and gave his companion a long embrace.

"And pray what am I to do," resumed Lizzie, wondering, rather proudly perhaps, at Jack's averted face, "while you are marching and countermarching in Virginia?"

"Your duty, of course," said Jack, in a steady voice, which belied a certain little conjecture of Lizzie's. "I think you will find the sun will rise in the east, my dear, just as it did before you were engaged."

"I'm sure I didn't suppose it wouldn't," says Lizzie.

"By duty I don't mean anything disagreeable, Liz," pursued the young man. "I hope you'll take your pleasure, too. I wish you might go to Boston, or even to Leatherborough, for a month or two."

"What for, pray?"

"What for? Why, for the fun of it: to 'go out,' as they say."

"Jack, do you think me capable of going to parties while you are in danger?"

"Why not? Why should I have all the fun?"

"Fun? I'm sure you're welcome to it all. As for me, I mean to make a new beginning."

"Of what?"

"Oh, of everything. In the first place, I shall begin to improve my mind. But don't you think it's horrid for women to be reasonable?"

"Hard, say you?"

"Horrid, — yes, and hard too. But I mean to become so. Oh, girls are such fools, Jack! I mean to learn to like boiled mutton and history and plain sewing, and all that. Yet, when a girl's engaged, she's not expected to do anything in particular."

Jack laughed, and said nothing; and Lizzie went on.

"I wonder what your mother will say to the news. I think I know."

"What?"

"She'll say you've been very unwise. No, she won't: she never speaks so to you. She'll say I've been very dishonest or indelicate, or something of that kind. No, she won't either: she doesn't say such things, though I'm sure she thinks them. I don't know what she'll say."

"No, I think not, Lizzie, if you indulge in such conjectures. My mother never speaks without thinking. Let us hope that she may

think favorably of our plan. Even if she doesn't" —

Jack did not finish his sentence, nor did Lizzie urge him. She had a great respect for his hesitations. But in a moment he began again.

"I was going to say this, Lizzie: I think for the present our engagement had better be kept quiet."

Lizzie's heart sank with a sudden disappointment. Imagine the feelings of the damsel in the fairytale, whom the disguised enchantress had just empowered to utter diamonds and pearls, should the old beldame have straightway added that for the present mademoiselle had better hold her tongue. Yet the disappointment was brief. I think this enviable young lady would have tripped home talking very hard to herself, and have been not ill pleased to find her little mouth turning into a tightly clasped jewel-casket. Nay, would she not on this occasion have been thankful for a large mouth, — a mouth huge and unnatural, — stretching from ear to ear? Who wish to cast their pearls before swine? The young lady of the pearls was, after all, but a barnyard miss. Lizzie was too proud of Jack to be vain. It's well enough to wear our own hearts upon our sleeves; but for those of others, when intrusted to our keeping, I think we had better find a more secluded lodging.

"You see, I think secrecy would leave us much freer," said Jack, — "leave *you* much freer."

"Oh, Jack, how can you?" cried Lizzie. "Yes, of course; I shall be falling in love with some one else. Freer! Thank you, Sir!"

"Nay, Lizzie, what I'm saying is really kinder than it sounds. Perhaps you *will* thank me one of these days."

"Doubtless! I've already taken a great fancy to George Mackenzie."

"Will you let me enlarge on my suggestion?"

"Oh, certainly! You seem to have your mind quite made up."

"I confess I like to take account of possibilities. Don't you know mathematics are my hobby? Did you ever study algebra? I always have an eye on the unknown quantity."

"No, I never studied algebra. I agree with you, that we had better not speak of our engagement."

"That's right, my dear. You're always right. But mind, I don't want to bind you to secrecy. Hang it, do as you please! Do what comes easiest to you, and you'll do the best thing. What made me speak is my dread of the horrible publicity which clings to all this business. Nowadays, when a girl's engaged, it's no longer, 'Ask mamma,' simply; but, 'Ask Mrs. Brown, and Mrs. Jones, and my large circle of acquaintance, — Mrs. Grundy, in short.' I say nowadays, but I suppose it's always been so."

"Very well, we'll keep it all nice and quiet," said Lizzie, who would have been ready to celebrate her nuptials according to the rites of the Esquimaux, had Jack seen fit to suggest it.

"I know it doesn't look well for a lover to be so cautious," pursued Jack; "but you understand me, Lizzie, don't you?"

"I don't entirely understand you, but I quite trust you."

"God bless you! My prudence, you see, is my best strength. Now, if ever, I need my strength. When a man's a-wooing, Lizzie, he is all feeling, or he ought to be; when he's accepted, then he begins to think."

"And to repent, I suppose you mean."

"Nay, to devise means to keep his sweetheart from repenting. Let me be frank. Is it the greatest fools only that are the best lovers? There's no telling what may happen, Lizzie. I want you to marry me with your eyes open. I don't want you to feel tied down or taken in. You're very young, you know. You're responsible to yourself of a year hence. You're at an age when no girl can count safely from year's end to year's end."

"And you, Sir!" cries Lizzie; "one would think you were a grandfather."

"Well, I'm on the way to it. I'm a pretty old boy. I mean what I say. I may not be entirely frank, but I think I'm sincere. It seems to me as if I'd been fibbing all my life before I told you that your affection was necessary to my happiness. I mean it out and out. I never loved any one before, and I never will again. If you had refused me half an hour ago, I should have died a bachelor. I have no fear for myself. But I have for you. You said a few min-

The Story of a Year

utes ago that you wanted me to be your adviser. Now you know the function of an adviser is to perfect his victim in the art of walking with his eyes shut. I sha'n't be so cruel."

Lizzie saw fit to view these remarks in a humorous light. "How disinterested!" quoth she: "how very self-sacrificing! Bachelor indeed! For my part, I think I shall become a Mormon!" — I verily believe the poor misinformed creature fancied that in Utah it is the ladies who are guilty of polygamy.

Before many minutes they drew near home. There stood Mrs. Ford at the garden-gate, looking up and down the road, with a letter in her hand.

"Something for you, John," said his mother, as they approached. "It looks as if it came from camp. — Why, Elizabeth, look at your skirts!"

"I know it," says Lizzie, giving the articles in question a shake. "What is it, Jack?"

"Marching orders!" cried the young man. "The regiment leaves day after to-morrow. I must leave by the early train in the morning. Hurray!" And he diverted a sudden gleeful kiss into a filial salute.

They went in. The two women were silent, after the manner of women who suffer. But Jack did little else than laugh and talk and circumnavigate the parlor, sitting first here and then there, — close beside Lizzie and on the opposite side of the room. After a while Miss Crowe joined in his laughter,

but I think her mirth might have been resolved into articulate heartbeats. After tea she went to bed, to give Jack opportunity for his last filial *épanchements*. How generous a man's intervention makes women! But Lizzie promised to see her lover off in the morning.

"Nonsense!" said Mrs. Ford. "You'll not be up. John will want to breakfast quietly."

"I shall see you off, Jack," repeated the young lady, from the threshold.

Elizabeth went up stairs buoyant with her young love. It had dawned upon her like a new life, — a life positively worth the living. Hereby she would subsist and cost nobody anything. In it she was boundlessly rich. She would make it the hidden spring of a hundred praiseworthy deeds. She would begin the career of duty: she would enjoy boundless equanimity: she would raise her whole being to the level of her sublime passion. She would practise charity, humility, piety, — in fine, all the virtues: together with certain *morceaux* of Beethoven and Chopin. She would walk the earth like one glorified. She would do homage to the best of men by inviolate secrecy. Here, by I know not what gentle transition, as she lay in the quiet darkness, Elizabeth covered her pillow with a flood of tears.

Meanwhile Ford, down-stairs, began in this fashion. He was lounging at his manly length on the sofa, in his slippers.

"May I light a pipe, mother?"

"Yes, my love. But please be

9

careful of your ashes. There's a newspaper."

"Pipes don't make ashes. — Mother, what do you think?" he continued, between the puffs of his smoking; "I've got a piece of news."

"Ah?" said Mrs. Ford, fumbling for her scissors; "I hope it's good news."

"I hope you'll think it so. I've been engaging myself" — puff, — puff — "to Lizzie Crowe." A cloud of puffs between his mother's face and his own. When they cleared away, Jack felt his mother's eyes. Her work was in her lap. "To be married, you know," he added.

In Mrs. Ford's view, like the king in that of the British Constitution, her only son could do no wrong. Prejudice is a stout bulwark against surprise. Moreover, Mrs. Ford's motherly instinct had not been entirely at fault. Still, it had by no means kept pace with fact. She had been silent, partly from doubt, partly out of respect for her son. As long as John did not doubt of himself, he was right. Should he come to do so, she was sure he would speak. And now, when he told her the matter was settled, she persuaded herself that he was asking her advice.

"I've been expecting it," she said, at last.

"You have? why didn't you speak?"

"Well, John, I can't say I've been hoping it."

"Why not?"

"I am not sure of Lizzie's heart," said Mrs. Ford, who, it may be well to add, was very sure of her own.

Jack began to laugh. "What's the matter with her heart?"

"I think Lizzie's shallow," said Mrs. Ford; and there was that in her tone which betokened some satisfaction with this adjective.

"Hang it! she is shallow," said Jack. "But when a thing's shallow, you can see to the bottom. Lizzie doesn't pretend to be deep. I want a wife, mother, that I can understand. That's the only wife I can love. Lizzie's the only girl I ever understood, and the first I ever loved. I love her very much, — more than I can explain to you."

"Yes, I confess it's inexplicable. It seems to me," she added, with a bad smile, "like infatuation."

Jack did not like the smile; he liked it even less than the remark. He smoked steadily for a few moments, and then he said, —

"Well, mother, love is notoriously obstinate, you know. We shall not be able to take the same view of this subject: suppose we drop it."

"Remember that this is your last evening at home, my son," said Mrs. Ford.

"I do remember. Therefore I wish to avoid disagreement."

There was a pause. The young man smoked, and his mother sewed, in silence.

"I think my position, as Lizzie's guardian," resumed Mrs. Ford, "entitles me to an interest in the matter."

"Certainly, I acknowledged your interest by telling you of our engagement."

Further pause.

"Will you allow me to say," said Mrs. Ford, after a while, "that I think this a little selfish?"

"Allow you? Certainly, if you particularly desire it. Though I confess it isn't very pleasant for a man to sit and hear his future wife pitched into, — by his own mother, too."

"John, I am surprised at your language."

"I beg your pardon," and John spoke more gently. "You mustn't be surprised at anything from an accepted lover. — I'm sure you misconceive her. In fact, mother, I don't believe you know her."

Mrs. Ford nodded, with an infinite depth of meaning; and from the grimness with which she bit off the end of her thread it might have seemed that she fancied herself to be executing a human vengeance.

"Ah, I know her only too well!"

"And you don't like her?"

Mrs. Ford performed another decapitation of her thread.

"Well, I'm glad Lizzie has one friend in the world," said Jack.

"Her best friend," said Mrs. Ford, "is the one who flatters her least. I see it all, John. Her pretty face has done the business."

The young man flushed impatiently.

"Mother," said he, "you are very much mistaken. I'm not a boy nor a fool. You trust me in a great many things; why not trust me in this?"

"My dear son, you are throwing yourself away. You deserve for your companion in life a higher character than that girl."

I think Mrs. Ford, who had been an excellent mother, would have liked to give her son a wife fashioned on her own model.

"Oh, come, mother," said he, "that's twaddle. I should be thankful, if I were half as good as Lizzie."

"It's the truth, John, and your conduct — not only the step you've taken, but your talk about it — is a great disappointment to me. If I have cherished any wish of late, it is that my darling boy should get a wife worthy of him. The household governed by Elizabeth Crowe is not the home I should desire for any one I love."

"It's one to which you should always be welcome, Ma'am," said Jack.

"It's not a place I should feel at home in," replied his mother.

"I'm sorry," said Jack. And he got up and began to walk about the room. "Well, well, mother," he said at last, stopping in front of Mrs. Ford, "we don't understand each other. One of these days we shall. For the present let us have done with discussion. I'm half sorry I told you."

"I'm glad of such a proof of your confidence. But if you hadn't, of course Elizabeth would have done so."

"No, Ma'am, I think not."

11

"Then she is even more reckless of her obligations than I thought her."

"I advised her to say nothing about it."

Mrs. Ford made no answer. She began slowly to fold up her work.

"I think we had better let the matter stand," continued her son. "I'm not afraid of time. But I wish to make a request of you: you won't mention this conversation to Lizzie, will you? nor allow her to suppose that you know of our engagement? I have a particular reason."

Mrs. Ford went on smoothing out her work. Then she suddenly looked up.

"No, my dear, I'll keep your secret. Give me a kiss."

II

I HAVE no intention of following Lieutenant Ford to the seat of war. The exploits of his campaign are recorded in the public journals of the day, where the curious may still peruse them. My own taste has always been for unwritten history, and my present business is with the reverse of the picture.

After Jack went off, the two ladies resumed their old homely life. But the homeliest life had now ceased to be repulsive to Elizabeth. Her common duties were no longer wearisome: for the first time, she experienced the delicious companionship of thought. Her chief task was still to sit by the window knitting soldiers' socks; but even Mrs. Ford could not help owning that she worked with a much greater diligence, yawned, rubbed her eyes, gazed up and down the road less, and indeed produced a much more comely article. Ah, me! if half the lovesome fancies that flitted through Lizzie's spirit in those busy hours could have found their way into the texture of the dingy yarn, as it was slowly wrought into shape, the eventual wearer of the socks would have been as light-footed as Mercury. I am afraid I should make the reader sneer, were I to rehearse some of this little fool's diversions. She passed several hours daily in Jack's old chamber: it was in this sanctuary, indeed, at the sunny south window, overlooking the long road, the wood-crowned heights, the gleaming river, that she worked with most pleasure and profit. Here she was removed from the untiring glance of the elder lady, from her jarring questions and commonplaces; here she was alone with her love, — that greatest commonplace in life. Lizzie felt in Jack's room a certain impress of his personality. The idle fancies of her mood were bodied forth in a dozen sacred relics. Some of these articles Elizabeth carefully cherished. It was rather late in the day for her to assert a literary taste, — her reading having begun and ended (naturally enough) with the ancient fiction of the "Scottish Chiefs." So she could hardly help smiling, herself, sometimes, at her interest in Jack's old college tomes. She carried several of them to her own apartment, and placed them at the foot of her little bed, on a bookshelf adorned, besides, with a pot of spring violets, a portrait of General McClellan, and a likeness of Lieutenant Ford. She had a vague belief that a loving study of their well-thumbed verses would remedy, in some degree, her sad intellectual deficiencies. She was sorry she knew so little: as sorry, that is, as she might be, for we know that she was shallow. Jack's omniscience was one of his most awful attributes. And yet she comforted herself with the thought, that, as he had forgiven her ignorance, she herself might surely forget it. Happy Lizzie, I envy you this easy path to knowledge! The volume she most frequently consulted was an old German "Faust," over which she used to fumble with a battered lexicon. The secret of this preference was in certain marginal notes in pencil, signed "J." I hope they were really of Jack's making.

Lizzie was always a small walker. Until she knew Jack, this had been quite an unsuspected pleasure. She was afraid, too, of the cows, geese, and sheep, — all the agricultural *spectra* of the feminine imagination. But now her terrors were over. Might she not play the soldier, too, in her own humble way? Often with a beating heart, I fear, but still with resolute, elastic steps, she revisited Jack's old haunts; she tried to love

Nature as he had seemed to love it; she gazed at his old sunsets; she fathomed his old pools with bright plummet glances, as if seeking some lingering trace of his features in their brown depths, stamped there as on a fond human heart; she sought out his dear name, scratched on the rocks and trees, — and when night came on, she studied, in her simple way, the great starlit canopy, under which, perhaps, her warrior lay sleeping; she wandered through the green glades, singing snatches of his old ballads in a clear voice, made tuneful with love, — and as she sang, there mingled with the everlasting murmur of the trees the faint sound of a muffled bass, borne upon the south wind like a distant drum-beat, responsive to a bugle. So she led for some months a very pleasant idyllic life, face to face with a strong, vivid memory, which gave everything and asked nothing. These were doubtless to be (and she half knew it) the happiest days of her life. Has life any bliss so great as this pensive ecstasy? To know that the golden sands are dropping one by one makes servitude freedom, and poverty riches.

In spite of a certain sense of loss, Lizzie passed a very blissful summer. She enjoyed the deep repose which, it is to be hoped, sanctifies all honest betrothals. Possible calamity weighed lightly upon her. We know that when the columns of battle-smoke leave the field, they journey through the heavy air to a thousand quiet homes, and play about the crackling blaze of as many firesides. But Lizzie's vision was never clouded. Mrs. Ford might gaze into the thickening summer dusk and wipe her spectacles; but her companion hummed her old ballad-ends with an unbroken voice. She no more ceased to smile under evil tidings than the brooklet ceases to ripple beneath the projected shadow of the roadside willow. The self-given promises of that tearful night of parting were forgotten. Vigilance had no place in Lizzie's scheme of heavenly idleness. The idea of moralizing in Elysium!

It must not be supposed that Mrs. Ford was indifferent to Lizzie's mood. She studied it watchfully, and kept note of all its variations. And among the things she learned was, that her companion knew of her scrutiny, and was, on the whole, indifferent to it. Of the full extent of Mrs. Ford's observation, however, I think Lizzie was hardly aware. She was like a reveller in a brilliantly lighted room, with a curtainless window, conscious, and yet heedless, of passers-by. And Mrs. Ford may not inaptly be compared to the chilly spectator on the dark side of the pane. Very few words passed on the topic of their common thoughts. From the first, as we have seen, Lizzie guessed at her guardian's probable view of her engagement: an abasement incurred by John. Lizzie lacked what is called a sense of duty; and, unlike the majority of such temperaments, which contrive to be buoyant on the glistening bubble of Dignity, she had likewise a modest estimate of her dues. Alack, my poor heroine had no pride! Mrs. Ford's silent censure awakened no resentment. It sounded in her ears like a dull, soporific hum. Lizzie was deeply enamored of what a French book terms her *aises intellectuelles*. Her mental comfort lay in the ignoring of problems. She possessed a certain native insight which revealed many of the horrent inequalities of her pathway; but she found it so cruel and disenchanting a faculty, that blindness was infinitely preferable. She preferred repose to order, and mercy to justice. She was speculative, without being critical. She was continually wondering, but she never inquired. This world was the riddle; the next alone would be the answer.

So she never felt any desire to have an "understanding" with Mrs. Ford. Did the old lady misconceive her? it was her own business. Mrs. Ford apparently felt no desire to set herself right. You see, Lizzie was ignorant of her friend's promise. There were moments when Mrs. Ford's tongue itched to speak. There were others, it is true, when she dreaded any explanation which would compel her to forfeit her displeasure. Lizzie's happy self-sufficiency was most irritating. She grudged the young girl the dignity of her secret; her own actual knowledge of it rather increased her jealousy, by showing her the importance of the scheme from which she was excluded. Lizzie, being in perfect good-humor with the world and with herself, abated no jot of her personal deference to Mrs. Ford. Of Jack, as a good friend and her guardian's son, she spoke very freely. But Mrs. Ford was mistrustful of this semi-confidence. She would not, she often said to herself, be wheedled against her principles. Her principles! Oh for some shining blade of purpose to hew down such stubborn stakes! Lizzie had no thought of flattering her companion. She never deceived any one but herself. She could not bring herself to value Mrs. Ford's good-will. She knew that Jack often suffered from his mother's obstinacy. So her unbroken humility shielded no unavowed purpose. She was patient and kindly from nature, from habit. Yet I think, that, if Mrs. Ford could have measured her benignity, she would have preferred, on the whole, the most open defiance. "Of all things," she would sometimes mutter, "to be patronized by that little piece!" It was very disagreeable, for instance, to have to listen to *portions* of her own son's letters.

These letters came week by week, flying out of the South like white-winged carrier-doves. Many and many a time, for very pride, Lizzie would have liked a larger audience. Portions of them certainly deserved publicity. They were far too good for her. Were they not better than that stupid war-correspondence in the "Times,"

which she so often tried in vain to read? They contained long details of movements, plans of campaigns, military opinions and conjectures, expressed with the emphasis habitual to young sub-lieutenants. I doubt whether General Halleck's despatches laid down the law more absolutely than Lieutenant Ford's. Lizzie answered in her own fashion. It must be owned that hers was a dull pen. She told her dearest, dearest Jack how much she loved and honored him, and how much she missed him, and how delightful his last letter was, (with those beautifully drawn diagrams,) and the village gossip, and how stout and strong his mother continued to be, — and again, how she loved, etc., etc., and that she remained his loving L. Jack read these effusions as became one so beloved. I should not wonder if he thought them very brilliant.

The summer waned to its close, and through myriad silent stages began to darken into autumn. Who can tell the story of those red months? I have to chronicle another silent transition. But as I can find no words delicate and fine enough to describe the multifold changes of Nature, so, too, I must be content to give you the spiritual facts in gross.

John Ford became a veteran down by the Potomac. And, to tell the truth, Lizzie became a veteran at home. That is, her love and hope grew to be an old story. She gave way, as the strongest must, as the wisest will, to time. The passion which, in her simple, shallow way, she had confided to the woods and waters reflected their outward variations; she thought of her lover less, and with less positive pleasure. The golden sands had run out. Perfect rest was over. Mrs. Ford's tacit protest began to be annoying. In a rather resentful spirit, Lizzie forbore to read any more letters aloud. These were as regular as ever. One of them contained a rough camp-photograph of Jack's newly bearded visage. Lizzie declared it was "too ugly for anything," and thrust it out of sight. She found herself skipping his military dissertations, which were still as long and written in as handsome a hand as ever. The "too good," which used to be uttered rather proudly, was now rather a wearisome truth. When Lizzie in certain critical moods tried to qualify Jack's temperament, she said to herself that he was too literal. Once he gave her a little scolding for not writing oftener. "Jack can make no allowances," murmured Lizzie. "He can understand no feelings but his own. I remember he used to say that moods were diseases. His mind is too healthy for such things; his heart is too stout for ache or pain. The night before he went off he told me that Reason, as he calls it, was the rule of life. I suppose he thinks it the rule of love, too. But his heart is younger than mine, — younger and better. He has lived through awful scenes of danger and bloodshed and cruelty, yet his heart is purer."

Lizzie had a horrible feeling of being *blasée* of this one affection. "Oh, God bless him!" she cried. She felt much better for the tears in which this soliloquy ended. I fear she had begun to doubt her ability to cry about Jack.

CHRISTMAS came. The Army of the Potomac had stacked its muskets and gone into winter-quarters. Miss Crowe received an invitation to pass the second fortnight in February at the great manufacturing town of Leatherborough. Leatherborough is on the railroad, two hours south of Glenham, at the mouth of the great river Tan, where this noble stream expands into its broadest smile, or gapes in too huge a fashion to be disguised by a bridge.

"Mrs. Littlefield kindly invites you for the last of the month," said Mrs. Ford, reading a letter behind the tea-urn.

It suited Mrs. Ford's purpose — a purpose which I have not space to elaborate — that her young charge should now go forth into society and pick up acquaintances.

Two sparks of pleasure gleamed in Elizabeth's eyes. But, as she had taught herself to do of late with her protectress, she mused before answering.

"It is my desire that you should go," said Mrs. Ford, taking silence for dissent.

The sparks went out.

"I intend to go," said Lizzie, rather grimly. "I am much obliged to Mrs. Littlefield."

Her companion looked up.

"I intend you shall. You will please to write this morning."

For the rest of the week the two stitched together over muslins and silks, and were very good friends. Lizzie could scarcely help wondering at Mrs. Ford's zeal on her behalf. Might she not have referred it to her guardian's principles? Her wardrobe, hitherto fashioned on the Glenham notion of elegance, was gradually raised to the Leatherborough standard of fitness. As she took up her bedroom candle the night before she left home, she said, —

"I thank you very much, Mrs. Ford, for having worked so hard for me, — for having taken so much interest in my outfit. If they ask me at Leatherborough who made my things, I shall certainly say it was you."

Mrs. Littlefield treated her young friend with great kindness. She was a good-natured, childless matron. She found Lizzie very ignorant and very pretty. She was glad to have so great a beauty and so many lions to show.

One evening Lizzie went to her room with one of the maids, carrying half a dozen candles between them. Heaven forbid that I should cross that virgin threshold — for the present! But we will wait. We will allow them two hours. At the end of that time, having gently knocked, we will enter the sanctuary. Glory of glories! The faithful attendant has done her work. Our lady is robed, crowned, ready for worshippers.

I trust I shall not be held to a minute description of our dear Lizzie's person and costume. Who is so great a recluse as never to have beheld young ladyhood in full dress? Many of us have sisters and daughters. Not a few of us, I hope, have female connections of another degree, yet no less dear. Others have looking-glasses. I give you my word for it that Elizabeth made as pretty a show as it is possible to see. She was of course well-dressed. Her skirt was of voluminous white, puffed and trimmed in wondrous sort. Her hair was profusely ornamented with curls and braids of its own rich substance. From her waist depended a ribbon, broad and blue. White with coral ornaments, as she wrote to Jack in the course of the week. Coral ornaments, forsooth! And pray, Miss, what of the other jewels with which your person was decorated, — the rubies, pearls, and sapphires? One by one Lizzie assumes her modest gimcracks: her bracelet, her gloves, her handkerchief, her fan, and then — her smile. Ah, that strange crowning smile!

An hour later, in Mrs. Littlefield's pretty drawing-room, amid music, lights, and talk, Miss Crowe was sweeping a grand curtsy before a tall, sallow man, whose name she caught from her hostess's redundant murmur as Bruce. Five minutes later, when the honest matron gave a glance at her newly started enterprise from the other side of the room, she said to herself that really, for a plain country-girl, Miss Crowe did this kind of thing very well. Her next glimpse of the couple showed them whirling round the room to the crashing thrum of the piano. At eleven o'clock she beheld them linked by their finger-tips in the dazzling mazes of the reel. At half-past eleven she discerned them charging shoulder to shoulder in the serried columns of the Lancers. At midnight she tapped her young friend gently with her fan.

"Your sash is unpinned, my dear. — I think you have danced often enough with Mr. Bruce. If he asks you again, you had better refuse. It's not quite the thing. — Yes, my dear, I know. — Mr. Simpson, will you be so good as to take Miss Crowe down to supper?"

I'm afraid young Simpson had rather a snappish partner.

After the proper interval, Mr. Bruce called to pay his respects to Mrs. Littlefield. He found Miss Crowe also in the drawing-room. Lizzie and he met like old friends. Mrs. Littlefield was a willing listener; but it seemed to her that she had come in at the second act of the play. Bruce went off with Miss Crowe's promise to drive with him in the afternoon. In the afternoon he swept up to the door in a prancing, tinkling sleigh. After some minutes of hoarse jesting and silvery laughter in the keen wintry air, he swept away again with Lizzie curled up in the buffalo-robe beside him, like a kitten in a rug. It was dark when they returned. When Lizzie came in to the sitting-room fire, she was congratulated by her hostess upon having made a "conquest."

"I think he's a most gentlemanly man," says Lizzie.

"So he is, my dear," said Mrs. Littlefield; "Mr. Bruce is a perfect gentleman. He's one of the finest young men I know. He's not so young either. He's a little too yellow for my taste; but he's beautifully educated. I wish you could hear his French accent. He has been abroad I don't know how many years. The firm of Bruce and Robertson does an immense business."

"And I'm so glad," cries Lizzie, "he's coming to Glenham in March! He's going to take his sister to the water-cure."

"Really? — poor thing! She has very good manners."

"What do you think of his looks?" asked Lizzie, smoothing her feather.

"I was speaking of Jane Bruce. I think Mr. Bruce has fine eyes."

"I must say I like tall men," says Miss Crowe.

"Then Robert Bruce is your man," laughs Mr. Littlefield. "He's as tall as a bell-tower. And he's got a bell-clapper in his head, too."

"I believe I will go and take off my things," remarks Miss Crowe, flinging up her curls.

Of course it behooved Mr. Bruce to call the next day and see how Miss Crowe had stood her drive. He set a veto upon her intended departure, and presented an invitation from his sister for the following week. At Mrs. Littlefield's instance, Lizzie accepted the invitation, despatched a laconic note to Mrs. Ford, and stayed over for Miss Bruce's party. It was a grand affair. Miss Bruce was a very great lady: she treated Miss Crowe with every attention. Lizzie was thought by some persons to look prettier than ever. The vaporous gauze, the sunny hair, the coral, the sapphires, the smile, were displayed with renewed success. The master of the house was unable to dance; he was summoned to sterner duties. Nor could Miss Crowe be induced to perform, having hurt her foot on the ice. This was of course a disappointment; let us hope that her entertainers made it up to her.

On the second day after the party, Lizzie returned to Glenham, Good Mr. Littlefield took her to the station, stealing a moment from his precious business-hours.

"There are your checks," said he; "be sure you don't lose them. Put them in your glove."

Lizzie gave a little scream of merriment.

"Mr. Littlefield, how can you? I've a reticule, Sir. But I really don't want you to stay."

"Well, I confess," said her companion. — "Hullo! there's your Scottish chief! I'll get him to stay with you till the train leaves. He may be going. Bruce!"

"Oh, Mr. Littlefield, don't!"

cries Lizzie. "Perhaps Mr. Bruce is engaged."

Bruce's tall figure came striding towards them. He was astounded to find that Miss Crowe was going by this train. Delightful! He had come to meet a friend who had not arrived.

"Littlefield," said he, "you can't be spared from your business. I will see Miss Crowe off."

When the elder gentleman had departed, Mr. Bruce conducted his companion into the car, and found her a comfortable seat, equidistant from the torrid stove and the frigid door. Then he stowed away her shawls, umbrella, and reticule. She would keep her muff? She did well. What a pretty fur!

"It's just like your collar," said Lizzie. "I wish I had a muff for my feet," she pursued, tapping on the floor.

"Why not use some of those shawls?" said Bruce; "let's see what we can make of them."

And he stooped down and arranged them as a rug, very neatly and kindly. And then he called himself a fool for not having used the next seat, which was empty; and the wrapping was done over again.

"I'm so afraid you'll be carried off!" said Lizzie. "What would you do?"

"I think I should make the best of it. And you?"

"I would tell you to sit down *there*"; and she indicated the seat facing her. He took it. "Now you'll be sure to," said Elizabeth.

"I'm afraid I shall, unless I put

the newspaper between us." And he took it out of his pocket. "Have you seen the news?"

"No," says Lizzie, elongating her bonnet-ribbons. "What is it? Just look at that party."

"There's not much news. There's been a scrimmage on the Rappahannock. Two of our regiments engaged, — the Fifteenth and the Twenty-Eighth. Didn't you tell me you had a cousin or something in the Fifteenth?"

"Not a cousin, no relation, but an intimate friend, — my guardian's son. What does the paper say, please?" inquires Lizzie, very pale.

Bruce cast his eye over the report. "It doesn't seem to have amounted to much; we drove back the enemy, and recrossed the river at our ease. Our loss only fifty. There are no names," he added, catching a glimpse of Lizzie's pallor, — "none in this paper at least."

In a few moments appeared a newsboy crying the New York journals.

"Do you think the New York papers would have any names?" asked Lizzie.

"We can try," said Bruce. And he bought a "Herald," and unfolded it. "Yes, there *is* a list," he continued, some time after he had opened out the sheet. "What's your friend's name?" he asked, from behind the paper.

"Ford, — John Ford, second lieutenant," said Lizzie.

There was a long pause.

At last Bruce lowered the sheet, and showed a face in which Lizzie's pallor seemed faintly reflected.

"There *is* such a name among the wounded," he said; and, folding the paper down, he held it out, and gently crossed to the seat beside her.

Lizzie took the paper, and held it close to her eyes. But Bruce could not help seeing that her temples had turned from white to crimson.

"Do you see it?" he asked; "I sincerely hope it's nothing very bad."

"*Severely,*" whispered Lizzie.

"Yes, but that proves nothing. Those things are most unreliable. *Do* hope for the best."

Lizzie made no answer. Meanwhile passengers had been brushing in, and the car was full. The engine began to puff, and the conductor to shout. The train gave a jog.

"You'd better go, Sir, or you'll be carried off," said Lizzie, holding out her hand, with her face still hidden.

"May I go on to the next station with you?" said Bruce.

Lizzie gave him a rapid look, with a deepened flush. He had fancied that she was shedding tears. But those eyes were dry; they held fire rather than water.

"No, no, Sir; you must not. I insist. Good bye."

Bruce's offer had cost him a blush, too. He had been prepared to back it with the assurance that he had business ahead, and, indeed, to make a little business in order to satisfy his conscience. But Lizzie's answer was final.

"Very well," said he, "*good* bye. You have my real sympathy, Miss Crowe. Don't despair. We shall meet again."

The train rattled away. Lizzie caught a glimpse of a tall figure with lifted hat on the platform. But she sat motionless, with her head against the window-frame, her veil down, and her hands idle.

She had enough to do to think, or rather to feel. It is fortunate that the utmost shock of evil tiding often comes first. After that everything is for the better. Jack's name stood printed in that fatal column like a stern signal for despair. Lizzie felt conscious of a crisis which almost arrested her breath. Night had fallen at midday: what was the hour? A tragedy had stepped into her life: was she spectator or actor? She found herself face to face with death: was it not her own soul masquerading in a shroud? She sat in a half-stupor. She had been aroused from a dream into a waking nightmare. It was like hearing a murder-shriek while you turn the page of your novel. But I cannot describe these things. In time the crushing sense of calamity loosened its grasp. Feeling lashed her pinions. Thought struggled to rise. Passion was still, stunned, floored. She had recoiled like a receding wave for a stronger onset. A hundred ghastly fears and fancies strutted a moment, pecking at the young girl's naked heart, like sand-pipers on the weltering beach. Then, as with a great murmurous rush, came the meaning of her grief. The flood-gates of emotion were opened.

At last passion exhausted itself, and Lizzie thought. Bruce's parting words rang in her ears. She did her best to hope. She reflected that wounds, even severe wounds, did not necessarily mean death. Death might easily be warded off. She would go to Jack; she would nurse him; she would watch by him; she would cure him. Even if Death had already beckoned, she would strike down his hand: if Life had already obeyed, she would issue the stronger mandate of Love. She would stanch his wounds; she would unseal his eyes with her kisses; she would call till he answered her.

Lizzie reached home and walked up the garden path. Mrs. Ford stood in the parlor as she entered, upright, pale, and rigid. Each read the other's countenance. Lizzie went towards her slowly and giddily. She must of course kiss her patroness. She took her listless hand and bent towards her stern lips. Habitually Mrs. Ford was the most undemonstrative of women. But as Lizzie looked closer into her face, she read the signs of a grief infinitely more potent than her own. The formal kiss gave way: the young girl leaned her head on the old woman's shoulder and burst into sobs. Mrs. Ford acknowledged those tears with a slow inclination of the head, full of a certain grim pathos: she put out her arms and pressed them closer to her heart.

At last Lizzie disengaged herself and sat down.

"I am going to him," said Mrs. Ford.

Lizzie's dizziness returned. Mrs. Ford was going, — and she, she?

"I am going to nurse him, and with God's help to save him."

"How did you hear?"

"I have a telegram from the surgeon of the regiment"; and Mrs. Ford held out a paper.

Lizzie took it and read: "Lieutenant Ford dangerously wounded in the action of yesterday. You had better come on."

"I should like to go myself," said Lizzie: "I think Jack would like to have me."

"Nonsense! A pretty place for a young girl! I am not going for sentiment; I am going for use."

Lizzie leaned her head back in her chair, and closed her eyes. From the moment they had fallen upon Mrs. Ford, she had felt a certain quiescence. And now it was a relief to have responsibility denied her. Like most weak persons, she was glad to step out of the current of life, now that it had begun to quicken into action. In emergencies, such persons are tacitly counted out; and they as tacitly consent to the arrangement. Even to the sensitive spirit there is a certain meditative rapture in standing on the quiet shore, (beside the ruminating cattle,) and watching the hurrying, eddying flood, which makes up for the loss of dignity. Lizzie's heart resumed

its peaceful throbs. She sat, almost dreamily, with her eyes shut.

"I leave in an hour," said Mrs. Ford. "I am going to get ready. — Do you hear?"

The young girl's silence was a deeper consent than her companion supposed.

IV

It was a week before Lizzie heard from Mrs. Ford. The letter, when it came, was very brief. Jack still lived. The wounds were three in number, and very serious; he was unconscious; he had not recognized her; but still the chances either way were thought equal. They would be much greater for his recovery nearer home; but it was impossible to move him. "I write from the midst of horrible scenes," said the poor lady. Subjoined was a list of necessary medicines, comforts, and delicacies, to be boxed up and sent.

For a while Lizzie found occupation in writing a letter to Jack, to be read in his first lucid moment, as she told Mrs. Ford. This lady's man-of-business came up from the village to superintend the packing of the boxes. Her directions were strictly followed; and in no point were they found wanting. Mr. Mackenzie bespoke Lizzie's admiration for their friend's wonderful clearness of memory and judgment. "I wish we had that woman at the head of affairs," said he. "Gad, I'd apply for a Brigadier-Generalship." — "I'd apply to be sent South," thought Lizzie. When the boxes and letter were despatched, she sat down to await more news. Sat down, say I? Sat down, and rose, and wondered, and sat down again. These were lonely, weary days. Very different are the idleness of love and the idleness of grief. Very different is it to be alone with your hope and alone with your despair. Lizzie failed to rally her musing. I do not mean to say that her sorrow was very poignant, although she fancied it was. Habit was a great force in her simple nature; and her chief trouble now was that habit refused to work. Lizzie had to grapple with the stern tribulation of a decision to make, a problem to solve. She felt that there was some spiritual barrier between herself and repose. So she began in her usual fashion to build up a false repose on the hither side of belief. She might as well have tried to float on the Dead Sea. Peace eluding her, she tried to resign herself to tumult. She drank deep at the well of self-pity, but found its waters brackish. People are apt to think that they may temper the penalties of misconduct by self-commiseration, just as they season the long after-taste of beneficence by a little spice of self-applause. But the Power of Good is a more grateful master than the Devil. What bliss to gaze into the smooth gurgling wake of a good deed, while the comely bark sails on with floating pennon! What

horror to look into the muddy sediment which floats round the piratic keel! Go, sinner, and dissolve it with your tears! And you, scoffing friend, there is the way out! Or would you prefer the window? I'm an honest man forevermore.

One night Lizzie had a dream, — a rather disagreeable one, — which haunted her during many waking hours. It seemed to her that she was walking in a lonely place, with a tall, dark-eyed man who called her wife. Suddenly, in the shadow of a tree, they came upon an unburied corpse. Lizzie proposed to dig him a grave. They dug a great hole and took hold of the corpse to lift him in; when suddenly he opened his eyes. Then they saw that he was covered with wounds. He looked at them intently for some time, turning his eyes from one to the other. At last he solemnly said, "Amen!" and closed his eyes. Then she and her companion placed him in the grave, and shovelled the earth over him, and stamped it down with their feet.

He of the dark eyes and he of the wounds were the two constantly recurring figures of Lizzie's reveries. She could never think of John without thinking of the courteous Leatherborough gentleman, too. These were the *data* of her problem. These two figures stood like opposing knights, (the black and the white,) foremost on the great chess-board of fate. Lizzie was the wearied, puzzled player. She would idly finger the other pieces, and shift them carelessly hither and thither; but it was of no avail: the game lay between the two knights. She would shut her eyes and long for some kind hand to come and tamper with the board; she would open them and see the two knights standing immovable, face to face. It was nothing new. A fancy had come in and offered defiance to a fact; they must fight it out. Lizzie generously inclined to the fancy, the unknown champion, with a reputation to make. Call her *blasée*, if you like, this little girl, whose record told of a couple of dances and a single lover, heartless, old before her time. Perhaps she deserves your scorn. I confess she thought herself ill-used. By whom? by what? wherein? These were questions Miss Crowe was not prepared to answer. Her intellect was unequal to the stern logic of human events. She expected two and two to make five: as why should they not for the nonce? She was like an actor who finds himself on the stage with a half-learned part and without sufficient wit to extemporize. Pray, where is the prompter? Alas, Elizabeth, that you had no mother! Young girls are prone to fancy that when once they have a lover, they have everything they need: a conclusion inconsistent with the belief entertained by many persons, that life begins with love. Lizzie's fortunes became old stories to her before she had half read them through. Jack's wounds and danger were an old story. Do not suppose that she had exhausted the lessons, the suggestions of these awful events, their inspirations, exhortations, — that she had wept as became the horror of the tragedy. No: the curtain had not yet fallen, yet our young lady had begun to yawn. To yawn? Ay, and to long for the afterpiece. Since the tragedy dragged, might she not divert herself with that well-bred man beside her?

Elizabeth was far from owning to herself that she had fallen away from her love. For my own part, I need no better proof of the fact than the dull persistency with which she denied it. What accusing voice broke out of the stillness? Jack's nobleness and magnanimity were the hourly theme of her clogged fancy. Again and again she declared to herself that she was unworthy of them, but that, if he would only recover and come home, she would be his eternal bond-slave. So she passed a very miserable month. Let us hope that her childish spirit was being tempered to some useful purpose. Let us hope so.

She roamed about the empty house with her footsteps tracked by an unlaid ghost. She cried aloud and said that she was very unhappy; she groaned and called herself wicked. Then, sometimes, appalled at her moral perplexities, she declared that she was neither wicked nor unhappy; she was contented, patient, and wise. Other girls had lost their lovers: it was the present way of life. Was she weaker than most women? Nay, but Jack was the best of men. If he would only come back directly, without delay, as he was, senseless, dying even, that she might look at him, touch him, speak to him! Then she would say that she could no longer answer for herself, and wonder (or pretend to wonder) whether she were not going mad. Suppose Mrs. Ford should come back and find her in an unswept room, pallid and insane? or suppose she should die of her troubles? What if she should kill herself? — dismiss the servants, and close the house, and lock herself up with a knife? Then she would cut her arm to escape from dismay at what she had already done; and then her courage would ebb away with her blood, and, having so far pledged herself to despair, her life would ebb away with her courage; and then, alone, in darkness, with none to help her, she would vainly scream, and thrust the knife into her temple, and swoon to death. And Jack would come back, and burst into the house, and wander through the empty rooms, calling her name, and for all answer get a deathscent! These imaginings were the more creditable or discreditable to Lizzie, that she had never read "Romeo and Juliet." At any rate, they served to dissipate time, — heavy, weary time, — the more heavy and weary as it bore dark foreshadowings of some momentous event. If that event would only come, whatever it was, and sever this Gordian knot of doubt! The days passed slowly: the leaden sands dropped one by one.

The roads were too bad for walking; so Lizzie was obliged to confine her restlessness to the narrow bounds of the empty house, or to an occasional journey to the village, where people sickened her by their dull indifference to her spiritual agony. Still they could not fail to remark how poorly Miss Crowe was looking. This was true, and Lizzie knew it. I think she even took a certain comfort in her pallor and in her failing interest in her dress. There was some satisfaction in displaying her white roses amid the apple-cheeked prosperity of Main Street. At last Miss Cooper, the Doctor's sister, spoke to her: —

"How is it, Elizabeth, you look so pale, and thin, and worn out? What you been doing with yourself? Falling in love, eh? It isn't right to be so much alone. Come down and stay with us awhile, — till Mrs. Ford and John come back," added Miss Cooper, who wished to put a cheerful face on the matter.

For Miss Cooper, indeed, any other face would have been difficult. Lizzie agreed to come. Her hostess was a busy, unbeautiful old maid, sister and housekeeper of the village physician. Her occupation here below was to perform the forgotten tasks of her fellowmen, — to pick up their dropped stitches, as she herself declared. She was never idle, for her general cleverness was commensurate with mortal needs. Her own story was, that she kept moving, so that folks couldn't see how ugly she was. And, in fact, her existence was manifest through her long train of good deeds, — just as the presence of a comet is shown by its tail. It was doubtless on the above principle that her visage was agitated by a perpetual laugh.

Meanwhile more news had been coming from Virginia. "What an absurdly long letter you sent John," wrote Mrs. Ford, in acknowledging the receipt of the boxes. "His first lucid moment would be very short, if he were to take upon himself to read your effusions. Pray keep your long stories till he gets well." For a fortnight the young soldier remained the same, — feverish, conscious only at intervals. Then came a change for the worse, which, for many weary days, however, resulted in nothing decisive. "If he could only be moved to Glenham, home, and old sights," said his mother, "I should have hope. But think of the journey!" By this time Lizzie had stayed out ten days of her visit.

One day Miss Cooper came in from a walk, radiant with tidings. Her face, as I have observed, wore a continual smile, being dimpled and punctured all over with merriment, — so that, when an unusual cheerfulness was super-diffused, it resembled a tempestuous little pool into which a great stone has been cast.

"Guess who's come," said she, going up to the piano, which Lizzie was carelessly fingering, and putting her hands on the young girl's shoulders. "Just guess!"

Lizzie looked up.

"Jack," she half gasped.

"Oh, dear, no, not that! How stupid of me! I mean Mr. Bruce, your Leatherborough admirer."

"Mr. Bruce! Mr. Bruce!" said Lizzie. "Really?"

"True as I live. He's come to bring his sister to the Water-Cure. I met them at the post-office."

Lizzie felt a strange sensation of good news. Her finger-tips were on fire. She was deaf to her companion's rattling chronicle. She broke into the midst of it with a fragment of some triumphant, jubilant melody. The keys rang beneath her flashing hands. And then she suddenly stopped, and Miss Cooper, who was taking off her bonnet at the mirror, saw that her face was covered with a burning flush.

That evening, Mr. Bruce presented himself at Doctor Cooper's, with whom he had a slight acquaintance. To Lizzie he was infinitely courteous and tender. He assured her, in very pretty terms, of his profound sympathy with her in her cousin's danger, — her cousin he still called him, — and it seemed to Lizzie that until that moment no one had begun to be kind. And then he began to rebuke her, playfully and in excellent taste, for her pale cheeks.

"Isn't it dreadful?" said Miss Cooper. "She looks like a ghost. I guess she's in love."

"He must be a good-for-nothing lover to make his mistress look so sad. If I were you, I'd give him up, Miss Crowe."

"I didn't know I looked sad," said Lizzie.

The Story of a Year

"You don't now," said Miss Cooper. "You're smiling and blushing. A'n't she blushing, Mr. Bruce?"

"I think Miss Crowe has no more than her natural color," said Bruce, dropping his eye-glass. "What have you been doing all this while since we parted?"

"All this while? it's only six weeks. I don't know. Nothing. What have you?"

"I've been doing nothing, too. It's hard work."

"Have you been to any more parties?"

"Not one."

"Any more sleigh-rides?"

"Yes. I took one more dreary drive all alone, — over that same road, you know. And I stopped at the farm-house again, and saw the old woman we had the talk with. She remembered us, and asked me what had become of the young lady who was with me before. I told her you were gone home, but that I hoped soon to go and see you. So she sent you her love" ——

"Oh, how nice!" exclaimed Lizzie.

"Wasn't it? And then she made a certain little speech; I won't repeat it, or we shall have Miss Cooper talking about your blushes again."

"I know," cried the lady in question: "she said she was very" ——

"Very what?" said Lizzie.

"Very h-a-n-d —— what every one says."

"Very handy?" asked Lizzie. "I'm sure no one ever said that."

"Of course," said Bruce; "and I answered what every one answers."

"Have you seen Mrs. Littlefield lately?"

"Several times. I called on her the day before I left town, to see if she had any messages for you."

"Oh, thank you! I hope she's well."

"Oh, she's as jolly as ever. She sent you her love, and hoped you would come back to Leatherborough very soon again. I told her, that, however it might be with the first message, the second should be a joint one from both of us."

"You're very kind. I should like very much to go again. — Do you like Mrs. Littlefield?"

"Like her? Yes. Don't you? She's thought a very pleasing woman."

"Oh, she's very nice. — I don't think she has much conversation."

"Ah, I'm afraid you mean she doesn't backbite. We've always found plenty to talk about."

"That's a very significant tone. What, for instance?"

"Well, we *have* talked about Miss Crowe."

"Oh, you have? Do you call that having plenty to talk about?"

"We *have* talked about Mr. Bruce, — haven't we, Elizabeth?" said Miss Cooper, who had her own notion of being agreeable.

It was not an altogether bad notion, perhaps; but Bruce found her interruptions rather annoying, and insensibly allowed them to shorten his visit. Yet, as it was, he sat till eleven o'clock, — a stay quite unprecedented at Glenham.

When he left the house, he went splashing down the road with a very elastic tread, springing over the starlit puddles, and trolling out some sentimental ditty. He reached the inn, and went up to his sister's sitting-room.

"Why, Robert, where have you been all this while?" said Miss Bruce.

"At Dr. Cooper's."

"Dr. Cooper's? I should think you had! Who's Dr. Cooper?"

"Where Miss Crowe's staying."

"Miss Crowe? Ah, Mrs. Little-field's friend! Is she as pretty as ever?"

"Prettier, — prettier, — prettier. *Tara-ta! tara-ta!*"

"Oh, Robert, do stop that singing! You'll rouse the whole house."

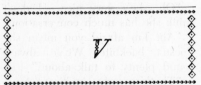

LATE one afternoon, at dusk, about three weeks after Mr. Bruce's arrival, Lizzie was sitting alone by the fire, in Miss Cooper's parlor, musing, as became the place and hour. The Doctor and his sister came in, dressed for a lecture.

"I'm sorry you won't go, my dear," said Miss Cooper. "It's a most interesting subject: 'A Year of the War.' All the battles and things described, you know."

"I'm tired of war," said Lizzie.

"Well, well, if you're tired of the war, we'll leave you in peace.

Kiss me good-bye. What's the matter? You look sick. You are homesick, a'n't you?"

"No, no, — I'm very well."

"Would you like me to stay at home with you?"

"Oh, no! pray, don't!"

"Well, we'll tell you all about it. Will they have programmes, James? I'll bring her a programme. — But you really feel as if you were going to be ill. Feel of her skin, James."

"No, you needn't, Sir," said Lizzie. "How queer of you, Miss Cooper! I'm perfectly well."

And at last her friends departed. Before long the servant came with the lamp, ushering Mr. Mackenzie.

"Good evening, Miss," said he. Bad news from Mrs. Ford."

"Bad news?"

"Yes, Miss. I've just got a letter stating that Mr. John is growing worse and worse, and that they look for his death from hour to hour. — It's very sad," he added, as Elizabeth was silent.

"Yes, it's very sad," said Lizzie.

"I thought you'd like to hear it."

"Thank you."

"He was a very noble young fellow," pursued Mr. Mackenzie. Lizzie made no response.

"There's the letter," said Mr. Mackenzie, handing it over to her. Lizzie opened it.

"How long she is reading it!" thought her visitor. "You can't see so far from the light, can you, Miss?"

"Yes," said Lizzie. — "His poor mother! Poor woman!"

"Ay, indeed, Miss, — she's the one to be pitied."

"Yes, she's the one to be pitied," said Lizzie. "Well!" and she gave him back the letter.

"I thought you'd like to see it," said Mackenzie, drawing on his gloves; and then, after a pause, — "I'll call again, Miss, if I hear anything more. Good night!"

Lizzie got up and lowered the light, and then went back to her sofa by the fire.

Half an hour passed; it went slowly; but it passed. Still lying there in the dark room on the sofa, Lizzie heard a ring at the doorbell, a man's voice and a man's tread in the hall. She rose and went to the lamp. As she turned it up, the parlor-door opened. Bruce came in.

"I was sitting in the dark," said Lizzie; "but when I heard you coming, I raised the light."

"Are you afraid of me?" said Bruce.

"Oh, no! I'll put it down again. Sit down."

"I saw your friends going out," pursued Bruce; "so I knew I should find you alone. — What are you doing here in the dark?"

"I've just received very bad news from Mrs. Ford about her son. He's much worse, and will probably not live."

"Is it possible?"

"I was thinking about that."

"Dear me! Well that's a sad subject. I'm told he was a very fine young man."

"He was, — very," said Lizzie.

Bruce was silent awhile. He was a stranger to the young officer, and felt that he had nothing to offer beyond the commonplace expressions of sympathy and surprise. Nor had he exactly the measure of his companion's interest in him.

"If he dies," said Lizzie, "it will be under great injustice."

"Ah! what do you mean?"

"There wasn't a braver man in the army."

"I suppose not."

"And, oh, Mr. Bruce," continued Lizzie, "he was so clever and good and generous! I wish you had known him."

"I wish I had. But what do you mean by injustice? Were these qualities denied him?"

"No indeed! Every one that looked at him could see that he was perfect."

"Where's the injustice, then? It ought to be enough for him that you should think so highly of him."

"Oh, he knew that," said Lizzie.

Bruce was a little puzzled by his companion's manner. He watched her, as she sat with her cheek on her hand, looking at the fire. There was a long pause. Either they were too friendly or too thoughtful for the silence to be embarrassing. Bruce broke it at last.

"Miss Crowe," said he, "on a certain occasion, some time ago, when you first heard of Mr. Ford's wounds, I offered you my company, with the wish to console you as far as I might for what seemed a considerable shock. It was, perhaps, a bold offer for so new a friend; but, nevertheless, in it even then my heart spoke. You turned me off. Will you let me repeat it? Now, with a better right, will you let me speak out all my heart?"

Lizzie heard this speech, which was delivered in a slow and hesitating tone, without looking up or moving her head, except, perhaps, at the words "turned me off." After Bruce had ceased, she still kept her position.

"You'll not turn me off now?" added her companion.

She dropped her hand, raised her head, and looked at him a moment: he thought he saw the glow of tears in her eyes. Then she sank back upon the sofa with her face in the shadow of the mantelpiece.

"I don't understand you, Mr. Bruce," said she.

"Ah, Elizabeth! am I such a poor speaker. How shall I make it plain? When I saw your friends leave home half an hour ago, and reflected that you would probably be alone, I determined to go right in and have a talk with you that I've long been wanting to have. But first I walked half a mile up the road, thinking hard, — thinking how I should say what I had to say. I made up my mind to nothing, but that somehow or other I should say it. I would trust, — I *do* trust to your frankness, kindness, and sympathy, to a feeling corresponding to my own. Do you understand that feeling? Do you know that I love you? I do, I do,

I do! You *must* know it. If you don't, I solemnly swear it. I solemnly ask you, Elizabeth, to take me for your husband."

While Bruce said these words, he rose, with their rising passion, and came and stood before Lizzie. Again she was motionless.

"Does it take you so long to think?" said he, trying to read her indistinct features; and he sat down on the sofa beside her and took her hand.

At last Lizzie spoke.

"Are you sure," said she, "that you love me?"

"As sure as that I breathe. Now, Elizabeth, make me as sure that I am loved in return."

"It seems very strange, Mr. Bruce," said Lizzie.

"What seems strange? Why should it? For a month I've been trying, in a hundred dumb ways, to make it plain; and now, when I swear it, it only seems strange!"

"What do you love me for?"

"For? For yourself, Elizabeth."

"Myself? I am nothing."

"I love you for what you are, — for your deep, kind heart, — for being so perfectly a woman."

Lizzie drew away her hand, and her lover rose and stood before her again. But now she looked up into his face, questioning when she should have answered, drinking strength from his entreaties for her replies. There he stood before her, in the glow of the firelight, in all his gentlemanhood, for her to accept or reject. She slowly rose and gave him the hand she had withdrawn.

The Story of a Year

"Mr. Bruce, I shall be very proud to love you," she said.

And then, as if this effort was beyond her strength, she half staggered back to the sofa again. And still holding her hand, he sat down beside her. And there they were still sitting when they heard the Doctor and his sister come in.

For three days Elizabeth saw nothing of Mr. Mackenzie. At last, on the fourth day, passing his office in the village, she went in and asked for him. He came out of his little back parlor with his mouth full and a beaming face.

"Good-day, Miss Crowe, and good news!"

"*Good* news?" cried Lizzie.

"Capital!" said he, looking hard at her, while he put on his spectacles. "She writes that Mr. John — won't you take a seat? — has taken a sudden and unexpected turn for the better. Now's the moment to save him; it's an equal risk. They were to start for the North the second day after date. The surgeon comes with them. So they'll be home — of course they'll travel slowly — in four or five days. Yes, Miss, it's a remarkable Providence. And that noble young man will be spared to the country, and to those who love him, as I do."

"I had better go back to the house and have it got ready," said Lizzie, for an answer.

"Yes, Miss, I think you had. In fact, Mrs. Ford made that request."

The request was obeyed. That same day Lizzie went home. For two days she found it her interest to overlook, assiduously, a general sweeping, scrubbing, and provisioning. She allowed herself no idle moment until bed-time. Then — But I would rather not be the chamberlain of her agony. It was the easier to work, as Mr. Bruce had gone to Leatherborough on business.

On the fourth evening, at twilight, John Ford was borne up to the door on his stretcher, with his mother stalking beside him in rigid grief, and kind, silent friends pressing about with helping hands.

"Home they brought her warrior dead,
She nor swooned nor uttered cry."

It was, indeed, almost a question, whether Jack was not dead. Death is not thinner, paler, stiller. Lizzie moved about like one in a dream. Of course, when there are so many sympathetic friends, a man's family has nothing to do, — except exercise a little self-control. The women huddled Mrs. Ford to bed; rest was imperative; she was killing herself. And it was significant of her weakness that she did not resent this advice. In greeting her, Lizzie felt as if she were embracing the stone image on the top of a sepulchre. She, too, had her cares anticipated. Good Doctor Cooper and his sister stationed themselves at the young man's couch.

The Doctor prophesied wondrous things of the change of climate; he was certain of a recovery. Lizzie found herself very shortly dealt with as an obstacle to this consummation. Access to John was prohibited. "Perfect stillness, you know, my dear," whispered Miss Cooper, opening his chamber-door on a crack, in a pair of very creaking shoes. So for the first evening that her old friend was at home Lizzie caught but a glimpse of his pale, senseless face, as she hovered outside the long train of his attendants. If we may suppose any of these kind people to have had eyes for aught but the sufferer, we may be sure that they saw another visage equally sad and white. The sufferer? It was hardly Jack, after all.

When Lizzie was turned from Jack's door, she took a covering from a heap of draperies that had been hurriedly tossed down in the hall: it was an old army-blanket. She wrapped it round her, and went out on the veranda. It was nine o'clock; but the darkness was filled with light. A great wanton wind — the ghost of the raw blast which travels by day — had arisen, bearing long, soft gusts of inland spring. Scattered clouds were hurrying across the white sky. The bright moon, careering in their midst, seemed to have wandered forth in frantic quest of the hidden stars.

Lizzie nestled her head in the blanket, and sat down on the steps. A strange earthly smell lingered in that faded old rug, and with it a faint perfume of tobacco. Instantly the young girl's senses were transported as they had never been before to those far-off Southern battle-fields. She saw men lying in swamps, puffing their kindly pipes, drawing their blankets closer, canopied with the same luminous dusk that shone down upon her comfortable weakness. Her mind wandered amid these scenes till recalled to the present by the swinging of the garden-gate. She heard a firm, well-known tread crunching the gravel. Mr. Bruce came up the path. As he drew near the steps, Lizzie arose. The blanket fell back from her head, and Bruce started at recognizing her.

"Hullo! You, Elizabeth? What's the matter?"

Lizzie made no answer.

"Are you one of Mr. Ford's watchers?" he continued, coming up the steps; "how is he?"

Still she was silent. Bruce put out his hands to take hers, and bent forward as if to kiss her. She half shook him off, and retreated toward the door.

"Good heavens!" cried Bruce; "what's the matter? Are you moon-struck? Can't you speak?"

"No, — no, — not to-night," said Lizzie, in a choking voice. "Go away, — go away!"

She stood holding the door-handle, and motioning him off. He hesitated a moment, and then advanced. She opened the door rapidly, and went in. He heard her lock it. He stood looking at it stupidly for some time, and then slowly turned round and walked down the steps.

The next morning Lizzie arose with the early dawn, and came down stairs. She went into the room where Jack lay, and gently opened the door. Miss Cooper was dozing in her chair. Lizzie crossed the threshold, and stole up to the bed. Poor Ford lay peacefully sleeping. There was his old face, after all, — his strong, honest features refined, but not weakened, by pain. Lizzie softly drew up a low chair, and sat down beside him. She gazed into his face, — the dear and honored face into which she had so often gazed in health. It was strangely handsomer: body stood for less. It seemed to Lizzie, that, as the fabric of her lover's soul was more clearly revealed, — the veil of the temple rent wellnigh in twain, — she could read the justification of all her old worship. One of Jack's hands lay outside the sheets, — those strong, supple fingers, once so cunning in workmanship, so frank in friendship, now thinner and whiter than her own. After looking at it for some time, Lizzie gently grasped it. Jack slowly opened his eyes. Lizzie's heart began to throb; it was as if the stillness of the sanctuary had given a sign. At first there was no recognition in the young man's gaze. Then the dull pupils began visibly to brighten. There came to his lips the commencement of that strange moribund smile which seems so ineffably satirical of the things of this world. O imposing spectacle of death! O blessed soul, marked for promotion! What earthly favor is like thine? Lizzie sank down on her knees, and, still clasping John's hand, bent closer over him.

"Jack, — dear, dear Jack," she whispered, "do you know me?"

The smile grew more intense. The poor fellow drew out his other hand, and slowly, feebly placed it on Lizzie's head, stroking down her hair with his fingers.

"Yes, yes," she murmured; "you know me, don't you? I am Lizzie, Jack. Don't you remember Lizzie?"

Ford moved his lips inaudibly, and went on patting her head.

"This is home, you know," said Lizzie; "this is Glenham. You haven't forgotten Glenham? You are with your mother and me and your friends. Dear, darling Jack!"

Still he went on, stroking her head; and his feeble lips tried to emit some sound. Lizzie laid her head down on the pillow beside his own, and still his hand lingered caressingly on her hair.

"Yes, you know me," she pursued; "you are with your friends now forever, — with those who will love and take care of you, oh, forever!"

"I'm very badly wounded," murmured Jack, close to her ear.

"Yes, yes, my dear boy, but your wounds are healing. I will love you and nurse you forever."

"Yes, Lizzie, our old promise," said Jack: and his hand fell upon her neck, and with its feeble pressure he drew her closer, and she wet his face with her tears.

Then Miss Cooper, awakening, rose and drew Lizzie away.

"I am sure you excite him, my dear. It is best he should have none of his family near him, — persons with whom he has associations, you know."

Here the Doctor was heard

gently tapping on the window, and Lizzie went round to the door to admit him.

She did not see Jack again all day. Two or three times she ventured into the room, but she was banished by a frown, or a finger raised to the lips. She waylaid the Doctor frequently. He was blithe and cheerful, certain of Jack's recovery. This good man used to exhibit as much moral elation at the prospect of a cure as an orthodox believer at that of a new convert: it was one more body gained from the Devil. He assured Lizzie that the change of scene and climate had already begun to tell: the fever was lessening, the worst symptoms disappearing. He answered Lizzie's reiterated desire to do something by directions to keep the house quiet and the sick-room empty.

Soon after breakfast, Miss Dawes, a neighbor, came in to relieve Miss Cooper, and this indefatigable lady transferred her attention to Mrs. Ford. Action was forbidden her. Miss Cooper was delighted for once to be able to lay down the law to her vigorous neighbor, of whose fine judgment she had always stood in awe. Having bullied Mrs. Ford into taking her breakfast in the little sitting-room, she closed the doors, and prepared for "a good long talk." Lizzie was careful not to break in upon this interview. She had bidden her patroness good morning, asked after her health, and received one of her temperate osculations. As she passed the invalid's door, Doctor Cooper came out and asked her to go and look for a certain roll of bandages, in Mr. John's trunk, which had been carried into another room. Lizzie hastened to perform this task. In fumbling through the contents of the trunk, she came across a packet of letters in a well-known feminine handwriting. She pocketed it, and, after disposing of the bandages, went to her own room, locked the door, and sat down to examine the letters. Between reading and thinking and sighing and (in spite of herself) smiling, this process took the whole morning. As she came down to dinner, she encountered Mrs. Ford and Miss Cooper, emerging from the sitting-room, the good long talk being only just concluded.

"How do you feel, Ma'am?" she asked of the elder lady, — "rested?"

For all answer Mrs. Ford gave a look — I had almost said a scowl — so hard, so cold, so reproachful, that Lizzie was transfixed. But suddenly its sickening meaning was revealed to her. She turned to Miss Cooper, who stood pale and fluttering beside the mistress, her everlasting smile glazed over with a piteous, deprecating glance; and I fear her eyes flashed out the same message of angry scorn they had just received. These telegraphic operations are very rapid. The ladies hardly halted: the next moment found them seated at the dinner-table with Miss Cooper scrutinizing her napkin-mark and Mrs. Ford saying grace.

Dinner was eaten in silence.

The Story of a Year

When it was over, Lizzie returned to her own room. Miss Cooper went home, and Mrs. Ford went to her son. Lizzie heard the firm low click of the lock as she closed the door. Why did she lock it? There was something fatal in the silence that followed. The plot of her little tragedy thickened. Be it so: she would act her part with the rest. For the second time in her experience, her mind was lightened by the intervention of Mrs. Ford. Before the scorn of her own conscience, (which never came,) before Jack's deepest reproach, she was ready to bow down, — but not before that long-faced Nemesis in black silk. The leaven of resentment began to work. She leaned back in her chair, and folded her arms, brave to await results. But before long she fell asleep. She was aroused by a knock at her chamber-door. The afternoon was far gone. Miss Dawes stood without.

"Elizabeth, Mr. John wants very much to see you, with his love. Come down very gently: his mother is lying down. Will you sit with him while I take my dinner? Better? Yes, ever so much."

Lizzie betook herself with trembling haste to Jack's bedside.

He was propped up with pillows. His pale cheeks were slightly flushed. His eyes were bright. He raised himself, and, for such feeble arms, gave Lizzie a long, strong embrace.

"I've not seen you all day, Lizzie," said he. "Where have you been?"

"Dear Jack, they wouldn't let me come near you. I begged and prayed. And I wanted so to go to you in the army; but I couldn't. I wish, I wish I had!"

"You wouldn't have liked it, Lizzie. I'm glad you didn't. It's a bad, bad place."

He lay quietly, holding her hands and gazing at her.

"Can I do anything for you, dear?" asked the young girl. "I would work my life out. I'm so glad you're better!"

It was some time before Jack answered, —

"Lizzie," said he, at last, "I sent for you to look at you. — You are more wondrously beautiful than ever. Your hair is brown, — like — like nothing; your eyes are blue; your neck is white. Well, well!"

He lay perfectly motionless, but for his eyes. They wandered over her with a kind of peaceful glee, like sunbeams playing on a statue. Poor Ford lay, indeed, not unlike an old wounded Greek, who at falling dusk has crawled into a temple to die, steeping the last dull interval in idle admiration of sculptured Artemis.

"Ah, Lizzie, this is already heaven!" he murmured.

"It will be heaven when you get well," whispered Lizzie.

He smiled into her eyes: —

"You say more than you mean. There should be perfect truth between us. Dear Lizzie, I am not going to get well. They are all very much mistaken. I am going to die. I've done my work. Death makes up for everything. My great

35

pain is in leaving you. But you, too, will die one of these days; remember that. In all pain and sorrow, remember that."

Lizzie was able to reply only by the tightening grasp of her hands.

"But there is something more," pursued Jack. "Life *is* as good as death. Your heart has found its true keeper; so we shall all three be happy. Tell him I bless him and honor him. Tell him God, too, blesses him. Shake hands with him for me," said Jack, feebly moving his pale fingers. "My mother," he went on, — "be very kind to her. She will have great grief, but she will not die of it. She'll live to great age. Now, Lizzie, I can't talk any more; I wanted to say farewell. You'll keep me farewell, — you'll stay with me awhile, —won't you? I'll look at you till the last. For a little while you'll be mine, holding my hands — so — until death parts us."

Jack kept his promise. His eyes were fixed in a firm gaze long after the sense had left them.

In the early dawn of the next day, Elizabeth left her sleepless bed, opened the window, and looked out on the wide prospect, still cool and dim with departing night. It offered freshness and peace to her hot head and restless heart. She dressed herself hastily, crept down stairs, passed the death-chamber, and stole out of the quiet house. She turned away from the still sleeping village and walked towards the open country. She went a long way without knowing it. The sun had risen high when she bethought herself to turn. As she came back along the brightening highway, and drew near home, she saw a tall figure standing beneath the budding trees of the garden, hesitating, apparently, whether to open the gate. Lizzie came upon him almost before he had seen her. Bruce's first movement was to put out his hands, as any lover might; but as Lizzie raised her veil, he dropped them.

"Yes, Mr. Bruce," said Lizzie, "I'll give you my hand once more, — in farewell."

"Elizabeth!" cried Bruce, half stupefied, "in God's name, what do you mean by these crazy speeches?"

"I mean well. I mean kindly and humanely to you. And I mean justice to my old — old love."

She went to him, took his listless hand, without looking into his wild smitten face, shook it passionately, and then, wrenching her own from his grasp, opened the gate and let it swing behind her. "No! no! no!" she almost shrieked, turning about in the path. "I forbid you to follow me!" But for all that, he went in.

THE EUROPEANS

A NARROW grave-yard in the heart of a bustling, indifferent city, seen from the windows of a gloomy-looking inn, is at no time an object of enlivening suggestion; and the spectacle is not at its best when the mouldy tombstones and funereal umbrage have received the ineffectual refreshment of a dull, moist snow-fall. If, while the air is thickened by this frosty drizzle, the calendar should happen to indicate that the blessed vernal season is already six weeks old, it will be admitted that no depressing influence is absent from the scene. This fact was keenly felt on a certain 12th of May, upwards of thirty years since, by a lady who stood looking out of one of the windows of the best hotel in the ancient city of Boston. She had stood there for half an hour — stood there, that is, at intervals; for from time to time she turned back into the room and measured its length with a restless step. In the chimney-place was a red-hot fire which emitted a small blue flame; and in front of the fire, at a table, sat a young man who was busily plying a pencil. He had a number of sheets of paper cut into small equal squares, and he was apparently covering them with pictorial designs — strange-looking figures. He worked rapidly and attentively, sometimes threw back his head and held out his drawing at arm's-length, and kept up a soft, gay-sounding humming and whistling. The lady brushed past him in her walk; her much-trimmed skirts were voluminous. She never dropped her eyes upon his work; she only turned them, occasionally, as she passed, to a mirror suspended above the toilet-table on the other side of the room. Here she paused a moment, gave a pinch to her waist with her two hands, or raised these members — they were very plump and pretty — to the multifold braids of her hair, with a movement half caressing, half corrective. An attentive observer might have fancied that during these periods of desultory self-inspection her face forgot its melancholy; but as soon as she neared the window again it began to proclaim that she was a very ill-pleased woman. And indeed, in what met her eyes there was little to be pleased with. The window-panes were battered by the sleet; the headstones in the grave-yard beneath seemed to be holding themselves askance to keep it out of their faces. A tall iron railing protected them from the street, and on the other side of the railing an assemblage of Bostonians were trampling about in the liquid snow. Many of them were looking up and down; they appeared to be waiting for something. From time to time a strange vehicle drew near to the place where they stood, — such a vehicle as the lady at the window, in spite of a considerable acquaintance with human inventions, had never seen before: a huge, low omnibus, painted in brilliant colors, and decorated apparently with jangling bells, attached to a species of groove in the pavement, through which it was dragged, with a great deal of rumbling, bouncing and scratching, by a couple of remarkably small horses. When it reached a certain point the people in front of the graveyard, of whom much the greater number were women, carrying satchel and parcels, projected themselves upon it in a compact body — a movement suggesting the scramble for places in a life-boat at sea — and were engulfed in its large interior. Then the life-boat — or the life-car, as the lady at the window of the hotel vaguely designated it — went bumping and jingling away upon its invisible wheels, with the helmsman (the man at the wheel) guiding its course incongruously from the prow. This phenomenon was repeated every three minutes, and the supply of eagerly-moving women in cloaks, bearing reticules and bundles, renewed itself in the most liberal manner. On the other side of the grave-yard was a row of small red brick houses, showing a series of homely, domestic-looking backs; at the end opposite the hotel a tall wooden church-spire, painted white, rose high into the vagueness of the snow-flakes. The lady at the window looked at it for some time; for reasons of her own she thought it the ugliest thing she had ever seen. She hated it, she despised it; it threw her into a state of irritation that was quite out of proportion to any sensible motives. She had never known herself to care so much about church-spires.

She was not pretty; but even when it expressed perplexed irritation her face was most interesting and agreeable. Neither was she in her first youth; yet, though slender, with a great deal of extremely well-fashioned roundness of contour — a suggestion both of maturity and flexibility — she carried her three and thirty years as a light-wristed Hebe might have carried a brimming wine-cup. Her complexion was fatigued, as the French say; her mouth was large, her lips too full, her teeth uneven, her chin rather commonly modeled; she had a thick nose, and when she smiled — she was constantly smiling — the lines beside it rose too high, toward her eyes. But these eyes were charming: gray in color, brilliant, quickly glancing, gently resting, full of intelligence. Her forehead was very low — it was her only handsome feature; and she had a great abundance of crisp dark hair, finely frizzled, which was always braided in a manner that suggested some Southern or Eastern, some remotely foreign, woman. She had a large collection of ear-rings, and wore them in alternation; and they seemed to give a point to her Oriental or exotic aspect. A compliment had once been paid her, which, being repeated to her, gave her greater pleasure than anything she had ever heard. "A pretty woman?" some one had said. "Why, her features are very bad." "I don't know about her features," a very discerning observer had answered; "but she carries her head like a pretty woman." You may imagine whether, after this, she carried her head less becomingly.

She turned away from the window at last, pressing her hand to her eyes. "It's too horrible!" she exclaimed. "I shall go back — I shall go back!" And she flung herself into a chair before the fire.

"Wait a little, dear child," said the young man softly, sketching away at his little scraps of paper.

The lady put out her foot; it was very small, and there was an immense rosette on her slipper. She fixed her eyes for a while on this ornament, and then she looked at the glowing bed of anthracite coal in the grate. "Did you ever see anything so hideous as that fire?" she demanded. "Did you ever see anything so — so *affreux* as — as everything?" She spoke English with perfect purity; but she brought out this French epithet in a manner that indicated that she was accustomed to using French epithets.

"I think the fire is very pretty," said the young man, glancing at it a moment. "Those little blue tongues, dancing on top of the crimson embers, are extremely picturesque. They are like a fire in an alchemist's laboratory."

"You are too good-natured, my dear," his companion declared.

The young man held out one of his drawings, with his head on one side. His tongue was gently moving along his under-lip. "Good-natured — yes. Too good-natured — no."

"You are irritating," said the lady, looking at her slipper.

He began to retouch his sketch. "I think you mean simply that you are irritated."

"Ah, for that, yes!" said his companion, with a little bitter laugh. "It's the darkest day of my life — and you know what that means."

"Wait till to-morrow," rejoined the young man.

"Yes, we have made a great mistake. If there is any doubt about it to-day, there certainly will be none to-morrow. Ce sera clair, au moins!"

The young man was silent a few moments, driving his pencil. Then at last, "There are no such things as mistakes," he affirmed.

"Very true — for those who are not clever enough to perceive them. Not to recognize one's mistakes — that would be happiness in life," the lady went on, still looking at her pretty foot.

"My dearest sister," said the young man, always intent upon

his drawing, "it's the first time you have told me I am not clever."

"Well, by your own theory I can't call it a mistake," answered his sister, pertinently enough.

The young man gave a clear, fresh laugh. "You, at least, are clever enough, dearest sister," he said.

"I was not so when I proposed this."

"Was it you who proposed it?" asked her brother.

She turned her head and gave him a little stare. "Do you desire the credit of it?"

"If you like, I will take the blame," he said, looking up with a smile.

"Yes," she rejoined in a moment, "you make no difference in these things. You have no sense of property."

The young man gave his joyous laugh again. "If that means I have no property, you are right!"

"Don't joke about your poverty," said his sister. "That is quite as vulgar as to boast about it."

"My poverty! I have just finished a drawing that will bring me fifty francs!"

"Voyons," said the lady, putting out her hand.

He added a touch or two, and then gave her his sketch. She looked at it, but she went on with her idea of a moment before. "If a woman were to ask you to marry her you would say, 'Certainly, my dear, with pleasure!' And you would marry her and be ridiculously happy. Then at the end of three months you would say to

her, 'You know that blissful day when I begged you to be mine!'"

The young man had risen from the table, stretching his arms a little; he walked to the window. "That is a description of a charming nature," he said.

"Oh, yes, you have a charming nature; I regard that as our capital. If I had not been convinced of that I should never have taken the risk of bringing you to this dreadful country."

"This comical country, this delightful country!" exclaimed the young man, and he broke into the most animated laughter.

"Is it those women scrambling into the omnibus?" asked his companion. "What do you suppose is the attraction?"

"I suppose there is a very good-looking man inside," said the young man.

"In each of them? They come along in hundreds, and the men in this country don't seem at all handsome. As for the women — I have never seen so many at once since I left the convent."

"The women are very pretty," her brother declared, "and the whole affair is very amusing. I must make a sketch of it." And he came back to the table quickly, and picked up his utensils — a small sketching-board, a sheet of paper, and three or four crayons. He took his place at the window with these things, and stood there glancing out, plying his pencil with an air of easy skill. While he worked he wore a brilliant smile. Brilliant is indeed the word at this moment for his strongly-lighted face. He was eight and twenty years old; he had a short, slight, well-made figure. Though he bore a noticeable resemblance to his sister, he was a better favored person: fair-haired, clear-faced, witty-looking, with a delicate finish of feature and an expression at once urbane and not at all serious, a warm blue eye, and eyebrow finely drawn and excessively arched — an eyebrow which, if ladies wrote sonnets to those of their lovers, might have been made the subject of such a piece of verse — and a light moustache that flourished upwards as if blown that way by the breath of a constant smile. There was something in his physiognomy at once benevolent and picturesque. But, as I have hinted, it was not at all serious. The young man's face was, in this respect, singular; it was not at all serious, and yet it inspired the liveliest confidence.

"Be sure you put in plenty of snow," said his sister. "Bonté divine, what a climate!"

"I shall leave the sketch all white, and I shall put in the little figures in black," the young man answered, laughing. "And I shall call it — what is that line in Keats? — Mid-May's Eldest Child!"

"I don't remember," said the lady, "that mamma ever told me it was like this."

"Mamma never told you anything disagreeable. And it's not like this — every day. You will see that to-morrow we shall have a splendid day."

"Qu'en savez-vous? To-morrow I shall go away."

"Where shall you go?"

"Anywhere away from here. Back to Silberstadt. I shall write to the Reigning Prince."

The young man turned a little and looked at her, with his crayon poised. "My dear Eugenia," he murmured, "were you so happy at sea?"

Eugenia got up; she still held in her hand the drawing her brother had given her. It was a bold, expressive sketch of a group of miserable people on the deck of a steamer, clinging together and clutching at each other, while the vessel lurched downward, at a terrific angle, into the hollow of a wave. It was extremely clever, and full of a sort of tragi-comical power. Eugenia dropped her eyes upon it and made a sad grimace. "How can you draw such odious scenes?" she asked. "I should like to throw it into the fire!" And she tossed the paper away. Her brother watched, quietly, to see where it went. It fluttered down to the floor, where he let it lie. She came toward the window, pinching in her waist. "Why don't you reproach me — abuse me?" she asked. "I think I should feel better then. Why don't you tell me that you hate me for bringing you here?"

"Because you would not believe it. I adore you, dear sister! I am delighted to be here, and I am charmed with the prospect."

"I don't know what had taken possession of me. I had lost my head," Eugenia went on.

The young man, on his side, went on plying his pencil. "It is evidently a most curious and interesting country. Here we are, and I mean to enjoy it."

His companion turned away with an impatient step, but presently came back. "High spirits are doubtless an excellent thing," she said; "but you give one too much of them, and I can't see that they have done you any good."

The young man stared, with lifted eyebrows, smiling; he tapped his handsome nose with his pencil. "They have made me happy!"

"That was the least they could do; they have made you nothing else. You have gone through life thanking fortune for such very small favors that she has never put herself to any trouble for you."

"She must have put herself to a little, I think, to present me with so admirable a sister."

"Be serious, Felix. You forget that I am your elder."

"With a sister, then, so elderly!" rejoined Felix, laughing. "I hoped we had left seriousness in Europe."

"I fancy you will find it here. Remember that you are nearly thirty years old, and that you are nothing but an obscure Bohemian — a penniless correspondent of an illustrated newspaper."

"Obscure as much as you please, but not so much of a Bohemian as you think. And not at all penniless! I have a hundred pounds in my pocket. I have an engagement to make fifty sketches, and I mean to paint the portraits of all our cousins, and of all *their* cousins, at a hundred dollars a head."

"You are not ambitious," said Eugenia.

"You are, dear Baroness," the young man replied.

The Baroness was silent a moment, looking out at the sleet-darkened grave-yard and the bumping horse-cars. "Yes, I am ambitious," she said at last. "And my ambition has brought me to this dreadful place!" She glanced about her — the room had a certain vulgar nudity; the bed and the window were curtainless — and she gave a little passionate sigh. "Poor old ambition!" she exclaimed. Then she flung herself down upon a sofa which stood near against the wall, and covered her face with her hands.

Her brother went on with his drawing, rapidly and skillfully; after some moments he sat down beside her and showed her his sketch. "Now, don't you think that's pretty good for an obscure Bohemian?" he asked. "I have knocked off another fifty francs."

Eugenia glanced at the little picture as he laid it on her lap. "Yes, it is very clever," she said. And in a moment she added, "Do you suppose our cousins do that?"

"Do what?"

"Get into those things, and look like that."

Felix meditated awhile. "I really can't say. It will be interesting to discover."

"Oh, the rich people can't!" said the Baroness.

"Are you very sure they are rich?" asked Felix, lightly.

His sister slowly turned in her place, looking at him. "Heavenly powers!" she murmured. "You have a way of bringing out things!"

"It will certainly be much pleasanter if they are rich," Felix declared.

"Do you suppose if I had not known they were rich I would ever have come?"

The young man met his sister's somewhat peremptory eye with his bright, contented glance. "Yes, it certainly will be pleasanter," he repeated.

"That is all I expect of them," said the Baroness. "I don't count upon their being clever or friendly — at first — or elegant or interesting. But I assure you I insist upon their being rich."

Felix leaned his head upon the back of the sofa and looked awhile at the oblong patch of sky to which the window served as frame. The snow was ceasing; it seemed to him that the sky had begun to brighten. "I count upon their being rich," he said at last, "and powerful, and clever, and friendly, and elegant, and interesting, and generally delightful! Tu vas voir." And he bent forward and kissed his sister. "Look there!" he went on. "As a portent, even while I speak, the sky is turning the color of gold; the day is going to be splendid."

And indeed, within five minutes the weather had changed. The sun broke out through the snow-clouds and jumped into the Baroness's

room. "Bonté divine," exclaimed this lady, "what a climate!"

"We will go out and see the world," said Felix.

And after a while they went out. The air had grown warm as well as brilliant; the sunshine had dried the pavements. They walked about the streets at hazard, looking at the people and the houses, the shops and the vehicles, the blazing blue sky and the muddy crossings, the hurrying men and the slow-strolling maidens, the fresh red bricks and the bright green trees, the extraordinary mixture of smartness and shabbiness. From one hour to another the day had grown vernal; even in the bustling streets there was an odor of earth and blossom. Felix was immensely entertained. He had called it a comical country, and he went about laughing at everything he saw. You would have said that American civilization expressed itself to his sense in a tissue of capital jokes. The jokes were certainly excellent, and the young man's merriment was joyous and genial. He possessed what is called the pictorial sense; and this first glimpse of democratic manners stirred the same sort of attention that he would have given to the movements of a lively young person with a bright complexion. Such attention would have been demonstrative and complimentary; and in the present case Felix might have passed for an undispirited young exile revisiting the haunts of his childhood. He kept looking at the violent blue of the sky, at the scintillating air, at the scattered and multiplied patches of color.

"Comme c'est bariolé, eh?" he said to his sister in that foreign tongue which they both appeared to feel a mysterious prompting occasionally to use.

"Yes, it is bariolé indeed," the Baroness answered. "I don't like the coloring; it hurts my eyes."

"It shows how extremes meet," the young man rejoined. "Instead of coming to the West we seem to have gone to the East. The way the sky touches the house-tops is just like Cairo; and the red and blue sign-boards patched over the face of everything remind one of Mahometan decorations."

"The young women are not Mahometan," said his companion. "They can't be said to hide their faces. I never saw anything so bold."

"Thank Heaven they don't hide their faces!" cried Felix. "Their faces are uncommonly pretty."

"Yes, their faces are often very pretty," said the Baroness, who was a very clever woman. She was too clever a woman not to be capable of a great deal of just and fine observation. She clung more closely than usual to her brother's arm; she was not exhilarated, as he was; she said very little, but she noted a great many things and made her reflections. She was a little excited; she felt that she had indeed come to a strange country, to make her fortune. Superficially, she was conscious of a good deal of irritation and displeasure; the Baroness was a very delicate and fastidious person. Of old, more than once, she had gone, for entertainment's sake and in brilliant company, to a fair in a provincial town. It seemed to her now that she was at an enormous fair — that the entertainment and the désagréments were very much the same. She found herself alternately smiling and shrinking; the show was very curious, but it was probable, from moment to moment, that one would be jostled. The Baroness had never seen so many people walking about before; she had never been so mixed up with people she did not know. But little by little she felt that this fair was a more serious undertaking. She went with her brother into a large public garden, which seemed very pretty, but where she was surprised at seeing no carriages. The afternoon was drawing to a close; the coarse, vivid grass and the slender tree-boles were gilded by the level sunbeams — gilded as with gold that was fresh from the mine. It was the hour at which ladies should come out for an airing and roll past a hedge of pedestrians, holding their parasols askance. Here, however, Eugenia observed no indications of this custom, the absence of which was more anomalous as there was a charming avenue of remarkably graceful, arching elms in the most convenient contiguity to a large, cheerful street, in which, evidently, among the more prosperous members of the bourgeoisie, a great deal of pedestrianism went forward. Our friends passed out into this well lighted promenade, and Felix noticed a great many more pretty girls and called his sister's attention to them. This latter measure, however, was superfluous; for the Baroness had inspected, narrowly, these charming young ladies.

"I feel an intimate conviction that our cousins are like that," said Felix.

The Baroness hoped so, but this is not what she said. "They are very pretty," she said, "but they are mere little girls. Where are the women — the women of thirty?"

"Of thirty-three, do you mean?" her brother was going to ask; for he understood often both what she said and what she did not say. But he only exclaimed upon the beauty of the sunset, while the Baroness, who had come to seek her fortune, reflected that it would certainly be well for her if the persons against whom she might need to measure herself should all be mere little girls. The sunset was superb; they stopped to look at it; Felix declared that he had never seen such a gorgeous mixture of colors. The Baroness also thought it splendid; and she was perhaps the more easily pleased from the fact that while she stood there she was conscious of much admiring observation on the part of various nice-looking people who passed that way, and to whom a distinguished, strikingly-dressed woman with a foreign air, exclaiming upon the beauties of nature on a Boston street corner in the French tongue, could not be an object of indifference. Eugenia's spirits rose. She surrendered herself to a certain tranquil gayety. If she had come to seek her fortune, it seemed to her that her fortune would be easy to find. There was a promise of it in the gorgeous purity of the western sky; there was an intimation in the mild, unimpertinent gaze of the passers of a certain natural facility in things.

"You will not go back to Silberstadt, eh?" asked Felix.

"Not to-morrow," said the Baroness.

"Nor write to the Reigning Prince?"

"I shall write to him that they evidently know nothing about him over here."

"He will not believe you," said the young man. "I advise you to let him alone."

Felix himself continued to be in high good humor. Brought up among ancient customs and in picturesque cities, he yet found plenty of local color in the little Puritan metropolis. That evening, after dinner, he told his sister that he should go forth early on the morrow to look up their cousins.

"You are very impatient," said Eugenia.

"What can be more natural," he asked, "after seeing all those pretty girls today? If one's cousins are of that pattern, the sooner one knows them the better."

"Perhaps they are not," said Eugenia. "We ought to have brought some letters — to some other people."

"The other people would not be our kinsfolk."

"Possibly they would be none the worse for that," the Baroness replied.

Her brother looked at her with his eyebrows lifted. "That was not what you said when you first proposed to me that we should come out here and fraternize with our relatives. You said that it was the prompting of natural affection; and when I suggested some reasons against it you declared that the *voix du sang* should go before everything."

"You remember all that?" asked the Baroness.

"Vividly! I was greatly moved by it."

She was walking up and down the room, as she had done in the morning; she stopped in her walk and looked at her brother. She apparently was going to say something, but she checked herself and resumed her walk. Then, in a few moments, she said something different, which had the effect of an explanation of the suppression of her earlier thought. "You will never be anything but a child, dear brother."

"One would suppose that you, madam," answered Felix, laughing, "were a thousand years old."

"I am — sometimes," said the Baroness.

"I will go, then, and announce to our cousins the arrival of a personage so extraordinary. They will immediately come and pay you their respects."

Eugenia paced the length of the room again, and then she stopped before her brother, laying her hand upon his arm. "They are not to come and see me," she said. "You are not to allow that. That is not the way I shall meet them first." And in answer to his interrogative glance she went on. "You will go and examine, and report. You will come back and tell me who they are and what they are; their number, gender, their respective ages — all about them. Be sure you observe everything; be ready to describe to me the locality, the accessories — how shall I say it? — the mise en scène. Then, at my own time, at my own hour, under circumstances of my own choosing, I will go to them. I will present myself — I will appear before them!" said the Baroness, this time phrasing her idea with a certain frankness.

"And what message am I to take to them?" asked Felix, who had a lively faith in the justness of his sister's arrangements.

She looked at him a moment — at his expression of agreeable veracity; and, with that justness that he admired, she replied, "Say what you please. Tell my story in the way that seems to you most — natural." And she bent her forehead for him to kiss.

II

THE NEXT day was splendid, as Felix had prophesied; if the winter had suddenly leaped into spring, the spring had for the moment as quickly leaped into summer. This was an observation made by a young girl who came out of a large square house in the country, and strolled about in the spacious garden which separated it from a muddy road. The flowering shrubs and the neatly-disposed plants were basking in the abundant light and warmth; the transparent shade of the great elms — they were magnificent trees — seemed to thicken by the hour; and the intensely habitual stillness offered a submissive medium to the sound of a distant church-bell. The young girl listened to the church-bell; but she was not dressed for church. She was bare-headed; she wore a white muslin waist, with an embroidered border, and the skirt of her dress was of colored muslin. She was a young lady of some two or three and twenty years of age, and though a young person of her sex walking bare-headed in a garden, of a Sunday morning in spring-time, can, in the nature of things, never be a dis-pleasing object, you would not have pronounced this innocent Sabbath-breaker especially pretty. She was tall and pale, thin and a little awkward; her hair was fair and perfectly straight; her eyes were dark, and they had the sin-gularity of seeming at once dull and restless — differing herein, as you see, fatally from the ideal "fine eyes," which we always im-agine to be both brilliant and tran-quil. The doors and windows of the large square house were all wide open, to admit the purifying sunshine, which lay in generous patches upon the floor of a wide, high, covered piazza adjusted to two sides of the mansion — a piazza on which several straw-bottomed rocking-chairs and half a dozen of those small cylindrical stools in green and blue porcelain, which suggest an affiliation between the residents and the Eastern trade, were symmetrically disposed. It was an ancient house — ancient in the sense of being eighty years old; it was built of wood, painted a clean, clear, faded gray, and adorned along the front, at inter-vals, with flat wooden pilasters, painted white. These pilasters ap-peared to support a kind of classic pediment, which was decorated in the middle by a large triple win-dow in a boldly carved frame, and in each of its smaller angles by a glazed circular aperture. A large white door, furnished with a high-ly-polished brass knocker, pre-sented itself to the rural-looking road, with which it was connected by a spacious pathway, paved with worn and cracked, but very clean, bricks. Behind it there were mead-ows and orchards, a barn and a pond; and facing it, a short dis-tance along the road, on the op-posite side, stood a smaller house, painted white, with external shut-ters painted green, a little garden on one hand and an orchard on the other. All this was shining in the morning air, through which the simple details of the picture ad-dressed themselves to the eye as distinctly as the items of a "sum" in addition.

A second young lady presently came out of the house, across the piazza, descended into the garden and approached the young girl of whom I have spoken. This second young lady was also thin and pale; but she was older than the other; she was shorter; she had dark, smooth hair. Her eyes, unlike the other's, were quick and bright; but they were not at all restless. She wore a straw bonnet with white ribbons, and a long, red, India scarf, which, on the front of her dress, reached to her feet. In her hand she carried a little key.

"Gertrude," she said, "are you very sure you had better not go to church?"

Gertrude looked at her a moment, plucked a small sprig from a lilac-bush, smelled it and threw it away. "I am not very sure of anything!" she answered.

The other young lady looked straight past her, at the distant pond, which lay shining between the long banks of fir-trees. Then she said in a very soft voice, "This is the key of the dining-room closet. I think you had better have it, if any one should want anything."

"Who is there to want anything?" Gertrude demanded. "I shall be all alone in the house."

"Some one may come," said her companion.

"Do you mean Mr. Brand?"

"Yes, Gertrude. He may like a piece of cake."

"I don't like men that are always eating cake!" Gertrude declared, giving a pull at the lilac-bush.

Her companion glanced at her, and then looked down on the ground. "I think father expected you would come to church," she said. "What shall I say to him?"

"Say I have a bad headache."

"Would that be true?" asked the elder lady, looking straight at the pond again.

"No, Charlotte," said the younger one simply.

Charlotte transferred her quiet eyes to her companion's face. "I am afraid you are feeling restless."

"I am feeling as I always feel," Gertrude replied, in the same tone.

Charlotte turned away; but she stood there a moment. Presently she looked down at the front of her dress. "Doesn't it seem to you, somehow, as if my scarf were too long?" she asked.

Gertrude walked half round her, looking at the scarf. "I don't think you wear it right," she said.

"How should I wear it, dear?"

"I don't know; differently from that. You should draw it differently over your shoulders, round your elbows; you should look differently behind."

"How should I look?" Charlotte inquired.

"I don't think I can tell you," said Gertrude, plucking out the scarf a little behind. "I could do it myself, but I don't think I can explain it."

48

Charlotte, by a movement of her elbows, corrected the laxity that had come from her companion's touch. "Well, some day you must do it for me. It doesn't matter now. Indeed, I don't think it matters," she added, "how one looks behind."

"I should say it mattered more," said Gertrude. "Then you don't know who may be observing you. You are not on your guard. You can't try to look pretty."

Charlotte received this declaration with extreme gravity. "I don't think one should ever try to look pretty," she rejoined, earnestly.

Her companion was silent. Then she said, "Well, perhaps it's not of much use."

Charlotte looked at her a little, and then kissed her. "I hope you will be better when we come back."

"My dear sister, I am very well!" said Gertrude.

Charlotte went down the large brick walk to the garden gate; her companion strolled slowly toward the house. At the gate Charlotte met a young man, who was coming in — a tall, fair young man, wearing a high hat and a pair of thread gloves. He was handsome, but rather too stout. He had a pleasant smile. "Oh, Mr. Brand!" exclaimed the young lady.

"I came to see whether your sister was not going to church," said the young man.

"She says she is not going; but I am very glad you have come. I think if you were to talk to her a little" . . . . And Charlotte lowered her voice. "It seems as if she were restless."

Mr. Brand smiled down on the young lady from his great height. "I shall be very glad to talk to her. For that I should be willing to absent myself from almost any occasion of worship, however attractive."

"Well, I suppose you know," said Charlotte, softly, as if positive acceptance of this proposition might be dangerous. "But I am afraid I shall be late."

"I hope you will have a pleasant sermon," said the young man.

"Oh, Mr. Gilman is always pleasant," Charlotte answered. And she went on her way.

Mr. Brand went into the garden, where Gertrude, hearing the gate close behind him, turned and looked at him. For a moment she watched him coming; then she turned away. But almost immediately she corrected this movement, and stood still, facing him. He took off his hat and wiped his forehead as he approached. Then he put on his hat again and held out his hand. His hat being removed, you would have perceived that his forehead was very large and smooth, and his hair abundant but rather colorless. His nose was too large, and his mouth and eyes were too small; but for all this he was, as I have said, a young man of striking appearance. The expression of his little clean-colored blue eyes was irresistibly gentle and serious; he looked, as the phrase is, as good as gold. The young girl, standing in the garden path, glanced, as he came up, at his thread gloves.

"I hoped you were going to church," he said. "I wanted to walk with you."

"I am very much obliged to you," Gertrude answered. "I am not going to church."

She had shaken hands with him; he held her hand a moment. "Have you any special reason for not going?"

"Yes, Mr. Brand," said the young girl.

"May I ask what it is?"

She looked at him smiling; and in her smile, as I have intimated, there was a certain dullness. But mingled with this dullness was something sweet and suggestive. "Because the sky is so blue!" she said.

He looked at the sky, which was magnificent, and then said, smiling too, "I have heard of young ladies staying at home for bad weather, but never for good. Your sister, whom I met at the gate, tells me you are depressed," he added.

"Depressed? I am never depressed."

"Oh, surely, sometimes," replied Mr. Brand, as if he thought this a regrettable account of one's self.

"I am never depressed," Gertrude repeated. "But I am sometimes wicked. When I am wicked I am in high spirits. I was wicked just now to my sister."

"What did you do to her?"

"I said things that puzzled her — on purpose."

"Why did you do that, Miss Gertrude?" asked the young man.

She began to smile again. "Because the sky is so blue!"

"You say things that puzzle *me*," Mr. Brand declared.

"I always know when I do it," proceeded Gertrude. "But people puzzle me more, I think. And they don't seem to know!"

"This is very interesting," Mr. Brand observed, smiling.

"You told me to tell you about my — my struggles," the young girl went on.

"Let us talk about them. I have so many things to say."

Gertrude turned away a moment; and then, turning back, "You had better go to church," she said.

"You know," the young man urged, "that I have always one thing to say."

Gertrude looked at him a moment. "Please don't say it now!"

"We are all alone," he continued, taking off his hat; "all alone in this beautiful Sunday stillness."

Gertrude looked around her, at the breaking buds, the shining distance, the blue sky to which she had referred as a pretext for her irregularities. "That's the reason," she said, "why I don't want you to speak. Do me a favor; go to church."

"May I speak when I come back?" asked Mr. Brand.

"If you are still disposed," she answered.

"I don't know whether you are wicked," he said, "but you are certainly puzzling."

50

She had turned away; she raised her hands to her ears. He looked at her a moment, and then he slowly walked to church.

She wandered for a while about the garden, vaguely and without purpose. The church-bell had stopped ringing; the stillness was complete. This young lady relished highly, on occasions, the sense of being alone — the absence of the whole family and the emptiness of the house. To-day, apparently, the servants had also gone to church; there was never a figure at the open windows; behind the house there was no stout negress in a red turban, lowering the bucket into the great shingle-hooded well. And the front door of the big, unguarded home stood open, with the trustfulness of the golden age; or what is more to the purpose, with that of New England's silvery prime. Gertrude slowly passed through it, and went from one of the empty rooms to the other — large, clear-colored rooms, with white wainscots, ornamented with thin-legged mahogany furniture, and, on the walls, with old-fashioned engravings, chiefly of scriptural subjects, hung very high. This agreeable sense of solitude, of having the house to herself, of which I have spoken, always excited Gertrude's imagination; she could not have told you why, and neither can her humble historian. It always seemed to her that she must do something particular — that she must honor the occasion; and while she roamed about, wondering what she could do, the occa-

sion usually came to an end. To-day she wondered more than ever. At last she took down a book; there was no library in the house, but there were books in all the rooms. None of them were forbidden books, and Gertrude had not stopped at home for the sake of a chance to climb to the inaccessible shelves. She possessed herself of a very obvious volume — one of the series of the Arabian Nights — and she brought it out into the portico and sat down with it in her lap. There, for a quarter of an hour, she read the history of the loves of the Prince Camaralzaman and the Princess Badoura. At last, looking up, she beheld, as it seemed to her, the Prince Camaralzaman standing before her. A beautiful young man was making her a very low bow — a magnificent bow, such as she had never seen before. He appeared to have dropped from the clouds; he was wonderfully handsome; he smiled — smiled as if he were smiling on purpose. Extreme surprise, for a moment, kept Gertrude sitting still; then she rose, without even keeping her finger in her book. The young man, with his hat in his hand, still looked at her, smiling and smiling. It was very strange.

"Will you kindly tell me," said the mysterious visitor, at last, "whether I have the honor of speaking to Miss Wentworth?"

"My name is Gertrude Wentworth," murmured the young woman.

"Then — then — I have the honor

— the pleasure — of being your cousin."

The young man had so much the character of an apparition that this announcement seemed to complete his unreality. "What cousin? Who are you?" said Gertrude.

He stepped back a few paces and looked up at the house; then glanced round him at the garden and the distant view. After this he burst out laughing. "I see it must seem to you very strange," he said. There was, after all, something substantial in his laughter. Gertrude looked at him from head to foot. Yes, he was remarkably handsome; but his smile was almost a grimace. "It is very still," he went on, coming nearer again. And as she only looked at him, for reply, he added, "Are you all alone?"

"Every one has gone to church," said Gertrude.

"I was afraid of that!" the young man exclaimed. "But I hope you are not afraid of me."

"You ought to tell me who you are," Gertrude answered.

"I am afraid of you!" said the young man. "I had a different plan. I expected the servant would take in my card, and that you would put your heads together, before admitting me, and make out my identity."

Gertrude had been wondering with a quick intensity which brought its results; and the result seemed an answer — a wondrous, delightful answer — to her vague wish that something would befall her. "I know — I know," she said. "You come from Europe."

"We came two days ago. You have heard of us, then — you believe in us?"

"We have known, vaguely," said Gertrude, "that we had relations in France."

"And have you ever wanted to see us?" asked the young man.

Gertrude was silent a moment. "I have wanted to see you."

"I am glad, then, it is you I have found. We wanted to see you, so we came."

"On purpose?" asked Gertrude.

The young man looked round him, smiling still. "Well, yes; on purpose. Does that sound as if we should bore you?" he added. "I don't think we shall — I really don't think we shall. We are rather fond of wandering, too; and we were glad of a pretext."

"And you have just arrived?"

"In Boston, two days ago. At the inn I asked for Mr. Wentworth. He must be your father. They found out for me where he lived; they seemed often to have heard of him. I determined to come, without ceremony. So, this lovely morning, they set my face in the right direction, and told me to walk straight before me, out of town. I came on foot because I wanted to see the country. I walked and walked, and here I am! It's a good many miles."

"It is seven miles and a half," said Gertrude, softly. Now that this handsome young man was proving himself a reality she found herself vaguely trembling; she was deeply excited. She had never in her life spoken to a foreigner, and she had often thought it would be delightful to do so. Here was one who had suddenly been engendered by the Sabbath stillness for her private use; and such a brilliant, polite, smiling one! She found time and means to compose herself, however: to remind herself that she must exercise a sort of official hospitality. "We are very — very glad to see you," she said. "Won't you come into the house?" And she moved toward the open door.

"You are not afraid of me, then?" asked the young man again, with his light laugh.

She wondered a moment, and then, "We are not afraid — here," she said.

"Ah, comme vous devez avoir raison!" cried the young man, looking all round him, appreciatively. It was the first time that Gertrude had heard so many words of French spoken. They gave her something of a sensation. Her companion followed her, watching, with a certain excitement of his own, this tall, interesting-looking girl, dressed in her clear, crisp muslin. He paused in the hall, where there was a broad white staircase with a white balustrade. "What a pleasant house!" he said. "It's lighter inside than it is out."

"It's pleasanter here," said Gertrude, and she led the way into the parlor, — a high, clean, rather empty-looking room. Here they stood looking at each other, — the young man smiling more than ever; Gertrude, very serious, trying to smile.

"I don't believe you know my name," he said. "I am called Felix Young. Your father is my uncle. My mother was his half sister, and older than he."

"Yes," said Gertrude, "and she turned Roman Catholic and married in Europe."

"I see you know," said the young man. "She married and she died. Your father's family didn't like her husband. They called him a foreigner; but he was not. My poor father was born in Sicily, but his parents were American."

"In Sicily?" Gertrude murmured.

"It is true," said Felix Young, "that they had spent their lives in Europe. But they were very patriotic. And so are we."

"And you are Sicilian," said Gertrude.

"Sicilian, no! Let's see. I was born at a little place — a dear little place — in France. My sister was born at Vienna."

"So you are French," said Gertrude.

"Heaven forbid!" cried the young man. Gertrude's eyes were fixed upon him almost insistently. He began to laugh again. "I can easily be French, if that will please you."

"You are a foreigner of some sort," said Gertrude.

"Of some sort — yes; I suppose so. But who can say of what sort? I don't think we have ever had occasion to settle the question. You know there are people like that. About their country, their religion, their profession, they can't tell."

Gertrude stood there gazing; she had not asked him to sit down. She had never heard of people like that; she wanted to hear. "Where do you live?" she asked.

"They can't tell that, either!" said Felix. "I am afraid you will think they are little better than vagabonds. I have lived anywhere — everywhere. I really think I have lived in every city in Europe." Gertrude gave a little long soft exhalation. It made the young man smile at her again; and his smile made her blush a little. To take refuge from blushing she asked him if, after his long walk, he was not hungry or thirsty. Her hand was in her pocket; she was fumbling with the little key that her sister had given her. "Ah, my dear young lady," he said, clasping his hands a little, "if you could give me, in charity, a glass of wine!"

Gertrude gave a smile and a little nod, and went quickly out of the room. Presently she came back with a very large decanter in one hand and a plate in the other, on which was placed a big, round cake with a frosted top. Gertrude, in taking the cake from the closet, had had a moment of acute consciousness that it composed the refection of which her sister had thought that Mr. Brand would like to partake. Her kinsman from across the seas was looking at the pale, high-hung engravings. When she came in he turned and smiled at her, as if they had been old friends meeting after a separation. "You wait upon me yourself?" he asked. "I am served like the gods!"

She had waited upon a great many people, but none of them had ever told her that. The observation added a certain lightness to the step with which she went to a little table where there were some curious red glasses — glasses covered with little gold sprigs, which Charlotte used to dust every morning with her own hands. Gertrude thought the glasses very handsome, and it was a pleasure to her to know that the wine was good; it was her father's famous madeira. Felix Young thought it excellent; he wondered why he had been told that there was no wine in America. She cut him an immense triangle out of the cake, and again she thought of Mr. Brand. Felix sat there, with his glass in one hand and his huge morsel of cake in the other — eating, drinking, smiling, talking. "I am very hungry," he said. "I am not at all tired; I am never tired. But I am very hungry."

"You must stay to dinner," said Gertrude. "At two o'clock. They will all have come back from church; you will see the others."

"Who are the others?" asked the young man. "Describe them all."

"You will see for yourself. It is you that must tell me; now, about your sister."

"My sister is the Baroness Münster," said Felix.

On hearing that his sister was a Baroness, Gertrude got up and walked about slowly, in front of him. She was silent a moment. She was thinking of it. "Why didn't she come, too?" she asked.

"She did come; she is in Boston, at the hotel."

"We will go and see her," said Gertrude, looking at him.

"She begs you will not!" the young man replied. "She sends you her love; she sent me to announce her. She will come and pay her respects to your father."

Gertrude felt herself trembling again. A Baroness Münster, who sent a brilliant young man to "announce" her; who was coming, as the Queen of Sheba came to Solomon, to pay her "respects" to quiet Mr. Wentworth — such a personage presented herself to Gertrude's vision with a most effective unexpectedness. For a moment she hardly knew what to say. "When will she come?" she asked at last.

"As soon as you will allow her — to-morrow. She is very impatient," answered Felix, who wished to be agreeable.

"To-morrow, yes," said Gertrude. She wished to ask more about her; but she hardly knew what could be predicated of a Baroness Münster. "Is she — is she — married?"

Felix had finished his cake and wine; he got up, fixing upon the young girl his bright, expressive eyes. "She is married to a German prince — Prince Adolf, of Silberstadt-Schreckenstein. He is not the reigning prince; he is a younger brother."

Gertrude gazed at her informant; her lips were slightly parted. "Is she a — a *Princess?*" she asked at last.

"Oh, no," said the young man; "her position is rather a singular one. It's a morganatic marriage."

"Morganatic?" These were new names and new words to poor Gertrude.

"That's what they call a marriage, you know, contracted between a scion of a ruling house and — and a common mortal. They made Eugenia a Baroness, poor woman; but that was all they could do. Now they want to dissolve the marriage. Prince Adolf, between ourselves, is a ninny; but his brother, who is a clever man, has plans for him. Eugenia, naturally enough, makes difficulties; not, however, that I think she cares much — she's a very clever woman; I'm sure you'll like her — but she wants to bother them. Just now everything is *en l'air.*"

The cheerful, off-hand tone in which her visitor related this darkly romantic tale seemed to Gertrude very strange; but it seemed also to convey a certain flattery to herself, a recognition of her wisdom and dignity. She felt a dozen impressions stirring within her, and presently the one that was uppermost found words. "They want to dissolve her marriage?" she asked.

"So it appears."

"And against her will?"

"Against her right."

"She must be very unhappy!" said Gertrude.

Her visitor looked at her, smiling; he raised his hand to the back of his head and held it there a moment. "So she says," he answered. "That's her story. She told me to tell it you."

"Tell me more," said Gertrude.

"No, I will leave that to her; she does it better."

Gertrude gave her little excited sigh again. "Well, if she is unhappy," she said, "I am glad she has come to us."

She had been so interested that she failed to notice the sound of a footstep in the portico; and yet it was a footstep that she always recognized. She heard it in the hall, and then she looked out of the window. They were all coming back from church — her father, her sister and brother, and their cousins, who always came to dinner on Sunday. Mr. Brand had come in first; he was in advance of the others, because, apparently, he was still disposed to say what she had not wished him to say an hour before. He came into the parlor, looking for Gertrude. He had two little books in his hand. On seeing Gertrude's companion he slowly stopped, looking at him.

"Is this a cousin?" asked Felix. Then Gertrude saw that she must introduce him; but her ears, and, by sympathy, her lips, were full of all that he had been telling her. "This is the Prince," she said, "the Prince of Silberstadt-Schreckenstein!"

Felix burst out laughing, and Mr. Brand stood staring, while the others, who had passed into the house, appeared behind him in the open door-way.

III

That evening at dinner Felix Young gave his sister, the Baroness Münster, an account of his impressions. She saw that he had come back in the highest possible spirits; but this fact, to her own mind, was not a reason for rejoicing. She had but a limited confidence in her brother's judgment; his capacity for taking rose-colored views was such as to vulgarize one of the prettiest of tints. Still, she supposed he could be trusted to give her the mere facts; and she invited him with some eagerness to communicate them. "I suppose, at least, they didn't turn you out from the door;" she said. "You have been away some ten hours."

"Turn me from the door!" Felix exclaimed. "They took me to their hearts; they killed the fatted calf."

"I know what you want to say: they are a collection of angels."

"Exactly," said Felix. "They are a collection of angels — simply."

"C'est bien vague," remarked the Baroness. "What are they like?"

"Like nothing you ever saw."

"I am sure I am much obliged; but that is hardly more definite. Seriously, they were glad to see you?"

"Enchanted. It has been the proudest day of my life. Never,

never have I been so lionized! I assure you, I was cock of the walk. My dear sister," said the young man, "nous n'avons qu'à nous tenir; we shall be great swells!"

Madame Münster looked at him, and her eye exhibited a slight responsive spark. She touched her lips to a glass of wine, and then she said, "Describe them. Give me a picture."

Felix drained his own glass. "Well, it's in the country, among the meadows and woods; a wild sort of place, and yet not far from here. Only, such a road, my dear! Imagine one of the Alpine glaciers reproduced in mud. But you will not spend much time on it, for they want you to come and stay, once for all."

"Ah," said the Baroness, "they want me to come and stay, once for all? Bon."

"It's intensely rural, tremendously natural; and all overhung with this strange white light, this far-away blue sky. There's a big wooden house — a kind of three-story bungalow; it looks like a magnified Nüremberg toy. There was a gentleman there that made a speech to me about it and called it a 'venerable mansion;' but it looks as if it had been built last night."

"Is it handsome — is it elegant?" asked the Baroness.

Felix looked at her a moment, smiling. "It's very clean! No splendors, no gilding, no troops of servants; rather straight-backed chairs. But you might eat off the floors,

and you can sit down on the stairs."

"That must be a privilege. And the inhabitants are straight-backed too, of course."

"My dear sister," said Felix, "the inhabitants are charming."

"In what style?"

"In a style of their own. How shall I describe it? It's primitive; it's patriarchal; it's the *ton* of the golden age."

"And have they nothing golden but their ton? Are there no symptoms of wealth?"

"I should say there was wealth without symptoms. A plain, homely way of life: nothing for show, and very little for — what shall I call it? — for the senses: but a great *aisance*, and a lot of money, out of sight, that comes forward very quietly for subscriptions to institutions, for repairing tenements, for paying doctor's bills; perhaps even for portioning daughters."

"And the daughters?" Madame Münster demanded. "How many are there?"

"There are two, Charlotte and Gertrude."

"Are they pretty?"

"One of them," said Felix.

"Which is that?"

The young man was silent, looking at his sister. "Charlotte," he said at last.

She looked at him in return. "I see. You are in love with Gertrude. They must be Puritans to their finger-tips; anything but gay!"

"No, they are not gay," Felix admitted. "They are sober; they

The Europeans

are even severe. They are of a pensive cast; they take things hard. I think there is something the matter with them; they have some melancholy memory or some depressing expectation. It's not the epicurean temperament. My uncle, Mr. Wentworth, is a tremendously high-toned old fellow; he looks as if he were undergoing martyrdom, not by fire, but by freezing. But we shall cheer them up; we shall do them good. They will take a good deal of stirring up; but they are wonderfully kind and gentle. And they are appreciative. They think one clever; they think one remarkable!"

"That is very fine, so far as it goes," said the Baroness. "But are we to be shut up to these three people, Mr. Wentworth and the two young women — what did you say their names were — Deborah and Hephzibah?"

"Oh, no; there is another little girl, a cousin of theirs, a very pretty creature; a thorough little American. And then there is the son of the house."

"Good!" said the Baroness. "We are coming to the gentlemen. What of the son of the house?"

"I am afraid he gets tipsy."

"He, then, has the epicurean temperament! How old is he?"

"He is a boy of twenty; a pretty young fellow, but I am afraid he has vulgar tastes. And then there is Mr. Brand — a very tall young man, a sort of lay-priest. They seem to think a good deal of him, but I don't exactly make him out."

"And is there nothing," asked the Baroness, "between these extremes — this mysterious ecclesiastic and that intemperate youth?"

"Oh, yes, there is Mr. Acton. I think," said the young man, with a nod at his sister, "that you will like Mr. Acton."

"Remember that I am very fastidious," said the Baroness. "Has he very good manners?"

"He will have them with you. He is a man of the world; he has been to China."

Madame Münster gave a little laugh. "A man of the Chinese world! He must be very interesting."

"I have an idea that he brought home a fortune," said Felix.

"That is always interesting. Is he young, good-looking, clever?"

"He is less than forty; he has a baldish head; he says witty things. I rather think," added the young man, "that he will admire the Baroness Münster."

"It is very possible," said this lady. Her brother never knew how she would take things; but shortly afterwards she declared that he had made a very pretty description and that on the morrow she would go and see for herself.

They mounted, accordingly, into a great barouche — a vehicle as to which the Baroness found nothing to criticise but the price that was asked for it and the fact that the coachman wore a straw hat. (At Silberstadt Madame Münster had had liveries of yellow and crimson.) They drove into the country, and the Baroness, leaning far back and swaying her lace-fringed parasol, looked to right and to left and surveyed the way-side objects. After a while she pronounced them "affreux." Her brother remarked that it was apparently a country in which the foreground was inferior to the *plans reculés:* and the Baroness rejoined that the landscape seemed to be all foreground. Felix had fixed with his new friends the hour at which he should bring his sister; it was four o'clock in the afternoon. The large, clean-faced house wore, to his eyes, as the barouche drove up to it, a very friendly aspect; the high, slender elms made lengthening shadows in front of it. The Baroness descended; her American kinsfolk were stationed in the portico. Felix waved his hat to them, and a tall, lean gentleman, with a high forehead and a clean shaven face, came forward toward the garden gate. Charlotte Wentworth walked at his side. Gertrude came behind, more slowly. Both of these young ladies wore rustling silk dresses. Felix ushered his sister into the gate. "Be very gracious," he said to her. But he saw the admonition was superfluous. Eugenia was prepared to be gracious as only Eugenia could be. Felix knew no keener pleasure than to be able to admire his sister unrestrictedly; for if the opportunity was frequent, it was not inveterate. When she desired to please she was to him, as to every one else, the most charming woman in the world. Then he forgot that she was ever anything else; that she was some-

times hard and perverse; that he was occasionally afraid of her. Now, as she took his arm to pass into the garden, he felt that she desired, that she proposed, to please, and this situation made him very happy. Eugenia would please.

The tall gentleman came to meet her, looking very rigid and grave. But it was a rigidity that had no illiberal meaning. Mr. Wentworth's manner was pregnant, on the contrary, with a sense of grand responsibility, of the solemnity of the occasion, of its being difficult to show sufficient deference to a lady at once so distinguished and so unhappy. Felix had observed on the day before his characteristic pallor; and now he perceived that there was something almost cadaverous in his uncle's high-featured white face. But so clever were this young man's quick sympathies and perceptions that he already learned that in these semimortuary manifestations there was no cause for alarm. His light imagination had gained a glimpse of Mr. Wentworth's spiritual mechanism, and taught him that, the old man being infinitely conscientious, the special operation of conscience within him announced itself by several of the indications of physical faintness.

The Baroness took her uncle's hand, and stood looking at him with her ugly face and her beautiful smile. "Have I done right to come?" she asked.

"Very right, very right," said Mr. Wentworth, solemnly. He had arranged in his mind a little speech; but now it quite faded away. He felt almost frightened. He had never been looked at in just that way — with just that fixed, intense smile — by any woman; and it perplexed and weighed upon him, now, that the woman who was smiling so and who had instantly given him a vivid sense of her possessing other unprecedented attributes, was his own niece, the child of his own father's daughter. The idea that his niece should be a German Baroness, married "morganatically" to a Prince, had already given him much to think about. Was it right, was it just, was it acceptable? He always slept badly, and the night before he had lain awake much more even than usual, asking himself these questions. The strange word "morganatic" was constantly in his ears; it reminded him of a certain Mrs. Morgan whom he had once known and who had been a bold, unpleasant woman. He had a feeling that it was his duty, so long as the Baroness looked at him, smiling in that way, to meet her glance with his own scrupulously adjusted, consciously frigid organs of vision; but on this occasion he failed to perform his duty to the last. He looked away toward his daughters. "We are very glad to see you," he had said. "Allow me to introduce my daughters — Miss Charlotte Wentworth, Miss Gertrude Wentworth."

The Baroness thought she had never seen people less demonstrative. But Charlotte kissed her and took her hand, looking at her sweetly and solemnly. Gertrude seemed to her almost funereal, though Gertrude might have found a source of gayety in the fact that Felix, with his magnificent smile, had been talking to her; he had greeted her as a very old friend. When she kissed the Baroness she had tears in her eyes. Madame Münster took each of these young women by the hand, and looked at them all over. Charlotte thought her very strange-looking and singularly dressed; she could not have said whether it was well or ill. She was glad, at any rate, that they had put on their silk gowns — especially Gertrude. "My cousins are very pretty," said the Baroness, turning her eyes from one to the other. "Your daughters are very handsome, sir."

Charlotte blushed quickly; she had never yet heard her personal appearance alluded to in a loud, expressive voice. Gertrude looked away — not at Felix; she was extremely pleased. It was not the compliment that pleased her; she did not believe it; she thought herself very plain. She could hardly have told you the source of her satisfaction; it came from something in the way the Baroness spoke, and it was not diminished — it was rather deepened, oddly enough — by the young girl's disbelief. Mr. Wentworth was silent; and then he asked, formally, "Won't you come into the house?"

"These are not all; you have some other children," said the Baroness.

"I have a son," Mr. Wentworth answered.

"And why doesn't he come to meet me?" Eugenia cried. "I am afraid he is not so charming as his sisters."

"I don't know; I will see about it," the old man declared.

"He is rather afraid of ladies," Charlotte said, softly.

"He is very handsome," said Gertrude, as loud as she could.

"We will go in and find him. We will draw him out of his *cachette*." And the Baroness took Mr. Wentworth's arm, who was not aware that he had offered it to her, and who, as they walked toward the house, wondered whether he ought to have offered it and whether it was proper for her to take it if it had not been offered. "I want to know you well," said the Baroness, interrupting these meditations, "and I want you to know me."

"It seems natural that we should know each other," Mr. Wentworth rejoined. "We are near relatives."

"Ah, there comes a moment in life when one reverts, irresistibly, to one's natural ties — to one's natural affections. You must have found that!" said Eugenia.

Mr. Wentworth had been told the day before by Felix that Eugenia was very clever, very brilliant, and the information had held him in some suspense. This was the cleverness, he supposed; the brilliancy was beginning. "Yes, the natural affections are very strong," he murmured.

"In some people," the Baroness declared. "Not in all." Charlotte was walking beside her; she took hold of her hand again, smiling always. "And you, *cousine*, where did you get that enchanting complexion?" she went on; "such lilies and roses?" The roses in poor Charlotte's countenance began speedily to predominate over the lilies, and she quickened her step and reached the portico. "This is the country of complexions," the Baroness continued, addressing herself to Mr. Wentworth. "I am convinced they are more delicate. There are very good ones in England — in Holland; but they are very apt to be coarse. There is too much red."

"I think you will find," said Mr. Wentworth, "that this country is superior in many respects to those you mention. I have been to England and Holland."

"Ah, you have been to Europe?" cried the Baroness. "Why didn't you come and see me? But it's better, after all, this way," she said. They were entering the house; she paused and looked round her. "I see you have arranged your house — your beautiful house — in the — in the Dutch taste!"

"The house is very old," remarked Mr. Wentworth. "General Washington once spent a week here."

"Oh, I have heard of Washington," cried the Baroness. "My father used to tell me of him."

Mr. Wentworth was silent a moment, and then, "I found he was very well known in Europe," he said.

Felix had lingered in the garden with Gertrude; he was standing before her and smiling, as he had done the day before. What had happened the day before seemed to her a kind of dream. He had been there and he had changed everything; the others had seen him, they had talked with him; but that he should come again, that he should be part of the future, part of her small, familiar, much-meditating life — this needed, afresh, the evidence of her senses. The evidence had come to her senses now; and her senses seemed to rejoice in it. "What do you think of Eugenia?" Felix asked. "Isn't she charming?"

"She is very brilliant," said Gertrude. "But I can't tell yet. She seems to me like a singer singing an air. You can't tell till the song is done."

"Ah, the song will never be done!" exclaimed the young man, laughing. "Don't you think her handsome?"

Gertrude had been disappointed in the beauty of the Baroness Münster; she had expected her, for mysterious reasons, to resemble a very pretty portrait of the Empress Josephine, of which there hung an engraving in one of the parlors, and which the younger Miss Wentworth had always greatly admired. But the Baroness was not at all like that — not at all. Though different, however, she was very wonderful, and Gertrude felt herself most suggestively cor-

rected. It was strange, nevertheless, that Felix should speak in that positive way about his sister's beauty. "I think I *shall* think her handsome," Gertrude said. "It must be very interesting to know her. I don't feel as if I ever could."

"Ah, you will know her well; you will become great friends," Felix declared, as if this were the easiest thing in the world.

"She is very graceful," said Gertrude, looking after the Baroness, suspended to her father's arm. It was a pleasure to her to say that any one was graceful.

Felix had been looking about him. "And your little cousin, of yesterday," he said, "who was so wonderfully pretty — what has become of her?"

"She is in the parlor," Gertrude answered. "Yes, she is very pretty." She felt as if it were her duty to take him straight into the house, to where he might be near her cousin. But after hesitating a moment she lingered still. "I didn't believe you would come back," she said.

"Not come back!" cried Felix, laughing. "You didn't know, then, the impression made upon this susceptible heart of mine."

She wondered whether he meant the impression her cousin Lizzie had made. "Well," she said, "I didn't think we should ever see you again."

"And pray what did you think would become of me?"

"I don't know. I thought you would melt away."

"That's a compliment to my

solidity! I melt very often," said Felix, "but there is always something left of me."

"I came and waited for you by the door, because the others did," Gertrude went on. "But if you had never appeared I should not have been surprised."

"I hope," declared Felix, looking at her, "that you would have been disappointed."

She looked at him a little, and shook her head. "No — no!"

"Ah, *par exemple!*" cried the young man. "You deserve that I should never leave you."

Going into the parlor they found Mr. Wentworth performing introductions. A young man was standing before the Baroness, blushing a good deal, laughing a little, and shifting his weight from one foot to the other — a slim, mild-faced young man, with neatly-arranged features, like those of Mr. Wentworth. Two other gentlemen, behind him, had risen from their seats, and a little apart, near one of the windows, stood a remarkably pretty young girl. The young girl was knitting a stocking; but, while her fingers quickly moved, she looked with wide, brilliant eyes at the Baroness.

"And what is your son's name?" said Eugenia, smiling at the young man.

"My name is Clifford Wentworth, ma'am," he said in a tremulous voice.

"Why didn't you come out to meet me, Mr. Clifford Wentworth?" the Baroness demanded, with her beautiful smile.

"I didn't think you would want me," said the young man, slowly sidling about.

"One always wants a *beau cousin,* — if one has one! But if you are very nice to me in future I won't remember it against you." And Madame Münster transferred her smile to the other persons present. It rested first upon the candid countenance and long-skirted figure of Mr. Brand, whose eyes were intently fixed upon Mr. Wentworth, as if to beg him not to prolong an anomalous situation. Mr. Wentworth pronounced his name. Eugenia gave him a very charming glance, and then looked at the other gentleman.

This latter personage was a man of rather less than the usual stature and the usual weight, with a quick, observant, agreeable dark eye, a small quantity of thin dark hair, and a small mustache. He had been standing with his hands in his pockets; and when Eugenia looked at him he took them out. But he did not, like Mr. Brand, look evasively and urgently at their host. He met Eugenia's eyes; he appeared to appreciate the privilege of meeting them. Madame Münster instantly felt that he was, intrinsically, the most important person present. She was not unconscious that this impression was in some degree manifested in the little sympathetic nod with which she acknowledged Mr. Wentworth's announcement, "My cousin, Mr. Acton!"

"Your cousin — not mine?" said the Baroness.

"It only depends upon you," Mr. Acton declared, laughing.

The Baroness looked at him a moment, and noticed that he had very white teeth. "Let it depend upon your behavior," she said. "I think I had better wait. I have cousins enough. Unless I can also claim relationship," she added, "with that charming young lady," and she pointed to the young girl at the window.

"That's my sister," said Mr. Acton. And Gertrude Wentworth put her arm round the young girl and led her forward. It was not, apparently, that she needed much leading. She came toward the Baroness with a light, quick step, and with perfect self-possession, rolling her stocking round its needles. She had dark blue eyes and dark brown hair; she was wonderfully pretty.

Eugenia kissed her, as she had kissed the other young women, and then held her off a little, looking at her. "Now this is quite another *type*," she said; she pronounced the word in the French manner. "This is a different outline, my uncle, a different character, from that of your own daughters. This, Felix," she went on, "is very much more what we have always thought of as the American type."

The young girl, during this exposition, was smiling askance at every one in turn, and at Felix out of turn. "I find only one type here!" cried Felix, laughing. "The type adorable!"

This sally was received in perfect silence, but Felix, who learned all things quickly, had already learned that the silences frequently observed among his new acquaintances were not necessarily restrictive or resentful. It was, as one might say, the silence of expectation, of modesty. They were all standing round his sister, as if they were expecting her to acquit herself of the exhibition of some peculiar faculty, some brilliant talent. Their attitude seemed to imply that she was a kind of conversational mountebank, attired, intellectually, in gauze and spangles. This attitude gave a certain ironical force to Madame Münster's next words. "Now this is your circle," she said to her uncle. "This is your *salon*. These are your regular habitués, eh? I am so glad to see you all together."

"Oh," said Mr. Wentworth, "they are always dropping in and out. You must do the same."

"Father," interposed Charlotte Wentworth, "they must do something more." And she turned her sweet, serious face, that seemed at once timid and placid, upon their interesting visitor. "What is your name?" she asked.

"Eugenia-Camilla-Dolores," said the Baroness, smiling. "But you needn't say all that."

"I will say Eugenia, if you will let me. You must come and stay with us."

The Baroness laid her hand upon Charlotte's arm very tenderly; but she reserved herself. She was wondering whether it would be possible to "stay" with these people. "It would be very charming — very charming," she said; and her eyes wandered over the company, over the room. She wished to gain time before committing herself. Her glance fell upon young Mr. Brand, who stood there, with his arms folded and his hand on his chin, looking at her. "The gentleman, I suppose, is a sort of ecclesiastic," she said to Mr. Wentworth, lowering her voice a little.

"He is a minister," answered Mr. Wentworth.

"A Protestant?" asked Eugenia.

"I am a Unitarian, madam," replied Mr. Brand, impressively.

"Ah, I see," said Eugenia, "Something new." She had never heard of this form of worship.

Mr. Acton began to laugh, and Gertrude looked anxiously at Mr. Brand.

"You have come very far," said Mr. Wentworth.

"Very far — very far," the Baroness replied, with a graceful shake of her head — a shake that might have meant many different things.

"That's a reason why you ought to settle down with us," said Mr. Wentworth, with that dryness of utterance which, as Eugenia was too intelligent not to feel, took nothing from the delicacy of his meaning.

She looked at him, and for an instant, in his cold, still face, she seemed to see a far-away likeness to the vaguely remembered image of her mother. Eugenia was a woman of sudden emotions, and now, unexpectedly, she felt one

rising in her heart. She kept looking round the circle; she knew that there was admiration in all the eyes that were fixed upon her. She smiled at them all.

"I came to look — to try — to ask," she said. "It seems to me I have done well. I am very tired; I want to rest." There were tears in her eyes. The luminous interior, the gentle, tranquil people, the simple, serious life — the sense of these things pressed upon her with an overmastering force, and she felt herself yielding to one of the most genuine emotions she had ever known. "I should like to stay here," she said. "Pray take me in."

Though she was smiling, there were tears in her voice as well as in her eyes. "My dear niece," said Mr. Wentworth, softly. And Charlotte put out her arms and drew the Baroness toward her; while Robert Acton turned away, with his hands stealing into his pockets.

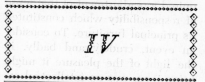

IV

A FEW days after the Baroness Münster had presented herself to her American kinsfolk she came, with her brother, and took up her abode in that small white house adjacent to Mr. Wentworth's own dwelling of which mention has already been made. It was on going with his daughters to return her visit that Mr. Wentworth placed this comfortable cottage at her

service; the offer being the result of a domestic colloquy, diffused through the ensuing twenty-
four hours, in the course of which
the two foreign visitors were discussed and analyzed with a great
deal of earnestness and subtlety.
The discussion went forward, as I
say, in the family circle; but that
circle on the evening following
Madame Münster's return to town,
as on many other occasions, included Robert Acton and his pretty
sister. If you had been present, it
would probably not have seemed
to you that the advent of these
brilliant strangers was treated as
an exhilarating occurrence, a pleasure the more in this tranquil
household, a prospective source of
entertainment. This was not Mr.
Wentworth's way of treating any
human occurrence. The sudden irruption into the well-ordered consciousness of the Wentworths of
an element not allowed for in its
scheme of usual obligations required a readjustment of that sense
of responsibility which constituted
its principal furniture. To consider
an event, crudely and badly, in
the light of the pleasure it might
bring them was an intellectual exercise with which Felix Young's
American cousins were almost
wholly unacquainted, and which
they scarcely supposed to be
largely pursued in any section of
human society. The arrival of Felix and his sister was a satisfaction, but it was a singularly joyless
and inelastic satisfaction. It was
an extension of duty, of the exercise of the more recondite virtues; but neither Mr. Wentworth,
nor Charlotte, nor Mr. Brand,
who, among these excellent people, was a great promoter of reflection and aspiration, frankly ad-
verted to it as an extension of
enjoyment. This function was ultimately assumed by Gertrude
Wentworth, who was a peculiar
girl, but the full compass of whose
peculiarities had not been exhibited before they very ingeniously
found their pretext in the presence
of these possibly too agreeable
foreigners. Gertrude, however, had
to struggle with a great accumulation of obstructions, both of the
subjective, as the metaphysicians
say, and of the objective, order;
and indeed it is no small part of
the purpose of this little history
to set forth her struggle. What
seemed paramount in this abrupt
enlargement of Mr. Wentworth's
sympathies and those of his daughters was an extension of the field
of possible mistakes; and the doctrine, as it may almost be called,
of the oppressive gravity of mistakes was one of the most cherished
traditions of the Wentworth family.

"I don't believe she wants to
come and stay in this house," said
Gertrude; Madame Münster, from
this time forward, receiving no
other designation than the personal pronoun. Charlotte and Gertrude acquired considerable facility in addressing her, directly, as
"Eugenia;" but in speaking of her
to each other they rarely called
her anything but "she."

"Doesn't she think it good

enough for her?" cried little Lizzie Acton, who was always asking unpractical questions that required, in strictness, no answer, and to which indeed she expected no other answer than such as she herself invariably furnished in a small, innocently-satirical laugh.

"She certainly expressed a willingness to come," said Mr. Wentworth.

"That was only politeness," Gertrude rejoined.

"Yes, she is very polite — very polite," said Mr. Wentworth.

"She is too polite," his son declared, in a softly growling tone which was habitual to him, but which was an indication of nothing worse than a vaguely humorous intention. "It is very embarrassing."

"That is more than can be said of you, sir," said Lizzie Acton, with her little laugh.

"Well, I don't mean to encourage her," Clifford went on.

"I'm sure I don't care if you do!" cried Lizzie.

"She will not think of you, Clifford," said Gertrude, gravely.

"I hope not!" Clifford exclaimed.

"She will think of Robert," Gertrude continued, in the same tone. Robert Acton began to blush; but there was no occasion for it, for every one was looking at Gertrude — every one, at least, save Lizzie, who, with her pretty head on one side, contemplated her brother.

"Why do you attribute motives, Gertrude?" asked Mr. Wentworth.

"I don't attribute motives, fa-

ther," said Gertrude. "I only say she will think of Robert; and she will!"

"Gertrude judges by herself!" Acton exclaimed, laughing. "Don't you, Gertrude? Of course the Baroness will think of me. She will think of me from morning till night."

"She will be very comfortable here," said Charlotte, with something of a housewife's pride. "She can have the large northeast room. And the French bedstead," Charlotte added, with a constant sense of the lady's foreignness.

"She will not like it," said Gertrude; "not even if you pin little tidies all over the chairs."

"Why not, dear?" asked Charlotte, perceiving a touch of irony here, but not resenting it.

Gertrude had left her chair; she was walking about the room; her stiff silk dress, which she had put on in honor of the Baroness, made a sound upon the carpet. "I don't know," she replied. "She will want something more — more private."

"If she wants to be private she can stay in her room," Lizzie Acton remarked.

Gertrude paused in her walk, looking at her. "That would not be pleasant," she answered. "She wants privacy and pleasure together."

Robert Acton began to laugh again. "My dear cousin, what a picture!"

Charlotte had fixed her serious eyes upon her sister; she wondered whence she had suddenly derived these strange notions. Mr.

Wentworth also observed his younger daughter.

"I don't know what her manner of life may have been," he said; "but she certainly never can have enjoyed a more refined and salubrious home."

Gertrude stood there looking at them all. "She is the wife of a Prince," she said.

"We are all princes here," said Mr. Wentworth; "and I don't know of any palace in this neighborhood that is to let."

"Cousin William," Robert Acton interposed, "do you want to do something handsome? Make them a present, for three months, of the little house over the way."

"You are very generous with other people's things!" cried his sister.

"Robert is very generous with his own things," Mr. Wentworth observed dispassionately, and looking, in cold meditation, at his kinsman.

"Gertrude," Lizzie went on, "I had an idea you were so fond of your new cousin."

"Which new cousin?" asked Gertrude.

"I don't mean the Baroness!" the young girl rejoined, with her laugh. "I thought you expected to see so much of him."

"Of Felix? I hope to see a great deal of him," said Gertrude, simply.

"Then why do you want to keep him out of the house?"

Gertrude looked at Lizzie Acton, and then looked away.

"Should you want me to live in the house with you, Lizzie?" asked Clifford.

"I hope you never will. I hate you!" Such was this young lady's reply.

"Father," said Gertrude, stopping before Mr. Wentworth and smiling, with a smile the sweeter, as her smile always was, for its rarity; "do let them live in the little house over the way. It will be lovely!"

Robert Acton had been watching her. "Gertrude is right," he said. "Gertrude is the cleverest girl in the world. If I might take the liberty, I should strongly recommend their living there."

"There is nothing there so pretty as the northeast room," Charlotte urged.

"She will make it pretty. Leave her alone!" Acton exclaimed.

Gertrude, at his compliment, had blushed and looked at him: it was as if some one less familiar had complimented her. "I am sure she will make it pretty. It will be very interesting. It will be a place to go to. It will be a foreign house."

"Are we very sure that we need a foreign house?" Mr. Wentworth inquired. "Do you think it desirable to establish a foreign house —in this quiet place?"

"You speak," said Acton, laughing, "as if it were a question of the poor Baroness opening a wine-shop or a gaming-table."

"It would be too lovely!" Gertrude declared again, laying her hand on the back of her father's chair.

"That she should open a gaming-table?" Charlotte asked, with great gravity.

Gertrude looked at her a moment, and then, "Yes, Charlotte," she said, simply.

"Gertrude is growing pert," Clifford Wentworth observed, with his humorous young growl. "That comes of associating with foreigners."

Mr. Wentworth looked up at his daughter, who was standing beside him; he drew her gently forward. "You must be careful," he said. "You must keep watch. Indeed, we must all be careful. This is a great change; we are to be exposed to peculiar influences. I don't say they are bad. I don't judge them in advance. But they may perhaps make it necessary that we should exercise a great deal of wisdom and self-control. It will be a different tone."

Gertrude was silent a moment, in deference to her father's speech; then she spoke in a manner that was not in the least an answer to it. "I want to see how they will live. I am sure they will have different hours. She will do all kinds of little things differently. When we go over there it will be like going to Europe. She will have a boudoir. She will invite us to dinner — very late. She will breakfast in her room."

Charlotte gazed at her sister again. Gertrude's imagination seemed to her to be fairly running riot. She had always known that Gertrude had a great deal of imagination — she had been very proud of it. But at the same time she had always felt that it was a dangerous and irresponsible faculty; and now, to her sense, for the moment, it seemed to threaten to make her sister a strange person who should come in suddenly, as from a journey, talking of the peculiar and possibly unpleasant things she had observed. Charlotte's imagination took no journeys whatever; she kept it, as it were, in her pocket, with the other furniture of this receptacle — a thimble, a little box of peppermint, and a morsel of court-plaster. "I don't believe she would have any dinner — or any breakfast," said Miss Wentworth. "I don't believe she knows how to do anything herself. I should have to get her ever so many servants, and she wouldn't like them."

"She has a maid," said Gertrude; "a French maid. She mentioned her."

"I wonder if the maid has a little fluted cap and red slippers," said Lizzie Acton. "There was a French maid in that play that Robert took me to see. She had pink stockings; she was very wicked."

"She was a *soubrette*," Gertrude announced, who had never seen a play in her life. "They call that a soubrette. It will be a great chance to learn French." Charlotte gave a little soft, helpless groan. She had a vision of a wicked, theatrical person, clad in pink stockings and red shoes, and speaking, with confounding volubility, an incomprehensible tongue, flitting through the sacred penetralia of that large, clean house. "That is one reason in favor of their coming here," Gertrude went on. "But we can make Eugenia speak French to us, and Felix. I mean to begin — the next time."

Mr. Wentworth had kept her standing near him, and he gave her his earnest, thin, unresponsive glance again. "I want you to make me a promise, Gertrude," he said.

"What is it?" she asked, smiling.

"Not to get excited. Not to allow these — these occurrences to be an occasion for excitement."

She looked down at him a moment, and then she shook her head. "I don't think I can promise that, father. I am excited already."

Mr. Wentworth was silent a while; they all were silent, as if in recognition of something audacious and portentous.

"I think they had better go to the other house," said Charlotte, quietly.

"I shall keep them in the other house," Mr. Wentworth subjoined, more pregnantly.

Gertrude turned away; then she looked across at Robert Acton. Her cousin Robert was a great friend of hers; she often looked at him this way instead of saying things. Her glance on this occasion, however, struck him as a substitute for a larger volume of diffident utterance than usual inviting him to observe, among other things, the inefficiency of her father's design — if design it was — for diminishing, in the interest of quiet nerves, their occasions of contact with their foreign relatives. But Acton immediately complimented Mr. Wentworth upon his liberality. "That's a very nice thing to do," he said, "giving them the little house. You will have treated them handsomely, and, whatever happens, you will be glad of it." Mr. Wentworth was liberal, and he knew he was liberal. It gave him pleasure to know it, to feel it, to see it recorded; and this pleasure is the only palpable form of self-indulgence with which the narrator of these incidents will be able to charge him.

"A three days' visit at most, over there, is all I should have found possible," Madame Münster remarked to her brother, after they had taken possession of the little white house. "It would have been too *intime* — decidedly too intime. Breakfast, dinner, and tea *en famille* — it would have been the end of the world if I could have reached the third day." And she made the same observation to her maid Augustine, an intelligent person, who enjoyed a liberal share of her confidence. Felix declared that he would willingly spend his life in the bosom of the Wentworth family; that they were the kindest, simplest, most amiable people in the world, and that he had taken a prodigious fancy to them all. The Baroness quite agreed with him that they were simple and kind; they were thoroughly nice people, and she liked them extremely. The girls were perfect ladies; it was impossible to be more of a lady than Charlotte Wentworth, in spite of her little village air. "But as for thinking them the best company in the world," said the Baroness, "that is another thing; and as for wishing to live *porte à porte* with them, I should as soon think of wishing myself back in the convent again, to wear a bombazine apron and sleep in a dormitory." And yet the Baroness was in high good humor; she had been very much pleased. With her lively perception and her refined imagination, she was capable of enjoying anything that was characteristic, anything that was good of its kind. The Wentworth household seemed to her very perfect in its kind — wonderfully peaceful and unspotted; pervaded by a sort of dove-colored freshness that had all the quietude and benevolence of what she deemed to be Quakerism, and yet seemed to be founded upon a degree of material abundance for which, in certain matters of detail, one might have looked in vain at the frugal little court of Silberstadt-Schreckenstein. She perceived immediately that her American relatives thought and talked very little about money; and this of itself made an impression upon Eugenia's imagination. She perceived at the same time that if Charlotte or Gertrude should ask their father for a very considerable sum he would at once place it in their hands; and this made a still greater impression. The greatest impression of all, perhaps, was made by another rapid induction. The Baron-

ess had an immediate conviction that Robert Acton would put his hand into his pocket every day in the week if that rattle-pated little sister of his should bid him. The men in this country, said the Baroness, are evidently very obliging. Her declaration that she was looking for rest and retirement had been by no means wholly untrue; nothing that the Baroness said was wholly untrue. It is but fair to add, perhaps, that nothing that she said was wholly true. She wrote to a friend in Germany that it was a return to nature; it was like drinking new milk, and she was very fond of new milk. She said to herself, of course, that it would be a little dull; but there can be no better proof of her good spirits than the fact that she thought she should not mind its being a little dull. It seemed to her, when from the piazza of her eleemosynary cottage she looked out over the soundless fields, the stony pastures, the clear-faced ponds, the rugged little orchards, that she had never been in the midst of so peculiarly intense a stillness; it was almost a delicate sensual pleasure. It was all very good, very innocent and safe, and out of it something good must come. Augustine, indeed, who had an unbounded faith in her mistress's wisdom and farsightedness, was a great deal perplexed and depressed. She was always ready to take her cue when she understood it; but she liked to understand it, and on this occasion comprehension failed. What, indeed, was the Baroness doing *dans cette galère?* what fish did she expect to land out of these very stagnant waters? The game was evidently a deep one. Augustine could trust her; but the sense of walking in the dark betrayed itself in the physiognomy of this spare, sober, sallow, middle-aged person, who had nothing in common with Gertrude Wentworth's conception of a soubrette, by the most ironical scowl that had ever rested upon the unpretending tokens of the peace and plenty of the Wentworths. Fortunately, Augustine could quench skepticism in action. She quite agreed with her mistress — or rather she quite outstripped her mistress — in thinking that the little white house was pitifully bare. "Il faudra," said Augustine, "lui faire un peu de toilette." And she began to hang up *portières* in the doorways; to place wax candles, procured after some research, in unexpected situations; to dispose anomalous draperies over the arms of sofas and the backs of chairs. The Baroness had brought with her to the New World a copious provision of the element of costume; and the two Miss Wentworths, when they came over to see her, were somewhat bewildered by the obtrusive distribution of her wardrobe. There were India shawls suspended, curtain-wise, in the parlor door, and curious fabrics, corresponding to Gertrude's metaphysical vision of an opera-cloak, tumbled about in the sitting-places. There were pink silk blinds in the windows, by which the

room was strangely bedimmed; and along the chimney-piece was disposed a remarkable band of velvet, covered with coarse, dirty-looking lace. "I have been making myself a little comfortable," said the Baroness, much to the confusion of Charlotte, who had been on the point of proposing to come and help her put her superfluous draperies away. But what Charlotte mistook for an almost culpably delayed subsidence Gertrude very presently perceived to be the most ingenious, the most interesting, the most romantic intention. "What is life, indeed, without curtains?" she secretly asked herself; and she appeared to herself to have been leading hitherto an existence singularly garish and totally devoid of festoons.

Felix was not a young man who troubled himself greatly about anything — least of all about the conditions of enjoyment. His faculty of enjoyment was so large, so unconsciously eager, that it may be said of it that it had a permanent advance upon embarrassment and sorrow. His sentient faculty was intrinsically joyous, and novelty and change were in themselves a delight to him. As they had come to him with a great deal of frequency, his life had been more agreeable than appeared. Never was a nature more perfectly fortunate. It was not a restless, apprehensive, ambitious spirit, running a race with the tyranny of fate,, but a temper so unsuspicious as to put Adversity off her guard, dodging and evading her with the easy, natural motion of a wind-shifted flower. Felix extracted entertainment from all things, and all his faculties — his imagination, his intelligence, his affections, his senses — had a hand in the game. It seemed to him that Eugenia and he had been very well treated; there was something absolutely touching in that combination of paternal liberality and social considerateness which marked Mr. Wentworth's deportment. It was most uncommonly kind of him, for instance, to have given them a house. Felix was positively amused at having a house of his own; for the little white cottage among the apple-trees — the chalet, as Madame Münster always called it — was much more sensibly his own than any domiciliary *quatrième*, looking upon a court, with the rent overdue. Felix had spent a good deal of his life in looking into courts, with a perhaps slightly tattered pair of elbows resting upon the ledge of a high-perched window, and the thin smoke of a cigarette rising into an atmosphere in which street-cries died away and the vibration of chimes from ancient belfries became sensible. He had never known anything so infinitely rural as these New England fields; and he took a great fancy to all their pastoral roughnesses. He had never had a greater sense of luxurious security; and at the risk of making him seem a rather sordid adventurer I must declare that he found an irresistible charm in the fact that he might dine every day at his uncle's. The charm was irresistible, however, because his fancy flung a rosy light over this homely privilege. He appreciated highly the fare that was set before him. There was a kind of fresh-looking abundance about it which made him think that people must have lived so in the mythological era, when they spread their tables upon the grass, replenished them from cornucopias, and had no particular need of kitchen stoves. But the great thing that Felix enjoyed was having found a family — sitting in the midst of gentle, generous people whom he might call by their first names. He had never known anything more charming than the attention they paid to what he said. It was like a large sheet of clean, fine-grained drawing-paper, all ready to be washed over with effective splashes of water-color. He had never had any cousins, and he had never before found himself in contact so unrestricted with young unmarried ladies. He was extremely fond of the society of ladies, and it was new to him that it might be enjoyed in just this manner. At first he hardly knew what to make of his state of mind. It seemed to him that he was in love, indiscriminately, with three girls at once. He saw that Lizzie Acton was more brilliantly pretty than Charlotte and 'Gertrude; but this was scarcely a superiority. His pleasure came from something they had in common — a part of which was, indeed, that physical delicacy which seemed to make it proper that they should always dress in thin materials and clear colors. But they were delicate in other ways, and it was most agreeable to him to feel that these latter delicacies were appreciable by contact, as it were. He had known, fortunately, many virtuous gentlewomen, but it now appeared to him that in his relations with them (especially when they were unmarried) he had been looking at pictures under glass. He perceived at present what a nuisance the glass had been — how it perverted and interfered, how it caught the reflection of other objects and kept you walking from side to side. He had no need to ask himself whether Charlotte and Gertrude, and Lizzie Acton, were in the right light; they were always in the right light. He liked everything about them: he was, for instance, not at all above liking the fact that they had very slender feet and high insteps. He liked their pretty noses; he liked their surprised eyes and their hesitating, not at all positive way of speaking; he liked so much knowing that he was perfectly at liberty to be alone for hours, anywhere, with either of them; that preference for one to the other, as a companion of solitude, remained a minor affair. Charlotte Wentworth's sweetly severe features were as agreeable as Lizzie Acton's wonderfully expressive blue eyes; and Gertrude's air of being always ready to walk about and listen was as charming as anything else, especially as she walked very gracefully. After a while Felix began to distinguish; but even then he would often wish, suddenly, that they were not all so sad. Even Lizzie Acton, in spite of her fine little chatter and laughter, appeared sad. Even Clifford Wentworth, who had extreme youth in his favor, and kept a buggy with enormous wheels and a little sorrel mare with the prettiest legs in the world — even this fortunate lad was apt to have an averted, uncomfortable glance, and to edge away from you at times, in the manner of a person with a bad conscience. The only person in the circle with no sense of oppression of any kind was, to Felix's perception, Robert Acton.

It might perhaps have been feared that after the completion of those graceful domiciliary embellishments which have been mentioned Madame Münster would have found herself confronted with alarming possibilities of *ennui*. But as yet she had not taken the alarm. The Baroness was a restless soul, and she projected her restlessness, as it may be said, into any situation that lay before her. Up to a certain point her restlessness might be counted upon to entertain her. She was always expecting something to happen, and, until it was disappointed, expectancy itself was a delicate pleasure. What the Baroness expected just now it would take some ingenuity to set forth; it is enough that while she looked about her she found something to

74

occupy her imagination. She assured herself that she was enchanted with her new relatives; she professed to herself that, like her brother, she felt it a sacred satisfaction to have found a family. It is certain that she enjoyed to the utmost the gentleness of her kinsfolk's deference. She had, first and last, received a great deal of admiration, and her experience of well-turned compliments was very considerable; but she knew that she had never been so real a power, never counted for so much, as now when, for the first time, the standard of comparison of her little circle was a prey to vagueness. The sense, indeed, that the good people about her had, as regards her remarkable self, no standard of comparison at all gave her a feeling of almost illimitable power. It was true, as she said to herself, that if for this reason they would be able to discover nothing against her, so they would perhaps neglect to perceive some of her superior points; but she always wound up her reflections by declaring that she would take care of that.

Charlotte and Gertrude were in some perplexity between their desire to show all proper attention to Madame Münster and their fear of being importunate. The little house in the orchard had hitherto been occupied during the summer months by intimate friends of the family, or by poor relations who found in Mr. Wentworth a landlord attentive to repairs and oblivious of quarter-day. Under these circumstances the open door of the small house and that of the large one, facing each other across their homely gardens, levied no tax upon hourly visits. But the Misses Wentworth received an impression that Eugenia was no friend to the primitive custom of "dropping in;" she evidently had no idea of living without a doorkeeper. "One goes into your house as into an inn — except that there are no servants rushing forward," she said to Charlotte. And she added that that was very charming. Gertrude explained to her sister that she meant just the reverse; she didn't like it at all. Charlotte inquired why she should tell an untruth, and Gertrude answered that there was probably some very good reason for it which they should discover when they knew her better. "There can surely be no good reason for telling an untruth," said Charlotte. "I hope she does not think so."

They had of course desired, from the first, to do everything in the way of helping her to arrange herself. It had seemed to Charlotte that there would be a great many things to talk about; but the Baroness was apparently inclined to talk about nothing.

"Write her a note, asking her leave to come and see her. I think that is what she will like," said Gertrude.

"Why should I give her the trouble of answering me?" Charlotte asked. "She will have to write a note and send it over."

"I don't think she will take any

75

trouble," said Gertrude, profoundly.

"What then will she do?"

"That is what I am curious to see," said Gertrude, leaving her sister with an impression that her curiosity was morbid.

They went to see the Baroness without preliminary correspondence; and in the little salon which she had already created, with its becoming light and its festoons, they found Robert Acton.

Eugenia was intensely gracious, but she accused them of neglecting her cruelly. "You see Mr. Acton has had to take pity upon me," she said. "My brother goes off sketching, for hours; I can never depend upon him. So I was to send Mr. Acton to beg you to come and give me the benefit of your wisdom."

Gertrude looked at her sister. She wanted to say, "*That* is what she would have done." Charlotte said that they hoped the Baroness would always come and dine with them; it would give them so much pleasure; and, in that case, she would spare herself the trouble of having a cook.

"Ah, but I must have a cook!" cried the Baroness. "An old negress in a yellow turban. I have set my heart upon that. I want to look out of my window and see her sitting there on the grass, against the background of those crooked, dusky little apple-trees, pulling the husks off a lapful of Indian corn. That will be local color, you know. There isn't much of it here — you don't mind my

saying that, do you? — so one must make the most of what one can get. I shall be most happy to dine with you whenever you will let me; but I want to be able to ask you sometimes. And I want to be able to ask Mr. Acton," added the Baroness.

"You must come and ask me at home," said Acton. "You must come and see me; you must dine with me first. I want to show you my place; I want to introduce you to my mother." He called again upon Madame Münster, two days later. He was constantly at the other house; he used to walk across the fields from his own place, and he appeared to have fewer scruples than his cousins with regard to dropping in. On this occasion he found that Mr. Brand had come to pay his respects to the charming stranger; but after Acton's arrival the young theologian said nothing. He sat in his chair with his two hands clasped, fixing upon his hostess a grave, fascinated stare. The Baroness talked to Robert Acton, but, as she talked, she turned and smiled at Mr. Brand, who never took his eyes off her. The two men walked away together; they were going to Mr. Wentworth's. Mr. Brand still said nothing; but after they had passed into Mr. Wentworth's garden he stopped and looked back for some time at the little white house. Then, looking at his companion, with his head bent a little to one side and his eyes somewhat contracted, "Now I suppose that's what is called conversation," he said; "real conversation."

"It's what I call a very clever woman," said Acton, laughing.

"It is most interesting," Mr. Brand continued. "I only wish she would speak French; it would seem more in keeping. It must be quite the style that we have heard about, that we have read about — the style of conversation of Madame de Staël, of Madame Récamier."

Acton also looked at Madame Münster's residence among its hollyhocks and apple-trees. "What I should like to know," he said, smiling, "is just what has brought Madame Récamier to live in that place!"

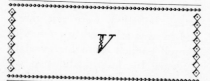

V

Mr. Wentworth, with his cane and his gloves in his hand, went every afternoon to call upon his niece. A couple of hours later she came over to the great house to tea. She had let the proposal that she should regularly dine there fall to the ground; she was in the enjoyment of whatever satisfaction was to be derived from the spectacle of an old negress in a crimson turban shelling peas under the apple-trees. Charlotte, who had provided the ancient negress, thought it must be a strange household, Eugenia having told her that Augustine managed everything, the ancient negress in-

cluded — Augustine who was naturally devoid of all acquaintance with the expurgatory English tongue. By far the most immoral sentiment which I shall have occasion to attribute to Charlotte Wentworth was a certain emotion of disappointment at finding that, in spite of these irregular conditions, the domestic arrangements at the small house were apparently not — from Eugenia's peculiar point of view — strikingly offensive. The Baroness found it amusing to go to tea; she dressed as if for dinner. The tea-table offered an anomalous and picturesque repast; and on leaving it they all sat and talked in the large piazza, or wandered about the garden in the starlight, with their ears full of those sounds of strange insects which, though they are supposed to be, all over the world, a part of the magic of summer nights, seemed to the Baroness to have beneath these western skies an incomparable resonance.

Mr. Wentworth, though, as I say, he went punctiliously to call upon her, was not able to feel that he was getting used to his niece. It taxed his imagination to believe that she was really his half-sister's child. His sister was a figure of his early years; she had been only twenty when she went abroad, never to return, making in foreign parts a willful and undesirable marriage. His aunt, Mrs. Whiteside, who had taken her to Europe for the benefit of the tour, gave, on her return, so lamentable an account of Mr. Adolphus

Young, to whom the headstrong girl had united her destiny, that it operated as a chill upon family feeling — especially in the case of the half-brothers. Catherine had done nothing subsequently to propitiate her family; she had not even written to them in a way that indicated a lucid appreciation of their suspended sympathy; so that it had become a tradition in Boston circles that the highest charity, as regards this young lady, was to think it well to forget her, and to abstain from conjecture as to the extent to which her aberrations were reproduced in her descendants. Over these young people — a vague report of their existence had come to his ears — Mr. Wentworth had not, in the course of years, allowed his imagination to hover. It had plenty of occupation nearer home, and though he had many cares upon his conscience the idea that he had been an unnatural uncle was, very properly, never among the number. Now that his nephew and niece had come before him, he perceived that they were the fruit of influences and circumstances very different from those under which his own familiar progeny had reached a vaguely-qualified maturity. He felt no provocation to say that these influences had been exerted for evil; but he was sometimes afraid that he should not be able to like his distinguished, delicate, lady-like niece. He was paralyzed and bewildered by her foreignness. She spoke, somehow, a different language.

There was something strange in her words. He had a feeling that another man, in his place, would accommodate himself to her tone; would ask her questions and joke with her, reply to those pleasantries of her own which sometimes seemed startling as addressed to an uncle. But Mr. Wentworth could not do these things. He could not even bring himself to attempt to measure her position in the world. She was the wife of a foreign nobleman who desired to repudiate her. This had a singular sound, but the old man felt himself destitute of the materials for a judgment. It seemed to him that he ought to find them in his own experience, as a man of the world and an almost public character; but they were not there, and he was ashamed to confess to himself — much more to reveal to Eugenia by interrogations possibly too innocent — the unfurnished condition of this repository.

It appeared to him that he could get much nearer, as he would have said, to his nephew; though he was not sure that Felix was altogether safe. He was so bright and handsome and talkative that it was impossible not to think well of him; and yet it seemed as if there were something almost impudent, almost vicious — or as if there ought to be — in a young man being at once so joyous and so positive. It was to be observed that while Felix was not at all a serious young man there was somehow more of him — he had more weight and volume and resonance

— than a number of young men who were distinctly serious. While Mr. Wentworth meditated upon this anomaly his nephew was admiring him unrestrictedly. He thought him a most delicate, generous, high-toned old gentleman, with a very handsome head, of the ascetic type, which he promised himself the profit of sketching. Felix was far from having made a secret of the fact that he wielded the paint-brush, and it was not his own fault if it failed to be generally understood that he was prepared to execute the most striking likenesses on the most reasonable terms. "He is an artist — my cousin is an artist," said Gertrude; and she offered this information to every one who would receive it. She offered it to herself, as it were, by way of admonition and reminder; she repeated to herself at odd moments, in lonely places, that Felix was invested with this sacred character. Gertrude had never seen an artist before; she had only read about such people. They seemed to her a romantic and mysterious class, whose life was made up of those agreeable accidents that never happened to other persons. And it merely quickened her meditations on this point that Felix should declare, as he repeatedly did, that he was really not an artist. "I have never gone into the thing seriously," he said. "I have never studied; I have had no training. I do a little of everything, and nothing well. I am only an amateur."

It pleased Gertrude even more to think that he was an amateur than to think that he was an artist; the former word, to her fancy, had an even subtler connotation. She knew, however, that it was a word to use more soberly. Mr. Wentworth used it freely; for though he had not been exactly familiar with it, he found it convenient as a help toward classifying Felix, who, as a young man extremely clever and active and apparently respectable and yet not engaged in any recognized business, was an importunate anomaly. Of course the Baroness and her brother — she was always spoken of first — were a welcome topic of conversation between Mr. Wentworth and his daughters and their occasional visitors.

"And the young man, your nephew, what is his profession?" asked an old gentleman — Mr. Broderip, of Salem — who had been Mr. Wentworth's classmate at Harvard College in the year 1809, and who came into his office in Devonshire Street. (Mr. Wentworth, in his later years, used to go but three times a week to his office, where he had a large amount of highly confidential trust-business to transact.)

"Well, he's an amateur," said Felix's uncle, with folded hands, and with a certain satisfaction in being able to say it. And Mr. Broderip had gone back to Salem with a feeling that this was probably a "European" expression for a broker or a grain exporter.

"I should like to do your head, sir," said Felix to his uncle one evening before them all—Mr. Brand and Robert Acton being also present. "I think I should make a very fine thing of it. It's an interesting head; it's very mediæval."

Mr. Wentworth looked grave; he felt awkwardly, as if all the company had come in and found him standing before the looking-glass. "The Lord made it," he said. "I don't think it is for man to make it over again."

"Certainly the Lord made it," replied Felix, laughing, "and he made it very well. But life has been touching up the work. It is a very interesting type of head. It's delightfully wasted and emaciated. The complexion is wonderfully bleached." And Felix looked round at the circle, as if to call their attention to these interesting points. Mr. Wentworth grew visibly paler. "I should like to do you as an old prelate, an old cardinal, or the prior of an order."

"A prelate, a cardinal?" murmured Mr. Wentworth. "Do you refer to the Roman Catholic priesthood?"

"I mean an old ecclesiastic who should have led a pure, abstinent life. Now I take it that has been the case with you, sir; one sees it in your face," Felix proceeded. "You have been very—a—very moderate. Don't you think one always sees that in a man's face?"

"You see more in a man's face than I should think of looking for," said Mr. Wentworth coldly.

The Baroness rattled her fan, and gave her brilliant laugh. "It is

a risk to look so close!" she exclaimed. "My uncle has some peccadilloes on his conscience." Mr. Wentworth looked at her, painfully at a loss; and in so far as the signs of a pure and abstinent life were visible in his face they were then probably peculiarly manifest. "You are a *beau vieillard*, dear uncle," said Madame Münster, smiling with her foreign eyes.

"I think you are paying me a compliment," said the old man.

"Surely, I am not the first woman that ever did so!" cried the Baroness.

"I think you are," said Mr. Wentworth gravely. And turning to Felix he added, in the same tone, "Please don't take my likeness. My children have my daguerreotype. That is quite satisfactory."

"I won't promise," said Felix, "not to work your head into something!"

Mr. Wentworth looked at him and then at all the others; then he got up and slowly walked away.

"Felix," said Gertrude, in the silence that followed, "I wish you would paint my portrait."

Charlotte wondered whether Gertrude was right in wishing this; and she looked at Mr. Brand as the most legitimate way of ascertaining. Whatever Gertrude did or said, Charlotte always looked at Mr. Brand. It was a standing pretext for looking at Mr. Brand — always, as Charlotte thought, in the interest of Gertrude's welfare. It is true that she felt a tremulous interest in Gertrude being right; for Charlotte, in her small, still way, was an heroic sister.

"We should be glad to have your portrait, Miss Gertrude," said Mr. Brand.

"I should be delighted to paint so charming a model," Felix declared.

"Do you think you are so lovely, my dear?" asked Lizzie Acton, with her little inoffensive pertness, biting off a knot in her knitting.

"It is not because I think I am beautiful," said Gertrude, looking all round. "I don't think I am beautiful, at all." She spoke with a sort of conscious deliberateness; and it seemed very strange to Charlotte to hear her discussing this question so publicly. "It is because I think it would be amusing to sit and be painted. I have always thought that."

"I am sorry you have not had better things to think about, my daughter," said Mr. Wentworth.

"You are very beautiful, cousin Gertrude," Felix declared.

"That's a compliment," said Gertrude. "I put all the compliments I receive into a little money-jug that has a slit in the side. I shake them up and down, and they rattle. There are not many yet — only two or three."

"No, it's not a compliment," Felix rejoined. "See; I am careful not to give it the form of a compliment. I didn't think you were beautiful at first. But you have come to seem so little by little."

"Take care, now, your jug doesn't burst!" exclaimed Lizzie.

"I think sitting for one's portrait is only one of the various forms of idleness," said Mr. Wentworth. "Their name is legion."

"My dear sir," cried Felix, "you can't be said to be idle when you are making a man work so!"

"One might be painted while one is asleep," suggested Mr. Brand, as a contribution to the discussion.

"Ah, do paint me while I am asleep," said Gertrude to Felix, smiling. And she closed her eyes a little. It had by this time become a matter of almost exciting anxiety to Charlotte what Gertrude would say or would do next.

She began to sit for her portrait on the following day — in the open air, on the north side of the piazza. "I wish you would tell me what you think of us — how we seem to you," she said to Felix, as he sat before his easel.

"You seem to me the best people in the world," said Felix.

"You say that," Gertrude resumed, "because it saves you the trouble of saying anything else."

The young man glanced at her over the top of his canvas. "What else should I say? It would certainly be a great deal of trouble to say anything different."

"Well," said Gertrude, "you have seen people before that you have liked, have you not?"

"Indeed I have, thank Heaven!"

"And they have been very different from us," Gertrude went on.

"That only proves," said Felix, "that there are a thousand different ways of being good company."

"Do you think us good company?" asked Gertrude.

"Company for a king!"

Gertrude was silent a moment; and then, "There must be a thousand different ways of being dreary," she said; "and sometimes I think we make use of them all."

Felix stood up quickly, holding up his hand. "If you could only keep that look on your face for half an hour — while I catch it!" he said. "It is uncommonly handsome."

"To look handsome for half an hour — that is a great deal to ask of me," she answered.

"It would be the portrait of a young woman who has taken some vow, some pledge, that she repents of," said Felix, "and who is thinking it over at leisure."

"I have taken no vow, no pledge," said Gertrude, very gravely; "I have nothing to repent of."

"My dear cousin, that was only a figure of speech. I am very sure that no one in your excellent family has anything to repent of."

"And yet we are always repenting!" Gertrude exclaimed. "That is what I mean by our being dreary. You know it perfectly well; you only pretend that you don't."

Felix gave a quick laugh. "The half hour is going on, and yet you are handsomer than ever. One must be careful what one says, you see."

"To me," said Gertrude, "you can say anything."

Felix looked at her, as an artist might, and painted for some time in silence.

"Yes, you seem to me different from your father and sister — from most of the people you have lived with," he observed.

"To say that one's self," Gertrude went on, "is like saying — by implication, at least — that one is better. I am not better; I am much worse. But they say themselves that I am different. It makes them unhappy."

"Since you accuse me of concealing my real impressions, I may admit that I think the tendency — among you generally — is to be made unhappy too easily."

"I wish you would tell that to my father," said Gertrude.

"It might make him more unhappy!" Felix exclaimed, laughing.

"It certainly would. I don't believe you have seen people like that."

"Ah, my dear cousin, how do you know what I have seen?" Felix demanded. "How can I tell you?"

"You might tell me a great many things, if you only would. You have seen people like yourself — people who are bright and gay and fond of amusement. We are not fond of amusement."

"Yes," said Felix, "I confess that rather strikes me. You don't seem to me to get all the pleasure out of life that you might. You don't seem to me to enjoy. . . . . Do you mind my saying this?" he asked, pausing.

"Please go on," said the girl, earnestly.

"You seem to me very well

placed for enjoying. You have money and liberty and what is called in Europe a 'position.' But you take a painful view of life, as one may say."

"One ought to think it bright and charming and delightful, eh?" asked Gertrude.

"I should say so — if one can. It is true it all depends upon that," Felix added.

"You know there is a great deal of misery in the world," said his model.

"I have seen a little of it," the young man rejoined. "But it was all over there — beyond the sea. I don't see any here. This is a paradise."

Gertrude said nothing; she sat looking at the dahlias and the currant-bushes in the garden, while Felix went on with his work. "To 'enjoy,'" she began at last, "to take life — not painfully, must one do something wrong?"

Felix gave his long, light laugh again. "Seriously, I think not. And for this reason, among others: you strike me as very capable of enjoying, if the chance were given you, and yet at the same time as incapable of wrong-doing."

"I am sure," said Gertrude, "that you are very wrong in telling a person that she is incapable of that. We are never nearer to evil than when we believe that."

"You are handsomer than ever," observed Felix, irrelevantly.

Gertrude had got used to hearing him say this. There was not so much excitement in it as at first. "What ought one to do?" she continued. "To give parties, to go to the theatre, to read novels, to keep late hours?"

"I don't think it's what one does or one doesn't do that promotes enjoyment," her companion answered. "It is the general way of looking at life."

"They look at it as a discipline — that's what they do here. I have often been told that."

"Well, that's very good. But there is another way," added Felix, smiling: "to look at it as an opportunity."

"An opportunity — yes," said Gertrude. "One would get more pleasure that way."

"I don't attempt to say anything better for it than that it has been my own way — and that is not saying much!" Felix had laid down his palette and brushes; he was leaning back, with his arms folded, to judge the effect of his work. "And you know," he said, "I am a very petty personage."

"You have a great deal of talent," said Gertrude.

"No — no," the young man rejoined, in a tone of cheerful impartiality, "I have not a great deal of talent. It is nothing at all remarkable. I assure you I should know if it were. I shall always be obscure. The world will never hear of me." Gertrude looked at him with a strange feeling. She was thinking of the great world which he knew and which she did not, and how full of brilliant talents it must be, since it could afford to make light of his abilities. "You needn't in general attach much importance to anything I tell you," he pursued; "but you may believe me when I say this, — that I am little better than a good-natured feather-head."

"A feather-head?" she repeated.

"I am a species of Bohemian."

"A Bohemian?" Gertrude had never heard this term before, save as a geographical denomination; and she quite failed to understand the figurative meaning which her companion appeared to attach to it. But it gave her pleasure.

Felix had pushed back his chair and risen to his feet; he slowly came toward her, smiling. "I am a sort of adventurer," he said, looking down at her.

She got up, meeting his smile. "An adventurer?" she repeated. "I should like to hear your adventures."

For an instant she believed that he was going to take her hand; but he dropped his own hands suddenly into the pockets of his painting-jacket. "There is no reason why you shouldn't," he said. "I have been an adventurer, but my adventures have been very innocent. They have all been happy ones; I don't think there are any I shouldn't tell. They were very pleasant and very pretty; I should like to go over them in memory. Sit down again, and I will begin," he added in a moment, with his naturally persuasive smile.

Gertrude sat down again on that day, and she sat down on several other days. Felix, while he plied his brush, told her a great many stories, and she listened with charmed avidity. Her eyes rested upon his lips; she was very serious; sometimes, from her air of wondering gravity, he thought she was displeased. But Felix never believed for more than a single moment in any displeasure of his own producing. This would have been fatuity if the optimism it expressed had not been much more a hope than a prejudice. It is beside the matter to say that he had a good conscience; for the best conscience is a sort of self-reproach, and this young man's brilliantly healthy nature spent itself in objective good intentions which were ignorant of any test save exactness in hitting their mark. He told Gertrude how he had walked over France and Italy with a painter's knapsack on his back, paying his way often by knocking off a flattering portrait of his host or hostess. He told her how he had played the violin in a little band of musicians — not of high celebrity — who traveled through foreign lands giving provincial concerts. He told her also how he had been a momentary ornament of a troupe of strolling actors, engaged in the arduous task of interpreting Shakespeare to French and German, Polish and Hungarian audiences.

While this periodical recital was going on, Gertrude lived in a fantastic world; she seemed to herself to be reading a romance that came out in daily numbers. She had known nothing so delightful since the perusal of "Nicholas Nickleby." One afternoon she went to see her cousin, Mrs. Acton,

84

Robert's mother, who was a great invalid, never leaving the house. She came back alone, on foot, across the fields — this being a short way which they often used. Felix had gone to Boston with her father, who desired to take the young man to call upon some of his friends, old gentlemen who remembered his mother — remembered her, but said nothing about her — and several of whom, with the gentle ladies their wives, had driven out from town to pay their respects at the little house among the apple-trees, in vehicles which reminded the Baroness, who received her visitors with discriminating civility, of the large, light, rattling barouche in which she herself had made her journey to this neighborhood. The afternoon was waning; in the western sky the great picture of a New England sunset, painted in crimson and silver, was suspended from the zenith; and the stony pastures, as Gertrude traversed them, thinking intently to herself, were covered with a light, clear glow. At the open gate of one of the fields she saw from the distance a man's figure; he stood there as if he were waiting for her, and as she came nearer she recognized Mr. Brand. She had a feeling as of not having seen him for some time; she could not have said for how long, for it yet seemed to her that he had been very lately at the house.

"May I walk back with you?" he asked. And when she had said that he might if he wanted, he ob-

served that he had seen her and recognized her half a mile away.

"You must have very good eyes," said Gertrude.

"Yes, I have very good eyes, Miss Gertrude," said Mr. Brand. She perceived that he meant something; but for a long time past Mr. Brand had constantly meant something, and she had almost got used to it. She felt, however, that what he meant had now a renewed power to disturb her, to perplex and agitate her. He walked beside her in silence for a moment, and then he added, "I have had no trouble in seeing that you are beginning to avoid me. But perhaps," he went on, "one needn't have had very good eyes to see that."

"I have not avoided you," said Gertrude, without looking at him.

"I think you have been unconscious that you were avoiding me," Mr. Brand replied. "You have not even known that I was there."

"Well, you are here now, Mr. Brand!" said Gertrude, with a little laugh. "I know that very well."

He made no rejoinder. He simply walked beside her slowly, as they were obliged to walk over the soft grass. Presently they came to another gate, which was closed. Mr. Brand laid his hand upon it, but he made no movement to open it; he stood and looked at his companion. "You are very much interested — very much absorbed," he said.

Gertrude glanced at him; she saw that he was pale and that he looked excited. She had never seen

Mr. Brand excited before, and she felt that the spectacle, if fully carried out, would be impressive, almost painful. "Absorbed in what?" she asked. Then she looked away at the illuminated sky. She felt guilty and uncomfortable, and yet she was vexed with herself for feeling so. But Mr. Brand, as he stood there looking at her with his small, kind, persistent eyes, represented an immense body of half-obliterated obligations, that were rising again into a certain distinctness.

"You have new interests, new occupations," he went on. "I don't know that I can say that you have new duties. We have always old ones, Gertrude," he added.

"Please open the gate, Mr. Brand," she said; and she felt as if, in saying so, she were cowardly and petulant. But he opened the gate, and allowed her to pass; then he closed it behind himself. Before she had time to turn away he put out his hand and held her an instant by the wrist.

"I want to say something to you," he said.

"I know what you want to say," she answered. And she was on the point of adding, "And I know just how you will say it;" but these words she kept back.

"I love you, Gertrude," he said. "I love you very much; I love you more than ever."

He said the words just as she had known he would; she had heard them before. They had no charm for her; she had said to herself before that it was very strange.

It was supposed to be delightful for a woman to listen to such words; but these seemed to her flat and mechanical. "I wish you would forget that," she declared.

"How can I — why should I?" he asked.

"I have made you no promise — given you no pledge," she said, looking at him, with her voice trembling a little.

"You have let me feel that I have an influence over you. You have opened your mind to me."

"I never opened my mind to you, Mr. Brand!" Gertrude cried, with some vehemence.

"Then you were not so frank as I thought — as we all thought."

"I don't see what any one else had to do with it!" cried the girl.

"I mean your father and your sister. You know it makes them happy to think you will listen to me."

She gave a little laugh. "It doesn't make them happy," she said. "Nothing makes them happy. No one is happy here."

"I think your cousin is very happy — Mr. Young," rejoined Mr. Brand, in a soft, almost timid tone.

"So much the better for him!" And Gertrude gave her little laugh again.

The young man looked at her a moment. "You are very much changed," he said.

"I am glad to hear it," Gertrude declared.

"I am not. I have known you a long time, and I have loved you as you were."

"I am much obliged to you,"

said Gertrude. "I must be going home."

He on his side, gave a little laugh.

"You certainly do avoid me — you see!"

"Avoid me, then," said the girl.

He looked at her again; and then, very gently, "No I will not avoid you," he replied; "but I will leave you, for the present, to yourself. I think you will remember — after a while — some of the things you have forgotten. I think you will come back to me; I have great faith in that."

This time his voice was very touching; there was a strong, reproachful force in what he said, and Gertrude could answer nothing. He turned away and stood there, leaning his elbows on the gate and looking at the beautiful sunset. Gertrude left him and took her way home again; but when she reached the middle of the next field she suddenly burst into tears. Her tears seemed to her to have been a long time gathering, and for some moments it was a kind of glee to shed them. But they presently passed away. There was something a little hard about Gertrude; and she never wept again.

VI

Going of an afternoon to call upon his niece, Mr. Wentworth more than once found Robert Acton sitting in her little drawing-room. This was in no degree, to Mr. Wentworth, a perturbing fact, for he had no sense of competing with his young kinsman for Eugenia's good graces. Madame Münster's uncle had the highest opinion of Robert Acton, who, indeed, in the family at large, was the object of a great deal of undemonstrative appreciation. They were all proud of him, in so far as the charge of being proud may be brought against people who were, habitually, distinctly guiltless of the misdemeanor known as "taking credit." They never boasted of Robert Acton, nor indulged in vainglorious reference to him; they never quoted the clever things he had said, nor mentioned the generous things he had done. But a sort of frigidly-tender faith in his unlimited goodness was a part of their personal sense of right; and there can, perhaps, be no better proof of the high esteem in which he was held than the fact that no explicit judgment was ever passed upon his actions. He was no more praised than he was blamed; but he was tacitly felt to be an ornament to his circle. He was the man of the world of the family. He had been to China and brought home a collection of curiosities; he had made a fortune — or rather he had quintupled a fortune already considerable; he was distinguished by that combination of celibacy, "property," and good humor which appeals to even the most subdued imaginations; and it was taken for granted that he would presently place these advantages at the disposal of some well-regulated young woman of his own "set." Mr. Wentworth was not a man to admit to himself that — his paternal duties apart — he liked any individual much better than all other individuals; but he thought Robert Acton extremely judicious; and this was perhaps as near an approach as he was capable of to the eagerness of preference, which his temperament repudiated as it would have disengaged itself from something slightly unchaste. Acton was, in fact, very judicious — and something more beside; and indeed it must be claimed for Mr. Wentworth that in the more illicit parts of his preference there hovered the vague adumbration of a belief that his cousin's final merit was a certain enviable capacity for whistling, rather gallantly, at the sanctions of mere judgment — for showing a larger courage, a finer quality of pluck, than common occasion demanded. Mr. Wentworth would never have risked the intimation that Acton was made, in the smallest degree, of the stuff of a hero; but this is small blame to him, for Robert would certainly never have risked it himself. Acton certainly exercised great discretion in all things — beginning with his estimate of himself. He knew that he was by no means so much of a man of the world as he was supposed to be in local circles; but it must be added that he knew also that his natural shrewdness had a reach of which he had never quite given local circles the measure. He was addicted to taking

the humorous view of things, and he had discovered that even in the narrowest circles such a disposition may find frequent opportunities. Such opportunities had formed for some time — that is, since his return from China, a year and a half before — the most active element in this gentleman's life, which had just now a rather indolent air. He was perfectly willing to get married. He was very fond of books, and he had a handsome library; that is, his books were much more numerous than Mr. Wentworth's. He was also very fond of pictures; but it must be confessed, in the fierce light of contemporary criticism, that his walls were adorned with several rather abortive masterpieces. He had got his learning — and there was more of it than commonly appeared — at Harvard College; and he took a pleasure in old associations, which made it a part of his daily contentment to live so near this institution that he often passed it in driving to Boston. He was extremely interested in the Baroness Münster.

She was very frank with him; or at least she intended to be. "I am sure you find it very strange that I should have settled down in this out-of-the-way part of the world!" she said to him three or four weeks after she had installed herself. "I am certain you are wondering about my motives. They are very pure." The Baroness by this time was an old inhabitant; the best society in Boston had called upon her, and Clifford Wentworth had taken her several times to drive in his buggy.

Robert Acton was seated near her, playing with a fan; there were always several fans lying about her drawing-room, with long ribbons of different colors attached to them, and Acton was always playing with one. "No, I don't find it at all strange," he said slowly, smiling. "That a clever woman should turn up in Boston, or its suburbs — that does not require so much explanation. Boston is a very nice place."

"If you wish to make me contradict you," said the Baroness, "*vous vous y prenez mal*. In certain moods there is nothing I am not capable of agreeing to. Boston is a paradise, and we are in the suburbs of Paradise."

"Just now I am not at all in the suburbs; I am in the place itself," rejoined Acton, who was lounging a little in his chair. He was, however, not always lounging; and when he was he was not quite so relaxed as he pretended. To a certain extent, he sought refuge from shyness in this appearance of relaxation; and like many persons in the same circumstances he somewhat exaggerated the appearance. Beyond this, the air of being much at his ease was a cover for vigilant observation. He was more than interested in this clever woman, who, whatever he might say, was clever not at all after the Boston fashion; she plunged him into a kind of excitement, held him in vague suspense. He was obliged to admit to himself that

he had never yet seen a woman just like this — not even in China. He was ashamed, for inscrutable reasons, of the vivacity of his emotion, and he carried it off, superficially, by taking, still superficially, the humorous view of Madame Münster. It was not at all true that he thought it very natural of her to have made this pious pilgrimage. It might have been said of him in advance that he was too good a Bostonian to regard in the light of an eccentricity the desire of even the remotest alien to visit the New England metropolis. This was an impulse for which, surely, no apology was needed; and Madame Münster was the fortunate possessor of several New England cousins. In fact, however, Madame Münster struck him as out of keeping with her little circle; she was at the best a very agreeable, a gracefully mystifying anomaly. He knew very well that it would not do to address these reflections too crudely to Mr. Wentworth; he would never have remarked to the old gentleman that he wondered what the Baroness was up to. And indeed he had no great desire to share his vague mistrust with any one. There was a personal pleasure in it; the greatest pleasure he had known at least since he had come from China. He would keep the Baroness, for better or worse, to himself; he had a feeling that he deserved to enjoy a monopoly of her, for he was certainly the person who had most adequately gauged her capacity for social intercourse. Before long it became apparent to him that the Baroness was disposed to lay no tax upon such a monopoly.

One day (he was sitting there again and playing with a fan) she asked him to apologize, should the occasion present itself, to certain people in Boston for her not having returned their calls. "There are half a dozen places," she said; "a formidable list. Charlotte Wentworth has written it out for me, in a terrifically distinct hand. There is no ambiguity on the subject; I know perfectly where I must go. Mr. Wentworth informs me that the carriage is always at my disposal, and Charlotte offers to go with me, in a pair of tight gloves and a very stiff petticoat. And yet for three days I have been putting it off. They must think me horribly vicious."

"You ask me to apologize," said Acton, "but you don't tell me what excuse I can offer."

"That is more," the Baroness declared, "than I am held to. It would be like my asking you to buy me a bouquet and giving you the money. I have no reason except that — somehow — it's too violent an effort. It is not inspiring. Wouldn't that serve as an excuse, in Boston? I am told they are very sincere; they don't tell fibs. And then Felix ought to go with me, and he is never in readiness. I don't see him. He is always roaming about the fields and sketching old barns, or taking ten-mile walks, or painting some one's portrait, or rowing on the pond, or flirting with Gertrude Wentworth."

"I should think it would amuse you to go and see a few people," said Acton. "You are having a very quiet time of it here. It's a dull life for you."

"Ah, the quiet, — the quiet!" the Baroness exclaimed. "That's what I like. It's rest. That's what I came here for. Amusement? I have had amusement. And as for seeing people — I have already seen a great many in my life. If it didn't sound ungracious I should say that I wish very humbly your people here would leave me alone!"

Acton looked at her a moment, and she looked at him. She was a woman who took being looked at remarkably well. "So you have come here for rest?" he asked.

"So I may say. I came for many of those reasons that are no reasons — don't you know? — and yet that are really the best: to come away, to change, to break with everything. When once one comes away one must arrive somewhere, and I asked myself why I shouldn't arrive here."

"You certainly had time on the way!" said Acton, laughing.

Madame Münster looked at him again; and then, smiling: "And I have certainly had time, since I got here, to ask myself why I came. However, I never ask myself idle questions. Here I am, and it seems to me you ought only to thank me."

"When you go away you will see the difficulties I shall put in your path."

"You mean to put difficulties in

my path?" she asked, rearranging the rosebud in her corsage.

"The greatest of all — that of having been so agreeable" —

"That I shall be unable to depart? Don't be too sure. I have left some very agreeable people over there."

"Ah," said Acton, "but it was to come here, where I am!"

"I didn't know of your existence. Excuse me for saying anything so rude; but, honestly speaking, I did not. No," the Baroness pursued, "it was precisely not to see you — such people as you — that I came."

"Such people as me?" cried Acton.

"I had a sort of longing to come into those natural relations which I knew I should find here. Over there I had only, as I may say, artificial relations. Don't you see the difference?"

"The difference tells against me," said Acton. "I suppose I am an artificial relation."

"Conventional," declared the Baroness; "very conventional."

"Well, there is one way in which the relation of a lady and a gentleman may always become natural," said Acton.

"You mean by their becoming lovers? That may be natural or not. And at any rate," rejoined Eugenia, *"nous n'en sommes pas là!"*

They were not, as yet; but a little later, when she began to go with him to drive, it might almost have seemed that they were. He came for her several times, alone, in his high "wagon," drawn by a pair of charming light-limbed horses. It was different, her having gone with Clifford Wentworth, who was her cousin, and so much younger. It was not to be imagined that she should have a flirtation with Clifford, who was a mere shame-faced boy, and whom a large section of Boston society supposed to be "engaged" to Lizzie Acton. Not, indeed, that it was to be conceived that the Baroness was a possible party to any flirtation whatever; for she was undoubtedly a married lady. It was generally known that her matrimonial condition was of the "morganatic" order; but in its natural aversion to suppose that this meant anything less than absolute wedlock, the conscience of the community took refuge in the belief that it implied something even more.

Acton wished her to think highly of American scenery, and he drove her to great distances, picking out the prettiest roads and the largest points of view. If we are good when we are contented, Eugenia's virtues should now certainly have been uppermost; for she found a charm in the rapid movement through a wild country, and in a companion who from time to time made the vehicle dip, with a motion like a swallow's flight, over roads of primitive construction, and who, as she felt, would do a great many things that she might ask him. Sometimes, for a couple of hours together, there were almost no houses; there were nothing but woods and rivers and lakes and horizons adorned with bright-looking mountains. It seemed to the Baroness very wild, as I have said, and lovely; but the impression added something to that sense of the enlargement of opportunity which had been born of her arrival in the New World.

One day — it was late in the afternoon — Acton pulled up his horses on the crest of a hill which commanded a beautiful prospect. He let them stand a long time to rest, while he sat there and talked with Madame Münster. The prospect was beautiful in spite of there being nothing human within sight. There was a wilderness of woods, and the gleam of a distant river, and a glimpse of half the hill-tops in Massachusetts. The road had a wide, grassy margin, on the further side of which there flowed a deep, clear brook; there were wild flowers in the grass, and beside the brook lay the trunk of a fallen tree. Acton waited a while; at last a rustic wayfarer came trudging along the road. Acton asked him to hold the horses — a service he consented to render, as a friendly turn to a fellow-citizen. Then he invited the Baroness to descend, and the two wandered away, across the grass, and sat down on the log beside the brook.

"I imagine it doesn't remind you of Silberstadt," said Acton. It was the first time that he had mentioned Silberstadt to her, for particular reasons. He knew she had a husband there, and this was disagreeable to him; and, further-

more, it had been repeated to him that this husband wished to put her away — a state of affairs to which even indirect reference was to be deprecated. It was true, nevertheless, that the Baroness herself had often alluded to Silberstadt; and Acton had often wondered why her husband wished to get rid of her. It was a curious position for a lady — this being known as a repudiated wife; and it is worthy of observation that the Baroness carried it off with exceeding grace and dignity. She had made it felt, from the first, that there were two sides to the question, and that her own side, when she should choose to present it, would be replete with touching interest.

"It does not remind me of the town, of course," she said, "of the sculptured gables and the Gothic churches, of the wonderful Schloss, with its moat and its clustering towers. But it has a little look of some other parts of the principality. One might fancy one's self among those grand old German forests, those legendary mountains; the sort of country one sees from the windows at Schreckenstein."

"What is Schreckenstein?" asked Acton.

"It is a great castle, — the summer residence of the Reigning Prince."

"Have you ever lived there?"

"I have stayed there," said the Baroness. Acton was silent; he looked a while at the uncastled landscape before him. "It is the first time you have ever asked me about Silberstadt," she said. "I should think you would want to know about my marriage; it must seem to you very strange."

Acton looked at her a moment. "Now you wouldn't like me to say that!"

"You Americans have such odd ways!" the Baroness declared. "You never ask anything outright; there seem to be so many things you can't talk about."

"We Americans are very polite," said Acton, whose national consciousness had been complicated by a residence in foreign lands, and who yet disliked to hear Americans abused. "We don't like to tread upon people's toes," he said. "But I should like very much to hear about your marriage. Now tell me how it came about."

"The Prince fell in love with me," replied the Baroness simply. "He pressed his suit very hard. At first he didn't wish me to marry him; on the contrary. But on that basis I refused to listen to him. So he offered me marriage — in so far as he might. I was young, and I confess I was rather flattered. But if it were to be done again now, I certainly should not accept him."

"How long ago was this?" asked Acton.

"Oh — several years," said Eugenia. "You should never ask a woman for dates."

"Why, I should think that when a woman was relating history" . . . . Acton answered. "And now he wants to break it off?"

"They want him to make a po-litical marriage. It is his brother's idea. His brother is very clever."

"They must be a precious pair!" cried Robert Acton.

The Baroness gave a little philosophic shrug. "Que voulez-vous? They are princes. They think they are treating me very well. Silberstadt is a perfectly despotic little state, and the Reigning Prince may annul the marriage by a stroke of his pen. But he has promised me, nevertheless, not to do so without my formal consent."

"And this you have refused?"

"Hitherto. It is an indignity, and I have wished at least to make it difficult for them. But I have a little document in my writing-desk which I have only to sign and send back to the Prince."

"Then it will be all over?"

The Baroness lifted her hand, and dropped it again. "Of course I shall keep my title; at least, I shall be at liberty to keep it if I choose. And I suppose I shall keep it. One must have a name. And I shall keep my pension. It is very small — it is wretchedly small; but it is what I live on."

"And you have only to sign that paper?" Acton asked.

The Baroness looked at him a moment. "Do you urge it?"

He got up slowly, and stood with his hands in his pockets. "What do you gain by not doing it?"

"I am supposed to gain this advantage — that if I delay, or temporize, the Prince may come back to me, may make a stand against his brother. He is very fond of me, and his brother has pushed him only little by little."

"If he were to come back to you," said Acton, "would you — would you take him back?"

The Baroness met his eyes; she colored just a little. Then she rose. "I should have the satisfaction of saying, 'Now it is my turn. I break with your serene highness!'"

They began to walk toward the carriage. "Well," said Robert Acton, "it's a curious story! How did you make his acquaintance?"

"I was staying with an old lady — an old Countess — in Dresden. She had been a friend of my father's. My father was dead; I was very much alone. My brother was wandering about the world in a theatrical troupe."

"Your brother ought to have stayed with you," Acton observed, "and kept you from putting your trust in princes."

The Baroness was silent a moment, and then, "He did what he could," she said. "He sent me money. The old Countess encouraged the Prince; she was even pressing. It seems to me," Madame Münster added, gently, "that — under the circumstances — I behaved very well."

Acton glanced at her, and made the observation — he had made it before — that a woman looks the prettier for having unfolded her wrongs or her sufferings. "Well," he reflected, audibly, "I should like to see you send his serene highness — somewhere!"

Madame Münster stooped and plucked a daisy from the grass.

"And not sign my renunciation?"

"Well, I don't know — I don't know," said Acton.

"In one case I should have my revenge; in another case I should have my liberty."

Acton gave a little laugh as he helped her into the carriage. "At any rate," he said, "take good care of that paper."

A couple of days afterward he asked her to come and see his house. The visit had already been proposed, but it had been put off in consequence of his mother's illness. She was a constant invalid, and she had passed these recent years, very patiently, in a great flowered arm-chair at her bedroom window. Lately, for some days, she had been unable to see any one; but now she was better, and she sent the Baroness a very civil message. Acton had wished their visitor to come to dinner; but Madame Münster preferred to begin with a simple call. She had reflected that if she should go to dinner Mr. Wentworth and his daughters would also be asked, and it had seemed to her that the peculiar character of the occasion would be best preserved in a *tête-à-tête* with her host. Why the occasion should have a peculiar character she explained to no one. As far as any one could see, it was simply very pleasant. Acton came for her and drove her to his door, an operation which was rapidly performed. His house the Baroness mentally pronounced a very good one; more articulately, she declared that it was enchanting. It was large and square and painted brown; it stood in a well-kept shrubbery, and was approached, from the gate, by a short drive. It was, moreover, a much more modern dwelling than Mr. Wentworth's, and was more redundantly upholstered and expensively ornamented. The Baroness perceived that her entertainer had analyzed material comfort to a sufficiently fine point. And then he possessed the most delightful *chinoiseries* — trophies of his sojourn in the Celestial Empire: pagodas of ebony and cabinets of ivory; sculptured monsters, grinning and leering on chimney-pieces, in front of beautifully figured hand-screens; porcelain dinner-sets, gleaming behind the glass doors of mahogany buffets; large screens, in corners, covered with tense silk and embroidered with mandarins and dragons. These things were scattered all over the house, and they gave Eugenia a pretext for a complete domiciliary visit. She liked it, she enjoyed it; she thought it a very nice place. It had a mixture of the homely and the liberal, and though it was almost a museum, the large, little-used rooms were as fresh and clean as a well-kept dairy. Lizzie Acton told her that she dusted all the pagodas and other curiosities every day with her own hands; and the Baroness answered that she was evidently a household fairy. Lizzie had not at all the look of a young lady who dusted things; she wore such pretty dresses and had such delicate fin-

gers that it was difficult to imagine her immersed in sordid cares. She came to meet Madame Münster on her arrival, but she said nothing, or almost nothing, and the Baroness again reflected — she had had occasion to do so before — that American girls had no manners. She disliked this little American girl, and she was quite prepared to learn that she had failed to commend herself to Miss Acton. Lizzie struck her as positive and explicit almost to pertness; and the idea of her combining the apparent incongruities of a taste for housework and the wearing of fresh, Parisian-looking dresses suggested the possession of a dangerous energy. It was a source of irritation to the Baroness that in this country it should seem to matter whether a little girl were a trifle less or a trifle more of a nonentity; for Eugenia had hitherto been conscious of no moral pressure as regards the appreciation of diminutive virgins. It was perhaps an indication of Lizzie's pertness that she very soon retired and left the Baroness on her brother's hands. Acton talked a great deal about his chinoiseries; he knew a good deal about porcelain and bric-a-brac. The Baroness, in her progress through the house, made, as it were, a great many stations. She sat down everywhere, confessed to being a little tired, and asked about the various objects with a curious mixture of alertness and inattention. If there had been any one to say it to she would have declared that she was positively in love with her host; but she could hardly make this declaration — even in the strictest confidence — to Acton himself. It gave her, nevertheless, a pleasure that had some of the charm of unwontedness to feel, with that admirable keenness with which she was capable of feeling things, that he had a disposition without any edges; that even his humorous irony always expanded toward the point. One's impression of his honesty was almost like carrying a bunch of flowers; the perfume was most agreeable, but they were occasionally an inconvenience. One could trust him, at any rate, round all the corners of the world; and, withal, he was not absolutely simple, which would have been excess; he was only relatively simple, which was quite enough for the Baroness.

Lizzie reappeared to say that her mother would now be happy to receive Madame Münster; and the Baroness followed her to Mrs. Acton's apartment. Eugenia reflected, as she went, that it was not the affectation of impertinence that made her dislike this young lady, for on that ground she could easily have beaten her. It was not an aspiration on the girl's part to rivalry, but a kind of laughing, childishly-mocking indifference to the results of comparison. Mrs. Acton was an emaciated, sweet-faced woman of five and fifty, sitting with pillows behind her, and looking out on a clump of hemlocks. She was very modest, very timid, and very ill; she made Eu-genia feel grateful that she herself was not like that — neither so ill, nor, possibly, so modest. On a chair, beside her, lay a volume of Emerson's Essays. It was a great occasion for poor Mrs. Acton, in her helpless condition, to be confronted with a clever foreign lady, who had more manner than any lady — any dozen ladies — that she had ever seen.

"I have heard a great deal about you," she said, softly, to the Baroness.

"From your son, eh?" Eugenia asked. "He has talked to me immensely of you. Oh, he talks of you as you would like," the Baroness declared; "as such a son *must* talk of such a mother!"

Mrs. Acton sat gazing; this was part of Madame Münster's "manner." But Robert Acton was gazing too, in vivid consciousness that he had barely mentioned his mother to their brilliant guest. He never talked of this still maternal presence, — a presence refined to such delicacy that it had almost resolved itself, with him, simply into the subjective emotion of gratitude. And Acton rarely talked of his emotions. The Baroness turned her smile toward him, and she instantly felt that she had been observed to be fibbing. She had struck a false note. But who were these people to whom such fibbing was not pleasing? If they were annoyed, the Baroness was equally so; and after the exchange of a few civil inquiries and low-voiced responses she took leave of Mrs. Acton. She begged Robert not to come home with her; she would get into the carriage alone; she preferred that. This was imperious, and she thought he looked disappointed. While she stood before the door with him — the carriage was turning in the gravel-walk — this thought restored her serenity.

When she had given him her hand in farewell she looked at him a moment. "I have almost decided to dispatch that paper," she said.

He knew that she alluded to the document that she had called her renunciation; and he assisted her into the carriage without saying anything. But just before the vehicle began to move he said, "Well, when you have in fact dispatched it, I hope you will let me know!"

VII

FELIX YOUNG finished Gertrude's portrait, and he afterwards transferred to canvas the features of many members of that circle of which it may be said that he had become for the time the pivot and the centre. I am afraid it must be confessed that he was a decidedly flattering painter, and that he imparted to his models a romantic grace which seemed easily and cheaply acquired by the payment of a hundred dollars to a young man who made "sitting" so entertaining. For Felix was paid for his pictures, making, as he did, no secret of the fact that in guiding

his steps to the Western world affectionate curiosity had gone hand in hand with a desire to better his condition. He took his uncle's portrait quite as if Mr. Wentworth had never averted himself from the experiment; and as he compassed his end only by the exercise of gentle violence, it is but fair to add that he allowed the old man to give him nothing but his time. He passed his arm into Mr. Wentworth's one summer morning — very few arms indeed had ever passed into Mr. Wentworth's — and led him across the garden and along the road into the studio which he had extemporized in the little house among the apple-trees. The grave gentleman felt himself more and more fascinated by his clever nephew, whose fresh, demonstrative youth seemed a compendium of experiences so strangely numerous. It appeared to him that Felix must know a great deal; he would like to learn what he thought about some of those things as regards which his own conversation had always been formal, but his knowledge vague. Felix had a confident, gayly trenchant way of judging human actions which Mr. Wentworth grew little by little to envy; it seemed like criticism made easy. Forming an opinion — say on a person's conduct — was, with Mr. Wentworth, a good deal like fumbling in a lock with a key chosen at hazard. He seemed to himself to go about the world with a big bunch of these ineffectual instruments at his girdle. His nephew, on the other hand, with a single turn of the wrist, opened any door as adroitly as a horse-thief. He felt obliged to keep up the convention that an uncle is always wiser than a nephew, even if he could keep it up no otherwise than by listening in serious silence to Felix's quick, light, constant discourse. But there came a day when he lapsed from consistency and almost asked his nephew's advice.

"Have you ever entertained the idea of settling in the United States?" he asked one morning, while Felix brilliantly plied his brush.

"My dear uncle," said Felix, "excuse me if your question makes me smile a little. To begin with, I have never entertained an idea. Ideas often entertain *me;* but I am afraid I have never seriously made a plan. I know what you are going to say; or rather, I know what you think, for I don't think you will say it — that this is very frivolous and loose-minded on my part. So it is; but I am made like that; I take things as they come, and somehow there is always some new thing to follow the last. In the second place, I should never propose to *settle.* I can't settle, my dear uncle; I'm not a settler. I know that is what strangers are supposed to do here; they always settle. But I haven't — to answer your question — entertained that idea."

"You intend to return to Europe and resume your irregular manner of life?" Mr. Wentworth inquired.

"I can't say I intend. But it's very likely I shall go back to Europe. After all, I am a European. I feel that, you know. It will depend a good deal upon my sister. She's even more of a European than I; here, you know, she's a picture out of her setting. And as for 'resuming,' dear uncle, I really have never given up my irregular manner of life. What, for me, could be more irregular than this?"

"Than what?" asked Mr. Wentworth, with his pale gravity.

"Well, than everything! Living in the midst of you, this way; this charming, quiet, serious family life; fraternizing with Charlotte and Gertrude; calling upon twenty young ladies and going out to walk with them; sitting with you in the evening on the piazza and listening to the crickets, and going to bed at ten o'clock."

"Your description is very animated," said Mr. Wentworth; "but I see nothing improper in what you describe."

"Neither do I, dear uncle. It is extremely delightful; I shouldn't like it if it were improper. I assure you I don't like improper things; though I dare say you think I do," Felix went on, painting away.

"I have never accused you of that."

"Pray don't," said Felix, "because, you see, at bottom I am a terrible Philistine."

"A Philistine?" repeated Mr. Wentworth.

"I mean, as one may say, a plain, God-fearing man." Mr. Wentworth looked at him reservedly, like a mystified sage, and Felix continued, "I trust I shall enjoy a venerable and venerated old age. I mean to live long. I can hardly call that a plan, perhaps; but it's a keen desire — a rosy vision. I shall be a lively, perhaps even a frivolous old man!"

"It is natural," said his uncle, sententiously, "that one should desire to prolong an agreeable life. We have perhaps a selfish indisposition to bring our pleasure to a close. But I presume," he added, "that you expect to marry."

"That too, dear uncle, is a hope, a desire, a vision," said Felix. It occurred to him for an instant that this was possibly a preface to the offer of the hand of one of Mr. Wentworth's admirable daughters. But in the name of decent modesty and a proper sense of the hard realities of this world, Felix banished the thought. His uncle was the incarnation of benevolence, certainly; but from that to accepting — much more postulating — the idea of a union between a young lady with a dowry presumptively brilliant and a penniless artist with no prospect of fame, there was a very long way. Felix had lately become conscious of a luxurious preference for the society — if possible unshared with others — of Gertrude Wentworth; but he had relegated this young lady, for the moment, to the coldly brilliant category of unattainable possessions. She was not the first woman for whom he had entertained an unpractical admiration.

He had been in love with duchesses and countesses, and he had made, once or twice, a perilously near approach to cynicism in declaring that the disinterestedness of women had been overrated. On the whole, he had tempered audacity with modesty; and it is but fair to him now to say explicitly that he would have been incapable of taking advantage of his present large allowance of familiarity to make love to the younger of his handsome cousins. Felix had grown up among traditions in the light of which such a proceeding looked like a grievous breach of hospitality. I have said that he was always happy, and it may be counted among the present sources of his happiness that he had as regards this matter of his relations with Gertrude a deliciously good conscience. His own deportment seemed to him suffused with the beauty of virtue — a form of beauty that he admired with the same vivacity with which he admired all other forms.

"I think that if you marry," said Mr. Wentworth presently, "it will conduce to your happiness."

"*Sicurissimo!*" Felix exclaimed; and then, arresting his brush, he looked at his uncle with a smile. "There is something I feel tempted to say to you. May I risk it?"

Mr. Wentworth drew himself up a little. "I am very safe; I don't repeat things." But he hoped Felix would not risk too much.

Felix was laughing at his answer.

"It's odd to hear you telling me

how to be happy. I don't think you know yourself, dear uncle. Now, does that sound brutal?"

The old man was silent a moment, and then, with a dry dignity that suddenly touched his nephew: "We may sometimes point out a road we are unable to follow."

"Ah, don't tell me you have had any sorrows," Felix rejoined. "I didn't suppose it, and I didn't mean to allude to them. I simply meant that you all don't amuse yourselves."

"Amuse ourselves? We are not children."

"Precisely not! You have reached the proper age. I was saying that the other day to Gertrude," Felix added. "I hope it was not indiscreet."

"If it was," said Mr. Wentworth, with a keener irony than Felix would have thought him capable of, "it was but your way of amusing yourself. I am afraid you have never had trouble."

"Oh, yes, I have!" Felix declared, with some spirit; "before I knew better. But you don't catch me at it again."

Mr. Wentworth maintained for a while a silence more expressive than a deep-drawn sigh. "You have no children," he said at last.

"Don't tell me," Felix exclaimed, "that your charming young people are a source of grief to you!"

"I don't speak of Charlotte." And then, after a pause, Mr. Wentworth continued, "I don't speak of Gertrude. But I feel considerable anxiety about Clifford. I will tell you another time."

The next time he gave Felix a sitting his nephew reminded him that he had taken him into his confidence. "How is Clifford today?" Felix asked. "He has always seemed to me a young man of remarkable discretion. Indeed, he is only too discreet; he seems on his guard against me — as if he thought me rather light company. The other day he told his sister — Gertrude repeated it to me — that I was always laughing at him. If I laugh it is simply from the impulse to try and inspire him with confidence. That is the only way I have."

"Clifford's situation is no laughing matter," said Mr. Wentworth. "It is very peculiar, as I suppose you have guessed."

"Ah, you mean his love affair with his cousin?"

Mr. Wentworth stared, blushing a little. "I mean his absence from college. He has been suspended. We have decided not to speak of it unless we are asked."

"Suspended?" Felix repeated.

"He has been requested by the Harvard authorities to absent himself for six months. Meanwhile he is studying with Mr. Brand. We think Mr. Brand will help him; at least we hope so."

"What befell him at college?" Felix asked. "He was too fond of pleasure? Mr. Brand certainly will not teach him any of those secrets!"

"He was too fond of something of which he should not have been fond. I suppose it is considered a pleasure."

Felix gave his light laugh. "My dear uncle, is there any doubt about its being a pleasure? *C'est de son âge*, as they say in France."

"I should have said rather it was a vice of later life — of disappointed old age."

Felix glanced at his uncle, with his lifted eyebrows, and then, "Of what are you speaking?" he demanded, smiling.

"Of the situation in which Clifford was found."

"Ah, he was found — he was caught?"

"Necessarily, he was caught. He couldn't walk; he staggered."

"Oh," said Felix, "he drinks! I rather suspected that, from something I observed the first day I came here. I quite agree with you that it is a low taste. It's not a vice for a gentleman. He ought to give it up."

"We hope for a good deal from Mr. Brand's influence," Mr. Wentworth went on. "He has talked to him from the first. And he never touches anything himself."

"I will talk to him — I will talk to him!" Felix declared, gayly.

"What will you say to him?" asked his uncle, with some apprehension.

Felix for some moments answered nothing. "Do you mean to marry him to his cousin?" he asked at last.

"Marry him?" echoed Mr. Wentworth. "I shouldn't think his cousin would want to marry him."

"You have no understanding, then, with Mrs. Acton?"

Mr. Wentworth stared, almost blankly. "I have never discussed such subjects with her."

"I should think it might be time," said Felix. "Lizzie Acton is admirably pretty, and if Clifford is dangerous . . . ."

"They are not engaged," said Mr. Wentworth. "I have no reason to suppose they are engaged."

"Par exemple!" cried Felix. "A clandestine engagement? Trust me, Clifford, as I say, is a charming boy. He is incapable of that. Lizzie Acton, then, would not be jealous of another woman."

"I certainly hope not," said the old man, with a vague sense of jealousy being an even lower vice than a love of liquor.

"The best thing for Clifford, then," Felix propounded, "is to become interested in some clever, charming woman." And he paused in his painting, and, with his elbows on his knees, looked with bright communicativeness at his uncle. "You see, I believe greatly in the influence of women. Living with women helps to make a man a gentleman. It is very true Clifford has his sisters, who are so charming. But there should be a different sentiment in play from the fraternal, you know. He has Lizzie Acton; but she, perhaps, is rather immature."

"I suspect Lizzie has talked to him, reasoned with him," said Mr. Wentworth.

"On the impropriety of getting tipsy — on the beauty of temperance? That is dreary work for a pretty young girl. No," Felix continued; "Clifford ought to frequent some agreeable woman, who, without ever mentioning such unsavory subjects, would give him a sense of its being very ridiculous to be fuddled. If he could fall in love with her a little, so much the better. The thing would operate as a cure."

"Well, now, what lady should you suggest?" asked Mr. Wentworth.

"There is a clever woman under your hand. My sister."

"Your sister — under my hand?" Mr. Wentworth repeated.

"Say a word to Clifford. Tell him to be bold. He is well disposed already; he has invited her two or three times to drive. But I don't think he comes to see her. Give him a hint to come — to come often. He will sit there of an afternoon, and they will talk. It will do him good."

Mr. Wentworth meditated. "You think she will exercise a helpful influence?"

"She will exercise a civilizing — I may call it a sobering — influence. A charming, clever, witty woman always does — especially if she is a little of a coquette. My dear uncle, the society of such women has been half my education. If Clifford is suspended, as you say, from college, let Eugenia be his preceptress."

Mr. Wentworth continued thoughtful. "You think Eugenia is a coquette?" he asked.

"What pretty woman is not?" Felix demanded in turn. But this, for Mr. Wentworth, could at the best have been no answer, for he did not think his niece pretty. "With Clifford," the young man pursued, "Eugenia will simply be enough of a coquette to be a little ironical. That's what he needs. So you recommend him to be nice with her, you know. The suggestion will come best from you."

"Do I understand," asked the old man, "that I am to suggest to my son to make a — a profession of — of affection to Madame Münster?"

"Yes, yes — a profession!" cried Felix sympathetically.

"But, as I understand it, Madame Münster is a married woman."

"Ah," said Felix, smiling, "of course she can't marry him. But she will do what she can."

Mr. Wentworth sat for some time with his eyes on the floor; at last he got up. "I don't think," he said, "that I can undertake to recommend my son any such course." And without meeting Felix's surprised glance he broke off his sitting, which was not resumed for a fortnight.

Felix was very fond of the little lake which occupied so many of Mr. Wentworth's numerous acres, and of a remarkable pine grove which lay upon the further side of it, planted upon a steep embankment and haunted by the summer breeze. The murmur of the air in the far off tree-tops had a strange distinctness; it was almost articulate. One afternoon the young man came out of his painting-room and passed the open door of Eugenia's little salon. Within, in the cool dimness, he saw his sister, dressed in white, buried in her arm-chair, and holding to her face an immense bouquet. Opposite to her sat Clifford Wentworth, twirling his hat. He had evidently just presented the bouquet to the Baroness, whose fine eyes, as she glanced at him over the big roses and geraniums, wore a conversational smile. Felix, standing on the threshold of the cottage, hesitated for a moment as to whether he should retrace his steps and enter the parlor. Then he went his way and passed into Mr. Wentworth's garden. That civilizing process to which he had suggested that Clifford should be subjected appeared to have come on of itself. Felix was very sure, at least, that Mr. Wentworth had not adopted his ingenious device for stimulating the young man's æsthetic consciousness. "Doubtless he supposes," he said to himself, after the conversation that has been narrated, "that I desire, out of fraternal benevolence, to procure for Eugenia the amusement of a flirtation — or, as he probably calls it, an intrigue — with the too susceptible Clifford. It must be admitted — and I have noticed it before — that nothing exceeds the license occasionally taken by the imagination of very rigid people." Felix, on his own side, had of course said nothing to Clifford; but he had observed to Eugenia that Mr. Wentworth was much mortified at his son's low tastes. "We ought to do something to help them, after all their kindness to us," he had added. "Encourage Clifford to come and see you, and inspire him with a taste for conversation. That will supplant the other, which only comes from his puerility, from his not taking his position in the world — that of a rich young man of ancient stock — seriously enough. Make him a little more serious. Even if he makes love to you it is no great matter."

"I am to offer myself as a superior form of intoxication — a substitute for a brandy bottle, eh?" asked the Baroness. "Truly, in this country one comes to strange uses."

But she had not positively declined to undertake Clifford's higher education, and Felix, who had not thought of the matter again, being haunted with visions of more personal profit, now reflected that the work of redemption had fairly begun. The idea in prospect had seemed of the happiest, but in operation it made him a trifle uneasy." What if Eugenia — what if Eugenia" — he asked himself softly; the question dying away in his sense of Eugenia's undetermined capacity. But before Felix had time either to accept or to reject its admonition, even in this vague form, he saw Robert Acton turn out of Mr. Wentworth's inclosure, by a distant gate, and come toward the cottage in the orchard. Acton had evidently walked from his own house along a shady by-way and was intending to pay a visit to

Madame Münster. Felix watched him a moment; then he turned away. Acton could be left to play the part of Providence and interrupt — if interruption were needed — Clifford's entanglement with Eugenia.

Felix passed through the garden toward the house and toward a postern gate which opened upon a path leading across the fields, beside a little wood, to the lake. He stopped and looked up at the house; his eyes rested more particularly upon a certain open window, on the shady side. Presently Gertrude appeared there, looking out into the summer light. He took off his hat to her and bade her good-day; he remarked that he was going to row across the pond, and begged that she would do him the honor to accompany him. She looked at him a moment; then, without saying anything, she turned away. But she soon reappeared below in one of those quaint and charming Leghorn hats, tied with white satin bows, that were worn at that period; she also carried a green parasol. She went with him to the edge of the lake, where a couple of boats were always moored; they got into one of them, and Felix, with gentle strokes, propelled it to the opposite shore. The day was the perfection of summer weather; the little lake was the color of sunshine; the plash of the oars was the only sound, and they found themselves listening to it. They disembarked, and, by a winding path, ascended the pine-crested mound which overlooked the water, whose white expanse glittered between the trees. The place was delightfully cool, and had the added charm that — in the softly sounding pine boughs — you seemed to hear the coolness as well as feel it. Felix and Gertrude sat down on the rust-colored carpet of pine-needles and talked of many things. Felix spoke at last, in the course of talk, of his going away; it was the first time he had alluded to it.

"You are going away?" said Gertrude, looking at him.

"Some day — when the leaves begin to fall. You know I can't stay forever."

Gertrude transferred her eyes to the outer prospect, and then, after a pause, she said, "I shall never see you again."

"Why not?" asked Felix. "We shall probably both survive my departure."

But Gertrude only repeated, "I shall never see you again. I shall never hear of you," she went on. "I shall know nothing about you. I knew nothing about you before, and it will be the same again."

"I knew nothing about you then, unfortunately," said Felix. "But now I shall write to you."

"Don't write to me. I shall not answer you," Gertrude declared.

"I should of course burn your letters," said Felix.

Gertrude looked at him again. "Burn my letters? You sometimes say strange things."

"They are not strange in themselves," the young man answered. "They are only strange as said to you. You will come to Europe."

"With whom shall I come?" She asked this question simply; she was very much in earnest. Felix was interested in her earnestness; for some moments he hesitated. "You can't tell me that," she pursued. "You can't say that I shall go with my father and my sister; you don't believe that."

"I shall keep your letters," said Felix, presently, for all answer.

"I never write. I don't know how to write." Gertrude, for some time, said nothing more; and her companion, as he looked at her, wished it had not been "disloyal" to make love to the daughter of an old gentleman who had offered one hospitality. The afternoon waned; the shadows stretched themselves; and the light grew deeper in the western sky. Two persons appeared on the opposite side of the lake, coming from the house and crossing the meadow. "It is Charlotte and Mr. Brand," said Gertrude. "They are coming over here." But Charlotte and Mr. Brand only came down to the edge of the water, and stood there, looking across; they made no motion to enter the boat that Felix had left at the mooring-place. Felix waved his hat to them; it was too far to call. They made no visible response, and they presently turned away and walked along the shore.

"Mr. Brand is not demonstrative," said Felix. "He is never demonstrative to me. He sits silent, with his chin in his hand, looking at me. Sometimes he looks away. Your father tells me he is so eloquent; and I should like to hear him talk. He looks like such a noble young man. But with me he will never talk. And yet I am so fond of listening to brilliant imagery!"

"He is very eloquent," said Gertrude; "but he has no brilliant imagery. I have heard him talk a great deal. I knew that when they saw us they would not come over here."

"Ah, he is making *la cour*, as they say, to your sister? They desire to be alone."

"No," said Gertrude, gravely, "they have no such reason as that for being alone."

"But why doesn't he make la cour to Charlotte?" Felix inquired. "She is so pretty, so gentle, so good."

Gertrude glanced at him, and then she looked at the distantly-seen couple they were discussing. Mr. Brand and Charlotte were walking side by side. They might have been a pair of lovers, and yet they might not. "They think I should not be here," said Gertrude.

"With me? I thought you didn't have those ideas."

"You don't understand. There are a great many things you don't understand."

"I understand my stupidity. But

why, then, do not Charlotte and Mr. Brand, who, as an elder sister and a clergyman, are free to walk about together, come over and make me wiser by breaking up the unlawful interview into which I have lured you?"

"That is the last thing they would do," said Gertrude.

Felix stared at her a moment, with his lifted eyebrows. "Je n'y comprends rien!" he exclaimed; then his eyes followed for a while the retreating figures of this critical pair. "You may say what you please," he declared; "it is evident to me that your sister is not indifferent to her clever companion. It is agreeable to her to be walking there with him. I can see that from here." And in the excitement of observation Felix rose to his feet.

Gertrude rose also, but she made no attempt to emulate her companion's discovery; she looked rather in another direction. Felix's words had struck her; but a certain delicacy checked her. "She is certainly not indifferent to Mr. Brand; she has the highest opinion of him."

"One can see it — one can see it," said Felix, in a tone of amused contemplation, with his head on one side. Gertrude turned her back to the opposite shore; it was disagreeable to her to look, but she hoped Felix would say something more. "Ah, they have wandered away into the wood," he added.

Gertrude turned round again. "She is *not* in love with him," she

said; it seemed her duty to say that.

"Then he is in love with her; or if he is not, he ought to be. She is such a perfect little woman of her kind. She reminds me of a pair of old-fashioned silver sugar-tongs; you know I am very fond of sugar. And she is very nice with Mr. Brand; I have noticed that; very gentle and gracious."

Gertrude reflected a moment. Then she took a great resolution. "She wants him to marry me," she said. "So of course she is nice."

Felix's eyebrows rose higher than ever. "To marry you! Ah, ah, this is interesting. And you think one must be very nice with a man to induce him to do that?"

Gertrude had turned a little pale, but she went on, "Mr. Brand wants it himself."

Felix folded his arms and stood looking at her. "I see — I see," he said quickly. "Why did you never tell me this before?"

"It is disagreeable to me to speak of it even now. I wished simply to explain to you about Charlotte."

"You don't wish to marry Mr. Brand, then?"

"No," said Gertrude, gravely.

"And does your father wish it?"

"Very much."

"And you don't like him — you have refused him?"

"I don't wish to marry him."

"Your father and sister think you ought to, eh?"

"It is a long story," said Gertrude. "They think there are good reasons. I can't explain it. They think I have obligations, and that I have encouraged him."

Felix smiled at her, as if she had been telling him an amusing story about some one else. "I can't tell you how this interests me," he said. "Now you don't recognize these reasons — these obligations?"

"I am not sure; it is not easy." And she picked up her parasol and turned away, as if to descend the slope.

"Tell me this," Felix went on, going with her: "are you likely to give in — to let them persuade you?"

Gertrude looked at him with the serious face that she had constantly worn, in opposition to his almost eager smile. "I shall never marry Mr. Brand," she said.

"I see!" Felix rejoined. And they slowly descended the hill together, saying nothing till they reached the margin of the pond. "It is your own affair," he then resumed; "but do you know, I am not altogether glad? If it were settled that you were to marry Mr. Brand I should take a certain comfort in the arrangement. I should feel more free. I have no right to make love to you myself, eh?" And he paused, lightly pressing his argument upon her.

"None whatever," replied Gertrude quickly — too quickly.

"Your father would never hear of it; I haven't a penny. Mr. Brand, of course, has property of his own, eh?"

"I believe he has some property; but that has nothing to do with it."

"With you, of course not; but with your father and sister it must have. So, as I say, if this were settled, I should feel more at liberty."

"More at liberty?" Gertrude repeated. "Please unfasten the boat."

Felix untwisted the rope and stood holding it. "I should be able to say things to you that I can't give myself the pleasure of saying now," he went on. "I could tell you how much I admire you, without seeming to pretend to that which I have no right to pretend to. I should make violent love to you," he added, laughing, "if I thought you were so placed as not to be offended by it."

"You mean if I were engaged to another man? That is strange reasoning!" Gertrude exclaimed.

"In that case you would not take me seriously."

"I take every one seriously," said Gertrude. And without his help she stepped lightly into the boat.

Felix took up the oars and sent it forward. "Ah, this is what you have been thinking about? It seemed to me you had something on your mind. I wish very much," he added, "that you would tell me some of these so-called reasons — these obligations."

"They are not real reasons — good reasons," said Gertrude, looking at the pink and yellow gleams in the water.

"I can understand that! Because a handsome girl has had a spark of coquetry, that is no reason."

"If you mean me, it's not that. I have not done that."

"It is something that troubles you, at any rate," said Felix.

"Not so much as it used to," Gertrude rejoined.

He looked at her, smiling always. "That is not saying much, eh?" But she only rested her eyes, very gravely, on the lighted water. She seemed to him to be trying to hide the signs of the trouble of which she had just told him. Felix felt, at all times, much the same impulse to dissipate visible melancholy that a good housewife feels to brush away dust. There was something he wished to brush away now; suddenly he stopped rowing and poised his oars. "Why should Mr. Brand have addressed himself to you, and not to your sister?" he asked. "I am sure she would listen to him."

Gertrude, in her family, was thought capable of a good deal of levity; but her levity had never gone so far as this. It moved her greatly, however, to hear Felix say that he was sure of something; so that, raising her eyes toward him, she tried intently, for some moments, to conjure up this wonderful image of a love-affair between her own sister and her own suitor. We know that Gertrude had an imaginative mind; so that it is not impossible that this effort should have been partially successful. But she only murmured, "Ah, Felix! ah, Felix!"

"Why shouldn't they marry? Try and make them marry!" cried Felix.

"Try and make them?"

"Turn the tables on them. Then they will leave you alone. I will help you as far as I can."

Gertrude's heart began to beat; she was greatly excited; she had never had anything so interesting proposed to her before. Felix had begun to row again, and he now sent the boat home with long strokes. "I believe she does care for him!" said Gertrude, after they had disembarked.

"Of course she does, and we will marry them off. It will make them happy; it will make every one happy. We shall have a wedding and I will write an epithalamium."

"It seems as if it would make me happy," said Gertrude.

"To get rid of Mr. Brand, eh? To recover your liberty?"

Gertrude walked on. "To see my sister married to so good a man."

Felix gave his light laugh. "You always put things on those grounds; you will never say anything for yourself. You are all so afraid, here, of being selfish. I don't think you know how," he went on. "Let me show you! It will make me happy for myself, and for just the reverse of what I told you a while ago. After that, when I make love to you, you will have to think I mean it."

"I shall never think you mean anything," said Gertrude. "You are too fantastic."

"Ah," cried Felix, "that's a license to say everything! Gertrude, I adore you!"

VIII

Charlotte and Mr. Brand had not returned when they reached the house; but the Baroness had come to tea, and Robert Acton also, who now regularly asked for a place at this generous repast or made his appearance later in the evening. Clifford Wentworth, with his juvenile growl, remarked upon it.

"You are always coming to tea nowadays, Robert," he said. "I should think you had drunk enough tea in China."

"Since when is Mr. Acton more frequent?" asked the Baroness.

"Since you came," said Clifford. "It seems as if you were a kind of attraction."

"I suppose I am a curiosity," said the Baroness. "Give me time and I will make you a salon."

"It would fall to pieces after you go!" exclaimed Acton.

"Don't talk about her going, in that familiar way," Clifford said. "It makes me feel gloomy."

Mr. Wentworth glanced at his son, and taking note of these words, wondered if Felix had been teaching him, according to the programme he had sketched out, to make love to the wife of a German prince.

Charlotte came in late with Mr. Brand; but Gertrude, to whom, at least, Felix had taught something, looked in vain, in her face, for the traces of a guilty passion. Mr. Brand sat down by Gertrude, and she presently asked him why they had not crossed the pond to join Felix and herself.

"It is cruel of you to ask me that," he answered, very softly. He had a large morsel of cake before him; but he fingered it without eating it. "I sometimes think you are growing cruel," he added.

Gertrude said nothing; she was afraid to speak. There was a kind of rage in her heart; she felt as if she could easily persuade herself that she was persecuted. She said to herself that it was quite right that she should not allow him to make her believe she was wrong. She thought of what Felix had said to her; she wished indeed Mr. Brand would marry Charlotte. She looked away from him and spoke no more. Mr. Brand ended by eating his cake, while Felix sat opposite, describing to Mr. Wentworth the students' duels at Heidelberg. After tea they all dispersed themselves, as usual, upon the piazza and in the garden; and Mr. Brand drew near to Gertrude again.

"I didn't come to you this afternoon because you were not alone," he began; "because you were with a newer friend."

"Felix? He is an old friend by this time."

Mr. Brand looked at the ground for some moments. "I thought I was prepared to hear you speak in that way," he resumed. "But I find it very painful."

"I don't see what else I can say," said Gertrude.

Mr. Brand walked beside her for a while in silence; Gertrude wished he would go away. "He is certainly very accomplished. But I think I ought to advise you."

"To advise me?"

"I think I know your nature."

"I think you don't," said Gertrude, with a soft laugh.

"You make yourself out worse than you are — to please him," Mr. Brand said, gently.

"Worse — to please him? What do you mean?" asked Gertrude, stopping.

Mr. Brand stopped also, and with the same soft straightforwardness, "He doesn't care for the things you care for — the great questions of life."

Gertrude, with her eyes on his, shook her head. "I don't care for the great questions of life. They are much beyond me."

"There was a time when you didn't say that," said Mr. Brand.

"Oh," rejoined Gertrude, "I think you made me talk a great deal of nonsense. And it depends," she added, "upon what you call the great questions of life. There are some things I care for."

"Are they the things you talk about with your cousin?"

"You should not say things to me against my cousin, Mr. Brand," said Gertrude. "That is dishonorable."

He listened to this respectfully; then he answered, with a little vibration of the voice, "I should be very sorry to do anything dishonorable. But I don't see why it is dishonorable to say that your cousin is frivolous."

"Go and say it to himself!"

"I think he would admit it," said Mr. Brand. "That is the tone he would take. He would not be ashamed of it."

"Then I am not ashamed of it!" Gertrude declared. "That is probably what I like him for. I am frivolous myself."

"You are trying, as I said just now, to lower yourself."

"I am trying for once to be natural!" cried Gertrude passionately. "I have been pretending, all my life; I have been dishonest; it is you that have made me so!" Mr. Brand stood gazing at her, and she went on, "Why shouldn't I be frivolous, if I want? One has a right to be frivolous, if it's one's nature. No, I don't care for the great questions. I care for pleasure — for amusement. Perhaps I am fond of wicked things; it is very possible!"

Mr. Brand remained staring; he was even a little pale, as if he had been frightened. "I don't think you know what you are saying!" he exclaimed.

"Perhaps not. Perhaps I am talking nonsense. But it is only with you that I talk nonsense. I never do so with my cousin."

"I will speak to you again, when you are less excited," said Mr. Brand.

"I am always excited when you speak to me. I must tell you that — even if it prevents you altogether, in future. Your speaking to me irritates me. With my cousin it is very different. That seems quiet and natural."

He looked at her, and then he looked away, with a kind of helpless distress, at the dusky garden and the faint summer stars. After which, suddenly turning back, "Gertrude, Gertrude!" he softly groaned. "Am I really losing you?"

She was touched — she was pained; but it had already occurred to her that she might do something better than say so. It would not have alleviated her companion's distress to perceive, just then, whence she had sympathetically borrowed this ingenuity. "I am not sorry for you," Gertrude said; "for in paying so much attention to me you are following a shadow — you are wasting something precious. There is something else you might have that you don't look at — something better than I am. That is a reality!" And then, with intention, she looked at him and tried to smile a little. He thought this smile of hers very strange; but she turned away and left him.

She wandered about alone in the garden wondering what Mr. Brand would make of her words, which it had been a singular pleasure for her to utter. Shortly after, passing in front of the house, she saw at a distance two persons standing near the garden gate. It was Mr. Brand going away and bidding good-night to Charlotte, who had walked down with him from the house. Gertrude saw that the parting was prolonged. Then she turned her back upon it. She had not gone very far, however, when she heard her sister slowly following her. She neither turned round nor waited for her; she knew what Charlotte was going to say. Charlotte, who at last overtook her, in fact presently began; she had passed her arm into Gertrude's.

"Will you listen to me, dear, if I say something very particular?"

"I know what you are going to say," said Gertrude. "Mr. Brand feels very badly."

"Oh, Gertrude, how can you treat him so?" Charlotte demanded. And as her sister made no answer she added, "After all he has done for you!"

"What has he done for me?"

"I wonder you can ask, Gertrude. He has helped you so. You told me so yourself, a great many times. You told me that he helped you to struggle with your — your peculiarities. You told me that he had taught you how to govern your temper."

For a moment Gertrude said nothing. Then, "Was my temper very bad?" she asked.

"I am not accusing you, Gertrude," said Charlotte.

"What are you doing, then?" her sister demanded, with a short laugh.

"I am pleading for Mr. Brand — reminding you of all you owe him."

"I have given it all back," said Gertrude, still with her little laugh. "He can take back the virtue he imparted! I want to be wicked again."

Her sister made her stop in the path, and fixed upon her, in the darkness, a sweet, reproachful gaze. "If you talk this way I shall almost believe it. Think of all we owe Mr. Brand. Think of how he has always expected something of you. Think how much he has been to us. Think of his beautiful influence upon Clifford."

"He is very good," said Gertrude, looking at her sister. "I know he is very good. But he shouldn't speak against Felix."

"Felix is good," Charlotte answered, softly but promptly. "Felix is very wonderful. Only he is so different. Mr. Brand is much nearer to us. I should never think of going to Felix with a trouble — with a question. Mr. Brand is much more to us, Gertrude."

"He is very — very good," Gertrude repeated. "He is more to you; yes, much more. Charlotte," she added suddenly, "you are in love with him!"

"Oh, Gertrude!" cried poor Charlotte; and her sister saw her blushing in the darkness.

Gertrude put her arm round her. "I wish he would marry you!" she went on.

Charlotte shook herself free. "You must not say such things!" she exclaimed, beneath her breath.

"You like him more than you say, and he likes you more than he knows."

"This is very cruel of you!" Charlotte Wentworth murmured.

But if it was cruel Gertrude continued pitiless. "Not if it's true," she answered. "I wish he would marry you."

"Please don't say that."

"I mean to tell him so!" said Gertrude.

"Oh, Gertrude, Gertrude!" her sister almost moaned.

"Yes, if he speaks to me again about myself. I will say, 'Why don't you marry Charlotte? She's a thousand times better than I.'"

"You *are* wicked; you *are* changed!" cried her sister.

"If you don't like it you can prevent it," said Gertrude. "You can prevent it by keeping him from speaking to me!" And with this she walked away, very conscious of what she had done; measuring it and finding a certain joy and a quickened sense of freedom in it.

Mr. Wentworth was rather wide of the mark in suspecting that Clifford had begun to pay unscrupulous compliments to his brilliant cousin; for the young man had really more scruples than he received credit for in his family. He had a certain transparent shamefacedness which was in itself a proof that he was not at his ease in dissipation. His collegiate peccadilloes had aroused a domestic murmur as disagreeable to the young man as the creaking of his boots would have been to a housebreaker. Only, as the housebreaker would have simplified matters by removing his *chaussures,* it had seemed to Clifford that the shortest cut to comfortable relations with people — relations which should make him cease to think that when they spoke to him they meant something improving — was to renounce all ambition toward a nefarious development. And, in fact, Clifford's ambition took the most commendable form. He thought of himself in the future as the well-known and much-liked Mr. Wentworth, of Boston, who should, in the natural course of prosperity, have married his pretty cousin, Lizzie Acton; should live in a wide-fronted house, in view of the Common; and should drive, behind a light wagon, over the damp autumn roads, a pair of beautifully matched sorrel horses. Clifford's vision of the coming years was very simple; its most definite features were this element of familiar matrimony and the duplication of his resources for trotting. He had not yet asked his cousin to marry him; but he meant to do so as soon as he had taken his degree. Lizzie was serenely conscious of his intention, and she had made up her mind that he would improve. Her brother, who was very fond of this light, quick, competent little Lizzie, saw on his side no reason to interpose. It seemed to him a graceful social law that Clifford and his sister should become engaged; he himself was not engaged, but every one else, fortunately, was not such a fool as he. He was fond of Clifford, as well, and had his own

way — of which it must be confessed he was a little ashamed — of looking at those aberrations which had led to the young man's compulsory retirement from the neighboring seat of learning. Acton had seen the world, as he said to himself; he had been to China and had knocked about among men. He had learned the essential difference between a nice young fellow and a mean young fellow, and was satisfied that there was no harm in Clifford. He believed — although it must be added that he had not quite the courage to declare it — in the doctrine of wild oats, and thought it a useful preventive of superfluous fears. If Mr. Wentworth and Charlotte and Mr. Brand would only apply it in Clifford's case, they would be happier; and Acton thought it a pity they should not be happier. They took the boy's misdemeanors too much to heart; they talked to him too solemnly; they frightened and bewildered him. Of course there was the great standard of morality, which forbade that a man should get tipsy, play at billiards for money, or cultivate his sensual consciousness; but what fear was there that poor Clifford was going to run a tilt at any great standard? It had, however, never occurred to Acton to dedicate the Baroness Münster to the redemption of a refractory collegian. The instrument, here, would have seemed to him quite too complex for the operation. Felix, on the other hand, had spoken in obedience to the belief that the more charming a woman is the more numerous, literally, are her definite social uses.

Eugenia herself, as we know, had plenty of leisure to enumerate her uses. As I have had the honor of intimating, she had come four thousand miles to seek her fortune; and it is not to be supposed that after this great effort she could neglect any apparent aid to advancement. It is my misfortune that in attempting to describe in a short compass the deportment of this remarkable woman I am obliged to express things rather brutally. I feel this to be the case, for instance, when I say that she had primarily detected such an aid to advancement in the person of Robert Acton, but that she had afterwards remembered that a prudent archer has always a second bowstring. Eugenia was a woman of finely-mingled motive, and her intentions were never sensibly gross. She had a sort of æsthetic ideal for Clifford which seemed to her a disinterested reason for taking him in hand. It was very well for a fresh-colored young gentleman to be ingenuous; but Clifford, really, was crude. With such a pretty face he ought to have prettier manners. She would teach him that, with a beautiful name, the expectation of a large property, and, as they said in Europe, a social position, an only son should know how to carry himself.

Once Clifford had begun to come and see her by himself and

for himself, he came very often. He hardly knew why he should come; he saw her almost every evening at his father's house; he had nothing particular to say to her. She was not a young girl, and fellows of his age called only upon young girls. He exaggerated her age; she seemed to him an old woman; it was happy that the Baroness, with all her intelligence, was incapable of guessing this. But gradually it struck Clifford that visiting old women might be, if not a natural, at least, as they say of some articles of diet, an acquired taste. The Baroness was certainly a very amusing old woman; she talked to him as no lady — and indeed no gentleman — had ever talked to him before.

"You should go to Europe and make the tour," she said to him one afternoon. "Of course, on leaving college you will go."

"I don't want to go," Clifford declared. "I know some fellows who have been to Europe. They say you can have better fun here."

"That depends. It depends upon your idea of fun. Your friends probably were not introduced."

"Introduced?" Clifford demanded.

"They had no opportunity of going into society; they formed no *relations*." This was one of a certain number of words that the Baroness often pronounced in the French manner.

"They went to a ball, in Paris; I know that," said Clifford.

"Ah, there are balls and balls; especially in Paris. No, you must go, you know; it is not a thing from which you can dispense yourself. You need it."

"Oh, I'm very well," said Clifford. "I'm not sick."

"I don't mean for your health, my poor child. I mean for your manners."

"I haven't got any manners!" growled Clifford.

"Precisely. You don't mind my assenting to that, eh?" asked the Baroness with a smile. "You must go to Europe and get a few. You can get them better there. It is a pity you might not have come while I was living in — in Germany. I would have introduced you; I had a charming little circle. You would perhaps have been rather young; but the younger one begins, I think, the better. Now, at any rate, you have no time to lose, and when I return you must immediately come to me."

All this, to Clifford's apprehension, was a great mixture — his beginning young, Eugenia's return to Europe, his being introduced to her charming little circle. What was he to begin, and what was her little circle? His ideas about her marriage had a good deal of vagueness; but they were in so far definite as that he felt it to be a matter not to be freely mentioned. He sat and looked all round the room; he supposed she was alluding in some way to her marriage.

"Oh, I don't want to go to Germany," he said; it seemed to him the most convenient thing to say.

She looked at him a while, smiling with her lips, but not with her eyes.

"You have scruples?" she asked.

"Scruples?" said Clifford.

"You young people, here, are very singular; one doesn't know where to expect you. When you are not extremely improper you are so terribly proper. I dare say you think that, owing to my irregular marriage, I live with loose people. You were never more mistaken. I have been all the more particular."

"Oh, no," said Clifford, honestly distressed. "I never thought such a thing as that."

"Are you very sure? I am convinced that your father does, and your sisters. They say to each other that here I am on my good behavior, but that over there — married by the left hand — I associate with light women."

"Oh, no," cried Clifford, energetically, "they don't say such things as that to each other!"

"If they think them they had better say them," the Baroness rejoined. "Then they can be contradicted. Please contradict that whenever you hear it, and don't be afraid of coming to see me on account of the company I keep. I have the honor of knowing more distinguished men, my poor child, than you are likely to see in a lifetime. I see very few women; but those are women of rank. So, my dear young Puritan, you needn't be afraid. I am not in the least one of those who think that the society of women who have lost their place in the *vrai monde* is necessary to form a young man. I have never taken that tone. I have kept my place myself, and I think we are a much better school than the others. Trust me, Clifford, and I will prove that to you," the Baroness continued, while she made the agreeable reflection that she could not, at least, be accused of perverting her young kinsman. "So if you ever fall among thieves don't go about saying I sent you to them."

Clifford thought it so comical that he should know—in spite of her figurative language—what she meant, and that she should mean what he knew, that he could hardly help laughing a little, although he tried hard. "Oh, no! oh, no!" he murmured.

"Laugh out, laugh out, if I amuse you!" cried the Baroness. "I am here for that!" And Clifford thought her a very amusing person indeed. "But remember," she said on this occasion, "that you are coming—next year—to pay me a visit over there."

About a week afterwards she said to him, point-blank, "Are you seriously making love to your little cousin?"

"Seriously making love"—these words, on Madame Münster's lips, had to Clifford's sense a portentous and embarrassing sound; he hesitated about assenting, lest he should commit himself to more than he understood. "Well, I shouldn't say it if I was!" he exclaimed.

"Why wouldn't you say it?" the Baroness demanded. "Those things ought to be known."

"I don't care whether it is known or not," Clifford rejoined. "But I don't want people looking at me."

"A young man of your importance ought to learn to bear observation—to carry himself as if he were quite indifferent to it. I won't say, exactly, unconscious," the Baroness explained. "No, he must seem to know he is observed, and to think it natural he should be; but he must appear perfectly used to it. Now you haven't that, Clifford; you haven't that at all. You must have that, you know. Don't tell me you are not a young man of importance," Eugenia added. "Don't say anything so flat as that."

"Oh, no, you don't catch me saying that!" cried Clifford.

"Yes, you must come to Germany," Madame Münster continued. "I will show you how people can be talked about, and yet not seem to know it. You will be talked about, of course, with me; it will be said you are my lover. I will show you how little one may mind that —how little I shall mind it."

Clifford sat staring, blushing and laughing. "I shall mind it a good deal!" he declared.

"Ah, not too much, you know; that would be uncivil. But I give you leave to mind it a little; especially if you have a passion for Miss Acton. *Voyons;* as regards that, you either have or you have not. It is very simple to say it."

"I don't see why you want to know," said Clifford.

"You ought to want me to know. If one is arranging a marriage, one tells one's friends."

"Oh, I'm not arranging anything," said Clifford.

"You don't intend to marry your cousin?"

"Well, I expect I shall do as I choose!"

The Baroness leaned her head upon the back of her chair and closed her eyes, as if she were tired. Then opening them again, "Your cousin is very charming!" she said.

"She is the prettiest girl in this place," Clifford rejoined.

" 'In this place' is saying little; she would be charming anywhere. I am afraid you are entangled."

"Oh, no, I'm not entangled."

"Are you engaged? At your age that is the same thing."

Clifford looked at the Baroness with some audacity. "Will you tell no one?"

"If it's as sacred as that — no."

"Well, then — we are not!" said Clifford.

"That's the great secret — that you are not, eh?" asked the Baroness, with a quick laugh. "I am very glad to hear it. You are altogether too young. A young man in your position must choose and compare; he must see the world first. Depend upon it," she added, "you should not settle that matter before you have come abroad and paid me that visit. There are several things I should like to call your attention to first."

"Well, I am rather afraid of that visit," said Clifford. "It seems to me it will be rather like going to school again."

The Baroness looked at him a moment.

"My dear child," she said, "there is no agreeable man who has not, at some moment, been to school to a clever woman — probably a little older than himself. And you must be thankful when you get your instructions gratis. With me you would get it gratis."

The next day Clifford told Lizzie Acton that the Baroness thought her the most charming girl she had ever seen.

Lizzie shook her head. "No, she doesn't!" she said.

"Do you think everything she says," asked Clifford, "is to be taken the opposite way?"

"I think that is!" said Lizzie.

Clifford was going to remark that in this case the Baroness must desire greatly to bring about a marriage between Mr. Clifford Wentworth and Miss Elizabeth Acton; but he resolved, on the whole, to suppress this observation.

IX

It seemed to Robert Acton, after Eugenia had come to his house, that something had passed between them which made them a good deal more intimate. It was hard to say exactly what, except her telling him that she had taken her resolution with regard to the

Prince Adolf; for Madame Mün- ster's visit had made no difference in their relations. He came to see her very often; but he had come to see her very often before. It was agreeable to him to find himself in her little drawing-room; but this was not a new discovery. There was a change, however, in this sense: that if the Baroness had been a great deal in Acton's thoughts before, she was now never out of them. From the first she had been personally fascinat- ing; but the fascination now had become intellectual as well. He was constantly pondering her words and motions; they were as interesting as the factors in an algebraic problem. This is saying a good deal; for Acton was ex- tremely fond of mathematics. He asked himself whether it could be that he was in love with her, and then hoped he was not; hoped it not so much for his own sake as for that of the amatory passion it- self. If this was love, love had been overrated. Love was a poetic impulse, and his own state of feel- ing with regard to the Baroness was largely characterized by that eminently prosaic sentiment — cu- riosity. It was true, as Acton with his quietly cogitative habit ob- served to himself, that curiosity, pushed to a given point, might become a romantic passion; and he certainly thought enough about this charming woman to make him restless and even a little melan- choly. It puzzled and vexed him at times to feel that he was not more ardent. He was not in the

least bent upon remaining a bach- elor. In his younger years he had been — or he had tried to be — of the opinion that it would be a good deal "jollier" not to marry, and he had flattered himself that his single condition was something of a citadel. It was a citadel, at all events, of which he had long since leveled the outworks. He had re- moved the guns from the ram- parts; he had lowered the draw- bridge across the moat. The draw-bridge had swayed lightly un- der Madame Münster's step; why should he not cause it to be raised again, so that she might be kept prisoner? He had an idea that she would become — in time at least, and on learning the conveniences of the place for making a lady comfortable — a tolerably patient captive. But the draw-bridge was never raised, and Acton's brilliant visitor was as free to depart as she had been to come. It was part of his curiosity to know why the deuce so susceptible a man was *not* in love with so charming a woman. If her various graces were, as I have said, the factors in an algebraic problem, the answer to this question was the indispensable unknown quantity. The pursuit of the unknown quantity was ex- tremely absorbing; for the present it taxed all Acton's faculties.

Toward the middle of August he was obliged to leave home for some days; an old friend, with whom he had been associated in China, had begged him to come to Newport, where he lay extremely ill. His friend got better, and at

118

the end of a week Acton was released. I use the word "released" advisedly; for in spite of his attachment to his Chinese comrade he had been but a half-hearted visitor. He felt as if he had been called away from the theatre during the progress of a remarkably interesting drama. The curtain was up all this time, and he was losing the fourth act; that fourth act which would have been so essential to a just appreciation of the fifth. In other words, he was thinking about the Baroness, who, seen at this distance, seemed a truly brilliant figure. He saw at Newport a great many pretty women, who certainly were figures as brilliant as beautiful light dresses could make them; but though they talked a great deal — and the Baroness's strong point was perhaps also her conversation — Madame Münster appeared to lose nothing by the comparison. He wished she had come to Newport too. Would it not be possible to make up, as they said, a party for visiting the famous watering-place and invite Eugenia to join it? It was true that the complete satisfaction would be to spend a fortnight at Newport with Eugenia alone. It would be a great pleasure to see her, in society, carry everything before her, as he was sure she would do. When Acton caught himself thinking these thoughts he began to walk up and down, with his hands in his pockets, frowning a little and looking at the floor. What did it prove — for it certainly proved something

— this lively disposition to be "off" somewhere with Madame Münster, away from all the rest of them? Such a vision, certainly, seemed a refined implication of matrimony, after the Baroness should have formally got rid of her informal husband. At any rate, Acton, with his characteristic discretion, forbore to give expression to whatever else it might imply, and the narrator of these incidents is not obliged to be more definite.

He returned home rapidly, and, arriving in the afternoon, lost as little time as possible in joining the familiar circle at Mr. Wentworth's. On reaching the house, however, he found the piazzas empty. The doors and windows were open, and their emptiness was made clear by the shafts of lamp-light from the parlors. Entering the house, he found Mr. Wentworth sitting alone in one of these apartments, engaged in the perusal of the "North American Review." After they had exchanged greetings and his cousin had made discreet inquiry about his journey, Acton asked what had become of Mr. Wentworth's companions.

"They are scattered about, amusing themselves as usual," said the old man. "I saw Charlotte, a short time since, seated, with Mr. Brand, upon the piazza. They were conversing with their customary animation. I suppose they have joined her sister, who, for the hundredth time, was doing the honors of the garden to her foreign cousin."

"I suppose you mean Felix,"

said Acton. And on Mr. Wentworth's assenting, he said, "And the others?"

"Your sister has not come this evening. You must have seen her at home," said Mr. Wentworth.

"Yes. I proposed to her to come. She declined."

"Lizzie, I suppose, was expecting a visitor," said the old man, with a kind of solemn slyness.

"If she was expecting Clifford, he had not turned up."

Mr. Wentworth, at this intelligence, closed the "North American Review" and remarked that he had understood Clifford to say that he was going to see his cousin. Privately, he reflected that if Lizzie Acton had had no news of his son, Clifford must have gone to Boston for the evening: an unnatural course of a summer night, especially when accompanied with disingenuous representations.

"You must remember that he has two cousins," said Acton, laughing. And then, coming to the point, "If Lizzie is not here," he added, "neither apparently is the Baroness."

Mr. Wentworth stared a moment, and remembered that queer proposition of Felix's. For a moment he did not know whether it was not to be wished that Clifford, after all, might have gone to Boston. "The Baroness has not honored us tonight," he said. "She has not come over for three days."

"Is she ill?" Acton asked.

"No; I have been to see her."

"What is the matter with her?"

"Well," said Mr. Wentworth, "I infer she has tired of us."

Acton pretended to sit down, but he was restless; he found it impossible to talk with Mr. Wentworth. At the end of ten minutes he took up his hat and said that he thought he would "go off." It was very late; it was ten o'clock.

His quiet-faced kinsman looked at him a moment. "Are you going home?" he asked.

Acton hesitated, and then answered that he had proposed to go over and take a look at the Baroness.

"Well, *you* are honest, at least," said Mr. Wentworth, sadly.

"So are you, if you come to that!" cried Acton, laughing. "Why shouldn't I be honest?"

The old man opened the "North American" again, and read a few lines. "If we have ever had any virtue among us, we had better keep hold of it now," he said. He was not quoting.

"We have a Baroness among us," said Acton. "That's what we must keep hold of!" He was too impatient to see Madame Münster again to wonder what Mr. Wentworth was talking about. Nevertheless, after he had passed out of the house and traversed the garden and the little piece of road that separated him from Eugenia's provisional residence, he stopped a moment outside. He stood in her little garden; the long window of her parlor was open, and he could see the white curtains, with the lamp-light shining through them, swaying softly to and fro in the warm night wind. There was a sort of excitement in the idea of seeing Madame Münster again; he became aware that his heart was beating rather faster than usual. It was this that made him stop, with a half-amused surprise. But in a moment he went along the piazza, and, approaching the open window, tapped upon its lintel with his stick. He could see the Baroness within; she was standing in the middle of the room. She came to the window and pulled aside the curtain; then she stood looking at him a moment. She was not smiling; she seemed serious.

"Mais entrez donc!" she said at last. Acton passed in across the window-sill; he wondered, for an instant, what was the matter with her. But the next moment she had begun to smile and had put out her hand. "Better late than never," she said. "It is very kind of you to come at this hour."

"I have just returned from my journey," said Acton.

"Ah, very kind, very kind," she repeated, looking about her where to sit.

"I went first to the other house," Acton continued. "I expected to find you there."

She had sunk into her usual chair; but she got up again, and began to move about the room. Acton had laid down his hat and stick; he was looking at her, conscious that there was in fact a great charm in seeing her again. "I don't know whether I ought to tell you to sit down," she said. "It is too late to begin a visit."

"It's too early to end one," Acton declared; "and we needn't mind the beginning."

She looked at him again, and, after a moment, dropped once more into her low chair, while he took a place near her. "We are in the middle, then?" she asked. "Was that where we were when you went away? No, I haven't been to the other house."

"Not yesterday, nor the day before, eh?"

"I don't know how many days it is."

"You are tired of it," said Acton.

She leaned back in her chair; her arms were folded. "That is a terrible accusation, but I have not the courage to defend myself."

"I am not attacking you," said Acton. "I expected something of this kind."

"It's a proof of extreme intelligence. I hope you enjoyed your journey."

"Not at all," Acton declared. "I would much rather have been here with you."

"Now you *are* attacking me," said the Baroness. "You are contrasting my inconstancy with your own fidelity."

"I confess I never get tired of people I like."

"Ah, you are not a poor wicked foreign woman, with irritable nerves and a sophisticated mind!"

"Something has happened to you since I went away," said Acton, changing his place.

"Your going away — that is what has happened to me."

"Do you mean to say that you have missed me?" he asked.

"If I had meant to say it, it would not be worth your making a note of. I am very dishonest and my compliments are worthless."

Acton was silent for some moments. "You have broken down," he said at last.

Madame Münster left her chair, and began to move about.

"Only for a moment. I shall pull myself together again."

"You had better not take it too hard. If you are bored, you needn't be afraid to say so — to me at least."

"You shouldn't say such things as that," the Baroness answered. "You should encourage me."

"I admire your patience; that is encouraging."

"You shouldn't even say that. When you talk of my patience you are disloyal to your own people. Patience implies suffering; and what have I had to suffer?"

"Oh, not hunger, not unkindness, certainly," said Acton, laughing. "Nevertheless, we all admire your patience."

"You all detest me!" cried the Baroness, with a sudden vehemence, turning her back toward him.

"You make it hard," said Acton, getting up, "for a man to say something tender to you." This evening there was something particularly striking and touching about her; an unwonted softness and a look of suppressed emotion.

He felt himself suddenly appreciating the fact that she had behaved very well. She had come to this quiet corner of the world under the weight of a cruel indignity, and she had been so gracefully, modestly thankful for the rest she found there. She had joined that simple circle over the way; she had mingled in its plain, provincial talk; she had shared its meagre and savorless pleasures. She had set herself a task, and she had rigidly performed it. She had conformed to the angular conditions of New England life, and she had had the tact and pluck to carry it off as if she liked them. Acton felt a more downright need than he had ever felt before to tell her that he admired her and that she struck him as a very superior woman. All along, hitherto, he had been on his guard with her; he had been cautious, observant, suspicious. But now a certain light tumult in his blood seemed to tell him that a finer degree of confidence in this charming woman would be its own reward. "We don't detest you," he went on. "I don't know what you mean. At any rate, I speak for myself; I don't know anything about the others. Very likely, you detest them for the dull life they make you lead. Really, it would give me a sort of pleasure to hear you say so."

Eugenia had been looking at the door on the other side of the room; now she slowly turned her eyes toward Robert Acton. "What can be the motive," she asked, "of a man like you — an honest man, a *galant homme* — in saying so base a thing as that?"

"Does it sound very base?" asked Acton, candidly. "I suppose it does, and I thank you for telling me so. Of course, I don't mean it literally."

The Baroness stood looking at him. "How do you mean it?" she asked.

This question was difficult to answer, and Acton, feeling the least bit foolish, walked to the open window and looked out. He stood there, thinking a moment, and then he turned back. "You know that document that you were to send to Germany," he said. "You called it your 'renunciation.' Did you ever send it?"

Madame Münster's eyes expanded; she looked very grave. "What a singular answer to my question!"

"Oh, it isn't an answer," said Acton. "I have wished to ask you, many times. I thought it probable you would tell me yourself. The question, on my part, seems abrupt now; but it would be abrupt at any time."

The Baroness was silent a moment; and then, "I think I have told you too much!" she said.

This declaration appeared to Acton to have a certain force; he had indeed a sense of asking more of her than he offered her. He returned to the window, and watched, for a moment, a little star that twinkled through the lattice of the piazza. There were at any rate offers enough he could

make; perhaps he had hitherto not been sufficiently explicit in doing so. "I wish you would ask something of me," he presently said. "Is there nothing I can do for you? If you can't stand this dull life any more, let me amuse you!"

The Baroness had sunk once more into a chair, and she had taken up a fan which she held, with both hands, to her mouth. Over the top of the fan her eyes were fixed on him. "You are very strange to-night," she said, with a little laugh.

"I will do anything in the world," he rejoined, standing in front of her. "Shouldn't you like to travel about and see something of the country? Won't you go to Niagara? You ought to see Niagara, you know."

"With you, do you mean?"

"I should be delighted to take you."

"You alone?"

Acton looked at her, smiling, and yet with a serious air. "Well, yes; we might go alone," he said.

"If you were not what you are," she answered, "I should feel insulted."

"How do you mean — what I am?"

"If you were one of the gentlemen I have been used to all my life. If you were not a queer Bostonian."

"If the gentlemen you have been used to have taught you to expect insults," said Acton, "I am glad I am what I am. You had much better come to Niagara."

"If you wish to 'amuse' me," the Baroness declared, "you need go to no further expense. You amuse me very effectually."

He sat down opposite to her; she still held her fan up to her face, with her eyes only showing above it. There was a moment's silence, and then he said, returning to his former question, "Have you sent that document to Germany?"

Again there was a moment's silence. The expressive eyes of Madame Münster seemed, however, half to break it.

"I will tell you — at Niagara!" she said.

She had hardly spoken when the door at the further end of the room opened — the door upon which, some minutes previous, Eugenia had fixed her gaze. Clifford Wentworth stood there, blushing and looking rather awkward. The Baroness rose, quickly, and Acton, more slowly, did the same. Clifford gave him no greeting; he was looking at Eugenia.

"Ah, you were here?" exclaimed Acton.

"He was in Felix's studio," said Madame Münster. "He wanted to see his sketches."

Clifford looked at Robert Acton, but said nothing; he only fanned himself with his hat. "You chose a bad moment," said Acton; "you hadn't much light."

"I hadn't any!" said Clifford, laughing.

"Your candle went out?" Eugenia asked. "You should have come back here and lighted it again."

Clifford looked at her a moment. "So I have — come back. But I have left the candle!"

Eugenia turned away. "You are very stupid, my poor boy. You had better go home."

"Well," said Clifford, "good night!"

"Haven't you a word to throw to a man when he has safely returned from a dangerous journey?" Acton asked.

"How do you do?" said Clifford. "I thought — I thought you were" — and he paused, looking at the Baroness again.

"You thought I was at Newport, eh? So I was — this morning."

"Good night, clever child!" said Madame Münster, over her shoulder.

Clifford stared at her — not at all like a clever child; and then, with one of his little facetious growls, took his departure.

"What is the matter with him?" asked Acton, when he was gone. "He seemed rather in a muddle."

Eugenia, who was near the window, glanced out, listening a moment. "The matter — the matter" — she answered. "But you don't say such things here."

"If you mean that he had been drinking a little, you can say that."

"He doesn't drink any more. I have cured him. And in return — he's in love with me."

It was Acton's turn to stare. He instantly thought of his sister; but he said nothing about her. He began to laugh. "I don't wonder at his passion! But I wonder at his

124

forsaking your society for that of your brother's paint-brushes."

Eugenia was silent a little. "He had not been in the studio. I invented that at the moment."

"Invented it? For what purpose?"

"He has an idea of being romantic. He has adopted the habit of coming to see me at midnight — passing only through the orchard and through Felix's painting-room, which has a door opening that way. It seems to amuse him," added Eugenia, with a little laugh.

Acton felt more surprise than he confessed to, for this was a new view of Clifford, whose irregularities had hitherto been quite without the romantic element. He tried to laugh again, but he felt rather too serious, and after a moment's hesitation his seriousness explained itself. "I hope you don't encourage him," he said. "He must not be inconstant to poor Lizzie."

"To your sister?"

"You know they are decidedly intimate," said Acton.

"Ah," cried Eugenia, smiling, "has she — has she" —

"I don't know," Acton interrupted, "what she has. But I always supposed that Clifford had a desire to make himself agreeable to her."

"Ah, par exemple!" the Baroness went on. "The little monster! The next time he becomes sentimental I will tell him that he ought to be ashamed of himself."

Acton was silent a moment. "You had better say nothing about it."

"I had told him as much already, on general grounds," said the Baroness. "But in this country, you know, the relations of young people are so extraordinary that one is quite at sea. They are not engaged when you would quite say they ought to be. Take Charlotte Wentworth, for instance, and that young ecclesiastic. If I were her father I should insist upon his marrying her; but it appears to be thought there is no urgency. On the other hand, you suddenly learn that a boy of twenty and a little girl who is still with her governess — your sister has no governess? Well, then, who is never away from her mamma — a young couple, in short, between whom you have noticed nothing beyond an exchange of the childish pleasantries characteristic of their age, are on the point of setting up as man and wife." The Baroness spoke with a certain exaggerated volubility which was in contrast with the languid grace that had characterized her manner before Clifford made his appearance. It seemed to Acton that there was a spark of irritation in her eye — a note of irony (as when she spoke of Lizzie being never away from her mother) in her voice. If Madame Münster was irritated, Robert Acton was vaguely mystified; she began to move about the room again, and he looked at her without saying anything. Presently she took out her watch, and, glancing at it, declared that it was three o'clock in the morning and that he must go.

"I have not been here an hour," he said, "and they are still sitting up at the other house. You can see the lights. Your brother has not come in."

"Oh, at the other house," cried Eugenia, "they are terrible people! I don't know what they may do over there. I am a quiet little humdrum woman; I have rigid rules and I keep them. One of them is not to have visitors in the small hours — especially clever men like you. So good night!"

Decidedly, the Baroness was incisive; and though Acton bade her good night and departed, he was still a good deal mystified.

The next day Clifford Wentworth came to see Lizzie, and Acton, who was at home and saw him pass through the garden, took note of the circumstance. He had a natural desire to make it tally with Madame Münster's account of Clifford's disaffection; but his ingenuity, finding itself unequal to the task, resolved at last to ask help of the young man's candor. He waited till he saw him going away, and then he went out and overtook him in the grounds.

"I wish very much you would answer me a question," Acton said. "What were you doing, last night, at Madame Münster's?"

Clifford began to laugh and to blush, by no means like a young man with a romantic secret. "What did she tell you?" he asked.

"That is exactly what I don't want to say."

"Well, I want to tell you the same," said Clifford; "and unless I know it perhaps I can't."

They had stopped in a garden path; Acton looked hard at his rosy young kinsman. "She said she couldn't fancy what had got into you; you appeared to have taken a violent dislike to her."

Clifford stared, looking a little alarmed. "Oh, come," he growled, "you don't mean that!"

"And that when — for common civility's sake — you came occasionally to the house you left her alone and spent your time in Felix's studio, under pretext of looking at his sketches."

"Oh, come!" growled Clifford, again.

"Did you ever know me to tell an untruth?"

"Yes, lots of them!" said Clifford, seeing an opening, out of the discussion, for his sarcastic powers. "Well," he presently added, "I thought you were my father."

"You knew some one was there?"

"We heard you coming in."

Acton meditated. "You had been with the Baroness, then?"

"I was in the parlor. We heard your step outside. I thought it was my father."

"And on that," asked Acton, "you ran away?"

"She told me to go — to go out by the studio."

Acton meditated more intensely; if there had been a chair at hand he would have sat down. "Why should she wish you not to meet your father?"

"Well," said Clifford, "father doesn't like to see me there."

Acton looked askance at his companion and forbore to make any comment upon this assertion. "Has he said so," he asked, "to the Baroness?"

"Well, I hope not," said Clifford. "He hasn't said so — in so many words — to me. But I know it worries him; and I want to stop worrying him. The Baroness knows it, and she wants me to stop, too."

"To stop coming to see her?"

"I don't know about that; but to stop worrying father. Eugenia knows everything," Clifford added, with an air of knowingness of his own.

"Ah," said Acton, interrogatively, "Eugenia knows everything?"

"She knew it was not father coming in."

"Then why did you go?"

Clifford blushed and laughed afresh. "Well, I was afraid it was. And besides, she told me to go, at any rate."

"Did she think it was I?" Acton asked.

"She didn't say so."

Again Robert Acton reflected. "But you didn't go," he presently said; "you came back."

"I couldn't get out of the studio," Clifford rejoined. "The door was locked, and Felix has nailed some planks across the lower half of the confounded windows to make the light come in from above. So they were no use. I waited there a good while, and then, suddenly, I felt ashamed. I didn't want to be hiding away from my own father. I couldn't stand it any

longer. I bolted out, and when I found it was you I was a little flurried. But Eugenia carried it off, didn't she?" Clifford added, in the tone of a young humorist whose perception had not been permanently clouded by the sense of his own discomfort.

"Beautifully!" said Acton. "Especially," he continued, "when one remembers that you were very imprudent and that she must have been a good deal annoyed."

"Oh," cried Clifford, with the indifference of a young man who feels that however he may have failed of felicity in behavior he is extremely just in his impressions, "Eugenia doesn't care for anything!"

Acton hesitated a moment. "Thank you for telling me this," he said at last. And then, laying his hand on Clifford's shoulder, he added, "Tell me one thing more: are you by chance a little in love with the Baroness?"

"No, sir!" said Clifford, almost shaking off his hand.

X

THE FIRST Sunday that followed Robert Acton's return from Newport witnessed a change in the brilliant weather that had long prevailed. The rain began to fall and the day was cold and dreary. Mr. Wentworth and his daughters put on overshoes and went to church, and Felix Young, without overshoes, went also, holding an umbrella over Gertrude. It is to be feared that, in the whole observance, this was the privilege he most highly valued. The Baroness remained at home; she was in neither a cheerful nor a devotional mood. She had, however, never been, during her residence in the United States, what is called a regular attendant at divine service; and on this particular Sunday morning of which I began with speaking she stood at the window of her little drawing-room, watching the long arm of a rose-tree that was attached to her piazza, but a portion of which had disengaged itself, sway to and fro, shake and gesticulate, against the dusky drizzle of the sky. Every now and then, in a gust of wind, the rose-tree scattered a shower of water-drops against the window-pane; it appeared to have a kind of human movement — a menacing, warning intention. The room was very cold; Madame Münster put on a shawl and walked about. Then she determined to have some fire; and summoning her ancient negress, the contrast of whose polished ebony and whose crimson turban had been at first a source of satisfaction to her, she made arrangements for the production of a crackling flame. This old woman's name was Azarina. The Baroness had begun by thinking that here would be a savory wildness in her talk, and, for amusement, she had encouraged her to chatter. But Azarina was dry and prim; her conversation was anything but African; she reminded Eugenia of the tiresome old ladies she met in society. She knew, however, how to make a fire; so that after she had laid the logs, Eugenia, who was terribly bored, found a quarter of an hour's entertainment in sitting and watching them blaze and sputter. She had thought it very likely Robert Acton would come and see her; she had not met him since that infelicitous evening. But the morning waned without his coming; several times she thought she heard his step on the piazza; but it was only a window-shutter shaking in a rain-gust. The Baroness, since the beginning of that episode in her career of which a slight sketch has been attempted in these pages, had had many moments of irritation. But to-day her irritation had a peculiar keenness; it appeared to feed upon itself. It urged her to do something; but it suggested no particularly profitable line of action. If she could have done something at the moment, on the spot, she would have stepped upon a European steamer and turned her back, with a kind of rapture, upon that profoundly mortifying failure, her visit to her American relations. It is not exactly apparent why she should have termed this enterprise a failure, inasmuch as she had been treated with the highest distinction for which allowance had been made in American institutions. Her irritation came, at bottom, from the sense, which, always present, had suddenly grown acute, that the social soil on this big, vague continent was somehow not adapted for growing those plants whose fragrance she especially inclined to inhale and by which she liked to see herself surrounded — a species of vegetation for which she carried a collection of seedlings, as we may say, in her pocket. She found her chief happiness in the sense of exerting a certain power and making a certain impression; and now she felt the annoyance of a rather wearied swimmer who, on nearing shore, to land, finds a smooth straight wall of rock when he had counted upon a clean firm beach. Her power, in the American air, seemed to have lost its prehensile attributes; the smooth wall of rock was insurmountable. "Surely je n'en suis pas là," she said to herself, "that I let it make me uncomfortable that a Mr. Robert Acton shouldn't honor me with a visit!" Yet she was vexed that he had not come; and she was vexed at her vexation.

Her brother, at least, came in, stamping in the hall and shaking the wet from his coat. In a moment he entered the room, with a glow in his cheek and half-a-dozen rain-drops glistening on his mustache. "Ah, you have a fire," he said.

"Les beaux jours sont passés," replied the Baroness.

"Never, never! They have only begun," Felix declared, planting himself before the hearth. He turned his back to the fire, placed his hands behind him, extended his legs and looked away through the window with an expression of face which seemed to denote the perception of rose-color even in the tints of a wet Sunday.

His sister, from her chair, looked up at him, watching him; and what she saw in his face was not grateful to her present mood. She was puzzled by many things, but her brother's disposition was a frequent source of wonder to her. I say frequent and not constant, for there were long periods during which she gave her attention to other problems. Sometimes she had said to herself that his happy temper, his eternal gayety, was an affection, a *pose;* but she was vaguely conscious that during the present summer he had been a highly successful comedian. They had never yet had an explanation; she had not known the need of one. Felix was presumably following the bent of his disinterested genius, and she felt that she had no advice to give him that he would understand. With this, there was always a certain element of comfort about Felix — the assurance that he would not interfere. He was very delicate, this pure-minded Felix; in effect, he was her brother, and Madame Münster felt that there was a great propriety, every way, in that. It is true that Felix was delicate; he was not fond of explanations with his sister; this was one of the very few things in the world about which he was uncomfortable. But now he was not thinking of anything uncomfortable.

"Dear brother," said Eugenia at

last, "do stop making *les yeux doux* at the rain."

"With pleasure. I will make them at you!" answered Felix.

"How much longer," asked Eugenia, in a moment, "do you propose to remain in this lovely spot?"

Felix stared. "Do you want to go away — already?"

" 'Already' is delicious. I am not so happy as you."

Felix dropped into a chair, looking at the fire. "The fact is I *am* happy," he said in his light, clear tone.

"And do you propose to spend your life in making love to Gertrude Wentworth?"

"Yes," said Felix, smiling sidewise at his sister.

The Baroness returned his glance, much more gravely; and then, "Do you like her?" she asked.

"Don't you?" Felix demanded.

The Baroness was silent a moment. "I will answer you in the words of the gentleman who was asked if he liked music: 'Je ne la crains pas!' "

"She admires you immensely," said Felix.

"I don't care for that. Other women should not admire one."

"They should dislike you?"

Again Madame Münster hesitated. "They should hate me! It's a measure of the time I have been losing here that they don't."

"No time is lost in which one has been happy!" said Felix, with a bright sententiousness which may well have been a little irritating.

"And in which," rejoined his sister, with a harsher laugh, "one

has secured the affections of a young lady with a fortune!"

Felix explained, very candidly and seriously. "I have secured Gertrude's affection, but I am by no means sure that I have secured her fortune. That may come — or it may not."

"Ah, well, it *may!* That's the great point."

"It depends upon her father. He doesn't smile upon our union. You know he wants her to marry Mr. Brand."

"I know nothing about it!" cried the Baroness. "Please to put on a log." Felix complied with her request and sat watching the quickening of the flames. Presently his sister added, "And you propose to elope with mademoiselle?"

"By no means. I don't wish to do anything that's disagreeable to Mr. Wentworth. He has been far too kind to us."

"But you must choose between pleasing yourself and pleasing him."

"I want to please every one!" exclaimed Felix, joyously. "I have a good conscience. I made up my mind at the outset that it was not my place to make love to Gertrude."

"So, to simplify matters, she made love to you!"

Felix looked at his sister with sudden gravity. "You say you are not afraid of her," he said. "But perhaps you ought to be — a little. She's a very clever person."

"I begin to see it!" cried the Baroness. Her brother, making no rejoinder, leaned back in his chair, and there was a long silence. At last, with an altered accent, Madame Münster put another question. "You expect, at any rate, to marry?"

"I shall be greatly disappointed if we don't."

"A disappointment or two will do you good!" the Baroness declared. "And, afterwards, do you mean to turn American?"

"It seems to me I am a very good American already. But we shall go to Europe. Gertrude wants extremely to see the world."

"Ah, like me, when I came here!" said the Baroness, with a little laugh.

"No, not like you," Felix rejoined, looking at his sister with a certain gentle seriousness. While he looked at her she rose from her chair, and he also got up. "Gertrude is not at all like you," he went on; "but in her own way she is almost as clever." He paused a moment; his soul was full of an agreeable feeling and of a lively disposition to express it. His sister, to his spiritual vision, was always like the lunar disk when only a part of it is lighted. The shadow on this bright surface seemed to him to expand and to contract; but whatever its proportions, he always appreciated the moonlight. He looked at the Baroness, and then he kissed her. "I am very much in love with Gertrude," he said. Eugenia turned away and walked about the room, and Felix continued. "She is very interesting, and very different from what she seems. She has never had a chance.

She is very brilliant. We will go to Europe and amuse ourselves."

The Baroness had gone to the window, where she stood looking out. The day was drearier than ever; the rain was doggedly falling. "Yes, to amuse yourselves," she said at last, "you had decidedly better go to Europe!" Then she turned round, looking at her brother. A chair stood near her; she leaned her hands upon the back of it. "Don't you think it is very good of me," she asked, "to come all this way with you simply to see you properly married — if properly it is?"

"Oh, it will be properly!" cried Felix, with light eagerness.

The Baroness gave a little laugh. "You are thinking only of yourself, and you don't answer my question. While you are amusing yourself — with the brilliant Gertrude — what shall I be doing?"

"Vous serez de la partie!" cried Felix.

"Thank you: I should spoil it." The Baroness dropped her eyes for some moments. "Do you propose, however, to leave me here?" she inquired.

Felix smiled at her. "My dearest sister, where you are concerned I never propose. I execute your commands."

"I believe," said Eugenia, slowly, "that you are the most heartless person living. Don't you see that I am in trouble?"

"I saw that you were not cheerful, and I gave you some good news."

"Well, let me give you some

news," said the Baroness. "You probably will not have discovered it for yourself. Robert Acton wants to marry me."

"No, I had not discovered that. But I quite understand it. Why does it make you unhappy?"

"Because I can't decide."

"Accept him, accept him!" cried Felix, joyously. "He is the best fellow in the world."

"He is immensely in love with me," said the Baroness.

"And he has a large fortune. Permit me in turn to remind you of that."

"Oh, I am perfectly aware of it," said Eugenia. "That's a great item in his favor. I am terribly candid." And she left her place and came nearer her brother, looking at him hard. He was turning over several things; she was wondering in what manner he really understood her.

There were several ways of understanding her: there was what she said, and there was what she meant, and there was something, between the two, that was neither. It is probable that, in the last analysis, what she meant was that Felix should spare her the necessity of stating the case more exactly and should hold himself commissioned to assist her by all honorable means to marry the best fellow in the world. But in all this it was never discovered what Felix understood.

"Once you have your liberty, what are your objections?" he asked.

"Well, I don't particularly like him."

"Oh, try a little."

"I am trying now," said Eugenia. "I should succeed better if he didn't live here. I could never live here."

"Make him go to Europe," Felix suggested.

"Ah, there you speak of happiness based upon violent effort," the Baroness rejoined. "That is not what I am looking for. He would never live in Europe."

"He would live anywhere, with you!" said Felix, gallantly.

His sister looked at him still, with a ray of penetration in her charming eyes; then she turned away again. "You see, at all events," she presently went on, "that if it had been said of me that I had come over here to seek my fortune it would have to be added that I have found it!"

"Don't leave it lying!" urged Felix, with smiling solemnity.

"I am much obliged to you for your interest," his sister declared, after a moment. "But promise me one thing: *pas de zèle!* If Mr. Acton should ask you to plead his cause, excuse yourself."

"I shall certainly have the excuse," said Felix, "that I have a cause of my own to plead."

"If he should talk of me — favorably," Eugenia continued, "warn him against dangerous illusions. I detest importunities; I want to decide at my leisure, with my eyes open."

"I shall be discreet," said Felix, "except to you. To you I will say, Accept him outright."

She had advanced to the open

door-way, and she stood looking at him. "I will go and dress and think of it," she said; and he heard her moving slowly to her apartments.

Late in the afternoon the rain stopped, and just afterwards there was a great flaming, flickering, trickling sunset. Felix sat in his painting-room and did some work; but at last, as the light, which had not been brilliant, began to fade, he laid down his brushes and came out to the little piazza of the cottage. Here he walked up and down for some time, looking at the splendid blaze of the western sky and saying, as he had often said before, that this was certainly the country of sunsets. There was something in these glorious deeps of fire that quickened his imagination; he always found images and promises in the western sky. He thought of a good many things — of roaming about the world with Gertrude Wentworth; he seemed to see their possible adventures, in a glowing frieze, between the cloud-bars; then of what Eugenia had just been telling him. He wished very much that Madame Münster would make a comfortable and honorable marriage. Presently, as the sunset expanded and deepened, the fancy took him of making a note of so magnificent a piece of coloring. He returned to his studio and fetched out a small panel, with his palette and brushes, and, placing the panel against a window-sill, he began to daub with great gusto. While he was so occupied he saw Mr. Brand,

in the distance, slowly come down from Mr. Wentworth's house, nursing a large folded umbrella. He walked with a joyless, meditative tread, and his eyes were bent upon the ground. Felix poised his brush for a moment, watching him; then, by a sudden impulse, as he drew nearer, advanced to the garden-gate and signaled to him — the palette and bunch of brushes contributing to this effect.

Mr. Brand stopped and started; then he appeared to decide to accept Felix's invitation. He came out of Mr. Wentworth's gate and passed along the road; after which he entered the little garden of the cottage. Felix had gone back to his sunset; but he made his visitor welcome while he rapidly brushed it in.

"I wanted so much to speak to you that I thought I would call you," he said, in the friendliest tone. "All the more that you have been to see me so little. You have come to see my sister; I know that. But you haven't come to see me — the celebrated artist. Artists are very sensitive, you know; they notice those things." And Felix turned round, smiling, with a brush in his mouth.

Mr. Brand stood there with a certain blank, candid majesty, pulling together the large flaps of his umbrella. "Why should I come to see you?" he asked. "I know nothing of Art."

"It would sound very conceited, I suppose," said Felix, "if I were to say that it would be a good little chance for you to learn something. You would ask me why you should learn; and I should have no answer to that. I suppose a minister has no need for Art, eh?"

"He has need for good temper, sir," said Mr. Brand, with decision.

Felix jumped up, with his palette on his thumb and a movement of the liveliest deprecation. "That's because I keep you standing there while I splash my red paint! I beg a thousand pardons! You see what bad manners Art gives a man; and how right you are to let it alone. I didn't mean you should stand, either. The piazza, as you see, is ornamented with rustic chairs; though indeed I ought to warn you that they have nails in the wrong places. I was just making a note of that sunset. I never saw such a blaze of different reds. It looks as if the Celestial City were in flames, eh? If that were really the case I suppose it would be the business of you theologians to put out the fire. Fancy me — an ungodly artist — quietly sitting down to paint it!"

Mr. Brand had always credited Felix Young with a certain impudence, but it appeared to him that on this occasion his impudence was so great as to make a special explanation — or even an apology — necessary. And the impression, it must be added, was sufficiently natural. Felix had at all times a brilliant assurance of manner which was simply the vehicle of his good spirits and his good will; but at present he had a special design, and as he would have

admitted that the design was audacious, so he was conscious of having summoned all the arts of conversation to his aid. But he was so far from desiring to offend his visitor that he was rapidly asking himself what personal compliment he could pay the young clergyman that would gratify him most. If he could think of it, he was prepared to pay it down. "Have you been preaching one of your beautiful sermons to-day?" he suddenly asked, laying down his palette. This was not what Felix had been trying to think of, but it was a tolerable stop-gap.

Mr. Brand frowned — as much as a man can frown who has very fair, soft eyebrows, and, beneath them, very gentle, tranquil eyes. "No, I have not preached any sermon to-day. Did you bring me over here for the purpose of making that inquiry?"

Felix saw that he was irritated, and he regretted it immensely; but he had no fear of not being, in the end, agreeable to Mr. Brand. He looked at him, smiling and laying his hand on his arm. "No, no, not for that — not for that. I wanted to ask you something; I wanted to tell you something. I am sure it will interest you very much. Only — as it is something rather private — we had better come into my little studio. I have a western window; we can still see the sunset. *Andiamo!*" And he gave a little pat to his companion's arm.

He led the way in; Mr. Brand stiffly and softly followed. The twilight had thickened in the little studio; but the wall opposite the western window was covered with a deep pink flush. There were a great many sketches and half-finished canvasses suspended in this rosy glow, and the corners of the room were vague and dusky. Felix begged Mr. Brand to sit down; then glancing round him, "By Jove, how pretty it looks!" he cried. But Mr. Brand would not sit down; he went and leaned against the window; he wondered what Felix wanted of him. In the shadow, on the darker parts of the wall, he saw the gleam of three or four pictures that looked fantastic and surprising. They seemed to represent naked figures. Felix stood there, with his head a little bent and his eyes fixed upon his visitor, smiling intensely, pulling his mustache. Mr. Brand felt vaguely uneasy. "It is very delicate — what I want to say," Felix began. "But I have been thinking of it for some time."

"Please to say it as quickly as possible," said Mr. Brand.

"It's because you are a clergyman, you know," Felix went on. "I don't think I should venture to say it to a common man."

Mr. Brand was silent a moment. "If it is a question of yielding to a weakness, of resenting an injury, I am afraid I am a very common man."

"My dearest friend," cried Felix, "this is not an injury; it's a benefit — a great service! You will like it extremely. Only it's so delicate!" And, in the dim light, he continued to smile intensely. "You

know I take a great interest in my cousins — in Charlotte and Gertrude Wentworth. That's very evident from my having traveled some five thousand miles to see them." Mr. Brand said nothing and Felix proceeded. "Coming into their society as a perfect stranger I received of course a great many new impressions, and my impressions had a great freshness, a great keenness. Do you know what I mean?"

"I am not sure that I do; but I should like you to continue."

"I think my impressions have always a good deal of freshness," said Mr. Brand's entertainer; "but on this occasion it was perhaps particularly natural that — coming in, as I say, from outside — I should be struck with things that passed unnoticed among yourselves. And then I had my sister to help me; and she is simply the most observant woman in the world."

"I am not surprised," said Mr. Brand, "that in our little circle two intelligent persons should have found food for observation. I am sure that, of late, I have found it myself!"

"Ah, but I shall surprise you yet!" cried Felix, laughing. "Both my sister and I took a great fancy to my cousin Charlotte."

"Your cousin Charlotte?" repeated Mr. Brand.

"We fell in love with her from the first!"

"You fell in love with Charlotte?" Mr. Brand murmured.

"*Dame!*" exclaimed Felix, "she's

a very charming person; and Eugenia was especially smitten." Mr. Brand stood staring, and he pursued, "Affection, you know, opens one's eyes, and we noticed something. Charlotte is not happy! Charlotte is in love." And Felix, drawing nearer, laid his hand upon his companion's arm.

There was something akin to an acknowledgment of fascination in the way Mr. Brand looked at him; but the young clergyman retained as yet quite enough self-possession to be able to say, with a good deal of solemnity, "She is not in love with you."

Felix gave a light laugh, and rejoined with the alacrity of a maritime adventurer who feels a puff of wind in his sail. "Ah, no; if she were in love with me I should know it! I am not so blind as you."

"As I?"

"My dear sir, you are stone blind. Poor Charlotte is dead in love with *you!*"

Mr. Brand said nothing for a moment; he breathed a little heavily. "Is that what you wanted to say to me?" he asked.

"I have wanted to say it these three weeks. Because of late she has been worse. I told you," added Felix, "it was very delicate."

"Well, sir" — Mr. Brand began; "well, sir" —

"I was sure you didn't know it," Felix continued. "But don't you see — as soon as I mention it — how everything is explained?"

Mr. Brand answered nothing; he looked for a chair and softly sat down. Felix could see that he was blushing; he had looked straight at his host hitherto, but now he looked away. The foremost effect of what he had heard had been a sort of irritation of his modesty. "Of course," said Felix, "I suggest nothing; it would be very presumptuous in me to advise you. But I think there is no doubt about the fact."

Mr. Brand looked hard at the floor for some moments; he was oppressed with a mixture of sensations. Felix, standing there, was very sure that one of them was profound surprise. The innocent young man had been completely unsuspicious of poor Charlotte's hidden flame. This gave Felix great hope; he was sure that Mr. Brand would be flattered. Felix thought him very transparent, and indeed he was so; he could neither simulate nor dissimulate. "I scarcely know what to make of this," he said at last, without looking up; and Felix was struck with the fact that he offered no protest or contradiction. Evidently Felix had kindled a train of memories — a retrospective illumination. It was making, to Mr. Brand's astonished eyes, a very pretty blaze; his second emotion had been a gratification of vanity.

"Thank me for telling you," Felix rejoined. "It's a good thing to know."

"I am not sure of that," said Mr. Brand.

136

"Ah, don't let her languish!" Felix murmured, lightly and softly.

"You *do* advise me, then?" And Mr. Brand looked up.

"I congratulate you!" said Felix, smiling. He had thought at first his visitor was simply appealing; but he saw he was a little ironical.

"It is in your interest; you have interfered with me," the young clergyman went on.

Felix still stood and smiled. The little room had grown darker, and the crimson glow had faded; but Mr. Brand could see the brilliant expression of his face. "I won't pretend not to know what you mean," said Felix at last. "But I have not really interfered with you. Of what you had to lose — with another person — you have lost nothing. And think what you have gained!"

"It seems to me I am the proper judge, on each side," Mr. Brand declared. He got up, holding the brim of his hat against his mouth and staring at Felix through the dusk.

"You have lost an illusion!" said Felix.

"What do you call an illusion?"

"The belief that you really know — that you have ever really known — Gertrude Wentworth. Depend upon that," pursued Felix. "I don't know her yet; but I have no illusions; I don't pretend to."

Mr. Brand kept gazing, over his hat. "She has always been a lucid, limpid nature," he said, solemnly.

"She has always been a dormant nature. She was waiting for a touchstone. But now she is beginning to awaken."

"Don't praise her to me!" said Mr. Brand, with a little quaver in his voice. "If you have the advantage of me that is not generous."

"My dear sir, I am melting with generosity!" exclaimed Felix. "And I am not praising my cousin. I am simply attempting a scientific definition of her. She doesn't care for abstractions. Now I think the contrary is what you have always fancied — is the basis on which you have been building. She is extremely preoccupied with the concrete. I care for the concrete, too. But Gertrude is stronger than I; she whirls me along!"

Mr. Brand looked for a moment into the crown of his hat. "It's a most interesting nature."

"So it is," said Felix. "But it pulls — it pulls — like a runaway horse. Now I like the feeling of a runaway horse; and if I am thrown out of the vehicle it is no great matter. But if *you* should be thrown, Mr. Brand" — and Felix paused a moment — "another person also would suffer from the accident."

"What other person?"

"Charlotte Wentworth!"

Mr. Brand looked at Felix for a moment sidewise, mistrustfully; then his eyes slowly wandered over the ceiling. Felix was sure he was secretly struck with the romance of the situation. "I think this is none of our business," the young minister murmured.

"None of mine, perhaps; but surely yours!"

Mr. Brand lingered still, looking at the ceiling; there was evidently something he wanted to say. "What do you mean by Miss Gertrude being strong?" he asked abruptly.

"Well," said Felix meditatively, "I mean that she has had a great deal of self-possession. She was waiting — for years; even when she seemed, perhaps, to be living in the present. She knew how to wait; she had a purpose. That's what I mean by her being strong."

"But what do you mean by her purpose?"

"Well — the purpose to see the world!"

Mr. Brand eyed his strange informant askance again; but he said nothing. At last he turned away, as if to take leave. He seemed bewildered, however; for instead of going to the door he moved toward the opposite corner of the room. Felix stood and watched him for a moment — almost groping about in the dusk; then he led him to the door, with a tender, almost fraternal movement. "Is that all you have to say?" asked Mr. Brand.

"Yes, it's all — but it will bear a good deal of thinking of."

Felix went with him to the garden-gate, and watched him slowly walk away into the thickening twilight with a relaxed rigidity that tried to rectify itself. "He is offended, excited, bewildered, perplexed — and enchanted!" Felix

said to himself. "That's a capital mixture."

XI

SINCE that visit paid by the Baroness Münster to Mrs. Acton, of which some account was given at an earlier stage of this narrative, the intercourse between these two ladies had been neither frequent nor intimate. It was not that Mrs. Acton had failed to appreciate Madame Münster's charms; on the contrary, her perception of the graces of manner and conversation of her brilliant visitor had been only too acute. Mrs. Acton was, as they said in Boston, very "intense," and her impressions were apt to be too many for her. The state of her health required the restriction of emotion; and this is why, receiving, as she sat in her eternal arm-chair, very few visitors, even of the soberest local type, she had been obliged to limit the number of her interviews with a lady whose costume and manner recalled to her imagination — Mrs. Acton's imagination was a marvel — all that she had ever read of the most stirring historical periods. But she had sent the Baroness a great many quaintly-worded messages and a great many nosegays from her garden and baskets of beautiful fruit. Felix had eaten the fruit, and the Baroness had arranged the flowers and returned the baskets and the messages. On the day that followed that rainy Sunday of which mention has been made, Eugenia determined to go and pay the beneficent invalid a *"visite d'adieux";* so it was that, to herself, she qualified her enterprise. It may be noted that neither on the Sunday evening nor on the Monday morning had she received that expected visit from Robert Acton. To his own consciousness, evidently he was "keeping away;" and as the Baroness, on her side, was keeping away from her uncle's, whither, for several days, Felix had been the unembarrassed bearer of apologies and regrets for absence, chance had not taken the cards from the hands of design. Mr. Wentworth and his daughters had respected Eugenia's seclusion; certain intervals of mysterious retirement appeared to them, vaguely, a natural part of the graceful, rhythmic movement of so remarkable a life. Gertrude especially held these periods in honor; she wondered what Madame Münster did at such times, but she would not have permitted herself to inquire too curiously.

The long rain had freshened the air, and twelve hours' brilliant sunshine had dried the roads; so that the Baroness, in the late afternoon, proposing to walk to Mrs. Acton's, exposed herself to no great discomfort. As with her charming undulating step she moved along the clean, grassy margin of the road, beneath the thickly-hanging boughs of the orchards, through the quiet of the

hour and place and the rich maturity of the summer, she was even conscious of a sort of luxurious melancholy. The Baroness had the amiable weakness of attaching herself to places — even when she had begun with a little aversion; and now, with the prospect of departure, she felt tenderly toward this well-wooded corner of the Western world, where the sunsets were so beautiful and one's ambitions were so pure. Mrs. Acton was able to receive her; but on entering this lady's large, freshly-scented room the Baroness saw that she was looking very ill. She was wonderfully white and transparent, and, in her flowered armchair, she made no attempt to move. But she flushed a little — like a young girl, the Baroness thought — and she rested her clear, smiling eyes upon those of her visitor. Her voice was low and monotonous, like a voice that had never expressed any human passions.

"I have come to bid you good-by," said Eugenia, "I shall soon be going away."

"When are you going away?"

"Very soon — any day."

"I am very sorry," said Mrs. Acton. "I hoped you would stay — always."

"Always?" Eugenia demanded.

"Well, I mean a long time," said Mrs. Acton, in her sweet, feeble tone. "They tell me you are so comfortable — that you have got such a beautiful little house."

Eugenia stared — that is, she smiled; she thought of her poor little *chalet* and she wondered whether her hostess were jesting. "Yes, my house is exquisite," she said; "though not to be compared to yours."

"And my son is so fond of going to see you," Mrs. Acton added. "I am afraid my son will miss you."

"Ah, dear madame," said Eugenia, with a little laugh, "I can't stay in America for your son!"

"Don't you like America?"

The Baroness looked at the front of her dress. "If I liked it — that would not be staying for your son!"

Mrs. Acton gazed at her with her grave, tender eyes, as if she had not quite understood. The Baroness at last found something irritating in the sweet, soft stare of her hostess; and if one were not bound to be merciful to great invalids she would almost have taken the liberty of pronouncing her, mentally, a fool. "I am afraid, then, I shall never see you again," said Mrs. Acton. "You know I am dying."

"Ah, dear madame," murmured Eugenia.

"I want to leave my children cheerful and happy. My daughter will probably marry her cousin."

"Two such interesting young people," said the Baroness, vaguely. She was not thinking of Clifford Wentworth.

"I feel so tranquil about my end," Mrs. Acton went on. "It is coming so easily, so surely." And she paused, with her mild gaze always on Eugenia's.

The Baroness hated to be reminded of death; but even in its imminence, so far as Mrs. Acton was concerned, she preserved her good manners. "Ah, madame, you are too charming an invalid," she rejoined.

But the delicacy of this rejoinder was apparently lost upon her hostess, who went on in her low, reasonable voice. "I want to leave my children bright and comfortable. You seem to me all so happy here — just as you are. So I wish you could stay. It would be so pleasant for Robert."

Eugenia wondered what she meant by its being pleasant for Robert; but she felt that she would never know what such a woman as that meant. She got up; she was afraid Mrs. Acton would tell her again that she was dying. "Good-by, dear madame," she said. "I must remember that your strength is precious."

Mrs. Acton took her hand and held it a moment. "Well, you *have* been happy here, haven't you? And you like us all, don't you? I wish you would stay," she added, "in your beautiful little house."

She had told Eugenia that her waiting-woman would be in the hall, to show her down-stairs; but the large landing outside her door was empty, and Eugenia stood there looking about. She felt irritated; the dying lady had not "*la main heureuse.*" She passed slowly down-stairs, still looking about. The broad staircase made a great bend, and in the angle was a high window, looking westward, with a deep bench, covered with a row of flowering plants in curious old pots of blue china-ware. The yellow afternoon light came in through the flowers and flickered a little on the white wainscots. Eugenia paused a moment; the house was perfectly still, save for the ticking, somewhere, of a great clock. The lower hall stretched away at the foot of the stairs, half covered over with a large Oriental rug. Eugenia lingered a little, noticing a great many things. "Comme c'est bien!" she said to herself; such a large, solid, irreproachable basis of existence the place seemed to her to indicate. And then she reflected that Mrs. Acton was soon to withdraw from it. The reflection accompanied her the rest of the way down-stairs, where she paused again, making more observations. The hall was extremely broad, and on either side of the front door was a wide, deeply-set window, which threw the shadows of everything back into the house. There were high-backed chairs along the wall and big Eastern vases upon tables, and, on either side, a large cabinet with a glass front and little curiosities within, dimly gleaming. The doors were open — into the darkened parlor, the library, the dining-room. All these rooms seemed empty. Eugenia passed along, and stopped a moment on the threshold of each. "Comme c'est bien!" she murmured again; she had thought of just such a house as this when she decided to come to America. She opened the front door for herself — her light tread had summoned none of the servants — and on the threshold she gave a last look. Outside, she was still in the humor for curious contemplation; so instead of going directly down the little drive, to the gate, she wandered away towards the garden, which lay to the right of the house. She had not gone many yards over the grass before she paused quickly; she perceived a gentleman stretched upon the level verdure, beneath a tree. He had not heard her coming, and he lay motionless, flat on his back, with his hands clasped under his head, staring up at the sky; so that the Baroness was able to reflect, at her leisure, upon the question of his identity. It was that of a person who had lately been much in her thoughts; but her first impulse, nevertheless, was to turn away; the last thing she desired was to have the air of coming in quest of Robert Acton. The gentleman on the grass, however, gave her no time to decide; he could not long remain unconscious of so agreeable a presence. He rolled back his eyes, stared, gave an exclamation, and then jumped up. He stood an instant, looking at her.

"Excuse my ridiculous position," he said.

"I have just now no sense of the ridiculous. But, in case you have, don't imagine I came to see you."

"Take care," rejoined Acton, "how you put it into my head! I was thinking of you."

"The occupation of extreme leisure!" said the Baroness. "To think of a woman when you are in that position is no compliment."

"I didn't say I was thinking well!" Acton affirmed, smiling.

She looked at him, and then she turned away. "Though I didn't come to see you," she said, "remember at least that I am within your gates."

"I am delighted — I am honored! Won't you come into the house?"

"I have just come out of it. I have been calling upon your mother. I have been bidding her farewell."

"Farewell?" Acton demanded.

"I am going away," said the Baroness. And she turned away again, as if to illustrate her meaning.

"When are you going?" asked Acton, standing a moment in his place. But the Baroness made no answer, and he followed her.

"I came this way to look at your garden," she said, walking back to the gate, over the grass. "But I must go."

"Let me at least go with you." He went with her, and they said nothing till they reached the gate. It was open, and they looked down the road which was darkened over with long bosky shadows. "Must you go straight home?" Acton asked.

But she made no answer. She said, after a moment, "Why have you not been to see me?" He said nothing and then she went on, "Why don't you answer me?"

"I am trying to invent an answer," Acton confessed.

"Have you none ready?"

"None that I can tell you," he said. "But let me walk with you now."

"You may do as you like."

She moved slowly along the road, and Acton went with her. Presently he said, "If I had done as I liked I would have come to see you several times."

"Is that invented?" asked Eugenia.

"No, that is natural. I stayed away because" —

"Ah, here comes the reason, then!"

"Because I wanted to think about you."

"Because you wanted to lie down!" said the Baroness. "I have seen you lie down — almost — in my drawing-room."

Acton stopped in the road, with a movement which seemed to beg her to linger a little. She paused, and he looked at her awhile; he thought her very charming. "You are jesting," he said; "but if you are really going away it is very serious."

"If I stay," and she gave a little laugh, "it is more serious still!"

"When shall you go?"

"As soon as possible."

"And why?"

"Why should I stay?"

"Because we all admire you so."

"That is not a reason. I am admired also in Europe." And she began to walk homeward again.

"What could I say to keep you?" asked Acton. He wanted to

142

keep her, and it was a fact that he had been thinking of her for a week. He was in love with her now; he was conscious of that, or he thought he was; and the only question with him was whether he could trust her.

"What you can say to keep me?" she repeated. "As I want very much to go it is not in my interest to tell you. Besides, I can't imagine."

He went on with her in silence; he was much more affected by what she had told him than appeared. Ever since that evening of his return from Newport her image had had a terrible power to trouble him. What Clifford Wentworth had told him — that had affected him, too, in an adverse sense; but it had not liberated him from the discomfort of a charm of which his intelligence was impatient. "She is not honest, she is not honest," he kept murmuring to himself. That is what he had been saying to the summer sky, ten minutes before. Unfortunately, he was unable to say it finally, definitively; and now that he was near her it seemed to matter wonderfully little. "She is a woman who will lie," he had said to himself. Now, as he went along, he reminded himself of this observation; but it failed to frighten him as it had done before. He almost wished he could make her lie and then convict her of it, so that he might see how he should like that. He kept thinking of this as he walked by her side, while she moved forward with her light,

graceful dignity. He had sat with her before; he had driven with her; but he had never walked with her.

"By Jove, how *comme il faut* she is!" he said, as he observed her sidewise. When they reached the cottage in the orchard she passed into the gate without asking him to follow; but she turned round, as he stood there, to bid him good-night.

"I asked you a question the other night which you never answered," he said. "Have you sent off that document — liberating yourself?"

She hesitated for a single moment — very naturally. Then, "Yes," she said, simply.

He turned away; he wondered whether that would do for his lie. But he saw her again that evening, for the Baroness reappeared at her uncle's. He had little talk with her, however; two gentlemen had driven out from Boston, in a buggy, to call upon Mr. Wentworth and his daughters, and Madame Münster was an object of absorbing interest to both of the visitors. One of them, indeed, said nothing to her; he only sat and watched with intense gravity, and leaned forward solemnly, presenting his ear (a very large one), as if he were deaf, whenever she dropped an observation. He had evidently been impressed with the idea of her misfortunes and reverses: he never smiled. His companion adopted a lighter, easier style; sat as near as possible to Madame Münster; attempted to draw her out, and proposed every few moments a new topic of conversation. Eugenia was less vividly responsive than usual and had less to say than, from her brilliant reputation, her interlocutor expected, upon the relative merits of European and American institutions; but she was inaccessible to Robert Acton, who roamed about the piazza with his hands in his pockets, listening for the grating sound of the buggy from Boston, as it should be brought round to the side-door. But he listened in vain, and at last he lost patience. His sister came to him and begged him to take her home, and he presently went off with her. Eugenia observed him leaving the house with Lizzie; in her present mood the fact seemed a contribution to her irritated conviction that he had several precious qualities. "Even that *mal-élevée* little girl," she reflected, "makes him do what she wishes."

She had been sitting just within one of the long windows that opened upon the piazza; but very soon after Acton had gone away she got up abruptly, just when the talkative gentleman from Boston was asking her what she thought of the "moral tone" of that city. On the piazza she encountered Clifford Wentworth, coming round from the other side of the house. She stopped him; she told him she wished to speak to him.

"Why didn't you go home with your cousin?" she asked.

Clifford stared. "Why, Robert has taken her," he said.

"Exactly so. But you don't usually leave that to him."

"Oh," said Clifford, "I want to see those fellows start off. They don't know how to drive."

"It is not, then, that you have quarreled with your cousin?"

Clifford reflected a moment, and then with a simplicity which had, for the Baroness, a singularly baffling quality, "Oh, no; we have made up!" he said.

She looked at him for some moments; but Clifford had begun to be afraid of the Baroness's looks, and he endeavored, now, to shift himself out of their range. "Why do you never come to see me any more?" she asked. "Have I displeased you?"

"Displeased me? Well, I guess not!" said Clifford, with a laugh.

"Why haven't you come, then?"

"Well, because I am afraid of getting shut up in that back room."

Eugenia kept looking at him. "I should think you would like that."

"Like it!" cried Clifford.

"I should, if I were a young man calling upon a charming woman."

"A charming woman isn't much use to me when I am shut up in that back room!"

"I am afraid I am not of much use to you anywhere!" said Madame Münster. "And yet you know how I have offered to be."

"Well," observed Clifford, by way of response, "there comes the buggy."

"Never mind the buggy. Do you know I am going away?"

"Do you mean now?"

"I mean in a few days. I leave this place."

"You are going back to Europe?"

"To Europe, where you are to come and see me."

"Oh, yes, I'll come out there," said Clifford.

"But before that," Eugenia declared, "you must come and see me here."

"Well, I shall keep clear of that back room!" rejoined her simple young kinsman.

The Baroness was silent a moment. "Yes, you must come frankly — boldly. That will be very much better. I see that now."

"I see it!" said Clifford. And then, in an instant, "What's the matter with that buggy?" His practiced ear had apparently detected an unnatural creak in the wheels of the light vehicle which had been brought to the portico, and he hurried away to investigate so grave an anomaly.

The Baroness walked homeward, alone, in the starlight, asking herself a question. Was she to have gained nothing — was she to have gained nothing?

Gertrude Wentworth had held a silent place in the little circle gathered about the two gentlemen from Boston. She was not interested in the visitors; she was watching Madame Münster, as she constantly watched her. She knew that Eugenia also was not interested — that she was bored; and Gertrude was absorbed in study of the problem how, in spite of her indifference and her absent attention, she managed to have such a charming manner. That was the manner Gertrude would have liked to have; she determined to cultivate it, and she wished that — to give her the charm — she might in future very often be bored. While she was engaged in these researches, Felix Young was looking for Charlotte, to whom he had something to say. For some time, now, he had had something to say to Charlotte, and this evening his sense of the propriety of holding some special conversation with her had reached the motive-point — resolved itself into acute and delightful desire. He wandered through the empty rooms on the large ground-floor of the house, and found her at last in a small apartment denominated, for reasons not immediately apparent, Mr. Wentworth's "office:" an extremely neat and well-dusted room, with an array of law-books, in time-darkened sheep-skin, on one of the walls; a large map of the United States on the other, flanked on either side by an old steel engraving of one of Raphael's Madonnas; and on the third several glass cases containing specimens of butterflies and beetles. Charlotte was sitting by a lamp, embroidering a slipper. Felix did not ask for whom the slipper was destined; he saw it was very large.

He moved a chair toward her and sat down, smiling as usual, but, at first, not speaking. She watched him, with her needle poised, and with a certain shy, fluttered look which she always

145

wore when he approached her. There was something in Felix's manner that quickened her modesty, her self-consciousness; if absolute choice had been given her she would have preferred never to find herself alone with him; and in fact, though she thought him a most brilliant, distinguished, and well-meaning person, she had exercised a much larger amount of tremulous tact than he had ever suspected, to circumvent the accident of *tête-à-tête*. Poor Charlotte could have given no account of the matter that would not have seemed unjust both to herself and to her foreign kinsman; she could only have said — or rather, she would never have said it — that she did not like so much gentleman's society at once. She was not reassured, accordingly, when he began, emphasizing his words with a kind of admiring radiance, "My dear cousin, I am enchanted at finding you alone."

"I am very often alone," Charlotte observed. Then she quickly added, "I don't mean I am lonely!"

"So clever a woman as you is never lonely," said Felix. "You have company in your beautiful work." And he glanced at the big slipper.

"I like to work," declared Charlotte, simply.

"So do I!" said her companion. "And I like to idle too. But it is not to idle that I have come in search of you. I want to tell you something very particular."

"Well," murmured Charlotte; "of course, if you must" —

"My dear cousin," said Felix, "it's nothing that a young lady may not listen to. At least I suppose it isn't. But *voyons;* you shall judge. I am terribly in love."

"Well, Felix," began Miss Wentworth, gravely. But her very gravity appeared to check the development of her phrase.

"I am in love with your sister; but in love, Charlotte — in love!" the young man pursued. Charlotte had laid her work in her lap; her hands were tightly folded on top of it; she was staring at the carpet. "In short, I'm in love, dear lady," said Felix. "Now I want you to help me."

"To help you?" asked Charlotte, with a tremor.

"I don't mean with Gertrude; she and I have a perfect understanding; and oh, how well she understands one! I mean with your father and with the world in general, including Mr. Brand."

"Poor Mr. Brand!" said Charlotte, slowly, but with a simplicity which made it evident to Felix that the young minister had not repeated to Miss Wentworth the talk that had lately occurred between them.

"Ah, now, don't say 'poor' Mr. Brand! I don't pity Mr. Brand at all. But I pity your father a little, and I don't want to displease him. Therefore, you see, I want you to plead for me. You don't think me very shabby, eh?"

"Shabby?" exclaimed Charlotte softly, for whom Felix represented the most polished and iridescent qualities of mankind.

"I don't mean in my appearance," rejoined Felix, laughing; for Charlotte was looking at his boots. "I mean in my conduct. You don't think it's an abuse of hospitality?"

"To — to care for Gertrude?" asked Charlotte.

"To have really expressed one's self. Because I *have* expressed myself, Charlotte; I must tell you the whole truth — I have! Of course I want to marry her — and here is the difficulty. I held off as long as I could; but she is such a terribly fascinating person! She's a strange creature, Charlotte; I don't believe you really know her." Charlotte took up her tapestry again, and again she laid it down. "I know your father has had higher views," Felix continued; "and I think you have shared them. You have wanted to marry her to Mr. Brand."

"Oh, no," said Charlotte, very earnestly. "Mr. Brand has always admired her. But we did not want anything of that kind."

Felix stared. "Surely, marriage was what you proposed."

"Yes; but we didn't wish to force her."

"A la bonne heure! That's very unsafe you know. With these arranged marriages there is often the deuce to pay."

"Oh, Felix," said Charlotte, "we didn't want to 'arrange.'"

"I am delighted to hear that. Because in such cases — even when the woman is a thoroughly good creature — she can't help looking for a compensation. A charming fellow comes along — and *voilà!*" Charlotte sat mutely staring at the floor, and Felix presently added, "Do go on with your slipper, I like to see you work."

Charlotte took up her variegated canvas, and began to draw vague blue stitches in a big round rose. "If Gertrude is so — so strange," she said, "why do you want to marry her?"

"Ah, that's it, dear Charlotte! I like strange women; I always have liked them. Ask Eugenia! And Gertrude is wonderful; she says the most beautiful things!"

Charlotte looked at him, almost for the first time, as if her meaning required to be severely pointed. "You have a great influence over her."

"Yes — and no!" said Felix. "I had at first, I think; but now it is six of one and half-a-dozen of the other; it is reciprocal. She affects me strongly — for she is so strong. I don't believe you know her; it's a beautiful nature."

"Oh, yes, Felix; I have always thought Gertrude's nature beautiful."

"Well, if you think so now," cried the young man, "wait and see! She's a folded flower. Let me pluck her from the parent tree and you will see her expand. I'm sure you will enjoy it."

"I don't understand you," murmured Charlotte. "I *can't*, Felix."

"Well, you can understand this — that I beg you to say a good word for me to your father. He regards me, I naturally believe, as a very light fellow, a Bohemian, an irregular character. Tell him I am not all this; if I ever was, I have forgotten it. I am fond of pleasure — yes; but of innocent pleasure. Pain is all one; but in pleasure, you know, there are tremendous distinctions. Say to him that Gertrude is a folded flower and that I am a serious man!"

Charlotte got up from her chair slowly rolling up her work. "We know you are very kind to every one, Felix," she said. "But we are extremely sorry for Mr. Brand."

"Of course you are — you especially! Because," added Felix hastily, "you are a woman. But I don't pity him. It ought to be enough for any man that you take an interest in him."

"It is not enough for Mr. Brand," said Charlotte, simply. And she stood there a moment, as if waiting conscientiously for anything more that Felix might have to say.

"Mr. Brand is not so keen about his marriage as he was," he presently said. "He is afraid of your sister. He begins to think she is wicked."

Charlotte looked at him now with beautiful, appealing eyes — eyes into which he saw the tears rising. "Oh, Felix, Felix," she cried, "what have you done to her?"

"I think she was asleep; I have waked her up!"

But Charlotte, apparently, was really crying, she walked straight out of the room. And Felix, standing there and meditating, had the apparent brutality to take satisfaction in her tears.

Late that night Gertrude, silent and serious, came to him in the garden; it was a kind of appointment. Gertrude seemed to like appointments. She plucked a handful of heliotrope and stuck it into the front of her dress, but she said nothing. They walked together along one of the paths, and Felix looked at the great, square, hospitable house, massing itself vaguely in the starlight, with all its windows darkened.

"I have a little of a bad conscience," he said. "I oughtn't to meet you this way till I have got your father's consent."

Gertrude looked at him for some time. "I don't understand you."

"You very often say that," he said. "Considering how little we understand each other, it is a wonder how well we get on!"

"We have done nothing but meet since you came here — but meet alone. The first time I ever saw you we were alone," Gertrude went on. "What is the difference now? Is it because it is at night?"

"The difference, Gertrude," said Felix, stopping in the path, "the difference is that I love you more — more than before!" And then they stood there, talking, in the warm stillness and in front of the closed dark house. "I have been talking to Charlotte — been trying to bespeak her interest with your father. She has a kind of sublime perversity; was ever a woman so bent upon cutting off her own head?"

"You are too careful," said Gertrude; "you are too diplomatic."

"Well," cried the young man, "I didn't come here to make any one unhappy!"

Gertrude looked round her awhile in the odorous darkness. "I will do anything you please," she said.

"For instance?" asked Felix, smiling.

"I will go away. I will do anything you please."

Felix looked at her in solemn admiration. "Yes, we will go away," he said. "But we will make peace first."

Gertrude looked about her again, and then she broke out, passionately, "Why do they try to make one feel guilty? Why do they make it so difficult? Why can't they understand?"

"I will make them understand!" said Felix. He drew her hand into his arm, and they wandered about in the garden, talking, for an hour.

XII

FELIX allowed Charlotte time to plead his cause; and then, on the third day, he sought an interview with his uncle. It was in the morning; Mr. Wentworth was in his office; and, on going in, Felix found that Charlotte was at that moment in conference with her father. She had, in fact, been constantly near him since her interview with Felix; she had made up her mind that it was her duty to repeat very literally her cousin's passionate plea. She had accordingly followed Mr. Wentworth about like a shadow, in order to find him at hand when she should have mustered sufficient composure to speak. For poor Charlotte, in this matter, naturally lacked composure; especially when she meditated upon some of Felix's intimations. It was not cheerful work, at the best, to keep giving small hammer-taps to the coffin in which one had laid away, for burial, the poor little acknowledged offspring of one's own misbehaving heart; and the occupation was not rendered more agreeable by the fact that the ghost of one's stifled dream had been summoned from the shades by the strange, bold words of a talkative young foreigner. What had Felix meant by saying that Mr. Brand was not so keen? To herself her sister's justly depressed suitor had shown no sign of faltering. Charlotte trembled all over when she allowed herself to believe for an instant now and then that, privately, Mr. Brand might have faltered; and as it seemed to give more force to Felix's words to repeat them to her father, she was waiting until she should have taught herself to be very calm. But she had now begun to tell Mr. Wentworth that she was extremely anxious. She was proceeding to develop this idea, to enumerate the objects of her anxiety, when Felix came in.

Mr. Wentworth sat there, with his legs crossed, lifting his dry, pure countenance from the Boston "Advertiser." Felix entered smiling, as if he had something particular to say, and his uncle looked at him as if he both expected and deprecated this event. Felix vividly expressing himself had come to be a formidable figure to his uncle, who had not yet arrived at definite views as to a proper tone. For the first time in his life, as I have said, Mr. Wentworth shirked a responsibility; he earnestly desired that it might not be laid upon him to determine how his nephew's lighter propositions should be treated. He lived under an apprehension that Felix might yet beguile him into assent to doubtful inductions, and his conscience instructed him that the best form of vigilance was the avoidance of discussion. He hoped that the pleasant episode of his nephew's visit would pass away without a further lapse of consistency.

Felix looked at Charlotte with an air of understanding, and then at Mr. Wentworth, and then at Charlotte again. Mr. Wentworth bent his refined eyebrows upon his nephew and stroked down the first page of the "Advertiser." "I ought to have brought a bouquet," said Felix, laughing. "In France they always do."

"We are not in France," observed Mr. Wentworth gravely, while Charlotte earnestly gazed at him.

"No, luckily, we are not in France, where I am afraid I should have a harder time of it. My dear Charlotte, have you rendered me that delightful service?" And Felix bent toward her as if some one had been presenting him.

Charlotte looked at him with almost frightened eyes; and Mr. Wentworth thought this might be the beginning of a discussion. "What is the bouquet for?" he inquired, by way of turning it off.

Felix gazed at him, smiling. "Pour la demande!" And then, drawing up a chair, he seated himself, hat in hand, with a kind of conscious solemnity.

Presently he turned to Charlotte again. "My good Charlotte, my admirable Charlotte," he murmured, "you have not played me false — you have not sided against me?"

Charlotte got up, trembling extremely, though imperceptibly. "You must speak to my father yourself," she said. "I think you are clever enough."

But Felix, rising too, begged her to remain. "I can speak better to an audience!" he declared.

"I hope it is nothing disagreeable," said Mr. Wentworth.

"It's something delightful, for me!" And Felix, laying down his hat, clasped his hands a little between his knees. "My dear uncle," he said, "I desire, very earnestly, to marry your daughter Gertrude." Charlotte sank slowly into her chair again, and Mr. Wentworth sat staring, with a light in his face that might have been flashed back from an iceberg. He stared and stared; he said nothing. Felix fell back, with his hands still clasped. "Ah — you don't like it. I was afraid!" He blushed deeply, and Charlotte noticed it — remarking to herself that it was the first time she had ever seen him blush. She began to blush herself and to reflect that he might be much in love.

"This is very abrupt," said Mr. Wentworth, at last.

"Have you never suspected it, dear uncle?" Felix inquired. "Well, that proves how discreet I have been. Yes, I thought you wouldn't like it."

"It is very serious, Felix," said Mr. Wentworth.

"You think it's an abuse of hospitality!" exclaimed Felix, smiling again.

"Of hospitality? — an abuse?" his uncle repeated very slowly.

"That is what Felix said to me," said Charlotte, conscientiously.

"Of course you think so; don't defend yourself!" Felix pursued. "It *is* an abuse, obviously; the most I can claim is that it is perhaps a pardonable one. I simply fell head over heels in love; one can hardly help that. Though you are Gertrude's progenitor I don't believe you know how attractive she is. Dear uncle, she contains the elements of a singularly — I may say a strangely — charming woman!"

"She has always been to me an object of extreme concern," said Mr. Wentworth. "We have always desired her happiness."

"Well, here it is!" Felix declared. "I will make her happy. She believes it, too. Now hadn't you noticed that?"

"I had noticed that she was much changed," Mr. Wentworth declared, in a tone whose unexpressive, unimpassioned quality appeared to Felix to reveal a profundity of opposition. "It may be that she is only becoming what you call a charming woman."

"Gertrude, at heart, is so earnest, so true," said Charlotte, very softly, fastening her eyes upon her father.

"I delight to hear you praise her!" cried Felix.

"She has a very peculiar temperament," said Mr. Wentworth.

"Eh, even that is praise!" Felix rejoined. "I know I am not the man you might have looked for. I have no position and no fortune; I can give Gertrude no place in the world. A place in the world — that's what she ought to have; that would bring her out."

"A place to do her duty!" remarked Mr. Wentworth.

"Ah, how charmingly she does it — her duty!" Felix exclaimed, with a radiant face. "What an exquisite conception she has of it! But she comes honestly by that, dear uncle." Mr. Wentworth and Charlotte both looked at him as if they were watching a greyhound doubling. "Of course with me she will hide her light under a bushel," he continued; "I being the bushel! Now I know you like me — you have certainly proved it. But you think I am frivolous and penniless and shabby! Granted — granted — a thousand times granted. I have been a loose fish — a fiddler, a painter, an actor. But there is this to be said: In the first place, I fancy you exaggerate; you lend me qualities I haven't had. I have been a Bohemian — yes; but in Bohemia I always passed for a gentleman. I wish you could see some of my old *camarades* — they would tell you! It was the liberty I liked, but not the opportunities! My sins were all peccadilloes; I always respected my neighbor's property — my neighbor's wife. Do you see, dear uncle?" Mr. Wentworth ought to have seen; his cold blue eyes were intently fixed. "And then, *c'est fini!* It's all over. Je me range. I have settled down to a jog-trot. I find I can earn my living — a very fair one — by going about the world and painting bad portraits. It's not a glorious profession, but it is a perfectly respectable one. You won't deny that, eh? Going about the world, I say? I must not deny that, for that I am afraid I shall always do — in quest of agreeable sitters. When I say agreeable, I mean susceptible of delicate flattery and prompt of payment. Gertrude declares she is willing to share my wanderings and help to pose my models. She even thinks it will be charming; and that brings me to my third point. Gertrude likes me. Encourage her a little and she will tell you so."

Felix's tongue obviously moved much faster than the imagination of his auditors; his eloquence, like the rocking of a boat in a deep, smooth lake, made long eddies of silence. And he seemed to be pleading and chattering still, with his brightly eager smile, his uplifted eyebrows, his expressive mouth, after he had ceased speaking, and while, with his glance quickly turning from the father to the daughter, he sat waiting for the effect of his appeal. "It is not your want of means," said Mr. Wentworth, after a period of severe reticence.

"Now it's delightful of you to say that! Only don't say it's my want of character. Because I have a character — I assure you I have; a small one, a little slip of a thing, but still something tangible."

"Ought you not to tell Felix that it is Mr. Brand, father?" Charlotte asked, with infinite mildness.

"It is not only Mr. Brand," Mr. Wentworth solemnly declared. And he looked at his knee for a long time. "It is difficult to explain," he said. He wished, evidently, to be very just. "It rests on moral grounds, as Mr. Brand says. It is the question whether it is the best thing for Gertrude."

"What is better — what is better, dear uncle?" Felix rejoined urgently, rising in his urgency and standing before Mr. Wentworth. His uncle had been looking at his knee; but when Felix moved he transferred his gaze to the handle of the door which faced him. "It is usually a fairly good thing for a girl to marry the man she loves!" cried Felix.

While he spoke, Mr. Wentworth saw the handle of the door begin to turn; the door opened and remained slightly ajar, until Felix had delivered himself of the cheerful axiom just quoted. Then it opened altogether and Gertrude stood there. She looked excited; there was a spark in her sweet, dull eyes. She came in slowly, but with an air of resolution, and, closing the door softly, looked round at the three persons present. Felix went to her with tender gallantry, holding out his hand, and Charlotte made a place for her on the sofa. But Gertrude put her hands behind her and made no motion to sit down.

"We are talking of you!" said Felix.

"I know it," she answered. "That's why I came." And she fastened her eyes on her father, who returned her gaze very fixedly. In his own cold blue eyes there was a kind of pleading, reasoning light.

"It is better you should be present," said Mr. Wentworth. "We are discussing your future."

"Why discuss it?" asked Gertrude. "Leave it to me."

"That is, to me!" cried Felix.

"I leave it, in the last resort, to a greater wisdom than ours," said the old man.

Felix rubbed his forehead gently. "But *en attendant* the last resort, your father lacks confidence," he said to Gertrude.

"Haven't you confidence in Felix?" Gertrude was frowning; there was something about her that her father and Charlotte had never seen. Charlotte got up and came to her, as if to put her arm round her; but suddenly, she seemed afraid to touch her.

Mr. Wentworth, however, was not afraid. "I have had more confidence in Felix than in you," he said.

"Yes, you have never had confidence in me — never, never! I don't know why."

"Oh sister, sister!" murmured Charlotte.

"You have always needed ad-vice," Mr. Wentworth declared. "You have had a difficult temperament."

"Why do you call it difficult? It might have been easy, if you had allowed it. You wouldn't let me be natural. I don't know what you wanted to make of me. Mr. Brand was the worst."

Charlotte at last took hold of her sister. She laid her two hands upon Gertrude's arm. "He cares so much for you," she almost whispered.

Gertrude looked at her intently an instant; then kissed her. "No, he does not," she said.

"I have never seen you so passionate," observed Mr. Wentworth, with an air of indignation mitigated by high principles.

"I am sorry if I offend you," said Gertrude.

"You offend me, but I don't think you are sorry."

"Yes, father, she is sorry," said Charlotte.

"I would even go further, dear uncle," Felix interposed. "I would question whether she really offends you. How can she offend you?"

To this Mr. Wentworth made no immediate answer. Then, in a moment, "She has not profited as we hoped."

"Profited? Ah *voilà!*" Felix exclaimed.

Gertrude was very pale; she stood looking down. "I have told Felix I would go away with him," she presently said.

"Ah, you have said some admirable things!" cried the young man.

"Go away, sister?" asked Charlotte.

"Away — away; to some strange country."

"That is to frighten you," said Felix, smiling at Charlotte.

"To — what do you call it?" asked Gertrude, turning an instant to Felix. "To Bohemia."

"Do you propose to dispense with preliminaries?" asked Mr. Wentworth, getting up.

"Dear uncle, *vous plaisantez!*" cried Felix. "It seems to me that these are preliminaries."

Gertrude turned to her father. "I *have* profited," she said. "You wanted to form my character. Well, my character is formed — for my age. I know what I want; I have chosen. I am determined to marry this gentleman."

"You had better consent, sir," said Felix very gently.

"Yes, sir, you had better consent," added a very different voice.

Charlotte gave a little jump, and the others turned to the direction from which it had come. It was the voice of Mr. Brand, who had stepped through the long window which stood open to the piazza. He stood patting his forehead with his pocket-handkerchief; he was very much flushed; his face wore a singular expression.

"Yes, sir, you had better consent," Mr. Brand repeated, coming forward. "I know what Miss Gertrude means."

"My dear friend!" murmured Felix, laying his hand caressingly on the young minister's arm.

Mr. Brand looked at him; then at Mr. Wentworth; lastly at Gertrude. He did not look at Charlotte. But Charlotte's earnest eyes were fastened to his own countenance; they were asking an immense question of it. The answer to this question could not come all at once; but some of the elements of it were there. It was one of the elements of it that Mr. Brand was very red, that he held his head very high, that he had a bright, excited eye and an air of embarrassed boldness — the air of a man who has taken a resolve, in the execution of which he apprehends the failure, not of his moral, but of his personal, resources. Charlotte thought he looked very grand; and it is incontestable that Mr. Brand felt very grand. This, in fact, was the grandest moment of his life; and it was natural that such a moment should contain opportunities of awkwardness for a large, stout, modest young man.

"Come in, sir," said Mr. Wentworth, with an angular wave of his hand. "It is very proper that you should be present."

"I know what you are talking about," Mr. Brand rejoined. "I heard what your nephew said."

"And he heard what you said!" exclaimed Felix, patting him again on the arm.

"I am not sure that I understood," said Mr. Wentworth, who had angularity in his voice as well as in his gestures.

Gertrude had been looking hard at her former suitor. She had been puzzled, like her sister; but her imagination moved more quickly than

Charlotte's. "Mr. Brand asked you to let Felix take me away," she said to her father.

The young minister gave her a strange look. "It is not because I don't want to see you any more," he declared, in a tone intended as it were for publicity.

"I shouldn't think you would want to see me any more," Gertrude answered, gently.

Mr. Wentworth stood staring. "Isn't this rather a change, sir?" he inquired.

"Yes, sir." And Mr. Brand looked anywhere; only still not at Charlotte. "Yes, sir," he repeated. And he held his handkerchief a few moments to his lips.

"Where are our moral grounds?" demanded Mr. Wentworth, who had always thought Mr. Brand would be just the thing for a younger daughter with a peculiar temperament.

"It is sometimes very moral to change, you know," suggested Felix.

Charlotte had softly left her sister's side. She had edged gently toward her father, and now her hand found its way into his arm. Mr. Wentworth had folded up the "Advertiser" into a surprisingly small compass, and, holding the roll with one hand, he earnestly clasped it with the other. Mr. Brand was looking at him; and yet, though Charlotte was so near, his eyes failed to meet her own. Gertrude watched her sister.

"It is better not to speak of change," said Mr. Brand. "In one sense there is no change. There was something I desired — something I asked of you; I desire something still — I ask it of you." And he paused a moment; Mr. Wentworth looked bewildered. "I should like, in my ministerial capacity, to unite this young couple."

Gertrude, watching her sister, saw Charlotte flushing intensely, and Mr. Wentworth felt her pressing upon his arm. "Heavenly Powers!" murmured Mr. Wentworth. And it was the nearest approach to profanity he had ever made.

"That is very nice; that is very handsome!" Felix exclaimed.

"I don't understand," said Mr. Wentworth; though it was plain that every one else did.

"That is very beautiful, Mr. Brand," said Gertrude, emulating Felix.

"I should like to marry you. It will give me great pleasure."

"As Gertrude says, it's a beautiful idea," said Felix.

Felix was smiling, but Mr. Brand was not even trying to. He himself treated his proposition very seriously. "I have thought of it, and I should like to do it," he affirmed.

Charlotte, meanwhile, was staring with expanded eyes. Her imagination, as I have said, was not so rapid as her sister's, but now it had taken several little jumps. "Father," she murmured, "consent!"

Mr. Brand heard her; he looked away. Mr. Wentworth, evidently, had no imagination at all. "I have always thought," he began, slowly, "that Gertrude's character required a special line of development."

"Father," repeated Charlotte, "*consent.*"

Then, at last, Mr. Brand looked at her. Her father felt her leaning more heavily upon his folded arm than she had ever done before; and this, with a certain sweet faintness in her voice, made him wonder what was the matter. He looked down at her and saw the encounter of her gaze with the young theologian's; but even this told him nothing, and he continued to be bewildered. Nevertheless, "I consent," he said at last, "since Mr. Brand recommends it."

"I should like to perform the ceremony very soon," observed Mr. Brand, with a sort of solemn simplicity.

"Come, come, that's charming!" cried Felix, profanely.

Mr. Wentworth sank into his chair. "Doubtless, when you understand it," he said, with a certain judicial asperity.

Gertrude went to her sister and led her away, and Felix having passed his arm into Mr. Brand's and stepped out of the long window with him, the old man was left sitting there in unillumined perplexity.

Felix did no work that day. In the afternoon, with Gertrude, he got into one of the boats and floated about with idly-dipping oars. They talked a good deal of Mr. Brand — though not exclusively.

"That was a fine stroke," said Felix. "It was really heroic."

Gertrude sat musing, with her eyes upon the ripples. "That was what he wanted to be; he wanted to do something fine."

"He won't be comfortable till he has married us," said Felix. "So much the better."

"He wanted to be magnanimous; he wanted to have a fine moral pleasure. I know him so well," Gertrude went on. Felix looked at her; she spoke slowly, gazing at the clear water. "He thought of it a great deal, night and day. He thought it would be beautiful. At last he made up his mind that it was his duty, his duty to do just that — nothing less than that. He felt exalted; he felt sublime. That's how he likes to feel. It is better for him than if I had listened to him."

"It's better for me," smiled Felix. "But do you know, as regards the sacrifice, that I don't believe he admired you when this decision was taken quite so much as he had done a fortnight before?"

"He never admired me. He admires Charlotte; he pitied me. I know him so well."

"Well, then, he didn't pity you so much."

Gertrude looked at Felix a little, smiling. "You shouldn't permit yourself," she said, "to diminish the splendor of his action. He admires Charlotte," she repeated.

"That's capital!" said Felix laughingly, and dipping his oars. I cannot say exactly to which member of Gertrude's phrase he alluded; but he dipped his oars again, and they kept floating about.

Neither Felix nor his sister, on that day, was present at Mr. Wentworth's at the evening repast. The two occupants of the chalet dined together, and the young man informed his companion that his marriage was now an assured fact. Eugenia congratulated him, and replied that if he were as reasonable a husband as he had been, on the whole, a brother, his wife would have nothing to complain of.

Felix looked at her a moment, smiling. "I hope," he said, "not to be thrown back on my reason."

"It is very true," Eugenia rejoined, "that one's reason is dismally flat. It's a bed with the mattress removed."

But the brother and sister, later in the evening, crossed over to the larger house, the Baroness desiring to compliment her prospective sister-in-law. They found the usual circle upon the piazza, with the exception of Clifford Wentworth and Lizzie Acton; and as every one stood up as usual to welcome the Baroness, Eugenia had an admiring audience for her compliment to Gertrude.

Robert Acton stood on the edge of the piazza, leaning against one of the white columns, so that he found himself next to Eugenia while she acquitted herself of a neat little discourse of congratulation.

"I shall be so glad to know you better," she said; "I have seen so much less of you than I should have liked. Naturally; now I see the reason why! You will love me

a little, won't you? I think I may say I gain on being known." And terminating these observations with the softest cadence of her voice, the Baroness imprinted a sort of grand official kiss upon Gertrude's forehead.

Increased familiarity had not, to Gertrude's imagination, diminished the mysterious impressiveness of Eugenia's personality, and she felt flattered and transported by this little ceremony. Robert Acton also seemed to admire it, as he admired so many of the gracious manifestations of Madame Münster's wit.

They had the privilege of making him restless, and on this occasion he walked away, suddenly, with his hands in his pockets, and then came back and leaned against his column. Eugenia was now complimenting her uncle upon his daughter's engagement, and Mr. Wentworth was listening with his usual plain yet refined politeness. It is to be supposed that by this time his perception of the mutual relations of the young people who surrounded him had become more acute; but he still took the matter very seriously, and he was not at all exhilarated.

"Felix will make her a good husband," said Eugenia. "He will be a charming companion; he has a great quality — indestructible gayety."

"You think that's a great quality?" asked the old man.

Eugenia meditated, with her eyes upon his. "You think one gets tired of it, eh?"

"I don't know that I am pre-pared to say that," said Mr. Wentworth.

"Well, we will say, then, that it is tiresome for others but delightful for one's self. A woman's husband, you know, is supposed to be her second self; so that, for Felix and Gertrude, gayety will be a common property."

"Gertrude was always very gay," said Mr. Wentworth. He was trying to follow this argument.

Robert Acton took his hands out of his pockets and came a little nearer to the Baroness. "You say you gain by being known," he said. "One certainly gains by knowing you."

"What have *you* gained?" asked Eugenia.

"An immense amount of wisdom."

"That's a questionable advantage for a man who was already so wise!"

Acton shook his head. "No, I was a great fool before I knew you!"

"And being a fool you made my acquaintance? You are very complimentary."

"Let me keep it up," said Acton, laughing. "I hope, for our pleasure, that your brother's marriage will detain you."

"Why should I stop for my brother's marriage when I would not stop for my own?" asked the Baroness.

"Why shouldn't you stop in either case, now that, as you say, you have dissolved that mechanical tie that bound you to Europe?"

The Baroness looked at him a moment. "As I say? You look as if you doubted it."

"Ah," said Acton, returning her glance, "that is a remnant of my old folly! We have other attractions," he added. "We are to have another marriage."

But she seemed not to hear him; she was looking at him still. "My word was never doubted before," she said.

"We are to have another marriage," Acton repeated, smiling.

Then she appeared to understand. "Another marriage?" And she looked at the others. Felix was chattering to Gertrude; Charlotte, at a distance, was watching them; and Mr. Brand, in quite another quarter, was turning his back to them, and, with his hands under his coat-tails and his large head on one side, was looking at the small, tender crescent of a young moon. "It ought to be Mr. Brand and Charlotte," said Eugenia, "but it doesn't look like it."

"There," Acton answered, "you must judge just now by contraries. There is more than there looks to be. I expect that combination one of these days; but that is not what I meant."

"Well," said the Baroness, "I never guess my own lovers; so I can't guess other people's."

Acton gave a loud laugh, and he was about to add a rejoinder when Mr. Wentworth approached his niece. "You will be interested to hear," the old man said, with a momentary aspiration toward jocosity, "of another matrimonial venture in our little circle."

"I was just telling the Baroness," Acton observed.

"Mr. Acton was apparently about to announce his own engagement," said Eugenia.

Mr. Wentworth's jocosity increased. "It is not exactly that; but it is in the family. Clifford, hearing this morning that Mr. Brand had expressed a desire to tie the nuptial knot for his sister, took it into his head to arrange that, while his hand was in, our good friend should perform a like ceremony for himself and Lizzie Acton."

The Baroness threw back her head and smiled at her uncle; then turning, with an intenser radiance, to Robert Acton, "I am certainly very stupid not to have thought of that," she said. Acton looked down at his boots, as if he thought he had perhaps reached the limits of legitimate experimentation, and for a moment Eugenia said nothing more. It had been, in fact, a sharp knock, and she needed to recover herself. This was done, however, promptly enough. "Where are the young people?" she asked.

"They are spending the evening with my mother."

"Is not the thing very sudden?"

Acton looked up. "Extremely sudden. There had been a tacit understanding; but within a day or two Clifford appears to have received some mysterious impulse to precipitate the affair."

"The impulse," said the Baroness, "was the charms of your very pretty sister."

"But my sister's charms were an old story; he had always known her." Acton had begun to experiment again.

Here, however, it was evident the Baroness would not help him. "Ah, one can't say! Clifford is very young; but he is a nice boy."

"He's a likeable sort of boy, and he will be a rich man." This was Acton's last experiment. Madame Münster turned away.

She made but a short visit and Felix took her home. In her little drawing-room she went almost straight to the mirror over the chimney-piece, and, with a candle uplifted, stood looking into it. "I shall not wait for your marriage," she said to her brother. "To-morrow my maid shall pack up."

"My dear sister," Felix exclaimed, "we are to be married immediately! Mr. Brand is too uncomfortable."

But Eugenia, turning and still holding her candle aloft, only looked about the little sitting-room at her gimcracks and curtains and cushions. "My maid shall pack up," she repeated. "*Bonté divine*, what rubbish! I feel like a strolling actress; these are my 'properties.'"

"Is the play over, Eugenia?" asked Felix.

She gave him a sharp glance. "I have spoken my part."

"With great applause!" said her brother.

"Oh, applause — applause!" she murmured. And she gathered up two or three of her dispersed draperies. She glanced at the beautiful brocade, and then, "I don't see how I can have endured it!" she said.

"Endure it a little longer. Come to my wedding."

"Thank you; that's your affair. My affairs are elsewhere."

"Where are you going?"

"To Germany — by the first ship."

"You have decided not to marry Mr. Acton?"

"I have refused him," said Eugenia.

Her brother looked at her in silence. "I am sorry," he rejoined at last. "But I was very discreet, as you asked me to be. I said nothing."

"Please continue, then, not to allude to the matter," said Eugenia.

Felix inclined himself gravely. "You shall be obeyed. But your position in Germany?" he pursued.

"Please to make no observations upon it."

"I was only going to say that I supposed it was altered."

"You are mistaken."

"But I thought you had signed" —

"I have not signed!" said the Baroness.

Felix urged her no further, and it was arranged that he should immediately assist her to embark. Mr. Brand was indeed, it appeared, very impatient to consummate his sacrifice and deliver the nuptial benediction which would set it off so handsomely; but Eugenia's impatience to withdraw from a country in which she had not found the fortune she had come to seek was even less to be mistaken. It is true she had not made any very various exertion; but she appeared to feel justified in generalizing — in deciding that the conditions of action on this provincial continent were not favorable to really superior women. The elder world was, after all, their natural field. The unembarrassed directness with which she proceeded to apply these intelligent conclusions appeared to the little circle of spectators who have figured in our narrative but the supreme exhibition of a character to which the experience of life had imparted an inimitable pliancy. It had a distinct effect upon Robert Acton, who, for the two days preceding her departure, was a very restless and irritated mortal. She passed her last evening at her uncle's, where she had never been more charming; and in parting with Clifford Wentworth's affianced bride she drew from her own finger a curious old ring and presented it to her with the prettiest speech and kiss. Gertrude, who as an affianced bride was also indebted to her gracious bounty, admired this little incident extremely, and Robert Acton almost wondered whether it did not give him the right, as Lizzie's brother and guardian, to offer in return a handsome present to the Baroness. It would have made him extremely happy to be able to offer a handsome present to the Baroness; but he abstained from this expression of his sentiments, and they were in consequence, at the very last, by so much the less comfortable. It was almost at the very last that he saw her — late the night before she went to Boston to embark.

"For myself, I wish you might have stayed," he said. "But not for your own sake."

"I don't make so many differences," said the Baroness. "I am simply sorry to be going."

"That's a much deeper difference than mine," Acton declared; "for you mean you are simply glad!"

Felix parted with her on the deck of the ship. "We shall often meet over there," he said.

"I don't know," she answered. "Europe seems to me much larger than America."

Mr. Brand, of course, in the days that immediately followed, was not the only impatient spirit; but it may be said that of all the young spirits interested in the event none rose more eagerly to the level of the occasion. Gertrude left her father's house with Felix Young; they were imperturbably happy and they went far away. Clifford and his young wife sought their felicity in a narrower circle, and the latter's influence upon her husband was such as to justify, strikingly, that theory of the elevating effect of easy intercourse with clever women which Felix had propounded to Mr. Wentworth. Gertrude was for a good while a distant figure, but she came back when Charlotte married Mr. Brand. She was present at the wedding feast, where Felix's gayety confessed to no change. Then she disappeared, and the echo of a gayety of her own, mingled with that of her husband, often came back to the home of her earlier years. Mr. Wentworth at last found himself listening for it; and Robert Acton, after his mother's death, married a particularly nice young girl.

161

WASHINGTON SQUARE

During a portion of the first half of the present century, and more particularly during the latter part of it, there flourished and practised in the city of New York a physician who enjoyed perhaps an exceptional share of the consideration which, in the United States, has always been bestowed upon distinguished members of the medical profession. This profession in America has constantly been held in honour, and more successfully than elsewhere has put forward a claim to the epithet of "liberal." In a country in which, to play a social part, you must either earn your income or make believe that you earn it, the healing art has appeared in a high degree to combine two recognised sources of credit. It belongs to the realm of the practical, which in the United States is a great recommendation; and it is touched by the light of science — a merit appreciated in a community in which the love of knowledge has not always been accompanied by leisure and opportunity. It was an element in Dr. Sloper's reputation that his learning and his skill were very evenly balanced; he was

what you might call a scholarly doctor, and yet there was nothing abstract in his remedies — he always ordered you to take something. Though he was felt to be extremely thorough, he was not uncomfortably theoretic, and if he sometimes explained matters rather more minutely than might seem of use to the patient, he never went so far (like some practitioners one has heard of) as to trust to the explanation alone, but always left behind him an inscrutable prescription. There were some doctors that left the prescription without offering any explanation at all; and he did not belong to that class either, which was, after all, the most vulgar. It will be seen that I am describing a clever man; and this is really the reason why Dr. Sloper had become a local celebrity. At the time at which we are chiefly concerned with him, he was some fifty years of age, and his popularity was at its height. He was very witty, and he passed in the best society of New York for a man of the world — which, indeed, he was, in a very sufficient degree. I hasten to add, to anticipate possible misconception, that he was not the least of a charlatan. He was a thoroughly honest man — honest in a degree of which he had perhaps lacked the opportunity to give the complete measure; and, putting aside the great good-nature of the circle in which he practised, which was rather fond of boasting that it possessed the "brightest" doctor in the country, he daily justified his claim to the talents attributed to him by the popular voice. He was an observer, even a philosopher, and to be bright was so natural to him, and (as the popular voice said) came so easily, that he never aimed at mere effect, and had none of the little tricks and pretensions of second-rate reputations. It must be confessed that fortune had favoured him, and that he had found the path to prosperity very soft to his tread. He had married at the age of twenty-seven, for love, a very charming girl, Miss Catherine Harrington, of New York, who, in addition to her charms, had brought him a solid dowry. Mrs. Sloper was amiable, graceful, accomplished, elegant, and in 1820 she had been one of the pretty girls of the small but promising capital which clustered about the Battery and overlooked the Bay, and of which the uppermost boundary was indicated by the grassy waysides of Canal Street. Even at the age of twenty-seven Austin Sloper had made his mark sufficiently to mitigate the anomaly of his having been chosen among a dozen suitors by a young woman of high fashion, who had ten thousand dollars of income and the most charming eyes in the island of Manhattan. These eyes, and some of their accompaniments, were for about five years a source of extreme satisfaction to the young physician, who was both a devoted and a very happy husband. The fact of his having married a rich woman made no difference in the line he had traced for himself, and he cultivated his profession with as definite a purpose as if he still had no other resources than his fraction of the modest patrimony which on his father's death he had shared with his brothers and sisters. This purpose had not been preponderantly to make money — it had been rather to learn something and to do something. To learn something interesting, and to do something useful — this was, roughly speaking, the programme he had sketched, and of which the accident of his wife having an income appeared to him in no degree to modify the validity. He was fond of his practice, and of exercising a skill of which he was agreeably conscious, and it was so patent a truth that if he were not a doctor there was nothing else he could be, that a doctor he persisted in being, in the best possible conditions. Of course his easy domestic situation saved him a good deal of drudgery, and his wife's affiliation to the "best people" brought him a good many of those patients whose symptoms are, if not more interesting in themselves than those of the lower orders, at least more consistently displayed. He desired experience, and in the course of twenty years he got a great deal. It must be added that it came to him in some forms which, whatever might have been their intrinsic value, made it the reverse of welcome. His first child, a little boy of extraordinary promise, as the Doctor, who was not addicted to easy enthusiasms, firmly believed, died at three years of age, in spite of everything that the mother's tenderness and the father's science could invent to save him. Two years later Mrs. Sloper gave birth to a second infant — an infant of a sex which rendered the poor child, to the Doctor's sense, an inadequate substitute for his lamented first-born, of whom he had promised himself to make an admirable man. The little girl was a disappointment; but this was not the worst. A week after her birth the young mother, who, as the phrase is, had been doing well, suddenly betrayed alarming symptoms, and before another week had elapsed Austin Sloper was a widower.

For a man whose trade was to keep people alive, he had certainly done poorly in his own family; and a bright doctor who within three years loses his wife and his little boy should perhaps be prepared to see either his skill or his affection impugned. Our friend, however, escaped criticism: that is, he escaped all criticism but his own, which was much the most competent and most formidable. He walked under the weight of this very private censure for the rest of his days, and bore forever the scars of a castigation to which the strongest hand he knew had treated him on the

night that followed his wife's death. The world, which, as I have said, appreciated him, pitied him too much to be ironical; his misfortune made him more interesting, and even helped him to be the fashion. It was observed that even medical families cannot escape the more insidious forms of disease, and that, after all, Dr. Sloper had lost other patients beside the two I have mentioned; which constituted an honourable precedent. His little girl remained to him, and though she was not what he had desired, he proposed to himself to make the best of her. He had on hand a stock of unexpended authority, by which the child, in its early years, profited largely. She had been named, as a matter of course, after her poor mother, and even in her most diminutive babyhood the Doctor never called her anything but Catherine. She grew up a very robust and healthy child, and her father, as he looked at her, often said to himself that, such as she was, he at least need have no fear of losing her. I say "such as she was," because, to tell the truth — But this is a truth of which I will defer the telling.

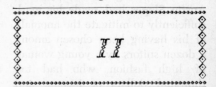

II

WHEN the child was about ten years old, he invited his sister, Mrs. Penniman, to come and stay with him. The Miss Slopers had been but two in number, and both of them had married early in life. The younger, Mrs. Almond by name, was the wife of a prosperous merchant, and the mother of a blooming family. She bloomed herself, indeed, and was a comely, comfortable, reasonable woman, and a favourite with her clever brother, who, in the matter of women, even when they were nearly related to him, was a man of distinct preferences. He preferred Mrs. Almond to his sister Lavinia, who had married a poor clergyman, of a sickly constitution and a flowery style of eloquence, and then, at the age of thirty-three, had been left a widow, without children, without fortune — with nothing but the memory of Mr. Penniman's flowers of speech, a certain vague aroma of which hovered about her own conversation. Nevertheless he had offered her a home under his own roof, which Lavinia accepted with the alacrity of a woman who had spent the ten years of her married life in the town of Poughkeepsie. The Doctor had not proposed to Mrs. Penniman to come and live with him indefinitely; he had suggested that she should make an asylum of his house while she looked about for unfurnished lodgings. It is uncertain whether Mrs. Penniman ever instituted a search for unfurnished lodgings, but it is beyond dispute that she never found them. She settled herself with her brother and never went away, and when Catherine was twenty years old her Aunt Lavinia was still one of the most striking features of her immediate *entourage*. Mrs. Penniman's own account of the matter was that she had remained to take charge of her niece's education. She had given this account, at least, to every one but the Doctor, who never asked for explanations which he could entertain himself any day with inventing. Mrs. Penniman, moreover, though she had a good deal of a certain sort of artificial assurance, shrank, for indefinable reasons, from presenting herself to her brother as a fountain of instruction. She had not a high sense of humour, but she had enough to prevent her from making this mistake; and her brother, on his side, had enough to excuse her, in her situation, for laying him under contribution during a considerable part of a lifetime. He therefore assented tacitly to the proposition which Mrs. Penniman had tacitly laid down, that it was of importance that the poor motherless girl should have a brilliant woman near her. His assent could only be tacit, for he had never been dazzled by his sister's intellectual lustre. Save when he fell in love with Catherine Harrington, he had never been dazzled, indeed, by any feminine characteristics whatever; and though he was to a certain extent what is called a ladies' doctor, his private opinion of the more complicated sex was not exalted. He regarded its complications as more curious than edifying, and he had an idea of the beauty of *reason*, which was, on the whole, meagrely gratified by what he observed in his female patients. His wife had been a reasonable woman, but she was a bright exception; among several things that he was sure of, this was perhaps the principal. Such a conviction, of course, did little either to mitigate or to abbreviate his widowhood; and it set a limit to his recognition, at the best, of Catherine's possibilities and of Mrs. Penniman's ministrations. He, nevertheless, at the end of six months, accepted his sister's permanent presence as an accomplished fact, and as Catherine grew older perceived that there were in effect good reasons why she should have a companion of her own imperfect sex. He was extremely polite to Lavinia, scrupulously, formally polite; and she had never seen him in anger but once in her life, when he lost his temper in a theological discussion with her late husband. With her he never discussed theology, nor, indeed, discussed anything; he contented himself with making known, very distinctly, in the form of a lucid ultimatum, his wishes with regard to Catherine.

Once, when the girl was about twelve years old, he had said to her:

"Try and make a clever woman of her, Lavinia; I should like her to be a clever woman."

Mrs. Penniman, at this, looked thoughtful a moment. "My dear Austin," she then inquired, "do you think it is better to be clever than to be good?"

"Good for what?" asked the Doctor. "You are good for nothing unless you are clever."

From this assertion Mrs. Penniman saw no reason to dissent; she possibly reflected that her own great use in the world was owing to her aptitude for many things.

"Of course I wish Catherine to be good," the Doctor said next day; "but she won't be any the less virtuous for not being a fool. I am not afraid of her being wicked; she will never have the salt of malice in her character. She is as good as good bread, as the French say; but six years hence I don't want to have to compare her to good bread and butter."

"Are you afraid she will turn insipid? My dear brother, it is I who supply the butter; so you needn't fear!" said Mrs. Penniman, who had taken in hand the child's accomplishments, overlooking her at the piano, where Catherine displayed a certain talent, and going with her to the dancing-class, where it must be confessed that she made but a modest figure.

Mrs. Penniman was a tall, thin, fair, rather faded woman, with a perfectly amiable disposition, a high standard of gentility, a taste for light literature, and a certain foolish indirectness and obliquity of character. She was romantic, she was sentimental, she had a passion for little secrets and mysteries — a very innocent passion, for her secrets had hitherto always been as unpractical as addled eggs. She was not absolutely veracious; but this defect was of no great consequence, for she had never had anything to conceal. She would have liked to have a lover, and to correspond with him under an assumed name in letters left at a shop; I am bound to say that her imagination never carried the intimacy farther than this. Mrs. Penniman had never had a lover, but her brother, who was very shrewd, understood her turn of mind. "When Catherine is about seventeen," he said to himself, "Lavinia will try and persuade her that some young man with a moustache is in love with her. It will be quite untrue; no young man, with a moustache or without, will ever be in love with Catherine. But Lavinia will take it up, and talk to her about it; perhaps, even, if her taste for clandestine operations doesn't prevail with her, she will talk to me about it. Catherine won't see it, and won't believe it, fortunately for her peace of mind; poor Catherine isn't romantic."

She was a healthy well-grown child, without a trace of her mother's beauty. She was not ugly; she had simply a plain, dull, gentle countenance. The most that had ever been said for her was that she had a "nice" face, and, though she was an heiress, no one had ever thought of regarding her as a belle. Her father's opinion of her moral purity was abundantly justified; she was excellently, imperturbably good; affectionate, docile, obedient, and much addict-

ed to speaking the truth. In her younger years she was a good deal of a romp, and, though it is an awkward confession to make about one's heroine, I must add that she was something of a glutton. She never, that I know of, stole raisins out of the pantry; but she devoted her pocket-money to the purchase of cream-cakes. As regards this, however, a critical attitude would be inconsistent with a candid reference to the early annals of any biographer. Catherine was decidedly not clever; she was not quick with her book, nor, indeed, with anything else. She was not abnormally deficient, and she mustered learning enough to acquit herself respectably in conversation with her contemporaries, among whom it must be avowed, however, that she occupied a secondary place. It is well known that in New York it is possible for a young girl to occupy a primary one. Catherine, who was extremely modest, had no desire to shine, and on most social occasions, as they are called, you would have found her lurking in the background. She was extremely fond of her father, and very much afraid of him; she thought him the cleverest and handsomest and most celebrated of men. The poor girl found her account so completely in the exercise of her affections that the little tremor of fear that mixed itself with her filial passion gave the thing an extra relish rather than blunted its edge. Her deepest desire was to please him, and her conception of happiness was to know that she had succeeded in pleasing him. She had never succeeded beyond a certain point. Though, on the whole, he was very kind to her, she was perfectly aware of this, and to go beyond the point in question seemed to her really something to live for. What she could not know, of course, was that she disappointed him, though on three or four occasions the Doctor had been almost frank about it. She grew up peacefully and prosperously, but at the age of eighteen Mrs. Penniman had not made a clever woman of her. Dr. Sloper would have liked to be proud of his daughter; but there was nothing to be proud of in poor Catherine. There was nothing, of course, to be ashamed of; but this was not enough for the Doctor, who was a proud man and would have enjoyed being able to think of his daughter as an unusual girl. There would have been a fitness in her being pretty and graceful, intelligent and distinguished; for her mother had been the most charming woman of her little day, and as regards her father, of course he knew his own value. He had moments of irritation at having produced a commonplace child, and he even went so far at times as to take a certain satisfaction in the thought that his wife had not lived to find her out. He was naturally slow in making this discovery himself, and it was not till Catherine had become a young lady grown that he regarded the matter as settled. He

gave her the benefit of a great many doubts; he was in no haste to conclude. Mrs. Penniman frequently assured him that his daughter had a delightful nature; but he knew how to interpret this assurance. It meant, to his sense, that Catherine was not wise enough to discover that her aunt was a goose — a limitation of mind that could not fail to be agreeable to Mrs. Penniman. Both she and her brother, however, exaggerated the young girl's limitations; for Catherine, though she was very fond of her aunt, and conscious of the gratitude she owed her, regarded her without a particle of that gentle dread which gave its stamp to her admiration of her father. To her mind there was nothing of the infinite about Mrs. Penniman; Catherine saw her all at once, as it were, and was not dazzled by the apparition; whereas her father's great faculties seemed, as they stretched away, to lose themselves in a sort of luminous vagueness, which indicated, not that they stopped, but that Catherine's own mind ceased to follow them.

It must not be supposed that Dr. Sloper visited his disappointment upon the poor girl, or ever let her suspect that she had played him a trick. On the contrary, for fear of being unjust to her, he did his duty with exemplary zeal, and recognised that she was a faithful and affectionate child. Besides, he was a philosopher; he smoked a good many cigars over his disappointment, and in the fulness of time he got used to it. He satisfied himself that he had expected nothing, though, indeed, with a certain oddity of reasoning. "I expect nothing," he said to himself, "so that if she gives me a surprise, it will be all clear again. If she doesn't, it will be no loss." This was about the time Catherine had reached her eighteenth year, so that it will be seen her father had not been precipitate. At this time she seemed not only incapable of giving surprises; it was almost a question whether she could have received one — she was so quiet and irresponsive. People who expressed themselves roughly called her stolid. But she was irresponsive because she was shy, uncomfortably, painfully shy. This was not always understood, and she sometimes produced an impression of insensibility. In reality she was the softest creature in the world.

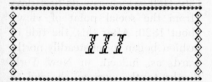

III

As a child she had promised to be tall, but when she was sixteen she ceased to grow, and her stature, like most other points in her composition, was not unusual. She was strong, however, and properly made, and, fortunately, her health was excellent. It has been noted that the Doctor was a philosopher, but I would not have answered for his philosophy if the poor girl had proved a sickly and suffering person. Her appearance of health constituted her principal claim to beauty, and her clear, fresh complexion, in which white and red were very equally distributed, was, indeed, an excellent thing to see. Her eye was small and quiet, her features were rather thick, her tresses brown and smooth. A dull, plain girl she was called by rigorous critics — a quiet, ladylike girl by those of the more imaginative sort; but by neither class was she very elaborately discussed. When it had been duly impressed upon her that she was a young lady — it was a good while before she could believe it — she suddenly developed a lively taste for dress: a lively taste is quite the expression to use. I feel as if I ought to write it very small, her judgement in this matter was by no means infallible; it was liable to confusions and embarrassments. Her great indulgence of it was really the desire of a rather inarticulate nature to manifest itself; she sought to be eloquent in her garments, and to make up for her diffidence of speech by a fine frankness of costume. But if she expressed herself in her clothes it is certain that people were not to blame for not thinking her a witty person. It must be added that though she had the expectation of a fortune — Dr. Sloper for a long time had been making twenty thousand dollars a year by his profession, and laying aside the half of it — the amount of money at her disposal was not greater than the allowance made to many poorer girls. In those days in New York there were still a few altar-fires flickering in the temple of Republican simplicity, and Dr. Sloper would have been glad to see his daughter present herself, with a classic grace, as a priestess of this mild faith. It made him fairly grimace, in private, to think that a child of his should be both ugly and overdressed. For himself, he was fond of the good things of life, and he made a considerable use of them; but he had a dread of vulgarity, and even a theory that it was increasing in the society that surrounded him. Moreover, the standard of luxury in the United States thirty years ago was carried by no means so high as at present, and Catherine's clever father took the old-fashioned view of the education of young persons. He had no particular theory on the subject; it had scarcely as yet become a necessity of self-defence to have a collection of theories. It simply appeared to him proper and reasonable that a well-bred young woman should not carry half her fortune on her back. Catherine's back was a broad one, and would have carried a good deal; but to the weight of the paternal displeasure she never ventured to expose it, and our heroine was twenty years old before she treated herself, for evening wear, to a red satin gown trimmed with gold fringe; though this was an article which, for many years, she had coveted in secret. It made her look, when she sported it, like a

woman of thirty; but oddly enough, in spite of her taste for fine clothes, she had not a grain of coquetry, and her anxiety when she put them on was as to whether they, and not she, would look well. It is a point on which history has not been explicit, but the assumption is warrantable; it was in the royal raiment just mentioned that she presented herself at a little entertainment given by her aunt, Mrs. Almond. The girl was at this time in her twenty-first year, and Mrs. Almond's party was the beginning of something very important.

Some three or four years before this Dr. Sloper had moved his household gods up town, as they say in New York. He had been living ever since his marriage in an edifice of red brick, with granite copings and an enormous fanlight over the door, standing in a street within five minutes' walk of the City Hall, which saw its best days (from the social point of view) about 1820. After this, the tide of fashion began to set steadily northward, as, indeed, in New York, thanks to the narrow channel in which it flows, it is obliged to do, and the great hum of traffic rolled farther to the right and left of Broadway. By the time the Doctor changed his residence the murmur of trade had become a mighty uproar, which was music in the ears of all good citizens interested in the commercial development, as they delighted to call it, of their fortunate isle. Dr. Sloper's interest in this phenomenon was only indirect — though, seeing that, as the years went on, half his patients came to be overworked men of business, it might have been more immediate — and when most of his neighbours' dwellings (also ornamented with granite copings and large fanlights) had been converted into offices, warehouses, and shipping agencies, and otherwise applied to the base uses of commerce, he determined to look out for a quieter home. The ideal of quiet and of genteel retirement, in 1835, was found in Washington Square, where the Doctor built himself a handsome, modern, wide-fronted house, with a big balcony before the drawing-room windows, and a flight of marble steps ascending to a portal which was also faced with white marble. This structure, and many of its neighbours, which it exactly resembled, were supposed, forty years ago, to embody the last results of architectural science, and they remain to this day very solid and honourable dwellings. In front of them was the Square, containing a considerable quantity of inexpensive vegetation, enclosed by a wooden paling, which increased its rural and accessible appearance; and round the corner was the more august precinct of the Fifth Avenue, taking its origin at this point with a spacious and confident air which already marked it for high destinies. I know not whether it is owing to the tenderness of early associations, but this portion of New York appears to many persons the most delectable. It has a

kind of established repose which is not of frequent occurrence in other quarters of the long, shrill city; it has a riper, richer, more honourable look than any of the upper ramifications of the great longitudinal thoroughfare — the look of having had something of a social history. It was here, as you might have been informed on good authority, that you had come into a world which appeared to offer a variety of sources of interest; it was here that your grandmother lived, in venerable solitude, and dispensed a hospitality which commended itself alike to the infant imagination and the infant palate; it was here that you took your first walks abroad, following the nursery-maid with unequal step and sniffing up the strange odour of the ailantus-trees which at that time formed the principal umbrage of the Square, and diffused an aroma that you were not yet critical enough to dislike as it deserved; it was here, finally, that your first school, kept by a broad-bosomed, broad-based old lady with a ferule, who was always having tea in a blue cup, with a saucer that didn't match, enlarged the circle both of your observations and your sensations. It was here, at any rate, that my heroine spent many years of her life; which is my excuse for this topographical parenthesis.

Mrs. Almond lived much farther up town, in an embryonic street with a high number — a region where the extension of the city began to assume a theoretic air, where poplars grew beside the pavement (when there was one), and mingled their shade with the steep roofs of desultory Dutch houses, and where pigs and chickens disported themelves in the gutter. These elements of rural picturesqueness have now wholly departed from New York street scenery; but they were to be found within the memory of middle-aged persons, in quarters which now would blush to be reminded of them. Catherine had a great many cousins, and with her Aunt Almond's children, who ended by being nine in number, she lived on terms of considerable intimacy. When she was younger they had been rather afraid of her; she was believed, as the phrase is, to be highly educated, and a person who lived in the intimacy of their Aunt Penniman had something of reflected grandeur. Mrs. Penniman, among the little Almonds, was an object of more admiration than sympathy. Her manners were strange and formidable, and her mourning robes — she dressed in black for twenty years after her husband's death, and then suddenly appeared one morning with pink roses in her cap — were complicated in odd, unexpected places with buckles, bugles, and pins, which discouraged familiarity. She took children too hard, both for good and for evil, and had an oppressive air of expecting subtle things of them, so that going to see her was a good deal like being taken to church and made to sit in a front pew. It was discovered after a while, however, that Aunt Penniman was but an accident in Catherine's existence, and not a part of its essence, and that when the girl came to spend a Saturday with her cousins, she was available for "follow-my-master," and even for leap-frog. On this basis an understanding was easily arrived at, and for several years Catherine fraternised with her young kinsmen. I say young kinsmen, because seven of the little Almonds were boys, and Catherine had a preference for those games which are most conveniently played in trousers. By degrees, however, the little Almonds' trousers began to lengthen, and the wearers to disperse and settle themselves in life. The elder children were older than Catherine, and the boys were sent to college or placed in counting-rooms. Of the girls, one married very punctually, and the other as punctually became engaged. It was to celebrate this latter event that Mrs. Almond gave the little party I have mentioned. Her daughter was to marry a stout young stock-broker, a boy of twenty; it was thought a very good thing.

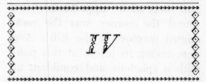

IV

MRS. PENNIMAN, with more buckles and bangles than ever, came, of course, to the entertainment, accompanied by her niece; the Doctor, too, had promised to look in later in the evening. There was to be a good deal of dancing, and before it had gone very far, Marian Almond came up to Catherine, in company with a tall young man. She introduced the young man as a person who had a great desire to make our heroine's acquaintance, and as a cousin of Arthur Townsend, her own intended.

Marion Almond was a pretty little person of seventeen, with a very small figure and a very big sash, to the elegance of whose manners matrimony had nothing to add. She already had all the airs of a hostess, receiving the company, shaking her fan, saying that with so many people to attend to she should have no time to dance. She made a long speech about Mr. Townsend's cousin, to whom she administered a tap with her fan before turning away to other cares. Catherine had not understood all that she said; her attention was given to enjoying Marian's ease of manner and flow of ideas, and to looking at the young man, who was remarkably handsome. She had succeeded, however, as she often failed to do when people were presented to her, in catching his name, which appeared to be the same as that of Marian's little stockbroker. Catherine was always agitated by an introduction; it seemed a difficult moment, and she wondered that some people — her new acquaintance at this moment, for instance — should mind it so little. She wondered what she ought to say, and what would be the conse-

quences of her saying nothing. The consequences at present were very agreeable. Mr. Townsend, leaving her no time for embarrassment, began to talk with an easy smile, as if he had known her for a year. "What a delightful party! What a charming house! What an interesting family! What a pretty girl your cousin is!"

These observations, in themselves of no great profundity, Mr. Townsend seemed to offer for what they were worth, and as a contribution to an acquaintance. He looked straight into Catherine's eyes. She answered nothing; she only listened, and looked at him; and he, as if expected no particular reply, went on to say many other things in the same comfortable and natural manner. Catherine, though she felt tongue-tied, was conscious of no embarrassment; it seemed proper that he should talk, and that she should simply look at him. What made it natural was that he was so handsome, or rather, as she phrased it to herself, so beautiful. The music had been silent for a while, but it suddenly began again; and then he asked her, with a deeper, intenser smile, if she would do him the honour of dancing with him. Even to this inquiry she gave no audible assent; she simply let him put his arm round her waist — as she did so it occurred to her more vividly than it had ever done before, that this was a singular place for a gentleman's arm to be — and in a moment he was guiding her round the room in the harmonious rotation of the polka. When they paused she felt that she was red; and then, for some moments, she stopped looking at him. She fanned herself, and looked at the flowers that were painted on her fan. He asked her if she would begin again, and she hesitated to answer, still looking at the flowers.

"Does it make you dizzy?" he asked, in a tone of great kindness.

Then Catherine looked up at him; he was certainly beautiful, and not at all red. "Yes," she said; she hardly knew why, for dancing had never made her dizzy.

"Ah, well, in that case," said Mr. Townsend, "we will sit still and talk. I will find a good place to sit."

He found a good place — a charming place; a little sofa that seemed meant only for two persons. The rooms by this time were very full; the dancers increased in number, and people stood close in front of them, turning their backs, so that Catherine and her companion seemed secluded and unobserved. "*We* will talk," the young man had said; but he still did all the talking. Catherine leaned back in her place, with her eyes fixed upon him, smiling and thinking him very clever. He had features like young men in pictures; Catherine had never seen such features — so delicate, so chiselled and finished — among the young New Yorkers whom she passed in the streets and met at parties. He was tall and slim, but he looked extremely strong. Catherine thought he looked like a statue. But a statue would not talk like that, and, above all, would not have eyes of so rare a colour. He had never been at Mrs. Almond's before; he felt very much like a stranger; and it was very kind of Catherine to take pity on him. He was Arthur Townsend's cousin — not very near; several times removed — and Arthur had brought him to present him to the family. In fact, he was a great stranger in New York. It was his native place; but he had not been there for many years. He had been knocking about the world, and living in far-away lands; he had only come back a month or two before. New York was very pleasant, only he felt lonely.

"You see, people forget you," he said, smiling at Catherine with his delightful gaze, while he leaned forward obliquely, turning towards her, with his elbows on his knees.

It seemed to Catherine that no one who had once seen him would ever forget him; but though she made this reflexion she kept it to herself, almost as you would keep something precious.

They sat there for some time. He was very amusing. He asked her about the people that were near them; he tried to guess who some of them were, and he made the most laughable mistakes. He criticised them very freely, in a positive, off-hand way. Catherine had never heard any one — especially any young man — talk just like that. It was the way a young man might talk in a novel; or better still, in a play, on the stage, close before the footlights, looking at the audience, and with every one looking at him, so that you wondered at his presence of mind. And yet Mr. Townsend was not like an actor; he seemed so sincere, so natural. This was very interesting; but in the midst of it Marian Almond came pushing through the crowd, with a little ironical cry, when she found these young people still together, which made every one turn round, and cost Catherine a conscious blush. Marian broke up their talk, and told Mr. Townsend — whom she treated as if she were already married, and he had become her cousin — to run away to her mother, who had been wishing for the last half-hour to introduce him to Mr. Almond.

"We shall meet again!" he said to Catherine as he left her, and Catherine thought it a very original speech.

Her cousin took her by the arm, and made her walk about. "I needn't ask you what you think of Morris!" the young girl exclaimed.

"Is that his name?"

"I don't ask you what you think of his name, but what you think of himself," said Marian.

"Oh, nothing particular!" Catherine answered, dissembling for the first time in her life.

"I have half a mind to tell him that!" cried Marian. "It will do him good. He's so terribly conceited."

"Conceited?" said Catherine, staring.

"So Arthur says, and Arthur knows about him."

"Oh, don't tell him!" Catherine murmured imploringly.

"Don't tell him he's conceited? I have told him so a dozen times."

At this profession of audacity Catherine looked down at her little companion in amazement. She supposed it was because Marian was going to be married that she took so much on herself; but she wondered too, whether, when she herself should become engaged, such exploits would be expected of her.

Half an hour later she saw her Aunt Penniman sitting in the embrasure of a window, with her head a little on one side, and her gold eye-glass raised to her eyes, which were wandering about the room. In front of her was a gentleman, bending forward a little, with his back turned to Catherine. She knew his back immediately, though she had never seen it; for when he had left her, at Marian's instigation, he had retreated in the best order, without turning round. Morris Townsend — the name had already become very familiar to her, as if some one had been repeating it in her ear for the last half-hour — Morris Townsend was giving his impressions of the company to her aunt, as he had done to herself; he was saying clever things, and Mrs. Penniman was smiling, as if she approved of them. As soon as Catherine had perceived this she moved away; she would not have liked him to turn round and see her. But it gave her pleasure — the whole thing. That he should talk with Mrs. Penniman, with whom she lived and whom she saw and talked with every day — that seemed to keep him near her, and to make him even easier to contemplate than if she herself had been the object of his civilities; and that Aunt Lavinia should like him, should not be shocked or startled by what he said, this also appeared to the girl a personal gain; for Aunt Lavinia's standard was extremely high, planted as it was over the grave of her late husband, in which, as she had convinced every one, the very genius of conversation was buried. One of the Almond boys, as Catherine called him, invited our heroine to dance a quadrille, and for a quarter of an hour her feet at least were occupied. This time she was not dizzy; her head was very clear. Just when the dance was over, she found herself in the crowd face to face with her father. Dr. Sloper had usually a little smile, never a very big one, and with his little smile playing in his clear eyes and on his neatly-shaved lips, he looked at his daughter's crimson gown.

"Is it possible that this magnificent person is my child?" he said.

You would have surprised him if you had told him so; but it is a literal fact that he almost never addressed his daughter save in the ironical form. Whenever he addressed her he gave her pleasure; but she had to cut her pleasure out of the piece, as it were. There were portions left over, light remnants and snippets of irony, which she never knew what to do with, which seemed too delicate for her own use; and yet Catherine, lamenting the limitations of her understanding, felt that they were too valuable to waste and had a belief that if they passed over her head they yet contributed to the general sum of human wisdom.

"I am not magnificent," she said mildly, wishing that she had put on another dress.

"You are sumptuous, opulent, expensive," her father rejoined. "You look as if you had eighty thousand a year."

"Well, so long as I haven't —— " said Catherine illogically. Her conception of her prospective wealth was as yet very indefinite.

"So long as you haven't you shouldn't look as if you had. Have you enjoyed your party?"

Catherine hesitated a moment; and then, looking away, "I am rather tired," she murmured. I have said that this entertainment was the beginning of something important for Catherine. For the second time in her life she made an indirect answer; and the beginning of a period of dissimulation is certainly a significant date. Catherine was not so easily tired as that.

Nevertheless, in the carriage, as they drove home, she was as quiet as if fatigue had been her portion. Dr. Sloper's manner of addressing his sister Lavinia had a good deal of resemblance to the tone he had adopted towards Catherine.

"Who was the young man that was making love to you?" he presently asked.

"Oh, my good brother!" murmured Mrs. Penniman, in deprecation.

"He seemed uncommonly tender. Whenever I looked at you, for half an hour, he had the most devoted air."

"The devotion was not to me," said Mrs. Penniman. "It was to Catherine; he talked to me of her."

Catherine had been listening with all her ears. "Oh, Aunt Penniman!" she exclaimed faintly.

"He is very handsome; he is very clever; he expressed himself with a great deal — a great deal of felicity," her aunt went on.

"He is in love with this regal creature, then?" the Doctor inquired humorously.

"Oh, father," cried the girl, still more faintly, devoutly thankful the carriage was dark.

"I don't know that; but he admired her dress."

Catherine did not say to herself in the dark, "My dress only?" Mrs. Penniman's announcement struck her by its richness, not by its meagreness.

"You see," said her father, "he thinks you have eighty thousand a year."

"I don't believe he thinks of that," said Mrs. Penniman; "he is too refined."

"He must be tremendously refined not to think of that!"

"Well, he is!" Catherine exclaimed, before she knew it.

"I thought you had gone to sleep," her father answered. "The hour has come!" he added to himself. "Lavinia is going to get up a romance for Catherine. It's a shame to play such tricks on the girl. What is the gentleman's name?" he went on, aloud.

"I didn't catch it, and I didn't like to ask him. He asked to be introduced to me," said Mrs. Penniman, with a certain grandeur; "but you know how indistinctly Jefferson speaks." Jefferson was Mr. Almond. "Catherine, dear, what was the gentleman's name?"

For a minute, if it had not been for the rumbling of the carriage, you might have heard a pin drop.

"I don't know, Aunt Lavinia," said Catherine, very softly. And, with all his irony, her father believed her.

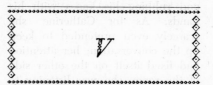

V

HE learned what he had asked some three or four days later, after Morris Townsend, with his cousin, had called in Washington Square. Mrs. Penniman did not tell her brother, on the drive home, that she had intimated to this agreeable young man, whose name she did not know, that, with her niece, she should be very glad to see him; but she was greatly pleased, and even a little flattered, when, late on a Sunday afternoon, the two gentlemen made their appearance. His coming with Arthur Townsend made it more natural

177

and easy; the latter young man was on the point of becoming connected with the family, and Mrs. Penniman had remarked to Catherine that, as he was going to marry Marian, it would be polite in him to call. These events came to pass late in the autumn, and Catherine and her aunt had been sitting together in the closing dusk, by the firelight, in the high back parlour.

Arthur Townsend fell to Catherine's portion, while his companion placed himself on the sofa, beside Mrs. Penniman. Catherine had hitherto not been a harsh critic; she was easy to please — she liked to talk with young men. But Marian's betrothed, this evening, made her feel vaguely fastidious; he sat looking at the fire and rubbing his knees with his hands. As for Catherine, she scarcely even pretended to keep up the conversation; her attention had fixed itself on the other side of the room; she was listening to what went on between the other Mr. Townsend and her aunt. Every now and then he looked over at Catherine herself and smiled, as if to show that what he said was for her benefit too. Catherine would have liked to change her place, to go and sit near them, where she might see and hear him better. But she was afraid of seeming bold — of looking eager; and, besides, it would not have been polite to Marian's little suitor. She wondered why the other gentleman had picked out her aunt — how he came to have so much to say to Mrs. Penniman, to whom, usually, young men were not especially devoted. She was not at all jealous of Aunt Lavinia, but she was a little envious, and above all she wondered; for Morris Townsend was an object on which she found that her imagination could exercise itself indefinitely. His cousin had been describing a house that he had taken in view of his union with Marian, and the domestic conveniences he meant to introduce into it; how Marian wanted a larger one, and Mrs. Almond recommended a smaller one, and how he himself was convinced that he had got the neatest house in New York.

"It doesn't matter," he said; "it's only for three or four years. At the end of three or four years we'll move. That's the way to live in New York — to move every three or four years. Then you always get the last thing. It's because the city's growing so quick — you've got to keep up with it. It's going straight up town — that's where New York's going. If I wasn't afraid Marian would be lonely, I'd go up there — right up to the top — and wait for it. Only have to wait ten years — they'd all come up after you. But Marian says she wants some neighbours — she doesn't want to be a pioneer. She says that if she's got to be the first settler she had better go out to Minnesota. I guess we'll move up little by little; when we get tired of one street we'll go higher. So you see we'll always have a new house; it's a great advantage to have a new house; you get all the latest improvements. They invent everything all over again about every five years, and it's a great thing to keep up with the new things. I always try and keep up with the new things of every kind. Don't you think that's a good motto for a young couple — to keep 'going higher'? That's the name of that piece of poetry — what do they call it? — *Excelsior!*"

Catherine bestowed on her junior visitor only just enough attention to feel that this was not the way Mr. Morris Townsend had talked the other night, or that he was talking now to her fortunate aunt. But suddenly his aspiring kinsman became more interesting. He seemed to have become conscious that she was affected by his companion's presence, and he thought it proper to explain it.

"My cousin asked me to bring him, or I shouldn't have taken the liberty. He seemed to want very much to come; you know he's awfully sociable. I told him I wanted to ask you first, but he said Mrs. Penniman had invited him. He isn't particular what he says when he wants to come somewhere! But Mrs. Penniman seems to think it's all right."

"We are very glad to see him," said Catherine. And she wished to talk more about him; but she hardly knew what to say. "I never saw him before," she went on presently.

Arthur Townsend stared.

"Why, he told me he talked with you for over half an hour the other night."

"I mean before the other night. That was the first time."

"Oh, he has been away from New York — he has been all round the world. He doesn't know many people here, but he's very sociable, and he wants to know every one."

"Every one?" said Catherine.

"Well, I mean all the good ones. All the pretty young ladies — like Mrs. Penniman!" and Arthur Townsend gave a private laugh.

"My aunt likes him very much," said Catherine.

"Most people like him — he's so brilliant."

"He's more like a foreigner," Catherine suggested.

"Well, I never knew a foreigner!" said young Townsend, in a tone which seemed to indicate that his ignorance had been optional.

"Neither have I," Catherine confessed, with more humility. "They say they are generally brilliant," she added vaguely.

"Well, the people of this city are clever enough for me. I know some of them that think they are too clever for me; but they ain't!"

"I suppose you can't be too clever," said Catherine, still with humility.

"I don't know. I know some people that call my cousin too clever."

Catherine listened to this statement with extreme interest, and a feeling that if Morris Townsend had a fault it would naturally be that one. But she did not commit herself, and in a moment she asked: "Now that he has come back, will he stay here always?"

"Ah," said Arthur, "if he can get something to do."

"Something to do?"

"Some place or other; some business."

"Hasn't he got any?" said Catherine, who had never heard of a young man — of the upper class — in this situation.

"No; he's looking round. But he can't find anything."

"I am very sorry," Catherine permitted herself to observe.

"Oh, he doesn't mind," said young Townsend. "He takes it easy — he isn't in a hurry. He is very particular."

Catherine thought he naturally would be, and gave herself up for some moments to the contemplation of this idea, in several of its bearings.

"Won't his father take him into his business — his office?" she at last inquired.

"He hasn't got any father — he has only got a sister. Your sister can't help you much."

It seemed to Catherine that if she were his sister she would disprove this axiom. "Is she — is she pleasant?" she asked in a moment.

"I don't know — I believe she's very respectable," said young Townsend. And then he looked across to his cousin and began to laugh. "Look here, we are talking about you," he added.

Morris Townsend paused in his conversation with Mrs. Penniman, and stared, with a little smile.

Then he got up, as if he were going.

"As far as you are concerned, I can't return the compliment," he said to Catherine's companion. "But as regards Miss Sloper, it's another affair."

Catherine thought this little speech wonderfully well turned; but she was embarrassed by it, and she also got up. Morris Townsend stood looking at her and smiling; he put out his hand for farewell. He was going, without having said anything to her; but even on these terms she was glad to have seen him.

"I will tell her what you have said — when you go!" said Mrs. Penniman, with an insinuating laugh.

Catherine blushed, for she felt almost as if they were making sport of her. What in the world could this beautiful young man have said? He looked at her still, in spite of her blush; but very kindly and respectfully.

"I have had no talk with you," he said, "and that was what I came for. But it will be a good reason for coming another time; a little pretext — if I am obliged to give one. I am not afraid of what your aunt will say when I go."

With this the two young men took their departure; after which Catherine, with her blush still lingering, directed a serious and interrogative eye to Mrs. Penniman. She was incapable of elaborate artifice, and she resorted to no jocular device — to no affectation of the belief that she had been maligned — to learn what she desired.

"What did you say you would tell me?" she asked.

Mrs. Penniman came up to her, smiling and nodding a little, looked at her all over, and gave a twist to the knot of ribbon in her neck. "It's a great secret, my dear child; but he is coming a-courting!"

Catherine was serious still. "Is that what he told you!"

"He didn't say so exactly. But he left me to guess it. I'm a good guesser."

"Do you mean a-courting me?"

"Not me, certainly, miss; though I must say he is a hundred times more polite to a person who has no longer extreme youth to recommend her than most of the young men. He is thinking of some one else." And Mrs. Penniman gave her niece a delicate little kiss. "You must be very gracious to him."

Catherine stared — she was bewildered. "I don't understand you," she said; "he doesn't know me."

"Oh yes, he does; more than you think. I have told him all about you."

"Oh, Aunt Penniman!" murmured Catherine, as if this had been a breach of trust. "He is a perfect stranger — we don't know him." There was infinite modesty in the poor girl's "we."

Aunt Penniman, however, took no account of it; she spoke even with a touch of acrimony. "My dear Catherine, you know very well that you admire him!"

"Oh, Aunt Penniman!" Catherine could only murmur again. It might very well be that she ad-

mired him — though this did not seem to her a thing to talk about. But that this brilliant stranger — this sudden apparition, who had barely heard the sound of her voice — took that sort of interest in her that was expressed by the romantic phrase of which Mrs. Penniman had just made use: this could only be a figment of the restless brain of Aunt Lavinia, whom every one knew to be a woman of powerful imagination.

VI

Mrs. Penniman even took for granted at times that other people had as much imagination as herself; so that when, half an hour later, her brother came in, she addressed him quite on this principle.

"He has just been here, Austin; it's such a pity you missed him."

"Whom in the world have I missed?" asked the Doctor.

"Mr. Morris Townsend; he has made us such a delightful visit."

"And who in the world is Mr. Morris Townsend?"

"Aunt Penniman means the gentleman — the gentleman whose name I couldn't remember," said Catherine.

"The gentleman at Elizabeth's party who was so struck with Catherine," Mrs. Penniman added.

"Oh, his name is Morris Townsend, is it? And did he come here to propose to you?"

"Oh, father," murmured the girl for all answer, turning away to the window, where the dusk had deepened to darkness.

"I hope he won't do that without your permission," said Mrs. Penniman, very graciously.

"After all, my dear, he seems to have yours," her brother answered.

Lavinia simpered, as if this might not be quite enough, and Catherine, with her forehead touching the window-panes, listened to this exchange of epigrams as reservedly as if they had not each been a pin-prick in her own destiny.

"The next time he comes," the Doctor added, "you had better call me. He might like to see me."

Morris Townsend came again, some five days afterwards; but Dr. Sloper was not called, as he was absent from home at the time. Catherine was with her aunt when the young man's name was brought in, and Mrs. Penniman, effacing herself and protesting, made a great point of her niece's going into the drawing-room alone.

"This time it's for you — for you only," she said. "Before, when he talked to me, it was only preliminary — it was to gain my confidence. Literally, my dear, I should not have the *courage* to show myself to-day."

And this was perfectly true. Mrs. Penniman was not a brave woman, and Morris Townsend had struck her as a young man of great force of character, and of remarkable powers of satire; a keen, resolute, brilliant nature, with which one must exercise a great deal of tact. She said to herself that he was "imperious," and she liked the word and the idea. She was not the least jealous of her niece, and she had been perfectly happy with Mr. Penniman, but in the bottom of her heart she permitted herself the observation: "That's the sort of husband I should have had!" He was certainly much more imperious — she ended by calling it imperial — than Mr. Penniman.

So Catherine saw Mr. Townsend alone, and her aunt did not come in even at the end of the visit. The visit was a long one; he sat there — in the front parlour, in the biggest armchair — for more than an hour. He seemed more at home this time — more familiar; lounging a little in the chair, slapping a cushion that was near him with his stick, and looking round the room a good deal, and at the objects it contained, as well as at Catherine; whom, however, he also contemplated freely. There was a smile of respectful devotion in his handsome eyes which seemed to Catherine almost solemnly beautiful; it made her think of a young knight in a poem. His talk, however, was not particularly knightly; it was light and easy and friendly; it took a practical turn, and he asked a number of questions about herself — what were her tastes — if she liked this and that — what were her habits. He said to her, with his charming smile, "Tell me about yourself; give me a little sketch." Catherine had very little to tell, and she had no talent for sketching; but before he went she had confided to him that she had a secret passion for the theatre, which had been but scantily gratified, and a taste for operatic music — that of Bellini and Donizetti, in especial (it must be remembered in extenuation of this primitive young woman that she held these opinions in an age of general darkness) — which she rarely had an occasion to hear, except on the hand-organ. She confessed that she was not particularly fond of literature. Morris Townsend agreed with her that books were tiresome things; only, as he said, you had to read a good many before you found it out. He had been to places that people had written books about, and they were not a bit like the descriptions. To see for yourself — that was the great thing; he always tried to see for himself. He had seen all the principal actors — he had been to all the best theatres in London and Paris. But the actors were always like the authors — they always exaggerated. He liked everything to be natural. Suddenly he stopped, looking at Catherine with his smile.

"That's what I like you for; you are so natural! Excuse me," he added; "you see I am natural myself!"

And before she had time to think whether she excused him or not — which afterwards, at leisure, she became conscious that she did — he began to talk about music, and to say that it was his greatest pleasure in life. He had heard all the great singers in Paris and London — Pasta and Rubini and Lablache — and when you had done that, you could say that you knew what singing was.

"I sing a little myself," he said; "some day I will show you. Not to-day, but some other time."

And then he got up to go; he had omitted, by accident, to say that he would sing to her if she would play to him. He thought of this after he got into the street; but he might have spared his compunction, for Catherine had not noticed the lapse. She was thinking only that "some other time" had a delightful sound; it seemed to spread itself over the future.

This was all the more reason, however, though she was ashamed and uncomfortable, why she should tell her father that Mr. Morris Townsend had called again. She announced the fact abruptly, almost violently, as soon as the Doctor came into the house; and having done so — it was her duty — she took measures to leave the room. But she could not leave it fast enough; her father stopped her just as she reached the door.

"Well, my dear, did he propose to you to-day?" the Doctor asked.

This was just what she had been afraid he would say; and yet she had no answer ready. Of course she would have liked to take it as a joke — as her father must have meant it; and yet she would have liked, also, in denying it, to be a little positive, a little sharp; so that he would perhaps not ask the question again. She didn't like it — it made her unhappy. But Catherine could never be sharp; and for a moment she only stood, with her hand on the door-knob, looking at her satiric parent, and giving a little laugh.

"Decidedly," said the Doctor to himself, "my daughter is not brilliant!"

But he had no sooner made this reflexion than Catherine found something; she had decided, on the whole, to take the thing as a joke.

"Perhaps he will do it the next time!" she exclaimed, with a repetition of her laugh. And she quickly got out of the room.

The Doctor stood staring; he wondered whether his daughter were serious. Catherine went straight to her own room, and by the time she reached it she bethought herself that there was something else — something better — she might have said. She almost wished, now, that her father would ask his question again, so that she might reply: "Oh yes, Mr. Morris Townsend proposed to me, and I refused him!"

The Doctor, however, began to put his questions elsewhere; it naturally having occurred to him that he ought to inform himself properly about this handsome young man who had formed the habit of running in and out of his house. He addressed himself to the younger of his sisters, Mrs. Almond — not going to her for the purpose; there was no such hurry as that — but having made a note of the

matter for the first opportunity. The Doctor was never eager, never impatient nor nervous; but he made notes of everything, and he regularly consulted his notes. Among them the information he obtained from Mrs. Almond about Morris Townsend took its place.

"Lavinia has already been to ask me," she said. "Lavinia is most excited; I don't understand it. It's not, after all, Lavinia that the young man is supposed to have designs upon. She is very peculiar."

"Ah, my dear," the Doctor replied, "she has not lived with me these twelve years without my finding it out!"

"She has got such an artificial mind," said Mrs. Almond, who always enjoyed an opportunity to discuss Lavinia's peculiarities with her brother. "She didn't want me to tell you that she had asked me about Mr. Townsend; but I told her I would. She always wants to conceal everything."

"And yet at moments no one blurts things out with such crudity. She is like a revolving lighthouse; pitch darkness alternating with a dazzling brilliancy! But what did you tell her?" the Doctor asked.

"What I tell you; that I know very little of him."

"Lavinia must have been disappointed at that," said the Doctor; "she would prefer him to have been guilty of some romantic crime. However, we must make the best of people. They tell me our gentleman is the cousin of the little boy to whom you are about to entrust the future of your little girl."

"Arthur is not a little boy; he is a very old man; you and I will never be so old. He is a distant relation of Lavinia's *protégé*. The name is the same, but I am given to understand that there are Townsends and Townsends. So Arthur's mother tells me; she talked about 'branches' — younger branches, elder branches, inferior branches — as if it were a royal house. Arthur, it appears, is of the reigning line, but poor Lavinia's young man is not. Beyond this, Arthur's mother knows very little about him; she has only a vague story that he has been 'wild.' But I know his sister a little, and she is a very nice woman. Her name is Mrs. Montgomery; she is a widow, with a little property and five children. She lives in the Second Avenue."

"What does Mrs. Montgomery say about him?"

"That he has talents by which he might distinguish himself."

"Only he is lazy, eh?"

"She doesn't say so."

"That's family pride," said the Doctor. "What is his profession?"

"He hasn't got any; he is looking for something. I believe he was once in the Navy."

"Once? What is his age?"

"I suppose he is upwards of thirty. He must have gone into the Navy very young. I think Arthur told me that he inherited a small property — which was perhaps the cause of his leaving the Navy — and that he spent it all in a few years. He travelled all over the world, lived abroad, amused himself. I believe it was a kind of system, a theory he had. He has lately come back to America, with the intention, as he tells Arthur, of beginning life in earnest."

"Is he in earnest about Catherine, then?"

"I don't see why you should be incredulous," said Mrs. Almond. "It seems to me that you have never done Catherine justice. You must remember that she has the prospect of thirty thousand a year."

The Doctor looked at his sister a moment, and then, with the slightest touch of bitterness: "You at least appreciate her," he said.

Mrs. Almond blushed.

"I don't mean that is her only merit; I simply mean that it is a great one. A great many young men think so; and you appear to me never to have been properly aware of that. You have always had a little way of alluding to her as an unmarriageable girl."

"My allusions are as kind as yours, Elizabeth," said the Doctor frankly. "How many suitors has Catherine had, with all her expectations — how much attention has she ever received? Catherine is not unmarriageable, but she is absolutely unattractive. What other reason is there for Lavinia being so charmed with the idea that there is a lover in the house? There has never been one before, and Lavinia, with her sensitive, sympathetic nature, is not used to the idea. It affects her imagina-

185

tion. I must do the young men of New York the justice to say that they strike me as very disinterested. They prefer pretty girls — lively girls — girls like your own. Catherine is neither pretty nor lively."

"Catherine does very well; she has a style of her own — which is more than my poor Marian has, who has no style at all," said Mrs. Almond. "The reason Catherine has received so little attention is that she seems to all the young men to be older than themselves. She is so large, and she dresses — so richly. They are rather afraid of her, I think; she looks as if she had been married already, and you know they don't like married women. And if our young men appear disinterested," the Doctor's wiser sister went on, "it is because they marry, as a general thing, so young, before twenty-five, at the age of innocence and sincerity, before the age of calculation. If they only waited a little, Catherine would fare better."

"As a calculation? Thank you very much," said the Doctor.

"Wait till some intelligent man of forty comes along, and he will be delighted with Catherine," Mrs. Aldmond continued.

"Mr. Townsend is not old enough, then; his motives may be pure."

"It is very possible that his motives are pure; I should be very sorry to take the contrary for granted. Lavinia is sure of it, and, as he is a very prepossessing youth, you might give him the benefit of the doubt."

Dr. Sloper reflected a moment. "What are his present means of subsistence?"

"I have no idea. He lives, as I say, with his sister."

"A widow, with five children? Do you mean he lives *upon* her?"

Mrs. Almond got up, and with a certain impatience: "Had you not better ask Mrs. Montgomery herself?" she inquired.

"Perhaps I may come to that," said the Doctor. "Did you say the Second Avenue?" He made a note of the Second Avenue.

VII

He was, however, by no means so much in earnest as this might seem to indicate; and, indeed, he was more than anything else amused with the whole situation. He was not in the least in a state of tension or of vigilance with regard to Catherine's prospects; he was even on his guard against the ridicule that might attach itself to the spectacle of a house thrown into agitation by its daughter and heiress receiving attentions unprecedented in its annals. More than this, he went so far as to promise himself some entertainment from the little drama — if drama it was — of which Mrs. Penniman desired to represent the ingenious Mr. Townsend as the hero. He had no intention, as yet, of regulating the *dénouement*. He was perfectly willing, as Elizabeth had suggested, to give the young man the benefit of every doubt. There was no great danger in it; for Catherine, at the age of twenty-two, was, after all, a rather mature blossom, such as could be plucked from the stem only by a vigorous jerk. The fact that Morris Townsend was poor — was not of necessity against him; the Doctor had never made up his mind that his daughter should marry a rich man. The fortune she would inherit struck him as a very sufficient provision for two reasonable persons, and if a penniless swain who could give a good account of himself should enter the lists, he should be judged quite upon his personal merits. There were other things besides. The Doctor thought it very vulgar to be precipitate in accusing people of mercenary motives, inasmuch as his door had as yet not been in the least besieged by fortune-hunters; and, lastly, he was very curious to see whether Catherine might really be loved for her moral worth. He smiled as he reflected that poor Mr. Townsend had been only twice to the house, and he said to Mrs. Penniman that the next time he should come she must ask him to dinner.

He came very soon again, and Mrs. Penniman had of course great pleasure in executing this mission. Morris Townsend accepted her invitation with equal good grace, and the dinner took place a few days later. The Doc-tor had said to himself, justly enough, that they must not have the young man alone; this would partake too much of the nature of encouragement. So two or three other persons were invited; but Morris Townsend, though he was by no means the ostensible, was the real, occasion of the feast. There is every reason to suppose that he desired to make a good impression; and if he fell short of this result, it was not for want of a good deal of intelligent effort. The Doctor talked to him very little during dinner; but he observed him attentively, and after the ladies had gone out he pushed him the wine and asked him several questions. Morris was not a young man who needed to be pressed, and he found quite enough encouragement in the superior quality of the claret. The Doctor's wine was admirable, and it may be communicated to the reader that while he sipped it Morris reflected that a cellar-full of good liquor — there was evidently a cellar-full here — would be a most attractive idiosyncrasy in a father-in-law. The Doctor was struck with his appreciative guest; he saw that he was not a common-place young man. "He has ability," said Catherine's father, "decided ability; he has a very good head if he chooses to use it. And he is uncommonly well turned out; quite the sort of figure that pleases the ladies. But I don't think I like him." The Doctor, however, kept his reflexions to himself, and talked to his visitors about foreign lands, concerning which Morris offered him more information than he was ready, as he mentally phrased it, to swallow. Dr. Sloper had travelled but little, and he took the liberty of not believing everything this anecdotical idler narrated. He prided himself on being something of a physiognomist, and while the young man, chatting with easy assurance, puffed his cigar and filled his glass again, the Doctor sat with his eyes quietly fixed on his bright, expressive face. "He has the assurance of the devil himself," said Morris's host; "I don't think I ever saw such assurance. And his powers of invention are most remarkable. He is very knowing; they were not so knowing as that in my time. And a good head, did I say? I should think so — after a bottle of Madeira and a bottle and a half of claret!"

After dinner Morris Townsend went and stood before Catherine, who was standing before the fire in her red satin gown.

"He doesn't like me — he doesn't like me at all!" said the young man.

"Who doesn't like you?" asked Catherine.

"Your father; extraordinary man!"

"I don't see how you know," said Catherine, blushing.

"I feel; I am very quick to feel."

"Perhaps you are mistaken."

"Ah, well; you ask him and you will see."

"I would rather not ask him, if there is any danger of his saying what you think."

Morris looked at her with an air of mock melancholy.

"It wouldn't give you any pleasure to contradict him?"

"I never contradict him," said Catherine.

"Will you hear me abused without opening your lips in my defence?"

"My father won't abuse you. He doesn't know you enough."

Morris Townsend gave a loud laugh, and Catherine began to blush again.

"I shall never mention you," she said, to take refuge from her confusion.

"That is very well; but it is not quite what I should have liked you to say. I should have liked you to say: 'If my father doesn't think well of you, what does it matter?'"

"Ah, but it would matter; I couldn't say that!" the girl exclaimed.

He looked at her for a moment, smiling a little; and the Doctor, if he had been watching him just then, would have seen a gleam of fine impatience in the sociable softness of his eye. But there was no impatience in his rejoinder — none, at least, save what was expressed in a little appealing sigh. "Ah, well, then, I must not give up the hope of bringing him round!"

He expressed it more frankly to Mrs. Penniman later in the evening. But before that he sang two or three songs at Catherine's timid request; not that he flattered himself that this would help to bring her father round. He had a sweet, light tenor voice, and when he had finished every one made some exclamation — every one, that is, save Catherine, who remained intensely silent. Mrs. Penniman declared that his manner of singing was "most artistic," and Dr. Sloper said it was "very taking — very taking indeed"; speaking loudly and distinctly, but with a certain dryness.

"He doesn't like me — he doesn't like me at all," said Morris Townsend, addressing the aunt in the same manner as he had done the niece. "He thinks I'm all wrong."

Unlike her niece, Mrs. Penniman asked for no explanation. She only smiled very sweetly, as if she understood everything; and, unlike Catherine too, she made no attempt to contradict him. "Pray, what does it matter?" she murmured softly.

"Ah, you say the right thing!" said Morris, greatly to the gratification of Mrs. Penniman, who prided herself on always saying the right thing.

The Doctor, the next time he saw his sister Elizabeth, let her know that he had made the acquaintance of Lavinia's *protégé*.

"Physically," he said, "he's uncommonly well set up. As an anatomist, it is really a pleasure to me to see such a beautiful structure; although, if people were all like him, I suppose there would be very little need for doctors."

"Don't you see anything in peo-ple but their bones?" Mrs. Almond rejoined. "What do you think of him as a father?"

"As a father? Thank Heaven I am not his father!"

"No; but you are Catherine's. Lavinia tells me she is in love."

"She must get over it. He is not a gentleman."

"Ah, take care! Remember that he is a branch of the Townsends."

"He is not what I call a gentleman. He has not the soul of one. He is extremely insinuating; but it's a vulgar nature. I saw through it in a minute. He is altogether too familiar — I hate familiarity. He is a plausible coxcomb."

"Ah, well," said Mrs. Almond; "if you make up your mind so easily, it's a great advantage."

"I don't make up my mind easily. What I tell you is the result of thirty years of observation; and in order to be able to form that judgement in a single evening, I have had to spend a lifetime in study."

"Very possibly you are right. But the thing is for Catherine to see it."

"I will present her with a pair of spectacles!" said the Doctor.

VIII

IF it were true that she was in love, she was certainly very quiet about it; but the Doctor was of course prepared to admit that her quietness might mean volumes.

She had told Morris Townsend that she would not mention him to her father, and she saw no reason to retract this vow of discretion. It was no more than decently civil, of course, that after having dined in Washington Square, Morris should call there again; and it was no more than natural that, having been kindly received on this occasion, he should continue to present himself. He had had plenty of leisure on his hands; and thirty years ago, in New York, a young man of leisure had reason to be thankful for aids to self-oblivion. Catherine said nothing to her father about these visits, though they had rapidly become the most important, the most absorbing thing in her life. The girl was very happy. She knew not as yet what would come of it; but the present had suddenly grown rich and solemn. If she had been told she was in love, she would have been a good deal surprised; for she had an idea that love was an eager and exacting passion, and her own heart was filled in these days with the impulse of self-effacement and sacrifice. Whenever Morris Townsend had left the house, her imagination projected itself, with all its strength, into the idea of his soon coming back; but if she had been told at such a moment that he would not return for a year, or even that he would never return, she would not have complained nor rebelled, but would have humbly accepted the decree, and sought for consolation in thinking over the times she had already seen him, the words he had spoken, the sound of his voice, of his tread, the expression of his face. Love demands certain things as a right; but Catherine had no sense of her rights; she had only a consciousness of immense and unexpected favours. Her very gratitude for these things had hushed itself; for it seemed to her that there would be something of impudence in making a festival of her secret. Her father suspected Morris Townsend's visits, and noted her reserve. She seemed to beg pardon for it; she looked at him constantly in silence, as if she meant to say that she said nothing because she was afraid of irritating him. But the poor girl's dumb eloquence irritated him more than anything else would have done, and he caught himself murmuring more than once that it was a grievous pity his only child was a simpleton. His murmurs, however, were inaudible; and for a while he said nothing to any one. He would have liked to know exactly how often young Townsend came; but he had determined to ask no questions of the girl herself — to say nothing more to her that would show that he watched her. The Doctor had a great idea of being largely just: he wished to leave his daughter her liberty, and interfere only when the danger should be proved. It was not in his manner to obtain information by indirect methods, and it never even occurred to him to question the servants. As for Lavinia, he hated to talk to her about the

Washington Square

matter; she annoyed him with her mock romanticism. But he had to come to this. Mrs. Penniman's convictions as regards the relations of her niece and the clever young visitor who saved appearances by coming ostensibly for both the ladies — Mrs. Penniman's convictions had passed into a riper and richer phase. There was to be no crudity in Mrs. Penniman's treatment of the situation; she had become as uncommunicative as Catherine herself. She was tasting of the sweets of concealment; she had taken up the line of mystery. "She would be enchanted to be able to prove to herself that she is persecuted," said the Doctor; and when at last he questioned her, he was sure she would contrive to extract from his words a pretext for this belief.

"Be so good as to let me know what is going on in the house," he said to her, in a tone which, under the circumstances, he himself deemed genial.

"Going on, Austin?" Mrs. Penniman exclaimed. "Why, I am sure I don't know! I believe that last night the old grey cat had kittens!"

"At her age?" said the Doctor. "The idea is startling — almost shocking. Be so good as to see that they are all drowned. But what else has happened?"

"Ah, the dear little kittens!" cried Mrs. Penniman. "I wouldn't have them drowned for the world!"

Her brother puffed his cigar a few moments in silence. "Your sympathy with kittens, Lavinia," he presently resumed, "arises from a feline element in your own character."

"Cats are very graceful, and very clean," said Mrs. Penniman, smiling.

"And very stealthy. You are the embodiment both of grace and of neatness; but you are wanting in frankness."

"You certainly are not, dear brother."

"I don't pretend to be graceful, though I try to be neat. Why haven't you let me know that Mr. Morris Townsend is coming to the house four times a week?"

Mrs. Penniman lifted her eyebrows. "Four times a week?"

"Five times, if you prefer it. I am away all day, and I see nothing. But when such things happen, you should let me know."

Mrs. Penniman, with her eyebrows still raised, reflected intently. "Dear Austin," she said at last, "I am incapable of betraying a confidence. I would rather suffer anything."

"Never fear; you shall not suffer. To whose confidence is it you allude? Has Catherine made you take a vow of eternal secrecy?"

"By no means. Catherine has not told me as much as she might. She has not been very trustful."

"It is the young man, then, who has made you his confidante? Allow me to say that it is extremely indiscreet of you to form secret alliances with young men. You don't know where they may lead you."

191

"I don't know what you mean by an alliance," said Mrs. Penniman. "I take a great interest in Mr. Townsend; I won't conceal that. But that's all."

"Under the circumstances, that is quite enough. What is the source of your interest in Mr. Townsend?"

"Why," said Mrs. Penniman, musing, and then breaking into her smile, "that he is so interesting!"

The Doctor felt that he had need of his patience. "And what makes him interesting? — his good looks?"

"His misfortunes, Austin."

"Ah, he has had misfortunes? That, of course, is always interesting. Are you at liberty to mention a few of Mr. Townsend's?"

"I don't know that he would like it," said Mrs. Penniman. "He has told me a great deal about himself — he has told me, in fact, his whole history. But I don't think I ought to repeat those things. He would tell them to you, I am sure, if he thought you would listen to him kindly. With kindness you may do anything with him."

The Doctor gave a laugh. "I shall request him very kindly, then, to leave Catherine alone."

"Ah!" said Mrs. Penniman, shaking her forefinger at her brother, with her little finger turned out, "Catherine had probably said something to him kinder than that."

"Said that she loved him? Do you mean that?"

Mrs. Penniman fixed her eyes on the floor. "As I tell you, Austin, she doesn't confide in me."

"You have an opinion, I suppose, all the same. It is that I ask you for; though I don't conceal from you that I shall not regard it as conclusive."

Mrs. Penniman's gaze continued to rest on the carpet; but at last she lifted it, and then her brother thought it very expressive. "I think Catherine is very happy; that is all I can say."

"Townsend is trying to marry her — is that what you mean?"

"He is greatly interested in her."

"He finds her such an attractive girl?"

"Catherine has a lovely nature, Austin," said Mrs. Penniman, "and Mr. Townsend has had the intelligence to discover that."

"With a little help from you, I suppose. My dear Lavinia," cried the Doctor, "you are an admirable aunt!"

"So Mr. Townsend says," observed Lavinia, smiling.

"Do you think he is sincere?" asked her brother.

"In saying that?"

"No; that's of course. But in his admiration for Catherine?"

"Deeply sincere. He has said to me the most appreciative, the most charming things about her. He would say them to you, if he were sure you would listen to him — gently."

"I doubt whether I can undertake it. He appears to require a great deal of gentleness."

"He is a sympathetic, sensitive nature," said Mrs. Penniman.

Her brother puffed his cigar again in silence. "These delicate qualities have survived his vicissitudes, eh? All this while you haven't told me about his misfortunes."

"It is a long story," said Mrs. Penniman, "and I regard it as a sacred trust. But I suppose there is no objection to my saying that he has been wild — he frankly confesses that. But he has paid for it."

"That's what has impoverished him, eh?"

"I don't mean simply in money. He is very much alone in the world."

"Do you mean that he has behaved so badly that his friends have given him up?"

"He has had false friends, who have deceived and betrayed him."

"He seems to have some good ones too. He has a devoted sister, and half-a-dozen nephews and nieces."

Mrs. Penniman was silent a minute. "The nephews and nieces are children, and the sister is not a very attractive person."

"I hope he doesn't abuse her to you," said the Doctor; "for I am told he lives upon her."

"Lives upon her?"

"Lives with her, and does nothing for himself; it is about the same thing."

"He is looking for a position — most earnestly," said Mrs. Penniman. "He hopes every day to find one."

"Precisely. He is looking for it here — over there in the front parlour. The position of husband of a weak-minded woman with a large fortune would suit him to perfection!"

Mrs. Penniman was truly amiable, but she now gave signs of temper. She rose with much animation, and stood for a moment looking at her brother. "My dear Austin," she remarked, "if you regard Catherine as a weak-minded woman, you are particularly mistaken!" And with this she moved majestically away.

IX

IT was a regular custom with the family in Washington Square to go and spend Sunday evening at Mrs. Almond's. On the Sunday after the conversation I have just narrated, this custom was not intermitted; and on this occasion, towards the middle of the evening, Dr. Sloper found reason to withdraw to the library, with his brother-in-law, to talk over a matter of business. He was absent some twenty minutes, and when he came back into the circle, which was enlivened by the presence of several friends of the family, he saw that Morris Townsend had come in and had lost as little time as possible in seating himself on a small sofa, beside Catherine. In the large room, where several different groups had been formed, and the hum of voices and of laughter was loud, these two young persons might confabulate, as the Doctor phrased it to himself, without attracting attention. He saw in a moment, however, that his daughter was painfully conscious of his own observation. She sat motionless, with her eyes bent down, staring at her open fan, deeply flushed, shrinking together as if to minimise the indiscretion of which she confessed herself guilty.

The Doctor almost pitied her. Poor Catherine was not defiant; she had no genius for bravado; and as she felt that her father viewed her companion's attentions with an unsympathising eye, there was nothing but discomfort for her in the accident of seeming to challenge him. The Doctor felt, indeed, so sorry for her that he turned away, to spare her the sense of being watched; and he was so intelligent a man that, in his thoughts, he rendered a sort of poetic justice to her situation.

"It must be deucedly pleasant for a plain inanimate girl like that to have a beautiful young fellow come and sit down beside her and whisper to her that he is her slave — if that is what this one whispers. No wonder she likes it, and that she thinks me a cruel tyrant; which of course she does, though she is afraid — she hasn't the animation necessary — to admit it to herself. Poor old Catherine!" mused the Doctor; "I verily believe she is capable of defending me when Townsend abuses me!"

And the force of this reflexion, for the moment, was such in making him feel the natural opposition between his point of view and that of an infatuated child, that he said to himself that he was perhaps, after all, taking things too hard and crying out before he was hurt. He must not condemn Morris Townsend unheard. He had a great aversion to taking things too hard; he thought that half the discomfort and many of the disappointments of life come from it; and for an instant he asked himself whether, possibly, he did not appear ridiculous to this intelligent young man, whose private perception of incongruities he suspected of being keen. At the end of a quarter of an hour Catherine had got rid of him, and Townsend was now standing before the fireplace in conversation with Mrs. Almond.

"We will try him again," said the Doctor. And he crossed the room and joined his sister and her companion, making her a sign that she should leave the young man to him. She presently did so, while Morris looked at him, smiling, without a sign of evasiveness in his affable eye.

"He's amazingly conceited!" thought the Doctor, and then he said aloud: "I am told you are looking out for a position."

"Oh, a position is more than I should presume to call it," Morris Townsend answered. "That sounds so fine. I should like some quiet work — something to turn an honest penny."

"What sort of thing should you prefer?"

Washington Square

"Do you mean what am I fit for? Very little, I am afraid. I have nothing but my good right arm, as they say in the melodramas."

"You are too modest," said the Doctor. "In addition to your good right arm, you have your subtle brain. I know nothing of you but what I see; but I see by your physiognomy that you are extremely intelligent."

"Ah," Townsend murmured, "I don't know what to answer when you say that! You advise me, then, not to despair?"

And he looked at his interlocutor as if the question might have a double meaning. The Doctor caught the look and weighed it a moment before he replied. "I should be very sorry to admit that a robust and well-disposed young man need ever despair. If he doesn't succeed in one thing, he can try another. Only, I should add, he should choose his line with discretion."

"Ah, yes, with discretion," Morris Townsend repeated sympathetically. "Well, I have been indiscreet, formerly; but I think I have got over it. I am very steady now." And he stood a moment, looking down at his remarkably neat shoes. Then at last, "Were you kindly intending to propose something for my advantage?" he inquired, looking up and smiling.

"Damn his impudence!" the Doctor exclaimed privately. But in a moment he reflected that he himself had, after all, touched first upon this delicate point, and that his words might have been construed as an offer of assistance. "I have no particular proposal to make," he presently said; "but it occurred to me to let you know that I have you in my mind. Sometimes one hears of opportunities. For instance — should you object to leaving New York — to going to a distance?"

"I am afraid I shouldn't be able to manage that. I must seek my fortune here or nowhere. You see," added Morris Townsend, "I have ties — I have responsibilities here. I have a sister, a widow, from whom I have been separated for a long time, and to whom I am almost everything. I shouldn't like to say to her that I must leave her. She rather depends upon me, you see."

"Ah, that's very proper; family feeling is very proper," said Dr. Sloper. "I often think there is not enough of it in our city. I think I have heard of your sister."

"It is possible, but I rather doubt it; she lives so very quietly."

"As quietly, you mean," the Doctor went on, with a short laugh, "as a lady may do who has several young children."

"Ah, my little nephews and nieces — that's the very point! I am helping to bring them up," said Morris Townsend. "I am a kind of amateur tutor; I give them lessons."

"That's very proper, as I say; but it is hardly a career."

"It won't make my fortune!" the young man confessed.

"You must not be too much

195

bent on a fortune," said the Doctor. "But I assure you I will keep you in mind; I won't lose sight of you!"

"If my situation becomes desperate I shall perhaps take the liberty of reminding you!" Morris rejoined, raising his voice a little, with a brighter smile, as his interlocutor turned away.

Before he left the house the Doctor had a few words with Mrs. Almond.

"I should like to see his sister," he said. "What do you call her? Mrs. Montgomery. I should like to have a little talk with her."

"I will try and manage it," Mrs. Almond responded. "I will take the first opportunity of inviting her, and you shall come and meet her. Unless, indeed," Mrs. Almond added, "she first takes it into her head to be sick and to send for you."

"Ah no, not that; she must have trouble enough without that. But it would have its advantages, for then I should see the children. I should like very much to see the children."

"You are very thorough. Do you want to catechise them about their uncle!"

"Precisely. Their uncle tells me he has charge of their education, that he saves their mother the expense of school-bills. I should like to ask them a few questions in the commoner branches."

"He certainly has not the cut of a schoolmaster!" Mrs. Almond said to herself a short time afterwards, as she saw Morris Townsend in a corner bending over her niece, who was seated.

And there was, indeed, nothing in the young man's discourse at this moment that savoured of the pedagogue.

"Will you meet me somewhere to-morrow or next day?" he said, in a low tone, to Catherine.

"Meet you?" she asked, lifting her frightened eyes.

"I have something particular to say to you — very particular."

"Can't you come to the house? Can't you say it there?"

Townsend shook his head gloomily. "I can't enter your doors again!"

"Oh, Mr. Townsend!" murmured Catherine. She trembled as she wondered what had happened, whether her father had forbidden it.

"I can't in self-respect," said the young man. "Your father has insulted me."

"Insulted you!"

"He has taunted me with my poverty."

"Oh, you are mistaken — you misunderstood him!" Catherine spoke with energy, getting up from her chair.

"Perhaps I am too proud — too sensitive. But would you have me otherwise?" he asked tenderly.

"Where my father is concerned, you must not be sure. He is full of goodness," said Catherine.

"He laughed at me for having no position! I took it quietly; but only because he belongs to you."

"I don't know," said Catherine; "I don't know what he thinks. I

196

am sure he means to be kind. You must not be too proud."

"I will be proud only of you," Morris answered. "Will you meet me in the Square in the afternoon?"

A great blush on Catherine's part had been the answer to the declaration I have just quoted. She turned away, heedless of his question.

"Will you meet me?" he repeated. "It is very quiet there; no one need see us — toward dusk?"

"It is you who are unkind, it is you who laugh, when you say such things as that."

"My dear girl!" the young man murmured.

"You know how little there is in me to be proud of. I am ugly and stupid."

Morris greeted this remark with an ardent murmur, in which she recognised nothing articulate but an assurance that she was his own dearest.

But she went on. "I am not even — I am not even —— " And she paused a moment.

"You are not what?"

"I am not even brave."

"Ah, then, if you are afraid, what shall we do?"

She hesitated a while; then at last — "You must come to the house," she said; "I am not afraid of that."

"I would rather it were in the Square," the young man urged. "You know how empty it is, often. No one will see us."

"I don't care who sees us! But leave me now."

He left her resignedly; he had got what he wanted. Fortunately he was ignorant that half an hour later, going home with her father and feeling him near, the poor girl, in spite of her sudden declaration of courage, began to tremble again. Her father said nothing; but she had an idea his eyes were fixed upon her in the darkness. Mrs. Penniman also was silent; Morris Townsend had told her that her niece preferred, unromantically, an interview in a chintz-covered parlour to a sentimental tryst beside a fountain sheeted with dead leaves, and she was lost in wonderment at the oddity — almost the perversity — of the choice.

X

CATHERINE received the young man the next day on the ground she had chosen — amid the chaste upholstery of a New York drawing-room furnished in the fashion of fifty years ago. Morris had swallowed his pride and made the effort necessary to cross the threshold of her too derisive parent — an act of magnanimity which could not fail to render him doubly interesting.

"We must settle something — we must take a line," he declared, passing his hand through his hair and giving a glance at the long narrow mirror which adorned the space between the two windows, and which had at its base a little gilded bracket covered by a thin slab of white marble, supporting in its turn a backgammon board folded together in the shape of two volumes, two shining folios inscribed in letters of greenish gilt, *History of England*. If Morris had been pleased to describe the master of the house as a heartless scoffer, it is because he thought him too much on his guard, and this was the easiest way to express his own dissatisfaction — a dissatisfaction which he had made a point of concealing from the Doctor. It will probably seem to the reader, however, that the Doctor's vigilance was by no means excessive, and that these two young people had an open field. Their intimacy was now considerable, and it may appear that for a shrinking and retiring person our heroine had been liberal of her favours. The young man, within a few days, had made her listen to things for which she had not supposed that she was prepared; having a lively foreboding of difficulties, he proceeded to gain as much ground as possible in the present. He remembered that fortune favours the brave, and even if he had forgotten it, Mrs. Penniman would have remembered it for him. Mrs. Penniman delighted of all things in a drama, and she flattered herself that a drama would now be enacted. Combining as she did the zeal of the prompter with the impatience of the spectator, she had long since done her utmost to pull up the curtain. She too expected to figure in the performance — to be the confidante, the Chorus, to speak the epilogue. It may even be said that there were times when she lost sight altogether of the modest heroine of the play, in the contemplation of certain great passages which would naturally occur between the hero and herself.

What Morris had told Catherine at last was simply that he loved her, or rather adored her. Virtually, he had made known as much already — his visits had been a series of eloquent intimations of it. But now he had affirmed it in lover's vows, and, as a memorable sign of it, he had passed his arm round the girl's waist and taken a kiss. This happy certitude had come sooner than Catherine expected, and she had regarded it, very naturally, as a priceless treasure. It may even be doubted whether she had ever definitely expected to possess it; she had not been waiting for it, and she had never said to herself that at a given moment it must come. As I have tried to explain, she was not eager and exacting; she took what was given her from day to day; and if the delightful custom of her lover's visits, which yielded her a happiness in which confidence and timidity were strangely blended, had suddenly come to an end, she would not only not have spoken of herself as one of the forsaken, but she would not have thought of herself as one of the disappointed. After Morris had kissed her, the last time he was with her, as a ripe assurance of his devotion, she begged him to go away, to leave her alone, to let her think. Morris went away, taking another kiss first. But Catherine's meditations had lacked a certain coherence. She felt his kisses on her lips and on her cheeks for a long time afterwards; the sensation was rather an obstacle than an aid to reflexion. She would have liked to see her situation all clearly before her, to make up her mind what she should do if, as she feared, her father should tell her that he disapproved of Morris Townsend. But all that she could see with any vividness was that it was terribly strange that any one should disapprove of him; that there must in that case be some mistake, some mystery, which in a little while would be set at rest. She put off deciding and choosing; before the vision of a conflict with her father she dropped her eyes and sat motionless, holding her breath and waiting. It made her heart beat, it was intensely painful. When Morris kissed her and said these things — that also made her heart beat; but this was worse, and it frightened her. Nevertheless, to-day, when the young man spoke of settling something, taking a line, she felt that it was the truth, and she answered very simply and without hesitating.

"We must do our duty," she said; "we must speak to my father. I will do it to-night; you must do it to-morrow."

"It is very good of you to do it first," Morris answered. "The young man — the happy lover — generally does that. But just as you please!"

It pleased Catherine to think that she should be brave for his sake, and in her satisfaction she even gave a little smile. "Women have more tact," she said; "they ought to do it first. They are more conciliating; they can persuade better."

"You will need all your powers of persuasion. But, after all," Morris added, "you are irresistible."

"Please don't speak that way — and promise me this. To-morrow, when you talk with father, you will be very gentle and respectful."

"As much so as possible," Morris promised. "It won't be much use, but I shall try. I certainly would rather have you easily than have to fight for you."

"Don't talk about fighting; we shall not fight."

"Ah, we must be prepared," Morris rejoined; "you especially, because for you it must come hardest. Do you know the first thing your father will say to you?"

"No, Morris; please tell me."

"He will tell you I am mercenary."

"Mercenary?"

"It's a big word; but it means a low thing. It means that I am after your money."

"Oh!" murmured Catherine softly.

The exclamation was so deprecating and touching that Morris indulged in another little demonstration of affection. "But he will be sure to say it," he added.

"It will be easy to be prepared for that," Catherine said. "I shall simply say that he is mistaken — that other men may be that way, but that you are not."

"You must make a great point of that, for it will be his own great point."

Catherine looked at her lover a minute, and then she said, "I shall persuade him. But I am glad we shall be rich," she added.

Morris turned away, looking into the crown of his hat. "No, it's a misfortune," he said at last. "It is from that our difficulty will come."

"Well, if it is the worst misfortune, we are not so unhappy. Many people would not think it so bad. I will persuade him, and after that we shall be very glad we have money."

Morris Townsend listened to this robust logic in silence. "I will leave my defence to you; it's a charge that a man has to stoop to defend himself from."

Catherine on her side was silent for a while; she was looking at him while he looked, with a good deal of fixedness, out of the window. "Morris," she said abruptly, "are you very sure you love me?"

He turned round, and in a moment he was bending over her. "My own dearest, can you doubt it?"

"I have only known it five days," she said; "but now it seems to me as if I could never do without it."

"You will never be called upon to try!" And he gave a little tender, reassuring laugh. Then, in a moment, he added, "There is something you must tell me, too." She had closed her eyes after the last word she uttered, and kept them closed; and at this she nodded her head, without opening them. "You must tell me," he went on, "that if your father is dead against me, if he absolutely forbids our marriage, you will still be faithful."

Catherine opened her eyes, gazing at him, and she could give no better promise than what he read there.

"You will cleave to me?" said Morris. "You know you are your own mistress — you are of age."

"Ah, Morris!" she murmured, for all answer. Or rather not for all; for she put her hand into his own. He kept it a while, and presently he kissed her again. This is all that need be recorded of their conversation; but Mrs. Penniman, if she had been present, would probably have admitted that it was as well it had not taken place beside the fountain in Washington Square.

XI

CATHERINE listened for her father when he came in that evening, and she heard him go to his study. She sat quiet, though her heart was beating fast, for nearly half an hour; then she went and knocked at his door — a ceremony without which she never crossed the threshold of this apartment. On entering it now she found him in his chair beside the fire, entertaining himself with a cigar and the evening paper.

"I have something to say to you," she began very gently; and she sat down in the first place that offered.

"I shall be very happy to hear it, my dear," said her father. He waited — waited, looking at her, while she stared, in a long silence, at the fire. He was curious and impatient, for he was sure she was going to speak of Morris Townsend; but he let her take her own time, for he was determined to be very mild.

"I am engaged to be married!" Catherine announced at last, still staring at the fire.

The Doctor was startled; the accomplished fact was more than he had expected. But he betrayed no surprise. "You do right to tell me," he simply said. "And who is the happy mortal whom you have honoured with your choice?"

"Mr. Morris Townsend." And as she pronounced her lover's name, Catherine looked at him. What she saw was her father's still grey eye and his clear-cut, definite smile. She contemplated these objects for a moment, and then she looked back at the fire; it was much warmer.

"When was this arrangement made?" the Doctor asked.

"This afternoon — two hours ago."

"Was Mr. Townsend here?"

"Yes, father; in the front parlour." She was very glad that she was not obliged to tell him that the ceremony of their betrothal had taken place out there under the bare ailantus-trees.

"Is it serious?" said the Doctor.

"Very serious, father."

Her father was silent a moment. "Mr. Townsend ought to have told me."

"He means to tell you to-morrow."

"After I know all about it from you? He ought to have told me before. Does he think I didn't care — because I left you so much liberty?"

"Oh no," said Catherine; "he knew you would care. And we have been so much obliged to you for — for the liberty."

The Doctor gave a short laugh. "You might have made a better use of it, Catherine."

"Please don't say that, father," the girl urged softly, fixing her dull and gentle eyes upon him.

He puffed his cigar awhile, meditatively. "You have gone very fast," he said at last.

"Yes," Catherine answered simply; "I think we have."

Her father glanced at her an instant, removing his eyes from the fire. "I don't wonder Mr. Townsend likes you. You are so simple and so good."

"I don't know why it is — but he *does* like me. I am sure of that."

"And are you very fond of Mr. Townsend?"

"I like him very much, of course

— or I shouldn't consent to marry him."

"But you have known him a very short time, my dear."

"Oh," said Catherine, with some eagerness, "it doesn't take long to like a person — when once you begin."

"You must have begun very quickly. Was it the first time you saw him — that night at your aunt's party?"

"I don't know, father," the girl answered. "I can't tell you about that."

"Of course; that's your own affair. You will have observed that I have acted on that principle. I have not interfered, I have left you your liberty, I have remembered that you are no longer a little girl — that you have arrived at years of discretion."

"I feel very old — and very wise," said Catherine, smiling faintly.

"I am afraid that before long you will feel older and wiser yet. I don't like your engagement."

"Ah!" Catherine exclaimed softly, getting up from her chair.

"No, my dear. I am sorry to give you pain; but I don't like it. You should have consulted me before you settled it. I have been too easy with you, and I feel as if you had taken advantage of my indulgence. Most decidedly, you should have spoken to me first."

Catherine hesitated a moment, and then — "It was because I was afraid you wouldn't like it!" she confessed.

"Ah, there it is! You had a bad conscience."

"No, I have not a bad conscience, father!" the girl cried out, with considerable energy. "Please don't accuse me of anything so dreadful." These words, in fact, represented to her imagination something very terrible indeed, something base and cruel, which she associated with malefactors and prisoners. "It was because I was afraid — afraid —— " she went on.

"If you were afraid, it was because you had been foolish!"

"I was afraid you didn't like Mr. Townsend."

"You were quite right. I don't like him."

"Dear father, you don't know him," said Catherine, in a voice so timidly argumentative that it might have touched him.

"Very true; I don't know him intimately. But I know him enough. I have my impression of him. You don't know him either."

She stood before the fire, with her hands lightly clasped in front of her; and her father, leaning back in his chair and looking up at her, made this remark with a placidity that might have been irritating.

I doubt, however, whether Catherine was irritated, though she broke into a vehement protest. "I don't know him?" she cried. "Why, I know him — better than I have ever known any one!"

"You know a part of him — what he has chosen to show you. But you don't know the rest."

"The rest? What is the rest?"

"Whatever it may be. There is sure to be plenty of it."

"I know what you mean," said Catherine, remembering how Morris had forewarned her. "You mean that he is mercenary."

Her father looked up at her still, with his cold, quiet reasonable eye. "If I meant it, my dear, I should say it! But there is an error I wish particularly to avoid — that of rendering Mr. Townsend more interesting to you by saying hard things about him."

"I won't think them hard if they are true," said Catherine.

"If you don't, you will be a remarkably sensible young woman!"

"They will be your reasons, at any rate, and you will want me to hear your reasons."

The Doctor smiled a little. "Very true. You have a perfect right to ask for them." And he puffed his cigar a few moments. "Very well, then, without accusing Mr. Townsend of being in love only with your fortune — and with the fortune that you justly expect — I will say that there is every reason to suppose that these good things have entered into his calculation more largely than a tender solicitude for your happiness strictly requires. There is, of course, nothing impossible in an intelligent young man entertaining a disinterested affection for you. You are an honest, amiable girl, and an intelligent young man might easily find it out. But the principal thing that we know about this young man — who is, indeed, very intelligent — leads us to suppose that, however much he may value your personal merits, he values your money more. The princi-

pal thing we know about him is that he has led a life of dissipation, and has spent a fortune of his own in doing so. That is enough for me, my dear. I wish you to marry a young man with other antecedents — a young man who could give positive guarantees. If Morris Townsend has spent his own fortune in amusing himself, there is every reason to believe that he would spend yours."

The Doctor delivered himself of these remarks slowly, deliberately, with occasional pauses and prolongations of accent, which made no great allowance for poor Catherine's suspense as to his conclusion. She sat down at last, with her head bent and her eyes still fixed upon him; and strangely enough — I hardly know how to tell it — even while she felt that what he said went so terribly against her, she admired his neatness and nobleness of expression. There was something hopeless and oppressive in having to argue with her father; but she too, on her side, must try to be clear. He was so quiet; he was not at all angry; and she too must be quiet. But her very effort to be quiet made her tremble.

"That is not the principal thing we know about him," she said; and there was a touch of her tremor in her voice. "There are other things — many other things. He has very high abilities — he wants so much to do something. He is kind, and generous, and true," said poor Catherine, who had not suspected hitherto the resources of her eloquence. "And his fortune — his fortune that he spent — was very small!"

"All the more reason he shouldn't have spent it," cried the Doctor, getting up, with a laugh. Then as Catherine, who had also risen to her feet again, stood there in her rather angular earnestness, wishing so much and expressing so little, he drew her towards him and kissed her. "You won't think me cruel?" he said, holding her a moment.

This question was not reassuring; it seemed to Catherine, on the contrary, to suggest possibilities which made her feel sick. But she answered coherently enough — "No, dear father; because if you knew how I feel — and you must know, you know everything — you would be so kind, so gentle."

"Yes, I think I know how you feel," the Doctor said. "I will be very kind — be sure of that. And I will see Mr. Townsend to-morrow. Meanwhile, and for the present, be so good as to mention to no one that you are engaged."

XII

On the morrow, in the afternoon, he stayed at home, awaiting Mr. Townsend's call — a proceeding by which it appeared to him (justly perhaps, for he was a very busy man) that he paid Catherine's suitor great honour, and gave both these young people so much the less to complain of. Morris pre-sented himself with a countenance sufficiently serene — he appeared to have forgotten the "insult" for which he had solicited Catherine's sympathy two evenings before, and Dr. Sloper lost no time in letting him know that he had been prepared for his visit.

"Catherine told me yesterday what has been going on between you," he said. "You must allow me to say that it would have been becoming of you to give me notice of your intentions before they had gone so far."

"I should have done so," Morris answered, "if you had not had so much the appearance of leaving your daughter at liberty. She seems to me quite her own mistress."

"Literally, she is. But she has not emancipated herself morally quite so far, I trust, as to choose a husband without consulting me. I have left her at liberty, but I have not been in the least indifferent. The truth is that your little affair has come to a head with a rapidity that surprises me. It was only the other day that Catherine made your acquaintance."

"It was not long ago, certainly," said Morris, with great gravity. "I admit that we have not been slow to — to arrive at an understanding. But that was very natural, from the moment we were sure of ourselves — and of each other. My interest in Miss Sloper began the first time I saw her."

"Did it not by chance precede your first meeting?" the Doctor asked.

Morris looked at him an instant.

"I certainly had already heard that she was a charming girl."

"A charming girl — that's what you think her?"

"Assuredly. Otherwise I should not be sitting here."

The Doctor meditated a moment. "My dear young man," he said at last, "you must be very susceptible. As Catherine's father, I have, I trust, a just and tender appreciation of her many good qualities; but I don't mind telling you that I have never thought of her as a charming girl, and never expected any one else to do so."

Morris Townsend received this statement with a smile that was not wholly devoid of deference. "I don't know what I might think of her if I were her father. I can't put myself in that place. I speak from my own point of view."

"You speak very well," said the Doctor; "but that is not all that is necessary. I told Catherine yesterday that I disapproved of her engagement."

"She let me know as much, and I was very sorry to hear it. I am greatly disappointed." And Morris sat in silence awhile, looking at the floor.

"Did you really expect I would say I was delighted, and throw my daughter into your arms?"

"Oh no; I had an idea you didn't like me."

"What gave you the idea?"

"The fact that I am poor."

"That has a harsh sound," said the Doctor, "but it is about the truth — speaking of you strictly as a son-in-law. Your absence of means, of a profession, of visible resources or prospects, places you in a category from which it would be imprudent for me to select a husband for my daughter, who is a weak young woman with a large fortune. In any other capacity I am perfectly prepared to like you. As a son-in-law, I abominate you!"

Morris Townsend listened respectfully. "I don't think Miss Sloper is a weak woman," he presently said.

"Of course you must defend her — it's the least you can do. But I have known my child twenty years, and you have known her six weeks. Even if she were not weak, however, you would still be a penniless man."

"Ah, yes; that is *my* weakness! And therefore, you mean, I am mercenary — I only want your daughter's money."

"I don't say that. I am not obliged to say it; and to say it, save under stress of compulsion, would be very bad taste. I say simply that you belong to the wrong category."

"But your daughter doesn't marry a category," Townsend urged, with his handsome smile. "She marries an individual — an individual whom she is so good as to say she loves."

"An individual who offers so little in return!"

"Is it possible to offer more than the most tender affection and a lifelong devotion?" the young man demanded.

"It depends how we take it. It is possible to offer a few other things besides; and not only is it possible, but it's usual. A lifelong devotion is measured after the fact; and meanwhile it is customary in these cases to give a few material securities. What are yours? A very handsome face and figure, and a very good manner. They are excellent as far as they go, but they don't go far enough."

"There is one thing you should add to them," said Morris; "the word of a gentleman!"

"The word of a gentleman that you will always love Catherine? You must be a very fine gentleman to be sure of that."

"The word of a gentleman that I am not mercenary; that my affection for Miss Sloper is as pure and disinterested a sentiment as was ever lodged in a human breast! I care no more for her fortune than for the ashes in that grate."

"I take note — I take note," said the Doctor. "But having done so, I turn to our category again. Even with that solemn vow on your lips, you take your place in it. There is nothing against you but an accident, if you will; but with my thirty years' medical practice, I have seen that accidents may have far-reaching consequences."

Morris smoothed his hat — it was already remarkably glossy — and continued to display a self-control which, as the Doctor was obliged to admit, was extremely creditable to him. But his disappointment was evidently keen.

"Is there nothing I can do to make you believe in me?"

"If there were I should be sorry to suggest it, for — don't you see? — I don't want to believe in you!" said the Doctor, smiling.

"I would go and dig in the fields."

"That would be foolish."

"I will take the first work that offers, to-morrow."

"Do so by all means — but for your own sake, not for mine."

"I see; you think I am an idler!" Morris exclaimed, a little too much in the tone of a man who has made a discovery. But he saw his error immediately, and blushed.

"It doesn't matter what I think, when once I have told you I don't think of you as a son-in-law."

But Morris persisted. "You think I would squander her money."

The Doctor smiled. "It doesn't matter, as I say; but I plead guilty to that."

"That's because I spent my own, I suppose," said Morris. "I frankly confess that. I have been wild. I have been foolish. I will tell you every crazy thing I ever did, if you like. There were some great follies among the number — I have never concealed that. But I have sown my wild oats. Isn't there some proverb about a reformed rake? I was not a rake, but I assure you I have reformed. It is better to have amused oneself for a while and have done with it. Your daughter would never care for a milksop; and I will take the liberty of saying that you would like one quite as little. Besides, between my money and hers there is a great difference. I spent my own; it was because it was my own that

I spent it. And I made no debts; when it was gone I stopped. I don't owe a penny in the world."

"Allow me to inquire what you are living on now — though I admit," the Doctor added, "that the question, on my part, is inconsistent."

"I am living on the remnants of my property," said Morris Townsend.

"Thank you!" the Doctor gravely replied.

Yes, certainly, Morris's self-control was laudable. "Even admitting I attach an undue importance to Miss Sloper's fortune," he went on, "would not that be in itself an assurance that I should take much care of it?"

"That you should take too much care would be quite as bad as that you should take too little. Catherine might suffer as much by your economy as by your extravagance."

"I think you are very unjust!" The young man made this declaration decently, civilly, without violence.

"It is your privilege to think so, and I surrender my reputation to you! I certainly don't flatter myself I gratify you."

"Don't you care a little to gratify your daughter? Do you enjoy the idea of making her miserable?"

"I am perfectly resigned to her thinking me a tyrant for a twelvemonth."

"For a twelvemonth!" exclaimed Morris, with a laugh.

"For a lifetime, then! She may

as well be miserable in that way as in the other."

Here at last Morris lost his temper. "Ah, you are not polite, sir!" he cried.

"You push me to it — you argue too much."

"I have a great deal at stake."

"Well, whatever it is," said the Doctor, "you have lost it!"

"Are you sure of that?" asked Morris; "are you sure your daughter will give me up?"

"I mean, of course, you have lost it as far as I am concerned. As for Catherine's giving you up — no, I am not sure of it. But as I shall strongly recommend it, as I have a great fund of respect and affection in my daughter's mind to draw upon, and as she has the sentiment of duty developed in a very high degree, I think it extremely possible."

Morris Townsend began to smooth his hat again. "I too have a fund of affection to draw upon!" he observed at last.

The Doctor at this point showed his own first symptoms of irritation. "Do you mean to defy me?"

"Call it what you please, sir! I mean not to give your daughter up."

The Doctor shook his head. "I haven't the least fear of your pining away your life. You are made to enjoy it."

Morris gave a laugh. "Your opposition to my marriage is all the more cruel, then! Do you intend to forbid your daughter to see me again?"

"She is past the age at which people are forbidden, and I am not a father in an old-fashioned novel. But I shall strongly urge her to break with you."

"I don't think she will," said Morris Townsend.

"Perhaps not. But I shall have done what I could."

"She has gone too far," Morris went on.

"To retreat? Then let her stop where she is."

"Too far to stop, I mean."

The Doctor looked at him a moment; Morris had his hand on the door. "There is a great deal of impertinence in your saying it."

"I will say no more, sir!" Morris answered; and, making his bow, he left the room.

XIII

It may be thought the Doctor was too positive, and Mrs. Almond intimated as much. But, as he said, he had his impression; it seemed to him sufficient, and he had no wish to modify it. He had passed his life in estimating people (it was part of the medical trade), and in nineteen cases out of twenty he was right.

"Perhaps Mr. Townsend is the twentieth case," Mrs. Almond suggested.

"Perhaps he is, though he doesn't look to me at all like a twentieth case. But I will give him the benefit of the doubt, and, to make sure, I will go and talk with Mrs. Montgomery. She will almost certainly tell me I have done right; but it is just possible that she will prove to me that I have made the greatest mistake of my life. If she does, I will beg Mr. Townsend's pardon. You needn't invite her to meet me, as you kindly proposed; I will write her a frank letter, telling her how matters stand, and asking leave to come and see her."

"I am afraid the frankness will be chiefly on your side. The poor little woman will stand up for her brother, whatever he may be."

"Whatever he may be? I doubt that. People are not always so fond of their brothers."

"Ah," said Mrs. Almond, "when it's a question of thirty thousand a year coming into a family——"

"If she stands up for him on account of the money, she will be a humbug. If she is a humbug I shall see it. If I see it, I won't waste time with her."

"She is not a humbug—she is an exemplary woman. She will not wish to play her brother a trick simply because he is selfish."

"If she is worth talking to, she will sooner play him a trick than that he should play Catherine one. Has she seen Catherine, by the way —does she know her?"

"Not to my knowledge. Mr. Townsend can have had no particular interest in bringing them together."

"If she is an exemplary woman, no. But we shall see to what extent she answers your description."

"I shall be curious to hear her

description of you!" said Mrs. Almond, with a laugh. "And, meanwhile, how is Catherine taking it?"

"As she takes everything — as a matter of course."

"Doesn't she make a noise? Hasn't she made a scene?"

"She is not scenic."

"I thought a love-lorn maiden was always scenic."

"A fantastic widow is more so. Lavinia has made me a speech; she thinks me very arbitrary."

"She has a talent for being in the wrong," said Mrs. Almond. "But I am very sorry for Catherine, all the same."

"So am I. But she will get over it."

"You believe she will give him up?"

"I count upon it. She has such an admiration for her father."

"Oh, we know all about that! But it only makes me pity her the more. It makes her dilemma the more painful, and the effort of choosing between you and her lover almost impossible."

"If she can't choose, all the better."

"Yes, but he will stand there entreating her to choose, and Lavinia will pull on that side."

"I am glad she is not on my side; she is capable of ruining an excellent cause. The day Lavinia gets into your boat it capsizes. But she had better be careful," said the Doctor. "I will have no treason in my house!"

"I suspect she will be careful; for she is at bottom very much afraid of you."

"They are both afraid of me — harmless as I am!" the Doctor answered. "And it is on that that I build — on the salutary terror I inspire!"

XIV

HE wrote his frank letter to Mrs. Montgomery, who punctually answered it, mentioning an hour at which he might present himself in the Second Avenue. She lived in a neat little house of red brick, which had been freshly painted, with the edges of the bricks very sharply marked out in white. It has now disappeared, with its companions, to make room for a row of structures more majestic. There were green shutters upon the windows, without slats, but pierced with little holes, arranged in groups; and before the house was a diminutive yard, ornamented with a bush of mysterious character, and surrounded by a low wooden paling, painted in the same green as the shutters. The place looked like a magnified baby-house, and might have been taken down from a shelf in a toy-shop. Dr. Sloper, when he went to call, said to himself, as he glanced at the objects I have enumerated, that Mrs. Montgomery was evidently a thrifty and self-respecting little person — the modest proportions of her dwelling seemed to indicate that she was of small stature — who took a virtuous satisfaction in keeping herself tidy, and had resolved that, since she might not be splendid, she would at least be immaculate. She received him in a little parlour, which was precisely the parlour he had expected: a small unspeckled bower, ornamented with a desultory foliage of tissue-paper, and with clusters of glass drops, amid which — to carry out the analogy — the temperature of the leafy season was maintained by means of a cast-iron stove, emitting a dry blue flame, and smelling strongly of varnish. The walls were embellished with engravings swathed in pink gauze, and the tables ornamented with volumes of extracts from the poets, usually bound in black cloth stamped with florid designs in jaundiced gilt. The Doctor had time to take cognisance of these details, for Mrs. Montgomery, whose conduct he pronounced under the circumstances inexcusable, kept him waiting some ten minutes before she appeared. At last, however, she rustled in, smoothing down a stiff poplin dress, with a little frightened flush in a gracefully-rounded cheek.

She was a small, plump, fair woman, with a bright, clear eye, and an extraordinary air of neatness and briskness. But these qualities were evidently combined with an unaffected humility, and the Doctor gave her his esteem as soon as he had looked at her. A brave little person, with lively perceptions, and yet a disbelief in her own talent for social, as distinguished from practical, affairs —

this was his rapid mental *résumé* of Mrs. Montgomery, who, as he saw, was flattered by what she regarded as the honour of his visit. Mrs. Montgomery, in her little red house in the Second Avenue, was a person for whom Dr. Sloper was one of the great men, one of the fine gentlemen of New York; and while she fixed her agitated eyes upon him, while she clasped her mittened hands together in her glossy poplin lap, she had the appearance of saying to herself that he quite answered her idea of what a distinguished guest would naturally be. She apologised for being late; but he interrupted her.

"It doesn't matter," he said; "for while I sat here I had time to think over what I wish to say to you, and to make up my mind how to begin."

"Oh, do begin!" murmured Mrs. Montgomery.

"It is not so easy," said the Doctor, smiling. "You will have gathered from my letter that I wish to ask you a few questions, and you may not find it very comfortable to answer them."

"Yes; I have thought what I should say. It is not very easy."

"But you must understand my situation — my state of mind. Your brother wishes to marry my daughter, and I wish to find out what sort of a young man he is. A good way to do so seemed to be to come and ask you; which I have proceeded to do."

Mrs. Montgomery evidently took the situation very seriously; she was in a state of extreme moral concentration. She kept her pretty eyes, which were illumined by a sort of brilliant modesty, attached to his own countenance, and evidently paid the most earnest attention to each of his words. Her expression indicated that she thought his idea of coming to see her a very superior conception, but that she was really afraid to have opinions on strange subjects.

"I am extremely glad to see you," she said, in a tone which seemed to admit, at the same time, that this had nothing to do with the question.

The Doctor took advantage of this admission. "I didn't come to see you for your pleasure; I came to make you say disagreeable things — and you can't like that. What sort of a gentleman is your brother?"

Mrs. Montgomery's illuminated gaze grew vague, and began to wander. She smiled a little, and for some time made no answer, so that the Doctor at last became impatient. And her answer, when it came, was not satisfactory. "It is difficult to talk about one's brother."

"Not when one is fond of him, and when one has plenty of good to say."

"Yes, even then, when a good deal depends on it," said Mrs. Montgomery.

"Nothing depends on it, for you."

"I mean for — for —— " and she hesitated.

"For your brother himself. I see!"

"I mean for Miss Sloper," said Mrs. Montgomery.

The Doctor liked this; it had the accent of sincerity. "Exactly; that's the point. If my poor girl should marry your brother, everything — as regards her happiness — would depend on his being a good fellow. She is the best creature in the world, and she could never do him a grain of injury. He, on the other hand, if he should not be all that we desire, might make her very miserable. That is why I want you to throw some light upon his character, you know. Of course you are not bound to do it. My daughter, whom you have never seen, is nothing to you; and I, possibly, am only an indiscreet and impertinent old man. It is perfectly open to you to tell me that my visit is in very bad taste and that I had better go about my business. But I don't think you will do this; because I think we shall interest you, my poor girl and I. I am sure that if you were to see Catherine, she would interest you very much. I don't mean because she is interesting in the usual sense of the word, but because you would feel sorry for her. She is so soft, so simple-minded, she would be such an easy victim! A bad husband would have remarkable facilities for making her miserable; for she would have neither the intelligence nor the resolution to get the better of him, and yet she would have an exaggerated power of suffering. I see," added the Doctor, with his most insinuating, his most professional laugh, "you are already interested!"

"I have been interested from the moment he told me he was engaged," said Mrs. Montgomery.

"Ah! he says that — he calls it an engagement?"

"Oh, he has told me you didn't like it."

"Did he tell you that I don't like *him*?"

"Yes, he told me that too. I said I couldn't help it!" added Mrs. Montgomery.

"Of course you can't. But what you can do is to tell me I am right — to give me an attestation, as it were." And the Doctor accompanied this remark with another professional smile.

Mrs. Montgomery, however, smiled not at all; it was obvious that she could not take the humorous view of his appeal. "That is a good deal to ask," she said at last.

"There can be no doubt of that; and I must, in conscience, remind you of the advantages a young man marrying my daughter would enjoy. She has an income of ten thousand dollars in her own right, left her by her mother; if she marries a husband I approve, she will come into almost twice as much more at my death."

Mrs. Montgomery listened in great earnestness to this splendid financial statement; she had never heard thousands of dollars so familiarly talked about. She flushed a little with excitement. "Your daughter will be immensely rich," she said softly.

"Precisely — that's the bother of it."

"And if Morris should marry her, he — he —— " And she hesitated timidly.

"He would be master of all that money? By no means. He would be master of the ten thousand a year that she has from her mother; but I should leave every penny of my own fortune, earned in the laborious exercise of my profession, to public institutions."

Mrs. Montgomery dropped her eyes at this, and sat for some time gazing at the straw matting which covered her floor.

"I suppose it seems to you," said the Doctor, laughing, "that in so doing I should play your brother a very shabby trick."

"Not at all. That is too much money to get possession of so easily, by marrying. I don't think it would be right."

"It's right to get all one can. But in this case your brother wouldn't be able. If Catherine marries without my consent, she doesn't get a penny from my own pocket."

"Is that certain?" asked Mrs. Montgomery, looking up.

"As certain as that I sit here!"

"Even if she should pine away?"

"Even if she should pine to a shadow, which isn't probable."

"Does Morris know this?"

"I shall be most happy to inform him!" the Doctor exclaimed.

Mrs. Montgomery resumed her meditations, and her visitor, who was prepared to give time to the affair, asked himself whether, in spite of her little conscientious air, she was not playing into her brother's hands. At the same time he was half ashamed of the ordeal to which he had subjected her, and was touched by the gentleness with which she bore it. "If she were a humbug," he said, "she would get angry; unless she be very deep indeed. It is not probable that she is as deep as that."

"What makes you dislike Morris so much?" she presently asked, emerging from her reflexions.

"I don't dislike him in the least as a friend, as a companion. He seems to me a charming fellow, and I should think he would be excellent company. I dislike him, exclusively, as a son-in-law. If the only office of a son-in-law were to dine at the paternal table, I should set a high value upon your brother. He dines capitally. But that is a small part of his function, which, in general, is to be a protector and caretaker of my child, who is singularly ill-adapted to take care of herself. It is there that he doesn't satisfy me. I confess I have nothing but my impression to go by; but I am in the habit of trusting my impression. Of course you are at liberty to contradict it flat. He strikes me as selfish and shallow."

Mrs. Montgomery's eyes expanded a little, and the Doctor fancied he saw the light of admiration in them. "I wonder you have discovered he is selfish!" she exclaimed.

"Do you think he hides it so well?"

"Very well indeed," said Mrs. Montgomery. "And I think we are all rather selfish," she added quickly.

"I think so too; but I have seen people hide it better than he. You see I am helped by a habit I have of dividing people into classes, into types. I may easily be mistaken about your brother as an individual, but his type is written on his whole person."

"He is very good-looking," said Mrs. Montgomery.

The Doctor eyed her a moment. "You women are all the same! But the type to which your brother belongs was made to be the ruin of you, and you were made to be its handmaids and victims. The sign of the type in question is the determination — sometimes terrible in its quiet intensity — to accept nothing of life but its pleasures, and to secure these pleasures chiefly by the aid of your complaisant sex. Young men of this class never do anything for themselves that they can get other people to do for them, and it is the infatuation, the devotion, the superstition of others that keeps them going. These others in ninety-nine cases out of a hundred are women. What our young friends chiefly insist upon is that some one else shall suffer for them; and women do that sort of thing, as you must know, wonderfully well." The Doctor paused a moment, and then he added abruptly, "You have suffered immensely for your brother!"

This exclamation was abrupt, as I say, but it was also perfectly calculated. The Doctor had been rather disappointed at not finding his compact and comfortable little hostess surrounded in a more visible degree by the ravages of Morris Townsend's immorality; but he had said to himself that this was not because the young man had spared her, but because she had contrived to plaster up her wounds. They were aching there, behind the varnished stove, the festooned engravings, beneath her own neat little poplin bosom; and if he could only touch the tender spot, she would make a movement that would betray her. The words I have just quoted were an attempt to put his finger suddenly upon the place; and they had some of the success that he looked for. The tears sprang for a moment to Mrs. Montgomery's eyes, and she indulged in a proud little jerk of the head.

"I don't know how you have found that out!" she exclaimed.

"By a philosophic trick — by what they call induction. You know you have always your option of contradicting me. But kindly answer me a question. Don't you give your brother money! I think you ought to answer that."

"Yes, I have given him money," said Mrs. Montgomery.

"And you have not had much to give him?"

She was silent a moment. "If you ask me for a confession of poverty, that is easily made. I am very poor."

"One would never suppose it from your — your charming house," said the Doctor. "I learned from my sister that your income was moderate, and your family numerous."

"I have five children," Mrs. Montgomery observed; "but I am happy to say I can bring them up decently."

"Of course you can — accomplished and devoted as you are! But your brother has counted them over, I suppose?"

"Counted them over?"

"He knows there are five, I mean. He tells me it is he that brings them up."

Mrs. Montgomery stared a moment, and then quickly — "Oh yes; he teaches them —— Spanish."

The Doctor laughed out. "That must take a great deal off your hands! Your brother also knows, of course, that you have very little money."

"I have often told him so!" Mrs. Montgomery exclaimed, more unreservedly than she had yet spoken. She was apparently taking some comfort in the Doctor's clairvoyancy.

"Which means that you have often occasion to, and that he often sponges on you. Excuse the crudity of my language; I simply express a fact. I don't ask you how much of your money he has had, it is none of my business. I have ascertained what I suspected — what I wished." And the Doctor got up, gently smoothing his hat. "Your brother lives on you," he said as he stood there.

Mrs. Montgomery quickly rose from her chair, following her visitor's movements with a look of fascination. But then, with a certain inconsequence — "I have never complained of him!" she said.

"You needn't protest — you have not betrayed him. But I advise you not to give him any more money."

"Don't you see it is in my interest that he should marry a rich person?" she asked. "If, as you say, he lives on me, I can only wish to get rid of him, and to put obstacles in the way of his marrying is to increase my own difficulties."

"I wish very much you would come to me with your difficulties," said the Doctor. "Certainly, if I throw him back on your hands, the least I can do is to help you to bear the burden. If you will allow me to say so, then, I shall take the liberty of placing in your hands, for the present, a certain fund for your brother's support."

Mrs. Montgomery stared; she evidently thought he was jesting; but she presently saw that he was not, and the complication of her feelings became painful. "It seems to me that I ought to be very much offended with you," she murmured.

"Because I have offered you money? That's a superstition," said the Doctor. "You must let me come and see you again, and we will talk about these things. I suppose that some of your children are girls."

"I have two little girls," said Mrs. Montgomery.

"Well, when they grow up, and begin to think of taking husbands, you will see how anxious you will be about the moral character of these gentlemen. Then you will understand this visit of mine!"

"Ah, you are not to believe that Morris's moral character is bad!"

The Doctor looked at her a little, with folded arms. "There is something I should greatly like — as a moral satisfaction. I should like to hear you say — 'He is abominably selfish!'"

The words came out with the grave distinctness of his voice, and they seemed for an instant to create, to poor Mrs. Montgomery's troubled vision, a material image. She gazed at it an instant, and then she turned away. "You distress me, sir!" she exclaimed. "He is, after all, my brother, and his talents, his talents —— " On these last words her voice quavered, and before he knew it she had burst into tears.

"His talents are first-rate!" said the Doctor. "We must find a proper field for them!" And he assured her most respectfully of his regret at having so greatly discomposed her. "It's all for my poor Catherine," he went on. "You must know her, and you will see."

Mrs. Montgomery brushed away her tears, and blushed at having shed them. "I should like to know your daughter," she answered; and then, in an instant — "Don't let her marry him!"

Dr. Sloper went away with the words gently humming in his ears — "Don't let her marry him!" They gave him the moral satisfaction of

which he had just spoken, and their value was the greater that they had evidently cost a pang to poor little Mrs. Montgomery's family pride.

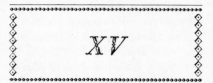

XV

HE had been puzzled by the way that Catherine carried herself; her attitude at this sentimental crisis seemed to him unnaturally passive. She had not spoken to him again after that scene in the library, the day before his interview with Morris; and a week had elapsed without making any change in her manner. There was nothing in it that appealed for pity, and he was even a little disappointed at her not giving him an opportunity to make up for his harshness by some manifestation of liberality which should operate as a compensation. He thought a little of offering to take her for a tour in Europe; but he was determined to do this only in case she should seem mutely to reproach him. He had an idea that she would display a talent for mute reproaches, and he was surprised at not finding himself exposed to these silent batteries. She said nothing, either tacitly or explicitly, and as she was never very talkative, there was now no especial eloquence in her reserve. And poor Catherine was not sulky — a style of behaviour for which she had too little histrionic talent; she was simply very patient. Of course she was thinking over her situation, and she was apparently doing so in a deliberate and unimpassioned manner, with a view of making the best of it.

"She will do as I have bidden her," said the Doctor, and he made the further reflexion that his daughter was not a woman of a great spirit. I know not whether he had hoped for a little more resistance for the sake of a little more entertainment; but he said to himself, as he had said before, that though it might have its momentary alarms, paternity was, after all, not an exciting vocation.

Catherine, meanwhile, had made a discovery of a very different sort; it had become vivid to her that there was a great excitement in trying to be a good daughter. She had an entirely new feeling, which may be described as a state of expectant suspense about her own actions. She watched herself as she would have watched another person, and wondered what she would do. It was as if this other person, who was both herself and not herself, had suddenly sprung into being, inspiring her with a natural curiosity as to the performance of untested functions.

"I am glad I have such a good daughter," said her father, kissing her, after the lapse of several days.

"I am trying to be good," she answered, turning away, with a conscience not altogether clear.

"If there is anything you would like to say to me, you know you must not hesitate. You needn't feel obliged to be so quiet. I shouldn't care that Mr. Townsend should be a frequent topic of conversation, but whenever you have anything particular to say about him I shall be very glad to hear it."

"Thank you," said Catherine; "I have nothing particular at present."

He never asked her whether she had seen Morris again, because he was sure that if this had been the case she would tell him. She had, in fact, not seen him, she had only written him a long letter. The letter at least was long for her; and, it may be added, that it was long for Morris; it consisted of five pages, in a remarkably neat and handsome hand. Catherine's handwriting was beautiful, and she was even a little proud of it; she was extremely fond of copying, and possessed volumes of extracts which testified to this accomplishment; volumes which she had exhibited one day to her lover, when the bliss of feeling that she was important in his eyes was exceptionally keen. She told Morris in writing that her father had expressed the wish that she should not see him again, and that she begged he would not come to the house until she should have "made up her mind." Morris replied with a passionate epistle, in which he asked to what, in Heaven's name, she wished to make up her mind. Had not her mind been made up two weeks before, and could it be possible that she entertained the idea of throwing

him off? Did she mean to break down at the very beginning of their ordeal, after all the promises of fidelity she had both given and extracted? And he gave an account of his own interview with her father — an account not identical at all points with that offered in these pages. "He was terribly violent," Morris wrote; "but you know my self-control. I have need of it all when I remember that I have it in my power to break in upon your cruel captivity." Catherine sent him, in answer to this, a note of three lines. "I am in great trouble; do not doubt of my affection, but let me wait a little and think." The idea of a struggle with her father, of setting up her will against his own, was heavy on her soul, and it kept her formally submissive, as a great physical weight keeps us motionless. It never entered into her mind to throw her lover off; but from the first she tried to assure herself that there would be a peaceful way out of their difficulty. The assurance was vague, for it contained no element of positive conviction that her father would change his mind. She only had an idea that if she should be very good, the situation would in some mysterious manner improve. To be good, she must be patient, respectful, abstain from judging her father too harshly, and from committing any act of open defiance. He was perhaps right, after all, to think as he did; by which Catherine meant not in the least that his judgement of Morris's motives in seeking to marry her was perhaps a just one, but that it was probably natural and proper that conscientious parents should be suspicious and even unjust. There were probably people in the world as bad as her father supposed Morris to be, and if there were the slightest chance of Morris being one of these sinister persons, the Doctor was right in taking it into account. Of course he could not know what she knew, how the purest love and truth were seated in the young man's eyes; but Heaven, in its time, might appoint a way of bringing him to such knowledge. Catherine expected a good deal of Heaven, and referred to the skies the initiative, as the French say, in dealing with her dilemma. She could not imagine herself imparting any kind of knowledge to her father, there was something superior even in his injustice and absolute in his mistakes. But she could at least be good, and if she were only good enough, Heaven would invent some way of reconciling all things — the dignity of her father's errors and the sweetness of her own confidence, the strict performance of her filial duties and the enjoyment of Morris Townsend's affection. Poor Catherine would have been glad to regard Mrs. Penniman as an illuminating agent, a part which this lady herself indeed was but imperfectly prepared to play. Mrs. Penniman took too much satisfaction in the sentimental shadows of this little drama to have, for the moment, any great interest in dissipating them. She wished the plot to thicken, and the advice that she gave her niece tended, in her own imagination, to produce this result. It was rather incoherent counsel, and from one day to another it contradicted itself; but it was pervaded by an earnest desire that Catherine should do something striking. "You must *act*, my dear; in your situation the great thing is to act," said Mrs. Penniman, who found her niece altogether beneath her opportunities. Mrs. Penniman's real hope was that the girl would make a secret marriage, at which she should officiate as brideswoman or duenna. She had a vision of this ceremony being performed in some subterranean chapel — subterranean chapels in New York were not frequent, but Mrs. Penniman's imagination was not chilled by trifles — and of the guilty couple — she liked to think of poor Catherine and her suitor as the guilty couple — being shuffled away in a fast-whirling vehicle to some obscure lodging in the suburbs, where she would pay them (in a thick veil) clandestine visits, where they would endure a period of romantic privation, and where ultimately, after she should have been their earthly providence, their intercessor, their advocate, and their medium of communication with the world, they should be reconciled to her brother in an artistic tableau, in which she herself should be somehow the central figure. She hesitated as yet to recommend this course to Catherine, but she attempted to draw an attractive picture of it to Morris Townsend. She was in daily communication with the young man, whom she kept informed by letters of the state of affairs in Washington Square. As he had been banished, as she said, from the house, she no longer saw him; but she ended by writing to him that she longed for an interview. This interview could take place only on neutral ground, and she bethought herself greatly before selecting a place of meeting. She had an inclination for Greenwood Cemetery, but she gave it up as too distant; she could not absent herself so long, as she said, without exciting suspicion. Then she thought of the Battery, but that was rather cold and windy, besides one's being exposed to intrusion from the Irish emigrants who at this point alight, with large appetites, in the New World; and at last she fixed upon an oyster saloon in the Seventh Avenue, kept by a negro — an establishment of which she knew nothing save that she had noticed it in passing. She made an appointment with Morris Townsend to meet him there, and she went to the tryst at dusk, enveloped in an impenetrable veil. He kept her waiting for half an hour — he had almost the whole width of the city to traverse — but she liked to wait, it seemed to intensify the situation. She ordered a cup of tea, which proved excessively bad, and this gave her a sense that she was suffering in a romantic cause. When

Morris at last arrived, they sat together for half an hour in the duskiest corner of a back shop; and it is hardly too much to say that this was the happiest half-hour that Mrs. Penniman had known for years. The situation was really thrilling, and it scarcely seemed to her a false note when her companion asked for an oyster stew, and proceeded to consume it before her eyes. Morris, indeed, needed all the satisfaction that stewed oysters could give him, for it may be intimated to the reader that he regarded Mrs. Penniman in the light of a fifth wheel to his coach. He was in a state of irritation natural to a gentleman of fine parts who had been snubbed in a benevolent attempt to confer a distinction upon a young woman of inferior characteristics, and the insinuating sympathy of this somewhat desiccated matron appeared to offer him no practical relief. He thought her a humbug, and he judged of humbugs with a good deal of confidence. He had listened and made himself agreeable to her at first, in order to get a footing in Washington Square; and at present he needed all his self-command to be decently civil. It would have gratified him to tell her that she was a fantastic old woman, and that he should like to put her into an omnibus and send her home. We know, however, that Morris possessed the virtue of self-control, and he had, moreover, the constant habit of seeking to be agreeable; so that, although Mrs. Penniman's demeanour only exasperated his already unquiet nerves, he listened to her with a sombre deference in which she found much to admire.

THEY had of course immediately spoken of Catherine. "Did she send me a message, or — or anything?" Morris asked. He appeared to think that she might have sent him a trinket or a lock of her hair.

Mrs. Penniman was slightly embarrassed, for she had not told her niece of her intended expedition. "Not exactly a message," she said; "I didn't ask her for one, because I was afraid to — to excite her."

"I am afraid she is not very excitable!" And Morris gave a smile of some bitterness.

"She is better than that. She is steadfast — she is true!"

"Do you think she will hold fast, then?"

"To the death!"

"Oh, I hope it won't come to that," said Morris.

"We must be prepared for the worst, and that is what I wish to speak to you about."

"What do you call the worst?"

"Well," said Mrs. Penniman, "my brother's hard, intellectual nature."

"Oh, the devil!"

"He is impervious to pity," Mrs. Penniman added, by way of explanation.

"Do you mean that he won't come round?"

"He will never be vanquished by argument. I have studied him. He will be vanquished only by the accomplished fact."

"The accomplished fact?"

"He will come round afterwards," said Mrs. Penniman, with extreme significance. "He cares for nothing but facts; he must be met by facts!"

"Well," rejoined Morris, "it is a fact that I wish to marry his daughter. I met him with that the other day, but he was not at all vanquished."

Mrs. Penniman was silent a little, and her smile beneath the shadow of her capacious bonnet, on the edge of which her black veil was arranged curtain-wise, fixed itself upon Morris's face with a still more tender brilliancy. "Marry Catherine first and meet him afterwards!" she exclaimed.

"Do you recommend that?" asked the young man, frowning heavily.

She was a little frightened, but she went on with considerable boldness. "That is the way I see it: a private marriage — a private marriage." She repeated the phrase because she liked it.

"Do you mean that I should carry Catherine off? What do they call it — elope with her?"

"It is not a crime when you are driven to it," said Mrs. Penniman. "My husband, as I have told you, was a distinguished clergyman; one of the most eloquent men of his day. He once married a young couple that had fled from the house of the young lady's father. He was so interested in their story. He had no hesitation, and everything came out beautifully. The father was afterwards reconciled, and thought everything of the young man. Mr. Penniman married them in the evening, about seven o'clock. The church was so dark, you could scarcely see; and Mr. Penniman was intensely agitated; he was so sympathetic. I don't believe he could have done it again."

"Unfortunately Catherine and I have not Mr. Penniman to marry us," said Morris.

"No, but you have me!" rejoined Mrs. Penniman expressively. "I can't perform the ceremony, but I can help you. I can watch."

"The woman's an idiot," thought Morris; but he was obliged to say something different. It was not, however, materially more civil. "Was it in order to tell me this that you requested I would meet you here?"

Mrs. Penniman had been conscious of a certain vagueness in her errand, and of not being able to offer him any very tangible reward for his long walk. "I thought perhaps you would like to see one who is so near to Catherine," she observed, with considerable majesty. "And also," she added, "that you would value an opportunity of sending her something."

Morris extended his empty hands with a melancholy smile. "I am greatly obliged to you, but I have nothing to send."

"Haven't you a *word?*" asked his companion, with her suggestive smile coming back.

Morris frowned again. "Tell her to hold fast," he said rather curtly.

"That is a good word — a noble word. It will make her happy for many days. She is very touching, very brave," Mrs. Penniman went on, arranging her mantle and preparing to depart. While she was so engaged she had an inspiration. She found the phrase that she could boldly offer as a vindication of the step she had taken. "If you marry Catherine at all risks," she said, "you will give my brother a proof of your being what he pretends to doubt."

"What he pretends to doubt?"

"Don't you know what that is?" Mrs. Penniman asked almost playfully.

"It does not concern me to know," said Morris grandly.

"Of course it makes you angry."

"I despise it," Morris declared.

"Ah, you know what it is, then?" said Mrs. Penniman, shaking her finger at him. "He pretends that you like — you like the money."

Morris hesitated a moment; and then, as if he spoke advisedly — "I *do* like the money!"

"Ah, but not — but not as he means it. You don't like it more than Catherine?"

He leaned his elbows on the table and buried his head in his hands. "You torture me!" he murmured. And, indeed, this was almost the effect of the poor lady's too importunate interest in his situation.

But she insisted on making her

point. "If you marry her in spite of him, he will take for granted that you expect nothing of him, and are prepared to do without it. And so he will see that you are disinterested."

Morris raised his head a little, following this argument, "And what shall I gain by that?"

"Why, that he will see that he has been wrong in thinking that you wished to get his money."

"And seeing that I wish he would go to the deuce with it, he will leave it to a hospital. Is that what you mean?" asked Morris.

"No, I don't mean that; though that would be very grand!" Mrs. Penniman quickly added. "I mean that having done you such an injustice, he will think it his duty, at the end, to make some amends."

Morris shook his head, though it must be confessed he was a little struck with this idea. "Do you think he is so sentimental?"

"He is not sentimental," said Mrs. Penniman; "but, to be perfectly fair to him, I think he has, in his own narrow way, a certain sense of duty."

There passed through Morris Townsend's mind a rapid wonder as to what he might, even under a remote contingency, be indebted to from the action of this principle in Dr. Sloper's breast, and the inquiry exhausted itself in his sense of the ludicrous. "Your brother has no duties to me," he said presently, "and I none to him."

"Ah, but he has duties to Catherine."

"Yes, but you see that on that principle Catherine has duties to him as well."

Mrs. Penniman got up, with a melancholy sigh, as if she thought him very unimaginative. "She has always performed them faithfully; and now, do you think she has no duties to *you?*" Mrs. Penniman always, even in conversation, italicised her personal pronouns.

"It would sound harsh to say so! I am so grateful for her love," Morris added.

"I will tell her you said that! And now, remember that if you need me, I am there." And Mrs. Penniman, who could think of nothing more to say, nodded vaguely in the direction of Washington Square.

Morris looked some moments at the sanded floor of the shop; he seemed to be disposed to linger a moment. At last, looking up with a certain abruptness, "It is your belief that if she marries me he will cut her off?" he asked.

Mrs. Penniman stared a little, and smiled. "Why, I have explained to you what I think would happen — that in the end it would be the best thing to do."

"You mean that, whatever she does, in the long run she will get the money?"

"It doesn't depend upon her, but upon you. Venture to appear as disinterested as you are!" said Mrs. Penniman ingeniously. Morris dropped his eyes on the sanded floor again, pondering this; and she pursued. "Mr. Penniman and I had nothing, and we were very happy. Catherine, moreover, has her mother's fortune, which, at the time my sister-in-law married, was considered a very handsome one."

"Oh, don't speak of that!" said Morris; and, indeed, it was quite superfluous, for he had contemplated the fact in all its lights.

"Austin married a wife with money — why shouldn't you?"

"Ah! but your brother was a doctor," Morris objected.

"Well, all young men can't be doctors!"

"I should think it an extremely loathsome profession," said Morris, with an air of intellectual independence. Then in a moment, he went on rather inconsequently, "Do you suppose there is a will already made in Catherine's favour?"

"I suppose so — even doctors must die; and perhaps a little in mine," Mrs. Penniman frankly added.

"And you believe he would certainly change it — as regards Catherine?"

"Yes; and then change it back again."

"Ah, but one can't depend on that!" said Morris.

"Do you want to *depend* on it?" Mrs. Penniman asked.

Morris blushed a little. "Well, I am certainly afraid of being the cause of an injury to Catherine."

"Ah! you must not be afraid. Be afraid of nothing, and everything will go well!"

And then Mrs. Penniman paid for her cup of tea, and Morris paid for his oyster stew, and they went out together into the dimly-lighted wilderness of the Seventh Avenue.

The dusk had closed in completely and the street lamps were separated by wide intervals of a pavement in which cavities and fissures played a disproportionate part. An omnibus, emblazoned with strange pictures, went tumbling over the dislocated cobble-stones.

"How will you go home?" Morris asked, following this vehicle with an interested eye. Mrs. Penniman had taken his arm.

She hesitated a moment. "I think this manner would be pleasant," she said; and she continued to let him feel the value of his support.

So he walked with her through the devious ways of the west side of the town, and through the bustle of gathering nightfall in populous streets, to the quiet precinct of Washington Square. They lingered a moment at the foot of Dr. Sloper's white marble steps, above which a spotless white door, adorned with a glittering silver plate, seemed to figure, for Morris, the closed portal of happiness; and then Mrs. Penniman's companion rested a melancholy eye upon a lighted window in the upper part of the house.

"That is my room — my dear little room!" Mrs. Penniman remarked.

Morris started. "Then I needn't come walking round the Square to gaze at it."

"That's as you please. But Catherine's is behind; two noble windows on the second floor. I think you can see them from the other street."

"I don't want to see them, ma'am!" And Morris turned his back to the house.

"I will tell her you have been *here,* at any rate," said Mrs. Penniman, pointing to the spot where they stood; "and I will give her your message — that she is to hold fast!"

"Oh, yes! of course. You know I write her all that."

"It seems to say more when it is spoken! And remember, if you need me, that I am *there";* and Mrs. Penniman glanced at the third floor.

On this they separated, and Morris, left to himself, stood looking at the house a moment; after which he turned away, and took a gloomy walk round the Square, on the opposite side, close to the wooden fence. Then he came back, and paused for a minute in front of Dr. Sloper's dwelling. His eyes travelled over it; they even rested on the ruddy windows of Mrs. Penniman's apartment. He thought it a devilish comfortable house.

XVII

MRS. PENNIMAN told Catherine that evening — the two ladies were sitting in the back parlour — that she had had an interview with Morris Townsend; and on receiving this news the girl started with a sense of pain. She felt angry for the moment; it was almost the first time she had ever felt angry.

It seemed to her that her aunt was meddlesome; and from this came a vague apprehension that she would spoil something.

"I don't see why you should have seen him. I don't think it was right," Catherine said.

"I was so sorry for him — it seemed to me some one ought to see him."

"No one but I," said Catherine, who felt as if she were making the most presumptuous speech of her life, and yet at the same time had an instinct that she was right in doing so.

"But you wouldn't, my dear," Aunt Lavinia rejoined; "and I didn't know what might have become of him."

"I have not seen him, because my father has forbidden it," Catherine said very simply.

There was a simplicity in this, indeed, which fairly vexed Mrs. Penniman. "If your father forbade you to go to sleep, I suppose you would keep awake!" she commented.

Catherine looked at her. "I don't understand you. You seem to be very strange."

"Well, my dear, you will understand me some day!" And Mrs. Penniman, who was reading the evening paper, which she perused daily from the first line to the last, resumed her occupation. She wrapped herself in silence; she was determined Catherine should ask her for an account of her interview with Morris. But Catherine was silent for so long, that she almost lost patience; and she was on the point of remarking to her that she was very heartless, when the girl at last spoke.

"What did he say?" she asked.

"He said he is ready to marry you any day, in spite of everything."

Catherine made no answer to this, and Mrs. Penniman almost lost patience again; owing to which she at last volunteered the information that Morris looked very handsome, but terribly haggard.

"Did he seem sad?" asked her niece.

"He was dark under the eyes," said Mrs. Penniman. "So different from when I first saw him; though I am not sure that if I had seen him in this condition the first time, I should not have been even more struck with him. There is something brilliant in his very misery."

This was, to Catherine's sense, a vivid picture, and though she disapproved, she felt herself gazing at it. "Where did you see him?" she asked presently.

"In — in the Bowery; at a confectioner's," said Mrs. Penniman, who had a general idea that she ought to dissemble a little.

"Whereabouts is the place?" Catherine inquired, after another pause.

"Do you wish to go there, my dear?" said her aunt.

"Oh no!" And Catherine got up from her seat and went to the fire, where she stood looking a while at the glowing coals.

"Why are you so dry, Catherine?" Mrs. Penniman said at last.

"So dry?"

"So cold — so irresponsive."

The girl turned very quickly. "Did *he* say that?"

Mrs. Penniman hesitated a moment. "I will tell you what he said. He said he feared only one thing — that you would be afraid."

"Afraid of what?"

"Afraid of your father."

Catherine turned back to the fire again, and then, after a pause, she said — "I *am* afraid of my father."

Mrs. Penniman got quickly up from her chair and approached her niece. "Do you mean to give him up, then?"

Catherine for some time never moved; she kept her eyes on the coals. At last she raised her head and looked at her aunt. "Why do you push me so?" she asked.

"I don't push you. When have I spoken to you before?"

"It seems to me that you have spoken to me several times."

"I am afraid it is necessary, then, Catherine," said Mrs. Penniman, with a good deal of solemnity. "I am afraid you don't feel the importance —— " She paused a little; Catherine was looking at her. "The importance of not disappointing that gallant young heart!" And Mrs. Penniman went back to her chair, by the lamp, and, with a little jerk, picked up the evening paper again.

Catherine stood there before the fire, with her hands behind her, looking at her aunt, to whom it seemed that the girl had never had just this dark fixedness in her gaze. "I don't think you understand — or that you know me," she said.

"If I don't, it is not wonderful; you trust me so little."

Catherine made no attempt to deny this charge, and for some time more nothing was said. But Mrs. Penniman's imagination was restless, and the evening paper failed on this occasion to enchain it.

"If you succumb to the dread of your father's wrath," she said, "I don't know what will become of us."

"Did *he* tell you to say these things to me?"

"He told me to use my influence."

"You must be mistaken," said Catherine. "He trusts me."

"I hope he may never repent of it!" And Mrs. Penniman gave a little sharp slap to her newspaper. She knew not what to make of her niece, who had suddenly become stern and contradictious.

This tendency on Catherine's part was presently even more apparent. "You had much better not make any more appointments with Mr. Townsend," she said. "I don't think it is right."

Mrs. Penniman rose with considerable majesty. "My poor child, are you jealous of me?" she inquired.

"Oh, Aunt Lavinia!" murmured Catherine, blushing.

"I don't think it is your place to teach me what is right."

On this point Catherine made no concession. "It can't be right to deceive."

"I certainly have not deceived *you!*"

"Yes; but I promised my father —— "

"I have no doubt you promised your father. But I have promised him nothing!"

Catherine had to admit this, and she did so in silence. "I don't believe Mr. Townsend himself likes it," she said at last.

"Doesn't like meeting me?"

"Not in secret."

"It was not in secret; the place was full of people."

"But it was a secret place — away off in the Bowery."

Mrs. Penniman flinched a little. "Gentlemen enjoy such things," she remarked presently. "I know what gentlemen like."

"My father wouldn't like it, if he knew."

"Pray, do you propose to inform him?" Mrs. Penniman inquired.

"No, Aunt Lavinia. But please don't do it again."

"If I do it again, you will inform him: is that what you mean? I do not share your dread of my brother; I have always known how to defend my own position. But I shall certainly never again take any step on your behalf; you are much too thankless. I knew you were not a spontaneous nature, but I believed you were firm, and I told your father that he would find you so. I am disappointed — but your father will not be!" And with this, Mrs. Penniman offered her niece a brief good-night, and withdrew to her own apartment.

XVIII

CATHERINE sat alone by the parlour fire — sat there for more than an hour, lost in her meditations. Her aunt seemed to her aggressive and foolish, and to see it so clearly — to judge Mrs. Penniman so positively — made her feel old and grave. She did not resent the imputation of weakness; it made no impression on her, for she had not the sense of weakness, and she was not hurt at not being appreciated. She had an immense respect for her father, and she felt that to displease him would be a misdemeanour analogous to an act of profanity in a great temple; but her purpose had slowly ripened, and she believed that her prayers had purified it of its violence. The evening advanced, and the lamp burned dim without her noticing it; her eyes were fixed upon her terrible plan. She knew her father was in his study — that he had been there all the evening; from time to time she expected to hear him move. She thought he would perhaps come, as he sometimes came, into the parlour. At last the clock struck eleven, and the house was wrapped in silence; the servants had gone to bed. Catherine got up and went slowly to the door of the library, where she waited a moment, motionless. Then she knocked, and then she waited again. Her father had answered her, but she had not the courage to turn the latch. What she had said to her aunt was true enough — she was afraid of him; and in saying that she had no sense of weakness she meant that she was not afraid of herself. She heard him move within, and he came and opened the door for her.

"What is the matter?" asked the Doctor. "You are standing there like a ghost."

She went into the room, but it was some time before she contrived to say what she had come to say. Her father, who was in his dressing-gown and slippers, had been busy at his writing-table, and after looking at her for some moments, and waiting for her to speak, he went and seated himself at his papers again. His back was turned to her — she began to hear the scratching of his pen. She remained near the door, with her heart thumping beneath her bodice; and she was very glad that his back was turned, for it seemed to her that she could more easily address herself to this portion of his person than to his face. At last she began, watching it while she spoke.

"You told me that if I should have anything more to say about Mr. Townsend you would be glad to listen to it."

"Exactly, my dear," said the Doctor, not turning round, but stopping his pen.

Catherine wished it would go on, but she herself continued. "I thought I would tell you that I have not seen him again, but that I should like to do so."

"To bid him good-bye?" asked the Doctor.

The girl hesitated a moment. "He is not going away."

The Doctor wheeled slowly round in his chair, with a smile that seemed to accuse her of an epigram; but extremes meet, and Catherine had not intended one. "It is not to bid him good-bye, then?" her father said.

"No, father, not that; at least, not for ever. I have not seen him again, but I should like to see him," Catherine repeated.

The Doctor slowly rubbed his under lip with the feather of his quill.

"Have you written to him?"

"Yes, four times."

"You have not dismissed him, then. Once would have done that."

"No," said Catherine; "I have asked him — asked him to wait."

Her father sat looking at her, and she was afraid he was going to break out into wrath; his eyes were so fine and cold.

"You are a dear, faithful child," he said at last. "Come here to your father." And he got up, holding out his hands toward her.

The words were a surprise, and they gave her an exquisite joy. She went to him, and he put his arm round her tenderly, soothingly; and then he kissed her. After this he said:

"Do you wish to make me very happy?"

"I should like to — but I am afraid I can't," Catherine answered.

"You can if you will. It all depends on your will."

"Is it to give him up?" said Catherine.

"Yes, it is to give him up."

And he held her still, with the same tenderness, looking into her face and resting his eyes on her averted eyes. There was a long silence; she wished he would release her.

"You are happier than I, father," she said, at last.

"I have no doubt you are unhappy just now. But it is better to be unhappy for three months and get over it, than for many years and never get over it."

"Yes, if that were so," said Catherine.

"It would be so; I am sure of that." She answered nothing, and he went on. "Have you no faith in my wisdom, in my tenderness, in my solicitude for your future?"

"Oh, father!" murmured the girl.

"Don't you suppose that I know something of men: their vices, their follies, their falsities?"

She detached herself, and turned upon him. "He is not vicious — he is not false!"

Her father kept looking at her with his sharp, pure eye. "You make nothing of my judgement, then?"

"I can't believe that!"

"I don't ask you to believe it, but to take it on trust."

Catherine was far from saying to herself that this was an ingenious sophism; but she met the appeal none the less squarely. "What has he done — what do you know?"

"He has never done anything — he is a selfish idler."

"Oh, father, don't abuse him!" she exclaimed pleadingly.

"I don't mean to abuse him; it would be a great mistake. You may do as you choose," he added, turning away.

"I may see him again?"

"Just as you choose."

"Will you forgive me?"

"By no means."

"It will only be for once."

"I don't know what you mean by once. You must either give him up or continue the acquaintance."

"I wish to explain — to tell him to wait."

"To wait for what?"

"Till you know him better — till you consent."

"Don't tell him any such nonsense as that. I know him well enough, and I shall never consent."

"But we can wait a long time," said poor Catherine, in a tone which was meant to express the humblest conciliation, but which had upon her father's nerves the effect of an iteration not characterised by tact.

The Doctor answered, however, quietly enough: "Of course you can wait till I die, if you like."

Catherine gave a cry of natural horror.

"Your engagement will have one delightful effect upon you; it will make you extremely impatient for that event."

Catherine stood staring, and the Doctor enjoyed the point he had made. It came to Catherine with the force — or rather with the vague impressiveness — of a logical axiom which it was not in her province to controvert; and yet, though it was a scientific truth, she felt wholly unable to accept it.

"I would rather not marry, if that were true," she said.

"Give me a proof of it, then; for it is beyond a question that by engaging yourself to Morris Townsend you simply wait for my death."

She turned away, feeling sick and faint; and the Doctor went on. "And if you wait for it with impatience, judge, if you please, what *his* eagerness will be!"

Catherine turned it over — her father's words had such an authority for her that her very thoughts were capable of obeying him. There was a dreadful ugliness in it, which seemed to glare at her through the interposing medium of her own feebler reason. Suddenly, however, she had an inspiration — she almost knew it to be an inspiration.

"If I don't marry before your death, I will not after," she said.

To her father, it must be admitted, this seemed only another epigram; and as obstinacy, in unaccomplished minds, does not usually select such a mode of expression, he was the more surprised at this wanton play of a fixed idea.

"Do you mean that for an impertinence?" he inquired; an inquiry of which, as he made it, he quite perceived the grossness.

"An impertinence? Oh, father, what terrible things you say!"

"If you don't wait for my death, you might as well marry immediately; there is nothing else to wait for."

For some time Catherine made no answer; but finally she said: "I think Morris — little by little — might persuade you."

"I shall never let him speak to me again. I dislike him too much."

Catherine gave a long, low sigh; she tried to stifle it, for she had made up her mind that it was wrong to make a parade of her trouble, and to endeavour to act upon her father by the meretricious aid of emotion. Indeed, she even thought it wrong — in the sense of being inconsiderate — to attempt to act upon his feelings at all; her part was to effect some gentle, gradual change in his intellectual perception of poor Morris's character. But the means of effecting such a change were at present shrouded in mystery, and she felt miserably helpless and hopeless. She had exhausted all arguments, all replies. Her father might have pitied her, and in fact he did so; but he was sure he was right.

"There is one thing you can tell Mr. Townsend when you see him again," he said: "that if you marry without my consent, I don't leave you a farthing of money. That will interest him more than anything else you can tell him."

"That would be very right," Catherine answered. "I ought not in that case to have a farthing of your money."

"My dear child," the Doctor observed, laughing, "your simplicity is touching. Make that remark, in that tone, and with that expression of countenance, to Mr. Townsend, and take a note of his answer. It won't be polite — it will express irritation; and I shall be glad of that, as it will put me in the right; unless, indeed — which is perfectly possible — you should like him the better for being rude to you."

"He will never be rude to me," said Catherine gently.

"Tell him what I say, all the same."

She looked at her father, and her quiet eyes filled with tears.

"I think I will see him, then," she murmured, in her timid voice.

"Exactly as you choose!" And he went to the door and opened it for her to go out. The movement gave her a terrible sense of his turning her off.

"It will be only once, for the present," she added, lingering a moment.

"Exactly as you choose," he repeated, standing there with his hand on the door. "I have told you what I think. If you see him, you will be an ungrateful, cruel child; you will have given your old father the greatest pain of his life."

This was more than the poor girl could bear; her tears overflowed, and she moved towards her grimly consistent parent with a pitiful cry. Her hands were raised in supplication, but he sternly evaded this appeal. Instead of letting her sob out her misery on his shoulder, he simply took her by the arm and directed her course across the threshold, closing the door gently but firmly behind her. After he had done so, he remained listening. For a long time there was no sound; he knew that she was standing outside. He was sorry for her, as I have said; but he was so sure he was right. At last he heard her move away, and then her footstep creaked faintly upon the stairs.

The Doctor took several turns round his study, with his hands in his pockets, and a thin sparkle, possibly of irritation, but partly also of something like humour, in his eye. "By Jove," he said to himself, "I believe she will stick — I believe she will stick!" And this idea of Catherine "sticking" appeared to have a comical side, and to offer a prospect of entertainment. He determined, as he said to himself, to see it out.

XIX

IT was for reasons connected with this determination that on the morrow he sought a few words of private conversation with Mrs. Penniman. He sent for her to the library, and he there informed her that he hoped very much that, as regarded this affair of Catherine's, she would mind her *p's* and *q's*.

"I don't know what you mean by such an expression," said his sister. "You speak as if I were learning the alphabet."

"The alphabet of common sense is something you will never learn," the Doctor permitted himself to respond.

"Have you called me here to insult me?" Mrs. Penniman inquired.

"Not at all. Simply to advise you. You have taken up young Townsend; that's your own affair. I have nothing to do with your sentiments, your fancies, your affections, your delusions; but what I request of you is that you will keep these things to yourself. I have explained my views to Catherine; she understands them perfectly, and anything that she does further in the way of encouraging Mr. Townsend's attentions will be in deliberate opposition to my wishes. Anything that you should do in the way of giving her aid and comfort will be — permit me the expression — distinctly treasonable. You know high treason is a capital offence; take care how you incur the penalty."

Mrs. Penniman threw back her head, with a certain expansion of the eye which she occasionally practised. "It seems to me that you talk like a great autocrat."

"I talk like my daughter's father."

"Not like your sister's brother!" cried Lavinia.

"My dear Lavinia," said the Doctor, "I sometimes wonder

whether I am your brother. We are so extremely different. In spite of differences, however, we can, at a pinch, understand each other; and that is the essential thing just now. Walk straight with regard to Mr. Townsend; that's all I ask. It is highly probable you have been corresponding with him for the last three weeks — perhaps even seeing him. I don't ask you — you needn't tell me." He had a moral conviction that she would contrive to tell a fib about the matter, which it would disgust him to listen to. "Whatever you have done, stop doing it. That's all I wish."

"Don't you wish also by chance to murder your child?" Mrs. Penniman inquired.

"On the contrary, I wish to make her live and be happy."

"You will kill her; she passed a dreadful night."

"She won't die of one dreadful night, nor of a dozen. Remember that I am a distinguished physician."

Mrs. Penniman hesitated a moment. Then she risked her retort. "Your being a distinguished physician has not prevented you from already losing *two members* of your family!"

She had risked it, but her brother gave her such a terribly incisive look — a look so like a surgeon's lancet — that she was frightened at her courage. And he answered her in words that corresponded to the look: "It may not prevent me, either, from losing the society of still another."

Mrs. Penniman took herself off,

with whatever air of depreciated merit was at her command, and repaired to Catherine's room, where the poor girl was closeted. She knew all about her dreadful night, for the two had met again, the evening before, after Catherine left her father. Mrs. Penniman was on the landing of the second floor when her niece came upstairs. It was not remarkable that a person of so much subtlety should have discovered that Catherine had been shut up with the Doctor. It was still less remarkable that she should have felt an extreme curiosity to learn the result of this interview, and that this sentiment, combined with her great amiability and generosity, should have prompted her to regret the sharp words lately exchanged between her niece and herself. As the unhappy girl came into sight, in the dusky corridor, she made a lively demonstration of sympathy. Catherine's bursting heart was equally oblivious. She only knew that her aunt was taking her into her arms. Mrs. Penniman drew her into Catherine's own room, and the two women sat there together, far into the small hours; the younger one with her head on the other's lap, sobbing and sobbing at first in a soundless, stifled manner, and then at last perfectly still. It gratified Mrs. Penniman to be able to feel conscientiously that this scene virtually removed the interdict which Catherine had placed upon her further communion with Morris Townsend. She was not gratified, however, when, in coming back to her niece's room before breakfast, she found that Catherine had risen and was preparing herself for this meal.

"You should not go to breakfast," she said; "you are not well enough, after your fearful night."

"Yes, I am very well, and I am only afraid of being late."

"I can't understand you!" Mrs. Penniman cried. "You should stay in bed for three days."

"Oh, I could never do that!" said Catherine, to whom this idea presented no attractions.

Mrs. Penniman was in despair, and she noted, with extreme annoyance, that the trace of the night's tears had completely vanished from Catherine's eyes. She had a most impracticable *physique*. "What effect do you expect to have upon your father," her aunt demanded, "if you come plumping down, without a vestige of any sort of feeling, as if nothing in the world had happened?"

"He would not like me to lie in bed," said Catherine simply.

"All the more reason for your doing it. How else do you expect to move him?"

Catherine thought a little. "I don't know how; but not in that way. I wish to be just as usual." And she finished dressing, and, according to her aunt's expression, went plumping down into the paternal presence. She was really too modest for consistent pathos.

And yet it was perfectly true that she had had a dreadful night. Even after Mrs. Penniman left her she had had no sleep. She lay staring at the uncomforting gloom, with her eyes and ears filled with the movement with which her father had turned her out of his room, and of the words in which he had told her that she was a heartless daughter. Her heart was breaking. She had heart enough for that. At moments it seemed to her that she believed him, and that to do what she was doing, a girl must indeed be bad. She *was* bad; but she couldn't help it. She would try to appear good, even if her heart were perverted; and from time to time she had a fancy that she might accomplish something by ingenious concessions to form, though she should persist in caring for Morris. Catherine's ingenuities were indefinite, and we are not called upon to expose their hollowness. The best of them perhaps showed itself in that freshness of aspect which was so discouraging to Mrs. Penniman, who was amazed at the absence of haggardness in a young woman who for a whole night had lain quivering beneath a father's curse. Poor Catherine was conscious of her freshness; it gave her a feeling about the future which rather added to the weight upon her mind. It seemed a proof that she was strong and solid and dense, and would live to a great age — longer than might be generally convenient; and this idea was depressing, for it appeared to saddle her with a pretension the more, just when the cultivation of any pretension was inconsistent with her doing right. She wrote that day to Morris Townsend, requesting him to come and see her on the morrow; using very few words, and explaining nothing. She would explain everything face to face.

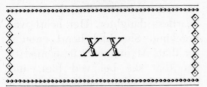

XX

ON the morrow, in the afternoon, she heard his voice at the door, and his step in the hall. She received him in the big, bright front parlour, and she instructed the servant that if any one should call she was particularly engaged. She was not afraid of her father's coming in, for at that hour he was always driving about town. When Morris stood there before her, the first thing that she was conscious of was that he was even more beautiful to look at than fond recollection had painted him; the next was that he had pressed her in his arms. When she was free again it appeared to her that she had now indeed thrown herself into the gulf of defiance, and even, for an instant, that she had been married to him.

He told her that she had been very cruel, and had made him very unhappy; and Catherine felt acutely the difficulty of her destiny, which forced her to give pain in such opposite quarters. But she wished that, instead of reproaches, however tender, he would give her help; he was certainly wise enough, and clever enough, to invent some issue from their troubles. She expressed this belief, and Morris received the assurance as if he thought it natural; but he interrogated, at first — as was natural too — rather than committed himself to marking out a course.

"You should not have made me wait so long," he said. "I don't know how I have been living; every hour seemed like years. You should have decided sooner."

"Decided?" Catherine asked.

"Decided whether you would keep me or give me up."

"Oh, Morris," she cried, with a long tender murmur, "I never thought of giving you up!"

"What, then, were you waiting for?" The young man was ardently logical.

"I thought my father might — might —— " and she hesitated.

"Might see how unhappy you were?"

"Oh no! But that he might look at it differently."

"And now you have sent for me to tell me that at last he does so. Is that it?"

This hypothetical optimism gave the poor girl a pang. "No, Morris," she said solemnly, "he looks at it still in the same way."

"Then why have you sent for me?"

"Because I wanted to see you!" cried Catherine piteously.

"That's an excellent reason, surely. But did you want to look at me only? Have you nothing to tell me?"

His beautiful persuasive eyes were fixed upon her face, and she wondered what answer would be noble enough to make to such a gaze as that. For a moment her own eyes took it in, and then — "I *did* want to look at you!" she said gently. But after this speech, most inconsistently, she hid her face.

Morris watched her for a moment, attentively. "Will you marry me to-morrow?" he asked suddenly.

"To-morrow?"

"Next week, then. Any time within a month."

"Isn't it better to wait?" said Catherine.

"To wait for what?"

She hardly knew for what; but this tremendous leap alarmed her. "Till we have thought about it a little more."

He shook his head, sadly and reproachfully. "I thought you had been thinking about it these three weeks. Do you want to turn it over in your mind for five years? You have given me more than time enough. My poor girl," he added in a moment, "you are not sincere!"

Catherine coloured from brow to chin, and her eyes filled with tears. "Oh, how can you say that?" she murmured.

"Why, you must take me or leave me," said Morris, very reasonably. "You can't please your father and me both; you must choose between us."

"I have chosen you!" she said passionately.

"Then marry me next week."

She stood gazing at him. "Isn't there any other way?"

"None that I know of for arriv-ing at the same result. If there is, I should be happy to hear of it."

Catherine could think of nothing of the kind, and Morris's luminosity seemed almost pitiless. The only thing she could think of was that her father might, after all, come round, and she articulated, with an awkward sense of her helplessness in doing so, a wish that this miracle might happen.

"Do you think it is in the least degree likely?" Morris asked.

"It would be, if he could only know you!"

"He can know me if he will. What is to prevent it?"

"His ideas, his reasons," said Catherine. "They are so — so terribly strong." She trembled with the recollection of them yet.

"Strong?" cried Morris. "I would rather you should think them weak."

"Oh, nothing about my father is weak!" said the girl.

Morris turned away, walking to the window, where he stood looking out. "You are terribly afraid of him!" he remarked at last.

She felt no impulse to deny it, because she had no shame in it; for if it was no honour to herself, at least it was an honour to him. "I suppose I must be," she said simply.

"Then you don't love me — not as I love you. If you fear your father more than you love me, then your love is not what I hoped it was."

"Ah, my friend!" she said, going to him.

"Do *I* fear anything?" he demanded, turning round on her. "For your sake what am I not ready to face?"

"You are noble — you are brave!" she answered, stopping short at a distance that was almost respectful.

"Small good it does me, if you are so timid."

"I don't think that I am — *really*," said Catherine.

"I don't know what you mean by 'really.' It is really enough to make us miserable."

"I should be strong enough to wait — to wait a long time."

"And suppose after a long time your father should hate me worse than ever?"

"He wouldn't — he couldn't!"

"He would be touched by my fidelity? Is that what you mean? If he is so easily touched, then why should you be afraid of him?"

This was much to the point, and Catherine was struck by it. "I will try not to be," she said. And she stood there submissively, the image, in advance, of a dutiful and responsible wife. This image could not fail to recommend itself to Morris Townsend, and he continued to give proof of the high estimation in which he held her. It could only have been at the prompting of such a sentiment that he presently mentioned to her that the course recommended by Mrs. Penniman was an immediate union, regardless of consequences.

"Yes, Aunt Penniman would like that," Catherine said simply — and yet with a certain shrewdness. It

must, however, have been in pure simplicity, and from motives quite untouched by sarcasm, that, a few moments after, she went on to say to Morris that her father had given her a message for him. It was quite on her conscience to deliver this message, and had the mission been ten times more painful she would have as scrupulously performed it. "He told me to tell you — to tell you very distinctly, and directly from himself, that if I marry without his consent, I shall not inherit a penny of his fortune. He made a great point of this. He seemed to think — he seemed to think —— "

Morris flushed, as any young man of spirit might have flushed at an imputation of baseness.

"What did he seem to think?"

"That it would make a difference."

"It *will* make a difference — in many things. We shall be by many thousands of dollars the poorer; and that is a great difference. But it will make none in my affection."

"We shall not want the money," said Catherine; "for you know I have a good deal myself."

"Yes, my dear girl, I know you have something. And he can't touch that!"

"He would never," said Catherine. "My mother left it to me."

Morris was silent a while. "He was very positive about this, was he?" he asked at last. "He thought such a message would annoy me terribly, and make me throw off the mask, eh?"

"I don't know what he thought," said Catherine wearily.

"Please tell him that I care for his message as much as for that!" And Morris snapped his fingers sonorously.

"I don't think I could tell him that."

"Do you know you sometimes disappoint me?" said Morris.

"I should think I might. I disappoint every one — father and Aunt Penniman."

"Well, it doesn't matter with me, because I am fonder of you than they are."

"Yes, Morris," said the girl, with her imagination — what there was of it — swimming in this happy truth, which seemed, after all, invidious to no one.

"Is it your belief that he will stick to it — stick to it for ever, to this idea of disinheriting you? — that your goodness and patience will never wear out his cruelty?"

"The trouble is that if I marry you, he will think I am not good. He will think that a proof."

"Ah, then, he will never forgive you!"

This idea, sharply expressed by Morris's handsome lips, renewed for a moment, to the poor girl's temporarily pacified conscience, all its dreadful vividness. "Oh, you must love me very much!" she cried.

"There is no doubt of that, my dear!" her lover rejoined. "You don't like that word 'disinherited,'" he added in a moment.

"It isn't the money; it is that he should — that he should feel so."

"I suppose it seems to you a kind of curse," said Morris. "It must be very dismal. But don't you think," he went on presently, "that if you were to try to be very clever, and to set rightly about it, you might in the end conjure it away? Don't you think," he continued further, in a tone of sympathetic speculation, "that a really clever woman, in your place, might bring him round at last? Don't you think —— "

Here, suddenly, Morris was interrupted; these ingenious inquiries had not reached Catherine's ears. The terrible word "disinheritance," with all its impressive moral reprobation, was still ringing there; seemed indeed to gather force as it lingered. The mortal chill of her situation struck more deeply into her child-like heart, and she was overwhelmed by a feeling of loneliness and danger. But her refuge was there, close to her, and she put out her hands to grasp it. "Ah, Morris," she said, with a shudder, "I will marry you as soon as you please." And she surrendered herself, leaning her head on his shoulder.

"My dear good girl!" he exclaimed, looking down at his prize. And then he looked up again, rather vaguely, with parted lips and lifted eyebrows.

XXI

DR. SLOPER very soon imparted his conviction to Mrs. Almond, in the same terms in which he had announced it to himself. "She's going to stick, by Jove! she's going to stick."

"Do you mean that she is going to marry him?" Mrs. Almond inquired.

"I don't know that; but she is not going to break down. She is going to drag out the engagement, in the hope of making me relent."

"And shall you not relent?"

"Shall a geometrical proposition relent? I am not so superficial."

"Doesn't geometry treat of surfaces?" asked Mrs. Almond, who, as we know, was clever, smiling.

"Yes; but it treats of them profoundly. Catherine and her young man are my surfaces; I have taken their measure."

"You speak as if it surprised you."

"It is immense; there will be a great deal to observe."

"You are shockingly cold-blooded!" said Mrs. Almond.

"I need to be with all this hot blood about me. Young Townsend indeed is cool; I must allow him that merit."

"I can't judge him," Mrs. Almond answered; "but I am not at all surprised at Catherine."

"I confess I am a little; she must have been so deucedly divided and bothered."

"Say it amuses you outright! I don't see why it should be such a joke that your daughter adores you."

"It is the point where the adoration stops that I find it interesting to fix."

"It stops where the other sentiment begins."

"Not at all — that would be simple enough. The two things are extremely mixed up, and the mixture is extremely odd. It will produce some third element, and that's what I am waiting to see. I wait with suspense — with positive excitement; and that is a sort of emotion that I didn't suppose Catherine would ever provide for me. I am really very much obliged to her."

"She will cling," said Mrs. Almond; "she will certainly cling."

"Yes; as I say, she will stick."

"Cling is prettier. That's what those very simple natures always do, and nothing could be simpler than Catherine. She doesn't take many impressions; but when she takes one she keeps it. She is like a copper kettle that receives a dent; you may polish up the kettle, but you can't efface the mark."

"We must try and polish up Catherine," said the Doctor. "I will take her to Europe."

"She won't forget him in Europe."

"He will forget her, then."

Mrs. Almond looked grave. "Should you really like that?"

"Extremely!" said the Doctor.

Mrs. Penniman, meanwhile, lost little time in putting herself again in communication with Morris Townsend. She requested him to favour her with another interview, but she did not on this occasion select an oyster saloon as the scene of their meeting. She proposed that he should join her at the door of a certain church, after service on Sunday afternoon, and she was careful not to appoint the place of worship which she usually visited, and where, as she said, the congregation would have spied upon her. She picked out a less elegant resort, and on issuing from its portal at the hour she had fixed she saw the young man standing apart. She offered him no recognition till she had crossed the street and he had followed her to some distance. Here, with a smile — "Excuse my apparent want of cordiality," she said. "You know what to believe about that. Prudence before everything." And on his asking her in what direction they should walk, "Where we shall be least observed," she murmured.

Morris was not in high good-humour, and his response to this speech was not particularly gallant. "I don't flatter myself we shall be much observed anywhere." Then he turned recklessly toward the centre of the town. "I hope you have come to tell me that he has knocked under," he went on.

"I am afraid I am not altogether a harbinger of good; and yet, too, I am to a certain extent a messenger of peace. I have been thinking a great deal, Mr. Townsend," said Mrs. Penniman.

"You think too much."

"I suppose I do; but I can't help it, my mind is so terribly active. When I give myself, I give my-

self. I pay the penalty in my headaches, my famous headaches — a perfect circlet of pain! But I carry it as a queen carries her crown. Would you believe that I have one now? I wouldn't, however, have missed our rendezvous for anything. I have something very important to tell you."

"Well, let's have it," said Morris.

"I was perhaps a little headlong the other day in advising you to marry immediately. I have been thinking it over, and now I see it just a little differently."

"You seem to have a great many different ways of seeing the same object."

"Their number is infinite!" said Mrs. Penniman, in a tone which seemed to suggest that this convenient faculty was one of her brightest attributes.

"I recommend you to take one way and stick to it," Morris replied.

"Ah! but it isn't easy to choose. My imagination is never quiet, never satisfied. It makes me a bad adviser, perhaps; but it makes me a capital friend!"

"A capital friend who gives bad advice!" said Morris.

"Not intentionally — and who hurries off, at every risk, to make the most humble excuses!"

"Well, what do you advise me now?"

"To be very patient; to watch and wait."

"And is that bad advice or good?"

"That is not for me to say," Mrs.

Penniman rejoined, with some dignity. "I only pretend it's sincere."

"And will you come to me next week and recommend something different and equally sincere?"

"I may come to you next week and tell you that I am in the streets!"

"In the streets?"

"I have had a terrible scene with my brother, and he threatens, if anything happens, to turn me out of the house. You know I am a poor woman."

Morris had a speculative idea that she had a little property; but he naturally did not press this.

"I should be very sorry to see you suffer martyrdom for me," he said. "But you make your brother out a regular Turk."

Mrs. Penniman hesitated a little.

"I certainly do not regard Austin as a satisfactory Christian."

"And am I to wait till he is converted?"

"Wait, at any rate, till he is less violent. Bide your time, Mr. Townsend; remember the prize is great!"

Morris walked along some time in silence, tapping the railings and gateposts very sharply with his stick.

"You certainly are devilish inconsistent!" he broke out at last. "I have already got Catherine to consent to a private marriage."

Mrs. Penniman was indeed inconsistent, for at this news she gave a little jump of gratification.

"Oh! when and where?" she cried. And then she stopped short.

Morris was a little vague about this.

"That isn't fixed; but she consents. It's deuced awkward, now, to back out."

Mrs. Penniman, as I say, had stopped short; and she stood there with her eyes fixed brilliantly on her companion.

"Mr. Townsend," she proceeded, "shall I tell you something? Catherine loves you so much that you may do anything."

This declaration was slightly ambiguous, and Morris opened his eyes.

"I am happy to hear it! But what do you mean by 'anything'?"

"You may postpone — you may change about; she won't think the worse of you."

Morris stood there still, with his raised eyebrows; then he said simply and rather dryly — "Ah!" After this he remarked to Mrs. Penniman that if she walked so slowly she would attract notice, and he succeeded, after a fashion, in hurrying her back to the domicile of which her tenure had become so insecure.

XXII

He had slightly misrepresented the matter in saying that Catherine had consented to take the great step. We left her just now declaring that she would burn her ships behind her; but Morris, after having elicited this declaration, had become conscious of good reasons for not taking it up. He avoided, gracefully enough, fixing a day, though he left her under the impression that he had his eye on one. Catherine may have had her difficulties; but those of her circumspect suitor are also worthy of consideration. The prize was certainly great; but it was only to be won by striking the happy mean between precipitancy and caution. It would be all very well to take one's jump and trust to Providence; Providence was more especially on the side of clever people, and clever people were known by an indisposition to risk their bones. The ultimate reward of a union with a young woman who was both unattractive and impoverished ought to be connected with immediate disadvantages by some very palpable chain. Between the fear of losing Catherine and her possible fortune altogether, and the fear of taking her too soon and finding this possible fortune as void of actuality as a collection of emptied bottles, it was not comfortable for Morris Townsend to choose; a fact that should be remembered by readers disposed to judge harshly of a young man who may have struck them as making but an indifferently successful use of fine natural parts. He had not forgotten that in any event Catherine had her own ten thousand a year; he had devoted an abundance of meditation to this circumstance. But with his fine parts he rated himself high, and he had a perfectly definite appreciation of his value, which seemed to him inadequately represented by the sum I have mentioned. At the same time he reminded himself that this sum was considerable, that everything is relative, and that if a modest income is less desirable than a large one, the complete absence of revenue is nowhere accounted an advantage. These reflexions gave him plenty of occupation, and made it necessary that he should trim his sail. Dr. Sloper's opposition was the unknown quantity in the problem he had to work out. The natural way to work it out was by marrying Catherine; but in mathematics there are many short cuts, and Morris was not without a hope that he should yet discover one. When Catherine took him at his word and consented to renounce the attempt to mollify her father, he drew back skilfully enough, as I have said, and kept the wedding-day still an open question. Her faith in his sincerity was so complete that she was incapable of suspecting that he was playing with her; her trouble just now was of another kind. The poor girl had an admirable sense of honour; and from the moment she had brought herself to the point of violating her father's wish, it seemed to her that she had no right to enjoy his protection. It was on her conscience that she ought to live under his roof only so long as she conformed to his wisdom. There was a great deal of glory in such a position, but poor Catherine felt that she had forfeited her claim to it. She had cast her lot with a young man against whom he had solemnly warned her, and broken the contract under which he provided her with a happy home. She could not give up the young man, so she must leave the home; and the sooner the object of her preference offered her another the sooner her situation would lose its awkward twist. This was close reasoning; but it was commingled with an infinite amount of merely instinctive penitence. Catherine's days at this time were dismal, and the weight of some of her hours was almost more than she could bear. Her father never looked at her, never spoke to her. He knew perfectly what he was about, and this was part of a plan. She looked at him as much as she dared (for she was afraid of seeming to offer herself to his observation), and she pitied him for the sorrow she had brought upon him. She held up her head and busied her hands, and went about her daily occupations; and when the state of things in Washington Square seemed intolerable, she closed her eyes and indulged herself with an intellectual vision of the man for whose sake she had broken a sacred law. Mrs. Penniman, of the three persons in Washington Square, had much the most of the manner that belongs to a great crisis. If Catherine was quiet, she was quietly quiet, as I may say, and her pathetic effects, which there was no one to notice, were entirely unstudied and unintended. If the Doctor was stiff and dry and absolutely indifferent to the presence of his companions, it was so lightly, neatly, easily done, that you would have had to know him well to discover that, on the whole, he rather enjoyed having to be so disagreeable. But Mrs. Penniman was elaborately reserved and significantly silent; there was a richer rustle in the very deliberate movements to which she confined herself, and when she occasionally spoke, in connexion with some very trivial event, she had the air of meaning something deeper than what she said. Between Catherine and her father nothing had passed since the evening she went to speak to him in his study. She had something to say to him — it seemed to her she ought to say it; but she kept it back, for fear of irritating him. He also had something to say to her; but he was determined not to speak first. He was interested, as we know, in seeing how, if she were left to herself, she would "stick." At last she told him she had seen Morris Townsend again, and that their relations remained quite the same.

"I think we shall marry — before very long. And probably, meanwhile, I shall see him rather often; about once a week, not more."

The Doctor looked at her coldly from head to foot, as if she had been a stranger. It was the first time his eyes had rested on her for a week, which was fortunate, if that was to be their expression. "Why not three times a day?" he asked. "What prevents your meeting as often as you choose?"

She turned away a moment; there were tears in her eyes. Then she said, "It is better once a week."

"I don't see how it is better. It is as bad as it can be. If you flatter yourself that I care for little modifications of that sort, you are very much mistaken. It is as wrong of you to see him once a week as it would be to see him all day long. Not that it matters to me, however."

Catherine tried to follow these words, but they seemed to lead towards a vague horror from which she recoiled. "I think we shall marry pretty soon," she repeated at last.

Her father gave her his dreadful look again, as if she were some one else. "Why do you tell me that? It's no concern of mine."

"Oh, father!" she broke out, "don't you care, even if you do feel so?"

"Not a button. Once you marry, it's quite the same to me when or where or why you do it; and if you think to compound for your folly by hoisting your flag in this way, you may spare yourself the trouble."

With this he turned away. But the next day he spoke to her of his own accord, and his manner was somewhat changed. "Shall you be married within the next four or five months?" he asked.

"I don't know, father," said Catherine, "It is not very easy for us to make up our minds."

"Put it off, then, for six months, and in the meantime I will take you to Europe. I should like you very much to go."

It gave her such delight, after his words of the day before, to hear that he should "like" her to do something, and that he still had in his heart any of the tenderness of preference, that she gave a little exclamation of joy. But then she became conscious that Morris was not included in this proposal, and that — as regards really going — she would greatly prefer to remain at home with him. But she blushed, none the less, more comfortably than she had done of late. "It would be delightful to go to Europe," she remarked, with a sense that the idea was not original, and that her tone was not all it might be.

"Very well, then, we will go. Pack up your clothes."

"I had better tell Mr. Townsend," said Catherine.

Her father fixed his cold eyes upon her. "If you mean that you had better ask his leave, all that remains to me is to hope he will give it."

The girl was sharply touched by the pathetic ring of the words; it was the most calculated, the most dramatic little speech the Doctor had ever uttered. She felt that it was a great thing for her, under the circumstances, to have this fine opportunity of showing him her respect; and yet there was something else that she felt

243

as well, and that she presently expressed. "I sometimes think that if I do what you dislike so much, I ought not to stay with you."

"To stay with me?"

"If I live with you, I ought to obey you."

"If that's your theory, it's certainly mine," said the Doctor, with a dry laugh.

"But if I don't obey you, I ought not to live with you — to enjoy your kindness and protection."

This striking argument gave the Doctor a sudden sense of having underestimated his daughter; it seemed even more than worthy of a young woman who had revealed the quality of unaggressive obstinacy. But it displeased him — displeased him deeply, and he signified as much. "That idea is in very bad taste," he said. "Did you get it from Mr. Townsend?"

"Oh no; it's my own!" said Catherine eagerly.

"Keep it to yourself, then," her father answered, more than ever determined she should go to Europe.

XXIII

IF Morris Townsend was not to be included in this journey, no more was Mrs. Penniman, who would have been thankful for an invitation, but who (to do her justice) bore her disappointment in a perfectly ladylike manner. "I should enjoy seeing the works of Raphael and the ruins — the ruins of the Pantheon," she said to Mrs. Almond; "but, on the other hand, I shall not be sorry to be alone and at peace for the next few months in Washington Square. I want rest; I have been through so much in the last four months." Mrs. Almond thought it rather cruel that her brother should not take poor Lavinia abroad; but she easily understood that, if the purpose of his expedition was to make Catherine forget her lover, it was not in his interest to give his daughter this young man's best friend as a companion. "If Lavinia had not been so foolish, she might visit the ruins of the Pantheon," she said to herself; and she continued to regret her sister's folly, even though the latter assured her that she had often heard the relics in question most satisfactorily described by Mr. Penniman. Mrs. Penniman was perfectly aware that her brother's motive in undertaking a foreign tour was to lay a trap for Catherine's constancy; and she imparted this conviction very frankly to her niece.

"He thinks it will make you forget Morris," she said (she always called the young man "Morris" now); "out of sight, out of mind, you know. He thinks that all the things you will see over there will drive him out of your thoughts."

Catherine looked greatly alarmed. "If he thinks that, I ought to tell him beforehand."

Mrs. Penniman shook her head. "Tell him afterwards, my dear! After he has had all the trouble and the expense! That's the way to serve him." And she added, in a softer key, that it must be delightful to think of those who love us among the ruins of the Pantheon.

Her father's displeasure had cost the girl, as we know, a great deal of deep-welling sorrow — sorrow of the purest and most generous kind, without a touch of resentment or rancour; but for the first time, after he had dismissed with such contemptuous brevity her apology for being a charge upon him, there was a spark of anger in her grief. She had felt his contempt; it had scorched her; that speech about her bad taste made her ears burn for three days. During this period she was less considerate; she had an idea — a rather vague one, but it was agreeable to her sense of injury — that now she was absolved from penance, and might do what she chose. She chose to write to Morris Townsend to meet her in the Square and take her to walk about the town. If she were going to Europe out of respect to her father, she might at least give herself this satisfaction. She felt in every way at present more free and more resolute; there was a force that urged her. Now at last, completely and unreservedly, her passion possessed her.

Morris met her at last, and they took a long walk. She told him immediately what had happened — that her father wished to take her away. It would be for six months, to Europe; she would do abso-

lutely what Morris should think best. She hoped inexpressibly that he would think it best she should stay at home. It was some time before he said what he thought: he asked, as they walked along, a great many questions. There was one that especially struck her; it seemed so incongruous.

"Should you like to see all those celebrated things over there?"

"Oh no, Morris!" said Catherine, quite deprecatingly.

"Gracious Heaven, what a dull woman!" Morris exclaimed to himself.

"He thinks I will forget you," said Catherine: "that all these things will drive you out of my mind."

"Well, my dear, perhaps they will!"

"Please don't say that," Catherine answered gently, as they walked along. "Poor father will be disappointed."

Morris gave a little laugh. "Yes, I verily believe that your poor father will be disappointed! But you will have seen Europe," he added humorously. "What a take-in!"

"I don't care for seeing Europe," Catherine said.

"You ought to care, my dear. And it may mollify your father."

Catherine, conscious of her obstinacy, expected little of this, and could not rid herself of the idea that in going abroad and yet remaining firm, she should play her father a trick. "Don't you think it would be a kind of deception?" she asked.

"Doesn't he want to deceive

you?" cried Morris. "It will serve him right! I really think you had better go."

"And not be married for so long?"

"Be married when you come back. You can buy your wedding clothes in Paris." And then Morris, with great kindness of tone, explained his view of the matter. It would be a good thing that she should go; it would put them completely in the right. It would show they were reasonable and willing to wait. Once they were so sure of each other, they could afford to wait — what had they to fear? If there was a particle of chance that her father would be favourably affected by her going, that ought to settle it; for, after all, Morris was very unwilling to be the cause of her being disinherited. It was not for himself, it was for her and for her children. He was willing to wait for her; it would be hard, but he could do it. And over there, among beautiful scenes and noble monuments, perhaps the old gentleman would be softened; such things were supposed to exert a humanising influence. He might be touched by her gentleness, her patience, her willingness to make any sacrifice but *that* one; and if she should appeal to him some day, in some celebrated spot — in Italy, say, in the evening; in Venice, in a gondola, by moonlight — if she should be a little clever about it and touch the right chord, perhaps he would fold her in his arms and tell her that he forgave her. Catherine was immensely struck with this conception of the affair, which seemed eminently worthy of her lover's brilliant intellect; though she viewed it askance in so far as it depended upon her own powers of execution. The idea of being "clever" in a gondola by moonlight appeared to her to involve elements of which her grasp was not active. But it was settled between them that she should tell her father that she was ready to follow him obediently anywhere, making the mental reservation that she loved Morris Townsend more than ever.

She informed the Doctor she was ready to embark, and he made rapid arrangements for this event. Catherine had many farewells to make, but with only two of them are we actively concerned. Mrs. Penniman took a discriminating view of her niece's journey; it seemed to her very proper that Mr. Townsend's destined bride should wish to embellish her mind by a foreign tour.

"You leave him in good hands," she said, pressing her lips to Catherine's forehead. (She was very fond of kissing people's foreheads; it was an involuntary expression of sympathy with the intellectual part.) "I shall see him often; I shall feel like one of the vestals of old, tending the sacred flame."

"You behave beautifully about not going with us," Catherine answered, not presuming to examine this analogy.

"It is my pride that keeps me up," said Mrs. Penniman, tapping the body of her dress, which always gave forth a sort of metallic ring.

Catherine's parting with her lover was short, and few words were exchanged.

"Shall I find you just the same when I come back?" she asked; though the question was not the fruit of scepticism.

"The same — only more so!" said Morris, smiling.

It does not enter into our scheme to narrate in detail Dr. Sloper's proceedings in the eastern hemisphere. He made the grand tour of Europe, travelled in considerable splendour, and (as was to have been expected in a man of his high cultivation) found so much in art and antiquity to interest him, that he remained abroad, not for six months, but for twelve. Mrs. Penniman, in Washington Square, accommodated herself to his absence. She enjoyed her uncontested dominion in the empty house, and flattered herself that she made it more attractive to their friends than when her brother was at home. To Morris Townsend, at least, it would have appeared that she made it singularly attractive. He was altogether her most frequent visitor, and Mrs. Penniman was very fond of asking him to tea. He had his chair — a very easy one at the fireside in the back parlour (when the great mahogany sliding-doors, with silver knobs and hinges, which divided this apartment from its more formal neighbour, were closed), and he used to smoke cigars in the Doctor's study, where he often spent an hour in turning over the curious collections of its absent proprietor. He thought Mrs. Penniman a goose, as we know; but he was no goose himself, and, as a young man of luxurious tastes and scanty resources, he found the house a perfect castle of indolence. It became for him a club with a single member. Mrs. Penniman saw much less of her sister than while the Doctor was at home; for Mrs. Almond had felt moved to tell her that she disapproved of her relations with Mr. Townsend. She had no business to be so friendly to a young man of whom their brother thought so meanly, and Mrs. Almond was surprised at her levity in foisting a most deplorable engagement upon Catherine.

"Deplorable?" cried Lavinia. "He will make her a lovely husband!"

"I don't believe in lovely husbands," said Mrs. Almond; "I only believe in good ones. If he marries her, and she comes into Austin's money, they may get on. He will be an idle, amiable, selfish, and doubtless tolerably good-natured fellow. But if she doesn't get the money and he finds himself tied to her, Heaven have mercy on her! He will have none. He will hate her for his disappointment, and take his revenge; he will be pitiless and cruel. Woe betide poor Catherine! I recommend you to talk a little with his sister; it's a pity Catherine can't marry *her!*"

Mrs. Penniman had no appetite whatever for conversation with Mrs. Montgomery, whose acquaintance she made no trouble to cultivate; and the effect of this alarming forecast of her niece's destiny was to make her think it indeed a thousand pities that Mr. Townsend's generous nature should be embittered. Bright enjoyment was his natural element, and how could he be comfortable if there should prove to be nothing to enjoy? It became a fixed idea with Mrs. Penniman that he should yet enjoy her brother's fortune, on which she had acuteness enough to perceive that her own claim was small.

"If he doesn't leave it to Catherine, it certainly won't be to leave it to me," she said.

XXIV

THE DOCTOR, during the first six months he was abroad, never spoke to his daughter of their little difference; partly on system, and partly because he had a great many other things to think about. It was idle to attempt to ascertain the state of her affections without direct inquiry, because, if she had not had an expressive manner among the familiar influences of home, she failed to gather animation from the mountains of Switzerland or the monuments of Italy. She was always her father's docile and reasonable associate —

going through their sight-seeing in deferential silence, never complaining of fatigue, always ready to start at the hour he had appointed over-night, making no foolish criticisms and indulging in no refinements of appreciation. "She is about as intelligent as the bundle of shawls," the Doctor said; her main superiority being that while the bundle of shawls sometimes got lost, or tumbled out of the carriage, Catherine was always at her post, and had a firm and ample seat. But her father had expected this, and he was not constrained to set down her intellectual limitations as a tourist to sentimental depression; she had completely divested herself of the characteristics of a victim, and during the whole time that they were abroad she never uttered an audible sigh. He supposed she was in correspondence with Morris Townsend; but he held his peace about it, for he never saw the young man's letters, and Catherine's own missives were always given to the courier to post. She heard from her lover with considerable regularity, but his letters came enclosed in Mrs. Penniman's; so that whenever the Doctor handed her a packet addressed in his sister's hand, he was an involuntary instrument of the passion he condemned. Catherine made this reflexion, and six months earlier she would have felt bound to give him warning; but now she deemed herself absolved. There was a sore spot in her heart that his own words had made when once she spoke to him as she thought honour prompted; she would try and please him as far as she could, but she would never speak that way again. She read her lover's letters in secret.

One day at the end of the summer, the two travellers found themselves in a lonely valley of the Alps. They were crossing one of the passes, and on the long ascent they had got out of the carriage and had wandered much in advance. After a while the Doctor descried a footpath which, leading through a transverse valley, would bring them out, as he justly supposed, at a much higher point of the ascent. They followed this devious way, and finally lost the path; the valley proved very wild and rough, and their walk became rather a scramble. They were good walkers, however, and they took their adventure easily; from time to time they stopped, that Catherine might rest; and then she sat upon a stone and looked about her at the hard-featured rocks and the glowing sky. It was late in the afternoon, in the last of August; night was coming on, and, as they had reached a great elevation, the air was cold and sharp. In the west there was a great suffusion of cold, red light, which made the sides of the little valley look only the more rugged and dusky. During one of their pauses, her father left her and wandered away to some high place, at a distance, to get a view. He was out of sight; she sat there alone, in the stillness, which was just touched by the vague murmur, somewhere, of a mountain brook. She thought of Morris Townsend, and the place was so desolate and lonely that he seemed very far away. Her father remained absent a long time; she began to wonder what had become of him. But at last he reappeared, coming towards her in the clear twilight, and she got up, to go on. He made no motion to proceed, however, but came close to her, as if he had something to say. He stopped in front of her and stood looking at her, with eyes that had kept the light of the flushing snow-summits on which they had just been fixed. Then, abruptly, in a low tone, he asked her an unexpected question:

"Have you given him up?"

The question was unexpected, but Catherine was only superficially unprepared.

"No, father!" she answered.

He looked at her again for some moments, without speaking.

"Does he write to you?" he asked.

"Yes — about twice a month."

The Doctor looked up and down the valley, swinging his stick; then he said to her, in the same low tone:

"I am very angry."

She wondered what he meant — whether he wished to frighten her. If he did, the place was well chosen; this hard, melancholy dell, abandoned by the summer light, made her feel her loneliness. She looked around her, and her heart grew cold; for a moment her fear was great. But she could think of nothing to say, save to murmur gently, "I am sorry."

"You try my patience," her father went on, "and you ought to know what I am, I am not a very good man. Though I am very smooth externally, at bottom I am very passionate; and I assure you I can be very hard."

She could not think why he told her these things. Had he brought her there on purpose, and was it part of a plan? What was the plan? Catherine asked herself. Was it to startle her suddenly into a retractation — to take an advantage of her by dread? Dread of what? The place was ugly and lonely, but the place could do her no harm. There was a kind of still intensity about her father, which made him dangerous, but Catherine hardly went so far as to say to herself that it might be part of his plan to fasten his hand — the neat, fine, supple hand of a distinguished physician — in her throat. Nevertheless, she receded a step. "I am sure you can be anything you please," she said. And it was her simple belief.

"I am very angry," he replied, more sharply.

"Why has it taken you so suddenly?"

"It has not taken me suddenly. I have been raging inwardly for the last six months. But just now this seemed a good place to flare out. It's so quiet, and we are alone."

"Yes, it's very quiet," said Catherine vaguely, looking about her.

"Won't you come back to the carriage?"

"In a moment. Do you mean that in all this time you have not yielded an inch?"

"I would if I could, father; but I can't."

The Doctor looked round him too. "Should you like to be left in such a place as this, to starve?"

"What do you mean?" cried the girl.

"That will be your fate — that's how he will leave you."

He would not touch her, but he had touched Morris. The warmth came back to her heart. "That is not true, father," she broke out, "and you ought not to say it! It is not right, and it's not true!"

He shook his head slowly. "No, it's not right, because you won't believe it. But it *is* true. Come back to the carriage."

He turned away, and she followed him; he went faster, and was presently much in advance. But from time to time he stopped, without turning round, to let her keep up with him, and she made her way forward with difficulty, her heart beating with the excitement of having for the first time spoken to him in violence. By this time it had grown almost dark, and she ended by losing sight of him. But she kept her course, and after a little, the valley making a sudden turn, she gained the road, where the carriage stood waiting. In it sat her father, rigid and silent; in silence, too, she took her place beside him. It seemed to her, later, in looking back upon all this, that for days afterwards not a word had been exchanged between them. The scene had been a strange one, but it had not permanently affected her feeling towards her father, for it was natural, after all, that he should occasionally make a scene of some kind, and he had let her alone for six months. The strangest part of it was that he had said he was not a good man; Catherine wondered a great deal what he had meant by that. The statement failed to appeal to her credence, and it was not grateful to any resentment that she entertained. Even in the utmost bitterness that she might feel, it would give her no satisfaction to think him less complete. Such a saying as that was a part of his great subtlety — men so clever as he might say anything and mean anything. And as to his being hard, that surely, in a man, was a virtue.

He let her alone for six months more — six months during which she accommodated herself without a protest to the extension of their tour. But he spoke again at the end of this time; it was at the very last, the night before they embarked for New York, in the hotel at Liverpool. They had been dining together in a great dim, musty sitting-room; and then the cloth had been removed, and the Doctor walked slowly up and down. Catherine at last took her candle to go to bed, but her father motioned her to stay.

"What do you mean to do when you get home?" he asked, while she stood there with her candle in her hand.

"Do you mean about Mr. Townsend?"

"About Mr. Townsend."

"We shall probably marry."

The Doctor took several turns again while she waited. "Do you hear from him as much as ever?"

"Yes; twice a month," said Catherine promptly.

"And does he always talk about marriage?"

"Oh yes! That is, he talks about other things too, but he always says something about that."

"I am glad to hear he varies his subjects; his letters might otherwise be monotonous."

"He writes beautifully," said Catherine, who was very glad of a chance to say it.

"They always write beautifully. However, in a given case that doesn't diminish the merit. So, as soon as you arrive, you are going off with him?"

This seemed a rather gross way of putting it, and something that there was of dignity in Catherine resented it. "I cannot tell you till we arrive," she said.

"That's reasonable enough," her father answered. "That's all I ask of you — that you *do* tell me, that you give me definite notice. When a poor man is to lose his only child, he likes to have an inkling of it beforehand."

"Oh, father, you will not lose me!" Catherine said, spilling her candle-wax.

"Three days before will do," he went on, "if you are in a position

251

to be positive then. He ought to be very thankful to me, do you know. I have done a mighty good thing for him in taking you abroad; your value is twice as great, with all the knowledge and taste that you have acquired. A year ago, you were perhaps a little limited — a little rustic; but now you have seen everything, and appreciated everything, and you will be a most entertaining companion. We have fattened the sheep for him before he kills it!" Catherine turned away, and stood staring at the blank door. "Go to bed," said her father; "and, as we don't go aboard till noon, you may sleep late. We shall probably have a most uncomfortable voyage."

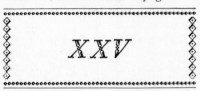

XXV

THE VOYAGE was indeed uncomfortable, and Catherine, on arriving in New York, had not the compensation of "going off," in her father's phrase, with Morris Townsend. She saw him, however, the day after she landed; and, in the meantime, he formed a natural subject of conversation between our heroine and her Aunt Lavinia, with whom, the night she disembarked, the girl was closeted for a long time before either lady retired to rest.

"I have seen a great deal of him," said Mrs. Penniman. "He is not very easy to know. I suppose you think you know him; but you don't, my dear. You will some day; but it will only be after you have lived with him. I may almost say *I* have lived with him," Mrs. Penniman proceeded, while Catherine stared. "I think I know him now; I have had such remarkable opportunities. You will have the same — or rather, you will have better!" and Aunt Lavinia smiled. "Then you will see what I mean. It's a wonderful character, full of passion and energy, and just as true!"

Catherine listened with a mixture of interest and apprehension. Aunt Lavinia was intensely sympathetic, and Catherine, for the past year, while she wandered through foreign galleries and churches, and rolled over the smoothness of posting roads, nursing the thoughts that never passed her lips, had often longed for the company of some intelligent person of her own sex. To tell her story to some kind woman — at moments it seemed to her that this would give her comfort, and she had more than once been on the point of taking the landlady, or the nice young person from the dressmaker's, into her confidence. If a woman had been near her she would on certain occasions have treated such a companion to a fit of weeping; and she had an apprehension that, on her return, this would form her response to Aunt Lavinia's first embrace. In fact, however, the two ladies had met, in Washington Square, without tears, and when they found themselves together a certain dryness fell upon the girl's emotion. It came over her with a greater force that Mrs. Penniman had enjoyed a whole year of her lover's society, and it was not a pleasure to her to hear her aunt explain and interpret the young man, speaking of him as if her own knowledge of him were supreme. It was not that Catherine was jealous; but her sense of Mrs. Penniman's innocent falsity, which had lain dormant, began to haunt her again, and she was glad that she was safely at home. With this, however, it was a blessing to be able to talk of Morris, to sound his name, to be with a person who was not unjust to him.

"You have been very kind to him," said Catherine. "He has written me that, often. I shall never forget that, Aunt Lavinia."

"I have done what I could; it has been very little. To let him come and talk to me, and give him his cup of tea — that was all. Your Aunt Almond thought it was too much, and used to scold me terribly; but she promised me, at least, not to betray me."

"To betray you?"

"Not to tell your father. He used to sit in your father's study!" said Mrs. Penniman, with a little laugh.

Catherine was silent a moment. This idea was disagreeable to her, and she was reminded again, with pain, of her aunt's secretive habits. Morris, the reader may be informed, had had the tact not to tell her that he sat in her father's study. He had known her but for a few months, and her aunt had known her for fifteen years; and yet he would not have made the mistake of thinking that Catherine would see the joke of the thing. "I am sorry you made him go into father's room," she said, after a while.

"I didn't make him go; he went himself. He liked to look at the books, and all those things in the glass cases. He knows all about them; he knows all about everything."

Catherine was silent again; then, "I wish he had found some employment," she said.

"He has found some employment! It's beautiful news, and he told me to tell you as soon as you arrived. He has gone into partnership with a commission merchant. It was all settled, quite suddenly, a week ago."

This seemed to Catherine indeed beautiful news; it had a fine prosperous air. "Oh, I'm so glad!" she said; and now, for a moment, she was disposed to throw herself on Aunt Lavinia's neck.

"It's much better than being under some one; and he has never been used to that," Mrs. Penniman went on. "He is just as good as his partner — they are perfectly equal! You see how right he was to wait. I should like to know what your father can say now! They have got an office in Duane Street, and little printed cards; he brought me one to show me. I have got it in my room, and you shall see it to-morrow. That's what he said to me the last time he was here — 'You see how right I was to wait!' He has got other people under him, instead of being a subordinate. He could never be a subordinate; I have often told him I could never think of him in that way."

Catherine assented to this proposition, and was very happy to know that Morris was his own master; but she was deprived of the satisfaction of thinking that she might communicate this news in triumph to her father. Her father would care equally little whether Morris were established in business or transported for life. Her trunks had been brought into her room, and further reference to her lover was for a short time suspended, while she opened them and displayed to her aunt some of the spoils of foreign travel. These were rich and abundant; and Catherine had brought home a present to every one — to every one save Morris, to whom she had brought simply her undiverted heart. To Mrs. Penniman she had been lavishly generous, and Aunt Lavinia spent half an hour in unfolding and folding again, with little ejaculations of gratitude and taste. She marched about for some time in a splendid cashmere shawl, which Catherine had begged her to accept, settling it on her shoulders, and twisting down her head to see how low the point descended behind.

"I shall regard it only as a loan," she said. "I will leave it to you again when I die; or rather," she added, kissing her niece again, "I will leave it to your first-born little girl!" And draped in her shawl, she stood there smiling.

"You had better wait till she comes," said Catherine.

"I don't like the way you say that," Mrs. Penniman rejoined, in a moment. "Catherine, are you changed?"

"No; I am the same."

"You have not swerved a line?"

"I am exactly the same," Catherine repeated, wishing her aunt were a little less sympathetic.

"Well, I am glad!" and Mrs. Penniman surveyed her cashmere in the glass. Then, "How is your father?" she asked in a moment, with her eyes on her niece. "Your letters were so meagre — I could never tell!"

"Father is very well."

"Ah, you know what I mean," said Mrs. Penniman, with a dignity to which the cashmere gave a richer effect. "Is he still implacable!"

"Oh yes!"

"Quite unchanged?"

"He is, if possible, more firm."

Mrs. Penniman took off her great shawl, and slowly folded it up. "That is very bad. You had no success with your little project?"

"What little project?"

"Morris told her all about it. The idea of turning the tables on him, in Europe; of watching him, when he was agreeably impressed by some celebrated sight — he pretends to be so artistic, you know — and then just pleading with him and bringing him round."

"I never tried it. It was Morris's idea; but if he had been with us, in Europe, he would have seen that father was never impressed in that way. He *is* artistic — tremendously artistic; but the more celebrated places we visited, and the more he admired them, the less use it would have been to plead with him. They seemed only to make him more determined — more terrible," said poor Catherine. "I shall never bring him round, and I expect nothing now."

"Well, I must say," Mrs. Penniman answered, "I never supposed you were going to give it up."

"I have given it up. I don't care now."

"You have grown very brave," said Mrs. Penniman, with a short laugh. "I didn't advise you to sacrifice your property."

"Yes, I am braver than I was. You asked me if I had changed; I have changed in that way. Oh," the girl went on, "I have changed very much. And it isn't my property. If *he* doesn't care for it, why should I?"

Mrs. Penniman hesitated. "Perhaps he does care for it."

"He cares for it for my sake, because he doesn't want to injure me. But he will know — he knows already — how little he need be afraid about that. Besides," said Catherine, "I have got plenty of money of my own. We shall be very well off; and now hasn't he got his business? I am delighted about that business." She went on talking, showing a good deal of excitement as she proceeded. Her aunt had never seen her with just this manner, and Mrs. Penniman, observing her, set it down to foreign travel, which had made her more positive, more mature. She thought also that Catherine had improved in appear-

ance; she looked rather handsome. Mrs. Penniman wondered whether Morris Townsend would be struck with that. While she was engaged in this speculation, Catherine broke out, with a certain sharpness, "Why are you so contradictory, Aunt Penniman? You seem to think one thing at one time, and another at another. A year ago, before I went away, you wished me not to mind about displeasing father; and now you seem to recommend me to take another line. You change about so."

This attack was unexpected, for Mrs. Penniman was not used, in any discussion, to seeing the war carried into her own country — possibly because the enemy generally had doubts of finding subsistence there. To her own consciousness, the flowery fields of her reason had rarely been ravaged by a hostile force. It was perhaps on this account that in defending them she was majestic rather than agile.

"I don't know what you accuse me of, save of being too deeply interested in your happiness. It is the first time I have been told I am capricious. That fault is not what I am usually reproached with."

"You were angry last year that I wouldn't marry immediately, and now you talk about my winning my father over. You told me it would serve him right if he should take me to Europe for nothing. Well, he has taken me for nothing, and you ought to be satisfied. Nothing is changed — nothing but my feeling about father. I don't mind nearly so much now. I have been as good as I could, but he doesn't care. Now I don't care either. I don't know whether I have grown bad; perhaps I have. But I don't care for that. I have come home to be married — that's all I know. That ought to please you, unless you have taken up some new idea; you are so strange. You may do as you please; but you must never speak to me again about pleading with father. I shall never plead with him for anything; that is all over. He has put me off. I am come home to be married."

This was a more authoritative speech than she had ever heard on her niece's lips, and Mrs. Penniman was proportionately startled. She was indeed a little awestruck, and the force of the girl's emotion and resolution left her nothing to reply. She was easily frightened, and she always carried off her discomfiture by a concession; a concession which was often accompanied, as in the present case, by a little nervous laugh.

XXVI

IF she had disturbed her niece's temper — she began from this moment forward to talk a good deal about Catherine's temper, an article which up to that time had never been mentioned in connexion with our heroine — Catherine had oppor-

tunity, on the morrow, to recover her serenity. Mrs. Penniman had given her a message from Morris Townsend, to the effect that he would come and welcome her home on the day after her arrival. He came in the afternoon; but, as may be imagined, he was not on this occasion made free of Dr. Sloper's study. He had been coming and going, for the past year, so comfortably and irresponsibly, that he had a certain sense of being wronged by finding himself reminded that he must now limit his horizon to the front parlour, which was Catherine's particular province.

"I am very glad you have come back," he said; "it makes me very happy to see you again." And he looked at her, smiling, from head to foot; though it did not appear, afterwards, that he agreed with Mrs. Penniman (who, womanlike, went more into details) in thinking her embellished.

To Catherine he appeared resplendent; it was some time before she could believe again that this beautiful young man was her own exclusive property. They had a great deal of characteristic lovers' talk — a soft exchange of inquiries and assurances. In these matters Morris had an excellent grace, which flung a picturesque interest even over the account of his début in the commission business — a subject as to which his companion earnestly questioned him. From time to time he got up from the sofa where they sat together, and walked about the room; after which he came back, smiling and passing his hand through his hair. He was unquiet, as was natural in a young man who has just been re-united to a long-absent mistress, and Catherine made the reflexion that she had never seen him so ex-cited. It gave her pleasure, some-how, to note this fact. He asked her questions about her travels, to some of which she was unable to reply, for she had forgotten the names of places, and the order of her father's journey. But for the moment she was so happy, so lifted up by the belief that her troubles at last were over, that she forgot to be ashamed of her meagre answers. It seemed to her now that she could marry him without the remnant of a scruple or a single tremor save those that belonged to joy. With-out waiting for him to ask, she told him that her father had come back in exactly the same state of mind — that he had not yielded an inch.

"We must not expect it now," she said, "and we must do without it."

Morris sat looking and smiling. "My poor dear girl!" he exclaimed.

"You mustn't pity me," said Catherine; "I don't mind it now — I am used to it."

Morris continued to smile, and then he got up and walked about again. "You had better let me try him!"

"Try to bring him over? You would only make him worse," Cath-erine answered resolutely.

"You say that because I managed it so badly before. But I should manage it differently now. I am much wiser; I have had a year to think of it. I have more tact."

"Is that what you have been thinking of for a year?"

"Much of the time. You see, the idea sticks in my crop. I don't like to be beaten."

"How are you beaten if we marry?"

"Of course, I am not beaten on the main issue; but I am, don't you see, on all the rest of it — on the question of my reputation, of my relations with your father, of my relations with my own children, if we should have any."

"We shall have enough for our children — we shall have enough for everything. Don't you expect to succeed in business?"

"Brilliantly, and we shall cer-tainly be very comfortable. But it isn't of the mere material comfort I speak; it is of the moral comfort," said Morris — "of the intellectual satisfaction!"

"I have great moral comfort now," Catherine declared, very simply.

"Of course you have. But with me it is different. I have staked my pride on proving to your father that he is wrong; and now that I am at the head of a flourishing business, I can deal with him as an equal. I have a capital plan — do let me go at him!"

He stood before her with his bright face, his jaunty air, his hands in his pockets; and she got up, with her eyes resting on his own. "Please don't, Morris; please don't," she said; and there was a certain mild, sad firmness in her tone which he heard for the first time. "We must ask no favours of him — we must ask nothing more. He won't relent, and nothing good will come of it. I know it now — I have a very good reason."

"And pray, what is your reason?"

She hesitated to bring it out, but at last it came. "He is not very fond of me!"

"Oh, bother!" cried Morris angrily.

"I wouldn't say such a thing without being sure. I saw it, I felt it, in England, just before he came away. He talked to me one night — the last night; and then it came over me. You can tell when a person feels that way. I wouldn't accuse him if he hadn't made me feel that way. I don't accuse him; I just tell you that that's how it is. He can't help it; we can't govern our affections. Do I govern mine? mightn't he say that to me? It's because he is so fond of my mother, whom we lost so long ago. She was beautiful, and very, very brilliant; he is always thinking of her. I am not at all like her; Aunt Penniman has told me that. Of course, it isn't my fault; but neither is it his fault. All I mean is, it's true; and it's a stronger reason for his never being reconciled than simply his dislike for you."

"'Simply?'" cried Morris, with a laugh, "I am much obliged for that!"

"I don't mind about his disliking you now; I mind everything less. I feel differently; I feel separated from my father."

"Upon my word," said Morris, "you are a queer family!"

"Don't say that — don't say anything unkind," the girl entreated. "You must be very kind to me now, because, Morris — because," and she hesitated a moment — "because I have done a great deal for you."

"Oh, I know that, my dear!"

She had spoken up to this moment without vehemence or outward sign of emotion, gently, reasoningly, only trying to explain. But her emotion had been ineffectually smothered, and it betrayed itself at last in the trembling of her voice. "It is a great thing to be separated like that from your father, when you have worshipped him before. It has made me very unhappy; or it would have made me so if I didn't love you. You can tell when a person speaks to you as if — as if —— "

"As if what?"

"As if they despised you!" said Catherine passionately. "He spoke that way the night before we sailed. It wasn't much, but it was enough, and I thought of it on the voyage, all the time. Then I made up my mind. I will never ask him for anything again, or expect anything from him. It would not be natural now. We must be very happy together, and we must not seem to depend upon his forgiveness. And Morris, Morris, you must never despise me!"

This was an easy promise to make, and Morris made it with fine

258

effect. But for the moment he undertook nothing more onerous.

XXVII

THE DOCTOR, of course, on his return, had a good deal of talk with his sisters. He was at no great pains to narrate his travels or to communicate his impressions of distant lands to Mrs. Penniman, upon whom he contented himself with bestowing a memento of his enviable experience, in the shape of a velvet gown. But he conversed with her at some length about matters nearer home, and lost no time in assuring her that he was still an inflexible father.

"I have no doubt you have seen a great deal of Mr. Townsend, and done your best to console him for Catherine's absence," he said. "I don't ask you, and you needn't deny it. I wouldn't put the question to you for the world, and expose you to the inconvenience of having to — a — excogitate an answer. No one has betrayed you, and there has been no spy upon your proceedings. Elizabeth has told no tales, and has never mentioned you except to praise your good looks and good spirits. The thing is simply an inference of my own — an induction, as the philosophers say. It seems to me likely that you would have offered an asylum to an interesting sufferer. Mr. Townsend has been a good deal in the house; there is something in the house that tells me so. We doctors, you know, end by acquiring fine perceptions, and it is impressed upon my sensorium that he has sat in these chairs, in a very easy attitude, and warmed himself at that fire. I don't grudge him the comfort of it; it is the only one he will ever enjoy at my expense. It seems likely, indeed, that I shall be able to economise at his own. I don't know what you may have said to him, or what you may say hereafter; but I should like you to know that if you have encouraged him to believe that he will gain anything by hanging on, or that I have budged a hair's-breadth from the position I took up a year ago, you have played him a trick for which he may exact reparation. I'm not sure that he may not bring a suit against you. Of course you have done it conscientiously; you have made yourself believe that I can be tired out. This is the most baseless hallucination that ever visited the brain of a genial optimist. I am not in the least tired; I am as fresh as when I started; I am good for fifty years yet. Catherine appears not to have budged an inch either; she is equally fresh; so we are about where we were before. This, however, you know as well as I. What I wish is simply to give you notice of my own state of mind! Take it to heart, dear Lavinia. Beware of the just resentment of a deluded fortune-hunter!"

"I can't say I expected it," said Mrs. Penniman. "And I had a sort of foolish hope that you would come home without that odious ironical tone with which you treat the most sacred subjects."

"Don't undervalue irony, it is often of great use. It is not, however, always necessary, and I will show you how gracefully I can lay it aside. I should like to know whether you think Morris Townsend will hang on."

"I will answer you with your own weapons," said Mrs. Penniman. "You had better wait and see!"

"Do you call such a speech as that one of my own weapons? I never said anything so rough."

"He will hang on long enough to make you very uncomfortable, then."

"My dear Lavinia," exclaimed the Doctor, "do you call that irony? I call it pugilism."

Mrs. Penniman, however, in spite of her pugilism, was a good deal frightened, and she took counsel of her fears. Her brother meanwhile took counsel, with many reservations, of Mrs. Almond, to whom he was no less generous than to Lavinia, and a good deal more communicative.

"I suppose she has had him there all the while," he said. "I must look into the state of my wine! You needn't mind telling me now; I have already said all I mean to say to her on the subject."

"I believe he was in the house a good deal," Mrs. Almond answered. "But you must admit that your leaving Lavinia quite alone was a great change for her, and

that it was natural she should want some society."

"I do admit that, and that is why I shall make no row about the wine; I shall set it down as compensation to Lavinia. She is capable of telling me that she drank it all herself. Think of the inconceivable bad taste, in the circumstances, of that fellow making free with the house — or coming there at all! If that doesn't describe him, he is indescribable."

"His plan is to get what he can. Lavinia will have supported him for a year," said Mrs. Almond. "It's so much gained."

"She will have to support him for the rest of his life, then!" cried the Doctor. "But without wine, as they say at the *tables d'hôte*."

"Catherine tells me he has set up a business, and is making a great deal of money."

The Doctor stared. "She has not told me that — and Lavinia didn't deign. Ah!" he cried, "Catherine has given me up. Not that it matters, for all that the business amounts to."

"She has not given up Mr. Townsend," said Mrs. Almond. "I saw that in the first half minute. She has come home exactly the same."

"Exactly the same; not a grain more intelligent. She didn't notice a stick or a stone all the while we were away — not a picture nor a view, not a statue nor a cathedral."

"How could she notice? She had other things to think of; they are never for an instant out of her mind. She touches me very much."

"She would touch me if she didn't irritate me. That's the effect she has upon me now. I have tried everything upon her; I really have been quite merciless. But it is of no use whatever; she is absolutely *glued*. I have passed, in consequence, into the exasperated stage. At first I had a good deal of a certain genial curiosity about it; I wanted to see if she really would stick. But, good Lord, one's curiosity is satisfied! I see she is capable of it, and now she can let go."

"She will never let go," said Mrs. Almond.

"Take care, or you will exasperate me too. If she doesn't let go, she will be shaken off — sent tumbling into the dust! That's a nice position for my daughter. She can't see that if you are going to be pushed you had better jump. And then she will complain of her bruises."

"She will never complain," said Mrs. Almond.

"That I shall object to even more. But the deuce will be that I can't prevent anything."

"If she is to have a fall," said Mrs. Almond, with a gentle laugh, "we must spread as many carpets as we can." And she carried out this idea by showing a great deal of motherly kindness to the girl.

Mrs. Penniman immediately wrote to Morris Townsend. The intimacy between these two was by this time consummate, but I must content myself with noting but a few of its features. Mrs. Penniman's own share in it was a singular sentiment, which might have been misinterpreted, but which in itself was not discreditable to the poor lady. It was a romantic interest in this attractive and unfortunate young man, and yet it was not such an interest as Catherine might have been jealous of. Mrs. Penniman had not a particle of jealousy of her niece. For herself, she felt as if she were Morris's mother or sister — a mother or sister of an emotional temperament — and she had an absorbing desire to make him comfortable and happy. She had striven to do so during the year that her brother left her an open field, and her efforts had been attended with the success that has been pointed out. She had never had a child of her own, and Catherine, whom she had done her best to invest with the importance that would naturally belong to a youthful Penniman, had only partly rewarded her zeal. Catherine, as an object of affection and solicitude, had never had that picturesque charm which (as it seemed to her) would have been a natural attribute of her own progeny. Even the maternal passion in Mrs. Penniman would have been romantic and factitious, and Catherine was not constituted to inspire a romantic passion. Mrs. Penniman was as fond of her as ever, but she had grown to feel that with Catherine she lacked opportunity. Sentimentally speaking, therefore, she had (though she had not disinherited her niece) adopted Morris Townsend, who gave her opportunity in abundance. She would have been very happy to have a handsome and tyrannical son, and would have taken an extreme interest in his love affairs. This was the light in which she had come to regard Morris, who had conciliated her at first, and made his impression by his delicate and calculated deference — a sort of exhibition to which Mrs. Penniman was particularly sensitive. He had largely abated his deference afterwards, for he economised his resources, but the impression was made, and the young man's very brutality came to have a sort of filial value. If Mrs. Penniman had had a son, she would probably have been afraid of him, and at this stage of our narrative she was certainly afraid of Morris Townsend. This was one of the results of his domestication in Washington Square. He took his ease with her — as, for that matter, he would certainly have done with his own mother.

XXVIII

THE LETTER was a word of warning; it informed him that the Doctor had come home more impracticable than ever. She might have reflected that Catherine would supply him with all the information he needed on this point; but we know that Mrs. Penniman's reflexions were rarely just; and,

moreover, she felt that it was not for her to depend on what Catherine might do. She was to do her duty, quite irrespective of Catherine. I have said that her young friend took his ease with her, and it is an illustration of the fact that he made no answer to her letter. He took note of it, amply; but he lighted his cigar with it, and he waited, in tranquil confidence that he should receive another. "His state of mind really freezes my blood," Mrs. Penniman had written, alluding to her brother; and it would have seemed that upon this statement she could hardly improve. Nevertheless, she wrote again, expressing herself with the aid of a different figure. "His hatred of you burns with a lurid flame — the flame that never dies," she wrote. "But it doesn't light up the darkness of your future. If my affection could do so, all the years of your life would be an eternal sunshine. I can extract nothing from C.; she is so terribly secretive, like her father. She seems to expect to be married very soon, and has evidently made preparations in Europe — quantities of clothing, ten pairs of shoes, etc. My dear friend, you cannot set up in married life simply with a few pairs of shoes, can you? Tell me what you think of this. I am intensely anxious to see you; I have so much to say. I miss you dreadfully; the house seems so empty wtihout you. What is the news down town? Is the business extending? That dear little business — I think it's so brave of you!

Couldn't I come to your office? — just for three minutes? I might pass for a customer — is that what you call them? I might come in to buy something — some shares or some railroad things. *Tell me what you think of this plan.* I would carry a little reticule, like a woman of the people."

In spite of the suggestion about the reticule, Morris appeared to think poorly of the plan, for he gave Mrs. Penniman no encouragement whatever to visit his office, which he had already represented to her as a place peculiarly and unnaturally difficult to find. But as she persisted in desiring an interview — up to the last, after months of intimate colloquy, she called these meetings "interviews" — he agreed that they should take a walk together, and was even kind enough to leave his office for this purpose, during the hours at which business might have been supposed to be liveliest. It was no surprise to him, when they met at a street corner, in a region of empty lots and undeveloped pavements (Mrs. Penniman being attired as much as possible like a "woman of the people"), to find that, in spite of her urgency, what she chiefly had to convey to him was the assurance of her sympathy. Of such assurances, however, he had already a voluminous collection, and it would not have been worth his while to forsake a fruitful avocation merely to hear Mrs. Penniman say, for the thousandth time, that she had made his cause her own. Morris had

something of his own to say. It was not an easy thing to bring out, and while he turned it over the difficulty made him acrimonious.

"Oh yes, I know perfectly that he combines the properties of a lump of ice and a red-hot coal," he observed. "Catherine has made it thoroughly clear, and you have told me so till I am sick of it. You needn't tell me again; I am perfectly satisfied. He will never give us a penny; I regard that as mathematically proved."

Mrs. Penniman at this point had an inspiration.

"Couldn't you bring a lawsuit against him?" She wondered that this simple expedient had never occurred to her before.

"I will bring a lawsuit against *you*," said Morris, "if you ask me any more such aggravating questions. A man should know when he is beaten," he added, in a moment. "I must give her up!"

Mrs. Penniman received this declaration in silence, though it made her heart beat a little. It found her by no means unprepared, for she had accustomed herself to the thought that, if Morris should decidedly not be able to get her brother's money, it would not do for him to marry Catherine without it. "It would not do" was a vague way of putting the thing; but Mrs. Penniman's natural affection completed the idea, which, though it had not as yet been so crudely expressed between them as in the form that Morris had just given it, had nevertheless been implied so often, in certain easy intervals of talk, as he sat stretching his legs in the Doctor's well-stuffed armchairs, that she had grown first to regard it with an emotion which she flattered herself was philosophic, and then to have a secret tenderness for it. The fact that she kept her tenderness secret proves, of course, that she was ashamed of it; but she managed to blink her shame by reminding herself that she was, after all, the official protector of her niece's marriage. Her logic would scarcely have passed muster with the Doctor. In the first place, Morris *must* get the money, and she would help him to it. In the second, it was plain it would never come to him, and it would be a grievous pity he should marry without it — a young man who might so easily find something better. After her brother had delivered himself, on his return from Europe, of that incisive little address that has been quoted, Morris's cause seemed so hopeless that Mrs. Penniman fixed her attention exclusively upon the latter branch of her argument. If Morris had been her son, she would certainly have sacrificed Catherine to a superior conception of his future; and to be ready to do so as the case stood was therefore even a finer degree of devotion. Nevertheless, it checked her breath a little to have the sacrificial knife, as it were, suddenly thrust into her hand.

Morris walked along a moment, and then he repeated harshly:

"I must give her up!"

"I think I understand you," said Mrs. Penniman gently.

"I certainly say it distinctly enough — brutally and vulgarly enough."

He was ashamed of himself, and his shame was uncomfortable; and as he was extremely intolerant of discomfort, he felt vicious and cruel. He wanted to abuse somebody, and he began, cautiously — for he was always cautious — with himself.

"Couldn't you take her down a little?" he asked.

"Take her down?"

"Prepare her — try and ease me off."

Mrs. Penniman stopped, looking at him very solemnly.

"My poor Morris, do you know how much she loves you?"

"No, I don't. I don't want to know. I have always tried to keep from knowing. It would be too painful."

"She will suffer much," said Mrs. Penniman.

"You must console her. If you are as good a friend to me as you pretend to be, you will manage it."

Mrs. Penniman shook her head sadly.

"You talk of my 'pretending' to like you; but I can't pretend to hate you. I can only tell her I think very highly of you; and how will that console her for losing you?"

"The Doctor will help you. He will be delighted at the thing being broken off, and, as he is a knowing fellow, he will invent something to comfort her."

"He will invent a new torture!" cried Mrs. Penniman. "Heaven deliver her from her father's comfort. It will consist of his crowing over her and saying, 'I always told you so!'"

Morris coloured a most uncomfortable red.

"If you don't console her any better than you console me, you certainly won't be of much use! It's a damned disagreeable necessity; I feel it extremely, and you ought to make it easy for me."

"I will be your friend for life!" Mrs. Penniman declared.

"Be my friend *now!*" And Morris walked on.

She went with him; she was almost trembling.

"Should you like me to tell her?" she asked.

"You mustn't tell her, but you can — you can —— " And he hesitated, trying to think what Mrs. Penniman could do. "You can explain to her why it is. It's because I can't bring myself to step in between her and her father — to give him the pretext he grasps at so eagerly (it's a hideous sight) for depriving her of her rights."

Mrs. Penniman felt with remarkable promptitude the charm of this formula.

"That's so like you," she said; "it's so finely felt."

Morris gave his stick an angry swing.

"Oh, botheration!" he exclaimed perversely.

Mrs. Penniman, however, was not discouraged.

"It may turn out better than you think. Catherine is, after all, so very peculiar." And she thought she might take it upon herself to assure him that, whatever happened, the girl would be very quiet — she wouldn't make a noise. They extended their walk, and, while they proceeded, Mrs. Penniman took upon herself other things besides, and ended by having assumed a considerable burden; Morris being ready enough, as may be imagined, to put everything off upon her. But he was not for a single instant the dupe of her blundering alacrity; he knew that of what she promised she was competent to perform but an insignificant fraction, and the more she professed her willingness to serve him, the greater fool he thought her.

"What will you do if you don't marry her?" she ventured to inquire in the course of this conversation.

"Something brilliant," said Morris. "Shouldn't you like me to do something brilliant?"

The idea gave Mrs. Penniman exceeding pleasure.

"I shall feel sadly taken in if you don't."

"I shall have to, to make up for this. This isn't at all brilliant, you know."

Mrs. Penniman mused a little, as if there might be some way of making out that it was; but she had to give up the attempt, and, to carry off the awkwardness of failure, she risked a new inquiry.

"Do you mean — do you mean another marriage?"

Morris greeted this question with a reflexion which was hardly the less impudent from being inaudible. "Surely, women are more crude than men!" And then he answered audibly:

"Never in the world!"

Mrs. Penniman felt disappointed and snubbed, and she relieved herself in a little vaguely-sarcastic cry. He was certainly perverse.

"I give her up, not for another woman, but for a wider career!" Morris announced.

This was very grand; but still Mrs. Penniman, who felt that she had exposed herself, was faintly rancorous.

"Do you mean never to come to see her again?" she asked, with some sharpness.

"Oh no, I shall come again; but what is the use of dragging it out? I have been four times since she came back, and it's terribly awkward work. I can't keep it up indefinitely; she oughtn't to expect that, you know. A woman should never keep a man dangling!" he added finely.

"Ah, but you must have your last parting!" urged his companion, in whose imagination the idea of last partings occupied a place inferior in dignity only to that of first meetings.

XXIX

He came again, without managing the last parting; and again and again, without finding that Mrs. Penniman had as yet done much to pave the path of retreat with flowers. It was devilish awkward, as he said, and he felt a lively animosity for Catherine's aunt, who, as he had now quite formed the habit of saying to himself, had dragged him into the mess and was bound in common charity to get him out of it. Mrs. Penniman, to tell the truth, had, in the seclusion of her own apartment — and, I may add, amid the suggestiveness of Catherine's, which wore in those days the appearance of that of a young lady laying out her *trousseau* — Mrs. Penniman had measured her responsibilities, and taken fright at their magnitude. The task of preparing Catherine and easing off Morris presented difficulties which increased in the execution, and even led the impulsive Lavinia to ask herself whether the modification of the young man's original project had been conceived in a happy spirit. A brilliant future, a wider career, a conscience exempt from the reproach of interference between a young lady and her natural rights — these excellent things might be too troublesomely purchased. From Catherine herself Mrs. Penniman received no assistance whatever; the poor girl was apparently without suspicion of her danger. She looked at her lover with eyes of undiminished trust, and though she had less confidence in her aunt than in a young man with whom she had exchanged so many tender vows, she gave her no han-

Washington Square

dle for explaining or confessing. Mrs. Penniman, faltering and wavering, declared Catherine was very stupid, put off the great scene, as she would have called it, from day to day, and wandered about very uncomfortably, primed, to repletion, with her apology, but unable to bring it to the light. Morris's own scenes were very small ones just now; but even these were beyond his strength. He made his visits as brief as possible, and while he sat with his mistress, found terribly little to talk about. She was waiting for him, in vulgar parlance, to name the day; and so long as he was unprepared to be explicit on this point it seemed a mockery to pretend to talk about matters more abstract. She had no airs and no arts; she never attempted to disguise her expectancy. She was waiting on his good pleasure, and would wait modestly and patiently; his hanging back at this supreme time might appear strange, but of course he must have a good reason for it. Catherine would have made a wife of the gentle old-fashioned pattern — regarding reasons as favours and windfalls, but no more expecting one every day than she would have expected a bouquet of camellias. During the period of her engagement, however, a young lady even of the most slender pretensions counts upon more bouquets than at other times; and there was a want of perfume in the air at this moment which at last excited the girl's alarm.

"Are you sick?" she asked of Morris. "You seem so restless, and you look pale."

"I am not at all well," said Morris; and it occurred to him that, if he could only make her pity him enough, he might get off.

"I am afraid you are overworked; you oughtn't to work so much."

"I must do that." And then he added, with a sort of calculated brutality, "I don't want to owe you everything!"

"Ah, how can you say that?"

"I am too proud," said Morris.

"Yes — you are too proud!"

"Well, you must take me as I am," he went on, "you can never change me."

"I don't want to change you," she said gently. "I will take you as you are!" And she stood looking at him.

"You know people talk tremendously about a man's marrying a rich girl," Morris remarked. "It's excessively disagreeable."

"But I am not rich?" said Catherine.

"You are rich enough to make me talked about!"

"Of course you are talked about. It's an honour!"

"It's an honour I could easily dispense with."

She was on the point of asking him whether it were not a compensation for this annoyance that the poor girl who had the misfortune to bring it upon him, loved him so dearly and believed in him so truly; but she hesitated, thinking that this would perhaps seem

267

an exacting speech, and while she hesitated, he suddenly left her.

The next time he came, however, she brought it out, and she told him again that he was too proud. He repeated that he couldn't change, and this time she felt the impulse to say that with a little effort he might change.

Sometimes he thought that if he could only make a quarrel with her it might help him; but the question was how to quarrel with a young woman who had such treasures of concession. "I suppose you think the effort is all on your side!" he was reduced to exclaiming. "Don't you believe that I have my own effort to make?"

"It's all yours now," she said. "My effort is finished and done with!"

"Well, mine is not."

"We must bear things together," said Catherine. "That's what we ought to do."

Morris attempted a natural smile. "There are some things which we can't very well bear together — for instance, separation."

"Why do you speak of separation?"

"Ah! you don't like it; I knew you wouldn't!"

"Where are you going, Morris?" she suddenly asked.

He fixed his eye on her for a moment, and for a part of that moment she was afraid of it. "Will you promise not to make a scene?"

"A scene! — do I make scenes?"

"All women do!" said Morris, with the tone of large experience.

"I don't. Where are you going?"

"If I should say I was going away on business, should you think it very strange?"

She wondered a moment, gazing at him. "Yes — no. Not if you will take me with you."

"Take you with me — on business?"

"What is your business? Your business is to be with me."

"I don't earn my living with you," said Morris. "Or rather," he cried with a sudden inspiration, "that's just what I do — or what the world says I do!"

This ought perhaps to have been a great stroke, but it miscarried. "Where are you going?" Catherine simply repeated.

"To New Orleans. About buying some cotton."

"I am perfectly willing to go to New Orleans," Catherine said.

"Do you suppose I would take you to a nest of yellow fever?" cried Morris. "Do you suppose I would expose you at such a time as this?"

"If there is yellow fever, why should you go? Morris, you must not go!"

"It is to make six thousand dollars," said Morris. "Do you grudge me that satisfaction?"

"We have no need of six thousand dollars. You think too much about money!"

"You can afford to say that? This is a great chance; we heard of it last night." And he explained to her in what the chance consisted; and told her a long story, going over more than once several of the details, about the remarkable stroke of business which he and his partner had planned between them.

But Catherine's imagination, for reasons best known to herself, absolutely refused to be fired. "If you can go to New Orleans, I can go," she said. "Why shouldn't you catch yellow fever quite as easily as I? I am every bit as strong as you, and not in the least afraid of any fever. When we were in Europe, we were in very unhealthy places; my father used to make me take some pills. I never caught anything, and I never was nervous. What will be the use of six thousand dollars if you die of a fever? When persons are going to be married they oughtn't to think so much about business. You shouldn't think about cotton, you should think about me. You can go to New Orleans some other time — there will always be plenty of cotton. It isn't the moment to choose — we have waited too long already." She spoke more forcibly and volubly than he had ever heard her, and she held his arm in her two hands.

"You said you wouldn't make a scene!" cried Morris. "I call this a scene."

"It's you that are making it! I have never asked you anything before. We have waited too long already." And it was a comfort to her to think that she had hitherto asked so little; it seemed to make her right to insist the greater now.

Morris bethought himself a little. "Very well, then; we won't talk about it any more. I will transact my business by letter." And he began to smooth his hat, as if to take leave.

"You won't go?" And she stood looking up at him.

He could not give up his idea of provoking a quarrel; it was so much the simplest way! He bent his eyes on her upturned face, with the darkest frown he could achieve. "You are not discreet. You mustn't bully me!"

But, as usual, she conceded everything. "No, I am not discreet; I know I am too pressing. But isn't it natural? It is only for a moment."

"In a moment you may do a great deal of harm. Try and be calmer the next time I come."

"When will you come?"

"Do you want to make conditions?" Morris asked. "I will come next Saturday."

"Come to-morrow," Catherine begged; "I want you to come to-morrow. I will be very quiet," she added; and her agitation had by this time become so great that the assurance was not becoming. A sudden fear had come over her; it was like the solid conjunction of a dozen disembodied doubts, and her imagination, at a single bound, had traversed an enormous distance. All her being, for the moment, centred in the wish to keep him in the room.

Morris bent his head and kissed her forehead. "When you are quiet, you are perfection," he said; "but when you are violent, you are not in character."

It was Catherine's wish that there should be no violence about her save the beating of her heart, which she could not help; and she went on, as gently as possible, "Will you promise to come to-morrow?"

"I said Saturday!" Morris answered, smiling. He tried a frown at one moment, a smile at another; he was at his wit's end.

"Yes, Saturday too," she answered, trying to smile. "But to-morrow first." He was going to the door, and she went with him quickly. She leaned her shoulder against it; it seemed to her that she would do anything to keep him.

"If I am prevented from coming to-morrow, you will say I have deceived you!" he said.

"How can you be prevented? You can come if you will."

"I am a busy man — I am not a dangler!" cried Morris sternly.

His voice was so hard and unnatural that, with a helpless look at him, she turned away; and then he quickly laid his hand on the door-knob. He felt as if he were absolutely running away from her. But in an instant she was close to him again, and murmuring in a tone none the less penetrating for being low, "Morris, you are going to leave me."

"Yes, for a little while."

"For how long?"

"Till you are reasonable again."

"I shall never be reasonable in that way!" And she tried to keep him longer; it was almost a struggle. "Think of what I have done!"

she broke out. "Morris, I have given up everything!"

"You shall have everything back!"

"You wouldn't say that if you didn't mean something. What is it? — what has happened? — what have I done? — what has changed you?"

"I will write to you — that is better," Morris stammered.

"Ah, you won't come back!" she cried, bursting into tears.

"Dear Catherine," he said, "don't believe that! I promise you that you shall see me again!" And he managed to get away and to close the door behind him.

XXX

It was almost her last outbreak of passive grief; at least, she never indulged in another that the world knew anything about. But this one was long and terrible; she flung herself on the sofa and gave herself up to her misery. She hardly knew what had happened; ostensibly she had only had a difference with her lover, as other girls had had before, and the thing was not only not a rupture, but she was under no obligation to regard it even as a menace. Nevertheless, she felt a wound, even if he had not dealt it; it seemed to her that a mask had suddenly fallen from his face. He had wished to get away from her; he had been angry and cruel, and said strange things, with strange looks. She was smothered and stunned; she buried her head in the cushions, sobbing and talking to herself. But at last she raised herself, with the fear that either her father or Mrs. Penniman would come in; and then she sat there, staring before her, while the room grew darker. She said to herself that perhaps he would come back to tell her he had not meant what he said; and she listened for his ring at the door, trying to believe that this was probable. A long time passed, but Morris remained absent; the shadows gathered; the evening settled down on the meagre elegance of the light, clear-coloured room; the fire went out. When it had grown dark, Catherine went to the window and looked out; she stood there for half an hour, on the mere chance that he would come up the steps. At last she turned away, for she saw her father come in. He had seen her at the window looking out, and he stopped a moment at the bottom of the white steps, and gravely, with an air of exaggerated courtesy, lifted his hat to her. The gesture was so incongruous to the condition she was in, this stately tribute of respect to a poor girl despised and forsaken was so out of place, that the thing gave her a kind of horror, and she hurried away to her room. It seemed to her that she had given Morris up.

She had to show herself half an hour later, and she was sustained at table by the immensity of her desire that her father should not perceive that anything had happened. This was a great help to her afterwards, and it served her (though never as much as she supposed) from the first. On this occasion Dr. Sloper was rather talkative. He told a great many stories about a wonderful poodle that he had seen at the house of an old lady whom he visited professionally. Catherine not only tried to appear to listen to the anecdotes of the poodle, but she endeavoured to interest herself in them, so as not to think of her scene with Morris. That perhaps was an hallucination; he was mistaken, she was jealous; people didn't change like that from one day to another. Then she knew that she had had doubts before — strange suspicions, that were at once vague and acute — and that he had been different ever since her return from Europe: whereupon she tried again to listen to her father, who told a story so remarkably well. Afterwards she went straight to her own room; it was beyond her strength to undertake to spend the evening with her aunt. All the evening, alone, she questioned herself. Her trouble was terrible; but was it a thing of her imagination, engendered by an extravagant sensibility, or did it represent a clearcut reality, and had the worst that was possible actually come to pass? Mrs. Penniman, with a degree of tact that was as unusual as it was commendable, took the line of leaving her alone. The truth is, that her suspicions having been aroused, she indulged a desire, natural to a timid person, that the explosion should be localised. So long as the air still vibrated she kept out of the way.

She passed and repassed Catherine's door several times in the course of the evening, as if she expected to hear a plaintive moan behind it. But the room remained perfectly still; and accordingly, the last thing before retiring to her own couch, she applied for admittance. Catherine was sitting up, and had a book that she pretended to be reading. She had no wish to go to bed, for she had no expectation of sleeping. After Mrs. Penniman had left her she sat up half the night, and she offered her visitor no inducement to remain. Her aunt came stealing in very gently, and approached her with great solemnity.

"I am afraid you are in trouble, my dear. Can I do anything to help you?"

"I am not in any trouble whatever, and do not need any help," said Catherine, fibbing roundly, and proving thereby that not only our faults, but our most involuntary misfortunes, tend to corrupt our morals.

"Has nothing happened to you?"

"Nothing whatever."

"Are you very sure, dear?"

"Perfectly sure."

"And can I really do nothing for you?"

"Nothing, aunt, but kindly leave me alone," said Catherine.

Mrs. Penniman, though she had been afraid of too warm a welcome before, was now disappointed at so cold a one; and in relating afterwards, as she did to many persons, and with considerable variations of detail, the history of the termination of her niece's engagement, she was usually careful to mention that the young lady, on a certain occasion, had "hustled" her out of the room. It was characteristic of Mrs. Penniman that she related this fact, not in the least out of malignity to Catherine, whom she very sufficiently pitied, but simply from a natural disposition to embellish any subject that she touched.

Catherine, as I have said, sat up half the night, as if she still expected to hear Morris Townsend ring at the door. On the morrow this expectation was less unreasonable; but it was not gratified by the reappearance of the young man. Neither had he written; there was not a word of explanation or reassurance. Fortunately for Catherine she could take refuge from her excitement, which had now become intense, in her determination that her father should see nothing of it. How well she deceived her father we shall have occasion to learn; but her innocent arts were of little avail before a person of the rare perspicacity of Mrs. Penniman. This lady easily saw that she was agitated, and if there was any agitation going forward, Mrs. Penniman was not a person to forfeit her natural share in it. She returned to the charge the next evening, and requested her niece to lean upon her — to unburden her heart. Perhaps she should be able to explain certain things that now seemed dark, and that she knew more about than Catherine supposed. If Catherine had been frigid the night before, to-day she was haughty.

"You are completely mistaken, and I have not the least idea what you mean. I don't know what you are trying to fasten on me, and I have never had less need of any one's explanations in my life."

In this way the girl delivered herself, and from hour to hour kept her aunt at bay. From hour to hour Mrs. Penniman's curiosity grew. She would have given her little finger to know what Morris had said and done, what tone he had taken, what pretext he had found. She wrote to him, naturally, to request an interview; but she received, as naturally, no answer to her petition. Morris was not in a writing mood; for Catherine had addressed him two short notes which met with no acknowledgment. These notes were so brief that I may give them entire. "Won't you give me some sign that you didn't mean to be so cruel as you seemed on Tuesday?" — that was the first; the other was a little longer. "If I was unreasonable or suspicious on Tuesday — if I annoyed you or troubled you in any way — I beg your forgiveness, and I promise never again to be so foolish. I am

punished enough, and I don't understand. Dear Morris, you are killing me!" These notes were despatched on the Friday and Saturday; but Saturday and Sunday passed without bringing the poor girl the satisfaction she desired. Her punishment accumulated; she continued to bear it, however, with a good deal of superficial fortitude. On Saturday morning the Doctor, who had been watching in silence, spoke to his sister Lavinia.

"The thing has happened — the scoundrel has backed out!"

"Never!" cried Mrs. Penniman, who had bethought herself what she should say to Catherine, but was not provided with a line of defence against her brother, so that indignant negation was the only weapon in her hands.

"He has begged for a reprieve, then, if you like that better!"

"It seems to make you very happy that your daughter's affections have been trifled with."

"It does," said the Doctor; "for I had foretold it! It's a great pleasure to be in the right."

"Your pleasures make one shudder!" his sister exclaimed.

Catherine went rigidly through her usual occupations; that is, up to the point of going with her aunt to church on Sunday morning. She generally went to afternoon service as well; but on this occasion her courage faltered, and she begged of Mrs. Penniman to go without her.

"I am sure you have a secret,"

said Mrs. Penniman, with great significance, looking at her rather grimly.

"If I have, I shall keep it!" Catherine answered, turning away.

Mrs. Penniman started for church; but before she had arrived, she stopped and turned back, and before twenty minutes had elapsed she re-entered the house, looked into the empty parlours, and then went upstairs and knocked at Catherine's door. She got no answer; Catherine was not in her room, and Mrs. Penniman presently ascertained that she was not in the house. "She has gone to him, she has fled!" Lavinia cried, clasping her hands with admiration and envy. But she soon perceived that Catherine had taken nothing with her — all her personal property in her room was intact — and then she jumped at the hypothesis that the girl had gone forth, not in tenderness, but in resentment. "She has followed him to his own door — she has burst upon him in his own apartment!" It was in these terms that Mrs. Penniman depicted to herself her niece's errand, which, viewed in this light, gratified her sense of the picturesque only a shade less strongly than the idea of a clandestine marriage. To visit one's lover, with tears and reproaches, at his own residence, was an image so agreeable to Mrs. Penniman's mind that she felt a sort of æsthetic disappointment at its lacking, in this case, the harmonious accompaniments of darkness and storm. A quiet Sunday afternoon appeared an inadequate setting for it; and, indeed, Mrs. Penniman was quite out of humour with the conditions of the time, which passed very slowly as she sat in the front parlour in her bonnet and her cashmere shawl, awaiting Catherine's return.

This event at last took place. She saw her — at the window — mount the steps, and she went to await her in the hall, where she pounced upon her as soon as she had entered the house, and drew her into the parlour, closing the door with solemnity. Catherine was flushed, and her eye was bright. Mrs. Penniman hardly knew what to think.

"May I venture to ask where you have been?" she demanded.

"I have been to take a walk," said Catherine. "I thought you had gone to church."

"I did go to church; but the service was shorter than usual. And pray, where did you walk?"

"I don't know!" said Catherine.

"Your ignorance is most extraordinary! Dear Catherine, you can trust me."

"What am I to trust you with?"

"With your secret — your sorrow."

"I have no sorrow!" said Catherine fiercely.

"My poor child," Mrs. Penniman insisted, "you can't deceive me. I know everything. I have been requested to — a — to converse with you."

"I don't want to converse!"

"It will relieve you. Don't you know Shakespeare's lines? — 'the grief that does not speak!' My dear girl, it is better as it is."

"What is better?" Catherine asked.

She was really too perverse. A certain amount of perversity was to be allowed for in a young lady whose lover had thrown her over; but not such an amount as would prove inconvenient to his apologists. "That you should be reasonable," said Mrs. Penniman, with some sternness. "That you should take counsel of worldly prudence, and submit to practical considerations. That you should agree to — a — separate."

Catherine had been ice up to this moment, but at this word she flamed up. "Separate? What do you know about our separating?"

Mrs. Penniman shook her head with a sadness in which there was almost a sense of injury. "Your pride is my pride, and your susceptibilities are mine. I see your side perfectly, but I also" — and she smiled with melancholy suggestiveness — "I also see the situation as a whole!"

This suggestiveness was lost upon Catherine, who repeated her violent inquiry. "Why do you talk about separation; what do you know about it?"

"We must study resignation," said Mrs. Penniman, hesitating, but sententious at a venture.

"Resignation to what?"

"To a change of — of our plans."

"My plans have not changed!" said Catherine, with a little laugh.

"Ah, but Mr. Townsend's have," her aunt answered very gently.

"What do you mean?"

There was an imperious brevity in the tone of this inquiry, against which Mrs. Penniman felt bound to protest; the information with which she had undertaken to supply her niece was, after all, a favour. She had tried sharpness, and she had tried sternness: but neither would do; she was shocked at the girl's obstinacy. "Ah, well," she said, "if he hasn't told you! . . ." and she turned away.

Catherine watched her a moment in silence; then she hurried after her, stopping her before she reached the door. "Told me what? What do you mean? What are you hinting at and threatening me with?"

"Isn't it broken off?" asked Mrs. Penniman.

"My engagement? Not in the least!"

"I beg your pardon in that case. I have spoken too soon!"

"Too soon! Soon or late," Catherine broke out, "you speak foolishly and cruelly!"

"What has happened between you, then?" asked her aunt, struck by the sincerity of this cry. "For something certainly has happened."

"Nothing has happened but that I love him more and more!"

Mrs. Penniman was silent an instant. "I suppose that's the reason you went to see him this afternoon."

Catherine flushed as if she had been struck. "Yes, I did go to see him! But that's my own business."

"Very well, then; we won't talk

about it." And Mrs. Penniman moved towards the door again. But she was stopped by a sudden imploring cry from the girl.

"Aunt Lavinia, *where* has he gone?"

"Ah, you admit, then, that he has gone away? Didn't they know at his house?"

"They said he had left town. I asked no more questions; I was ashamed," said Catherine, simply enough.

"You needn't have taken so compromising a step if you had had a little more confidence in me," Mrs. Penniman observed, with a good deal of grandeur.

"Is it to New Orleans?" Catherine went on irrelevantly.

It was the first time Mrs. Penniman had heard of New Orleans in this connexion; but she was averse to letting Catherine know that she was in the dark. She attempted to strike an illumination from the instructions she had received from Morris. "My dear Catherine," she said, "when a separation has been agreed upon, the farther he goes away the better."

"Agreed upon? Has he agreed upon it with you?" A consummate sense of her aunt's meddlesome folly had come over her during the last five minutes, and she was sickened at the thought that Mrs. Penniman had been let loose, as it were, upon her happiness.

"He certainly has sometimes advised with me," said Mrs. Penniman.

"Is it you, then, that have changed him and made him so unnatural?" Catherine cried. "Is it you that have worked on him and taken him from me? He doesn't belong to you, and I don't see how you have anything to do with what is between us! Is it you that have made this plot and told him to leave me? How could you be so wicked, so cruel? What have I ever done to you; why can't you leave me alone? I was afraid you would spoil everything; for you *do* spoil everything you touch; I was afraid of you all the time we were abroad; I had no rest when I thought that you were always talking to him." Catherine went on with growing vehemence, pouring out in her bitterness and in the clairvoyance of her passion (which suddenly, jumping all processes, made her judge her aunt finally and without appeal) the uneasiness which had lain for so many months upon her heart.

Mrs. Penniman was scared and bewildered; she saw no prospect of introducing her little account of the purity of Morris's motives. "You are a most ungrateful girl!" she cried. "Do you scold me for talking with him? I am sure we never talked of anything but you!"

"Yes; and that was the way you worried him; you made him tired of my very name! I wish you had never spoken of me to him; I never asked your help!"

"I am sure if it hadn't been for me he would never have come to the house, and you would never have known what he thought of you," Mrs. Penniman rejoined, with a good deal of justice.

"I wish he never had come to the house, and that I never had known it! That's better than this," said poor Catherine.

"You are a very ungrateful girl," Aunt Lavinia repeated.

Catherine's outbreak of anger and the sense of wrong gave her, while they lasted, the satisfaction that comes from all assertion of force; they hurried her along, and there is always a sort of pleasure in cleaving the air. But at the bottom she hated to be violent, and she was conscious of no aptitude for organised resentment. She calmed herself with a great effort, but with great rapidity, and walked about the room a few moments, trying to say to herself that her aunt had meant everything for the best. She did not succeed in saying it with much conviction, but after a little she was able to speak quietly enough.

"I am not ungrateful, but I am very unhappy. It's hard to be grateful for that," she said. "Will you please tell me where he is?"

"I haven't the least idea; I am not in secret correspondence with him!" And Mrs. Penniman wished indeed that she were, so that she might let him know how Catherine abused her, after all she had done.

"Was it a plan of his, then, to break off —— ?" By this time Catherine had become completely quiet.

Mrs. Penniman began again to

have a glimpse of her chance for explaining. "He shrank — he shrank," she said. "He lacked courage, but it was the courage to injure you! He couldn't bear to bring down on you your father's curse."

Catherine listened to this with her eyes fixed upon her aunt, and continued to gaze at her for some time afterwards. "Did he tell you to say that?"

"He told me to say many things — all so delicate, so discriminating. And he told me to tell you he hoped you wouldn't despise him."

"I don't," said Catherine. And then she added: "And will he stay away for ever?"

"Oh, for ever is a long time. Your father, perhaps, won't live for ever."

"Perhaps not."

"I am sure you appreciate — you understand — even though your heart bleeds," said Mrs. Penniman. "You doubtless think him too scrupulous. So do I, but I respect his scruples. What he asks of you is that you should do the same."

Catherine was still gazing at her aunt, but she spoke at last, as if she had not heard or not understood her. "It has been a regular plan, then. He has broken it off deliberately; he has given me up."

"For the present, dear Catherine. He has put it off only."

"He has left me alone," Catherine went on.

"Haven't you *me?*" asked Mrs. Penniman, with much expression. Catherine shook her head slowly. "I don't believe it!" and she left the room.

XXXI

THOUGH she had forced herself to be calm, she preferred practising this virtue in private, and she forbore to show herself at tea — a repast which, on Sundays, at six o'clock, took the place of dinner. Dr. Sloper and his sister sat face to face, but Mrs. Penniman never met her brother's eye. Late in the evening she went with him, but without Catherine, to their sister Almond's, where, between the two ladies, Catherine's unhappy situation was discussed with a frankness that was conditioned by a good deal of mysterious reticence on Mrs. Penniman's part.

"I am delighted he is not to marry her," said Mrs. Almond, "but he ought to be horsewhipped all the same."

Mrs. Penniman, who was shocked at her sister's coarseness, replied that he had been actuated by the noblest of motives — the desire not to impoverish Catherine.

"I am very happy that Catherine is not to be impoverished — but I hope he may never have a penny too much! And what does the poor girl say to *you?*" Mrs. Almond asked.

"She says I have a genius for consolation," said Mrs. Penniman.

This was the account of the matter that she gave to her sister, and

it was perhaps with the consciousness of genius that, on her return that evening to Washington Square, she again presented herself for admittance at Catherine's door. Catherine came and opened it; she was apparently very quiet.

"I only want to give you a little word of advice," she said. "If your father asks you, say that everything is going on."

Catherine stood there, with her hand on the knob, looking at her aunt, but not asking her to come in. "Do you think he will ask me?"

"I am sure he will. He asked me just now, on our way home from your Aunt Elizabeth's. I explained the whole thing to your Aunt Elizabeth. I said to your father I know nothing about it."

"Do you think he will ask me when he sees — when he sees —— ?" But here Catherine stopped.

"The more he sees the more disagreeable he will be," said her aunt.

"He shall see as little as possible!" Catherine declared.

"Tell him you are to be married."

"So I am," said Catherine softly; and she closed the door upon her aunt.

She could not have said this two days later — for instance, on Tuesday, when she at last received a letter from Morris Townsend. It was an epistle of considerable length, measuring five large square pages, and written at Philadelphia. It was an explanatory document, and it explained a great many things, chief among which were the considerations that had led the writer to take advantage of an urgent "professional" absence to try and banish from his mind the image of one whose path he had crossed only to scatter it with ruins. He ventured to expect but partial success in this attempt, but he could promise her that, whatever his failure, he would never again interpose between her generous heart and her brilliant prospects and filial duties. He closed with an intimation that his professional pursuits might compel him to travel for some months, and with the hope that when they should each have accommodated themselves to what was sternly involved in their respective positions — even should this result not be reached for years — they should meet as friends, as fellow-sufferers, as innocent but philosophic victims of a great social law. That her life should be peaceful and happy was the dearest wish of him who ventured still to subscribe himself her most obedient servant. The letter was beautifully written, and Catherine, who kept it for many years after this, was able, when her sense of the bitterness of its meaning and the hollowness of its tone had grown less acute, to admire its grace of expression. At present, for a long time after she received it, all she had to help her was the determination, daily more rigid, to make no appeal to the compassion of her father.

He suffered a week to elapse,

and then one day, in the morning, at an hour at which she rarely saw him, he strolled into the back parlour. He had watched his time, and he found her alone. She was sitting with some work, and he came and stood in front of her. He was going out, he had on his hat and was drawing on his gloves.

"It doesn't seem to me that you are treating me just now with all the consideration I deserve," he said in a moment.

"I don't know what I have done," Catherine answered, with her eyes on her work.

"You have apparently quite banished from your mind the request I made you at Liverpool, before we sailed; the request that you would notify me in advance before leaving my house."

"I have not left your house!" said Catherine.

"But you intend to leave it, and by what you gave me to understand, your departure must be impending. In fact, though you are still here in body, you are already absent in spirit. Your mind has taken up its residence with your prospective husband, and you might quite as well be lodged under the conjugal roof, for all the benefit we get from your society."

"I will try and be more cheerful!" said Catherine.

"You certainly ought to be cheerful, you ask a great deal if you are not. To the pleasure of marrying a brilliant young man, you add that of having your own way; you strike me as a very lucky young lady!"

Catherine got up; she was suffocating. But she folded her work, deliberately and correctly, bending her burning face upon it. Her father stood where he had planted himself; she hoped he would go, but he smoothed and buttoned his gloves, and then he rested his hands upon his hips.

"It would be a convenience to me to know when I may expect to have an empty house," he went on. "When you go, your aunt marches."

She looked at him at last, with a long silent gaze, which, in spite of her pride and her resolution, uttered part of the appeal she had tried not to make. Her father's cold grey eye sounded her own, and he insisted on his point.

"Is it to-morrow? Is it next week, or the week after?"

"I shall not go away!" said Catherine.

The Doctor raised his eyebrows. "Has he backed out?"

"I have broken off my engagement."

"Broken it off?"

"I have asked him to leave New York, and he has gone away for a long time."

The Doctor was both puzzled and disappointed, but he solved his perplexity by saying to himself that his daughter simply misrepresented — justifiably, if one would, but nevertheless misrepresented — the facts; and he eased off his disappointment, which was that of a man losing a chance for a little triumph that he had rather counted on, by a few words that he uttered aloud.

"How does he take his dismissal?"

"I don't know!" said Catherine, less ingeniously than she had hitherto spoken.

"You mean you don't care? You are rather cruel, after encouraging him and playing with him for so long!"

The Doctor had his revenge, after all.

XXXII

OUR story has hitherto moved with very short steps, but as it approaches its termination it must take a long stride. As time went on, it might have appeared to the Doctor that his daughter's account of her rupture with Morris Townsend, mere bravado as he had deemed it, was in some degree justified by the sequel. Morris remained as rigidly and unremittingly absent as if he had died of a broken heart, and Catherine had apparently buried the memory of this fruitless episode as deep as if it had terminated by her own choice. We know that she had been deeply and incurably wounded, but the Doctor had no means of knowing it. He was certainly curious about it, and would have given a good deal to discover the exact truth; but it was his punishment that he never knew — his punishment, I mean, for the abuse of sarcasm in his relations with his daughter. There was a good deal of effective sarcasm in her keeping him in the dark, and the rest of the world conspired with her, in this sense, to be sarcastic. Mrs. Penniman told him nothing, partly because he never questioned her — he made too light of Mrs. Penniman for that — and partly because she flattered herself that a tormenting reserve, and a serene profession of ignorance, would avenge her for his theory that she had meddled in the matter. He went two or three times to see Mrs. Montgomery, but Mrs. Montgomery had nothing to impart. She simply knew that her brother's engagement was broken off, and now that Miss Sloper was out of danger she preferred not to bear witness in any way against Morris. She had done so before — however unwillingly — because she was sorry for Miss Sloper; but she was not sorry for Miss Sloper now — not at all sorry. Morris had told her nothing about his relations with Miss Sloper at the time, and he had told her nothing since. He was always away, and he very seldom wrote to her; she believed he had gone to California. Mrs. Almond had, in her sister's phrase, "taken up" Catherine violently since the recent catastrophe; but though the girl was very grateful to her for her kindness, she revealed no secrets, and the good lady could give the Doctor no satisfaction. Even, however, had she been able to narrate to him the private history of his daughter's unhappy love affair, it would have given her a certain comfort to leave him in ignorance; for Mrs. Almond was at this time not altogether in sympathy with her brother. She had guessed for herself that Catherine had been cruelly jilted — she knew nothing from Mrs. Penniman, for Mrs. Penniman had not ventured to lay the famous explanation of Morris's motives before Mrs. Almond, though she had thought it good enough for Catherine — and she pronounced her brother too consistently indifferent to what the poor creature must have suffered and must still be suffering. Dr. Sloper had his theory, and he rarely altered his theories. The marriage would have been an abominable one, and the girl had had a blessed escape. She was not to be pitied for that, and to pretend to condole with her would have been to make concessions to the idea that she had ever had a right to think of Morris.

"I put my foot on this idea from the first, and I keep it there now," said the Doctor. "I don't see anything cruel in that; one can't keep it there too long." To this Mrs. Almond more than once replied that if Catherine had got rid of her incongruous lover, she deserved the credit of it, and that to bring herself to her father's enlightened view of the matter must have cost her an effort that he was bound to appreciate.

"I am by no means sure she has got rid of him," the Doctor said. "There is not the smallest probability that, after having been as obstinate as a mule for two years, she suddenly became amenable to reason. It is infinitely more probable that he got rid of her."

"All the more reason you should be gentle with her."

"I *am* gentle with her. But I can't do the pathetic; I can't pump up tears, to look graceful, over the most fortunate thing that ever happened to her."

"You have no sympathy," said Mrs. Almond; "that was never your strong point. You have only to look at her to see that, right or wrong, and whether the rupture came from herself or from him, her poor little heart is grievously bruised."

"Handling bruises — and even dropping tears on them — doesn't make them any better! My business is to see she gets no more knocks, and that I shall carefully attend to. But I don't at all recognise your description of Catherine. She doesn't strike me in the least as a young woman going about in search of a moral poultice. In fact, she seems to me much better than while the fellow was hanging about. She is perfectly comfortable and blooming; she eats and sleeps, takes her usual exercise, and overloads herself, as usual, with finery. She is always knitting some purse or embroidering some handkerchief, and it seems to me she turns these articles out about

as fast as ever. She hasn't much to say; but when had she anything to say? She had her little dance, and now she is sitting down to rest. I suspect that, on the whole, she enjoys it."

"She enjoys it as people enjoy getting rid of a leg that has been crushed. The state of mind after amputation is doubtless one of comparative repose."

"If your leg is a metaphor for young Townsend, I can assure you he has never been crushed. Crushed? Not he! He is alive and perfectly intact, and that's why I am not satisfied."

"Should you have liked to kill him?" asked Mrs. Almond.

"Yes, very much. I think it is quite possible that it is all a blind."

"A blind?"

"An arrangement between them. *Il fait le mort,* as they say in France; but he is looking out of the corner of his eye. You can depend upon it he has not burned his ships; he has kept one to come back in. When I am dead, he will set sail again, and then she will marry him."

"It is interesting to know that you accuse your only daughter of being the vilest of hypocrites," said Mrs. Almond.

"I don't see what difference her being my only daughter makes. It is better to accuse one than a dozen. But I don't accuse any one. There is not the smallest hypocrisy about Catherine, and I deny that she even pretends to be miserable."

The Doctor's idea that the thing

was a "blind" had its intermissions and revivals; but it may be said on the whole to have increased as he grew older; together with his impression of Catherine's blooming and comfortable condition. Naturally, if he had not found grounds for viewing her as a love-lorn maiden during the year or two that followed her great trouble, he found none at a time when she had completely recovered her self-possession. He was obliged to recognise the fact that if the two young people were waiting for him to get out of the way, they were at least waiting very patiently. He had heard from time to time that Morris was in New York; but he never remained there long, and, to the best of the Doctor's belief, had no communication with Catherine. He was sure they never met, and he had reason to suspect that Morris never wrote to her. After the letter that has been mentioned, she heard from him twice again, at considerable intervals; but on none of these occasions did she write herself. On the other hand, as the Doctor observed, she averted herself rigidly from the idea of marrying other people. Her opportunities for doing so were not numerous, but they occurred often enough to test her disposition. She refused a widower, a man with a genial temperament, a handsome fortune, and three little girls (he had heard that she was very fond of children, and he pointed to his own with some confidence); and she turned a deaf ear to the solicitations of a clever

young lawyer, who, with the prospect of a great practice, and the reputation of a most agreeable man, had had the shrewdness, when he came to look about him for a wife, to believe that she would suit him better than several younger and prettier girls. Mr. Macalister, the widower, had desired to make a marriage of reason, and had chosen Catherine for what he supposed to be her latent matronly qualities; but John Ludlow, who was a year the girl's junior, and spoken of always as a young man who might have his "pick," was seriously in love with her. Catherine, however, would never look at him; she made it plain to him that she thought he came to see her too often. He afterwards consoled himself, and married a very different person, little Miss Sturtevant, whose attractions were obvious to the dullest comprehension. Catherine, at the time of these events, had left her thirtieth year well behind her, and had quite taken her place as an old maid. Her father would have preferred she should marry, and he once told her that he hoped she would not be too fastidious. "I should like to see you an honest man's wife before I die," he said. This was after John Ludlow had been compelled to give it up, though the Doctor had advised him to persevere. The Doctor exercised no further pressure, and had the credit of not "worrying" at all over his daughter's singleness. In fact he worried rather more than appeared, and there were considerable periods during which he felt sure that Morris Townsend was hidden behind some door. "If he is not, why doesn't she marry?" he asked himself. "Limited as her intelligence may be, she must understand perfectly well that she is made to do the usual thing." Catherine, however, became an admirable old maid. She formed habits, regulated her days upon a system of her own, interested herself in charitable institutions, asylums, hospitals, and aid societies; and went generally, with an even and noiseless step, about the rigid business of her life. This life had, however, a secret history as well as a public one — if I may talk of the public history of a mature and diffident spinster for whom publicity had always a combination of terrors. From her own point of view the great facts of her career were that Morris Townsend had trifled with her affection, and that her father had broken its spring. Nothing could ever alter these facts; they were always there, like her name, her age, her plain face. Nothing could ever undo the wrong or cure the pain that Morris had inflicted on her, and nothing could ever make her feel towards her father as she felt in her younger years. There was something dead in her life, and her duty was to try and fill the void. Catherine recognised this duty to the utmost; she had a great disapproval of brooding and moping. She had, of course, no faculty for quenching memory in dissipation; but she mingled freely in the usual gaieties of the town, and she became at last an inevitable figure at all respectable entertainments. She was greatly liked, and as time went on she grew to be a sort of kindly maiden aunt to the younger portion of society. Young girls were apt to confide to her their love affairs (which they never did to Mrs. Penniman), and young men to be fond of her without knowing why. She developed a few harmless eccentricities; her habits, once formed, were rather stiffly maintained; her opinions, on all moral and social matters, were extremely conservative; and before she was forty she was regarded as an old-fashioned person, and an authority on customs that had passed away. Mrs. Penniman, in comparison, was quite a girlish figure; she grew younger as she advanced in life. She lost none of her relish for beauty and mystery, but she had little opportunity to exercise it. With Catherine's later wooers she failed to establish relations as intimate as those which had given her so many interesting hours in the society of Morris Townsend. These gentlemen had an indefinable mistrust of her good offices, and they never talked to her about Catherine's charms. Her ringlets, her buckles and bangles, glistened more brightly with each succeeding year, and she remained quite the same officious and imaginative Mrs. Penniman, and the odd mixture of impetuosity and circumspection, that we have hitherto known. As regards one point,

284

however, her circumspection prevailed, and she must be given due credit for it. For upwards of seventeen years she never mentioned Morris Townsend's name to her niece. Catherine was grateful to her, but this consistent silence, so little in accord with her aunt's character, gave her a certain alarm, and she could never wholly rid herself of a suspicion that Mrs. Penniman sometimes had news of him.

XXXIII

LITTLE by little Dr. Sloper had retired from his profession; he visited only those patients in whose symptoms he recognised a certain originality. He went again to Europe, and remained two years; Catherine went with him, and on this occasion Mrs. Penniman was of the party. Europe apparently had few surprises for Mrs. Penniman, who frequently remarked, in the most romantic sites — "You know I am very familiar with all this." It should be added that such remarks were usually not addressed to her brother, or yet to her niece, but to fellow-tourists who happened to be at hand, or even to the cicerone or the goatherd in the foreground.

One day, after his return from Europe, the Doctor said something to his daughter that made her start — it seemed to come from so far out of the past.

"I should like you to promise me something before I die."

"Why do you talk about your dying?" she asked.

"Because I am sixty-eight years old."

"I hope you will live a long time," said Catherine.

"I hope I shall! But some day I shall take a bad cold, and then it will not matter much what any one hopes. That will be the manner of my exit, and when it takes place, remember I told you so. Promise me not to marry Morris Townsend after I am gone."

This was what made Catherine start, as I have said; but her start was a silent one, and for some moments she said nothing. "Why do you speak of him?" she asked at last.

"You challenge everything I say. I speak of him because he's a topic, like any other. He's to be seen, like any one else, and he is still looking for a wife — having had one and got rid of her, I don't know by what means. He has lately been in New York, and at your cousin Marian's house; your Aunt Elizabeth saw him there."

"They neither of them told me," said Catherine.

"That's their merit; it's not yours. He has grown fat and bald, and he has not made his fortune. But I can't trust those facts alone to steel your heart against him, and that's why I ask you to promise."

"Fat and bald": these words presented a strange image to Catherine's mind, out of which the memory of the most beautiful young man in the world had never faded. "I don't think you understand," she said. "I very seldom think of Mr. Townsend."

"It will be very easy for you to go on, then. Promise me, after my death, to do the same."

Again, for some moments, Catherine was silent; her father's request deeply amazed her; it opened an old wound and made it ache afresh. "I don't think I can promise that," she answered.

"It would be a great satisfaction," said her father.

"You don't understand. I can't promise that."

The Doctor was silent a minute. "I ask you for a particular reason. I am altering my will."

This reason failed to strike Catherine; and indeed she scarcely understood it. All her feelings were merged in the sense that he was trying to treat her as he had treated her years before. She had suffered from it then; and now all her experience, all her acquired tranquillity and rigidity, protested. She had been so humble in her youth that she could now afford to have a little pride, and there was something in this request, and in her father's thinking himself so free to make it, that seemed an injury to her dignity. Poor Catherine's dignity was not aggressive; it never sat in state; but if you pushed far enough you could find it. Her father had pushed very far.

"I can't promise," she simply repeated.

"You are very obstinate," said the Doctor.

"I don't think you understand."

"Please explain, then."

"I can't explain," said Catherine. "And I can't promise."

"Upon my word," her father explained, "I had no idea how obstinate you are!"

She knew herself that she was obstinate, and it gave her a certain joy. She was now a middle-aged woman.

About a year after this, the accident that the Doctor had spoken of occurred; he took a violent cold. Driving out to Bloomingdale one April day to see a patient of unsound mind, who was confined in a private asylum for the insane, and whose family greatly desired a medical opinion from an eminent source, he was caught in a spring shower, and being in a buggy, without a hood, he found himself soaked to the skin. He came home with an ominous chill, and on the morrow he was seriously ill. "It is congestion of the lungs," he said to Catherine; "I shall need very good nursing. It will make no difference, for I shall not recover; but I wish everything to be done, to the smallest detail, as if I should. I hate an ill-conducted sick-room; and you will be so good as to nurse me on the hypothesis that I shall get well." He told her which of his fellow-physicians to send for, and gave her a multitude of minute directions; it was quite on the optimistic hypothesis that she nursed him. But he had never been wrong in his life, and he was not wrong now. He was touching his seventieth year, and though he had a very well-tempered constitution, his hold upon life had lost its firmness. He died after three weeks' illness, during which Mrs. Penniman, as well as his daughter, had been assiduous at his bedside.

On his will being opened after a decent interval, it was found to consist of two portions. The first of these dated from ten years back, and consisted of a series of dispositions by which he left the great mass of property to his daughter, with becoming legacies to his two sisters. The second was a codicil, of recent origin, maintaining the annuities to Mrs. Penniman and Mrs. Almond, but reducing Catherine's share to a fifth of what he had first bequeathed her. "She is amply provided for from her mother's side," the document ran, "never having spent more than a fraction of her income from this source; so that her fortune is already more than sufficient to attract those unscrupulous adventurers whom she has given me reason to believe that she persists in regarding as an interesting class." The large remainder of his property, therefore, Dr. Sloper had divided into seven unequal parts, which he left, as endowments, to as many different hospitals and schools of medicine, in various cities of the Union.

To Mrs. Penniman it seemed monstrous that a man should play such tricks with other people's money; for after his death, of course, as she said, it was other people's. "Of course, you will dispute the will," she remarked, fatuously, to Catherine.

"Oh, no," Catherine answered, "I like it very much. Only I wish it had been expressed a little differently!"

XXXIV

It was her habit to remain in town very late in the summer; she preferred the house in Washington Square to any other habitation whatever, and it was under protest that she used to go to the seaside for the month of August. At the sea she spent her month at an hotel. The year that her father died she intermitted this custom altogether, not thinking it consistent with deep mourning; and the year after that she put off her departure till so late that the middle of August found her still in the heated solitude of Washington Square. Mrs. Penniman, who was fond of a change, was usually eager for a visit to the country; but this year she appeared quite content with such rural impressions as she could gather, at the parlour window, from the ailantus-trees behind the wooden paling. The peculiar fragrance of this vegetation used to diffuse itself in the evening air, and Mrs. Penniman, on the warm nights of July, often sat at the open window and inhaled it. This was a happy moment for Mrs. Penniman; after the death of her brother she felt more free to obey her impulses. A vague oppression had disappeared from her life, and she enjoyed a sense of freedom of which she had not been conscious since the memorable time, so long ago, when the Doctor went abroad with Catherine and left her at home to entertain Morris Townsend. The year that had elapsed since her brother's death reminded her of that happy time, because, although Catherine, in growing older, had become a person to be reckoned with, yet her society was a very different thing, as Mrs. Penniman said, from that of a tank of cold water. The elder lady hardly knew what use to make of this larger margin of her life; she sat and looked at it very much as she had often sat, with her poised needle in her hand, before her tapestry frame. She had a confident hope, however, that her rich impulses, her talent for embroidery, would still find their application, and this confidence was justified before many months had elapsed.

Catherine continued to live in her father's house in spite of its being represented to her that a maiden lady of quiet habits might find a more convenient abode in one of the smaller dwellings, with brown stone fronts, which had at this time begun to adorn the transverse thoroughfares in the upper part of the town. She liked the earlier structure — it had begun by this time to be called an "old" house — and proposed to herself to end her days in it. If it was too large for a pair of unpretending gentlewomen, this was better than the opposite fault; for Catherine had no desire to find herself in closer quarters with her aunt. She expected to spend the rest of her life in Washington Square, and to enjoy Mrs. Penniman's society for the whole of this period; as she had a conviction that, long as she might live, her aunt would live at least as long, and always retain her brilliancy and activity. Mrs. Penniman suggested to her the idea of a rich vitality.

On one of those warm evenings in July of which mention has been made, the two ladies sat together at an open window, looking out on the quiet Square. It was too hot for lighted lamps, for reading, or for work; it might have appeared too hot even for conversation, Mrs. Penniman having long been speechless. She sat forward in the window, half on the balcony, humming a little song. Catherine was within the room, in a low rocking-chair, dressed in white, and slowly using a large palmetto fan. It was in this way, at this season, that the aunt and niece, after they had had tea, habitually spent their evenings.

"Catherine," said Mrs. Penniman at last, "I am going to say something that will surprise you."

"Pray do," Catherine answered; "I like surprises. And it is so quiet now."

"Well, then, I have seen Morris Townsend."

If Catherine was surprised, she checked the expression of it; she gave neither a start nor an exclamation. She remained, indeed, for some moments intensely still, and this may very well have been a symptom of emotion. "I hope he was well," she said at last.

"I don't know; he is a great deal changed. He would like very much to see you."

"I would rather not see him," said Catherine quickly.

"I was afraid you would say that. But you don't seem surprised!"

"I am — very much."

"I met him at Marian's," said Mrs. Penniman. "He goes to Marian's, and they are so afraid you will meet him there. It's my belief that that's why he goes. He wants so much to see you." Catherine made no response to this, and Mrs. Penniman went on. "I didn't know him at first; he is so remarkably changed. But he knew me in a minute. He says I am not in the least changed. You know how polite he always was. He was coming away when I came, and we walked a little distance together. He is still very handsome, only, of course, he looks older, and he is not so — so animated as he used to be. There was a touch of sadness about him; but there was a touch of sadness about him before — especially when he went away. I am afraid he has not been

very successful — that he has never got thoroughly established. I don't suppose he is sufficiently plodding, and that, after all, is what succeeds in this world." Mrs. Penniman had not mentioned Morris Townsend's name to her niece for upwards of the fifth of a century; but now that she had broken the spell, she seemed to wish to make up for lost time, as if there had been a sort of exhilaration in hearing herself talk of him. She proceeded, however, with considerable caution, pausing occasionally to let Catherine give some sign. Catherine gave no other sign than to stop the rocking of her chair and the swaying of her fan; she sat motionless and silent. "It was on Tuesday last," said Mrs. Penniman, "and I have been hesitating ever since about telling you. I didn't know how you might like it. At last I thought that it was so long ago that you would probably not have any particular feeling. I saw him again, after meeting him at Marian's. I met him in the street, and he went a few steps with me. The first thing he said was about you; he asked ever so many questions. Marian didn't want me to speak to you; she didn't want you to know that they receive him. I told him I was sure that after all these years you couldn't have any feeling about that; you couldn't grudge him the hospitality of his own cousin's house. I said you would be bitter indeed if you did that. Marian has the most extraordinary ideas about what happened between you; she seems to think he behaved in some very unusual manner. I took the liberty of reminding her of the real facts, and placing the story in its true light. *He* has no bitterness, Catherine, I can assure you; and he might be excused for it, for things have not gone well with him. He has been all over the world, and tried to establish himself everywhere; but his evil star was against him. It is most interesting to hear him talk of his evil star. Everything failed; everything but his — you know, you remember — his proud, high spirit. I believe he married some lady somewhere in Europe. You know they marry in such a peculiar matter-of-course way in Europe; a marriage of reason they call it. She died soon afterwards; as he said to me, she only flitted across his life. He has not been in New York for ten years; he came back a few days ago. The first thing he did was to ask me about you. He had heard you had never married; he seemed very much interested about that. He said you had been the real romance of his life."

Catherine had suffered her companion to proceed from point to point, and pause to pause, without interrupting her; she fixed her eyes on the ground and listened. But the last phrase I have quoted was followed by a pause of peculiar significance, and then, at last, Catherine spoke. It will be observed that before doing so she had received a good deal of information about Morris Townsend. "Please say no more; please don't follow up that subject."

"Doesn't it interest you?" asked Mrs. Penniman, with a certain timorous archness.

"It pains me," said Catherine.

"I was afraid you would say that. But don't you think you could get used to it? He wants so much to see you."

"Please don't, Aunt Lavinia," said Catherine, getting up from her seat. She moved quickly away, and went to the other window, which stood open to the balcony; and here, in the embrasure, concealed from her aunt by the white curtains, she remained a long time, looking out into the warm darkness. She had had a great shock; it was as if the gulf of the past had suddenly opened, and a spectral figure had risen out of it. There were some things she believed she had got over, some feelings that she had thought of as dead; but apparently there was a certain vitality in them still. Mrs. Penniman had made them stir themselves. It was but a momentary agitation, Catherine said to herself; it would presently pass away. She was trembling, and her heart was beating so that she could feel it; but this also would subside. Then, suddenly, while she waited for a return of her calmness, she burst into tears. But her tears flowed very silently, so that Mrs. Penniman had no observation of them. It was perhaps, however, because Mrs. Penniman suspected them that she said no more that evening about Morris Townsend.

XXXV

HER refreshed attention to this gentleman had not those limits of which Catherine desired, for herself, to be conscious; it lasted long enough to enable her to wait another week before speaking of him again. It was under the same circumstances that she once more attacked the subject. She had been sitting with her niece in the evening; only on this occasion, as the night was not so warm, the lamp had been lighted, and Catherine had placed herself near it with a morsel of fancy-work. Mrs. Penniman went and sat alone for half an hour on the balcony; then she came in, moving vaguely about the room. At last she sank into a seat near Catherine, with clasped hands, and a little look of excitement.

"Shall you be angry if I speak to you again about *him?*" she asked.

Catherine looked up at her quietly. "Who is *he?*"

"He whom you once loved."

"I shall not be angry, but I shall not like it."

"He sent you a message," said Mrs. Penniman. "I promised him to deliver it, and I must keep my promise."

In all these years Catherine had had time to forget how little she had to thank her aunt for in the season of her misery; she had long ago forgiven Mrs. Penniman for taking too much upon herself. But for a moment this attitude of interposition and disinterestedness, this carrying of messages and redeeming of promises, brought back the sense that her companion was a dangerous woman. She had said she would not be angry; but for an instant she felt sore. "I don't care what you do with your promise!" she answered.

Mrs. Penniman, however, with her high conception of the sanctity of pledges, carried her point. "I have gone too far to retreat," she said, though precisely what this meant she was not at pains to explain. "Mr. Townsend wishes most particularly to see you, Catherine; he believes that if you knew how much, and why, he wishes it, you would consent to do so."

"There can be no reason," said Catherine; "no good reason."

"His happiness depends upon it. Is not that a good reason?" asked Mrs. Penniman impressively.

"Not for me. My happiness does not."

"I think you will be happier after you have seen him. He is going away again — going to resume his wanderings. It is a very lonely, restless, joyless life. Before he goes he wishes to speak to you; it is a fixed idea with him — he is always thinking of you. He believes that you never understood him — that you never judged him rightly, and the belief has always weighed upon him terribly. He wishes to justify himself; he believes that in a very few words he could do so. He wishes to meet you as a friend."

Catherine listened to this wonderful speech without pausing in her work; she had now had several days to accustom herself to think of Morris Townsend again as an actuality. When it was over she said simply, "Please say to Mr. Townsend that I wish he would leave me alone."

She had hardly spoken when a sharp, firm ring at the door vibrated through the summer night. Catherine looked up at the clock; it marked a quarter-past nine — a very late hour for visitors, especially in the empty condition of the town. Mrs. Penniman at the same moment gave a little start, and then Catherine's eyes turned quickly to her aunt. They met Mrs. Penniman's and sounded them for a moment, sharply. Mrs. Penniman was blushing; her look was a conscious one; it seemed to confess something. Catherine guessed its meaning, and rose quickly from her chair.

"Aunt Penniman," she said, in a tone that scared her companion, "have you taken the *liberty* . . . ?"

"My dearest Catherine," stammered Mrs. Penniman, "just wait till you see him!"

Catherine had frightened her aunt, but she was also frightened herself; she was on the point of rushing to give orders to the servant, who was passing to the door, to admit no one; but the fear of meeting her visitor checked her.

"Mr. Morris Townsend."

This was what she heard, vaguely but recognisably articulated by the domestic, while she hesitated. She had her back turned to the door of the parlour, and for some moments she kept it turned, feeling that he had come in. He had not spoken, however, and at last she faced about. Then she saw a gentleman standing in the middle of the room, from which her aunt had discreetly retired.

She would never have known him. He was forty-five years old, and his figure was not that of the straight, slim young man she remembered. But it was a very fine person, and a fair and lustrous beard, spreading itself upon a well-presented chest, contributed to its effect. After a moment Catherine recognised the upper half of the face, which, though her visitor's clustering locks had grown thin, was still remarkably handsome. He stood in a deeply deferential attitude, with his eyes on her face. "I have ventured — I have ventured," he said; and then he paused, looking about him, as if he expected her to ask him to sit down. It was the old voice, but it had not the old charm. Catherine, for a minute, was conscious of a distinct determination not to invite him to take a seat. Why had he come? It was wrong of him to come. Morris was embarrassed, but Catherine gave him no help. It was not that she was glad of his embarrassment; on the contrary, it excited all her own liabil ities of this kind, and gave her great pain. But how could she welcome him when she felt so vividly that he ought not to have come? "I wanted so much — I was determined," Morris went on. But he stopped again; it was not easy. Catherine still said nothing, and he may well have recalled with apprehension her ancient faculty of silence. She continued to look at him, however, and as she did so she made the strangest observation. It seemed to be he, and yet not he; it was the man who had been everything, and yet this person was nothing. How long ago it was — how old she had grown — how much she had lived! She had lived on something that was connected with *him,* and she had consumed it in doing so. This person did not look unhappy. He was fair and well-preserved, perfectly dressed, mature and complete. As Catherine looked at him, the story of his life defined itself in his eyes; he had made himself comfortable, and he had never been caught. But even while her perception opened itself to this, she had no desire to catch him; his presence was painful to her, and she only wished he would go.

"Will you not sit down?" he asked.

"I think we had better not," said Catherine.

"I offend you by coming?" He was very grave; he spoke in a tone of the richest respect.

"I don't think you ought to have come."

"Did not Mrs. Penniman tell you — did she not give you my message?"

"She told me something, but I did not understand."

"I wish you would let *me* tell you — let me speak for myself."

"I don't think it is necessary," said Catherine.

"Not for you, perhaps, but for me. It would be a great satisfaction — and I have not many." He seemed to be coming nearer; Catherine turned away. "Can we not be friends again?" he said.

"We are not enemies," said Catherine. "I have none but friendly feelings to you."

"Ah, I wonder whether you know the happiness it gives me to hear you say that!" Catherine uttered no intimation that she measured the influence of her words; and he presently went on, "You have not changed — the years have passed happily for you."

"They have passed very quietly," said Catherine.

"They have left no marks; you are admirably young." This time he succeeded in coming nearer — he was close to her; she saw his glossy perfumed beard, and his eyes above it looking strange and hard. It was very different from his old — from his young — face. If she had first seen him this way she would not have liked him. It seemed to her that he was smiling, or trying to smile. "Catherine," he said, lowering his voice, "I have never ceased to think of you."

"Please don't say those things," she answered.

"Do you hate me?"

"Oh no," said Catherine.

Something in her tone discouraged him, but in a moment he recovered himself. "Have you still some kindness for me, then?"

"I don't know why you have come here to ask me such things!" Catherine exclaimed.

"Because for many years it has been the desire of my life that we should be friends again."

"That is impossible."

"Why so? Not if you will allow it."

"I will not allow it!" said Catherine.

He looked at her again in silence. "I see; my presence troubles you and pains you. I will go away; but you must give me leave to come again."

"Please don't come again," she said.

"Never? — never?"

She made a great effort; she wished to say something that would make it impossible he should ever again cross her threshold. "It is wrong of you. There is no propriety in it — no reason for it."

"Ah, dearest lady, you do me injustice!" cried Morris Townsend. "We have only waited, and now we are free."

"You treated me badly," said Catherine.

"Not if you think of it rightly. You had your quiet life with your father — which was just what I could not make up my mind to rob you of."

"Yes; I had that."

Morris felt it to be a considerable damage to his cause that he could not add that she had had something more besides; for it is needless to say that he had learnt the contents of Dr. Sloper's will. He was nevertheless not at a loss. "There are worse fates than that!" he exclaimed, with expression; and he might have been supposed to refer to his own unprotected situation. Then he added, with a deeper tenderness, "Catherine, have you never forgiven me?"

"I forgave you years ago, but it is useless for us to attempt to be friends."

"Not if we forget the past. We have still a future, thank God!"

"I can't forget — I don't forget," said Catherine. "You treated me too badly. I felt it very much; I felt it for years." And then she went on, with her wish to show him that he must not come to her this way. "I can't begin again — I can't take it up. Everything is dead and buried. It was too serious; it made a great change in my life. I never expected to see you here."

"Ah, you are angry!" cried Morris, who wished immensely that he could extort some flash of passion from her mildness. In that case he might hope.

"No, I am not angry. Anger does not last, that way, for years. But there are other things. Impressions last, when they have been strong. But I can't talk."

Morris stood stroking his beard, with a clouded eye. "Why have you never married?" he asked abruptly. "You have had opportunities."

"I didn't wish to marry."

"Yes, you are rich, you are free; you had nothing to gain."

"I had nothing to gain," said Catherine.

Morris looked vaguely round him, and gave a deep sigh. "Well, I was in hopes that we might still have been friends."

"I meant to tell you, by my aunt, in answer to your message — if you had waited for an answer — that it was unnecessary for you to come in that hope."

"Good-bye, then," said Morris. "Excuse my indiscretion."

He bowed, and she turned away — standing there, averted, with her eyes on the ground, for some moments after she had heard him close the door of the room.

In the hall he found Mrs. Penniman, fluttered and eager; she appeared to have been hovering there under the irreconcilable promptings of her curiosity and her dignity.

"That was a precious plan of yours!" said Morris, clapping on his hat.

"Is she so hard?" asked Mrs. Penniman.

"She doesn't care a button for me — with her confounded little dry manner."

"Was it very dry?" pursued Mrs. Penniman, with solicitude.

Morris took no notice of her question; he stood musing an instant, with his hat on. "But why the deuce, then, would she never marry?"

"Yes — why indeed?" sighed Mrs. Penniman. And then, as if from a sense of the inadequacy of this explanation, "But you will not despair — you will come back?"

"Come back? Damnation!" And Morris Townsend strode out of the house, leaving Mrs. Penniman staring.

Catherine, meanwhile, in the parlour, picking up her morsel of fancy work, had seated herself with it again — for life, as it were.

THE POINT OF VIEW

FROM MISS AURORA
CHURCH AT SEA TO MISS WHITE-
SIDE IN PARIS

September 1880
. . . MY dear child, the bromide
of sodium (if that's what you call
it) proved perfectly useless. I
don't mean that it did me no
good, but that I never had occasion to take the bottle out of my
bag. It might have done wonders
for me if I had needed it; but I
didn't, simply because I've been
a wonder myself. Will you believe
that I've spent the whole voyage
on deck, in the most animated
conversation and exercise? Twelve
times round the deck make a mile,
I believe; and by this measure-
ment I've been walking twenty
miles a day. And down to every
meal, if you please, where I've
displayed the appetite of a fish-
wife. Of course the weather has
been lovely; so there's no great
merit. The wicked old Atlantic has
been as blue as the sapphire in my
only ring — rather a good one —
and as smooth as the slippery floor
of Madame Galopin's dining-
room. We've been for the last
three hours in sight of land, and
are soon to enter the Bay of New

York which is said to be exquisitely beautiful. But of course you
recall it, though they say everything changes so fast over here.
I find I don't remember anything,
for my recollections of our voyage to Europe so many years ago
are exceedingly dim; I've only a
painful impression that mamma
shut me up for an hour every day
in the stateroom and made me
learn by heart some religious
poem. I was only five years old
and I believe that as a child I
was extremely timid; on the other
hand mamma, as you know, had
what she called a method with
me. She has it to this day; only
I've become indifferent; I've been
so pinched and pushed — morally
speaking, *bien entendu*. It's true,
however, that there are children
of five on the vessel to-day who
have been extremely conspicuous
— ranging all over the ship and always under one's feet. Of course
they're little compatriots, which
means that they're little barbari-
ans. I don't mean to pronounce *all*
our compatriots barbarous; they
seem to improve somehow after
their first communion. I don't
know whether it's that ceremony
that improves them, especially as
so few of them go in for it; but
the women are certainly nicer
than the little girls; I mean of
course in proportion, you know.
You warned me not to generalise,

and you see I've already begun, before we've arrived. But I suppose there's no harm in it so long as it's favourable.

Isn't it favourable when I say I've had the most lovely time? I've never had so much liberty in my life, and I've been out alone, as you may say, every day of the voyage. If it's a foretaste of what's to come I shall take very kindly to that. When I say I've been out alone I mean we've always been two. But we two were alone, so to speak, and it wasn't like always having mamma or Madame Galopin, or some lady in the pension or the temporary cook. Mamma has been very poorly; she's so very well on land that it's a wonder to see her at all taken down. She says, however, that it isn't the being at sea; it's on the contrary approaching the land. She's not in a hurry to arrive; she keeps well before her that great disillusions await us. I didn't know she *had* any illusions — she has too many opinions, I should think, for that: she discriminates, as she's always saying, from morning till night. Where would the poor illusions find room? She's meanwhile very serious; she sits for hours in perfect silence, her eyes fixed on the horizon. I heard her say yesterday to an English gentleman — a very odd Mr. Antrobus, the only person with whom she converses — that she was afraid she shouldn't like her native land, and that she shouldn't like not liking it. But this is a mistake; she'll like that immensely — I mean the not liking it. If it should

prove at all agreeable she'll be furious, for that will go against her system. You know all about mamma's system; I've explained it so often. It goes against her system that we should come back at all; that was *my* system — I've had at last to invent one! She consented to come only because she saw that, having no *dot,* I should never marry in Europe; and I pretended to be immensely pre-occupied with this idea in order to make her start. In reality *cela m'est parfaitement égal.* I'm only afraid I shall like it too much — I don't mean marriage, of course, but the sense of a native land. Say what you will, it's a charming thing to go out alone, and I've given notice that I mean to be always *en course.* When I tell mamma this she looks at me in the same silence; her eyes dilate and then she slowly closes them. It's as if the sea were affecting her a little, though it's so beautifully calm. I ask her if she'll try my bromide, which is there in my bag; but she motions me off and I begin to walk again, tapping my little boot-soles on the smooth clean deck. This allusion to my boot-soles, by the way, isn't prompted by vanity; but it's a fact that at sea one's feet and one's shoes assume the most extraordinary importance, so that one should take the precaution to have nice ones. They're all you seem to see as the people walk about the deck; you get to know them intimately and to dislike some of them so much. I'm afraid you'll think that I've already broken

297

loose; and for aught I know I'm writing as a demoiselle bien-éle-vée shouldn't write. I don't know whether it's the American air; if it is, all I can say is that the American air's very charming. It makes me impatient and restless, and I sit scribbling here because I'm so eager to arrive and the time passes better if I occupy myself.

I'm in the saloon, where we have our meals, and opposite me is a big round porthole, wide open to let in the smell of the land. Every now and then I rise a little and look through it to see if we're arriving. I mean in the Bay, you know, for we shall not come up to the city till dark. I don't want to lose the Bay; it appears it's so wonderful. I don't exactly understand what it contains except some beautiful islands; but I suppose you'll know all about that. It's easy to see that these are the last hours, for all the people about me are writing letters to put into the post as soon as we come up to the dock. I believe they're dreadful at the custom-house, and you'll remember how many new things you persuaded mamma that — with my pre-occupation of marriage — I should take to this country, where even the prettiest girls are expected not to go unadorned. We ruined ourselves in Paris — that's partly accountable for mamma's solemnity — *mais au moins je serai belle!* Moreover I believe that mamma's prepared to say or to do anything that may be necessary for escaping from their odious duties; as she very justly remarks she can't afford to be ruined twice. I don't know how one approaches these terrible *douaniers,* but I mean to invent something very charming. I mean to say "Voyons, Messieurs, a young girl like me, brought up in the strictest foreign traditions, kept always in the background by a very superior mother — *la voilà;* you can see for yourself! — what is it possible that she should attempt to smuggle in? Nothing but a few simple relics of her convent!" I won't tell them my convent was called the Magasin du Bon Marché. Mamma began to scold me three days ago for insisting on so many trunks, and the truth is that between us we've not fewer than seven. For relics, that's a good many! We're all writing very long letters — or at least we're writing a great number. There's no news of the Bay as yet. Mr. Antrobus, mamma's friend, opposite to me, is beginning on his ninth. He's a Right Honourable and a Member of Parliament; he has written during the voyage about a hundred letters and seems greatly alarmed at the number of stamps he'll have to buy when he arrives. He's full of information, but he hasn't enough, for he asks as many questions as mamma when she goes to hire apartments. He's going to "look into" various things; he speaks as if they had a little hole for the purpose. He walks almost as much as I, and has enormous shoes. He asks questions even of me, and I tell him again and again that I know nothing about Amer-

298

ica. But it makes no difference; he always begins again, and indeed it's not strange he should find my ignorance incredible. "Now how would it be in one of your Southwestern States?" — that's his favourite way of opening conversation. Fancy me giving an account of one of "my" Southwestern States! I tell him he had better ask mamma — a little to tease that lady, who knows no more about such places than I. Mr. Antrobus is very big and black; he speaks with a sort of brogue; he has a wife and ten children; he doesn't say — apart from his talking — anything at all to me. But he has lots of letters to people *là-bas* — I forget that we're just arriving — and mamma, who takes an interest in him in spite of his views (which are dreadfully advanced, and not at all like mamma's own) has promised to give him the entrée to the best society. I don't know what she knows about the best society over here today, for we've not kept up our connexions at all, and no one will know — or, I am afraid, care — anything about us. She has an idea we shall be immensely recognised; but really, except the poor little Rucks, who are bankrupt and, I'm told, in no society at all, I don't know on whom we can count. C'est égal, mamma has an idea that, whether or no we appreciate America ourselves, we shall at least be universally appreciated. It's true we have begun to be, a little; you would see that from the way Mr. Cockerel and

Mr. Louis Leverett are always inviting me to walk. Both of these gentlemen, who are Americans, have asked leave to call on me in New York, and I've said *Mon Dieu oui,* if it's the custom of the country. Of course I've not dared to tell this to mamma, who flatters herself that we've brought with us in our trunks a complete set of customs of our own and that we shall only have to shake them out a little and put them on when we arrive. If only the two gentlemen I just spoke of don't call at the same time I don't think I shall be too much frightened. If they do, on the other hand, I won't answer for it. They've a particular aversion to each other and are ready to fight about poor little me. I'm only the pretext, however; for, as Mr. Leverett says, it's really the opposition of temperaments. I hope they won't cut each other's throats, for I'm not crazy about either of them. They're very well for the deck of a ship, but I shouldn't care about them in a salon; they're not at all distinguished. They think they are, but they're not; at least Mr. Louis Leverett does; Mr. Cockerel doesn't appear to care so much. They're extremely different — with their opposed temperaments — and each very amusing for a while; but I should get dreadfully tired of passing my life with either. Neither has proposed that as yet; but it's evidently what they're coming to. It will be in a great measure to spite each other, for I think that au fond they don't quite believe in me. If they don't, it's the only point on which they agree. They hate each other awfully; they take such different views. That is Mr. Cockerel hates Mr. Leverett — he calls him a sickly little ass; he pronounces his opinions half affectation and the other half dyspepsia. Mr. Leverett speaks of Mr. Cockerel as a "strident savage," but he allows he finds him most diverting. He says there's nothing in which we can't find a certain entertainment if we only look at it in the right way, and that we have no business with either hating or loving: we ought only to strive to understand. He "claims" — he's always claiming — that to understand is to forgive. Which is very pretty, but I don't like the suppression of our affections, though I've no desire to fix mine upon Mr. Leverett. He's very artistic and talks like an article in some review. He has lived a great deal in Paris, and Mr. Cockerel, who doesn't believe in Paris, says it's what has made him such an idiot.

That's not complimentary to you, dear Louisa, and still less to your brilliant brother; for Mr. Cockerel explains that he means it (the bad effect of Paris) chiefly of men. In fact he means the bad effect of Europe altogether. This, however, is compromising to mamma; and I'm afraid there's no doubt that, from what I've told him, he thinks mamma also an idiot. (I'm not responsible, you know — I've always wanted to go home.) If mamma knew him, which she doesn't, for she always closes her eyes when I pass on his arm, she would think him disgusting. Mr. Leverett meanwhile assures me he's nothing to what we shall see yet. He's from Philadelphia (Mr. Cockerel); he insists that we shall go and see Philadelphia, but mamma says she saw it in 1855 and it was then *affreux*. Mr. Cockerel says that mamma's evidently not familiar with the rush of improvement in this country; he speaks of 1855 as if it were a hundred years ago. Mamma says she knows it goes only too fast, the rush — it goes so fast that it has time to do nothing well; and then Mr. Cockerel, who, to do him justice, is perfectly good-natured, remarks that she had better wait till she has been ashore and seen the improvements. Mamma retorts that she sees them from here, the awful things, and that they give her a sinking of the heart. (This little exchange of ideas is carried on through me; they've never spoken to each other.) Mr. Cockerel, as I say, is extremely good-natured, and he bears out what I've heard said about the men in America being very considerate of the women. They evidently listen to them a great deal; they don't contradict them, but it seems to me this is rather negative. There's very little gallantry in not contradicting one; and it strikes me that there are some things the men don't express. There are others on the ship whom I've noticed. It's as if they were all one's brothers or one's cousins. The extent to which one isn't in danger from them — my dear, my dear! But I promised you not to generalise, and perhaps there will be more expression when we arrive. Mr. Cockerel returns to America, after a general tour, with a renewed conviction that this is the only country. I left him on deck an hour ago looking at the coast-line with an opera-glass and saying it was the prettiest thing he had seen in all his travels. When I remarked that the coast seemed rather low he said it would be all the easier to get ashore. Mr. Leverett at any rate doesn't seem in a hurry to get ashore, he's sitting within sight of me in a corner of the saloon — writing letters, I suppose, but looking, from the way he bites his pen and rolls his eyes about, as if he were composing a sonnet and waiting for a rhyme. Perhaps the sonnet's addressed to me; but I forget that he suppresses the affections! The only person in whom mamma takes much interest is the great French critic, M. Lejaune, whom we have the honour to carry with us. We've read a few of his works, though mamma disapproves of his tendencies and thinks him a dreadful materialist. We've read them for the style; you know he's one of the new Academicians. He's a Frenchman like any other, except that he's rather more quiet; he has a grey moustache and the ribbon of the Legion of Honour. He's the first French writer of distinction who has been to America since De Tocqueville; the

French, in such matters, are not very enterprising. Also he has the air of wondering what he's doing *dans cette galère*. He has come with his beau-frère, who's an engineer and is looking after some mines, and he talks with scarcely any one else, as he speaks no English and appears to take for granted that no one speaks French. Mamma would be delighted to convince him of the contrary; she has never conversed with an Academician. She always makes a little vague inclination, with a smile, when he passes her, and he answers with a most respectful bow; but it goes no further, to mamma's disappointment. He's always with the beau-frère, a rather untidy fat bearded man — decorated too, always smoking and looking at the feet of the ladies, whom mamma (though she has very good feet) has not the courage to *aborder*. I believe M. Lejaune is going to write a book about America, and Mr. Leverett says it will be terrible. Mr. Leverett has made his acquaintance and says M. Lejaune will put him into his book; he says the movement of the French intellect is superb. As a general thing he doesn't care for Academicians, but M. Lejaune's an exception — he's so living, so remorseless, so personal.

I've asked Mr. Cockerel meanwhile what he thinks of M. Lejaune's plan of writing a book, and he answers that he doesn't see what it matters to him that a Frenchman the more should make the motions of a monkey — on that side poor Mr. Cockerel is *de cette force*. I asked him why he hadn't written a book about Europe, and he says that in the first place Europe isn't worth writing about, and that in the second if he said what he thought people would call it a joke. He says they're very superstitious about Europe over here; he wants people in America to behave as if Europe didn't exist. I told this to Mr. Leverett, and he answered that if Europe didn't exist America wouldn't, for Europe keeps us alive by buying our corn. He said also that the trouble with America in the future will be that she'll produce things in such enormous quantities that there won't be enough people in the rest of the world to buy them, and that we shall be left with our productions — most of them very hideous — on our hands. I asked him if he thought corn a hideous production, and he replied that there's nothing more unbeautiful than too much food. I think that to feed the world too well, however, will be after all a *beau rôle*. Of course I don't understand these things, and I don't believe Mr. Leverett does; but Mr. Cockerel seems to know what he's talking about, and he describes America as complete in herself. I don't know exactly what he means, but he speaks as if human affairs had somehow moved over to this side of the world. It may be a very good place for them, and heaven knows I'm extremely tired of Europe, which mamma has always insisted

so on my appreciating; but I don't think I like the idea of our being so completely cut off. Mr. Cockerel says it is not we that are cut off, but Europe, and he seems to think Europe has somehow deserved it. That may be; our life over there was sometimes extremely tiresome, though mamma says it's now that our real fatigues will begin. I like to abuse those dreadful old countries myself, but I'm not sure I'm pleased when others do the same. We had some rather pretty moments there after all, and at Piacenza we certainly lived for four francs a day. Mamma's already in a terrible state of mind about the expenses here; she's frightened by what people on the ship (the few she has spoken to) have told her. There's one comfort at any rate — we've spent so much money in coming that we shall have none left to get away. I'm scribbling along, as you see, to occupy me till we get news of the islands. Here comes Mr. Cockerel to bring it. Yes, they're in sight; he tells me they're lovelier than ever and that I must come right up right away. I suppose you'll think I'm already begining to use the language of the country. It's certain that at the end of the month I shall speak nothing else. I've picked up every dialect, wherever we've travelled; you've heard my Platt-Deutsch and my Neapolitan. But, *voyons un peu* the Bay! I've just called to Mr. Leverett to remind him of the islands. "The islands — the islands? Ah my dear young lady,

I've seen Capri, I've seen Ischia!"
Well, so have I, but that doesn't
prevent . . . (*A little later.*) I've
seen the islands — they're rather
queer.

II

MRS. CHURCH IN NEW
YORK TO MADAME GALOPIN AT
GENEVA

October 1880

IF I felt far away from you in the
middle of that deplorable Atlantic,
chère Madame, how do I feel
now, in the heart of this extraordinary city? We've arrived —
we've arrived, dear friend; but I
don't know whether to tell you
that I consider that an advantage.
If we had been given our choice
of coming safely to land or going
down to the bottom of the sea I
should doubtless have chosen the
former course; for I hold, with your
noble husband and in opposition
to the general tendency of modern thought, that our lives are not
our own to dispose of, but a sacred trust from a higher power by
whom we shall be held responsible. Nevertheless if I had foreseen more vividly some of the impressions that awaited me here
I'm not sure that, for my daughter at least, I shouldn't have preferred on the spot to hand in our
account. Should I not have been
less (rather than more) guilty in
presuming to dispose of *her* destiny than of my own? There's a
nice point for dear M. Galopin to
settle — one of those points I've
heard him discuss in the pulpit
with such elevation. We're safe,
however, as I say; by which I
mean we're physically safe. We've
taken up the thread of our familiar pension-life, but under
strikingly different conditions.
We've found a refuge in a boarding-house which has been highly
recommended to me and where
the arrangements partake of the
barbarous magnificence that in
this country is the only alternative from primitive rudeness. The
terms per week are as magnificent as all the rest. The landlady
wears diamond ear-rings and the
drawing rooms are decorated with
marble statues. I should indeed
be sorry to let you know how I've
allowed myself to be rançonnée;
and I should be still more sorry
that it should come to the ears of
any of my good friends in Geneva, who know me less well than
you and might judge me more
harshly. There's no wine given for
dinner, and I've vainly requested
the person who conducts the establishment to garnish her table
more liberally. She says I may
have all the wine I want if I will
order it at the merchant's and settle the matter with himself. But
I've never, as you know, consented to regard our modest allowance of eau rougie as an extra; indeed, I remember that it's
largely to your excellent advice
that I've owed my habit of being
firm on this point.

There are, however, greater difficulties than the question of what we shall drink for dinner, chère Madame. Still, I've never lost courage and I shall not lose it now. At the worst we can re-embark again and seek repose and refreshment on the shores of your beautiful lake. (There's absolutely no scenery here!) We shall not perhaps in that case have achieved what we desired, but we shall at least have made an honourable retreat. What we desire — I know it's just this that puzzles you, dear friend; I don't think you ever really comprehended my motives in taking this formidable step, though you were good enough, and your magnanimous husband was good enough, to press my hand at parting in a way that seemed to tell me you'd still be with me even were I wrong. To be very brief, I wished to put an end to the ceaseless reclamations of my daughter. Many Americans had assured her that she was wasting her belle jeunesse in those historic lands which it was her privilege to see so intimately, and this unfortunate conviction had taken possession of her. "Let me at least see for myself," she used to say; "if I should dislike it over there as much as you promise me, so much the better for you. In that case we'll come back and make a new arrangement at Stuttgart." The experiment's a terribly expensive one, but you know how my devotion never has shrunk from an ordeal. There's another point moreover which, from a mother to a mother, it would be affectation not to touch upon. I remember the just satisfaction with which you announced to me the fiançailles of your charming Cécile. You know with what earnest care my Aurora has been educated — how thoroughly she's acquainted with the principal results of modern research. We've always studied together, we've always enjoyed together. It will perhaps surprise you to hear that she makes these very advantages a reproach to me — represents them as an injury to herself. "In this country," she says, "the gentlemen have not those accomplishments; they care nothing for the results of modern research. Therefore it won't help a young person to be sought in marriage that she can give an account of the latest German presentation of Pessimism." That's possible, and I've never concealed from her that it wasn't for this country I had educated her. If she marries in the United States it's of course my intention that my son-in-law shall accompany us to Europe. But when she calls my attention more and more to these facts I feel that we're moving in a different world. This is more and more the country of the many; the few find less and less place for them; and the individual — well, the individual has quite ceased to be recognised. He's recognised as a voter, but he's not recognised as a gentleman — still less as a lady. My daughter and I of course can only pretend to constitute a *few!*

You know that I've never for

a moment remitted my pretensions as an individual, though among the agitations of pension-life I've sometimes needed all my energy to uphold them. "Oh yes, I may be poor," I've had occasion to say, "I may be unprotected, I may be reserved, I may occupy a small apartment au quatrième and be unable to scatter unscrupulous bribes among the domestics; but at least I'm a *person* and have personal rights." In this country the people have rights, but the person has none. You'd have perceived that if you had come with me to make arrangements at this establishment. The very fine lady who condescends to preside over it kept me waiting twenty minutes and then came sailing in without a word of apology. I had sat very silent, with my eyes on the clock; Aurora amused herself with a false admiration of the room, a wonderful drawing-room with magenta curtains, frescoed walls and photographs of the landlady's friends — as if one cares for her friends! When this exalted personage came in she simply remarked that she had just been trying on a dress — that it took so long to get a skirt to hang. "It seems to take very long indeed!" I answered; "but I hope the skirt's right at last. You might have sent for us to come up and look at it!" She evidently didn't understand, and when I asked her to show us her rooms she handed us over to a negro as dégingandé as herself. While we looked at them I heard her sit

down to the piano in the drawing-room; she began to sing an air from a comic opera. I felt certain we had gone quite astray; I didn't know in what house we could be, and was only reassured by seeing a Bible in every room. When we come down our musical hostess expressed no hope the rooms had pleased us, she seemed grossly indifferent to our taking them. She wouldn't consent moreover to the least diminution and was inflexible, as I told you, on the article of our common beverage. When I pushed this point she was so good as to observe that she didn't keep a cabaret. One's not in the least considered; there's no respect for one's privacy, for one's preferences, for one's reserves. The familiarity's without limits, and I've already made a dozen acquaintances, of whom I know, and wish to know, nothing. Aurora tells me she's the "belle of the boarding-house." It appears that this is a great distinction.

It brings me back to my poor child and her prospects. She takes a very critical view of them herself — she tells me I've given her a false education and that no one will marry her to-day. No American will marry her because she's too much of a foreigner, and no foreigner will marry her because she's too much of an American. I remind her how scarcely a day passes that a foreigner, usually of distinction, doesn't — as perversely as you will indeed — select an American bride, and she answers me that in these cases the young lady isn't married for her fine eyes. Not always, I reply; and then she declares that she'll marry no foreigner who shall not be one of the first of the first. You'll say doubtless that she should content herself with advantages that haven't been deemed insufficient for Cécile; but I'll not repeat to you the remark she made when I once employed this argument. You'll doubtless be surprised to hear that I've ceased to argue; but it's time I should confess that I've at last agreed to let her act for herself. She's to live for three months à l'Américaine and I'm to be a mere passive spectator. You'll feel with me that this is a cruel position for a cœur de mère. I count the days till our three months are over, and I know you'll join with me in my prayers. Aurora walks the streets alone; she goes out in the tramway: a voiture de place costs five francs for the least little *course*. (I beseech you not to let it be known that I've sometimes had the weakness.) My daughter's frequently accompanied by a gentleman — by a dozen gentlemen; she remains out for hours and her conduct excites no surprise in this establishment. I know but too well the emotions it will excite in your quiet home. If you betray us, chère Madame, we're lost; and why, after all, should any one know of these things in Geneva? Aurora pretends she has been able to persuade herself that she doesn't care who knows them; but there's a strange expression in her face which proves that her conscience isn't at rest. I watch her, I let her go, but I sit with my hands clasped. There's a peculiar custom in this country — I shouldn't know how to express it in Genevese: it's called "being attentive," and young girls are the object of the futile process. It hasn't necessarily anything to do with projects of marriage — though it's the privilege only of the unmarried and though at the same time (fortunately, and this may surprise you) it has no relation to other projects. It's simply an invention by which young persons of the two sexes pass large parts of their time together with no questions asked. How shall I muster courage to tell you that Aurora now constitutes the main apparent recreation of several gentlemen? Though it has no relation to marriage the practice happily doesn't exclude it, and marriages have been known to take place in consequence (or in spite) of it. It's true that even in this country a young lady may marry but one husband at a time, whereas she may receive at once the attentions of several gentlemen, who are equally entitled "admirers." My daughter then has admirers to an indefinite number. You'll think I'm joking perhaps when I tell you that I'm unable to be exact — I who was formerly l'exactitude même.

Two of these gentlemen are to a certain extent old friends, having been passengers on the steamer which carried us so far from you. One of them, still young, is typical of the American character, but a respectable person and a lawyer considerably launched. Every one in this country follows a profession, but it must be admitted that the professions are more highly remunerated than chez vous. Mr. Cockerel, even while I write you, is in not undisputed, but temporarily triumphant, possession of my child. He called for her an hour ago in a "boghey" — a strange unsafe rickety vehicle, mounted on enormous wheels, which holds two persons very near together; and I watched her from the window take her place at his side. Then he whirled her away behind two little horses with terribly thin legs; the whole equipage — and most of all her being in it — was in the most questionable taste. But she'll return — return positively very much as she went. It's the same when she goes down to Mr. Louis Leverett, who has no vehicle and who merely comes and sits with her in the front salon. He has lived a great deal in Europe and is very fond of the arts, and though I'm not sure I agree with him in his views of the relation of art to life and life to art, and in his interpretation of some of the great works that Aurora and I have studied together, he seems to me a sufficiently serious and intelligent young man. I don't regard him as intrinsically dangerous, but on the other hand he offers absolutely no guarantees. I've no means whatever of ascertaining his pecuniary situation. There's a vagueness on these points which

is extremely embarrassing, and it never occurs to young men to offer you a reference. In Geneva I shouldn't be at a loss; I should come to you, chère Madame, with my little enquiry, and what you shouldn't be able to tell me wouldn't be worth my knowing. But no one in New York can give me the smallest information about the état de fortune of Mr. Louis Leverett. It's true that he's a native of Boston, where most of his friends reside; I can't, however, go to the expense of a journey to Boston simply to learn perhaps that Mr. Leverett (the young Louis) has an income of five thousand francs. As I say indeed, he doesn't strike me as dangerous. When Aurora comes back to me after having passed an hour with him she says he has described to her his emotions on visiting the home of Shelley or discussed some of the differences between the Boston temperament and that of the Italians of the Renaissance. You'll not enter into these rapprochements, and I can't blame you. But you won't betray me, chère Madame?

FROM MISS STURDY AT NEWPORT TO MRS. DRAPER AT OUCHY

September 1880

I PROMISED to tell you how I like it, but the truth is I've gone to and fro so often that I've ceased to like and dislike. Nothing strikes me as unexpected; I expect everything in its order. Then too, you know, I'm not a critic; I've no talent for keen analysis, as the magazines say; I don't go into the reasons of things. It's true I've been for a longer time than usual on the wrong side of the water, and I admit that I feel a little out of training for American life. They're breaking me in very fast, however. I don't mean that they bully me — I absolutely decline to be bullied. I say what I think, because I believe I've on the whole the advantage of knowing what I think — when I think anything; which is half the battle. Sometimes indeed I think nothing at all. They don't like that over here; they like you to have impressions. That they like these impressions to be favourable appears to me perfectly natural; I don't make a crime to them of this; it seems to me on the contrary a very amiable point. When individuals betray it we call them sympathetic; I don't see why we shouldn't give nations the same benefit. But there are things I haven't the least desire to have an opinion about. The privilege of indifference is the dearest we possess, and I hold that intelligent people are known by the way they exercise it. Life is full of rubbish, and we have at least our share of it over here. When you wake up in the morning you find that during the night a cartload has been deposited in your front garden. I decline, however, to have any of it in my premises; there are thousands of things I want to know nothing about. I've outlived the necessity of being hypocritical; I've nothing to gain and everything to lose. When one's fifty years old — single stout and red in the face — one has outlived a good many necessities. They tell me over here that my increase of weight's extremely marked, and though they don't tell me I'm coarse I feel they think me so. There's very little coarseness here — not quite enough, I think — though there's plenty of vulgarity, which is a very different thing. On the whole the country becomes much more agreeable. It isn't that the people are charming, for that they always were (the best of them, I mean — it isn't true of the others), but that places and things as well recognise the possibility of pleasing. The houses are extremely good and look extraordinarily fresh and clean. Many European interiors seem in comparison musty and gritty. We have a great deal of taste; I shouldn't wonder if we should end by inventing something pretty; we only need a little time. Of course as yet it's all imitation, except, by the way, these delicious piazzas. I'm sitting on one now; I'm writing to you with my portfolio on my knees. This broad light *loggia* surrounds the house with a movement as free as the expanded wings of a bird, and the wandering airs

The Point of View

come up from the deep sea, which murmurs on the rocks at the end of the lawn.

Newport's more charming even than you remember it; like everything else over here it has improved. It's very exquisite to-day; it's indeed, I think, in all the world the only exquisite watering-place, for I detest the whole genus. The crowd has left it now, which makes it all the better, though plenty of talkers remain in these large light luxurious houses which are planted with a kind of Dutch definiteness all over the green carpet of the cliff. This carpet's very neatly laid and wonderfully well swept, and the sea, just at hand, is capable of prodigies of blue. Here and there a pretty woman strolls over one of the lawns, which all touch each other, you know, without hedges or fences; the light looks intense as it plays on her brilliant dress; her large parasol shines like a silver dome. The long lines of the far shores are soft and pure, though they are places one hasn't the least desire to visit. Altogether the effect's very delicate, and anything that's delicate counts immensely over here; for delicacy, I think, is as rare as coarseness. I'm talking to you of the sea, however, without having told you a word of my voyage. It was very comfortable and amusing; I should like to take another next month. You know I'm almost offensively well at sea — I breast the weather and brave the storm. We had no storm

fortunately, and I had brought with me a supply of light literature; so I passed nine days on deck in my sea-chair with my heels up — passed them reading Tauchnitz novels. There was a great lot of people, but no one in particular save some fifty American girls. You know all about the American girl, however, having been one yourself. They're on the whole very nice, but fifty's too many; there are always too many. There was an enquiring Briton, a radical M.P., by name Mr. Antrobus, who entertained me as much as any one else. He's an excellent man; I even asked him to come down here and spend a couple of days. He looked rather frightened till I told him he shouldn't be alone with me, that the house was my brother's and that I gave the invitation in his name. He came a week ago; he goes everywhere; we've heard of him in a dozen places. The English are strangely simple, or at least they seem so over here. Their old measurements and comparisons desert them; they don't know whether it's all a joke or whether it's too serious by half. We're quicker than they, though we talk so much more slowly. We think fast, and yet we talk as deliberately as if we were speaking a foreign language. They toss off their sentences with an air of easy familiarity with the tongue, and yet they misunderstand two thirds of what people say to them. Perhaps after all it is only *our* thoughts they think slowly; they

The Point of View

think their own often to a lively tune enough.

Mr. Antrobus arrived here in any case at eight o'clock in the morning; I don't know how he managed it; it appears to be his favourite hour; wherever we've heard of him he has come in with the dawn. In England he would arrive at 5.30 P.M. He asks innumerable questions, but they're easy to answer, for he has a sweet credulity. He made me rather ashamed; he's a better American than so many of us; he takes us more seriously than we take ourselves. He seems to think we've an oligarchy of wealth growing up which he advised me to be on my guard against. I don't know exactly what I can do, but I promised him to look out. He's fearfully energetic; the energy of the people here is nothing to that of the enquiring Briton. If we should devote half the zeal to building up our institutions that they devote to obtaining information about them we should have a very satisfactory country. Mr. Antrobus seemed to think very well of us — which surprised me on the whole, since, say what one will, it's far from being so agreeable as England. It's very horrid that this should be; and it's delightful, when one thinks of it, that some things in England are after all so hateful. At the same time Mr. Antrobus appeared to be a good deal preoccupied with our dangers. I don't understand quite what they are; they seem to me

so few on a Newport piazza this bright still day. Yet alas what one sees on a Newport piazza isn't America; it's only the back of Europe. I don't mean to say I haven't noticed any dangers since my return; there are two or three that seem to me very serious, but they aren't those Mr. Antrobus apprehends. One, for instance, is that we shall cease to speak the English language, which I prefer so to any other. It's less and less spoken; American's crowding it out. All the children speak American, which as a child's language is dreadfully rough. It's exclusively in use in the schools; all the magazines and newspapers are in American. Of course a people of fifty millions who have invented a new civilisation have a right to a language of their own; that's what they tell me, and I can't quarrel with it. But I wish they had made it as pretty as the mother-tongue, from which, when all's said, it's more or less derived. We ought to have invented something as noble as our country. They tell me it's more expressive, and yet some admirable things have been said in the Queen's English. There can be no question of the Queen over here of course, and American no doubt is the music of the future. Poor dear future, how "expressive" you'll be! For women and children, as I say, it strikes one as very rough; and moreover they don't speak it well, their own though it be. My small nephews, when I first came home, hadn't

310

gone back to school, and it distressed me to see that, though they're charming children, they had the vocal inflexions of little news-boys. My niece is sixteen years old; she has the sweetest nature possible; she's extremely well-bred and is dressed to perfection. She chatters from morning till night; but its helplessness breaks my heart. These little persons are in the opposite case from so many English girls who know how to speak but don't know how to talk. My niece knows how to talk but doesn't know how to speak.

If I allude to the young people, that's our other danger; the young people are eating us up — there's nothing in America but the young people. The country's made for the rising generation; life's arranged for them; they're the destruction of society. People talk of them, consider them, defer to them, bow down to them. They're always present, and whenever they're present nothing else of the smallest interest is. They're often very pretty, and physically are wonderfully looked after; they're scoured and brushed, they wear hygienic clothes, they go every week to the dentist's. But the little boys kick your shins and the little girls offer to slap your face. There's an immense literature entirely addressed to them in which the kicking of shins and the slapping of faces carries the day. As a woman of fifty I protest, I insist on being judged by my peers. It's too late, however, for several

millions of little feet are actively engaged in stamping out conversation, and I don't see how they can long fail to keep it under. The future's theirs; adult forms will evidently be at an increasing discount. Longfellow wrote a charming little poem called "The Children's Hour," but he ought to have called it "The Children's Century." And by children I naturally don't mean simple infants; I mean everything of less than twenty. The social importance of the young American increases steadily up to that age and then suddenly stops. The little girls of course are more important than the lads, but the lads are very important too. I'm struck with the way they're known and talked about; they're small celebrities; they have reputations and pretensions; they're taken very seriously. As for the little girls, as I just said, they're ever so much too many. You'll say perhaps that my fifty years and my red face are jealous of them. I don't think so, because I don't suffer; my red face doesn't frighten people away, and I always find plenty of talkers. The young things themselves, I believe, like me very much, and I delight in the young things. They're often very pretty; not so pretty as people say in the magazines, but pretty enough. The magazines rather overdo that; they make a mistake. I've seen no great beauties, but the level of prettiness is high, and occasionally one sees a woman completely handsome. (As a general thing, a pretty person here means a person with a pretty face. The figure's rarely mentioned, though there are several good ones.) The level of prettiness is high, but the level of conversation is low; that's one of the signs of its being a young ladies' country. There are a good many things young ladies can't talk about, but think of all the things they can when they are as clever as most of these. Perhaps one ought to content one's self with that measure, but it's difficult if one has lived long by a larger one. This one's decidedly narrow — I stretch it sometimes till it cracks. Then it is they call me coarse, which I undoubtedly am, thank goodness.

What it comes to, obviously, is that people's talk is much less conveniently free than in Europe; I'm struck with that wherever I go. There are certain things that are never said at all, certain allusions that are never made. There are no light stories, no propos risqués. I don't know exactly what people find to bite into, for the supply of scandal's small and it's little more than twaddle at that. They don't seem, however, to lack topics. The little girls are always there; they keep the gates of conversation; very little passes that's not innocent. I find we do very well without wickedness, and for myself, as I take my ease, I don't miss my liberties. You remember what I thought of the tone of your table in Florence last year, and how surprised you were when I asked you why you allowed such things. You said they were like the courses of the seasons; one couldn't prevent them; also that to change the tone of your table you'd have to change so many other things. Of course in your house one never saw a little girl; I was the only spinster and no one was afraid of me. Likewise if talk's more innocent in this country manners are so to begin with. The liberty of the young people is the strongest proof of it. The little girls are let loose in the world, and the world gets more good of it than ces demoiselles get harm. In your world — pardon me, but you know what I mean — this wouldn't do at all. Your world's a sad affair — the young ladies would encounter all sorts of horrors. Over here, considering the way they knock about, they remain wonderfully simple, and the reason is that society protects them instead of setting them traps. There's almost no gallantry as you understand it; the flirtations are child's play. People have no time for making love; the men in particular are extremely busy. I'm told that sort of thing consumes hours; I've never had any time for it myself. If the leisure class should increase here considerably there may possibly be a change; but I doubt it, for the women seem to me in all essentials exceedingly reserved. Great superficial frankness, but an extreme dread of complications. The men strike me as very good fellows. I find them at bottom better than the women, who if not inverately hard haven't at least the European, the (as I heard some one once call it) chemical softness. They're not so nice to the men as the men are to them; I mean of course in proportion, you know. But women aren't so nice as men "anyway," as they say here.

The men at any rate are professional, commercial; there are very few gentlemen pure and simple. This personage needs to be very well done, however, to be of great utility; and I suppose you won't pretend he's always well done in your countries. When he's not, the less of him the better. It's very much the same indeed with the system on which the female young are brought up. (You see I have to come back to the female young.) When it succeeds they're the most charming creatures possible; when it doesn't the failure's disastrous. If a girl's a very nice girl the American method brings her to great completeness — makes all her graces flower; but if she isn't nice it plays the devil with any possible compromise or *biais* in the interest of social convenience. In a word the American girl's rarely negative, and when she isn't a great success she's a great warning. In nineteen cases out of twenty, among the people who know how to live — I won't say what *their* proportion is — the results are highly satisfactory. The girls aren't shy, but I don't know why they should be, for there's really nothing here to be afraid of. Manners are very gentle, very humane; the democratic system deprives people of weapons that every one doesn't equally possess. No one's formidable; no one's on stilts; no one has great pretensions or any recognised right to be arrogant. I think there's not much wickedness, and there's certainly less human or social cruelty — less than in "good" (that is in more amusing) society. Every one can sit — no one's kept standing. One's much less liable to be snubbed, which you will say is a pity. I think it is — to a certain extent; but on the other hand folly's less fatuous in form than in your countries; and as people generally have fewer revenges to take there's less need of their being squashed in advance. The general good nature, the social equality, deprive them of triumphs on the one hand and of grievances on the other. There's extremely little impertinence, there's almost none. You'll say I'm describing a terrible world, a world without great figures or great social prizes. You've hit it, my dear — there are no great figures. (The great prize of course in Europe is the opportunity to *be* a great figure.) You'd miss these things a good deal — you who delight to recognise greatness; and my advice to you therefore is never to come back. You'd miss the small people even more than the great; every one's middle-sized, and you can never have that

313

momentary sense of profiting by the elevation of your class which is so agreeable in Europe. I needn't add that you don't, either, languish with its depression. There are at all events no brilliant types — the most important people seem to lack dignity. They're very bourgeois; they make little jokes; on occasion they make puns; they've no form; they're too good-natured. The men have no style; the women, who are fidgety and talk too much, have it only in their tournures, where they have it superabundantly.

Well, I console myself — since consolation is needed — with the greater bonhomie. Have you ever arrived at an English country-house in the dusk of a winter's day? Have you ever made a call in London when you knew nobody but the hostess? People here are more expressive, more demonstrative; and it's a pleasure, when one comes back — if one happens, like me, to be no one in particular — to feel one's merely personal and unclassified value rise. They attend to you more; they have you on their mind; they talk to you; they listen to you. That is the men do; the women listen very little — not enough. They interrupt, they prattle, one feels their presence too much as importunate and untrained sound. I imagine this is partly because their wits are quick and they think of a good many things to say; not indeed that they always say such wonders! Perfect repose, after all, is not *all* self-control; it's also partly

stupidity. American women, however, make too many vague exclamations — say too many indefinite things, have in short still a great deal of nature. The American order or climate or whatever gives them a nature they *can* let loose. Europe has to protect itself with more art. On the whole I find very little affectation, though we shall probably have more as we improve. As yet people haven't the assurance that carries those things off; they know too much about each other. The trouble is that over here we've all been brought up together. You'll think this a picture of a dreadfully insipid society; but I hasten to add that it's not all so tame as that. I've been speaking of the people that one meets socially, and these're the smallest part of American life. The others — those one meets on a basis of mere convenience — are much more exciting; they keep one's temper in healthy exercise. I mean the people in the shops and on the railroads; the servants, the hack-men, the labourers, the conductors; every one of whom you buy anything or have occasion to make an enquiry. With them you need all your best manners, for you must always have enough for two. If you think we're *too* democratic taste a little of American life in these walks and you'll be reassured. This is the region of inequality, and you'll find plenty of people to make your curtsey to. You see it from below — the weight of inequality's on your own back. You asked me to tell you about prices. They're unspeakable.

FROM THE RIGHT HON. ED-
WARD ANTROBUS M.P. IN BOSTON
TO THE HONOURABLE MRS. ANTRO-
BUS

November 1880

MY DEAR SUSAN

I sent you a post-card on the 13th and a native newspaper yesterday; I really have had no time to write. I sent you the newspaper partly because it contained a report — extremely incorrect — of some remarks I made at the meeting of the Association of the Teachers of New England; partly because it's so curious that I thought it would interest you and the children. I cut out some portions I didn't think it well the children should go into — the passages remaining contain the most striking features. Please point out to the children the peculiar orthography, which probably will be adopted in England by the time they are grown up; the amusing oddities of expression and the like. Some of them are intentional; you'll have heard of the celebrated American humour — remind me, by the way, on my return to Thistleton, to give you a few of the examples of it that my own experience supplies. Certain other of the journalistic eccentricities I speak of are unconscious and are perhaps on that account the more diverting. Point out to the children the difference — in so far as you're sure that you yourself perceive it. You must excuse me if these lines are not very legible; I'm writing them by the light of a railway lamp which rattles above my left ear; it being only at odd moments that I can find time to extend my personal researches. You'll say this is a very odd moment indeed when I tell you I'm in bed in a sleeping-car. I occupy the upper berth (I will explain to you the arrangement when I return) while the lower forms the couch — the jolts are fearful — of an unknown female. You'll be very anxious for my explanation, but I assure you that the circumstance I mention is the custom of the country. I myself am assured that a lady may travel in this manner all over the Union (the Union of States) without a loss of consideration. In case of her occupying the upper berth I presume it would be different, but I must make enquiries on this point. Whether it be the fact that a mysterious being of another sex has retired to rest behind the same curtains, or whether it be the swing of the train, which rushes through the air with very much the same movement as the tail of a kite, the situation is at the best so anomalous that I'm unable to sleep. A ventilator's open just over my head, and a lively draught, mingled with a drizzle of cinders, pours in through this dubious advantage. (I will describe to you its mechanism on my return.) If I had occupied the lower berth I should have had a whole window to myself, and by drawing back the blind — a safe proceeding at the dead of night — I should have been able, by the light of an extraordinary brilliant moon, to see a little better what I write. The question occurs to me, however, would the lady below me in that case have ascended to the upper berth? (You know my old taste for hypothetic questions.) I incline to think (from what I have seen) that she would simply have requested me to evacuate my own couch. (The ladies in this country ask for anything they want.) In this case, I suppose, I should have had an extensive view of the country, which, from what I saw of it before I turned in (while the sharer of my privacy was going to bed) offered a rather ragged expanse dotted with little white wooden houses that resembled in the moonshine large pasteboard boxes. I've been unable to ascertain as precisely as I should wish by whom these modest residences are occupied; for they are too small to be the homes of country gentlemen, there's no peasantry here, and (in New England, for all the corn comes from the far West) there are no yeomen nor farmers. The information one receives in this country is apt to be rather conflicting, but I'm determined to sift the mystery to the bottom.

I've already noted down a multitude of facts bearing on the points that interest me most — the operation of the school-boards, the co-education of the sexes, the elevation of the tone of the lower classes, the participation of the latter in political life. Political life indeed is almost wholly confined to the lower middle class and the upper section of the lower class. In fact in some of the large towns the lowest order of all participates considerably — a very interesting phase, to which I shall give more attention. It's very gratifying to see the taste for public affairs pervading so many social strata, but the indifference of the gentry is a fact not to be lightly considered. It may be objected perhaps that there are no gentry; and it's very true that I've not yet encountered a character of the type of Lord Bottomley — a type which I'm free to confess I should be sorry to see disappear from our English system, if system it may be called where so much is the growth of blind and incoherent forces. It's nevertheless obvious that an idle and luxurious class exists in this country and that it's less exempt than in our own from the reproach of preferring inglorious ease to the furtherance of liberal ideas. It's rapidly increasing, and I'm not sure that the indefinite growth of the dilettante spirit, in connexion with large and lavishly-expended wealth, is an unmixed good even in a society in which freedom of development has obtained so many interesting triumphs. The fact that this body is not represented in the governing class is perhaps as much the

The Point of View

result of the jealousy with which it is viewed by the more earnest workers as of its own (I dare not perhaps apply a harsher term than) levity. Such at least is the impression made on me in the Middle States and in New England; in the Southwest, the Northwest and the far West it will doubtless be liable to correction. These divisions are probably new to you; but they are the general denomination of large and flourishing communities, with which I hope to make myself at least superficially acquainted. The fatigue of traversing, as I habitually do, three or four hundred miles at a bound, is of course considerable; but there is usually much to feed the mind by the way. The conductors of the trains, with whom I freely converse, are often men of vigorous and original views and even of some social eminence. One of them a few days ago gave me a letter of introduction to his brother-in-law, who's president of a Western University. Don't have any fear therefore that I'm not in the best society!

The arrangements for travelling are as a general thing extremely ingenious, as you will probably have inferred from what I told you above; but it must at the same time be conceded that some of them are more ingenious than happy. Some of the facilities with regard to luggage, the transmission of parcels and the like are doubtless very useful when thoroughly mastered, but I've not yet succeeded in availing myself of them without disaster. There are on the other hand no cabs and no porters, and I've calculated that I've myself carried my *impedimenta* — which, you know, are somewhat numerous, and from which I can't bear to be separated — some seventy or eighty miles. I have sometimes thought it was a great mistake not to bring Plummeridge — he would have been useful on such occasions. On the other hand the startling question would have presented itself of who would have carried Plummeridge's portmanteau? He would have been useful indeed for brushing and packing my clothes and getting me my tub; I travel with a large tin one — there are none to be obtained at the inns — and the transport of this receptacle often presents the most insoluble difficulties. It is often too an object of considerable embarrassment in arriving at private houses, where the servants have less reserve of manner than in England; and to tell you the truth I'm by no means certain at the present moment that the tub has been placed in the train with me. "On board" the train is the consecrated phrase here; it's an allusion to the tossing and pitching of the concatenation of cars, so similar to that of a vessel in a storm. As I was about to enquire, however, Who would get Plummeridge *his* tub and attend to his little comforts? We couldn't very well make our appearance, on arriving for a visit, with *two* of the utensils I've named; even if as regards a single one I have had the courage, as I may say, of a life long habit. It would hardly be expected that we should both use the same; though there have been occasions in my travels as to which I see no way of blinking the fact that Plummeridge would have had to sit down to dinner with me. Such a contingency would completely have unnerved him, so that on the whole it was doubtless the wiser part to leave him respectfully touching his hat on the tender in the Mersey. No one touches his hat over here, and, deem this who will the sign of a more advanced social order, I confess that when I see poor Plummeridge again that familiar little gesture — familiar I mean only in the sense of one's immemorial acquaintance with it — will give me a measurable satisfaction. You'll see from what I tell you that democracy is not a mere word in this country, and I could give you many more instances of its universal reign. This, however, is what we come here to look at and, in so far as there appears proper occasion, to admire; though I'm by no means sure that we can hope to establish within an appreciable time a corresponding change in the somewhat rigid fabric of English manners. I'm not even inclined to believe such a change desirable; you know this is one of the points on which I don't as yet see my way to going so far as Lord B. I've always held that there's a certain social ideal of inequality as well as of equality, and

if I've found the people of this country, as a general thing, quite equal to each other, I'm not quite ready to go so far as to say that, as a whole, they're equal to — pardon that dreadful blot! The movement of the train and the precarious nature of the light — it is close to my nose and most offensive — would, I flatter myself, long since have got the better of a less resolute diarist!

What I was distinctly *not* prepared for is the very considerable body of aristocratic feeling that lurks beneath this republican simplicity. I've on several occasions been made the confidant of these romantic but delusive vagaries, of which the stronghold appears to be the Empire City — a slang name for the rich and predominant, but unprecedentedly maladministered and disillusioned New York. I was assured in many quarters that this great desperate eternally-swindled city at least is ripe, everything else failing, for the monarchical experiment or revolution, and that if one of the Queen's sons would come over to sound the possibilities he would meet with the highest encouragement. This information was given me in strict confidence, with closed doors, as it were; it reminded me a good deal of the dreams of the old Jacobites when they whispered their messages to the king across the water. I doubt, however, whether these less excusable visionaries will be able to secure the services of a Pretender, for I

The Point of View

fear that in such a case he would encounter a still more fatal Culloden. I have given a good deal of time, as I told you, to the educational system, and have visited no fewer than one hundred and forty-three schools and colleges. It's extraordinary the number of persons who are being educated in this country; and yet at the same time the tone of the people is less scholarly than one might expect. A lady a few days since described to me her daughter as being always "on the go," which I take to be a jocular way of saying that the young lady was very fond of paying visits. Another person, the wife of a United States Senator, informed me that if I should go to Washington in January I should be quite "in the swim." I don't regard myself as slow to grasp new meanings, however whimsical; but in this case the lady's explanation made her phrase rather more than less ambiguous. To say that I'm on the go describes very accurately my own situation. I went yesterday to the Poganuc High School, to hear fifty-seven boys and girls recite in unison a most remarkable ode to the American flag, and shortly afterward attended a ladies' luncheon at which some eighty or ninety of the sex were present. There was only one individual in trousers — his trousers, by the way, though he brought several pair, begin to testify to the fury of his movements! The men in America absent themselves systematically from this meal, at which ladies assemble in large numbers to discuss religious, political and social topics.

Immense female symposia at which every delicacy is provided are one of the most striking features of American life, and would seem to prove that our sex is scarcely so indispensable in the scheme of creation as it sometimes supposes. I've been admitted on the footing of an Englishman — "just to show you some of our bright women," the hostess yesterday remarked. ("Bright" here has the meaning of *intellectually remarkable*.) I noted indeed the frequency of the predominantly cerebral — as they call it here "brainy" — type. These rather oddly invidious banquets are organised according to age, for I've also been present as an enquiring stranger at several "girls' lunches," from which married ladies are rigidly excluded, but here the fair revellers were equally numerous and equally "bright." There's a good deal I should like to tell you about my study of the educational question, but my position's now somewhat cramped, and I must dismiss the subject briefly. My leading impression is that the children are better educated (in proportion of course) than the adults. The position of a child is on the whole one of great distinction. There's a popular ballad of which the refrain, if I'm not mistaken, is "Make me a child again just for to-night!" and which seems to express the sentiment of regret for lost privileges. At all events they are a powerful and independent class, and have organs, of immense circulation, in the press. They are often extremely "bright." I've talked with a great many teachers, most of them lady-teachers, as they are here called. The phrase doesn't mean teachers of ladies, as you might suppose, but applies to the sex of the instructress, who often has large classes of young men under her control. I was lately introduced to a young woman of twenty-three who occupies the chair of Moral Philosophy and Belles-Lettres in a Western University and who told me with the utmost frankness that she's "just adored" by the undergraduates. This young woman was the daughter of a petty trader in one of the Southwestern States and had studied at Amanda College in Missourah, an institution at which young people of the two sexes pursue their education together. She was very pretty and modest, and expressed a great desire to see something of English country life, in consequence of which I made her promise to come down to Thistleton in the event of her crossing the Atlantic. She's not the least like Gwendolen or Charlotte, and I'm not prepared to say how they would get on with her; the boys would probably do better. Still, I think her acquaintance would be of value to dear Miss Gulp, and the two might pass their time very pleasantly in the school-room. I grant you freely

that those I have seen here are much less comfortable than the school-room at Thistleton. Has Charlotte, by the way, designed any more texts for the walls? I've been extremely interested in my visit to Philadelphia, where I saw several thousand little red houses with white steps, occupied by intelligent artisans and arranged (in streets) on the rectangular system. Improved cooking-stoves, rosewood pianos, gas and hot water, æsthetic furniture and complete sets of the British Essayists. A tramway through every street; every block of exactly equal length; blocks and houses economically lettered and numbered. There's absolutely no loss of time and no need of looking for, or indeed *at,* anything. The mind always on one's object; it's very delightful.

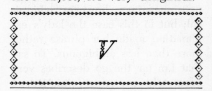

From Louis Leverett in Boston to Harvard Tremont in Paris

November 1880

The scales have turned, my sympathetic Harvard, and the beam that has lifted you up has dropped me again on this terribly hard spot. I'm extremely sorry to have missed you in London, but I received your little note and took due heed of your injunction to let you know how I got on. I don't get on at all, my dear Harvard — I'm consumed with the love of the further shore. I've been so long away that I've dropped out of my place in this little Boston world and the shallow tides of New England life have closed over it. I'm a stranger here and find it hard to believe I ever was a native. It's very hard, very cold, very vacant. I think of your warm rich Paris; I think of the Boulevard Saint-Michel on the mild spring evenings; I see the little corner by the window (of the Café de la Jeunesse) where I used to sit: the doors are open, the soft deep breath of the great city comes in. The sense is of a supreme splendour and an incomparable arrangement, yet there's a kind of tone, of body, in the radiance; the mighty murmur of the ripest civilisation in the world comes in; the dear old *peuple de Paris*, the most interesting people in the world, pass by. I've a little book in my pocket; it's exquisitely printed, a modern Elzevir. It consists of a lyric cry from the heart of young France and is full of the sentiment of form. There's no form here, dear Harvard; I had no idea how little form there is. I don't know what I shall do; I feel so undraped, so uncurtained, so uncushioned; I feel as if I were sitting in the centre of a mighty "reflector." A terrible crude glare is over everything; the earth looks peeled and excoriated; the raw heavens seem to bleed with the quick hard light.

I've not got back my rooms in West Cedar Street; they're occupied by a mesmeric healer. I'm staying at an hotel and it's all very dreadful. Nothing for one's self, nothing for one's preferences and habits. No one to receive you when you arrive; you push in through a crowd, you edge up to a counter, you write your name in a horrible book where every one may come and stare at it and finger it. A man behind the counter stares at you in silence; his stare seems to say "What the devil do *you* want?" But after this stare he never looks at you again. He tosses down a key at you; he presses a bell; a savage Irishman arrives. "Take him away," he seems to say to the Irishman; but it's all done in silence; there's no answer to your own wild wail — "What's to be done with me, please?" "Wait and you'll see" the awful silence seems to say. There's a great crowd round you, but there's also a great stillness; every now and then you hear some one expectorate. There are a thousand people in this huge and hideous structure; they feed together in a big white-walled room. It's lighted by a thousand gas-jets and heated by cast-iron screens which vomit forth torrents of scorching air. The temperature's terrible; the atmosphere's more so; the furious light and heat seem to intensify the dreadful definiteness. When things are so ugly they shouldn't be so definite, and they're terribly ugly here. There's no mystery in the corners, there's no light and shade in the types. The people are haggard and joyless; they look as if they had no passions, no tastes, no senses. They sit feeding in silence under the dry hard light; occasionally I hear the high firm note of a child. The servants are black and familiar; their faces shine as they shuffle about; there are blue tones in their dark masks. They've no manners; they address but don't answer you; they plant themselves at your elbow (it rubs their clothes as you eat) and watch you as if your proceedings were strange. They deluge you with iced water; it's the only thing they'll bring you; if you look round to summon them they've gone for more. If you read the newspaper — which I don't, gracious heaven, I can't! — they hang over your shoulder and peruse it also. I always fold it up and present it to them; the newspapers here are indeed for an African taste.

Then there are long corridors defended by gusts of hot air; down the middle swoops a pale little girl on parlour skates. "Get out of my way!" she shrieks as she passes; she has ribbons in her hair and frills on her dress; she makes the tour of the immense hotel. I think of Puck, who put a girdle round the earth in forty minutes, and wonder what *he* said as he flitted by. A black waiter marches past me bearing a tray that he thrusts into my spine as he goes. It's laden with large white jugs; they tinkle as he moves, and I recognise the unconsoling fluid. We're dying of iced water, of hot air, of flaring gas. I sit in my room thinking of these things — this room of mine which

is a chamber of pain. The walls are white and bare, they shine in the rays of a horrible chandelier of imitation bronze which depends from the middle of the ceiling. It flings a patch of shadow on a small table covered with white marble, of which the genial surface supports at the present moment the sheet of paper I thus employ for you; and when I go to bed (I like to read in bed, Harvard) it becomes an object of mockery and torment. It dangles at inaccessible heights; it stares me in the face; it flings the light on the covers of my book but not upon the page — the little French Elzevir I love so well. I rise and put out the gas — when my room becomes even lighter than before. Then a crude illumination from the hall, from the neighbouring room, pours through the glass openings that surmount the two doors of my apartment. It covers my bed, where I toss and groan; it beats in through my closed lids; it's accompanied by the most vulgar, though the most human, sounds. I spring up to call for some help, some remedy; but there's no bell and I feel desolate and weak. There's only a strange orifice in the wall, through which the traveller in distress may transmit his appeal. I fill it with incoherent sounds, and sounds more incoherent yet come back to me. I gather at last their meaning; they appear to constitute an awful enquiry. A hollow impersonal voice wishes to know what I want, and the very question paralyses me. I want everything — yet I want nothing, nothing this hard impersonality can give! I want my little corner of Paris; I want the rich, the deep, the dark Old World; I want to be out of this horrible place. Yet I can't confide all this to that mechanical tube; it would be of no use; a barbarous laugh would come up from the office. Fancy appealing in these sacred, these intimate moments to an "office"; fancy calling out into indifferent space for a candle, for a curtain! I pay incalculable sums in this dreadful house, and yet haven't a creature to assist me. I fling myself back on my couch and for a long time afterwards the orifice in the wall emits strange murmurs and rumblings. It seems unsatisfied and indignant and is evidently scolding me for my vagueness. My vagueness indeed, dear Harvard! I loathe their horrible arrangements — isn't that definite enough?

You asked me to tell you whom I see and what I think of my friends. I haven't very many; I don't feel at all *en rapport*. The people are very good, very serious, very devoted to their work; but there's a terrible absence of variety of type. Every one's Mr. Jones, Mr. Brown, and every one looks like Mr. Jones and Mr. Brown. They're thin, they're diluted in the great tepid bath of Democracy! They lack completeness of identity; they're quite without modelling. No, they're not beautiful, my poor Harvard; it must be whispered that they're not

beautiful. You may say that they're as beautiful as the French, as the Germans; but I can't agree with you there. The French, the Germans, have the greatest beauty of all, the beauty of their ugliness — the beauty of the strange, the grotesque. These people are not even ugly — they're only plain. Many of the girls are pretty, but to be only pretty is (to my sense) to be plain. Yet I've had some talk. I've seen a young woman. She was on the steamer, and I afterwards saw her in New York — a mere maiden thing, yet a peculiar type, a real personality: a great deal of modelling, a great deal of colour, and withal something elusive and ambiguous. She was not, however, of this country; she was a compound of far-off things. But she was looking for something here — like me. We found each other, and for a moment that was enough. I've lost her now; I'm sorry, because she liked to listen to me. She has passed away; I shall not see her again. She liked to listen to me; she almost understood.

VI

FROM M. GUSTAVE LE- JAUNE OF THE FRENCH ACADEMY IN WASHINGTON TO M. ADOLPHE BOUCHE IN PARIS

December 1880

I GIVE you my little notes; you must make allowances for haste, for bad inns, for the perpetual scram-

ble, for ill-humour. Everywhere the
same impression — the platitude of
unbalanced democracy intensified
by the platitude of the spirit of
commerce. Everything on an immense scale — everything illustrated
by millions of examples. My
brother-in-law is always busy; he
has appointments, inspections, interviews, disputes. The people, it
appears, are incredibly sharp in
conversation, in argument; they
wait for you in silence at the corner of the road and then suddenly
discharge their revolver. If you
fall they empty your pockets; the
only chance is to shoot them first.
With this no amenities, no preliminaries, no manners, no care for
the appearance. I wander about
while my brother's occupied; I
lounge along the streets; I stop at
the corners; I look into the shops;
je regarde passer les femmes. It's
an easy country to see; one sees
everything there is; the civilisation's skin deep; you don't have
to dig. This positive practical
pushing bourgeoisie is always
about its business; it lives in the
street, in the hotel, in the train;
one's always in a crowd — there
are seventy-five people in the
tramway. They sit in your lap;
they stand on your toes; when
they wish to pass they simply
push you. Everything in silence;
they know that silence is golden
and they've the worship of gold.
When the conductor wishes your
fare he gives you a poke, very
serious, without a word. As for
the types — but there's only one,
they're all variations of the same

— the commis-voyageur *minus* the
gaiety. The women are often
pretty; you meet the young ones
in the streets, in the trains, in
search of a husband. They look at
you frankly coldly judicially, to
see if you'll serve; but they don't
want what you might think (*du
moins on me l'assure*); they only
want the husband. A Frenchman
may mistake; he needs to be sure
he's right, and I always make sure.
They begin at fifteen; the mother
sends them out; it lasts all day
(with an interval for dinner at a
pastry-cook's); sometimes it goes
on for ten years. If they haven't
by that time found him they give
it up; they make place for the
cadettes, as the number of women
is enormous. No salons, no society,
no conversation; people don't receive at home; the young girls
have to look for the husband
where they can. It's no disgrace
not to find him — several have
never done so. They continue to
go about unmarried — from the
force of habit, from the love of
movement, without hopes, without
regrets. There's no imagination, no
sensibility, no desire for the convent.

We've made several journeys —
few of less than three hundred
miles. Enormous trains, enormous
wagons, with beds and lavatories,
with negroes who brush you with
a big broom, as if they were groom-
ing a horse. A bounding movement, a roaring noise, a crowd of
people who look horribly tired, a
boy who passes up and down hurl-
ing pamphlets and sweetmeats into

your face: that's an American journey. There are windows in the
wagons — enormous like everything
else; but there's nothing to see.
The country's a void — no features, no objects, no details, nothing to show you that you're in one
place more than another. *Aussi*
you're not in one place, you're everywhere, anywhere; the train
goes a hundred miles an hour. The
cities are all the same; little houses
ten feet high or else big ones
two hundred; tramways, telegraph-
poles, enormous signs, holes in the
pavement, oceans of mud, commis-
voyageurs, young ladies looking
for the husband. On the other hand
no beggars and no *cocottes* — none
at least that you see. A colossal
mediocrity, except (my brother-
in-law tells me) in the machinery,
which is magnificent. Naturally no
architecture (they make houses of
wood and of iron), no art, no literature, no theatre. I've opened
some of the books — *ils ne se lais-
sent pas lire*. No form, no matter,
no style, no general ideas: they
seem written for children and
young ladies. The most successful
ful (those that they praise most)
are the facetious; they sell in thousands of editions. I've looked into
some of the most *vantés;* but you
need to be forewarned to know
they're amusing; grins through a
horse-collar, burlesques of the Bible, *des plaisanteries de croque-
mort.* They've a novelist with pretensions to literature who writes
about the chase for the husband
and the adventures of the rich
Americans in our corrupt old Europe, where their primeval candour puts the Europeans to shame.
C'est proprement écrit, but it's
terribly pale. What isn't pale is
the newspapers — enormous, like
everything else (fifty columns of
advertisements), and full of the
commérages of a continent. And
such a tone, *grand Dieu!* The
amenities, the personalities, the
recriminations, are like so many
coups de revolver. Headings six
inches tall; correspondences from
places one never heard of; telegrams from Europe about Sarah
Bernhardt; little paragraphs about
nothing at all — the *menu* of the
neighbour's dinner; articles on the
European situation *à pouffer de
rire;* all the *tripotage* of local politics. The *reportage* is incredible;
I'm chased up and down by the
interviewers. The matrimonial in-
felicities of M. and Madame X.
(they give the name) *tout au long,*
with every detail — not in six lines,
discreetly veiled, with an art of
insinuation, as with us; but with
all the facts (or the fictions), the
letters, the dates, the places, the
hours. I open a paper at hazard
and find *au beau milieu,* apropos
of nothing, the announcement:
"Miss Susan Green has the longest nose in Western New York."
Miss Susan Green (*je me ren-
seigne*) is a celebrated authoress,
and the Americans have the
reputation of spoiling their wom-
en. They spoil them *à coups de
poing.*

We've seen few interiors (no
one speaks French); but if the
newspapers give an idea of the

domestic *mœurs*, the *mœurs* must be curious. The passport's abolished, but they've printed my *signalement* in these sheets — perhaps for the young ladies who look for the husband. We went one night to the theatre; the piece was French (they are the only ones) but the acting American — too American; we came out in the middle. The want of taste is incredible. An Englishman whom I met tells me that even the language corrupts itself from day to day; the Englishman ceases to understand. It encourages me to find I'm not the only one. There are things every day that one can't describe. Such is Washington, where we arrived this morning, coming from Philadelphia. My brother-in-law wishes to see the Bureau of Patents, and on our arrival he went to look at his machines while I walked about the streets and visited the Capitol! The human machine is what interests me most. I don't even care for the political — for that's what they call their Government here, "the machine." It operates very roughly and some day evidently will explode. It is true that you'd never suspect they *have* a government; this is the principal seat, but, save for three or four big buildings, most of them *affreux*, it looks like a settlement of negroes. No movement, no officials, no authority, no embodiment of the State. Enormous streets, *comme toujours*, lined with little red houses where nothing ever passes but the tramway. The Capitol — a vast structure, false classic, white marble, iron and stucco, which has *assez grand air* — must be seen to be appreciated. The goddess of liberty on the top, dressed in a bear's skin; their liberty over here is the liberty of bears. You go into the Capitol as you would into a railway-station; you walk about as you would in the Palais Royal. No functionaries, no doorkeepers, no officers, no uniforms, no badges, no reservations, no authority — nothing but a crowd of shabby people circulating in a labyrinth of spittoons. We're too much governed perhaps in France; but at least we have a certain incarnation of the national conscience, of the national dignity. The dignity's absent here, and I'm told the public conscience is an abyss. *"L'état c'est moi"* even — I like that better than the spittoons. These implements are architectural, monumental; they're the only monuments. *En somme* the country's interesting, now that we too have the Republic; it is the biggest illustration, the biggest warning. It's the last word of democracy, and that word is — platitude. It's very big, very rich, and perfectly ugly. A Frenchman couldn't live here; for life with us, after all, at the worst, is a sort of appreciation. Here one has nothing to appreciate. As for the people, they're the English *minus* the conventions. You can fancy what remains. The women, *pourtant*, are sometimes rather well turned. There was one at Philadelphia — I made her acquaintance by accident — whom it's probable I shall see again. She's not looking for the husband; she has already got one. It was at the hotel; I think the husband doesn't matter. A Frenchman, as I've said, may mistake, and he needs to be sure he's right. *Aussi* I always make sure!

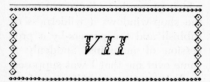

VII

FROM MARCELLUS COCKEREL IN WASHINGTON TO MRS. COOLER NÉE COCKEREL AT OAKLAND CALIFORNIA

October 1880

I OUGHT to have written you long before this, for I've had your last excellent letter these four months in my hands. The first half of that time I was still in Europe, the last I've spent on my native soil. I think accordingly my silence is owing to the fact that over there I was too miserable to write and that here I've been too happy. I got back the 1st of September — you'll have seen it in the papers. Delightful country where one sees everything in the papers — the big familiar vulgar good-natured delightful papers, none of which has any reputation to keep up for anything but getting the news! I really think that has had as much to do as anything else with my satisfaction at getting home — the difference in what they call the "tone of the press." In Europe it's too dreary — the sapience, the solemnity, the false respectability, the verbosity, the long disquisitions on superannuated subjects. Here the newspapers are like the railroad-trains which carry everything that comes to the station and have only the religion of punctuality. As a woman, however, you probably detest them; you think they're (the great word) vulgar. I admitted it just now, and I'm very happy to have an early opportunity to announce to you that that idea has quite ceased to have any terrors for me. There are some conceptions to which the female mind can never rise. Vulgarity's a stupid superficial question-begging accusation, which has become today the easiest refuge of mediocrity. Better than anything else it saves people the trouble of thinking, and anything which does that succeeds. You must know that in these last three years in Europe I've become terribly vulgar myself; that's one service my travels have rendered me. By three years in Europe I mean three years in foreign parts altogether, for I spent several months of that time in Japan, India and the rest of the East. Do you remember when you bade me good-bye in San Francisco the night before I embarked for Yokohama? You foretold that I'd take such a fancy to foreign life that America would never see me more, and that if *you* should wish to see me (an event you were good enough to regard as possible) you'd have to make a rendezvous in Paris or in Rome. I think we made one — which you never kept;

but I shall never make another for those cities. It was in Paris, however, that I got your letter; I remember the moment as well as if it were (to my honour) much more recent. You must know that among many places I dislike Paris carries the palm. I'm bored to death there; it's the home of every humbug. The life is full of that false comfort which is worse than discomfort, and the small fat irritable people give me the shivers.

I had been making these reflexions even more devoutly than usual one very tiresome evening toward the beginning of last summer when, as I re-entered my hotel at ten o'clock, the little reptile of a portress handed me your gracious lines. I was in a villainous humour. I had been having an overdressed dinner in a stuffy restaurant and had gone from there to a suffocating theatre, where, by way of amusement, I saw a play in which blood and lies were the least of the horrors. The theatres over there are insupportable; the atmosphere's pestilential. People sit with their elbows in your sides; they squeeze past you every half-hour. It was one of my bad moments — I have a great many in Europe. The conventional mechanical play, all in falsetto, which I seemed to have seen a thousand times; the horrible faces of the people, the pushing bullying *ouvreuse* with her false politeness and her real rapacity, drove me out of the place at the end of an hour; and as it was too early to go home, I sat down before a café on the Boulevard, where they served me a glass of sour watery beer. There on the Boulevard, in the summer night, life itself was even uglier than the play, and it wouldn't do for me to tell you what I saw. Besides, I was sick of the Boulevard, with its eternal grimace and the deadly sameness of the *article de Paris,* which pretends to be so various — the shop-windows a wilderness of rubbish and the passers-by a procession of manikins. Suddenly it came over me that I was supposed to be amusing myself — my face was a yard long — and that you probably at that moment were saying to your husband: "He stays away so long! What a good time he must be having!" The idea was the first thing that had made me smile for a month; I got up and walked home, reflecting as I went that I was "seeing Europe" and that after all one *must* see Europe. It was because I had been convinced of this that I had come out, and it's because the operation has been brought to a close that I've been so happy for the last eight weeks. I was very conscientious about it, and, though your letter that night made me abominably homesick, I held out to the end, knowing it to be once for all. I shan't trouble Europe again; I shall see America for the rest of my days. My long delay has had the advantage that now at least I can give you my impressions — I don't mean of Europe; impressions of Europe are easy to get — but of this country as it strikes the reinstated exile.

Very likely you'll think them queer; but keep my letter and twenty years hence they'll be quite commonplace. They won't even be vulgar. It was very deliberate, my going round the world. I knew that one ought to see for one's self and that I should have eternity, so to speak, to rest. I travelled energetically; I went everywhere and saw everything; took as many letters as possible and made as many acquaintances. In short I held my nose to the grindstone and here I am back.

Well, the upshot of it all is that I've got rid of a superstition. We have so many that one the less — perhaps the biggest of all — makes a real difference in one's comfort. The one in question — of course you have it — is that there's no salvation but through Europe. Our salvation is here, if we have eyes to see it, and the salvation of Europe into the bargain; that is if Europe's to be saved, which I rather doubt. Of course you'll call me a bird of freedom, a vulgar patriot, a waver of the stars and stripes; but I'm in the delightful position of not minding in the least what any one calls me. I haven't a mission; I don't want to preach; I've simply arrived at a state of mind. I've got Europe off my back. You've no idea how it simplifies things and how jolly it makes me feel. Now I can live, now I can talk. If we wretched Americans could only say once for all "Oh Europe be hanged!" we should attend much better to our proper business. We've simply to

mind that business and the rest will look after itself. You'll probably enquire what it is I like better over here, and I'll answer that it's simply — life. Disagreeables for disagreeables I prefer our own. The way I've been bored and bullied in foreign parts, and the way I've had to say I found it pleasant! For a good while this appeared to be a sort of congenital obligation, but one fine day it occurred to me that there was no obligation at all and that it would ease me immensely to admit to myself that (for me at least) all those things had no importance. I mean the things they rub into you over there; the tiresome international topics, the petty politics, the stupid social customs, the baby-house scenery. The vastness and freshness of this American world, the great scale and great pace of our development, the good sense and good nature of the people, console me for there being no cathedrals and no Titians. I hear nothing about Prince Bismarck and Gambetta, about the Emperor William and the Czar of Russia, about Lord Beaconsfield and the Prince of Wales. I used to get so tired of their Mumbo-Jumbo of a Bismarck, of his secrets and surprises, his mysterious intentions and oracular words. They revile us for our party politics; but what are all the European jealousies and rivalries, their armaments and their wars, their rapacities and their mutual lies, but the intensity of the spirit of party? What question, what interest, what idea, what need of mankind, is involved in any of these things? Their big pompous armies drawn up in great silly rows, their gold lace, their salaams, their hierarchies, seem a pastime for children: there's a sense of humour and of reality over here that laughs at all that.

Yes, we're nearer the reality, nearer what they'll all have to come to. The questions of the future are social questions, which the Bismarcks and Beaconsfields are very much afraid to see settled; and the sight of a row of supercilious potentates holding their peoples like their personal property and bristling all over, to make a mutual impression, with feathers and sabres, strikes us as a mixture of the grotesque and the abominable. What do we care for the mutual impressions of potentates who amuse themselves with sitting on people? Those things are their own affair, and they ought to be shut up in a dark room to have it out together. Once one feels, over here, that the great questions of the future are social questions, that a mighty tide is sweeping the world to democracy, and that this country is the biggest stage on which the drama can be enacted, the fashionable European topics seem petty and parochial. They talk about things that we've settled ages ago, and the solemnity with which they propound to you their little domestic embarrassments makes a heavy draft on one's good nature. In England they were talking about the Hares and Rabbits Bill, about the extension of the County Franchise, about the Dissenters' Burials, about the Deceased Wife's Sister, about the abolition of the House of Lords, about heaven knows what ridiculous little measure for the propping-up of their ridiculous little country. And they call *us* provincial! It's hard to sit and look respectable while people discuss the utility of the House of Lords and the beauty of a State Church, and it's only in a dowdy civilisation that you'll find them doing such things. The lightness and clearness of the social air — *that's* the great relief in these parts. The gentility of bishops, the propriety of parsons, even the impressiveness of a restored cathedral, give less of a charm to life than that. I used to be furious with the bishops and beadles, with the humbuggery of the whole affair, which every one was conscious of but which people agreed not to expose because they'd be compromised all round. The convenience of life in our conditions, the quick and simple arrangements, the absence of the spirit of routine, are a blessed change from the stupid stiffness with which I struggled for two long years. There were people with swords and cockades who used to order me about; for the simplest operation of life I had to kootoo to some bloated official. When it was a question of my doing a little differently from others the bloated official gasped as if I had given him a blow on the stomach; he needed to take a week to think of it.

On the other hand it's impossible to take an American by surprise; he's ashamed to confess he hasn't the wit to do a thing another man has had the wit to think of. Besides being as good as his neighbour he must therefore be as clever — which is an affliction only to people who are afraid he may be cleverer. If this general efficiency and spontaneity of the people — the union of the sense of freedom with the love of knowledge — isn't the very essence of a high civilisation I don't know what a high civilisation is. I felt this greater ease on my first railroad journey — felt the blessing of sitting in a train where I could move about, where I could stretch my legs and come and go, where I had a seat and a window to myself, where there were chairs and tables and food and drink. The villainous little boxes on the European trains, in which you're stuck down in a corner with doubled-up knees, opposite to a row of people, often most offensive types, who stare at you for ten hours on end — these were part of my two years' ordeal. The large free way of doing things here is everywhere a pleasure. In London, at my hotel, they used to come to me on Saturday to make me order my Sunday's dinner, and when I asked for a sheet of paper they put it into the bill. The meagreness, the stinginess, the perpetual expectation of a sixpence, used to exasperate me. Of course

I saw a great many people who were pleasant; but as I'm writing to you and not to one of them I may say that they were dreadfully apt to be dull. The imagination among the people I see here is more flexible, and then they have the advantage of a larger horizon. It's not bounded on the north by the British aristocracy and on the south by the *scrutin de liste*. (I mix up the countries a little, but they're not worth the keeping apart.) The absence of little conventional measurements, of little cut-and-dried judgements, is an immense refreshment. We're more analytic, more discriminating, more familiar with realities. As for manners, there are bad manners everywhere, but an aristocracy is bad manners organised. (I don't mean that they mayn't be polite among themselves, but they're rude to every one else.) The sight of all these growing millions simply minding their business is impressive to me — more so than all the gilt buttons and padded chests of the Old World; and there's a certain powerful type of "practical" American (you'll find him chiefly in the West) who doesn't "blow" as I do (I'm not practical) but who quietly feels that he has the Future in his vitals — a type that strikes me more than any I met in your favourite countries.

Of course you'll come back to the cathedrals and Titians, but there's a thought that helps one to do without them — the thought that, though we've an immense deal of pie-eating plainness, we've little misery, little squalor, little degradation. There's no regular wife-beating class, and there are none of the stultified peasants of whom it takes so many to make a European noble. The people here are more conscious of things; they invent, they act, they answer for themselves; they're not (I speak of social matters) tied up by authority and precedent. We shall have all the Titians by and by, and we shall move over a few cathedrals. You had better stay here if you want to have the best. Of course I'm a roaring Yankee; but you'll call me that if I say the least, so I may as well take my ease and say the most. Washington's a most entertaining place; and here at least, at the seat of government, one isn't overgoverned. In fact there's no government at all to speak of; it seems too good to be true. The first day I was here I went to the Capitol, and it took me ever so long to figure to myself that I had as good a right there as any one else — that the whole magnificent pile (it *is* magnificent, by the way) was in fact my own. In Europe one doesn't rise to such conceptions, and my spirit had been broken in Europe. The doors were gaping wide — I walked all about; there were no door-keepers, no officers nor flunkeys, there wasn't even a policeman to be seen. It seemed strange not to see a uniform, if only as a patch of colour. But this isn't government by livery. The absence of these things is odd at first; you seem to miss something,

to fancy the machine has stopped. It hasn't, though; it only works without fire and smoke. At the end of three days this simple negative impression, the fact that there are no soldiers nor spies, nothing but plain black coats, begins to affect the imagination, becomes vivid majestic symbolic. It ends by being more impressive than the biggest review I saw in Germany. Of course I'm a roaring Yankee; but one has to take a big brush to copy a big model. The future's here of course, but it isn't only that — the present's here as well. You'll complain that I don't give you any personal news, but I'm more modest for myself than for my country. I spent a month in New York and while there saw a good deal of a rather interesting girl who came over with me in the steamer and whom for a day or two I thought I should like to marry. But I shouldn't. She has been spoiled by Europe — and yet the prime stuff struck me as so right.

VIII

From Miss Aurora Church in New York to Miss Whiteside in Paris

January 1881
I told you (after we landed) about my agreement with mamma — that I was to have my liberty for three months and that if at the end of this time I shouldn't have

made a good use of it I was to give it back to her. Well, the time's up to-day, and I'm very much afraid I haven't made a good use of it. In fact I haven't made any use of it at all — I haven't got married, for that's what mamma meant by our little bargain. She has been trying to marry me in Europe for years, without a *dot*, and as she has never (to the best of my knowledge) even come near it, she thought at last that if she were to leave it to me I might possibly do better. I couldn't certainly do worse. Well, my dear, I've done very badly — that is I haven't done at all. I haven't even tried. I had an idea that the *coup* in question came of itself over here; but it hasn't come to *me*. I won't say I'm disappointed, for I haven't on the whole seen any one I should like to marry. When you marry people in these parts they expect you to love them, and I haven't seen any one I should like to love. I don't know what the reason is, but they're none of them what I've thought of. It may be that I've thought of the impossible; and yet I've seen people in Europe whom I should have liked to marry. It's true they were almost always married to some one else. What I *am* disappointed in is simply having to give back my liberty. I don't wish particularly to be married, and I do wish to do as I like — as I've been doing for the last month. All the same I'm sorry for poor mamma, since nothing has happened that she wished to happen. To begin with we're not appreciated, not even by the Rucks, who have disappeared in the strange way in which people over here seem to vanish from the world. We've made no sensation; my new dresses count for nothing (they all have better ones); our philological and historical studies don't show. We've been told we might do better in Boston; but on the other hand mamma hears that in Boston the people only marry their cousins. Then mamma's out of sorts because the country's exceedingly dear and we've spent all our money. Moreover, I've neither eloped, nor been insulted, nor been talked about, nor — so far as I know — deteriorated in manners or character; so that she's wrong in all her previsions. I think she would have rather liked me to be insulted. But I've been insulted as little as I've been adored. They don't adore you over here; they only make you think they're going to.

Do you remember the two gentlemen who were on the ship and who after we arrived came to see me *à tour de rôle?* At first I never dreamed they were making love to me, though mamma was sure it must be that; then, as it went on a good while, I thought perhaps it *was* that — after which I ended by seeing it wasn't anything! It was simply conversation — and conversation a precocious child might have listened to at that. Mr. Leverett and Mr. Cockerel disappeared one fine day without the smallest pretension to having broken my heart, I'm sure — though it only depended on me to think they must have tried to. All the gentlemen are like that; you can't tell what they mean; the "passions" don't rage, the appearances don't matter — nobody believes them. Society seems oddly to consist of a sort of innocent jilting. I think on the whole I *am* a little disappointed — I don't mean about one's not marrying; I mean about the life generally. It looks so different at first that you expect it will be very exciting; and then you find that after all, when you've walked out for a week or two by yourself and driven out with a gentleman in a buggy, that's about all there is to it, as they say here. Mamma's very angry at not finding more to dislike; she admitted yesterday that, once one has got a little settled, the country hasn't even the merit of being hateful. This has evidently something to do with her suddenly proposing three days ago that we should "go West." Imagine my surprise at such an idea coming from mamma! The people in the pension — who, as usual, wish immensely to get rid of her — have talked to her about the West, and she has taken it up with a kind of desperation. You see we must do something; we can't simply remain here. We're rapidly being ruined and we're not — so to speak — getting married. Perhaps it will be easier in the West; at any rate it will be cheaper and the country will have the advantage of being more hateful. It's a question between that and returning to Europe, and for the moment mamma's balancing. I say nothing: I'm really indifferent; perhaps I shall marry a pioneer. I'm just thinking how I shall give back my liberty. It really won't be possible; I haven't got it any more; I've given it away to others. Mamma may get it back if she can from *them!* She comes in at this moment to announce that we must push further — she has decided for the West. Wonderful mamma! It appears that my real chance is for a pioneer — they've sometimes millions. But fancy us at Oshkosh!

A NEW ENGLAND WINTER

MRS. DAINTRY stood on her steps a moment, to address a parting injunction to her little domestic, whom she had induced a few days before, by earnest and friendly argument, — the only coercion or persuasion this enlightened mistress was ever known to use, — to crown her ruffled tresses with a cap; and then, slowly and with deliberation, she descended to the street. As soon as her back was turned, her maid-servant closed the door, not with violence, but inaudibly, quickly, and firmly; so that when she reached the bottom of the steps and looked up again at the front, — as she always did before leaving it, to assure herself that everything was well, — the folded wings of her portal were presented to her, smooth and shining, as wings should be, and ornamented with the large silver plate on which the name of her late husband was inscribed, — which she had brought with her when, taking the inevitable course of good Bostonians, she had transferred her household goods from the "hill" to the "new land," and the exhibition of which, as an act of conjugal fidelity, she preferred

— how much, those who knew her could easily understand — to the more distinguished modern fashion of suppressing the domiciliary label. She stood still for a minute on the pavement, looking at the closed aperture of her dwelling and asking herself a question; not that there was anything extraordinary in that, for she never spared herself in this respect. She would greatly have preferred that her servant should not shut the door till she had reached the sidewalk, and dismissed her, as it were, with that benevolent, that almost maternal, smile with which it was a part of Mrs. Daintry's religion to encourage and reward her domestics. She liked to know that her door was being held open behind her until she should pass out of sight of the young woman standing in the hall. There was a want of respect in shutting her out so precipitately; it was almost like giving her a push down the steps. What Mrs. Daintry asked herself was, whether she should not do right to ascend the steps again, ring the bell, and request Beatrice, the parlor-maid, to be so good as to wait a little longer. She felt that this would have been a proceeding of some importance, and she presently decided against it. There were a good many reasons, and she thought them over as she took her way slowly up Newbury

335

Street, turning as soon as possible into Commonwealth Avenue; for she was very fond of the south side of this beautiful prospect, and the autumn sunshine to-day was delightful. During the moment that she paused, looking up at her house, she had had time to see that everything was as fresh and bright as she could desire. It looked a little too new, perhaps, and Florimond would not like that; for of course his great fondness was for the antique, which was the reason for his remaining year after year in Europe, where, as a young painter of considerable, if not of the highest, promise, he had opportunities to study the most dilapidated buildings. It was a comfort to Mrs. Daintry, however, to be able to say to herself that he would be struck with her living really very nicely, — more nicely, in many ways, than he could possibly be accommodated — that she was sure of — in a small dark *appartement de garçon* in Paris, on the uncomfortable side of the Seine. Her state of mind at present was such that she set the highest value on anything that could possibly help to give Florimond a pleasant impression. Nothing could be too small to count, she said to herself; for she knew that Florimond was both fastidious and observant. Everything that would strike him agreeably would contribute to detain him, so that if there were only enough agreeable things he would perhaps stay four or five months, instead of three, as he had prom-

ised, — the three that were to date from the day of his arrival in Boston, not from that (an important difference) of his departure from Liverpool, which was about to take place.

It was Florimond that Mrs. Daintry had had in mind when, on emerging from the little vestibule, she gave the direction to Beatrice about the position of the door-mat, — in which the young woman, so carefully selected, as a Protestant, from the British Provinces, had never yet taken the interest that her mistress expected from such antecedents. It was Florimond also that she had thought of in putting before her parlor-maid the question of donning a badge of servitude in the shape of a neat little muslin coif, adorned with pink ribbon and stitched together by Mrs. Daintry's own beneficent fingers. Naturally there was no obvious connection between the parlor-maid's coiffure and the length of Florimond's stay; that detail was to be only a part of the general effect of American life. It was still Florimond that was uppermost as his mother, on her way up the hill, turned over in her mind that question of the ceremony of the front-door. He had been living in a country in which servants observed more forms, and he would doubtless be shocked at Beatrice's want of patience. An accumulation of such anomalies would at last undermine his loyalty. He would not care for them for himself, of course, but he would care about them for her; coming from France, where, as she knew by his letters, and indeed by her own reading, — for she made a remarkably free use of the Athenæum, — that the position of a mother was one of the most exalted, he could not fail to be *froissé* at any want of consideration for his surviving parent. As an artist, he could not make up his mind to live in Boston; but he was a good son for all that. He had told her frequently that they might easily live together if she would only come to Paris; but of course she could not do that, with Joanna and her six children round in Clarendon Street, and her responsibilities to her daughter multiplied in the highest degree. Besides, during that winter she spent in Paris, when Florimond was definitely making up his mind, and they had in the evening the most charming conversations, interrupted only by the repeated care of winding up the lamp or applying the bellows to the obstinate little fire, — during that winter she had felt that Paris was not her element. She had gone to the lectures at the Sorbonne, and she had visited the Louvre as few people did it, catalogue in hand, taking the catalogue volume by volume; but all the while she was thinking of Joanna and her new baby, and how the other three (that was the number then) were getting on while their mother was so much absorbed with the last. Mrs. Daintry, familiar as she was with these anxieties, had not the step of a

grandmother; for a mind that was always intent had the effect of refreshing and brightening her years. Responsibility with her was not a weariness, but a joy, — at least it was the nearest approach to a joy that she knew, and she did not regard her life as especially cheerless; there were many others that were more denuded than hers. She moved with circumspection, but without reluctance, holding up her head and looking at every one she met with a clear, unaccusing gaze. This expression showed that she took an interest, as she ought, in everything that concerned her fellow-creatures; but there was that also in her whole person which indicated that she went no farther than Christian charity required. It was only with regard to Joanna and that vociferous houseful, — so fertile in problems, in opportunities for devotion, — that she went really very far. And now to-day, of course, in this matter of Florimond's visit, after an absence of six years; which was perhaps more on her mind than anything had ever been. People who met Mrs. Daintry after she had traversed the Public Garden — she always took that way — and begun to ascend the charming slope of Beacon Street, would never, in spite of the relaxation of her pace as she measured this eminence, have mistaken her for a little old lady who should have crept out, vaguely and timidly, to inhale one of the last mild days. It was easy to see that she was not without a duty, or at least a reason, — and indeed Mrs. Daintry had never in her life been left in this predicament. People who knew her ever so little would have felt that she was going to call on a relation; and if they had been to the manner born they would have added a mental hope that her relation was prepared for her visit. No one would have doubted this, however, who had been aware that her steps were directed to the habitation of Miss Lucretia Daintry. Her sister-in-law, her husband's only sister, lived in that commodious nook which is known as Mount Vernon Place; and Mrs. Daintry therefore turned off at Joy Street. By the time she did so, she had quite settled in her mind the question of Beatrice's behavior in connection with the front-door. She had decided that it would never do to make a formal remonstrance, for it was plain that, in spite of the Old-World training which she hoped the girl might have imbibed in Nova Scotia (where, until lately, she learned, there had been an English garrison), she would in such a case expose herself to the danger of desertion; Beatrice would not consent to stand there holding the door open for nothing. And after all, in the depths of her conscience Mrs. Daintry was not sure that she ought to; she was not sure that this was an act of homage that one human being had a right to exact of another, simply because this other happened to wear a little muslin cap with pink ribbons.

It was a service that ministered to her importance, to her dignity, not to her hunger or thirst; and Mrs. Daintry, who had had other foreign advantages besides her winter in Paris, was quite aware that in the United States the machinery for that former kind of tribute was very undeveloped. It was a luxury that one ought not to pretend to enjoy, — it was a luxury, indeed, that she probably ought not to presume to desire. At the bottom of her heart Mrs. Daintry suspected that such hankerings were criminal. And yet, turning the thing over, as she turned everything, she could not help coming back to the idea that it would be very pleasant, it would be really delightful, if Beatrice herself, as a result of the growing refinement of her taste, her transplantation to a society after all more elaborate than that of Nova Scotia, should perceive the fitness, the felicity, of such an attitude. This perhaps was too much to hope; but it did not much matter, for before she had turned into Mount Vernon Place Mrs. Daintry had invented a compromise. She would continue to talk to her parlor-maid until she should reach the bottom of her steps, making earnestly one remark after the other over her shoulder, so that Beatrice would be obliged to remain on the threshold. It is true that it occurred to her that the girl might not attach much importance to these Parthian observations, and would perhaps not trouble herself to wait for their natural term; but this idea was too fraught with embarrassment to be long entertained. It must be added that this was scarcely a moment for Mrs. Daintry to go much into the ethics of the matter, for she felt that her call upon her sister-in-law was the consequence of a tolerably unscrupulous determination.

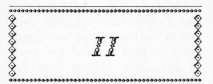

LUCRETIA DAINTRY was at home, for a wonder; but she kept her visitor waiting a quarter of an hour, during which this lady had plenty of time to consider her errand afresh. She was a little ashamed of it; but she did not so much mind being put to shame by Lucretia, for Lucretia did things that were much more ambiguous than any she should have thought of doing. It was even for this that Mrs. Daintry had picked her out, among so many relations, as the object of an appeal in its nature somewhat precarious. Nevertheless, her heart beat a little faster than usual as she sat in the quiet parlor, looking about her for the thousandth time at Lucretia's "things," and observing that she was faithful to her old habit of not having her furnace lighted until long after every one. else. Miss Daintry had her own habits, and she was the only person her sister-in-law knew who had more reasons than herself. Her taste was of

the old fashion, and her drawing-room embraced neither festoons nor Persian rugs, nor plates and *plaques* upon the wall, nor faded stuffs suspended from unexpected projections. Most of the articles it contained dated from the year 1830; and a sensible, reasonable, rectangular arrangement of them abundantly answered to their owner's conception of the decorative. A rosewood sofa against the wall, surmounted by an engraving from Kaulbach; a neatly drawn carpet, faded, but little worn, and sprigged with a floral figure; a chimney-piece of black marble, veined with yellow, garnished with an empire clock and antiquated lamps; half a dozen large mirrors, with very narrow frames; and an immense glazed screen representing in the livid tints of early worsted-work a ruined temple overhanging a river, — these were some of the more obvious of Miss Daintry's treasures. Her sister-in-law was a votary of the newer school, and had made sacrifices to have everything in black and gilt; but she could not fail to see that Lucretia had some very good pieces. It was a wonder how she made them last, for Lucretia had never been supposed to know much about the keeping of a house, and no one would have thought of asking her how she treated the marble floor of her vestibule, or what measures she took in the spring with regard to her curtains. Her work in life lay outside. She took an interest in questions and institutions, sat on committees, and had views on Female Suffrage, — a movement which she strongly opposed. She even wrote letters sometimes to the "Transcript," not "chatty" and jocular, and signed with a fancy name, but "over" her initials, as the phrase was, — every one recognized them, — and bearing on some important topic. She was not, however, in the faintest degree slipshod or dishevelled, like some of the ladies of the newspaper and the forum; she had no ink on her fingers, and she wore her bonnet as scientifically poised as the dome of the State House. When you rang at her door-bell you were never kept waiting and when you entered her dwelling you were not greeted with those culinary odors which, pervading halls and parlors, had in certain other cases been described as the right smell in the wrong place. If Mrs. Daintry was made to wait some time before her hostess appeared, there was nothing extraordinary in this, for none of her friends came down directly, and she never did herself. To come down directly would have seemed to her to betray a frivolous eagerness for the social act. The delay, moreover, not only gave her, as I have said, opportunity to turn over her errand afresh, but enabled her to say to herself, as she had often said before, that though Lucretia had no taste, she had some very good things, and to wonder both how she had kept them so well, and how she had originally got them. Mrs. Daintry knew that they proceeded from her mother and her aunts, who had been supposed to distribute among the children of the second generation the accumulations of the old house in Federal Street, where many Daintrys had been born in the early part of the century. Of course she knew nothing of the principles on which the distribution had been made, but all she could say was that Lucretia had evidently been first in the field. There was apparently no limit to what had come to her. Mrs. Daintry was not obliged to look, to assure herself that there was another clock in the back parlor, — which would seem to indicate that all the clocks had fallen to Lucretia. She knew of four other timepieces in other parts of the house, for of course in former years she had often been up stairs; it was only in comparatively recent times that she had renounced that practice. There had been a period when she ascended to the second story as a matter of course, without asking leave. On seeing that her sister-in-law was in neither of the parlors, she mounted and talked with Lucretia at the door of her bedroom, if it happened to be closed. And there had been another season when she stood at the foot of the staircase, and, lifting her voice, inquired of Miss Daintry — who called down with some shrillness in return — whether she might climb, while the maid-servant, wandering away with a vague cachinnation, left her to her own devices. But both of these phases belonged to the past. Lucretia never came into *her* bedroom to-day, nor did she presume to penetrate into Lucretia's; so that she did not know for a long time whether she had renewed her chintz, nor whether she had hung in that bower the large photograph of Florimond, presented by Mrs. Daintry herself to his aunt, which had been placed in neither of the parlors. Mrs. Daintry would have given a good deal to know whether this memento had been honored with a place in her sister-in-law's "chamber," — it was by this name, on each side, that these ladies designated their sleeping-apartment; but she could not bring herself to ask directly, for it would be embarrassing to learn — what was possible — that Lucretia had not paid the highest respect to Florimond's portrait. The point was cleared up by its being revealed to her accidentally that the photograph, — an expensive and very artistic one, taken in Paris, — had been relegated to the spare-room, or guest-chamber. Miss Daintry was very hospitable, and constantly had friends of her own sex staying with her. They were very apt to be young women in their twenties; and one of them had remarked to Mrs. Daintry that her son's portrait — he must be wonderfully handsome — was the first thing she saw when she woke up in the morning. Certainly Florimond was handsome; but his mother had a lurking suspicion that, in spite of his beauty, his aunt was not fond of him. She doubtless thought he ought to come back and settle down in Boston; he was the first of the Daintrys who had had so much in common with Paris. Mrs. Daintry knew as a fact that, twenty-eight years before, Lucretia, whose opinions even at that period were already wonderfully formed, had not approved of the romantic name which, in a moment of pardonable weakness, she had conferred upon her rosy babe. The spinster (she had been as much of a spinster at twenty as she was to-day) had accused her of making a fool of the child. Every one was reading old ballads in Boston then, and Mrs. Daintry had found the name in a ballad. It doubled any anxiety she might feel with regard to her present business to think that, as certain foreign newspapers which her son sent her used to say about ambassadors, Florimond was perhaps not a *persona grata* to his aunt. She reflected, however, that if his fault were in his absenting himself, there was nothing that would remedy it so effectively as his coming home. She reflected, too, that if she and Lucretia no longer took liberties with each other, there was still something a little indiscreet in her purpose this morning. But it fortified and consoled her for everything to remember, as she sat looking at the empire clock, which was a very handsome one, that her husband at least had been disinterested.

Miss Daintry found her visitor in this attitude, and thought it was an expression of impatience; which led her to explain that she had been on the roof of her house with a man who had come to see about repairing it. She had walked all over it, and peeped over the cornice, and not been in the least dizzy; and had come to the conclusion that one ought to know a great deal more about one's roof than was usual.

"I am sure you have never been over yours," she said to her sister-in-law.

Mrs. Daintry confessed with some embarrassment that she had not, and felt, as she did so, that she was superficial and slothful. It annoyed her to reflect that while she supposed, in her new house, she had thought of everything, she had not thought of this important feature. There was no one like Lucretia for giving one such reminders.

"I will send Florimond up when he comes," she said; "he will tell me all about it."

"Do you suppose he knows about roofs, except tumbledown ones, in his little pictures? I am afraid it will make him giddy." This had been Miss Daintry's rejoinder, and the tone of it was not altogether reassuring. She was nearly fifty years old; she had a plain, fresh, delightful face, and in whatever part of the world she might have been met, an attentive observer of American life would not have had the least difficulty in guessing what phase of it she represented. She represented the various and enlightened activities which cast their rapid shuttle — in the comings and goings of eager workers — from one side to the other of Boston Common. She had in an eminent degree the physiognomy, the accent, the costume, the conscience, and the little eye-glass, of her native place. She had never sacrificed to the graces, but she inspired unlimited confidence. Moreover, if she was thoroughly in sympathy with the New England capital, she reserved her liberty; she had a great charity, but she was independent and witty; and if she was as earnest as other people, she was not quite so serious. Her voice was a little masculine; and it had been said of her that she didn't care in the least how she looked. This was far from true, for she would not for the world have looked better than she thought was right for so plain a woman.

Mrs. Daintry was fond of calculating consequences; but she was not a coward, and she arrived at her business as soon as possible.

"You know that Florimond sails on the 20th of this month. He will get home by the 1st of December."

"Oh, yes, my dear, I know it; everybody is talking about it. I have heard it thirty times. That's where Boston is so small," Lucretia Daintry remarked.

"Well, it's big enough for me," said her sister-in-law. "And of course people notice his coming back; it shows that everything that has been said is false, and that he really does like us."

"He likes his mother, I hope; about the rest I don't know that it matters."

"Well, it certainly will be pleasant to have him," said Mrs. Daintry, who was not content with her companion's tone, and wished to extract from her some recognition of the importance of Florimond's advent. "It will prove how unjust so much of the talk has been."

"My dear woman, I don't know anything about the talk. We make too much fuss about everything. Florimond was an infant when I last saw him."

This was open to the interpretation that too much fuss had been made about Florimond, — an idea that accorded ill with the project that had kept Mrs. Daintry waiting a quarter of an hour while her hostess walked about on the roof. But Miss Daintry continued, and in a moment gave her sister-in-law the best opportunity she could have hoped for. "I don't suppose he will bring with him either salvation or the other thing; and if he has decided to winter among the bears, it will matter much more to him than to any one else. But I shall be very glad to see him if he behaves himself; and I needn't tell you that if there is anything I can do for him — " and Miss Daintry, tightening her lips together a little, paused, suiting her action to the idea that professions were usually humbug.

"There is indeed something you can do for him," her sister-in-law hastened to respond; "or some-thing you can do for me, at least," she added, more discreetly.

"Call it for both of you. What is it?" and Miss Daintry put on her eyeglass.

"I know you like to do kindnesses, when they are *real* ones; and you almost always have some one staying with you for the winter."

Miss Daintry stared. "Do you want to put him to live with me?"

"No, indeed! Do you think I could part with him? It's another person, — a lady!"

"A lady! Is he going to bring a woman with him?"

"My dear Lucretia, you won't wait. I want to make it as pleasant for him as possible. In that case he may stay longer. He has promised three months; but I should so like to keep him till the summer. It would make me very happy."

"Well, my dear, keep him, then, if you can."

"But I can't, unless I am helped."

"And you want me to help you? Tell me what I must do. Should you wish me to make love to him?"

Mrs. Daintry's hesitation at this point was almost as great as if she had found herself obliged to say yes. She was well aware that what she had come to suggest was very delicate; but it seemed to her at the present moment more delicate than ever. Still, her cause was good, because it was the cause of maternal devotion. "What I should like you to do would be to ask

Rachel Torrance to spend the winter with you."

Miss Daintry had not sat so much on committees without getting used to queer proposals, and she had long since ceased to waste time in expressing a vain surprise. Her method was Socratic; she usually entangled her interlocutor in a net of questions.

"Ah, do you want *her* to make love to him?"

"No, I don't want any love at all. In such a matter as that I want Florimond to be perfectly free. But Rachel is such an attractive girl; she is so artistic and so bright."

"I don't doubt it; but I can't invite all the attractive girls in the country. Why don't you ask her yourself?"

"It would be too marked. And then Florimond might not like her in the same house; he would have too much of her. Besides, she is no relation of mine, you know; the cousinship — such as it is, it is not very close — is on your side. I have reason to believe she would like to come; she knows so little of Boston, and admires it so much. It is astonishing how little idea the New York people have. She would be different from any one here, and that would make a pleasant change for Florimond. She was in Europe so much when she was young. She speaks French perfectly, and Italian, I think, too; and she was brought up in a kind of artistic way. Her father never did anything; but even when he hadn't bread to give his children,

he always arranged to have a studio, and they gave musical parties. That's the way Rachel was brought up. But they tell me that it hasn't in the least spoiled her; it has only made her very familiar with life."

"Familiar with humbug!" Miss Daintry ejaculated.

"My dear Lucretia, I assure you she is a very good girl, or I never would have proposed such a plan as this. She paints very well herself, and tries to sell her pictures. They are dreadfully poor, — I don't mean the pictures, but Mrs. Torrance and the rest, — and they live in Brooklyn, in some second-rate boarding-house. With that, Rachel has everything about her that would enable her to appreciate Boston. Of course it would be a real kindness, because there would be one less to pay for at the boarding-house. You haven't a son, so you can't understand how a mother feels. I want to prepare everything, to have everything pleasantly arranged. I want to deprive him of every pretext for going away before the summer; because in August — I don't know whether I have told you — I have a kind of idea of going back with him myself. I am so afraid he will miss the artistic side. I don't mind saying that to you, Lucretia, for I have heard you say yourself that you thought it had been left out here. Florimond might go and see Rachel Torrance every day if he liked; of course, being his cousin, and calling her Rachel, it couldn't attract any particular attention. I shouldn't much care if it did," Mrs. Daintry went on, borrowing a certain bravado, that in calmer moments was eminently foreign to her nature, from the impunity with which she had hitherto proceeded. Her project, as she heard herself unfold it, seemed to hang together so well that she felt something of the intoxication of success. "I shouldn't care if it did," she repeated, "so long as Florimond had a little of the conversation that he is accustomed to, and I was not in perpetual fear of his starting off."

Miss Daintry had listened attentively while her sister-in-law spoke, with eager softness, passing from point to point with a *crescendo* of lucidity, like a woman who had thought it all out, and had the consciousness of many reasons on her side. There had been momentary pauses, of which Lucretia had not taken advantage, so that Mrs. Daintry rested at last in the enjoyment of a security that was almost complete, and that her companion's first question was not of a nature to dispel.

"It's so long since I have seen her. Is she pretty?" Miss Daintry inquired.

"She is decidedly striking; she has magnificent hair!" her visitor answered, almost with enthusiasm.

"Do you want Florimond to marry her?"

This, somehow, was less pertinent. "Ah, no, my dear," Mrs. Daintry rejoined, very judicially. "That is not the kind of education — the kind of *milieu* — one would

wish for the wife of one's son." She knew, moreover, that her sister-in-law knew her opinion about the marriage of young people. It was a sacrament more high and holy than any words could express, the propriety and timeliness of which lay deep in the hearts of the contracting parties, below all interference from parents and friends; it was an inspiration from above, and she would no more have thought of laying a train to marry her son, than she would have thought of breaking open his letters. More relevant even than this, however, was the fact that she did not believe he would wish to make a wife of a girl from a slipshod family in Brooklyn, however little he might care to lose sight of the artistic side. It will be observed that she gave Florimond the credit of being a very discriminating young man; and she indeed discriminated for him in cases in which she would not have presumed to discriminate for herself.

"My dear Susan, you are simply the most immoral woman in Boston!" These were the words of which, after a moment, her sister-in-law delivered herself.

Mrs. Daintry turned a little pale. "Don't you think it would be right?" she asked quickly.

"To sacrifice the poor girl to Florimond's amusement? What has she done that you should wish to play her such a trick?" Miss Daintry did not look shocked: she never looked shocked, for even when she was annoyed she was never frightened; but after a moment she broke into a loud, uncompromising laugh, — a laugh which her sister-in-law knew of old, and regarded as a peculiarly dangerous form of criticism.

"I don't see why she should be sacrificed. She would have a lovely time if she were to come on. She would consider it the greatest kindness to be asked."

"To be asked to come and amuse Florimond?"

Mrs. Daintry hesitated a moment. "I don't see why she should object to that. Florimond is certainly not beneath a person's notice. Why, Lucretia, you speak as if there were something disagreeable about Florimond."

"My dear Susan," said Miss Daintry, "I am willing to believe that he is the first young man of his time; but, all the same, it isn't a thing to do."

"Well, I have thought of it in every possible way, and I haven't seen any harm in it. It isn't as if she were giving up anything to come."

"You have thought of it too much, perhaps. Stop thinking for a while. I should have imagined you were more scrupulous."

Mrs. Daintry was silent a moment; she took her sister-in-law's asperity very meekly, for she felt that if she had been wrong in what she proposed, she deserved a severe judgment. But why was she wrong? She clasped her hands in her lap and rested her eyes with extreme seriousness upon Lucre-

tia's little *pince-nez*, inviting her to judge her, and too much interested in having the question of her culpability settled to care whether or no she were hurt. "It is very hard to know what is right," she said presently. "Of course it is only a plan; I wondered how it would strike you."

"You had better leave Florimond alone," Miss Daintry answered. "I don't see why you should spread so many carpets for him. Let him shift for himself. If he doesn't like Boston, Boston can spare him."

"You are not nice about him; no, you are not, Lucretia!" Mrs. Daintry cried, with a slight tremor in her voice.

"Of course I am not as nice as you, — he is not my son; but I am trying to be nice about Rachel Torrance."

"I am sure she would like him, — she would delight in him," Mrs. Daintry broke out.

"That's just what I'm afraid of; I couldn't stand that."

"Well, Lucretia, I am not convinced," Mrs. Daintry said, rising, with perceptible coldness. "It is very hard to be sure one is not unjust. Of course I shall not expect you to send for her; but I shall think of her with a good deal of compassion, all winter, in that dingy place in Brooklyn. And if you have some one else with you — and I am sure you will, because you always do, unless you remain alone on purpose, this year, to put me in the wrong, — if you have some one else I shall keep saying to myself: 'Well, after all, it might have been Rachel!' "

Miss Daintry gave another of her loud laughs at the idea that she might remain alone "on purpose." "I shall have a visitor, but it will be some one who will not amuse Florimond in the least. If he wants to go away, it won't be for anything in this house that he will stay."

"I really don't see why you should hate him," said poor Mrs. Daintry.

"Where do you find that? On the contrary, I appreciate him very highly. That's just why I think it very possible that a girl like Rachel Torrance — an odd, uninstructed girl, who hasn't had great advantages — may fall in love with him and break her heart."

Mrs. Daintry's clear eyes expanded. "Is *that* what you are afraid of?"

"Do you suppose my solicitude is for Florimond? An accident of that sort — if she were to show him her heels at the end — might perhaps do him good. But I am thinking of the girl, since you say you don't want him to marry her."

"It was not for that that I suggested what I did. I don't want him to marry any one — I have no plans for that," Mrs. Daintry said, as if she were resenting an imputation.

"Rachel Torrance least of all!" and Miss Daintry indulged still again in that hilarity, so personal to herself, which sometimes made the subject look so little jocular to others. "My dear Susan, I don't

blame you," she said; "for I suppose mothers are necessarily unscrupulous. But that is why the rest of us should hold them in check."

"It's merely an assumption, that she would fall in love with him," Mrs. Daintry continued, with a certain majesty; "there is nothing to prove it, and I am not bound to take it for granted."

"In other words, you don't care if she should! Precisely; that, I suppose, is your *rôle*. I am glad I haven't any children; it's very sophisticating. For so good a woman, you are very bad. Yes, you *are* good, Susan; and you *are* bad."

"I don't know that I pretend to be particularly good," Susan remarked, with the warmth of one who had known something of the burden of such a reputation, as she moved toward the door.

"You have a conscience, and it will wake up," her companion returned. "It will come over you in the watches of the night that your idea was — as I have said — immoral."

Mrs. Daintry paused in the hall, and stood there looking at Lucretia. It was just possible that she was being laughed at, for Lucretia's deepest mirth was sometimes silent, — that is, one heard the laughter several days later. Suddenly she colored to the roots of her hair, as if the conviction of her error had come over her. Was it possible she had been corrupted by an affection in itself so pure? "I only want to do right," she said, softly. "I would rather he should never come home, than that I should go too far."

She was turning away, but her sister-in-law held her a moment and kissed her. "You are a delightful woman, but I won't ask Rachel Torrance!" This was the understanding on which they separated.

III

Miss Daintry, after her visitor had left her, recognized that she had been a little brutal; for Susan's proposition did not really strike her as so heinous. Her eagerness to protect the poor girl in Brooklyn was not a very positive quantity, inasmuch as she had an impression that this young lady was on the whole very well able to take care of herself. What her talk with Mrs. Daintry had really expressed was the lukewarmness of her sentiment with regard to Florimond. She had no wish to help his mother lay carpets for him, as she said. Rightly or wrongly, she had a conviction that he was selfish, that he was spoiled, that he was conceited; and she thought Lucretia Daintry meant for better things than the service of sugaring for the young man's lips the pill of a long-deferred visit to Boston. It was quite indifferent to her that he should be conscious, in that city, of unsatisfied needs. At bottom, she had never forgiven him for having

sought another way of salvation. Moreover she had a strong sense of humor, and it amused her more than a little that her sister-in-law — of all women in Boston — should have come to her on that particular errand. It completed the irony of the situation that one should frighten Mrs. Daintry — just a little — about what she had undertaken; and more than once that day Lucretia had, with a smile, the vision of Susan's countenance as she remarked to her that she was immoral. In reality, and speaking seriously, she did not consider Mrs. Daintry's inspiration unpardonable; what was very positive was simply that she had no wish to invite Rachel Torrance for the benefit of her nephew. She was by no means sure that she should like the girl for her own sake, and it was still less apparent that she should like her for that of Florimond. With all this, however, Miss Daintry had a high love of justice; she revised her social accounts from time to time, to see that she had not cheated any one. She thought over her interview with Mrs. Daintry the next day, and it occurred to her that she had been a little unfair. But she scarcely knew what to do to repair her mistake, by which Rachel Torrance also had suffered, perhaps; for after all, if it had not been wicked of her sister-in-law to ask such a favor, it had at least been cool; and the penance that presented itself to Lucretia Daintry did not take the form of despatching a letter to Brooklyn. An accident came to her help, and four days after the conversation I have narrated she wrote her a note, which explains itself, and which I will presently transcribe. Meanwhile Mrs. Daintry, on her side, had held an examination of her heart; and though she did not think she had been very civilly treated, the result of her reflections was to give her a fit of remorse. Lucretia was right: she had been anything but scrupulous; she had skirted the edge of an abyss. Questions of conduct had long been familiar to her; and the cardinal rule of life in her eyes was that before one did anything which involved in any degree the happiness or the interest of another, one should take one's motives out of the closet in which they are usually laid away and give them a thorough airing. This operation, undertaken before her visit to Lucretia, had been cursory and superficial; for now that she repeated it, she discovered among the recesses of her spirit a number of nut-like scruples which she was astonished to think she should have overlooked. She had really been very wicked, and there was no doubt about *her* proper penance. It consisted of a letter to her sister-in-law, in which she completely disavowed her little project, attributing it to a momentary intermission of her reason. She saw it would never do, and she was quite ashamed of herself. She did not exactly thank Miss Daintry for the manner in which she had admonished her, but she spoke as one saved from a great danger, and assured her relative of Mount Vernon Place that she should not soon again expose herself. This letter crossed with Miss Daintry's missive, which ran as follows: —

"My Dear Susan, — I have been thinking over our conversation of last Tuesday, and I am afraid I went rather too far in my condemnation of your idea with regard to Rachel Torrance. If I expressed myself in a manner to wound your feelings, I can assure you of my great regret. Nothing could have been farther from my thoughts than the belief that you are wanting in delicacy. I know very well that you were prompted by the highest sense of duty. It is possible, however, I think, that your sense of duty to poor Florimond is a little too high. You think of him too much as that famous dragon of antiquity, — wasn't it in Crete, or somewhere? — to whom young virgins had to be sacrificed. It may relieve your mind, however, to hear that this particular virgin will probably, during the coming winter, be provided for. Yesterday, at Doll's, where I had gone in to look at the new pictures (there is a striking Appleton Brown) I met Pauline Mesh, whom I had not seen for ages, and had half an hour's talk with her. She seems to me to have come out very much this winter, and to have altogether a higher tone. In short, she is much enlarged, and seems to want to take an interest in something.

A New England Winter

Of course you will say: Has she not her children? But, somehow, they don't seem to fill her life. You must remember that they are very small as yet, to fill anything. Anyway, she mentioned to me her great disappointment in having had to give up her sister, who was to have come on from Baltimore to spend the greater part of the winter. Rosalie is very pretty, and Pauline expected to give a lot of Germans, and make things generally pleasant. I shouldn't wonder if she thought something might happen that would make Rosalie a fixture in our city. She would have liked this immensely; for, whatever Pauline's faults may be, she has plenty of family feeling. But her sister has suddenly got engaged in Baltimore (I believe it's much easier than here), so that the visit has fallen through. Pauline seemed to be quite in despair, for she had made all sorts of beautifications in one of her rooms, on purpose for Rosalie; and not only had she wasted her labor (you know how she goes into those things, whatever we may think, sometimes, of her taste), but she spoke as if it would make a great difference in her winter; said she should suffer a great deal from loneliness. She says Boston is no place for a married woman, standing on her own merits; she can't have any sort of time unless she hitches herself to some attractive girl who will help her to pull the social car. You know that isn't what every one says, and how much talk there has

been the last two or three winters about the frisky young matrons. Well, however that may be, I don't pretend to know much about it, not being in the married set. Pauline spoke as if she were really quite high and dry, and I felt so sorry for her that it suddenly occurred to me to say something about Rachel Torrance. I remembered that she is related to Donald Mesh in about the same degree as she is to me, — a degree nearer, therefore, than to Florimond. Pauline didn't seem to think much of the relationship, — it's so remote; but when I told her that Rachel (strange as it might appear) would probably be thankful for a season in Boston, and might be a good substitute for Rosalie, why she quite jumped at the idea. She has never seen her, but she knows who she is, — fortunately, for I could never begin to explain. She seems to think such a girl will be quite a novelty in this place. I don't suppose Pauline can do her any particular harm, from what you tell me of Miss Torrance, and, on the other hand, I don't know that she could injure Pauline. She is certainly very kind (Pauline, of course), and I have no doubt she will immediately write to Brooklyn, and that Rachel will come on. Florimond won't, of course, see as much of her as if she were staying with me, and I don't know that he will particularly care about Pauline Mesh, who, you know, is intensely American; but they will go out a great deal, and he will meet them (if he takes the trouble), and I have no doubt that Rachel will take the edge off the east wind for him. At any rate I have perhaps done her a good turn. I must confess to you — and it won't surprise you — that I was thinking of her, and not of him, when I spoke to Pauline. Therefore I don't feel that I have taken a risk, but I don't much care if I have. I have my views, but I never worry. I recommend you not to do so either, — for you go, I know, from one extreme to the other. I have told you my little story; it was on my mind. Aren't you glad to see the lovely snow? Ever affectionately yours, L. D.

"P.S. The more I think of it, the more convinced I am that you *will* worry now about the danger for Rachel. Why did I drop the poison into your mind? Of course I didn't say a word about you or Florimond."

This epistle reached Mrs. Daintry, as I have intimated, about an hour after her letter to her sister-in-law had been posted; but it is characteristic of her that she did not for a moment regret having made a retractation rather humble in form, and which proved, after all, scarcely to have been needed. The delight of having done that duty carried her over the sense of having given herself away. Her sister-in-law spoke from knowledge when she wrote that phrase about Susan's now beginning to worry from the opposite point of view. Her conscience, like the good Homer, might sometimes nod; but

when it woke, it woke with a start; and for many a day afterward its vigilance was feverish. For the moment, her emotions were mingled. She thought Lucretia very strange, and that *she* was scarcely in a position to talk about one's going from one extreme to the other. It was good news to her that Rachel Torrance would probably be on the ground after all, and she was delighted that on Lucretia the responsibility of such a fact should rest. This responsibility she now already, after her revulsion, as we know, regarded as grave; she exhaled an almost luxurious sigh when she thought of having herself escaped from it. What she did not quite understand was Lucretia's apology, and her having, even if Florimond's happiness were not her motive, taken almost the very step which three days before she had so severely criticised. This was puzzling, for Lucretia was usually so consistent. But all the same Mrs. Daintry did not repent of her own penance; on the contrary, she took more and more comfort in it. If, with that, Rachel Torrance should be really useful, it would be delightful.

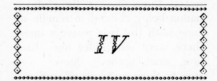

IV

FLORIMOND DAINTRY had stayed at home for three days after his arrival; he had sat close to the fire in his slippers, every now and then casting a glance over his shoulders at the hard white world which seemed to glare at him from the other side of the window-panes. He was very much afraid of the cold, and he was not in a hurry to go out and meet it. He had met it, on disembarking in New York, in the shape of a wave of frozen air, which had travelled from some remote point in the west (he was told) on purpose, apparently, to smite him in the face. That portion of his organism tingled yet with it, though the gasping, bewildered look which sat upon his features during the first few hours had quite left it. I am afraid it will be thought he was a young man of small courage; and on a point so delicate I do not hold myself obliged to pronounce. It is only fair to add that it was delightful to him to be with his mother, and that they easily spent three days in talking. Moreover he had the company of Joanna and her children, who, after a little delay, occasioned apparently by their waiting to see whether he would not first come to them, had arrived in a body and had spent several hours. As regards the majority of them, they had repeated this visit several times in the three days, Joanna being obliged to remain at home with the two younger ones. There were four older ones, and their grandmother's house was open to them as a second nursery. The first day, their Uncle Florimond thought them charming; and as he had brought a French toy for each, it is probable that this impression was mutual. The second day, their little ruddy bodies and woollen clothes seemed to him to have a positive odor of the cold, — it was disagreeable to him, and he spoke to his mother about their "wintry smell." The third day they had become very familiar; they called him "Florry"; and he had made up his mind that, to let them loose in that way on his mother, Joanna must be rather wanting in delicacy, — not mentioning this deficiency, however, as yet, for he saw that his mother was not prepared for it. She evidently thought it proper, or at least it seemed inevitable, either that she should be round at Joanna's, or the children should be round in Newbury Street; for "Joanna's" evidently represented primarily the sound of small, loud voices, and the hard breathing that signalized the intervals of romps. Florimond was rather disappointed in his sister, seeing her after a long separation; he remarked to his mother that she seemed completely submerged. As Mrs. Daintry spent most of her time under the waves with her daughter, she had grown to regard this element as sufficiently favorable to life, and was rather surprised when Florimond said to her that he was sorry to see she and his sister appeared to have been converted into a pair of *bonnes d'enfants*. Afterward, however, she perceived what he meant; she was not aware, until he called her attention to it, that the little Merrimans took up an enormous place in the intellec-

A New England Winter

tual economy of two households. "You ought to remember that they exist for you, and not you for them," Florimond said to her in a tone of friendly admonition; and he remarked on another occasion that the perpetual presence of children was a great injury to conversation, — it kept it down so much; and that in Boston they seemed to be present even when they were absent, inasmuch as most of the talk was about them. Mrs. Daintry did not stop to ask herself what her son knew of Boston, leaving it years before as a boy, and not having so much as looked out of the window since his return; she was taken up mainly with noting certain little habits of speech which he evidently had formed, and in wondering how they would strike his fellow-citizens. He was very definite and trenchant; he evidently knew perfectly what he thought; and though his manner was not defiant, — he had, perhaps, even too many of the forms of politeness, as if sometimes, for mysterious reasons, he were playing upon you, — the tone in which he uttered his opinions did not appear exactly to give you the choice. And then apparently he had a great many; there was a moment when Mrs. Daintry vaguely foresaw that the little house in Newbury Street would be more crowded with Florimond's views than it had ever been with Joanna's children. She hoped very much people would like him, and she hardly could see why they should fail to find him

agreeable. To herself he was sweeter than any grandchild; he was as kind as if he had been a devoted parent. Florimond had but a small acquaintance with his brother-in-law; but after he had been at home forty-eight hours he found that he bore Arthur Merriman a grudge, and was ready to think rather ill of him, — having a theory that he ought to have held up Joanna and interposed to save her mother. Arthur Merriman was a young and brilliant commission-merchant, who had not married Joanna Daintry for the sake of Florimond, and, doing an active business all day in East Boston, had a perfectly good conscience in leaving his children's mother and grandmother to establish their terms of intercourse.

Florimond, however, did not particularly wonder why his brother-in-law had not been round to bid him welcome. It was for Mrs. Daintry that this anxiety was reserved; and what made it worse was her uncertainty as to whether she should be justified in mentioning the subject to Joanna. It might wound Joanna to suggest to her that her husband was derelict, — especially if she did not think so, and she certainly gave her mother no opening; and on the other hand, Florimond might have ground for complaint if Arthur should continue not to notice him. Mrs. Daintry earnestly desired that nothing of this sort should happen, and took refuge in the hope that Florimond would have adopted the foreign theory of visiting, in accordance with which the newcomer was to present himself first. Meanwhile the young man, who had looked upon a meeting with his brother-in-law as a necessity rather than a privilege, was simply conscious of a reprieve; and up in Clarendon Street, as Mrs. Daintry said, it never occurred to Arthur Merriman to take this social step, nor to his wife to propose it to him. Mrs. Merriman simply took for granted that her brother would be round early some morning to see the children. A day or two later the couple dined at her mother's, and that virtually settled the question. It is true that Mrs. Daintry, in later days, occasionally recalled the fact that, after all, Joanna's husband never had called upon Florimond; and she even wondered why Florimond, who sometimes said bitter things, had not made more of it. The matter came back at moments when, under the pressure of circumstances which, it must be confessed, were rare, she found herself giving assent to an axiom that sometimes reached her ears. This axiom, it must be added, did not justify her in the particular case I have mentioned, for the full purport of it was that the queerness of Bostonians was collective, not individual.

There was no doubt, however, that it was Florimond's place to call first upon his aunt, and this was a duty of which she could not hesitate to remind him. By the time he took his way across the long expanse of the new land and

up the charming hill, which constitutes as it were, the speaking face of Boston, the temperature either had relaxed, or he had got used, even in his mother's hot little house, to his native air. He breathed the bright cold sunshine with pleasure; he raised his eyes to the arching blueness, and thought he had never seen a dome so magnificently painted. He turned his head this way and that, as he walked (now that he had recovered his legs, he foresaw that he should walk a good deal), and freely indulged his most valued organ, the organ that had won him such reputation as he already enjoyed. In the little artistic circle in which he moved in Paris, Florimond Daintry was thought to have a great deal of eye. His power of rendering was questioned, his execution had been called pretentious and feeble; but a conviction had somehow been diffused that he saw things with extraordinary intensity. No one could tell better than he what to paint, and what not to paint, even though his interpretation were sometimes rather too sketchy. It will have been guessed that he was an impressionist; and it must be admitted that this was the character in which he proceeded on his visit to Miss Daintry. He was constantly shutting one eye, to see the better with the other, making a little telescope by curving one of his hands together, waving these members in the air with vague pictorial gestures, pointing at things which, when people turned to follow his direction, seemed to mock the vulgar vision by eluding it. I do not mean that he practised these devices as he walked along Beacon Street, into which he had crossed shortly after leaving his mother's house; but now that he had broken the ice, he acted quite in the spirit of the reply he had made to a friend in Paris, shortly before his departure, who asked him why he was going back to America, — "I am going to see how it looks." He was of course very conscious of his eye; and his effort to cultivate it was both intuitive and deliberate. He spoke of it freely, as he might have done of a valuable watch or a horse. He was always trying to get the visual impression; asking himself, with regard to such and such an object or a place, of what its "character" would consist. There is no doubt he really saw with great intensity; and the reader will probably feel that he was welcome to this ambiguous privilege. It was not important for him that things should be beautiful; what he sought to discover was their identity, — the signs by which he should know them. He began this inquiry as soon as he stepped into Newbury Street from his mother's door, and he was destined to continue it for the first few weeks of his stay in Boston. As time went on, his attention relaxed; for one couldn't do more than see, as he said to his mother and another person; and he had seen. Then the novelty wore off, — the novelty which is often so absurdly great in the eyes of the American who returns to his native land after a few years spent in the foreign element, — an effect to be accounted for only on the supposition that in the secret parts of his mind he recognizes the aspect of life in Europe as, through long heredity, the more familiar; so that superficially, having no interest to oppose it, it quickly supplants the domestic type, which, upon his return, becomes supreme, but with its credit in many cases appreciably and permanently diminished. Florimond painted a few things while he was in America, though he had told his mother he had come home to rest; but when, several months later, in Paris, he showed his "notes," as he called them, to a friend, the young Frenchman asked him if Massachusetts were really so much like Andalusia.

There was certainly nothing Andalusian in the prospect as Florimond traversed the artificial bosom of the Back Bay. He had made his way promptly into Beacon Street, and he greatly admired that vista. The long straight avenue lay airing its newness in the frosty day, and all its individual façades, with their neat, sharp ornaments, seemed to have been scoured, with a kind of friction, by the hard, salutary light. Their brilliant browns and drabs, their rosy surfaces of brick, made a variety of fresh, violent tones, such as Florimond liked to memorize, and the large clear windows of their curved fronts faced each other, across the street, like candid, inevitable eyes. There was something almost terrible in the windows; Florimond had forgotten how vast and clean they were, and how, in their sculptured frames, the New England air seemed, like a zealous housewife, to polish and preserve them. A great many ladies were looking out, and groups of children, in the drawing-rooms, were flattening their noses against the transparent plate. Here and there, behind it, the back of a statuette or the symmetry of a painted vase, erect on a pedestal, presented itself to the street, and enabled the passer to construct, more or less, the room within, — its frescoed ceilings, its new silk sofas, its untarnished fixtures. This continuity of glass constituted a kind of exposure, within and without, and gave the street the appearance of an enormous corridor, in which the public and the private were familiar and intermingled. But it was all very cheerful and commodious, and seemed to speak of diffused wealth, of intimate family life, of comfort constantly renewed. All sorts of things in the region of the temperature had happened during the few days that Florimond had been in the country. The cold wave had spent itself, a snowstorm had come and gone, and the air, after this temporary relaxation, had renewed its keenness. The snow, which had fallen in but moderate abundance, was heaped along the side of the pavement; it formed a radiant cornice on the housetops, and crowned the windows with a plain white cap. It deepened the color of everything else, made all surfaces look ruddy, and at a distance sent into the air a thin, delicate mist, — a tinted exhalation, — which occasionally softened an edge. The upper part of Beacon Street seemed to Florimond charming, — the long, wide, sunny slope, the uneven line of the older houses, the contrasted, differing, bulging fronts, the painted bricks, the tidy facings, the immaculate doors, the burnished silver plates, the denuded twigs of the far extent of the Common, on the other side; and to crown the eminence and complete the picture, high in the air, poised in the right place, over everything that clustered below, the most felicitous object in Boston, — the gilded dome of the State House. It was in the shadow of this monument, as we know, that Miss Daintry lived; and Florimond, who was always lucky, had the good fortune to find her at home.

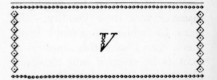

V

IT may seem that I have assumed on the part of the reader too great a curiosity about the impressions of this young man, who was not very remarkable, and who has not even the recommendation of being the hero of our perhaps too descriptive tale. The reader will already have discovered that a hero fails us here; but if I go on at all risks to say a few words about Florimond, he will perhaps understand the better why this part has not been filled. Miss Daintry's nephew was not very original; it was his own illusion that he had in a considerable degree the value of rareness. Even this youthful conceit was not rare, for it was not of heroic proportions, and was liable to lapses and discouragements. He was a fair, slim, civil young man, and you would never have guessed from his appearance that he was an impressionist. He was neat and sleek and quite anti-Bohemian, and in spite of his looking about him as he walked, his figure was much more in harmony with the Boston landscape than he supposed. He was a little vain, a little affected, a little pretentious, a little good-looking, a little amusing, a little spoiled, and at times a little tiresome. If he was disagreeable, however, it was also only a little; he did not carry anything to a very high pitch; he was accomplished, industrious, successful, — all in the minor degree. He was fond of his mother and fond of himself; he also liked the people who liked him. Such people could belong only to the class of good listeners, for Florimond, with the least encouragement (he was very susceptible to that), would chatter by the hour. As he was very observant, and knew a great many stories, his talk was often entertaining, especially to women, many of whom thought him wonderfully sympathetic. It may be added that he was still very young and fluid, and neither his defects nor his virtues had a great consistency. He was fond of the society of women, and had an idea that he knew a great deal about that element of humanity. He believed himself to know everything about art, and almost everything about life, and he expressed himself as much as possible in the phrases that are current in studios. He spoke French very well, and it had rubbed off on his English.

His aunt listened to him attentively, with her nippers on her nose. She had been a little restless at first, and, to relieve herself, had vaguely punched the sofa-cushion which lay beside her, — a gesture that her friends always recognized; they knew it to express a particular emotion. Florimond, whose egotism was candid and confiding, talked for an hour about himself, — about what he had done, and what he intended to do, what he had said and what had been said to him; about his habits, tastes, achievements, peculiarities, which were apparently so numerous; about the decorations of his studio in Paris; about the character of the French, the works of Zola, the theory of art for art, the American type, the "stupidity" of his mother's new house, — though of course it had some things that were knowing, — the pronunciation of Joanna's children, the effect of the commission business on Arthur Merriman's conversation, the effect of everything on his mother, Mrs. Daintry, and the effect of Mrs. Daintry on her son Florimond. The young man had an epithet, which he constantly introduced, to express disapproval; when he spoke of the architecture of his mother's house, over which she had taken great pains (she remembered the gabled fronts of Nuremberg), he said that a certain effect had been dreadfully missed, that the character of the doorway was simply "crass." He expressed, however, a lively sense of the bright cleanness of American interiors. "Oh, as for that," he said, "the place is kept, — it's kept;" and, to give an image of this idea, he put his gathered fingers to his lips an instant, seemed to kiss them or blow upon them, and then opened them into the air. Miss Daintry had never encountered this gesture before; she had heard it described by travelled persons; but to see her own nephew in the very act of it led her to administer another thump to the sofa-cushion. She finally got this article under control, and sat more quiet, with her hands clasped upon it, while her visitor continued to discourse. In pursuance of his character as an impressionist, he gave her a great many impressions; but it seemed to her that as he talked, he simply exposed himself, — exposed his egotism, his little pretensions. Lucretia Daintry, as we know, had a love of justice, and though her opinions were apt to be very positive, her charity was great and her judgments were not harsh; more-

over, there was in her composition not a drop of acrimony. Nevertheless, she was, as the phrase is, rather hard on poor little Florimond; and to explain her severity we are bound to assume that in the past he had in some way offended her. To-day, at any rate, it seemed to her that he patronized his maiden aunt. He scarcely asked about her health, but took for granted on her part an unlimited interest in his own sensations. It came over her afresh that his mother had been absurd in thinking that the usual resources of Boston would not have sufficed to maintain him; and she smiled a little grimly at the idea that a special provision should have been made. This idea presently melted into another, over which she was free to regale herself only after her nephew had departed. For the moment she contented herself with saying to him, when a pause in his young eloquence gave her a chance, — "You will have a great many people to go and see. You pay the penalty of being a Bostonian; you have several hundred cousins. One pays for everything."

Florimond lifted his eyebrows. "I pay for that every day of my life. Have I got to go and see them all?"

"All — every one," said his aunt, who in reality did not hold this obligation in the least sacred.

"And to say something agreeable to them all?" the young man went on.

"Oh, no, that is not necessary," Miss Daintry rejoined, with more exactness. "There are one or two, however, who always appreciate a pretty speech." She added in an instant, "Do you remember Mrs. Mesh?"

"Mrs. Mesh?" Florimond apparently did not remember.

"The wife of Donald Mesh; your grandfathers were first cousins. I don't mean her grandfather, but her husband's. If you don't remember her, I suppose he married her after you went away."

"I remember Donald; but I never knew he was a relation. He was single then, I think."

"Well, he's double now," said Miss Daintry; "he's triple, I may say, for there are two ladies in the house."

"If you mean he's a polygamist — are there Mormons even here?" Florimond, leaning back in his chair, with his elbow on the arm, and twisting with his gloved fingers the point of a small fair mustache, did not appear to have been arrested by this account of Mr. Mesh's household; for he almost immediately asked, in a large, detached way, — "Are there any nice women here?"

"It depends on what you mean by nice women; there are some very sharp ones."

"Oh, I don't like sharp ones," Florimond remarked, in a tone which made his aunt long to throw her sofa-cusion at his head. "Are there any pretty ones?"

She looked at him a moment, hesitating. "Rachel Torrance is pretty, in a strange, unusual way, — black hair and blue eyes, a ser-

pentine figure, old coins in her tresses; that sort of thing."

"I have seen a good deal of that sort of thing," said Florimond, a little confusedly.

"That I know nothing about. I mention Pauline Mesh's as one of the houses that you ought to go to, and where I know you are expected."

"I remember now that my mother has said something about that. But who is the woman with coins in her hair? — what has she to do with Pauline Mesh?"

"Rachel is staying with her; she came from New York a week ago, and I believe she means to spend the winter. She isn't a woman, she's a girl."

"My mother didn't speak of her," said Florimond; "but I don't think she would recommend me a girl with a serpentine figure."

"Very likely not," Miss Daintry answered, dryly. "Rachel Torrance is a far-away cousin of Donald Mesh, and consequently of mine and of yours. She's an artist, like yourself; she paints flowers on little panels and *plaques*."

"Like myself? — I never painted a *plaque* in my life!" exclaimed Florimond, staring.

"Well, she's a model also; you can paint her if you like; she has often been painted, I believe."

Florimond had begun to caress the other tip of his mustache. "I don't care for women who have been painted before. I like to find them out. Besides, I want to rest this winter."

His aunt was disappointed; she

wished to put him into relation with Rachel Torrance, and his indifference was an obstacle. The meeting was sure to take place sooner or later, but she would have him glad to precipitate it, and, above all, to quicken her nephew's susceptibilities. "Take care you are not found out yourself!" she exclaimed, tossing away her sofa-cushion and getting up.

Florimond did not see what she meant, and he accordingly bore her no rancor; but when, before he took his leave, he said to her, rather irrelevantly, that if he should find himself in the mood during his stay in Boston, he should like to do her portrait, — she had such a delightful face, — she almost thought the speech a deliberate impertinence. "Do you mean that you have discovered me, — that no one has suspected it before?" she inquired with a laugh, and a little flush in the countenance that he was so good as to appreciate.

Florimond replied, with perfect coolness and good-nature, that he didn't know about this, but that he was sure no one had seen her in just the way he saw her; and he waved his hand in the air with strange circular motions, as if to evoke before him the image of a canvas, with a figure just rubbed in. He repeated this gesture, or something very like it, by way of farewell, when he quitted his aunt, and she thought him insufferably patronizing.

This is why she wished him, without loss of time, to make the acquaintance of Rachel Torrance, whose treatment of his pretensions she thought would be salutary. It may now be communicated to the reader — after a delay proportionate to the momentousness of the fact — that this had been the idea which suddenly flowered in her brain as she sat face to face with her irritating young visitor. It had vaguely shaped itself after her meeting with that strange girl from Brooklyn, whom Mrs. Mesh, all gratitude, — for she liked strangeness, — promptly brought to see her; and her present impression of her nephew rapidly completed it. She had not expected to take an interest in Rachel Torrance, and could not see why, through a freak of Susan's, she should have been called upon to think so much about her; but, to her surprise, she perceived that Mrs. Daintry's proposed victim was not the usual forward girl. She perceived at the same time that it had been ridiculous to think of Rachel as a victim, — to suppose that she was in danger of vainly fixing her affections upon Florimond. She was much more likely to triumph than to suffer; and if her visit to Boston were to produce bitter fruits, it would not be she who should taste them. She had a striking, oriental head, a beautiful smile, a manner of dressing which carried out her exotic type, and a great deal of experience and wit. She evidently knew the world, as one knows it when one has to live by its help. If she had an aim in life, she would draw her bow well

above the tender breast of Florimond Daintry. With all this, she
certainly was an honest, obliging
girl, and had a sense of humor
which was a fortunate obstacle to
her falling into a *pose*. Her coins
and amulets and seamless garments were, for her, a part of the
general joke of one's looking like
a Circassian or a Smyrniote, — an
accident for which Nature was responsible; and it may be said of
her that she took herself much
less seriously than other people
took her. This was a defect for
which Lucretia Daintry had a
great kindness; especially as she
quickly saw that Rachel was not
of an insipid paste, as even triumphant coquettes sometimes are.
In spite of her poverty and the
opportunities her beauty must
have brought her, she had not yet
seen fit to marry, — which was a
proof that she was clever as well
as disinterested. It looks dreadfully cold-blooded as I write it
here, but the notion that this capable creature might administer
poetic justice to Florimond gave
a measurable satisfaction to Miss
Daintry. He was in distinct need
of a snub, for down in Newbury
Street his mother was perpetually
swinging the censer; and no young
nature could stand that sort of
thing, — least of all such a nature
as Florimond's. She said to herself that such a "putting in his
place" as he might receive from
Rachel Torrance would probably
be a permanent correction. She
wished his good, as she wished
the good of every one; and that

desire was at the bottom of her
vision. She knew perfectly what
she should like: she should like
him to fall in love with Rachel, as
he probably would, and to have
no doubt of her feeling immensely
honored. She should like Rachel
to encourage him just enough —
just so far as she might, without
being false. A little would do, for
Florimond would always take his
success for granted. To this point
did the study of her nephew's
moral regeneration bring the excellent woman, who a few days
before had accused his mother of
a lack of morality. His mother was
thinking only of his pleasure; *she*
was thinking of his immortal spirit.
She should like Rachel to tell him
at the end that he was a presumptuous little boy, and that since it
was his business to render "impressions," he might see what he
could do with that of having been
jilted. This extraordinary flight of
fancy on Miss Daintry's part was
caused in some degree by the
high spirits which sprang from her
conviction, after she met the young
lady, that Mrs. Mesh's companion
was not in danger; for even when
she wrote to her sister-in-law in
the manner the reader knows, her
conscience was not wholly at rest.
There was still a risk, and she
knew not why she should take
risks for Florimond. Now, however, she was prepared to be perfectly happy when she should hear
that the young man was constantly
in Arlington Street; and at the end
of a little month she enjoyed this
felicity.

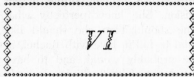

Mrs. Mesh sat on one side of the fire, and Florimond on the other; he had by this time acquired the privilege of a customary seat. He had taken a general view of Boston. It was like a first introduction, for before his going to live in Paris he had been too young to judge; and the result of this survey was the conviction that there was nothing better than Mrs. Mesh's drawing-room. She was one of the few persons whom one was certain to find at home after five o'clock; and the place itself was agreeable to Florimond, who was very fastidious about furniture and decorations. He was willing to concede that Mrs. Mesh (the relationship had not yet seemed close enough to justify him in calling her Pauline) knew a great deal about such matters; though it was clear that she was indebted for some of her illumination to Rachel Torrance, who had induced her to make several changes. These two ladies, between them, represented a great fund of taste; with a difference that was a result of Rachel's knowing clearly beforehand what she liked (Florimond called her, at least, by her baptismal name), and Mrs. Mesh's only knowing it after a succession of experiments, of transposings and drapings, all more or less ingenious and expen-

sive. If Florimond liked Mrs. Mesh's drawing-room better than any other corner of Boston, he also had his preference in regard to its phases and hours. It was most charming in the winter twilight, by the glow of the fire, before the lamps had been brought in. The ruddy flicker played over many objects, making them look more mysterious than Florimond had supposed anything could look in Boston, and, among others, upon Rachel Torrance, who, when she moved about the room in a desultory way (never so much *enfoncée*, as Florimond said, in a chair as Mrs. Mesh was) certainly attracted and detained the eye. The young man, from his corner (he was almost as much *enfoncé* as Mrs. Mesh), used to watch her; and he could easily see what his aunt had meant by saying she had a serpentine figure. She was slim and flexible, she took attitudes which would have been awkward in other women, but which her charming pliancy made natural. She reminded him of a celebrated actress in Paris, who was the ideal of tortuous thinness. Miss Torrance used often to seat herself for a short time at the piano; and though she never had been taught this art (she played only by ear), her musical feeling was such that she charmed the twilight hour. Mrs. Mesh sat on one side of the fire, as I have said, and Florimond on the other; the two might have been found in this relation, — listening, face to face, — almost any day in the week. Mrs. Mesh raved

362

about her new friend, as they said in Boston, — I mean about Rachel Torrance, not about Florimond Daintry. She had at last got hold of a mind that understood her own (Mrs. Mesh's mind contained depths of mystery), and she sacrificed herself, generally, to throw her companion into relief. Her sacrifice was rewarded, for the girl was universally liked and admired; she was a new type altogether; she was the lioness of the winter. Florimond had an opportunity to see his native town in one of its fits of enthusiasm. He had heard of the infatuations of Boston, literary and social; of its capacity for giving itself with intensity to a temporary topic; and he was now conscious, on all sides, of the breath of New England discussion. Some one had said to him, — or had said to some one, who repeated it, — that there was no place like Boston for taking up with such seriousness a second-rate spinster from Brooklyn. But Florimond himself made no criticism; for, as we know, he speedily fell under the charm of Rachel Torrance's personality. He was perpetually talking with Mrs. Mesh about it; and when Mrs. Mesh herself descanted on the subject, he listened with the utmost attention. At first, on his return, he rather feared the want of topics; he foresaw that he should miss the talk of the studios, of the theatres, of the boulevard, of a little circle of "naturalists" (in literature and art) to which he belonged, without sharing all its views. But he

presently perceived that Boston, too, had its actualities, and that it even had this in common with Paris, — that it gave its attention most willingly to a female celebrity. If he had had any hope of being himself the lion of the winter, it had been dissipated by the spectacle of his cousin's success. He saw that while she was there, he could only be a subject of secondary reference. He bore her no grudge for this. I must hasten to declare that from the pettiness of this particular jealousy poor Florimond was quite exempt. Moreover, he was swept along by the general chorus; and he perceived that when one changes one's sky, one inevitably changes, more or less, one's standard. Rachel Torrance was neither an actress, nor a singer, nor a beauty, nor one of the ladies who were chronicled in the "Figaro," nor the author of a successful book, nor a person of the great world; she had neither a future, nor a past, nor a position, nor even a husband, to make her identity more solid; she was a simple American girl, of the class that lived in *pensions* (a class of which Florimond had ever entertained a theoretic horror); and yet she had profited to the degree of which our young man was witness, by those treasures of sympathy constantly in reserve in the American public (as has already been intimated) for the youthful-feminine. If Florimond was struck with all this, it may be imagined whether or no his mother thought she had been clever when it occurred to her (before any one else) that Rachel would be a resource for the term of hibernation. She had forgotten all her scruples and hesitations; she only knew she had seen very far. She was proud of her prescience, she was even amused with it; and for the moment she held her head rather high. No one knew of it but Lucretia, — for she had never confided it to Joanna, of whom she would have been more afraid in such a connection even than of her sister-in-law; but Mr. and Mrs. Merriman perceived an unusual lightness in her step, a fitful sparkle in her eye. It was of course easy for them to make up their mind that she was exhilarated to this degree by the presence of her son; especially as he seemed to be getting on beautifully in Boston.

"She stays out longer every day; she is scarcely ever home to tea," Mrs. Mesh remarked, looking up at the clock on the chimney-piece.

Florimond could not fail to know to whom she alluded, for it has been intimated that between these two there was much conversation about Rachel Torrance. "It's funny, the way the girls run about alone here," he said, in the amused, contemplative tone in which he frequently expressed himself on the subject of American life. "Rachel stays out after dark, and no one thinks any the worse of her."

"Oh, well, she's old enough," Mrs. Mesh rejoined, with a little sigh, which seemed to suggest that Rachel's age was really affecting.

Her eyes had been opened by Florimond to many of the peculiarities of the society that surrounded her; and though she had spent only as many months in Europe as her visitor had spent years, she now sometimes spoke as if she thought the manners of Boston more odd even than he could pretend to do. She was very quick at picking up an idea, and there was nothing she desired more than to have the last on every subject. This winter, from her two new friends, Florimond and Rachel, she had extracted a great many that were new to her; the only trouble was that, coming from different sources, they sometimes contradicted each other. Many of them, however, were very vivifying; they added a new zest to that prospect of life which had always, in winter, the denuded bushes, the solid pond, and the plank-covered walks, the exaggerated bridge, the patriotic statues, the dry, hard texture of the Public Garden for its foreground, and for its middle distance, the pale, frozen twigs, stiff in the windy sky, that whistled over the Common, the domestic dome of the State House, familiar in the untinted air, and the competitive spires of a liberal faith. Mrs. Mesh had an active imagination, and plenty of time on her hands. Her two children were young, and they slept a good deal; she had explained to Florimond, who observed that she was a great deal less in the nursery than his sister, that she pretended only to give her attention to their waking hours. "I have people for the rest of the time," she said; and the rest of the time was considerable; so that there were very few obstacles to her cultivation of ideas. There was one in her mind now, and I may as well impart it to the reader without delay. She was not quite so delighted with Rachel Torrance as she had been a month ago; it seemed to her that the young lady took up — socially speaking — too much room in the house; and she wondered how long she intended to remain, and whether it would be possible, without a direct request, to induce her to take her way back to Brooklyn. This last was the conception with which she was at present engaged; she was at moments much pressed by it, and she had thoughts of taking Florimond Daintry into her confidence. This, however, she determined not to do, lest he should regard it as a sign that she was jealous of her companion. I know not whether she was, but this I know, — that Mrs. Mesh was a woman of a high ideal, and would not for the world have appeared so. If she was jealous, this would imply that she thought Florimond was in love with Rachel; and she could only object to that on the ground of being in love with him herself. She was not in love with him, and had no intention of being; of this the reader, possibly alarmed, may definitely rest assured. Moreover, she did not think him in love with Rachel; as to her reason for this reserve, I need not,

perhaps, be absolutely outspoken. She was not jealous, she would have said; she was only oppressed — she was a little over-ridden. Rachel pervaded her house, pervaded her life, pervaded Boston; every one thought it necessary to talk to her about Rachel, to rave about her in the Boston manner, which seemed to Mrs. Mesh, in spite of the Puritan tradition, very much more unbridled than that of Baltimore. They thought it would give her pleasure; but by this time she knew everything about Rachel. The girl had proved rather more of a figure than she expected; and though she could not be called pretentious, she had the air, in staying with Pauline Mesh, of conferring rather more of a favor than she received. This was absurd for a person who was, after all, though not in her first youth, only a girl, and who, as Mrs. Mesh was sure, from her biography, — for Rachel had related every item, — had never before had such unrestricted access to the fleshpots. The fleshpots were full, under Donald Mesh's roof, and his wife could easily believe that the poor girl would not be in a hurry to return to her boarding-house in Brooklyn. For that matter there were lots of people in Boston who would be delighted that she should come to them. It was doubtless an inconsistency on Mrs. Mesh's part that if she was overdone with the praises of Rachel Torrance which fell from every lip, she should not herself have forborne to broach the topic. But I have sufficiently intimated that it had a perverse fascination for her; it is true she did not speak of Rachel only to praise her. Florimond, in truth, was a little weary of the young lady's name; he had plenty of topics of his own, and he had his own opinion about Rachel Torrance. He did not take up Mrs. Mesh's remark as to her being old enough.

"You must wait till she comes in. Please ring for tea," said Mrs. Mesh, after a pause. She had noticed that Florimond was comparing his watch with her clock; it occurred to her that he might be going.

"Oh, I always wait, you know; I like to see her when she has been anywhere. She tells one all about it, and describes everything so well."

Mrs. Mesh looked at him a moment. "She sees a great deal more in things than I am usually able to discover. She sees the most extraordinary things in Boston."

"Well, so do I," said Florimond, placidly.

"Well, I don't, I must say!" She asked him to ring again; and then, with a slight irritation, accused him of not ringing hard enough; but before he could repeat the operation, she left her chair and went herself to the bell. After this she stood before the fire a moment, gazing into it; then suggested to Florimond that he should put on a log.

"Is it necessary, — when your servant is coming in a moment?" the young man asked, unexpect-edly, without moving. In an instant, however, he rose; and then he explained that this was only his little joke.

"Servants are too stupid," said Mrs. Mesh. "But I spoil you. What would your mother say?" She watched him while he placed the log. She was plump, and she was not tall; but she was a very pretty woman. She had round brown eyes, which looked as if she had been crying a little, — she had nothing in life to cry about; and dark, wavy hair, which, here and there, in short, crisp tendrils, escaped artfully from the form in which it was dressed. When she smiled, she showed very pretty teeth; and the combination of her touching eyes and her parted lips was at such moments almost bewitching. She was accustomed to express herself in humorous superlatives, in pictorial circumlocutions; and had acquired in Boston the rudiments of a social dialect which, to be heard in perfection, should be heard on the lips of a native. Mrs. Mesh had picked it up; but it must be confessed that she used it without originality. It was an accident that on this occasion she had not expressed her wish for her tea by saying that she should like a pint or two of that Chinese fluid.

"My mother believes I can't be spoiled," said Florimond, giving a little push with his toe to the stick that he had placed in the embers; after which he sank back into his chair, while Mrs. Mesh resumed possession of her own. "I am ever fresh, — ever pure."

"You are ever conceited. I don't see what you find so extraordinary in Boston," Mrs. Mesh added, reverting to his remark of a moment before.

"Oh, everything! the ways of the people, their ideas, their peculiar *cachet*. The very expression of their faces amuses me."

"Most of them have no expression at all."

"Oh, you are used to it," Florimond said. "You have become one of themselves; you have ceased to notice."

"I am more of a stranger than you; I was born beneath other skies. Is it possible that you don't know yet that I am a native of Baltimore? 'Maryland, my Maryland!'"

"Have they got so much expression in Maryland? No, I thank you; no tea. Is it possible!" Florimond went on, with the familiarity of pretended irritation, — "is it possible that you haven't noticed yet that I never take it? *Boisson fade, écœurante,* as Balzac calls it."

"Ah, well, if you don't take it on account of Balzac!" said Mrs. Mesh. "I never saw a man who had such fantastic reasons. Where, by the way, is the volume of that depraved old author which you promised to bring me?"

"When do you think he flourished? You call everything old, in this country, that isn't in the morning paper. I haven't brought you the volume, because I don't want to bring you presents," Florimond said; "I want you to love me for myself, as they say in Paris."

"Don't quote what they say in Paris! Don't sully this innocent bower with those fearful words!" Mrs. Mesh rejoined, with a jocose intention. "Dear lady, your son is not everything we could wish!" she added in the same mock dramatic tone, as the curtain of the door was lifted, and Mrs. Daintry rather timidly advanced. Mrs. Daintry had come to satisfy a curiosity, after all quite legitimate; she could no longer resist the impulse to ascertain for herself, so far as she might, how Rachel Torrance and Florimond were getting on. She had had no definite expectation of finding Florimond at Mrs. Mesh's; but she supposed that at this hour of the afternoon, — it was already dark, and the ice, in many parts of Beacon Street, had a polish which gleamed through the dusk, — she should find Rachel. "Your son has lived too long in far-off lands; he has dwelt among outworn things," Mrs. Mesh went on, as she conducted her visitor to a chair. "Dear lady, you are not as Balzac was; do you start at the mention of his name? — therefore you will have some tea in a little painted cup."

Mrs. Daintry was not bewildered, though it may occur to the reader that she might have been; she was only a little disappointed. She had hoped she might have occasion to talk about Florimond;

but the young man's presence was a denial of this privilege. "I am afraid Rachel is not at home," she remarked. "I am afraid she will think I have not been very attentive."

"She will be in in a moment; we are waiting for her," Florimond said. "It's impossible she should think any harm of you. I have told her too much good."

"Ah, Mrs. Daintry, don't build too much on what he has told her! He's a false and faithless man!" Pauline Mesh interposed; while the good lady from Newbury Street, smiling at this adjuration, but looking a little grave, turned from one of her companions to the other. Florimond had relapsed into his chair by the fireplace; he sat contemplating the embers, and fingering the tip of his mustache. Mrs. Daintry imbibed her tea, and told how often she had slipped coming down the hill. These expedients helped her to wear a quiet face; but in reality she was nervous, and she felt rather foolish. It came over her that she was rather dishonest; she had presented herself at Mrs. Mesh's in the capacity of a spy. The reader already knows she was subject to sudden revulsions of feeling. There is an adage about repenting at leisure; but Mrs. Daintry always repented in a hurry. There was something in the air — something impalpable, magnetic — that told her she had better not have come; and even while she conversed with Mrs. Mesh she wondered what this mystic element could be. Of course she had been greatly preoccupied, these last weeks; for it had seemed to her that her plan with regard to Rachel Torrance was succeeding only too well. Florimond had frankly accepted her in the spirit in which she had been offered, and it was very plain that she was helping him to pass his winter. He was constantly at the house, — Mrs. Daintry could not tell exactly how often; but she knew very well that in Boston, if one saw anything of a person, one saw a good deal. At first he used to speak of it; for two or three weeks, he had talked a good deal about Rachel Torrance. More lately, his allusions had become few; yet to the best of Mrs. Daintry's belief his step was often in Arlington Street. This aroused her suspicions, and at times it troubled her conscience; there were moments when she wondered whether, in arranging a genial winter for Florimond, she had also prepared a season of torment for herself. Was he in love with the girl, or had he already discovered that the girl was in love with him? The delicacy of either situation would account for his silence. Mrs. Daintry said to herself that it would be a grim joke if she should prove to have plotted only too well. It was her sister-in-law's warning in especial that haunted her imagination, and she scarcely knew, at times, whether more to hope that Florimond might have been smitten, or to pray that Rachel might remain indifferent. It was impossible for Mrs. Daintry to shake off the sense of responsibility; she could not shut her eyes to the fact that she had been the prime mover. It was all very well to say that the situation, as it stood, was of Lucretia's making; the thing never would have come into Lucretia's head if she had not laid it before her. Unfortunately, with the quiet life she led, she had very little chance to observe; she went out so little, that she was reduced to guessing what the manner of the two young persons might be to each other when they met in society, and she should have thought herself wanting in delicacy if she had sought to be intimate with Rachel Torrance. Now that her plan was in operation, she could make no attempt to foster it, to acknowledge it in the face of Heaven. Fortunately, Rachel had so many attentions, that there was no fear of her missing those of Newbury Street. She had dined there once, in the first days of her sojourn, without Pauline and Donald, who had declined, and with Joanna and Joanna's husband for all "company." Mrs. Daintry had noticed nothing particular then, save that Arthur Merriman talked rather more than usual, — though he was always a free talker, — and had bantered Rachel rather more familiarly than was perhaps necessary (considering that he, after all, was not her cousin) on her ignorance of Boston, and her thinking that Pauline Mesh could tell her anything about it. On this occasion Florimond talked very little; of course he could not say much when Arthur was in such extraordinary spirits. She knew by this time all that Florimond thought of his brother-in-law, and she herself had to confess that she liked Arthur better in his jaded hours, even though then he was a little cynical. Mrs. Daintry had been perhaps a little disappointed in Rachel, whom she saw for the first time in several years. The girl was less peculiar than she remembered her being, savored less of the old studio, the musical parties, the creditors waiting at the door. However, people in Boston found her unusual, and Mrs. Daintry reflected, with a twinge at her depravity, that perhaps she had expected something too dishevelled. At any rate, several weeks had elapsed since then, and there had been plenty of time for Miss Torrance to attach herself to Florimond. It was less than ever Mrs. Daintry's wish that he should (even in this case) ask her to be his wife. It seemed to her less than ever the way her son should marry, — because he had got entangled with a girl in consequence of his mother's rashness. It occurred to her, of course, that she might warn the young man; but when it came to the point she could not bring herself to speak. She had never discussed the question of love with him, and she didn't know what ideas he might have brought with him from Paris. It was too delicate; it might put notions into his head. He might say something strange and French, which she shouldn't like; and then perhaps she should feel bound to warn Rachel herself, — a complication from which she absolutely shrank. It was part of her embarrassment now, as she sat in Mrs. Mesh's drawing-room, that she should probably spoil Florimond's entertainment for this afternoon, and that such a crossing of his inclination would make him the more dangerous. He had told her that he was waiting for Rachel to come in; and at the same time, in view of the lateness of the hour and her being on foot, when she herself should take her leave he would be bound in decency to accompany her. As for remaining after Rachel should come in, that was an indiscretion which scarcely seemed to her possible. Mrs. Daintry was an American mother, and she knew what the elder generation owes to the younger. If Florimond had come there to call on a young lady, he didn't, as they used to say, want any mothers round. She glanced covertly at her son, to try and find some comfort in his countenance; for her perplexity was heavy. But she was struck only with his looking very handsome, as he lounged there in the firelight, and with his being very much at home. This did not lighten her burden, and she expressed all the weight of it — in the midst of Mrs. Mesh's flights of comparison — in an irrelevant little sigh. At such a time her only comfort could be the thought that at all events she had not betrayed herself to Lucretia. She had

scarcely exchanged a word with Lucretia about Rachel since that young lady's arrival; and she had observed in silence that Miss Daintry now had a guest in the person of a young woman who had lately opened a kindergarten. This reticence might surely pass for natural.

Rachel came in before long, but even then Mrs. Daintry ventured to stay a little. The visitor from Brooklyn embraced Mrs. Mesh, who told her that, prodigal as she was, there was no fatted calf for her return; she must content herself with cold tea. Nothing could be more charming than her manner, which was full of native archness; and it seemed to Mrs. Daintry that she directed her pleasantries at Florimond with a grace that was intended to be irresistible. The relation between them· was a relation of "chaff," and consisted, on one side and the other, in alternations of attack and defence. Mrs. Daintry reflected that she should not wish her son to have a wife who should be perpetually turning him into a joke; for it seemed to her, perhaps, that Rachel Torrance put in her thrusts rather faster than Florimond could parry them. She was evidently rather wanting in the faculty of reverence, and Florimond panted a little. They presently went into an adjoining room, where the lamplight was brighter; Rachel wished to show the young man an old painted fan, which she had brought back from the repairer's. They remained there ten minutes.

Mrs. Daintry, as she sat with Mrs. Mesh, heard their voices much intermingled. She wished very much to confide herself a little to Pauline, — to ask her whether she thought Rachel was in love with Florimond. But she had a foreboding that this would not be safe; Pauline was capable of repeating her question to the others, of calling out to Rachel to come back and answer it. She contented herself, therefore, with asking her hostess about the little Meshes, and regaling her with anecdotes of Joanna's progeny.

"Don't you ever have your little ones with you at this hour?" she inquired. "You know this is what Longfellow calls the children's hour."

Mrs. Mesh hesitated a moment. "Well, you know, one can't have everything at once. I have my social duties now; I have my guests. I have Miss Torrance, — you see she is not a person one can overlook."

"I suppose not," said poor Mrs. Daintry, remembering how little she herself had overlooked her.

"Have you done brandishing that superannuated relic?" Mrs. Mesh asked of Rachel and Florimond, as they returned to the fireside. "I should as soon think of fanning myself with the fireshovel!"

"He has broken my heart," Rachel said. "He tells me it is not a Watteau."

"Do you believe everything he tells you, my dear? His word is the word of the betrayer."

"Well, I know Watteau didn't paint fans," Florimond remarked, "any more than Michael Angelo."

"I suppose you think he painted ceilings," said Rachel Torrance. "I have painted a great many myself."

"A great many ceilings? I should like to see that!" Florimond exclaimed.

Rachel Torrance, with her usual promptness, adopted this fantasy. "Yes, I have decorated half the churches in Brooklyn; you know how many there are."

"If you mean fans, I wish men carried them," the young man went on; "I should like to have one *de votre façon.*"

"You're cool enough as you are; I should be sorry to give you anything that would make you cooler!"

This retort, which may not strike the reader by its originality, was pregnant enough for Mrs. Daintry; it seemed to her to denote that the situation was critical; and she proposed to retire. Florimond walked home with her; but it was only as they reached their door that she ventured to say to him what had been on her tongue's end since they left Arlington Street.

"Florimond, I want to ask you something. I think it is important, and you mustn't be surprised. Are you in love with Rachel Torrance?"

Florimond stared, in the light of the street-lamp. The collar of his overcoat was turned up; he stamped a little as he stood still; the breath of the February evening pervaded the empty vistas of

the "new land." "In love with Rachel Torrance? *Jamais de la vie!*
What put that into your head?"

"Seeing you with her, that way,
this evening. You know you are
very attentive."

"How do you mean, attentive?"

"You go there very often. Isn't
it almost every day?"

Florimond hesitated, and, in
spite of the frigid dusk, his mother
could see that there was irritation
in his eye. "Where else can I go,
in this precious place? It's the
pleasantest house here."

"Yes, I suppose it's very pleasant," Mrs. Daintry murmured.
"But I would rather have you return to Paris than go there too
often," she added, with sudden
energy.

"How do you mean, too often?
*Qu'est-ce qui vous prend, ma
mère?*" said Florimond.

"Is Rachel — Rachel in love
with *you?*" she inquired solemnly.
She felt that this question, though
her heart beat as she uttered it,
should not be mitigated by a circumlocution.

"Good heavens! mother, fancy
talking about love in this temperature!" Florimond exclaimed. "Let
one at least get into the house."

Mrs. Daintry followed him re-
luctantly; for she always had a
feeling that if anything disagreeable were to be done, one should
not make it less drastic by selecting agreeable conditions. In the
drawing-room, before the fire, she
returned to her inquiry. "My son,
you have not answered me about
Rachel."

"Is she in love with me? Why,
very possibly!"

"Are you serious, Florimond?"

"Why shouldn't I be? I have
seen the way women go off."

Mrs. Daintry was silent a moment. "Florimond, is it true?" she
said, presently.

"Is what true? I don't see where
you want to come out?"

"Is it true that that girl has
fixed her affections — " and Mrs.
Daintry's voice dropped.

"Upon me, *ma mère?* I don't
say it's true, but I say it's possible.
You ask me, and I can only answer
you. I am not swaggering, I am
simply giving you decent satisfaction. You wouldn't have me think
it impossible that a woman should
fall in love with me? You know
what women are, and how there
is nothing, in that way, too queer
for them to do."

Mrs. Daintry, in spite of the
knowledge of her sex that she
might be supposed to possess, was
not prepared to rank herself on
the side of this axiom. "I wished
to warn you," she simply said; "do
be very careful."

"Yes, I'll be careful; but I can't
give up the house."

"There are other houses, Florimond."

"Yes, but there is a special
charm there."

"I would rather you should return to Paris than do any harm."

"Oh, I sha'n't do any harm;
don't worry, *ma mère,*" said Florimond.

It was a relief to Mrs. Daintry
to have spoken, and she endeav-

ored not to worry. It was doubtless this effort that, for the rest of the winter, gave her a somewhat rigid, anxious look. People who met her in Beacon Street missed something from her face. It was her usual confidence in the clearness of human duty; and some of her friends explained the change by saying that she was disappointed about Florimond, — she was afraid he was not particularly liked.

VII

By the first of March this young man had received a good many optical impressions, and had noted in water-colors several characteristic winter effects. He had perambulated Boston in every direction, he had even extended his researches to the suburbs; and if his eye had been curious, his eye was now almost satisfied. He perceived that even amid the simple civilization of New England there was material for the naturalist; and in Washington Street of a winter's afternoon, it came home to him that it was a fortunate thing the impressionist was not exclusively preoccupied with the beautiful. He became familiar with the slushy streets, crowded with thronging pedestrians and obstructed horse-cars, bordered with strange, promiscuous shops, which seemed at once violent and indifferent, overhung with

snowbanks from the housetops; the avalanche that detached itself at intervals, fell with an enormous thud amid the dense processions of women, made for a moment a clear space, splashed with whiter snow, on the pavement, and contributed to the gayety of the Puritan capital. Supreme in the thoroughfare was the rigid groove of the railway, where oblong receptacles, of fabulous capacity, governed by familiar citizens, jolted and jingled eternally, close on each other's rear, absorbing and emitting innumerable specimens of a single type. The road on either side, buried in mounds of pulverized, mud-colored ice, was ploughed across by laboring vehicles, and traversed periodically by the sisterhood of "shoppers," laden with satchels and parcels, and protected by a round-backed policeman. Florimond looked at the shops, saw the women disgorged, surging, ebbing, dodged the avalanches, squeezed in and out of the horse-cars, made himself, on their little platforms, where flatness was enforced, as perpendicular as possible. The horses steamed in the sunny air, the conductor punched the tickets and poked the passengers, some of whom were under and some above, and all alike stabled in trampled straw. They were precipitated, collectively, by stoppages and starts; the tight, silent interior stuffed itself more and more, and the whole machine heaved and reeled in its interrupted course. Florimond had forgotten the look of many things, the details of American publicity; in some cases, indeed, he only pretended to himself that he had forgotten them, because it helped to entertain him. The houses — a bristling, jagged line of talls and shorts, a particolored surface, expressively commercial — were spotted with staring signs, with labels and pictures, with advertisements familiar, colloquial, vulgar; the air was traversed with the tangle of the telegraph, with festoons of bunting, with banners not of war, with inexplicable loops and ropes; the shops, many of them enormous, had heterogeneous fronts, with queer juxtapositions in the articles that peopled them, and incompleteness of array, the stamp of the latest modern ugliness. They had pendent stuffs in the doorways, and flapping tickets outside. Every fifty yards there was a "candy store;" in the intervals was the painted panel of a chiropodist, representing him in his professional attitude. Behind the plates of glass, in the hot interiors, behind the counters, were pale, familiar, delicate, tired faces of women, with polished hair and glazed complexions. Florimond knew their voices; he knew how women would speak when their hair was "treated," as they said in the studios, like that. But the women that passed through the streets were the main spectacle. Florimond had forgotten their extraordinary numerosity, and the impression that they produced of a deluge of petticoats. He could see that they were perfectly at home on the road; they had an air of possession, of perpetual equipment, a look, in the eyes, of always meeting the gaze of crowds, always seeing people pass, noting things in shop-windows, and being on the watch at crossings; many of them evidently passed most of their time in these conditions, and Florimond wondered what sort of *intérieurs* they could have. He felt at moments that he was in a city of women, in a country of women. The same impression came to him *dans le monde,* as he used to say, for he made the most incongruous application of his little French phrases to Boston. The talk, the social life, were so completely in the hands of the ladies, the masculine note was so subordinate, that on certain occasions he could have believed himself (putting the brightness aside) in a country stricken by a war, where the men had all gone to the army, or in a seaport half depopulated by the absence of its vessels. This idea had intermissions; for instance, when he walked out to Cambridge. In this little excursion he often indulged; he used to go and see one of his college mates, who was now a tutor at Harvard. He stretched away across the long, mean bridge that spans the mouth of the Charles, — a mile of wooden piles, supporting a brick pavement, a roadway deep in mire, and a rough timber fence, over which the pedestrian enjoys a view of the frozen bay, the backs

374

of many new houses, and a big brown marsh. The horse-cars bore him company, relieved here of the press of the streets, though not of their internal congestion, and constituting the principal feature of the wide, blank avenue, where the puddles lay large across the bounding rails. He followed their direction through a middle region, in which the small wooden houses had an air of tent-like impermanence, and the February mornings, splendid and indiscreet, stared into bare windows and seemed to make civilization transparent. Further, the suburb remained wooden, but grew neat, and the painted houses looked out on the car-track with an expression almost of superiority. At Harvard, the buildings were square and fresh; they stood in a yard planted with slender elms, which the winter had reduced to spindles; the town stretched away from the horizontal palings of the collegiate precinct, low, flat, and immense, with vague, featureless spaces and the air of a clean encampment. Florimond remembered that when the summer came in, the whole place was transformed. It was pervaded by verdure and dust, the slender elms became profuse, arching over the unpaved streets, the green shutters bowed themselves before the windows, the flowers and creeping-plants bloomed in the small gardens, and on the piazzas, in the gaps of dropped awnings, light dresses arrested the eye. At night, in the warm darkness, — for Cambridge is not festooned with lamps, — the bosom of nature would seem to palpitate, there would be a smell of earth and vegetation, — a smell more primitive than the odor of Europe, — and the air would vibrate with the sound of insects. All this was in reserve, if one would have patience, especially from March to June; but for the present the seat of the University struck our poor little critical Florimond as rather hard and bare. As the winter went on, and the days grew longer, he knew that Mrs. Daintry often believed him to be in Arlington Street when he was walking out to see his friend the tutor, who had once spent a winter in Paris and who never tired of talking about it. It is to be feared that he did not undeceive her so punctually as he might; for, in the first place, he was at Mrs. Mesh's very often; in the second, he failed to understand how worried his mother was; and in the third, the idea that he should be thought to have the peace of mind of a brilliant girl in his keeping was not disagreeable to him.

One day his Aunt Lucretia found him in Arlington Street; it occurred to her about the middle of the winter that, considering she liked Rachel Torrance so much, she had not been to see her very often. She had little time for such indulgences; but she caught a moment in its flight, and was told at Mrs. Mesh's door that this lady had not yet come in, but that her companion was accessible. Florimond was in his customary chair by the chimney corner (his aunt perhaps did not know quite how customary it was), and Rachel, at the piano, was regaling him with a composition of Schubert. Florimond, up to this time, had not become very intimate with his aunt, who had not, as it were, given him the key of her house, and in whom he detected a certain want of interest in his affairs. He had a limited sympathy with people who were interested only in their own, and perceived that Miss Daintry belonged to this preoccupied and ungraceful class. It seemed to him that it would have been more becoming to her to feign at least a certain attention to the professional and social prospects of the most promising of her nephews. If there was one thing that Florimond disliked more than another, it was an eager self-absorption; and he could not see that it was any better for people to impose their personality upon committees and charities than upon general society. He would have modified this judgment of his kinswoman, with whom he had dined but once, if he could have guessed with what anxiety she watched for the symptoms of that salutary change which she expected to see wrought in him by the fascinating independence of Rachel Torrance. If she had dared, she would have prompted the girl a little; she would have confided to her this secret desire. But the matter was

delicate; and Miss Daintry was shrewd enough to see that everything must be spontaneous. When she paused at the threshold of Mrs. Mesh's drawing-room, looking from one of her young companions to the other, she felt a slight pang, for she feared they were getting on too well. Rachel was pouring sweet music into the young man's ears, and turning to look at him over her shoulder while she played; and he with his head tipped back and his eyes on the ceiling hummed an accompaniment which occasionally became an articulate remark. Harmonious intimacy was stamped upon the scene; and poor Miss Daintry was not struck with its being in any degree salutary. She was not reassured when, after ten minutes, Florimond took his departure; she could see that he was irritated by the presence of a third person; and this was a proof that Rachel had not yet begun to do her duty by him. It is possible that when the two ladies were left together, her disappointment would have led her to betray her views, had not Rachel almost immediately said to her: "My dear cousin, I am so glad you have come; I might not have seen you again. I go away in three days."

"Go away? Where do you go to?"

"Back to Brooklyn," said Rachel, smiling sweetly.

"Why on earth — I thought you had come here to stay for six months?"

"Oh, you know, six months would be a terrible visit for these good people; and of course no time was fixed. That would have been very absurd. I have been here an immense time already. It was to be as things should go."

"And haven't they gone well?"

"Oh yes, they have gone beautifully."

"Then why in the world do you leave?"

"Well, you know, I have duties at home. My mother coughs a good deal, and they write me dismal letters."

"They are ridiculous, selfish people. You are going home because your mother coughs? I don't believe a word of it!" Miss Daintry cried. "You have some other reason. Something has happened here; it has become disagreeable. Be so good as to tell me the whole story."

Rachel answered that there was not any story to tell, and that her reason consisted entirely of conscientious scruples as to absenting herself so long from her domestic circle. Miss Daintry esteemed conscientious scruples when they were well placed, but she thought poorly on the present occasion of those of Mrs. Mesh's visitor; they interfered so much with her own sense of fitness. "Has Florimond been making love to you?" she suddenly inquired. "You mustn't mind that — beyond boxing his ears."

Her question appeared to amuse Miss Torrance exceedingly; and

the girl, a little inarticulate with her mirth, answered very positively that the young man had done her no such honor.

"I am very sorry to hear it," said Lucretia; "I was in hopes he would give you a chance to take him down. He needs it very much. He's dreadfully puffed up."

"He's an amusing little man!"

Miss Daintry put on her nippers. "Don't tell me it's you that are in love!"

"Oh, dear no! I like big, serious men, not small, Frenchified gentlemen, like Florimond. Excuse me if he's your nephew, but you began it. Though I am fond of art," the girl added, "I don't think I am fond of artists."

"Do you call Florimond an artist?"

Rachel Torrance hesitated a little, smiling. "Yes, when he poses for Pauline Mesh."

This rejoinder for a moment left Miss Daintry in visible perplexity; then a sudden light seemed to come to her. She flushed a little; what she found was more than she was looking for. She thought of many things quickly, and among others she thought that she had accomplished rather more than she intended. "Have you quarrelled with Pauline?" she said presently.

"No, but she is tired of me."

"Everything has not gone well, then, and you *have* another reason for going home than your mother's cough?"

"Yes, if you must know, Pauline wants me to go. I didn't feel free to tell you that; but since you guess it — " said Rachel, with her rancorless smile.

"Has she asked you to decamp?"

"Oh, dear no! for what do you take us? But she absents herself from the house; she stays away all day. I have to play to Florimond to console him."

"So you *have* been fighting about him?" Miss Daintry remarked, perversely.

"Ah, my dear cousin, what have you got in your head? Fighting about sixpence! if you knew how Florimond bores me! I play to him to keep him silent. I have heard everything he has to say, fifty times over!"

Miss Daintry sank back in her chair; she was completely out of her reckoning. "I think he might have made love to you a little!" she exclaimed incoherently.

"So do I! but he didn't — not a crumb. He is afraid of me — thank Heaven!"

"It isn't for you he comes, then?" Miss Daintry appeared to cling to her theory.

"No, my dear cousin, it isn't!"

"Just now, as he sat there, one could easily have supposed it. He didn't at all like my interruption."

"That was because he was waiting for Pauline to come in. He will wait that way an hour. You may imagine whether he likes me for boring her so that, as I tell you, she can't stay in the house. I am out myself as much as possible. But there are days when I drop with fatigue; then I must

rest. I can assure you that it's fortunate that I go so soon."

"Is Pauline in love with him?" Miss Daintry asked, gravely.

"Not a grain. She is the best little woman in the world."

"Except for being a goose. Why, then, does she object to your company — after being so enchanted with you?"

"Because even the best little woman in the world must object to something. She has everything in life, and nothing to complain of. Her children sleep all day, and her cook is a jewel. Her husband adores her, and she is perfectly satisfied with Mr. Mesh. I act on her nerves, and I think she believes I regard her as rather silly to care so much for Florimond. Excuse me again!"

"You contradict yourself. She *does* care for him, then?"

"Oh, as she would care for a new *coupé!* She likes to have a young man of her own — fresh from Paris — quite to herself. She has everything else — why shouldn't she have that? She thinks your nephew very original, and he thinks her what she is, — the prettiest woman in Boston. They have an idea that they are making a 'celebrated friendship,' — like Horace Walpole and Madame du Deffand. They sit there face to face — they are as innocent as the shovel and tongs. But, all the same, I am in the way, and Pauline is provoked that I am not jealous."

Miss Daintry got up with energy. "She's a vain, hollow, silly little creature, and you are quite right to go away; you are worthy of better company. Only you will not go back to Brooklyn, in spite of your mother's cough; you will come straight to Mount Vernon Place."

Rachel hesitated to agree to this. She appeared to think it was her duty to quit Boston altogether; and she gave as a reason that she had already refused other invitations. But Miss Daintry had a better reason than this, — a reason that glowed in her indignant breast. It was she who had been the cause of the girl's being drawn into this sorry adventure; it was she who should charge herself with the reparation. The conversation I have related took place on a Tuesday; and it was settled that on the Friday Miss Torrance should take up her abode for the rest of the winter under her Cousin Lucretia's roof. This lady left the house without having seen Mrs. Mesh.

On Thursday she had a visit from her sister-in-law, the motive of which was not long in appearing. All winter Mrs. Daintry had managed to keep silent on the subject of her doubts and fears. Discretion and dignity recommended this course; and the topic was a painful one to discuss with Lucretia, for the bruises of their primary interview still occasionally throbbed. But at the first sign of alleviation the excellent woman overflowed, and she lost no time in announcing to Lucretia, as a Heaven-sent piece of news, that Rachel had been called away by the illness of poor Mrs. Torrance, and was to leave Boston from one day to the other. Florimond had given her this information the evening before; and it had made her so happy, that she couldn't help coming to let Lucretia know that they were safe. Lucretia listened to her announcement in silence, fixing her eyes on her sister-in-law with an expression that the latter thought singular; but when Mrs. Daintry, expanding still further, went on to say that she had spent a winter of misery, that the harm the two together (she and Lucretia) might have done was never out of her mind, for Florimond's assiduity in Arlington Street had become notorious, and she had been told that the most cruel things were said, — when Mrs. Daintry, expressing herself to this effect, added that from the present moment she breathed, the danger was over, the sky was clear, and her conscience might take a holiday, — her hostess broke into the most prolonged, the most characteristic, and most bewildering fit of laughter in which she had ever known her to indulge. They were safe, Mrs. Daintry had said? For Lucretia this was true, now, of herself, at least; she was secure from the dangers of her irritation; her sense of the whole affair had turned to hilarious music. The contrast that rose before her between her visitor's anxieties and the real position of the parties, her quick vision of poor Susan's dismay in case *that* reality should meet her eyes, among the fragments of her squandered scruples, — these things smote the chords of mirth in Miss Daintry's spirit, and seemed to her in their high comicality to offer a sufficient reason for everything that had happened. The picture of her sister-in-law sitting all winter with her hands clasped and her eyes fixed on the wrong object was an image that would abide with her always; and it would render her an inestimable service, — it would cure her of the tendency to worry. As may be imagined, it was eminently open to Mrs. Daintry to ask her what on earth she was laughing at; and there was a color in the cheek of Florimond's mother that brought her back to propriety. She suddenly kissed this lady very tenderly — to the latter's great surprise, there having been no kissing since her visit in November — and told her that she would reveal to her some day, later, the cause of so much merriment. She added that Miss Torrance was leaving Arlington Street, yes; but only to go as far as Mount Vernon Place. She was engaged to spend three months in that very house. Mrs. Daintry's countenance, at this, fell several inches, and her joy appeared completely to desert her. She gave her sister-in-law a glance of ineffable reproach, and in a moment she exclaimed: "Then nothing is gained! it will all go on here!"

"Nothing will go on here. If you mean that Florimond will pursue the young lady into this mountain fastness, you may simply be quiet. He is not fond enough of me to wear out my threshold."

"Are you very sure?" Mrs. Daintry murmured, dubiously.

"I know what I say. Hasn't he told you he hates me?"

Mrs. Daintry colored again, and hesitated. "I don't know how you think we talk," she said.

"Well, he does, and he will leave us alone."

Mrs. Daintry sprang up with an elasticity that was comical. "That's all I ask!" she exclaimed.

"I believe you hate me too!" Lucretia said, laughing; but at any risk, she kissed her sister-in-law again before they separated.

Three weeks later Mrs. Daintry paid her another visit; and this time she looked very serious. "It's very strange. I don't know what to think. But perhaps you know it already?" This was her *entrée en matière*, as the French say. "Rachel's leaving Arlington Street has made no difference. He goes there as much as ever. I see no change at all. Lucretia, I have not the peace that I thought had come," said poor Mrs. Daintry, whose voice had failed below her breath.

"Do you mean that he goes to see Pauline Mesh?"

"I'm afraid so, every day."

"Well, my dear, what's the harm?" Miss Daintry asked. "He can't hurt *her* by not marrying her."

Mrs. Daintry stared; she was amazed at her sister-in-law's tone.

"But it makes one suppose that all winter, for so many weeks, it has been for *her* that he has gone!" and the image of the *tête-à-tête* in which she had found them immured that day, rose again before her; she could interpret it now.

"You wanted some one; why may not Pauline have served?"

Mrs. Daintry was silent, with the same expanded eyes. "Lucretia, it is not right!"

"My dear Susan, you are touching," Lucretia said.

Mrs. Daintry went on without heeding her. "It appears that people are talking about it; they have noticed it for ever so long. Joanna never hears anything, or she would have told me. The children are too much. I have been the last to know."

"I knew it a month ago," said Miss Daintry, smiling.

"And you never told me?"

"I knew that you wanted to detain him. Pauline will detain him a year."

Mrs. Daintry gathered herself together. "Not a day, not an hour, that I can help! He shall go, if I have to take him."

"My dear Susan," murmured her sister-in-law on the threshold. Miss Daintry scarcely knew what to say; she was almost frightened at the rigidity of her face.

"My dear Lucretia, it is not right!" This ejaculation she solemnly repeated, and she took her departure as if she were decided upon action.

She had found so little sympathy in her sister-in-law, that she made no answer to a note Miss Daintry wrote her that evening, to remark that she was really unjust to Pauline, who was silly, vain, and flattered by the development of her ability to monopolize an impressionist, but a perfectly innocent little woman and incapable of a serious flirtation. Miss Daintry had been careful to add to these last words no comment that could possibly shock Florimond's mother. Mrs. Daintry announced, about the 10th of April, that she had made up her mind she needed a change, and had determined to go abroad for the summer; and she looked so tired that people could see there was reason in it. Her summer began early; she embarked on the 20th of the month, accompanied by Florimond. Miss Daintry, who had not been obliged to dismiss the young lady of the kindergarten to make room for Rachel Torrance, never knew what had passed between the mother and the son, and she was disappointed at Mrs. Mesh's coolness in the face of this catastrophe. She disapproved of her flirtation with Florimond, and yet she was vexed at Pauline's pert resignation; it proved her to be so superficial. She disposed of everything with her absurd little phrases, that were half slang and half quotation. Mrs. Daintry was a native of Salem, and this gave Pauline, as a Baltimorean and a descendant of the Cavaliers, an obvious opportunity. Rachel repeated her words to Miss Daintry, for she had spoken to Rachel of Florimond's departure, the day after he embarked. "Oh yes, he's in the midst of the foam, the cruel, crawling foam! I 'kind of' miss him, afternoons; he was so useful round the fire. It's his mother that charmed him away; she's a most uncanny old party. I don't care for Salem witches, anyway; she has worked on him with philters and spells!" Lucretia was obliged to recognize a grain of truth in this last assertion; she felt that her sister-in-law must indeed have worked upon Florimond, and she smiled to think that the conscientious Susan should have descended, in the last resort, to an artifice, to a pretext. She had probably persuaded him she was tired of Joanna's children.

PANDORA

I

It has long been the custom of the North German Lloyd steamers, which convey passengers from Bremen to New York, to anchor for several hours in the pleasant port of Southampton, where their human cargo receives many additions. An intelligent young German, Count Otto Vogelstein, hardly knew a few years ago whether to condemn this custom or approve it. He leaned over the bulwarks of the *Donau* as the American passengers crossed the plank — the travelers who embark at Southampton are mainly of that nationality — and curiously, indifferently, vaguely, through the smoke of his cigar, saw them absorbed in the huge capacity of the ship, where he had the agreeable consciousness that his own nest was comfortably made. To watch from such a point of vantage the struggles of those less fortunate than ourselves — of the uninformed, the unprovided, the belated, the bewildered — is an occupation not devoid of sweetness, and there was nothing to mitigate the complacency with which our young friend gave himself up to it; nothing, that is, save a natural benevolence which had not yet been extinguished by the consciousness of official greatness. For Count Vogelstein was official, as I think you would have seen from the straightness of his back, the lustre of his light elegant spectacles, and something discreet and diplomatic in the curve of his moustache, which looked as if it might well contribute to the principal function, as cynics say, of the lips — the active concealment of thought. He had been appointed to the secretaryship of the German legation at Washington and in these first days of the autumn was about to take possession of his post. He was a model character for such a purpose — serious civil ceremonious curious stiff, stuffed with knowledge and convinced that, as lately rearranged, the German Empire places in the most striking light the highest of all the possibilities of the greatest of all the peoples. He was quite aware, however, of the claims to economic and other consideration of the United States, and that this quarter of the globe offered a vast field for study.

The process of enquiry had already begun for him, in spite of his having as yet spoken to none of his fellow passengers; the case being that Vogelstein enquired not only with his tongue, but with his eyes — that is with his spectacles — with his ears, with his nose, with his palate, with all his senses and organs. He was a highly upright young man, whose only fault was that his sense of comedy, or of the humour of things, had never been specifically disengaged from his several other senses. He vaguely felt that something should be done about this, and in a general manner proposed to do it, for he was on his way to explore a society abounding in comic aspects. This consciousness of a missing measure gave him a certain mistrust of what might be said of him; and if circumspection is the essence of diplomacy our young aspirant promised well. His mind contained several millions of facts, packed too closely together for the light breeze of the imagination to draw through the mass. He was impatient to report himself to his superior in Washington, and the loss of time in an English port could only incommode him, inasmuch as the study of English institutions was no part of his mission. On the other hand the day was charming; the blue sea, in Southampton Water, pricked all over with light, had no movement but that of its infinite shimmer. Moreover he was by no means sure that he should be happy in the United States, where doubtless he should find himself soon enough disembarked. He knew that this was not an important question and that happiness was an unscientific term, such as a man of his education should be ashamed to use even

in the silence of his thoughts. Lost none the less in the inconsiderate crowd and feeling himself neither in his own country nor in that to which he was in a manner accredited, he was reduced to his mere personality; so that during the hour, to save his importance, he cultivated such ground as lay in sight for a judgement of this delay to which the German steamer was subjected in English waters. Mightn't it be proved, facts, figures and documents — or at least watch — in hand, considerably greater than the occasion demanded?

Count Vogelstein was still young enough in diplomacy to think it necessary to have opinions. He had a good many indeed which had been formed without difficulty; they had been received ready-made from a line of ancestors who knew what they liked. This was of course — and under pressure, being candid, he would have admitted it — an unscientific way of furnishing one's mind. Our young man was a stiff conservative, a Junker of Junkers; he thought modern democracy a temporary phase and expected to find many arguments against it in the great Republic. In regard to these things it was a pleasure to him to feel that, with his complete training, he had been taught thoroughly to appreciate the nature of evidence. The ship was heavily laden with German emigrants, whose mission in the United States differed considerably from Count Otto's. They hung over the bulwarks, densely grouped; they leaned forward on their elbows for hours, their shoulders kept on a level with their ears; the men in furred caps, smoking long-bowled pipes, the women with babies hidden in remarkably ugly shawls. Some were yellow Germans and some were black, and all looked greasy and matted with the sea-damp. They were destined to swell still further the huge current of the Western democracy; and Count Vogelstein doubtless said to himself that they wouldn't improve its quality. Their numbers, however, were striking, and I know not what he thought of the nature of this particular evidence.

The passengers who came on board at Southampton were not of the greasy class; they were for the most part American families who had been spending the summer, or a longer period, in Europe. They had a great deal of luggage, innumerable bags and rugs and hampers and sea-chairs, and were composed largely of ladies of various ages, a little pale with anticipation, wrapped also in striped shawls, though in prettier ones than the nursing mothers of the steerage, and crowned with very high hats and feathers. They darted to and fro across the gangway, looking for each other and for their scattered parcels; they separated and reunited, they exclaimed and declared, they eyed with dismay the occupants of the forward quarter, who seemed numerous enough to sink the vessel, and their voices sounded faint and

far as they rose to Vogelstein's ear over the latter's great tarred sides. He noticed that in the new contingent there were many young girls, and he remembered what a lady in Dresden had once said to him — that America was the country of the Mädchen. He wondered whether he should like that, and reflected that it would be an aspect to study, like everything else. He had known in Dresden an American family in which there were three daughters who used to skate with the officers, and some of the ladies now coming on board struck him as of that same habit, except that in the Dresden days feathers weren't worn quite so high.

At last the ship began to creak and slowly budge, and the delay at Southampton came to an end. The gangway was removed and the vessel indulged in the awkward evolutions that were to detach her from the land. Count Vogelstein had finished his cigar, and he spent a long time in walking up and down the upper deck. The charming English coast passed before him, and he felt this to be the last of the old world. The American coast also might be pretty — he hardly knew what one would expect of an American coast; but he was sure it would be different. Differences, however, were notoriously half the charm of travel, and perhaps even most when they couldn't be expressed in figures, numbers, diagrams or the other merely useful symbols. As yet indeed there were very few among the objects presented to sight on the steamer. Most of his fellow passengers appeared of one and the same persuasion, and that persuasion the least to be mistaken. They were Jews and commercial to a man. And by this time they had lighted their cigars and put on all manner of seafaring caps, some of them with big ear-lappets which somehow had the effect of bringing out their peculiar facial type. At last the new voyagers began to emerge from below and to look about them, vaguely, with that suspicious expression of face always to be noted in the newly embarked and which, as directed to the receding land, resembles that of a person who begins to perceive himself the victim of a trick. Earth and ocean, in such glances, are made the subject of a sweeping objection, and many travellers, in the general plight, have an air at once duped and superior, which seems to say that they could easily go ashore if they would.

It still wanted two hours of dinner, and by the time Vogelstein's long legs had measured three or four miles on the deck he was ready to settle himself in his sea-chair and draw from his pocket a Tauchnitz novel by an American author whose pages, he had been assured, would help to prepare him for some of the oddities. On the back of his chair his name was painted in rather large letters, this being a precaution taken at the recommendation of a friend who had told him that on

the American steamers the passengers — especially the ladies — thought nothing of pilfering one's little comforts. His friend had even hinted at the correct reproduction of his coronet. This marked man of the world had added that the Americans are greatly impressed by a coronet. I know not whether it was scepticism or modesty, but Count Vogelstein had omitted every pictured plea for his rank; there were others of which he might have made use. The precious piece of furniture which on the Atlantic voyage is trusted never to flinch among universal concussions was emblazoned simply with his title and name. It happened, however, that the blazonry was huge; the back of the chair was covered with enormous German characters. This time there can be no doubt: it was modesty that caused the secretary of legation, in placing himself, to turn this portion of his seat outward, away from the eyes of his companions — to present it to the balustrade of the deck. The ship was passing the Needles — the beautiful uttermost point of the Isle of Wight. Certain tall white cones of rock rose out of the purple sea; they flushed in the afternoon light and their vague rosiness gave them a human expression in face of the cold expanse towards which the prow was turned; they seemed to say farewell, to be the last note of a peopled world. Vogelstein saw them very comfortably from his place and after a while turned his eyes to the other quarter, where the elements of air and water managed to make between them so comparatively poor an opposition. Even his American novelist was more amusing than that, and he prepared to return to this author. In the great curve which it described, however, his glance was arrested by the figure of a young lady who had just ascended to the deck and who paused at the mouth of the companionway.

This was not in itself an extraordinary phenomenon; but what attracted Vogelstein's attention was the fact that the young person appeared to have fixed her eyes on him. She was slim, brightly dressed, rather pretty; Vogelstein remembered in a moment that he had noticed her among the people on the wharf at Southampton. She was soon aware he had observed her; whereupon she began to move along the deck with a step that seemed to indicate a purpose of approaching him. Vogelstein had time to wonder whether she could be one of the girls he had known at Dresden; but he presently reflected that they would now be much older than that. It was true they were apt to advance, like this one, straight upon their victim. Yet the present specimen was no longer looking at him, and though she passed near him it was now tolerably clear she had come above but to take a general survey. She was a quick handsome competent girl, and she simply wanted to see what one could think of the ship, of the weather, of the

appearance of England, from such a position as that; possibly even of one's fellow passengers. She satisfied herself promptly on these points, and then she looked about, while she walked, as if in keen search of a missing object; so that Vogelstein finally arrived at a conviction of her real motive. She passed near him again and this time almost stopped, her eyes bent upon him attentively. He thought her conduct remarkable even after he had gathered that it was not at his face, with its yellow moustache, she was looking, but at the chair on which he was seated. Then those words of his friend came back to him — the speech about the tendency of the people, especially of the ladies, on the American steamers to take to themselves one's little belongings. Especially the ladies, he might well say; for here was one who apparently wished to pull from under him the very chair he was sitting on. He was afraid she would ask him for it, so he pretended to read, systematically avoiding her eye. He was conscious she hovered near him, and was moreover curious to see what she would do. It seemed to him strange that such a nice-looking girl — for her appearance was really charming — should endeavour by arts so flagrant to work upon the quiet dignity of a secretary of legation. At last it stood out that she was trying to look round a corner, as it were — trying to see what was written on the back of his chair. "She wants to find out my name; she wants to see who I am!" This reflexion passed through his mind and caused him to raise his eyes. They rested on her own — which for an appreciable moment she didn't withdraw. The latter were brilliant and expressive, and surmounted a delicate aquiline nose, which, though pretty, was perhaps just a trifle too hawk-like. It was the oddest coincidence in the world; the story Vogelstein had taken up treated of a flighty forward little American girl who plants herself in front of a young man in the garden of an hotel. Wasn't the conduct of this young lady a testimony to the truthfulness of the tale, and wasn't Vogelstein himself in the position of the young man in the garden? That young man — though with more, in such connexions in general, to go upon — ended by addressing himself to his aggressor, as she might be called, and after a very short hesitation Vogelstein followed his example. "If she wants to know who I am she's welcome," he said to himself; and he got out of the chair, seized it by the back and, turning it round, exhibited the superscription to the girl. She coloured slightly, but smiled and read his name, while Vogelstein raised his hat.

"I'm much obliged to you. That's all right," she remarked as if the discovery had made her very happy.

It affected him indeed as all right that he should be Count Otto Vogelstein; this appeared even rather a flippant mode of dis-posing of the fact. By way of rejoinder he asked her if she desired of him the surrender of his seat.

"I'm much obliged to you; of course not. I thought you had one of our chairs, and I didn't like to ask you. It looks exactly like one of ours; not so much now as when you sit in it. Please sit down again. I don't want to trouble you. We've lost one of ours, and I've been looking for it everywhere. They look so much alike; you can't tell till you see the back. Of course I see there will be no mistake about yours," the young lady went on with a smile of which the serenity matched her other abundance. "But we've got such a small name — you can scarcely see it," she added with the same friendly intention. "Our name's just Day — you mightn't think it *was* a name, might you? if we didn't make the most of it. If you see that on anything, I'd be so obliged if you'd tell me. It isn't for myself, it's for my mother; she's so dependent on her chair, and that one I'm looking for pulls out so beautifully. Now that you sit down again and hide the lower part it does look just like ours. Well, it must be somewhere. You must excuse me; I wouldn't disturb you."

This was a long and even confidential speech for a young woman, presumably unmarried, to make to a perfect stranger; but Miss Day acquitted herself of it with perfect simplicity and self-possession. She held up her head and stepped away, and Vogelstein could see that the foot she pressed upon the clean smooth deck was slender and shapely. He watched her disappear through the trap by which she had ascended, and he felt more than ever like the young man in his American tale. The girl in the present case was older and not so pretty, as he could easily judge, for the image of her smiling eyes and speaking lips still hovered before him. He went back to his book with the feeling that it would give him some information about her. This was rather illogical, but it indicated a certain amount of curiosity on the part of Count Vogelstein. The girl in the book had a mother, it appeared, and so had this young lady; the former had also a brother, and he now remembered that he had noticed a young man on the wharf — a young man in a high hat and a white overcoat — who seemed united to Miss Day by this natural tie. And there was some one else too, as he gradually recollected, an older man, also in a high hat, but in a black overcoat — in black altogether — who completed the group and who was presumably the head of the family. These reflexions would indicate that Count Vogelstein read his volume of Tauchnitz rather interruptedly. Moreover they represented but the loosest economy of consciousness; for wasn't he to be afloat in an oblong box for ten days with such people, and could it be doubted he should see at least enough of them?

It may as well be written with-

out delay that he saw a great deal of them. I have sketched in some detail the conditions in which he made the acquaintance of Miss Day, because the event had a certain importance for this fair square Teuton; but I must pass briefly over the incidents that immediately followed it. He wondered what it was open to him, after such an introduction, to do in relation to her, and he determined he would push through his American tale and discover what the hero did. But he satisfied himself in a very short time that Miss Day had nothing in common with the heroine of that work save certain signs of habitat and climate — and save, further, the fact that the male sex wasn't terrible to her. The local stamp sharply, as he gathered, impressed upon her he estimated indeed rather in a borrowed than in a natural light, for if she was native to a small town in the interior of the American continent one of their fellow passengers, a lady from New York with whom he had a good deal of conversation, pronounced her "atrociously" provincial. How the lady arrived at this certitude didn't appear, for Vogelstein observed that she held no communication with the girl. It was true she gave it the support of her laying down that certain Americans could tell immediately who other Americans were, leaving him to judge whether or no she herself belonged to the critical or only to the criticised half of the nation. Mrs. Dangerfield was a handsome confidential insinuating woman, with whom Vogelstein felt his talk take a very wide range indeed. She convinced him rather effectually that even in a great democracy there are human differences, and that American life was full of social distinctions, of delicate shades, which foreigners often lack the intelligence to perceive. Did he suppose every one knew every one else in the biggest country in the world, and that one wasn't as free to choose one's company there as in the most monarchical and most exclusive societies? She laughed such delusions to scorn as Vogelstein tucked her beautiful furred coverlet — they reclined together a great deal in their elongated chairs — well over her feet. How free an American lady was to choose her company she abundantly proved by not knowing any one on the steamer but Count Otto.

He could see for himself that Mr. and Mrs. Day had not at all her grand air. They were fat plain serious people who sat side by side on the deck for hours and looked straight before them. Mrs. Day had a white face, large cheeks and small eyes; her forehead was surrounded with a multitude of little tight black curls; her lips moved as if she had always a lozenge in her mouth. She wore entwined about her head an article which Mrs. Dangerfield spoke of as a "nuby," a knitted pink scarf concealing her hair, encircling her neck and having among its convolutions a hole for her perfectly expressionless face. Her hands were folded on her stomach, and in her still, swathed figure her little bead-like eyes, which occasionally changed their direction, alone represented life. Her husband had a stiff grey beard on his chin and a bare spacious upper lip, to which constant shaving had imparted a hard glaze. His eyebrows were thick and his nostrils wide, and when he was uncovered, in the saloon, it was visible that his grizzled hair was dense and perpendicular. He might have looked rather grim and truculent hadn't it been for the mild familiar accommodating gaze with which his large light-coloured pupils — the leisurely eyes of a silent man — appeared to consider surrounding objects. He was evidently more friendly than fierce, but he was more diffident than friendly. He liked to have you in sight, but wouldn't have pretended to understand you much or to classify you, and would have been sorry it should put you under an obligation. He and his wife spoke sometimes, but seldom talked, and there was something vague and patient in them, as if they had become victims of a wrought spell. The spell however was of no sinister cast; it was the fascination of prosperity, the confidence of security, which sometimes makes people arrogant, but which had had such a different effect on this simple satisfied pair, in whom further development of every kind appeared to have been happily arrested.

Mrs. Dangerfield made it known to Count Otto that every morning

390

after breakfast, the hour at which he wrote his journal in his cabin, the old couple were guided upstairs and installed in their customary corner by Pandora. This she had learned to be the name of their elder daughter, and she was immensely amused by her discovery. "Pandora" — that was in the highest degree typical; it placed them in the social scale if other evidence had been wanting; you could tell that a girl was from the interior, the mysterious interior about which Vogelstein's imagination was now quite excited, when she had such a name as that. This young lady managed the whole family, even a little the small beflounced sister, who, with bold pretty innocent eyes, a torrent of fair silky hair, a crimson fez, such as is worn by male Turks, very much askew on top of it, and a way of galloping and straddling about the ship in any company she could pick up — she had long thin legs, very short skirts and stockings of every tint — was going home, in elegant French clothes, to resume an interrupted education. Pandora overlooked and directed her relatives; Vogelstein could see this for himself, could see she was very active and decided, that she had in a high degree the sentiment of responsibility, settling on the spot most of the questions that could come up for a family from the interior.

The voyage was remarkably fine, and day after day it was possible to sit there under the salt sky and feel one's self rounding the great curves of the globe. The long deck made a white spot in the sharp black circle of the ocean and in the intense sea-light, while the shadow of the smoke-streamers trembled on the familiar floor, the shoes of fellow passengers, distinctive now, and in some cases irritating, passed and repassed, accompanied, in the air so tremendously "open," that rendered all voices weak and most remarks rather flat, by fragments of opinion on the run of the ship. Vogelstein by this time had finished his little American story and now definitely judged that Pandora Day was not at all like the heroine. She was of quite another type; much more serious and strenuous, and not at all keen, as he had supposed, about making the acquaintance of gentlemen. Her speaking to him that first afternoon had been, he was bound to believe, an incident without importance for herself; in spite of her having followed it up the next day by the remark, thrown at him as she passed, with a smile that was almost fraternal: "It's all right, sir! I've found that old chair." After this she hadn't spoken to him again and had scarcely looked at him. She read a great deal, and almost always French books, in fresh yellow paper; not the lighter forms of that literature, but a volume of Sainte-Beuve, of Renan or at the most, in the way of dissipation, of Alfred de Musset. She took frequent exercise and almost always walked alone, apparently not having made many friends on the ship and being without the resource of her parents, who, as has been related, never budged out of the cosey corner in which she planted them for the day.

Her brother was always in the smoking-room, where Vogelstein observed him, in very tight clothes, his neck encircled with a collar like a palisade. He had a sharp little face, which was not disagreeable; he smoked enormous cigars and began his drinking early in the day: but his appearance gave no sign of these excesses. As regards euchre and poker and the other distractions of the place he was guilty of none. He evidently understood such games in perfection, for he used to watch the players and even at moments impartially advise them; but Vogelstein never saw the cards in his hand. He was referred to as regards disputed points, and his opinion carried the day. He took little part in the conversation, usually much relaxed, that prevailed in the smoking-room, but from time to time he made, in his soft flat youthful voice, a remark which every one paused to listen to and which was greeted with roars of laughter. Vogelstein, well as he knew English, could rarely catch the joke; but he could see at least that these must be choice specimens of that American humour admired and practised by a whole continent and yet to be rendered accessible to a trained diplomatist, clearly, but by some special and incalculable revelation. The young man, in his way, was very re-

markable, for, as Vogelstein heard some one say once after the laughter had subsided, he was only nineteen. If his sister didn't resemble the dreadful little girl in the tale already mentioned, there was for Vogelstein at least an analogy between young Mr. Day and a certain small brother — a candy-loving Madison, Hamilton or Jefferson — who was, in the Tauchnitz volume, attributed to that unfortunate maid. This was what the little Madison would have grown up to at nineteen, and the improvement was greater than might have been expected.

The days were long, but the voyage was short, and it had almost come to an end before Count Otto yielded to an attraction peculiar in its nature and finally irresistible and, in spite of Mrs. Dangerfield's emphatic warning, sought occasion for a little continuous talk with Miss Pandora. To mention that this impulse took effect without mentioning sundry other of his current impressions with which it had nothing to do is perhaps to violate proportion and give a false idea; but to pass it by would be still more unjust. The Germans, as we know, are a transcendental people, and there was at last an irresistible appeal for Vogelstein in this quick bright silent girl who could smile and turn vocal in an instant, who imparted a rare originality to the filial character and whose profile was delicate as she bent it over a volume which she cut as she read, or presented it in musing attitudes, at the side of the ship, to the horizon they had left behind. But he felt it to be a pity, as regards a possible acquaintance with her, that her parents should be heavy little burghers, that her brother should not correspond to his conception of a young man of the upper class and that her sister should be a Daisy Miller *en herbe*. Repeatedly admonished by Mrs. Dangerfield, the young diplomatist was doubly careful as to the relations he might form at the beginning of his sojourn in the United States. That lady reminded him, and he had himself made the observation in other capitals, that the first year, and even the second, is the time for prudence. One was ignorant of proportions and values; one was exposed to mistakes and thankful for attention, and one might give one's self away to people who would afterwards be as a millstone round one's neck: Mrs. Dangerfield struck and sustained that note, which resounded in the young man's imagination. She assured him that if he didn't "look out" he would be committing himself to some American girl with an impossible family. In America, when one committed one's self there was nothing to do but march to the altar, and what should he say for instance to finding himself a near relation of Mr. and Mrs. P. W. Day? – since such were the initials inscribed on the back of the two chairs of that couple. Count Otto felt the peril, for he could immediately think of a dozen men he knew who had mar-

ried American girls. There appeared now to be a constant danger of marrying the American girl; it was something one had to reckon with, like the railway, the telegraph, the discovery of dynamite, the Chassepôt rifle, the Socialistic spirit: it was one of the complications of modern life.

It would doubtless be too much to say that he feared being carried away by a passion for a young woman who was not strikingly beautiful and with whom he had talked, in all, but ten minutes. But, as we recognise, he went so far as to wish that the human belongings of a person whose high spirit appeared to have no taint either of fastness, as they said in England, or of subversive opinion, and whose mouth had charming lines, should not be a little more distinguished. There was an effect of drollery in her behaviour to these subjects of her zeal, whom she seemed to regard as a care, but not as an interest; it was as if they had been entrusted to her honour and she had engaged to convey them safe to a certain point; she was detached and inadvertent, and then suddenly remembered, repented and came back to tuck them into their blankets, to alter the position of her mother's umbrella, to tell them something about the run of the ship. These little offices were usually performed deftly, rapidly, with the minimum of words, and when their daughter drew near them Mr. and Mrs. Day closed their eyes after the fashion of a

pair of household dogs who expect to be scratched.

One morning she brought up
the Captain of the ship to present
to them; she appeared to have a
private and independent acquaintance with this officer, and the introduction to her parents had the
air of a sudden happy thought. It
wasn't so much an introduction as
an exhibition, as if she were saying to him: "This is what they
look like; see how comfortable I
make them. Aren't they rather
queer and rather dear little people? But they leave me perfectly
free. Oh I can assure you of that.
Besides, you must see it for yourself." Mr. and Mrs. Day looked up
at the high functionary who thus
unbent to them with very little
change of countenance; then
looked at each other in the same
way. He saluted, he inclined himself a moment; but Pandora shook
her head, she seemed to be answering for them; she made little
gestures as if in explanation to the
good Captain of some of their peculiarities, as for instance that he
needn't expect them to speak.
They closed their eyes at last; she
appeared to have a kind of mesmeric influence on them, and Miss
Day walked away with the important friend, who treated her with
evident consideration, bowing very
low, for all his importance, when
the two presently after separated.
Vogelstein could see she was capable of making an impression;
and the moral of our little matter
is that in spite of Mrs. Dangerfield, in spite of the resolutions of

his prudence, in spite of the limits
of such acquaintance as he had
momentarily made with her, in
spite of Mr. and Mrs. Day and the
young man in the smoking-room,
she had fixed his attention.

It was in the course of the evening after the scene with the Captain that he joined her, awkwardly,
abruptly, irresistibly, on the deck,
where she was pacing to and fro
alone, the hour being auspiciously
mild and the stars remarkably fine.
There were scattered talkers and
smokers and couples, unrecognise-
able, that moved quickly through
the gloom. The vessel dipped with
long regular pulsations; vague and
spectral under the low stars, its
swaying pinnacles spotted here
and there with lights, it seemed to
rush through the darkness faster
than by day. Count Otto had come
up to walk, and as the girl brushed
past him he distinguished Pandora's face — with Mrs. Dangerfield he always spoke of her as
Pandora — under the veil worn to
protect it from the sea-damp. He
stopped, turned, hurried after her,
threw away his cigar — then asked
her if she would do him the honour to accept his arm. She declined his arm but accepted his
company, and he allowed her to
enjoy it for an hour. They had a
great deal of talk, and he was to
remember afterwards some of the
things she had said. There was
now a certainty of the ship's getting into dock the next morning
but one, and this prospect afforded an obvious topic. Some of
Miss Day's expressions struck him

as singular, but of course, as he was aware, his knowledge of English was not nice enough to give him a perfect measure.

"I'm not in a hurry to arrive; I'm very happy here," she said. "I'm afraid I shall have such a time putting my people through."

"Putting them through?"

"Through the Custom-House. We've made so many purchases. Well, I've written to a friend to come down, and perhaps he can help us. He's very well acquainted with the head. Once I'm chalked I don't care. I feel like a kind of blackboard by this time anyway. We found them awful in Germany."

Count Otto wondered if the friend she had written to were her lover and if they had plighted their troth, especially when she alluded to him again as "that gentleman who's coming down." He asked her about her travels, her impressions, whether she had been long in Europe and what she liked best, and she put it to him that they had gone abroad, she and her family, for a little fresh experience. Though he found her very intelligent he suspected she gave this as a reason because he was a German and she had heard the Germans were rich in culture. He wondered what form of culture Mr. and Mrs. Day had brought back from Italy, Greece and Palestine — they had travelled for two years and been everywhere — especially when their daughter said: "I wanted father and mother to see the best things. I kept them

three hours on the Acropolis. I guess they won't forget that!" Perhaps it was of Phidias and Pericles they were thinking, Vogelstein reflected, as they sat ruminating in their rugs. Pandora remarked also that she wanted to show her little sister everything while she was comparatively unformed ("comparatively!" he mutely gasped); remarkable sights made so much more impression when the mind was fresh: she had read something of that sort somewhere in Goethe. She had wanted to come herself when she was her sister's age; but her father was in business then and they couldn't leave Utica. The young man thought of the little sister frisking over the Parthenon and the Mount of Olives and sharing for two years, the years of the schoolroom, this extraordinary pilgrimage of her parents; he wondered whether Goethe's dictum had been justified in this case. He asked Pandora if Utica were the seat of her family, if it were an important or typical place, if it would be an interesting city for him, as a stranger, to see. His companion replied frankly that this was a big question, but added that all the same she would ask him to "come and visit us at our home," if it weren't that they should probably soon leave it.

"Ah you're going to live elsewhere?" Vogelstein asked as if that fact too would be typical.

"Well, I'm working for New York. I flatter myself I've loosened them while we've been away," the

Pandora

girl went on. "They won't find in Utica the same charm; that was my idea. I want a big place, and of course Utica — !" She broke off as before a complex statement.

"I suppose Utica is inferior — ?" Vogelstein seemed to see his way to suggest.

"Well no, I guess I can't have you call Utica inferior. It isn't supreme — that's what's the matter with it, and I hate anything middling," said Pandora Day. She gave a light dry laugh, tossing back her head a little as she made this declaration. And looking at her askance in the dusk, as she trod the deck that vaguely swayed, he recognised something in her air and port that matched such a pronouncement.

"What's her social position?" he enquired of Mrs. Dangerfield the next day. "I can't make it out at all — it's so contradictory. She strikes me as having much cultivation and much spirit. Her appearance, too, is very neat. Yet her parents are complete little burghers. That's easily seen."

"Oh social position," and Mrs. Dangerfield nodded two or three times portentously. "What big expressions you use! Do you think everybody in the world has a social position? That's reserved for an infinitely small majority of mankind. You can't have a social position at Utica any more than you can have an opera-box. Pandora hasn't got one; where, if you please, should she have got it? Poor girl, it isn't fair of you to

make her the subject of such questions as that."

"Well," said Vogelstein, "if she's of the lower class it seems to me very — very — " And he paused a moment, as he often paused in speaking English, looking for his word.

"Very what, dear Count?"

"Very significant, very representative."

"Oh dear, she isn't of the lower class," Mrs. Dangerfield returned with an irritated sense of wasted wisdom. She liked to explain her country, but that somehow always required two persons.

"What is she then?"

"Well, I'm bound to admit that since I was at home last she's a novelty. A girl like that with such people — it *is* a new type."

"I like novelties" — and Count Otto smiled with an air of considerable resolution. He couldn't however be satisfied with a demonstration that only begged the question; and when they disembarked in New York he felt, even amid the confusion of the wharf and the heaps of disembowelled baggage, a certain acuteness of regret at the idea that Pandora and her family were about to vanish into the unknown. He had a consolation however: it was apparent that for some reason or other — illness or absence from town — the gentleman to whom she had written had not, as she said, come down. Vogelstein was glad — he couldn't have told you why — that this sympathetic person had failed her; even though without him Pandora

396

had to engage single-handed with
the United States Custom-House.
Our young man's first impression
of the Western world was received
on the landing-place of the German steamers at Jersey City — a
huge wooden shed covering a
wooden wharf which resounded
under the feet, an expanse pali-
saded with rough-hewn piles that
leaned this way and that, and bestrewn with masses of heterogeneous luggage. At one end, toward
the town, was a row of tall painted
palings, behind which he could
distinguish a press of hackney-
coachmen, who brandished their
whips and awaited their victims,
while their voices rose, incessant,
with a sharp strange sound, a challenge at once fierce and familiar.
The whole place, behind the
fence, appeared to bristle and re-
sound. Out there was America,
Count Otto said to himself, and he
looked toward it with a sense that
he should have to muster resolution. On the wharf people were
rushing about amid their trunks,
pulling their things together, trying to unite their scattered parcels.
They were heated and angry, or
else quite bewildered and discouraged. The few that had succeeded
in collecting their battered boxes
had an air of flushed indifference
to the efforts of their neighbours,
not even looking at people with
whom they had been fondly intimate on the steamer. A detachment of the officers of the Customs
was in attendance, and energetic
passengers were engaged in attempts to drag them toward their

luggage or to drag heavy pieces
toward them. These functionaries
were good-natured and taciturn,
except when occasionally they remarked to a passenger whose open
trunk stared up at them, eloquent,
imploring, that they were afraid
the voyage had been "rather
glassy." They had a friendly leisurely speculative way of dis-
charging their duty, and if they
perceived a victim's name written
on the portmanteau they addressed
him by it in a tone of old acquaintance. Vogelstein found however
that if they were familiar they
weren't indiscreet. He had heard
that in America all public functionaries were the same, that there
wasn't a different *tenue,* as they
said in France, for different positions, and he wondered whether
at Washington the President and
ministers, whom he expected to
see — to *have* to see — a good deal
of, would be like that.

He was diverted from these
speculations by the sight of Mr.
and Mrs. Day seated side by side
upon a trunk and encompassed apparently by the accumulations of
their tour. Their faces expressed
more consciousness of surrounding objects than he had hitherto
recognised, and there was an air
of placid expansion in the mysterious couple which suggested that
this consciousness was agreeable.
Mr. and Mrs. Day were, as they
would have said, real glad to get
back. At a little distance, on the
edge of the dock, our observer remarked their son, who had found
a place where, between the sides

of two big ships, he could see the ferry-boats pass; the large pyramidal low-laden ferry-boats of American waters. He stood there, patient and considering, with his small neat foot on a coil of rope, his back to everything that had been disembarked, his neck elongated in its polished cylinder, while the fragrance of his big cigar mingled with the odour of the rotting piles and his little sister, beside him, hugged a huge post and tried to see how far she could crane over the water without falling in. Vogelstein's servant was off in search of an examiner; Count Otto himself had got his things together and was waiting to be released, fully expecting that for a person of his importance the ceremony would be brief. Before it began he said a word to young Mr. Day, raising his hat at the same time to the little girl, whom he had not yet greeted and who dodged his salute by swinging herself boldly outward to the dangerous side of the pier. She was indeed still unformed, but was evidently as light as a feather.

"I see you're kept waiting like me. It's very tiresome," Count Otto said.

The young American answered without looking behind him. "As soon as we're started we'll go all right. My sister has written to a gentleman to come down."

"I've looked for Miss Day to bid her good-bye," Vogelstein went on; "but I don't see her."

"I guess she has gone to meet that gentleman; he's a great friend of hers."

"I guess he's her lover!" the little girl broke out. "She was always writing to him in Europe."

Her brother puffed his cigar in silence a moment. "That was only for this. I'll tell on you, sis," he presently added.

But the younger Miss Day gave no heed to his menace; she addressed herself only, though with all freedom, to Vogelstein. "This is New York; I like it better than Utica.

He had no time to reply, for his servant had arrived with one of the dispensers of fortune; but as he turned away he wondered, in the light of the child's preference, about the towns of the interior. He was naturally exempt from the common doom. The officer who took him in hand and who had a large straw hat and a diamond breastpin, was quite a man of the world and in reply to the Count's formal declarations only said "Well, I guess it's all right; I guess I'll just pass you"; distributing chalk-marks as if they had been so many love-pats. The servant had done some superfluous unlocking and unbuckling, and while he closed the pieces the officer stood there wiping his forehead and conversing with Vogelstein. "First visit to our country, sir? — quite alone — no ladies? Of course the ladies are what we're most after." It was in this manner he expressed himself while the young diplomatist wondered what he was

Pandora

waiting for and whether he ought to slip something into his palm. But this representative of order left our friend only a moment in suspense; he presently turned away with the remark, quite paternally uttered, that he hoped the Count would make quite a stay; upon which the young man saw how wrong he should have been to offer a tip. It was simply the American manner, which had a finish of its own after all. Vogelstein's servant had secured a porter with a truck, and he was about to leave the place when he saw Pandora Day dart out of the crowd and address herself with much eagerness to the functionary who had just liberated him. She had an open letter in her hand which she gave him to read and over which he cast his eyes, thoughtfully stroking his beard. Then she led him away to where her parents sat on their luggage. Count Otto sent off his servant with the porter and followed Pandora, to whom he really wished to address a word of farewell. The last thing they had said to each other on the ship was that they should meet again on shore. It seemed improbable however that the meeting would occur anywhere but just here on the dock; inasmuch as Pandora was decidedly not in society, where Vogelstein would be of course, and as, if Utica — he had her sharp little sister's word for it — was worse than what was about him there, he'd be hanged if he'd go to Utica. He overtook Pandora quickly; she

was in the act of introducing the representative of order to her parents, quite in the same manner in which she had introduced the Captain of the ship. Mr. and Mrs. Day got up and shook hands with him and they evidently all prepared to have a little talk. "I should like to introduce you to my brother and sister," he heard the girl say, and he saw her look about for these appendages. He caught her eye as she did so, and advanced with his hand outstretched, reflecting the while that evidently the Americans, whom he had always heard described as silent and practical, rejoiced to extravagance in the social graces. They dawdled and chattered like so many Neapolitans.

"Good-bye, Count Vogelstein," said Pandora, who was a little flushed with her various exertions but didn't look the worse for it. "I hope you'll have a splendid time and appreciate our country."

"I hope you'll get through all right," Vogelstein answered, smiling and feeling himself already more idiomatic.

"That gentleman's sick that I wrote to," she rejoined; "isn't it too bad? But he sent me down a letter to a friend of his — one of the examiners — and I guess we won't have any trouble. Mr. Lansing, let me make you acquainted with Count Vogelstein," she went on, presenting to her fellow passenger the wearer of the straw hat and the breastpin, who shook hands with the young German as

399

if he had never seen him before. Vogelstein's heart rose for an instant to his throat; he thanked his stars he hadn't offered a tip to the friend of a gentleman who had often been mentioned to him and who had also been described by a member of Pandora's family as Pandora's lover.

"It's a case of ladies this time," Mr. Lansing remarked to him with a smile which seemed to confess surreptitiously, and as if neither party could be eager, to recognition.

"Well, Mr. Bellamy says you'll do anything for *him*," Pandora said, smiling very sweetly at Mr. Lansing. "We haven't got much; we've been gone only two years."

Mr. Lansing scratched his head a little behind, with a movement that sent his straw hat forward in the direction of his nose. "I don't know as I'd do anything for him that I wouldn't do for you," he responded with an equal geniality. "I guess you'd better open that one" — and he gave a little affectionate kick to one of the trunks.

"Oh mother, isn't he lovely? It's only your sea-things," Pandora cried, stooping over the coffer with the key in her hand.

"I don't know as I like showing them," Mrs. Day modestly murmured.

Vogelstein made his German salutation to the company in general, and to Pandora he offered an audible good-bye, which she returned in a bright friendly voice, but without looking round as she fumbled at the lock of her trunk.

"We'll try another, if you like," said Mr. Lansing good-humouredly.

"Oh no, it has got to be this one! Good-bye, Count Vogelstein. I hope you'll judge us correctly!"

The young man went his way and passed the barrier of the dock. Here he was met by his English valet with a face of consternation which led him to ask if a cab weren't forthcoming.

"They call 'em 'acks 'ere, sir," said the man, "and they're beyond everything. He wants thirty shillings to take you to the inn."

Vogelstein hesitated a moment. "Couldn't you find a German?"

"By the way he talks he *is* a German!" said the man; and in a moment Count Otto began his career in America by discussing the tariff of hackney-coaches in the language of the fatherland.

II

He went wherever he was asked, on principle, partly to study American society and partly because in Washington pastimes seemed to him not so numerous that one could afford to neglect occasions. At the end of two winters he had naturally had a good many of various kinds — his study of American society had yielded considerable fruit. When, however, in April, during the second year of his residence, he presented himself at a large party given by Mrs. Bonnycastle and of which it was believed that it would be the last serious affair of the season, his being there (and still more his looking very fresh and talkative) was not the consequence of a rule of conduct. He went to Mrs. Bonnycastle's simply because he liked the lady, whose receptions were the pleasantest in Washington, and because if he didn't go there he didn't know what he should do; that absence of alternatives having become familiar to him by the waters of the Potomac. There were a great many things he did because if he didn't do them he didn't know what he should do. It must be added that in this case even if there had been an alternative he would still have decided to go to Mrs. Bonnycastle's. If her house wasn't the pleasantest there it was at least difficult to say which was pleasanter; and the complaint sometimes made of it that it was too limited, that it left out, on the whole, more people than it took in, applied with much less force when it was thrown open for a general party. Toward the end of the social year, in those soft scented days of the Washington spring when the air began to show a southern glow and the Squares and Circles (to which the wide empty avenues converged according to a plan so ingenious, yet so bewildering) to flush with pink blossom and to make one wish to sit on benches — under this magic of expansion and condonation Mrs. Bonnycastle, who during the winter had been a good

deal on the defensive, relaxed her vigilance a little, became whimsically wilful, vernally reckless, as it were, and ceased to calculate the consequences of an hospitality which a reference to the back files or even to the morning's issue of the newspapers might easily prove a mistake. But Washington life, to Count Otto's apprehension, was paved with mistakes; he felt himself in a society founded on fundamental fallacies and triumphant blunders. Little addicted as he was to the sportive view of existence, he had said to himself at an early stage of his sojourn that the only way to enjoy the great Republic would be to burn one's standards and warm one's self at the blaze. Such were the reflexions of a theoretic Teuton who now walked for the most part amid the ashes of his prejudices.

Mrs. Bonnycastle had endeavoured more than once to explain to him the principles on which she received certain people and ignored certain others; but it was with difficulty that he entered into her discriminations. American promiscuity, goodness knew, had been strange to him, but it was nothing to the queerness of American criticism. This lady would discourse to him *à perte de vue* on differences where he only saw resemblances, and both the merits and the defects of a good many members of Washington society, as this society was interpreted to him by Mrs. Bonnycastle, he was often at a loss to understand. Fortunately she had a fund of good humour which, as I have inti- mated, was apt to come upper- most with the April blossoms and which made the people she didn't invite to her house almost as amus- ing to her as those she did. Her husband was not in politics, though politics were much in him; but the couple had taken upon themselves the responsibilities of an active patriotism; they thought it right to live in America, differ- ing therein from many of their ac- quaintances who only, with some grimness, thought it inevitable. They had that burdensome herit- age of foreign reminiscence with which so many Americans were saddled; but they carried it more easily than most of their country- people, and one knew they had lived in Europe only by their pres- ent exultation, never in the least by their regrets. Their regrets, that is, were only for their ever having lived there, as Mrs. Bonnycastle once told the wife of a foreign minister. They solved all their problems successfully, including those of knowing none of the peo- ple they didn't wish to, and of finding plenty of occupation in a society supposed to be meagerly provided with resources for that body which Vogelstein was to hear invoked, again and again, with the mixture of desire and of deprecation that might have at- tended the mention of a secret vice, under the name of a leisure- class. When as the warm weather approached they opened both the wings of their house-door, it was because they thought it would en-

tertain them and not because they were conscious of a pressure. Al- fred Bonnycastle all winter indeed chafed a little at the definiteness of some of his wife's reserves; it struck him that for Washington their society was really a little too good. Vogelstein still remembered the puzzled feeling — it had cleared up somewhat now — with which, more than a year before, he had heard Mr. Bonnycastle exclaim one evening, after a dinner in his own house, when every guest but the German secretary (who often sat late with the pair) had de- parted: "Hang it, there's only a month left; let us be vulgar and have some fun — let us invite the President."

This was Mrs. Bonnycastle's car- nival, and on the occasion to which I began my chapter by re- ferring the President had not only been invited but had signified his intention of being present. I has- ten to add that this was not the same august ruler to whom Alfred Bonnycastle's irreverent allusion had been made. The White House had received a new tenant — the old one was then just leaving it — and Count Otto had had the ad- vantage, during the first eighteen months of his stay in America, of seeing an electoral campaign, a presidential inauguration and a distribution of spoils. He had been bewildered during those first weeks by finding that at the na- tional capital, in the houses he supposed to be the best, the head of the State was not a coveted guest; for this could be the only explanation of Mr. Bonnycastle's whimsical suggestion of their inviting him, as it were, in carnival. His successor went out a good deal for a President.

The legislative session was over, but this made little difference in the aspect of Mrs. Bonnycastle's rooms, which even at the height of the congressional season could scarce be said to overflow with the representatives of the people. They were garnished with an occasional Senator, whose movements and utterances often appeared to be regarded with a mixture of alarm and indulgence, as if they would be disappointing if they weren't rather odd and yet might be dangerous if not carefully watched. Our young man had come to entertain a kindness for these conscript fathers of invisible families, who had something of the toga in the voluminous folds of their conversation, but were otherwise rather bare and bald, with stony wrinkles in their faces, like busts and statues of ancient law-givers. There seemed to him something chill and exposed in their being at once so exalted and so naked; there were frequent lonesome glances in their eyes, as if in the social world their legislative consciousness longed for the warmth of a few comfortable laws ready-made. Members of the House were very rare, and when Washington was new to the enquiring secretary he used sometimes to mistake them, in the halls and on the staircases where he met them, for the functionaries engaged, under stress, to usher in guests and wait at supper. It was only a little later that he perceived these latter public characters almost always to be impressive and of that rich racial hue which of itself served as a livery. At present, however, such confounding figures were much less to be met than during the months of winter, and indeed they were never frequent at Mrs. Bonnycastle's. At present the social vistas of Washington, like the vast fresh flatness of the lettered and numbered streets, which at this season seemed to Vogelstein more spacious and vague than ever, suggested but a paucity of political phenomena. Count Otto that evening knew every one or almost every one. There were often enquiring strangers, expecting great things, from New York and Boston, and to them, in the friendly Washington way, the young German was promptly introduced. It was a society in which familiarity reigned and in which people were liable to meet three times a day, so that their ultimate essence really became a matter of importance.

"I've got three new girls," Mrs. Bonnycastle said. "You must talk to them all."

"All at once?" Vogelstein asked, reversing in fancy a position not at all unknown to him. He had so repeatedly heard himself addressed in even more than triple simultaneity.

"Oh no; you must have something different for each; you can't get off that way. Haven't you discovered that the American girl expects something especially adapted to herself? It's very well for Europe to have a few phrases that will do for any girl. The American girl isn't *any* girl; she's a remarkable specimen in a remarkable species. But you must keep the best this evening for Miss Day."

"For Miss Day!"—and Vogelstein had a stare of intelligence. "Do you mean for Pandora?"

Mrs. Bonnycastle broke on her side into free amusement. "One would think you had been looking for her over the globe! So you know her already—and you call her by her pet name?"

"Oh no, I don't know her; that is I haven't seen her or thought of her from that day to this. We came to America in the same ship."

"Isn't she an American then?"

"Oh yes; she lives at Utica—in the interior."

"In the interior of Utica? You can't mean my young woman then, who lives in New York, where she's a great beauty and a great belle and has been immensely admired this winter."

"After all," said Count Otto, considering and a little disappointed, "the name's not so uncommon; it's perhaps another. But has she rather strange eyes, a little yellow, but very pretty, and a nose a little arched?"

"I can't tell you all that; I haven't seen her. She's staying with Mrs. Steuben. She only came a day or two ago, and Mrs. Steu-

ben's to bring her. When she wrote to me to ask leave she told me what I tell you. They haven't come yet."

Vogelstein felt a quick hope that the subject of this correspondence might indeed be the young lady he had parted from on the dock at New York, but the indications seemed to point another way, and he had no wish to cherish an illusion. It didn't seem to him probable that the energetic girl who had introduced him to Mr. Lansing would have the entrée of the best house in Washington; besides, Mrs. Bonnycastle's guest was described as a beauty and belonging to the brilliant city.

"What's the social position of Mrs. Steuben?" it occurred to him to ask while he meditated. He had an earnest artless literal way of putting such a question as that; you could see from it that he was very thorough.

Mrs. Bonnycastle met it, however, but with mocking laughter. "I'm sure I don't know! What's your own?"—and she left him to turn to her other guests, to several of whom she repeated his question. Could they tell her what was the social position of Mrs. Steuben? There was Count Vogelstein who wanted to know. He instantly became aware of course that he oughtn't so to have expressed himself. Wasn't the lady's place in the scale sufficiently indicated by Mrs. Bonnycastle's acquaintance with her? Still there were fine degrees, and he felt a little unduly snubbed. It was perfectly true, as he told his hostess, that with the quick wave of new impressions that had rolled over him after his arrival in America the image of Pandora was almost completely effaced; he had seen innumerable things that were quite as remarkable in their way as the heroine of the *Donau,* but at the touch of the idea that he might see her and hear her again at any moment she became as vivid in his mind as if they had parted the day before: he remembered the exact shade of the eyes he had described to Mrs. Bonnycastle as yellow, the tone of her voice when at the last she expressed the hope he might judge America correctly. *Had* he judged America correctly? If he were to meet her again she doubtless would try to ascertain. It would be going much too far to say that the idea of such an ordeal was terrible to Count Otto; but it may at least be said that the thought of meeting Pandora Day made him nervous. The fact is certainly singular, but I shall not take on myself to explain it; there are some things that even the most philosophic historian isn't bound to account for.

He wandered into another room, and there, at the end of five minutes, he was introduced by Mrs. Bonnycastle to one of the young ladies of whom she had spoken. This was a very intelligent girl who came from Boston and showed much acquaintance with Spielhagen's novels. "Do you like them?" Vogelstein asked rather vaguely,

not taking much interest in the matter, as he read works of fiction only in case of a sea-voyage. The young lady from Boston looked pensive and concentrated; then she answered that she liked *some* of them *very* much, but that there were others she didn't like — and she enumerated the works that came under each of these heads. Spielhagen is a voluminous writer, and such a catalogue took some time; at the end of it moreover Vogelstein's question was not answered, for he couldn't have told us whether she liked Spielhagen or not.

On the next topic, however, there was no doubt about her feelings. They talked about Washington as people talk only in the place itself, revolving about the subject in widening and narrowing circles, perching successively on its many branches, considering it from every point of view. Our young man had been long enough in America to discover that after half a century of social neglect Washington had become the fashion and enjoyed the great advantage of being a new resource in conversation. This was especially the case in the months of spring, when the inhabitants of the commercial cities came so far southward to escape, after the long winter, that final affront. They were all agreed that Washington was fascinating, and none of them were better prepared to talk it over than the Bostonians. Vogelstein originally had been rather out of step with them; he hadn't seized their point of view, hadn't known with what they compared this object of their infatuation. But now he knew everything; he had settled down to the pace; there wasn't a possible phase of the discussion that could find him at a loss. There was a kind of Hegelian element in it; in the light of these considerations the American capital took on the semblance of a monstrous mystical infinite *Werden*. But they fatigued Vogelstein a little, and it was his preference, as a general thing, not to engage the same evening with more than one newcomer, one visitor in the freshness of initiation. This was why Mrs. Bonnycastle's expression of a wish to introduce him to three young ladies had startled him a little; he saw a certain process, in which he flattered himself that he had become proficient, but which was after all tolerably exhausting, repeated for each of the damsels. After separating from his judicious Bostonian he rather evaded Mrs. Bonnycastle, contenting himself with the conversation of old friends, pitched for the most part in a lower and easier key.

At last he heard it mentioned that the President had arrived, had been some half-hour in the house, and he went in search of the illustrious guest, whose whereabouts at Washington parties was never indicated by a cluster of courtiers. He made it a point, whenever he found himself in company with the President, to pay him his respects, and he had not been dis-

couraged by the fact that there was no association of ideas in the eye of the great man as he put out his hand presidentially and said "Happy to meet you, sir." Count Otto felt himself taken for a mere loyal subject, possibly for an office-seeker; and he used to reflect at such moments that the monarchical form had its merits: it provided a line of heredity for the faculty of quick recognition. He had now some difficulty in finding the chief magistrate, and ended by learning that he was in the tea-room, a small apartment devoted to light refection near the entrance of the house. Here our young man presently perceived him seated on a sofa and in conversation with a lady. There were a number of people about the table, eating, drinking, talking; and the couple on the sofa, which was not near it but against the wall, in a shallow recess, looked a little withdrawn, as if they had sought seclusion and were disposed to profit by the diverted attention of the others. The President leaned back; his gloved hands, resting on either knee, made large white spots. He looked eminent, but he looked relaxed, and the lady beside him ministered freely and without scruple, it was clear, to this effect of his comfortably unbending. Vogelstein caught her voice as he approached. He heard her say "Well now, remember; I consider it a promise." She was beautifully dressed, in rose-colour; her hands were clasped in her lap and her eyes attached to the presidential profile.

"Well, madam, in that case it's about the fiftieth promise I've given to-day."

It was just as he heard these words, uttered by her companion in reply, that Count Otto checked himself, turned away and pretended to be looking for a cup of tea. It wasn't usual to disturb the President, even simply to shake hands, when he was sitting on a sofa with a lady, and the young secretary felt it in this case less possible than ever to break the rule, for the lady on the sofa was none other than Pandora Day. He had recognised her without her appearing to see him, and even with half an eye, as they said, had taken in that she was now a person to be reckoned with. She had an air of elation, of success; she shone, to intensity, in her rose-coloured dress; she was extracting promises from the ruler of fifty millions of people. What an odd place to meet her, her old shipmate thought, and how little one could tell, after all, in America, who people were! He didn't want to speak to her yet; he wanted to wait a little and learn more; but meanwhile there was something attractive in the fact that she was just beyond him, a few yards off, that if he should turn he might see her again. It was she Mrs. Bonnycastle had meant, it was she who was so much admired in New York. Her face was the same, yet he had made out in a moment that she was vaguely prettier; he had recognised the arch of her nose, which suggested a fine ambition. He took some tea, which he hadn't desired, in order not to go away. He remembered her *entourage* on the steamer; her father and mother, the silent senseless burghers, so little "of the world," her infant sister, so much of it, her humorous brother with his tall hat and his influence in the smoking-room. He remembered Mrs. Dangerfield's warnings — yet her perplexities too — and the letter from Mr. Bellamy, and the introduction to Mr. Lansing, and the way Pandora had stooped down on the dirty dock, laughing and talking, mistress of the situation, to open her trunk for the Customs. He was pretty sure she had paid no duties that day; this would naturally have been the purpose of Mr. Bellamy's letter. Was she still in correspondence with that gentleman, and had he got over the sickness interfering with their reunion? These images and these questions coursed through Count Otto's mind, and he saw it must be quite in Pandora's line to be mistress of the situation, for there was evidently nothing on the present occasion that could call itself her master. He drank his tea and as he put down his cup heard the President, behind him, say: "Well, I guess my wife will wonder why I don't come home."

"Why didn't you bring her with you?" Pandora benevolently asked.

"Well, she doesn't go out much. Then she has got her sister staying with her — Mrs. Runkle, from Natchez. She's a good deal of an invalid, and my wife doesn't like to leave her."

"She must be a very kind woman" — and there was a high mature competence in the way the girl sounded the note of approval.

"Well, I guess she isn't spoiled — yet."

"I should like very much to come and see her," said Pandora.

"Do come round. Couldn't you come some night?" the great man responded.

"Well, I'll come some time. And I shall remind you of your promise."

"All right. There's nothing like keeping it up. Well," said the President, "I must bid good-bye to these bright folks."

Vogelstein heard him rise from the sofa with his companion; after which he gave the pair time to pass out of the room before him. They did it with a certain impressive deliberation, people making way for the ruler of fifty millions and looking with a certain curiosity at the striking pink person at his side. When a little later he followed them across the hall, into one of the other rooms, he saw the host and hostess accompany the President to the door and two foreign ministers and a judge of the Supreme Court address themselves to Pandora Day. He resisted the impulse to join this circle: if he should speak to her at all he would

somehow wish it to be in more privacy. She continued nevertheless to occupy him, and when Mrs. Bonnycastle came back from the hall he immediately approached her with an appeal. "I wish you'd tell me something more about that girl — that one opposite and in pink."

"The lovely Day — that's what they call her, I believe? I wanted you to talk with her."

"I find she is the one I've met. But she seems to be so different here. I can't make it out," said Count Otto.

There was something in his expression that again moved Mrs. Bonnycastle to mirth. "How we do puzzle you Europeans! You look quite bewildered."

"I'm sorry I look so — I try to hide it. But of course we're very simple. Let me ask then a simple earnest childlike question. Are her parents also in society?"

"Parents in society? D'où tombez-vous? Did you ever hear of the parents of a triumphant girl in rose-colour, with a nose all her own, in society?"

"Is she then all alone?" he went on with a strain of melancholy in his voice.

Mrs. Bonnycastle launched at him all her laughter. "You're too pathetic. Don't you know what she is? I supposed of course you knew."

"It's exactly what I'm asking you."

"Why she's the new type. It has only come up lately. They have had articles about it in the papers. That's the reason I told Mrs. Steuben to bring her."

"The new type? *What* new type, Mrs. Bonnycastle?" he returned pleadingly — so conscious was he that all types in America were new.

Her laughter checked her reply a moment, and by the time she had recovered herself the young lady from Boston, with whom Vogelstein had been talking, stood there to take leave. This, for an American type, was an old one, he was sure; and the process of parting between the guest and her hostess had an ancient elaboration. Count Otto waited a little; then he turned away and walked up to Pandora Day, whose group of interlocutors had now been re-enforced by a gentleman who had held an important place in the cabinet of the late occupant of the presidential chair. He had asked Mrs. Bonnycastle if she were "all alone"; but there was nothing in her present situation to show her for solitary. She wasn't sufficiently alone for our friend's taste; but he was impatient and he hoped she'd give him a few words to himself. She recognised him without a moment's hesitation and with the sweetest smile, a smile matching to a shade the tone in which she said: "I was watching you. I wondered if you weren't going to speak to me."

"Miss Day was watching him!" one of the foreign ministers exclaimed; "and we flattered our-

selves that her attention was all with us."

"I mean before," said the girl, "while I was talking with the President."

At which the gentlemen began to laugh, one of them remarking that this was the way the absent were sacrificed, even the great; while another put on record that he hoped Vogelstein was duly flattered.

"Oh I was watching the President too," said Pandora. "I've got to watch *him*. He has promised me something."

"It must be the mission to England," the judge of the Supreme Court suggested. "A good position for a lady; they've got a lady at the head over there."

"I wish they would send you to *my* country," one of the foreign ministers suggested. "I'd immediately get recalled."

"Why perhaps in your country I wouldn't speak to you! It's only because you're here," the ex-heroine of the *Donau* returned with a gay familiarity which evidently ranked with her but as one of the arts of defence. "You'll see what mission it is when it comes out. But I'll speak to Count Vogelstein anywhere," she went on. "He's an older friend than any right here. I've known him in difficult days."

"Oh, yes, on the great ocean," the young man smiled. "On the watery waste, in the tempest!"

"Oh I don't mean that so much; we had a beautiful voyage and there wasn't any tempest. I mean when I was living in Utica. That's a watery waste if you like, and a tempest there would have been a pleasant variety."

"Your parents seemed to me so peaceful!" her associate in the other memories sighed with a vague wish to say something sympathetic.

"Oh you haven't seen them ashore! At Utica they were very lively. But that's no longer our natural home. Don't you remember I told you I was working for New York? Well, I worked — I had to work hard. But we've moved."

Count Otto clung to his interest. "And I hope they're happy."

"My father and mother? Oh they will be, in time. I must give them time. They're very young yet, they've years before them. And you've been always in Washington?" Pandora continued. "I suppose you've found out everything about everything."

"Oh no — there are some things I *can't* find out."

"Come and see me and perhaps I can help you. I'm very different from what I was in that phase. I've advanced a great deal since then."

"Oh how was Miss Day in that phase?" asked a cabinet minister of the last administration.

"She was delightful of course," Count Otto said.

"He's very flattering; I didn't open my mouth!" Pandora cried. "Here comes Mrs. Steuben to take me to some other place. I believe it's a literary party near the Capitol. Everything seems so separate

in Washington. Mrs. Steuben's going to read a poem. I wish she'd read it here; wouldn't it do as well?"

This lady, arriving, signified to her young friend the necessity of their moving on. But Miss Day's companions had various things to say to her before giving her up. She had a vivid answer for each, and it was brought home to Vogelstein while he listened that this would be indeed, in her development, as she said, another phase. Daughter of small burghers as she might be she was really brilliant. He turned away a little and while Mrs. Steuben waited put her a question. He had made her half an hour before the subject of that enquiry to which Mrs. Bonnycastle returned so ambiguous an answer; but this wasn't because he failed of all direct acquaintance with the amiable woman or of any general idea of the esteem in which she was held. He had met her in various places and had been at her house. She was the widow of a commodore, was a handsome mild soft swaying person, whom every one liked, with glossy bands of black hair and a little ringlet depending behind each ear. Some one had said that she looked like the *vieux jeu* idea of the queen in "Hamlet." She had written verses which were admired in the South, wore a full-length portrait of the commodore on her bosom and spoke with the accent of Savannah. She had about her a positive strong odour of Washington. It had certainly been very superfluous in our young man to question Mrs. Bonnycastle about her social position.

"Do kindly tell me," he said, lowering his voice, "what's the type to which that young lady belongs? Mrs. Bonnycastle tells me it's a new one."

Mrs. Steuben for a moment fixed her liquid eyes on the secretary of legation. She always seemed to be translating the prose of your speech into the finer rhythms with which her own mind was familiar. "Do you think anything's really new?" she then began to flute. "I'm very fond of the old; you know that's a weakness of we Southerners." The poor lady, it will be observed, had another weakness as well. "What we often take to be the new is simply the old under some novel form. Were there not remarkable natures in the past? If you doubt it you should visit the South, where the past still lingers."

Vogelstein had been struck before this with Mrs. Steuben's pronunciation of the word by which her native latitudes were designated; transcribing it from her lips you would have written it (as the nearest approach) the Sooth. But at present he scarce heeded this peculiarity; he was wondering rather how a woman could be at once so copious and so uninforming. What did he care about the past or even about the Sooth? He was afraid of starting her again. He looked at her, discouraged and helpless, as bewildered almost as Mrs. Bonnycastle had found him

half an hour before; looked also at the commodore, who, on her bosom, seemed to breathe again with his widow's respirations. "Call it an old type then if you like," he said in a moment. "All I want to know is what type it *is!* It seems impossible," he gasped, "to find out."

"You can find out in the newspapers. They've had articles about it. They write about everything now. But it isn't true about Miss Day. It's one of the first families. Her great-grandfather was in the Revolution." Pandora by this time had given her attention again to Mrs. Steuben. She seemed to signify that she was ready to move on. "Wasn't your great-grandfather in the Revolution?" the elder lady asked. "I'm telling Count Vogelstein about him."

"Why are you asking about my ancestors?" the girl demanded of the young German with untempered brightness. "Is that the thing you said just now that you can't find out? Well, if Mrs. Steuben will only be quiet you never will."

Mrs. Steuben shook her head rather dreamily. "Well, it's no trouble for we of the South to be quiet. There's a kind of languor in our blood. Besides, we have to be to-day. But I've got to show some energy to-night. I've got to get you to the end of Pennsylvania Avenue."

Pandora gave her hand to Count Otto and asked him if he thought they should meet again. He answered that in Washington people were always meeting again and that at any rate he shouldn't fail to wait upon her. Hereupon, just as the two ladies were detaching themselves, Mrs. Steuben remarked that if the Count and Miss Day wished to meet again the picnic would be a good chance — the picnic she was getting up for the following Thursday. It was to consist of about twenty bright people, and they'd go down the Potomac to Mount Vernon. The Count answered that if Mrs. Steuben thought him bright enough he should be delighted to join the party; and he was told the hour for which the tryst was taken.

He remained at Mrs. Bonnycastle's after every one had gone, and then he informed this lady of his reason for waiting. Would she have mercy on him and let him know, in a single word, before he went to rest — for without it rest would be impossible — what was this famous type to which Pandora Day belonged?

"Gracious, you don't mean to say you've not found out that type yet!" Mrs. Bonnycastle exclaimed with a return of her hilarity. "What have you been doing all the evening? You Germans may be thorough, but you certainly are not quick!"

It was Alfred Bonnycastle who at last took pity on him. "My dear Vogelstein, she's the latest freshest fruit of our great American evolution. She's the self-made girl!"

Count Otto gazed a moment. "The fruit of the great American Revolution? Yes, Mrs. Steuben told me her great-grandfather — " but the rest of his sentence was lost in a renewed explosion of Mrs. Bonnycastle's sense of the ridiculous. He bravely pushed his advantage, such as it was, however, and, desiring his host's definition to be defined, enquired what the self-made girl might be.

"Sit down and we'll tell you all about it," Mrs. Bonnycastle said. "I like talking this way, after a party's over. You can smoke if you like, and Alfred will open another window. Well, to begin with, the self-made girl's a new feature. That, however, you know. In the second place she isn't self-made at all. We all help to make her — we take such an interest in her."

"That's only after she's made!" Alfred Bonnycastle broke in. "But it's Vogelstein that takes an interest. What on earth has started you up so on the subject of Miss Day?"

The visitor explained as well as he could that it was merely the accident of his having crossed the ocean in the steamer with her; but he felt the inadequacy of this account of the matter, felt it more than his hosts, who could know neither how little actual contact he had had with her on the ship, how much he had been affected by Mrs. Dangerfield's warnings, nor how much observation at the same time he had lavished on her. He sat there half an hour, and the warm dead stillness of the Washington night — nowhere are the nights so silent — came in at the open window, mingled with a soft sweet earthy smell, the smell of growing things and in particular, as he thought, of Mrs. Steuben's Sooth. Before he went away he had heard all about the self-made girl, and there was something in the picture that strongly impressed him. She was possible doubtless only in America; American life had smoothed the way for her. She was not fast, nor emancipated, nor crude, nor loud, and there wasn't in her, of necessity at least, a grain of the stuff of which the adventuress is made. She was simply very successful, and her success was entirely personal. She hadn't been born with the silver spoon of social opportunity; she had grasped it by honest exertion. You knew her by many different signs, but chiefly, infallibly, by the appearance of her parents. It was her parents who told her story; you always saw how little her parents could have made her. Her attitude with regard to them might vary in different ways. As the great fact on her own side was that she had lifted herself from a lower social plane, done it all herself, and done it by the simple lever of her personality, it was naturally to be expected that she would leave the authors of her mere material being in the shade. Sometimes she had them in her wake, lost in the bubbles and the foam that showed where she had passed; sometimes, as Alfred Bonnycastle said, she let them slide altogether; sometimes she kept them in close confinement, resorting to them under cover of night and with every precaution; sometimes she exhibited them to the public in discreet glimpses, in prearranged attitudes. But the general characteristic of the self-made girl was that, though it was frequently understood that she was privately devoted to her kindred, she never attempted to impose them on society, and it was striking that, though in some of her manifestations a bore, she was at her worst less of a bore than they. They were almost always solemn and portentous, and they were for the most part of a deathly respectability. She wasn't necessarily snobbish, unless it was snobbish to want the best. She didn't cringe, she didn't make herself smaller than she was; she took on the contrary a stand of her own and attracted things to herself. Naturally she was possible only in America — only in a country where whole ranges of competition and comparison were absent. The natural history of this interesting creature was at last completely laid bare to the earnest stranger, who, as he sat there in the animated stillness, with the fragrant breath of the Western world in his nostrils, was convinced of what he had already suspected, that conversation in the great Republic was more yearningly, not to say gropingly, psychological than elsewhere. Another thing, as he learned, that you knew the self-made girl by was her culture, which was perhaps a little too restless and obvious. She had usually got into society more or less by reading, and her conversation was apt to be garnished with literary allusions, even with familiar quota-

413

tions. Vogelstein hadn't had time to observe this element as a developed form in Pandora Day; but Alfred Bonnycastle hinted that he wouldn't trust her to keep it under in a *tête-à-tête*. It was needless to say that these young persons had always been to Europe; that was usually the first place they got to. By such arts they sometimes entered society on the other side before they did so at home; it was to be added at the same time that this resource was less and less valuable, for Europe, in the American world, had less and less prestige and people in the Western hemisphere now kept a watch on that roundabout road. All of which quite applied to Pandora Day — the journey to Europe, the culture (as exemplified in the books she read on the ship), the relegation, the effacement, of the family. The only thing that was exceptional was the rapidity of her march; for the jump she had taken since he left her in the hands of Mr. Lansing struck Vogelstein, even after he had made all allowance for the abnormal homogeneity of the American mass, as really considerable. It took all her cleverness to account for such things. When she "moved" from Utica — mobilised her commissariat — the battle appeared virtually to have been gained.

Count Otto called the next day, and Mrs. Steuben's blackamoor informed him, in the communicative manner of his race, that the ladies had gone out to pay some visits and look at the Capitol.

Pandora apparently had not hitherto examined this monument, and our young man wished he had known, the evening before, of her omission, so that he might have offered to be her initiator. There is too obvious a connexion for us to fail of catching it between his regret and the fact that in leaving Mrs. Steuben's door he reminded himself that he wanted a good walk, and that he thereupon took his way along Pennsylvania Avenue. His walk had become fairly good by the time he reached the great white edifice that unfolds its repeated colonnades and uplifts its isolated dome at the end of a long vista of saloons and tobacco-shops. He slowly climbed the great steps, hesitating a little, even wondering why he had come. The superficial reason was obvious enough, but there was a real one behind it that struck him as rather wanting in the solidity which should characterise the motives of an emissary of Prince Bismarck. The superficial reason was a belief that Mrs. Steuben would pay her visit first — it was probably only a question of leaving cards — and bring her young friend to the Capitol at the hour when the yellow afternoon light would give a tone to the blankness of its marble walls. The Capitol was a splendid building, but it was rather wanting in tone. Vogelstein's curiosity about Pandora Day had been much more quickened than checked by the revelations made to him in Mrs. Bonnycastle's drawing-room. It was a relief to have the creature

414

classified; but he had a desire, of which he had not been conscious before, to see really to the end how well, in other words how completely and artistically, a girl could make herself. His calculations had been just, and he had wandered about the rotunda for only ten minutes, looking again at the paintings, commemorative of the national annals, which occupy its lower spaces, and at the simulated sculptures, so touchingly characteristic of early American taste, which adorn its upper reaches, when the charming women he had been counting on presented themselves in charge of a licensed guide. He went to meet them and didn't conceal from them that he had marked them for his very own. The encounter was happy on both sides, and he accompanied them through the queer and endless interior, through labyrinths of bleak bare development, into legislative and judicial halls. He thought it a hideous place; he had seen it all before and asked himself what senseless game he was playing. In the lower House were certain bedaubed walls, in the basest style of imitation, which made him feel faintly sick, not to speak of a lobby adorned with artless prints and photographs of eminent defunct Congressmen that was all too serious for a joke and too comic for a Valhalla. But Pandora was greatly interested; she thought the Capitol very fine; it was easy to criticise the details, but as a whole it was the most impressive build-

ing she had ever seen. She proved a charming fellow tourist; she had constantly something to say, but never said it too much; it was impossible to drag in the wake of a *cicerone* less of a lengthening or an irritating chain. Vogelstein could see too that she wished to improve her mind; she looked at the historical pictures, at the uncanny statues of local worthies, presented by the different States — they were of different sizes, as if they had been "numbered," in a shop — she asked questions of the guide and in the chamber of the Senate requested him to show her the chairs of the gentlemen from New York. She sat down in one of them, though Mrs. Steuben told her *that* Senator (she mistook the chair, dropping into another State) was a horrid old thing.

Throughout the hour he spent with her Vogelstein seemed to see how it was she had made herself. They walked about afterwards on the splendid terrace that surrounds the Capitol, the great marble floor on which it stands, and made vague remarks — Pandora's were the most definite — about the yellow sheen of the Potomac, the hazy hills of Virginia, the far-gleaming pediment of Arlington, the raw confused-looking country. Washington was beneath them, bristling and geometrical; the long lines of its avenues seemed to stretch into national futures. Pandora asked Count Otto if he had ever been to Athens and, on his admitting so much, sought to know whether the eminence on which they stood didn't give him an idea of the Acropolis in its prime. Vogelstein deferred the satisfaction of this appeal to their next meeting; he was glad — in spite of the appeal — to make pretexts for seeing her again. He did so on the morrow; Mrs. Steuben's picnic was still three days distant. He called on Pandora a second time, also met her each evening in the Washington world. It took very little of this to remind him that he was forgetting both Mrs. Dangerfield's warnings and the admonitions — long familiar to him — of his own conscience. Was he in peril of love? Was he to be sacrificed on the altar of the American girl, an altar at which those other poor fellows had poured out some of the bluest blood in Germany and he had himself taken oath he would never seriously worship? He decided that he wasn't in real danger, that he had rather clinched his precautions. It was true that a young person who had succeeded so well for herself might be a great help to her husband; but this diplomatic aspirant preferred on the whole that his success should be his own: it wouldn't please him to have the air of being pushed by his wife. Such a wife as that would wish to push him, and he could hardly admit to himself that this was what fate had in reserve for him — to be propelled in his career by a young lady who would perhaps attempt to talk to the Kaiser as he had heard her the other night talk to the President. Would she consent to discontinue rela-

tions with her family, or would she wish still to borrow plastic relief from that domestic background? That her family was so impossible was to a certain extent an advantage; for if they had been a little better the question of a rupture would be less easy. He turned over these questions in spite of his security, or perhaps indeed because of it. The security made them speculative and disinterested.

They haunted him during the excursion to Mount Vernon, which took place according to traditions long established. Mrs. Steuben's confederates assembled on the steamer and were set afloat on the big brown stream which had already seemed to our special traveller to have too much bosom and too little bank. Here and there, however, he became conscious of a shore where there was something to look at, even though conscious at the same time that he had of old lost great opportunities of an idyllic cast in not having managed to be more "thrown with" a certain young lady on the deck of the North German Lloyd. The two turned round together to hang over Alexandria, which for Pandora, as she declared, was a picture of Old Virginia. She told Vogelstein that she was always hearing about it during the Civil War, ages before. Little girl as she had been at the time she remembered all the names that were on people's lips during those years of reiteration. This historic spot had a touch of the romance of rich de-

Pandora

cay, a reference to older things, to a dramatic past. The past of Alexandria appeared in the vista of three or four short streets sloping up a hill and lined with poor brick warehouses erected for merchandise that had ceased to come or go. It looked hot and blank and sleepy, down to the shabby waterside where tattered darkies dangled their bare feet from the edge of rotting wharves. Pandora was even more interested in Mount Vernon — when at last its wooded bluff began to command the river — than she had been in the Capitol, and after they had disembarked and ascended to the celebrated mansion she insisted on going into every room it contained. She "claimed for it," as she said — some of her turns were so characteristic both of her nationality and her own style — the finest situation in the world, and was distinct as to the shame of their not giving it to the President for his country-seat. Most of her companions had seen the house often, and were now coupling themselves in the grounds according to their sympathies, so that it was easy for Vogelstein to offer the benefit of his own experience to the most inquisitive member of the party. They were not to lunch for another hour, and in the interval the young man roamed with his first and fairest acquaintance. The breath of the Potomac, on the boat, had been a little harsh, but on the softly-curving lawn, beneath the clustered trees, with the river relegated to a mere shining

presence far below and in the distance, the day gave out nothing but its mildness, the whole scene became noble and genial.

Count Otto could joke a little on great occasions, and the present one was worthy of his humour. He maintained to his companion that the shallow painted mansion resembled a false house, a "wing" or structure of daubed canvas, on the stage; but she answered him so well with certain economical palaces she had seen in Germany, where, as she said, there was nothing but china stoves and stuffed birds, that he was obliged to allow the home of Washington to be after all really *gemüthlich*. What he found so in fact was the soft texture of the day, his personal situation, the sweetness of his suspense. For suspense had decidedly become his portion; he was under a charm that made him feel he was watching his own life and that his susceptibilities were beyond his control. It hung over him that things might take a turn, from one hour to the other, which would make them very different from what they had been yet; and his heart certainly beat a little faster as he wondered what that turn might be. Why did he come to picnics on fragrant April days with American girls who might lead him too far? Wouldn't such girls be glad to marry a Pomeranian count? And *would* they, after all, talk that way to the Kaiser? If he were to marry one of them he should have to give her several thorough lessons.

417

Pandora

In their little tour of the house our young friend and his companion had had a great many fellow visitors, who had also arrived by the steamer and who had hitherto not left them an ideal privacy. But the others gradually dispersed; they circled about a kind of showman who was the authorised guide, a big slow genial vulgar heavily-bearded man, with a whimsical edifying patronising tone, a tone that had immense success when he stopped here and there to make his points — to pass his eyes over his listening flock, then fix them quite above it with a meditative look and bring out some ancient pleasantry as if it were a sudden inspiration. He made a cheerful thing, an echo of the platform before the booth of a country fair, even of a visit to the tomb of the *pater patriæ*. It is enshrined in a kind of grotto in the grounds, and Vogelstein remarked to Pandora that he was a good man for the place, but was too familiar. "Oh he'd have been familiar with Washington," said the girl with the bright dryness with which she often uttered amusing things. Vogelstein looked at her a moment, and it came over him, as he smiled, that she herself probably wouldn't have been abashed even by the hero with whom history has taken fewest liberties. "You look as if you could hardly believe that," Pandora went on. "You Germans are always in such awe of great people." And it occurred to her critic that perhaps after all Washington would have liked her manner, which was wonderfully fresh and natural. The man with the beard was an ideal minister to American shrines; he played on the curiosity of his little band with the touch of a master, drawing them at the right moment away to see the classic ice-house where the old lady had been found weeping in the belief it was Washington's grave. While this monument was under inspection our interesting couple had the house to themselves, and they spent some time on a pretty terrace where certain windows of the second floor opened — a little roofless verandah which overhung, in a manner, obliquely, all the magnificence of the view; the immense sweep of the river, the artistic plantations, the last-century garden with its big box hedges and remains of old espaliers. They lingered here for nearly half an hour, and it was in this retirement that Vogelstein enjoyed the only approach to intimate conversation appointed for him, as was to appear, with a young woman in whom he had been unable to persuade himself that he was not absorbed. It's not necessary, and it's not possible, that I should reproduce this colloquy; but I may mention that it began — as they leaned against the parapet of the terrace and heard the cheerful voice of the showman wafted up to them from a distance — with his saying to her rather abruptly that he couldn't make out why they hadn't had more talk together when they crossed the Atlantic.

"Well, I can if you can't," said Pandora. "I'd have talked quick enough if you had spoken to me. I spoke to you first."

"Yes, I remember that" — and it affected him awkwardly.

"You listened too much to Mrs. Dangerfield."

He feigned a vagueness. "To Mrs. Dangerfield?"

"That woman you were always sitting with; she told you not to speak to me. I've seen her in New York; she speaks to me now herself. She recommended you to have nothing to do with me."

"Oh how can you say such dreadful things?" Count Otto cried with a very becoming blush.

"You know you can't deny it. You weren't attracted by my family. They're charming people when you know them. I don't have a better time anywhere than I have at home," the girl went on loyally. "But what does it matter? My family are very happy. They're getting quite used to New York. Mrs. Dangerfield's a vulgar wretch — next winter she'll call on me."

"You are unlike any Mädchen I've ever seen — I don't understand you," said poor Vogelstein with the colour still in his face.

"Well, you never *will* understand me — probably; but what difference does it make?"

He attempted to tell her what difference, but I've no space to follow him here. It's known that when the German mind attempts to explain things it doesn't always reduce them to simplicity, and Pandora was first mystified, then amused, by some of the Count's revelations. At last I think she was a little frightened, for she remarked irrelevantly, with some decision, that luncheon would be ready and that they ought to join Mrs. Steuben. Her companion walked slowly, on purpose, as they left the house together, for he knew the pang of a vague sense that he was losing her.

"And shall you be in Washington many days yet?" he appealed as they went.

"It will all depend. I'm expecting important news. What I shall do will be influenced by that."

The way she talked about expecting news — and important! — made him feel somehow that she had a career, that she was active and independent, so that he could scarcely hope to stop her as she passed. It was certainly true that he had never seen any girl like her. It would have occurred to him that the news she was expecting might have reference to the favour she had begged of the President, if he hadn't already made up his mind — in the calm of meditation after that talk with the Bonnycastles — that this favour must be a pleasantry. What she had said to him had a discouraging, a somewhat chilling effect; nevertheless it was not without a certain ardour that he enquired of her whether, so long as she stayed in Washington, he mightn't pay her certain respectful attentions.

"As many as you like — and as respectful ones; but you won't keep them up for ever!"

"You try to torment me," said Count Otto.

She waited to explain. "I mean that I may have some of my family."

"I shall be delighted to see them again."

Again she just hung fire. "There are some you've never seen."

In the afternoon, returning to Washington on the steamer, Vogelstein received a warning. It came from Mrs. Bonnycastle and constituted, oddly enough, the second juncture at which an officious female friend had, while sociably afloat with him, advised him on the subject of Pandora Day.

"There's one thing we forgot to tell you the other night about the self-made girl," said the lady of infinite mirth. "It's never safe to fix your affections on her, because she has almost always an impediment somewhere in the background."

He looked at her askance, but smiled and said: "I should understand your information — for which I'm so much obliged — a little better if I knew what you mean by an impediment."

"Oh I mean she's always engaged to some young man who belongs to her earlier phase."

"Her earlier phase?"

"The time before she had made herself — when she lived unconscious of her powers. A young man from Utica, say. They usually have to wait; he's probably in a store. It's a long engagement."

Count Otto somehow preferred to understand as little as possible. "Do you mean a betrothal — to take effect?"

"I don't mean anything German and moonstruck. I mean that piece of peculiarly American enterprise a premature engagement — to take effect, but too complacently, at the end of time."

Vogelstein very properly reflected that it was no use his having entered the diplomatic career if he weren't able to bear himself as if this interesting generalisation had no particular message for him. He did Mrs. Bonnycastle moreover the justice to believe that she wouldn't have approached the question with such levity if she had supposed she should make him wince. The whole thing was, like everything else, but for her to laugh at, and the betrayal moreover of a good intention. "I see, I see — the self-made girl has of course always had a past. Yes, and the young man in the store — from Utica — is part of her past."

"You express it perfectly," said Mrs. Bonnycastle. "I couldn't say it better myself."

"But with her present, with her future, when they change like this young lady's, I suppose everything else changes. How do you say it in America? She lets him slide."

"We don't say it at all!" Mrs. Bonnycastle cried. "She does nothing of the sort; for what do you take her? She sticks to him; that at least is what we *expect* her to do," she added with less assurance. "As I tell you, the type's new and the case under consideration. We haven't yet had time for complete study."

"Oh of course I hope she sticks to him," Vogelstein declared simply and with his German accent more audible, as it always was when he was slightly agitated. For the rest of the trip he was rather restless. He wandered about the boat, talking little with the returning picnickers. Toward the last, as they drew near Washington and the white dome of the Capitol hung aloft before them, looking as simple as a suspended snowball, he found himself, on the deck, in proximity to Mrs. Steuben. He reproached himself with having rather neglected her during an entertainment for which he was indebted to her bounty, and he sought to repair his omission by a proper deference. But the only act of homage that occurred to him was to ask her as by chance whether Miss Day were, to her knowledge, engaged.

Mrs. Steuben turned her Southern eyes upon him with a look of almost romantic compassion. "To my knowledge? Why of course I'd know! I should think you'd know too. Didn't you know she was engaged? Why she has been engaged since she was sixteen."

Count Otto gazed at the dome of the Capitol. "To a gentleman from Utica?"

"Yes, a native of her place. She's expecting him soon."

"I'm so very glad to hear it," said Vogelstein, who decidedly, for his career, had promise. "And is she going to marry him?"

"Why what do people fall in love with each other *for?* I presume they'll marry when she gets round to it. Ah if she had only been from the Sooth — !"

At this he broke quickly in: "But why have they never brought it off, as you say, in so many years?"

"Well, at first she was too young, and then she thought her family ought to see Europe — of course they could see it better *with* her — and they spent some time there. And then Mr. Bellamy had some business difficulties that made him feel as if he didn't want to marry just then. But he has given up business and I presume feels more free. Of course it's rather long, but all the while they've been engaged. It's a true, true love," said Mrs. Steuben, whose sound of the adjective was that of a feeble flute.

"Is his name Mr. Bellamy?" the Count asked with his haunting reminiscence. "D. F. Bellamy, so? And has he been in a store?"

"I don't know what kind of business it was: it was some kind of business in Utica. I think he had a branch in New York. He's one of the leading gentlemen of Utica and very highly educated. He's a good deal older than Miss Day. He's a very fine man — I presume a college man. He stands very high in Utica. I don't know why you look as if you doubted it."

Vogelstein assured Mrs. Steuben that he doubted nothing, and indeed what she told him was probably the more credible for seeming to him eminently strange. Bellamy had been the name of the gentleman who, a year and a half before, was to have met Pandora on the arrival of the German steamer; it was in Bellamy's name that she had addressed herself with such effusion to Bellamy's friend, the man in the straw hat who was about to fumble in her mother's old clothes. This was a fact that seemed to Count Otto to finish the picture of her contradictions; it wanted at present no touch to be complete. Yet even as it hung there before him it continued to fascinate him, and he stared at it, detached from surrounding things and feeling a little as if he had been pitched out of an overturned vehicle, till the boat bumped against one of the outstanding piles of the wharf at which Mrs. Steuben's party was to disembark. There was some delay in getting the steamer adjusted to the dock, during which the passengers watched the process over its side and extracted what entertainment they might from the appearance of the various persons collected to receive it. There were darkies and loafers and hackmen, and also vague individuals, the loosest and blankest he had ever seen anywhere, with tufts on their chins, toothpicks in their mouths, hands in their pockets, rumination in their jaws and diamond pins in their shirt-fronts, who looked as if they had sauntered over from

Pennsylvania Avenue to while away half an hour, forsaking for that interval their various slanting postures in the porticoes of the hotels and the doorways of the saloons.

"Oh I'm so glad! How sweet of you to come down!" It was a voice close to Count Otto's shoulder that spoke these words, and he had no need to turn to see from whom it proceeded. It had been in his ears the greater part of the day, though, as he now perceived, without the fullest richness of expression of which it was capable. Still less was he obliged to turn to discover to whom it was addressed, for the few simple words I have quoted had been flung across the narrowing interval of water, and a gentleman who had stepped to the edge of the dock without our young man's observing him tossed back an immediate reply.

"I got here by the three o'clock train. They told me in K Street where you were, and I thought I'd come down and meet you."

"Charming attention!" said Pandora Day with the laugh that seemed always to invite the whole of any company to partake in it; though for some moments after this she and her interlocutor appeared to continue the conversation only with their eyes. Meanwhile Vogelstein's also were not idle. He looked at her visitor from head to foot, and he was aware that she was quite unconscious of his own proximity. The gentleman before him was tall, good-looking, well-dressed; evidently he would stand well not only at Utica, but, judging from the way he had planted himself on the dock, in any position that circumstances might compel him to take up. He was about forty years old; he had a black moustache and he seemed to look at the world over some counter-like expanse on which he invited it all warily and pleasantly to put down first its idea of the terms of a transaction. He waved a gloved hand at Pandora as if, when she exclaimed "Gracious, ain't they long!" to urge her to be patient. She was patient several seconds and then asked him if he had any news. He looked at her briefly, in silence, smiling, after which he drew from his pocket a large letter with an official-looking seal and shook it jocosely above his head. This was discreetly, covertly done. No one but our young man appeared aware of how much was taking place — and poor Count Otto mainly felt it in the air. The boat was touching the wharf and the space between the pair inconsiderable.

"Department of State?" Pandora very prettily and soundlessly mouthed across at him.

"That's what they call it."

"Well, what country?"

"What's your opinion of the Dutch?" the gentleman asked for answer.

"Oh gracious!" cried Pandora.

"Well, are you going to wait for the return trip?" said the gentleman.

Our silent sufferer turned away, and presently Mrs. Steuben and her companion disembarked together. When this lady entered a carriage with Miss Day the gentleman who had spoken to the girl followed them; the others scattered, and Vogelstein, declining with thanks a "lift" from Mrs. Bonnycastle, walked home alone and in some intensity of meditation. Two days later he saw in a newspaper an announcement that the President had offered the post of Minister to Holland to Mr. D. F. Bellamy of Utica; and in the course of a month he heard from Mrs. Steuben that Pandora, a thousand other duties performed, had finally "got round" to the altar of her own nuptials. He communicated this news to Mrs. Bonnycastle, who had not heard it but who, shrieking at the queer face he showed her, met it with the remark that there was now ground for a new induction as to the self-made girl.

THE BOSTONIANS

"OLIVE will come down in about ten minutes; she told me to tell you that. About ten; that is exactly like Olive. Neither five nor fifteen, and yet not ten exactly, but either nine or eleven. She didn't tell me to say she was glad to see you, because she doesn't know whether she is or not, and she wouldn't for the world expose herself to telling a fib. She is very honest, is Olive Chancellor; she is full of rectitude. Nobody tells fibs in Boston; I don't know what to make of them all. Well, I am very glad to see you, at any rate."

These words were spoken with much volubility by a fair, plump, smiling woman who entered a narrow drawing-room in which a visitor, kept waiting for a few moments, was already absorbed in a book. The gentleman had not even needed to sit down to become interested: apparently he had taken up the volume from a table as soon as he came in, and, standing there, after a single glance round the apartment, had lost himself in its pages. He threw it down at the approach of Mrs. Luna, laughed, shook hands with her, and said in answer to her last remark, "You imply that you do tell fibs. Perhaps that is one."

"Oh no; there is nothing wonderful in my being glad to see you," Mrs. Luna rejoined, "when I tell you that I have been three long weeks in this unprevaricating city."

"That has an unflattering sound for me," said the young man. "I pretend not to prevaricate."

"Dear me, what's the good of being a Southerner?" the lady asked. "Olive told me to tell you she hoped you will stay to dinner. And if she said it, she does really hope it. She is willing to risk that."

"Just as I am?" the visitor inquired, presenting himself with rather a work-a-day aspect.

Mrs. Luna glanced at him from head to foot, and gave a little smiling sigh, as if he had been a long sum in addition. And, indeed, he was very long, Basil Ransom, and he even looked a little hard and discouraging, like a column of figures, in spite of the friendly face which he bent upon his hostess's deputy, and which, in its thinness, had a deep dry line, a sort of premature wrinkle, on either side of the mouth. He was tall and lean, and dressed throughout in black; his shirt-collar was low and wide, and the triangle of linen, a little crumpled, exhibited by the opening of his waistcoat, was adorned by a pin containing a small red stone. In spite of this decoration the young man looked poor — as poor as a young man could look who had such a fine head and such magnificent eyes. Those of Basil Ransom were dark, deep, and glowing; his head had a character of elevation which fairly added to his stature; it was a head to be seen above the level of a crowd, on some judicial bench or political platform, or even on a bronze medal. His forehead was high and broad, and his thick black hair, perfectly straight and glossy, and without any division, rolled back from it in a leonine manner. These things, the eyes especially, with their smouldering fire, might have indicated that he was to be a great American statesman; or, on the other hand, they might simply have proved that he came from Carolina or Alabama. He came, in fact, from Mississippi, and he spoke very perceptibly with the accent of that country. It is not in my power to reproduce by any combination of characters this charming dialect; but the initiated reader will have no difficulty in evoking the sound, which is to be associated in the present instance with nothing vulgar or vain. This lean, pale, sallow, shabby, striking young man, with his superior head, his sedentary shoulders, his expression of bright grimness and hard enthusiasm, his provincial, distinguished appearance, is, as a representative of his sex, the most important personage in my narrative; he played · a very active part

in the events I have undertaken in some degree to set forth. And yet the reader who likes a complete image, who desires to read with the senses as well as with the reason, is entreated not to forget that he prolonged his consonants and swallowed his vowels, that he was guilty of elisions and interpolations which were equally unexpected, and that his discourse was pervaded by something sultry and vast, something almost African in its rich, basking tone, something that suggested the teeming expanse of the cotton-field. Mrs. Luna looked up at all this, but saw only a part of it; otherwise she would not have replied in a bantering manner, in answer to his inquiry: "Are you ever different from this?" Mrs. Luna was familiar — intolerably familiar.

Basil Ransom coloured a little. Then he said: "Oh yes; when I dine out I usually carry a six-shooter and a bowie-knife." And he took up his hat vaguely — a soft black hat with a low crown and an immense straight brim. Mrs. Luna wanted to know what he was doing. She made him sit down; she assured him that her sister quite expected him, would feel as sorry as she could ever feel for anything — for she was a kind of fatalist, anyhow — if he didn't stay to dinner. It was an immense pity — she herself was going out; in Boston you must jump at invitations. Olive, too, was going somewhere after dinner, but he mustn't mind that; perhaps he would like to go with her. It wasn't a party — Olive didn't go to parties; it was one of those weird meetings she was so fond of.

"What kind of meetings do you refer to? You speak as if it were a rendezvous of witches on the Brocken."

"Well, so it is; they are all witches and wizards, mediums, and spirit-rappers, and roaring radicals."

Basil Ransom stared; the yellow light in his brown eyes deepened. "Do you mean to say your sister's a roaring radical?"

"A radical? She's a female Jacobin — she's a nihilist. Whatever is, is wrong, and all that sort of thing. If you are going to dine with her, you had better know it."

"Oh, murder!" murmured the young man vaguely, sinking back in his chair with his arms folded. He looked at Mrs. Luna with intelligent incredulity. She was sufficiently pretty; her hair was in clusters of curls, like bunches of grapes; her tight bodice seemed to crack with her vivacity; and from beneath the stiff plaits of her petticoat a small fat foot protruded, resting upon a stilted heel. She was attractive and impertinent, especially the latter. He seemed to think it was a great pity, what she had told him; but he lost himself in this consideration, or, at any rate, said nothing for some time, while his eyes wandered over Mrs. Luna, and he probably wondered what body of doctrine *she* represented, little as she might partake of the nature of her sister. Many things were strange to Basil Ransom; Boston especially was strewn with surprises, and he was a man who liked to understand. Mrs. Luna was drawing on her gloves; Ransom had never seen any that were so long; they reminded him of stockings, and he wondered how she managed without garters above the elbow. "Well, I suppose I might have known that," he continued, at last.

"You might have known what?"

"Well, that Miss Chancellor would be all that you say. She was brought up in the city of reform."

"Oh, it isn't the city; it's just Olive Chancellor. She would reform the solar system if she could get hold of it. She'll reform you, if you don't look out. That's the way I found her when I returned from Europe."

"Have you been in Europe?" Ransom asked.

"Mercy, yes! Haven't you?"

"No, I haven't been anywhere. Has your sister?"

"Yes; but she stayed only an hour or two. She hates it; she would like to abolish it. Didn't you know I had been to Europe?" Mrs. Luna went on, in the slightly aggrieved tone of a woman who discovers the limits of her reputation.

Ransom reflected he might answer her that until five minutes ago he didn't know she existed; but he remembered that this was not the way in which a Southern gentleman spoke to ladies, and he contented himself with saying that he must condone his Bœotian ignorance (he was fond of an elegant phrase); that he lived in a part of the country where they didn't think much about Europe, and that he had always supposed she was domiciled in New York. This last remark he made at a venture, for he had, naturally, not devoted any supposition whatever to Mrs. Luna. His dishonesty, however, only exposed him the more.

"If you thought I lived in New York, why in the world didn't you come and see me?" the lady inquired.

"Well, you see, I don't go out much, except to the courts."

"Do you mean the law-courts? Every one has got some profession over here! Are you very ambitious? You look as if you were."

"Yes, very," Basil Ransom replied, with a smile, and the curious feminine softness with which Southern gentlemen enunciate that adverb.

Mrs. Luna explained that she had been living in Europe for several years — ever since her husband died — but had come home a month before, come home with her little boy, the only thing she had in the world, and was paying a visit to her sister, who, of course, was the nearest thing after the child. "But it isn't the same," she said. "Olive and I disagree so much."

"While you and your little boy don't," the young man remarked.

"Oh no, I never differ from Newton!" And Mrs. Luna added that now she was back she didn't know what she should do. That

was the worst of coming back; it was like being born again, at one's age — one had to begin life afresh. One didn't even know what one had come back for. There were people who wanted one to spend the winter in Boston; but she couldn't stand that — she knew, at least, what she had not come back for. Perhaps she should take a house in Washington; did he ever hear of that little place? They had invented it while she was away. Besides, Olive didn't want her in Boston, and didn't go through the form of saying so. That was one comfort with Olive; she never went through any forms.

Basil Ransom had got up just as Mrs. Luna made this last declaration; for a young lady had glided into the room, who stopped short as it fell upon her ears. She stood there looking, consciously and rather seriously, at Mr. Ransom; a smile of exceeding faintness played about her lips — it was just perceptible enough to light up the native gravity of her face. It might have been likened to a thin ray of moonlight resting upon the wall of a prison.

"If that were true," she said, "I shouldn't tell you that I am very sorry to have kept you waiting."

Her voice was low and agreeable — a cultivated voice — and she extended a slender white hand to her visitor, who remarked with some solemnity (he felt a certain guilt of participation in Mrs. Luna's indiscretion) that he was intensely happy to make her acquaintance. He observed that Miss

Chancellor's hand was at once cold and limp; she merely placed it in his, without exerting the smallest pressure. Mrs. Luna explained to her sister that her freedom of speech was caused by his being a relation — though, indeed, he didn't seem to know much about them. She didn't believe he had ever heard of her, Mrs. Luna, though he pretended, with his Southern chivalry, that he had. She must be off to her dinner now, she saw the carriage was there, and in her absence Olive might give any version of her she chose.

"I have told him you are a radical, and you may tell him, if you like, that I am a painted Jezebel. Try to reform him; a person from Mississippi is sure to be all wrong. I shall be back very late; we are going to a theatre-party; that's why we dine so early. Good-bye, Mr. Ransom," Mrs. Luna continued, gathering up the feathery white shawl which added to the volume of her fairness. "I hope you are going to stay a little, so that you may judge us for yourself. I should like you to see Newton, too; he is a noble little nature, and I want some advice about him. You only stay tomorrow? Why, what's the use of that? Well, mind you come and see me in New York; I shall be sure to be part of the winter there. I shall send you a card; I won't let you off. Don't come out; my sister has the first claim. Olive, why don't you take him to your female convention?" Mrs. Luna's familiarity extended even to her sister; she remarked to Miss Chancellor that

she looked as if she were got up for a sea-voyage. "I am glad I haven't opinions that prevent my dressing in the evening!" she declared from the doorway. "The amount of thought they give to their clothing, the people who are afraid of looking frivolous!"

Chapter II

WHETHER much or little consideration had been directed to the result, Miss Chancellor certainly would not have incurred this reproach. She was habited in a plain dark dress, without any ornaments, and her smooth, colourless hair was confined as carefully as that of her sister was encouraged to stray. She had instantly seated herself, and while Mrs. Luna talked she kept her eyes on the ground, glancing even less toward Basil Ransom than toward that woman of many words. The young man was therefore free to look at her; a contemplation which showed him that she was agitated and trying to conceal it. He wondered why she was agitated, not foreseeing that he was destined to discover, later, that her nature was like a skiff in a stormy sea. Even after her sister had passed out of the room she sat there with her eyes turned away, as if there had been a spell upon her which forbade her to raise them. Miss Olive Chancellor, it may be confided to the reader, to whom in the

The Bostonians

course of our history I shall be under the necessity of imparting much occult information, was subject to fits of tragic shyness, during which she was unable to meet even her own eyes in the mirror. One of these fits had suddenly seized her now, without any obvious cause, though, indeed, Mrs. Luna had made it worse by becoming instantly so personal. There was nothing in the world so personal as Mrs. Luna; her sister could have hated her for it if she had not forbidden herself this emotion as directed to individuals. Basil Ransom was a young man of first-rate intelligence, but conscious of the narrow range, as yet, of his experience. He was on his guard against generalisations which might be hasty; but he had arrived at two or three that were of value to a gentleman lately admitted to the New York bar and looking out for clients. One of them was to the effect that the simplest division it is possible to make of the human race is into the people who take things hard and the people who take them easy. He perceived very quickly that Miss Chancellor belonged to the former class. This was written so intensely in her delicate face that he felt an unformulated pity for her before they had exchanged twenty words. He himself, by nature, took things easy; if he had put on the screw of late, it was after reflection, and because circumstances pressed him close. But this pale girl, with her light-green eyes, her pointed features and nervous man-

ner, was visibly morbid; it was as plain as day that she was morbid. Poor Ransom anounced this fact to himself as if he had made a great discovery; but in reality he had never been so "Bœotian" as at that moment. It proved nothing of any importance, with regard to Miss Chancellor, to say that she was morbid; any sufficient account of her would lie very much to the rear of that. Why was she morbid, and why was her morbidness typical? Ransom might have exulted if he had gone back far enough to explain that mystery. The women he had hitherto known had been mainly of his own soft clime, and it was not often they exhibited the tendency he detected (and cursorily deplored) in Mrs. Luna's sister. That was the way he liked them — not to think too much, not to feel any responsibility for the government of the world, such as he was sure Miss Chancellor felt. If they would only be private and passive, and have no feeling but for that, and leave publicity to the sex of tougher hide! Ransom was pleased with the vision of that remedy; it must be repeated that he was very provincial.

These considerations were not present to him as definitely as I have written them here; they were summed up in the vague compassion which his cousin's figure excited in his mind, and which was yet accompanied with a sensible reluctance to know her better, obvious as it was that with such a face as that she must be remarkable. He was sorry for her, but he

429

saw in a flash that no one could help her: that was what made her tragic. He had not, seeking his fortune, come away from the blighted South, which weighed upon his heart, to look out for tragedies; at least he didn't want them outside of his office in Pine Street. He broke the silence ensuing upon Mrs. Luna's departure by one of the courteous speeches to which blighted regions may still encourage a tendency, and presently found himself talking comfortably enough with his hostess. Though he had said to himself that no one could help her, the effect of his tone was to dispel her shyness; it was her great advantage (for the career she had proposed to herself) that in certain conditions she was liable suddenly to become bold. She was reassured at finding that her visitor was peculiar; the way he spoke told her that it was no wonder he had fought on the Southern side. She had never yet encountered a personage so exotic, and she always felt more at her ease in the presence of anything strange. It was the usual things of life that filled her with silent rage; which was natural enough, inasmuch as, to her vision, almost everything that was usual was iniquitous. She had no difficulty in asking him now whether he would not stay to dinner — she hoped Adeline had given him her message. It had been when she was upstairs with Adeline, as his card was brought up, a sudden and very abnormal inspiration to offer him this (for her) really ultimate favour; nothing could be further from her common habit than to entertain alone, at any repast, a gentleman she had never seen.

It was the same sort of impulse that had moved her to write to Basil Ransom, in the spring, after hearing accidentally that he had come to the North and intended, in New York, to practise his profession. It was her nature to look out for duties, to appeal to her conscience for tasks. This attentive organ, earnestly consulted, had represented to her that he was an offshoot of the old slave-holding oligarchy which, within her own vivid remembrance, had plunged the country into blood and tears, and that, as associated with such abominations, he was not a worthy object of patronage for a person whose two brothers — her only ones — had given up life for the Northern cause. It reminded her, however, on the other hand, that he too had been much bereaved, and, moreover, that he had fought and offered his own life, even if it had not been taken. She could not defend herself against a rich admiration — a kind of tenderness of envy — of any one who had been so happy as to have that opportunity. The most secret, the most sacred hope of her nature was that she might some day have such a chance, that she might be a martyr and die for something. Basil Ransom had lived, but she knew he had lived to see bitter hours. His family was ruined; they had lost their slaves, their property, their friends and relations, their home; had tasted of all the cruelty of defeat. He had tried for a while to carry on the plantation himself, but he had a millstone of debt round his neck, and he longed for some work which would transport him to the haunts of men. The State of Mississippi seemed to him the state of despair; so he surrendered the remnants of his patrimony to his mother and sisters, and, at nearly thirty years of age, alighted for the first time in New York, in the costume of his province, with fifty dollars in his pocket and a gnawing hunger in his heart.

That this incident had revealed to the young man his ignorance of many things — only, however, to make him say to himself, after the first angry blush, that here he would enter the game and here he would win it — so much Olive Chancellor could not know; what was sufficient for her was that he had rallied, as the French say, had accepted the accomplished fact, had admitted that North and South were a single, indivisible political organism. Their cousinship — that of Chancellors and Ransoms — was not very close; it was the kind of thing that one might take up or leave alone, as one pleased. It was "in the female line," as Basil Ransom had written, in answering her letter with a good deal of form and flourish; he spoke as if they had been royal houses. Her mother had wished to take it up; it was only the fear of seeming patronising to people in misfortune that had prevented her from writing to Mississippi. If it had been possible to send Mrs. Ransom money, or even clothes, she would have liked that; but she had no means of ascertaining how such an offering would be taken. By the time Basil came to the North — making advances, as it were — Mrs. Chancellor had passed away; so it was for Olive, left alone in the little house in Charles Street (Adeline being in Europe), to decide.

She knew what her mother would have done, and that helped her decision; for her mother always chose the positive course. Olive had a fear of everything, but her greatest fear was of being afraid. She wished immensely to be generous, and how could one be generous unless one ran a risk? She had erected it into a sort of rule of conduct that whenever she saw a risk she was to take it; and she had frequent humiliations at finding herself safe after all. She was perfectly safe after writing to Basil Ransom; and, indeed, it was difficult to see what he could have done to her except thank her (he was only exceptionally superlative) for her letter, and assure her that he would come and see her the first time his business (he was beginning to get a little) should take him to Boston. He had now come, in redemption of his grateful vow, and even this did not make Miss Chancellor feel that she had courted danger. She saw (when once she had looked at him) that he would not put those worldly interpretations on things which, with her, it was both an impulse and a principle to defy. He was too simple — too Mississippian — for that; she was almost disappointed. She certainly had not hoped that she might have struck him as making unwomanly overtures (Miss Chancellor hated this epithet almost as much as she hated its opposite); but she had a presentiment that he would be too good-natured, primitive to that degree. Of all things in the world contention was most sweet to her (though why it is hard to imagine, for it always cost her tears, headaches, a day or two in bed, acute emotion), and it was very possible Basil Ransom would not care to contend. Nothing could be more displeasing than this indifference when people didn't agree with you. That he should agree she did not in the least expect of him; how could a Mississippian agree? If she had supposed he would agree, she would not have written to him.

Chapter III

WHEN he had told her that if she would take him as he was he should be very happy to dine with her, she excused herself a moment and went to give an order in the dining-room. The young man, left alone, looked about the parlour — the two parlours which, in their prolonged, adjacent narrowness, formed evidently one apartment — and wandered to the windows at the back, where there was a view of the water; Miss Chancellor having the good fortune to dwell on that side of Charles Street toward which, in the rear, the afternoon sun slants redly, from an horizon indented at empty intervals with wooden spires, the masts of lonely boats, the chimneys of dirty "works," over a brackish expanse of anomalous character, which is too big for a river and too small for a bay. The view seemed to him very picturesque, though in the gathered dusk little was left of it save a cold yellow streak in the west, a gleam of brown water, and the reflection of the lights that had begun to show themselves in a row of houses, impressive to Ransom in their extreme modernness, which overlooked the same lagoon from a long embankment on the left, constructed of stones roughly piled. He thought this prospect, from a city-house, almost romantic; and he turned from it back to the interior (illuminated now by a lamp which the parlour-maid had placed on a table while he stood at the window) as to something still more genial and interesting. The artistic sense in Basil Ransom had not been highly cultivated; neither (though he had passed his early years as the son of a rich man) was his conception of material comfort very definite; it consisted mainly of the vision of plenty of cigars and brandy and water and newspapers, and a cane-bottomed arm-chair of the right inclination, from which he could stretch his legs. Nevertheless it seemed to him he had never seen an interior that was so much an interior as this queer corridor-shaped drawing-room of his new-found kinswoman; he had never felt himself in the presence of so much organised privacy or of so many objects that spoke of habits and tastes. Most of the people he had hitherto known had no tastes; they had a few habits, but these were not of a sort that required much upholstery. He had not as yet been in many houses in New York, and he had never before seen so many accessories. The general character of the place struck him as Bostonian; this was, in fact, very much what he had supposed Boston to be. He had always heard Boston was a city of culture, and now there was culture in Miss Chancellor's tables and sofas, in the books that were everywhere, on little shelves like brackets (as if a book were a statuette), in the photographs and water-colours that covered the walls, in the curtains that were festooned rather stiffly in the doorways. He looked at some of the books and saw that his cousin read German; and his impression of the importance of this (as a symptom of superiority) was not diminished by the fact that he himself had mastered the tongue (knowing it contained a large literature of jurisprudence) during a long, empty, deadly summer on the plantation. It is a curious proof of a certain crude modesty inherent in Basil Ransom that the main effect of his observing his cousin's German books was to give him an idea of the natural energy of Northerners. He had no-

ticed it often before; he had already told himself that he must count with it. It was only after much experience he made the discovery that few Northerners were, in their secret soul, so energetic as he. Many other persons had made it before that. He knew very little about Miss Chancellor; he had come to see her only because she wrote to him; he would never have thought of looking her up, and since then there had been no one in New York he might ask about her. Therefore he could only guess that she was a rich young woman; such a house, inhabited in such a way by a quiet spinster, implied a considerable income. How much? he asked himself; five thousand, ten thousand, fifteen thousand a year? There was richness to our panting young man in the smallest of these figures. He was not of a mercenary spirit, but he had an immense desire for success, and he had more than once reflected that a moderate capital was an aid to achievement. He had seen in his younger years one of the biggest failures that history commemorates, an immense national *fiasco*, and it had implanted in his mind a deep aversion to the ineffectual. It came over him, while he waited for his hostess to reappear, that she was unmarried as well as rich, that she was sociable (her letter answered for that) as well as single; and he had for a moment a whimsical vision of becoming a partner in so flourishing a firm. He ground his teeth a little as he thought of the contrasts of the human lot; this cushioned feminine nest made him feel unhoused and underfed. Such a mood, however, could only be momentary, for he was conscious at bottom of a bigger stomach than all the culture of Charles Street could fill.

Afterwards, when his cousin had come back and they had gone down to dinner together, where he sat facing her at a little table decorated in the middle with flowers, a position from which he had another view, through a window where the curtain remained undrawn by her direction (she called his attention to this — it was for his benefit), of the dusky, empty river, spotted with points of light — at this period, I say, it was very easy for him to remark to himself that nothing would induce him to make love to such a type as that. Several months later, in New York, in conversation with Mrs. Luna, of whom he was destined to see a good deal, he alluded by chance to this repast, to the way her sister had placed him at table, and to the remark with which she had pointed out the advantage of his seat.

"That's what they call in Boston being very 'thoughtful,'" Mrs. Luna said, "giving you the Back Bay (don't you hate the name?) to look at, and then taking credit for it."

This, however, was in the future; what Basil Ransom actually perceived was that Miss Chancellor was a signal old maid. That was her quality, her destiny; nothing could be more distinctly written. There are women who are unmarried by accident, and others who are unmarried by option; but Olive Chancellor was unmarried by every implication of her being. She was a spinster as Shelley was a lyric poet, or as the month of August is sultry. She was so essentially a celibate that Ransom found himself thinking of her as old, though when he came to look at her (as he said to himself) it was apparent that her years were fewer than his own. He did not dislike her, she had been so friendly; but, little by little, she gave him an uneasy feeling — the sense that you could never be safe with a person who took things so hard. It came over him that it was because she took things hard she had sought his acquaintance; it had been because she was strenuous, not because she was genial; she had had in her eye — and what an extraordinary eye it was! — not a pleasure, but a duty. She would expect him to be strenuous in return; but he couldn't — in private life, he couldn't; privacy for Basil Ransom consisted entirely in what he called "laying off." She was not so plain on further acquaintance as she had seemed to him at first; even the young Mississippian had culture enough to see that she was refined. Her white skin had a singular look of being drawn tightly across her face; but her features, though sharp and irregular, were delicate in a fashion that suggested good breeding. Their line was perverse, but it was not poor.

The curious tint of her eyes was a living colour; when she turned it upon you, you thought vaguely of the glitter of green ice. She had absolutely no figure, and presented a certain appearance of feeling cold. With all this, there was something very modern and highly developed in her aspect; she had the advantages as well as the drawbacks of a nervous organisation. She smiled constantly at her guest, but from the beginning to the end of dinner, though he made several remarks that he thought might prove amusing, she never once laughed. Later, he saw that she was a woman without laughter; exhilaration, if it ever visited her, was dumb. Once only, in the course of his subsequent acquaintance with her, did it find a voice; and then the sound remained in Ransom's ear as one of the strangest he had heard.

She asked him a great many questions, and made no comment on his answers, which only served to suggest to her fresh inquiries. Her shyness had quite left her, it did not come back; she had confidence enough to wish him to see that she took a great interest in him. Why should she? he wondered. He couldn't believe he was one of *her* kind; he was conscious of much Bohemianism — he drank beer, in New York, in cellars, knew no ladies, and was familiar with a "variety" actress. Certainly, as she knew him better, she would disapprove of him, though, of course, he would never mention the actress, nor even, if necessary, the

beer. Ransom's conception of vice was purely as a series of special cases, of explicable accidents. Not that he cared; if it were a part of the Boston character to be inquiring, he would be to the last a courteous Mississippian. He would tell her about Mississippi as much as she liked; he didn't care how much he told her that the old ideas in the South were played out. She would not understand him any the better for that; she would not know how little his own views could be gathered from such a limited admission. What her sister imparted to him about her mania for "reform" had left in his mouth a kind of unpleasant aftertaste; he felt, at any rate, that if she had the religion of humanity — Basil Ransom had read Comte, he had read everything — she would never understand him. He, too, had a private vision of reform, but the first principle of it was to reform the reformers. As they drew to the close of a meal which, in spite of all latent incompatibilities, had gone off brilliantly, she said to him that she should have to leave him after dinner, unless perhaps he should be inclined to accompany her. She was going to a small gathering at the house of a friend who had asked a few people, "interested in new ideas," to meet Mrs. Farrinder.

"Oh, thank you," said Basil Ransom. "Is it a party? I haven't been to a party since Mississippi seceded."

"No; Miss Birdseye doesn't give parties. She's an ascetic."

435

"Oh, well, we have had our dinner," Ransom rejoined, laughing.

His hostess sat silent a moment, with her eyes on the ground; she looked at such times as if she were hesitating greatly between several things she might say, all so important that it was difficult to choose.

"I think it might interest you," she remarked presently. "You will hear some discussion, if you are fond of that. Perhaps you wouldn't agree," she added, resting her strange eyes on him.

"Perhaps I shouldn't — I don't agree with everything," he said, smiling and stroking his leg.

"Don't you care for human progress?" Miss Chancellor went on.

"I don't know — I never saw any. Are you going to show me some?"

"I can show you an earnest effort towards it. That's the most one can be sure of. But I am not sure you are worthy."

"Is it something very Bostonian? I should like to see that," said Basil Ransom.

"There are movements in other cities. Mrs. Farrinder goes everywhere; she may speak to-night."

"Mrs. Farrinder, the celebrated —— ?"

"Yes, the celebrated; the great apostle of the emancipation of women. She is a great friend of Miss Birdseye."

"And who is Miss Birdseye?"

"She is one of our celebrities. She is the woman in the world, I suppose, who has laboured most for every wise reform. I think I ought to tell you," Miss Chancellor went on in a moment, "she was one of the earliest, one of the most passionate, of the old Abolitionists."

She had thought, indeed, she ought to tell him that, and it threw her into a little tremor of excitement to do so. Yet, if she had been afraid he would show some irritation at this news, she was disappointed at the geniality with which he exclaimed:

"Why, poor old lady — she must be quite mature!"

It was therefore with some severity that she rejoined:

"She will never be old. She is the youngest spirit I know. But if you are not in sympathy, perhaps you had better not come," she went on.

"In sympathy with what, dear madam?" Basil Ransom asked, failing still, to her perception, to catch the tone of real seriousness. "If, as you say, there is to be a discussion, there will be different sides, and of course one can't sympathise with both."

"Yes, but every one will, in his way — or in her way — plead the cause of the new truths. If you don't care for them, you won't go with us."

"I tell you I haven't the least idea what they are! I have never yet encountered in the world any but old truths — as old as the sun and moon. How can I know? But *do* take me; it's such a chance to see Boston."

"It isn't Boston — it's humanity!" Miss Chancellor, as she made this remark, rose from her chair, and her movement seemed to say that she consented. But before she quitted her kinsman to get ready, she observed to him that she was sure he knew what she meant; he was only pretending he didn't.

"Well, perhaps, after all, I have a general idea," he confessed; "but don't you see how this little re-union will give me a chance to fix it?"

She lingered an instant, with her anxious face. "Mrs. Farrinder will fix it!" she said; and she went to prepare herself.

It was in this poor young lady's nature to be anxious, to have scruple within scruple and to forecast the consequences of things. She returned in ten minutes, in her bonnet, which she had apparently assumed in recognition of Miss Birdseye's asceticism. As she stood there drawing on her gloves — her visitor had fortified himself against Mrs. Farrinder by another glass of wine — she declared to him that she quite repented of having proposed to him to go; something told her that he would be an unfavourable element.

"Why, is it going to be a spiritual *séance?*" Basil Ransom asked.

"Well, I have heard at Miss Birdseye's some inspirational speaking." Olive Chancellor was determined to look him straight in the face as she said this; her sense of the way it might strike him operated as a cogent, not as a deterrent, reason.

"Why, Miss Olive, it's just got up on purpose for me!" cried the young Mississippian, radiant, and clasping his hands. She thought him very handsome as he said this, but reflected that unfortunately men didn't care for the truth, especially the new kinds, in proportion as they were good-looking. She had, however, a moral resource that she could always fall back upon; it had already been a comfort to her, on occasions of acute feeling, that she hated men, as a class, anyway. "And I want so much to see an old Abolitionist; I have never laid eyes on one," Basil Ransom added.

"Of course you couldn't see one in the South; you were too afraid of them to let them come there!" She was now trying to think of something she might say that would be sufficiently disagreeable to make him cease to insist on accompanying her; for, strange to record — if anything, in a person of that intense sensibility, be stranger than any other — her second thought with regard to having asked him had deepened with the elapsing moments into an unreasoned terror of the effect of his presence. "Perhaps Miss Birdseye won't like you," she went on, as they waited for the carriage.

"I don't know; I reckon she will," said Basil Ransom good-humouredly. He evidently had no intention of giving up his opportunity.

From the window of the dining-room, at that moment, they heard the carriage drive up. Miss Birdseye lived at the South End; the distance was considerable, and Miss Chancellor had ordered a

437

hackney-coach, it being one of the advantages of living in Charles Street that stables were near. The logic of her conduct was none of the clearest; for if she had been alone she would have proceeded to her destination by the aid of the street-car; not from economy (for she had the good fortune not to be obliged to consult it to that degree), and not from any love of wandering about Boston at night (a kind of exposure she greatly disliked), but by reason of a theory she devotedly nursed, a theory which bade her put off invidious differences and mingle in the common life. She would have gone on foot to Boylston Street, and there she would have taken the public conveyance (in her heart she loathed it) to the South End. Boston was full of poor girls who had to walk about at night and to squeeze into horse-cars in which every sense was displeased; and why should she hold herself superior to these? Olive Chancellor regulated her conduct on lofty principles, and this is why, having to-night the advantage of a gentleman's protection, she sent for a carriage to obliterate that patronage. If they had gone together in the common way she would have seemed to owe it to him that she should be so daring, and he belonged to a sex to which she wished to be under no obligations. Months before, when she wrote to him, it had been with the sense, rather, of putting *him* in debt. As they rolled toward the South End, side by side, in a good deal of silence,

bouncing and bumping over the railway-tracks very little less, after all, than if their wheels had been fitted to them, and looking out on either side at rows of red houses, dusky in the lamplight, with protuberant fronts, approached by ladders of stone; as they proceeded, with these contemplative undulations, Miss Chancellor said to her companion, with a concentrated desire to defy him, as a punishment for having thrown her (she couldn't tell why) into such a tremor:

"Don't you believe, then, in the coming of a better day — in its being possible to do something for the human race?"

Poor Ransom perceived the defiance, and he felt rather bewildered; he wondered what type, after all, he *had* got hold of, and what game was being played with him. Why had she made advances, if she wanted to pinch him this way? However, he was good for any game — that one as well as another — and he saw that he was "in" for something of which he had long desired to have a nearer view. "Well, Miss Olive," he answered, putting on again his big hat, which he had been holding in his lap, "what strikes me most is that the human race has got to bear its troubles."

"That's what men say to women, to make them patient in the position they have made for them."

"Oh, the position of women!" Basil Ransom exclaimed. "The position of women is to make fools of men. I would change my position for yours any day," he went on.

438

"That's what I said to myself as I sat there in your elegant home."

He could not see, in the dimness of the carriage, that she had flushed quickly, and he did not know that she disliked to be reminded of certain things which, for her, were mitigations of the hard feminine lot. But the passionate quaver with which, a moment later, she answered him sufficiently assured him that he had touched her at a tender point.

"Do you make it a reproach to me that I happen to have a little money? The dearest wish of my heart is to do something with it for others — for the miserable."

Basil Ransom might have greeted this last declaration with the sympathy it deserved, might have commended the noble aspirations of his kinswoman. But what struck him, rather, was the oddity of so sudden a sharpness of pitch in an intercourse which, an hour or two before, had begun in perfect amity, and he burst once more into an irrepressible laugh. This made his companion feel, with intensity, how little she was joking. "I don't know why I should care what you think," she said.

"Don't care — don't care. What does it matter? It is not of the slightest importance."

He might say that, but it was not true; she felt that there were reasons why she should care. She had brought him into her life, and she should have to pay for it. But she wished to know the worst at once. "Are you against our emancipation?" she asked, turning a

white face on him in the momentary radiance of a street-lamp.

"Do you mean your voting and preaching and all that sort of thing?" He made this inquiry, but seeing how seriously she would take his answer, he was almost frightened, and hung fire. "I will tell you when I have heard Mrs. Farrinder."

They had arrived at the address given by Miss Chancellor to the coachman, and their vehicle stopped with a lurch. Basil Ransom got out; he stood at the door with an extended hand, to assist the young lady. But she seemed to hesitate; she sat there with her spectral face. "You hate it!" she exclaimed, in a low tone.

"Miss Birdseye will convert me," said Ransom, with intention; for he had grown very curious, and he was afraid that now, at the last, Miss Chancellor would prevent his entering the house. She alighted without his help, and behind her he ascended the high steps of Miss Birdseye's residence. He had grown very curious, and among the things he wanted to know was why in the world this ticklish spinster had written to him.

Chapter IV

SHE had told him before they started that they should be early; she wished to see Miss Birdseye alone, before the arrival of any one else. This was just for the pleasure of seeing her — it was an opportunity; she was always so taken up with others. She received Miss Chancellor in the hall of the mansion, which had a salient front, an enormous and very high number — 756 — painted in gilt on the glass light above the door, a tin sign bearing the name of a doctress (Mary J. Prance) suspended from one of the windows of the basement, and a peculiar look of being both new and faded — a kind of modern fatigue — like certain articles of commerce which are sold at a reduction as shopworn. The hall was very narrow; a considerable part of it was occupied by a large hat-tree, from which several coats and shawls already depended; the rest offered space for certain lateral demonstrations on Miss Birdseye's part. She sidled about her visitors, and at last went round to open for them a door of further admission, which happened to be locked inside. She was a little old lady, with an enormous head; that was the first thing Ransom noticed — the vast, fair, protuberant, candid, ungarnished brow, surmounting a pair of weak, kind, tired-looking eyes, and ineffectually balanced in the rear by a cap which had the air of falling backward, and which Miss Birdseye suddenly felt for while she talked, with unsuccessful irrelevant movements. She had a sad, soft, pale face, which (and it was the effect of her whole head) looked as if it had been soaked, blurred, and made vague

by exposure to some slow dissolvent. The long practice of philanthropy had not given accent to her features; it had rubbed out their transitions, their meanings. The waves of sympathy, of enthusiasm, had wrought upon them in the same way in which the waves of time finally modify the surface of old marble busts, gradually washing away their sharpness, their details. In her large countenance her dim little smile scarcely showed. It was a mere sketch of a smile, a kind of instalment, or payment on account; it seemed to say that she would smile more if she had time, but that you could see, without this, that she was gentle and easy to beguile.

She always dressed in the same way: she wore a loose black jacket, with deep pockets, which were stuffed with papers, memoranda of a voluminous correspondence; and from beneath her jacket depended a short stuff dress. The brevity of this simple garment was the one device by which Miss Birdseye managed to suggest that she was a woman of business, that she wished to be free for action. She belonged to the Short-Skirts League, as a matter of course; for she belonged to any and every league that had been founded for almost any purpose whatever. This did not prevent her being a confused, entangled, inconsequent, discursive old woman, whose charity began at home and ended nowhere, whose credulity kept pace with it, and who knew less about her fellow-creatures, if possible, after fifty years of humanitary zeal, than on the day she had gone into the field to testify against the iniquity of most arrangements. Basil Ransom knew very little about such a life as hers, but she seemed to him a revelation of a class, and a multitude of socialistic figures, of names and episodes that he had heard of, grouped themselves behind her. She looked as if she had spent her life on platforms, in audiences, in conventions, in phalansteries, in *séances;* in her faded face there was a kind of reflection of ugly lecture-lamps; with its habit of an upward angle, it seemed turned toward a public speaker, with an effort of respiration in the thick air in which social reforms are usually discussed. She talked continually, in a voice of which the spring seemed broken, like that of an over-worked bell-wire; and when Miss Chancellor explained that she had brought Mr. Ransom because he was so anxious to meet Mrs. Farrinder, she gave the young man a delicate, dirty, democratic little hand, looking at him kindly, as she could not help doing, but without the smallest discrimination as against others who might not have the good fortune (which involved, possibly, an injustice) to be present on such an interesting occasion. She struck him as very poor, but it was only afterward that he learned she had never had a penny in her life. No one had an idea how she lived; whenever money was given her she gave it away to a negro or a refugee. No woman could be less invidious, but on the whole she preferred these two classes of the human race. Since the Civil War much of her occupation was gone; for before that her best hours had been spent in fancying that she was helping some Southern slave to escape. It would have been a nice question whether, in her heart of hearts, for the sake of this excitement, she did not sometimes wish the blacks back in bondage. She had suffered in the same way by the relaxation of many European despotisms, for in former years much of the romance of her life had been in smoothing the pillow of exile for banished conspirators. Her refugees had been very precious to her; she was always trying to raise money for some cadaverous Pole, to obtain lessons for some shirtless Italian. There was a legend that an Hungarian had once possessed himself of her affections, and had disappeared after robbing her of everything she possessed. This, however, was very apocryphal, for she had never possessed anything, and it was open to grave doubt that she could have entertained a sentiment so personal. She was in love, even in those days, only with causes, and she languished only for emancipations. But they had been the happiest days, for when causes were embodied in foreigners (what else were the Africans?), they were certainly more appealing.

She had just come down to see Doctor Prance — to see whether she wouldn't like to come up. But

441

she wasn't in her room, and Miss Birdseye guessed she had gone out to her supper; she got her supper at a boarding-table about two blocks off. Miss Birdseye expressed the hope that Miss Chancellor had had hers; she would have had plenty of time to take it, for no one had come in yet; she didn't know what made them all so late. Ransom perceived that the garments suspended to the hat-rack were not a sign that Miss Birdseye's friends had assembled; if he had gone a little further still he would have recognised the house as one of those in which mysterious articles of clothing are always hooked to something in the hall. Miss Birdseye's visitors, those of Doctor Prance, and of other tenants — for Number 756 was the common residence of several persons, among whom there prevailed much vagueness of boundary — used to leave things to be called for; many of them went about with satchels and reticules, for which they were always looking for places of deposit. What completed the character of this interior was Miss Birdseye's own apartment, into which her guests presently made their way, and where they were joined by various other members of the good lady's circle. Indeed, it completed Miss Birdseye herself, if anything could be said to render that office to this essentially formless old woman, who had no more outline than a bundle of hay. But the bareness of her long, loose, empty parlour (it was shaped exactly like Miss Chancel-

lor's) told that she had never had any needs but moral needs, and that all her history had been that of her sympathies. The place was lighted by a small hot glare of gas, which made it look white and featureless. It struck even Basil Ransom with its flatness, and he said to himself that his cousin must have a very big bee in her bonnet to make her like such a house. He did not know then, and he never knew, that she mortally disliked it, and that in a career in which she was constantly exposing herself to offence and laceration, her most poignant suffering came from the injury of her taste. She had tried to kill that nerve, to persuade herself that taste was only frivolity in the disguise of knowledge; but her susceptibility was constantly blooming afresh and making her wonder whether an absence of nice arrangements were a necessary part of the enthusiasm of humanity. Miss Birdseye was always trying to obtain employment, lessons in drawing, orders for portraits, for poor foreign artists, as to the greatness of whose talent she pledged herself without reserve; but in point of fact she had not the faintest sense of the scenic or plastic side of life.

Toward nine o'clock the light of her hissing burners smote the majestic person of Mrs. Farrinder, who might have contributed to answer that question of Miss Chancellor's in the negative. She was a copious, handsome woman, in whom angularity had been corrected by the air of success; she had a rustling dress (it was evident what *she* thought about taste), abundant hair of a glossy blackness, a pair of folded arms, the expression of which seemed to say that rest, in such a career as hers, was as sweet as it was brief, and a terrible regularity of feature. I apply that adjective to her fine placid mask because she seemed to face you with a question of which the answer was preordained, to ask you how a countenance could fail to be noble of which the measurements were so correct. You could contest neither the measurements nor the nobleness, and had to feel that Mrs. Farrinder imposed herself. There was a lithographic smoothness about her, and a mixture of the American matron and the public character. There was something public in her eye, which was large, cold, and quiet; it had acquired a sort of exposed reticence from the habit of looking down from a lecture-desk, over a sea of heads, while its distinguished owner was eulogised by a leading citizen. Mrs. Farrinder, at almost any time, had the air of being introduced by a few remarks. She talked with great slowness and distinctness, and evidently a high sense of responsibility; she pronounced every syllable of every word and insisted on being explicit. If, in conversation with her, you attempted to take anything for granted, or to jump two or three steps at a time, she paused, looking at you with a cold patience, as if she knew that trick,

and then went on at her own measured pace. She lectured on temperance and the rights of women; the ends she laboured for were to give the ballot to every woman in the country and to take the flowing bowl from every man. She was held to have a very fine manner, and to embody the domestic virtues and the graces of the drawing-room; to be a shining proof, in short, that the forum, for ladies, is not necessarily hostile to the fireside. She had a husband, and his name was Amariah.

Doctor Prance had come back from supper and made her appearance in response to an invitation that Miss Birdseye's relaxed voice had tinkled down to her from the hall over the banisters, with much repetition, to secure attention. She was a plain, spare young woman, with short hair and an eye-glass; she looked about her with a kind of near-sighted deprecation, and seemed to hope that she should not be expected to generalise in any way, or supposed to have come up for any purpose more social than to see what Miss Birdseye wanted this time. By nine o'clock twenty other persons had arrived, and had placed themselves in the chairs that were ranged along the sides of the long, bald room, in which they ended by producing the similitude of an enormous street-car. The apartment contained little else but these chairs, many of which had a borrowed aspect, an implication of bare bedrooms in the upper regions; a table or two with a discoloured marble top, a few books, and a collection of newspapers piled up in corners. Ransom could see for himself that the occasion was not crudely festive; there was a want of convivial movement, and, among most of the visitors, even of mutual recognition. They sat there as if they were waiting for something; they looked obliquely and silently at Mrs. Farrinder, and were plainly under the impression that, fortunately, they were not there to amuse themselves. The ladies, who were much the more numerous, wore their bonnets, like Miss Chancellor; the men were in the garb of toil, many of them in weary-looking overcoats. Two or three had retained their overshoes, and as you approached them the odour of the india-rubber was perceptible. It was not, however, that Miss Birdseye ever noticed anything of that sort; she neither knew what she smelled nor tasted what she ate. Most of her friends had an anxious, haggard look, though there were sundry exceptions — half a dozen placid, florid faces. Basil Ransom wondered who they all were; he had a general idea they were mediums, communists, vegetarians. It was not, either, that Miss Birdseye failed to wander about among them with repetitions of inquiry and friendly absences of attention; she sat down near most of them in turn, saying "Yes, yes," vaguely and kindly, to remarks they made to her, feeling for the papers in the pockets of her loosened bodice, recovering her cap and sacrificing her spectacles, wondering most of all what had been her idea in convoking these people. Then she remembered that it had been connected in some way with Mrs. Farrinder; that this eloquent woman had promised to favour the company with a few reminiscences of her last campaign; to sketch even, perhaps, the lines on which she intended to operate during the coming winter. This was what Olive Chancellor had come to hear; this would be the attraction for the dark-eyed young man (he looked like a genius) she had brought with her. Miss Birdseye made her way back to the great lecturess, who was bending an indulgent attention on Miss Chancellor; the latter compressed into a small space, to be near her, and sitting with clasped hands and a concentration of inquiry which by contrast made Mrs. Farrinder's manner seem large and free. In her transit, however, the hostess was checked by the arrival of fresh pilgrims; she had no idea she had mentioned the occasion to so many people — she only remembered, as it were, those she had forgotten — and it was certainly a proof of the interest felt in Mrs. Farrinder's work. The people who had just come in. were Doctor and Mrs. Tarrant and their daughter Verena; he was a mesmeric healer and she was of old Abolitionist stock. Miss Birdseye rested her dim, dry smile upon the daughter, who was new to her, and it floated before her that she would probably be remarkable as a genius; her parentage was an implication of that. There was a genius for Miss Birdseye in every bush. Selah Tarrant had effected wonderful cures; she knew so many people — if they would only try him. His wife was a daughter of Abraham Greenstreet; she had kept a runaway slave in her house for thirty days. That was years before, when this girl must have been a child; but hadn't it thrown a kind of rainbow over her cradle, and wouldn't she naturally have some gift? The girl was very pretty, though she had red hair.

Chapter V

MRS. FARRINDER, meanwhile, was not eager to address the assembly. She confessed as much to Olive Chancellor, with a smile which asked that a temporary lapse of promptness might not be too harshly judged. She had addressed so many assemblies, and she wanted to hear what other people had to say. Miss Chancellor herself had thought so much on the vital subject; would not she make a few remarks and give them some of her experiences? How did the ladies on Beacon Street feel about the ballot? Perhaps she could speak for *them* more than for some others. That was a branch of the question on which, it might be, the leaders had not information enough; but they wanted to take

in everything, and why shouldn't Miss Chancellor just make that field her own? Mrs. Farrinder spoke in the tone of one who took views so wide that they might easily, at first, before you could see how she worked round, look almost meretricious; she was conscious of a scope that exceeded the first flight of your imagination. She urged upon her companion the idea of labouring in the world of fashion, appeared to attribute to her familiar relations with that mysterious realm, and wanted to know why she shouldn't stir up some of her friends down there on the Mill-dam?

Olive Chancellor received this appeal with peculiar feelings. With her immense sympathy for reform, she found herself so often wishing that reformers were a little different. There was something grand about Mrs. Farrinder; it lifted one up to be with her: but there was a false note when she spoke to her young friend about the ladies in Beacon Street. Olive hated to hear that fine avenue talked about as if it were such a remarkable place, and to live there were a proof of worldly glory. All sorts of inferior people lived there, and so brilliant a woman as Mrs. Farrinder, who lived at Roxbury, ought not to mix things up. It was, of course, very wretched to be irritated by such mistakes; but this was not the first time Miss Chancellor had observed that the possession of nerves was not by itself a reason for embracing the new truths. She knew her place in the Boston hierarchy, and it was not what Mrs. Farrinder supposed; so that there was a want of perspective in talking to her as if she had been a representative of the aristocracy. Nothing could be weaker, she knew very well, than (in the United States) to apply that term too literally; nevertheless, it would represent a reality if one were to say that, by distinction, the Chancellors belonged to the *bourgeoisie* – the oldest and best. They might care for such a position or not (as it happened, they were very proud of it), but there they were, and it made Mrs. Farrinder seem provincial (there was something provincial, after all, in the way she did her hair too) not to understand. When Miss Birdseye spoke as if one was a "leader of society," Olive could forgive her even that odious expression, because, of course, one never pretended that she, poor dear, had the smallest sense of the real. She was heroic, she was sublime, the whole moral history of Boston was reflected in her displaced spectacles; but it was a part of her originality, as it were, that she was deliciously provincial. Olive Chancellor seemed to herself to have privileges enough without being affiliated to the exclusive set and having invitations to the smaller parties, which were the real test; it was ·a mercy for her that she had not that added immorality on her conscience. The ladies Mrs. Farrinder meant (it was to be supposed she meant some particular ones) might speak for themselves. She wished to

work in another field; she had long been preoccupied with the romance of the people. She had an immense desire to know intimately some *very* poor girl. This might seem one of the most accessible of pleasures; but, in point of fact, she had not found it so. There were two or three pale shop-maidens whose acquaintance she had sought; but they had seemed afraid of her, and the attempt had come to nothing. She took them more tragically than they took themselves; they couldn't make out what she wanted them to do, and they always ended by being odiously mixed up with Charlie. Charlie was a young man in a white overcoat and a paper collar; it was for him, in the last analysis, that they cared much the most. They cared far more about Charlie than about the ballot. Olive Chancellor wondered how Mrs. Farrinder would treat that branch of the question. In her researches among her young townswomen she had always found this obtrusive swain planted in her path, and she grew at last to dislike him extremely. It filled her with exasperation to think that he should be necessary to the happiness of his victims (she had learned that whatever they might talk about with her, it was of him and him only that they discoursed among themselves), and one of the main recommendations of the evening club for her fatigued, underpaid sisters, which it had long been her dream to establish, was that it would in some degree undermine his position — distinct as her prevision might be that he would be in waiting at the door. She hardly knew what to say to Mrs. Farrinder when this momentarily misdirected woman, still preoccupied with the Mill-dam, returned to the charge.

"We want labourers in that field, though I know two or three lovely women — sweet *home-women* — moving in circles that are for the most part closed to every new voice, who are doing their best to help on the fight. I have several names that might surprise you, names well known on State Street. But we can't have too many recruits, especially among those whose refinement is generally acknowledged. If it be necessary, we are prepared to take certain steps to conciliate the shrinking. Our movement is for all — it appeals to the most delicate ladies. Raise the standard among them, and bring me a thousand names. I know several that I should like to have. I look after the details as well as the big currents," Mrs. Farrinder added, in a tone as explanatory as could be expected of such a woman, and with a smile of which the sweetness was thrilling to her listener.

"I can't talk to those people, I can't!" said Olive Chancellor, with a face which seemed to plead for a remission of responsibility. "I want to give myself up to others; I want to know everything that lies beneath and out of sight, don't you know? I want to enter into the lives of women who are lonely, who are piteous. I want to be near to them — to help them. I want to do something — oh, I should like so to speak!"

"We should be glad to have you make a few remarks at present," Mrs. Farrinder declared, with a punctuality which revealed the faculty of presiding.

"Oh, dear, no, I can't speak; I have none of that sort of talent. I have no self-possession, no eloquence; I can't put three words together. But I do want to contribute."

"What *have* you got?" Mrs. Farrinder inquired, looking at her interlocutress, up and down, with the eye of business, in which there was a certain chill. "Have you got money?"

Olive was so agitated for the moment with the hope that this great woman would approve of her on the financial side that she took no time to reflect that some other quality might, in courtesy, have been suggested. But she confessed to possessing a certain capital, and the tone seemed rich and deep in which Mrs. Farrinder said to her, "Then contribute that!" She was so good as to develop this idea, and her picture of the part Miss Chancellor might play by making liberal donations to a fund for the diffusion among the women of America of a more adequate conception of their public and private rights — a fund her adviser had herself lately inaugurated — this bold, rapid sketch had the vividness which characterised the speaker's most successful public efforts. It placed Olive under the spell; it made her feel almost inspired. If her life struck others in that way — especially a woman like Mrs. Farrinder, whose horizon was so full — then there must be something for her to do. It was one thing to choose for herself, but now the great representative of the enfranchisement of their sex (from every form of bondage) had chosen for her.

The barren, gas-lighted room grew richer and richer to her earnest eyes; it seemed to expand, to open itself to the great life of humanity. The serious, tired people, in their bonnets and overcoats, began to glow like a company of heroes. Yes, she would do something, Olive Chancellor said to herself; she would do something to brighten the darkness of that dreadful image that was always before her, and against which it seemed to her at times that she had been born to lead a crusade — the image of the unhappiness of women. The unhappiness of women! The voice of their silent suffering was always in her ears, the ocean of tears that they had shed from the beginning of time seemed to pour through her own eyes. Ages of oppression had rolled over them; uncounted millions had lived only to be tortured, to be crucified. They were her sisters, they were her own, and the day of their delivery had dawned. This was the only sacred cause; this was the great, the just revolution. It must triumph, it must sweep everything before it; it must exact from the other, the brutal, bloodstained, ravening race, the last particle of expiation! It would be the greatest change the world had seen; it would be a new era for the human family, and the names of those who had helped to show the way and lead the squadrons would be the brightest in the tables of fame. They would be names of women weak, insulted, persecuted, but devoted in every pulse of their being to the cause, and asking no better fate than to die for it. It was not clear to this interesting girl in what manner such a sacrifice (as this last) would be required of her, but she saw the matter through a kind of sunrise-mist of emotion which made danger as rosy as success. When Miss Birdseye approached, it transfigured her familiar, her comical shape, and made the poor little humanitary hack seem already a martyr. Olive Chancellor looked at her with love, remembered that she had never, in her long, unrewarded, weary life, had a thought or an impulse for herself. She had been consumed by the passion of sympathy; it had crumpled her into as many creases as an old glazed, distended glove. She had been laughed at, but she never knew it; she was treated as a bore, but she never cared. She had nothing in the world but the clothes on her back, and when she should go down into the grave she would leave nothing behind her but her grotesque, undistinguished, pathetic little name. And yet people said that women were vain, that they were personal, that they were interested! While Miss Birdseye stood there, asking Mrs. Farrinder if she wouldn't say something, Olive Chancellor tenderly fastened a small battered brooch which confined her collar and which had half detached itself.

Chapter VI

"OH thank you," said Miss Birdseye, "I shouldn't like to lose it; it was given me by Mirandola!" He had been one of her refugees in the old time, when two or three of her friends, acquainted with the limits of his resources, wondered how he had come into possession of the trinket. She had been diverted again, after her greeting with Doctor and Mrs. Tarrant, by stopping to introduce the tall, dark young man whom Miss Chancellor had brought with her to Doctor Prance. She had become conscious of his somewhat sombre figure, uplifted against the wall, near the door; he was leaning there in solitude, unacquainted with opportunities which Miss Birdseye felt to be, collectively, of value, and which were really, of course, what strangers came to Boston for. It did not occur to her to ask herself why Miss Chancellor didn't talk to him, since she had brought him; Miss Birdseye was incapable of a speculation of this kind. Olive, in fact, had remained vividly conscious of her kinsman's isolation

until the moment when Mrs. Farrinder lifted her, with a word, to a higher plane. She watched him across the room; she saw that he might be bored. But she proposed to herself not to mind that; she had asked him, after all, not to come. Then he was no worse off than others; he was only waiting, like the rest; and before they left she would introduce him to Mrs. Farrinder. She might tell that lady who he was first; it was not every one that would care to know a person who had borne such a part in the Southern disloyalty. It came over our young lady that when she sought the acquaintance of her distant kinsman she had indeed done a more complicated thing than she suspected. The sudden uneasiness that he flung over her in the carriage had not left her, though she felt it less now she was with others, and especially that she was close to Mrs. Farrinder, who was such a fountain of strength. At any rate, if he was bored, he could speak to some one; there were excellent people near him, even if they *were* ardent reformers. He could speak to that pretty girl who had just come in — the one with red hair — if he liked; Southerners were supposed to be so chivalrous!

Miss Birdseye reasoned much less, and did not offer to introduce him to Verena Tarrant, who was apparently being presented by her parents to a group of friends at the other end of the room. It came back to Miss Birdseye, in this connection, that, sure enough,

Verena had been away for a long time — for nearly a year; had been on a visit to friends in the West, and would therefore naturally be a stranger to most of the Boston circle. Doctor Prance was looking at her — at Miss Birdseye — with little, sharp, fixed pupils; and the good lady wondered whether she were angry at having been induced to come up. She had a general impression that when genius was original its temper was high, and all this would be the case with Doctor Prance. She wanted to say to her that she could go down again if she liked; but even to Miss Birdseye's unsophisticated mind this scarcely appeared, as regards a guest, an adequate formula of dismissal. She tried to bring the young Southerner out; she said to him that she presumed they would have some entertainment soon — Mrs. Farrinder could be interesting when she tried! And then she bethought herself to introduce him to Doctor Prance; it might serve as a reason for having brought her up. Moreover, it would do her good to break up her work now and then; she pursued her medical studies far into the night, and Miss Birdseye, who was nothing of a sleeper (Mary Prance, precisely, had wanted to treat her for it), had heard her, in the stillness of the small hours, with her open windows (she had fresh air on the brain), sharpening instruments (it was Miss Birdseye's mild belief that she dissected), in a little physiological laboratory which she had set up in her back room, the room which, if she hadn't been a doctor, might have been her "chamber," and perhaps was, even with the dissecting, Miss Birdseye didn't know! She explained her young friends to each other, a trifle incoherently, perhaps, and then went to stir up Mrs. Farrinder.

Basil Ransom had already noticed Doctor Prance; he had not been at all bored, and had observed every one in the room, arriving at all sorts of ingenious inductions. The little medical lady struck him as a perfect example of the "Yankee female" — the figure which, in the unregenerate imagination of the children of the cotton-States, was produced by the New England school-system, the Puritan code, the ungenial climate, the absence of chivalry. Spare, dry, hard, without a curve, an inflection or a grace, she seemed to ask no odds in the battle of life and to be prepared to give none. But Ransom could see that she was not an enthusiast, and after his contact with his cousin's enthusiasm this was rather a relief to him. She looked like a boy, and not even like a good boy. It was evident that if she had been a boy, she would have "cut" school, to try private experiments in mechanics or to make researches in natural history. It was true that if she had been a boy she would have borne some relation to a girl, whereas Doctor Prance appeared to bear none whatever. Except her intelligent eye, she had no features to speak of. Ransom asked her if she were acquainted with the lioness, and on her staring at him, without response, explained that he meant the renowned Mrs. Farrinder.

"Well, I don't know as I ought to say that I'm acquainted with her; but I've heard her on the platform. I have paid my half-dollar," the doctor added, with a certain grimness.

"Well, did she convince you?" Ransom inquired.

"Convince me of what, sir?"

"That women are so superior to men."

"Oh, deary me!" said Doctor Prance, with a little impatient sigh; "I guess I know more about women than she does."

"And that isn't your opinion, I hope," said Ransom, laughing.

"Men and women are all the same to me," Doctor Prance remarked. "I don't see any difference. There is room for improvement in both sexes. Neither of them is up to the standard." And on Ransom's asking her what the standard appeared to her to be, she said, "Well, they ought to live better; that's what they ought to do." And she went on to declare, further, that she thought they all talked too much. This had so long been Ransom's conviction that his heart quite warmed to Doctor Prance, and he paid homage to her wisdom in the manner of Mississippi — with a richness of compliment that made her turn her acute, suspicious eye upon him. This checked him; she was capable of thinking that *he* talked too

much — she herself having, apparently, no general conversation. It was german to the matter, at any rate, for him to observe that he believed they were to have a lecture from Mrs. Farrinder — he didn't know why she didn't begin. "Yes," said Doctor Prance, rather drily, "I suppose that's what Miss Birdseye called me up for. She seemed to think I wouldn't want to miss that."

"Whereas, I infer, you could console yourself for the loss of the oration," Ransom suggested.

"Well, I've got some work. I don't want any one to teach me what a woman can do!" Doctor Prance declared. "She can find out some things, if she tries. Besides, I am familiar with Mrs. Farrinder's system; I know all she has got to say."

"Well, what is it, then, since she continues to remain silent?"

"Well, what it amounts to is just that women want to have a better time. That's what it comes to in the end. I am aware of that, without her telling me."

"And don't you sympathise with such an aspiration?"

"Well, I don't know as I cultivate the sentimental side," said Doctor Prance. "There's plenty of sympathy without mine. If they want to have a better time, I suppose it's natural; so do men too, I suppose. But I don't know as it appeals to me — to make sacrifices for it; it ain't such a wonderful time — the best you *can* have!"

This little lady was tough and technical; she evidently didn't care for great movements; she became more and more interesting to Basil Ransom, who, it is to be feared, had a fund of cynicism. He asked her if she knew his cousin, Miss Chancellor, whom he indicated, beside Mrs. Farrinder; *she* believed, on the contrary, in wonderful times (she thought they were coming); she had plenty of sympathy, and he was sure she was willing to make sacrifices.

Doctor Prance looked at her across the room for a moment; then she said she didn't know her, but she guessed she knew others like her — she went to see them when they were sick. "She's having a private lecture to herself," Ransom remarked; whereupon Doctor Prance rejoined, "Well, I guess she'll have to pay for it!" She appeared to regret her own half-dollar, and to be vaguely impatient of the behaviour of her sex. Ransom became so sensible of this that he felt it was indelicate to allude further to the cause of woman, and, for a change, endeavoured to elicit from his companion some information about the gentlemen present. He had given her a chance, vainly, to start some topic herself; but he could see that she had no interests beyond the researches from which, this evening, she had been torn, and was incapable of asking him a personal question. She knew two or three of the gentlemen; she had seen them before at Miss Birdseye's. Of course she knew principally ladies; the time hadn't come when a lady-doctor was sent for

by a gentleman, and she hoped it never would, though some people seemed to think that this was what lady-doctors were working for. She knew Mr. Pardon; that was the young man with the "side-whiskers" and the white hair; he was a kind of editor, and he wrote, too, "over his signature" — perhaps Basil had read some of his works; he was under thirty, in spite of his white hair. He was a great deal thought of in magazine circles. She believed he was very bright — but she hadn't read anything. She didn't read much — not for amusement; only the "Transcript." She believed Mr. Pardon sometimes wrote in the "Transcript"; well, she supposed he *was* very bright. The other that she knew — only she didn't know him (she supposed Basil would think that queer) — was the tall, pale gentleman, with the black moustache and the eye-glass. She knew him because she had met him in society; but she didn't know him — well, because she didn't want to. If he should come and speak to her — and he looked as if he were going to work around that way — she should just say to him, "Yes, sir," or "No, sir," very coldly. She couldn't help it if he did think her dry; if *he* were a little more dry, it might be better for him. What was the matter with him? Oh, she thought she had mentioned that; he was a mesmeric healer, he made miraculous cures. She didn't believe in his system or disbelieve in it, one way or the other; she only knew that she had been called to see ladies he had worked on, and she found that he had made them lose a lot of valuable time. He talked to them — well, as if he didn't know what he was saying. She guessed he was quite ignorant of physiology, and she didn't think he ought to go round taking responsibilities. She didn't want to be narrow, but she thought a person ought to know something. She supposed Basil would think her very uplifted; but he had put the question to her, as she might say. All she could say was she didn't want him to be laying his hands on any of *her* folks; it was all done with the hands — what wasn't done with the tongue! Basil could see that Doctor Prance was irritated; that this extreme candour of allusion to her neighbour was probably not habitual to her, as a member of a society in which the casual expression of strong opinion generally produced waves of silence. But he blessed her irritation, for him it was so illuminating; and to draw further profit from it he asked her who the young lady was with the red hair — the pretty one, whom he had only noticed during the last ten minutes. She was Miss Tarrant, the daughter of the healer; hadn't she mentioned his name? Selah Tarrant; if he wanted to send for him. Doctor Prance wasn't acquainted with her, beyond knowing that she was the mesmerist's only child, and having heard something about her having some gift — she couldn't remember which it was. Oh, if she was his child, she would be sure to have some gift — if it was only the gift of the g—— well, she didn't mean to say that; but a talent for conversation. Perhaps she could die and come to life again; perhaps she would show them her gift, as no one seemed inclined to do anything. Yes, she was pretty-appearing, but there was a certain indication of anæmia, and Doctor Prance would be surprised if she didn't eat too much candy. Basil thought she had an engaging exterior; it was his private reflection, coloured doubtless by "sectional" prejudice, that she was the first pretty girl he had seen in Boston. She was talking with some ladies at the other end of the room; and she had a large red fan, which she kept constantly in movement. She was not a quiet girl; she fidgeted, was restless, while she talked, and had the air of a person who, whatever she might be doing, would wish to be doing something else. If people watched her a good deal, she also returned their contemplation, and her charming eyes had several times encountered those of Basil Ransom. But they wandered mainly in the direction of Mrs. Farrinder — they lingered upon the serene solidity of the great oratress. It was easy to see that the girl admired this beneficent woman, and felt it a privilege to be near her. It was apparent, indeed, that she was excited by the company in which she found herself; a fact to be explained by a reference to that recent period of exile in the West, of which we have had a hint, and

The Bostonians

in consequence of which the present occasion may have seemed to her a return to intellectual life. Ransom secretly wished that his cousin — since fate was to reserve for him a cousin in Boston — had been more like that.

By this time a certain agitation was perceptible; several ladies, impatient of vain delay, had left their places, to appeal personally to Mrs. Farrinder, who was presently surrounded with sympathetic remonstrants. Miss Birdseye had given her up; it had been enough for Miss Birdseye that she should have said, when pressed (so far as her hostess, muffled in laxity, could press) on the subject of the general expectation, that she could only deliver her message to an audience which she felt to be partially hostile. There was no hostility there; they were all only too much in sympathy. "I don't require sympathy," she said, with a tranquil smile, to Olive Chancellor; "I am only myself, I only rise to the occasion, when I see prejudice, when I see bigotry, when I see injustice, when I see conservatism, massed before me like an army. Then I feel — I feel as I imagine Napoleon Bonaparte to have felt on the eve of one of his great victories. I *must* have unfriendly elements — I like to win them over."

Olive thought of Basil Ransom, and wondered whether he would do for an unfriendly element. She mentioned him to Mrs. Farrinder, who expressed an earnest hope that if he were opposed to the

principles which were so dear to the rest of them, he might be induced to take the floor and testify on his own account. "I should be so happy to answer him," said Mrs. Farrinder, with supreme softness. "I should be so glad, at any rate, to exchange ideas with him." Olive felt a deep alarm at the idea of a public dispute between these two vigorous people (she had a perception that Ransom would be vigorous), not because she doubted of the happy issue, but because she herself would be in a false position, as having brought the offensive young man, and she had a horror of false positions. Miss Birdseye was incapable of resentment; she had invited forty people to hear Mrs. Farrinder speak, and now Mrs. Farrinder wouldn't speak. But she had such a beautiful reason for it! There was something martial and heroic in her pretext, and, besides, it was so characteristic, so free, that Miss Birdseye was quite consoled, and wandered away, looking at her other guests vaguely, as if she didn't know them from each other, while she mentioned to them, at a venture, the excuse for their disappointment, confident, evidently, that they would agree with her it was very fine. "But we can't pretend to be on the other side, just to start her up, can we?" she asked of Mr. Tarrant, who sat there beside his wife with a rather conscious but by no means complacent air of isolation from the rest of the company.

"Well, I don't know — I guess

454

we are all solid here," this gentleman replied, looking round him with a slow, deliberate smile, which made his mouth enormous, developed two wrinkles, as long as the wings of a bat, on either side of it, and showed a set of big, even, carnivorous teeth.

"Selah," said his wife, laying her hand on the sleeve of his water-proof, "I wonder whether Miss Birdseye would be interested to hear Verena."

"Well, if you mean she sings, it's a shame I haven't got a piano," Miss Birdseye took upon herself to respond. It came back to her that the girl had a gift.

"She doesn't want a piano — she doesn't want anything," Selah remarked, giving no apparent attention to his wife. It was a part of his attitude in life never to appear to be indebted to another person for a suggestion, never to be surprised or unprepared.

"Well, I don't know that the interest in singing is so general," said Miss Birdseye, quite unconscious of any slackness in preparing a substitute for the entertainment that had failed her.

"It isn't singing, you'll see," Mrs. Tarrant declared.

"What is it, then?"

Mr. Tarrant unfurled his wrinkles, showed his back teeth. "It's inspirational."

Miss Birdseye gave a small vague, unsceptical laugh. "Well, if you can guarantee that —— "

"I think it would be acceptable," said Mrs. Tarrant; and putting up a half-gloved, familiar hand, she drew Miss Birdseye down to her, and the pair explained in alternation what it was their child could do.

Meanwhile, Basil Ransom confessed to Doctor Prance that he was, after all, rather disappointed. He had expected more of a programme; he wanted to hear some of the new truths. Mrs. Farrinder, as he said, remained within her tent, and he had hoped not only to see these distinguished people but also to listen to them.

"Well, I ain't disappointed," the sturdy little doctress replied. "If any question had been opened, I suppose I should have had to stay."

"But I presume you don't propose to retire."

"Well, I've got to pursue my studies some time. I don't want the gentlemen-doctors to get ahead of me."

"Oh, no one will ever get ahead of you, I'm very sure. And there is that pretty young lady going over to speak to Mrs. Farrinder. She's going to beg her for a speech — Mrs. Farrinder can't resist that."

"Well, then, I'll just trickle out before she begins. Good-night, sir," said Doctor Prance, who by this time had begun to appear to Ransom more susceptible of domestication, as if she had been a small forest-creature, a catamount or a ruffled doe, that had learned to stand still while you stroked it, or even to extend a paw. She ministered to health, and she was healthy herself; if his cousin could have been even of this type Basil would have felt himself more fortunate.

"Good-night, Doctor," he replied. "You haven't told me, after all, your opinion of the capacity of the ladies."

"Capacity for what?" said Doctor Prance. "They've got a capacity for making people waste time. All I know is that I don't want any one to tell *me* what a lady can do!" And she edged away from him softly, as if she had been traversing a hospital-ward, and presently he saw her reach the door, which, with the arrival of the later comers, had remained open. She stood there an instant, turning over the whole assembly a glance like a flash of a watchman's bull's-eye, and then quickly passed out. Ransom could see that she was impatient of the general question and bored with being reminded, even for the sake of her rights, that she was a woman — a detail that she was in the habit of forgetting, having as many rights as she had time for. It was certain that whatever might become of the movement at large, Doctor Prance's own little revolution was a success.

Chapter VII

SHE had no sooner left him than Olive Chancellor came towards him with eyes that seemed to say, "I don't care whether you are here now or not — I'm all right!" But what her lips said was much more gracious; she asked him if she mightn't have the pleasure of introducing him to Mrs. Farrinder. Ransom consented, with a little of his Southern flourish, and in a moment the lady got up to receive him from the midst of the circle that now surrounded her. It was an occasion for her to justify her reputation of an elegant manner, and it must be impartially related that she struck Ransom as having a dignity in conversation and a command of the noble style which could not have been surpassed by a daughter — one of the most accomplished, most far-descended daughters — of his own latitude. It was as if she had known that he was not eager for the changes she advocated, and wished to show him that, especially to a Southerner who had bitten the dust, her sex could be magnanimous. This knowledge of his secret heresy seemed to him to be also in the faces of the other ladies, whose circumspect glances, however (for he had not been introduced), treated it as a pity rather than as a shame. He was conscious of all these middle-aged feminine eyes, conscious of curls, rather limp, that depended from dusky bonnets, of heads poked forward, as if with a waiting, listening, familiar habit, of no one being very bright or gay — no one, at least, but that girl he had noticed before, who had a brilliant head, and who now hovered on the edge of the conclave. He met her eye again; she was watching him too.

It had been in his thought that Mrs. Farrinder, to whom his cousin might have betrayed or misrepresented him, would perhaps defy him to combat, and he wondered whether he could pull himself together (he was extremely embarrassed) sufficiently to do honour to such a challenge. If she would fling down the glove on the temperance question, it seemed to him that it would be in him to pick it up; for the idea of a meddling legislation on this subject filled him with rage; the taste of liquor being good to him, and his conviction strong that civilisation itself would be in danger if it should fall into the power of a herd of vociferating women (I am but the reporter of his angry *formulæ*) to prevent a gentleman from taking his glass. Mrs. Farrinder proved to him that she had not the eagerness of insecurity; she asked him if he wouldn't like to give the company some account of the social and political condition of the South. He begged to be excused, expressing at the same time a high sense of the honour done him by such a request, while he smiled to himself at the idea of his extemporising a lecture. He smiled even while he suspected the meaning of the look Miss Chancellor gave him: "Well, you are not of much account after all!" To talk to those people about the South — if they could have guessed how little he cared to do it! He had a passionate tenderness for his own country, and a sense of intimate connection with it which would have made it as impossible for him to take a roomful of Northern fanatics into his confidence as to read aloud his mother's or his mistress's letters. To be quiet about the Southern land, not to touch her with vulgar hands, to leave her alone with her wounds and her memories, not prating in the market-place either of her troubles or her hopes, but waiting as a man should wait, for the slow process, the sensible beneficence, of time — this was the desire of Ransom's heart, and he was aware of how little it could minister to the entertainment of Miss Birdseye's guests.

"We know so little about the women of the South; they are very voiceless," Mrs. Farrinder remarked. "How much can we count upon them? in what numbers would they flock to our standard? I have been recommended not to lecture in the Southern cities."

"Ah, madam, that was very cruel advice — for us!" Basil Ransom exclaimed, with gallantry.

"*I* had a magnificent audience last spring in St. Louis," a fresh young voice announced, over the heads of the gathered group — a voice which, on Basil's turning, like every one else, for an explanation, appeared to have proceeded from the pretty girl with red hair. She had coloured a little with the effort of making this declaration, and she stood there smiling at her listeners.

Mrs. Farrinder bent a benignant brow upon her, in spite of her being, evidently, rather a surprise.

"Oh, indeed; and your subject, my dear young lady?"

"The past history, the present condition, and the future prospects of our sex."

"Oh, well, St. Louis — that's scarcely the South," said one of the ladies.

"I'm sure the young lady would have had equal success at Charleston or New Orleans," Basil Ransom interposed.

"Well, I wanted to go farther," the girl continued, "but I had no friends. I have friends in St. Louis."

"You oughtn't to want for them anywhere," said Mrs. Farrinder, in a manner which, by this time, had quite explained her reputation. "I am acquainted with the loyalty of St. Louis."

"Well, after that, you must let me introduce Miss Tarrant; she's perfectly dying to know you, Mrs. Farrinder." These words emanated from one of the gentlemen, the young man with white hair, who had been mentioned to Ransom by Doctor Prance as a celebrated magazinist. He, too, up to this moment, had hovered in the background, but he now gently clove the assembly (several of the ladies made way for him), leading in the daughter of the mesmerist.

She laughed and continued to blush — her blush was the faintest pink; she looked very young and slim and fair as Mrs. Farrinder made way for her on the sofa which Olive Chancellor had quitted. "I *have* wanted to know you; I admire you so much; I hoped so

you would speak to-night. It's too lovely to see you, Mrs. Farrinder." So she expressed herself, while the company watched the encounter with a look of refreshed inanition. "You don't know who I am, of course; I'm just a girl who wants to thank you for all you have done for us. For you have spoken for us girls, just as much as — just as much as —— " She hesitated now, looking about with enthusiastic eyes at the rest of the group, and meeting once more the gaze of Basil Ransom.

"Just as much as for the old women," said Mrs. Farrinder, genially. "You seem very well able to speak for yourself."

"She speaks so beautifully — if she would only make a little address," the young man who had introduced her remarked. "It's a new style, quite original," he added. He stood there with folded arms, looking down at his work, the conjunction of the two ladies, with a smile; and Basil Ransom, remembering what Miss Prance had told him, and enlightened by his observation in New York of some of the sources from which newspapers are fed, was immediately touched by the conviction that he perceived in it the material of a paragraph.

"My dear child, if you'll take the floor, I'll call the meeting to order," said Mrs. Farrinder.

The girl looked at her with extraordinary candour and confidence. "If I could only hear you first — just to give me an atmosphere."

"I've got no atmosphere; there's

very little of the Indian summer about *me!* I deal with facts — hard facts," Mrs. Farrinder replied. "Have you ever heard me? If so, you know how crisp I am."

"Heard you? I've lived on you! It's so much to me to see you. Ask mother if it ain't!" She had expressed herself, from the first word she uttered, with a promptness and assurance which gave almost the impression of a lesson rehearsed in advance. And yet there was a strange spontaneity in her manner, and an air of artless enthusiasm, of personal purity. If she was theatrical, she was naturally theatrical. She looked up at Mrs. Farrinder with all her emotion in her smiling eyes. This lady had been the object of many ovations; it was familiar to her that the collective heart of her sex had gone forth to her; but, visibly, she was puzzled by this unforeseen embodiment of gratitude and fluency, and her eyes wandered over the girl with a certain reserve, while, within the depth of her eminently public manner, she asked herself whether Miss Tarrant were a remarkable young woman or only a forward minx. She found a response which committed her to neither view; she only said, "We want the young — of course we want the young!"

"Who is that charming creature?" Basil Ransom heard his cousin ask, in a grave, lowered tone, of Matthias Pardon, the young man who had brought Miss Tarrant forward. He didn't know whether Miss Chancellor knew him, or whether her curiosity had pushed her to boldness. Ransom was near the pair, and had the benefit of Mr. Pardon's answer.

"The daughter of Doctor Tarrant, the mesmeric healer — Miss Verena. She's a high-class speaker."

"What do you mean?" Olive asked. "Does she give public addresses?"

"Oh yes, she has had quite a career in the West. I heard her last spring at Topeka. They call it inspirational. I don't know what it is — only it's exquisite; so fresh and poetical. She has to have her father to start her up. It seems to pass into her." And Mr. Pardon indulged in a gesture intended to signify the passage.

Olive Chancellor made no rejoinder save a low, impatient sigh; she transferred her attention to the girl, who now held Mrs. Farrinder's hand in both her own, and was pleading with her just to prelude a little. "I want a starting-point — I want to know where I am," she said. "Just two or three of your grand old thoughts."

Basil stepped nearer to his cousin; he remarked to her that Miss Verena was very pretty. She turned an instant, glanced at him, and then said, "Do you think so?" An instant later she added, "How you must hate this place!"

"Oh, not now, we are going to have some fun," Ransom replied good-humouredly, if a trifle coarsely; and the declaration had a point, for Miss Birdseye at this moment reappeared, followed by the mesmeric healer and his wife.

"Ah, well, I see you are drawing her out," said Miss Birdseye to Mrs. Farrinder; and at the idea that this process had been necessary Basil Ransom broke into a smothered hilarity, a spasm which indicated that, for him, the fun had already begun, and procured him another grave glance from Miss Chancellor. Miss Verena seemed to him as far "out" as a young woman could be. "Here's her father, Doctor Tarrant — he has a wonderful gift — and her mother — she was a daughter of Abraham Greenstreet." Miss Birdseye presented her companion; she was sure Mrs. Farrinder would be interested; she wouldn't want to lose an opportunity, even if for herself the conditions were not favourable. And then Miss Birdseye addressed herself to the company more at large, widening the circle so as to take in the most scattered guests, and evidently feeling that after all it was a relief that one happened to have an obscurely inspired maiden on the premises when greater celebrities had betrayed the whimsicality of genius. It was a part of this whimsicality that Mrs. Farrinder — the reader may find it difficult to keep pace with her variations — appeared now to have decided to utter a few of her thoughts, so that her hostess could elicit a general response to the remark that it would be delightful to have both the old school and the new.

"Well, perhaps you'll be disappointed in Verena," said Mrs. Tarrant, with an air of dolorous resignation to any event, and seating herself, with her gathered mantle, on the edge of a chair, as if she, at least, were ready, whoever else might keep on talking.

"It isn't *me*, mother," Verena rejoined, with soft gravity, rather detached now from Mrs. Farrinder, and sitting with her eyes fixed thoughtfully on the ground. With deference to Mrs. Tarrant, a little more talk was necessary, for the young lady had as yet been insufficiently explained. Miss Birdseye felt this, but she was rather helpless about it, and delivered herself, with her universal familiarity, which embraced every one and everything, of a wandering, amiable tale, in which Abraham Greenstreet kept reappearing, in which Doctor Tarrant's miraculous cures were specified, with all the facts wanting, and in which Verena's successes in the West were related, not with emphasis or hyperbole, in which Miss Birdseye never indulged, but as accepted and recognised wonders, natural in an age of new revelations. She had heard of these things in detail only ten minutes before, from the girl's parents, but her hospitable soul had needed but a moment to swallow and assimilate them. If her account of them was not very lucid, it should be said in excuse for her that it was impossible to have any idea of Verena Tarrant unless one had heard her, and therefore still more impossible to give an idea to others. Mrs. Farrinder was perceptibly irritated; she appeared to have made up her mind, after her first hesitation, that the Tarrant family were fantastical and compromising. She had bent an eye of coldness on Selah and his wife — she might have regarded them all as a company of mountebanks.

"Stand up and tell us what you have to say," she remarked, with some sternness, to Verena, who only raised her eyes to her, silently now, with the same sweetness, and then rested them on her father. This gentleman seemed to respond to an irresistible appeal; he looked around at the company with all his teeth, and said that these flattering allusions were not so embarrassing as they might otherwise be, inasmuch as any success that he and his daughter might have had was so thoroughly impersonal: he insisted on that word. They had just heard her say, "It is not *me,* mother," and he and Mrs. Tarrant and the girl herself were all equally aware it was not she. It was some power outside — it seemed to flow through her; he couldn't pretend to say why his daughter should be called, more than any one else. But it seemed as if she *was* called. When he just calmed her down by laying his hand on her a few moments, it seemed to come. It so happened that in the West it had taken the form of a considerable eloquence. She had certainly spoken with great facility to cultivated and high-minded audiences. She had long followed with sympathy the movement for the liberation of her sex from every sort of bondage; it had been her principal interest even as a child (he might mention that at the age of nine she had christened her favourite doll Eliza P. Moseley, in memory of a great precursor whom they all reverenced), and now the inspiration, if he might call it so, seemed just to flow in that channel. The voice that spoke from her lips seemed to want to take that form. It didn't seem as if it *could* take any other. She let it come out just as it would — she didn't pretend to have any control. They could judge for themselves whether the whole thing was not quite unique. That was why he was willing to talk about his own child that way, before a gathering of ladies and gentlemen; it was because they took no credit — they felt it was a power outside. If Verena felt she was going to be stimulated that evening, he was pretty sure they would be interested. Only he should have to request a few moments' silence, while she listened for the voice.

Several of the ladies declared that they should be delighted — they hoped that Miss Tarrant was in good trim; whereupon they were corrected by others, who reminded them that it wasn't *her* — she had nothing to do with it — so her trim didn't matter; and a gentleman added that he guessed there were many present who had conversed with Eliza P. Moseley. Meanwhile Verena, more and more withdrawn into herself, but perfectly undisturbed by the public discussion of her mystic faculty, turned yet again, very prettily, to Mrs. Farrinder, and asked her if she wouldn't strike out — just to give her courage. By this time Mrs. Farrinder was in a condition of overhanging gloom; she greeted the charming suppliant with the frown of Juno. She disapproved completely of Doctor Tarrant's little speech, and she had less and less disposition to be associated with a miracle-monger. Abraham Greenstreet was very well, but Abraham Greenstreet was in his grave; and Eliza P. Moseley, after all, had been very tepid. Basil Ransom wondered whether it were effrontery or innocence that enabled Miss Tarrant to meet with such complacency the aloofness of the elder lady. At this moment he heard Olive Chancellor, at his elbow, with the tremor of excitement in her tone, suddenly exclaim: "Please begin, please begin! A voice, a human voice, is what we want."

"I'll speak after you, and if you're a humbug, I'll expose you!" Mrs. Farrinder said. She was more majestic than facetious.

"I'm sure we are all solid, as Doctor Tarrant says. I suppose we want to be quiet," Miss Birdseye remarked.

Chapter VIII

VERENA TARRANT got up and went to her father in the middle of the room; Olive Chancellor crossed and resumed her place beside Mrs. Farrinder on the sofa the girl had quitted; and Miss Birdseye's visitors, for the rest, settled themselves attentively in chairs or leaned against the bare sides of the parlour. Verena took her father's hands, held them for a moment, while she stood before him, not looking at him, with her eyes towards the company; then, after an instant, her mother, rising, pushed forward, with an interesting sigh, the chair on which she had been sitting. Mrs. Tarrant was provided with another seat, and Verena, relinquishing her father's grasp, placed herself in the chair, which Tarrant put in position for her. She sat there with closed eyes, and her father now rested his long, lean hands upon her head. Basil Ransom watched these proceedings with much interest, for the girl amused and pleased him. She had far more colour than any one there, for whatever brightness was to be found in Miss Birdseye's rather faded and dingy human collection had gathered itself into this attractive but ambiguous young person. There was nothing ambiguous, by the way, about her confederate; Ransom simply loathed him, from the moment he opened his mouth; he was intensely familiar — that is, his type was; he was simply the detested carpet-bagger. He was false, cunning, vulgar, ignoble; the cheapest kind of human product. That he should be the father of a delicate, pretty girl, who was apparently clever too, whether she had a gift or no, this was an annoying, disconcerting fact. The white,

462

puffy mother, with the high forehead, in the corner there, looked more like a lady; but if she were one, it was all the more shame to her to have mated with such a varlet, Ransom said to himself, making use, as he did generally, of terms of opprobrium extracted from the older English literature. He had seen Tarrant, or his equivalent, often before; he had "whipped" him, as he believed, controversially, again and again, at political meetings in blighted Southern towns, during the horrible period of reconstruction. If Mrs. Farrinder had looked at Verena Tarrant as if she were a mountebank, there was some excuse for it, inasmuch as the girl made much the same impression on Basil Ransom. He had never seen such an odd mixture of elements; she had the sweetest, most unworldly face, and yet, with it, an air of being on exhibition, of belonging to a troupe, of living in the gaslight, which pervaded even the details of her dress, fashioned evidently with an attempt at the histrionic. If she had produced a pair of castanets or a tambourine, he felt that such accessories would have been quite in keeping.

Little Doctor Prance, with her hard good sense, had noted that she was anæmic, and had intimated that she was a deceiver. The value of her performance was yet to be proved, but she was certainly very pale, white as women are who have that shade of red hair; they look as if their blood had gone into it. There was, however, something rich in the fairness of this young lady; she was strong and supple, there was colour in her lips and eyes, and her tresses, gathered into a complicated coil, seemed to glow with the brightness of her nature. She had curious, radiant, liquid eyes (their smile was a sort of reflection, like the glisten of a gem), and though she was not tall, she appeared to spring up, and carried her head as if it reached rather high. Ransom would have thought she looked like an Oriental, if it were not that Orientals are dark; and if she had only had a goat she would have resembled Esmeralda, though he had but a vague recollection of who Esmeralda had been. She wore a light-brown dress, of a shape that struck him as fantastic, a yellow petticoat, and a large crimson sash fastened at the side; while round her neck, and falling low upon her flat young chest, she had a double chain of amber beads. It must be added that, in spite of her melodramatic appearance, there was no symptom that her performance, whatever it was, would be of a melodramatic character. She was very quiet now, at least (she had folded her big fan), and her father continued the mysterious process of calming her down. Ransom wondered whether he wouldn't put her to sleep; for some minutes her eyes had remained closed; he heard a lady near him, apparently familiar with phenomena of this class, remark that she was going off. As yet the exhibition was not exciting, though it was certainly pleasant to have such a pretty girl placed there before one, like a moving statue. Doctor Tarrant looked at no one as he stroked and soothed his daughter; his eyes wandered round the cornice of the room, and he grinned upward, as if at an imaginary gallery. "Quietly — quietly," he murmured, from time to time. "It will come, my good child, it will come. Just let it work — just let it gather. The spirit, you know; you've got to let the spirit come out when it will." He threw up his arms at moments, to rid himself of the wings of his long waterproof, which fell forward over his hands. Basil Ransom noticed all these things, and noticed also, opposite, the waiting face of his cousin, fixed, from her sofa, upon the closed eyes of the young prophetess. He grew more impatient at last, not of the delay of the edifying voice (though some time had elapsed), but of Tarrant's grotesque manipulations, which he resented as much as if he himself had felt their touch, and which seemed a dishonour to the passive maiden. They made him nervous, they made him angry, and it was only afterwards that he asked himself wherein they concerned him, and whether even a carpet-bagger hadn't a right to do what he pleased with his daughter. It was a relief to him when Verena got up from her chair, with a movement which made Tarrant drop into the background as if his part were now over. She stood there with a quiet face, serious and sightless; then, after a short further delay, she began to speak.

She began incoherently, almost inaudibly, as if she were talking in a dream. Ransom could not understand her; he thought it very queer, and wondered what Doctor Prance would have said. "She's just arranging her ideas, and trying to get in report; she'll come out all right." This remark he heard dropped in a low tone by the mesmeric healer; "in report" was apparently Tarrant's version of *en rapport*. His prophecy was verified, and Verena did come out, after a little; she came out with a great deal of sweetness — with a very quaint and peculiar effect. She proceeded slowly, cautiously, as if she were listening for the prompter, catching, one by one, certain phrases that were whispered to her a great distance off, behind the scenes of the world. Then memory, or inspiration, returned to her, and presently she was in possession of her part. She played it with extraordinary simplicity and grace; at the end of ten minutes Ransom became aware that the whole audience — Mrs. Farrinder, Miss Chancellor, and the tough subject from Mississippi — were under the charm. I speak of ten minutes, but to tell the truth the young man lost all sense of time. He wondered afterwards how long she had spoken; then he counted that her strange, sweet, crude, absurd, enchanting improvisation must have lasted half an hour. It was not what she said; he didn't care for that, he scarcely understood it; he could only see that it was all about the gentleness and goodness of women, and how, during the long ages of history, they had been trampled under the iron heel of man. It was about their equality — perhaps even (he was not definitely conscious) about their superiority. It was about their day having come at last, about the universal sisterhood, about their duty to themselves and to each other. It was about such matters as these, and Basil Ransom was delighted to observe that such matters as these didn't spoil it. The effect was not in what she said, though she said some such pretty things, but in the picture and figure of the half-bedizened damsel (playing, now again, with her red fan), the visible freshness and purity of the little effort. When she had gained confidence she opened her eyes, and their shining softness was half the effect of her discourse. It was full of school-girl phrases, of patches of remembered eloquence, of childish lapses of logic, of flights of fancy which might indeed have had success at Topeka; but Ransom thought that if it had been much worse it would have been quite as good, for the argument, the doctrine, had absolutely nothing to do with it. It was simply an intensely personal exhibition, and the person making it happened to be fascinating. She might have offended the taste of certain people — Ransom could imagine that there were other Boston circles in which she would be thought pert; but for himself all

he could feel was that to *his* starved senses she irresistibly appealed. He was the stiffest of conservatives, and his mind was steeled against the inanities she uttered — the rights and wrongs of women, the equality of the sexes, the hysterics of conventions, the further stultification of the suffrage, the prospect of conscript mothers in the national Senate. It made no difference; she didn't mean it, she didn't know what she meant, she had been stuffed with this trash by her father, and she was neither more nor less willing to say it than to say anything else; for the necessity of her nature was not to make converts to a ridiculous cause, but to emit those charming notes of her voice, to stand in those free young attitudes, to shake her braided locks like a naiad rising from the waves, to please every one who came near her, and to be happy that she pleased. I know not whether Ransom was aware of the bearings of this interpretation, which attributed to Miss Tarrant a singular hollowness of character; he contented himself with believing that she was as innocent as she was lovely, and with regarding her as a vocalist of exquisite faculty, condemned to sing bad music. How prettily, indeed, she made some of it sound!

"Of course I only speak to women — to my own dear sisters; I don't speak to men, for I don't expect them to like what I say. They pretend to admire us very much, but I should like them to admire us a little less and to trust us a little more. I don't know what we have ever done to them that they should keep us out of everything. We have trusted *them* too much, and I think the time has come now for us to judge them, and say that by keeping us out we don't think they have done so well. When I look around me at the world, and at the state that men have brought it to, I confess I say to myself, 'Well, if women had fixed it this way I should like to know what they would think of it!' When I see the dreadful misery of mankind and think of the suffering of which at any hour, at any moment, the world is full, I say that if this is the best they can do by themselves, they had better let us come in a little and see what *we* can do. We couldn't possibly make it worse, could we? If we had done only this, we shouldn't boast of it. Poverty, and ignorance, and crime; disease, and wickedness, and wars! Wars, always more wars, and always more and more. Blood, blood — the world is drenched with blood! To kill each other, with all sorts of expensive and perfected instruments, that is the most brilliant thing they have been able to invent. It seems to me that we might stop it, we might invent something better. The cruelty — the cruelty; there is so much, so much! Why shouldn't tenderness come in? Why should our woman's hearts be so full of it, and all so wasted and withered, while armies and prisons and helpless miseries grow greater all the while? I am only a girl, a simple American girl, and of course I haven't seen much, and there is a great deal of life that I don't know anything about. But there are some things I feel — it seems to me as if I had been born to feel them; they are in my ears in the stillness of the night and before my face in the visions of the darkness. It is what the great sisterhood of women might do if they should all join hands, and lift up their voices above the brutal uproar of the world, in which it is so hard for the plea of mercy or of justice, the moan of weakness and suffering, to be heard. We should quench it, we should make it still, and the sound of our lips would become the voice of universal peace! For this we must trust one another, we must be true and gentle and kind. We must remember that the world is ours too, ours — little as we have ever had to say about anything! — and that the question is *not* yet definitely settled whether it shall be a place of injustice or a place of love!"

It was with this that the young lady finished her harangue, which was not followed by her sinking exhausted into her chair or by any of the traces of a laboured climax. She only turned away slowly towards her mother, smiling over her shoulder at the whole room, as if it had been a single person, without a flush in her whiteness, or the need of drawing a longer breath. The performance had evidently been very easy to her, and there might have been a kind of impertinence in her air of not having suffered from an exertion which had wrought so powerfully on every one else. Ransom broke into a genial laugh, which he instantly swallowed again, at the sweet grotesqueness of this virginal creature's standing up before a company of middle-aged people to talk to them about "love," the note on which she had closed her harangue. It was the most charming touch in the whole thing, and the most vivid proof of her innocence. She had had immense success, and Mrs. Tarrant, as she took her into her arms and kissed her, was certainly able to feel that the audience was not disappointed. They were exceedingly affected; they broke into exclamations and murmurs. Selah Tarrant went on conversing ostentatiously with his neighbours, slowly twirling his long thumbs and looking up at the cornice again, as if there could be nothing in the brilliant manner in which his daughter had acquitted herself to surprise *him*, who had heard her when she was still more remarkable, and who, moreover, remembered that the affair was so impersonal. Miss Birdseye looked round at the company with dim exultation; her large mild cheeks were shining with unwiped tears. Young Mr. Pardon remarked, in Ransom's hearing, that he knew parties who, if they had been present, would want to engage Miss Verena at a high figure for the winter campaign. And Ransom heard him add in a lower tone: "There's money for some one in

that girl; you see if she don't have quite a run!" As for our Mississippian he kept his agreeable sensation for himself, only wondering whether he might not ask Miss Birdseye to present him to the heroine of the evening. Not immediately, of course, for the young man mingled with his Southern pride a shyness which often served all the purpose of humility. He was aware how much he was an outsider in such a house as that, and he was ready to wait for his coveted satisfaction till the others, who all hung together, should have given her the assurance of an approval which she would value, naturally, more than anything he could say to her. This episode had imparted animation to the assembly; a certain gaiety, even, expressed in a higher pitch of conversation, seemed to float in the heated air. People circulated more freely, and Verena Tarrant was presently hidden from Ransom's sight by the close-pressed ranks of the new friends she had made. "Well, I never heard it put *that* way!" Ransom heard one of the ladies exclaim; to which another replied that she wondered one of their bright women hadn't thought of it before. "Well, it *is* a gift, and no mistake," and "Well, they may call it what they please, it's a pleasure to listen to it" — these genial tributes fell from the lips of a pair of ruminating gentlemen. It was affirmed within Ransom's hearing that if they had a few more like that the matter would soon be fixed; and it was rejoined that they couldn't expect to have a great many — the style was so peculiar. It was generally admitted that the style was peculiar, but Miss Tarrant's peculiarity was the explanation of her success.

Chapter IX

RANSOM approached Mrs. Farrinder again, who had remained on her sofa with Olive Chancellor; and as she turned her face to him he saw that she had felt the universal contagion. Her keen eye sparkled, there was a flush on her matronly cheek, and she had evidently made up her mind what line to take. Olive Chancellor sat motionless; her eyes were fixed on the floor with the rigid, alarmed expression of her moments of nervous diffidence; she gave no sign of observing her kinsman's approach. He said something to Mrs. Farrinder, something that imperfectly represented his admiration of Verena; and this lady replied with dignity that it was no wonder the girl spoke so well — she spoke in such a good cause. "She is very graceful, has a fine command of language; her father says it's a natural gift." Ransom saw that he should not in the least discover Mrs. Farrinder's real opinion, and her dissimulation added to his impression that she was a woman with a policy. It was none of his business whether in her heart she thought Verena a parrot or a gen-

ius; it was perceptible to him that she saw she would be effective, would help the cause. He stood almost appalled for a moment, as he said to himself that she would take her up and the girl would be ruined, would force her note and become a screamer. But he quickly dodged this vision, taking refuge in a mechanical appeal to his cousin, of whom he inquired how she liked Miss Verena. Olive made no answer; her head remained averted, she bored the carpet with her conscious eyes. Mrs. Farrinder glanced at her askance, and then said to Ransom serenely:

"You praise the grace of your Southern ladies, but you have had to come North to see a human gazelle. Miss Tarrant is of the best New England stock — what I call the best!"

"I'm sure from what I have seen of the Boston ladies, no manifestation of grace can excite my surprise," Ransom rejoined, looking, with his smile, at his cousin.

"She has been powerfully affected," Mrs. Farrinder explained, very slightly dropping her voice, as Olive, apparently, still remained deaf.

Miss Birdseye drew near at this moment; she wanted to know if Mrs. Farrinder didn't want to express some acknowledgment, on the part of the company at large, for the real stimulus Miss Tarrant had given them. Mrs. Farrinder said: Oh yes, she would speak now with pleasure; only she must have a glass of water first. Miss Birdseye replied that there was some coming in a moment; one of the ladies had asked for it, and Mr. Pardon had just stepped down to draw some. Basil took advantage of this intermission to ask Miss Birdseye if she would give him the great privilege of an introduction to Miss Verena. "Mrs. Farrinder will thank her for the company," he said, laughing, "but she won't thank her for me."

Miss Birdseye manifested the greatest disposition to oblige him; she was so glad he had been impressed. She was proceeding to lead him toward Miss Tarrant when Olive Chancellor rose abruptly from her chair and laid her hand, with an arresting movement, on the arm of her hostess. She explained to her that she must go, that she was not very well, that her carriage was there; also that she hoped Miss Birdseye, if it was not asking too much, would accompany her to the door.

"Well, you are impressed too," said Miss Birdseye, looking at her philosophically. "It seems as if no one had escaped."

Ransom was disappointed; he saw he was going to be taken away, and, before he could suppress it, an exclamation burst from his lips — the first exclamation he could think of that would perhaps check his cousin's retreat: "Ah, Miss Olive, are you going to give up Mrs. Farrinder?"

At this Miss Olive looked at him, showed him an extraordinary face, a face he scarcely understood or even recognised. It was portentously grave, the eyes were en-larged, there was a red spot in each of the cheeks, and as directed to him, a quick, piercing question, a kind of leaping challenge, in the whole expression. He could only answer this sudden gleam with a stare, and wonder afresh what trick his Northern kinswoman was destined to play him. Impressed too? He should think he had been! Mrs. Farrinder, who was decidedly a woman of the world, came to his assistance, or to Miss Chancellor's, and said she hoped very much Olive wouldn't stay — she felt these things too much. "If you stay, I won't speak," she added; "I should upset you altogether." And then she continued, tenderly, for so preponderantly intellectual a nature: "When women feel as you do, how can I doubt that we shall come out all right?"

"Oh, we shall come out all right, I guess," murmured Miss Birdseye.

"But you must remember Beacon Street," Mrs. Farrinder subjoined. "You must take advantage of your position — you must wake up the Back Bay!"

"I'm sick of the Back Bay!" said Olive fiercely; and she passed to the door with Miss Birdseye, bidding good-bye to no one. She was so agitated that, evidently, she could not trust herself, and there was nothing for Ransom but to follow. At the door of the room, however, he was checked by a sudden pause on the part of the two ladies: Olive stopped and stood there hesitating. She looked round the room and spied out Verena, where she sat with her mother, the centre of a gratified group; then, throwing back her head with an air of decision, she crossed over to her. Ransom said to himself that now, perhaps, was his chance, and he quickly accompanied Miss Chancellor. The little knot of reformers watched her as she arrived; their faces expressed a suspicion of her social importance, mingled with conscientious scruples as to whether it were right to recognise it. Verena Tarrant saw that she was the object of this manifestation, and she got up to meet the lady whose approach was so full of point. Ransom perceived, however, or thought he perceived, that she recognised nothing; she had no suspicions of social importance. Yet she smiled with all her radiance, as she looked from Miss Chancellor to him; smiled because she liked to smile, to please, to feel her success — or was it because she was a perfect little actress, and this was part of her training? She took the hand that Olive put out to her; the others, rather solemnly, sat looking up from their chairs.

"You don't know me, but I want to know you," Olive said. "I can thank you now. Will you come and see me?"

"Oh yes; where do you live?" Verena answered, in the tone of a girl for whom an invitation (she hadn't so many) was always an invitation.

Miss Chancellor syllabled her address, and Mrs. Tarrant came forward, smiling. "I know about you, Miss Chancellor. I guess your father knew my father — Mr. Greenstreet. Verena will be very glad to visit you. We shall be very happy to see you in *our* home."

Basil Ransom, while the mother spoke, wanted to say something to the daughter, who stood there so near him, but he could think of nothing that would do; certain words that came to him, his Mississippi phrases, seemed patronising and ponderous. Besides, he didn't wish to assent to what she had said; he wished simply to tell her she was delightful, and it was difficult to mark that difference. So he only smiled at her in silence, and she smiled back at him — a smile that seemed to him quite for himself.

"Where do you live?" Olive asked; and Mrs. Tarrant replied that they lived at Cambridge, and that the horse-cars passed just near their door. Whereupon Olive insisted "Will you come very soon?" and Verena said, Oh yes, she would come very soon, and repeated the number in Charles Street, to show that she had taken heed of it. This was done with childlike good faith. Ransom saw that she would come and see any one who would ask her like that, and he regretted for a minute that he was not a Boston lady, so that he might extend to her such an invitation. Olive Chancellor held her hand a moment longer, looked at her in farewell, and then, saying, "Come, Mr. Ransom," drew him out of the room. In the hall

470

they met Mr. Pardon, coming up from the lower regions with a jug of water and a tumbler. Miss Chancellor's hackney-coach was there, and when Basil had put her into it she said to him that she wouldn't trouble him to drive with her — his hotel was not near Charles Street. He had so little desire to sit by her side — he wanted to smoke — that it was only after the vehicle had rolled off that he reflected upon her coolness, and asked himself why the deuce she had brought him away. She *was* a very odd cousin, was this Boston cousin of his. He stood there a moment, looking at the light in Miss Birdseye's windows and greatly minded to re-enter the house, now he might speak to the girl. But he contented himself with the memory of her smile, and turned away with a sense of relief, after all, at having got out of such wild company, as well as with (in a different order) a vulgar consciousness of being very thirsty.

Chapter X

VERENA TARRANT came in the very next day from Cambridge to Charles Street; that quarter of Boston is in direct communication with the academic suburb. It hardly seemed direct to poor Verena, perhaps, who, in the crowded street-car which deposited her finally at Miss Chancellor's door, had to stand up all the way, half suspended by a leathern strap from the glazed roof of the stifling vehicle, like some blooming cluster dangling in a hothouse. She was used, however, to these perpendicular journeys, and though, as we have seen, she was not inclined to accept without question the social arrangements of her time, it never would have occurred to her to criticise the railways of her native land. The promptness of her visit to Olive Chancellor had been an idea of her mother's, and Verena listened open-eyed while this lady, in the seclusion of the little house in Cambridge, while Selah Tarrant was "off," as they said, with his patients, sketched out a line of conduct for her. The girl was both submissive and unworldly, and she listened to her mother's enumeration of the possible advantages of an intimacy with Miss Chancellor as she would have listened to any other fairytale. It was still a part of the fairy-tale when this zealous parent put on with her own hands Verena's smart hat and feather, buttoned her little jacket (the buttons were immense and gilt), and presented her with twenty cents to pay her car-fare.

There was never any knowing in advance how Mrs. Tarrant would take a thing, and even Verena, who, filially, was much less argumentative than in her civic and, as it were, public capacity, had a perception that her mother was queer. She was queer, indeed — a flaccid, relaxed, unhealthy, whimsical woman, who still had a capacity to cling. What she clung to was "society," and a position in the world which a secret whisper told her she had never had and a voice more audible reminded her she was in danger of losing. To keep it, to recover it, to reconsecrate it, was the ambition of her heart; this was one of the many reasons why Providence had judged her worthy of having so wonderful a child. Verena was born not only to lead their common sex out of bondage, but to remodel a visiting-list which bulged and contracted in the wrong places, like a country-made garment. As the daughter of Abraham Greenstreet, Mrs. Tarrant had passed her youth in the first Abolitionist circles, and she was aware how much such a prospect was clouded by her union with a young man who had begun life as an itinerant vendor of lead-pencils (he had called at Mr. Greenstreet's door in the exercise of this function), had afterwards been for a while a member of the celebrated Cayuga community, where there were no wives, or no husbands, or something of that sort (Mrs. Tarrant could never remember), and had still later (though before the development of the healing faculty) achieved distinction in the spiritualistic world. (He was an extraordinarily favoured medium, only he had had to stop for reasons of which Mrs. Tarrant possessed her version.) Even in a society much occupied with the effacement of prejudice there had been

certain dim presumptions against this versatile being, who naturally had not wanted arts to ingratiate himself with Miss Greenstreet, her eyes, like his own, being fixed exclusively on the future. The young couple (he was considerably her elder) had gazed on the future together until they found that the past had completely forsaken them and that the present offered but a slender foothold. Mrs. Tarrant, in other words, incurred the displeasure of her family, who gave her husband to understand that, much as they desired to remove the shackles from the slave, there were kinds of behaviour which struck them as too unfettered. These had prevailed, to their thinking, at Cayuga, and they naturally felt it was no use for him to say that his residence there had been (for him — the community still existed) but a momentary episode, inasmuch as there was little more to be urged for the spiritual picnics and vegetarian camp-meetings in which the discountenanced pair now sought consolation.

Such were the narrow views of people hitherto supposed capable of opening their hearts to all salutary novelties, but now put to a genuine test, as Mrs. Tarrant felt. Her husband's tastes rubbed off on her soft, moist moral surface, and the couple lived in an atmosphere of novelty, in which, occasionally, the accommodating wife encountered the fresh sensation of being in want of her dinner. Her father died, leaving, after all, very little money; he had spent his modest fortune upon the blacks. Selah Tarrant and his companion had strange adventures; she found herself completely enrolled in the great irregular army of nostrum-mongers, domiciled in humanitary Bohemia. It absorbed her like a social swamp; she sank into it a little more every day, without measuring the inches of her descent. Now she stood there up to her chin; it may probably be said of her that she had touched bottom. When she went to Miss Birdseye's it seemed to her that she re-entered society. The door that admitted her was not the door that admitted some of the others (she should never forget the tipped-up nose of Mrs. Farrinder), and the superior portal remained ajar, disclosing possible vistas. She had lived with long-haired men and short-haired women, she had contributed a flexible faith and an irremediable want of funds to a dozen social experiments, she had partaken of the comfort of a hundred religions, had followed innumerable dietary reforms, chiefly of the negative order, and had gone of an evening to a *séance* or a lecture as regularly as she had eaten her supper. Her husband always had tickets for lectures; in moments of irritation at the want of a certain sequence in their career, she had remarked to him that it was the only thing he did have. The memory of all the winter nights they had tramped through the slush (the tickets, alas! were not car-tickets) to hear Mrs. Ada T. P. Foat discourse on the "Summer-land," came back to her with bitterness. Selah was quite enthusiastic at one time about Mrs. Foat, and it was his wife's belief that he had been "associated" with her (that was Selah's expression in referring to such episodes) at Cayuga. The poor woman, matrimonially, had a great deal to put up with; it took, at moments, all her belief in his genius to sustain her. She knew that he was very magnetic (that, in fact, was his genius), and she felt that it was his magnetism that held her to him. He had carried her through things where she really didn't know what to think; there were moments when she suspected that she had lost the strong moral sense for which the Greenstreets were always so celebrated.

Of course a woman who had had the bad taste to marry Selah Tarrant would not have been likely under any circumstances to possess a very straight judgment; but there is no doubt that this poor lady had grown dreadfully limp. She had blinked and compromised and shuffled; she asked herself whether, after all, it was any more than natural that she should have wanted to help her husband, in those exciting days of his mediumship, when the table, sometimes, would rise from the ground, the sofa wouldn't float through the air, and the soft hand of a lost loved one was not so alert as it might have been to visit the circle. Mrs. Tarrant's hand was soft enough for the most supernatural effect, and she consoled her conscience on such occasions by reflecting that she ministered to a belief in immortality. She was glad, somehow, for Verena's sake, that they had emerged from the phase of spirit-intercourse; her ambition for her daughter took another form than desiring that she, too, should minister to a belief in immortality. Yet among Mrs. Tarrant's multifarious memories these reminiscences of the darkened room, the waiting circle, the little taps on table and wall, the little touches on cheek and foot, the music in the air, the rain of flowers, the sense of something mysteriously flitting, were most tenderly cherished. She hated her husband for having magnetised her so that she consented to certain things, and even did them, the thought of which to-day would suddenly make her face burn; hated him for the manner in which, somehow, as she felt, he had lowered her social tone; yet at the same time she admired him for an impudence so consummate that it had ended (in the face of mortifications, exposures, failures, all the misery of a hand-to-mouth existence) by imposing itself on her as a kind of infallibility. She knew he was an awful humbug, and yet her knowledge had this imperfection, that he had never confessed it — a fact that was really grand when one thought of his opportunities for doing so. He had never allowed that he wasn't straight; the pair had so often been in the position of the two augurs behind the al-

tar, and yet he had never given her a glance that the whole circle mightn't have observed. Even in the privacy of domestic intercourse he had phrases, excuses, explanations, ways of putting things, which, as she felt, were too sublime for just herself; they were pitched, as Selah's nature was pitched, altogether in the key of public life.

So it had come to pass, in her distended and demoralised conscience, that with all the things she despised in her life and all the things she rather liked, between being worn out with her husband's inability to earn a living and a kind of terror of his consistency (he had a theory that they lived delightfully), it happened, I say, that the only very definite criticism she made of him to-day was that he didn't know how to speak. That was where the shoe pinched — that was where Selah was slim. He couldn't hold the attention of an audience, he was not acceptable as a lecturer. He had plenty of thoughts, but it seemed as if he couldn't fit them into each other. Public speaking had been a Greenstreet tradition, and if Mrs. Tarrant had been asked whether in her younger years she had ever supposed she should marry a mesmeric healer, she would have replied: "Well, I never thought I should marry a gentleman who would be silent on the platform!" This was her most general humiliation; it included and exceeded every other, and it was a poor consolation that Selah possessed as a substitute — his career as a healer, to speak of none other, was there to prove it — the eloquence of the hand. The Greenstreets had never set much store on manual activity; they believed in the influence of the lips. It may be imagined, therefore, with what exultation, as time went on, Mrs. Tarrant found herself the mother of an inspired maiden, a young lady from whose lips eloquence flowed in streams. The Greenstreet tradition would not perish, and the dry places of her life would, perhaps, be plentifully watered. It must be added that, of late, this sandy surface had been irrigated, in moderation, from another source. Since Selah had addicted himself to the mesmeric mystery, their home had been a little more what the home of a Greenstreet should be. He had "considerable many" patients, he got about two dollars a sitting, and he had effected some most gratifying cures. A lady in Cambridge had been so much indebted to him that she had recently persuaded them to take a house near her, in order that Doctor Tarrant might drop in at any time. He availed himself of this convenience — they had taken so many houses that another, more or less, didn't matter — and Mrs. Tarrant began to feel as if they really had "struck" something.

Even to Verena, as we know, she was confused and confusing; the girl had not yet had an opportunity to ascertain the princi-

ples on which her mother's limpness was liable suddenly to become rigid. This phenomenon occurred when the vapours of social ambition mounted to her brain, when she extended an arm from which a crumpled dressing-gown fluttered back to seize the passing occasion. Then she surprised her daughter by a volubility of exhortation as to the duty of making acquaintances, and by the apparent wealth of her knowledge of the mysteries of good society. She had, in particular, a way of explaining confidentially — and in her desire to be graphic she often made up the oddest faces — the interpretation that you must sometimes give to the manners of the best people, and the delicate dignity with which you should meet them, which made Verena wonder what secret sources of information she possessed. Verena took life, as yet, very simply; she was not conscious of so many differences of social complexion. She knew that some people were rich and others poor, and that her father's house had never been visited by such abundance as might make one ask one's self whether it were right, in a world so full of the disinherited, to roll in luxury. But except when her mother made her slightly dizzy by a resentment of some slight that she herself had never perceived, or a flutter over some opportunity that appeared already to have passed (while Mrs. Tarrant was looking for something to "put on"),

Verena had no vivid sense that she was not as good as any one else, for no authority appealing really to her imagination had fixed the place of mesmeric healers in the scale of fashion. It was impossible to know in advance how Mrs. Tarrant would take things. Sometimes she was abjectly indifferent; at others she thought that every one who looked at her wished to insult her. At moments she was full of suspicion of the ladies (they were mainly ladies) whom Selah mesmerised; then again she appeared to have given up everything but her slippers and the evening-paper (from this publication she derived inscrutable solace), so that if Mrs. Foat in person had returned from the summer-land (to which she had some time since taken her flight), she would not have disturbed Mrs. Tarrant's almost cynical equanimity.

It was, however, in her social subtleties that she was most beyond her daughter; it was when she discovered extraordinary though latent longings on the part of people they met to make their acquaintance, that the girl became conscious of how much she herself had still to learn. All her desire was to learn, and it must be added that she regarded her mother, in perfect good faith, as a wonderful teacher. She was perplexed sometimes by her worldliness; that, somehow, was not a part of the higher life which every one in such a house as theirs must wish above all things to lead; and it was not involved in the reign of justice, which they were all trying to bring about, that such a strict account should be kept of every little snub. Her father seemed to Verena to move more consecutively on the high plane; though his indifference to old-fashioned standards, his perpetual invocation of the brighter day, had not yet led her to ask herself whether, after all, men are more disinterested than women. Was it interest that prompted her mother to respond so warmly to Miss Chancellor, to say to Verena, with an air of knowingness, that the thing to do was to go in and see her *immediately?* No italics can represent the earnestness of Mrs. Tarrant's emphasis. Why hadn't she said, as she had done in former cases, that if people wanted to see them they could come out to their home; that she was not so low down in the world as not to know there was such a ceremony as leaving cards? When Mrs. Tarrant began on the question of ceremonies she was apt to go far; but she had waived it in this case; it suited her more to hold that Miss Chancellor had been very gracious, that she was a most desirable friend, that she had been more affected than any one by Verena's beautiful outpouring; that she would open to her the best saloons in Boston; that when she said "Come soon" she meant the very next day, that this was the way to take it, anyhow (one must know when to go forward gracefully); and that in short she, Mrs. Tarrant, knew what she was talking about.

Verena accepted all this, for she was young enough to enjoy any journey in a horse-car, and she was ever-curious about the world; she only wondered a little how her mother knew so much about Miss Chancellor just from looking at her once. What Verena had mainly observed in the young lady who came up to her that way the night before was that she was rather dolefully dressed, that she looked as if she had been crying (Verena recognised that look quickly, she had seen it so much), and that she was in a hurry to get away. However, if she was as remarkable as her mother said, one would very soon see it; and meanwhile there was nothing in the girl's feeling about herself, in her sense of her importance, to make it a painful effort for her to run the risk of a mistake. She had no particular feeling about herself; she only cared, as yet, for outside things. Even the development of her "gift" had not made her think herself too precious for mere experiments; she had neither a particle of diffidence nor a particle of vanity. Though it would have seemed to you eminently natural that a daughter of Selah Tarrant and his wife should be an inspirational speaker, yet, as you knew Verena better, you would have wondered immensely how she came to issue from such a pair. Her ideas of enjoyment were very simple; she enjoyed putting on her new hat, with its redundancy of feather, and twenty cents appeared to her a very large sum.

Chapter XI

"I WAS certain you would come — I have felt it all day — something told me!" It was with these words that Olive Chancellor greeted her young visitor, coming to her quickly from the window, where she might have been waiting for her arrival. Some weeks later she explained to Verena how definite this prevision had been, how it had filled her all day with a nervous agitation so violent as to be painful. She told her that such forebodings were a peculiarity of her organisation, that she didn't know what to make of them, that she had to accept them; and she mentioned, as another example, the sudden dread that had come to her the evening before in the carriage, after proposing to Mr. Ransom to go with her to Miss Birdseye's. This had been as strange as it had been instinctive, and the strangeness, of course, was what must have struck Mr. Ransom; for the idea that he might come had been hers, and yet she suddenly veered round. She couldn't help it; her heart had begun to throb with the conviction that if he crossed that threshold some harm would come of it for her. She hadn't prevented him, and now she didn't care, for now, as she intimated, she had the interest of Verena, and that made her indifferent to every danger, to every ordinary pleasure. By this time Verena had learned how peculiarly her friend was constituted, how nervous and serious she was, how personal, how exclusive, what a force of will she had, what a concentration of purpose. Olive had taken her up, in the literal sense of the phrase, like a bird of the air, had spread an extraordinary pair of wings, and carried her through the dizzying void of space. Verena liked it, for the most part; liked to shoot upward without an effort of her own and look down upon all creation, upon all history, from such a height. From this first interview she felt that she was seized, and she gave herself up, only shutting her eyes a little, as we do whenever a person in whom we have perfect confidence proposes, with our assent, to subject us to some sensation.

"I want to know you," Olive said, on this occasion; "I felt that I must last night, as soon as I heard you speak. You seem to me very wonderful. I don't know what to make of you. I think we ought to be friends; so I just asked you to come to me straight off, without preliminaries, and I believed you would come. It is so *right* that you have come, and it proves how right I was." These remarks fell from Miss Chancellor's lips one by one, as she caught her breath, with the tremor that was always in her voice, even when she was the least excited, while she made Verena sit down near her on the sofa, and

looked at her all over in a manner that caused the girl to rejoice at having put on the jacket with the gilt buttons. It was this glance that was the beginning; it was with this quick survey, omitting nothing, that Olive took possession of her. "You are very remarkable; I wonder if you know how remarkable!" she went on, murmuring the words as if she were losing herself, becoming inadvertent in admiration.

Verena sat there smiling, without a blush, but with a pure, bright look which, for her, would always make protests unnecessary. "Oh, it isn't me, you know; it's something outside!" She tossed this off lightly, as if she were in the habit of saying it, and Olive wondered whether it were a sincere disclaimer or only a phrase of the lips. The question was not a criticism, for she might have been satisfied that the girl was a mass of fluent catch-words and yet scarcely have liked her the less. It was just as she was that she liked her; she was so strange, so different from the girls one usually met, seemed to belong to some queer gipsy-land or transcendental Bohemia. With her bright, vulgar clothes, her salient appearance, she might have been a rope-dancer or a fortune-teller; and this had the immense merit, for Olive, that it appeared to make her belong to the "people," threw her into the social dusk of that mysterious democracy which Miss Chancellor held that the fortunate classes know so little about, and with which (in a future possibly very near) they will have to count. Moreover, the girl had moved her as she had never been moved, and the power to do that, from whatever source it came, was a force that one must admire. Her emotion was still acute, however much she might speak to her visitor as if everything that had happened seemed to her natural; and what kept it, above all, from subsiding was her sense that she found here what she had been looking for so long — a friend of her own sex with whom she might have a union of soul. It took a double consent to make a friendship, but it was not possible that this intensely sympathetic girl would refuse. Olive had the penetration to discover in a moment that she was a creature of unlimited generosity. I know not what may have been the reality of Miss Chancellor's other premonitions, but there is no doubt that in this respect she took Verena's measure on the spot. This was what she wanted; after that the rest didn't matter; Miss Tarrant might wear gilt buttons from head to foot, her soul could not be vulgar.

"Mother told me I had better come right in," said Verena, looking now about the room, very glad to find herself in so pleasant a place, and noticing a great many things that she should like to see in detail.

"Your mother saw that I meant what I said; it isn't everybody that does me the honour to perceive that. She saw that I was shaken from head to foot. I could only say three words — I couldn't have spoken more! What a power — what a power, Miss Tarrant!"

"Yes, I suppose it is a power. If it wasn't a power, it couldn't do much with me!"

"You are so simple — so much like a child," Olive Chancellor said. That was the truth, and she wanted to say it because, quickly, without forms or circumlocutions, it made them familiar. She wished to arrive at this; her impatience was such that before the girl had been five minutes in the room she jumped to her point — inquired of her, interrupting herself, interrupting everything: "Will you be my friend, my friend of friends, beyond every one, everything, forever and forever?" Her face was full of eagerness and tenderness.

Verena gave a laugh of clear amusement, without a shade of embarrassment or confusion. "Perhaps you like me too much."

"Of course I like you too much! When I like, I like too much. But of course it's another thing, your liking me," Olive Chancellor added. "We must wait — we must wait. When I care for anything, I can be patient." She put out her hand to Verena, and the movement was at once so appealing and so confident that the girl instinctively placed her own in it. So, hand in hand, for some moments, these two young women sat looking at each other. "There is so much I want to ask you," said Olive.

"Well, I can't say much except

when father has worked on me," Verena answered, with an ingenuousness beside which humility would have seemed pretentious.

"I don't care anything about your father," Olive Chancellor rejoined very gravely, with a great air of security.

"He is very good," Verena said simply. "And he's wonderfully magnetic."

"It isn't your father, and it isn't your mother; I don't think of them, and it's not them I want. It's only you — just as you are."

Verena dropped her eyes over the front of her dress. "Just as she was" seemed to her indeed very well.

"Do you want me to give up —— ?" she demanded, smiling.

Olive Chancellor drew in her breath for an instant, like a creature in pain; then, with her quavering voice, touched with a vibration of anguish, she said: "Oh, how can I ask you to give up? I will give up — I will give up everything!"

Filled with the impression of her hostess's agreeable interior, and of what her mother had told her about Miss Chancellor's wealth, her position in Boston society, Verena, in her fresh, diverted scrutiny of the surrounding objects, wondered what could be the need of this scheme of renunciation. Oh no, indeed, she hoped she wouldn't give up — at least not before she, Verena, had had a chance to see. She felt, however, that for the present there would be no answer for her save in the mere pressure of Miss Chancellor's eager nature, that intensity of emotion which made her suddenly exclaim, as if in a nervous ecstasy of anticipation, "But we must wait! Why do we talk of this? We must wait! All will be right," she added more calmly, with great sweetness.

Verena wondered afterward why she had not been more afraid of her — why, indeed, she had not turned and saved herself by darting out of the room. But it was not in this young woman's nature to be either timid or cautious; she had as yet to make acquaintance with the sentiment of fear. She knew too little of the world to have learned to mistrust sudden enthusiasms, and if she had had a suspicion it would have been (in accordance with common worldly knowledge) the wrong one — the suspicion that such a whimsical liking would burn itself out. She could not have that one, for there was a light in Miss Chancellor's magnified face which seemed to say that a sentiment, with her, might consume its object, might consume Miss Chancellor, but would never consume itself. Verena, as yet, had no sense of being scorched; she was only agreeably warmed. She also had dreamed of a friendship, though it was not what she had dreamed of most, and it came over her that this was the one which fortune might have been keeping. She never held back.

"Do you live here all alone?" she asked of Olive.

480

"I shouldn't if you would come and live with me!"

Even this really passionate rejoinder failed to make Verena shrink; she thought it so possible that in the wealthy class people made each other such easy proposals. It was a part of the romance, the luxury, of wealth; it belonged to the world of invitations, in which she had had so little share. But it seemed almost a mockery when she thought of the little house in Cambridge, where the boards were loose in the steps of the porch.

"I must stay with my father and mother," she said. "And then I have my work, you know. That's the way I must live now."

"Your work?" Olive repeated, not quite understanding.

"My gift," said Verena, smiling.

"Oh yes, you must use it. That's what I mean; you must move the world with it; it's divine."

It was so much what she meant that she had lain awake all night thinking of it, and the substance of her thought was that if she could only rescue the girl from the danger of vulgar exploitation, could only constitute herself her protectress and devotee, the two, between them, might achieve the great result. Verena's genius was a mystery, and it might remain a mystery; it was impossible to see how this charming, blooming, simple creature, all youth and grace and innocence, got her extraordinary powers of reflection. When her gift was not in exercise she appeared anything but reflective,

and as she sat there now, for instance, you would never have dreamed that she had had a vivid revelation. Olive had to content herself, provisionally, with saying that her precious faculty had come to her just as her beauty and distinction (to Olive she was full of that quality) had come; it had dropped straight from heaven, without filtering through her parents, whom Miss Chancellor decidedly did not fancy. Even among reformers she discriminated; she thought all wise people wanted great changes, but the votaries of change were not necessarily wise. She remained silent a little, after her last remark, and then she repeated again, as if it were the solution of everything, as if it represented with absolute certainty some immense happiness in the future — "We must wait, we must wait!" Verena was perfectly willing to wait, though she did not exactly know what they were to wait for, and the aspiring frankness of her assent shone out of her face, and seemed to pacify their mutual gaze. Olive asked her innumerable questions; she wanted to enter into her life. It was one of those talks which people remember afterwards, in which every word has been given and taken, and in which they see the signs of a beginning that was to be justified. The more Olive learnt of her visitor's life the more she wanted to enter into it, the more it took her out of herself. Such strange lives are led in America, she always knew that; but this was queerer than anything she had dreamed of, and the queerest part was that the girl herself didn't appear to think it queer. She had been nursed in darkened rooms, and suckled in the midst of manifestations; she had begun to "attend lectures," as she said, when she was quite an infant, because her mother had no one to leave her with at home. She had sat on the knees of somnambulists, and had been passed from hand to hand by trance-speakers; she was familiar with every kind of "cure," and had grown up among lady-editors of newspapers advocating new religions, and people who disapproved of the marriage-tie. Verena talked of the marriage-tie as she would have talked of the last novel — as if she had heard it as frequently discussed; and at certain times, listening to the answers she made to her questions, Olive Chancellor closed her eyes in the manner of a person waiting till giddiness passed. Her young friend's revelations actually gave her a vertigo; they made her perceive everything from which she should have rescued her. Verena was perfectly uncontaminated, and she would never be touched by evil; but though Olive had no views about the marriage-tie except that she should hate it for herself — that particular reform she did not propose to consider — she didn't like the "atmosphere" of circles in which such institutions were called into question. She had no wish now to enter into an examination of that particular one; neverthe-less, to make sure, she would just ask Verena whether she disapproved of it.

"Well, I must say," said Miss Tarrant, "I prefer free unions."

Olive held her breath an instant; such an idea was so disagreeable to her. Then, for all answer, she murmured, irresolutely, "I wish you would let me help you!" Yet it seemed, at the same time, that Verena needed little help, for it was more and more clear that her eloquence, when she stood up that way before a roomful of people, was literally inspiration. She answered all her friend's questions with a good-nature which evidently took no pains to make things plausible, an effort to oblige, not to please; but, after all, she could give very little account of herself. This was very visible when Olive asked her where she had got her "intense realisation" of the suffering of women; for her address at Miss Birdseye's showed that she, too (like Olive herself), had had that vision in the watches of the night. Verena thought a moment, as if to understand what her companion referred to, and then she inquired, always smiling, where Joan of Arc had got her idea of the suffering of France. This was so prettily said that Olive could scarcely keep from kissing her; she looked at the moment as if, like Joan, she might have had visits from the saints. Olive, of course, remembered afterwards that it had not literally answered the question; and she also reflected on something that made an answer seem more difficult — the fact that the girl had grown up among lady-doctors, lady-mediums, lady-editors, lady-preachers, lady-healers, women who, having rescued themselves from a passive existence, could illustrate only partially the misery of the sex at large. It was true that they might have illustrated it by their talk, by all they had "been through" and all they could tell a younger sister; but Olive was sure that Verena's prophetic impulse had not been stirred by the chatter of women (Miss Chancellor knew that sound as well as any one); it had proceeded rather out of their silence. She said to her visitor that whether or no the angels came down to her in glittering armour, she struck her as the only person she had yet encountered who had exactly the same tenderness, the same pity, for women that she herself had. Miss Birdseye had something of it, but Miss Birdseye wanted passion, wanted keenness, was capable of the weakest concessions. Mrs. Farrinder was not weak, of course, and she brought a great intellect to the matter; but she was not personal enough — she was too abstract. Verena was not abstract; she seemed to have lived in imagination through all the ages. Verena said she *did* think she had a certain amount of imagination; she supposed she couldn't be so effective on the platform if she hadn't a rich fancy. Then Olive said to her, taking her hand again, that she wanted her to assure her of this — that it was the only thing

in all the world she cared for, the redemption of women, the thing she hoped under Providence to give her life to. Verena flushed a little at this appeal, and the deeper glow of her eyes was the first sign of exaltation she had offered. "Oh yes — I want to give my life!" she exclaimed, with a vibrating voice; and then she added gravely, "I want to do something great!"

"You will, you will, we both will!" Olive Chancellor cried, in rapture. But after a little she went on: "I wonder if you know what it means, young and lovely as you are — giving your life!"

Verena looked down for a moment in meditation.

"Well," she replied, "I guess I have thought more than I appear."

"Do you understand German? Do you know 'Faust'?" said Olive. "'Entsagen sollst du, sollst entsagen!'"

"I don't know German; I should like so to study it; I want to know everything."

"We will work at it together — we will study everything," Olive almost panted; and while she spoke the peaceful picture hung before her of still winter evenings under the lamp, with falling snow outside, and tea on a little table, and successful renderings, with a chosen companion, of Goethe, almost the only foreign author she cared about; for she hated the writing of the French, in spite of the importance they have given to women. Such a vision as this was the highest indulgence she could offer herself; she had it only at considerable intervals. It seemed as if Verena caught a glimpse of it too, for her face kindled still more, and she said she should like that ever so much. At the same time she asked the meaning of the German words.

"'Thou shalt renounce, refrain, abstain!' That's the way Bayard Taylor has translated them," Olive answered.

"Oh, well, I guess I can abstain!" Verena exclaimed, with a laugh. And she got up rather quickly, as if by taking leave she might give a proof of what she meant. Olive put out her hands to hold her, and at this moment one of the *portières* of the room was pushed aside, while a gentleman was ushered in by Miss Chancellor's little parlour-maid.

Chapter XII

VERENA recognised him; she had seen him the night before at Miss Birdseye's, and she said to her hostess, "Now I must go — you have got another caller!" It was Verena's belief that in the fashionable world (like Mrs. Farrinder, she thought Miss Chancellor belonged to it — thought that, in standing there, she herself was in it) — in the highest social walks it was the custom of a prior guest to depart when another friend arrived. She had been told at people's doors that she could not be received because the lady of the

house had a visitor, and she had retired on these occasions with a feeling of awe much more than a sense of injury. They had not been the portals of fashion, but in this respect, she deemed, they had emulated such bulwarks. Olive Chancellor offered Basil Ransom a greeting which she believed to be consummately lady-like, and which the young man, narrating the scene several months later to Mrs. Luna, whose susceptibilities he did not feel himself obliged to consider (she considered his so little), described by saying that she glared at him. Olive had thought it very possible he would come that day if he was to leave Boston; though she was perfectly mindful that she had given him no encouragement at the moment they separated. If he should not come she should be annoyed, and if he should come she should be furious; she was also sufficiently mindful of that. But she had a foreboding that, of the two grievances, fortune would confer upon her only the less; the only one she had as yet was that he had responded to her letter — a complaint rather wanting in richness. If he came, at any rate, he would be likely to come shortly before dinner, at the same hour as yesterday. He had now anticipated this period considerably, and it seemed to Miss Chancellor that he had taken a base advantage of her, stolen a march upon her privacy. She was startled, disconcerted, but as I have said, she was rigorously lady-like. She was determined not again to be fantastic, as she had been about his coming to Miss Birdseye's. The strange dread associating itself with that was something which, she devoutly trusted, she had felt once for all. She didn't know what he could do to her; he hadn't prevented, on the spot though he was, one of the happiest things that had befallen her for so long — this quick, confident visit of Verena Tarrant. It was only just at the last that he had come in, and Verena must go now; Olive's detaining hand immediately relaxed itself.

It is to be feared there was no disguise of Ransom's satisfaction at finding himself once more face to face with the charming creature with whom he had exchanged that final speechless smile the evening before. He was more glad to see her than if she had been an old friend, for it seemed to him that she had suddenly become a new one. "The delightful girl," he said to himself; "she smiles at me as if she liked me!" He could not know that this was fatuous, that she smiled so at every one; the first time she saw people she treated them as if she recognised them. Moreover, she did not seat herself again in his honour; she let it be seen that she was still going. The three stood there together in the middle of the long, characteristic room, and, for the first time in her life, Olive Chancellor chose not to introduce two persons who met under her roof. She hated Europe, but she could be European if it were necessary. Neither of her

companions had an idea that in leaving them simply planted face to face (the terror of the American heart) she had so high a warrant; and presently Basil Ransom felt that he didn't care whether he were introduced or not, for the greatness of an evil didn't matter if the remedy were equally great.

"Miss Tarrant won't be surprised if I recognise her — if I take the liberty to speak to her. She is a public character; she must pay the penalty of her distinction." These words he boldly addressed to the girl, with his most gallant Southern manner, saying to himself meanwhile that she was prettier still by daylight.

"Oh, a great many gentlemen have spoken to me," Verena said. "There were quite a number at Topeka — " And her phrase lost itself in her look at Olive, as if she were wondering what was the matter with her.

"Now, I am afraid you are going the very moment I appear," Ransom went on. "Do you know that's very cruel to me? I know what your ideas are — you expressed them last night in such beautiful language; of course you convinced me. I am ashamed of being a man; but I am, and I can't help it, and I'll do penance any way you may prescribe. *Must* she go, Miss Olive?" he asked of his cousin. "Do you flee before the individual male?" And he turned again to Verena.

This young lady gave a laugh that resembled speech in liquid

The Bostonians

fusion. "Oh no; I like the individual!"

As an incarnation of a "movement," Ransom thought her more and more singular, and he wondered how she came to be closeted so soon with his kinswoman, to whom, only a few hours before, she had been a complete stranger. These, however, were doubtless the normal proceedings of women. He begged her to sit down again; he was sure Miss Chancellor would be sorry to part with her. Verena, looking at her friend, not for permission, but for sympathy, dropped again into a chair, and Ransom waited to see Miss Chancellor do the same. She gratified him after a moment, because she could not refuse without appearing to put a hurt upon Verena; but it went hard with her, and she was altogether discomposed. She had never seen any one so free in her own drawing-room as this loud Southerner, to whom she had so rashly offered a footing; he extended invitations to her guests under her nose. That Verena should do as he asked her was a signal sign of the absence of that "home-culture" (it was so that Miss Chancellor expressed the missing quality) which she never supposed the girl possessed: fortunately, as it would be supplied to her in abundance in Charles Street. (Olive of course held that home-culture was perfectly compatible with the widest emancipation.) It was with a perfectly good conscience that Verena complied with Basil Ransom's request; but

it took her quick sensibility only a moment to discover that her friend was not pleased. She scarcely knew what had ruffled her, but at the same instant there passed before her the vision of the anxieties (of this sudden, unexplained sort, for instance, and much worse) which intimate relations with Miss Chancellor might entail.

"Now, I want you to tell me this," Basil Ransom said, leaning forward towards Verena, with his hands on his knees, and completely oblivious to his hostess. "Do you really believe all that pretty moonshine you talked last night? I could have listened to you for another hour; but I never heard such monstrous sentiments. I must protest — I must, as a calumniated, misrepresented man. Confess you meant it as a kind of *reductio ad absurdum* — a satire on Mrs. Farrinder?" He spoke in a tone of the freest pleasantry, with his familiar, friendly Southern cadence.

Verena looked at him with eyes that grew large. "Why, you don't mean to say you don't believe in our cause?"

"Oh, it won't do — it won't do!" Ransom went on, laughing. "You are on the wrong tack altogether. Do you really take the ground that your sex has been without influence? Influence? Why, you have led us all by the nose to where we are now! Wherever we are, it's all you. You are at the bottom of everything."

"Oh yes, and we want to be at the top," said Verena.

"Ah, the bottom is a better

486

place, depend on it, when from there you move the whole mass! Besides, you are on the top as well; you are everywhere, you are everything. I am of the opinion of that historical character — wasn't he some king? — who thought there was a lady behind everything. Whatever it was, he held, you have only to look for her; she is the explanation. Well, I always look for her, and I always find her; of course, I am always delighted to do so; but it proves she is the universal cause. Now, you don't mean to deny that power, the power of setting men in motion. You are at the bottom of all the wars."

"Well, I am like Mrs. Farrinder; I like opposition," Verena exclaimed, with a happy smile.

"That proves, as I say, how in spite of your expressions of horror you delight in the shock of battle. What do you say to Helen of Troy and the fearful carnage she excited? It is well known that the Empress of France was at the bottom of the last war in that country. And as for our four fearful years of slaughter, of course you won't deny that there the ladies were the great motive power. The Abolitionists brought it on, and were not the Abolitionists principally females? Who was that celebrity that was mentioned last night? — Eliza P. Moseley. I regard Eliza as the cause of the biggest war of which history preserves the record."

Basil Ransom enjoyed his humour the more because Verena ap-

peared to enjoy it; and the look with which she replied to him, at the end of this little tirade, "Why, sir, you ought to take the platform too; we might go round together as poison and antidote!" — this made him feel that he had convinced her, for the moment, quite as much as it was important he should. In Verena's face, however, it lasted but an instant — an instant after she had glanced at Olive Chancellor, who, with her eyes fixed intently on the ground (a look she was to learn to know so well), had a strange expression. The girl slowly got up; she felt that she must go. She guessed Miss Chancellor didn't like this handsome joker (it was so that Basil Ransom struck her); and it was impressed upon her ("in time," as she thought) that her new friend would be more serious even than she about the woman-question, serious as she had hitherto believed herself to be.

"I should like so much to have the pleasure of seeing you again," Ransom continued. "I think I should be able to interpret history for you by a new light."

"Well, I should be very happy to see you in my home." These words had barely fallen from Verena's lips (her mother told her they were, in general, the proper thing to say when people expressed such a desire as that; she must not let it be assumed that she would come first to them) — she had hardly uttered this hospitable speech when she felt the hand of her hostess upon her arm and became aware that a passionate appeal sat in Olive's eyes.

"You will just catch the Charles Street car," that young woman murmured, with muffled sweetness.

Verena did not understand further than to see that she ought already to have departed; and the simplest response was to kiss Miss Chancellor, an act which she briefly performed. Basil Ransom understood still less, and it was a melancholy commentary on his contention that men are not inferior, that this meeting could not come, however rapidly, to a close without his plunging into a blunder which necessarily aggravated those he had already made. He had been invited by the little prophetess, and yet he had not been invited; but he did not take that up, because he must absolutely leave Boston on the morrow, and, besides, Miss Chancellor appeared to have something to say to it. But he put out his hand to Verena and said, "Good-bye, Miss Tarrant; are we not to have the pleasure of hearing you in New York? I am afraid we are sadly sunk."

"Certainly, I should like to raise my voice in the biggest city," the girl replied.

"Well, try to come on. I won't refute you. It would be a very stupid world, after all, if we always knew what women were going to say."

Verena was conscious of the approach of the Charles Street car, as well as of the fact that Miss Chancellor was in pain; but she lingered long enough to remark that she could see he had the old-fashioned ideas — he regarded woman as the toy of man.

"Don't say the toy — say the joy!" Ransom exclaimed. "There is one statement I will venture to advance; I am quite as fond of you as you are of each other!"

"Much he knows about that!" said Verena, with a side-long smile at Olive Chancellor.

For Olive, it made her more beautiful than ever; still, there was no trace of this mere personal elation in the splendid sententiousness with which, turning to Mr. Ransom, she remarked: "What women may be, or may not be, to each other, I won't attempt just now to say; but what *the truth* may be to a human soul, I think perhaps even a woman may faintly suspect!"

"The truth? My dear cousin, your truth is a most vain thing!"

"Gracious me!" cried Verena Tarrant; and the gay vibration of her voice as she uttered this simple ejaculation was the last that Ransom heard of her. Miss Chancellor swept her out of the room, leaving the young man to extract a relish from the ineffable irony with which she uttered the words "even a woman." It was to be supposed, on general grounds, that she would reappear, but there was nothing in the glance she gave him, as she turned her back, that was an earnest of this. He stood there a moment, wondering; then his wonder spent itself on the page of a book which, according to his habit at such times, he had mechanically taken up, and in which he speedily became interested. He read it for five minutes in an uncomfortable-looking attitude, and quite forgot that he had been forsaken. He was recalled to this fact by the entrance of Mrs. Luna, arrayed as if for the street, and putting on her gloves again — she seemed always to be putting on her gloves. She wanted to know what in the world he was doing there alone — whether her sister had not been notified.

"Oh yes," said Ransom, "she has just been with me, but she has gone downstairs with Miss Tarrant."

"And who in the world is Miss Tarrant?"

Ransom was surprised that Mrs. Luna should not know of the intimacy of the two young ladies, in spite of the brevity of their acquaintance, being already so great. But, apparently, Miss Olive had not mentioned her new friend. "Well, she is an inspirational speaker — the most charming creature in the world!"

Mrs. Luna paused in her manipulations, gave an amazed, amused stare, then caused the room to ring with her laughter. "You don't mean to say you are converted — already?"

"Converted to Miss Tarrant, decidedly."

"You are not to belong to any Miss Tarrant; you are to belong to me," Mrs. Luna said, having thought over her Southern kins-man during the twenty-four hours, and made up her mind that he would be a good man for a lone woman to know. Then she added: "Did you come here to meet her — the inspirational speaker?"

"No; I came to bid your sister good-bye."

"Are you really going? I haven't made you promise half the things I want yet. But we will settle that in New York. How do you get on with Olive Chancellor?" Mrs. Luna continued, making her points, as she always did, with eagerness, though her roundness and her dimples had hitherto prevented her from being accused of that vice. It was her practice to speak of her sister by her whole name, and you would have supposed, from her usual manner of alluding to her, that Olive was much the older, instead of having been born ten years later than Adeline. She had as many ways as possible of marking the gulf that divided them; but she bridged it over lightly now by saying to Basil Ransom: "Isn't she a dear old thing?"

This bridge, he saw, would not bear his weight, and her question seemed to him to have more audacity than sense. Why should she be so insincere? She might know that a man couldn't recognise Miss Chancellor in such a description as that. She was not old — she was sharply young; and it was inconceivable to him, though he had just seen the little prophetess kiss her, that she should ever become any one's "dear." Least of all was she a "thing"; she was intensely fearfully, a person. He hesitated a moment, and then he replied: "She's a very remarkable woman."

"Take care — don't be reckless!" cried Mrs. Luna. "Do you think she is very dreadful?"

"Don't say anything against my cousin," Basil answered; and at that moment Miss Chancellor re-entered the room. She murmured some request that he would excuse her absence, but her sister interrupted her with an inquiry about Miss Tarrant.

"Mr. Ransom thinks her wonderfully charming. Why didn't you show her to me? Do you want to keep her all to yourself?"

Olive rested her eyes for some moments upon Mrs. Luna, without speaking. Then she said: "Your veil is not put on straight, Adeline."

"I look like a monster — that, evidently, is what you mean!" Adeline exclaimed, going to the mirror to rearrange the peccant tissue.

Miss Chancellor did not again ask Ransom to be seated; she appeared to take it for granted that he would leave her now. But instead of this he returned to the subject of Verena; he asked her whether she supposed the girl would come out in public — would go about like Mrs. Farrinder?

"Come out in public!" Olive repeated; "in public? Why, you don't imagine that pure voice is to be hushed?"

"Oh, hushed, no! it's too sweet for that. But not raised to a scream; not forced and cracked and

ruined. She oughtn't to become like the others. She ought to remain apart."

"Apart — *apart?*" said Miss Chancellor; "when we shall all be looking to her, gathering about her, praying for her!" There was an exceeding scorn in her voice. "If *I* can help her, she shall be an immense power for good."

"An immense power for quackery, my dear Miss Olive!" This broke from Basil Ransom's lips in spite of a vow he had just taken not to say anything that should "aggravate" his hostess, who was in a state of tension it was not difficult to detect. But he had lowered his tone to friendly pleading, and the offensive word was mitigated by his smile.

She moved away from him, backwards, as if he had given her a push. "Ah, well, now you are reckless," Mrs. Luna remarked, drawing out her ribbons before the mirror.

"I don't think you would interfere if you knew how little you understand us," Miss Chancellor said to Ransom.

"Whom do you mean by 'us' — your whole delightful sex? I don't understand *you*, Miss Olive."

"Come away with me, and I'll explain her as we go," Mrs. Luna went on, having finished her toilet.

Ransom offered his hand in farewell to his hostess; but Olive found it impossible to do anything but ignore the gesture. She could not have let him touch her. "Well, then, if you must exhibit her to the multitude, bring her on to New York," he said, with the same attempt at a light treatment.

"You'll have *me* in New York — you don't want any one else!" Mrs. Luna ejaculated, coquettishly. "I have made up my mind to winter there now."

Olive Chancellor looked from one to the other of her two relatives, one near and the other distant, but each so little in sympathy with her, and it came over her that there might be a kind of protection for her in binding them together, entangling them with each other. She had never had an idea of that kind in her life before, and that this sudden subtlety should have gleamed upon her as a momentary talisman gives the measure of her present nervousness.

"If I could take her to New York, I would take her farther," she remarked, hoping she was enigmatical.

"You talk about 'taking' her, as if you were a lecture-agent. Are you going into that business?" Mrs. Luna asked.

Ransom could not help noticing that Miss Chancellor would not shake hands with him, and he felt, on the whole, rather injured. He paused a moment before leaving the room — standing there with his hand on the knob of the door. "Look here, Miss Olive, what did you write to me to come and see you for?" He made this inquiry with a countenance not destitute of gaiety, but his eyes showed something of that yellow light — just momentarily lurid — of which

mention has been made. Mrs. Luna was on her way downstairs, and her companions remained face to face.

"Ask my sister — I think she will tell you," said Olive, turning away from him and going to the window. She remained there, looking out; she heard the door of the house close, and saw the two cross the street together. As they passed out of sight her fingers played, softly, a little air upon the pane; it seemed to her that she had had an inspiration.

Basil Ransom, meanwhile, put the question to Mrs. Luna. "If she was not going to like me, why in the world did she write to me?"

"Because she wanted you to know me — she thought *I* would like you!" And apparently she had not been wrong; for Mrs. Luna, when they reached Beacon Street, would not hear of his leaving her to go her way alone, would not in the least admit his plea that he had only an hour or two more in Boston (he was to travel, economically, by the boat) and must devote the time to his business. She appealed to his Southern chivalry, and not in vain; practically, at least, he admitted the rights of women.

Chapter XIII

MRS. TARRANT was delighted, as may be imagined, with her daughter's account of Miss Chancellor's interior, and the reception the girl had found there; and Verena, for the next month, took her way very often to Charles Street. "Just you be as nice to her as you know how," Mrs. Tarrant had said to her; and she reflected with some complacency that her daughter did know — she knew how to do everything of that sort. It was not that Verena had been taught; that branch of the education of young ladies which is known as "manners and deportment" had not figured, as a definite head, in Miss Tarrant's curriculum. She had been told, indeed, that she must not lie nor steal; but she had been told very little else about behaviour; her only great advantage, in short, had been the parental example. But her mother liked to think that she was quick and graceful, and she questioned her exhaustively as to the progress of this interesting episode; she didn't see why, as she said, it shouldn't be a permanent "stand-by" for Verena. In Mrs. Tarrant's meditations upon the girl's future she had never thought of a fine marriage as a reward of effort; she would have deemed herself very immoral if she had endeavoured to capture for her child a rich husband. She had not, in fact, a very vivid sense of the existence of such agents of fate; all the rich men she had seen already had wives, and the unmarried men, who were generally very young, were distinguished from each other not so much by the figure of their income, which came little into question, as by the degree of

their interest in regenerating ideas. She supposed Verena would marry some one, some day, and she hoped the personage would be connected with public life — which meant, for Mrs. Tarrant, that his name would be visible, in the lamplight, on a coloured poster, in the doorway of Tremont Temple. But she was not eager about this vision, for the implications of matrimony were for the most part wanting in brightness — consisted of a tired woman holding a baby over a furnace-register that emitted lukewarm air. A real lovely friendship with a young woman who had, as Mrs. Tarrant expressed it, "prop' ty," would occupy agreeably such an interval as might occur before Verena should meet her sterner fate; it would be a great thing for her to have a place to run into when she wanted a change, and there was no knowing but what it might end in her having two homes. For the idea of the home, like most American women of her quality, Mrs. Tarrant had an extreme reverence; and it was her candid faith that in all the vicissitudes of the past twenty years she had preserved the spirit of this institution. If it should exist in duplicate for Verena, the girl would be favoured indeed.

All this was as nothing, however, compared with the fact that Miss Chancellor seemed to think her young friend's gift *was* inspirational, or at any rate, as Selah had so often said, quite unique. She couldn't make out very exactly, by Verena, what she thought; but if the way Miss Chancellor had taken hold of her didn't show that she believed she could rouse the people, Mrs. Tarrant didn't know what it showed. It was a satisfaction to her that Verena evidently responded freely; she didn't think anything of what she spent in car-tickets, and indeed she had told her that Miss Chancellor wanted to stuff her pockets with them. At first she went in because her mother liked to have her; but now, evidently, she went because she was so much drawn. She expressed the highest admiration of her new friend; she said it took her a little while to see into her, but now that she did, well, she was perfectly splendid. When Verena wanted to admire she went ahead of every one, and it was delightful to see how she was stimulated by the young lady in Charles Street. They thought everything of each other — that was very plain; you could scarcely tell which thought most. Each thought the other so noble, and Mrs. Tarrant had a faith that between them they *would* rouse the people. What Verena wanted was some one who would know how to handle her (her father hadn't handled anything except the healing, up to this time, with real success), and perhaps Miss Chancellor would take hold better than some that made more of a profession.

"It's beautiful, the way she draws you out," Verena had said to her mother; "there's something so searching that the first time I visited her it quite realised my idea of the Day of Judgment. But she seems to show all that's in herself at the same time, and then you see how lovely it is. She's just as pure as she can live; you see if she is not, when you know her. She's so noble herself that she makes you feel as if you wouldn't want to be less so. She doesn't care for anything but the elevation of our sex; if she can work a little toward that, it's all she asks. I can tell you, she kindles me; she does, mother, really. She doesn't care a speck what she wears — only to have an elegant parlour. Well, she *has* got that; it's a regular dream-like place to sit. She's going to have a tree in, next week; she says she wants to see me sitting under a tree. I believe it's some oriental idea; it has lately been introduced in Paris. She doesn't like French ideas as a general thing; but she says this has more nature than most. She has got so many of her own that I shouldn't think she would require to borrow any. I'd sit in a forest to hear her bring some of them out," Verena went on, with characteristic raciness. "She just quivers when she describes what our sex has been through. It's so interesting to me to hear what I have always felt. If she wasn't afraid of facing the public, she would go far ahead of me. But she doesn't want to speak herself; she only wants to call me out. Mother, if she doesn't attract attention to me there isn't any attention to be attracted. She says I have got the gift of expression — it doesn't matter where it comes from. She says it's a great advantage to a movement to be personified in a bright young figure. Well, of course I'm young, and I feel bright enough when once I get started. She says my serenity while exposed to the gaze of hundreds is in itself a qualification; in fact, she seems to thing my serenity is quite God-given. She hasn't got much of it herself; she's the most emotional woman I have met, up to now. She wants to know how I can speak the way I do unless I feel; and of course I tell her I do feel, so far as I realise. She seems to be realising all the time; I never saw any one that took so little rest. She says I ought to do something great, and she makes me feel as if I should. She says I ought to have a wide influence, if I can obtain the ear of the public; and I say to her that if I do it will be all her influence."

Selah Tarrant looked at all this from a higher standpoint than his wife; at least such an altitude on his part was to be inferred from his increased solemnity. He committed himself to no precipitate elation at the idea of his daughter's being taken up by a patroness of movements who happened to have money; he looked at his child only from the point of view of the service she might render to humanity. To keep her ideal pointing in the right direction, to guide and animate her moral life — this was a duty more imperative for a parent so closely identified with revelations and panaceas than see-

ing that she formed profitable worldly connections. He was "off," moreover, so much of the time that he could keep little account of her comings and goings, and he had an air of being but vaguely aware of whom Miss Chancellor, the object now of his wife's perpetual reference, might be. Verena's initial appearance in Boston, as he called her performance at Miss Birdseye's, had been a great success; and this reflection added, as I say, to his habitually sacerdotal expression. He looked like the priest of a religion that was passing through the stage of miracles; he carried his responsibility in the general elongation of his person, of his gestures (his hands were now always in the air, as if he were being photographed in postures), of his words and sentences, as well as in his smile, as noiseless as a patent hinge, and in the folds of his eternal waterproof. He was incapable of giving an off-hand answer or opinion on the simplest occasion, and his tone of high deliberation increased in proportion as the subject was trivial or domestic. If his wife asked him at dinner if the potatoes were good, he replied that they were strikingly fine (he used to speak of the newspaper as "fine" — he applied this term to objects the most dissimilar), and embarked on a parallel worthy of Plutarch, in which he compared them with other specimens of the same vegetable. He produced, or would have liked to produce, the impression of looking above and beyond everything, of not caring for the immediate, of reckoning only with the long run. In reality he had one all-absorbing solicitude — the desire to get paragraphs put into the newspapers, paragraphs of which he had hitherto been the subject, but of which he was now to divide the glory with his daughter. The newspapers were his world, the richest expression, in his eyes, of human life; and, for him, if a diviner day was to come upon earth, it would be brought about by copious advertisement in the daily prints. He looked with longing for the moment when Verena should be advertised among the "personals," and to his mind the supremely happy people were those (and there were a good many of them) of whom there was some journalistic mention every day in the year. Nothing less than this would really have satisfied Selah Tarrant; his ideal of bliss was to be as regularly and indispensably a component part of the newspaper as the title and date, or the list of fires, or the column of Western jokes. The vision of that publicity haunted his dreams, and he would gladly have sacrificed to it the innermost sanctities of home. Human existence to him, indeed, was a huge publicity, in which the only fault was that it was sometimes not sufficiently effective. There had been a Spiritualist paper of old which he used to pervade; but he could not persuade himself that through this medium his personality had attracted general attention; and, moreover, the

sheet, as he said, was played out anyway. Success was not success so long as his daughter's *physique*, the rumour of her engagement, were not included in the "Jottings," with the certainty of being extensively copied.

The account of her exploits in the West had not made their way to the seaboard with the promptitude that he had looked for; the reason of this being, he supposed, that the few addresses she had made had not been lectures, announced in advance, to which tickets had been sold, but incidents, of abrupt occurrence, of certain multitudinous meetings, where there had been other performers better known to fame. They had brought in no money; they had been delivered only for the good of the cause. If it could only be known that she spoke for nothing, that might deepen the reverberation; the only trouble was that her speaking for nothing was not the way to remind him that he had a remunerative daughter. It was not the way to stand out so very much either, Selah Tarrant felt; for there were plenty of others that knew how to make as little money as she would. To speak — that was the one thing that most people were willing to do for nothing; it was not a line in which it was easy to appear conspicuously disinterested. Disinterestedness, too, was incompatible with receipts; and receipts were what Selah Tarrant was, in his own parlance, after. He wished to bring about the day when they would flow in freely; the reader perhaps sees the gesture with which, in his colloquies with himself, he accompanied this mental image.

It seemed to him at present that the fruitful time was not far off; it had been brought appreciably nearer by that fortunate evening at Miss Birdseye's. If Mrs. Farrinder could be induced to write an "open letter" about Verena, that would do more than anything else. Selah was not remarkable for delicacy of perception, but he knew the world he lived in well enough to be aware that Mrs. Farrinder was liable to rear up, as they used to say down in Pennsylvania, where he lived before he began to peddle lead-pencils. She wouldn't always take things as you might expect, and if it didn't meet her views to pay a public tribute to Verena, there wasn't any way known to Tarrant's ingenious mind of getting round her. If it was a question of a favour from Mrs. Farrinder, you just had to wait for it, as you would for a rise in the thermometer. He had told Miss Birdseye what he would like, and she seemed to think, from the way their celebrated friend had been affected, that the idea might take her some day of just letting the public know all she had felt. She was off somewhere now (since that evening), but Miss Birdseye had an idea that when she was back in Roxbury she would send for Verena and give her a few points. Meanwhile, at any rate, Selah was sure he had a card; he felt there was money in the air. It

might already be said there were receipts from Charles Street; that rich, peculiar young woman seemed to want to lavish herself. He pretended, as I have intimated, not to notice this; but he never saw so much as when he had his eyes fixed on the cornice. He had no doubt that if he should make up his mind to take a hall some night, she would tell him where the bill might be sent. That was what he was thinking of now, whether he had better take a hall right away, so that Verena might leap at a bound into renown, or wait till she had made a few more appearances in private, so that curiosity might be worked up.

These meditations accompanied him in his multifarious wanderings through the streets and the suburbs of the New England capital. As I have also mentioned, he was absent for hours — long periods during which Mrs. Tarrant, sustaining nature with a hard-boiled egg and a doughnut, wondered how in the world he stayed his stomach. He never wanted anything but a piece of pie when he came in; the only thing about which he was particular was that it should be served up hot. She had a private conviction that he partook, at the houses of his lady patients, of little lunches; she applied this term to any episodical repast, at any hour of the twenty-four. It is but fair to add that once, when she betrayed her suspicion, Selah remarked that the only refreshment *he* ever wanted was the sense that he was doing some good. This effort with him had many forms; it involved, among other things, a perpetual perambulation of the streets, a haunting of horse-cars, railway-stations, shops that were "selling off." But the places that knew him best were the offices of the newspapers and the vestibules of the hotels — the big marble-paved chambers of informal reunion which offer to the streets, through high glass plates, the sight of the American citizen suspended by his heels. Here, amid the piled-up luggage, the convenient spittoons, the elbowing loungers, the disconsolate "guests," the truculent Irish porters, the rows of shaggy-backed men in strange hats, writing letters at a table inlaid with advertisements, Selah Tarrant made innumerable contemplative stations. He could not have told you, at any particular moment, what he was doing; he only had a general sense that such places were national nerve-centres, and that the more one looked in, the more one was "on the spot." The *penetralia* of the daily press were, however, still more fascinating, and the fact that they were less accessible, that here he found barriers in his path, only added to the zest of forcing an entrance. He abounded in pretexts; he even sometimes brought contributions; he was persistent and penetrating, he was known as the irrepressible Tarrant. He hung about, sat too long, took up the time of busy people, edged into the printing-rooms when he had been eliminated from the office,

talked with the compositors till they set up his remarks by mistake, and to the newsboy when the compositors had turned their backs. He was always trying to find out what was "going in"; he would have liked to go in himself, bodily, and, failing in this, he hoped to get advertisements inserted gratis. The wish of his soul was that he might be interviewed; that made him hover at the editorial elbow. Once he thought he had been, and the headings, five or six deep, danced for days before his eyes; but the report never appeared. He expected his revenge for this the day after Verena should have burst forth; he saw the attitude in which he should receive the emissaries who would come after his daughter.

Chapter XIV

"We ought to have some one to meet her," Mrs. Tarrant said; "I presume she wouldn't care to come out just to see us." "She," between the mother and the daughter, at this period, could refer only to Olive Chancellor, who was discussed in the little house at Cambridge at all hours and from every possible point of view. It was never Verena now who began, for she had grown rather weary of the topic; she had her own ways of thinking of it, which were not her mother's, and if she lent herself to this lady's extensive considerations it was because that was the best way of keeping her thoughts to herself.

Mrs. Tarrant had an idea that she (Mrs. Tarrant) liked to study people, and that she was now engaged in an analysis of Miss Chancellor. It carried her far, and she came out at unexpected times with her results. It was still her purpose to interpret the world to the ingenuous mind of her daughter, and she translated Miss Chancellor with a confidence which made little account of the fact that she had seen her but once, while Verena had this advantage nearly every day. Verena felt that by this time she knew Olive very well, and her mother's most complicated versions of motive and temperament (Mrs. Tarrant, with the most imperfect idea of the meaning of the term, was always talking about people's temperament), rendered small justice to the phenomena it was now her privilege to observe in Charles Street. Olive was much more remarkable than Mrs. Tarrant suspected, remarkable as Mrs. Tarrant believed her to be. She had opened Verena's eyes to extraordinary pictures, made the girl believe that she had a heavenly mission, given her, as we have seen, quite a new measure of the interest of life. These were larger consequences than the possibility of meeting the leaders of society at Olive's house. She had met no one, as yet, but Mrs. Luna; her new friend seemed to wish to keep her quite for herself. This was the only reproach that Mrs. Tarrant directed to the new friend

as yet; she was disappointed that Verena had not obtained more insight into the world of fashion. It was one of the prime articles of her faith that the world of fashion was wicked and hollow, and, moreover, Verena told her that Miss Chancellor loathed and despised it. She could not have informed you wherein it would profit her daughter (for the way those ladies shrank from any new gospel was notorious); nevertheless she was vexed that Verena shouldn't come back to her with a little more of the fragrance of Beacon Street. The girl herself would have been the most interested person in the world if she had not been the most resigned; she took all that was given her and was grateful, and missed nothing that was withheld; she was the most extraordinary mixture of eagerness and docility. Mrs. Tarrant theorised about temperaments and she loved her daughter; but she was only vaguely aware of the fact that she had at her side the sweetest flower of character (as one might say) that had ever bloomed on earth. She was proud of Verena's brightness, and of her special talent; but the commonness of her own surface was a non-conductor of the girl's quality. Therefore she thought that it would add to her success in life to know a few high-flyers, if only to put them to shame; as if anything could add to Verena's success, as if it were not supreme success simply to have been made as she was made.

Mrs. Tarrant had gone into town to call upon Miss Chancellor; she carried out this resolve, on which she had bestowed infinite consideration, independently of Verena. She had decided that she had a pretext; her dignity required one, for she felt that at present the antique pride of the Greenstreets was terribly at the mercy of her curiosity. She wished to see Miss Chancellor again, and to see her among her charming appurtenances, which Verena had described to her with great minuteness. The pretext that she would have valued most was wanting — that of Olive's having come out to Cambridge to pay the visit that had been solicited from the first; so she had to take the next best — she had to say to herself that it was her duty to see what she should think of a place where her daughter spent so much time. To Miss Chancellor she would appear to have come to thank her for her hospitality; she knew, in advance, just the air she should take (or she fancied she knew, it — Mrs. Tarrant's airs were not always what she supposed), just the *nuance*, (she had also an impression she knew a little French) of her tone. Olive, after the lapse of weeks, still showed no symptoms of presenting herself, and Mrs. Tarrant rebuked Verena with some sternness for not having made her feel that this attention was due to the mother of her friend. Verena could scarcely say to her she guessed Miss Chancellor didn't think much of that personage, true as it was that the girl had discerned this angular fact, which she attributed to Olive's extraordinary comprehensiveness of view. Verena herself did not suppose that her mother occupied a very important place in the universe; and Miss Chancellor never looked at anything smaller than that. Nor was she free to report (she was certainly now less frank at home, and, moreover, the suspicion was only just becoming distinct to her) that Olive would like to detach her from her parents altogether, and was therefore not interested in appearing to cultivate relations with them. Mrs. Tarrant, I may mention, had a further motive: she was consumed with the desire to behold Mrs. Luna. This circumstance may operate as a proof that the aridity of her life was great, and if it should have that effect I shall not be able to gainsay it. She had seen all the people who went to lectures, but there were hours when she desired, for a change, to see some who didn't go; and Mrs. Luna, from Verena's description of her, summed up the characteristics of this eccentric class.

Verena had given great attention to Olive's brilliant sister; she had told her friend everything now — everything but one little secret, namely, that if she could have chosen at the beginning she would have liked to resemble Mrs. Luna. This lady fascinated her, carried off her imagination to strange lands; she should enjoy so much a long evening with her alone, when she might ask her ten thousand questions. But she never saw her alone, never saw her at all but in glimpses. Adeline flitted in and out, dressed for dinner and concerts, always saying something worldly to the young woman from Cambridge, and something to Olive that had a freedom which she herself would probably never arrive at (a failure of foresight on Verena's part). But Miss Chancellor never detained her, never gave Verena a chance to see her, never appeared to imagine that she could have the least interest in such a person; only took up the subject again after Adeline had left them — the subject, of course, which was always the same, the subject of what they should do together for their suffering sex. It was not that Verena was not interested in that — gracious, no; it opened up before her, in those wonderful colloquies with Olive, in the most inspiring way; but her fancy would make a dart to right or left when other game crossed their path, and her companion led her, intellectually, a dance in which her feet — that is, her head — failed her at times for weariness. Mrs. Tarrant found Miss Chancellor at home, but she was not gratified by even the most transient glimpse of Mrs. Luna; a fact which, in her heart, Verena regarded as fortunate, inasmuch as (she said to herself) if her mother, returning from Charles Street, began to explain Miss Chancellor to her

with fresh energy, and as if she (Verena) had never seen her, and up to this time they had had nothing to say about her, to what developments (of the same sort) would not an encounter with Adeline have given rise?

When Verena at last said to her friend that she thought she ought to come out to Cambridge — she didn't understand why she didn't — Olive expressed her reasons very frankly, admitted that she was jealous, that she didn't wish to think of the girl's belonging to any one but herself. Mr. and Mrs. Tarrant would have authority, opposed claims, and she didn't wish to see them, to remember that they existed. This was true, so far as it went; but Olive could not tell Verena everything — could not tell her that she hated that dreadful pair at Cambridge. As we know, she had forbidden herself this emotion as regards individuals; and she flattered herself that she considered the Tarrants as a type, a deplorable one, a class that, with the public at large, discredited the cause of the new truths. She had talked them over with Miss Birdseye (Olive was always looking after her now and giving her things — the good lady appeared at this period in wonderful caps and shawls — for she felt she couldn't thank her enough), and even Doctor Prance's fellowlodger, whose animosity to flourishing evils lived in the happiest (though the most illicit) union with the mania for finding excuses, even Miss Birdseye was obliged to confess that if you came to examine his record, poor Selah didn't amount to so very much. How little he amounted to Olive perceived after she had made Verena talk, as the girl did immensely, about her father and mother — quite unconscious, meanwhile, of the conclusions she suggested to Miss Chancellor. Tarrant was a moralist without moral sense — that was very clear to Olive as she listened to the history of his daughter's childhood and youth, which Verena related with an extraordinary artless vividness. This narrative, tremendously fascinating to Miss Chancellor, made her feel in all sort of ways — prompted her to ask herself whether the girl was also destitute of the perception of right and wrong. No, she was only supremely innocent; she didn't understand, she didn't interpret nor see the *portée* of what she described; she had no idea whatever of judging her parents. Olive had wished to "realise" the conditions in which her wonderful young friend (she thought her more wonderful every day) had developed, and to this end, as I have related, she prompted her to infinite discourse. But now she was satisfied, the realisation was complete, and what she would have liked to impose on the girl was an effectual rupture with her past. That past she by no means absolutely deplored, for it had the merit of having initiated Verena (and her patroness, through her

agency) into the miseries and mysteries of the People. It was her theory that Verena (in spite of the blood of the Greenstreets, and, after all, who were they?) was a flower of the great Democracy, and that it was impossible to have had an origin less distinguished than Tarrant himself. His birth, in some unheard-of place in Pennsylvania, was quite inexpressibly low, and Olive would have been much disappointed if it had been wanting in this defect. She liked to think that Verena, in her childhood, had known almost the extremity of poverty, and there was a kind of ferocity in the joy with which she reflected that there had been moments when this delicate creature came near (if the pinch had only lasted a little longer) to literally going without food. These things added to her value for Olive; they made that young lady feel that their common undertaking would, in consequence, be so much more serious. It is always supposed that revolutionists have been goaded, and the goading would have been rather deficient here were it not for such happy accidents in Verena's past. When she conveyed from her mother a summons to Cambridge for a particular occasion, Olive perceived that the great effort must now be made. Great efforts were nothing new to her — it was a great effort to live at all — but this one appeared to her exceptionally cruel. She determined, however, to make it, promising herself that her first visit to Mrs. Tarrant should also be her last. Her only consolation was that she expected to suffer intensely; for the prospect of suffering was always, spiritually speaking, so much cash in her pocket. It was arranged that Olive should come to tea (the repast that Selah designated as his supper), when Mrs. Tarrant, as we have seen, desired to do her honour by inviting another guest. This guest, after much deliberation between that lady and Verena, was selected, and the first person Olive saw on entering the little parlour in Cambridge was a young man with hair prematurely, or, as one felt that one should say, precociously white, whom she had a vague impression she had encountered before, and who was introduced to her as Mr. Matthias Pardon.

She suffered less than she had hoped — she was so taken up with the consideration of Verena's interior. It was as bad as she could have desired; desired in order to feel that (to take her out of such a *milieu* as that) she should have a right to draw her altogether to herself. Olive wished more and more to extract some definite pledge from her; she could hardly say what it had best be as yet; she only felt that it must be something that would have an absolute sanctity for Verena and would bind them together for life. On this occasion it seemed to shape itself in her mind; she began to see what it ought to be, though she also saw that she would per-

haps have to wait awhile. Mrs. Tarrant, too, in her own house, became now a complete figure; there was no manner of doubt left as to her being vulgar. Olive Chancellor despised vulgarity, had a scent for it which she followed up in her own family, so that often, with a rising flush, she detected the taint even in Adeline. There were times, indeed, when every one seemed to have it, every one but Miss Birdseye (who had nothing to do with it — she was an antique) and the poorest, humblest people. The toilers and spinners, the very obscure, these were the only persons who were safe from it. Miss Chancellor would have been much happier if the movements she was interested in could have been carried on only by the people she liked, and if revolutions, somehow, didn't always have to begin with one's self — with internal convulsions, sacrifices, executions. A common end, unfortunately, however fine as regards a special result, does not make community impersonal.

Mrs. Tarrant, with her soft corpulence, looked to her guest very bleached and tumid; her complexion had a kind of withered glaze; her hair, very scanty, was drawn off her forehead *à la Chinoise;* she had no eyebrows, and her eyes seemed to stare, like those of a figure of wax. When she talked and wished to insist, and she was always insisting, she puckered and distorted her face, with an effort to express the inexpressible, which turned out, after all, to be nothing. She had a kind of doleful elegance, tried to be confidential, lowered her voice and looked as if she wished to establish a secret understanding, in order to ask her visitor if she would venture on an apple-fritter. She wore a flowing mantle, which resembled her husband's waterproof — a garment which, when she turned to her daughter or talked about her, might have passed for the robe of a sort of priestess of maternity. She endeavoured to keep the conversation in a channel which would enable her to ask sudden incoherent questions of Olive, mainly as to whether she knew the principal ladies (the expression was Mrs. Tarrant's), not only in Boston, but in the other cities which, in her nomadic course, she herself had visited. Olive knew some of them, and of some of them had never heard; but she was irritated, and pretended a universal ignorance (she was conscious that she had never told so many fibs), by which her hostess was much disconcerted, although her questions had apparently been questions pure and simple, leading nowhither and without bearings on any new truth.

Chapter XV

TARRANT, however, kept an eye in that direction; he was solemnly civil to Miss Chancellor, handed her the dishes at table over and over again, and ventured to intimate that the apple-fritters were very fine; but, save for this, alluded to do nothing more trivial than the regeneration of humanity and the strong hope he felt that Miss Birdseye would again have one of her delightful gatherings. With regard to this latter point he explained that it was not in order that he might again present his daughter to the company, but simply because on such occasions there was a valuable interchange of hopeful thought, a contact of mind with mind. If Verena had anything suggestive to contribute to the social problem, the opportunity would come — that was part of their faith. They couldn't reach out for it and try and push their way; if they were wanted, their hour would strike; if they were not, they would just keep still and let others press forward who seemed to be called. If they were called, they would know it; and if they weren't, they could just hold on to each other as they had always done. Tarrant was very fond of alternatives, and he mentioned several others; it was never his fault if his listeners failed to think him impartial. They hadn't much, as Miss Chancellor could see; she could tell by their manner of life that they hadn't raked in the dollars; but they had faith that, whether one raised one's voice or simply worked on in silence, the principal difficulties would straighten themselves out; and they had also a considerable experience of great questions. Tarrant spoke as if, as a family, they were prepared to take charge of them on moderate terms. He always said "ma'am" in speaking to Olive, to whom, moreover, the air had never been so filled with the sound of her own name. It was always in her ear, save when Mrs. Tarrant and Verena conversed in prolonged and ingenuous asides; this was still for her benefit, but the pronoun sufficed them. She had wished to judge Doctor Tarrant (not that she believed he had come honestly by his title), to make up her mind. She had done these things now, and she expressed to herself the kind of man she believed him to be in reflecting that if she should offer him ten thousand dollars to renounce all claim to Verena, keeping — he and his wife — clear of her for the rest of time, he would probably say, with his fearful smile, "Make it twenty, money down, and I'll do it." Some image of this transaction, as one of the possibilities of the future, outlined itself for Olive among the moral incisions of that evening. It seemed implied in the very place, the bald bareness of Tarrant's temporary lair, a wooden cottage, with a rough front yard, a little naked piazza, which seemed rather to expose than to protect, facing upon an unpaved road, in which the footway was overlaid with a strip of planks. These planks were embedded in ice or in liquid thaw, according to the momentary mood of the weather, and the advancing pedestrian traversed them in the attitude, and with a good deal of the suspense, of a rope-dancer. There was nothing in the house to speak of; nothing, to Olive's sense, but a smell of kerosene; though she had a consciousness of sitting down somewhere — the object creaked and rocked beneath her — and of the table at tea being covered with a cloth stamped in bright colours.

As regards the pecuniary transaction with Selah, it was strange how she should have seen it through the conviction that Verena would never give up her parents. Olive was sure that she would never turn her back upon them, would always share with them. She would have despised her had she thought her capable of another course; yet it baffled her to understand why, when parents were so trashy, this natural law should not be suspended. Such a question brought her back, however, to her perpetual enigma, the mystery she had already turned over in her mind for hours together — the wonder of such people being Verena's progenitors at all. She had explained it, as we explain all exceptional things, by making the part, as the French say, of the miraculous. She had come to consider the girl as a wonder of wonders, to hold that no human origin, however congruous it might superficially appear, would sufficiently account for her; that her springing up between Selah and his wife was an exquisite whim of the creative force; and that in such a case a few shades more or less of the inexplicable didn't matter. It was notorious that great beauties, great geniuses, great characters, take their own times and places for coming into the world, leaving the gaping spectators to make them "fit in," and holding from far-off ancestors, or even, perhaps, straight from the divine generosity, much more than from their ugly or stupid progenitors. They were incalculable phenomena, anyway, as Selah would have said. Verena, for Olive, was the very type and model of the "gifted being;" her qualities had not been bought and paid for; they were like some brilliant birthday-present, left at the door by an unknown messenger, to be delightful for ever as an inexhaustible legacy, and amusing for ever from the obscurity of its source. They were superabundantly crude as yet — happily for Olive, who promised herself, as we know, to train and polish them — but they were as genuine as fruit and flowers, as the glow of the fire or the plash of water. For her scrutinising friend Verena had the disposition of the artist, the spirit to which all charming forms come easily and naturally. It required an effort at first to imagine an artist so untaught, so mistaught, so poor in experience; but then it required an effort also to imagine people like the old Tarrants, or a life so full as her life had been of ugly things. Only an exquisite creature could have resisted such associations, only a girl who had some natural

light, some divine spark of taste. There were people like that, fresh from the hand of Omnipotence; they were far from common, but their existence was as incontestable as it was beneficent.

Tarrant's talk about his daughter, her prospects, her enthusiasm, was terribly painful to Olive; it brought back to her what she had suffered already from the idea that he laid his hands upon her to make her speak. That he should be mixed up in any way with this exercise of her genius was a great injury to the cause, and Olive had already determined that in future Verena should dispense with his co-operation. The girl had virtually confessed that she lent herself to it only because it gave him pleasure, and that anything else would do as well, anything that would make her quiet a little before she began to "give out." Olive took upon herself to believe that *she* could make her quiet, though, certainly, she had never had that effect upon any one; she would mount the platform with Verena if necessary, and lay her hands upon her head. Why in the world had a perverse fate decreed that Tarrant should take an interest in the affairs of Woman — as if she wanted *his* aid to arrive at her goal; a charlatan of the poor, lean, shabby sort, without the humour, brilliancy, prestige, which sometimes throw a drapery over shallowness? Mr. Pardon evidently took an interest as well, and there was something in his appearance that seemed to say that his sympathy

505

would not be dangerous. He was much at his ease, plainly, beneath the roof of the Tarrants, and Olive reflected that though Verena had told her much about him, she had not given her the idea that he was as intimate as that. What she had mainly said was that he sometimes took her to the theatre. Olive could enter, to a certain extent, into that; she herself had had a phase (some time after her father's death — her mother's had preceded his — when she bought the little house in Charles Street and began to live alone), during which she accompanied gentlemen to respectable places of amusement. She was accordingly not shocked at the idea of such adventures on Verena's part; than which, indeed, judging from her own experience, nothing could well have been less adventurous. Her recollections of these expeditions were as of something solemn and edifying — of the earnest interest in her welfare exhibited by her companion (there were few occasions on which the young Bostonian appeared to more advantage), of the comfort of other friends sitting near, who were sure to know whom she was with, of serious discussion between the acts in regard to the behaviour of the characters in the piece, and of the speech at the end with which, as the young man quitted her at her door, she rewarded his civility — "I must thank you for a very pleasant evening." She always felt that she made that too prim; her lips stiffened themselves as she spoke. But the whole affair had always a

primness; this was discernible even to Olive's very limited sense of humour. It was not so religious as going to evening-service at King's Chapel; but it was the next thing to it. Of course all girls didn't do it; there were families that viewed such a custom with disfavour. But this was where the girls were of the romping sort; there had to be some things they were known not to do. As a general thing, moreover, the practice was confined to the decorous; it was a sign of culture and quiet tastes. All this made it innocent for Verena, whose life had exposed her to much worse dangers; but the thing referred itself in Olive's mind to a danger which cast a perpetual shadow there — the possibility of the girl's embarking with some ingenuous youth on an expedition that would last much longer than an evening. She was haunted, in a word, with the fear that Verena would marry, a fate to which she was altogether unprepared to surrender her; and this made her look with suspicion upon all male acquaintance.

Mr. Pardon was not the only one she knew; she had an example of the rest in the persons of two young Harvard law-students, who presented themselves after tea on this same occasion. As they sat there Olive wondered whether Verena had kept something from her, whether she were, after all (like so many other girls in Cambridge), a college-"belle," an object of frequentation to undergraduates. It was natural that at the seat of a big university there should be girls like that, with students dangling after them, but she didn't want Verena to be one of them. There were some that received the Seniors and Juniors; others that were accessible to Sophomores and Freshmen. Certain young ladies distinguished the professional students; there was a group, even, that was on the best terms with the young men who were studying for the Unitarian ministry in that queer little barrack at the end of Divinity Avenue. The advent of the new visitors made Mrs. Tarrant bustle immensely; but after she had caused every one to change places two or three times with every one else the company subsided into a circle which was occasionally broken by wandering movements on the part of her husband, who, in the absence of anything to say on any subject whatever, placed himself at different points in listening attitudes, shaking his head slowly up and down, and gazing at the carpet with an air of supernatural attention. Mrs. Tarrant asked the young men from the Law School about their studies, and whether they meant to follow them up seriously; said she thought some of the laws were very unjust, and she hoped they meant to try and improve them. She had suffered by the laws herself, at the time her father died; she hadn't got half the prop'ty she should have got if they had been different. She thought they should be for public matters, not for people's private affairs; the idea always seemed to her to keep you

down if you *were* down, and to hedge you in with difficulties. Sometimes she thought it was a wonder how she had developed in the face of so many; but it was a proof that freedom was everywhere, if you only knew how to look for it.

The two young men were in the best humour; they greeted these sallies with a merriment of which, though it was courteous in form, Olive was by no means unable to define the spirit. They talked naturally more with Verena than with her mother; and while they were so engaged Mrs. Tarrant explained to her who they were, and how one of them, the smaller, who was not quite so spruce, had brought the other, his particular friend, to introduce him. This friend, Mr. Burrage, was from New York; he was very fashionable, he went out a great deal in Boston ("I have no doubt you know some of the places," said Mrs. Tarrant); his "fam'ly" was very rich.

"Well, he knows plenty of that sort," Mrs. Tarrant went on, "but he felt unsatisfied; he didn't know any one like *us*. He told Mr. Gracie (that's the little one) that he felt as if he *must;* it seemed as if he couldn't hold out. So we told Mr. Gracie, of course, to bring him right round. Well, I hope he'll get something from us, I'm sure. He has been reported to be engaged to Miss Winkworth; I have no doubt you know who I mean. But Mr. Gracie says he hasn't looked at her more than twice. That's the way rumours fly round in that set,

I presume. Well, I am glad we are not in it, wherever we are! Mr. Gracie is very different; he is intensely plain, but I believe he is very learned. You don't think him plain? Oh, you don't know? Well, I suppose you don't care, you must see so many. But I must say, when a young man looks like that, I call him painfully plain. I heard Doctor Tarrant make the remark the last time he was here. I don't say but what the plainest are the best. Well, I had no idea we were going to have a party when I asked you. I wonder whether Verena hadn't better hand the cake; we generally find the students enjoy it so much."

This office was ultimately delegated to Selah, who, after a considerable absence, reappeared with a dish of dainties, which he presented successively to each member of the company. Olive saw Verena lavish her smiles on Mr. Gracie and Mr. Burrage; the liveliest relation had established itself, and the latter gentleman in especial abounded in appreciative laughter. It might have been fancied, just from looking at the group, that Verena's vocation was to smile and talk with young men who bent towards her; might have been fancied, that is, by a person less sure of the contrary than Olive, who had reason to know that a "gifted being" is sent into the world for a very different purpose, and that making the time pass pleasantly for conceited young men is the last duty you are bound to think of if you happen to have

a talent for embodying a cause. Olive tried to be glad that her friend had the richness of nature that makes a woman gracious without latent purposes; she reflected that Verena was not in the smallest degree a flirt, that she was only enchantingly and universally genial, that nature had given her a beautiful smile, which fell impartially on every one, man and woman, alike. Olive may have been right, but it shall be confided to the reader that in reality she never knew, by any sense of her own, whether Verena were a flirt or not. This young lady could not possibly have told her (even if she herself knew, which she didn't), and Olive, destitute of the quality, had no means of taking the measure in another of the subtle feminine desire to please. She could see the difference between Mr. Gracie and Mr. Burrage; her being bored by Mrs. Tarrant's attempting to point it out is perhaps a proof of that. It was a curious incident of her zeal for the regeneration of her sex that manly things were, perhaps on the whole, what she understood best. Mr. Burrage was rather a handsome youth, with a laughing, clever face, a certain sumptuosity of apparel, an air of belonging to the "fast set" — a precocious, good-natured man of the world, curious of new sensations and containing, perhaps, the making of a *dilettante*. Being, doubtless, a little ambitious, and liking to flatter himself that he appreciated worth in lowly forms, he had associated himself with the

The Bostonians

ruder but at the same time acuter personality of a genuine son of New England, who had a harder head than his own and a humour in reality more cynical, and who, having earlier knowledge of the Tarrants, had undertaken to show him something indigenous and curious, possibly even fascinating. Mr. Gracie was short, with a big head; he wore eye-glasses, looked unkempt, almost rustic, and said good things with his ugly lips. Verena had replies for a good many of them, and a pretty colour came into her face as she talked. Olive could see that she produced herself quite as well as one of these gentlemen had foretold the other that she would. Miss Chancellor knew what had passed between them as well as if she had heard it; Mr. Gracie had promised that he would lead her on, that she should justify his description and prove the raciest of her class. They would laugh about her as they went away, lighting their cigars, and for many days afterwards their discourse would be enlivened with quotations from the "women's rights girl."

It was amazing how many ways men had of being antipathetic; these two were very different from Basil Ransom, and different from each other, and yet the manner of each conveyed an insult to one's womanhood. The worst of the case was that Verena would be sure not to perceive this outrage — not to dislike them in consequence. There were so many things that she hadn't yet learned to dislike,

in spite of her friend's earnest efforts to teach her. She had the idea vividly (that was the marvel) of the cruelty of man, of his immemorial injustice; but it remained abstract, platonic; she didn't detest him in consequence. What was the use of her having that sharp, inspired vision of the history of the sex (it was, as she had said herself, exactly like Joan of Arc's absolutely supernatural apprehension of the state of France), if she wasn't going to carry it out, if she was going to behave as the ordinary pusillanimous, conventional young lady? It was all very well for her to have said that first day that she would renounce: did she look, at such a moment as this, like a young woman who had renounced? Suppose this glittering, laughing Burrage youth, with his chains and rings and shining shoes, should fall in love with her and try to bribe her, with his great possessions, to practise renunciations of another kind — to give up her holy work and to go with him to New York, there to live as his wife, partly bullied, partly pampered, in the accustomed Burrage manner? There was as little comfort for Olive as there had been on the whole alarm in the recollection of that off-hand speech of Verena's about her preference for "free unions." This had been mere maiden flippancy; she had not known the meaning of what she said. Though she had grown up among people who took for granted all sorts of queer laxities, she had

509

kept the consummate innocence of the American girl, that innocence which was the greatest of all, for it had survived the abolition of walls and locks; and of the various remarks that had dropped from Verena expressing this quality that startling observation certainly expressed it most. It implied, at any rate, that unions of some kind or other had her approval, and did not exclude the dangers that might arise from encounters with young men in search of sensations.

Chapter XVI

MR. PARDON, as Olive observed, was a little out of this combination; but he was not a person to allow himself to droop. He came and seated himself by Miss Chancellor and broached a literary subject; he asked her if she were following any of the current "serials" in the magazines. On her telling him that she never followed anything of that sort, he undertook a defence of the serial system, which she presently reminded him that she had not attacked. He was not discouraged by this retort, but glided gracefully off to the question of Mount Desert; conversation on some subject or other being evidently a necessity of his nature. He talked very quickly and softly, with words, and even sentences, imperfectly formed; there was a certain amiable flatness in his tone, and he abounded in exclama-

tions — "Goodness gracious!" and "Mercy on us!" — not much in use among the sex whose profanity is apt to be coarse. He had small, fair features, remarkably neat, and pretty ones, and a moustache that he caressed, and an air of juvenility much at variance with his grizzled locks, and the free familiar reference in which he was apt to indulge to his career as a journalist. His friends knew that in spite of his delicacy and his prattle he was what they called a live man; his appearance was perfectly reconcilable with a large degree of literary enterprise. It should be explained that for the most part they attached to this idea the same meaning as Selah Tarrant — a state of intimacy with the newspapers, the cultivation of the great arts of publicity. For this ingenuous son of his age all distinction between the person and the artist had ceased to exist; the writer was personal, the person food for newsboys, and everything and every one were every one's business. All things, with him, referred themselves to print, and print meant simply infinite reporting, a promptitude of announcement, abusive when necessary, or even when not, about his fellow-citizens. He poured contumely on their private life, on their personal appearance, with the best conscience in the world. His faith, again, was the faith of Selah Tarrant — that being in the newspapers is a condition of bliss, and that it would be fastidious to question the terms of the privilege. He was an *en-*

510

fant de la balle, as the French say; he had begun his career, at the age of fourteen, by going the rounds of the hotels, to cull flowers from the big, greasy registers which lie on the marble counters; and he might flatter himself that he had contributed in his measure, and on behalf of a vigilant public opinion, the pride of a democratic State, to the great end of preventing the American citizen from attempting clandestine journeys. Since then he had ascended other steps of the same ladder; he was the most brilliant young interviewer on the Boston press. He was particularly successful in drawing out the ladies; he had condensed into shorthand many of the most celebrated women of his time — some of these daughters of fame were very voluminous — and he was supposed to have a remarkably insinuating way of waiting upon *prime donne* and actresses the morning after their arrival, or sometimes the very evening, while their luggage was being brought up. He was only twenty-eight years old, and, with his hoary head, was a thoroughly modern young man; he had no idea of not taking advantage of all the modern conveniences. He regarded the mission of mankind upon earth as a perpetual evolution of telegrams; everything to him was very much the same, he had no sense of proportion or quality; but the newest thing was what came nearest exciting in his mind the sentiment of respect. He was an object of extreme admiration to Selah Tarrant, who believed that he had mastered all the secrets of success, and who, when Mrs. Tarrant remarked (as she had done more than once) that it looked as if Mr. Pardon was really coming after Verena, declared that if he was, he was one of the few young men he should want to see in that connection, one of the few he should be willing to allow to handle her. It was Tarrant's conviction that if Matthias Pardon should seek Verena in marriage, it would be with a view to producing her in public; and the advantage for the girl of having a husband who was at the same time reporter, interviewer, manager, agent, who had the command of the principal "dailies," would write her up and work her, as it were, scientifically — the attraction of all this was too obvious to be insisted on. Matthias had a mean opinion of Tarrant, thought him quite second-rate, a votary of played-out causes. It was his impression that he himself was in love with Verena, but his passion was not a jealous one, and included a remarkable disposition to share the object of his affection with the American people.

He talked some time to Olive about Mount Desert, told her that in his letters he had described the company at the different hotels. He remarked, however, that a correspondent suffered a good deal to-day from the competition of the "lady-writers"; the sort of article they produced was sometimes more acceptable to the papers. He supposed she would be glad to

511

hear that — he knew she was so interested in woman's having a free field. They certainly made lovely correspondents; they picked up something bright before you could turn round; there wasn't much you could keep away from them; you had to be lively if you wanted to get there first. Of course, they were naturally more chatty, and that was the style of literature that seemed to take most to-day; only they didn't write much but what ladies would want to read. Of course, he knew there were millions of lady-readers, but he intimated that *he* didn't address himself exclusively to the gynecæum; he tried to put in something that would interest all parties. If you read a lady's letter you knew pretty well in advance what you would find. Now, what he tried for was that you shouldn't have the least idea; he always tried to have something that would make you jump. Mr. Pardon was not conceited more, at least, than is proper when youth and success go hand in hand, and it was natural he should not know in what spirit Miss Chancellor listened to him. Being aware that she was a woman of culture his desire was simply to supply her with the pabulum that she would expect. She thought him very inferior; she had heard he was intensely bright, but there was probably some mistake; there couldn't be any danger for Verena from a mind that took merely a gossip's view of great tendencies. Besides, he wasn't half educated, and it was her belief,

or at least her hope, that an educative process was now going on for Verena (under her own direction), which would enable her to make such a discovery for herself. Olive had a standing quarrel with the levity, the good-nature, of the judgments of the day; many of them seemed to her weak to imbecility, losing sight of all measures and standards, lavishing superlatives, delighted to be fooled. The age seemed to her relaxed and demoralised, and I believe she looked to the influx of the great feminine element to make it feel and speak more sharply.

"Well, it's a privilege to hear you two talk together," Mrs. Tarrant said to her; "it's what I call real conversation. It isn't often we have anything so fresh; it makes me feel as if I wanted to join in. I scarcely know whom to listen to most; Verena seems to be having such a time with those gentlemen. First I catch one thing and then another; it seems as if I couldn't take it all in. Perhaps I ought to pay more attention to Mr. Burrage; I don't want him to think we are not so cordial as they are in New York."

She decided to draw nearer to the trio on the other side of the room, for she had perceived (as she devoutly hoped Miss Chancellor had not), that Verena was endeavouring to persuade either of her companions to go and talk to her dear friend, and that these unscrupulous young men, after a glance over their shoulder, appeared to plead for remission, to

512

intimate that this was not what they had come round for. Selah wandered out of the room again with his collection of cakes, and Mr. Pardon began to talk to Olive about Verena, to say that he felt as if he couldn't say all he did feel with regard to the interest she had shown in her. Olive could not imagine why he was called upon to say or to feel anything, and she gave him short answers; while the poor young man, unconscious of his doom, remarked that he hoped she wasn't going to exercise any influence that would prevent Miss Tarrant from taking the rank that belonged to her. He thought there was too much hanging back; he wanted to see her in a front seat; he wanted to see her name in the biggest kind of bills and her portrait in the windows of the stores. She had genius, there was no doubt of that, and she would take a new line altogether. She had charm, and there was a great demand for that nowadays in connection with new ideas. There were so many that seemed to have fallen dead for want of it. She ought to be carried straight ahead; she ought to walk right up to the top. There was a want of bold action; he didn't see what they were waiting for. He didn't suppose they were waiting till she was fifty years old; there were old ones enough in the field. He knew that Miss Chancellor appreciated the advantage of her girlhood, because Miss Verena had told him so. Her father was dreadfully slack, and the winter was ebbing away. Mr. Par-

don went so far as to say that if Dr. Tarrant didn't see his way to do something, he should feel as if he should want to take hold himself. He expressed a hope at the same time that Olive had not any views that would lead her to bring her influence to bear to make Miss Verena hold back; also that she wouldn't consider that he pressed in too much. He knew that was a charge that people brought against newspaper-men — that they were rather apt to cross the line. He only worried because he thought those who were no doubt nearer to Miss Verena than he could hope to be were not sufficiently alive. He knew that she had appeared in two or three parlours since that evening at Miss Birdseye's, and he had heard of the delightful occasion at Miss Chancellor's own house, where so many of the first families had been invited to meet her. (This was an allusion to a small luncheon-party that Olive had given, when Verena discoursed to a dozen matrons and spinsters, selected by her hostess with infinite consideration and many spiritual scruples; a report of the affair, presumably from the hand of the young Matthias, who naturally had not been present, appeared with extraordinary promptness in an evening-paper.) That was very well so far as it went, but he wanted something on another scale, something so big that people would have to go round if they wanted to get past. Then lowering his voice a little, he mentioned what it was: a lecture in the Music Hall, at fifty cents a ticket, without her father, right there on her own basis. He lowered his voice still more and revealed to Miss Chancellor his innermost thought, having first assured himself that Selah was still absent and that Mrs. Tarrant was inquiring of Mr. Burrage whether he visited much on the new land. The truth was, Miss Verena wanted to "shed" her father altogether; she didn't want him pawing round her that way before she began; it didn't add in the least to the attraction. Mr. Pardon expressed the conviction that Miss Chancellor agreed with him in this, and it required a great effort of mind on Olive's part, so small was her desire to act in concert with Mr. Pardon, to admit to herself that she did. She asked him, with a certain lofty coldness — he didn't make her shy, now, a bit — whether he took a great interest in the improvement of the position of women. The question appeared to strike the young man as abrupt and irrelevant, to come down on him from a height with which he was not accustomed to hold intercourse. He was used to quick operations, however, and he had only a moment of bright blankness before replying:

"Oh, there is nothing I wouldn't do for the ladies; just give me a chance and you'll see."

Olive was silent a moment. "What I mean is — is your sympathy a sympathy with our sex, or a particular interest in Miss Tarrant?"

"Well, sympathy is just sympathy — that's all I can say. It takes in Miss Verena and it takes in all others — except the lady-correspondents," the young man added, with a jocosity which, as he perceived even at the moment, was lost on Verena's friend. He was not more successful when he went on: "It takes in even you, Miss Chancellor!"

Olive rose to her feet, hesitating; she wanted to go away, and yet she couldn't bear to leave Verena to be exploited, as she felt that she would be after her departure, that indeed she had already been, by those offensive young men. She had a strange sense, too, that her friend had neglected her for the last half-hour, had not been occupied with her, had placed a barrier between them — a barrier of broad male backs, of laughter that verged upon coarseness, of glancing smiles directed across the room, directed to Olive, which seemed rather to disconnect her with what was going forward on that side than to invite her to take part in it. If Verena recognised that Miss Chancellor was not in report, as her father said, when jocose young men ruled the scene, the discovery implied no great penetration; but the poor girl might have reflected further that to see it taken for granted that she was unadapted for such company could scarcely be more agreeable to Olive than to be dragged into it. This young lady's worst apprehensions were now justified by Mrs. Tarrant's crying to her that she must not go, as Mr. Burrage and Mr. Gracie were trying to persuade Verena to give them a little specimen of inspirational speaking, and she was sure her daughter would comply in a moment if Miss Chancellor would just tell her to compose herself. They had got to own up to it, Miss Chancellor could do more with her than any one else; but Mr. Gracie and Mr. Burrage had excited her so that she was afraid it would be rather an unsuccessful effort. The whole group had got up, and Verena came to Olive with her hands outstretched and no signs of a bad conscience in her bright face.

"I know you like me to speak so much — I'll try to say something if you want me to. But I'm afraid there are not enough people; I can't do much with a small audience."

"I wish we had brought some of our friends — they would have been delighted to come if we had given them a chance," said Mr. Burrage. "There is an immense desire throughout the University to hear you, and there is no such sympathetic audience as an audience of Harvard men. Gracie and I are only two, but Gracie is a host in himself, and I am sure he will say as much of me." The young man spoke these words freely and lightly, smiling at Verena, and even a little at Olive, with the air of one to whom a mastery of clever "chaff" was commonly attributed.

"Mr. Burrage listens even bet-

ter than he talks," his companion declared. "We have the habit of attention at lectures, you know. To be lectured by you would be an advantage indeed. We are sunk in ignorance and prejudice."

"Ah, my prejudices," Burrage went on; "if you could see them — I assure you they are something monstrous!"

"Give them a regular ducking and make them gasp," Matthias Pardon cried. "If you want an opportunity to act on Harvard College, now's your chance. These gentlemen will carry the news; it will be the narrow end of the wedge."

"I can't tell what you like," Verena said, still looking into Olive's eyes.

"I'm sure Miss Chancellor likes everything here," Mrs. Tarrant remarked, with a noble confidence. Selah had reappeared by this time; his lofty, contemplative person was framed by the doorway. "Want to try a little inspiration?" he inquired, looking round on the circle with an encouraging inflection.

"I'll do it alone, if you prefer," Verena said, soothingly to her friend. "It might be a good chance to try without father."

"You don't mean to say you ain't going to be supported?" Mrs. Tarrant exclaimed, with dismay.

"Ah, I beseech you, give us the whole programme — don't omit any leading feature!" Mr. Burrage was heard to plead.

"My only interest is to draw her out," said Selah, defending his in-

515

tegrity. "I will drop right out if I don't seem to vitalise. I have no desire to draw attention to my own poor gifts." This declaration appeared to be addressed to Miss Chancellor.

"Well, there will be more inspiration if you don't touch her," Matthias Pardon said to him. "It will seem to come right down from — well, wherever it does come from."

"Yes, we don't pretend to say that," Mrs. Tarrant murmured.

This little discussion had brought the blood to Olive's face; she felt that every one present was looking at her — Verena most of all — and that here was a chance to take a more complete possession of the girl. Such chances were agitating; moreover, she didn't like, on any occasion, to be so prominent. But everything that had been said was benighted and vulgar; the place seemed thick with the very atmosphere out of which she wished to lift Verena. They were treating her as a show, as a social resource, and the two young men from the College were laughing at her shamelessly. She was not meant for that, and Olive would save her. Verena was so simple, she couldn't see herself; she was the only pure spirit in the odious group.

"I want you to address audiences that are worth addressing — to convince people who are serious and sincere." Olive herself, as she spoke, heard the great shake in her voice. "Your mission is not to

exhibit yourself as a pastime for individuals, but to touch the heart of communities, of nations."

"Dear madam, I'm sure Miss Tarrant will touch my heart!" Mr. Burrage objected, gallantly.

"Well, I don't know but she judges you young men fairly," said Mrs. Tarrant, with a sigh.

Verena, diverted a moment from her communion with her friend, considered Mr. Burrage with a smile. "I don't believe you have got any heart, and I shouldn't care much if you had!"

"You have no idea how much the way you say that increases my desire to hear you speak."

"Do as you please, my dear," said Olive, almost inaudibly. "My carriage must be there — I must leave you, in any case."

"I can see you don't want it," said Verena, wondering. "You would stay if you liked it, wouldn't you?"

"I don't know what I should do. Come out with me!" Olive spoke almost with fierceness.

"Well, you'll send them away no better than they came," said Matthias Pardon.

"I guess you had better come round some other night," Selah suggested pacifically, but with a significance which fell upon Olive's ear.

Mr. Gracie seemed inclined to make the sturdiest protest. "Look here, Miss Tarrant; do you want to save Harvard College, or do you not?" he demanded, with a humorous frown.

"I didn't know *you* were Harvard College!" Verena returned as humorously.

"I am afraid you are rather disappointed in your evening if you expected to obtain some insight into our ideas," said Mrs. Tarrant, with an air of impotent sympathy, to Mr. Gracie.

"Well, good-night, Miss Chancellor," she went on; "I hope you've got a warm wrap. I suppose you'll think we go a good deal by what you say in this house. Well, most people don't object to that. There's a little hole right there in the porch; it seems as if Doctor Tarrant couldn't remember to go for the man to fix it. I am afraid you'll think we're too much taken up with all these new hopes. Well, we *have* enjoyed seeing you in our home; it quite raises my appetite for social intercourse. Did you come out on wheels? I can't stand a sleigh myself; it makes me sick."

This was her hostess's response to Miss Chancellor's very summary farewell, uttered as the three ladies proceeded together to the door of the house. Olive had got herself out of the little parlour with a sort of blind, defiant dash; she had taken no perceptible leave of the rest of the company. When she was calm she had very good manners, but when she was agitated she was guilty of lapses, every one of which came back to her, magnified, in the watches of the night. Sometimes they excited remorse, and sometimes triumph;

in the latter case she felt that she could not have been so justly vindictive in cold blood. Tarrant wished to guide her down the steps, out of the little yard, to her carriage; he reminded her that they had had ashes sprinkled on the planks on purpose. But she begged him to let her alone, she almost pushed him back; she drew Verena out into the dark freshness, closing the door of the house behind her. There was a splendid sky, all blue-black and silver — a sparkling wintry vault, where the stars were like a myriad points of ice. The air was silent and sharp, and the vague snow looked cruel. Olive knew now very definitely what the promise was that she wanted Verena to make; but it was too cold, she could keep her there bareheaded but an instant. Mrs. Tarrant, meanwhile, in the parlour, remarked that it seemed as if she couldn't trust Verena with her own parents; and Selah intimated that, with a proper invitation, his daughter would be very happy to address Harvard College at large. Mr. Burrage and Mr. Gracie said they would invite her on the spot, in the name of the University; and Matthias Pardon reflected (and asserted) with glee that this would be the newest thing yet. But he added that they would have a high time with Miss Chancellor first, and this was evidently the conviction of the company.

"I can see you are angry at something," Verena said to Olive, as the two stood there in the starlight. "I hope it isn't me. What have I done?"

"I am not angry — I am anxious. I am so afraid I shall lose you. Verena, don't fail me — don't fail me!" Olive spoke low, with a kind of passion.

"Fail you? How can I fail?"

"You can't, of course you can't. Your star is above you. But don't listen to *them*."

"To whom do you mean, Olive? To my parents?"

"Oh no, not your parents," Miss Chancellor replied, with some sharpness. She paused a moment, and then she said: "I don't care for your parents. I have told you that before; but now that I have seen them — as they wished, as you wished, and I didn't — I don't care for them; I must repeat it, Verena. I should be dishonest if I let you think I did."

"Why, Olive Chancellor!" Verena murmured, as if she were trying, in spite of the sadness produced by this declaration, to do justice to her friend's impartiality.

"Yes, I am hard; perhaps I am cruel; but we must be hard if we wish to triumph. Don't listen to young men when they try to mock and muddle you. They don't care for you; they don't care for *us*. They care only for their pleasure, for what they believe to be the right of the stronger. The stronger? I am not so sure!"

"Some of them care so much — are supposed to care too much — for us," Verena said, with a smile that looked dim in the darkness.

"Yes, if we will give up every-

thing. I have asked you before — are you prepared to give up?"

"Do you mean, to give *you* up?"

"No, all our wretched sisters — all our hopes and purposes — all that we think sacred and worth living for!"

"Oh, they don't want that, Olive." Verena's smile became more distinct, and she added: "They don't want so much as that!"

"Well, then, go in and speak for them — and sing for them — and dance for them!"

"Olive, you are cruel!"

"Yes, I am. But promise me one thing, and I shall be — oh, so tender!"

"What a strange place for promises," said Verena, with a shiver, looking about her into the night.

"Yes, I am dreadful; I know it. But promise." And Olive drew the girl nearer to her, flinging over her with one hand the fold of a cloak that hung ample upon her own meagre person, and holding her there with the other, while she looked at her, suppliant but half hesitating. "Promise!" she repeated.

"Is is something terrible?"

"Never to listen to one of them, never to be bribed —— "

At this moment the house-door was opened again, and the light of the hall projected itself across the little piazza. Matthias Pardon stood in the aperture, and Tarrant and his wife, with the two other visitors, appeared to have come forward as well, to see what detained Verena.

"You seem to have started a kind of lecture out here," Mr. Pardon said. "You ladies had better look out, or you'll freeze together!"

Verena was reminded by her mother that she would catch her death, but she had already heard sharply, low as they were spoken, five last words from Olive, who now abruptly released her and passed swiftly over the path from the porch to her waiting carriage. Tarrant creaked along, in pursuit, to assist Miss Chancellor; the others drew Verena into the house. "Promise me not to marry!" — that was what echoed in her startled mind, and repeated itself there when Mr. Burrage returned to the charge, asking her if she wouldn't at least appoint some evening when they might listen to her. She knew that Olive's injunction ought not to have surprised her; she had already felt it in the air; she would have said at any time, if she had been asked, that she didn't suppose Miss Chancellor would want her to marry. But the idea, uttered as her friend had uttered it, had a new solemnity, and the effect of that quick, violent colloquy was to make her nervous and impatient, as if she had had a sudden glimpse of futurity. That was rather awful, even if it represented the fate one would like.

When the two young men from the College pressed their petition, she asked, with a laugh that surprised them, whether they wished to "mock and muddle" her. They went away, assenting to Mrs. Tarrant's last remark: "I am afraid you'll feel that you don't quite understand us yet." Matthias Pardon

remained; her father and mother, expressing their perfect confidence that he would excuse them, went to bed and left him sitting there. He stayed a good while longer, nearly an hour, and said things that made Verena think that *he*, perhaps, would like to marry her. But while she listened to him, more abstractedly than her custom was, she remarked to herself that there could be no difficulty in promising Olive so far as he was concerned. He was very pleasant, and he knew an immense deal about everything, or, rather, about every one, and he would take her right into the midst of life. But she didn't wish to marry him, all the same, and after he had gone she reflected that, once she came to think of it, she didn't want to marry any one. So it would be easy, after all, to make Olive that promise, and it would give her so much pleasure!

Chapter XVII

THE NEXT time Verena saw Olive, she said to her that she was ready to make the promise she had asked the other night; but, to her great surprise, this young woman answered her by a question intended to check such rashness. Miss Chancellor raised a warning finger; she had an air of dissuasion almost as solemn as her former pressure; her passionate impatience appeared to have given way to other considerations, to be replaced by the resignation that comes with deeper reflection. It was tinged in this case, indeed, by such bitterness as might be permitted to a young lady who cultivated the brightness of a great faith.

"Don't you want any promise at present?" Verena asked. "Why, Olive, how you change!"

"My dear child, you are so young — so strangely young. I am a thousand years old; I have lived through generations — through centuries. I know what I know by experience; you know it by imagination. That is consistent with your being the fresh, bright creature that you are. I am constantly forgetting the difference between us — that you are a mere child as yet, though a child destined for great things. I forgot it the other night, but I have remembered it since. You must pass through a certain phase, and it would be very wrong in me to pretend to suppress it. That is all clear to me now; I see it was my jealousy that spoke — my restless, hungry jealousy. I have far too much of that; I oughtn't to give any one the right to say that it's a woman's quality. I don't want your signature; I only want your confidence — only what springs from that. I hope with all my soul that you won't marry; but if you don't it must not be because you have promised me. You know what I think — that there is something noble done when one makes a sacrifice for a great good. Priests — when they were real priests — never married, and what you and I dream of doing demands of us a kind of priesthood. It seems to me very poor, when friendship and faith and charity and the most interesting occupation in the world — when such a combination as this doesn't seem, by itself, enough to live for. No man that I have ever seen cares a straw in his heart for what we are trying to accomplish. They hate it; they scorn it; they will try to stamp it out whenever they can. Oh yes, I know there are men who pretend to care for it; but they are not really men, and I wouldn't be sure even of them! Any man that one would look at — with him, as a matter of course, it is war upon us to the knife. I don't mean to say there are not some male beings who are willing to patronise us a little; to pat us on the back and recommend a few moderate concessions; to say that there *are* two or three little points in which society has not been quite just to us. But any man who pretends to accept our programme *in toto,* as you and I understand it, of his own free will, before he is forced to — such a person simply schemes to betray us. There are gentlemen in plenty who would be glad to stop your mouth by kissing you! If you become dangerous some day to their selfishness, to their vested interests, to their immorality — as I pray heaven every day, my dear friend, that you may! — it will be a grand thing for one of them if he can persuade you that he loves you. Then you will see what he will do with you, and how far his love will take him! It would be a sad day for you and for me and for all of us, if you were to believe something of that kind. You see I am very calm now; I have thought it all out."

Verena had listened with earnest eyes. "Why, Olive, you are quite a speaker yourself!" she exclaimed. "You would far surpass me if you would let yourself go."

Miss Chancellor shook her head with a melancholy that was not devoid of sweetness. "I can speak to *you;* but that is no proof. The very stones of the street — all the dumb things of nature — might find a voice to talk to you. I have no facility; I am awkward and embarrassed and dry." When this young lady, after a struggle with the winds and waves of emotion, emerged into the quiet stream of a certain high reasonableness, she presented her most graceful aspect; she had a tone of softness and sympathy, a gentle dignity, a serenity of wisdom, which sealed the appreciation of those who knew her well enough to like her, and which always impressed Verena as something almost august. Such moods, however, were not often revealed to the public at large; they belonged to Miss Chancellor's very private life. One of them had possession of her at present, and she went on to explain the inconsequence which had puzzled her friend with the same quiet clearness, the detachment from error, of a woman whose self-scrutiny has been as sharp as her deflection.

"Don't think me capricious if I say I would rather trust you without a pledge. I owe you, I owe every one, an apology for my rudeness and fierceness at your mother's. It came over me — just seeing those young men — how exposed you are; and the idea made me (for the moment) frantic. I see your danger still, but I see other things too, and I have recovered my balance. You must be safe, Verena — you must be saved; but your safety must not come from your having tied your hands. It must come from the growth of your perception; from your seeing things, of yourself, sincerely and with conviction, in the light in which I see them; from your feeling that for your work your freedom is essential, and that there is no freedom for you and me save in religiously *not* doing what you will often be asked to do — and I never!" Miss Chancellor brought out these last words with a proud jerk which was not without its pathos. "Don't promise, don't promise!" she went on. "I would far rather you didn't. But don't fail me — don't fail me, or I shall die!"

Her manner of repairing her inconsistency was altogether feminine: she wished to extract a certainty at the same time that she wished to deprecate a pledge, and she would have been delighted to put Verena into the enjoyment of that freedom which was so important for her by preventing her exercising it in a particular direction. The girl was now completely under her influence; she had latent curiosities and distractions — left to herself, she was not always thinking of the unhappiness of women; but the touch of Olive's tone worked a spell, and she found something to which at least a portion of her nature turned with eagerness in her companion's wider knowledge, her elevation of view. Miss Chancellor was historic and philosophic; or, at any rate, she appeared so to Verena, who felt that through such an association one might at last intellectually command all life. And there was a simpler impulse; Verena wished to please her if only because she had such a dread of displeasing her. Olive's displeasures, disappointments, disapprovals were tragic, truly memorable; she grew white under them, not shedding many tears, as a general thing, like inferior women (she cried when she was angry, not when she was hurt), but limping and panting, morally, as if she had received a wound that she would carry for life. On the other hand, her commendations, her satisfactions were as soft as a west wind; and she had this sign, the rarest of all, of generosity, that she liked obligations of gratitude when they were not laid upon her by men. Then, indeed, she scarcely recognised them. She considered men in general as so much in the debt of the opposite sex that any individual woman had an unlimited credit with them; she could not possibly overdraw the general feminine account. The unexpected temperance

of her speech on this subject of Verena's accessibility to matrimonial error seemed to the girl to have an antique beauty, a wisdom purged of worldly elements; it reminded her of qualities that she believed to have been proper to Electra or Antigone. This made her wish the more to do something that would gratify Olive; and in spite of her friend's dissuasion she declared that she should like to promise. "I will promise, at any rate, not to marry any of those gentlemen that were at the house," she said. "Those seemed to be the ones you were principally afraid of."

"You will promise not to marry any one you don't like," said Olive. "That would be a great comfort!"

"But I do like Mr. Burrage and Mr. Gracie."

"And Mr. Matthias Pardon? What a name!"

"Well, he knows how to make himself agreeable. He can tell you everything you want to know."

"You mean everything you don't! Well, if you like every one, I haven't the least objection. It would only be preferences that I should find alarming. I am not the least afraid of your marrying a repulsive man; your danger would come from an attractive one."

"I'm glad to hear you admit that some *are* attractive!" Verena exclaimed, with the light laugh which her reverence for Miss Chancellor had not yet quenched. "It sometimes seems as if there weren't any you could like!"

"I can imagine a man I should like very much," Olive replied, after a moment. "But I don't like those I see. They seem to me poor creatures." And, indeed, her uppermost feeling in regard to them was a kind of cold scorn; she thought most of them palterers and bullies. The end of the colloquy was that Verena, having assented, with her usual docility, to her companion's optimistic contention that it was a "phase," this taste for evening-calls from collegians and newspaper-men, and would consequently pass away with the growth of her mind, remarked that the injustice of men might be an accident or might be a part of their nature, but at any rate she should have to change a good deal before she should want to marry.

About the middle of December, Miss Chancellor received a visit from Matthias Pardon, who had come to ask her what she meant to do about Verena. She had never invited him to call upon her, and the appearance of a gentleman whose desire to see her was so irrepressible as to dispense with such a preliminary was not in her career an accident frequent enough to have taught her equanimity. She thought Mr. Pardon's visit a liberty; but, if she expected to convey this idea to him by withholding any suggestion that he should sit down, she was greatly mistaken, inasmuch as he cut the ground from under her feet by himself offering her a chair. His manner represented hospitality enough for both of them, and she was obliged to listen, on the edge of her sofa (she could at least seat herself where she liked), to his extraordinary inquiry. Of course she was not obliged to answer it, and indeed she scarcely understood it. He explained that it was prompted by the intense interest he felt in Miss Verena; but that scarcely made it more comprehensible, such a sentiment (on his part) being such a curious mixture. He had a sort of enamel of good humour which showed that his indelicacy was his profession; and he asked for revelations of the *vie intime* of his victims with the bland confidence of a fashionable physician inquiring about symptoms. He wanted to know what Miss Chancellor meant to do, because if she didn't mean to do anything, he had an idea — which he wouldn't conceal from her — of going into the enterprise himself. "You see, what I should like to know is this: do you consider that she belongs to you, or that she belongs to the people? If she belongs to you, why don't you bring her out?"

He had no purpose and no consciousness of being impertinent; he only wished to talk over the matter sociably with Miss Chancellor. He knew, of course, that there was a presumption she would not be sociable, but no presumption had yet deterred him from presenting a surface which he believed to be polished till it shone; there was always a larger one in favour of his power to penetrate and of the majesty of the "great dailies." Indeed, he took so many things for granted that Olive remained dumb while she regarded them; and he availed himself of what he considered as a fortunate opening to be really very frank. He reminded her that he had known Miss Verena a good deal longer than she; he had travelled out to Cambridge the other winter (when he could get an off-night), with the thermometer at ten below zero. He had always thought her attractive, but it wasn't till this season that his eyes had been fully opened. Her talent had matured, and now he had no hesitation in calling her brilliant. Miss Chancellor could imagine whether, as an old friend, he could watch such a beautiful unfolding with indifference. She would fascinate the people, just as she had fascinated her (Miss Chancellor), and, he might be permitted to add, himself. The fact was, she was a great card, and some one ought to play it. There never had been a more attractive female speaker before the American public; she would walk right past Mrs. Farrinder, and Mrs. Farrinder knew it. There was room for both, no doubt, they had such a different style; anyhow, what he wanted to show was that there was room for Miss Verena. She didn't want any more tuning-up, she wanted to break right out. Moreover, he felt that any gentleman who should lead her to success would win her esteem; he might even attract her more powerfully — who could tell? If Miss Chancellor wanted to attach her permanently, she ought to push her right forward. He gathered from what Miss Verena had told him that she wanted to make her study up the subject a while longer — follow some kind of course. Well, now, he could assure her that there was no preparation so good as just seeing a couple of thousand people down there before you who have paid their money to have you tell them something. Miss Verena was a natural genius, and he hoped very much she wasn't going to take the nature out of her. She could study up as she went along; she had got the great thing that you couldn't learn, a kind of divine afflatus, as the ancients used to say, and she had better just begin on that. He wouldn't deny what was the matter with *him;* he was quite under the spell, and his admiration made him want to see her where she belonged. He shouldn't care so much how she got there, but it would certainly add to his pleasure if he could show her up to her place. Therefore, would Miss Chancellor just tell him this: How long did she expect to hold her back; how long did she expect a humble admirer to wait? Of course he hadn't come there to cross-question her; there was one thing he trusted he always kept clear of; when he was indiscreet he wanted to know it. He had come with a proposal of his own, and he hoped it would seem a sufficient warrant for his visit. Would Miss Chancellor be willing to divide a — the — well, he might call it the responsibilities? Couldn't they run Miss Verena together? In this case, every one would be satisfied. She could travel round with her as her companion, and he would see that the American people walked up. If Miss Chancellor would just let her go a little, he would look after the rest. He wanted no odds; he only wanted her for about an hour and a half three or four evenings a week.

Olive had time, in the course of this appeal, to make her faculties converge, to ask herself what she could say to this prodigious young man that would make him feel as how base a thing she held his proposal that they should constitute themselves into a company for drawing profit from Verena. Unfortunately, the most sarcastic inquiry that could occur to her as a response was also the most obvious one, so that he hesitated but a moment with his rejoinder after she had asked him how many thousand of dollars he expected to make.

"For Miss Verena? It depends upon the time. She'd run for ten years, at least. I can't figure it up till all the States have been heard from," he said, smiling.

"I don't mean for Miss Tarrant, I mean for you," Olive returned, with the impression that she was looking him straight in the eye.

"Oh, as many as you'll leave me!" Matthias Pardon answered, with a laugh that contained all, and more than all, the jocularity of the American press. "To speak seriously," he added, "I don't want to make money out of it."

"What do you want to make, then?"

"Well, I want to make history! I want to help the ladies."

"The ladies?" Olive murmured. "What do you know about ladies?" she was on the point of adding, when his promptness checked her.

"All over the world. I want to work for their emancipation. I regard it as the great modern question."

Miss Chancellor got up now; this was rather too strong. Whether, eventually, she was successful in what she attempted, the reader of her history will judge; but at this moment she had not that promise of success which resides in a willingness to make use of every aid that offers. Such is the penalty of being of a fastidious, exclusive, uncompromising nature; of seeing things not simply and sharply, but in perverse relations, in intertwisted strands. It seemed to our young lady that nothing could be less attractive than to owe her emancipation to such a one as Matthias Pardon; and it is curious that those qualities which he had in common with Verena, and which in her seemed to Olive romantic and touching — her having sprung from the "people," had an acquaintance with poverty, a hand-to-mouth development, and an experience of the seamy side of life — availed in no degree to conciliate Miss Chancellor. I suppose it was because he was a man. She told him that she was much

The Bostonians

obliged to him for his offer, but that he evidently didn't understand Verena and herself. No, not even Miss Tarrant, in spite of his long acquaintance with her. They had no desire to be notorious; they only wanted to be useful. They had no wish to make money; there would always be plenty of money for Miss Tarrant. Certainly, she should come before the public, and the world would acclaim her and hang upon her words; but crude, precipitate action was what both of them least desired. The change in the dreadful position of women was not a question for to-day simply, or for to-morrow, but for many years to come; and there would be a great deal to think of, to map out. One thing they were determined upon — that men shouldn't taunt them with being superficial. When Verena should appear it would be armed at all points, like Joan of Arc (this analogy had lodged itself in Olive's imagination); she should have facts and figures; she should meet men on their own ground. "What we mean to do, we mean to do well," Miss Chancellor said to her visitor, with considerable sternness; leaving him to make such an application to himself as his fancy might suggest.

This announcement had little comfort for him; he felt baffled and disheartened — indeed, quite sick. Was it not sickening to hear her talk of this dreary process of preparation? — as if any one cared

about that, and would know whether Verena were prepared or not! Had Miss Chancellor no faith in her girlhood? didn't she know what a card that would be? This was the last inquiry Olive allowed him the opportunity of making. She remarked to him that they might talk for ever without coming to an agreement — their points of view were so far apart. Besides, it was a woman's question; what they wanted was for women, and it should be by women. It had happened to the young Matthias more than once to be shown the way to the door, but the path of retreat had never yet seemed to him so unpleasant. He was naturally amiable, but it had not hitherto befallen him to be made to feel that he was not — and could not be — a factor in contemporary history: here was a rapacious woman who proposed to keep that favourable setting for herself. He let her know that she was rightdown selfish, and that if she chose to sacrifice a beautiful nature to her antediluvian theories and love of power, a vigilant daily press — whose business it was to expose wrong-doing — would demand an account from her. She replied that, if the newspapers chose to insult her, that was their own affair; one outrage the more to the sex in her person was of little account. And after he had left her she seemed to see the glow of dawning success; the battle had begun, and something of the ecstasy of the martyr.

526

Chapter XVIII

VERENA told her, a week after this, that Mr. Pardon wanted so much she should say she would marry him; and she added, with evident pleasure at being able to give her so agreeable a piece of news, that she had declined to say anything of the sort. She thought that now, at least, Olive must believe in her; for the proposal was more attractive than Miss Chancellor seemed able to understand. "He does place things in a very seductive light," Verena said; "he says that if I become his wife I shall be carried straight along by a force of excitement of which at present I have no idea. I shall wake up famous, if I marry him; I have only got to give out my feelings, and he will take care of the rest. He says every hour of my youth is precious to me, and that we should have a lovely time travelling round the country. I think you ought to allow that all that is rather dazzling — for I am not naturally concentrated, like you!"

"He promises you success. What do you call success?" Olive inquired, looking at her friend with a kind of salutary coldness — a suspension of sympathy — with which Verena was now familiar (though she liked it no better than at first), and which made

approbation more gracious when approbation came.

Verena reflected a moment, and then answered, smiling, but with confidence: "Producing a pressure that shall be irresistible. Causing certain laws to be repealed by Congress and by the State legislatures, and others to be enacted." She repeated the words as if they had been part of a catechism committed to memory, while Olive saw that this mechanical tone was in the nature of a joke that she could not deny herself; they had had that definition so often before, and Miss Chancellor had had occasion so often to remind her what success *really* was. Of course it was easy to prove to her now that Mr. Pardon's glittering bait was a very different thing; was a mere trap and lure, a bribe to vanity and impatience, a device for making her give herself away — let alone fill his pockets while she did so. Olive was conscious enough of the girl's want of continuity; she had seen before how she could be passionately serious at times, and then perversely, even if innocently, trivial — as just now, when she seemed to wish to convert one of their most sacred formulas into a pleasantry. She had already quite recognised, however, that it was not of importance that Verena should be just like herself; she was all of one piece, and Verena was of many pieces, which had, where they fitted together, little capricious chinks, through which mocking inner lights seemed sometimes to gleam. It was a part of Verena's being unlike her that she should feel Mr. Pardon's promise of eternal excitement to be a brilliant thing, should indeed consider Mr. Pardon with any tolerance at all. But Olive tried afresh to allow for such aberrations, as a phase of youth and suburban culture; the more so that, even when she tried most, Verena reproached her — so far as Verena's incurable softness could reproach — with not allowing enough. Olive didn't appear to understand that, while Matthias Pardon drew that picture and tried to hold her hand (this image was unfortunate), she had given one long, fixed, wistful look, through the door he opened, at the bright tumult of the world, and then had turned away, solely for her friend's sake, to an austerer probation and a purer effort; solely for her friend's, that is, and that of the whole enslaved sisterhood. The fact remained, at any rate, that Verena had made a sacrifice; and this thought, after a while, gave Olive a greater sense of security. It seemed almost to seal the future; for Olive knew that the young interviewer would not easily be shaken off, and yet she was sure that Verena would never yield to him.

It was true that at present Mr. Burrage came a great deal to the little house at Cambridge; Verena told her about that, told her so much that it was almost as good as if she had told her all. He came without Mr. Gracie now; he could find his way alone, and he seemed to wish that there should be no one else. He had made himself so pleasant to her mother that she almost always went out of the room; that was the highest proof Mrs. Tarrant could give of her appreciation of a "gentleman-caller." They knew everything about him by this time; that his father was dead, his mother very fashionable and prominent, and he himself in possession of a handsome patrimony. They thought ever so much of him in New York. He collected beautiful things, pictures and antiques and objects that he sent for to Europe on purpose, many of which were arranged in his rooms at Cambridge. He had intaglios and Spanish altar-cloths and drawings by the old masters. He was different from most others; he seemed to want so much to enjoy life, and to think you easily could if you would only let yourself go. Of course — judging by what *he* had — he appeared to think you required a great many things to keep you up. And then Verena told Olive — she could see it was after a little delay — that he wanted her to come round to his place and see his treasures. He wanted to show them to her, he was so sure she would admire them. Verena was sure also, but she wouldn't go alone, and she wanted Olive to go with her. They would have tea, and there would be other ladies, and Olive would tell her what she thought of a life that was so crowded with beauty. Miss Chancellor made her reflections on all this, and the first of them was that it was happy for her that she had determined for the present to accept these accidents, for otherwise might she not now have had a deeper alarm? She wished to heaven that conceited young men with time on their hands would leave Verena alone; but evidently they wouldn't, and her best safety was in seeing as many as should turn up. If the type should become frequent, she would very soon judge it. If Olive had not been so grim, she would have had a smile to spare for the frankness with which the girl herself adopted this theory. She was eager to explain that Mr. Burrage didn't seem at all to want what poor Mr. Pardon had wanted; he made her talk about her views far more than that gentleman, but gave no sign of offering himself either as a husband or as a lecture-agent. The furthest he had gone as yet was to tell her that he liked her for the same reason that he liked old enamels and old embroideries; and when she said that she didn't see how she resembled such things, he had replied that it was because she was so peculiar and so delicate. She might be peculiar, but she had protested against the idea that she was delicate; it was the last thing that she wanted to be thought; and Olive could see from this how far she was from falling in with everything he said. When Miss Chancellor asked if she respected Mr. Burrage (and how solemn Olive could make that word she by this time knew),

she answered, with her sweet, vain laugh, but apparently with perfect good faith, that it didn't matter whether she did or not, for what was the whole thing but simply a phase — the very one they had talked about? The sooner she got through it the better, was it not? — and she seemed to think that her transit would be materially quickened by a visit to Mr. Burrage's rooms. As I say, Verena was pleased to regard the phase as quite inevitable, and she had said more than once to Olive that if their struggle was to be with men, the more they knew about them the better. Miss Chancellor asked her why her mother should not go with her to see the curiosities, since she mentioned that their possessor had not neglected to invite Mrs. Tarrant; and Verena said that this, of course, would be very simple — only her mother wouldn't be able to tell her so well as Olive whether she ought to respect Mr. Burrage. This decision as to whether Mr. Burrage should be respected assumed in the life of these two remarkable young women, pitched in so high a moral key, the proportions of a momentous event. Olive shrank at first from facing it — not, indeed, the decision — for we know that her own mind had long since been made up in regard to the quantity of esteem due to almost any member of the other sex — but the incident itself, which, if Mr. Burrage should exasperate her further, might expose her to the danger of appearing to Verena to be unfair to him. It was her belief that he was playing a deeper game than the young Matthias, and she was very willing to watch him; but she thought it prudent not to attempt to cut short the phase (she adopted that classification) prematurely — an imputation she should incur if, without more delay, she were to "shut down," as Verena said, on the young connoisseur.

It was settled, therefore, that Mrs. Tarrant should, with her daughter, accept Mr. Burrage's invitation; and in a few days these ladies paid a visit to his apartments. Verena subsequently, of course, had much to say about it, but she dilated even more upon her mother's impressions than upon her own. Mrs. Tarrant had carried away a supply which would last her all winter; there had been some New York ladies present who were "on" at that moment, and with whom her intercourse was rich in emotions. She had told them all that she should be happy to see them in her home, but they had not yet picked their way along the little planks of the front yard. Mr. Burrage, at all events, had been quite lovely, and had talked about his collections, which were wonderful, in the most interesting manner. Verena inclined to think he was to be respected. He admitted that he was not really studying law at all; he had only come to Cambridge for the form; but she didn't see why it wasn't enough when you made yourself as pleasant as that. She went so far as to ask Olive whether taste and art were not something, and her friend could see that she was certainly very much involved in the phase. Miss Chancellor, of course, had her answer ready. Taste and art were good when they enlarged the mind, not when they narrowed it. Verena assented to this, and said it remained to be seen what effect they had had upon Mr. Burrage — a remark which led Olive to fear that at such a rate much would remain, especially when Verena told her, later, that another visit to the young man's rooms was projected, and that this time she must come, he having expressed the greatest desire for the honour, and her own wish being greater still that they should look at some of his beautiful things together.

A day or two after this, Mr. Henry Burrage left a card at Miss Chancellor's door, with a note in which he expressed the hope that she would take tea with him on a certain day on which he expected the company of his mother. Olive responded to this invitation, in conjunction with Verena; but in doing so she was in the position, singular for her, of not quite understanding what she was about. It seemed to her strange that Verena should urge her to take such a step when she was free to go without her, and it proved two things: first, that she was much interested in Mr. Henry Burrage, and second, that her nature was extraordinarily beautiful. Could anything, in effect, be less underhand than such an indifference to what she supposed to be the best opportunities for carrying on a flirtation? Verena wanted to know the truth, and it was clear that by this time she believed Olive Chancellor to have it, for the most part, in her keeping. Her insistence, therefore, proved, above all, that she cared more for her friend's opinion of Henry Burrage than for her own — a reminder, certainly, of the responsibility that Olive had incurred in undertaking to form this generous young mind, and of the exalted place that she now occupied in it. Such revelations ought to have been satisfactory; if they failed to be completely so, it was only on account of the elder girl's regret that the subject as to which her judgement was wanted should be a young man destitute of the worst vices. Henry Burrage had contributed to throw Miss Chancellor into a "state," as these young ladies called it, the night she met him at Mrs. Tarrant's; but it had none the less been conveyed to Olive by the voices of the air that he was a gentleman and a good fellow.

This was painfully obvious when the visit to his rooms took place; he was so good-humoured, so amusing, so friendly and considerate, so attentive to Miss Chancellor, he did the honours of his bachelor-nest with so easy a grace, that Olive, part of the time, sat dumbly shaking her conscience, like a watch that wouldn't go, to make it tell her some better reason why she shouldn't like him. She saw that there would be no difficulty in disliking his mother; but that, unfortunately, would not serve her purpose nearly so well. Mrs. Burrage had come to spend a few days near her son; she was staying at an hotel in Boston. It presented itself to Olive that after this entertainment it would be an act of courtesy to call upon her; but here, at least, was the comfort that she could cover herself with the general absolution extended to the Boston temperament and leave her alone. It was slightly provoking, indeed, that Mrs. Burrage should have so much the air of a New Yorker who didn't particularly notice whether a Bostonian called or not; but there is ever an imperfection, I suppose, in even the sweetest revenge. She was a woman of society, large and voluminous, fair (in complexion) and regularly ugly, looking as if she ought to be slow and rather heavy, but disappointing this expectation by a quick, amused utterance, a short, bright, summary laugh, with which she appeared to dispose of the joke (whatever it was) for ever, and an air of recognising on the instant everything she saw and heard. She was evidently accustomed to talk, and even to listen, if not kept waiting too long for details and parentheses; she was not continuous, but frequent, as it were, and you could see that she hated explanations, though it was not to be supposed that she had anything to fear from them. Her favours were general, not particular; she was civil enough to every one, but not in any case endearing, and perfectly genial without being confiding, as people were in Boston when (in moments of exaltation) they wished to mark that they were not suspicious. There was something in her whole manner which seemed to say to Olive that she belonged to a larger world than hers; and our young lady was vexed at not hearing that she had lived for a good many years in Europe, as this would have made it easy to classify her as one of the corrupt. She learned, almost with a sense of injury, that neither the mother nor the son had been longer beyond the seas than she herself; and if they were to be judged as triflers they must be dealt with individually. Was it an aid to such a judgment to see that Mrs. Burrage was very much pleased with Boston, with Harvard College, with her son's interior, with her cup of tea (it was old Sèvres), which was not half so bad as she had expected, with the company he had asked to meet her (there were three or four gentlemen, one of whom was Mr. Gracie), and, last, not least, with Verena Tarrant, whom she addressed as a celebrity, kindly, cleverly, but without maternal tenderness or anything to mark the difference in their age? She spoke to her as if they were equals in that respect, as if Verena's genius and fame would make up the disparity, and the girl had no need of encouragement and patronage. She made no direct allusion, however, to her particular views, and asked her no question about her "gift" —

an omission which Verena thought strange, and, with the most speculative candour, spoke of to Olive afterwards. Mrs. Burrage seemed to imply that every one present had some distinction and some talent, that they were all good company together. There was nothing in her manner to indicate that she was afraid of Verena on her son's account; she didn't resemble a person who would like him to marry the daughter of a mesmeric healer, and yet she appeared to think it charming that he should have such a young woman there to give gusto to her hour at Cambridge. Poor Olive was, in the nature of things, entangled in contradictions; she had a horror of the idea of Verena's marrying Mr. Burrage, and yet she was angry when his mother demeaned herself as if the little girl with red hair, whose freshness she enjoyed, could not be a serious danger. She saw all this through the blur of her shyness, the conscious, anxious silence to which she was so much of the time condemned. It may therefore be imagined how sharp her vision would have been could she only have taken the situation more simply; for she was intelligent enough not to have needed to be morbid, even for purposes of self-defence.

I must add, however, that there was a moment when she came near being happy — or, at any rate, reflected that it was a pity she could not be so. Mrs. Burrage asked her son to play "some little thing," and he sat down to his piano and revealed a talent that might well have gratified that lady's pride. Olive was extremely susceptible to music, and it was impossible to her not to be soothed and beguiled by the young man's charming art. One "little thing" succeeded another; his selections were all very happy. His guests sat scattered in the red firelight, listening, silent, in comfortable attitudes; there was a faint fragrance from the burning logs, which mingled with the perfume of Schubert and Mendelssohn; the covered lamps made a glow here and there, and the cabinets and brackets produced brown shadows, out of which some precious object gleamed — some ivory carving or cinque-cento cup. It was given to Olive, under these circumstances, for half an hour, to surrender herself, to enjoy the music, to admit that Mr. Burrage played with exquisite taste, to feel as if the situation were a kind of truce. Her nerves were calmed, her problems — for the time — subsided. Civilisation, under such an influence, in such a setting, appeared to have done its work; harmony ruled the scene; human life ceased to be a battle. She went so far as to ask herself why one should have a quarrel with it; the relations of men and women, in that picturesque grouping, had not the air of being internecine. In short, she had an interval of unexpected rest, during which she kept her eyes mainly on Verena, who sat near Mrs. Burrage, letting herself go, evidently, more completely than

Olive. To her, too, music was a delight, and her listening face turned itself to different parts of the room, unconsciously, while her eyes vaguely rested on the *bibelots* that emerged into the firelight. At moments Mrs. Burrage bent her countenance upon her and smiled, at random, kindly; and then Verena smiled back, while her expression seemed to say that, oh yes, she was giving up everything, all principles, all projects. Even before it was time to go, Olive felt that they were both (Verena and she) quite demoralised, and she only summoned energy to take her companion away when she heard Mrs. Burrage propose to her to come and spend a fortnight in New York. Then Olive exclaimed to herself, "Is it a plot? Why in the world can't they let her alone?" and prepared to throw a fold of her mantle, as she had done before, over her young friend. Verena answered, somewhat impetuously, that she should be delighted to visit Mrs. Burrage; then checked her impetuosity, after a glance from Olive, by adding that perhaps this lady wouldn't ask her if she knew what strong ground she took on the emancipation of women. Mrs. Burrage looked at her son and laughed; she said she was perfectly aware of Verena's views, and that it was impossible to be more in sympathy with them than she herself. She took the greatest interest in the emancipation of women; she thought there was so much to be done. These were the only remarks that passed in reference to the great subject; and nothing more was said to Verena, either by Henry Burrage or by his friend Gracie, about her addressing the Harvard students. Verena had told her father that Olive had put her veto upon that, and Tarrant had said to the young men that it seemed as if Miss Chancellor was going to put the thing through in her own way. We know that he thought this way very circuitous; but Miss Chancellor made him feel that she was in earnest, and that idea frightened the resistance out of him — it had such terrible associations. The people he had ever seen who were most in earnest were a committee of gentlemen who had investigated the phenomena of the "materialisation" of spirits, some ten years before, and had bent the fierce light of the scientific method upon him. To Olive it appeared that Mr. Burrage and Mr. Gracie had ceased to be jocular; but that did not make them any less cynical. Henry Burrage said to Verena, as she was going, that he hoped she would think seriously of his mother's invitation; and she replied that she didn't know whether she should have much time in the future to give to people who already approved of her views: she expected to have her hands full with the others, who didn't.

"Does your scheme of work exclude all distraction, all recreation, then?" the young man inquired; and his look expressed real suspense.

Verena referred the matter, as usual, with her air of bright, ungrudging deference, to her companion. "Does it, should you say — our scheme of work?"

"I am afraid the distraction we have had this afternoon must last us for a long time," Olive said, without harshness, but with considerable majesty.

"Well, now, *is* he to be respected?" Verena demanded, as the two young women took their way through the early darkness, pacing quietly side by side, in their winter-robes, like women consecrated to some holy office.

Olive turned it over a moment. "Yes, very much — as a pianist!"

Verena went into town with her in the horse-car — she was staying in Charles Street for a few days — and that evening she startled Olive by breaking out into a reflection very similar to the whimsical falterings of which she herself had been conscious while they sat in Mr. Burrage's pretty rooms, but against which she had now violently reacted.

"It would be very nice to do that always — just to take men as they are, and not to have to think about their badness. It would be very nice not to have so many questions, but to think they were all comfortably answered, so that one could sit there on an old Spanish leather chair, with the curtains drawn and keeping out the cold, the darkness, all the big, terrible, cruel world — sit there and listen for ever to Schubert and Mendelssohn. *They* didn't care anything about female suffrage! And I didn't feel the want of a vote to-day at all, did you?" Verena inquired, ending, as she always ended in these few speculations, with an appeal to Olive.

This young lady thought it necessary to give her a very firm answer. "I always feel it — everywhere — night and day. I feel it *here;*" and Olive laid her hand solemnly on her heart. "I feel it as a deep, unforgetable wrong; I feel it as one feels a stain that is on one's honour."

Verena gave a clear laugh, and after that a soft sigh, and then said, "Do you know, Olive, I sometimes wonder whether, if it wasn't for you, I should feel it so very much!"

"My own friend," Olive replied, "you have never yet said anything to me which expressed so clearly the closeness and sanctity of our union."

"You do keep me up," Verena went on. "You are my conscience."

"I should like to be able to say that you are my form — my envelope. But you are too beautiful for that!" So Olive returned her friend's compliment; and later she said that, of course, it would be far easier to give up everything and draw the curtains to and pass one's life in an artificial atmosphere, with rose-coloured lamps. It would be far easier to abandon the struggle, to leave all the unhappy women of the world to their immemorial misery, to lay down one's burden, close one's eyes to the whole dark picture, and, in short, simply expire. To this Ve-

rena objected that it would not be easy for her to expire at all; that such an idea was darker than anything the world contained; that she had not done with life yet, and that she didn't mean to allow her responsibilities to crush her. And then the two young women concluded, as they had concluded before, by finding themselves completely, inspiringly in agreement, full of the purpose to live indeed, and with high success; to become great, in order not to be obscure, and powerful, in order not to be useless. Olive had often declared before that her conception of life was as something sublime or as nothing at all. The world was full of evil, but she was glad to have been born before it had been swept away, while it was still there to face, to give one a task and a reward. When the great reforms should be consummated, when the day of justice should have dawned, would not life perhaps be rather poor and pale? She had never pretended to deny that the hope of fame, of the very highest distinction, was one of her strongest incitements; and she held that the most effective way of protesting against the state of bondage of women was for an individual member of the sex to become illustrious. A person who might have overheard some of the talk of this possibly infatuated pair would have been touched by their extreme familiarity with the idea of earthly glory. Verena had not invented it, but she had taken it eagerly from her friend, and she returned it with interest. To Olive it appeared that just this partnership of their two minds — each of them, by itself, lacking an important group of facets — made an organic whole which, for the work in hand, could not fail to be brilliantly effective. Verena was often far more irresponsible than she liked to see her; but the happy thing in her composition was that, after a short contact with the divine idea — Olive was always trying to flash it at her, like a jewel in an uncovered case — she kindled, flamed up, took the words from her friend's less persuasive lips, resolved herself into a magical voice, became again the pure young sibyl. Then Olive perceived how fatally, without Verena's tender notes, her crusade would lack sweetness, what the Catholics call unction; and, on the other hand, how weak Verena would be on the statistical and logical side if she herself should not bring up the rear. Together, in short, they would be complete, they would have everything, and together they would triumph.

Chapter XIX

THIS idea of their triumph, a triumph as yet ultimate and remote, but preceded by the solemn vista of an effort so religious as never to be wanting in ecstasy, became tremendously familiar to the two friends, but especially to Olive, during the winter of 187–, a season which ushered in the most momentous period of Miss Chancellor's life. About Christmas a step was taken which advanced her affairs immensely, and put them, to her apprehension, on a regular footing. This consisted in Verena's coming in to Charles Street to stay with her, in pursuance of an arrangement on Olive's part with Selah Tarrant and his wife that she should remain for many months. The coast was now perfectly clear. Mrs. Farrinder had started on her annual grand tour; she was rousing the people, from Maine to Texas; Matthias Pardon (it was to be supposed) had received, temporarily at least, his quietus; and Mrs. Luna was established in New York, where she had taken a house for a year, and whence she wrote to her sister that she was going to engage Basil Ransom (with whom she was in communication for this purpose) to do her law-business. Olive wondered what law-business Adeline could have, and hoped she would get into a pickle with her landlord or her milliner, so that repeated interviews with Mr. Ransom might become necessary. Mrs. Luna let her know very soon that these interviews had begun; the young Mississippian had come to dine with her; he hadn't got started much, by what she could make out, and she was even afraid that he didn't dine every day. But he wore a tall hat now, like a Northern gentleman, and Adeline intimated that she found him really attractive. He had been very nice to Newton, told him all about the war (quite the Southern version, of course, but Mrs. Luna didn't care anything about American politics, and she wanted her son to know all sides), and Newton did nothing but talk about him, calling him "Rannie," and imitating his pronunciation of certain words. Adeline subsequently wrote that she had made up her mind to put her affairs into his hands (Olive sighed, not unmagnanimously, as she thought of her sister's "affairs"), and later still she mentioned that she was thinking strongly of taking him to be Newton's tutor. She wished this interesting child to be privately educated, and it would be more agreeable to have in that relation a person who was already, as it were, a member of the family. Mrs. Luna wrote as if he were prepared to give up his profession to take charge of her son, and Olive was pretty sure that this was only a part of her grandeur, of the habit she had contracted, especially since living in Europe, of speaking as if in every case she required special arrangements.

In spite of the difference in their age, Olive had long since judged her, and made up her mind that Adeline lacked every quality that a person needed to be interesting in her eyes. She was rich (or sufficiently so), she was conventional and timid, very fond of attentions from men (with whom indeed she was reputed bold, but Olive scorned such boldness as that), given up to a merely personal, egotistical, instinctive life, and as unconscious of the tendencies of the age, the revenges of the future, the new truths and the great social questions, as if she had been a mere bundle of dress-trimmings, which she very nearly was. It was perfectly observable that she had no conscience, and it irritated Olive deeply to see how much trouble a woman was spared when she was constructed on that system. Adeline's "affairs," as I have intimated, her social relations, her views of Newton's education, her practice and her theory (for she had plenty of that, such as it was, heaven save the mark!), her spasmodic disposition to marry again, and her still sillier retreats in the presence of danger (for she had not even the courage of her frivolity), these things had been a subject of tragic consideration to Olive ever since the return of the elder sister to America. The tragedy was not in any particular harm that Mrs. Luna could do her (for she did her good, rather, that is, she did her honour, by laughing at her), but in the spectacle itself, the drama, guided by the hand of fate, of which the small, ignoble scenes unrolled themselves so logically. The *dénouement* would of course be in keeping, and would consist simply of the spiritual death of Mrs. Luna, who would end by understanding no common speech of Olive's at all, and would sink into mere worldly plumpness, into the last complacency, the supreme imbecility, of petty, genteel conserva-

The Bostonians

tism. As for Newton, he would be more utterly odious, if possible, as he grew up, than he was already; in fact, he would not grow up at all, but only grow down, if his mother should continue her infatuated system with him. He was insufferably forward and selfish; under the pretext of keeping him, at any cost, refined, Adeline had coddled and caressed him, having him always in her petticoats, remitting his lessons when he pretended he had an earache, drawing him into the conversation, letting him answer her back, with an impertinence beyond his years, when she administered the smallest check. The place for him, in Olive's eyes, was one of the public schools, where the children of the people would teach him his small importance, teach it, if necessary, by the aid of an occasional drubbing; and the two ladies had a grand discussion on this point before Mrs. Luna left Boston — a scene which ended in Adeline's clutching the irrepressible Newton to her bosom (he came in at the moment), and demanding of him a vow that he would live and die in the principles of his mother. Mrs. Luna declared that if she must be trampled upon — and very likely it was her fate! — she would rather be trampled upon by men than by women, and that if Olive and her friends should get possession of the government they would be worse despots than those who were celebrated in history. Newton took an infant oath that he would never be a destructive,

impious radical, and Olive felt that after this she needn't trouble herself any more about her sister, whom she simply committed to her fate. That fate might very properly be to marry an enemy of her country, a man who, no doubt, desired to treat women with the lash and manacles, as he and his people had formerly treated the wretched coloured race. If she was so fond of the fine old institutions of the past, he would supply them to her in abundance; and if she wanted so much to be a conservative, she could try first how she liked being a conservative's wife. If Olive troubled herself little about Adeline, she troubled herself more about Basil Ransom; she said to herself that since he hated women who respected themselves (and each other), destiny would use him rightly in hanging a person like Adeline round his neck. That would be the way poetic justice ought to work, for him — and the law that our prejudices, when they act themselves out, punish us in doing so. Olive considered all this, as it was her effort to consider everything, from a very high point of view, and ended by feeling sure it was not for the sake of any nervous personal security that she desired to see her two relations in New York get mixed up together. If such an event as their marriage would gratify her sense of fitness, it would be simply as an illustration of certain laws. Olive, thanks to the philosophic cast of her mind, was exceedingly fond of illustrations of laws.

538

I hardly know, however, what illumination it was that sprang from her consciousness (now a source of considerable comfort), that Mrs. Farrinder was carrying the war into distant territories, and would return to Boston only in time to preside at a grand Female Convention, already advertised to take place in Boston in the month of June. It was agreeable to her that this imperial woman should be away; it made the field more free, the air more light; it suggested an exemption from official criticism. I have not taken space to mention certain episodes of the more recent intercourse of these ladies, and must content myself with tracing them, lightly, in their consequences. These may be summed up in the remark, which will doubtless startle no one by its freshness, that two imperial women are scarcely more likely to hit it off together, as the phrase is, than two imperial men. Since that party at Miss Birdseye's, so important in its results for Olive, she had had occasion to approach Mrs. Farrinder more nearly, and those overtures brought forth the knowledge that the great leader of the feminine revolution was the one person (in that part of the world) more concentrated, more determined, than herself. Miss Chancellor's aspirations, of late, had been immensely quickened; she had begun to believe in herself to a livelier tune than she had ever listened to before; and she now perceived that when spirit meets spirit there must either be mutual ab-

sorption or a sharp concussion. It had long been familiar to her that she should have to count with the obstinacy of the world at large, but she now discovered that she should have to count also with certain elements in the feminine camp. This complicated the problem, and such a complication, naturally, could not make Mrs. Farrinder appear more easy to assimilate. If Olive's was a high nature and so was hers, the fault was in neither; it was only an admonition that they were not needed as landmarks in the same part of the field. If such perceptions are delicate as between men, the reader need not be reminded of the exquisite form they may assume in natures more refined. So it was that Olive passed, in three months, from the stage of veneration to that of competition; and the process had been accelerated by the introduction of Verena into the fold. Mrs. Farrinder had behaved in the strangest way about Verena. First she had been struck with her, and then she hadn't; first she had seemed to want to take her in, then she had shied at her unmistakably — intimating to Olive that there were enough of that kind already. Of "that kind" indeed! — the phrase reverberated in Miss Chancellor's resentful soul. Was it possible she didn't know the kind Verena was of, and with what vulgar aspirants to notoriety did she confound her? It had been Olive's original desire to obtain Mrs. Farrinder's stamp for her *protégée;* she wished her to hold a commission from the commander-in-chief. With this view the two young women had made more than one pilgrimage to Roxbury, and on one of these occasions the sibylline mood (in its most charming form) had descended upon Verena. She had fallen into it, naturally and gracefully, in the course of talk, and poured out a stream of eloquence even more touching than her regular discourse at Miss Birdseye's. Mrs. Farrinder had taken it rather drily, and certainly it didn't resemble her own style of oratory, remarkable and cogent as this was. There had been considerable question of her writing a letter to the New York "Tribune," the effect of which should be to launch Miss Tarrant into renown; but this beneficent epistle never appeared, and now Olive saw that there was no favour to come from the prophetess of Roxbury. There had been primnesses, pruderies, small reserves, which ended by staying her pen. If Olive didn't say at once that she was jealous of Verena's more attractive manner, it was only because such a declaration was destined to produce more effect a little later. What she did say was that evidently Mrs. Farrinder wanted to keep the movement in her own hands — viewed with suspicion certain romantic, æsthetic elements which Olive and Verena seemed to be trying to introduce into it. They insisted so much, for instance, on the historic unhappiness of women; but Mrs. Farrinder didn't appear to care anything for that, or indeed to know much about history at all. She seemed to begin just to-day, and she demanded their rights for them whether they were unhappy or not. The upshot of this was that Olive threw herself on Verena's neck with a movement which was half indignation, half rapture; she exclaimed that they would have to fight the battle without human help, but, after all, it was better so. If they were all in all to each other, what more could they want? They would be isolated, but they would be free; and this view of the situation brought with it a feeling that they had almost already begun to be a force. It was not, indeed, that Olive's resentment faded quite away; for not only had she the sense, doubtless very presumptuous, that Mrs. Farrinder was the only person thereabouts of a stature to judge her (a sufficient cause of antagonism in itself, for if we like to be praised by our betters we prefer that censure should come from the other sort), but the kind of opinion she had unexpectedly betrayed, after implying such esteem in the earlier phase of their intercourse, made Olive's cheeks occasionally flush. She prayed heaven that *she* might never become so personal, so narrow. She was frivolous, worldly, an amateur, a trifler, a frequenter of Beacon Street; her taking up Verena Tarrant was only a kind of elderly, ridiculous doll-dressing: this was the light in which Miss Chancellor had reason to believe that it now suited Mrs. Farrinder to regard her! It was fortunate, perhaps, that the misrepresentation was so gross; yet, none the less, tears of wrath rose more than once to Olive's eyes when she reflected that this particular wrong had been put upon her. Frivolous, worldly, Beacon Street! She appealed to Verena to share in her pledge that the world should know in due time how much of that sort of thing there was about her. As I have already hinted, Verena at such moments quite rose to the occasion; she had private pangs at committing herself to give the cold shoulder to Beacon Street for ever; but she was now so completely in Olive's hands that there was no sacrifice to which she would not have consented in order to prove that her benefactress was not frivolous.

The matter of her coming to stay for so long in Charles Street was arranged during a visit that Selah Tarrant paid there at Miss Chancellor's request. This interview, which had some curious features, would be worth describing, but I am forbidden to do more than mention the most striking of these. Olive wished to have an understanding with him; wished the situation to be clear, so that, disagreeable as it would be to her to receive him, she sent him a summons for a certain hour — an hour at which she had planned that Verena should be out of the house. She withheld this incident from the girl's knowledge, rejecting with some solemnity that it was the first deception (for Olive her silence was a deception) that she had yet practised on her friend, and wondering whether she should have to practise others in the future. She then and there made up her mind that she would not shrink from others should they be necessary. She notified Tarrant that she should keep Verena a long time, and Tarrant remarked that it was certainly very pleasant to see her so happily located. But he also intimated that he should like to know what Miss Chancellor laid out to do with her; and the tone of this suggestion made Olive feel how right she had been to foresee that their interview would have the stamp of business. It assumed that complexion very definitely when she crossed over to her desk and wrote Mr. Tarrant a cheque for a very considerable amount. "Leave us alone — entirely alone — for a year, and then I will write you another:" it was with these words she handed him the little strip of paper that meant so much, feeling, as she did so, that surely Mrs. Farrinder herself could not be less amateurish than that. Selah looked at the cheque, at Miss Chancellor, at the cheque again, at the ceiling, at the floor, at the clock, and once more at his hostess; then the document disappeared beneath the folds of his waterproof, and she saw that he was putting it into some queer place on his queer person. "Well, if I didn't believe you were going to help her to develop," he remarked; and he stopped, while his hands continued to fumble, out of sight, and he treated Olive to his large joyless smile. She assured him that he need have no fear on that score; Verena's development was the thing in the world in which she took most interest; she should have every opportunity for a free expansion. "Yes, that's the great thing," Selah said; "it's more important than attracting a crowd. That's all we shall ask of you; let her act out her nature. Don't all the trouble of humanity come from our being pressed back? Don't shut down the cover, Miss Chancellor; just let her overflow!" And again Tarrant illuminated his inquiry, his metaphor, by the strange and silent lateral movement of his jaws. He added, presently, that he supposed he should have to fix it with Mis' Tarrant; but Olive made no answer to that; she only looked at him with a face in which she intended to express that there was nothing that need detain him longer. She knew it had been fixed with Mrs. Tarrant; she had been over all that with Verena, who had told her that her mother was willing to sacrifice her for her highest good. She had reason to know (not through Verena, of course), that Mrs. Tarrant had embraced, tenderly, the idea of a pecuniary compensation, and there was no fear of her making a scene when Tarrant should come back with a cheque in his pocket. "Well, I trust she *may* develop, richly, and that you may accomplish what you desire; it seems as if we had only a little way to go further," that worthy observed, as he erected himself for departure.

"It's not a little way; it's a very long way," Olive replied, rather sternly.

Tarrant was on the threshold; he lingered a little, embarrassed by her grimness, for he himself had always inclined to rose-coloured views of progress, of the march of truth. He had never met any one so much in earnest as this definite, literal young woman, who had taken such an unhoped-for fancy to his daughter; whose longing for the new day had such perversities of pessimism, and who, in the midst of something that appeared to be terribly searching in her honesty, was willing to corrupt him, as a father, with the most extravagant orders on her bank. He hardly knew in what language to speak to her; it seemed as if there was nothing soothing enough, when a lady adopted that tone about a movement which was thought by some of the brightest to be so promising. "Oh, well, I guess there's some kind of mysterious law . . ." he murmured, almost timidly; and so he passed from Miss Chancellor's sight.

Chapter XX

SHE hoped she should not soon see him again, and there appeared to be no reason she should, if their intercourse was to be conducted by means of cheques. The understanding with Verena was, of course, complete; she had promised to stay with her friend as long as her friend should require it. She had said at first that she couldn't give up her mother, but she had been made to feel that there was no question of giving up. She should be as free as air, to go and come; she could spend hours and days with her mother, whenever Mrs. Tarrant required her attention; all that Olive asked of her was that, for the time, she should regard Charles Street as her home. There was no struggle about this, for the simple reason that by the time the question came to the front Verena was completely under the charm. The idea of Olive's charm will perhaps make the reader smile; but I use the word not in its derived, but in its literal sense. The fine web of authority, of dependence, that her strenuous companion had woven about her, was now as dense as a suit of golden mail; and Verena was thoroughly interested in their great undertaking; she saw it in the light of an active, enthusiastic faith. The benefit that her father desired for her was now assured; she expanded, developed, on the most liberal scale. Olive saw the difference, and you may imagine how she rejoiced in it; she had never known a greater pleasure. Verena's former attitude had been girlish submission, grateful, curious sympathy. She had given herself, in her young, amused surprise, because Olive's stronger will and the incisive proceedings with which she pointed her purpose drew her on. Besides, she was held by hospitality, the vision of new social horizons, the sense of novelty, and the love of change. But now the girl was disinterestedly attached to the precious things they were to do together; she cared about them for themselves, believed in them ardently, had them constantly in mind. Her share in the union of the two young women was no longer passive, purely appreciative; it was passionate, too, and it put forth a beautiful energy. If Olive desired to get Verena into training, she could flatter herself that the process had already begun, and that her colleague enjoyed it almost as much as she. Therefore she could say to herself, without the imputation of heartlessness, that when she left her mother it was for a noble, a sacred use. In point of fact, she left her very little, and she spent hours in jingling, aching, jostled journeys between Charles Street and the stale suburban cottage. Mrs. Tarrant sighed and grimaced, wrapped herself more than ever in her mantle, said she didn't know as she was fit to struggle alone, and that, half the time, if Verena was away, she wouldn't have the nerve to answer the doorbell; she was incapable, of course, of neglecting such an opportunity to posture as one who paid with her heart's blood for leading the van of human progress. But Verena had an inner sense (she judged her mother now, a little, for the first time), that she would be sorry to be taken at her word, and that she felt safe enough in trusting to her daughter's generosity. She could not divest herself of the faith — even now that Mrs. Luna was gone, leaving no trace, and the gray walls of a sedentary winter were apparently closing about the two young women — she could not renounce the theory that a residence in Charles Street must at least produce some contact with the brilliant classes. She was vexed at her daughter's resignation to not going to parties and to Miss Chancellor's not giving them; but it was nothing new for her to have to practise patience, and she could feel, at least, that it was just as handy for Mr. Burrage to call on the child in town, where he spent half his time, sleeping constantly at Parker's.

It was a fact that this fortunate youth called very often, and Verena saw him with Olive's full concurrence whenever she was at home. It had now been quite agreed between them that no artificial limits should be set to the famous phase; and Olive had, while it lasted, a sense of real heroism in steeling herself against uneasiness. It seemed to her, moreover, only justice that she should make some concession; if Verena made a great sacrifice of filial duty in coming to live with her (this, of course, should be permanent — she would buy off the Tarrants from year to year), she must not incur the imputation (the world would judge her, in that case, ferociously) of keeping her from forming common social ties. The friendship of a young man and a young woman was, according to the pure code of New England, a common social tie; and as the weeks elapsed Miss Chancellor saw no reason to repent of her temerity. Verena was not falling in love; she felt that she should know it, should guess it on the spot. Verena was fond of human intercourse; she was essentially a sociable creature; she liked to shine and smile and talk and listen; and so far as Henry Burrage was concerned he introduced an element of easy and convenient relaxation into a life now a good deal stiffened (Olive was perfectly willing to own it) by great civic purposes. But the girl was being saved, without interference, by the simple operation of her interest in those very designs. From this time there was no need of putting pressure on her; her own springs were working; the fire with which she glowed came from within. Sacredly, brightly single she would remain; her only espousals would be at the altar of a great cause. Olive always absented herself when Mr. Burrage was announced; and when Verena afterwards attempted to give some account of his conversation she checked her, said she would rather know nothing about it — all with a very solemn mildness; this made her feel very superior, truly noble. She knew by this time (I scarcely can tell how, since Verena could give her no report), exactly what sort of a youth Mr. Burrage was: he was weakly pretentious, softly original, cultivated eccentricity, patronised progress, liked to have mysteries, sudden appointments to keep, anonymous persons to visit, the air of leading a double life, of being devoted to a girl whom people didn't know, or at least didn't meet. Of course he liked to make an impression on Verena; but what he mainly liked was to play her off upon the other girls, the daughters of fashion, with whom he danced at Papanti's. Such were the images that proceeded from Olive's rich moral consciousness. "Well, he *is* greatly interested in our movement:" so much Verena once managed to announce; but the words rather irritated Miss Chancellor, who, as we know, did not care to allow for accidental exceptions in the great masculine conspiracy.

In the month of March Verena told her that Mr. Burrage was offering matrimony — offering it with much insistence, begging that she would at least wait and think of it before giving him a final answer. Verena was evidently very glad to be able to say to Olive that she had assured him she couldn't think of it, and that if he expected this he had better not come any more. He continued to come, and it was therefore to be supposed that he had ceased to count on such a concession; it was now Olive's opinion that he really didn't desire it. She had a theory that he proposed to almost any girl who was not likely to accept him — did it because he was making a collection of such episodes — a mental album of declarations, blushes, hesitations, refusals that just missed imposing themselves as acceptances, quite as he collected enamels and Cremona violins. He would be very sorry indeed to ally himself to the house of Tarrant; but such a fear didn't prevent him from holding it becoming in a man of taste to give that encouragement to low-born girls who were pretty, for one looked out for the special cases in which, for reasons (even the lowest might have reasons), they wouldn't "rise." "I told you I wouldn't marry him, and I won't," Verena said, delightedly, to her friend; her tone suggested that a certain credit belonged to her for the way she carried out her assurance. "I never thought you would, if you didn't want to," Olive replied to this; and Verena could have no rejoinder but the good-humour that sat in her eyes, unable as she was to say that she had wanted to. They had a little discussion, however, when she intimated that she pitied him for his discomfiture, Olive's contention being that, selfish, conceited, pampered and insincere, he might properly be left now to digest his affront. Miss Chancellor felt none of the remorse now that she would have felt six months before at standing in the way of such a chance for Verena, and she would have been very angry if any one had asked her if she were not afraid of taking too much upon herself. She would have said, moreover, that she stood in no one's way, and that even if she were not there Verena would never think seriously of a frivolous little man who fiddled while Rome was burning. This did not prevent Olive from making up her mind that they had better go to Europe in the spring; a year's residence in that quarter of the globe would be highly agreeable to Verena, and might even contribute to the evolution of her genius. It cost Miss Chancellor an effort to admit that any virtue still lingered in the elder world, and that it could have any important lesson for two such good Americans as her friend and herself; but it suited her just then to make this assumption, which was not altogether sincere. It was recommended by the idea that it would get her companion out of the way — out of the way of officious fellow-citizens — till she should be absolutely firm on her feet, and would also give greater intensity to their own long conversation. On that continent of strangers they would cleave more closely still to each other. This, of course, would be to fly before the inevitable "phase," much more than to face it; but Olive decided that if they should reach unscathed the term of their delay (the first of July) she should have faced it as much as either justice or generosity demanded. I may as well say at once that she traversed most of this period without further serious alarms and with a great many little thrills of bliss and hope.

Nothing happened to dissipate the good omens with which her partnership with Verena Tarrant was at present surrounded. They threw themselves into study; they had innumerable big books from the Athenæum, and consumed the midnight oil. Henry Burrage, after Verena had shaken her head at him so sweetly and sadly, returned to New York, giving no sign; they only heard that he had taken refuge under the ruffled maternal wing. (Olive, at least, took for granted the wing was ruffled; she could fancy how Mrs. Burrage would be affected by the knowledge that her son had been refused by the daughter of a mesmeric healer. She would be almost as angry as if she had learnt that he had been accepted.) Matthias Pardon had not yet taken his revenge in the newspapers; he was perhaps nursing his thunderbolts; at any rate, now that the operatic season had begun, he was much occupied in interviewing the principal singers, one of whom he described in one of the leading journals (Olive, at least, was sure it was only he who could write like that), as "a dear little woman with baby dimples and kittenish movements." The Tarrants were apparently given up to a measure of sensual ease with which they had not hitherto been familiar, thanks to the increase of income that they drew from their eccentric protectress. Mrs. Tarrant now enjoyed the ministrations of a "girl"; it was partly her pride (at any rate, she chose to give it this turn), that her house had for many years been conducted without the element — so debasing on both sides — of

The Bostonians

servile, mercenary labour. She wrote to Olive (she was perpetually writing to her now, but Olive never answered), that she was conscious of having fallen to a lower plane, but she admitted that it was a prop to her wasted spirit to have some one to converse with when Selah was off. Verena, of course, perceived the difference, which was inadequately explained by the theory of a sudden increase of her father's practice (nothing of her father's had ever increased like that), and ended by guessing the cause of it — a discovery which did not in the least disturb her equanimity. She accepted the idea that her parents should receive a pecuniary tribute from the extraordinary friend whom she had encountered on the threshold of womanhood, just as she herself accepted that friend's irresistible hospitality. She had no worldly pride, no traditions of independence, no ideas of what was done and what was not done; but there was only one thing that equalled this perfectly gentle and natural insensibility to favours — namely, the inveteracy of her habit of not asking them. Olive had had an apprehension that she would flush a little at learning the terms on which they should now be able to pursue their career together; but Verena never changed colour; it was either not new or not disagreeble to her that the authors of her being should be bought off, silenced by money, treated as the troublesome of the lower orders are treated when they are not locked

up; so that her friend had a perception, after this, that it would probably be impossible in any way ever to offend her. She was too rancourless, too detached from conventional standards, too free from private self-reference. It was too much to say of her that she forgave injuries, since she was not conscious of them; there was in forgiveness a certain arrogance of which she was incapable, and her bright mildness glided over the many traps that life sets for our consistency. Olive had always held that pride was necessary to character, but there was no peculiarity of Verena's that could make her spirit seem less pure. The added luxuries in the little house at Cambridge, which even with their help was still such a penal settlement, made her feel afresh that before she came to the rescue the daughter of that house had traversed a desert of sordid misery. She had cooked and washed and swept and stitched; she had worked harder than any of Miss Chancellor's servants. These things had left no trace upon her person or her mind; everything fresh and fair renewed itself in her with extraordinary facility, everything ugly and tiresome evaporated as soon as it touched her; but Olive deemed that, being what she was, she had a right to immense compensations. In the future she should have exceeding luxury and ease, and Miss Chancellor had no difficulty in persuading herself that persons doing the high intellectual and moral work to which the two young la-

547

dies in Charles Street were now committed owed it to themselves, owed it to the groaning sisterhood, to cultivate the best material conditions. She herself was nothing of a sybarite, and she had proved, visiting the alleys and slums of Boston in the service of the Associated Charities, that there was no foulness of disease or misery she feared to look in the face; but her house had always been thoroughly well regulated, she was passionately clean, and she was an excellent woman of business. Now, however, she elevated daintiness to a religion; her interior shone with superfluous friction, with punctuality, with winter roses. Among these soft influences Verena herself bloomed like the flower that attains such perfection in Boston. Olive had always rated high the native refinement of her countrywomen, their latent "adaptability," their talent for accommodating themselves at a glance to changed conditions; but the way her companion rose with the level of the civilisation that surrounded her, the way she assimilated all delicacies and absorbed all traditions, left this friendly theory halting behind. The winter days were still, indoors, in Charles Street, and the winter nights secure from interruption. Our two young women had plenty of duties, but Olive had never favoured the custom of running in and out. Much conference on social and reformatory topics went forward under her roof, and she received her colleagues — she be-

longed to twenty associations and committees — only at preappointed hours, which she expected them to observe rigidly. Verena's share in these proceedings was not active; she hovered over them, smiling, listening, dropping occasionally a fanciful though never an idle word, like some gently animated image placed there for good omen. It was understood that her part was before the scenes, not behind; that she was not a prompter, but (potentially, at least) a "popular favourite," and that the work over which Miss Chancellor presided so efficiently was a general preparation of the platform on which, later, her companion would execute the most striking steps.

The western windows of Olive's drawing-room, looking over the water, took in the red sunsets of winter; the long, low bridge that crawled, on its staggering posts, across the Charles; the casual patches of ice and snow; the desolate suburban horizons, peeled and made bald by the rigour of the season; the general hard, cold void of the prospect; the extrusion, at Charlestown, at Cambridge, of a few chimneys and steeples, straight, sordid tubes of factories and engine-shops, or spare, heavenward finger of the New England meeting-house. There was something inexorable in the poverty of the scene, shameful in the meanness of its details, which gave a collective impression of boards and tin and frozen earth, sheds and rotting piles, railway-lines striding flat across a thor oughfare of puddles, and tracks of the humbler, the universal horse-car, traversing obliquely this path of danger; loose fences, vacant lots, mounds of refuse, yards bestrewn with iron pipes, telegraph poles, and bare wooden backs of places. Verena thought such a view lovely, and she was by no means without excuse when, as the afternoon closed, the ugly picture was tinted with a clear, cold rosiness. The air, in its windless chill, seemed to tinkle like a crystal, the faintest gradations of tone were perceptible in the sky, the west became deep and delicate, everything grew doubly distinct before taking on the dimness of evening. There were pink flushes on snow, "tender" reflections in patches of stiffened marsh, sounds of car-bells, no longer vulgar, but almost silvery, on the long bridge, lonely outlines of distant dusky undulations against the fading glow. These agreeable effects used to light up that end of the drawing-room, and Olive often sat at the window with her companion before it was time for the lamp. They admired the sunsets, they rejoiced in the ruddy spots projected upon the parlour-wall, they followed the darkening perspective in fanciful excursions. They watched the stellar points come out at last in a colder heaven, and then, shuddering a little, arm in arm, they turned away, with a sense that the winter night was even more cruel than the tyranny of men — turned back to drawn curtains and a brighter fire and a glittering tea-tray and more and more talk about the long martyrdom of women, a subject as to which Olive was inexhaustible and really most interesting. There were some nights of deep snowfall, when Charles Street was white and muffled and the door-bell foredoomed to silence, which seemed little islands of lamplight, of enlarged and intensified vision. They read a great deal of history together, and read it ever with the same thought — that of finding confirmation in it for this idea that their sex had suffered inexpressibly, and that at any moment in the course of human affairs the state of the world would have been so much less horrible (history seemed to them in every way horrible), if women had been able to press down the scale. Verena was full of suggestions which stimulated discussions; it was she, oftenest, who kept in view the fact that a good many women in the past had been intrusted with power and had not always used it amiably, who brought up the wicked queens, the profligate mistresses of kings. These ladies were easily disposed of between the two, and the public crimes of Bloody Mary, the private misdemeanours of Faustina, wife of the pure Marcus Aurelius, were very satisfactorily classified. If the influence of women in the past accounted for every act of virtue that men had happened to achieve, it only made the matter balance properly that the influence of men should explain the casual irregularities of the other sex. Ol-

The Bostonians

ive could see how few books had passed through Verena's hands, and how little the home of the Tarrants had been a house of reading; but the girl now traversed the fields of literature with her characteristic lightness of step. Everything she turned to or took up became an illustration of the facility, the "giftedness," which Olive, who had so little of it, never ceased to wonder at and prize. Nothing frightened her; she always smiled at it, she could do anything she tried. As she knew how to do other things, she knew how to study; she read quickly and remembered infallibly; could repeat, days afterward, passages that she appeared only to have glanced at. Olive, of course, was more and more happy to think that their cause should have the services of an organisation so rare.

All this doubtless sounds rather dry, and I hasten to add that our friends were not always shut up in Miss Chancellor's strenuous parlour. In spite of Olive's desire to keep her precious inmate to herself and to bend her attention upon their common studies, in spite of her constantly reminding Verena that this winter was to be purely educative and that the platitudes of the satisfied and unregenerate would have little to teach her, in spite, in short, of the severe and constant duality of our young women, it must not be supposed that their life had not many personal confluents and tributaries. Individual and original as Miss Chancellor was universally ac-

knowledged to be, she was yet a typical Bostonian, and as a typical Bostonian she could not fail to belong in some degree to a "set." It had been said of her that she was in it but not of it; but she was of it enough to go occasionally into other houses and to receive their occupants in her own. It was her belief that she filled her tea-pot with the spoon of hospitality, and made a good many select spirits feel that they were welcome under her roof at convenient hours. She had a preference for what she called *real* people, and there were several whose reality she had tested by arts known to herself. This little society was rather suburban and miscellaneous; it was prolific in ladies who trotted about, early and late, with books from the Athenæum nursed behind their muff, or little nosegays of exquisite flowers that they were carrying as presents to each other. Verena, who, when Olive was not with her, indulged in a good deal of desultory contemplation at the window, saw them pass the house in Charles Street, always apparently straining a little, as if they might be too late for something. At almost any time, for she envied their preoccupation, she would have taken the chance with them. Very often, when she described them to her mother, Mrs. Tarrant didn't know who they were; there were even days (she had so many discouragements) when it seemed as if she didn't want to know. So long as they were not some one else, it seemed to be no use that they

550

were themselves; whoever they were, they were sure to have that defect. Even after all her mother's disquisitions Verena had but vague ideas as to whom she would have liked them to be; and it was only when the girl talked of the concerts, to all of which Olive subscribed and conducted her inseparable friend, that Mrs. Tarrant appeared to feel in any degree that her daughter was living up to the standard formed for her in their Cambridge home. As all the world knows, the opportunities in Boston for hearing good music are numerous and excellent, and it had long been Miss Chancellor's practice to cultivate the best. She went in, as the phrase is, for the superior programmes, and that high, dim, dignified Music Hall, which has echoed in its time to so much eloquence and so much melody, and of which the very proportions and colour seem to teach respect and attention, shed the protection of its illuminated cornice, this winter, upon no faces more intelligently upturned than those of the young women for whom Bach and Beethoven only repeated, in a myriad forms, the idea that was always with them. Symphonies and fugues only stimulated their convictions, excited their revolutionary passion, led their imagination further in the direction in which it was always pressing. It lifted them to immeasurable heights; and as they sat looking at the great florid, sombre organ, overhanging the bronze statue of Beethoven, they felt that this was the only temple in which the votaries of their creed could worship.

And yet their music was not their greatest joy, for they had two others which they cultivated at least as zealously. One of these was simply the society of old Miss Birdseye, of whom Olive saw more this winter than she had ever seen before. It had become apparent that her long and beautiful career was drawing to a close, her earnest, unremitting work was over, her old-fashioned weapons were broken and dull. Olive would have liked to hang them up as venerable relics of a patient fight, and this was what she seemed to do when she made the poor lady relate her battles — never glorious and brilliant, but obscure and wastefully heroic — call back the figures of her companions in arms, exhibit her medals and scars. Miss Birdseye knew that her uses were ended; she might pretend still to go about the business of unpopular causes, might fumble for papers in her immemorial satchel and think she had important appointments, might sign petitions, attend conventions, say to Doctor Prance that if she would only make her sleep she should live to see a great many improvements yet; she ached and was weary, growing almost as glad to look back (a great anomaly for Miss Birdseye) as to look forward. She let herself be coddled now by her friends of the new generation; there were days when she seemed to want nothing better than to sit by Olive's fire and ramble on about the old struggles, with a vague, comfortable sense — no physical rapture of Miss Birdseye's could be very acute — of immunity from wet feet, from the draughts that prevail at thin meetings, of independence of street-cars that would probably arrive overflowing; and also a pleased perception, not that she was an example to these fresh lives which began with more advantages than hers, but that she was in some degree an encouragement, as she helped them to measure the way the new truths had advanced — being able to tell them of such a different state of things when she was a young lady, the daughter of a very talented teacher (indeed her mother had been a teacher too), down in Connecticut. She had always had for Olive a kind of aroma of martyrdom, and her battered, unremunerated, unpensioned old age brought angry tears, springing from depths of outraged theory, into Miss Chancellor's eyes. For Verena, too, she was a picturesque humanitary figure. Verena had been in the habit of meeting martyrs from her childhood up, but she had seen none with so many reminiscences as Miss Birdseye, or who had been so nearly scorched by penal fires. She had had escapes, in the early days of abolitionism, which it was a marvel she could tell with so little implication that she had shown courage. She had roamed through certain parts of the South, carrying the Bible to the slave; and more than one of her companions, in the

course of these expeditions, had been tarred and feathered. She herself, at one season, had spent a month in a Georgian jail. She had preached temperance in Irish circles where the doctrine was received with missiles; she had interfered between wives and husbands mad with drink; she had taken filthy children, picked up in the street, to her own poor rooms, and had removed their pestilent rags and washed their sore bodies with slippery little hands. In her own person she appeared to Olive and Verena a representative of suffering humanity; the pity they felt for her was part of their pity for all who were weakest and most hardly used; and it struck Miss Chancellor (more especially) that this frumpy little missionary was the last link in a tradition, and that when she should be called away the heroic age of New England life — the age of plain living and high thinking, of pure ideals and earnest effort, of moral passion and noble experiment — would effectually be closed. It was the perennial freshness of Miss Birdseye's faith that had had such a contagion for these modern maidens, the unquenched flame of her transcendentalism, the simplicity of her vision, the way in which, in spite of mistakes, deceptions, the changing fashions of reform, which make the remedies of a previous generation look as ridiculous as their bonnets, the only thing that was still actual for her was the elevation of the species by the reading of Emerson and the frequentation of Tremont Temple. Olive had been active enough, for years, in the city-missions; she too had scoured dirty children, and, in squalid lodging-houses, had gone into rooms where the domestic situation was strained and the noises made the neighbours turn pale. But she reflected that after such exertions she had the refreshment of a pretty house, a drawing-room full of flowers, a crackling hearth, where she threw in pine-cones and made them snap, an imported tea-service, a Chickering piano, and the *Deutsche Rundschau;* whereas Miss Birdseye had only a bare, vulgar room, with a hideous flowered carpet (it looked like a dentist's), a cold furnace, the evening-paper, and Doctor Prance. Olive and Verena were present at another of her gatherings before the winter ended; it resembled the occasion that we described at the beginning of this history, with the difference that Mrs. Farrinder was not there to oppress the company with her greatness, and that Verena made a speech without the co-operation of her father. This young lady had delivered herself with even finer effect than before, and Olive could see how much she had gained, in confidence and range of allusion, since the educative process in Charles Street began. Her *motif* was now a kind of unprepared tribute to Miss Birdseye, the fruit of the occasion and of the unanimous tenderness of the younger members of the circle, which made her a willing mouth-piece. She pictured her la-

borious career, her early associates (Eliza P. Moseley was not neglected as Verena passed), her difficulties and dangers and triumphs, her humanising effect upon so many, her serene and honoured old age — expressed, in short, as one of the ladies said, just the very way they all felt about her. Verena's face brightened and grew triumphant as she spoke, but she brought tears into the eyes of most of the others. It was Olive's opinion that nothing could be more graceful and touching, and she saw that the impression made was now deeper than on the former evening. Miss Birdseye went about with her eighty years of innocence, her undiscriminating spectacles, asking her friends if it wasn't perfectly splendid; she took none of it to herself, she regarded it only as a brilliant expression of Verena's gift. Olive thought, afterwards, that if a collection could only be taken up on the spot, the good lady would be made easy for the rest of her days; then she remembered that most of her guests were as impecunious as herself.

I have intimated that our young friends had a source of fortifying emotion which was distinct from the hours they spent with Beethoven and Bach, or in hearing Miss Birdseye describe Concord as it used to be. This consisted in the wonderful insight they had obtained into the history of feminine anguish. They perused that chapter perpetually and zealously, and they derived from it the purest part of their mission. Olive had pored over it so long, so earnestly, that she was now in complete possession of the subject; it was the one thing in life which she felt she had really mastered. She was able to exhibit it to Verena with the greatest authority and accuracy, to lead her up and down, in and out, through all the darkest and most tortuous passages. We know that she was without belief in her own eloquence, but she was very eloquent when she reminded Verena how the exquisite weakness of women had never been their defence, but had only exposed them to sufferings more acute than masculine grossness can conceive. Their odious partner had trampled upon them from the beginning of time, and their tenderness, their abnegation, had been his opportunity. All the bullied wives, the stricken mothers, the dishonoured, deserted maidens who have lived on the earth and longed to leave it, passed and repassed before her eyes, and the interminable dim procession seemed to stretch out a myriad hands to her. She sat with them at their trembling vigils, listened for the tread, the voice, at which they grew pale and sick, walked with them by the dark waters that offered to wash away misery and shame, took with them, even, when the vision grew intense, the last shuddering leap. She had analysed to an extraordinary fineness their susceptibility, their softness; she knew (or she thought she knew) all the possible tortures of anxiety, of suspense and dread; and she had made up her mind that it was women, in the end, who had paid for everything. In the last resort the whole burden of the human lot came upon them; it pressed upon them far more than on the others, the intolerable load of fate. It was they who sat cramped and chained to receive it; it was they who had done all the waiting and taken all the wounds. The sacrifices, the blood, the tears, the terrors were theirs. Their organism was in itself a challenge to suffering, and men had practised upon it with an impudence that knew no bounds. As they were the weakest most had been wrung from them, and as they were the most generous they had been most deceived. Olive Chancellor would have rested her case, had it been necessary, on those general facts; and her simple and comprehensive contention was that the peculiar wretchedness which had been the very essence of the feminine lot was a monstrous artificial imposition, crying aloud for redress. She was willing to admit that women, too, could be bad; that there were many about the world who were false, immoral, vile. But their errors were as nothing to their sufferings; they had expiated, in advance, an eternity, if need be, of misconduct. Olive poured forth these views to her listening and responsive friend; she presented them again and again, and there was no light in which they did not seem to palpitate with truth. Verena was immensely wrought upon; a subtle fire passed into her;

she was not so hungry for revenge as Olive, but at the last, before they went to Europe (I shall take no place to describe the manner in which she threw herself into that project), she quite agreed with her companion that after so many ages of wrong (it would also be after the European journey) men must take *their* turn, men must pay!

Chapter XXI

BASIL RANSOM lived in New York, rather far to the eastward, and in the upper reaches of the town; he occupied two small shabby rooms in a somewhat decayed mansion which stood next to the corner of the Second Avenue. The corner itself was formed by a considerable grocer's shop, the near neighbourhood of which was fatal to any pretensions Ransom and his fellow-lodgers might have had in regard to gentility of situation. The house had a red, rusty face, and faded green shutters, of which the slats were limp and at variance with each other. In one of the lower windows was suspended a fly-blown card, with the words "Table Board" affixed in letters cut (not very neatly) out of coloured paper, of graduated tints, and surrounded with a small band of stamped gilt. The two sides of the shop were protected by an immense pent-house shed, which projected over a greasy pavement and was supported by wooden posts fixed in the curbstone. Beneath it, on the dislocated flags, barrels and baskets were freely and picturesquely grouped; an open cellarway yawned beneath the feet of those who might pause to gaze too fondly on the savoury wares displayed in the window; a strong odour of smoked fish, combined with a fragrance of molasses, hung about the spot; the pavement, toward the gutters, was fringed with dirty panniers, heaped with potatoes, carrots, and onions; and a smart, bright waggon, with the horse detached from the shafts, drawn up on the edge of the abominable road (it contained holes and ruts a foot deep, and immemorial accumulations of stagnant mud), imparted an idle, rural, pastoral air to a scene otherwise perhaps expressive of a rank civilisation. The establishment was of the kind known to New Yorkers as a Dutch grocery; and red-faced, yellow-haired, bare-armed vendors might have been observed to lounge in the doorway. I mention it not on account of any particular influence it may have had on the life or the thoughts of Basil Ransom, but for old acquaintance sake and that of local colour; besides which, a figure is nothing without a setting, and our young man came and went every day, with rather an indifferent, unperceiving step, it is true, among the objects I have briefly designated. One of his rooms was directly above the street-door of the house; such a dormitory, when it is so exiguous, is called in the nomenclature of New York a "hall bedroom." The sitting-room, beside it, was slightly larger, and they both commanded a row of tenements no less degenerate than Ransom's own habitation — houses built forty years before, and already sere and superannuated. These were also painted red, and the bricks were accentuated by a white line; they were garnished, on the first floor, with balconies covered with small tin roofs, striped in different colours, and with an elaborate iron lattice-work, which gave them a repressive, cage-like appearance, and caused them slightly to resemble the little boxes for peeping unseen into the street, which are a feature of oriental towns. Such posts of observation commanded a view of the grocery on the corner, of the relaxed and disjointed roadway, enlivened at the curbstone with an occasional ash-barrel or with gas-lamps drooping from the perpendicular, and westward, at the end of the truncated vista, of the fantastic skeleton of the Elevated Railway, overhanging the transverse longitudinal street, which it darkened and smothered with the immeasurable spinal column and myriad clutching paws of an antediluvian monster. If the opportunity were not denied me here, I should like to give some account of Basil Ransom's interior, of certain curious persons of both sexes, for the most part not favourites of fortune, who had found an obscure asylum there; some picture of the crumpled little *table d'hôte,* at two dollars and a half a week, where everything felt sticky, which went forward in the low-ceiled basement, under the conduct of a couple of shuffling negresses, who mingled in the conversation and indulged in low, mysterious chuckles when it took a facetious turn. But we need, in strictness, concern ourselves with it no further than to gather the implication that the young Mississippian, even a year and a half after that momentous visit of his to Boston, had not made his profession very lucrative.

He had been diligent, he had been ambitious, but he had not yet been successful. During the few weeks preceding the moment at which we meet him again, he had even begun to lose faith altogether in his earthly destiny. It became much of a question with him whether success in any form was written there; whether for a hungry young Mississippian, without means, without friends, wanting, too, in the highest energy, the wisdom of the serpent, personal arts and national prestige, the game of life was to be won in New York. He had been on the point of giving it up and returning to the home of his ancestors, where, as he had heard from his mother, there was still just a sufficient supply of hot corn-cake to support existence. He had never believed much in his luck, but during the last year it had been guilty of aberrations surprising even to a constant, an imperturbable, victim of fate. Not only had he not extended his con-

The Bostonians

nection, but he had lost most of the little business which was an object of complacency to him a twelvemonth before. He had had none but small jobs, and he had made a mess of more than one of them. Such accidents had not had a happy effect upon his reputation; he had been able to perceive that this fair flower may be nipped when it is so tender a bud as scarcely to be palpable. He had formed a partnership with a person who seemed likely to repair some of his deficiencies — a young man from Rhode Island, acquainted, according to his own expression, with the inside track. But this gentleman himself, as it turned out, would have been better for a good deal of remodelling, and Ransom's principal deficiency, which was, after all, that of cash, was not less apparent to him after his colleague, prior to a sudden and unexplained departure for Europe, had drawn the slender accumulations of the firm out of the bank. Ransom sat for hours in his office, waiting for clients who either did not come, or, if they did come, did not seem to find him encouraging, as they usually left him with the remark that they would think what they would do. They thought to little purpose, and seldom reappeared, so that at last he began to wonder whether there were not a prejudice against his Southern complexion. Perhaps they didn't like the way he spoke. If they could show him a better way, he was willing to adopt it; but the manner of New York could

not be acquired by precept, and example, somehow, was not in this case contagious. He wondered whether he were stupid and unskilled, and he was finally obliged to confess to himself that he was unpractical.

This confession was in itself a proof of the fact, for nothing could be less fruitful than such a speculation, terminating in such a way. He was perfectly aware that he cared a great deal for the theory, and so his visitors must have thought when they found him, with one of his long legs twisted round the other, reading a volume of De Tocqueville. That was the kind of reading he liked; he had thought a great deal about social and economical questions, forms of government and the happiness of peoples. The convictions he had arrived at were not such as mix gracefully with the time-honoured verities a young lawyer looking out for business is in the habit of taking for granted; but he had to reflect that these doctrines would probably not contribute any more to his prosperity in Mississippi than in New York. Indeed, he scarcely could think of the country where they would be a particular advantage to him. It came home to him that his opinions were stiff, whereas in comparison his effort was lax; and he accordingly began to wonder whether he might not make a living by his opinions. He had always had a desire for public life; to cause one's ideas to be embodied in national conduct appeared to him the high-

557

est form of human enjoyment. But there was little enough that was public in his solitary studies, and he asked himself what was the use of his having an office at all, and why he might not as well carry on his profession at the Astor Library, where, in his spare hours and on chance holidays, he did an immense deal of suggestive reading. He took copious notes and memoranda, and these things sometimes shaped themselves in a way that might possibly commend them to the editors of periodicals. Readers perhaps would come, if clients didn't; so he produced, with a great deal of labour, half a dozen articles, from which, when they were finished, it seemed to him that he had omitted all the points he wished most to make, and addressed them to the powers that preside over weekly and monthly publications. They were all declined with thanks, and he would have been forced to believe that the accent of his languid clime brought him luck as little under the pen as on the lips, had not another explanation been suggested by one of the more explicit of his oracles, in relation to a paper on the rights of minorities. This gentleman pointed out that his doctrines were about three hundred years behind the age; doubtless some magazine of the sixteenth century would have been very happy to print them. This threw light on his own suspicion that he was attached to causes that could only, in the nature of things, be unpopular. The disagreeable editor was right about his being out of date, only he had got the time wrong. He had come centuries too soon; he was not too old, but too new. Such an impression, however, would not have prevented him from going into politics, if there had been any other way to represent constituencies than by being elected. People might be found eccentric enough to vote for him in Mississippi, but meanwhile where should he find the twenty-dollar greenbacks which it was his ambition to transmit from time to time to his female relations, confined so constantly to a farinaceous diet? It came over him with some force that his opinions would not yield interest, and the evaporation of this pleasing hypothesis made him feel like a man in an open boat, at sea, who should just have parted with his last rag of canvas.

I shall not attempt a complete description of Ransom's ill-starred views, being convinced that the reader will guess them as he goes, for they had a frolicsome, ingenious way of peeping out of the young man's conversation. I shall do them sufficient justice in saying that he was by natural disposition a good deal of a stoic, and that, as the result of a considerable intellectual experience, he was, in social and political matters, a reactionary. I suppose he was very conceited, for he was much addicted to judging his age. He thought it talkative, querulous, hysterical, maudlin, full of false ideas, of unhealthy germs, of extravagant, dissipated habits, for which a great reckoning was in store. He was an immense admirer of the late Thomas Carlyle, and was very suspicious of the encroachments of modern democracy. I know not exactly how these queer heresies had planted themselves, but he had a longish pedigree (it had flowered at one time with English royalists and cavaliers), and he seemed at moments to be inhabited by some transmitted spirit of a robust but narrow ancestor, some broad-faced wigwearer or sword-bearer, with a more primitive conception of manhood than our modern temperament appears to require, and a programme of human felicity much less varied. He liked his pedigree, he revered his forefathers, and he rather pitied those who might come after him. In saying so, however, I betray him a little, for he never mentioned such feelings as these. Though he thought the age too talkative, as I have hinted, he liked to talk as well as any one; but he could hold his tongue, if that were more expressive, and he usually did so when his perplexities were greatest. He had been sitting for several evenings in a beer-cellar, smoking his pipe with a profundity of reticence. This attitude was so unbroken that it marked a crisis — the complete, the acute consciousness of his personal situation. It was the cheapest way he knew of spending an evening. At this particular establishment the *Schoppen* were very tall and the beer was very good; and

as the host and most of the guests were German, and their colloquial tongue was unknown to him, he was not drawn into any undue expenditure of speech. He watched his smoke and he thought, thought so hard that at last he appeared to himself to have exhausted the thinkable. When this moment of combined relief and dismay arrived (on the last of the evenings that we are concerned with), he took his way down Third Avenue and reached his humble dwelling. Till within a short time there had been a resource for him at such an hour and in such a mood; a little variety-actress, who lived in the house, and with whom he had established the most cordial relations, was often having her supper (she took it somewhere, every night, after the theatre), in the dim, close dining-room, and he used to drop in and talk to her. But she had lately married, to his great amusement, and her husband had taken her on a wedding-tour, which was to be at the same time professional. On this occasion he mounted, with rather a heavy tread, to his rooms, where (on the rickety writing-table in the parlour) he found a note from Mrs. Luna. I need not reproduce it *in extenso;* a pale reflection of it will serve. She reproached him with neglecting her, wanted to know what had become of him, whether he had grown too fashionable for a person who cared only for serious society. She accused him of having changed, and inquired as to the reason of his coldness. Was it too much to ask whether he could tell her at least in what manner she had offended him? She used to think they were so much in sympathy — he expressed her own ideas about everything so vividly. She liked intellectual companionship, and she had none now. She hoped very much he would come and see her — as he used to do six months before — the following evening; and however much she might have sinned or he might have altered, she was at least always his affectionate cousin Adeline.

"What the deuce does she want of me now?" It was with this somewhat ungracious exclamation that he tossed away his cousin Adeline's missive. The gesture might have indicated that he meant to take no notice of her; nevertheless, after a day had elapsed, he presented himself before her. He knew what she wanted of old — that is, a year ago; she had wanted him to look after her property and to be tutor to her son. He had lent himself, good-naturedly, to this desire — he was touched by so much confidence — but the experiment had speedily collapsed. Mrs. Luna's affairs were in the hands of trustees, who had complete care of them, and Ransom instantly perceived that his function would be simply to meddle in things that didn't concern him. The levity with which she had exposed him to the derision of the lawful guardians of her fortune opened his eyes to some of the dangers of cousinship; nevertheless

he said to himself that he might turn an honest penny by giving an hour or two every day to the education of her little boy. But this, too, proved a brief illusion. Ransom had to find his time in the afternoon; he left his business at five o'clock and remained with his young kinsman till the hour of dinner. At the end of a few weeks he thought himself lucky in retiring without broken shins. That Newton's little nature was remarkable had often been insisted on by his mother; but it was remarkable, Ransom saw, for the absence of any of the qualities which attach a teacher to a pupil. He was in truth an insufferable child, entertaining for the Latin language a personal, physical hostility, which expressed itself in convulsions of rage. During these paroxysms he kicked furiously at every one and everything — at poor "Rannie," at his mother, at Messrs. Andrews and Stoddard, at the illustrious men of Rome, at the universe in general, to which, as he lay on his back on the carpet, he presented a pair of singularly active little heels. Mrs. Luna had a way of being present at his lessons, and when they passed, as sooner or later they were sure to, into the stage I have described, she interceded for her overwrought darling, reminded Ransom that these were the signs of an exquisite sensibility, begged that the child might be allowed to rest a little, and spend the remainder of the time in conversation with the preceptor. It came to seem to him, very soon, that he was not earning his fee; besides which, it was disagreeable to him to have pecuniary relations with a lady who had not the art of concealing from him that she liked to place him under obligations. He resigned his tutorship, and drew a long breath, having a vague feeling that he had escaped a danger. He could not have told you exactly what it was, and he had a certain sentimental, provincial respect for women which even prevented him from attempting to give a name to it in his own thoughts. He was addicted with the ladies to the old forms of address and of gallantry; he held that they were delicate, agreeable creatures, whom Providence had placed under the protection of the bearded sex; and it was not merely a humorous idea with him that whatever might be the defects of Southern gentlemen, they were at any rate remarkable for their chivalry. He was a man who still, in a slangy age, could pronounce that word with a perfectly serious face.

This boldness did not prevent him from thinking that women were essentially inferior to men, and infinitely tiresome when they declined to accept the lot which men had made for them. He had the most definite notions about their place in nature, in society, and was perfectly easy in his mind as to whether it excluded them from any proper homage. The chivalrous man paid that tax with alacrity. He admitted their rights; these consisted in a standing claim to the generosity and tenderness of the stronger race. The exercise of such feelings was full of advantage for both sexes, and they flowed most freely, of course, when women were gracious and grateful. It may be said that he had a higher conception of politeness than most of the persons who desired the advent of female lawmakers. When I have added that he hated to see women eager and argumentative, and thought that their softness and docility were the inspiration, the opportunity (the highest) of man, I shall have sketched a state of mind which will doubtless strike many readers as painfully crude. It had prevented Basil Ransom, at any rate, from putting the dots on his *i*'s, as the French say, in this gradual discovery that Mrs. Luna was making love to him. The process went on a long time before he became aware of it. He had perceived very soon that she was a tremendously familiar little woman — that she took, more rapidly than he had ever known, a high degree of intimacy for granted. But as she had seemed to him neither very fresh nor very beautiful, so he could not easily have represented to himself why she should take it into her head to marry (it would never have occurred to him to doubt that she wanted marriage), an obscure and penniless Mississippian, with womenkind of his own to provide for. He could not guess that he answered to a certain secret ideal of Mrs. Luna's, who loved the landed gentry even when landless, who adored a

561

Southerner under any circumstances, who thought her kinsman a fine, manly, melancholy, disinterested type, and who was sure that her views of public matters, the questions of the age, the vulgar character of modern life would meet with a perfect response in his mind. She could see by the way he talked that he was a conservative, and this was the motto inscribed upon her own silken banner. She took this unpopular line both by temperament and by reaction from her sister's "extreme" views, the sight of the dreadful people that they brought about her. In reality, Olive was distinguished and discriminating, and Adeline was the dupe of confusions in which the worse was apt to be mistaken for the better. She talked to Ransom about the inferiority of republics, the distressing persons she had met abroad in the legations of the United States, the bad manners of servants and shopkeepers in that country, the hope she entertained that "the good old families" would make a stand; but he never suspected that she cultivated these topics (her treatment of them struck him as highly comical), for the purpose of leading him to the altar, of beguiling the way. Least of all could he suppose that she would be indifferent to his want of income — a point in which he failed to do her justice; for, thinking the fact that he had remained poor a proof of delicacy in that shopkeeping age, it gave her much pleasure to reflect that, as Newton's little

property was settled on him (with safeguards which showed how long-headed poor Mr. Luna had been, and large-hearted, too, since to what he left *her* no disagreeable conditions, such as eternal mourning, for instance, were attached) — that as Newton, I say, enjoyed the pecuniary independence which befitted his character, her own income was ample even for two, and she might give herself the luxury of taking a husband who should owe her something. Basil Ransom did not divine all this, but he divined that it was not for nothing that Mrs. Luna wrote him little notes every other day, that she proposed to drive him in the Park at unnatural hours, and that when he said he had his business to attend to, she replied: "Oh, a plague on your business! I am sick of that word — one hears of nothing else in America. There are ways of getting on without business, if you would only take them!" He seldom answered her notes, and he disliked extremely the way in which, in spite of her love of form and order, she attempted to clamber in at the window of one's house when one had locked the door; so that he began to interspace his visits considerably, and at last made them very rare. When I reflect on his habits of almost superstitious politeness to women, it comes over me that some very strong motive must have operated to make him give his friendly — his only too friendly — cousin the cold shoulder. Nevertheless, when he received her reproachful letter (after it had had time to work a little), he said to himself that he had perhaps been unjust and even brutal, and as he was easily touched by remorse of this kind, he took up the broken thread.

Chapter XXII

As he sat with Mrs. Luna, in her little back drawing-room, under the lamp, he felt rather more tolerant than before of the pressure she could not help putting upon him. Several months had elapsed, and he was no nearer to the sort of success he had hoped for. It stole over him gently that there was another sort, pretty visibly open to him, not so elevated nor so manly, it is true, but on which he should after all, perhaps, be able to reconcile it with his honour to fall back. Mrs. Luna had had an inspiration; for once in her life she had held her tongue. She had not made him a scene, there had been no question of an explanation; she had received him as if he had been there the day before, with the addition of a spice of mysterious melancholy. She might have made up her mind that she had lost him as what she had hoped, but that it was better than desolation to try and keep him as a friend. It was as if she wished him to see now how she tried. She was subdued and consolatory, she waited upon him, moved away a

screen that intercepted the fire, remarked that he looked very tired, and rang for some tea. She made no inquiry about his affairs, never asked if he had been busy and prosperous; and this reticence struck him as unexpectedly delicate and discreet; it was as if she had guessed, by a subtle feminine faculty, that his professional career was nothing to boast of. There was a simplicity in him which permitted him to wonder whether she had not improved. The lamp-light was soft, the fire crackled pleasantly, everything that surrounded him betrayed a woman's taste and touch; the place was decorated and cushioned in perfection, delightfully private and personal, the picture of a well-appointed home. Mrs. Luna had complained of the difficulties of installing one's self in America, but Ransom remembered that he had received an impression similar to this in her sister's house in Boston, and reflected that these ladies had, as a family-trait, the art of making themselves comfortable. It was better for a winter's evening than the German beer-cellar (Mrs. Luna's tea was excellent), and his hostess herself appeared to-night almost as amiable as the variety-actress. At the end of an hour he felt, I will not say almost marriageable, but almost married. Images of leisure played before him, leisure in which he saw himself covering foolscap paper with his views on several subjects, and with favourable illustrations of Southern eloquence. It became tolerably vivid to him that if editors wouldn't print one's lucubrations, it would be a comfort to feel that one was able to publish them at one's own expense.

He had a moment of almost complete illusion. Mrs. Luna had taken up her bit of crochet; she was sitting opposite to him, on the other side of the fire. Her white hands moved with little jerks as she took her stitches, and her rings flashed and twinkled in the light of the hearth. Her head fell a little to one side, exhibiting the plumpness of her chin and neck, and her dropped eyes (it gave her a little modest air), rested quietly on her work. A silence of a few moments had fallen upon their talk, and Adeline — who decidedly *had* improved — appeared also to feel the charm of it, not to wish to break it. Basil Ransom was conscious of all this, and at the same time he was vaguely engaged in a speculation. If it gave one time, if it gave one leisure, was not that in itself a high motive? Thorough study of the question he cared for most — was not the chance for *that* an infinitely desirable good? He seemed to see himself, to feel himself, in that very chair, in the evenings of the future, reading some indispensable book in the still lamp-light — Mrs. Luna knew where to get such pretty mellowing shades. Should he not be able to act in that way upon the public opinion of his time, to check certain tendencies, to point out certain dangers, to indulge in much salutary criticism? Was it not one's

duty to put one's self in the best conditions for such action? And as the silence continued he almost fell to musing on his duty, almost persuaded himself that the moral law commanded him to marry Mrs. Luna. She looked up presently from her work, their eyes met, and she smiled. He might have believed she had guessed what he was thinking of. This idea startled him, alarmed him a little, so that when Mrs. Luna said, with her sociable manner, "There is nothing I like so much, of a winter's night, as a cosy *tête-à-tête* by the fire. It's quite like Darby and Joan; what a pity the kettle has ceased singing!" — when she uttered these insinuating words he gave himself a little imperceptible shake, which was, however, enough to break the spell, and made no response more direct than to ask her, in a moment, in a tone of cold, mild curiosity, whether she had lately heard from her sister, and how long Miss Chancellor intended to remain in Europe.

"Well, you *have* been living in your hole!" Mrs. Luna exclaimed. "Olive came home six weeks ago. How long did you expect her to endure it?"

"I am sure I don't know; I have never been there," Ransom replied.

"Yes, that's what I like you for," Mrs. Luna remarked sweetly. "If a man is nice without it, it's such a pleasant change."

The young man started, then gave a natural laugh. "Lord, how few reasons there must be!"

"Oh, I mention that one because I can tell it. I shouldn't care to tell the others."

"I am glad you have some to fall back upon, the day I should go," Ransom went on. "I thought you thought so much of Europe."

"So I do; but it isn't everything," said Mrs. Luna philosophically. "You had better go there with me," she added, with a certain inconsequence.

"One would go to the end of the world with so irresistible a lady!" Ransom exclaimed, falling into the tone which Mrs. Luna always found so unsatisfactory. It was a part of his Southern gallantry — his accent always came out strongly when he said anything of that sort — and it committed him to nothing in particular. She had had occasion to wish, more than once, that he wouldn't be so beastly polite, as she used to hear people say in England. She answered that she didn't care about ends, she cared about beginnings; but he didn't take up the declaration; he returned to the subject of Olive, wanted to know what she had done over there, whether she had worked them up much.

"Oh, of course, she fascinated every one," said Mrs. Luna. "With her grace and beauty, her general style, how could she help that?"

"But did she bring them round, did she swell the host that is prepared to march under her banner?"

"I suppose she saw plenty of the strong-minded, plenty of vicious old maids, and fanatics, and frumps. But I haven't the least idea what she accomplished — what they call 'wonders,' I suppose."

"Didn't you see her when she returned?" Basil Ransom asked.

"How could I see her? I can see pretty far, but I can't see all the way to Boston." And then, in explaining that it was at this port that her sister had disembarked, Mrs. Luna further inquired whether he could imagine Olive doing anything in a first-rate way, as long as there were inferior ones. "Of course she likes bad ships — Boston steamers — just as she likes common people, and red-haired hoydens, and preposterous doctrines."

Ransom was silent a moment. "Do you mean the — a — rather striking young lady whom I met in Boston a year ago last October? What was her name? — Miss Tarrant? Does Miss Chancellor like her as much as ever?"

"Mercy! don't you know she took her to Europe? It was to form *her* mind she went. Didn't I tell you that last summer? You used to come to see me then."

"Oh yes, I remember," Ransom said, rather musingly. "And did she bring her back?"

"Gracious, you don't suppose she would leave her! Olive thinks she's born to regenerate the world."

"I remember you telling me that, too. It comes back to me. Well, is her mind formed?"

"As I haven't seen it, I cannot tell you."

"Aren't you going on there to see —— "

"To see whether Miss Tarrant's mind is formed?" Mrs. Luna broke in. "I will go if you would like me to. I remember your being immensely excited about her that time you met her. Don't you recollect that?"

Ransom hesitated an instant. "I can't say I do. It is too long ago."

"Yes, I have no doubt that's the way you change, about women! Poor Miss Tarrant, if she thinks she made an impression on you!"

"She won't think about such things as that, if her mind has been formed by your sister," Ransom said. "It does come back to me now, what you told me about the growth of their intimacy. And do they mean to go on living together for ever?"

"I suppose so — unless some one should take it into his head to marry Verena."

"Verena — is that her name?" Ransom asked.

Mrs. Luna looked at him with a suspended needle. "Well! have you forgotten that too? You told me yourself you thought it so pretty, that time in Boston, when you walked me up the hill." Ransom declared that he remembered that walk, but didn't remember everything he had said to her; and she suggested, very satirically, that perhaps he would like to marry Verena himself — he seemed so interested in her. Ransom shook his head sadly, and said he was afraid he was not in a position to marry; whereupon Mrs. Luna asked him what he meant — did he mean (after a moment's hesitation) that he was too poor?

"Never in the world — I am very rich; I make an enormous income!" the young man exclaimed; so that, remarking his tone, and the slight flush of annoyance that rose to his face, Mrs. Luna was quick enough to judge that she had overstepped the mark. She remembered (she ought to have remembered before), that he had never taken her in the least into his confidence about his affairs. That was not the Southern way, and he was at least as proud as he was poor. In this surmise she was just; Basil Ransom would have despised himself if he had been capable of confessing to a woman that he couldn't make a living. Such questions were none of their business (their business was simply to be provided for, practise the domestic virtues, and be charmingly grateful), and there was, to his sense, something almost indecent in talking about them. Mrs. Luna felt doubly sorry for him as she perceived that he denied himself the luxury of sympathy (that is, of hers), and the vague but comprehensive sigh that passed her lips as she took up her crochet again was unusually expressive of helplessness. She said that of course she knew how great his talents were — he could do anything he wanted; and Basil Ransom wondered for a moment whether, if she were to ask him point-blank to marry her, it would

566

be consistent with the high courtesy of a Southern gentleman to refuse. After she should be his wife he might of course confess to her that he was too poor to marry, for in that relation even a Southern gentleman of the highest tone must sometimes unbend. But he didn't in the least long for this arrangement, and was conscious that the most pertinent sequel to her conjecture would be for him to take up his hat and walk away.

Within five minutes, however, he had come to desire to do this almost as little as to marry Mrs. Luna. He wanted to hear more about the girl who lived with Olive Chancellor. Something had revived in him — an old curiosity, an image half effaced — when he learned that she had come back to America. He had taken a wrong impression from what Mrs. Luna said, nearly a year before, about her sister's visit to Europe; he had supposed it was to be a long absence, that Miss Chancellor wanted perhaps to get the little prophetess away from her parents, possibly even away from some amorous entanglement. Then, no doubt, they wanted to study up the woman-question with the facilities that Europe would offer; he didn't know much about Europe, but he had an idea that it was a great place for facilities. His knowledge of Miss Chancellor's departure, accompanied by her young companion, had checked at the time, on Ransom's part, a certain habit of idle but none the less entertaining retrospect. His life, on the whole,

had not been rich in episode, and that little chapter of his visit to his queer, clever, capricious cousin, with his evening at Miss Birdseye's, and his glimpse, repeated on the morrow, of the strange, beautiful, ridiculous, red-haired young *improvisatrice*, unrolled itself in his memory like a page of interesting fiction. The page seemed to fade, however, when he heard that the two girls had gone, for an indefinite time, to unknown lands; this carried them out of his range, spoiled the perspective, diminished their actuality; so that for several months past, with his increase of anxiety about his own affairs, and the low pitch of his spirits, he had not thought at all about Verena Tarrant. The fact that she was once more in Boston, with a certain contiguity that it seemed to imply between Boston and New York, presented itself now as important and agreeable. He was conscious that this was rather an anomaly, and his consciousness made him, had already made him, dissimulate slightly. He did not pick up his hat to go; he sat in his chair taking his chance of the tax which Mrs. Luna might lay upon his urbanity. He remembered that he had not made, as yet, any very eager inquiry about Newton, who at this late hour had succumbed to the only influence that tames the untamable and was sleeping the sleep of childhood, if not of innocence. Ransom repaired his neglect in a manner which elicited the most copious response from his hostess. The boy had had a good many tutors since Ransom gave him up, and it could not be said that his education languished. Mrs. Luna spoke with pride of the manner in which he went through them; if he did not master his lessons, he mastered his teachers, and she had the happy conviction that she gave him every advantage. Ransom's delay was diplomatic, but at the end of ten minutes, he returned to the young ladies in Boston; he asked why, with their aggressive programme, one hadn't begun to feel their onset, why the echoes of Miss Tarrant's eloquence hadn't reached his ears. Hadn't she come out yet in public? was she not coming to stir them up in New York? He hoped she hadn't broken down.

"She didn't seem to break down last summer, at the Female Convention," Mrs. Luna replied. "Have you forgotten that too? Didn't I tell you of the sensation she produced there, and of what I heard from Boston about it? Do you mean to say I didn't give you that 'Transcript,' with the report of her great speech? It was just before they sailed for Europe; she went off with flying colours, in a blaze of fireworks." Ransom protested that he had not heard this affair mentioned till that moment, and then, when they compared dates, they found it had taken place just after his last visit to Mrs. Luna. This, of course, gave her a chance to say that he had treated her even worse than she supposed; it had been her impression, at any rate, that they had

talked together about Verena's sudden bound into fame. Apparently she confounded him with some one else, that was very possible; he was not to suppose that he occupied such a distinct place in her mind, especially when she might die twenty deaths before he came near her. Ransom demurred to the implication that Miss Tarrant was famous; if she were famous, wouldn't she be in the New York papers? He hadn't seen her there, and he had no recollection of having encountered any mention at the time (last June, was it?) of her exploits at the Female Convention. A local reputation doubtless she had, but that had been the case a year and a half before, and what was expected of her then was to become a first-class national glory. He was willing to believe that she had created some excitement in Boston, but he shouldn't attach much importance to that till one began to see her photograph in the stores. Of course, one must give her time, but he had supposed Miss Chancellor was going to put her through faster.

If he had taken a contradictious tone on purpose to draw Mrs. Luna out, he could not have elicited more of the information he desired. It was perfectly true that he had seen no reference to Verena's performances in the preceding June; there were periods when the newspapers seemed to him so idiotic that for weeks he never looked at one. He learned from Mrs. Luna that it was not

Olive who had sent her the "Transcript" and in letters had added some private account of the doings at the convention to the testimony of that amiable sheet; she had been indebted for this service to a "gentleman-friend," who wrote her everything that happened in Boston, and what every one had every day for dinner. Not that it was necessary for her happiness to know; but the gentleman she spoke of didn't know what to invent to please her. A Bostonian couldn't imagine that one didn't want to know, and that was their idea of ingratiating themselves, or, at any rate, it was his, poor man. Olive would never have gone into particulars about Verena; she regarded her sister as quite too much one of the profane, and knew Adeline couldn't understand why, when she took to herself a bosom-friend, she should have been at such pains to select her in just the most dreadful class in the community. Verena was a perfect little adventuress, and quite third-rate into the bargain; but, of course, she was a pretty girl enough, if one cared for hair of the colour of cochineal. As for her people, they were too absolutely awful; it was exactly as if she, Mrs. Luna, had struck up an intimacy with the daughter of her chiropodist. It took Olive to invent such monstrosities, and to think she was doing something great for humanity when she did so; though, in spite of her wanting to turn everything over, and put the lowest highest, she could be just as con-

temptuous and invidious, when it came to really mixing, as if she were some grand old duchess. She must do her the justice to say that she hated the Tarrants, the father and mother; but, all the same, she let Verena run to and fro between Charles Street and the horrible hole they lived in, and Adeline knew from that gentleman who wrote so copiously that the girl now and then spent a week at a time at Cambridge. Her mother, who had been ill for some weeks, wanted her to sleep there. Mrs. Luna knew further, by her correspondent, that Verena had — or had had the winter before — a great deal of attention from gentlemen. She didn't know how she worked that into the idea that the female sex was sufficient to itself; but she had grounds for saying that this was one reason why Olive had taken her abroad. She was afraid Verena would give in to some man, and she wanted to make a break. Of course, any such giving in would be very awkward for a young woman who shrieked out on platforms that old maids were the highest type. Adeline guessed Olive had perfect control of her now, unless indeed she used the expeditions to Cambridge as a cover for meeting gentlemen. She was an artful little minx, and cared as much for the rights of women as she did for the Panama Canal; the only right of a woman she wanted was to climb up on top of something, where the men could look at her. She would stay with Olive as long as it served her purpose, because Olive, with her great respectability, could push her, and counteract the effect of her low relations, to say nothing of paying all her expenses and taking her the tour of Europe. "But, mark my words," said Mrs. Luna, "she will give Olive the greatest cut she has ever had in her life. She will run off with some lion-tamer; she will marry a circus-man!" And Mrs. Luna added that it would serve Olive Chancellor right. But she would take it hard; look out for tantrums then!

Basil Ransom's emotions were peculiar while his hostess delivered herself, in a manner at once casual and emphatic, of these rather insidious remarks. He took them all in, for they represented to him certain very interesting facts; but he perceived at the same time that Mrs. Luna didn't know what she was talking about. He had seen Verena Tarrant only twice in his life, but it was no use telling him that she was an adventuress — though, certainly, it *was* very likely she would end by giving Miss Chancellor a cut. He chuckled, with a certain grimness, as this image passed before him; it was not unpleasing, the idea that he should be avenged (for it would avenge him to know it), upon the wanton young woman who had invited him to come and see her in order simply to slap his face. But he had an odd sense of having lost something in not knowing of the other girl's appearance at the Women's Convention — a vague feeling that he had been

cheated and trifled with. The complaint was idle, inasmuch as it was not probable he could have gone to Boston to listen to her; but it represented to him that he had not shared, even dimly and remotely, in an event which concerned her very closely. Why should he share, and what was more natural than that the things which concerned her closely should not concern him at all? This question came to him only as he walked home that evening; for the moment it remained quite in abeyance: therefore he was free to feel also that his imagination had been rather starved by his ignorance of the fact that she was near him again (comparatively), that she was in the dimness of the horizon (no longer beyond the curve of the globe), and yet he had not perceived it. This sense of personal loss, as I have called it, made him feel, further, that he had something to make up, to recover. He could scarcely have told you how he would go about it; but the idea, formless though it was, led him in a direction very different from the one he had been following a quarter of an hour before. As he watched it dance before him he fell into another silence, in the midst of which Mrs. Luna gave him another mystic smile. The effect of it was to make him rise to his feet; the whole landscape of his mind had suddenly been illuminated. Decidedly, it was *not* his duty to marry Mrs. Luna, in order to have means to pursue his studies; he jerked himself back, as if he had been on the point of it.

"You don't mean to say you are going already? I haven't said half I wanted to!" she exclaimed.

He glanced at the clock, saw it was not yet late, took a turn about the room, then sat down again in a different place, while she followed him with her eyes, wondering what was the matter with him. Ransom took good care not to ask her what it was she had still to say, and perhaps it was to prevent her telling him that he now began to talk, freely, quickly, in quite a new tone. He stayed half an hour longer, and made himself very agreeable. It seemed to Mrs. Luna now that he had every distinction (she had known he had most), that he was really a charming man. He abounded in conversation, till at last he took up his hat in earnest; he talked about the state of the South, its social peculiarities, the ruin wrought by the war, the dilapidated gentry, the queer types of superannuated fire-eaters, ragged and unreconciled, all the pathos and all the comedy of it, making her laugh at one moment, almost cry at another, and say to herself throughout that when he took it into his head there was no one who could make a lady's evening pass so pleasantly. It was only afterwards that she asked herself why he had not taken it into his head till the last, so quickly. She delighted in the dilapidated gentry; her taste was completely different from her sister's, who took an interest only in the lower class, as it struggled to rise; what Adeline cared for was the fallen aristocracy (it seemed to be falling everywhere very much; was not Basil Ransom an example of it? was he not like a French *gentilhomme de province* after the Revolution? or an old monarchical *émigré* from the Languedoc?), the despoiled patriciate, I say, whose attitude was noble and touching, and toward whom one might exercise a charity as discreet as their pride was sensitive. In all Mrs. Luna's visions of herself, her discretion was the leading feature. "Are you going to let ten years elapse again before you come?" she asked, as Basil Ransom bade her good-night. "You must let me know, because between this and your next visit I shall have time to go to Europe and come back. I shall take care to arrive the day before."

Instead of answering this sally, Ransom said, "Are you not going one of these days to Boston? Are you not going to pay your sister another visit?"

Mrs. Luna stared. "What good will that do *you?* Excuse my stupidity," she added; "of course, it gets me away. Thank you very much!"

"I don't want you to go away; but I want to hear more about Miss Olive."

"Why in the world? You know you loathe her!" Here, before Ransom could reply, Mrs. Luna again overtook herself. "I verily believe that by Miss Olive you mean Miss Verena!" Her eyes charged him a moment with this perverse intention; then she exclaimed, "Basil Ransom, *are* you in love with that creature?"

He gave a perfectly natural laugh, not pleading guilty, in order to practise on Mrs. Luna, but expressing the simple state of the case. "How should I be? I have seen her but twice in my life."

"If you had seen her more, I shouldn't be afraid! Fancy your wanting to pack me off to Boston!" his hostess went on. "I am in no hurry to stay with Olive again; besides, that girl takes up the whole house. You had better go there yourself."

"I should like nothing better," said Ransom.

"Perhaps you would like me to ask Verena to spend a month with me — it might be a way of attracting you to the house," Adeline went on, in the tone of exuberant provocation.

Ransom was on the point of replying that it would be a better way than any other, but he checked himself in time; he had never yet, even in joke, made so crude, so rude a speech to a lady. You only knew when he was joking with women by his superadded civility. "I beg you to believe there is nothing I would do for any woman in the world that I wouldn't do for you," he said, bending, for the last time, over Mrs. Luna's plump hand.

"I shall remember that and keep you up to it!" she cried after him, as he went. But even with this rather lively exchange of vows he

felt that he had got off rather easily. He walked slowly up Fifth Avenue, into which, out of Adeline's cross-street, he had turned, by the light of a fine winter moon; and at every corner he stopped a minute, lingered in meditation, while he exhaled a soft, vague sigh. This was an unconscious, involuntary expression of relief, such as a man might utter who had seen himself on the point of being run over and yet felt that he was whole. He didn't trouble himself much to ask what had saved him; whatever it was it had produced a reaction, so that he felt rather ashamed of having found his lookout of late so blank. By the time he reached his lodgings, his ambition, his resolution, had rekindled; he had remembered that he formerly supposed he was a man of ability, that nothing particular had occurred to make him doubt it (the evidence was only negative, not positive), and that at any rate he was young enough to have another try. He whistled that night as he went to bed.

Chapter XXIII

THREE weeks afterward he stood in front of Olive Chancellor's house, looking up and down the street and hesitating. He had told Mrs. Luna that he should like nothing better than to make another journey to Boston; and it was not simply because he liked it that he had come. I was on the point of saying that a happy chance had favoured him, but it occurs to me that one is under no obligation to call chances by flattering epithets when they have been waited for so long. At any rate, the darkest hour is before the dawn; and a few days after that melancholy evening I have described, which Ransom spent in his German beer-cellar, before a single glass, soon emptied, staring at his future with an unremunerated eye, he found that the world appeared to have need of him yet. The "party," as he would have said (I cannot pretend that his speech was too heroic for that), for whom he had transacted business in Boston so many months before, and who had expressed at the time but a limited appreciation of his services (there had been between the lawyer and his client a divergence of judgment), observing, apparently, that they proved more fruitful than he expected, had reopened the affair and presently requested Ransom to transport himself again to the sister city. His errand demanded more time than before, and for three days he gave it his constant attention. On the fourth he found he was still detained; he should have to wait till the evening — some important papers were to be prepared. He determined to treat the interval as a holiday, and he wondered what one could do in Boston to give one's morning a festive complexion. The weather was brilliant enough to minister to any illusion, and he strolled along the streets, taking it in. In front of the Music Hall and of Tremont Temple he stopped, looking at the posters in the doorway; for was it not possible that Miss Chancellor's little friend might be just then addressing her fellow-citizens? Her name was absent, however, and this resource seemed to mock him. He knew no one in the place but Olive Chancellor, so there was no question of a visit to pay. He was perfectly resolved that he would never go near *her* again; she was doubtless a very superior being, but she had been too rough with him to tempt him further. Politeness, even a largely-interpreted "chivalry," required nothing more than he had already done; he had quitted her, the other year, without telling her that she was a vixen, and that reticence was chivalrous enough. There was also Verena Tarrant, of course; he saw no reason to dissemble when he spoke of her to himself, and he allowed himself the entertainment of feeling that he should like very much to see her again. Very likely she wouldn't seem to him the same; the impression she had made upon him was due to some accident of mood or circumstance; and, at any rate, any charm she might have exhibited then had probably been obliterated by the coarsening effect of publicity and the tonic influence of his kinswoman. It will be observed that in this reasoning of Basil Ransom's the impression was freely recognised, and recognised as a

The Bostonians

phenomenon still present. The attraction might have vanished, as he said to himself, but the mental picture of it was yet vivid. The greater the pity that he couldn't call upon Verena (he called her by her name in his thoughts, it was so pretty), without calling upon Olive, and that Olive was so disagreeable as to place that effort beyond his strength. There was another consideration, with Ransom, which eminently belonged to the man; he believed that Miss Chancellor had conceived, in the course of those few hours, and in a manner that formed so absurd a sequel to her having gone out of her way to make his acquaintance, such a dislike to him that it would be odious to her to see him again within her doors; and he would have felt indelicate in taking warrant from her original invitation (before she had seen him), to inflict on her a presence which he had no reason to suppose the lapse of time had made less offensive. She had given him no sign of pardon or penitence in any of the little ways that are familiar to women — by sending him a message through her sister, or even a book, a photograph, a Christmas card, or a newspaper, by the post. He felt, in a word, not at liberty to ring at her door; he didn't know what kind of a fit the sight of his long Mississippian person would give her, and it was characteristic of him that he should wish so to spare the sensibilities of a young lady whom he had not found tender; being ever as willing to let

women off easily in the particular case as he was fixed in the belief that the sex in general requires watching.

Nevertheless, he found himself, at the end of half an hour, standing on the only spot in Charles Street which had any significance for him. It had occurred to him that if he couldn't call upon Verena without calling upon Olive, he should be exempt from that condition if he called upon Mrs. Tarrant. It was not her mother, truly, who had asked him, it was the girl herself; and he was conscious, as a candid young American, that a mother is always less accessible, more guarded by social prejudice, than a daughter. But he was at a pass in which it was permissible to strain a point, and he took his way in the direction in which he knew that Cambridge lay, remembering that Miss Tarrant's invitation had reference to that quarter and that Mrs. Luna had given him further evidence. Had she not said that Verena often went back there for visits of several days — that her mother had been ill and she gave her much care? There was nothing inconceivable in her being engaged at that hour (it was getting to be one o'clock), in one of those expeditions — nothing impossible in the chance that he might find her in Cambridge. The chance, at any rate, was worth taking; Cambridge, moreover, was worth seeing, and it was as good a way as another of keeping his holiday. It occurred to him, indeed, that Cambridge was a big place, and that he had no particular address. This reflection overtook him just as he reached Olive's house, which oddly enough, he was obliged to pass on his way to the mysterious suburb. That is partly why he paused there; he asked himself for a moment why he shouldn't ring the bell and obtain his needed information from the servant, who would be sure to be able to give it to him. He had just dismissed this method, as of questionable taste, when he heard the door of the house open, within the deep embrasure in which, in Charles Street, the main portals are set, and which are partly occupied by a flight of steps protected at the bottom by a second door, whose upper half, in either wing, consists of a sheet of glass. It was a minute before he could see who had come out, and in that minute he had time to turn away and then to turn back again, and to wonder which of the two inmates would appear to him, or whether he should behold neither or both.

The person who had issued from the house descended the steps very slowly, as if on purpose to give him time to escape; and when at last the glass doors were divided they disclosed a little old lady. Ransom was disappointed; such an apparition was so scantily to his purpose. But the next minute his spirits rose again, for he was sure that he had seen the little old lady before. She stopped on the side-walk, and looked vaguely about her, in the manner of a person waiting for an omnibus or a street-car; she had a dingy, loosely-habited air, as if she had worn her clothes for many years and yet was even now imperfectly acquainted with them; a large, benignant face, caged in by the glass of her spectacles, which seemed to cover it almost equally everywhere, and a fat, rusty satchel, which hung low at her side, as if it wearied her to carry it. This gave Ransom time to recognize her; he knew in Boston no such figure as that save Miss Birdseye. Her party, her person, the exalted account Miss Chancellor gave of her, had kept a very distinct place in his mind; and while she stood there in dim circumspection she came back to him as a friend of yesterday. His necessity gave a point to the reminiscences she evoked; it took him only a moment to reflect that she would be able to tell him where Verena Tarrant was at that particular time, and where, if need be, her parents lived. Her eyes rested on him, and as she saw that he was looking at her she didn't go through the ceremony (she had broken so completely with all conventions), of removing them; he evidently represented nothing to her but a sentient fellow-citizen in the enjoyment of his rights, which included that of staring. Miss Birdseye's modesty had never pretended that it was not to be publicly challenged; there were so many bright new motives and ideas in the world that there might even be reasons for looking at her.

When Ransom approached her and, raising his hat with a smile, said, "Shall I stop this car for you, Miss Birdseye?" she only looked at him more vaguely, in her complete failure to seize the idea that this might be simply Fame. She had trudged about the streets of Boston for fifty years, and at no period had she received that amount of attention from dark-eyed young men. She glanced, in an unprejudiced way, at the big parti-coloured human van which now jingled toward them from out of the Cambridge road. "Well, I should like to get into it, if it will take me home," she answered. "Is this a South End car?"

The vehicle had been stopped by the conductor, on his perceiving Miss Birdseye; he evidently recognised her as a frequent passenger. He went, however, through none of the forms of reassurance beyond remarking, "You want to get right in here — quick," but stood with his hand raised, in a threatening way, to the cord of his signal-bell.

"You must allow me the honour of taking you home, madam; I will tell you who I am," Basil Ransom said, in obedience to a rapid reflection. He helped her into the car, the conductor pressed a fraternal hand upon her back, and in a moment the young man was seated beside her, and the jingling had recommenced. At that hour of the day the car was almost empty, and they had it virtually to themselves.

"Well, I know you are some one; I don't think you belong round here," Miss Birdseye declared, as they proceeded.

"I was once at your house — on a very interesting occasion. Do you remember a party you gave, a year ago last October, to which Miss Chancellor came, and another young lady, who made a wonderful speech?"

"Oh yes! when Verena Tarrant moved us all so! There were a good many there; I don't remember all."

"I was one of them," Basil Ransom said; "I came with Miss Chancellor, who is a kind of relation of mine, and you were very good to me."

"What did I do?" asked Miss Birdseye, candidly. Then, before he could answer her, she recognised him. "I remember you now, and Olive bringing you! You're a Southern gentleman — she told me about you afterwards. You don't approve of our great struggle — you want us to be kept down." The old lady spoke with perfect mildness, as if she had long ago done with passion and resentment. Then she added, "Well, I presume we can't have the sympathy of all."

"Doesn't it look as if you had my sympathy, when I get into a car on purpose to see you home — one of the principal agitators?" Ransom inquired, laughing.

"Did you get in on purpose?"

"Quite on purpose. I am not so bad as Miss Chancellor thinks me."

"Oh, I presume you have your ideas," said Miss Birdseye. "Of course, Southerners have peculiar views. I suppose they retain more than one might think. I hope you won't ride too far — I know my way round Boston."

"Don't object to me, or think me officious," Ransom replied. "I want to ask you something."

Miss Birdseye looked at him again. "Oh, yes, I place you now; you conversed some with Doctor Prance."

"To my great edification!" Ransome exclaimed. "And I hope Doctor Prance is well."

"She looks after every one's health but her own," said Miss Birdseye, smiling. "When I tell her that, she says she hasn't got any to look after. She says she's the only woman in Boston that hasn't got a doctor. She was determined she wouldn't be a patient, and it seemed as if the only way not to be one was to be a doctor. She is trying to make me sleep; that's her principal occupation."

"Is it possible you don't sleep yet?" Ransom asked, almost tenderly.

"Well, just a little. But by the time I get to sleep I have to get up. I can't sleep when I want to live."

"You ought to come down South," the young man suggested. "In that languid air you would doze deliciously!"

"Well, I don't want to be languid," said Miss Birdseye. "Besides, I have been down South, in the old times, and I can't say they let me sleep very much; they were always round after me!"

"Do you mean on account of the negroes?"

"Yes, I couldn't think of anything else then. I carried them the Bible."

Ransom was silent a moment; then he said, in a tone which evidently was carefully considerate, "I should like to hear all about that!"

"Well, fortunately, we are not required now; we are required for something else." And Miss Birdseye looked at him with a wandering, tentative humour, as if he would know what she meant.

"You mean for the other slaves!" he exclaimed, with a laugh. "You can carry them all the Bibles you want."

"I want to carry them the Statute-book; that must be our Bible now."

Ransom found himself liking Miss Birdseye very much, and it was quite without hypocrisy or a tinge too much of the local quality in his speech that he said: "Wherever you go, madam, it will matter little what you carry. You will always carry your goodness."

For a minute she made no response. Then she murmured: "That's the way Olive Chancellor told me you talked."

"I am afraid she has told you little good of me."

"Well, I am sure she thinks she is right."

"Thinks it?" said Ransom. "Why, she knows it, with supreme certainty! By the way, I hope she is well."

Miss Birdseye stared again.

"Haven't you seen her? Are you not visiting?"

"Oh, no, I am not visiting! I was literally passing her house when I met you."

"Perhaps you live here now," said Miss Birdseye. And when he had corrected this impression, she added, in a tone which showed with what positive confidence he had now inspired her, "Hadn't you better drop in?"

"It would give Miss Chancellor no pleasure," Basil Ransom rejoined. "She regards me as an enemy in the camp."

"Well, she is very brave."

"Precisely. And I am very timid."

"Didn't you fight once?"

"Yes; but it was in such a good cause!"

Ransom meant this allusion to the great Secession and, by comparison, to the attitude of the resisting male (laudable even as that might be), to be decently jocular; but Miss Birdseye took it very seriously, and sat there for a good while as speechless as if she meant to convey that she had been going on too long now to be able to discuss the propriety of the late rebellion. The young man felt that he had silenced her, and he was very sorry; for, with all deference to the disinterested Southern attitude toward the unprotected female, what he had got into the car with her for was precisely to make her talk. He had wished for general, as well as for particular, news of Verena Tarrant; it was a topic on which he had proposed to draw Miss Birdseye out. He preferred not to broach it himself, and he waited awhile for another opening. At last, when he was on the point of exposing himself by a direct inquiry (he reflected that the exposure would in any case not be long averted), she anticipated him by saying, in a manner which showed that her thoughts had continued in the same train, "I wonder very much that Miss Tarrant didn't affect you that evening!"

"Ah, but she did!" Ransom said, with alacrity. "I thought her very charming!"

"Didn't you think her very reasonable?"

"God forbid, madam! I consider women have no business to be reasonable."

His companion turned upon him, slowly and mildly, and each of her glasses, in her aspect of reproach, had the glitter of an enormous tear. "Do you regard us, then, simply as lovely baubles?"

The effect of this question, as coming from Miss Birdseye, and referring in some degree to her own venerable identity, was such as to move him to irresistible laughter. But he controlled himself quickly enough to say, with genuine expression, "I regard you as the dearest thing in life, the only thing which makes it worth living!"

"Worth living for — you! But for us?" suggested Miss Birdseye.

"It's worth any woman's while to be admired as I admire you. Miss Tarrant, of whom we were speaking, affected me, as you say, in this way — that I think more highly still, if possible, of the sex which produced such a delightful young lady."

"Well, we think everything of her here," said Miss Birdseye. "It seems as if it were a real gift."

"Does she speak often — is there any chance of my hearing her now?"

"She raises her voice a good deal in the places round — like Framingham and Billerica. It seems as if she were gathering strength, just to break over Boston like a wave. In fact she did break, last summer. She is a growing power since her great success at the convention."

"Ah! her success at the convention was very great?" Ransom inquired, putting discretion into his voice.

Miss Birdseye hesitated a moment, in order to measure her response by the bounds of righteousness. "Well," she said, with the tenderness of a long retrospect, "I have seen nothing like it since I last listened to Eliza P. Moseley."

"What a pity she isn't speaking somewhere to-night!" Ransom exclaimed.

"Oh, to-night she's out in Cambridge. Olive Chancellor mentioned that."

"Is she making a speech there?"

"No; she's visiting her home."

"I thought her home was in Charles Street?"

"Well, no; that's her residence — her principal one — since she became so united to your cousin. Isn't Miss Chancellor your cousin?"

"We don't insist on the relationship," said Ransom, smiling. "Are they very much united, the two young ladies?"

"You would say so if you were to see Miss Chancellor when Verena rises to eloquence. It's as if the chords were strung across her own heart; she seems to vibrate, to echo with every word. It's a very close and very beautiful tie, and we think everything of it here. They will work together for a great good!"

"I hope so," Ransom remarked. "But in spite of it Miss Tarrant spends a part of her time with her father and mother."

"Yes, she seems to have something for every one. If you were to see her at home, you would think she was all the daughter. She leads a lovely life!" said Miss Birdseye.

"See her at home? That's exactly what I want!" Ransom rejoined, feeling that if he was to come to this he needn't have had scruples at first. "I haven't forgotten that she invited me, when I met her."

"Oh, of course she attracts many visitors," said Miss Birdseye, limiting her encouragement to this statement.

"Yes; she must be used to admirers. And where, in Cambridge, do her family live?"

"Oh, it's on one of those little streets that don't seem to have very much of a name. But they do call it — they do call it —— " she meditated, audibly.

This process was interrupted by

an abrupt allocution from the conductor. "I guess you change here for *your* place. You want one of them blue cars." ·

The good lady returned to a sense of the situation, and Ransom helped her out of the vehicle, with the aid, as before, of a certain amount of propulsion from the conductor. Her road branched off to the right, and she had to wait on the corner of a street, there being as yet no blue car within hail. The corner was quiet and the day favourable to patience — a day of relaxed rigour and intense brilliancy. It was as if the touch of the air itself were gloved, and the street-colouring had the richness of a superficial thaw. Ransom, of course, waited with his philanthropic companion, though she now protested more vigorously against the idea that a gentleman from the South should pretend to teach an old abolitionist the mysteries of Boston. He promised to leave her when he should have consigned her to the blue car; and meanwhile they stood in the sun, with their backs against an apothecary's window, and she tried again, at his suggestion, to remember the name of Doctor Tarrant's street. "I guess if you ask for Doctor Tarrant, any one can tell you," she said; and then suddenly the address came to her — the residence of the mesmeric healer was in Monadnoc Place.

"But you'll have to ask for that, so it comes to the same," she went on. After this she added, with a friendliness more personal, "Ain't you going to see your cousin too?"

"Not if I can help it!"

Miss Birdseye gave a little ineffectual sigh. "Well, I suppose every one must act out their ideal. That's what Olive Chancellor does. She's a very noble character."

"Oh yes, a glorious nature."

"You know their opinions are just the same — hers and Verena's," Miss Birdseye placidly continued. "So why should you make a distinction?"

"My dear madam," said Ransom, "does a woman consist of nothing but her opinions? I like Miss Tarrant's lovely face better, to begin with."

"Well, she *is* pretty-looking." And Miss Birdseye gave another sigh, as if she had had a theory submitted to her — that one about a lady's opinions — which, with all that was unfamiliar and peculiar lying behind it, she was really too old to look into much. It might have been the first time she really felt her age. "There's a blue car," she said, in a tone of mild relief.

"It will be some moments before it gets here. Moreover, I don't believe that at bottom they *are* Miss Tarrant's opinions," Ransom added.

"You mustn't think she hasn't a strong hold of them," his companion exclaimed, more briskly. "If you think she is not sincere, you are very much mistaken. Those views are just her life."

"Well, *she* may bring me round to them," said Ransom, smiling.

Miss Birdseye had been watching her blue car, the advance of which was temporarily obstructed. At this, she transferred her eyes to him, gazing at him solemnly out of the pervasive window of her spectacles. "Well, I shouldn't wonder if she did! Yes, that will be a good thing. I don't see how you can help being a good deal shaken by her. She has acted on so many."

"I see; no doubt she will act on me." Then it occurred to Ransom to add: "By the way, Miss Birdseye, perhaps you will be so kind as not to mention this meeting of ours to my cousin, in case of your seeing her again. I have a perfectly good conscience in not calling upon her, but I shouldn't like her to think that I announced my slighting intention all over the town. I don't want to offend her, and she had better not know that I have been in Boston. If you don't tell her, no one else will."

"Do you wish me to conceal ——?" murmured Miss Birdseye, panting a little.

"No, I don't want you to conceal anything. I only want you to let this incident pass — to say nothing."

"Well, I never did anything of that kind."

"Of what kind?" Ransom was half vexed, half touched by her inability to enter into his point of view, and her resistance made him hold to his idea the more. "It is very simple, what I ask of you. You are under no obligation to tell Miss Chancellor everything that happens to you, are you?"

His request seemed still something of a shock to the poor old lady's candour. "Well, I see her very often, and we talk a great deal. And then — won't Verena tell her?"

"I have thought of that — but I hope not."

"She tells her most everything. Their union is so close."

"She won't want her to be wounded," Ransom said, ingeniously.

"Well, you *are* considerate." And Miss Birdseye continued to gaze at him. "It's a pity you can't sympathise."

"As I tell you, perhaps Miss Tarrant will bring me round. You have before you a possible convert," Ransom went on, without, I fear, putting up the least little prayer to heaven that his dishonesty might be forgiven.

"I should be very happy to think that — after I have told you her address in this secret way." A smile of infinite mildness glimmered in Miss Birdseye's face, and she added: "Well, I guess that will be your fate. She *has* affected so many. I would keep very quiet if I thought that. Yes, she will bring you round."

"I will let you know as soon as she does," Basil Ransom said. "Here is your car at last."

"Well, I believe in the victory of the truth. I won't say anything." And she suffered the young man to lead her to the car, which had now stopped at their corner.

"I hope very much I shall see you again," he remarked, as they went.

"Well, I am always round the streets, in Boston." And while, lifting and pushing, he was helping again to insert her into the oblong receptacle, she turned a little and repeated, "She *will* affect you! If that's to be your secret, I will keep it," Ransom heard her subjoin. He raised his hat and waved her a farewell, but she didn't see him; she was squeezing further into the car and making the discovery that this time it was full and there was no seat for her. Surely, however, he said to himself, every man in the place would offer his own to such an innocent old dear.

Chapter XXIV

A LITTLE more than an hour after this he stood in the parlour of Doctor Tarrant's suburban residence, in Monadnoc Place. He had induced a juvenile maid-servant, by an appeal somewhat impassioned, to let the ladies know that he was there; and she had returned, after a long absence, to say that Miss Tarrant would come down to him in a little while. He possessed himself, according to his wont, of the nearest book (it lay on the table, with an old magazine and a little japanned tray containing Tarrant's professional cards — his denomination as a mesmeric healer), and spent ten minutes in turning it over. It was a biography of Mrs. Ada T. P. Foat,

the celebrated trance-lecturer, and was embellished by a portrait representing the lady with a surprised expression and innumerable ringlets. Ransom said to himself, after reading a few pages, that much ridicule had been cast upon Southern literature; but if that was a fair specimen of Northern! — and he threw it back upon the table with a gesture almost as contemptuous as if he had not known perfectly, after so long a residence in the North, that it was not, while he wondered whether this was the sort of thing Miss Tarrant had been brought up on. There was no other book to be seen, and he remembered to have read the magazine; so there was finally nothing for him, as the occupants of the house failed still to appear, but to stare before him, into the bright, bare, common little room, which was so hot that he wished to open a window, and of which an ugly, undraped cross-light seemed to have taken upon itself to reveal the poverty. Ransom, as I have mentioned, had not a high standard of comfort, and noticed little, usually, how people's houses were furnished — it was only when they were very pretty that he observed; but what he saw while he waited at Doctor Tarrant's made him say to himself that it was no wonder Verena liked better to live with Olive Chancellor. He even began to wonder whether it were for the sake of that superior softness she had cultivated Miss Chancellor's favour, and whether Mrs. Luna had been right about her being

582

mercenary and insincere. So many minutes elapsed before she appeared that he had time to remember he really knew nothing to the contrary, as well as to consider the oddity (so great when one did consider it), of his coming out to Cambridge to see her, when he had only a few hours in Boston to spare, a year and a half after she had given him her very casual invitation. She had not refused to receive him, at any rate; she was free to, if it didn't please her. And not only this, but she was apparently making herself fine in his honour, inasmuch as he heard a rapid footstep move to and fro above his head, and even, through the slightness which in Monadnoc Place did service for an upper floor, the sound of drawers and presses opened and closed. Some one was "flying round," as they said in Mississippi. At last the stairs creaked under a light tread, and the next moment a brilliant person came into the room.

His reminiscence of her had been very pretty; but now that she had developed and matured, the little prophetess was prettier still. Her splendid hair seemed to shine; her cheek and chin had a curve which struck him by its fineness; her eyes and lips were full of smiles and greetings. She had appeared to him before as a creature of brightness, but now she lighted up the place, she irradiated, she made everything that surrounded her of no consequence; dropping upon the shabby sofa with an effect as charming as if she had been a nymph sinking on a leopard-skin, and with the native sweetness of her voice forcing him to listen till she spoke again. It was not long before he perceived that this added lustre was simply success; she was young and tender still, but the sound of a great applauding audience had been in her ears; it formed an element in which she felt buoyant and floated. Still, however, her glance was as pure as it was direct, and that fantastic fairness hung about her which had made an impression on him of old, and which reminded him of unworldly places — he didn't know where — convent-cloisters or vales of Arcady. At that other time she had been parti-coloured and bedizened, and she had always an air of costume, only now her costume was richer and more chastened. It was her line, her condition, part of her expression. If at Miss Birdseye's, and afterwards in Charles Street, she might have been a rope-dancer, to-day she made a "scene" of the mean little room in Monadnoc Place, such a scene as a prima donna makes of daubed canvas and dusty boards. She addressed Basil Ransom as if she had seen him the other week and his merits were fresh to her, though she let him, while she sat smiling at him, explain in his own rather ceremonious way why it was he had presumed to call upon her on so slight an acquaintance — on an invitation which she herself had had more than time to forget. His explanation, as a finished and satisfactory thing, quite broke down; there was no more impressive reason than that he had simply wished to see her. He became aware that this motive loomed large, and that her listening smile, innocent as it was, in the Arcadian manner, of mockery, seemed to accuse him of not having the courage of his inclination. He had alluded especially to their meeting at Miss Chancellor's; there it was that she had told him she should be glad to see him in her home.

"Oh yes, I remember perfectly, and I remember quite as well seeing you at Miss Birdseye's the night before. I made the speech — don't you remember? That was delightful."

"It was delightful indeed," said Basil Ransom.

"I don't mean my speech; I mean the whole thing. It was then I made Miss Chancellor's acquaintance. I don't know whether you know how we work together. She has done so much for me."

"Do you still make speeches?" Ransom asked, conscious, as soon as he had uttered it, that the question was below the mark.

"Still? Why, I should hope so; it's all I'm good for! It's my life — or it's going to be. And it's Miss Chancellor's too. We are determined to do something."

"And does she make speeches too?"

"Well, she makes mine — or the best part of them. She tells me what to say — the real things, the strong things. It's Miss Chancellor as much as me!" said the singular girl, with a generous complacency which was yet half ludicrous.

"I should like to hear you again," Basil Ransom rejoined.

"Well, you must come some night. You will have plenty of chances. We are going on from triumph to triumph."

Her brightness, her self-possession, her air of being a public character, her mixture of the girlish and the comprehensive, startled and confounded her visitor, who felt that if he had come to gratify his curiosity he should be in danger of going away still more curious than satiated. She added in her gay, friendly, trustful tone — the tone of facile intercourse, the tone in which happy, flower-crowned maidens may have talked to sunburnt young men in the golden age — "I am very familiar with your name; Miss Chancellor has told me all about you."

"All about me?" Ransom raised his black eyebrows. "How could she do that? She doesn't know anything about me!"

"Well, she told me you are a great enemy to our movement. Isn't that true? I think you expressed some unfavourable idea that day I met you at her house."

"If you regard me as an enemy, it's very kind of you to receive me."

"Oh, a great many gentlemen call," Verena said, calmly and brightly. "Some call simply to inquire. Some call because they have heard of me, or been present on some occasion when I have moved them. Every one is so interested."

"And you have been in Europe," Ransom remarked, in a moment.

"Oh yes, we went over to see if they were in advance. We had a magnificent time — we saw all the leaders."

"The leaders?" Ransom repeated.

"Of the emancipation of our sex. There are gentlemen there, as well as ladies. Olive had splendid introductions in all countries, and we conversed with all the earnest people. We heard much that was suggestive. And as for Europe!" — and the young lady paused, smiling at him and ending in a happy sigh, as if there were more to say on the subject than she could attempt on such short notice.

"I suppose it's very attractive," said Ransom, encouragingly.

"It's just a dream!"

"And did you find that they were in advance?"

"Well, Miss Chancellor thought they were. She was surprised at some things we observed, and concluded that perhaps she hadn't done the Europeans justice — she has got such an open mind, it's as wide as the sea! — while I incline to the opinion that on the whole *we* make the better show. The state of the movement there reflects their general culture, and their general culture is higher than ours (I mean taking the term in its broadest sense). On the other hand, the *special* condition — moral, social, personal — of our sex seems to me to be superior in this country; I mean regarded in relation — in proportion as it were — to the social phase at large. I must add that we did see some noble specimens over there. In England we met some lovely women, highly cultivated, and of immense organising power. In France we saw some wonderful, contagious types; we passed a delightful evening with the celebrated Marie Verneuil; she was released from prison, you know, only a few weeks before. Our total impression was that it is only a question of time — the future is ours. But everywhere we heard one cry — 'How long, O Lord, how long?'"

Basil Ransom listened to this considerable statement with a feeling which, as the current of Miss Tarrant's facile utterance flowed on, took the form of an hilarity charmed into stillness by the fear of losing something. There was indeed a sweet comicality in seeing this pretty girl sit there and, in answer to a casual, civil inquiry, drop into oratory as a natural thing. Had she forgotten where she was, and did she take him for a full house? She had the same turns and cadences, almost the same gestures, as if she had been on the platform; and the great queerness of it was that, with such a manner, she should escape being odious. She was not odious, she was delightful; she was not dogmatic, she was genial. No wonder she was a success, if she speechified as a bird sings! Ransom could see, too, from her easy lapse, how the lecture-tone was the thing in the world with which, by education, by association, she was most familiar. He didn't know what to make of her; she was an astounding young phenomenon. The other time came back to him afresh, and how she had stood up at Miss Birdseye's; it occurred to him that an element, here, had been wanting. Several moments after she had ceased speaking he became conscious that the expression of his face presented a perceptible analogy to a broad grin. He changed his posture, saying the first thing that came into his head. "I presume you do without your father now."

"Without my father?"

"To set you going, as he did that time I heard you."

"Oh, I see; you thought I had begun a lecture!" And she laughed, in perfect good humour. "They tell me I speak as I talk, so I suppose I talk as I speak. But you mustn't put me on what I saw and heard in Europe. That's to be the title of an address I am now preparing, by the way. Yes, I don't depend on father any more," she went on, while Ransom's sense of having said too sarcastic a thing was deepened by her perfect indifference to it. "He finds his patients draw off about enough, any way. But I owe him everything; if it hadn't been for him, no one would ever have known I had a gift — not even myself. He started me so, once for all, that I now go alone."

"You go beautifully," said Ransom, wanting to say something agreeable, and even respectfully tender, to her, but troubled by the fact that there was nothing he could say that didn't sound rather like chaff. There was no resentment in her, however, for in a moment she said to him, as quickly as it occurred to her, in the manner of a person repairing an accidental omission, "It was very good of you to come so far."

This was a sort of speech it was never safe to make to Ransom; there was no telling what retribution it might entail. "Do you suppose any journey is too great, too wearisome, when it's a question of so great a pleasure?" On this occasion it was not worse than that.

"Well, people *have* come from other cities," Verena answered, not with pretended humility, but with pretended pride. "Do you know Cambridge?"

"This is the first time I have ever been here."

"Well, I suppose you have heard of the university; it's so celebrated."

"Yes — even in Mississippi. I suppose it's very fine."

"I presume it is," said Verena; "but you can't expect me to speak with much admiration of an institution of which the doors are closed to our sex."

"Do you then advocate a system of education in common?"

"I advocate equal rights, equal opportunities, equal privileges. So does Miss Chancellor," Verena added, with just a perceptible air of feeling that her declaration needed support.

"Oh, I thought what she wanted was simply a different inequality — simply to turn out the men altogether," Ransom said.

"Well, she thinks we have great arrears to make up. I do tell her, sometimes, that what she desires is not only justice but vengeance. I think she admits that," Verena continued, with a certain solemnity. The subject, however, held her but an instant, and before Ransom had time to make any comment, she went on, in a different tone: "You don't mean to say you live in Mississippi *now?* Miss Chancellor told me when you were in Boston before, that you had located in New York." She persevered in this reference to himself, for when he had assented to her remark about New York, she asked him whether he had quite given up the South.

"Given it up — the poor, dear, desolate, old South? Heaven forbid!" Basil Ransom exclaimed.

She looked at him for a moment with an added softness. "I presume it is natural you should love your home. But I am afraid you think I don't love mine much; I have been here — for so long — so little. Miss Chancellor *has* absorbed me — there is no doubt about that. But it's a pity I wasn't with her to-day." Ransom made no answer to this; he was incapable of telling Miss Tarrant that if she had been he would not have called upon her. It was not, indeed, that he was incapable of

hypocrisy, for when she had asked him if he had seen his cousin the night before, and he had replied that he hadn't seen her at all, and she had exclaimed with a candour which the next minute made her blush, "Ah, you don't mean to say you haven't forgiven her!" — after this he put on a look of innocence sufficient to carry off the inquiry, "Forgiven her for what?"

Verena coloured at the sound of her own words. "Well, I could see how much she felt, that time at her house."

"What did she feel?" Basil Ransom asked, with the natural provokingness of a man.

I know not whether Verena was provoked, but she answered with more spirit than sequence: "Well, you know you *did* pour contempt on us, ever so much; I could see how it worked Olive up. Are you not going to see her at all?"

"Well, I shall think about that; I am here only for three or four days," said Ransom, smiling as men smile when they are perfectly unsatisfactory.

It is very possible that Verena was provoked, inaccessible as she was, in a general way, to irritation; for she rejoined in a moment, with a little deliberate air: "Well, perhaps it's as well you shouldn't go, if you haven't changed at all."

"I haven't changed at all," said the young man, smiling still, with his elbows on the arms of his chair, his shoulders pushed up a little, and his thin brown hands interlocked in front of him.

"Well, I have had visitors who were quite opposed!" Verena announced, as if such news could not possibly alarm her. Then she added, "How then did you know I was out here?"

"Miss Birdseye told me."

"Oh, I am so glad you went to see *her!*" the girl cried, speaking again with the impetuosity of a moment before.

"I didn't go to see her. I met her in the street, just as she was leaving Miss Chancellor's door. I spoke to her, and accompanied her some distance. I passed that way because I knew it was the direct way to Cambridge — from the Common — and I was coming out to see you any way — on the chance."

"On the chance?" Verena repeated.

"Yes; Mrs. Luna, in New York, told me you were sometimes here, and I wanted, at any rate, to make the attempt to find you."

It may be communicated to the reader that it was very agreeable to Verena to learn that her visitor had made this arduous pilgrimage (for she knew well enough how people in Boston regarded a winter journey to the academic suburb) with only half the prospect of a reward; but her pleasure was mixed with other feelings, or at least with the consciousness that the whole situation was rather less simple than the elements of her life had been hitherto. There was the germ of disorder in this invidious distinction which Mr. Ransom had suddenly made between Ol-

ive Chancellor, who was related to him by blood, and herself, who had never been related to him in any way whatever. She knew Olive by this time well enough to wish not to reveal it to her, and yet it would be something quite new for her to undertake to conceal such an incident as her having spent an hour with Mr. Ransom during a flying visit he had made to Boston. She had spent hours with other gentlemen, whom Olive didn't see; but that was different, because her friend knew about her doing it and didn't care, in regard to the persons — didn't care, that is, as she would care in this case. It was vivid to Verena's mind that now Olive *would* care. She had talked about Mr. Burrage, and Mr. Pardon, and even about some gentlemen in Europe, and she had not (after the first few days, a year and a half before) talked about Mr. Ransom.

Nevertheless there were reasons, clear to Verena's view, for wishing either that he would go and see Olive or would keep away from *her;* and the responsibility of treating the fact that he had not so kept away as a secret seemed the greater, perhaps, in the light of this other fact, that so far as simply seeing Mr. Ransom went — why, she quite liked it. She had remembered him perfectly after their two former meetings, superficial as their contact then had been; she had thought of him at moments and wondered whether she should like him if she were to know him better. Now, at the end of twenty minutes, she did know him better, and found that he had rather a curious, but still a pleasant way. There he was, at any rate, and she didn't wish his call to be spoiled by any uncomfortable implication of consequences. So she glanced off, at the touch of Mrs. Luna's name; it seemed to afford relief. "Oh, yes, Mrs. Luna — isn't she fascinating?"

Ransom hesitated a little. "Well, no, I don't think she is."

"You ought to like her — she hates our movement!" And Verena asked, further, numerous questions about the brilliant Adeline; whether he saw her often, whether she went out much, whether she was admired in New York, whether he thought her very handsome. He answered to the best of his ability, but soon made the reflection that he had not come out to Monadnoc Place to talk about Mrs. Luna; in consequence of which, to change the subject (as well as to acquit himself of a social duty), he began to speak of Verena's parents, to express regret that Mrs. Tarrant had been sick, and fear that he was not to have the pleasure of seeing her. "She is a great deal better," Verena said; "but she's lying down; she lies down a great deal when she has got nothing else to do. Mother's very peculiar," she added in a moment; "she lies down when she feels well and happy, and when she's sick she walks about — she roams all round the house. If you hear her on the stairs a good deal, you can be pretty sure she's very

bad. She'll be very much interested to hear about you after you have left."

Ransom glanced at his watch. "I hope I am not staying too long — that I am not taking you away from her."

"Oh no; she likes visitors, even when she can't see them. If it didn't take her so long to rise, she would have been down here by this time. I suppose you think she has missed me, since I have been so absorbed. Well, so she has, but she knows it's for my good. She would make any sacrifice for affection."

The fancy suddenly struck Ransom of asking, in response to this, "And you? would you make any?"

Verena gave him a bright natural stare. "Any sacrifice for affection?" She thought a moment, and then she said: "I don't think I have a right to say, because I have never been asked. I don't remember ever to have had to make a sacrifice — not an important one."

"Lord! you must have had a happy life!"

"I have been very fortunate, I know that. I don't know what to do when I think how some women — how most women — suffer. But I must not speak of that," she went on, with her smile coming back to her. "If you oppose our movement, you won't want to hear of the suffering of women!"

"The suffering of women is the suffering of all humanity," Ransom returned. "Do you think any movement is going to stop that — or all the lectures from now to doomsday? We are born to suffer — and to bear it, like decent people."

"Oh, I adore heroism!" Verena interposed.

"And as for women," Ransom went on, "they have one source of happiness that is closed to us — the consciousness that their presence here below lifts half the load of *our* suffering."

Verena thought this very graceful, but she was not sure it was not rather sophistical; she would have liked to have Olive's judgment upon it. As that was not possible for the present, she abandoned the question (since learning that Mr. Ransom had passed over Olive, to come to her, she had become rather fidgety), and inquired of the young man, irrelevantly, whether he knew any one else in Cambridge.

"Not a creature; as I tell you, I have never been here before. Your image alone attracted me; this charming interview will be henceforth my only association with the place."

"It's a pity you couldn't have a few more," said Verena, musingly.

"A few more interviews? I should be unspeakably delighted!"

"A few more associations. Did you see the colleges as you came?"

"I had a glimpse of a large enclosure, with some big buildings. Perhaps I can look at them better as I go back to Boston."

"Oh yes, you ought to see them — they have improved so much of late. The inner life, of course, is the greatest interest, but there is some fine architecture, if you are not familiar with Europe." She paused a moment, looking at him with an eye that seemed to brighten, and continued quickly, like a person who had collected herself for a little jump, "If you would like to walk round a little, I shall be very glad to show you."

"To walk round — with you to show me?" Ransom repeated. "My dear Miss Tarrant, it would be the greatest privilege — the greatest happiness — of my life. What a delightful idea — what an ideal guide!"

Verena got up; she would go and put on her hat; he must wait a little. Her offer had a frankness and a friendliness which gave him a new sensation, and he could not know that as soon as she had made it (though she had hesitated too, with a moment of intense reflection), she seemed to herself strangely reckless. An impulse pushed her; she obeyed it with her eyes open. She felt as a girl feels when she commits her first conscious indiscretion. She had done many things before which many people would have called indiscreet, but that quality had not even faintly belonged to them in her own mind; she had done them in perfect good faith and with a remarkable absence of palpitation. This superficially ingenuous proposal to walk around the colleges with Mr. Ransom had really another colour; it deepened the ambiguity of her position, by reason of a prevision which I shall presently mention. If Olive was not to know that she had seen him, this extension of their interview would double her secret. And yet, while she saw it grow — this monstrous little mystery — she couldn't feel sorry that she was going out with Olive's cousin. As I have already said, she had become nervous. She went to put on her hat, but at the door of the room she stopped, turned round, and presented herself to her visitor with a small spot in either cheek, which had appeared there within the instant. "I have suggested this, because it seems to me I ought to do something for you — in return," she said. "It's nothing, simply sitting there with me. And we haven't got anything else. This is our only hospitality. And the day seems so splendid."

The modesty, the sweetness, of this little explanation, with a kind of intimated desire, constituting almost an appeal, for rightness, which seemed to pervade it, left a fragrance in the air after she had vanished. Ransom walked up and down the room, with his hands in his pockets, under the influence of it, without taking up even once the book about Mrs. Foat. He occupied the time in asking himself by what perversity of fate or of inclination such a charming creature was ranting upon platforms and living in Olive Chancellor's pocket, or how a ranter and sycophant could possibly be so engaging. And she was so disturbingly beautiful, too. This last fact was not less evident when she came

down arranged for their walk. They left the house, and as they proceeded he remembered that he had asked himself earlier how he could do honour to such a combination of leisure and ethereal mildness as he had waked up to that morning — a mildness that seemed the very breath of his own latitude. This question was answered now; to do exactly what he was doing at that moment was an observance sufficiently festive.

Chapter XXV

THEY passed through two or three small, short streets, which, with their little wooden houses, with still more wooden door-yards, looked as if they had been constructed by the nearest carpenter and his boy — a sightless, soundless, interspaced, embryonic region — and entered a long avenue which, fringed on either side with fresh villas, offering themselves trustfully to the public, had the distinction of a wide pavement of neat red brick. The new paint on the square detached houses shone afar off in the transparent air: they had, on top, little cupolas and belvederes, in front a pillared piazza, made bare by the indoor life of winter, on either side a bow-window or two, and everywhere an embellishment of scallops, brackets, cornices, wooden flourishes. They stood, for the most part, on small eminences, lifted above the impertinence of hedge or paling, well up before the world, with all the good conscience which in many cases came, as Ransom saw (and he had noticed the same ornament when he traversed with Olive the quarter of Boston inhabited by Miss Birdseye), from a silvered number, affixed to the glass above the door, in figures huge enough to be read by the people who, in the periodic horse-cars, travelled along the middle of the avenue. It was to these glittering badges that many of the houses on either side owed their principal identity. One of the horse-cars now advanced in the straight, spacious distance; it was almost the only object that animated the prospect, which, in its large cleanness, its implication of strict business-habits on the part of all the people who were not there, Ransom thought very impressive. As he went on with Verena he asked her about the Women's Convention, the year before; whether it had accomplished much work and she had enjoyed it.

"What do you care about the work it accomplished?" said the girl. "You don't take any interest in that."

"You mistake my attitude. I don't like it, but I greatly fear it."

In answer to this Verena gave a free laugh. "I don't believe you fear much!"

"The bravest men have been afraid of women. Won't you even tell me whether you enjoyed it? I am told you made an immense sensation there — that you leaped into fame."

Verena never waved off an allusion to her ability, her eloquence; she took it seriously, without any flutter or protest, and had no more manner about it than if it concerned the goddess Minerva. "I believe I attracted considerable attention; of course, that's what Olive wants — it paves the way for future work. I have no doubt I reached many that wouldn't have been reached otherwise. They think that's my great use — to take hold of the outsiders, as it were; of those who are prejudiced or thoughtless, or who don't care about anything unless it's amusing. I wake up the attention."

"That's the class to which I belong," Ransom said. "Am I not an outsider? I wonder whether you would have reached me — or waked up my attention!"

Verena was silent awhile, as they walked; he heard the light click of her boots on the smooth bricks. Then — "I think I *have* waked it up a little," she replied, looking straight before her.

"Most assuredly! You have made me wish tremendously to contradict you."

"Well, that's a good sign."

"I suppose it was very exciting — your convention," Ransom went on, in a moment; "the sort of thing you would miss very much if you were to return to the ancient fold."

"The ancient fold, you say very well, where women were slaughtered like sheep! Oh, last June, for a week, we just quivered! There were delegates from every State and every city; we lived in a crowd of people and of ideas; the heat was intense, the weather magnificent, and great thoughts and brilliant sayings flew round like darting fire-flies. Olive had six celebrated, high-minded women staying in her house — two in a room; and in the summer evenings we sat in the open windows, in her parlour, looking out on the bay, with the lights gleaming in the water, and talked over the doings of the morning, the speeches, the incidents, the fresh contributions to the cause. We had some tremendously earnest discussions, which it would have been a benefit to you to hear, or any man who doesn't think that we can rise to the highest point. Then we had some refreshment — we consumed quantities of ice-cream!" said Verena, in whom the note of gaiety alternated with that of earnestness, almost of exaltation, in a manner which seemed to Basil Ransom absolutely and fascinatingly original. "Those were great nights!" she added, between a laugh and a sigh.

Her description of the convention put the scene before him vividly; he seemed to see the crowded, overheated hall, which he was sure was filled with carpet-baggers, to hear flushed women, with loosened bonnet-strings, forcing thin voices into ineffectual shrillness. It made him angry, and all the more angry, that he hadn't a

reason, to think of the charming creature at his side being mixed up with such elements, pushed and elbowed by them, conjoined with them in emulation, in unsightly strainings and clappings and shoutings, in wordy, windy iteration of inanities. Worst of all was the idea that she should have expressed such a congregation to itself so acceptably, have been acclaimed and applauded by hoarse throats, have been lifted up, to all the vulgar multitude, as the queen of the occasion. He made the reflection, afterwards, that he was singularly ill-grounded in his wrath, inasmuch as it was none of his business what use Miss Tarrant chose to make of her energies, and, in addition to this, nothing else was to have been expected of her. But that reflection was absent now, and in its absence he saw only the fact that his companion had been odiously perverted. "Well, Miss Tarrant," he said, with a deeper seriousness than showed in his voice, "I am forced to the painful conclusion that you are simply ruined."

"Ruined! Ruined yourself!"

"Oh, I know the kind of women that Miss Chancellor had at her house, and what a group you must have made when you looked out at the Back Bay! It depresses me very much to think of it."

"We made a lovely, interesting group, and, if we had had a spare minute we would have been photographed," Verena said.

This led him to ask her if she had ever subjected herself to the

593

process; and she answered that a photographer had been after her as soon as she got back from Europe, and that she had sat for him, and that there were certain shops in Boston where her portrait could be obtained. She gave him this information very simply, without pretence of vagueness of knowledge, spoke of the matter rather respectfully, indeed, as if it might be of some importance; and when he said that he should go and buy one of the little pictures as soon as he returned to town, contented herself with replying, "Well, be sure you pick out a good one!" He had not been altogether without a hope that she would offer to give him one, with her name written beneath, which was a mode of acquisition he would greatly have preferred; but this, evidently, had not occurred to her, and now, as they went further, her thought was following a different train. That was proved by her remarking, at the end of a silence, inconsequently, "Well, it showed I have a great use!" As he stared, wondering what she meant, she explained that she referred to the brilliancy of her success at the convention. "It proved I have a great use," she repeated, "and that is all I care for!"

"The use of a truly amiable woman is to make some honest man happy," Ransom said, with a sententiousness of which he was perfectly aware.

It was so marked that it caused her to stop short in the middle of the broad walk, while she looked at him with shining eyes. "See here, Mr. Ransom, do you know what strikes me?" she exclaimed. "The interest you take in me isn't really controversial — a bit. It's quite personal!" She was the most extraordinary girl; she could speak such words as those without the smallest look of added consciousness coming into her face, without the least supposable intention of coquetry, or any visible purpose of challenging the young man to say more.

"My interest in you — my interest in you," he began. Then hesitating, he broke off suddenly. "It is certain your discovery doesn't make it any less!"

"Well, that's better," she went on; "for we needn't dispute."

He laughed at the way she arranged it, and they presently reached the irregular group of heterogeneous buildings — chapels, dormitories, libraries, halls — which, scattered among slender trees, over a space reserved by means of a low rustic fence, rather than inclosed (for Harvard knows nothing either of the jealousy or the dignity of high walls and guarded gateways), constitutes the great university of Massachusetts. The yard, or college-precinct, is traversed by a number of straight little paths, over which, at certain hours of the day, a thousand undergraduates, with books under their arm and youth in their step, flit from one school to another. Verena Tarrant knew her way round, as she said to her companion; it was not the first time she had taken an admiring visitor to see the local monuments. Basil Ransom, walking with her from point to point, admired them all, and thought several of them exceedingly quaint and venerable. The rectangular structures of old red brick especially gratified his eye; the afternoon sun was yellow on their homely faces; their windows showed a peep of flower-pots and bright-coloured curtains; they wore an expression of scholastic quietude, and exhaled for the young Mississippian a tradition, an antiquity. "This is the place where I ought to have been," he said to his charming guide. "I should have had a good time if I had been able to study here."

"Yes; I presume you feel yourself drawn to any place where ancient prejudices are garnered up," she answered, not without archness. "I know by the stand you take about our cause that you share the superstitions of the old bookmen. You ought to have been at one of those really mediæval universities that we saw on the other side, at Oxford, or Göttingen, or Padua. You would have been in perfect sympathy with their spirit."

"Well, I don't know much about those old haunts," Ransom rejoined. "I reckon this is good enough for me. And then it would have had the advantage that your residence isn't far, you know."

"Oh, I guess we shouldn't have seen you much at my residence! As you live in New York, you come, but here you wouldn't; that is always the way." With this light philosophy Verena beguiled the transit to the library, into which she introduced her companion with the air of a person familiar with the sanctified spot. This edifice, a diminished copy of the chapel of King's College, at the greater Cambridge, is a rich and impressive institution; and as he stood there, in the bright, heated stillness, which seemed suffused with the odour of old print and old bindings, and looked up into the high, light vaults that hung over quiet book-laden galleries, alcoves and tables, and glazed cases where rarer treasures gleamed more vaguely, over busts of benefactors and portraits of worthies, bowed heads of working students and the gentle creak of passing messengers — as he took possession, in a comprehensive glance, of the wealth and wisdom of the place, he felt more than ever the soreness of an opportunity missed; but he abstained from expressing it (it was too deep for that), and in a moment Verena had introduced him to a young lady, a friend of hers, who, as she explained, was working on the catalogue, and whom she had asked for on entering the library, at a desk where another young lady was occupied. Miss Catching, the first-mentioned young lady, presented herself with promptness, offered Verena a low-toned but appreciative greeting, and, after a little, undertook to explain to Ransom the mysteries of the catalogue, which consisted of a myriad little cards, disposed

595

alphabetically in immense chests of drawers. Ransom was deeply interested, and as, with Verena, he followed Miss Catching about (she was so good as to show them the establishment in all its ramifications), he considered with attention the young lady's fair ringlets and refined, anxious expression, saying to himself that this was in the highest degree a New England type. Verena found an opportunity to mention to him that she was wrapped up in the cause, and there was a moment during which he was afraid that his companion would expose him to her as one of its traducers; but there was that in Miss Catching's manner (and in the influence of the lofty halls), which deprecated loud pleasantry, and seemed to say, moreover, that if she were treated to such a revelation she should not know under what letter to range it.

"Now there is one place where perhaps it would be indelicate to take a Mississippian," Verena said, after this episode. "I mean the great place that towers above the others — that big building with the beautiful pinnacles, which you see from every point." But Basil Ransom had heard of the great Memorial Hall; he knew what memories it enshrined, and the worst that he should have to suffer there; and the ornate, overtopping structure, which was the finest piece of architecture he had ever seen, had moreover solicited his enlarged curiosity for the last half-hour. He thought there was rather too much brick about it, but it was buttressed, cloistered, turreted, dedicated, superscribed, as he had never seen anything; though it didn't look old, it looked significant; it covered a large area, and it sprang majestic into the winter air. It was detached from the rest of the collegiate group, and stood in a grassy triangle of its own. As he approached it with Verena she suddenly stopped, to decline responsibility. "Now mind, if you don't like what's inside, it isn't my fault."

He looked at her an instant, smiling. "Is there anything against Mississippi?"

"Well, no, I don't think she is mentioned. But there is great praise of our young men in the war."

"It says they were brave, I suppose."

"Yes, it says so in Latin."

"Well, so they were — I know something about that," Basil Ransom said. "I must be brave enough to face them — it isn't the first time." And they went up the low steps and passed into the tall doors. The Memorial Hall of Harvard consists of three main divisions: one of them a theatre, for academic ceremonies; another a vast refectory, covered with a timbered roof, hung about with portraits and lighted by stained windows, like the halls of the colleges of Oxford; and the third, the most interesting, a chamber high, dim, and severe, consecrated to the sons of the university who fell in the long Civil War. Ransom and his companion wandered from one part of the building to another, and stayed their steps at several impressive points; but they lingered longest in the presence of the white, ranged tablets, each of which, in its proud, sad clearness, is inscribed with the name of a student-soldier. The effect of the place is singularly noble and solemn, and it is impossible to feel it without a lifting of the heart. It stands there for duty and honour, it speaks of sacrifice and example, seems a kind of temple to youth, manhood, generosity. Most of them were young, all were in their prime, and all of them had fallen; this simple idea hovers before the visitor and makes him read with tenderness each name and place — names often without other history, and forgotten Southern battles. For Ransom these things were not a challenge nor a taunt; they touched him with respect, with the sentiment of beauty. He was capable of being a generous foeman, and he forgot, now, the whole question of sides and parties; the simple emotion of the old fighting-time came back to him, and the monument around him seemed an embodiment of that memory; it arched over friends as well as enemies, the victims of defeat as well as the sons of triumph.

"It is very beautiful — but I think it is very dreadful!" This remark, from Verena, called him back to the present. "It's a real sin to put up such a building, just to glorify a lot of bloodshed. If it wasn't so majestic, I would have it pulled down."

"That is delightful feminine logic!" Ransom answered. "If, when women have the conduct of affairs, they fight as well as they reason, surely for them too we shall have to set up memorials."

Verena retorted that they would reason so well they would have no need to fight — they would usher in the reign of peace. "But this is very peaceful too," she added, looking about her; and she sat down on a low stone ledge, as if to enjoy the influence of the scene. Ransom left her alone for ten minutes; he wished to take another look at the inscribed tablets, and read again the names of the various engagements, at several of which he had been present. When he came back to her she greeted him abruptly, with a question which had no reference to the solemnity of the spot. "If Miss Birdseye knew you were coming out to see me, can't *she* easily tell Olive? Then won't Olive make her reflections about your neglect of herself?"

"I don't care for her reflections. At any rate, I asked Miss Birdseye, as a favour, not to mention to her that she had met me," Ransom added.

Verena was silent a moment. "Your logic is almost as good as a woman's. Do change your mind and go to see her now," she went on. "She will probably be at home by the time you get to Charles Street. If she was a little strange, a little stiff with you before (I know just how she must have been), all that will be different to-day."

"Why will it be different?"

"Oh, she will be easier, more genial, much softer."

"I don't believe it," said Ransom; and his scepticism seemed none the less complete because it was light and smiling.

"She is much happier now — she can afford not to mind you."

"Not to mind me? That's a nice inducement for a gentleman to go and see a lady!"

"Well, she will be more gracious, because she feels now that she is more successful."

"You mean because she has brought you out? Oh, I have no doubt that has cleared the air for her immensely, and you have improved her very much. But I have got a charming impression out here, and I have no wish to put another — which won't be charming, anyhow you arrange it — on top of it."

"Well, she will be sure to know you have been round here, at any rate," Verena rejoined.

"How will she know, unless you tell her?"

"I tell her everything," said the girl; and now as soon as she had spoken, she blushed. He stood before her, tracing a figure on the mosaic pavement with his cane, conscious that in a moment they had become more intimate. They were discussing their affairs, which had nothing to do with the heroic symbols that surrounded them; but their affairs had suddenly grown so serious that there was no want of decency in their lingering there for the purpose. The implication that his visit might remain as a secret between them made them both feel it differently. To ask her to keep it so would have been, as it seemed to Ransom, a liberty, and, moreover, he didn't care so much as that; but if she were to prefer to do so such a preference would only make him consider the more that his expedition had been a success.

"Oh, then, you can tell her this!" he said in a moment.

"If I shouldn't, it would be the first —— " And Verena checked herself.

"You must arrange that with your conscience," Ransom went on, laughing.

They came out of the hall, passed down the steps, and emerged from the Delta, as that portion of the college precinct is called. The afternoon had begun to wane, but the air was filled with a pink brightness, and there was a cool, pure smell, a vague breath of spring.

"Well, if I don't tell Olive, then you must leave me here," said Verena, stopping in the path and putting out a hand of farewell.

"I don't understand. What has that to do with it? Besides I thought you said you *must* tell," Ransom added. In playing with the subject this way, in enjoying her visible hesitation, he was slightly conscious of a man's brutality — of being pushed by an impulse to test her good-nature, which seemed to have no limit. It showed no sign of perturbation as she answered:

"Well, I want to be free — to do as I think best. And, if there is a chance of my keeping it back, there mustn't be anything more — there must not, Mr. Ransom, really."

"Anything more? Why, what are you afraid there will be — if I should simply walk home with you?"

"I must go alone, I must hurry back to mother," she said, for all reply. And she again put out her hand, which he had not taken before.

Of course he took it now, and even held it a moment; he didn't like being dismissed, and was thinking of pretexts to linger. "Miss Birdseye said you would convert me, but you haven't yet," it came into his head to say.

"You can't tell yet; wait a little. My influence is peculiar; it sometimes comes out a long time afterwards!" This speech, on Verena's part, was evidently perfunctory, and the grandeur of her self-reference jocular; she was much more serious when she went on quickly, "Do you mean to say Miss Birdseye promised you that?"

"Oh yes. Talk about influence! you should have seen the influence I obtained over her."

"Well, what good will it do, if I'm going to tell Olive about your visit?"

"Well, you see, I think she hopes you won't. She believes you are going to convert me privately — so that I shall blaze forth, suddenly, out of the darkness of Mississippi, as a first-class proselyte: very effective and dramatic."

Verena struck Basil Ransom as constantly simple, but there were moments when her candour seemed to him preternatural. "If I thought that would be the effect, I might make an exception," she remarked, speaking as if such a result were, after all, possible.

"Oh, Miss Tarrant, you will convert me enough, any way," said the young man.

"Enough? What do you mean by enough?"

"Enough to make me terribly unhappy."

She looked at him a moment, evidently not understanding; but she tossed him a retort at a venture, turned away, and took her course homeward. The retort was that if he should be unhappy it would serve him right — a form of words that committed her to nothing. As he returned to Boston he saw how curious he should be to learn whether she had betrayed him, as it were, to Miss Chancellor. He might learn through Mrs. Luna; that would almost reconcile him to going to see her again. Olive would mention it in writing to her sister, and Adeline would repeat the complaint. Perhaps she herself would even make him a scene about it; that would be, for him, part of the unhappiness he had foretold to Verena Tarrant.

Chapter XXVI

"MRS. HENRY BURRAGE, at home Wednesday evening, March 26th, at half-past nine o'clock." It was in consequence of having received a card with these words inscribed upon it that Basil Ransom presented himself, on the evening she had designated, at the house of a lady he had never heard of before. The account of the relation of effect to cause is not complete, however, unless I mention that the card bore, furthermore, in the left-hand lower corner, the words: "An Address from Miss Verena Tarrant." He had an idea (it came mainly from the look and even the odour of the engraved pasteboard), that Mrs. Burrage was a member of the fashionable world, and it was with considerable surprise that he found himself in such an element. He wondered what had induced a denizen of that fine air to send him an invitation; then he said to himself that, obviously, Verena Tarrant had simply requested that this should be done. Mrs. Henry Burrage, whoever she might be, had asked her if she shouldn't like some of her own friends to be present, and she had said, Oh yes, and mentioned him in the happy group. She had been able to give Mrs. Burrage his address, for had it not been contained in the short letter he despatched to Monadnoc Place soon after his return from Boston, in which he thanked Miss Tarrant afresh for the charming hour she had enabled him to spend at Cambridge? She had not answered his letter at the time, but Mrs. Burrage's card was a very good answer. Such a missive deserved a rejoinder, and it was by way of rejoinder that he entered the street-car which, on the evening of March 26th, was to deposit him at a corner adjacent to Mrs. Burrage's dwelling. He almost never went to evening parties (he knew scarcely any one who gave them, though Mrs. Luna had broken him in a little), and he was sure this occasion was of festive intention, would have nothing in common with the nocturnal "exercises" at Miss Birdseye's; but he would have exposed himself to almost any social discomfort in order to see Verena Tarrant on the platform. The platform it evidently was to be — private if not public — since one was admitted by a ticket given away if not sold. He took his in his pocket, quite ready to present it at the door. It would take some time for me to explain the contradiction to the reader; but Basil Ransom's desire to be present at one of Verena's regular performances was not diminished by the fact that he detested her views and thought the whole business a poor perversity. He understood her now very well (since his visit to Cambridge); he saw she was honest and natural; she had queer, bad lecture-blood in her veins, and a comically false idea

600

of the aptitude of little girls for conducting movements; but her enthusiasm was of the purest, her illusions had a fragrance, and so far as the mania for producing herself personally was concerned, it had been distilled into her by people who worked her for ends which to Basil Ransom could only appear insane. She was a touching, ingenuous victim, unconscious of the pernicious forces which were hurrying her to her ruin. With this idea of ruin there had already associated itself in the young man's mind, the idea — a good deal more dim and incomplete — of rescue; and it was the disposition to confirm himself in the view that her charm was her own, and her fallacies, her absurdity, a mere reflection of unlucky circumstance, that led him to make an effort to behold her in the position in which he could least bear to think of her. Such a glimpse was all that was wanted to prove to him that she was a person for whom he might open an unlimited credit of tender compassion. He expected to suffer — to suffer deliciously.

By the time he had crossed Mrs. Burrage's threshold there was no doubt whatever in his mind that he was in the fashionable world. It was embodied strikingly in the stout, elderly, ugly lady, dressed in a brilliant colour, with a twinkle of jewels and a bosom much uncovered, who stood near the door of the first room, and with whom the people passing in before him were shaking hands. Ransom made her a Mississippian

bow, and she said she was delighted to see him, while people behind him pressed him forward. He yielded to the impulsion, and found himself in a great saloon, amid lights and flowers, where the company was dense, and there were more twinkling, smiling ladies, with uncovered bosoms. It was certainly the fashionable world, for there was no one there whom he had ever seen before. The walls of the room were covered with pictures — the very ceiling was painted and framed. The people pushed each other a little, edged about, advanced and retreated, looking at each other with differing faces — sometimes blandly, unperceivingly, sometimes with a harshness of contemplation, a kind of cruelty, Ransom thought; sometimes with sudden nods and grimaces, inarticulate murmurs, followed by a quick reaction, a sort of gloom. He was now absolutely certain that he was in the best society. He was carried further and further forward, and saw that another room stretched beyond the one he had entered, in which there was a sort of little stage, covered with a red cloth, and an immense collection of chairs, arranged in rows. He became aware that people looked at him, as well as at each other, rather more, indeed, than at each other, and he wondered whether it were very visible in his appearance that his being there was a kind of exception. He didn't know how much his head looked over the heads of others, or that his brown complexion, fuliginous eye, and straight black hair, the leonine fall of which I mentioned in the first pages of this narrative, gave him that relief which, in the best society, has the great advantage of suggesting a topic. But there were other topics besides, as was proved by a fragment of conversation, between two ladies, which reached his ear while he stood rather wistfully wondering where Verena Tarrant might be.

"Are you a member?" one of the ladies said to the other. "I didn't know you had joined."

"Oh, I haven't; nothing would induce me."

"That's not fair; you have all the fun and none of the responsibility."

"Oh, the fun — the fun!" exclaimed the second lady.

"You needn't abuse us, or I will never invite you," said the first.

"Well, I thought it was meant to be improving; that's all I mean; very good for the mind. Now, this woman to-night; isn't she from Boston?"

"Yes, I believe they have brought her on, just for this."

"Well, you must be pretty desperate, when you have got to go to Boston for your entertainment."

"Well, there's a similar society there, and I never heard of their sending to New York."

"Of course not, they think they have got everything. But doesn't it make your life a burden, thinking what you can possibly have?"

"Oh dear, no. I am going to have Professor Gougenheim — all about the Talmud. You must come."

"Well, I'll come," said the second lady; "but nothing would induce me to be a regular member."

Whatever the mystic circle might be, Ransom agreed with the second lady that regular membership must have terrors, and he admired her independence in such an artificial world. A considerable part of the company had now directed itself to the further apartment — people had begun to occupy the chairs, to confront the empty platform. He reached the wide doors, and saw that the place was a spacious music-room, decorated in white and gold, with a polished floor and marble busts of composers, on brackets attached to the delicate panels. He forebore to enter, however, being shy about taking a seat, and seeing that the ladies were arranging themselves first. He turned back into the first room, to wait till the audience had massed itself, conscious that even if he were behind every one he should be able to make a long neck; and here, suddenly, in a corner, his eyes rested upon Olive Chancellor. She was seated a little apart, in an angle of the room, and she was looking straight at him; but as soon as she perceived that he saw her she dropped her eyes, giving no sign of recognition. Ransom hesitated a moment, but the next he went straight over to her. It had been in his mind that if Verena Tarrant was there, *she* would be there; an instinct told him that Miss Chancellor would not allow her dear friend to come to New York without her. It was very possible she meant to "cut" him — especially if she knew of his having cut her, the other week, in Boston; but it was his duty to take for granted she would speak to him, until the contrary should be definitely proved. Though he had seen her only twice he remembered well how acutely shy she was capable of being, and he thought it possible one of these spasms had seized her at the present time.

When he stood before her he found his conjecture perfectly just; she was white with the intensity of her self-consciousness; she was altogether in a very uncomfortable state. She made no response to his offer to shake hands with her, and he saw that she would never go through that ceremony again. She looked up at him when he spoke to her, and her lips moved; but her face was intensely grave and her eye had almost a feverish light. She had evidently got into her corner to be out of the way; he recognised in her the air of an interloper, as he had felt it in himself. The small sofa on which she had placed herself had the form to which the French give the name of *causeuse;* there was room on it for just another person, and Ransom asked her, with a cheerful accent, if he might sit down beside her. She turned towards him when he had done so, turned everything but her eyes, and opened and shut her fan while she waited for her fit of diffidence to pass away. Ransom himself did not wait; he took a jocular tone about their encounter, asking her if she had come to New York to rouse the people. She glanced round the room; the backs of Mrs. Burrage's guests, mainly, were presented to them, and their position was partly masked by a pyramid of flowers which rose from a pedestal close to Olive's end of the sofa and diffused a fragrance in the air.

"Do you call these the 'people'?" she asked.

"I haven't the least idea. I don't know who any of them are, not even who Mrs. Henry Burrage is. I simply received an invitation."

Miss Chancellor gave him no information on the point he had mentioned; she only said, in a moment: "Do you go wherever you are invited?"

"Why, I go if I think I may find you there," the young man replied, gallantly. "My card mentioned that Miss Tarrant would give an address, and I knew that wherever she is you are not far off. I have heard you are inseparable, from Mrs. Luna."

"Yes, we are inseparable. That is exactly why I am here."

"It's the fashionable world, then, you are going to stir up."

Olive remained for some time with her eyes fastened to the floor; then she flashed them up at her interlocutor. "It's a part of our life to go anywhere — to carry our work where it seems most needed. We have taught ourselves to stifle repulsion, distaste."

"Oh, I think this is very amusing," said Ransom. "It's a beautiful house, and there are some very pretty faces. We haven't anything so brilliant in Mississippi."

To everything he said Olive offered at first a momentary silence, but the worst of her shyness was apparently leaving her.

"Are you successful in New York? do you like it?" she presently asked, uttering the inquiry in a tone of infinite melancholy, as if the eternal sense of duty forced it from her lips.

"Oh, successful! I am not successful as you and Miss Tarrant are; for (to my barbaric eyes) it is a great sign of prosperity to be the heroines of an occasion like this."

"Do I look like the heroine of an occasion?" asked Olive Chancellor, without an intention of humour, but with an effect that was almost comical.

"You would if you didn't hide yourself away. Are you not going into the other room to hear the speech? Everything is prepared."

"I am going when I am notified — when I am invited."

There was considerable majesty in her tone, and Ransom saw that something was wrong, that she felt neglected. To see that she was as ticklish with others as she had been with him made him feel forgiving, and there was in his manner a perfect disposition to forget their differences as he said, "Oh,

there is plenty of time; the place isn't half full yet."

She made no direct rejoinder to this, but she asked him about his mother and sisters, what news he received from the South. "Have they any happiness?" she inquired, rather as if she warned him to take care not to pretend they had. He neglected her warning to the point of saying that there was one happiness they always had — that of having learned not to think about it too much, and to make the best of their circumstances. She listened to this with an air of great reserve, and apparently thought he had wished to give her a lesson; for she suddenly broke out, "You mean that you have traced a certain line for them, and that that's all you know about it!"

Ransom stared at her, surprised; he felt, now, that she would always surprise him. "Ah, don't be rough with me," he said, in his soft Southern voice; "don't you remember how you knocked me about when I called on you in Boston?"

"You hold us in chains, and then, when we writhe in our agony, you say we don't behave prettily!" These words, which did not lessen Ransom's wonderment, were the young lady's answer to his deprecatory speech. She saw that he was honestly bewildered and that in a moment more he would laugh at her, as he had done a year and a half before (she remembered it as if it had been yesterday); and to stop that off, at

any cost, she went on hurriedly —
"If you listen to Miss Tarrant, you
will know what I mean."

"Oh, Miss Tarrant — Miss Tarrant!" And Basil Ransom's laughter came.

She had not escaped that mockery, after all, and she looked at
him sharply now, her embarrassment having quite cleared up.
"What do you know about her?
What observation have you had?"

Ransom met her eye, and for a
moment they scrutinised each other. Did she know of his interview
with Verena a month before, and
was her reserve simply the wish
to place on him the burden of declaring that he had been to Boston since they last met, and yet
had not called in Charles Street?
He thought there was suspicion in
her face; but in regard to Verena
she would always be suspicious. If
he had done at that moment just
what would gratify him he would
have said to her that he knew a
great deal about Miss Tarrant,
having lately had a long walk and
talk with her; but he checked himself, with the reflection that if Verena had not betrayed him it would
be very wrong in him to betray
her. The sweetness of the idea that
she should have thought the episode of his visit to Monadnoc Place
worth placing under the rose, was
quenched for the moment in his
regret at not being able to let his
disagreeable cousin know that he
had passed *her* over. "Don't you
remember my hearing her speak
that night at Miss Birdseye's?" he
said, presently. "And I met her

the next day at your house, you
know."

"She has developed greatly since
then," Olive remarked drily; and
Ransom felt sure that Verena had
held her tongue.

At this moment a gentleman
made his way through the clusters
of Mrs. Burrage's guests and presented himself to Olive. "If you
will do me the honour to take my
arm I will find a good seat for you
in the other room. It's getting to
be time for Miss Tarrant to reveal
herself. I have been taking her
into the picture-room; there were
some things she wanted to see. She
is with my mother now," he added, as if Miss Chancellor's grave
face constituted a sort of demand
for an explanation of her friend's
absence. "She said she was a little nervous; so I thought we would
just move about."

"It's the first time I have ever
heard of that!" said Miss Chancellor, preparing to surrender herself
to the young man's guidance. He
told her that he had reserved the
best seat for her; it was evidently
his desire to conciliate her, to treat
her as a person of importance. Before leading her away, he shook
hands with Ransom and remarked
that he was very glad to see him;
and Ransom saw that he must be
the master of the house, though he
could scarcely be the son of the
stout lady in the doorway. He was
a fresh, pleasant, handsome young
man, with a bright friendly manner; he recommended Ransom to
take a seat in the other room,
without delay; if he had never

heard Miss Tarrant he would have one of the greatest pleasures of his life.

"Oh, Mr. Ransom only comes to ventilate his prejudices," Miss Chancellor said, as she turned her back to her kinsman. He shrank from pushing into the front of the company, which was now rapidly filling the music-room, and contented himself with lingering in the doorway, where several gentlemen were stationed. The seats were all occupied; all, that is, save one, towards which he saw Miss Chancellor and her companion direct themselves, squeezing and edging past the people who were standing up against the walls. This was quite in front, close to the little platform; every one noticed Olive as she went, and Ransom heard a gentleman near him say to another — "I guess she's one of the same kind." He looked for Verena, but she was apparently keeping out of sight. Suddenly he felt himself smartly tapped on the back, and, turning around, perceived Mrs. Luna, who had been prodding him with her fan.

Chapter XXVII

"You won't speak to me in my own house — that I have almost grown used to; but if you are going to pass me over in public I think you might give me warning first." This was only her archness, and he knew what to make of that

now; she was dressed in yellow and looked very plump and gay. He wondered at the unerring instinct by which she had discovered his exposed quarter. The outer room was completely empty; she had come in at the further door and found the field free for her operations. He offered to find her a place where she could see and hear Miss Tarrant, to get her a chair to stand on, even, if she wished to look over the heads of the gentlemen in the doorway; a proposal which she greeted with the inquiry — "Do you suppose I came here for the sake of that chatterbox? haven't I told you what I think of her?"

"Well, you certainly did not come here for my sake," said Ransom, anticipating this insinuation; "for you couldn't possibly have known I was coming."

"I guessed it — a presentiment told me!" Mrs. Luna declared; and she looked up at him with searching, accusing eyes. "I know what you have come for," she cried in a moment. "You never mentioned to me that you knew Mrs. Burrage!"

"I don't — I never had heard of her till she asked me."

"Then why in the world did she ask you?"

Ransom had spoken a trifle rashly; it came over him, quickly, that there were reasons why he had better not have said that. But almost as quickly he covered up his mistake. "I suppose your sister was so good as to ask for a card for me."

"My sister? My grandmother! I know how Olive loves you. Mr. Ransom, you are very deep." She had drawn him well into the room, out of earshot of the group in the doorway, and he felt that if she should be able to compass her wish she would organise a little entertainment for herself, in the outer drawing-room, in opposition to Miss Tarrant's address. "Please come and sit down here a moment; we shall be quite undisturbed. I have something very particular to say to you." She led the way to the little sofa in the corner, where he had been talking with Olive a few minutes before, and he accompanied her, with extreme reluctance, grudging the moments that he should be obliged to give to her. He had quite forgotten that he once had a vision of spending his life in her society, and he looked at his watch as he made the observation:

"I haven't the least idea of losing any of the sport in there, you know."

He felt, the next instant, that he oughtn't to have said that either; but he was irritated, disconcerted, and he couldn't help it. It was in the nature of a gallant Mississippian to do everything a lady asked him, and he had never, remarkable as it may appear, been in the position of finding such a request so incompatible with his own desires as now. It was a new predicament, for Mrs. Luna evidently meant to keep him if she could. She looked round the room, more and more pleased at their having it to themselves, and for the moment said nothing more about the singularity of his being there. On the contrary, she became freshly jocular, remarked that now they had got hold of him they wouldn't easily let him go, they would make him entertain them, induce him to give a lecture — on the "Lights and Shadows of Southern Life," or the "Social Peculiarities of Mississippi" — before the Wednesday Club.

"And what in the world is the Wednesday Club? I suppose it's what those ladies were talking about," Ransom said.

"I don't know your ladies, but the Wednesday Club is this thing. I don't mean you and me here together, but all those deluded beings in the other room. It is New York trying to be like Boston. It is the culture, the good form, of the metropolis. You might not think it, but it is. It's the 'quiet set'; they *are* quiet enough; you might hear a pin drop, in there. Is some one going to offer up a prayer? How happy Olive must be, to be taken so seriously! They form an association for meeting at each other's houses, every week, and having some performance, or some paper read, or some subject explained. The more dreary it is and the more fearful the subject, the more they think it is what it ought to be. They have an idea this is the way to make New York society intellectual. There's a sumptuary law — isn't that what you call it? — about suppers, and they restrict themselves to a kind of Spartan broth. When it's made by their French cooks it isn't bad. Mrs. Burrage is one of the principal members — one of the founders, I believe; and when her turn has come round, formerly — it comes only once in the winter for each — I am told she has usually had very good music. But that is thought rather a base evasion, a begging of the question; the vulgar set can easily keep up with them on music. So Mrs. Burrage conceived the extraordinary idea" — and it was wonderful to hear how Mrs. Luna pronounced that adjective — "of sending on to Boston for that girl. It was her son, of course, who put it into her head; he has been at Cambridge for some years — that's where Verena lived, you know — and he was as thick with her as you please out there. Now that he is no longer there it suits him very well to have her here. She is coming on a visit to his mother when Olive goes. I asked them to stay with me, but Olive declined, majestically; she said they wished to be in some place where they would be free to receive 'sympathising friends.' So they are staying at some extraordinary kind of New Jerusalem boarding-house, in Tenth Street; Olive thinks it's her duty to go to such places. I was greatly surprised that she should let Verena be drawn into such a worldly crowd as this; but she told me they had made up their minds not to let *any* occasion slip, that they could sow the seed of truth in drawing-rooms as well as in workshops, and that if a single person was brought round to their ideas they should have been justified in coming on. That's what they are doing in there — sowing the seed; but you shall not be the one that's brought round, I shall take care of that. Have you seen my delightful sister yet? The way she *does* arrange herself when she wants to protest against frills! She looks as if she thought it pretty barren ground round here, now she has come to see it. I don't think she thinks you can be saved in a French dress, anyhow. I must say I call it a *very* base evasion of Mrs. Burrage's producing Verena Tarrant; it's worse than the meretricious music. Why didn't she honestly send for a *ballerina* from Niblo's — if she wanted a young woman capering about on a platform? They don't care a fig about poor Olive's ideas; it's only because Verena has strange hair, and shiny eyes, and gets herself up like a prestidigitator's assistant. I have never understood how Olive can reconcile herself to Verena's really low style of dress. I suppose it's only because her clothes are so fearfully made. You look as if you didn't believe me — but I assure you that the cut is revolutionary; and that's a salve to Olive's conscience."

Ransom was surprised to hear that he looked as if he didn't believe her, for he had found himself, after his first uneasiness, listening with considerable interest to her account of the circumstances under which Miss Tarrant was visiting New York. After a moment, as the result of some private reflection, he propounded this question: "Is the son of the lady of the house a handsome young man, very polite, in a white vest?"

"I don't know the colour of his vest — but he has a kind of fawning manner. Verena judges from that that he is in love with her."

"Perhaps he is," said Ransom. "You say it was his idea to get her to come on."

"Oh, he likes to flirt; that is highly probable."

"Perhaps she has brought him round."

"Not to where she wants, I think. The property is very large; he will have it all one of these days."

"Do you mean she wishes to impose on him the yoke of matrimony?" Ransom asked, with Southern languor.

"I believe she thinks matrimony an exploded superstition; but there is here and there a case in which it is still the best thing; when the gentleman's name happens to be Burrage and the young lady's Tarrant. I don't admire 'Burrage' so much myself. But I think she would have captured this present scion if it hadn't been for Olive. Olive stands between them — she wants to keep her in the single sisterhood; to keep her, above all, for herself. Of course she won't listen to her marrying, and she has put a spoke in the wheel. She has

brought her to New York; that may seem against what I say; but the girl pulls hard, she has to humour her, to give her her head sometimes, to throw something overboard, in short, to save the rest. You may say, as regards Mr. Burrage, that it's a queer taste in a gentleman; but there is no arguing about that. It's queer taste in a lady, too; for she is a lady, poor Olive. You can see that to-night. She is dressed like a book-agent, but she is more distinguished than any one here. Verena, beside her, looks like a walking advertisement."

When Mrs. Luna paused, Basil Ransom became aware that, in the other room, Verena's address had begun; the sound of her clear, bright, ringing voice, an admirable voice for public uses, came to them from the distance. His eagerness to stand where he could hear her better, and see her into the bargain, made him start in his place, and this movement produced an outgush of mocking laughter on the part of his companion. But she didn't say — "Go, go, deluded man, I take pity on you!" she only remarked, with light impertinence, that he surely wouldn't be so wanting in gallantry as to leave a lady absolutely alone in a public place — it was so Mrs. Luna was pleased to qualify Mrs. Burrage's drawing-room — in the face of her entreaty that he would remain with her. She had the better of poor Ransom, thanks to the superstitions of Mississippi.

The Bostonians

It was in his simple code a gross rudeness to withdraw from conversation with a lady at a party before another gentleman should have come to take one's place; it was to inflict on the lady a kind of outrage. The other gentlemen, at Mrs. Burrage's, were all too well occupied; there was not the smallest chance of one of them coming to his rescue. He couldn't leave Mrs. Luna, and yet he couldn't stay with her and lose the only thing he had come so much out of his way for. "Let me at least find you a place over there, in the doorway. You can stand upon a chair — you can lean on me."

"Thank you very much; I would much rather lean on this sofa. And I am much too tired to stand on chairs. Besides, I wouldn't for the world that either Verena or Olive should see me craning over the heads of the crowd — as if I attached the smallest importance to their perorations!"

"It isn't time for the peroration yet," Ransom said, with savage dryness; and he sat forward, with his elbow on his knees, his eyes on the ground, a flush in his sallow cheek.

"It's never time to say such things as those," Mrs. Luna remarked, arranging her laces.

"How do you know what she is saying?"

"I can tell by the way her voice goes up and down. It sounds so silly."

Ransom sat there five minutes longer — minutes which, he felt, the recording angel ought to write down to his credit — and asked himself how Mrs. Luna could be such a goose as not to see that she was making him hate her. But she was goose enough for anything. He tried to appear indifferent, and it occurred to him to doubt whether the Mississippi system could be right, after all. It certainly hadn't foreseen such a case as this. "It's as plain as day that Mr. Burrage intends to marry her — if he can," he said in a minute; that remark being better calculated than any other he could thing of to dissimulate his real state of mind.

It drew no rejoinder from his companion, and after an instant he turned his head a little and glanced at her. The result of something that silently passed between them was to make her say, abruptly: "Mr. Ransom, my sister never sent you an invitation to this place. Didn't it come from Verena Tarrant?"

"I haven't the least idea."

"As you hadn't the least acquaintance with Mrs. Burrage, who else could it have come from?"

"If it came from Miss Tarrant, I ought at least to recognise her courtesy by listening to her."

"If you rise from this sofa I will tell Olive what I suspect. She will be perfectly capable of carrying Verena off to China — or anywhere out of your reach."

"And pray what is it you suspect?"

"That you two have been in correspondence."

610

"Tell her whatever you like, Mrs. Luna," said the young man, with the grimness of resignation. "You are quite unable to deny it, I see."

"I never contradict a lady."

"We shall see if I can't make you tell a fib. Haven't you been seeing Miss Tarrant, too?"

"Where should I have seen her? I can't see all the way to Boston, as you said the other day."

"Haven't you been there — on secret visits?"

Ransom started just perceptibly; but to conceal it, the next instant, he stood up.

"They wouldn't be secret if I were to tell you."

Looking down at her he saw that her words were a happy hit, not the result of definite knowledge. But she appeared to him vain, egotistical, grasping, odious.

"Well, I shall give the alarm," she went on; "that is, I will if you leave me. Is that the way a Southern gentleman treats a lady? Do as I wish, and I will let you off!"

"You won't let me off from staying with you."

"It is such a *corvée*? I never heard of such rudeness!" Mrs. Luna cried. "All the same, I am determined to keep you if I can!"

Ransom felt that she must be in the wrong, and yet superficially she seemed (and it was quite intolerable), to have right on her side. All this while Verena's golden voice, with her words indistinct, solicited, tantalised his ear. The question had evidently got on Mrs.

Luna's nerves; she had reached that point of feminine embroilment when a woman is perverse for the sake of perversity, and even with a clear vision of bad consequences.

"You have lost your head," he relieved himself by saying, as he looked down at her.

"I wish you would go and get me some tea."

"You say that only to embarrass me." He had hardly spoken when a great sound of applause, the clapping of many hands, and the cry from fifty throats of "Brava, brava!" floated in and died away. All Ransom's pulses throbbed, he flung his scruples to the winds, and after remarking to Mrs. Luna — still with all due ceremony — that he feared he must resign himself to forfeiting her good opinion, turned his back upon her and strode away to the open door of the music-room. "Well, I have never been so insulted!" he heard her exclaim, with exceeding sharpness, as he left her; and, glancing back at her, as he took up his position, he saw her still seated on her sofa — alone in the lamp-lit desert — with her eyes making, across the empty space, little vindictive points. Well, she could come where he was, if she wanted him so much; he would support her on an ottoman, and make it easy for her to see. But Mrs. Luna was uncompromising; he became aware, after a minute, that she had withdrawn, majestically, from the place, and he did not see her again that evening.

Chapter XXVIII

HE could command the music-room very well from where he stood, behind a thick outer fringe of intently listening men. Verena Tarrant was erect on her little platform, dressed in white, with flowers in her bosom. The red cloth beneath her feet looked rich in the light of lamps placed on high pedestals on either side of the stage; it gave her figure a setting of colour which made it more pure and salient. She moved freely in her exposed isolation, yet with great sobriety of gesture; there was no table in front of her, and she had no notes in her hand, but stood there like an actress before the footlights, or a singer spinning vocal sounds to a silver thread. There was such a risk that a slim provincial girl, pretending to fascinate a couple of hundred *blasé* New Yorkers by simply giving them her ideas, would fail of her effect, that at the end of a few moments Basil Ransom became aware that he was watching her in very much the same excited way as if she had been performing, high above his head, on the trapeze. Yet, as one listened, it was impossible not to perceive that she was in perfect possession of her faculties, her subject, her audience; and he remembered the other time at Miss Birdseye's well enough to be able to measure the ground she had travelled since then. This exhibition was much more complete, her manner much more assured; she seemed to speak and survey the whole place from a much greater height. Her voice, too, had developed; he had forgotten how beautiful it could be when she raised it to its full capacity. Such a tone as that, so pure and rich, and yet so young, so natural, constituted in itself a talent; he didn't wonder that they had made a fuss about her at the Female Convention, if she filled their hideous hall with such a music. He had read, of old, of the *improvisatrice* of Italy, and this was a chastened, modern, American version of the type, a New England Corinna, with a mission instead of a lyre. The most graceful part of her was her earnestness, the way her delightful eyes, wandering over the "fashionable audience" (before which she was so perfectly unabashed), as if she wished to resolve it into a single sentient personality, seemed to say that the only thing in life she cared for was to put the truth into a form that would render conviction irresistible. She was as simple as she was charming, and there was not a glance or motion that did not seem part of the pure, still-burning passion that animated her. She had indeed — it was manifest — reduced the company to unanimity their attention was anything but languid; they smiled back at her when she smiled; they were noiseless, motionless when she was solemn; and it was evident that th

The Bostonians

entertainment which Mrs. Burrage had had the happy thought of offering to her friends would be memorable in the annals of the Wednesday Club. It was agreeable to Basil Ransom to think that Verena noticed him in his corner; her eyes played over her listeners so freely that you couldn't say they rested in one place more than another; nevertheless, a single rapid ray, which, however, didn't in the least strike him as a deviation from her ridiculous, fantastic, delightful argument, let him know that he had been missed and now was particularly spoken to. This glance was a sufficient assurance that his invitation had come to him by the girl's request. He took for granted the matter of her speech was ridiculous; how could it help being, and what did it signify if it was? She was none the less charming for that, and the moonshine she had been plied with was none the less moonshine for her being charming. After he had stood there a quarter of an hour he became conscious that he should not be able to repeat a word she had said; he had not definitely heeded it, and yet he had not lost a vibration of her voice. He had discovered Olive Chancellor by this time; she was in the front row of chairs, at the end, on the left; her back was turned to him, but he could see half her sharp profile, bent down a little and absolutely motionless. Even across the wide interval her attitude expressed to him a kind of rapturous stillness, the concentration of triumph. There were several irrepressible effusions of applause, instantly self-checked, but Olive never looked up, at the loudest, and such a calmness as that could only be the result of passionate volition. Success was in the air, and she was tasting it; she tasted it, as she did everything, in a way of her own. Success for Verena was success for her, and Ransom was sure that the only thing wanting to her triumph was that he should have been placed in the line of her vision, so that she might enjoy his embarrassment and confusion, might say to him, in one of her dumb, cold flashes — "*Now* do you think our movement is not a force — *now* do you think that women are meant to be slaves?" Honestly, he was not conscious of any confusion; it subverted none of his heresies to perceive that Verena Tarrant had even more power to fix his attention than he had hitherto supposed. It was fixed in a way it had not been yet, however, by his at last understanding her speech, feeling it reach his inner sense through the impediment of mere dazzled vision. Certain phrases took on a meaning for him — an appeal she was making to those who still resisted the beneficent influence of the truth. They appeared to be mocking, cynical men, mainly; many of whom were such triflers and idlers, so heartless and brainless that it didn't matter much what they thought on any subject; if the old tyranny needed to be propped up by *them* it

613

showed it was in a pretty bad way. But there were others whose prejudice was stronger and more cultivated, pretended to rest upon study and argument. To those she wished particularly to address herself; she wanted to waylay them, to say, "Look here, you're all wrong; you'll be so much happier when I have convinced you. Just give me five minutes," she should like to say; "just sit down here and let me ask a simple question. Do you think any state of society can come to good that is based upon an organised wrong?" That was the simple question that Verena desired to propound, and Basil smiled across the room at her with an amused tenderness as he gathered that she conceived it to be a poser. He didn't think it would frighten him much if she were to ask him that, and he would sit down with her for as many minutes as she liked.

He, of course, was one of the systematic scoffers, one of those to whom she said — "Do you know how you strike me? You strike me as men who are starving to death while they have a cupboard at home, all full of bread and meat and wine; or as blind, demented beings who let themselves be cast into a debtor's prison, while in their pocket they have the key of vaults and treasure-chests heaped up with gold and silver. The meat and wine, the gold and silver," Verena went on, "are simply the suppressed and wasted force, the precious sovereign remedy, of which society insanely deprives itself — the genius, the intelligence, the inspiration of women. It is dying, inch by inch, in the midst of old superstitions which it invokes in vain, and yet it has the elixir of life in its hands. Let it drink but a draught, and it will bloom once more; it will be refreshed, radiant; it will find its youth again. The heart, the heart is cold, and nothing but the touch of woman can warm it, make it act. We *are* the Heart of humanity, and let us have the courage to insist on it! The public life of the world will move in the same barren, mechanical vicious circle — the circle of egotism, cruelty, ferocity, jealousy, greed, of blind striving to do things only for *some*, at the cost of others, instead of trying to do everything for all. All, all? Who dares to say "all" when we are not there? We are an equal, a splendid, an inestimable part. Try us and you'll see — you will wonder how, without us, society has ever dragged itself even this distance — so wretchedly small compared with what it might have been — on its painful earthly pilgrimage. That is what I should like above all to pour into the ears of those who still hold out, who stiffen their necks and repeat hard, empty formulas, which are as dry as a broken gourd that has been flung away in the desert. I would take them by their selfishness, their indolence, their interest. am not here to recriminate, nor t deepen the gulf that already yawr between the sexes, and I don't ac cept the doctrine that they ar natural enemies, since my plea is for a union far more intimate — provided it be equal — than any that the sages and philosophers of former times have ever dreamed of. Therefore I shall not touch upon the subject of men's being most easily influenced by considerations of what is most agreeable and profitable for *them; I* shall simply assume that they *are* so influenced, and I shall say to them that our cause would long ago have been gained if their vision were not so dim, so veiled, even in matters in which their own interests are concerned. If they had the same quick sight as women, if they had the intelligence of the heart, the world would be very different now; and I assure you that half the bitterness of our lot is to see so clearly and not to be able to do! Good gentlemen all, if I could make you believe how much brighter and fairer and sweeter the garden of life would be for you, if you would only let us help you to keep it in order! You would like so much better to walk there, and you would find grass and trees and flowers that would make you think you were in Eden. That is what I should like to press home to each of you, personally, individually — to give him the vision of the world as it hangs perpetually before me, redeemed, transfigured, by a new moral tone. There would be generosity, tenderness, sympathy, where there is now only brute force and sordid rivalry. But you really do strike me as stupid even about your own welfare! Some of you say that we have already all the influence we can possibly require, and talk as if we ought to be grateful that we are allowed even to breathe. Pray, who shall judge what we require if not we ourselves? We require simply freedom; we require the lid to be taken off the box in which we have been kept for centuries. You say it's a very comfortable, cozy, convenient box, with nice glass sides, so that we can see out, and that all that's wanted is to give another quiet turn to the key. That is very easily answered. Good gentlemen, you have never been in the box, and you haven't the least idea how it feels!"

The historian who has gathered these documents together does not deem it necessary to give a larger specimen of Verena's eloquence, especially as Basil Ransom, through whose ears we are listening to it, arrived, at this point, at a definite conclusion. He had taken her measure as a public speaker, judged her importance in the field of discussion, the cause of reform. Her speech, in itself, had about the value of a pretty essay, committed to memory and delivered by a bright girl at an "academy;" it was, vague, thin, rambling, a tissue of generalities that glittered agreeably enough in Mrs. Burrage's veiled lamplight. From any serious point of view it was neither worth answering nor worth considering, and Basil Ransom made his reflections on the crazy character of the age in which such a performance as that was treated as an intellectual effort, a contribution to a question. He asked himself what either he or any one else would think of it if Miss Chancellor — or even Mrs. Luna — had been on the platform instead of the actual declaimer. Nevertheless, its importance was high, and consisted precisely, in part, of the fact that the voice was not the voice of Olive or of Adeline. Its importance was that Verena was unspeakably attractive, and this was all the greater for him in the light of the fact, which quietly dawned upon him as he stood there, that he was falling in love with her. It had tapped at his heart for recognition, and before he could hesitate or challenge, the door had sprung open and the mansion was illuminated. He gave no outward sign; he stood gazing as at a picture; but the room wavered before his eyes, even Verena's figure danced a little. This did not make the sequel of her discourse more clear to him; her meaning faded again into the agreeable vague, and he simply felt her presence, tasted her voice. Yet the act of reflection was not suspended; he found himself rejoicing that she was so weak in argument, so inevitably verbose. The idea that she was brilliant, that she counted as a factor only because the public mind was in a muddle, was not an humiliation but a delight to him; it was a proof that her apostleship was all nonsense, the most passing of fashions, the veriest of delusions, and

that she was meant for something divinely different — for privacy, for him, for love. He took no measure of the duration of her talk; he only knew, when it was over and succeeded by a clapping of hands, an immense buzz of voices and shuffling of chairs, that it had been capitally bad, and that her personal success, wrapping it about with a glamour like the silver mist that surrounds a fountain, was such as to prevent its badness from being a cause of mortification to her lover. The company — such of it as did not immediately close together around Verena — filed away into the other rooms, bore him in its current into the neighbourhood of a table spread for supper, where he looked for signs of the sumptuary law mentioned to him by Mrs. Luna. It appeared to be embodied mainly in the glitter of crystal and silver, and the fresh tints of mysterious viands and jellies, which looked desirable in the soft circle projected by lace-fringed lamps. He heard the popping of corks, he felt a pressure of elbows, a thickening of the crowd, perceived that he was glowered at, squeezed against the table, by contending gentlemen who observed that he usurped space, was neither feeding himself nor helping others to feed. He had lost sight of Verena; she had been borne away in clouds of compliment; but he found himself thinking — almost paternally — that she must be hungry after so much chatter, and he hoped some one was getting her something to eat.

616

After a moment, just as he was edging away, for his own opportunity to sup much better than usual was not what was uppermost in his mind, this little vision was suddenly embodied — embodied by the appearance of Miss Tarrant, who faced him, in the press, attached to the arm of a young man now recognisable to him as the son of the house — the smiling, fragrant youth who an hour before had interrupted his colloquy with Olive. He was leading her to the table, while people made way for them, covering Verena with gratulations of word and look. Ransom could see that, according to a phrase which came back to him just then, oddly, out of some novel or poem he had read of old, she was the cynosure of every eye. She looked beautiful, and they were a beautiful couple. As soon as she saw him, she put out her left hand to him — the other was in Mr. Burrage's arm — and said: "Well, don't you think it's all true?"

"No, not a word of it!" Ransom answered, with a kind of joyous sincerity. "But it doesn't make any difference."

"Oh, it makes a great deal of difference to me!" Verena cried.

"I mean to me. I don't care in the least whether I agree with you," Ransom said, looking askance at young Mr. Burrage, who had detached himself and was getting something for Verena to eat.

"Ah, well, if you are so indifferent!"

"It's not because I'm indiffer-

ent!" His eyes came back to her own, the expression of which had changed before they quitted them. She began to complain to her companion, who brought her something very dainty on a plate, that Mr. Ransom was "standing out," that he was about the hardest subject she had encountered yet. Henry Burrage smiled upon Ransom in a way that was meant to show he remembered having already spoken to him, while the Mississippian said to himself that there was nothing on the face of it to make it strange there should be between these fair, successful young persons some such question of love or marriage as Mrs. Luna had tattled about. Mr. Burrage was successful, he could see that in the turn of an eye; not perhaps as having a commanding intellect or a very strong character, but as being rich, polite, handsome, happy, amiable, and as wearing a splendid camellia in his buttonhole. And that *he*, at any rate, thought Verena had succeeded was proved by the casual, civil tone, and the contented distraction of eye, with which he exclaimed, "You don't mean to say you were not moved by that! It's my opinion that Miss Tarrant will carry everything before her." He was so pleased himself, and so safe in his conviction, that it didn't matter to him what any one else thought; which was, after all, just Basil Ransom's own state of mind.

"Oh! I didn't say I wasn't moved," the Mississippian remarked.

"Moved the wrong way!" said Verena. "Never mind; you'll be left behind."

"If I am, you will come back to console me."

"*Back?* I shall never come back!" the girl replied, gaily.

"You'll be the very first!" Ransom went on, feeling himself now, and as if by a sudden clearing up of his spiritual atmosphere, no longer in the vein for making the concessions of chivalry, and yet conscious that his words were an expression of homage.

"Oh, I call that presumptuous!" Mr. Burrage exclaimed, turning away to get a glass of water for Verena, who had refused to accept champagne, mentioning that she had never drunk any in her life and that she associated a kind of iniquity with it. Olive had no wine in her house (not that Verena gave this explanation), but her father's old madeira and a little claret; of the former of which liquors Basil Ransom had highly approved the day he dined with her.

"Does he believe in all those lunacies?" he inquired, knowing perfectly what to think about the charge of presumption brought by Mr. Burrage.

"Why, he's crazy about our movement," Verena responded. "He's one of my most gratifying converts."

"And don't you despise him for it?"

"Despise him? Why, you seem to think I swing round pretty often!"

"Well, I have an idea that I shall see you swing round yet," Ransom remarked, in a tone in which it would have appeared to Henry Burrage, had he heard these words, that presumption was pushed to fatuity.

On Verena, however, they produced no impression that prevented her from saying simply, without the least rancour, "Well, if you expect to draw me back five hundred years, I hope you won't tell Miss Birdseye." And as Ransom did not seize immediately the reason of her allusion, she went on, "You know she is convinced it will be just the other way. I went to see her after you had been at Cambridge — almost immediately."

"Darling old lady — I hope she's well," the young man said.

"Well, she's tremendously interested."

"She's always interested in something, isn't she?"

"Well, this time it's in our relations, yours and mine," Verena replied, in a tone in which only Verena could say a thing like that. "You ought to see how she throws herself into them. She is sure it will all work round for your good."

"All what, Miss Tarrant?" Ransom asked.

"Well, what I told her. She is sure you are going to become one of our leaders, that you are very gifted for treating great question and acting on masses of people that you will become quite enthu siastic about our uprising, and tha when you go up to the top as on of our champions it will all have been through me."

Ransom stood there, smiling at her; the dusky glow in his eyes expressed a softness representing no prevision of such laurels, but which testified none the less to Verena's influence. "And what you want is that I shouldn't undeceive her?"

"Well, I don't want you to be hypocritical — if you shouldn't take our side; but I do think that it would be sweet if the dear old thing could just cling to her illusion. She won't live so very long, probably; she told me the other day she was ready for her final rest; so it wouldn't interfere much with your freedom. She feels quite romantic about it — your being a Southerner and all, and not naturally in sympathy with Boston ideas, and your meeting her that way in the street and making yourself known to her. She won't believe but what I shall move you."

"Don't fear, Miss Tarrant, she shall be satisfied," Ransom said, with a laugh which he could see she but partially understood. He was prevented from making his meaning more clear by the return of Mr. Burrage, bringing not only Verena's glass of water but a smooth-faced, rosy, smiling old gentleman, who had a velvet waistcoat, and thin white hair, brushed effectively, and whom he introduced to Verena under a name which Ransom recognised as that of a rich and venerable citizen, conspicuous for his public spirit and his large almsgiving.

Ransom had lived long enough in New York to know that a request from this ancient worthy to be made known to Miss Tarrant would mark her for the approval of the respectable, stamp her as a success of no vulgar sort; and as he turned away, a faint, inaudible sigh passed his lips, dictated by the sense that he himself belonged to a terribly small and obscure minority. He turned away because, as we know, he had been taught that a gentleman talking to a lady must always do that when a new gentleman is presented; though he observed, looking back, after a minute, that young Mr. Burrage evidently had no intention of abdicating in favour of the eminent philanthropist. He thought he had better go home; he didn't know what might happen at such a party as that, nor when the proceedings might be supposed to terminate; but after considering it a minute he dismissed the idea that there was a chance of Verena's speaking again. If he was a little vague about this, however, there was no doubt in his mind as to the obligation he was under to take leave first of Mrs. Burrage. He wished he knew where Verena was staying; he wanted to see her alone, not in a supper-room crowded with millionaires. As he looked about for the hostess it occurred to him that she would know, and that if he were able to quench a certain shyness sufficiently to ask her, she would tell him. Having satisfied himself presently that she was not in the supper-room, he made his way back to the parlours, where the company now was much diminished. He looked again into the music-room, tenanted only by half-a-dozen couples, who were cultivating privacy among the empty chairs, and here he perceived Mrs. Burrage sitting in conversation with Olive Chancellor (the latter, apparently, had not moved from her place), before the deserted scene of Verena's triumph. His search had been so little for Olive that at the sight of her he faltered a moment; then he pulled himself together, advancing with a consciousness of the Mississippi manner. He felt Olive's eyes receiving him; she looked at him as if it was just the hope that she shouldn't meet him again that had made her remain where she was. Mrs. Burrage got up, as he bade her good-night, and Olive followed her example.

"So glad you were able to come. Wonderful creature, isn't she? She can do anything she wants."

These words from the elder lady Ransom received at first with a reserve which, as he trusted, suggested extreme respect; and it was a fact that his silence had a kind of Southern solemnity in it. Then he said, in a tone equally expressive of great deliberation:

"Yes, madam, I think I never was present at an exhibition, an entertainment of any kind, which held me more completely under the charm."

"Delighted you liked it. I didn't know what in the world to have,

and this has proved an inspiration — for me as well as for Miss Tarrant. Miss Chancellor has been telling me how they have worked together; it's really quite beautiful. Miss Chancellor is Miss Tarrant's great friend and colleague. Miss Tarrant assures me that she couldn't do anything without her." After which explanation, turning to Olive, Mrs. Burrage murmured: "Let me introduce Mr. —— introduce Mr. —— "

But she had forgotten poor Ransom's name, forgotten who had asked her for a card for him; and, perceiving it, he came to her rescue with the observation that he was a kind of cousin of Miss Olive's, if she didn't repudiate him, and that he knew what a tremendous partnership existed between the two young ladies. "When I applauded I was applauding the firm — that is, you too," he said, smiling, to his kinswoman.

"Your applause? I confess I don't understand it," Olive replied, with much promptitude.

"Well, to tell the truth, I didn't myself!"

"Oh yes, of course I know; that's why — that's why —— " And this further speech of Mrs. Burrage's, in reference to the relationship between the young man and her companion, faded also into vagueness. She had been on the point of saying it was the reason why he was in her house; but she had bethought herself in time that this ought to pass as a matter of course. Basil Ransom could see she was a woman who could carry off an awkwardness like that, and he considered her with a sense of her importance. She had a brisk, familiar, slightly impatient way, and if she had not spoken so fast, and had more of the softness of the Southern matron, she would have reminded him of a certain type of woman he had seen of old, before the changes in his own part of the world — the clever, capable, hospitable proprietress, widowed or unmarried, of a big plantation carried on by herself. "If you are her cousin, do take Miss Chancellor to have some supper — instead of going away," she went on, with her infelicitous readiness.

At this Olive instantly seated herself again.

"I am much obliged to you; I never touch supper. I shall not leave this room — I like it."

"Then let me send you something — or let Mr. ——, your cousin, remain with you."

Olive looked at Mrs. Burrage with a strange beseechingness, "I am very tired, I must rest. These occasions leave me exhausted."

"Ah yes, I can imagine that. Well, then, you shall be quite quiet — I shall come back to you." And with a smile of farewell for Basil Ransom, Mrs. Burrage moved away.

Basil lingered a moment, though he saw that Olive wished to get rid of him. "I won't disturb you further than to ask you a single question," he said. "Where are you staying? I want to come and see Miss Tarrant. I don't say I want to come and see you, because I

have an idea that it would give you no pleasure." It had occurrred to him that he might obtain their address from Mrs. Luna — he only knew vaguely it was Tenth Street; much as he had displeased her she couldn't refuse him that; but suddenly the greater simplicity and frankness of applying directly to Olive, even at the risk of appearing to brave her, recommended itself. He couldn't, of course, call upon Verena without her knowing it, and she might as well make her protest (since he proposed to pay no heed to it), sooner as later. He had seen nothing, personally, of their life together, but it had come over him that what Miss Chancellor most disliked in him (had she not, on the very threshold of their acquaintance, had a sort of mystical foreboding of it?) was the possibility that he would interfere. It was quite on the cards that he might; yet it was decent, all the same, to ask her rather than any one else. It was better that his interference should be accompanied with all the forms of chivalry.

Olive took no notice of his remark as to how she herself might be affected by his visit; but she asked in a moment why he should think it necessary to call on Miss Tarrant. "You know you are not in sympathy," she added, in a tone which contained a really touching element of entreaty that he would not even pretend to prove he was.

I know not whether Basil was touched, but he said, with every appearance of a conciliatory purpose — "I wish to thank her for all the interesting information she has given me this evening."

"If you think it generous to come and scoff at her, of course she has no defence; you will be glad to know that."

"Dear Miss Chancellor, if you are not a defence — a battery of many guns!" Ransom exclaimed.

"Well, she at least is not mine!" Olive returned, springing to her feet. She looked round her as if she were really pressed too hard, panting like a hunted creature.

"Your defence is your certain immunity from attack. Perhaps if you won't tell me where you are staying, you will kindly ask Miss Tarrant herself to do so. Would she send me a word on a card?"

"We are in West Tenth Street," Olive said; and she gave the number. "Of course you are free to come."

"Of course I am! Why shouldn't I be? But I am greatly obliged to you for the information. I will ask her to come out, so that you won't see us." And he turned away, with the sense that it was really insufferable, her attempt always to give him the air of being in the wrong. If that was the kind of spirit in which women were going to act when they had more power!

Chapter XXIX

MRS. LUNA was early in the field the next day and her sister wondered to what she owed the honour of a visit from her at eleven o'clock in the morning. She very soon saw, when Adeline asked her whether it had been she who procured for Basil Ransom an invitation to Mrs. Burrage's.

"Me — why in the world should it have been me?" Olive asked, feeling something of a pang at the implication that it had not been Adeline, as she supposed.

"I didn't know — but you took him up so."

"Why, Adeline Luna, when did I ever —— ?" Miss Chancellor exclaimed, staring and intensely grave.

"You don't mean to say you have forgotten how you brought him on to see you, a year and a half ago!"

"I didn't bring him on — I said if he happened to be there."

"Yes, I remember how it was: he did happen, and then you happened to hate him, and tried to get out of it."

Miss Chancellor saw, I say, why Adeline had come to her at the hour she knew she was always writing letters, after having given her all the attention that was necessary the day before; she had come simply to make herself disagreeable, as Olive knew, of old, the spirit sometimes moved her irresistibly to do. It seemed to her that Adeline had been disagreeable enough in not having beguiled Basil Ransom into a marriage, according to that memorable calculation of probabilities in which she indulged (with a licence that she scarcely liked definitely to recall), when the pair made acquaintance under her eyes in Charles Street, and Mrs. Luna seemed to take to him as much as she herself did little. She would gladly have accepted him as a brother-in-law, for the harm such a relation could do one was limited and definite; whereas in his general capacity of being at large in her life the ability of the young Mississippian to injure her seemed somehow immense. "I wrote to him — that time — for a perfectly definite reason," she said. "I thought mother would have liked us to know him. But it was a mistake."

"How do you know it was a mistake? Mother would have liked him, I dare say."

"I mean my acting as I did; it was a theory of duty which I allowed to press me too much. I always do. Duty should be obvious; one shouldn't hunt round for it."

"Was it very obvious when it brought you on here?" asked Mrs. Luna, who was distinctly out of humour.

Olive looked for a moment at the toe of her shoe. "I had an idea that you would have married him by this time," she presently remarked.

"Marry him yourself, my dear! What put such an idea into your head?"

"You wrote to me at first so much about him. You told me he was tremendously attentive, and that you liked him."

"His state of mind is one thing

and mine is another. How can I marry every man that hangs about me — that dogs my footsteps? I might as well become a Mormon at once!" Mrs. Luna delivered herself of this argument with a certain charitable air, as if her sister could not be expected to understand such a situation by her own light.

Olive waived the discussion, and simply said: "I took for granted *you* had got him the invitation."

"I, my dear? That would be quite at variance with my attitude of discouragement."

"Then she simply sent it herself."

"Whom do you mean by 'she'?"

"Mrs. Burrage, of course."

"I thought that you might mean Verena," said Mrs. Luna, casually.

"Verena — to him? Why in the world——?" And Olive gave the cold glare with which her sister was familiar.

"Why in the world not — since she knows him?"

"She had seen him twice in her life before last night, when she met him for the third time and spoke to him."

"Did she tell you that?"

"She tells me everything."

"Are you very sure?"

"Adeline Luna, what *do* you mean?" Miss Chancellor murmured.

"Are you very sure that last night was only the third time?" Mrs. Luna went on.

Olive threw back her head and swept her sister from her bonnet to her lowest flounce. "You have no right to hint at such a thing as that unless you know!"

"Oh, I know — I know, at any rate, more than you do!" And then Mrs. Luna, sitting with her sister, much withdrawn, in one of the windows of the big, hot, faded parlour of the boarding-house in Tenth Street, where there was a rug before the chimney representing a Newfoundland dog saving a child from drowning, and a row of chromo-lithographs on the walls, imparted to her the impression she had received the evening before — the impression of Basil Ransom's keen curiosity about Verena Tarrant. Verena must have asked Mrs. Burrage to send him a card, and asked it without mentioning the fact to Olive — for wouldn't Olive certainly have remembered it? It was no use her saying that Mrs. Burrage might have sent it of her own movement, because she wasn't aware of his existence, and why should she be? Basil Ransom himself had told her he didn't know Mrs. Burrage. Mrs. Luna knew whom he knew and whom he didn't, or at least the sort of people, and they were not the sort that belonged to the Wednesday Club. That was one reason why she didn't care about him for any intimate relation — that he didn't seem to have any taste for making nice friends. Olive would know what *her* taste was in this respect, though it wasn't that young woman's own any more than his. It was positive that the

suggestion about the card could only have come from Verena. At any rate Olive could easily ask, or if she was afraid of her telling a fib she could ask Mrs. Burrage. It was true Mrs. Burrage might have been put on her guard by Verena, and would perhaps invent some other account of the matter; therefore Olive had better just believe what *she* believed, that Verena had secured his presence at the party and had had private reasons for doing so. It is to be feared that Ransom's remark to Mrs. Luna the night before about her having lost her head was near to the mark; for if she had not been blinded by her rancour she would have guessed the horror with which she inspired her sister when she spoke in that off-hand way of Verena's lying and Mrs. Burrage's lying. Did people lie like that in Mrs. Luna's set? It was Olive's plan of life not to lie, and attributing a similar disposition to people she liked, it was impossible for her to believe that Verena had had the intention of deceiving her. Mrs. Luna, in a calmer hour, might also have divined that Olive would make her private comments on the strange story of Basil Ransom's having made up to Verena out of pique at Adeline's rebuff; for this was the account of the matter that she now offered to Miss Chancellor. Olive did two things: she listened intently and eagerly, judging there was distinct danger in the air (which, however, she had not wanted Mrs.

Luna to tell her, having perceived it for herself the night before); and she saw that poor Adeline was fabricating fearfully, that the "rebuff" was altogether an invention. Mr. Ransom was evidently preoccupied with Verena, but he had not needed Mrs. Luna's cruelty to make him so. So Olive maintained an attitude of great reserve; she did not take upon herself to announce that her own version was that Adeline, for reasons absolutely imperceptible to others, had tried to catch Basil Ransom, had failed in her attempt, and, furious at seeing Verena preferred to a person of her importance (Olive remembered the *spretæ injuria formæ*), now wished to do both him and the girl an ill turn. This would be accomplished if she could induce Olive to interfere. Miss Chancellor was conscious of an abundant readiness to interfere, but it was not because she cared for Adeline's mortification. I am not sure, even, that she did not think her *fiasco* but another illustration of her sister's general uselessness, and rather despise her for it; being perfectly able at once to hold that nothing is baser than the effort to entrap a man, and to think it very ignoble to have to renounce it because you can't. Olive kept these reflections to herself, but she went so far as to say to her sister that she didn't see where the "pique" came in. How could it hurt Adeline that he should turn his attention to Verena? What was Verena to her?

"Why, Olive Chancellor, how can you ask?" Mrs. Luna boldly responded. "Isn't Verena everything to you, and aren't you everything to me, and wouldn't an attempt — a successful one — to take Verena away from you knock you up fearfully, and shouldn't I suffer, as you know I suffer, by sympathy?"

I have said that it was Miss Chancellor's plan of life not to lie, but such a plan was compatible with a kind of consideration for the truth which led her to shrink from producing it on poor occasions. So she didn't say, "Dear me, Adeline, what humbug! you know you hate Verena and would be very glad if she were drowned!" She only said, "Well, I see; but it's very roundabout." What she did see was that Mrs. Luna was eager to help her to stop off Basil Ransom from "making head," as the phrase was; and the fact that her motive was spite, and not tenderness for the Bostonians, would not make her assistance less welcome if the danger were real. She herself had a nervous dread, but she had that about everything; still, Adeline had perhaps seen something, and what in the world did she mean by her reference to Verena's having had secret meetings? When pressed on this point, Mrs. Luna could only say that she didn't pretend to give definite information, and she wasn't a spy anyway, but that the night before he had positively flaunted in her face his admiration for the girl, his enthusiasm for her way of standing up there. Of course he hated her ideas, but he was quite conceited enough to think she would give them up. Perhaps it was all directed at *her* — as if she cared! It would depend a good deal on the girl herself; certainly, if there was any likelihood of Verena's being affected, she should advise Olive to look out. She knew best what to do; it was only Adeline's duty to give her the benefit of her own impression, whether she was thanked for it or not. She only wished to put her on her guard, and it was just like Olive to receive such information so coldly; she was the most disappointing woman she knew.

Miss Chancellor's coldness was not diminished by this rebuke; for it had come over her that, after all, she had never opened herself at that rate to Adeline, had never let her see the real intensity of her desire to keep the sort of danger there was now a question of away from Verena, had given her no warrant for regarding her as her friend's keeper; so that she was taken aback by the flatness of Mrs. Luna's assumption that she was ready to enter into a conspiracy to circumvent and frustrate the girl. Olive put on all her majesty to dispel this impression, and if she could not help being aware that she made Mrs. Luna still angrier, on the whole, than at first, she felt that she would much rather disappoint her than give herself away to her — especially as she was intensely eager to profit by her warning!

Chapter XXX

MRS. LUNA would have been still less satisfied with the manner in which Olive received her proffered assistance had she known how many confidences that reticent young woman might have made her in return. Olive's whole life now was a matter for whispered communications; she felt this herself, as she sought the privacy of her own apartment after her interview with her sister. She had for the moment time to think; Verena having gone out with Mr. Burrage, who had made an appointment the night before to call for her to drive at that early hour. They had other engagements in the afternoon — the principal of which was to meet a group of earnest people at the house of one of the great local promoters. Olive would whisk Verena off to these appointments directly after lunch; she flattered herself that she could arrange matters so that there would not be half an hour in the day during which Basil Ransom, complacently calling, would find the Bostonians in the house. She had had this well in mind when, at Mrs. Burrage's, she was driven to give him their address; and she had had it also in mind that she would ask Verena, as a special favour, to accompany her back to Boston on the next day but one, which was the morning of the morrow. There had been considerable talk of her staying a few days with Mrs. Burrage — staying on after her own departure; but Verena backed out of it spontaneously, seeing how the idea worried her friend. Olive had accepted the sacrifice, and their visit to New York was now cut down, in intention, to four days, one of which, the moment she perceived whither Basil Ransom was tending, Miss Chancellor promised herself also to suppress. She had not mentioned that to Verena yet; she hesitated a little, having a slightly bad conscience about the concessions she had already obtained from her friend. Verena made such concessions with a generosity which caused one's heart to ache for admiration, even while one asked for them; and never once had Olive known her to demand the smallest credit for any virtue she showed in this way, or to bargain for an instant about any effort she made to oblige. She had been delighted with the idea of spending a week under Mrs. Burrage's roof; she had said, too, that she believed her mother would die happy (not that there was the least prospect of Mrs. Tarrant's dying), if she could hear of her having such an experience as that; and yet, perceiving how solemn Olive looked about it, how she blanched and brooded at the prospect, she had offered to give it up, with a smile sweeter, if possible, than any that had ever sat in her eyes. Olive knew what that meant for her, knew what a pow-

er of enjoyment she still had, in spite of the tension of their common purpose, their vital work, which had now, as they equally felt, passed into the stage of realisation, of fruition; and that is why her conscience rather pricked her for consenting to this further act of renunciation, especially as their position seemed really so secure, on the part of one who had already given herself away so sublimely.

Secure as their position might be, Olive called herself a blind idiot for having, in spite of all her first shrinkings, agreed to bring Verena to New York. Verena had jumped at the invitation, the very unexpectedness of which on Mrs. Burrage's part — it was such an odd idea to have come to a mere worldling — carried a kind of persuasion with it. Olive's immediate sentiment had been an instinctive general fear; but, later, she had dismissed that as unworthy; she had decided (and such a decision was nothing new), that where their mission was concerned they ought to face everything. Such an opportunity would contribute too much to Verena's reputation and authority to justify a refusal at the bidding of apprehensions which were after all only vague. Olive's specific terrors and dangers had by this time very much blown over; Basil Ransom had given no sign of life for ages, and Henry Burrage had certainly got his quietus before they went to Europe. If it had occurred to his mother that she might convert Verena into the animating principle of a big soirée, she was at least acting in good faith, for it could be no more her wish to-day that he should marry Selah Tarrant's daughter than it was her wish a year before. And then they should do some good to the benighted, the most benighted, the fashionable benighted; they should perhaps make them furious — there was always some good in that. Lastly, Olive was conscious of a personal temptation in the matter; she was not insensible to the pleasure of appearing in a distinguished New York circle as a representative woman, an important Bostonian, the prompter, colleague, associate of one of the most original girls of the time. Basil Ransom was the person she had least expected to meet at Mrs. Burrage's; it had been her belief that they might easily spend four days in a city of more than a million of inhabitants without that disagreeable accident. But it had occurred; nothing was wanting to make it seem serious; and, setting her teeth, she shook herself, morally, hard, for having fallen into the trap of fate. Well, she would scramble out, with only a scare, probably. Henry Burrage was very attentive, but somehow she didn't fear him now; and it was only natural he should feel that he couldn't be polite enough, after they had consented to be exploited in that worldly way by his mother. The other danger was the worst; the palpitation of her strange dread, the night of Miss Birdseye's party, came back to her.

Mr. Burrage seemed, indeed, a protection; she reflected, with relief, that it had been arranged that after taking Verena to drive in the Park and see the Museum of Art in the morning, they should in the evening dine with him at Delmonico's (he was to invite another gentleman), and go afterwards to the German opera. Olive had kept all this to herself, as I have said; revealing to her sister neither the vividness of her prevision that Basil Ransom would look blank when he came down to Tenth Street and learned they had flitted, nor the eagerness of her desire just to find herself once more in the Boston train. It had been only this prevision that sustained her when she gave Mr. Ransom their number.

Verena came to her room shortly before luncheon, to let her know she had returned; and while they sat there, waiting to stop their ears when the gong announcing the repast was beaten, at the foot of the stairs, by a negro in a white jacket, she narrated to her friend her adventures with Mr. Burrage — expatiated on the beauty of the Park, the splendour and interest of the Museum, the wonder of the young man's acquaintance with everything it contained, the swiftness of his horses, the softness of his English cart, the pleasure of rolling at that pace over roads as firm as marble, the entertainment he promised them for the evening. Olive listened in serious silence; she saw Verena was quite carried away; of course she hadn't gone so far with her without knowing that phase.

"Did Mr. Burrage try to make love to you?" Miss Chancellor inquired at last, without a smile.

Verena had taken off her hat to arrange her feather, and as she placed it on her head again, her uplifted arms making a frame for her face, she said: "Yes, I suppose it was meant for love."

Olive waited for her to tell more, to tell how she had treated him, kept him in his place, made him feel that that question was over long ago; but as Verena gave her no farther information she did not insist, conscious as she always was that in such a relation as theirs there should be a great respect on either side for the liberty of each. She had never yet infringed on Verena's, and of course she wouldn't begin now. Moreover, with the request that she meant presently to make of her she felt that she must be discreet. She wondered whether Henry Burrage were really going to begin again; whether his mother had only been acting in his interest in getting them to come on. Certainly, the bright spot in such a prospect was that if she listened to him she couldn't listen to Basil Ransom; and he *had* told Olive herself last night, when he put them into their carriage, that he hoped to prove to her yet that he had come round to her gospel. But the old sickness stole upon her again, the faintness of discouragement, as she asked herself why in the name of pity Verena should listen to any one at

all but Olive Chancellor. Again it came over her, when she saw the brightness, the happy look, the girl brought back, as it had done in the earlier months, that the great trouble was that weak spot of Verena's, that sole infirmity and subtle flaw, which she had expressed to her very soon after they began to live together, in saying (she remembered it through the ineffaceable impression made by her friend's avowal), "I'll tell you what is the matter with you — you don't dislike men as a class!" Verena had replied on this occasion, "Well, no, I don't dislike them when they are pleasant!" As if organised atrociousness could ever be pleasant! Olive disliked them most when they were least unpleasant. After a little, at present, she remarked, referring to Henry Burrage: "It is not right of him, not decent, after your making him feel how, while he was at Cambridge, he wearied you, tormented you."

"Oh, I didn't show anything," said Verena, gaily. "I am learning to dissimulate," she added in a moment. "I suppose you have to as you go along. I pretend not to notice."

At this moment the gong sounded for luncheon, and the two young women covered up their ears, face to face, Verena with her quick smile, Olive with her pale patience. When they could hear themselves speak, the latter said abruptly:

"How did Mrs. Burrage come to invite Mr. Ransom to her party?

He told Adeline he had never seen her before."

"Oh, I asked her to send him an invitation — after she had written to me, to thank me, when it was definitely settled we should come on. She asked me in her letter if there were any friends of mine in the city to whom I should like her to send cards, and I mentioned Mr. Ransom."

Verena spoke without a single instant's hesitation, and the only sign of embarrassment she gave was that she got up from her chair, passing in this manner a little out of Olive's scrutiny. It was easy for her not to falter, because she was glad of the chance. She wanted to be very simple in all her relations with her friend, and of course it was not simple so soon as she began to keep things back. She could at any rate keep back as little as possible, and she felt as if she were making up for a dereliction when she answered Olive's inquiry so promptly.

"You never told me of that," Miss Chancellor remarked, in a low tone.

"I didn't want to. I know you don't like him, and I thought it would give you pain. Yet I wanted him to be there — I wanted him to hear."

"What does it matter — why should you care about him?"

"Well, because he is so awfully opposed!"

"How do you know that, Verena?"

At this point Verena began to hesitate. It was not, after all, so easy to keep back only a little; it appeared rather as if one must either tell everything or hide everything. The former course had already presented itself to her as unduly harsh; it was because it seemed so that she had ended by keeping the incident of Basil Ransom's visit to Monadnoc Place buried in unspoken, in unspeakable, considerations, the only secret she had in the world — the only thing that was all her own. She was so glad to say what she could without betraying herself that it was only after she had spoken that she perceived there was a danger of Olive's pushing the inquiry to the point where, to defend herself as it were, she should be obliged to practise a positive deception; and she was conscious at the same time that the moment her secret was threatened it became dearer to her. She began to pray silently that Olive might not push; for it would be odious, it would be impossible, to defend herself by a lie. Meanwhile, however, she had to answer, and the way she answered was by exclaiming, much more quickly than the reflections I note might have appeared to permit, "Well, if you can't tell from his appearance! He's the type of the reactionary."

Verena went to the toilet-glass to see that she had put on her hat properly, and Olive slowly got up, in the manner of a person not in the least eager for food. "Let him react as he likes — for heaven's sake don't mind him!" That was Miss Chancellor's rejoinder, and

Verena felt that it didn't say all that was in her mind. She wished she would come down to luncheon, for she, at least, was honestly hungry. She even suspected Olive had an idea she was afraid to express, such distress it would bring with it. "Well, you know, Verena, this isn't our *real* life — it isn't our work," Olive went on.

"Well, no, it isn't, certainly," said Verena, not pretending at first that she did not know what Olive meant. In a moment, however, she added, "Do you refer to this social intercourse with Mr. Burrage?"

"Not to that only." Then Olive asked abruptly, looking at her, "How did you know his address?"

"His address?"

"Mr. Ransom's — to enable Mrs. Burrage to invite him?"

They stood for a moment interchanging a gaze. "It was in a letter I got from him."

At these words there came into Olive's face an expression which made her companion cross over to her directly and take her by the hand. But the tone was different from what Verena expected when she said, with cold surprise: "Oh, you are in correspondence!" It showed an immense effort of self-control.

"He wrote to me once — I never told you," Verena rejoined, smiling. She felt that her friend's strange, uneasy eyes searched very far; a little more and they would go to the very bottom. Well, they might go if they would; she didn't, after all, care so much about her

secret as that. For the moment, however, Verena did not learn what Olive had discovered, inasmuch as she only remarked presently that it was really time to go down. As they descended the staircase she put her arm into Miss Chancellor's and perceived that she was trembling.

Of course there were plenty of people in New York interested in the uprising, and Olive had made appointments, in advance, which filled the whole afternoon. Everybody wanted to meet them, and wanted everybody else to do so, and Verena saw they could easily have quite a vogue, if they only chose to stay and work that vein. Very likely, as Olive said, it wasn't their real life, and people didn't seem to have such a grip of the movement as they had in Boston; but there was something in the air that carried one along, and a sense of vastness and variety, of the infinite possibilities of a great city, which — Verena hardly knew whether she ought to confess it to herself — might in the end make up for the want of the Boston earnestness. Certainly, the people seemed very much alive, and there was no other place where so many cheering reports could flow in, owing to the number of electric feelers that stretched away everywhere. The principal centre appeared to be Mrs. Croucher's, on Fifty-sixth Street, where there was an informal gathering of sympathisers who didn't seem as if they could forgive her when they learned that she had been speaking the night before in a circle in which none of them were acquainted. Certainly, they were very different from the group she had addressed at Mrs. Burrage's, and Verena heaved a thin, private sigh, expressive of some helplessness, as she thought what a big, complicated world it was, and how it evidently contained a little of everything. There was a general demand that she should repeat her address in a more congenial atmosphere; to which she replied that Olive made her engagements for her, and that as the address had been intended just to lead people on, perhaps she would think Mrs. Croucher's friends had reached a higher point. She was as cautious as this because she saw that Olive was now just straining to get out of the city; she didn't want to say anything that would tie them. When she felt her trembling that way before luncheon it made her quite sick to realise how much her friend was wrapped up in her — how terribly she would suffer from the least deviation. After they had started for their round of engagements the very first thing Verena spoke of in the carriage (Olive had taken one, in her liberal way, for the whole time), was the fact that her correspondence with Mr. Ransom, as her friend had called it, had consisted on his part of only one letter. It was a very short one, too; it had come to her a little more than a month before. Olive knew she got letters from gentlemen; she didn't see why she should at-

tach such importance to this one. Miss Chancellor was leaning back in the carriage, very still, very grave, with her head against the cushioned surface, only turning her eyes towards the girl.

"You attach importance yourself; otherwise you would have told me."

"I knew you wouldn't like it — because you don't like *him*."

"I don't think of him," said Olive; "he's nothing to me." Then she added, suddenly, "Have you noticed that I am afraid to face what I don't like?"

Verena could not say that she had, and yet it was not just on Olive's part to speak as if she were an easy person to tell such a thing to: the way she lay there, white and weak, like a wounded creature, sufficiently proved the contrary. "You have such a fearful power of suffering," she replied in a moment.

To this at first Miss Chancellor made no rejoinder; but after a little she said, in the same attitude, "Yes, *you* could make me."

Verena took her hand and held it awhile. "I never will, till I have been through everything myself."

"*You* were not made to suffer — you were made to enjoy," Olive said, in very much the same tone in which she had told her that what was the matter with her was that she didn't dislike men as a class — a tone which implied that the contrary would have been much more natural and perhaps rather higher. Perhaps it would; but Verena was unable to rebut

The Bostonians

the charge; she felt this, as she looked out of the window of the carriage at the bright, amusing city, where the elements seemed so numerous, the animation so immense, the shops so brilliant, the women so strikingly dressed, and knew that these things quickened her curiosity, all her pulses.

"Well, I suppose I mustn't presume on it," she remarked, glancing back at Olive with her natural sweetness, her uncontradicting grace.

That young lady lifted her hand to her lips — held it there a moment; the movement seemed to say, "When you are so divinely docile, how can I help the dread of losing you?" This idea, however, was unspoken, and Olive Chancellor's uttered words, as the carriage rolled on, were different.

"Verena, I don't understand why he wrote to you."

"He wrote to me because he likes me. Perhaps you'll say you don't understand why he likes me," the girl continued, laughing. "He liked me the first time he saw me."

"Oh, that time!" Olive murmured.

"And still more the second."

"Did he tell you that in his letter?" Miss Chancellor inquired.

"Yes, my dear, he told me that. Only he expressed it more gracefully." Verena was very happy to say that; a written phrase of Basil Ransom's sufficiently justified her.

"It was my intuition — it was my foreboding!" Olive exclaimed, closing her eyes.

"I thought you said you didn't dislike him."

"It isn't dislike — it's simple dread. Is that all there is between you?"

"Why, Olive Chancellor, what do you think?" Verena asked, feeling now distinctly like a coward. Five minutes afterwards she said to Olive that if it would give her pleasure they would leave New York on the morrow, without taking a fourth day; and as soon as she had done so she felt better, especially when she saw how gratefully Olive looked at her for the concession, how eagerly she rose to the offering in saying, "Well, if you *do* feel that it isn't our own life — our very own!" It was with these words, and others besides, and with an unusually weak, indefinite kiss, as if she wished to protest that, after all, a single day didn't matter, and yet accepted the sacrifice and was a little ashamed of it — it was in this manner that the agreement as to an immediate retreat was sealed. Verena could not shut her eyes to the fact that for a month she had been less frank, and if she wished to do penance this abbreviation of their pleasure in New York, even if it made her almost completely miss Basil Ransom, was easier than to tell Olive just now that the letter was *not* all, that there had been a long visit, a talk, and a walk besides, which she had been covering up for ever so many weeks. And of what consequence, anyway, was the missing? Was it such a pleasure to converse with

633

a gentleman who only wanted to let you know — and why he should want it so much Verena couldn't guess — that he thought you quite preposterous? Olive took her from place to place, and she ended by forgetting everything but the present hour, and the bigness and variety of New York, and the entertainment of rolling about in a carriage with silk cushions, and meeting new faces, new expressions of curiosity and sympathy, assurances that one was watched and followed. Mingled with this was a bright consciousness, sufficient for the moment, that one was moreover to dine at Delmonico's and go to the German opera. There was enough of the epicurean in Verena's composition to make it easy for her in certain conditions to live only for the hour.

Chapter XXXI

WHEN she returned with her companion to the establishment in Tenth Street she saw two notes lying on the table in the hall; one of which she perceived to be addressed to Miss Chancellor, the other to herself. The hand was different, but she recognised both. Olive was behind her on the steps, talking to the coachman about sending another carriage for them in half an hour (they had left themselves but just time to dress); so that she simply possessed herself of her own note and ascended to her room. As she did so she felt that all the while she had known it would be there, and was conscious of a kind of treachery, an unfriendly wilfulness, in not being more prepared for it. If she could roll about New York the whole afternoon and forget that there might be difficulties ahead, that didn't alter the fact that there *were* difficulties, and that they might even become considerable — might not be settled by her simply going back to Boston. Half an hour later, as she drove up the Fifth Avenue with Olive (there seemed to be so much crowded into that one day), smoothing her light gloves, wishing her fan were a little nicer, and proving by the answering, familiar brightness with which she looked out on the lamp-lighted streets that, whatever theory might be entertained as to the genesis of her talent and her personal nature, the blood of the lecture-going, night-walking Tarrants did distinctly flow in her veins; as the pair proceeded, I say, to the celebrated restaurant, at the door of which Mr. Burrage had promised to be in vigilant expectancy of their carriage. Verena found a sufficiently gay and natural tone of voice for remarking to her friend that Mr. Ransom had called upon her while they were out, and had left a note in which there were many compliments for Miss Chancellor.

"That's wholly your own affair, my dear," Olive replied, with a melancholy sigh, gazing down the vista of Fourteenth Street (which they happened just then to be traversing, with much agitation), toward the queer barrier of the elevated railway.

It was nothing new to Verena that if the great striving of Olive's life was for justice she yet sometimes failed to arrive at it in particular cases; and she reflected that it was rather late for her to say, like that, that Basil Ransom's letters were only his correspondent's business. Had not his kinswoman quite made the subject her own during their drive that afternoon? Verena determined now that her companion should hear all there was to be heard about the letter; asking herself whether, if she told her at present more than she cared to know, it wouldn't make up for her hitherto having told her less. "He brought it with him, written, in case I should be out. He wants to see me to-morrow — he says he has ever so much to say to me. He proposes an hour — says he hopes it won't be inconvenient for me to see him about eleven in the morning; thinks I may have no other engagements so early as that. Of course our return to Boston settles it," Verena added, with serenity.

Miss Chancellor said nothing for a moment; then she replied, "Yes, unless you invite him to come on with you in the train."

"Why, Olive, how bitter you are!" Verena exclaimed, in genuine surprise.

Olive could not justify her bitterness by saying that her companion had spoken as if she were disappointed, because Verena had not. So she simply remarked, "I don't see what he can have to say to you — that would be worth your hearing."

"Well, of course, it's the other side. He has got it on the brain!" said Verena, with a laugh which seemed to relegate the whole matter to the category of the unimportant.

"If we should stay, would you see him — at eleven o'clock?" Olive inquired.

"Why do you ask that — when I have given it up?"

"Do you consider it such a tremendous sacrifice?"

"No," said Verena good-naturedly; "but I confess I am curious."

"Curious — how do you mean?"

"Well, to hear the other side."

"Oh heaven!" Olive Chancellor murmured, turning her face upon her.

"You must remember I have never heard it." And Verena smiled into her friend's wan gaze.

"Do you want to hear all the infamy that is in the world?"

"No, it isn't that; but the more he should talk the better chance he would give me. I guess I can meet him."

"Life is too short. Leave him as he is."

"Well," Verena went on, "there are many I haven't cared to move at all, whom I might have been more interested in than in him. But to make him give in just at two or three points — that I should like better than anything I have done."

"You have no business to enter upon a contest that isn't equal; and it wouldn't be, with Mr. Ransom."

"The inequality would be that I have right on my side."

"What is that — for a man? For what was their brutality given them, but to make that up?"

"I don't think he's brutal; I should like to see," said Verena gaily.

Olive's eyes lingered a little on her own; then they turned away, vaguely, blindly, out of the carriage-window, and Verena made the reflection that she looked strangely little like a person who was going to dine at Delmonico's. How terribly she worried about everything, and how tragical was her nature; how anxious, suspicious, exposed to subtle influences! In their long intimacy Verena had come to revere most of her friend's peculiarities; they were a proof of her depth and devotion, and were so bound up with what was noble in her that she was rarely provoked to criticise them separately. But at present, suddenly, Olive's earnestness began to appear as inharmonious with the scheme of the universe as if it had been a broken saw; and she was positively glad she had not told her about Basil Ransom's appearance in Monadnoc Place. If she worried so about what she knew, how much would she not have worried about the rest! Verena had by this time made up her mind that her acquaintance with Mr. Ransom was the most episodical, most superficial, most unimportant of all possible relations.

Olive Chancellor watched Henry Burrage very closely that evening; she had a special reason for doing so, and her entertainment, during the successive hours, was derived much less from the delicate little feast over which this insinuating proselyte presided, in the brilliant public room of the establishment, where French waiters flitted about on deep carpets and parties at neighbouring tables excited curiosity and conjecture, or even from the magnificent music of "Lohengrin," than from a secret process of comparison and verification, which shall presently be explained to the reader. As some discredit has possibly been thrown upon her impartiality it is a pleasure to be able to say that on her return from the opera she took a step dictated by an earnest consideration of justice — of the promptness with which Verena had told her of the note left by Basil Ransom in the afternoon. She drew Verena into her room with her. The girl, on the way back to Tenth Street, had spoken only of Wagner's music, of the singers, the orchestra, the immensity of the house, her tremendous pleasure. Olive could see how fond she might become of New York, where that kind of pleasure was so much more in the air.

"Well, Mr. Burrage was certainly very kind to us — no one could have been more thoughtful," Olive said; and she coloured a little at the look with which Verena greeted this tribute of appreciation from Miss Chancellor to a single gentleman.

"I am so glad you were struck with that, because I do think we have been a little rough to him." Verena's *we* was angelic. "He was particularly attentive to you, my dear; he has got over me. He looked at you so sweetly. Dearest Olive, if you marry him —— !" And Miss Tarrant, who was in high spirits, embraced her companion, to check her own silliness.

"He wants you to stay there, all the same. They haven't given *that* up," Olive remarked, turning to a drawer, out of which she took a letter.

"Did he tell you that, pray? He said nothing more about it to me."

"When we came in this afternoon I found this note from Mrs. Burrage. You had better read it." And she presented the document, open, to Verena.

The purpose of it was to say that Mrs. Burrage could really not reconcile herself to the loss of Verena's visit, on which both she and her son had counted so much. She was sure they would be able to make it as interesting to Miss Tarrant as it would be to themselves. She, Mrs. Burrage, moreover, felt as if she hadn't heard half she wanted about Miss Tarrant's views, and there were so many more who were present at the address, who

had come to her that afternoon (losing not a minute, as Miss Chancellor could see), to ask how in the world they too could learn more — how they could get at the fair speaker and question her about certain details. She hoped so much, therefore, that even if the young ladies should be unable to alter their decision about the visit they might at least see their way to staying over long enough to allow her to arrange an informal meeting for some of these poor thirsty souls. Might she not at least talk over the question with Miss Chancellor? She gave her notice that she would attack her on the subject of the visit too. Might she not see her on the morrow, and might she ask of her the very great favour that the interview should be at Mrs. Burrage's own house? She had something very particular to say to her, as regards which perfect privacy was a great consideration, and Miss Chancellor would doubtless recognize that this would be best secured under Mrs. Burrage's roof. She would therefore send her carriage for Miss Chancellor at any hour that would be convenient to the latter. She really thought much good might come from their having a satisfactory talk.

Verena read this epistle with much deliberation; it seemed to her mysterious, and confirmed the idea she had received the night before — the idea that she had not got quite a correct impression of this clever, worldly, curious woman on the occasion of her visit to

Cambridge, when they met her at her son's rooms. As she gave the letter back to Olive she said, "That's why he didn't seem to believe we are really leaving to-morrow. He knows she had written that, and he thinks it will keep us."

"Well, if I were to say it may — should you think me too miserably changeful?"

Verena stared, with all her candour, and it was so very queer that Olive should now wish to linger that the sense of it, for the moment, almost covered the sense of its being pleasant. But that came out after an instant, and she said, with great honesty, "You needn't drag me away for consistency's sake. It would be absurd for me to pretend that I don't like being here."

"I think perhaps I ought to see her." Olive was very thoughtful.

"How lovely it must be to have a secret with Mrs. Burrage!" Verena exclaimed.

"It won't be a secret from you."

"Dearest, you needn't tell me unless you want," Verena went on, thinking of her own unimparted knowledge.

"I thought it was our plan to divide everything. It was certainly mine."

"Ah, don't talk about plans!" Verena exclaimed, rather ruefully. "You see, if we *are* going to stay to-morrow, how foolish it was to have any. There is more in her letter than is expressed," she added, as Olive appeared to be studying in her face the reasons for and against making this concession to Mrs. Burrage, and that was rather embarrassing.

"I thought it over all the evening — so that if now you will consent we will stay."

"Darling — what a spirit you have got! All through all those dear little dishes — all through 'Lohengrin!' As I haven't thought it over at all, you must settle it. You know I am not difficult."

"And would you go and stay with Mrs. Burrage, after all, if she should say anything to me that seems to make it desirable?"

Verena broke into a laugh. "You know it's not our real life!"

Olive said nothing for a moment; then she replied: "Don't think *I* can forget that. If I suggest a deviation, it's only because it sometimes seems to me that perhaps, after all, almost anything is better than the form reality *may* take with us." This was slightly obscure, as well as very melancholy, and Verena was relieved when her companion remarked, in a moment, "You must think me strangely inconsequent;" for this gave her a chance to reply, sooth-ingly:

"Why, you don't suppose I expect you to keep always screwed up! I will stay a week with Mrs. Burrage, or a fortnight, or a month, or anything you like," she pursued; "anything it may seem to you best to tell her after you have seen her."

"Do you leave it all to me? You don't give me much help," Olive said.

"Help to what?"

"Help to help *you*."

"I don't want any help; I am quite strong enough!" Verena cried, gaily. The next moment she inquired, in an appeal half comical, half touching, "My dear colleague, why do you make me say such conceited things?"

"And if you do stay — just even to-morrow — shall you be — very much of the time — with Mr. Ransom?"

As Verena for the moment appeared ironically-minded, she might have found a fresh subject for hilarity in the tremulous, tentative tone in which Olive made this inquiry. But it had not that effect; it produced the first manifestation of impatience — the first, literally, and the first note of reproach — that had occurred in the course of their remarkable intimacy. The colour rose to Verena's cheek, and her eye for an instant looked moist.

"I don't know what you always think, Olive, nor why you don't seem able to trust me. You didn't, from the first, with gentlemen. Perhaps you were right then — I don't say; but surely it is very different now. I don't think I ought to be suspected so much. Why have you a manner as if I had to be watched, as if I wanted to run away with every man that speaks to me? I should think I had proved how little I care. I thought you had discovered by this time that I am serious; that I have dedicated my life; that there is something unspeakably dear to me. But you begin again, every time — you don't do me justice. I must take every-

thing that comes. I mustn't be afraid. I thought we had agreed that we were to do our work in the midst of the world, facing everything, keeping straight on, always taking hold. And now that it all opens out so magnificently, and victory is really sitting on our banners, it is strange of you to doubt of me, to suppose I am not more wedded to all our old dreams than ever. I told you the first time I saw you that I could renounce, and knowing better to-day, perhaps, what that means, I am ready to say it again. That I can, that I will! Why, Olive Chancellor," Verena cried, panting, a moment, with her eloquence, and with the rush of a culminating idea, "haven't you discovered by this time that I *have* renounced?"

The habit of public speaking, the training, the practice, in which she had been immersed, enabled Verena to unroll a coil of propositions dedicated even to a private interest with the most touching, most cumulative effect. Olive was completely aware of this, and she stilled herself, while the girl uttered one soft, pleading sentence after another, into the same rapt attention she was in the habit of sending up from the benches of an auditorium. She looked at Verena fixedly, felt that she was stirred to her depths, that she was exquisitely passionate and sincere, that she was a quivering, spotless, consecrated maiden, that she really had renounced, that they were both safe, and that her own injustice and indelicacy had been great.

She came to her slowly, took her in her arms and held her long — giving her a silent kiss. From which Verena knew that she believed her.

Chapter XXXII

THE HOUR that Olive proposed to Mrs. Burrage, in a note sent early the next morning, for the interview to which she consented to lend herself, was the stroke of noon; this period of the day being chosen in consequence of a prevision of many subsequent calls upon her time. She remarked in her note that she did not wish any carriage to be sent for her, and she surged and swayed up the Fifth Avenue on one of the convulsive, clattering omnibuses which circulate in that thoroughfare. One of her reasons for mentioning twelve o'clock had been that she knew Basil Ransom was to call at Tenth Street at eleven, and (as she supposed he didn't intend to stay all day) this would give her time to see him come and go. It had been tacitly agreed between them, the night before, that Verena was quite firm enough in her faith to submit to his visit, and that such a course would be much more dignified than dodging it. This understanding passed from one to the other during that dumb embrace which I have described as taking place before they separated for the night. Shortly before noon, Olive, passing out of the house, looked into the big, sunny double parlour, where, in the morning, with all the husbands absent for the day and all the wives and spinsters launched upon the town, a young man desiring to hold a debate with a young lady might enjoy every advantage in the way of a clear field. Basil Ransom was still there; he and Verena, with the place to themselves, were standing in the recess of a window, their backs presented to the door. If he had got up, perhaps he was going, and Olive, softly closing the door again, waited a little in the hall, ready to pass into the back part of the house if she should hear him coming out. No sound, however, reached her ear; apparently he did mean to stay all day, and she should find him there on her return. She left the house, knowing they were looking at her from the window as she descended the steps, but feeling she could not bear to see Basil Ransom's face. As she walked, averting her own, towards the Fifth Avenue, on the sunny side, she was barely conscious of the loveliness of the day, the perfect weather, all suffused and tinted with spring, which sometimes descends upon New York when the winds of March have been stilled; she was given up only to the remembrance of that moment when she herself had stood at a window (the second time he came to see her in Boston), and watched Basil Ransom pass out with Adeline — with Adeline who had seemed capable then of getting such a hold on him but

640

had proved as ineffectual in this respect as she was in every other. She recalled the vision she had allowed to dance before her as she saw the pair cross the street together, laughing and talking, and how it seemed to interpose itself against the fears which already then — so strangely — haunted her. Now that she saw it so fruitless — and that Verena, moreover, had turned out really so great — she was rather ashamed of it; she felt associated, however remotely, in the reasons which had made Mrs. Luna tell her so many fibs the day before, and there could be nothing elevating in that. As for the other reasons why her fidgety sister had failed and Mr. Ransom had held his own course, naturally Miss Chancellor didn't like to think of them.

If she had wondered what Mrs. Burrage wished so particularly to talk about, she waited some time for the clearing-up of the mystery. During this interval she sat in a remarkably pretty boudoir, where there were flowers and faiences and little French pictures, and watched her hostess revolve round the subject in circles the vagueness of which she tried to dissimulate. Olive believed she was a person who never could enjoy asking a favour, especially of a votary of the new ideas; and that was evidently what was coming. She had asked one already, but that had been handsomely paid for; the note from Mrs. Burrage which Verena found awaiting her in Tenth Street, on her arrival, contained the largest cheque this young woman had ever received for an address. The request that hung fire had reference to Verena too, of course; and Olive needed no prompting to feel that her friend's being a young person who took money could not make Mrs. Burrage's present effort more agreeable. To this taking of money (for when it came to Verena it was as if it came to her as well), she herself was now completely inured; money was a tremendous force, and when one wanted to assault the wrong with every engine one was happy not to lack the sinews of war. She liked her hostess better this morning than she had liked her before; she had more than ever the air of taking all sorts of sentiments and views for granted between them; which could only be flattering to Olive so long as it was really Mrs. Burrage who made each advance, while her visitor sat watchful and motionless. She had a light, clever, familiar way of traversing an immense distance with a very few words, as when she remarked, "Well then, it is settled that she will come, and will stay till she is tired."

Nothing of the kind had been settled, but Olive helped Mrs. Burrage (this time) more than she knew by saying, "Why do you want her to visit you, Mrs. Burrage? why do you want her socially? Are you not aware that your son, a year ago, desired to marry her?"

"My dear Miss Chancellor, that is just what I wish to talk to you about. I am aware of everything; I don't believe you ever met any one who is aware of more things than I." And Olive had to believe this, as Mrs. Burrage held up, smiling, her intelligent, proud, good-natured, successful head. "I knew a year ago that my son was in love with your friend, I know that he has been so ever since, and that in consequence he would like to marry her to-day. I daresay you don't like the idea of her marrying at all; it would break up a friendship which is so full of interest" (Olive wondered for a moment whether she had been going to say "so full of profit"), "for you. This is why I hesitated; but since you are willing to talk about it, that is just what I want."

"I don't see what good it will do," Olive said.

"How can we tell till we try? I never give a thing up till I have turned it over in every sense."

It was Mrs. Burrage, however, who did most of the talking; Olive only inserted from time to time an inquiry, a protest, a correction, an ejaculation tinged with irony. None of these things checked or diverted her hostess; Olive saw more and more that she wished to please her, to win her over, to smooth matters down, to place them in a new and original light. She was very clever and (little by little Olive said to herself), absolutely unscrupulous, but she didn't think she was clever enough for what she had undertaken. This was neither more nor less, in the first place, than to persuade Miss Chancellor that she and her son were consumed with sympathy for the movement to which Miss Chancellor had dedicated her life. But how could Olive believe that, when she saw the type to which Mrs. Burrage belonged — a type into which nature herself had inserted a face turned in the very opposite way from all earnest and improving things? People like Mrs. Burrage lived and fattened on abuses, prejudices, privileges, on the petrified, cruel fashions of the past. It must be added, however, that if her hostess was a humbug, Olive had never met one who provoked her less; she was such a brilliant, genial, artistic one, with such a recklessness of perfidy, such a willingness to bribe you if she couldn't deceive you. She seemed to be offering Olive all the kingdoms of the earth if she would only exert herself to bring about a state of feeling on Verena Tarrant's part which would lead the girl to accept Henry Burrage.

"We know it's you — the whole business; that you can do what you please. You could decide it to-morrow with a word."

She had hesitated at first, and spoken of her hesitation, and it might have appeared that she would need all her courage to say to Olive, that way, face to face, that Verena was in such subjection to her. But she didn't look afraid; she only looked as if it were an infinite pity Miss Chancellor couldn't understand what immense advantages and rewards there would be for her in striking an alliance with the house of Burrage. Olive was so impressed with this, so occupied, even, in wondering what these mystic benefits might be, and whether after all there might not be a protection in them (from something worse), a fund of some sort that she and Verena might convert to a large use, setting aside the mother and son when once they had got what they had to give — she was so arrested with the vague daze of this vision, the sense of Mrs. Burrage's full hands, her eagerness, her thinking it worth while to flatter and conciliate, whatever her pretexts and pretensions might be, that she was almost insensible, for the time, to the strangeness of such a woman's coming round to a positive desire for a connection with the Tarrants. Mrs. Burrage had indeed explained this partly by saying that her son's condition was wearing her out, and that she would enter into anything that would make him happier, make him better. She was fonder of him than of the whole world beside, and it was an anguish to her to see him yearning for Miss Tarrant only to lose her. She made that charge about Olive's power in the matter in such a way that it seemed at the same time a tribute to her force of character.

"I don't know on what terms you suppose me to be with my friend," Olive returned, with considerable majesty. "She will do exactly as she likes, in such a case as the one you allude to. She is absolutely free; you speak as if I were her keeper!"

Then Mrs. Burrage explained that of course she didn't mean that Miss Chancellor exercised a conscious tyranny; but only that Verena had a boundless admiration for her, saw through her eyes, took the impress of all her opinions, preferences. She was sure that if Olive would only take a favourable view of her son Miss Tarrant would instantly throw herself into it. "It's very true that you may ask me," added Mrs. Burrage, smiling, "how you can take a favourable view of a young man who wants to marry the very person in the world you want most to keep unmarried!"

This description of Verena was of course perfectly correct; but it was not agreeable to Olive to have the fact in question so clearly perceived, even by a person who expressed it with an air intimating that there was nothing in the world *she* couldn't understand.

"Did your son know that you were going to speak to me about this?" Olive asked, rather coldly, waiving the question of her influence on Verena and the state in which she wished her to remain.

"Oh, yes, poor dear boy; we had a long talk yesterday, and I told him I would do what I could for him. Do you remember the little visit I paid to Cambridge last spring, when I saw you at his rooms? Then it was I began to perceive how the wind was setting; but yesterday we had a real *éclaircissement*. I didn't like it at all, at first; I don't mind telling you that, now — now that I am really enthusiastic about it. When a girl is as charming, as original, as Miss Tarrant, it doesn't in the least matter who she is; she makes herself the standard by which you measure her; she makes her own position. And then Miss Tarrant has such a future!" Mrs. Burrage added, quickly, as if that were the last thing to be overlooked. "The whole question has come up again — the feeling that Henry tried to think dead, or at least dying, has revived, through the — I hardly know what to call it, but I really may say the unexpectedly great effect of her appearance here. She was really wonderful on Wednesday evening; prejudice, conventionality, every presumption there might be against her, had to fall to the ground. I expected a success, but I didn't expect what you gave us," Mrs. Burrage went on, smiling, while Olive noted her "you." "In short, my poor boy flamed up again; and now I see that he will never again care for any girl as he cares for that one. My dear Miss Chancellor, *j'en ai pris mon parti*, and perhaps you know my way of doing that sort of thing. I am not at all good at resigning myself, but I am excellent at taking up a craze. I haven't renounced, I have only changed sides. For or against, I must be a partisan. Don't you know that kind of nature? Henry has put the affair into my hands, and you see I put it into yours. Do help me; let us work together."

This was a long, explicit speech for Mrs. Burrage, who dealt, usually, in the cursory and allusive; and she may very well have expected that Miss Chancellor would recognise its importance. What Olive did, in fact, was simply to inquire, by way of rejoinder: "Why did you ask us to come on?"

If Mrs. Burrage hesitated now, it was only for twenty seconds. "Simply because we are so interested in your work."

"That surprises me," said Olive, thoughtfully.

"I daresay you don't believe it; but such a judgment is superficial. I am sure we give proof in the offer we make," Mrs. Burrage remarked, with a good deal of point. "There are plenty of girls — without any views at all — who would be delighted to marry my son. He is very clever, and he has a large fortune. Add to that that he's an angel!"

That was very true, and Olive felt all the more that the attitude of these fortunate people, for whom the world was so well arranged just as it was, was very curious. But as she sat there it came over her that the human spirit has many variations, that the influence of the truth is great, and that there are such things in life as happy surprises, quite as well as disagreeable ones. Nothing, certainly, forced such people to fix their affections on the daughter of a "healer"; it would be very clumsy to pick her out of her generation only for the purpose of frustrating her. Moreover, her observation of their young host at Delmonico's and in the spacious box at the Academy of Music, where they had privacy and ease, and murmured words could pass without making neighbours more given up to the stage turn their heads — her consideration of Henry Burrage's manner, suggested to her that she had measured him rather scantily the year before, that he was as much in love as the feebler passions of the age permitted (for though Miss Chancellor believed in the amelioration of humanity, she thought there was too much water in the blood of all of us), that he prized Verena for her rarity, which was her genius, her gift, and would therefore have an interest in promoting it, and that he was of so soft and fine a paste that his wife might do what she liked with him. Of course there would be the mother-in-law to count with; but unless she was perjuring herself shamelessly Mrs. Burrage really had the wish to project herself into the new atmosphere, or at least to be generous personally; so that, oddly enough, the fear that most glanced before Olive was not that this high, free matron, slightly irritable with cleverness and at the same time good-natured with prosperity, would bully her son's bride, but rather that she might take too fond a possession of her. It was a fear which may be described as a presentiment of jealousy. It occurred, accordingly, to Miss Chancellor's quick conscience that, possibly, the proposal which presented itself in circumstances so complicated and anomalous was simply a magnificent chance, an improvement on the very best, even, that

she had dreamed of for Verena. It meant a large command of money — much larger than her own; the association of a couple of clever people who simulated conviction very well, whether they felt it or not, and who had a hundred useful worldly ramifications, and a kind of social pedestal from which she might really shine afar. The conscience I have spoken of grew positively sick as it thought of having such a problem as that to consider, such an ordeal to traverse. In the presence of such a contingency the poor girl felt grim and helpless; she could only vaguely wonder whether she were called upon in the name of duty to lend a hand to the torture of her own spirit.

"And if she should marry him, how could I be sure that — afterwards — you would care so much about the question which has all our thoughts, hers and mine?" This inquiry evolved itself from Olive's rapid meditation; but even to herself it seemed a little rough.

Mrs. Burrage took it admirably. "You think we are feigning an interest, only to get hold of her? That's not very nice of you, Miss Chancellor; but of course you have to be tremendously careful. I assure you my son tells me he firmly believes your movement is the great question of the immediate future, that it has entered into a new phase; into what does he call it? the domain of practical politics. As for me, you don't suppose I don't want everything we poor women can get, or that I would

The Bostonians

refuse any privilege or advantage
that's offered me? I don't rant or
rave about anything, but I have
— as I told you just now — my own
quiet way of being zealous. If you
had no worse partisan than I, you
would do very well. My son has
talked to me immensely about your
ideas; and even if I should enter
into them only because he does, I
should do so quite enough. You
may say you don't see Henry dangling about after a wife who gives
public addresses; but I am convinced that a great many things are
coming to pass — very soon, too —
that we don't see in advance. Henry is a gentleman to his finger-tips,
and there is not a situation in
which he will not conduct himself
with tact."

Olive could see that they really
wanted Verena immensely, and it
was impossible for her to believe
that if they were to get her they
would not treat her well. It came
to her that they would even over-
indulge her, flatter her, spoil her;
she was perfectly capable, for the
moment, of assuming that Verena
was susceptible of deterioration
and that her own treatment of her
had been discriminatingly severe.
She had a hundred protests, objections, replies; her only embarrassment could be as to which she
should use first.

"I think you have never seen
Doctor Tarrant and his wife," she
remarked, with a calmness which
she felt to be very pregnant.

"You mean they are absolutely
fearful? My son has told me they
are quite impossible, and I am

quite prepared for that. Do you
ask how we should get on with
them? My dear young lady, we
should get on as you do!"

If Olive had answers, so had
Mrs. Burrage; she had still an answer when her visitor, taking up
the supposition that it was in her
power to dispose in any manner
whatsoever of Verena, declared
that she didn't know why Mrs.
Burrage addressed herself to *her*,
that Miss Tarrant was free as air,
that her future was in her own
hands, that such a matter as this
was a kind of thing with which it
could never occur to one to interfere. "Dear Miss Chancellor, we
don't ask you to interfere. The
only thing we ask of you is simply
not to interfere."

"And have you sent for me only
for that?"

"For that, and for what I hinted
at in my note; that you would really exercise your influence with
Miss Tarrant to induce her to
come to us now for a week or two.
That is really, after all, the main
thing I ask. Lend her to us, here,
for a little while, and we will take
care of the rest. That sounds conceited — but she *would* have a good
time."

"She doesn't live for that," said
Olive.

"What I mean is that she should
deliver an address every night!"
Mrs. Burrage returned, smiling.

"I think you try to prove too
much. You do believe — though
you pretend you don't — that I control her actions, and as far as possible her desires, and that I am

jealous of any other relations she may possibly form. I can imagine that we may perhaps have that air, though it only proves how little such an association as ours is understood, and how superficial is still" — Olive felt that her "still" was really historical — "the interpretation of many of the elements in the activity of women, how much the public conscience with regard to them needs to be educated. Your conviction with respect to my attitude being what I believe it to be," Miss Chancellor went on, "I am surprised at your not perceiving how little it is in my interest to deliver my — my victim up to you."

If we were at this moment to take, in a single glance, an inside view of Mrs. Burrage (a liberty we have not yet ventured on), I suspect we should find that she was considerably exasperated at her visitor's superior tone, at seeing herself regarded by this dry, shy, obstinate, provincial young woman as superficial. If she liked Verena very nearly as much as she tried to convince Miss Chancellor, she was conscious of disliking Miss Chancellor more than she should probably ever be able to reveal to Verena. It was doubtless partly her irritation that found a voice as she said, after a self-administered pinch of caution not to say too much, "Of course it would be absurd in us to assume that Miss Tarrant would find my son irresistible, especially as she has already refused him. But even if she should remain obdurate, should you con-

sider yourself quite safe as regards others?"

The manner in which Miss Chancellor rose from her chair on hearing these words showed her hostess that if she had wished to take a little revenge by frightening her, the experiment was successful. "What others do you mean?" Olive asked, standing very straight, and turning down her eyes as from a great height.

Mrs. Burrage — since we have begun to look into her mind we may continue the process — had not meant any one in particular; but a train of association was suddenly kindled in her thought by the flash of the girl's resentment. She remembered the gentleman who had come up to her in the music-room, after Miss Tarrant's address, while she was talking with Olive, and to whom that young lady had given so cold a welcome. "I don't mean any one in particular; but, for instance, there is the young man to whom she asked me to send an invitation to my party, and who looked to me like a possible admirer." Mrs. Burrage also got up; then she stood a moment, closer to her visitor. "Don't you think it's a good deal to expect that, young, pretty, attractive, clever, charming as she is, you should be able to keep her always, to exclude other affections, to cut off a whole side of life, to defend her against dangers — if you call them dangers — to which every young woman who is not positively repulsive is exposed? My dear young lady, I wonder if

I might give you three words of advice?" Mrs. Burrage did not wait till Olive had answered this inquiry; she went on quickly, with her air of knowing exactly what she wanted to say and feeling at the same time that, good as it might be, the manner of saying it, like the manner of saying most other things, was not worth troubling much about. "Don't attempt the impossible. You have got hold of a good thing; don't spoil it by trying to stretch it too far. If you don't take the better, perhaps you will have to take the worse; if it's safety you want I should think she was much safer with my son — for with us you know the worst — than as a possible prey to adventurers, to exploiters, or to people who, once they had got hold of her, would shut her up altogether."

Olive dropped her eyes; she couldn't endure Mrs. Burrage's horrible expression of being near the mark, her look of worldly cleverness, of a confidence born of much experience. She felt that nothing would be spared her, that she should have to go to the end, that this ordeal also must be faced, and that, in particular, there was a detestable wisdom in her hostess's advice. She was conscious, however, of no obligation to recognise it then and there; she wanted to get off, and even to carry Mrs. Burrage's sapient words along with her — to hurry to some place where she might be alone and think. "I don't know why you have thought it right to send for me only to say this. I take no interest whatever in your son — in his settling in life." And she gathered her mantle more closely about her, turning away.

"It is exceedingly kind of you to have come," said Mrs. Burrage, imperturbably. "Think of what I have said; I am sure you won't feel that you have wasted your hour."

"I have a great many things to think of!" Olive exclaimed, insincerely; for she knew that Mrs. Burrage's ideas would haunt her.

"And tell her that if she will make us the little visit, all New York shall sit at her feet!"

That was what Olive wanted, and yet it seemed a mockery to hear Mrs. Burrage say it. Miss Chancellor retreated, making no response even when her hostess declared again that she was under great obligations to her for coming. When she reached the street she found she was deeply agitated, but not with a sense of weakness; she hurried along, excited and dismayed, feeling that her insufferable conscience was bristling like some irritated animal, that a magnificent offer had really been made to Verena, and that there was no way for her to persuade herself she might be silent about it. Of course, if Verena should be tempted by the idea of being made so much of by the Burrages, the danger of Basil Ransom getting any kind of hold on her would cease to be pressing. That was what was present to Olive as she walked along, and that was what made her nervous, conscious only of this problem that had suddenly turned the bright day to grayness, heedless of the sophisticated-looking people who passed her on the wide Fifth Avenue pavement. It had risen in her mind the day before, planted first by Mrs. Burrage's note; and then, as we know, she had vaguely entertained the conception, asking Verena whether she would make the visit if it were again to be pressed upon them. It had been pressed, certainly, and the terms of the problem were now so much sharper that they seemed cruel. What had been in her own mind was that if Verena should appear to lend herself to the Burrages Basil Ransom might be discouraged — might think that, shabby and poor, there was no chance for him as against people with every advantage of fortune and position. She didn't see him relax his purpose so easily; she knew she didn't believe he was of that pusillanimous fibre. Still, it was a chance, and any chance that might help her had been worth considering. At present she saw it was a question not of Verena's lending herself, but of a positive gift, or at least of a bargain in which the terms would be immensely liberal. It would be impossible to use the Burrages as a shelter on the assumption that they were not dangerous, for they became dangerous from the moment they set up as sympathisers, took the ground that what they offered the girl was simply a boundless opportunity. It came back to Olive, again and again, that this was, and could only be, fantastic and false; but it

was always possible that Verena might not think it so, might trust them all the way. When Miss Chancellor had a pair of alternatives to consider, a question of duty to study, she put a kind of passion into it — felt, above all, that the matter must be settled that very hour, before anything in life could go on. It seemed to her at present that she couldn't re-enter the house in Tenth Street without having decided first whether she might trust the Burrages or not. By "trust" them, she meant trust them to fail in winning Verena over, while at the same time they put Basil Ransom on a false scent. Olive was able to say to herself that he probably wouldn't have the hardihood to push after her into those gilded saloons, which, in any event, would be closed to him as soon as the mother and son should discover what he wanted. She even asked herself whether Verena would not be still better defended from the young Southerner in New York, amid complicated hospitalities, than in Boston with a cousin of the enemy. She continued to walk down the Fifth Avenue, without noticing the cross-streets, and after a while became conscious that she was approaching Washington Square. By this time she had also definitely reasoned it out that Basil Ransom and Henry Burrage could not both capture Miss Tarrant, that therefore there could not be two dangers, but only one; that this was a good deal gained, and that it behooved her to determine which peril had most reality, in order that she might deal with that one only. She held her way to the Square, which, as all the world knows, is of great extent and open to the encircling street. The trees and grass-plats had begun to bud and sprout, the fountains plashed in the sunshine, the children of the quarter, both the dingier types from the south side, who played games that required much chalking of the paved walks, and much sprawling and crouching there, under the feet of passers, and the little curled and feathered people who drove their hoops under the eyes of French nursemaids — all the infant population filled the vernal air with small sounds which had a crude, tender quality, like the leaves and the thin herbage. Olive wandered through the place, and ended by sitting down on one of the continuous benches. It was a long time since she had done anything so vague, so wasteful. There were a dozen things which, as she was staying over in New York, she ought to do; but she forgot them, or, if she thought of them, felt that they were now of no moment. She remained in her place an hour, brooding, tremulous, turning over and over certain thoughts. It seemed to her that she was face to face with a crisis of her destiny, and that she must not shrink from seeing it exactly as it was. Before she rose to return to Tenth Street she had made up her mind that there was no menace so great as the menace of Basil Ransom; she had accepted in thought any arrangement which

would deliver her from that. If the Burrages were to take Verena they would take her from Olive immeasurably less than he would do; it was from him, from him they would take her most. She walked back to her boarding house, and the servant who admitted her said, in answer to her inquiry as to whether Verena were at home, that Miss Tarrant had gone out with the gentleman who called in the morning, and had not yet come in. Olive stood staring; the clock in the hall marked three.

Chapter XXXIII

"Come out with me, Miss Tarrant; come out with me. *Do* come out with me." That was what Basil Ransom had been saying to Verena when they stood where Olive perceived them, in the embrasure of the window. It had of course taken considerable talk to lead up to this; for the tone, even more than the words, indicated a large increase of intimacy. Verena was mindful of this when he spoke; and it frightened her a little, made her uneasy, which was one of the reasons why she got up from her chair and went to the window — an inconsequent movement, inasmuch as her wish was to impress upon him that it was impossible she should comply with his request. It would have served this end much better for her to sit, very firmly, in her place. He made

650

her nervous and restless; she was beginning to perceive that he produced a peculiar effect upon her. Certainly, she had been out with him at home the very first time he called upon her; but it seemed to her to make an important difference that she herself should then have proposed the walk — simply because it was the easiest thing to do when a person came to see you in Monadnoc Place.

They had gone out that time because she wanted to, not because he did. And then it was one thing for her to stroll with him round Cambridge, where she knew every step and had the confidence and freedom which came from being on her own ground, and the pretext, which was perfectly natural, of wanting to show him the colleges, and quite another thing to go wandering with him through the streets of this great strange city, which, attractive, delightful as it was, had not the suitableness even of being his home, not his real one. He wanted to show her something, he wanted to show her everything; but she was not sure now — after an hour's talk — that she particularly wanted to see anything more that he could show her. He had shown her a great deal while he sat there, especially what balderdash he thought it — the whole idea of women's being equal to men. He seemed to have come only for that, for he was all the while revolving round it; she couldn't speak of anything but what he brought it back to the question of some new truth like

that. He didn't say so in so many words; on the contrary, he was tremendously insinuating and satirical, and pretended to think she had proved all and a great deal more than she wanted to prove; but his exaggeration, and the way he rung all the changes on two or three of the points she had made at Mrs. Burrage's, were just the sign that he was a scoffer of scoffers. He wouldn't do anything but laugh; he seemed to think that he might laugh at her all day without her taking offence. Well, he might if it amused him; but she didn't see why she should ramble round New York with him to give him his opportunity.

She had told him, and she had told Olive, that she was determined to produce some effect on him; but now, suddenly, she felt differently about that — she ceased to care whether she produced any effect or not. She didn't see why she should take him so seriously, when he wouldn't take her so; that is, wouldn't take her ideas. She had guessed before that he didn't want to discuss them; this had been in her mind when she said to him at Cambridge that his interest in her was personal, not controversial. Then she had simply meant that, as an inquiring young Southerner, he had wanted to see what a bright New England girl was like; but since then it had become a little more clear to her — her short talk with Ransom at Mrs. Burrage's threw some light upon the question — what the personal interest of a young Southerner (however inquiring merely) might amount to. Did he too want to make love to her? This idea made Verena rather impatient, weary in advance. The thing she desired least in the world was to be put into the wrong with Olive; for she had certainly given her ground to believe (not only in their scene the night before, which was a simple repetition, but all along, from the very first), that she really had an interest which would transcend any attraction coming from such a source as that. If yesterday it seemed to her that she should like to struggle with Mr. Ransom, to refute and convince him, she had this morning gone into the parlour to receive him with the idea that, now they were alone together in a quiet, favourable place, he would perhaps take up the different points of her address one by one, as several gentlemen had done after hearing her on other occasions. There was nothing she liked so well as that, and Olive never had anything to say against it. But he hadn't taken up anything; he had simply laughed and chaffed, and unrolled a string of queer fancies about the delightful way women would fix things when, as she said in her address, they should get out of their box. He kept talking about the box; he seemed as if he wouldn't let go that simile. He said that he had come to look at her through the glass sides, and if he wasn't afraid of hurting her he would smash them in. He was determined to find the key that would open it, if he had to look for it all

over the world; it was tantalising only to be able to talk to her through the keyhole. If he didn't want to take up the subject, he at least wanted to take *her* up — to keep his hand upon her as long as he could. Verena had had no such sensation since the first day she went in to see Olive Chancellor, when she felt herself plucked from the earth and borne aloft.

"It's the most lovely day, and I should like so much to show you New York, as you showed me your beautiful Harvard," Basil Ransom went on, pressing her to accede to his proposal. "You said that was the only thing you could do for me then, and so this is the only thing I can do for you here. It would be odious to see you go away, giving me nothing but this stiff little talk in a boarding-house parlour."

"Mercy, if you call this stiff!" Verena exclaimed, laughing, while at that moment Olive passed out of the house and descended the steps before her eyes.

"My poor cousin's stiff; she won't turn her head a hair's breadth to look at us," said the young man. Olive's figure, as she went by, was, for Verena, full of a queer, touching, tragic expression, saying ever so many things, both familiar and strange; and Basil Ransom's companion privately remarked how little men knew about women, or indeed about what was really delicate, that he, without any cruel intention, should attach an idea of ridicule to such an incarnation of the pathetic, should speak rough, derisive words about it. Ransom, in truth, to-day, was not disposed to be very scrupulous, and he only wanted to get rid of Olive Chancellor, whose image, at last, decidedly bothered and bored him. He was glad to see her go out; but that was not sufficient, she would come back quick enough; the place itself contained her, expressed her. For to-day he wanted to take possession of Verena, to carry her to a distance, to reproduce a little the happy conditions they had enjoyed the day of his visit to Cambridge. And the fact that in the nature of things it could only be for to-day made his desire more keen, more full of purpose. He had thought over the whole question in the last forty-eight hours, and it was his belief that he saw things in their absolute reality. He took a greater interest in her than he had taken in any one yet, but he proposed, after to-day, not to let that accident make any difference. This was precisely what gave its high value to the present limited occasion. He was too shamefully poor, too shabbily and meagrely equipped, to have the right to talk of marriage to a girl in Verena's very peculiar position. He understood now how good that position was, from a worldly point of view; her address at Mrs. Burrage's gave him something definite to go upon, showed him what she could do, that people would flock in thousands to an exhibition so charming (and small blame to them); that she might easily have a big

career, like that of a distinguished actress or singer, and that she would make money in quantities only slightly smaller than performers of that kind. Who wouldn't pay half a dollar for such an hour as he had passed at Mrs. Burrage's? The sort of thing she was able to do, to say, was an article for which there was more and more demand — fluent, pretty, third-rate palaver, conscious or unconscious, perfected humbug; the stupid, gregarious, gullible public, the enlightened democracy of his native land, could swallow unlimited draughts of it. He was sure she could go, like that, for several years, with her portrait in the druggists' windows and her posters on the fences, and during that time would make a fortune sufficient to keep her in affluence for evermore. I shall perhaps expose our young man to the contempt of superior minds if I say that all this seemed to him an insuperable impediment to his making up to Verena. His scruples were doubtless begotten of a false pride, a sentiment in which there was a thread of moral tinsel, as there was in the Southern idea of chivalry; but he felt ashamed of his own poverty, the positive flatness of his situation, when he thought of the gilded nimbus that surrounded the protégée of Mrs. Burrage. This shame was possible to him even while he was conscious of what a mean business it was to practise upon human imbecility, how much better it was even to be seedy and obscure, discouraged about one's self. He had been born to the prospect of a fortune, and in spite of the years of misery that followed the war had never rid himself of the belief that a gentleman who desired to unite himself to a charming girl couldn't yet ask her to come and live with him in sordid conditions. On the other hand it was no possible basis of matrimony that Verena should continue for his advantage the exercise of her remunerative profession; if he should become her husband he should know a way to strike her dumb. In the midst of this an irrepressible desire urged him on to taste, for once, deeply, all that he was condemned to lose, or at any rate forbidden to attempt to gain. To spend a day with her and not to see her again — that presented itself to him at once as the least and the most that was possible. He did not need even to remind himself that young Mr. Burrage was able to offer her everything *he* lacked, including the most amiable adhesion to her views.

"It will be charming in the Park to-day. Why not take a stroll with me there as I did with you in the little park at Harvard?" he asked, when Olive had disappeared.

"Oh, I've seen it, very well, in every corner. A friend of mine kindly took me to drive there yesterday," Verena said.

"A friend? — do you mean Mr. Burrage?" And Ransom stood looking at her with his extraordinary eyes. "Of course, I haven't a vehicle to drive you in; but we can sit on a bench and talk." She didn't

say it was Mr. Burrage, but she was unable to say it was not, and something in her face showed him that he had guessed. So he went on: "Is it only with him you can go out? Won't he like it, and may you only do what he likes? Mrs. Luna told me he wants to marry you, and I saw at his mother's how he stuck to you. If you are going to marry him, you can drive with him every day in the year, and that's just a reason for your giving me an hour or two now, before it becomes impossible." He didn't mind much what he said — it had been his plan not to mind much to-day — and so long as he made her do what he wanted he didn't care much how he did it. But he saw that his words brought the colour to her face; she stared, surprised at his freedom and familiarity. He went on, dropping the hardness, the irony of which he was conscious, out of his tone. "I know it's no business of mine whom you marry, or even whom you drive with, and I beg your pardon if I seem indiscreet and obtrusive; but I would give anything just to detach you a little from your ties, your belongings, and feel for an hour or two, as if — as if —— " And he paused.

"As if what?" she asked, very seriously.

"As if there were no such person as Mr. Burrage — as Miss Chancellor — in the whole place." This had not been what he was going to say; he used different words.

"I don't know what you mean,

654

why you speak of other persons. I can do as I like, perfectly. But I don't know why you should take so for granted that *that* would be it!" Verena spoke these words not out of coquetry, or to make him beg her more for a favour, but because she was thinking, and she wanted to gain a moment. His allusion to Henry Burrage touched her, his belief that she had been in the Park under circumstances more agreeable than those he proposed. They were not; somehow, she wanted him to know that. To wander there with a companion, slowly stopping, lounging, looking at the animals as she had seen the people do the day before; to sit down in some out-of-the-way part where there were distant views, which she had noticed from her high perch beside Henry Burrage — she had to look down so, it made her feel unduly fine: that was much more to her taste, much more her idea of true enjoyment. It came over her that Mr. Ransom had given up his work to come to her at such an hour; people of his kind, in the morning, were always getting their living, and it was only for Mr. Burrage that it didn't matter, inasmuch as he had no profession. Mr. Ransom simply wanted to give up his whole day. That pressed upon her; she was, as the most good-natured girl in the world, too entirely tender not to feel any sacrifice that was made for her; she had always done everything that people asked. Then, if Olive should make that strange arrangement for her to go to Mrs.

Burrage's he would take it as a proof that there was something serious between her and the gentleman of the house, in spite of anything she might say to the contrary; moreover, if she should go she wouldn't be able to receive Mr. Ransom there. Olive would trust her not to, and she must certainly, in future, not disappoint Olive nor keep anything back from her, whatever she might have done in the past. Besides, she didn't want to do that; she thought it much better not. It was this idea of the episode which was possibly in store for her in New York, and from which her present companion would be so completely excluded, that worked upon her now with a rapid transition, urging her to grant him what he asked, so that in advance she should have made up for what she might not do for him later. But most of all she disliked his thinking she was engaged to some one. She didn't know, it is true, why she should mind it; and indeed, at this moment, our young lady's feelings were not in any way clear to her. She did not see what was the use of letting her acquaintance with Mr. Ransom become much closer (since his interest did really seem personal); and yet she presently asked him why he wanted her to go out with him, and whether there was anything particular he wanted to say to her (there was no one like Verena for making speeches apparently flirtatious, with the best faith and the most innocent intention in the world); as if that would not be precisely a reason to make it well she should get rid of him altogether.

"Of course I have something particular to say to you — I have a tremendous lot to say to you!" the young man exclaimed. "Far more than I can say in this stuck-up, confined room, which is public, too, so that any one may come in from one moment to another. Besides," he added, sophistically, "it isn't proper for me to pay a visit of three hours."

Verena did not take up the sophistry, nor ask him whether it would be more proper for her to ramble about the city with him for an equal period; she only said, "Is it something that I shall care to hear, or that will do me any good?"

"Well, I hope it will do you good; but I don't suppose you will care much to hear it." Basil Ransom hesitated a moment, smiling at her; then he went on: "It's to tell you, once for all, how much I really do differ from you!" He said this at a venture, but it was a happy inspiration.

If it was only that, Verena thought she might go, for that was not personal. "Well, I'm glad you care so much," she answered, musingly. But she had another scruple still, and she expressed it in saying that she should like Olive very much to find her when she came in.

"That's all very well," Ransom returned; "but does she think that she only has a right to go out? Does she expect you to keep the house because she's abroad? If she stays out long enough, she will find you when she comes in."

"Her going out that way — it proves that she trusts me," Verena said, with a candour which alarmed her as soon as she had spoken.

Her alarm was just, for Basil Ransom instantly caught up her words, with a great mocking amazement. "Trusts you? and why shouldn't she trust you? Are you a little girl of ten and she your governess? Haven't you any liberty at all, and is she always watching you and holding you to an account? Have you such vagabond instincts that you are only thought safe when you are between four walls?" Ransom was going on to speak, in the same tone, of her having felt it necessary to keep Olive in ignorance of his visit to Cambridge — a fact they had touched on, by implication, in their short talk at Mrs. Burrage's; but in a moment he saw that he had said enough. As for Verena, she had said more than she meant, and the simplest way to unsay it was to go and get her bonnet and jacket and let him take her where he liked. Five minutes later he was walking up and down the parlour, waiting while she prepared herself to go out.

They went up to the Central Park by the elevated railway, and Verena reflected, as they proceeded, that anyway Olive was probably disposing of her somehow at Mrs. Burrage's, and that therefore there wasn't much harm in her just taking this little run on her own responsibility, especially as she should only be out an hour — which would be just the duration of Olive's absence. The beauty of the "elevated" was that it took you up to the Park and brought you back in a few minutes, and you had all the rest of the hour to walk about and see the place. It was so pleasant now that one was glad to see it twice over. The long, narrow inclosure, across which the houses in the streets that border it look at each other with their glittering windows, bristled with the raw delicacy of April, and, in spite of its rockwork grottoes and tunnels, its pavilions and statues, its too numerous paths and pavements, lakes too big for the landscape and bridges too big for the lakes, expressed all the fragrance and freshness of the most charming moment of the year. Once Verena was fairly launched the spirit of the day took possession of her; she was glad to have come, she forgot about Olive, enjoyed the sense of wandering in the great city with a remarkable young man who would take beautiful care of her, while no one else in the world knew where she was. It was very different from her drive yesterday with Mr. Burrage, but it was more free, more intense, more full of amusing incident and opportunity. She could stop and look at everything now, and indulge all her curiosities, even the most childish; she could feel as if she were out for the day, though she was not really — as she had not done since she was a little girl, when in the country, once or twice, when her father and mother had

drifted into summer quarters, gone out of town like people of fashion, she had, with a chance companion, strayed far from home, spent hours in the woods and fields, looking for raspberries and playing she was a gipsy. Basil Ransom had begun with proposing, strenuously, that she should come somewhere and have luncheon; he had brought her out half an hour before that meal was served in West Tenth Street, and he maintained that he owed her the compensation of seeing that she was properly fed; he knew a very quiet, luxurious French restaurant, near the top of the Fifth Avenue: he didn't tell her that he knew it through having once lunched there in company with Mrs. Luna. Verena for the present declined his hospitality — said she was going to be out so short a time that it wasn't worth the trouble; she should not be hungry, luncheon to her was nothing, she would eat when she went home. When he pressed her she said she would see later, perhaps, if she should find she wanted something. She would have liked immensely to go with him to an eating-house, and yet, with this, she was afraid, just as she was rather afraid, at bottom, and in the intervals of her quick pulsations of amusement, of the whole expedition, not knowing why she had come, though it made her happy, and reflecting that there was really nothing Mr. Ransom could have to say to her that would concern her closely enough. He knew what he intended about her sharing the noonday repast with him somehow; it had been part of his plan that she should sit opposite him at a little table, taking her napkin out of its curious folds — sit there smiling back at him while he said to her certain things that hummed, like memories of tunes, in his fancy, and they waited till something extremely good, and a little vague, chosen out of a French *carte,* was brought them. That was not at all compatible with her going home at the end of half an hour, as she seemed to expect to. They visited the animals in the little zoological garden which forms one of the attractions of the Central Park; they observed the swans in the ornamental water, and they even considered the question of taking a boat for half an hour, Ransom saying that they needed this to make their visit complete. Verena replied that she didn't see why it should be complete, and after having threaded the devious ways of the Ramble, lost themselves in the Maze, and admired all the statues and busts of great men with which the grounds are decorated, they contented themselves with resting on a sequestered bench, where, however, there was a pretty glimpse of the distance and an occasional stroller creaked by on the asphalt walk.

They had had by this time a great deal of talk, none of which, nevertheless, had been serious to Verena's view. Mr. Ransom continued to joke about everything, including the emancipation of women; Verena, who had always lived with people who took the world very earnestly, had never encountered such a power of disparagement or heard so much sarcasm levelled at the institutions of her country and the tendencies of the age. At first she replied to him, contradicted, showed a high spirit of retort, turning his irreverence against himself; she was too quick and ingenious not to be able to think of something to oppose — talking in a fanciful strain — to almost everything he said. But little by little she grew weary and rather sad; brought up, as she had been, to admire new ideas, to criticise the social arrangements that one met almost everywhere, and to disapprove of a great many things, she had yet never dreamed of such a wholesale arraignment as Mr. Ransom's, so much bitterness as she saw lurking beneath his exaggerations, his misrepresentations. She knew he was an intense conservative, but she didn't know that being a conservative could make a person so aggressive and unmerciful. She thought conservatives were only smug and stubborn and self-complacent, satisfied with what actually existed; but Mr. Ransom didn't seem any more satisfied with what existed than with what she wanted to exist, and he was ready to say worse things about some of those whom she would have supposed to be on his own side than she thought it right to say about almost any one. She ceased after a while to care to argue with him, and wondered what could have happened to him to make him so perverse. Probably something had gone wrong in his life — he had had some misfortune that coloured his whole view of the world. He was a cynic; she had often heard about that state of mind, though she had never encountered it, for all the people she had seen only cared, if possible, too much. Of Basil Ransom's personal history she knew only what Olive had told her, and that was but a general outline, which left plenty of room for private dramas, secret disappointments and sufferings. As she sat there beside him she thought of some of these things, asked herself whether they were what he was thinking of when he said, for instance, that he was sick of all the modern cant about freedom and had no sympathy with those who wanted an extension of it. What was needed for the good of the world was that people should make a better use of the liberty they possessed. Such declarations as this took Verena's breath away; she didn't suppose you could hear any one say such a thing as that in the nineteenth century, even the least advanced. It was of a piece with his denouncing the spread of education; he thought the spread of education a gigantic farce — people stuffing their heads with a lot of empty catchwords that prevented them from doing their work quietly and honestly. You had a right to an education only if you had an intelligence, and if you looked at the matter with any desire to see things as they are you soon perceived that an intelligence was a very rare luxury, the attribute of one person in a hundred. He seemed to take a pretty low view of humanity, anyway. Verena hoped that something really bad had happened to him — not by way of gratifying any resentment he aroused in her nature, but to help herself to forgive him for so much contempt and brutality. She wanted to forgive him, for after they had sat on their bench half an hour and his jesting mood had abated a little, so that he talked with more consideration (as it seemed), and more sincerity, a strange feeling came over her, a perfect willingness not to keep insisting on her own side and a desire not to part from him with a mere accentuation of their differences. Strange I call the nature of her reflections, for they softly battled with each other as she listened, in the warm, still air, touched with the far-away hum of the immense city, to his deep, sweet, distinct voice, expressing monstrous opinions with exotic cadences and mild, familiar laughs, which, as he leaned towards her, almost tickled her cheek and ear. It seemed to her strangely harsh, almost cruel, to have brought her out only to say to her things which, after all, free as she was to contradict them and tolerant as she always tried to be, could only give her pain; yet there was a spell upon her as she listened; it was in her nature to be easily submissive, to like being overborne. She could be silent when people insisted, and silent without acrimony. Her whole relation to Olive was a kind of tacit, tender assent to passionate insistence, and if this had ended by being easy and agreeable to her (and indeed had never been anything else), it may be supposed that the struggle of yielding to a will which she felt to be stronger even than Olive's was not of long duration. Ransom's will had the effect of making her linger even while she knew the afternoon was going on, that Olive would have come back and found her still absent, and would have been submerged again in the bitter waves of anxiety. She saw her, in fact, as she must be at that moment, posted at the window of her room in Tenth Street, watching for some sign of her return, listening for her step on the staircase, her voice in the hall. Verena looked at this image as at a painted picture, perceived all it represented, every detail. If it didn't move her more, make her start to her feet, dart away from Basil Ransom and hurry back to her friend, this was because the very torment to which she was conscious of subjecting that friend made her say to herself that it must be the very last. This was the last time she could ever sit by Mr. Ransom and hear him express himself in a manner that interfered so with her life; the ordeal had been so personal and so complete that she forgot, for the moment, it was also the first time it had occurred. It might have been going on for months. She was perfectly aware that it could bring them to nothing, for one must lead one's own life; it was impossible to lead the life of another, especially when that other was so different, so arbitrary and unscrupulous.

Chapter XXXIV

"I PRESUME you are the only person in this country who feels as you do," she observed at last.

"Not the only person who feels so, but very possibly the only person who thinks so. I have an idea that my convictions exist in a vague, unformulated state in the minds of a great many of my fellow-citizens. If I should succeed some day in giving them adequate expression I should simply put into shape the slumbering instincts of an important minority."

"I am glad you admit it's a minority!" Verena exclaimed. "That's fortunate for us poor creatures. And what do you call adequate expression? I presume you would like to be President of the United States?"

"And breathe forth my views in glowing messages to a palpitating Senate? That is exactly what I should like to be; you read my aspirations wonderfully well."

"Well, do you consider that you have advanced far in that direction, as yet?" Verena asked.

This question, with the tone in which it happened to be uttered, seemed to the young man to project rather an ironical light upon his present beggarly condition, so that for a moment he said nothing; a moment during which if his neighbour had glanced round at his face she would have seen it ornamented by an incipient blush. Her words had for him the effect of a sudden, though, on the part of a young woman who had of course every right to defend herself, a perfectly legitimate taunt. They appeared only to repeat in another form (so at least his exaggerated Southern pride, his hot sensibility, interpreted the matter), the idea that a gentleman so dreadfully backward in the path of fortune had no right to take up the time of a brilliant, successful girl, even for the purpose of satisfying himself that he renounced her. But the reminder only sharpened his wish to make her feel that if he had renounced, it was simply on account of that same ugly, accidental, outside backwardness; and if he had not, he went so far as to flatter himself, he might triumph over the whole accumulation of her prejudices — over all the bribes of her notoriety. The deepest feeling in Ransom's bosom in relation to her was the conviction that she was made for love, as he had said to himself while he listened to her at Mrs. Burrage's. She was profoundly unconscious of it, and another ideal, crude and thin and artificial, had interposed itself; but in the presence of a man she should really care for, this false, flimsy structure would rattle to her feet, and the emancipation of Ol-

ive Chancellor's sex (what sex was it, great heaven? he used profanely to ask himself), would be relegated to the land of vapours, of dead phrases. The reader may imagine whether such an impression as this made it any more agreeable to Basil to have to believe it would be indelicate in him to try to woo her. He would have resented immensely the imputation that he had done anything of that sort yet. "Ah, Miss Tarrant, my success in life is one thing — my ambition is another!" he exclaimed, presently, in answer to her inquiry. "Nothing is more possible than that I may be poor and unheard of all my days; and in that case no one but myself will know the vision of greatness I have stifled and buried."

"Why do you talk of being poor and unheard of? Aren't you getting on quite well in this city?"

This question of Verena's left him no time, or at least no coolness, to remember that to Mrs. Luna and to Olive he had put a fine face on his prospects, and that any impression the girl might have about them was but the natural echo of what these ladies believed. It had to his ear such a subtly mocking, defiant, unconsciously injurious quality, that the only answer he could make to it seemed to him for the moment to be an outstretched arm, which, passing round her waist, should draw her so close to him as to enable him to give her a concise account of his situation in the form of a deliberate kiss. If the moment I speak of had lasted a few seconds longer I know not what monstrous proceeding of this kind it would have been my difficult duty to describe; it was fortunately arrested by the arrival of a nursery-maid pushing a perambulator and accompanied by an infant who toddled in her wake. Both the nurse and her companion gazed fixedly, and it seemed to Ransom even sternly, at the striking couple on the bench; and meanwhile Verena, looking with a quickened eye at the children (she adored children), went on —

"It sounds too flat for you to talk about your remaining unheard of. Of course you are ambitious; any one can see that, to look at you. And once your ambition is excited in any particular direction, people had better look out. With your will!" she added, with a curious mocking candour.

"What do you know about my will?" he asked, laughing a little awkwardly, as if he had really attempted to kiss her — in the course of the second independent interview he had ever had with her — and been rebuffed.

"I know it's stronger than mine. It made me come out, when I thought I had much better not, and it keeps me sitting here long after I should have started for home."

"Give me the day, dear Miss Tarrant, give me the day," Basil Ransom murmured; and as she turned her face upon him, moved by the expression of his voice, he added — "Come and dine with me,

since you wouldn't lunch. Are you really not faint and weak?"

"I am faint and weak at all the horrible things you have said; I have lunched on abominations. And now you want me to dine with you? Thank you; I think you're cool!" Verena cried, with a laugh which her chronicler knows to have been expressive of some embarrassment, though Basil Ransom did not.

"You must remember that I have, on two different occasions, listened to you for an hour, in speechless, submissive attention, and that I shall probably do it a great many times more."

"Why should you ever listen to me again, when you loathe my ideas?"

"I don't listen to your ideas; I listen to your voice."

"Ah, I told Olive!" said Verena, quickly, as if his words had confirmed an old fear; which was general, however, and did not relate particularly to him.

Ransom still had an impression that he was not making love to her, especially when he could observe, with all the superiority of a man — "I wonder whether you have understood ten words I have said to you?"

"I should think you had made it clear enough — you had rubbed it in!"

"What have you understood, then?"

"Why, that you want to put us back further than we have been at any period."

"I have been joking; I have been

piling it up," Ransom said, making that concession unexpectedly to the girl. Every now and then he had an air of relaxing himself, becoming absent, ceasing to care to discuss.

She was capable of noticing this, and in a moment she asked — "Why don't you write out your ideas?"

This touched again upon the matter of his failure; it was curious how she couldn't keep off it, hit it every time. "Do you mean for the public? I have written many things, but I can't get them printed."

"Then it would seem that there are not so many people — so many as you said just now — who agree with you."

"Well," said Basil Ransom, "editors are a mean, timorous lot, always saying they want something original, but deadly afraid of it when it comes."

"Is it for papers, magazines?" As it sank into Verena's mind more deeply that the contributions of this remarkable young man had been rejected — contributions in which, apparently, everything she held dear was riddled with scorn — she felt a strange pity and sadness, a sense of injustice. "I am very sorry you can't get published," she said, so simply that he looked up at her, from the figure he was scratching on the asphalt with his stick, to see whether such a tone as that, in relation to such a fact, were not "put on." But it was evidently genuine, and Verena added that she supposed getting pub-

lished was very difficult always; she remembered, though she didn't mention, how little success her father had when he tried. She hoped Mr. Ransom would keep on; he would be sure to succeed at last. Then she continued, smiling, with more irony: "You may denounce me by name if you like. Only please don't say anything about Olive Chancellor."

"How little you understand what I want to achieve!" Basil Ransom exclaimed. "There you are — you women — all over; always meaning yourselves, something personal, and always thinking it is meant by others!"

"Yes, that's the charge they make," said Verena, gaily.

"I don't want to touch you, or Miss Chancellor, or Mrs. Farrinder, or Miss Birdseye, or the shade of Eliza P. Moseley, or any other gifted and celebrated being on earth — or in heaven."

"Oh, I suppose you want to destroy us by neglect, by silence!" Verena exclaimed, with the same brightness.

"No, I don't want to destroy you, any more than I want to save you. There has been far too much talk about you, and I want to leave you alone altogether. My interest is in my own sex; yours evidently can look after itself. That's what I want to save."

Verena saw that he was more serious now than he had been before, that he was not piling it up satirically, but saying really and a trifle wearily, as if suddenly he were tired of much talk, what he meant. "To save it from what?" she asked.

"From the most damnable feminisation! I am so far from thinking, as you set forth the other night, that there is not enough woman in our general life, that it has long been pressed home to me that there is a great deal too much. The whole generation is womanised; the masculine tone is passing out of the world; it's a feminine, a nervous, hysterical, chattering, canting age, an age of hollow phrases and false delicacy and exaggerated solicitudes and coddled sensibilities, which, if we don't soon look out, will usher in the reign of mediocrity, of the feeblest and flattest and the most pretentious that has ever been. The masculine character, the ability to dare and endure, to know and yet not fear reality, to look the world in the face and take it for what it is — a very queer and partly very base mixture — that is what I want to preserve, or rather, as I may say, to recover; and I must tell you that I don't in the least care what becomes of you ladies while I make the attempt!"

The poor fellow delivered himself of these narrow notions (the rejection of which by leading periodicals was certainly not a matter for surprise), with low, soft earnestness, bending towards her so as to give out his whole idea, yet apparently forgetting for the moment how offensive it must be to her now that it was articulated in that calm, severe way, in which no allowance was to be made for hyperbole. Verena did not remind herself of this; she was too much impressed by his manner and by the novelty of a man taking that sort of religious tone about such a cause. It told her on the spot, from one minute to the other and once for all, that the man who could give her that impression would never come round. She felt cold, slightly sick, though she replied that now he summed up his creed in such a distinct, lucid way, it was much more comfortable — one knew with what one was dealing; a declaration much at variance with the fact, for Verena had never felt less gratified in her life. The ugliness of her companion's profession of faith made her shiver; it would have been difficult to her to imagine anything more crudely profane. She was determined, however, not to betray any shudder that could suggest weakness, and the best way she could think of to disguise her emotion was to remark in a tone which, although not assumed for that purpose, was really the most effective revenge, inasmuch as it always produced on Ransom's part (it was not peculiar, among women, to Verena), an angry helplessness — "Mr. Ransom, I assure you this is an age of conscience."

"That's a part of your cant. It's an age of unspeakable shams, as Carlyle says."

"Well," returned Verena, "it's all very comfortable for you to say that you wish to leave us alone. But you can't leave us alone. We are here, and we have got to be dis-

The Bostonians

posed of. You have got to put us somewhere. It's a remarkable social system that has no place for *us!*" the girl went on, with her most charming laugh.

"No place in public. My plan is to keep you at home and have a better time with you there than ever."

"I'm glad it's to be better; there's room for it. Woe to American womanhood when you start a movement for being more — what you like to be — at home!"

"Lord, how you're perverted; you, the very genius!" Basil Ransom murmured, looking at her with the kindest eyes.

She paid no attention to this, she went on, "And those who have got no home (there are millions, you know), what are you going to do with *them?* You must remember that women marry — are given in marriage — less and less; that isn't their career, as a matter of course, any more. You can't tell them to go and mind their husband and children, when they have no husband and children to mind."

"Oh," said Ransom, "that's a detail! And for myself, I confess, I have such a boundless appreciation of your sex in private life that I am perfectly ready to advocate a man's having a half a dozen wives."

"The civilisation of the Turks, then, strikes you as the highest?"

"The Turks have a second-rate religion; they are fatalists, and that keeps them down. Besides, their women are not nearly so charm-ing as ours — or as ours would be if this modern pestilence were eradicated. Think what a confession you make when you say that women are less and less sought in marriage; what a testimony that is to the pernicious effect on their manners, their person, their nature, of this fatuous agitation."

"That's very complimentary to me!" Verena broke in, lightly.

But Ransom was carried over her interruption by the current of his argument. "There are a thousand ways in which any woman, all women, married or single, may find occupation. They may find it in making society agreeable."

"Agreeable to men, of course."

"To whom else, pray? Dear Miss Tarrant, what is most agreeable to women is to be agreeable to men! That is a truth as old as the human race, and don't let Olive Chancellor persuade you that she and Mrs. Farrinder have invented any that can take its place, or that is more profound, more durable."

Verena waived this point of the discussion; she only said: "Well, I am glad to hear you are prepared to see the place all choked up with old maids!"

"I don't object to the *old* old maids; they were delightful; they had always plenty to do, and didn't wander about the world crying out for a vocation. It is the new old maid that you have invented from whom I pray to be delivered." He didn't say he meant Olive Chancellor, but Verena looked at him as if she suspected him of doing so; and to put her off

665

that scent he went on, taking up what she had said a moment before: "As for its not being complimentary to you, my remark about the effect on the women themselves of this pernicious craze, my dear Miss Tarrant, you may be quite at your ease. You stand apart, you are unique, extraordinary; you constitute a category by yourself. In you the elements have been mixed in a manner so felicitous that I regard you as quite incorruptible. I don't know where you come from nor how you come to be what you are, but you are outside and above all vulgarising influences. Besides, you ought to know," the young man proceeded, in the same cool, mild, deliberate tone, as if he were demonstrating a mathematical solution, "you ought to know that your connection with all these rantings and ravings is the most unreal, accidental, illusory thing in the world. You think you care about them, but you don't at all. They were imposed upon you by circumstances, by unfortunate associations, and you accepted them as you would have accepted any other burden, on account of the sweetness of your nature. You always want to please some one, and now you go lecturing about the country, and trying to provoke demonstrations, in order to please Miss Chancellor, just as you did it before to please your father and mother. It isn't *you*, the least in the world, but an inflated little figure (very remarkable in its way too), whom you have invented

and set on its feet, pulling strings, behind it, to make it move and speak, while you try to conceal and efface yourself there. Ah, Miss Tarrant, if it's a question of pleasing, how much you might please some one else by tipping your preposterous puppet over and standing forth in your freedom as well as in your loveliness!"

While Basil Ransom spoke — and he had not spoken just that way yet — Verena sat there deeply attentive, with her eyes on the ground; but as soon as he ceased she sprang to her feet — something made her feel that their association had already lasted quite too long. She turned away from him as if she wished to leave him, and indeed were about to attempt to do so. She didn't desire to look at him now, or even to have much more conversation with him. "Something," I say, made her feel so, but it was partly his curious manner — so serene and explicit, as if he knew the whole thing to an absolute certainty — which partly scared her and partly made her feel angry. She began to move along the path to one of the gates, as if it were settled that they should immediately leave the place. He laid it all out so clearly; if he had had a revelation he couldn't speak otherwise. That description of herself as something different from what she was trying to be, the charge of want of reality, made her heart beat with pain; she was sure, at any rate, it was her real self that was there with him now, where she oughtn't to be. In a moment he was at her side again, going with her; and as they walked it came over her that some of the things he had said to her were far beyond what Olive could have imagined as the very worst possible. What would be her state now, poor forsaken friend, if some of them had been borne to her in the voices of the air? Verena had been affected by her companion's speech (his manner had changed so; it seemed to express something quite different), in a way that pushed her to throw up the discussion and determine that as soon as they should get out of the park she would go off by herself; but she still had her wits about her sufficiently to think it important she should give no sign of discomposure, of confessing that she was driven from the field. She appeared to herself to notice and reply to his extraordinary observations enough, without taking them up too much, when she said, tossing the words over her shoulder at Ransom, while she moved quickly: "I presume, from what you say, that you don't think I have much ability."

He hesitated before answering, while his long legs easily kept pace with her rapid step — her charming, touching, hurrying step, which expressed all the trepidation she was anxious to conceal. "Immense ability, but not in the line in which you most try to have it. In a very different line, Miss Tarrant! Ability is no word for it; it's genius!"

She felt his eyes on her face — ever so close and fixed there — after he had chosen to reply to her question that way. She was beginning to blush; if he had kept them longer, and on the part of any one else, she would have called such a stare impertinent. Verena had been commended of old by Olive for her serenity "while exposed to the gaze of hundreds"; but a change had taken place, and she was now unable to endure the contemplation of an individual. She wished to detach him, to lead him off again into the general; and for this purpose, at the end of a moment, she made another inquiry: "I am to understand, then, as your last word that you regard us as quite inferior?"

"For public, civic uses, absolutely — perfectly weak and second-rate. I know nothing more indicative of the muddled sentiment of the time than that any number of men should be found to pretend that they regard you in any other light. But privately, personally, it's another affair. In the realm of family life and the domestic affections ——"

At this Verena broke in, with a nervous laugh, "Don't say that; it's only a phrase!"

"Well, it's a better one than any of yours," said Basil Ransom, turning with her out of one of the smaller gates — the first they had come to. They emerged into the species of *plaza* formed by the numbered street which constitutes the southern extremity of the park and the termination of the Sixth Avenue. The glow of the splendid afternoon was over everything, and the day seemed to Ransom still in its youth. The bowers and boskages stretched behind them, the artificial lakes and cockneyfied landscapes, making all the region bright with the sense of air and space, and raw natural tints, and vegetation too diminutive to overshadow. The chocolate-coloured houses, in tall, new rows, surveyed the expanse; the street-cars rattled in the foreground, changing horses while the horses steamed, and absorbing and emitting passengers; and the beer-saloons, with exposed shoulders and sides, which in New York do a good deal towards representing the picturesque, the "bit" appreciated by painters, announced themselves in signs of large lettering to the sky. Groups of the unemployed, the children of disappointment from beyond the seas, propped themselves against the low, sunny wall of the park; and on the other side the commercial vista of the Sixth Avenue stretched away with a remarkable absence of aerial perspective.

"I must go home; good-bye," Verena said, abruptly, to her companion.

"Go home? You won't come and dine, then?"

Verena knew people who dined at midday and others who dined in the evening, and others still who never dined at all; but she knew no one who dined at half-past three. Ransom's attachment to this idea therefore struck her as queer and infelicitous, and she supposed it betrayed the habits of Mississippi. But that couldn't make it any more acceptable to her, in spite of his looking so disappointed — with his dimly-glowing eyes — that he was heedless for the moment that the main fact connected with her return to Tenth Street was that she wished to go alone.

"I must leave you, right away," she said. "Please don't ask me to stay; you wouldn't if you knew how little I want to!" Her manner was different now, and her face as well, and though she smiled more than ever she had never seemed to him more serious.

"Alone, do you mean? Really I can't let you do that," Ransom replied, extremely shocked at this sacrifice being asked of him. "I have brought you this immense distance, I am responsible for you, and I must place you where I found you."

"Mr. Ransom, I must, I will!" she exclaimed, in a tone he had not yet heard her use; so that, a good deal amazed, puzzled and pained, he saw that he should make a mistake if he were to insist. He had known that their expedition must end in a separation which could not be sweet, but he had counted on making some of the terms of it himself. When he expressed the hope that she would at least allow him to put her into a car, she replied that she wished no car; she wanted to walk. This image of her "streaking off" by herself, as he figured it, did not mend the matter; but in the presence of her sudden nervous impatience he felt that here was a feminine mystery which must be allowed to take its course.

"It costs me more than you probably suspect, but I submit. Heaven guard you and bless you, Miss Tarrant!"

She turned her face away from him as if she were straining at a leash; then she rejoined, in the most unexpected manner: "I hope very much you *will* get printed."

"Get my articles published?" He stared, and broke out: "Oh, you delightful being!"

"Good-bye," she repeated; and now she gave him her hand. As he held it a moment, and asked her if she were really leaving the city so soon that she mightn't see him again, she answered: "If I stay it will be at a place to which you mustn't come. They wouldn't let you see me."

He had not intended to put that question to her; he had set himself a limit. But the limit had suddenly moved on. "Do you mean at that house where I heard you speak?"

"I may go there for a few days."

"If it's forbidden to me to go and see you there, why did you send me a card?"

"Because I wanted to convert you then."

"And now you give me up?"

"No, no; I want you to remain as you are!"

She looked strange, with her more mechanical smile, as she said this, and he didn't know what idea was in her head. She had already left him, but he called after her,

"If you do stay, I will come!" She neither turned nor made an answer, and all that was left to him was to watch her till she passed out of sight. Her back, with its charming young form, seemed to repeat that last puzzle, which was almost a challenge.

For this, however, Verena Tarrant had not meant it. She wanted, in spite of the greater delay and the way Olive would wonder, to walk home, because it gave her time to think, and think again, how glad she was (really, positively, *now*), that Mr. Ransom was on the wrong side. If he had been on the right——! She did not finish this proposition. She found Olive waiting for her in exactly the manner she had foreseen; she turned to her, as she came in, a face sufficiently terrible. Verena instantly explained herself, related exactly what she had been doing; then went on, without giving her friend time for question or comment: "And you — you paid your visit to Mrs. Burrage?"

"Yes, I went through that."

"And did she press the question of my coming there?"

"Very much indeed."

"And what did you say?"

"I said very little, but she gave me such assurances——"

"That you thought I ought to go?"

Olive was silent a moment; then she said: "She declares they are devoted to the cause, and that New York will be at your feet."

Verena took Miss Chancellor's shoulders in each of her hands, and gave her back, for an instant, her gaze, her silence. Then she broke out, with a kind of passion: "I don't care for her assurances — I don't care for New York! I won't go to them — I won't — do you understand?" Suddenly her voice changed, she passed her arms round her friend and buried her face in her neck. "Olive Chancellor, take me away, take me away!" she went on. In a moment Olive felt that she was sobbing and that the question was settled, the question she herself had debated in anguish a couple of hours before.

Chapter XXXV

THE AUGUST night had gathered by the time Basil Ransom, having finished his supper, stepped out upon the piazza of the little hotel. It was a very little hotel and of a very slight and loose construction; the tread of a tall Mississippian made the staircase groan and the windows rattle in their frames. He was very hungry when he arrived, having not had a moment, in Boston, on his way through, to eat even the frugal morsel with which he was accustomed to sustain nature between a breakfast that consisted of a cup of coffee and a dinner that consisted of a cup of tea. He had had his cup of tea now, and very bad it was, brought him by a pale round-backed young lady, with auburn ringlets, a fancy belt, and an expression of limited

tolerance for a gentleman who could not choose quickly between fried fish, fried steak, and baked beans. The train for Marmion left Boston at four o'clock in the afternoon, and rambled fitfully toward the southern cape, while the shadows grew long in the stony pastures and the slanting light gilded the straggling, shabby, woods, and painted the ponds and marshes with yellow gleams. The ripeness of summer lay upon the land, and yet there was nothing of the country Basil Ransom traversed that seemed susceptible of maturity; nothing but the apples in the little tough, dense orchards, which gave a suggestion of sour fruition here and there, and the tall, bright golden-rod at the bottom of the bare stone dykes. There were no fields of yellow grain; only here and there a crop of brown hay. But there was a kind of soft scrubbiness in the landscape, and a sweetness begotten of low horizons, of mild air, with a possibility of summer haze, of unregarded inlets where on August mornings the water must be brightly blue. Ransom had heard that the Cape was the Italy, so to speak, of Massachusetts; it had been described to him as the drowsy Cape, the languid Cape, the Cape not of storms, but of eternal peace. He knew that the Bostonians had been drawn thither, for the hot weeks, by its sedative influence, by the conviction that its toneless air would minister to perfect rest. In a career in which there was so much nervous excitement as in theirs they had no wish to be wound up when they went out of town; they were sufficiently wound up at all times by the sense of all their sex had been through. They wanted to live idly, to unbend and lie in hammocks, and also to keep out of the crowd, the rush of the watering-place. Ransom could see there was no crowd at Marmion, as soon as he got there, though indeed there was a rush, which directed itself to the only vehicle in waiting outside of the small, lonely, hut-like station, so distant from the village that, as far as one looked along the sandy, sketchy road which was supposed to lead to it, one saw only an empty land on either side. Six or eight men, in "dusters," carrying parcels and handbags, projected themselves upon the solitary, rickety carry-all, so that Ransom could read his own fate, while the ruminating conductor of the vehicle, a lean shambling citizen, with a long neck and a tuft on his chin, guessed that if he wanted to get to the hotel before dusk he would have to strike out. His valise was attached in a precarious manner to the rear of the carry-all. "Well, I'll chance it," the driver remarked, sadly, when Ransom protested against its insecure position. He recognised the southern quality of that picturesque fatalism — judged that Miss Chancellor and Verena Tarrant must be pretty thoroughly relaxed if they had given themselves up to the genius of the place. This was what he hoped for and counted on, as he took his way, the sole pedestrian in the group that

had quitted the train, in the wake of the overladen carry-all. It helped him to enjoy the first country walk he had had for many months, for more than months, for years, that the reflection was forced upon him as he went (the mild, vague scenery, just beginning to be dim with twilight, suggested it at every step), that the two young women who constituted, at Marmion, his whole prefigurement of a social circle, must, in such a locality as that, be taking a regular holiday. The sense of all the wrongs they had still to redress must be lighter there than it was in Boston; the ardent young man had, for the hour, an ingenuous hope that they had left their opinions in the city. He liked the very smell of the soil as he wandered along; cool, soft whiffs of evening met him at bends of the road which disclosed very little more — unless it might be a band of straight-stemmed woodland, keeping, a little, the red glow from the west, or (as he went further) an old house, shingled all over, gray and slightly collapsing, which looked down at him from a steep bank, at the top of wooden steps. He was already refreshed; he had tasted the breath of nature, measured his long grind in New York, without a vacation, with the repetition of the daily movement up and down the long, straight, maddening city, like a bucket in a well or a shuttle in a loom.

He lit his cigar in the office of the hotel — a small room on the right of the door, where a "register," meagrely inscribed, led a

The Bostonians

terribly public life on the little bare desk, and got its pages dogs'-eared before they were covered. Local worthies, of a vague identity, used to lounge there, as Ransom perceived the next day, by the hour. They tipped back their chairs against the wall, seldom spoke, and might have been supposed, with their converging vision, to be watching something out of the window, if there had been anything in Marmion to watch. Sometimes one of them got up and went to the desk, on which he leaned his elbows, hunching a pair of sloping shoulders to an uncollared neck. For the fiftieth time he perused the fly-blown page of the recording volume, where the names followed each other with such jumps of date. The others watched him while he did so — or contemplated in silence some "guest" of the hostelry, when such a personage entered the place with an air of appealing from the general irresponsibility of the establishment and found no one but the village-philosophers to address himself to. It was an establishment conducted by invisible, elusive agencies; they had a kind of stronghold in the dining-room, which was kept locked at all but sacramental hours. There was a tradition that a "boy" exercised some tutelary function as regards the crumpled register; but when he was inquired about, it was usually elicited from the impartial circle in the office either that he was somewhere round or that he

had gone a-fishing. Except the haughty waitress who had just been mentioned as giving Ransom his supper, and who only emerged at meal-times from her mystic seclusion, this impalpable youth was the single person on the premises who represented domestic service. Anxious lady-boarders, wrapped in shawls, were seen waiting for him, as if he had been the doctor, on horse-hair rocking-chairs, in the little public parlour; others peered vaguely out of back doors and windows, thinking that if he were somewhere round they might see him. Sometimes people went to the door of the dining-room and tried it, shaking it a little, timidly, to see if it would yield; then, finding it fast, came away, looking, if they had been observed, shy and snubbed, at their fellows. Some of them went so far as to say that they didn't think it was a very good hotel.

Ransom, however, didn't much care whether it were good or not; he hadn't come to Marmion for the love of the hotel. Now that he had got there, however, he didn't know exactly what to do; his course seemed rather less easy than it had done when, suddenly, the night before, tired, sick of the city-air, and hungry for a holiday, he decided to take the next morning's train to Boston, and there take another to the shores of Buzzard's Bay. The hotel itself offered few resources; the inmates were not numerous; they moved about a little outside, on the small piazza and

672

in the rough yard which interposed between the house and the road, and then they dropped off into the unmitigated dusk. This element, touched only in two or three places by a far-away dim glimmer, presented itself to Ransom as his sole entertainment. Though it was pervaded by that curious, pure, earthy smell which in New England, in summer, hangs in the nocturnal air, Ransom bethought himself that the place might be a little dull for persons who had not come to it, as he had, to take possession of Verena Tarrant. The unfriendly inn, which suggested dreadfully to Ransom (he despised the practice), an early bed-time, seemed to have no relation to anything, not even to itself; but a fellow-tenant of whom he made an inquiry told him the village was sprinkled round. Basil presently walked along the road in search of it, under the stars, smoking one of the good cigars which constituted his only tribute to luxury. He reflected that it would hardly do to begin his attack that night; he ought to give the Bostonians a certain amount of notice of his appearance on the scene. He thought it very possible, indeed, that they might be addicted to the vile habit of "retiring" with the cocks and hens. He was sure that was one of the things Olive Chancellor would do so long as he should stay — on purpose to spite him; she would make Verena Tarrant go to bed at unnatural hours, just to deprive him of his evenings. He walked some dis-

tance without encountering a creature or discerning an habitation; but he enjoyed the splendid starlight, the stillness, the shrill melancholy of the crickets, which seemed to make all the vague forms of the country pulsate around him; the whole impression was a bath of freshness after the long strain of the preceding two years, and his recent sweltering weeks in New York. At the end of ten minutes (his stroll had been slow), a figure drew near him, at first indistinct, but presently defining itself as that of a woman. She was walking apparently without purpose, like himself, or without other purpose than that of looking at the stars, which she paused for an instant, throwing back her head, to contemplate, as he drew nearer to her. In a moment he was very close; he saw her look at him, through the clear gloom, as they passed each other. She was small and slim; he made out her head and face, saw that her hair was cropped; had an impression of having seen her before. He noticed that as she went by she turned as well as himself, and that there was a sort of recognition in her movement. Then he felt sure that he had seen her elsewhere, and before she had added to the distance that separated them he stopped short, looking after her. She noticed his halt, paused equally, and for a moment they stood there face to face, at a certain interval, in the darkness.

"I beg your pardon — is it Doctor Prance?" he found himself demanding.

For a minute there was no answer; then came the voice of the little lady:

"Yes, sir; I am Doctor Prance. Any one sick at the hotel?"

"I hope not; I don't know," Ransom said, laughing.

Then he took a few steps, mentioned his name, recalled his having met her at Miss Birdseye's, ever so long before (nearly two years), and expressed the hope that she had not forgotten that.

She thought it over a little — she was evidently addicted neither to empty phrases nor to unconsidered assertions. "I presume you mean that night Miss Tarrant launched out so."

"That very night. We had a very interesting conversation."

"Well, I remember I lost a good deal," said Doctor Prance.

"Well, I don't know; I have an idea you made it up in other ways," Ransom returned, laughing still.

He saw her bright little eyes engage with his own. Staying, apparently, in the village, she had come out, bareheaded, for an evening walk, and if it had been possible to imagine Doctor Prance bored and in want of recreation, the way she lingered there as if she were quite willing to have another talk might have suggested to Basil Ransom this condition. "Why, don't you consider her career very remarkable?"

"Oh yes; everything is remarkable nowadays; we live in an age

of wonders!" the young man replied, much amused to find himself discussing the object of his adoration in this casual way, in the dark, on a lonely country-road, with a short-haired female physician. It was astonishing how quickly Doctor Prance and he had made friends again. "I suppose, by the way, you know Miss Tarrant and Miss Chancellor are staying down here?" he went on.

"Well, yes, I suppose I know it. I am visiting Miss Chancellor," the dry little woman added.

"Oh indeed? I am delighted to hear it!" Ransom exclaimed, feeling that he might have a friend in the camp. "Then you can inform me where those ladies have their house."

"Yes, I guess I can tell in the dark. I will show you round now, if you like."

"I shall be glad to see it, though I am not sure I shall go in immediately. I must reconnoitre a little first. That makes me so very happy to have met you. I think it's very wonderful — your knowing me."

Doctor Prance did not repudiate this compliment, but she presently observed: "You didn't pass out of my mind entirely, because I have heard about you since, from Miss Birdseye."

"Ah yes, I saw her in the spring. I hope she is in health and happiness."

"She is always in happiness, but she can't be said to be in health. She is very weak; she is failing."

"I am very sorry for that."

"She is also visiting Miss Chan

cellor," Doctor Prance observed, after a pause which was an illustration of an appearance she had of thinking that certain things didn't at all imply some others.

"Why, my cousin has got all the distinguished women!" Basil Ransom exclaimed.

"Is Miss Chancellor your cousin? There isn't much family resemblance. Miss Birdseye came down for the benefit of the country air, and I came down to see if I could help her to get some good from it. She wouldn't much, if she were left to herself. Miss Birdseye has a very fine character, but she hasn't much idea of hygiene." Doctor Prance was evidently more and more disposed to be chatty. Ransom appreciated this fact, and said he hoped she, too, was getting some good from the country-air — he was afraid she was very much confined to her profession, in Boston; to which she replied — "Well, I was just taking a little exercise along the road. I presume you don't realise what it is to be one of four ladies grouped together in a small frame-house."

Ransom remembered how he had liked her before, and he felt that, as the phrase was, he was going to like her again. He wanted to express his good-will to her, and would greatly have enjoyed being at liberty to offer her a cigar. He didn't know what to offer her or what to do, unless he should invite her to sit with him on a fence. He did realise perfectly what the situation in the small frame-house must be, and entered with instant

sympathy into the feelings which had led Doctor Prance to detach herself from the circle and wander forth under the constellations, all of which he was sure she knew. He asked her permission to accompany her on her walk, but she said she was not going much further in that direction; she was going to turn around. He turned round with her, and they went back together to the village, in which he at last began to discover a certain consistency, signs of habitation, houses disposed with a rough resemblance to a plan. The road wandered among them with a kind of accommodating sinuosity, and there were even cross-streets, and an oil-lamp on a corner, and here and there the small sign of a closed shop, with an indistinctly countrified lettering. There were lights now in the windows of some of the houses, and Doctor Prance mentioned to her companion several of the inhabitants of the little town, who appeared all to rejoice in the prefix of captain. They were retired shipmasters; there was quite a little nest of these worthies, two or three of whom might be seen lingering in their dim doorways, as if they were conscious of a want of encouragement to sit up, and yet remembered the nights in faraway waters when they would not have thought of turning in at all. Marmion called itself a town, but it was a good deal shrunken since the decline in the shipbuilding interest; it turned out a good many vessels every year, in the palmy days, before the war. There were shipyards still, where you could almost pick up the old shavings, the old nails and rivets, but they were grass-grown now, and the water lapped them without anything to interfere. There was a kind of arm of the sea put in; it went up some way, it wasn't the real sea, but very quiet, like a river; that was more attractive to some. Doctor Prance didn't say the place was picturesque, or quaint, or weird; but he could see that was what she meant when she said it was mouldering away. Even under the mantle of night he himself gathered the impression that it had had a larger life, seen better days. Doctor Prance made no remark designed to elicit from him an account of his motives in coming to Marmion; she asked him neither when he had arrived nor how long he intended to stay. His allusion to his cousinship with Miss Chancellor might have served to her mind as a reason; yet, on the other hand, it would have been open to her to wonder why, if he had come to see the young ladies from Charles Street, he was not in more of a hurry to present himself. It was plain Doctor Prance didn't go into that kind of analysis. If Ransom had complained to her of a sore throat she would have inquired with precision about his symptoms; but she was incapable of asking him any question with a social bearing. Sociably enough, however, they continued to wander through the principal street of the little town, darkened in places by immense old elms, which made

a blackness overhead. There was a salt smell in the air, as if they were nearer the water; Doctor Prance said that Olive's house was at the other end.

"I shall take it as a kindness if, for this evening, you don't mention that you have happened to meet me," Ransom remarked, after a little. He had changed his mind about giving notice.

"Well, I wouldn't," his companion replied; as if she didn't need any caution in regard to making vain statements.

"I want to keep my arrival a little surprise for to-morrow. It will be a great pleasure to me to see Miss Birdseye," he went on, rather hypocritically, as if that at bottom had been to his mind the main attraction of Marmion.

Doctor Prance did not reveal her private comment, whatever it was, on this intimation; she only said, after some hesitation — "Well, I presume the old lady will take quite an interest in your being here."

"I have no doubt she is capable even of that degree of philanthropy."

"Well, she has charity for all, but she does — even she — prefer her own side. She regards you as quite an acquisition."

Ransom could not but feel flattered at the idea that he had been a subject of conversation — as this implied — in the little circle at Miss Chancellor's; but he was at a loss, for the moment, to perceive what he had done up to this time to gratify the senior member of the group. "I hope she will find me an acquisition after I have been here a few days," he said, laughing.

"Well, she thinks you are one of the most important converts yet," Doctor Prance replied, in a colourless way, as if she would not have pretended to explain why.

"A convert — me? Do you mean of Miss Tarrant's?" It had come over him that Miss Birdseye, in fact, when he was parting with her after their meeting in Boston, had assented to his request for secrecy (which at first had struck her as somewhat unholy), on the ground that Verena would bring him into the fold. He wondered whether the young lady had been telling her old friend that she had succeeded with him. He thought this improbable; but it didn't matter, and he said, gaily, "Well, I can easily let her suppose so!"

It was evident that it would be no easier for Doctor Prance to subscribe to a deception than it had been for her venerable patient; but she went so far as to reply, "Well, I hope you won't let her suppose you are where you were that time I conversed with you. I could see where you were then!"

"It was in about the same place you were, wasn't it?"

"Well," said Doctor Prance, with a small sigh, "I am afraid I have moved back, if anything!" Her sigh told him a good deal; it seemed a thin, self-controlled protest against the tone of Miss Chancellor's interior, of which it was her present fortune to form a part: and the way she hovered round, indistinct in the gloom, as if she were rather loath to resume her place there, completed his impression that the little doctress had a line of her own.

"That, at least, must distress Miss Birdseye," he said, reproachfully.

"Not much, because I am not of importance. They think women the equals of men; but they are a great deal more pleased when a man joins than when a woman does."

Ransom complimented Doctor Prance on the lucidity of her mind, and then he said: "Is Miss Birdseye really sick? Is her condition very precarious?"

"Well, she is very old, and very — very gentle," Doctor Prance answered, hesitating a moment for her adjective. "Under those circumstances a person may flicker out."

"We must trim the lamp," said Ransom; "I will take my turn, with pleasure, in watching the sacred flame."

"It will be a pity if she doesn't live to hear Miss Tarrant's great effort," his companion went on.

"Miss Tarrant's? What's that?"

"Well, it's the principle interest, in there." And Doctor Prance now vaguely indicated, with a movement of her head, a small white house, much detached from its neighbours, which stood on their left, with its back to the water, at a little distance from the road. It exhibited more signs of animation than any of its fellows; several windows, notably those of the ground floor, were open to the warm evening, and a large shaft of light was projected upon the grassy wayside in front of it. Ransom, in his determination to be discreet, checked the advance of his companion, who added presently, with a short, suppressed laugh — "You can see it is, from that!" He listened, to ascertain what she meant, and after an instant a sound came to his ear — a sound he knew already well, which carried the accents of Verena Tarrant, in ample periods and cadences, out into the stillness of the August night.

"Murder, what a lovely voice!" he exclaimed, involuntarily.

Doctor Prance's eye gleamed towards him a moment, and she observed, humorously (she was relaxing immensely), "Perhaps Miss Birdseye is right!" Then, as he made no rejoinder, only listening to the vocal inflections that floated out of the house, she went on — "She's practising her speech."

"Her speech? Is she going to deliver one here?"

"No, as soon as they go back to town — at the Music Hall."

Ransom's attention was now transferred to his companion. "Is that why you call it her great effort?"

"Well, so they think it, I believe. She practises that way every night; she reads portions of it aloud to Miss Chancellor and Miss Birdseye."

"And that's the time you choose for your walk?" Ransom said, smiling.

"Well, it's the time my old lady has least need of me; she's too absorbed."

Doctor Prance dealt in facts; Ransom had already discovered that; and some of her facts were very interesting.

"The Music Hall — isn't that your great building?" he asked.

"Well, it's the biggest we've got; it's pretty big, but it isn't so big as Miss Chancellor's ideas," added Doctor Prance. "She has taken it to bring out Miss Tarrant before the general public — she has never appeared that way in Boston — on a great scale. She expects her to make a big sensation. It will be a great night, and they are preparing for it. They consider it her real beginning."

"And this is the preparation?" Basil Ransom said.

"Yes; as I say, it's their principal interest."

Ransom listened, and while he listened he meditated. He had thought it possible Verena's principles might have been shaken by the profession of faith to which he treated her in New York; but this hardly looked like it. For some moments Doctor Prance and he stood together in silence.

"You don't hear the words," the doctor remarked, with a smile which, in the dark, looked Mephistophelean.

"Oh, I know the words!" the young man exclaimed, with rather a groan, as he offered her his hand for good-night.

Chapter XXXVI

A CERTAIN prudence had determined him to put off his visit till the morning; he thought it more probable that at that time he should be able to see Verena alone, whereas in the evening the two young women would be sure to be sitting together. When the morrow dawned, however, Basil Ransom felt none of the trepidation of the procrastinator; he knew nothing of the reception that awaited him, but he took his way to the cottage designated to him overnight by Doctor Prance, with the step of a man much more conscious of his own purpose than of possible obstacles. He made the reflection, as he went, that to see a place for the first time at night is like reading a foreign author in a translation. At the present hour — it was getting towards eleven o'clock — he felt that he was dealing with the original. The little straggling, loosely-clustered town lay along the edge of a blue inlet, on the other side of which was a low, wooded shore, with a gleam of white sand where it touched the water. The narrow bay carried the vision outward to a picture that seemed at once bright and dim — a shining, slumbering summer-sea, and a far-off, circling line of coast, which, under the August sun, was hazy and delicate. Ransom regarded the place as a town because Doctor Prance had called it one; but it was a town where you smelt the breath of the hay in the streets and you might gather blackberries in the principal square. The houses looked at each other across the grass — low, rusty, crooked, distended houses, with dry, cracked faces and the dim eyes of small-paned, stiffly-sliding windows. Their little door-yards bristled with rank, old-fashioned flowers, mostly yellow; and on the quarter that stood back from the sea the fields sloped upward, and the woods in which they presently lost themselves looked down over the roofs. Bolts and bars were not a part of the domestic machinery of Marmion, and the responsive menial, receiving the visitor on the threshold, was a creature rather desired than definitely possessed; so that Basil Ransom found Miss Chancellor's house-door gaping wide (as he had seen it the night before), and destitute even of a knocker or a bell-handle. From where he stood in the porch he could see the whole of the little sitting-room on the left of the hall — see that it stretched straight through to the back windows; that it was garnished with photographs of foreign works of art, pinned upon the walls, and enriched with a piano and other little extemporised embellishments, such as ingenious women lavish upon the houses they hire for a few weeks. Verena told him afterwards that Olive had taken her cottage furnished, but that the paucity of chairs and tables and bedsteads was such that their little party used almost to sit down, to lie down, in turn. On the other hand they had all George Eliot's writings, and two photographs of the Sistine Madonna. Ransom rapped with his stick on the lintel of the door, but no one came to receive him; so he made his way into the parlour, where he observed that his cousin Olive had as many German books as ever lying about. He dipped into this literature, momentarily, according to his wont, and then remembered that this was not what he had come for and that as he waited at the door he had seen, through another door, opening at the opposite end of the hall, signs of a small verandah attached to the other face of the house. Thinking the ladies might be assembled there in the shade, he pushed aside the muslin curtain of the back window, and saw that the advantages of Miss Chancellor's summer-residence were in this quarter. There was a verandah, in fact, to which a wide, horizontal trellis, covered with an ancient vine, formed a kind of extension. Beyond the trellis was a small, lonely garden; beyond the garden was a large, vague, woody space, where a few piles of old timber were disposed, and which he afterwards learned to be a relic of the shipbuilding era described to him by Doctor Prance; and still beyond this again was the charming lake-like estuary he had already admired. His eyes did not rest upon the distance; they were attracted by a figure seated under the trellis, where the chequers of sun, in the interstices of the vine-leaves, fell upon a bright-coloured rug spread out on the ground. The floor of the roughly-constructed verandah was so low that there was virtually no difference in the level. It took Ransom only a moment to recognise Miss Birdseye, though her back was turned to the house. She was alone; she sat there motionless (she had a newspaper in her lap, but her attitude was not that of a reader), looking at the shimmering bay. She might be asleep; that was why Ransom moderated the process of his long legs as he came round through the house to join her. This precaution represented his only scruple. He stepped across the verandah and stood close to her, but she did not appear to notice him. Visibly, she was dozing, or presumably, rather, for her head was enveloped in an old faded straw-hat, which concealed the upper part of her face. There were two or three other chairs near her, and a table on which were half a dozen books and periodicals, together with a glass containing a colourless liquid, on the top of which a spoon was laid. Ransom desired only to respect her repose, so he sat down in one of the chairs and waited till she should become aware of his presence. He thought Miss Chancellor's back-garden a delightful spot, and his jaded senses tasted the breeze — the idle, wandering summer-wind — that stirred the vine-leaves over his head. The hazy shores on the other side of the water, which had tints more delicate than the street-vistas of New York (they seemed powdered with silver, a sort of mid-summer light), suggested to him a land of dreams, a country in a picture. Basil Ransom had seen very few pictures, there were none in Mississippi; but he had a vision at times of something that would be more refined than the real world, and the situation in which he now found himself pleased him almost as much as if it had been a striking work of art. He was un-able to see, as I have said, wheth-er Miss Birdseye were taking in the prospect through open or only, im-agination aiding (she had plenty of that), through closed, tired, dazzled eyes. She appeared to him, as the minutes elapsed and he sat beside her, the incarnation of well-earned rest, of patient, submissive superannuation. At the end of her long day's work she might have been placed there to enjoy this dim prevision of the peaceful riv-er, the gleaming shores, of the par-adise her unselfish life had cer-tainly qualified her to enter, and which, apparently, would so soon be opened to her. After a while she said, placidly, without turning: "I suppose it's about time I should take my remedy again. It does seem as if she had found the right thing; don't you think so?"

"Do you mean the contents of that tumbler? I shall be delighted to give it to you, and you must tell me how much you take." And Basil Ransom, getting up, possessed him-self of the glass on the table.

At the sound of his voice Miss Birdseye pushed back her straw-hat by a movement that was fa-miliar to her, and twisting about her muffled figure a little (even in August she felt the cold, and had to be much covered up to sit out), directed at him a speculative, un-astonished gaze.

"One spoonful — two?" Ransom asked, stirring the dose and smil-ing.

"Well, I guess I'll take two this time."

"Certainly, Doctor Prance couldn't help finding the right thing," Ransom said, as he admin-istered the medicine; while the movement with which she extend-ed her face to take it made her seem doubly childlike.

He put down the glass, and she relapsed into her position; she seemed to be considering. "It's homœopathic," she remarked, in a moment.

"Oh, I have no doubt of that; I presume you wouldn't take any-thing else."

"Well, it's generally admitted now to be the true system."

Ransom moved closer to her, placed himself where she could see him better. "It's a great thing to have the true system," he said, bending towards her in a friendly way; "I'm sure you have it in ev-erything." He was not often hypo-critical; but when he was he went all lengths.

"Well, I don't know that any one has a right to say that. I thought you were Verena," she added in a moment, taking him in again with her mild, deliberate vision.

"I have been waiting for you to recognise me; of course you didn't know I was here — I only arrived last night."

"Well, I'm glad you have come to see Olive now."

"You remember that I wouldn't do that when I met you last?"

"You asked me not to mention to her that I had met you; that's what I principally recall."

"And don't you remember what I told you I wanted to do? I wanted to go out to Cambridge and see Miss Tarrant. Thanks to the information that you were so good as to give me, I was able to do so."

"Yes, she gave me quite a little description of your visit," said Miss Birdseye, with a smile and a vague sound in her throat — a sort of pensive, private reference to the idea of laughter — of which Ransom never learned the exact significance, though he retained for a long time afterwards a kindly memory of the old lady's manner at the moment.

"I don't know how much she enjoyed it, but it was an immense pleasure to me; so great a one that, as you see, I have come to call upon her again."

"Then I presume, she *has* shaken you?"

"She has shaken me tremendously!" said Ransom, laughing.

"Well, you'll be a great addition," Miss Birdseye returned. "And this time your visit is also for Miss Chancellor?"

"That depends on whether she will receive me."

"Well, if she knows you are shaken, that will go a great way," said Miss Birdseye, a little musingly, as if even to her unsophisticated mind it had been manifested that one's relations with Miss Chancellor might be ticklish. "But she can't receive you now — can she? — because she's out. She has gone to the post-office for the Boston letters, and they get so many every day that she had to take Verena with her to help her carry them home. One of them wanted to stay with me, because Doctor Prance has gone fishing, but I said I presumed I could be left alone for about seven minutes. I know how they love to be together; it seems as if one *couldn't* go out without the other. That's what they came down here for, because it's quiet, and it didn't look as if there was any one else they would be much drawn to. So it would be a pity for me to come down after them just to spoil it!"

"I am afraid I shall spoil it, Miss Birdseye."

"Oh, well, a gentleman," murmured the ancient woman.

"Yes, what can you expect of a gentleman? I certainly shall spoil it if I can."

"You had better go fishing with Doctor Prance," said Miss Birdseye, with a serenity which showed that she was far from measuring the sinister quality of the announcement he had just made.

"I shan't object to that at all. The days here must be very long

— very full of hours. Have you got the doctor with you?" Ransom inquired, as if he knew nothing at all about her.

"Yes, Miss Chancellor invited us both; she is very thoughtful. She is not merely a theoretic philanthropist — she goes into details," said Miss Birdseye, presenting her large person, in her chair, as if she herself were only an item. "It seems as if we were not so much wanted in Boston, just in August."

"And here you sit and enjoy the breeze, and admire the view," the young man remarked, wondering when the two messengers, whose seven minutes must long since have expired, would return from the post-office.

"Yes, I enjoy everything in this little old-world place; I didn't suppose I should be satisfied to be so passive. It's a great contrast to my former exertions. But somehow it doesn't seem as if there were any trouble or any wrong round here; and if there should be, there are Miss Chancellor and Miss Tarrant to look after it. They seem to think I had better fold my hands. Besides, when helpful, generous minds begin to flock in from *your* part of the country," Miss Birdseye continued, looking at him from under the distorted and discoloured canopy of her hat with a benignity which completed the idea in any cheerful sense he chose.

He felt by this time that he was committed to rather a dishonest part; he was pledged not to give a shock to her optimism. This might cost him, in the coming days, a good deal of dissimulation, but he was now saved from any further expenditure of ingenuity by certain warning sounds which admonished him that he must keep his wits about him for a purpose more urgent. There were voices in the hall of the house, voices he knew, which came nearer, quickly; so that before he had time to rise one of the speakers had come out with the exclamation — "Dear Miss Birdseye, here are seven letters for you!" The words fell to the ground, indeed, before they were fairly spoken, and when Ransom got up, turning, he saw Olive Chancellor standing there, with the parcel from the post-office in her hand. She stared at him in sudden horror; for the moment her self-possession completely deserted her. There was so little of any greeting in her face save the greeting of dismay, that he felt there was nothing for him to say to her, nothing that could mitigate the odious fact of his being there. He could only let her take it in, let her divine that, this time, he was not to be got rid of. In an instant — to ease off the situation — he held out his hand for Miss Birdseye's letters, and it was a proof of Olive's having turned rather faint and weak that she gave them up to him. He delivered the packet to the old lady, and now Verena had appeared in the doorway of the house. As soon as she saw him, she blushed crimson; but she did not, like Olive, stand voiceless.

"Why, Mr. Ransom," she cried out, "where in the world were *you* washed ashore?" Miss Birdseye, meanwhile, taking her letters, had no appearance of observing that the encounter between Olive and her visitor was a kind of concussion.

It was Verena who eased off the situation; her gay challenge rose to her lips as promptly as if she had had no cause for embarrassment. She was not confused even when she blushed, and her alertness may perhaps be explained by the habit of public speaking. Ransom smiled at her while she came forward, but he spoke first to Olive, who had already turned her eyes away from him and gazed at the blue sea-view as if she were wondering what was going to happen to her at last.

"Of course you are very much surprised to see me; but I hope to be able to induce you to regard me not absolutely in the light of an intruder. I found your door open, and I walked in, and Miss Birdseye seemed to think I might stay. Miss Birdseye, I put myself under your protection; I invoke you; I appeal to you," the young man went on. "Adopt me, answer for me, cover me with the mantle of your charity!"

Miss Birdseye looked up from her letters, as if at first she had only faintly heard his appeal. She turned her eyes from Olive to Verena; then she said, "Doesn't it seem as if we had room for all? When I remember what I have seen in the South, Mr. Ransom's being here strikes me as a great triumph."

Olive evidently failed to understand, and Verena broke in with eagerness, "It was by my letter, of course, that you knew we were here. The one I wrote just before we came, Olive," she went on. "Don't you remember I showed it to you?"

At the mention of this act of submission on her friend's part Olive started, flashing her a strange look; then she said to Basil that she didn't see why he should explain so much about his coming; every one had a right to come. It was a very charming place; it ought to do any one good. "But it will have one defect for you," she added; "three-quarters of the summer residents are women!"

This attempted pleasantry on Miss Chancellor's part, so unexpected, so incongruous, uttered with white lips and cold eyes, struck Ransom to that degree by its oddity that he could not resist exchanging a glance of wonder with Verena, who, if she had had the opportunity, could probably have explained to him the phenomenon. Olive had recovered herself, reminded herself that she was safe, that her companion in New York had repudiated, denounced her pursuer; and, as a proof to her own sense of her security, as well as a touching mark to Verena that now, after what had passed, she had no fear, she felt that a certain light mockery would be effective.

"Ah, Miss Olive, don't pretend to think I love your sex so little, when you know that what you really object to in me is that I love it too much!" Ransom was not brazen, he was not impudent, he was really a very modest man; but he was aware that whatever he said or did he was condemned to seem impudent now, and he argued within himself that if he was to have the dishonour of being thought brazen he might as well have the comfort. He didn't care a straw, in truth, how he was judged or how he might offend; he had a purpose which swallowed up such inanities as that, and he was so full of it that it kept him firm, balanced him, gave him an assurance that might easily have been confounded with a cold detachment. "This place will do me good," he pursued; "I haven't had a holiday for more than two years, I couldn't have gone another day; I was finished. I would have written to you beforehand that I was coming, but I only started at a few hours' notice. It occurred to me that this would be just what I wanted; I remembered what Miss Tarrant had said in her note, that it was a place where people could lie on the ground and wear their old clothes. I delight to lie on the ground, and all my clothes are old. I hope to be able to stay three or four weeks."

Olive listened till he had done speaking; she stood a single moment longer, and then, without a word, a glance, she rushed into the house. Ransom saw that Miss Birdseye was immersed in her letters; so he went straight to Verena and stood before her, looking far into her eyes. He was not smiling now, as he had been in speaking

to Olive. "Will you come somewhere apart, where I can speak to you alone?"

"Why have you done this? It was not right in you to come!" Verena looked still as if she were blushing, but Ransom perceived he must allow for her having been delicately scorched by the sun.

"I have come because it is necessary — because I have something very important to say to you. A great number of things."

"The same things you said in New York? I don't want to hear them again — they were horrible!"

"No, not the same — different ones. I want you to come out with me, away from here."

"You always want me to come out! We can't go out here; we *are* out, as much as we can be!" Verena laughed. She tried to turn it off — feeling that something really impended.

"Come down into the garden, and out beyond there — to the water, where we can speak. It's what I have come for; it was not for what I told Miss Olive!"

He had lowered his voice, as if Miss Olive might still hear them, and there was something strangely grave — altogether solemn, indeed — in its tone. Verena looked around her, at the splendid summer day, at the much-swathed, formless figure of Miss Birdseye, holding her letter inside her hat. "Mr. Ransom!" she articulated then, simply; and as her eyes met him again they showed him a couple of tears.

"It's not to make you suffer, I honestly believe. I don't want to say anything that will hurt you. How can I possibly hurt you, when I feel to you as I do?" he went on, with suppressed force.

She said no more, but all her face entreated him to let her off, to spare her; and as this look deepened, a quick sense of elation and success began to throb in his heart, for it told him exactly what he wanted to know. It told him that she was afraid of him, that she had ceased to trust herself, that the way he had read her nature was the right way (she was tremendously open to attack, she was meant for love, she was meant for him), and that his arriving at the point at which he wished to arrive was only a question of time. This happy consciousness made him extraordinarily tender to her; he couldn't put enough reassurance into his smile, his low murmur, as he said: "Only give me ten minutes; don't receive me by turning me away. It's my holiday — my poor little holiday; don't spoil it."

Three minutes later Miss Birdseye, looking up from her letter, saw them move together through the bristling garden and traverse a gap in the old fence which inclosed the further side of it. They passed into the ancient ship-yard which lay beyond, and which was now a mere vague, grass-grown approach to the waterside, bestrewn with a few remnants of supererogatory timber. She saw them stroll forward to the edge of the bay and stand there, taking the soft breeze in their faces. She watched them a little, and it warmed her heart to see the stiff-necked young Southerner led captive by a daughter of New England trained in the right school, who would impose her opinions in their integrity. Considering how prejudiced he must have been he was certainly behaving very well; even at that distance Miss Birdseye dimly made out that there was something positively humble in the way he invited Verena Tarrant to seat herself on a low pile of weather-blackened planks, which constituted the principal furniture of the place, and something, perhaps, just a trifle too expressive of righteous triumph in the manner in which the girl put the suggestion by and stood where she liked, a little proudly, turning a good deal away from him. Miss Birdseye could see as much as this, but she couldn't hear, so that she didn't know what it was that made Verena turn suddenly back to him, at something he said. If she had known, perhaps his observation would have struck her as less singular — under the circumstances in which these two young persons met — than it may appear to the reader.

"They have accepted one of my articles; I think it's the best." These were the first words that passed Basil Ransom's lips after the pair had withdrawn as far as it was possible to withdraw (in that direction) from the house.

"Oh, is it printed — when does it appear?" Verena asked that question instantly; it sprang from her lips in a manner that completely belied the air of keeping herself at a distance from him which she had worn a few moments before.

He didn't tell her again this time, as he had told her when, on the occasion of their walk together in New York, she expressed an inconsequent hope that his fortune as a rejected contributor would take a turn — he didn't remark to her once more that she was a delightful being; he only went on (as if her revulsion were a matter of course), to explain everything he could, so that she might as soon as possible know him better and see how completely she could trust him. "That was, at bottom, the reason I came here. The essay in question is the most important thing I have done in the way of a literary attempt, and I determined to give up the game or to persist, according as I should be able to bring it to the light or not. The other day I got a letter from the editor of the 'Rational Review,' telling me that he should be very happy to print it, that he thought it very remarkable, and that he should be glad to hear from me again. He shall hear from me again — he needn't be afraid! It contained a good many of the opinions I have expressed to you, and a good many more besides. I really believe it will attract some attention. At any rate, the simple fact that it is to be published makes an era in my life. This will seem pitiful to you, no doubt, who publish yourself, have been before the world these several years, and are flushed with every kind of triumph; but to me it's simply a tremendous affair. It makes me believe I may do something; it has changed the whole way I look at my future. I have been building castles in the air, and I have put you in the biggest and fairest of them. That's a great change, and, as I say, it's really why I came on."

Verena lost not a word of this gentle, conciliatory, explicit statement; it was full of surprises for her, and as soon as Ransom had stopped speaking she inquired: "Why, didn't you feel satisfied about your future before?"

Her tone made him feel how little she had suspected he could have the weakness of a discouragement, how little of a question it must have seemed to her that he would one day triumph on his own erratic line. It was the sweetest tribute he had yet received to the idea that he might have ability; the letter of the editor of the "Rational Review" was nothing to it. "No, I felt very blue; it didn't seem to me at all clear that there was a place for me in the world."

"Gracious!" said Verena Tarrant.

A quarter of an hour later Miss Birdseye, who had returned to her letters (she had a correspondent at Framingham who usually wrote fifteen pages), became aware that Verena, who was now alone, was re-entering the house. She stopped her on her way, and said she hoped she hadn't pushed Mr. Ransom overboard.

"Oh, no; he has gone off — round the other way."

"Well. I hope he is going to speak for us soon."

Verena hesitated a moment. "He speaks with the pen. He has written a very fine article — for the 'Rational Review.'"

Miss Birdseye gazed at her young friend complacently; the sheets of her interminable letter fluttered in the breeze. "Well, it's delightful to see the way it goes on, isn't it?"

Verena scarcely knew what to say; then, remembering that Doctor Prance had told her that they might lose their dear old companion any day, and confronting it with something Basil Ransom had just said — that the "Rational Review" was a quarterly and the editor had notified him that his article would appear only in the number after the next — she reflected that perhaps Miss Birdseye wouldn't be there, so many months later, to see how it was her supposed consort had spoken. She might, therefore, be left to believe what she liked to believe, without fear of a day of reckoning. Verena committed herself to nothing more confirmatory than a kiss, however, which the old lady's displaced head-gear enabled her to imprint upon her forehead and which caused Miss Birdseye to exclaim, "Why, Verena Tarrant, how cold your lips are!" It was not surprising to Verena to hear that her lips were cold; a mortal chill had crept over her, for she knew that this time she should have a tremendous scene with Olive.

She found her in her room, to which she had fled on quitting Mr. Ransom's presence; she sat in the window, having evidently sunk into a chair the moment she came in, a position from which she must have seen Verena walk through the garden and down to the water with the intruder. She remained as she had collapsed, quite prostrate; her attitude was the same as that other time Verena had found her waiting, in New York. What Olive was likely to say to her first the girl scarcely knew; her mind, at any rate, was full of an intention of her own. She went straight to her and fell on her knees before her, taking hold of the hands which were clasped together, with nervous intensity, in Miss Chancellor's lap. Verena remained a moment, looking up at her, and then said: "There is something I want to tell you now, without a moment's delay; something I didn't tell you at the time it happened, nor afterwards. Mr. Ransom came out to see me once, at Cambridge, a little while before we went to New York. He spent a couple of hours with me; we took a walk together and saw the colleges. It was after that that he wrote to me — when I answered his letter, as I told you in New York. I didn't tell you then of his visit. We had a great deal of talk about him, and I kept that back. I did so on purpose; I can't explain why, except that I didn't like to tell you, and that I thought it better. But now I want you to know everything; when you know that, you *will* know everything. It was only one visit — about two hours. I enjoyed it very much — he seemed so much interested. One reason I didn't tell you was that I didn't want you to know that he had come on to Boston, and called on me in Cambridge, without going to see you. I thought it might affect you disagreeably. I suppose you will think I deceived you; certainly I left you with a wrong impression. But now I want you to know all — all!"

Verena spoke with breathless haste and eagerness; there was a kind of passion in the way she tried to expiate her former want of candour. Olive listened, staring; at first she seemed scarcely to understand. But Verena perceived that she understood sufficiently when she broke out: "You deceived me — you deceived me! Well, I must say I like your deceit better than such dreadful revelations! And what does anything matter when he has come after you now? What does he want — what has he come for?"

"He has come to ask me to be his wife."

Verena said this with the same eagerness, with as determined an air of not incurring any reproach this time. But as soon as she had spoken she buried her head in Olive's lap.

Olive made no attempt to raise it again, and returned none of the pressure of her hands; she only sat silent for a time, during which Verena wondered that the idea of the

episode at Cambridge, laid bare only after so many months, should not have struck her more deeply. Presently she saw it was because the horror of what had just happened drew her off from it. At last Olive asked: "Is that what he told you, off there by the water?"

"Yes" — and Verena looked up — "he wanted me to know it right away. He says it's only fair to you that he should give notice of his intentions. He wants to try and make me like him — so he says. He wants to see more of me, and he wants me to know him better."

Olive lay back in her chair, with dilated eyes and parted lips. "Verena Tarrant, what *is* there between you? what *can* I hold on to, what *can* I believe? Two hours, in Cambridge, before we went to New York?" The sense that Verena had been perfidious there — perfidious in her reticence — now began to roll over her. "Mercy of heaven, how you did act!"

"Olive, it was to spare you."

"To spare me? If you really wished to spare me he wouldn't be here now!"

Miss Chancellor flashed this out with a sudden violence, a spasm which threw Verena off and made her rise to her feet. For an instant the two young women stood confronted, and a person who had seen them at that moment might have taken them for enemies rather than friends. But any such opposition could last but a few seconds. Verena replied, with a tremor in her voice which was not that of passion, but of charity: "Do you mean that I expected him, that I brought him? I never in my life was more surprised at anything than when I saw him there."

"Hasn't he the delicacy of one of his own slave-drivers? Doesn't he know you loathe him?"

Verena looked at her friend with a degree of majesty which, with her, was rare. "I don't loathe him — I only dislike his opinions."

"Dislike! Oh, misery!" And Olive turned away to the open window, leaning her forehead against the lifted sash.

Verena hesitated, then went to her, passing her arm round her. "Don't scold me! help me — help me!" she murmured.

Olive gave her a sidelong look; then, catching her up and facing her again — "Will you come away, now, by the next train?"

"Flee from him again, as I did in New York? No, no, Olive Chancellor, that's not the way," Verena went on, reasoningly, as if all the wisdom of the ages were seated on her lips. "Then how can we leave Miss Birdseye, in her state? We must stay here — we must fight it out here."

"Why not be honest, if you have been false — really honest, not only half so? Why not tell him plainly that you love him?"

"Love him, Olive? why, I scarcely know him."

"You'll have a chance, if he stays a month!"

"I don't dislike him, certainly, as you do. But how can I love him when he tells me he wants me to give up everything, all our work, our faith, our future, never to give another address, to open my lips in public? How can I consent to that?" Verena went on, smiling strangely.

"He asks you that, just that way?"

"No; it's not that way. It's very kindly."

"Kindly? Heaven help you, don't grovel! Doesn't he know it's my house?" Olive added, in a moment.

"Of course he won't come into it, if you forbid him."

"So that you may meet him in other places — on the shore, in the country?"

"I certainly shan't avoid him, hide away from him," said Verena, proudly. "I thought I made you believe, in New York, that I really cared for our aspirations. The way for me then is to meet him, feeling conscious of my strength. What if I do like him? what does it matter? I like my work in the world, I like everything I believe in, better."

Olive listened to this, and the memory of how, in the house in Tenth Street, Verena had rebuked her doubts, professed her own faith anew, came back to her with a force which made the present situation appear slightly less terrific. Nevertheless, she gave no assent to the girl's logic; she only replied: "But you didn't meet him there; you hurried away from New York, after I was willing you should stay. He affected you very much there; you were not so calm when you came back to me from your expedition to the park as you pretend to be now. To get away from him you gave up all the rest."

"I know I wasn't so calm. But now I have had three months to think about it — about the way he affected me there. I take it very quietly."

"No, you don't; you are not calm now!"

Verena was silent a moment, while Olive's eyes continued to search her, accuse her, condemn her. "It's all the more reason you shouldn't give me stab after stab," she replied, with a gentleness which was infinitely touching.

It had an instant effect upon Olive; she burst into tears, threw herself on her friend's bosom. "Oh, don't desert me — don't desert me, or you'll kill me in torture," she moaned, shuddering.

"You must help me — you must help me!" cried Verena, imploringly too.

Chapter XXXVII

BASIL RANSOM spent nearly a month at Marmion; in announcing this fact I am very conscious of its extraordinary character. Poor Olive may well have been thrown back into her alarms by his presenting himself there; for after her return from New York she took to her soul the conviction that she had really done with him. Not only did the impulse of revulsion under which Verena had demand-

ed that their departure from Tenth Street should be immediate appear to her a proof that it had been sufficient for her young friend to touch Mr. Ransom's moral texture with her finger, as it were, in order to draw back for ever; but what she had learned from her companion of his own manifestations, his apparent disposition to throw up the game, added to her feeling of security. He had spoken to Verena of their little excursion as his last opportunity, let her know that he regarded it not as the beginning of a more intimate acquaintance but as the end even of such relations as already existed between them. He gave her up, for reasons best known to himself; if he wanted to frighten Olive he judged that he had frightened her enough: his Southern chivalry suggested to him perhaps that he ought to let her off before he had worried her to death. Doubtless, too, he had perceived how vain it was to hope to make Verena abjure a faith so solidly founded; and though he admired her enough to wish to possess her on his own terms, he shrank from the mortification which the future would have in keeping for him — that of finding that, after six months of courting and in spite of all her sympathy, her desire to do what people expected of her, she despised his opinions as much as the first day. Olive Chancellor was able to a certain extent to believe what she wished to believe, and that was one reason why she had twisted Verena's flight from New

York, just after she let her friend see how much she should like to drink deeper of the cup, into a warrant for living in a fool's paradise. If she had been less afraid, she would have read things more clearly; she would have seen that we don't run away from people unless we fear them and that we don't fear them unless we know that we are unarmed. Verena feared Basil Ransom now (though this time she declined to run); but now she had taken up her weapons, she had told Olive she was exposed, she had asked *her* to be her defence. Poor Olive was stricken as she had never been before, but the extremity of her danger gave her a desperate energy. The only comfort in her situation was that this time Verena had confessed her peril, had thrown herself into her hands. "I like him, I can't help it — I do like him. I don't want to marry him, I don't want to embrace his ideas, which are unspeakably false and horrible; but I like him better than any gentleman I have seen." So much as this the girl announced to her friend as soon as the conversation of which I have just given a sketch was resumed, as it was very soon, you may be sure, and very often, in the course of the next few days. That was her way of saying that a great crisis had arrived in her life, and the statement needed very little amplification to stand as a shy avowal that she too had succumbed to the universal passion. Olive had had her suspicions, her terrors, before; but she perceived

now how idle and foolish they had been, and that this was a different affair from any of the "phases" of which she had hitherto anxiously watched the development. As I say, she felt it to be a considerable mercy that Verena's attitude was frank, for it gave her something to take hold of; she could no longer be put off with sophistries about receiving visits from handsome and unscrupulous young men for the sake of the opportunities it gave one to convert them. She took hold, accordingly, with passion, with fury; after the shock of Ransom's arrival had passed away she determined that he should not find her chilled into dumb submission. Verena had told her that she wanted her to hold her tight, to rescue her; and there was no fear that, for an instant, she should sleep at her post.

"I like him — I like him; but I want to hate ——"

"You want to hate him!" Olive broke in.

"No, I want to hate my liking. I want you to keep before me all the reasons why I should — many of them so fearfully important. Don't let me lose sight of anything! Don't be afraid I shall not be grateful when you remind me."

That was one of the singular speeches that Verena made in the course of their constant discussion of the terrible question, and it must be confessed that she made a great many. The strangest of all was when she protested, as she did again and again to Olive, against the idea of their seeking safety in retreat. She said there was a want of dignity in it — that she had been ashamed, afterwards, of what she had done in rushing away from New York. This care for her moral appearance was, on Verena's part, something new; inasmuch as, though she had struck that note on previous occasions — had insisted on its being her duty to face the accidents and alarms of life — she had never erected such a standard in the face of a disaster so sharply possible. It was not her habit either to talk or to think about her dignity, and when Olive found her taking that tone she felt more than ever that the dreadful, ominous, fatal part of the situation was simply that now, for the first time in all the history of their sacred friendship, Verena was not sincere. She was not sincere when she told her that she wanted to be helped against Mr. Ransom — when she exhorted her, that way, to keep everything that was salutary and fortifying before her eyes. Olive did not go so far as to believe that she was playing a part in putting her off with words which, glossing over her treachery, only made it more cruel; she would have admitted that that treachery was as yet unwitting, that Verena deceived herself first of all, thinking she really wished to be saved. Her phrases about her dignity were insincere, as well as her pretext that they must stay to look after Miss Birdseye: as if Doctor Prance were not abundantly able to discharge that function and would not be enchanted to get them out of the house! Olive had perfectly divined by this time that Doctor Prance had no sympathy with their movement, no general ideas; that she was simply shut up to petty questions of physiological science and of her own professional activity. She would never have invited her down if she had realised this in advance so much as the doctor's dry detachment from all their discussions, their readings and practisings, her constant expeditions to fish and botanise, subsequently enabled her to do. She was very narrow, but it did seem as if she knew more about Miss Birdseye's peculiar physical conditions — they were *very* peculiar — than any one else, and this was a comfort at a time when that admirable woman seemed to be suffering a loss of vitality.

"The great point is that it must be met some time, and it will be a tremendous relief to have it over. He is determined to have it out with me, and if the battle doesn't come off to-day we shall have to fight it to-morrow. I don't see why this isn't as good a time as any other. My lecture for the Music Hall is as good as finished, and I haven't got anything else to do; so I can give all my attention to our personal struggle. It requires a good deal, you would admit, if you knew how wonderfully he can talk. If we should leave this place to-morrow he would come after us to the very next one. He would follow us everywhere. A little while ago we could have escaped him, because he says that then he had no money. He hasn't got much now, but he has got enough to pay his way. He is so encouraged by the reception of his article by the editor of the 'Rational Review,' that he is sure that in future his pen will be a resource."

These remarks were uttered by Verena after Basil Ransom had been three days at Marmion, and when she reached this point her companion interrupted her with the inquiry, "Is that what he proposes to support you with — his pen?"

"Oh, yes; of course he admits we should be terribly poor."

"And this vision of a literary career is based entirely upon an article that hasn't yet seen the light? I don't see how a man of any refinement can approach a woman with so beggarly an account of his position in life."

"He says he wouldn't — he would have been ashamed — three months ago; that was why, when we were in New York, and he felt, even then — well (so he says) all he feels now, he made up his mind not to persist, to let me go. But just lately a change has taken place; his state of mind altered completely, in the course of a week, in consequence of the letter that editor wrote him about his contribution, and his paying for it right off. It was a remarkably flattering letter. He says he believes in his future now; he has before him a vision of distinction, of influence, and of fortune, not great, perhaps, but sufficient to make life

tolerable. He doesn't think life is very delightful, in the nature of things; but one of the best things a man can do with it is to get hold of some woman (of course, she must please him very much, to make it worth while), whom he may draw close to him."

"And couldn't he get hold of any one but you — among all the exposed millions of our sex?" poor Olive groaned. "Why must he pick you out, when everything he knew about you showed you to be, exactly, the very last?"

"That's just what I have asked him, and he only remarks that there is no reasoning about such things. He fell in love with me that first evening, at Miss Birdseye's. So you see there was some ground for that mystic apprehension of yours. It seems as if I pleased him more than any one."

Olive flung herself over on the couch, burying her face in the cushions, which she tumbled in her despair, and moaning out that he didn't love Verena, he never had loved her, it was only his hatred of their cause that made him pretend it; he wanted to do that an injury, to do it the worst he could think of. He didn't love her, he hated her, he only wanted to smother her, to crush her, to kill her — as she would infallibly see that he would if she listened to him. It was because he knew that her voice had magic in it, and from the moment he caught its first note he had determined to destroy it. It was not tenderness that moved him — it was devilish ma-

The Bostonians

lignity; tenderness would be incapable of requiring the horrible sacrifice that he was not ashamed to ask, of requiring her to commit perjury and blasphemy, to desert a work, an interest, with which her very heart-strings were interlaced, to give the lie to her whole young past, to her purest, holiest ambitions. Olive put forward no claim of her own, breathed, at first, at least, not a word of remonstrance in the name of her personal loss, of their blighted union; she only dwelt upon the unspeakable tragedy of a defection from their standard, of a failure on Verena's part to carry out what she had undertaken, of the horror of seeing her bright career blotted out with darkness and tears, of the joy and elation that would fill the breast of all their adversaries at this illustrious, consummate proof of the fickleness, the futility, the predestined servility, of women. A man had only to whistle for her, and she who had pretended most was delighted to come and kneel at his feet. Olive's most passionate protest was summed up in her saying that if Verena were to forsake them it would put back the emancipation of women a hundred years. She did not, during these dreadful days, talk continuously; she had long periods of pale, intensely anxious, watchful silence, interrupted by outbreaks of passionate argument, entreaty, invocation. It was Verena who talked incessantly, Verena who was in a state entirely new to her, and, as any one could see, in an attitude

entirely unnatural and overdone. If she was deceiving herself, as Olive said, there was something very affecting in her effort, her ingenuity. If she tried to appear to Olive impartial, coldly judicious, in her attitude with regard to Basil Ransom, and only anxious to see, for the moral satisfaction of the thing, how good a case, as a lover, he might make out for himself and how much he might touch her susceptibilities, she endeavoured, still more earnestly, to practise this fraud upon her own imagination. She abounded in every proof that she should be in despair if she should be overborne, and she thought of arguments even more convincing, if possible, than Olive's, why she should hold on to her old faith, why she should resist even at the cost of acute temporary suffering. She was voluble, fluent, feverish; she was perpetually bringing up the subject, as if to encourage her friend, to show how she kept possession of her judgment, how independent she remained.

No stranger situation can be imagined than that of these extraordinary young women at this juncture; it was so singular on Verena's part, in particular, that I despair of presenting it to the reader with the air of reality. To understand it, one must bear in mind her peculiar frankness, natural and acquired, her habit of discussing questions, sentiments, moralities, her education, in the atmosphere of lecture-rooms, of *séances*, her familiarity with the vocabulary of

695

emotion, the mysteries of "the spiritual life." She had learned to breathe and move in a rarefied air, as she would have learned to speak Chinese if her success in life had depended upon it; but this dazzling trick, and all her artlessly artful facilities, were not a part of her essence, an expression of her innermost preferences. What *was* a part of her essence was the extraordinary generosity with which she would expose herself, give herself away, turn herself inside out, for the satisfaction of a person who made demands of her. Olive, as we know, had made the reflection that no one was naturally less preoccupied with the idea of her dignity and though Verena put it forward as an excuse for remaining where they were, it must be admitted that in reality she was very deficient in the desire to be consistent with herself. Olive had contributed with all her zeal to the development of Verena's gift; but I scarcely venture to think now, what she may have said to herself, in the secrecy of deep meditation, about the consequences of cultivating an abundant eloquence. Did she say that Verena was attempting to smother her now in her own phrases? did she view with dismay the fatal effect of trying to have an answer for everything? From Olive's condition during these lamentable weeks there is a certain propriety — a delicacy enjoined by the respect for misfortune — in averting our head. She neither ate nor slept; she could scarcely speak without bursting into tears; she felt so implacably, insidiously baffled. She remembered the magnanimity with which she had declined (the winter before the last) to receive the vow of eternal maidenhood which she had at first demanded and then put by as too crude a test, but which Verena, for a precious hour, for ever flown, would *then* have been willing to take. She repented of it with bitterness and rage; and then she asked herself, more desperately still, whether even if she held that pledge she should be brave enough to enforce it in the face of actual complications. She believed that if it were in her power to say, "No, I won't let you off; I have your solemn word, and I won't!" Verena would bow to that decree and remain with her; but the magic would have passed out of her spirit for ever, the sweetness out of their friendship, the efficacy out of their work. She said to her again and again that she had utterly changed since that hour she came to her, in New York, after her morning with Mr. Ransom, and sobbed out that they must hurry away. Then she had been wounded, outraged, sickened, and in the interval nothing had happened, nothing but that one exchange of letters, which she knew about, to bring her round to a shameless tolerance. Shameless Verena admitted it to be; she assented over and over to this proposition, and explained, as eagerly each time as if it were the first, what it was that had come to pass, what it was that had brought her round. It had simply come over her that she liked him, that this was the true point of view, the only one from which one could consider the situation in a way that would lead to what she called a *real* solution — a permanent rest. On this particular point Verena never responded, in the liberal way I have mentioned, without asseverating at the same time that what she desired most in the world was to prove (the picture Olive had held up from the first), that a woman *could* live on persistently, clinging to a great, vivifying, redemptory idea, without the help of a man. To testify to the end against the stale superstition — mother of every misery — that those gentry were as indispensable as they had proclaimed themselves on the house-tops — that, she passionately protested, was as inspiring a thought in the present poignant crisis as it had ever been.

The one grain of comfort that Olive extracted from the terrors that pressed upon her was that now she knew the worst; she knew it since Verena had told her, after so long and so ominous a reticence, of the detestable episode at Cambridge. That seemed to her the worst, because it had been thunder in a clear sky; the incident had sprung from a quarter from which, months before, all symptoms appeared to have vanished. Though Verena had now done all she could to make up for her perfidious silence by repeating everything that passed between them as she sat with Mr. Ransom in Monadnoc Place or strolled with him through the colleges, it imposed itself upon Olive that that occasion was the key of all that happened since, that he had then obtained an irremediable hold upon her. If Verena had spoken at the time, she would never have let her go to New York; the sole compensation for that hideous mistake was that the girl, recognising it to the full, evidently deemed now that she couldn't be communicative enough. There were certain afternoons in August, long, beautiful and terrible, when one felt that the summer was rounding its curve, and the rustle of the full-leaved trees in the slanting golden light, in the breeze that ought to be delicious, seemed the voice of the coming autumn, of the warnings and dangers of life — portentous, insufferable hours when, as she sat under the softly swaying vine-leaves of the trellis with Miss Birdseye and tried, in order to still her nerves, to read something aloud to her guest, the sound of her own quavering voice made her think more of that baleful day at Cambridge than even of the fact that at that very moment Verena was "off" with Mr. Ransom — had gone to take the little daily walk with him to which it had been arranged that their enjoyment of each other's society should be reduced. Arranged, I say; but that is not exactly the word to describe the compromise arrived at by a kind of tacit exchange of tearful entreaty and tightened grasp, after Ransom had made it definite to

Verena that he was indeed going to stay a month and she had promised that she would not resort to base evasions, to flight (which would avail her nothing, he notified her), but would give him a chance, would listen to him a few minutes every day. He had insisted that the few minutes should be an hour, and the way to spend it was obvious. They wandered along the waterside to a rocky, shrub-covered point, which made a walk of just the right duration. Here all the homely languor of the region, the mild, fragrant Cape-quality, the sweetness of white sands, quiet waters, low promontories where there were paths among the barberries and tidal pools gleamed in the sunset — here all the spirit of a ripe summer-afternoon seemed to hang in the air. There were wood-walks too; they sometimes followed bosky uplands, where accident had grouped the trees with odd effects of "style," and where in grassy intervals and fragrant nooks of rest they came out upon sudden patches of Arcady. In such places Verena listened to her companion with her watch in her hand, and she wondered, very sincerely, how he could care for a girl who made the conditions of courtship so odious. He had recognised, of course, at the very first, that he could not inflict himself again upon Miss Chancellor, and after that awkward morning-call I have described he did not again, for the first three weeks of his stay at Marmion, penetrate into the cottage whose back windows overlooked the deserted shipyard. Olive, as may be imagined, made, on this occasion, no protest for the sake of being ladylike or of preventing him from putting her apparently in the wrong. The situation between them was too grim; it was war to the knife, it was a question of which should pull hardest. So Verena took a tryst with the young man as if she had been a maid-servant and Basil Ransom a "follower." They met a little way from the house; beyond it, outside the village.

Chapter XXXVIII

OLIVE thought she knew the worst, as we have perceived; but the worst was really something she could not know, inasmuch as up to this time Verena chose as little to confide to her on that one point as she was careful to expatiate with her on every other. The change that had taken place in the object of Basil Ransom's merciless devotion since the episode in New York was, briefly, just this change — that the words he had spoken to her there about her genuine vocation, as distinguished from the hollow and factitious ideal with which her family and her association with Olive Chancellor had saddled her — these words, the most effective and penetrating he had uttered, had sunk into her soul and worked and fermented there. She had come at last to believe them, and that was the alteration, the transformation. They had kindled a light in which she saw herself afresh and, strange to say, liked herself better than in the old exaggerated glamour of the lecture-lamps. She could not tell Olive this yet, for it struck at the root of everything, and the dreadful, delightful sensation filled her with a kind of awe at all that it implied and portended. She was to burn everything she had adored; she was to adore everything she had burned. The extraordinary part of it was that though she felt the situation to be, as I say, tremendously serious, she was not ashamed of the treachery which she — yes, decidedly, by this time she must admit it to herself — she meditated. It was simply that the truth had changed sides; that radiant image began to look at her from Basil Ransom's expressive eyes. She loved, she was in love — she felt it in every throb of her being. Instead of being constituted by nature for entertaining that sentiment in an exceptionally small degree (which had been the implication of her whole crusade, the warrant for her offer of old to Olive to renounce), she was framed, apparently, to allow it the largest range, the highest intensity. It was always passion, in fact; but now the object was other. Formerly she had been convinced that the fire of her spirit was a kind of double flame, one half of which was responsive friendship for a most extraordinary person, and the other pity for the sufferings of women

in general. Verena gazed aghast at the colourless dust into which, in three short months (counting from the episode in New York), such a conviction as that could crumble; she felt it must be a magical touch that could bring about such a cataclysm. Why Basil Ransom had been deputed by fate to exercise this spell was more than she could say — poor Verena, who up to so lately had flattered herself that she had a wizard's wand in her own pocket.

When she saw him a little way off, about five o'clock — the hour she usually went out to meet him — waiting for her at a bend of the road which lost itself, after a winding, straggling mile or two, in the indented, insulated "point," where the wandering bee droned through the hot hours with a vague, misguided flight, she felt that his tall, watching figure, with the low horizon behind, represented well the importance, the towering eminence he had in her mind — the fact that he was just now, to her vision, the most definite and upright, the most incomparable, object in the world. If he had not been at his post when she expected him she would have had to stop and lean against something, for weakness; her whole being would have throbbed more painfully than it throbbed at present, though finding him there made her nervous enough. And who was he, what was he? she asked herself. What did he offer her besides a chance (in which there was no compensation of brilliancy or fashion), to falsify, in a conspicuous manner, every hope and pledge she had hitherto given? He allowed her, certainly, no illusion on the subject of the fate she should meet as his wife; he flung over it no rosiness of promised ease; he let her know that she should be poor, withdrawn from view, a partner of his struggle, of his severe, hard, unique stoicism. When he spoke of such things as these, and bent his eyes on her, she could not keep the tears from her own; she felt that to throw herself into his life (bare and arid as for the time it was), was the condition of happiness for her, and yet that the obstacles were terrible, cruel. It must not be thought that the revolution which was taking place in her was unaccompanied with suffering. She suffered less than Olive certainly, for her bent was not, like her friend's, in that direction; but as the wheel of her experience went round she had the sensation of being ground very small indeed. With her light, bright texture, her complacent responsiveness, her genial, graceful, ornamental cast, her desire to keep on pleasing others at the time when a force she had never felt before was pushing her to please herself, poor Verena lived in these days in a state of moral tension — with a sense of being strained and aching — which she didn't betray more only because it was absolutely not in her power to look desperate. An immense pity for Olive sat in her heart, and she asked herself how far it was necessary to go in the path of self-sacrifice. Nothing was wanting to make the wrong she should do her com-

plete; she had deceived her up to the very last; only three months earlier she had reasserted her vows, given her word, with every show of fidelity and enthusiasm. There were hours when it seemed to Verena that she must really push her inquiry no further, but content herself with the conclusion that she loved as deeply as a woman could love and that it didn't make any difference. She felt Olive's grasp too clinching, too terrible. She said to herself that she should never dare, that she might as well give up early as late; that the scene, at the end, would be something she couldn't face; that she had no right to blast the poor creature's whole future. She had a vision of those dreadful years; she knew that Olive would never get over the disappointment. It would touch her in the point where she felt everything most keenly; she would be incurably lonely and eternally humiliated. It was a very peculiar thing, their friendship; it had elements which made it probably as complete as any (between women) that had ever existed. Of course it had been more on Olive's side than on hers, she had always known that; but that, again, didn't make any difference. It was of no use for her to tell herself that Olive had begun it entirely and she had only responded out of a kind of charmed politeness, at first, to a tremendous appeal. She had lent herself, given herself, utterly, and she ought to have known better if she didn't mean to abide by it. At the end of the three weeks she felt that her inquiry was complete, but that after all nothing was gained except an immense interest in Basil Ransom's views and the prospect of an eternal heartache. He had told her he wanted her to know him, and now she knew him pretty thoroughly. She knew him and she adored him, but it didn't make any difference. To give him up or to give Olive up — this effort would be the greater of the two.

If Basil Ransom had the advantage, as far back as that day in New York, of having struck a note which was to reverberate, it may easily be imagined that he did not fail to follow it up. If he had projected a new light into Verena's mind, and made the idea of giving herself to a man more agreeable to her than that of giving herself to a movement, he found means to deepen this illumination, to drag her former standard in the dust. He was in a very odd situation indeed, carrying on his siege with his hands tied. As he had to do everything in an hour a day, he perceived that he must confine himself to the essential. The essential was to show her how much he loved her, and then to press, to press, always to press. His hovering about Miss Chancellor's habitation without going in was a strange regimen to be subjected to, and he was sorry not to see more of Miss Birdseye, besides often not knowing what to do with himself in the mornings and evenings. Fortunately he had brought plenty of books (volumes of rusty aspect, picked up at New York

bookstalls), and in such an affair as this he could take the less when the more was forbidden him. For the mornings, sometimes, he had the resource of Doctor Prance, with whom he made a great many excursions on the water. She was devoted to boating and an ardent fisherwoman, and they used to pull out into the bay together, cast their lines, and talk a prodigious amount of heresy. She met him, as Verena met him, "in the environs," but in a different spirit. He was immensely amused at her attitude, and saw that nothing in the world could, as he expressed it, make her wink. She would never blench nor show surprise; she had an air of taking everything abnormal for granted; betrayed no consciousness of the oddity of Ransom's situation; said nothing to indicate she had noticed that Miss Chancellor was in a frenzy or that Verena had a daily appointment. You might have supposed from her manner that it was as natural for Ransom to sit on a fence half a mile off as in one of the red rocking-chairs, of the so-called "Shaker" species, which adorned Miss Chancellor's back verandah. The only thing our young man didn't like about Doctor Prance was the impression she gave him (out of the crevices of her reticence he hardly knew how it leaked), that she thought Verena rather slim. She took an ironical view of almost any kind of courtship, and he could see she didn't wonder women were such featherheads, so long as, whatever brittle follies they cultivated, they could get men to come and sit on fences for them. Doctor Prance told him Miss Birdseye noticed nothing; she had sunk, within a few days, into a kind of transfigured torpor; she didn't seem to know whether Mr. Ransom were anywhere round or not. She guessed she thought he had just come down for a day and gone off again; she probably supposed he just wanted to get toned up a little by Miss Tarrant. Sometimes, out in the boat, when she looked at him in vague, sociable silence, while she waited for a bite (she delighted in a bite), she had an expression of diabolical shrewdness. When Ransom was not scorching there beside her (he didn't mind the sun of Massachusetts), he lounged about in the pastoral land which hung (at a very moderate elevation), above the shore. He always had a book in his pocket, and he lay under whispering trees and kicked his heels and made up his mind on what side he should take Verena the next time. At the end of a fortnight he had succeeded (so he believed, at least), far better than he had hoped, in this sense, that the girl had now the air of making much more light of her "gift." He was indeed quite appalled at the facility with which she threw it over, gave up the idea that it was useful and precious. That had been what he wanted her to do, and the fact of the sacrifice (once she had fairly looked at it), costing her so little only proved his contention, only made it clear that it was not

necessary to her happiness to spend half her life ranting (no matter how prettily), in public. All the same he said to himself that, to make up for the loss of whatever was sweet in the reputation of the thing, he should have to be tremendously nice to her in all the coming years. During the first week he was at Marmion she made of him an inquiry which touched on this point.

"Well, if it's all a mere delusion, why should this facility have been given me — why should I have been saddled with a superfluous talent? I don't care much about it — I don't mind telling you that; but I confess I should like to know what is to become of all that part of me, if I retire into private life, and live, as you say, simply to be charming for you. I shall be like a singer with a beautiful voice (you have told me yourself my voice is beautiful), who has accepted some decree of never raising a note. Isn't that a great waste, a great violation of nature? Were not our talents given us to use, and have we any right to smother them and deprive our fellow-creatures of such pleasure as they may confer? In the arrangement you propose" (that was Verena's way of speaking of the question of their marriage), "I don't see what provision is made for the poor faithful, dismissed servant. It is all very well to be charming to you, but there are people who have told me that once I get on a platform I am charming to all the world. There is no harm in my speaking of that,

because you have told me so yourself. Perhaps you intend to have a
platform erected in our front parlour, where I can address you every evening, and put you to sleep
after your work. I say our *front*
parlour, as if it were certain we
should have two! It doesn't look
as if our means would permit that
— and we must have some place to
dine, if there is to be a platform in
our sitting-room."

"My dear young woman, it will
be easy to solve the difficulty: the
dining-table itself shall be our platform, and you shall mount on top
of that." This was Basil Ransom's
sportive reply to his companion's
very natural appeal for light, and
the reader will remark that if it led
her to push her investigation no
further, she was very easily satisfied. There was more reason, however, as well as more appreciation
of a very considerable mystery, in
what he went on to say. "Charming to me, charming to all the
world? What will become of your
charm? — is that what you want to
know? It will be about five thousand times greater than it is now;
that's what will become of it. We
shall find plenty of room for your
facility; it will lubricate our whole
existence. Believe me, Miss Tarrant, these things will take care of
themselves. You won't sing in the
Music Hall, but you will sing to
me; you will sing to every one who
knows you and approaches you.
Your gift is indestructible; don't
talk as if I either wanted to wipe
it out or should be able to make it
a particle less divine. I want to

give it another direction, certainly;
but I don't want to stop your activity. Your gift is the gift of expression, and there is nothing I
can do for you that will make you
less expressive. It won't gush out
at a fixed hour and on a fixed day,
but it will irrigate, it will fertilise,
it will brilliantly adorn your conversation. Think how delightful it
will be when your influence becomes really social. Your facility,
as you call it, will simply make
you, in conversation, the most
charming woman in America."

It is to be feared, indeed, that
Verena was easily satisfied (convinced, I mean, not that she ought
to succumb to him, but that there
were lovely, neglected, almost unsuspected truths on his side); and
there is further evidence on the
same head in the fact that after
the first once or twice she found
nothing to say to him (much as
she was always saying to herself),
about the cruel effect her apostasy
would have upon Olive. She forebore to plead that reason after she
had seen how angry it made him,
and with how almost savage a contempt he denounced so flimsy a
pretext. He wanted to know since
when it was more becoming to
take up with a morbid old maid
than with an honourable young
man; and when Verena pronounced
the sacred name of friendship he
inquired what fanatical sophistry
excluded him from a similar privilege. She had told him, in a moment of expansion (Verena believed she was immensely on her
guard, but her guard was very apt

to be lowered), that his visits to Marmion cast in Olive's view a remarkable light upon his chivalry; she chose to regard his resolute pursuit of Verena as a covert persecution of herself. Verena repented, as soon as she had spoken, of having given further currency to this taunt; but she perceived the next moment no harm was done, Basil Ransom taking in perfectly good part Miss Chancellor's reflections on his delicacy, and making them the subject of much free laughter. She could not know, for in the midst of his hilarity the young man did not compose himself to tell her, that he had made up his mind on this question before he left New York — as long ago as when he wrote her the note (subsequent to her departure from that city), to which allusion has already been made, and which was simply the fellow of the letter addressed to her after his visit to Cambridge: a friendly, respectful, yet rather pregnant sign that, decidedly, on second thoughts, separation didn't imply for him the intention of silence. We know a little about his second thoughts, as much as is essential, and especially how the occasion of their springing up had been the windfall of an editor's encouragement. The importance of that encouragement, to Basil's imagination, was doubtless much augmented by his desire for an excuse to take up again a line of behaviour which he had forsworn (small as had, as yet, been his opportunity to indulge in it), very much less than he supposed;

still, it worked an appreciable revolution in his view of his case, and made him ask himself what amount of consideration he should (from the most refined Southern point of view), owe Miss Chancellor in the event of his deciding to go after Verena Tarrant in earnest. He was not slow to decide that he owed her none. Chivalry had to do with one's relations with people one hated, not with those one loved. He didn't hate poor Miss Olive, though she might make him yet; and even if he did, any chivalry was all moonshine which should require him to give up the girl he adored in order that his third cousin should see he could be gallant. Chivalry was forbearance and generosity with regard to the weak; and there was nothing weak about Miss Olive, she was a fighting woman, and she would fight him to the death, giving him not an inch of odds. He felt that she was fighting there all day long, in her cottage-fortress; her resistance was in the air he breathed, and Verena came out to him sometimes quite limp and pale from the tussle.

It was in the same jocose spirit with which he regarded Olive's view of the sort of standard a Mississippian should live up to that he talked to Verena about the lecture she was preparing for her great exhibition at the Music Hall. He learned from her that she was to take the field in the manner of Mrs. Farrinder, for a winter campaign, carrying with her a tremendous big gun. Her engagements were all made, her route was marked out; she expected to repeat her lecture in about fifty different places. It was to be called "A Woman's Reason," and both Olive and Miss Birdseye thought it, so far as they could tell in advance, her most promising effort. She wasn't going to trust to inspiration this time; she didn't want to meet a big Boston audience without knowing where she was. Inspiration, moreover, seemed rather to have faded away; in consequence of Olive's influence she had read and studied so much that it seemed now as if everything must take form beforehand. Olive was a splendid critic, whether he liked her or not, and she had made her go over every word of her lecture twenty times. There wasn't an intonation she hadn't made her practise; it was very different from the old system, when her father had worked her up. If Basil considered women superficial, it was a pity he couldn't see what Olive's standard of preparation was, or be present at their rehearsals, in the evening, in their little parlour. Ransom's state of mind in regard to the affair at the Music Hall was simply this — that he was determined to circumvent it if he could. He covered it with ridicule, in talking of it to Verena, and the shafts he levelled at it went so far that he could see she thought he exaggerated his dislike to it. In point of fact he could not have overstated that; so odious did the idea seem to him that she was soon to be launched in a more infatuated ca-

reer. He vowed to himself that she should never take that fresh start which would commit her irretrievably if she should succeed (and she would succeed — he had not the slightest doubt of her power to produce a sensation in the Music Hall), to the acclamations of the newspapers. He didn't care for her engagements, her campaigns, or all the expectancy of her friends; to "squelch" all that, at a stroke, was the dearest wish of his heart. It would represent to him his own success, it would symbolise his victory. It became a fixed idea with him, and he warned her again and again. When she laughed and said she didn't see how he could stop her unless he kidnapped her, he really pitied her for not perceiving, beneath his ominous pleasantries, the firmness of his resolution. He felt almost capable of kidnapping her. It was palpably in the air that she would become "widely popular," and that idea simply sickened him. He felt as differently as possible about it from Mr. Matthias Pardon.

One afternoon, as he returned with Verena from a walk which had been accomplished completely within the prescribed conditions, he saw, from a distance, Doctor Prance, who had emerged bareheaded from the cottage, and, shading her eyes from the red, declining sun, was looking up and down the road. It was part of the regulation that Ransom should separate from Verena before reaching the house, and they had just paused to exchange their last words (which every day promoted the situation more than any others), when Doctor Prance began to beckon to them with much animation. They hurried forward, Verena pressing her hand to her heart, for she had instantly guessed that something terrible had happened to Olive — she had given out, fainted away, perhaps fallen dead, with the cruelty of the strain. Doctor Prance watched them come, with a curious look in her face; it was not a smile, but a kind of exaggerated intimation that she noticed nothing. In an instant she had told them what was the matter. Miss Birdseye had had a sudden weakness; she had remarked abruptly that she was dying, and her pulse, sure enough, had fallen to nothing. She was down on the piazza with Miss Chancellor and herself, and they had tried to get her up to bed. But she wouldn't let them move her; she was passing away, and she wanted to pass away just there, in such a pleasant place, in her customary chair, looking at the sunset. She asked for Miss Tarrant, and Miss Chancellor told her she was out — walking with Mr. Ransom. Then she wanted to know if Mr. Ransom was still there — she supposed he had gone. (Basil knew, by Verena, apart from this, that his name had not been mentioned to the old lady since the morning he saw her.) She expressed a wish to see him — she had something to say to him; and Miss Chancellor told her that he would be back soon, with Verena, and that they would bring

him in. Miss Birdseye said she hoped they wouldn't be long, because she was sinking; and Doctor Prance now added, like a person who knew what she was talking about, that it was, in fact, the end. She had darted out two or three times to look for them, and they must step right in. Verena had scarcely given her time to tell her story; she had already rushed into the house. Ransom followed with Doctor Prance, conscious that for him the occasion was doubly solemn; inasmuch as if he was to see poor Miss Birdseye yield up her philanthropic soul, he was on the other hand doubtless to receive from Miss Chancellor a reminder that *she* had no intention of quitting the game.

By the time he had made this reflection he stood in the presence of his kinswoman and her venerable guest, who was sitting just as he had seen her before, muffled and bonneted, on the back piazza of the cottage. Olive Chancellor was on one side of her, holding one of her hands, and on the other was Verena, who had dropped on her knees, close to her, bending over those of the old lady. "Did you ask for me — did you want me?" the girl said, tenderly. "I will never leave you again."

"Oh, I won't keep you long. I only wanted to see you once more." Miss Birdseye's voice was very low, like that of a person breathing with difficulty; but it had no painful nor querulous note — it expressed only the cheerful weariness which had marked all this last period of her life, and which seemed to make it now as blissful as it was suitable that she should pass away. Her head was thrown back against the top of the chair, the ribbon which confined her ancient hat hung loose, and the late afternoon-light covered her octogenarian face and gave it a kind of fairness, a double placidity. There was, to Ransom, something almost august in the trustful renunciation of her countenance; something in it seemed to say that she had been ready long before, but as the time was not ripe she had waited, with her usual faith that all was for the best; only, at present, since the right conditions met, she couldn't help feeling that it was quite a luxury, the greatest she had ever tasted. Ransom knew why it was that Verena had tears in her eyes as she looked up at her patient old friend; she had spoken to him, often, during the last three weeks, of the stories Miss Birdseye had told her of the great work of her life, her mission, repeated year after year, among the Southern blacks. She had gone among them with every precaution, to teach them to read and write; she had carried them Bibles and told them of the friends they had in the North who prayed for their deliverance. Ransom knew that Verena didn't reproduce these legends with a view to making him ashamed of his Southern origin, his connection with people who, in a past not yet remote, had made that kind of apostleship necessary; he knew this because she had heard what he thought of all that chapter himself; he had given her a kind of historical summary of the slavery-question which left her no room to say that he was more tender to that particular example of human imbecility than he was to any other. But she had told him that this was what *she* would have liked to do — to wander, alone, with her life in her hand, on an errand of mercy, through a country in which society was arrayed against her; she would have liked it much better than simply talking about the right from the gas-lighted vantage of the New England platform. Ransome had replied simply "Balderdash!" it being his theory, as we have perceived, that he knew much more about Verena's native bent than the young lady herself. This did not, however, as he was perfectly aware, prevent her feeling that she had come too late for the heroic age of New England life, and regarding Miss Birdseye as a battered, immemorial monument of it. Ransom could share such an admiration as that, especially at this moment; he had said to Verena, more than once, that he wished he might have met the old lady in Carolina or Georgia before the war — shown her round among the negroes and talked over New England ideas with her; there were a good many he didn't care much about now, but at that time they would have been tremendously refreshing. Miss Birdseye had given herself away so lavishly all her life that it was rather odd there was anything left of her for the supreme surrender. When he looked at Olive he saw that she meant to ignore him; and during the few minutes he remained on the spot his kinswoman never met his eye. She turned away, indeed, as soon as Doctor Prance said, leaning over Miss Birdseye, "I have brought Mr. Ransom to you. Don't you remember you asked for him?"

"I am very glad to see you again," Ransom remarked. "It was very good of you to think of me." At the sound of his voice Olive rose and left her place; she sank into a chair at the other end of the piazza, turning round to rest her arms on the back and bury her head in them.

Miss Birdseye looked at the young man still more dimly than she had ever done before. "I thought you were gone. You never came back."

"He spends all his time in long walks; he enjoys the country so much," Verena said.

"Well, it's very beautiful, what I see from here. I haven't been strong enough to move round since the first days. But I am going to move now." She smiled when Ransom made a gesture as if to help her, and added: "Oh, I don't mean I am going to move out of my chair."

"Mr. Ransom has been out in a boat with me several times. I have been showing him how to cast a line," said Doctor Prance, who appeared to deprecate a sentimental tendency.

"Oh, well, then, you have been one of our party; there seems to

be every reason why you should feel that you belong to us." Miss Birdseye looked at the visitor with a sort of misty earnestness, as if she wished to communicate with him further; then her glance turned slightly aside; she tried to see what had become of Olive. She perceived that Miss Chancellor had withdrawn herself, and, closing her eyes, she mused, ineffectually, on the mystery she had not grasped, the peculiarity of Basil Ransom's relations with her hostess. She was visibly too weak to concern herself with it very actively; she only felt, now that she seemed really to be going, a desire to reconcile and harmonise. But she presently exhaled a low, soft sigh — a kind of confession that it was too mixed, that she gave it up. Ransom had feared for a moment that she was about to indulge in some appeal to Olive, some attempt to make him join hands with that young lady, as a supreme satisfaction to herself. But he saw that her strength failed her, and that, besides, things were getting less clear to her, to his considerable relief, inasmuch as, though he would not have objected to joining hands, the expression of Miss Chancellor's figure and her averted face, with their desperate collapse, showed him well enough how *she* would have met such a proposal. What Miss Birdseye clung to, with benignant perversity, was the idea that, in spite of his exclusion from the house, which was perhaps only the result of a certain high-strung jealousy on Olive's part of her friend's other personal ties, Verena had drawn him in, and made him sympathise with the great reform and desire to work for it. Ransom saw no reason why such an illusion should be dear to Miss Birdseye; his contact with her in the past had been so momentary that he could not account for her taking an interest in his views, in his throwing his weight into the right scale. It was part of the general desire for justice that fermented within her, the passion for progress; and it was also in some degree her interest in Verena — a suspicion, innocent and idyllic, as any such suspicion on Miss Birdseye's part must be, that there was something between them, that the closest of all unions (as Miss Birdseye at least supposed it was), was preparing itself. Then his being a Southerner gave a point to the whole thing; to bring round a Southerner would be a real encouragement for one who had seen, even at a time when she was already an old woman, what was the tone of opinion in the cotton States. Ransom had no wish to discourage her, and he bore well in mind the caution Doctor Prance had given him about destroying her last theory. He only bowed his head very humbly, not knowing what he had done to earn the honour of being the subject of it. His eyes met Verena's as she looked up at him from her place at Miss Birdseye's feet, and he saw she was following his thought, throwing herself into it, and trying to communicate to him a wish. The wish touched him immensely; she was dreadfully afraid he would betray her to Miss Birdseye — let her know how she had cooled off. Verena was ashamed of that now, and trembled at the danger of exposure; her eyes adjured him to be careful of what he said. Her tremor made him glow a little in return, for it seemed to him the fullest confession of his influence she had yet made.

"We have been a very happy little party," she said to the old lady. "It is delightful that you should have been able to be with us all these weeks."

"It has been a great rest. I am very tired. I can't speak much. It has been a lovely time. I have done so much — so many things."

"I guess I wouldn't talk much, Miss Birdseye," said Doctor Prance, who had now knelt down on the other side of her. "We know how much you have done. Don't you suppose every one knows *your* life?"

"It isn't much — only I tried to take hold. When I look back from here, from where we've sat, I can measure the progress. That's what I wanted to say to you and Mr. Ransom — because I'm going fast. Hold on to me, that's right; but you can't keep me. I don't want to stay now; I presume I shall join some of the others that we lost long ago. Their faces come back to me now, quite fresh. It seems as if they might be waiting; as if they were all there; as if they wanted to hear. You mustn't think there's no progress because you don't see

it all right off; that's what I wanted to say. It isn't till you have gone
a long way that you can feel what's
been done. That's what I see when
I look back from here; I see that
the community wasn't half waked
up when I was young."

"It is you that have waked it up
more than any one else, and it's
for that we honour you, Miss Birdseye!" Verena cried, with a sudden
violence of emotion. "If you were
to live for a thousand years, you
would think only of others — you
would think only of helping on humanity. You are our heroine, you
are our saint, and there has never
been anyone like you!" Verena had
no glance for Ransom now, and
there was neither deprecation nor
entreaty in her face. A wave of
contrition, of shame, had swept
over her — a quick desire to atone
for her secret swerving by a renewed recognition of the nobleness of such a life as Miss Birdseye's.

"Oh, I haven't effected very
much; I have only cared and
hoped. You will do more than I
have ever done — you and Olive
Chancellor, because you are young
and bright, brighter than I ever
was; and besides, everything has
got started."

"Well, you've got started, Miss
Birdseye," Doctor Prance remarked, with raised eyebrows, protesting drily but kindly, and putting forward, with an air as if,
after all, it didn't matter much, an
authority that had been superseded. The manner in which this
competent little woman indulged

her patient showed sufficiently that
the good lady was sinking fast.

"We will think of you always,
and your name will be sacred to
us, and that will teach us singleness and devotion," Verena went
on, in the same tone, still not meeting Ransom's eyes again, and
speaking as if she were trying now
to stop herself, to tie herself by a
vow.

"Well, it's the thing you and Olive have given your lives to that
has absorbed me most, of late
years. I did want to see justice
done — to us. I haven't seen it, but
you will. And Olive will. Where is
she — why isn't she near me, to bid
me farewell? And Mr. Ransom will
— and he will be proud to have
helped."

"Oh, mercy, mercy!" cried Verena, burying her head in Miss
Birdseye's lap.

"You are not mistaken if you
think I desire above all things that
your weakness, your generosity,
should be protected," Ransom
said, rather ambiguously, but with
pointed respectfulness. "I shall remember you as an example of
what women are capable of," he
added; and he had no subsequent
compunctions for the speech, for
he thought poor Miss Birdseye, for
all her absence of profile, essentially feminine.

A kind of frantic moan from
Olive Chancellor responded to
these words, which had evidently
struck her as an insolent sarcasm;
and at the same moment Doctor
Prance sent Ransom a glance
which was an adjuration to depart.

"Good-bye, Olive Chancellor," Miss Birdseye murmured. "I don't want to stay, though I should like to see what you will see."

"I shall see nothing but shame and ruin!" Olive shrieked, rushing across to her old friend, while Ransom discreetly quitted the scene.

Chapter XXXIX

HE met Doctor Prance in the village the next morning, and as soon as he looked at her he saw that the event which had been impending at Miss Chancellor's had taken place. It was not that her aspect was funereal; but it contained, somehow, an announcement that she had, for the present, no more thought to give to casting a line. Miss Birdseye had quietly passed away, in the evening, an hour or two after Ransom's visit. They had wheeled her chair into the house; there had been nothing to do but wait for complete extinction. Miss Chancellor and Miss Tarrant had sat by her there, without moving, each of her hands in theirs, and she had just melted away, towards eight o'clock. It was a lovely death; Doctor Prance intimated that she had never seen any that she thought more seasonable. She added that she was a good woman — one of the old sort; and that was the only funeral oration that Basil Ransom was destined to hear pronounced upon Miss Birdseye. The impression of the simplicity and humility of her end remained with him, and he reflected more than once, during the days that followed, that the absence of pomp and circumstance which had marked her career marked also the consecration of her memory. She had been almost celebrated, she had been active, earnest, ubiquitous beyond any one else, she had given herself utterly to charities and creeds and causes; and yet the only persons, apparently, to whom her death made a real difference were three young women in a small "frame-house" on Cape Cod. Ransom learned from Doctor Prance that her mortal remains were to be committed to their rest in the little cemetery at Marmion, in sight of the pretty sea-view she loved to gaze at, among old mossy headstones of mariners and fisher-folk. She had seen the place when she first came down, when she was able to drive out a little, and she had said she thought it must be pleasant to lie there. It was not an injunction, a definite request; it had not occurred to Miss Birdseye, at the end of her days, to take an exacting line or to make, for the first time in eighty years, a personal claim. But Olive Chancellor and Verena had put their construction on her appreciation of the quietest corner of the striving, suffering world so weary a pilgrim of philanthropy had ever beheld.

In the course of the day Ransom received a note of five lines from Verena, the purport of which was to tell him that he must not expect to see her again for the present; she wished to be very quiet and think things over. She added the recommendation that he should leave the neighbourhood for three or four days; there were plenty of strange old places to see in that part of the country. Ransom meditated deeply on this missive, and perceived that he should be guilty of very bad taste in not immediately absenting himself. He knew that to Olive Chancellor's vision his conduct already wore that stain, and it was useless, therefore, for him to consider how he could displease her either less or more. But he wished to convey to Verena the impression that he would do anything in the wide world to gratify *her* except give her up, and as he packed his valise he had an idea that he was both behaving beautifully and showing the finest diplomatic sense. To go away proved to himself how secure he felt, what a conviction he had that however she might turn and twist in his grasp he held her fast. The emotion she had expressed as he stood there before poor Miss Birdseye was only one of her instinctive contortions; he had taken due note of that — said to himself that a good many more would probably occur before she would be quiet. A woman that listens is lost, the old proverb says; and what had Verena done for the last three weeks but listen? — not very long each day, but with a degree of attention of which her not withdrawing from Marmion was the measure. She had not told him that Olive want-

ed to whisk her away, but he had not needed this confidence to know that if she stayed on the field it was because she preferred to. She probably had an idea she was fighting, but if she should fight no harder than she had fought up to now he should continue to take the same view of his success. She meant her request that he should go away for a few days as something combative; but, decidedly, he scarcely felt the blow. He liked to think that he had great tact with women, and he was sure Verena would be struck with this quality in reading, in the note he presently addressed her in reply to her own, that he had determined to take a little run to Provincetown. As there was no one under the rather ineffectual roof which sheltered him to whose hand he could intrust the billet — at the Marmion hotel one had to be one's own messenger — he walked to the village post-office to request that his note should be put into Miss Chancellor's box. Here he met Doctor Prance, for a second time that day; she had come to deposit the letters by which Olive notified a few of Miss Birdseye's friends of the time and place of her obsequies. This young lady was shut up with Verena, and Doctor Prance was transacting all their business for them. Ransom felt that he made no admission that would impugn his estimate of the sex to which she in a manner belonged, in reflecting that she would acquit herself of these delegated duties with the greatest rapidity and accuracy.

He told her he was going to absent himself for a few days, and expressed a friendly hope that he should find her at Marmion on his return.

Her keen eye gauged him a moment, to see if he were joking; then she said, "Well, I presume you think I can do as I like. But I can't."

"You mean you have got to go back to work?"

"Well, yes; my place is empty in the city."

"So is every other place. You had better remain till the end of the season."

"It's all one season to me. I want to see my office-slate. I wouldn't have stayed so long for any one but her."

"Well, then, good-bye," Ransom said. "I shall always remember our little expeditions. And I wish you every professional distinction."

"That's why I want to go back," Doctor Prance replied, with her flat, limited manner. He kept her a moment; he wanted to ask her about Verena. While he was hesitating how to form his question she remarked, evidently wishing to leave him a little memento of her sympathy, "Well, I hope you will be able to follow up your views."

"My views, Miss Prance? I am sure I have never mentioned them to you!" Then Ransom added, "How is Miss Tarrant to-day? is she more calm?"

"Oh no, she isn't calm at all," Doctor Prance answered, very definitely.

"Do you mean she's excited, emotional?"

"Well, she doesn't talk, she's perfectly still, and so is Miss Chancellor. They're as still as two watchers — they don't speak. But you can hear the silence vibrate."

"Vibrate?"

"Well, they are very nervous."

Ransom was confident, as I say, yet the effort that he made to extract a good omen from this characterisation of the two ladies at the cottage was not altogether successful. He would have liked to ask Doctor Prance whether she didn't think he might count on Verena in the end; but he was too shy for this, the subject of his relations with Miss Tarrant never yet having been touched upon between them; and, besides, he didn't care to hear himself put a question which was more or less an implication of a doubt. So he compromised, with a sort of oblique and general inquiry about Olive; that might draw some light. "What do you think of Miss Chancellor — how does she strike you?"

Doctor Prance reflected a little, with an apparent consciousness that he meant more than he asked. "Well, she's losing flesh," she presently replied; and Ransom turned away, not encouraged, and feeling that, no doubt, the little doctress had better go back to her office-slate.

He did the thing handsomely, remained at Provincetown a week, inhaling the delicious air, smoking innumerable cigars, and lounging among the ancient wharves, where

713

the grass grew thick and the impression of fallen greatness was still stronger than at Marmion. Like his friends the Bostonians he was very nervous; there were days when he felt that he must rush back to the margin of that mild inlet; the voices of the air whispered to him that in his absence he was being outwitted. Nevertheless he stayed the time he had determined to stay; quieting himself with the reflection that there was nothing they could do to elude him unless, perhaps, they should start again for Europe, which they were not likely to do. If Miss Olive tried to hide Verena away in the United States he would undertake to find her — though he was obliged to confess that a flight to Europe would baffle him, owing to his want of cash for pursuit. Nothing, however, was less probable than that they would cross the Atlantic on the eve of Verena's projected *début* at the Music Hall. Before he went back to Marmion he wrote to this young lady, to announce his reappearance there and let her know that he expected she would come out to meet him the morning after. This conveyed the assurance that he intended to take as much of the day as he could get; he had had enough of the system of dragging through all the hours till a mere fraction of time was left before night, and he couldn't wait so long, at any rate, the day after his return. It was the afternoon-train that had brought him back from Provincetown, and in the evening he ascertained that the Bostonians

had not deserted the field. There were lights in the windows of the house under the elms, and he stood where he had stood that evening with Doctor Prance and listened to the waves of Verena's voice, as she rehearsed her lecture. There were no waves this time, no sounds, and no sign of life but the lamps; the place had apparently not ceased to be given over to the conscious silence described by Doctor Prance. Ransom felt that he gave an immense proof of chivalry in not calling upon Verena to grant him an interview on the spot. She had not answered his last note, but the next day she kept the tryst, at the hour he had proposed; he saw her advance along the road, in a white dress, under a big parasol, and again he found himself liking immensely the way she walked. He was dismayed, however, at her face and what it portended; pale, with red eyes, graver than she had ever been before, she appeared to have spent the period of his absence in violent weeping. Yet that it was not for him she had been crying was proved by the very first words she spoke.

"I only came out to tell you definitely it's impossible! I have thought over everything, taking plenty of time — over and over; and that is my answer, finally, positively. You must take it — you shall have no other."

Basil Ransom gazed, frowning fearfully. "And why not, pray?"

"Because I can't, I can't, I can't, I can't!" she repeated, passionately, with her altered, distorted face.

"Damnation!" murmured the young man. He seized her hand, drew it into his arm, forcing her to walk with him along the road.

That afternoon Olive Chancellor came out of her house and wandered for a long time upon the shore. She looked up and down the bay, at the sails that gleamed on the blue water, shifting in the breeze and the light; they were a source of interest to her that they had never been before. It was a day she was destined never to forget; she felt it to be the saddest, the most wounding of her life. Unrest and haunting fear had not possession of her now, as they had held her in New York when Basil Ransom carried off Verena, to mark her for his own, in the park. But an immeasurable load of misery seemed to sit upon her soul; she ached with the bitterness of her melancholy, she was dumb and cold with despair. She had spent the violence of her terror, the eagerness of her belief, and now she was too weary to struggle with fate. She appeared to herself almost to have accepted it, as she wandered forth in the beautiful afternoon with the knowledge that the "ten minutes" which Verena had told her she meant to devote to Mr. Ransom that morning had developed suddenly into an embarkation for the day. They had gone out in a boat together; one of the village-worthies, from whom small craft were to be hired, had, at Verena's request, sent his little son to Miss Chancellor's cottage with that information. She had not understood whether they had taken the boatman with them. Even when the information came (and it came at a moment of considerable reassurance), Olive's nerves were not ploughed up by it as they had been, for instance, by the other expedition, in New York; and she could measure the distance she had traversed since then. It had not driven her away on the instant to pace the shore in frenzy, to challenge every boat that passed, and beg that the young lady who was sailing somewhere in the bay with a dark gentleman with long hair, should be entreated immediately to return. On the contrary, after the first quiver of pain inflicted by the news she had been able to occupy herself, to look after her house, to write her morning's letters, to go into her accounts, which she had had some time on her mind. She had wanted to put off thinking, for she knew to what hideous recognitions that would bring her round again. These were summed up in the fact that Verena was now not to be trusted for an hour. She had sworn to her the night before, with a face like a lacerated angel's, that her choice was made, that their union and their work were more to her than any other life could ever be, and that she deeply believed that should she forswear these holy things she should simply waste away, in the end, with remorse and shame. She would see Mr. Ransom just once more, for ten minutes, to utter one or two supreme truths to him, and then they would take up their old, happy, active, fruitful days again, would throw themselves more than ever into their splendid effort. Olive had seen how Verena was moved by Miss Birdseye's death, how at the sight of that unique woman's majestically simple withdrawal from a scene in which she had held every vulgar aspiration, every worldly standard and lure, so cheap, the girl had been touched again with the spirit of their most confident hours, had flamed up with the faith that no narrow personal joy could compare in sweetness with the idea of doing something for those who had always suffered and who waited still. This helped Olive to believe that she might begin to count upon her again, conscious as she was at the same time that Verena had been strangely weakened and strained by her odious ordeal. Oh, Olive knew that she loved him — knew what the passion was with which the wretched girl had to struggle; and she did her the justice to believe that her professions were sincere, her effort was real. Harassed and embittered as she was, Olive Chancellor still proposed to herself to be rigidly just, and that is why she pitied Verena now with an unspeakable pity, regarded her as the victim of an atrocious spell, and reserved all her execration and contempt for the author of their common misery. If Verena had stepped into a boat with him half an hour after declaring that she would give him his dismissal in twenty words, that was because he

had ways, known to himself and other men, of creating situations without an issue, of forcing her to do things she could do only with sharp repugnance, under the menace of pain that would be sharper still. But all the same, what actually stared her in the face was that Verena was not to be trusted, even after rallying again as passionately as she had done during the days that followed Miss Birdseye's death. Olive would have liked to know the pang of penance that *she* would have been afraid, in her place, to incur; to see the locked door which *she* would not have managed to force open!

This inexpressibly mournful sense that, after all, Verena, in her exquisite delicacy and generosity, was appointed only to show how women had from the beginning of time been the sport of men's selfishness and avidity, this dismal conviction accompanied Olive on her walk, which lasted all the afternoon, and in which she found a kind of tragic relief. She went very far, keeping in the lonely places, unveiling her face to the splendid light, which seemed to make a mock of the darkness and bitterness of her spirit. There were little sandy coves, where the rocks were clean, where she made long stations, sinking down in them as if she hoped she should never rise again. It was the first time she had been out since Miss Birdseye's death, except the hour when, with the dozen sympathisers who came from Boston, she stood by the tired old woman's grave. Since then, for three days, she had been writing letters, narrating, describing to those who hadn't come; there were some, she thought, who might have managed to do so, instead of despatching her pages of diffuse reminiscence and asking her for all particulars in return. Selah Tarrant and his wife had come, obtrusively, as she thought, for they never had had very much intercourse with Miss Birdseye; and if it was for Verena's sake, Verena was there to pay every tribute herself. Mrs. Tarrant had evidently hoped Miss Chancellor would ask her to stay on at Marmion, but Olive felt how little she was in a state for such heroics of hospitality. It was precisely in order that she should not have to do that sort of thing that she had given Selah such considerable sums, on two occasions, at a year's interval. If the Tarrants wanted a change of air they could travel all over the country — their present means permitted it; they could go to Saratoga or Newport if they liked. Their appearance showed that they could put their hands into their pockets (or into hers); at least Mrs. Tarrant's did. Selah still sported (on a hot day in August), his immemorial waterproof; but his wife rustled over the low tombstones at Marmion in garments of which (little as she was versed in such inquiries), Olive could see that the cost had been large. Besides, after Doctor Prance had gone (when all was over), she felt what a relief it was that Verena and she could be just together — together with the monstrous wedge of a question that had come up between them. That was company enough, great heaven! and she had not got rid of such an inmate as Doctor Prance only to put Mrs. Tarrant in her place.

Did Verena's strange aberration, on this particular day, suggest to Olive that it was no use striving, that the world was all a great trap or trick, of which women were ever the punctual dupes, so that it was the worst of the curse that rested upon them that they must most humiliate those who had most their cause at heart? Did she say to herself that their weakness was not only lamentable but hideous — hideous their predestined subjection to man's larger and grosser insistence? Did she ask herself why she should give up her life to save a sex which, after all, didn't wish to be saved, and which rejected the truth even after it had bathed them with its auroral light and they had pretended to be fed and fortified? These are mysteries into which I shall not attempt to enter, speculations with which I have no concern; it is sufficient for us to know that all human effort had never seemed to her so barren and thankless as on that fatal afternoon. Her eyes rested on the boats she saw in the distance, and she wondered if in one of them Verena were floating to her fate; but so far from straining forward to beckon her home she almost wished that she might glide away for ever, that *she* might never see her again, never undergo the horrible details of a more deliberate separation. Olive lived over, in her miserable musings, her life for the last two years; she knew, again, how noble and beautiful her scheme had been, but how it had all rested on an illusion of which the very thought made her feel faint and sick. What was before her now was the reality, with the beautiful, indifferent sky pouring down its complacent rays upon it. The reality was simply that Verena had been more to her than she ever was to Verena, and that, with her exquisite natural art, the girl had cared for their cause only because, for the time, no interest, no fascination, was greater. Her talent, the talent which was to achieve such wonders, was nothing to her; it was too easy, she could leave it alone, as she might close her piano, for months; it was only to Olive that it was everything. Verena had submitted, she had responded, she had lent herself to Olive's incitement and exhortation, because she was sympathetic and young and abundant and fanciful; but it had been a kind of hothouse loyalty, the mere contagion of example, and a sentiment springing up from within had easily breathed a chill upon it. Did Olive ask herself whether, for so many months, her companion had been only the most unconscious and most successful of humbugs? Here again I must plead a certain incompetence to give an answer. Positive it is that she spared herself none of the inductions of a reverie that seemed to dry up the mists and ambigui-

ties of life. These hours of backward clearness come to all men and women, once at least, when they read the past in the light of the present, with the reasons of things, like unobserved fingerposts, protruding where they never saw them before. The journey behind them is mapped out and figured, with its false steps, its wrong observations, all its infatuated, deluded geography. They understand as Olive understood, but it is probable that they rarely suffer as she suffered. The sense of regret for her baffled calculations burned within her like a fire, and the splendour of the vision over which the curtain of mourning now was dropped brought to her eyes slow, still tears, tears that came one by one, neither easing her nerves nor lightening her load of pain. She thought of her innumerable talks with Verena, of the pledges they had exchanged, of their earnest studies, their faithful work, their certain reward, the winter-nights under the lamp, when they thrilled with previsions as just and a passion as high as had ever found shelter in a pair of human hearts. The pity of it, the misery of such a fall after such a flight, could express itself only, as the poor girl prolonged the vague pauses of her unnoticed ramble, in a low, inarticulate murmur of anguish.

The afternoon waned, bringing with it the slight chill which, at the summer's end, begins to mark the shortening days. She turned her face homeward, and by this time became conscious that if Verena's companion had not yet brought her back there might be ground for uneasiness as to what had happened to them. It seemed to her that no sail-boat could have put into the town without passing more or less before her eyes and showing her whom it carried; she had seen a dozen, freighted only with the figures of men. An accident was perfectly possible (what could Ransom, with his plantation-habits, know about the management of a sail?), and once that danger loomed before her — the signal loveliness of the weather had prevented its striking her before — Olive's imagination hurried, with a bound, to the worst. She saw the boat overturned and drifting out to sea, and (after a week of nameless horror) the body of an unknown young woman, defaced beyond recognition, but with long auburn hair and in a white dress, washed up in some far-away cove. An hour before, her mind had rested with a sort of relief on the idea that Verena should sink for ever beneath the horizon, so that their tremendous trouble might never be; but now, with the lateness of the hour, a sharp, immediate anxiety took the place of that intended resignation; and she quickened her step, with a heart that galloped too as she went. Then it was, above all, that she felt how *she* had understood friendship, and how never again to see the face of the creature she had taken to her soul would be for her as the stroke of blindness. The

twilight had become thick by the time she reached Marmion and paused for an instant in front of her house, over which the elms that stood on the grassy wayside appeared to her to hang a blacker curtain than ever before.

There was no candle in any window, and when she pushed in and stood in the hall, listening a moment, her step awakened no answering sound. Her heart failed her; Verena's staying out in a boat from ten o'clock in the morning till nightfall was too unnatural, and she gave a cry, as she rushed into the low, dim parlour (darkened on one side, at that hour, by the wide-armed foliage, and on the other by the verandah and trellis), which expressed only a wild personal passion, a desire to take her friend in her arms again on any terms, even the most cruel to herself. The next moment she started back, with another and a different exclamation, for Verena was in the room, motionless, in a corner — the first place in which she had seated herself on re-entering the house — looking at her with a silent face which seemed strange, unnatural, in the dusk. Olive stopped short, and for a minute the two women remained as they were, gazing at each other in the dimness. After that, too, Olive still said nothing; she only went to Verena and sat down beside her. She didn't know what to make of her manner; she had never been like that before. She was unwilling to speak; she seemed crushed and humbled. This was almost the worst — if anything could be worse

719

than what had gone before; and
Olive took her hand with an irresistible impulse of compassion and
reassurance. From the way it lay
in her own she guessed her whole
feeling — saw it was a kind of
shame, shame for her weakness,
her swift surrender, her insane gy-
ration, in the morning. Verena expressed it by no protest and no explanation; she appeared not even
to wish to hear the sound of her
own voice. Her silence itself was
an appeal — an appeal to Olive to
ask no questions (she could trust
her to inflict no spoken reproach);
only to wait till she could lift up
her head again. Olive understood,
or thought she understood, and the
wofulness of it all only seemed the
deeper. She would just sit there
and hold her hand; that was all she
could do; they were beyond each
other's help in any other way now.
Verena leaned her head back and
closed her eyes, and for an hour, as
nightfall settled in the room, neither of the young women spoke.
Distinctly, it was a kind of shame.
After a while the parlour-maid,
very casual, in the manner of the
servants at Marmion, appeared on
the threshold with a lamp; but Olive motioned her frantically away.
She wished to keep the darkness.
It was a kind of shame.

The next morning Basil Ransom
rapped loudly with his walking-
stick on the lintel of Miss Chancellor's house-door, which, as usual
on fine days, stood open. There
was no need he should wait till
the servant had answered his summons; for Olive, who had reason

to believe he would come, and
who had been lurking in the sitting-room for a purpose of her
own, stepped forth into the little
hall.

"I am sorry to disturb you; I had
the hope that — for a moment — I
might see Miss Tarrant." That was
the speech with which (and a
measured salutation), he greeted
his advancing kinswoman. She
faced him an instant, and her
strange green eyes caught the light.

"It's impossible. You may believe that when I say it."

"Why is it impossible?" he
asked, smiling in spite of an inward displeasure. And as Olive
gave him no answer, only gazing
at him with a cold audacity which
he had not hitherto observed in
her, he added a little explanation.
"It is simply to have seen her
before I go — to have said five
words to her. I want her to know
that I have made up my mind
— since yesterday — to leave this
place; I shall take the train at
noon."

It was not to gratify Olive Chancellor that he had determined to
go away, or even that he told her
this; yet he was surprised that his
words brought no expression of
pleasure to her face. "I don't think
it is of much importance whether
you go away or not. Miss Tarrant
herself has gone away."

"Miss Tarrant — gone away?"
This announcement was so much
at variance with Verena's apparent
intentions the night before that his
ejaculation expressed chagrin as
well as surprise, and in doing so it

gave Olive a momentary advantage. It was the only one she had ever had, and the poor girl may be excused for having enjoyed it — so far as enjoyment was possible to her. Basil Ransom's visible discomfiture was more agreeable to her than anything had been for a long time.

"I went with her myself to the early train; and I saw it leave the station." And Olive kept her eyes unaverted, for the satisfaction of seeing how he took it.

It must be confessed that he took it rather ill. He had decided it was best he should retire, but Verena's retiring was another matter. "And where is she gone?" he asked, with a frown.

"I don't think I am obliged to tell you."

"Of course not! Excuse my asking. It is much better that I should find it out for myself, because if I owed the information to you I should perhaps feel a certain delicacy as regards profiting by it."

"Gracious heaven!" cried Miss Chancellor, at the idea of Ransom's delicacy. Then she added more deliberately: "You will not find out for yourself."

"You think not?"

"I am sure of it!" And her enjoyment of the situation becoming acute, there broke from her lips a shrill, unfamiliar, troubled sound, which performed the office of a laugh, a laugh of triumph, but which, at a distance, might have passed almost as well for a wail of despair. It rang in Ransom's ears as he quickly turned away.

Chapter XL

IT was Mrs. Luna who received him, as she had received him on the occasion of his first visit to Charles Street; by which I do not mean quite in the same way. She had known very little about him then, but she knew too much for her happiness to-day, and she had with him now a little invidious, contemptuous manner, as if everything he should say or do could be a proof only of abominable duplicity and perversity. She had a theory that he had treated her shamefully; and he knew it — I do not mean the fact, but the theory: which led him to reflect that her resentments were as shallow as her opinions, inasmuch as if she really believed in her grievance, or if it had had any dignity, she would not have consented to see him. He had not presented himself at Miss Chancellor's door without a very good reason, and having done so he could not turn away so long as there was any one in the house of whom he might have speech. He had sent up his name to Mrs. Luna, after being told that she was staying there, on the mere chance that she would see him; for he thought a refusal a very possible sequel to the letters she had written him during the past four or five months — letters he had scarcely read, full of allusions of the most cutting sort to proceed-

721

ings of his, in the past, of which he had no recollection whatever. They bored him, for he had quite other matters in his mind.

"I don't wonder you have the bad taste, the crudity," she said, as soon as he came into the room, looking at him more sternly than he would have believed possible to her.

He saw that this was an allusion to his not having been to see her since the period of her sister's visit to New York; he having conceived for her, the evening of Mrs. Burrage's party, a sentiment of aversion which put an end to such attentions. He didn't laugh, he was too worried and preoccupied; but he replied, in a tone which apparently annoyed her as much as any indecent mirth: "I thought it very possible you wouldn't see me."

"Why shouldn't I see you, if I should take it into my head? Do you suppose I care whether I see you or not?"

"I suppose you wanted to, from your letters."

"Then why did you think I would refuse?"

"Because that's the sort of thing women do."

"Women — women! You know much about them!"

"I am learning something every day."

"You haven't learned yet, apparently, to answer their letters. It's rather a surprise to me that you don't pretend not to have received mine."

Ransom could smile now; the opportunity to vent the exaspera-

tion that had been consuming him almost restored his good humour. "What could I say? You overwhelmed me. Besides, I did answer one of them."

"One of them? You speak as if I had written you a dozen!" Mrs. Luna cried.

"I thought that was your contention — that you had done me the honour to address me so many. They were crushing, and when a man's crushed, it's all over."

"Yes, you look as if you were in very small pieces! I am glad I shall never see you again."

"I can see now why you received me — to tell me that," Ransom said.

"It is a kind of pleasure. I am going back to Europe."

"Really? for Newton's education?"

"Ah, I wonder you can have the face to speak of that — after the way you deserted him!"

"Let us abandon the subject, then, and I will tell you what I want."

"I don't in the least care what you want," Mrs. Luna remarked. "And you haven't even the grace to ask me where I am going — over there."

"What difference does that make to me — once you leave these shores?"

Mrs. Luna rose to her feet. "Ah, chivalry, chivalry!" she exclaimed. And she walked away to the window — one of the windows from which Ransom had first enjoyed, at Olive's solicitation, the view of the Back Bay. Mrs. Luna looked forth at it with little of the air of a person who was sorry to be about to lose it. "I am determined you shall know where I am going," she said in a moment. "I am going to Florence."

"Don't be afraid!" he replied. "I shall go to Rome."

"And you'll carry there more impertinence than has been seen there since the old emperors."

"Were the emperors impertinent, in addition to their other vices? I am determined, on my side, that you shall know what I have come for," Ransom said. "I wouldn't ask you if I could ask any one else; but I am very hard pressed, and I don't know who can help me."

Mrs. Luna turned on him a face of the frankest derision. "Help you? Do you remember the last time I asked you to help me?"

"That evening at Mrs. Burrage's? Surely I wasn't wanting then; I remember urging on your acceptance a chair, so that you might stand on it, to see and to hear."

"To see and to hear what, please? Your disgusting infatuation!"

"It's just about that I want to speak to you," Ransom pursued. "As you already know all about it, you have no new shock to receive, and I therefore venture to ask you ——"

"Where tickets for her lecture to-night can be obtained? Is it possible she hasn't sent you one?"

"I assure you I didn't come to Boston to hear it," said Ransom, with a sadness which Mrs. Luna evidently regarded as a refinement of outrage. "What I should like to ascertain is where Miss Tarrant may be found at the present moment."

"And do you think that's a delicate inquiry to make of *me?*"

"I don't see why it shouldn't be, but I know you don't think it is, and that is why, as I say, I mention the matter to you only because I can imagine absolutely no one else who is in a position to assist me. I have been to the house of Miss Tarrant's parents, in Cambridge, but it is closed and empty, destitute of any sign of life. I went there first, on arriving this morning, and rang at this door only when my journey to Monadnoc Place had proved fruitless. Your sister's servant told me that Miss Tarrant was not staying here, but she added that Mrs. Luna was. No doubt you won't be pleased at having been spoken of as a sort of equivalent; and I didn't say to myself — or to the servant — that you would do as well; I only reflected that I could at least try you. I didn't even ask for Miss Chancellor, as I am sure she would give me no information whatever."

Mrs. Luna listened to this candid account of the young man's proceedings with her head turned a little over her shoulder at him, and her eyes fixed as unsympathetically as possible upon his own. "What you propose, then, as I understand it," she said in a moment, "is that I should betray my sister to you."

"Worse than that; I propose that

you should betray Miss Tarrant herself."

"What do I care about Miss Tarrant? I don't know what you are talking about."

"Haven't you really any idea where she is living? Haven't you seen her here? Are Miss Olive and she not constantly together?"

Mrs. Luna, at this, turned full round upon him, and, with folded arms and her head tossed back, exclaimed: "Look here, Basil Ransom, I never thought you were a fool, but it strikes me that since we last met you have lost your wits!"

"There is no doubt of that," Ransom answered, smiling.

"Do you mean to tell me you don't know everything about Miss Tarrant that can be known?"

"I have neither seen her nor heard of her for the last ten weeks; Miss Chancellor has hidden her away."

"Hidden her away, with all the walls and fences of Boston flaming to-day with her name?"

"Oh yes, I have noticed that, and I have no doubt that by waiting till this evening I shall be able to see her. But I don't want to wait till this evening; I want to see her now, and not in public — in private."

"Do you indeed? — how interesting!" cried Mrs. Luna, with rippling laughter. "And pray what do you want to do with her?"

Ransom hesitated a little. "I think I would rather not tell you."

"Your charming frankness, then, has its limits! My poor cousin, you are really too *naïf*. Do you suppose it matters a straw to me?"

Ransom made no answer to this appeal, but after an instant he broke out: "Honestly, Mrs. Luna, can you give me no clue?"

"Lord, what terrible eyes you make, and what terrible words you use! 'Honestly,' quoth he! Do you think I am so fond of the creature that I want to keep her all to myself?"

"I don't know; I don't understand," said Ransom, slowly and softly, but still with his terrible eyes.

"And do you think I understand any better? You are not a very edifying young man," Mrs. Luna went on; "but I really think you have deserved a better fate than to be jilted and thrown over by a girl of that class."

"I haven't been jilted. I like her very much, but she never encouraged me."

At this Mrs. Luna broke again into articulate scoffing. "It is very odd that at your age you should be so little a man of the world!"

Ransom made her no other answer than to remark, thoughtfully and rather absently: "Your sister is really very clever."

"By which you mean, I suppose, that I am not!" Mrs. Luna suddenly changed her tone, and said, with the greatest sweetness and humility: "God knows, I have never pretended to be!"

Ransom looked at her a moment, and guessed the meaning of this altered note. It had suddenly come over her that with her portrait in half the shop-fronts, her advertisement on all the fences, and the great occasion on which she was to reveal herself to the country at large close at hand, Verena had become so conscious of high destinies that her dear friend's Southern kinsman really appeared to her very small game, and she might therefore be regarded as having cast him off. If this were the case, it would perhaps be well for Mrs. Luna still to hold on. Basil's induction was very rapid, but it gave him time to decide that the best thing to say to his interlocutress was: "On what day do you sail for Europe?"

"Perhaps I shall not sail at all," Mrs. Luna replied, looking out of the window.

"And in that case — poor Newton's education?"

"I should try to content myself with a country which has given you yours."

"Don't you want him, then, to be a man of the world?"

"Ah, the world, the world!" she murmured, while she watched, in the deepening dusk, the lights of the town begin to reflect themselves in the Back Bay. "Has it been such a source of happiness to me that I belong to it?"

"Perhaps, after all, I shall be able to go to Florence!" said Ransom, laughing.

She faced him once more, this time slowly, and declared that she had never known anything so strange as his state of mind — she would be so glad to have an explanation of it. With the opinions he professed (it was for them she had liked him — she didn't like his character), why on earth should he be running after a little fifth-rate *poseuse,* and in such a frenzy to get hold of her? He might say it was none of her business, and of course she would have no answer to that; therefore she admitted that she asked simply out of intellectual curiosity, and because one always was tormented at the sight of a painful contradiction. With the things she had heard him say about his convictions and theories, his view of life and the great questions of the future, she should have thought he would find Miss Tarrant's attitudinising absolutely nauseous. Were not her views the same as Olive's, and hadn't Olive and he signally failed to hit it off together? Mrs. Luna only asked because she was really quite puzzled. "Don't you know that some minds, when they see a mystery, can't rest till they clear it up?"

"You can't be more puzzled than I am," said Ransom. "Apparently the explanation is to be found in a sort of reversal of the formula you were so good, just now, as to apply to me. You like my opinions, but you entertain a different sentiment for my character. I deplore Miss Tarrant's opinions, but her character — well, her character pleases me."

Mrs. Luna stared, as if she were waiting, the explanation surely not being complete. "But as much as that?" she inquired.

"As much as what?" said Ransom, smiling. Then he added, "Your sister has beaten me."

"I thought she had beaten some one of late; she has seemed so gay and happy. I didn't suppose it was *all* because I was going away."

"Has she seemed very gay?" Ransom inquired, with a sinking of the heart. He wore such a long face, as he asked this question, that Mrs. Luna was again moved to audible mirth, after which she explained:

"Of course I mean gay for her. Everything is relative. With her impatience for this lecture of her friend's to-night, she's in an unspeakable state! She can't sit still for three minutes, she goes out fifteen times a day, and there has been enough arranging and interviewing, and discussing and telegraphing and advertising, enough wire-pulling and rushing about, to put an army in the field. What is it they are always doing to the armies in Europe? — mobilising them? Well, Verena has been mobilised, and this has been headquarters."

"And shall you go to the Music Hall to-night?"

"For what do you take me? I have no desire to be shrieked at for an hour."

"No doubt, no doubt, Miss Olive must be in a state," Ransom went on, rather absently. Then he said, with abruptness, in a different tone: "If this house has been, as you say, headquarters, how comes it you haven't seen her?"

"Seen Olive? I have seen nothing else!"

"I mean Miss Tarrant. She must be somewhere — in the place — if she's to speak to-night."

"Should you like me to go out and look for her? *Il ne manquerait plus que cela!*" cried Mrs. Luna. "What's the matter with you, Basil Ransom, and what are you after?" she demanded, with considerable sharpness. She had tried haughtiness and she had tried humility, but they brought her equally face to face with a competitor whom she couldn't take seriously, yet who was none the less objectionable for that.

I know not whether Ransom would have attempted to answer her question had an obstacle not presented itself; at any rate, at the moment she spoke, the curtain in the doorway was pushed aside, and a visitor crossed the threshold. "Mercy! how provoking!" Mrs. Luna exclaimed, audibly enough; and without moving from her place she bent an uncharitable eye upon the invader, a gentleman whom Ransom had the sense of having met before. He was a young man with a fresh face and abundant locks, prematurely white; he stood smiling at Mrs. Luna, quite undaunted by the absence of any demonstration in his favour. She looked as if she didn't know him, while Ransom prepared to depart, leaving them to settle it together.

"I'm afraid you don't remember me, though I have seen you before," said the young man, very amiably. "I was here a week ago, and Miss Chancellor presented me to you."

"Oh, yes; she's not at home now," Mrs. Luna returned, vaguely.

"So I was told — but I didn't let that prevent me." And the young man included Basil Ransom in the smile with which he made himself more welcome than Mrs. Luna appeared to be disposed to make him, and by which he seemed to call attention to his superiority. "There is a matter on which I want very much to obtain some information, and I have no doubt you will be so good as to give it to me."

"It comes back to me — you have something to do with the newspapers," said Mrs. Luna; and Ransom too, by this time, had placed the young man among his reminiscences. He had been at Miss Birdseye's famous party, and Doctor Prance had there described him as a brilliant journalist.

It was quite with the air of such a personage that he accepted Mrs. Luna's definition, and he continued to radiate towards Ransom (as if, in return, he remembered *his* face), while he dropped, confidentially, the word that expressed everything — " 'The Vesper,' don't you know?" Then he went on: "Now, Mrs. Luna, I don't care, I'm not going to let you off! We want the last news about Miss Verena, and it has got to come out of this house."

"Oh murder!" Ransom muttered, beneath his breath, taking up his hat.

"Miss Chancellor has hidden her away; I have been scouring the city in search of her, and her own father hasn't seen her for a week. We have got his ideas; they are very easy to get, but that isn't what we want."

"And what do you want?" Ransom was now impelled to inquire, as Mr. Pardon (even the name at present came back to him), appeared sufficiently to have introduced himself.

"We want to know how she feels about to-night; what report she makes of her nerves, her anticipations; how she looked, what she had on, up to six o'clock. Gracious! if I could see her I should know what I wanted, and so would she, I guess!" Mr. Pardon exclaimed. "You must know something, Mrs. Luna; it isn't natural you shouldn't. I won't inquire any further where she is, because that might seem a little pushing, if she does wish to withdraw herself — though I am bound to say I think she makes a mistake; we could work up these last hours for her! But can't you tell me any little personal items — the sort of thing the people like? What is she going to have for supper? or is she going to speak — a — without previous nourishment?"

"Really, sir, I don't know, and I don't in the least care; I have nothing to do with the business!" Mrs. Luna cried, angrily.

The reporter stared; then, eagerly, "You have nothing to do with it — you take an unfavorable view, you protest?" And he was already feeling in a side-pocket for his note-book.

"Mercy on us! are you going to

put *that* in the paper?" Mrs. Luna
exclaimed; and in spite of the
sense, detestable to him, that everything he wished most to avert
was fast closing over the girl, Ransome broke into cynical laughter.

"Ah, but do protest, madam; let
us at least have that fragment!"
Mr. Pardon went on. "A protest
from this house would be a charming note. We *must* have it — we've
got nothing else! The public are almost as much interested in your
sister as they are in Miss Verena;
they know to what extent she has
backed her: and I should be so
delighted (I see the heading, from
here, so attractive!) just to take
down 'What Miss Chancellor's
Family Think about It!' "

Mrs. Luna sank into the nearest
chair, with a groan, covering her
face with her hands. "Heaven help
me, I am glad I am going to Europe!"

"That is another little item — everything counts," said Matthias
Pardon, making a rapid entry in
his tablets. "May I inquire whether
you are going to Europe in consequence of your disapproval of your
sister's views?"

Mrs. Luna sprang up again, almost snatching the memoranda out
of his hand. "If you have the impertinence to publish a word about
me, or to mention my name in
print, I will come to your office and
make such a scene!"

"Dearest lady, that would be a
godsend!" Mr. Pardon cried, en-
thusiastically; but he put his notebook back into his pocket.

"Have you made an exhaustive
search for Miss Tarrant?" Basil
Ransom asked of him. Mr. Pardon,
at this inquiry, eyed him with a
sudden, familiar archness, expressive of the idea of competition; so
that Ransom aded: "You needn't
be afraid, I'm not a reporter."

"I didn't know but what you
had come on from New York."

"So I have — but not as the representative of a newspaper."

"Fancy his taking you——"
Mrs. Luna murmured, with indignation.

"Well, I have been everywhere
I could think of," Mr. Pardon remarked. "I have been hunting
round after your sister's agent, but
I haven't been able to catch up
with him; I suppose he has been
hunting on his side. Miss Chancellor told me — Mrs. Luna may remember it — that she shouldn't be
here at all during the week, and
that she preferred not to tell me either where or how she was to spend
her time until the momentous evening. Of course I let her know that
I should find out if I could, and you
may remember," he said to Mrs.
Luna, "the conversation we had on
the subject. I remarked, candidly,
that if they didn't look out they
would overdo the quietness. Doctor
Tarrant has felt very low about it.
However, I have done what I
could with the material at my
command, and the 'Vesper' has let
the public know that her whereabouts was the biggest mystery of
the season. It's difficult to get
round the 'Vesper.' "

"I am almost afraid to open my
lips in your presence," Mrs. Luna

The Bostonians

broke in, "but I must say that I think my sister was strangely communicative. She told you ever so much that I wouldn't have breathed."

"I should like to try you with something you know!" Matthias Pardon returned, imperturbably. "This isn't a fair trial, because you don't know. Miss Chancellor came round — came round considerably, there's no doubt of that; because a year or two ago she was terribly unapproachable. If I have mollified her, madam, why shouldn't I mollify you? She realises that I can help her now, and as I ain't rancorous I am willing to help her all she'll let me. The trouble is, she won't let me enough, yet; it seems as if she couldn't believe it of me. At any rate," he pursued, addressing himself more particularly to Ransom, "half an hour ago, at the Hall, they knew nothing whatever about Miss Tarrant, beyond the fact that about a month ago she came there, with Miss Chancellor, to try her voice, which rang all over the place, like silver, and that Miss Chancellor guaranteed her absolute punctuality to-night."

"Well, that's all that is required," said Ransom, at hazard; and he put out his hand, in farewell, to Mrs. Luna.

"Do you desert me already?" she demanded, giving him a glance which would have embarrassed any spectator but a reporter of the "Vesper."

"I have fifty things to do; you must excuse me." He was nervous, restless, his heart was beating much faster than usual; he couldn't stand still, and he had no compunction whatever about leaving her to get rid, by herself, of Mr. Pardon.

This gentleman continued to mix in the conversation, possibly from the hope that if he should linger either Miss Tarrant or Miss Chancellor would make her appearance. "Every seat in the Hall is sold; the crowd is expected to be immense. When our Boston public *does* take an idea!" Mr. Pardon exclaimed.

Ransom only wanted to get away, and in order to facilitate his release by implying that in such a case he should see her again, he said to Mrs. Luna, rather hypocritically, from the threshold, "You had really better come to-night."

"I am not like the Boston public — I don't take an idea!" she replied.

"Do you mean to say you are not going?" cried Mr. Pardon, with widely-open eyes, clapping his hand again to his pocket. "Don't you regard her as a wonderful genius?"

Mrs. Luna was sorely tried, and the vexation of seeing Ransom slip away from her with his thoughts visibly on Verena, leaving her face to face with the odious newspaperman, whose presence made passionate protest impossible — the annoyance of seeing everything and every one mock at her and fail to compensate her was such that she lost her head, while rashness leaped to her lips and jerked out the answer — "No indeed; I think her a vulgar idiot!"

"Ah, madam, I should never

permit myself to print that!" Ransom heard Mr. Pardon rejoin, reproachfully, as he dropped the *portière* of the drawing-room.

Chapter XLI

He walked about for the next two hours, walked all over Boston, heedless of his course, and conscious only of an unwillingness to return to his hotel and an inability to eat his dinner or rest his weary legs. He had been roaming in very much the same desperate fashion, at once eager and purposeless, for many days before he left New York, and he knew that his agitation and suspense must wear themselves out. At present they pressed him more than ever; they had become tremendously acute. The early dusk of the last half of November had gathered thick, but the evening was fine and the lighted streets had the animation and variety of a winter that had begun with brilliancy. The shop-fronts glowed through frosty panes, the passers bustled on the pavement, the bells of the street-cars jangled in the cold air, the newsboys hawked the evening-papers, the vestibules of the theatres, illuminated and flanked with coloured posters and the photographs of actresses, exhibited seductively their swinging doors of red leather or baize, spotted with little brass nails. Behind great plates of glass the interior of the hotels became visible, with marble-paved lobbies, white with electric lamps, and columns, and Westerners on divans stretching their legs, while behind a counter, set apart and covered with an array of periodicals and novels in paper covers, little boys, with the faces of old men, showing plans of the play-houses and offering librettos, sold orchestra-chairs at a premium. When from time to time Ransom paused at a corner, hesitating which way to drift, he looked up and saw the stars, sharp and near, scintillating over the town. Boston seemed to him big and full of nocturnal life, very much awake and preparing for an evening of pleasure.

He passed and repassed the Music Hall, saw Verena immensely advertised, gazed down the vista, the approach for pedestrians, which leads out of School Street, and thought it looked expectant and ominous. People had not begun to enter yet, but the place was ready, lighted and open, and the interval would be only too short. So it appeared to Ransom, while at the same time he wished immensely the crisis were over. Everything that surrounded him referred itself to the idea with which his mind was palpitating, the question whether he might not still intervene as against the girl's jump into the abyss. He believed that all Boston was going to hear her, or that at least every one was whom he saw in the streets; and there was a kind of incentive and inspiration in his thought. The vision of wresting her from the mighty multitude set him off again, to stride through the population that would fight for her. It was not too late, for he felt strong; it would not be too late even if she should already stand there before thousands of converging eyes. He had had his ticket since the morning, and now the time was going on. He went back to his hotel at last for ten minutes, and refreshed himself by dressing a little and by drinking a glass of wine. Then he took his way once more to the Music Hall, and saw that people were beginning to go in — the first drops of the great stream, among whom there were many women. Since seven o'clock the minutes had moved fast — before that they had dragged — and now there was only half an hour. Ransom passed in with the others; he knew just where his seat was; he had chosen it, on reaching Boston, from the few that were left, with what he believed to be care. But now, as he stood beneath the far-away panelled roof, stretching above the line of little tongues of flame which marked its junction with the walls, he felt that this didn't matter much, since he certainly was not going to subside into his place. He was not one of the audience; he was apart, unique, and had come on a business altogether special. It wouldn't have mattered if, in advance, he had got no place at all and had just left himself to pay for standing-room at the last. The people came pouring in, and in a very short time there would only be standing-room left. Ransom had no

definite plan; he had mainly wanted to get inside of the building, so that, on a view of the field, he might make up his mind. He had never been in the Music Hall before, and its lofty vaults and rows of overhanging balconies made it to his imagination immense and impressive. There were two or three moments during which he felt as he could imagine a young man to feel who, waiting in a public place, has made up his mind, for reasons of his own, to discharge a pistol at the king or the president.

The place struck him with a kind of Roman vastness; the doors which opened out of the upper balconies, high aloft, and which were constantly swinging to and fro with the passage of spectators and ushers, reminded him of the *vomitoria* that he had read about in descriptions of the Colosseum. The huge organ, the background of the stage — a stage occupied with tiers of seats for choruses and civic worthies — lifted to the dome its shining pipes and sculptured pinnacles, and some genius of music or oratory erected himself in monumental bronze at the base. The hall was so capacious and serious, and the audience increased so rapidly without filling it, giving Ransom a sense of the numbers it would contain when it was packed, that the courage of the two young women, face to face with so tremendous an ordeal, hovered before him as really sublime, especially the conscious tension of poor Olive, who would have been spared none of the anxieties and tremors, none of the previsions of accident or calculations of failure. In the front of the stage was a slim, high desk, like a music-stand, with a cover of red velvet, and near it was a light ornamental chair, on which he was sure Verena would not seat herself, though he could fancy her leaning at moments on the back. Behind this was a kind of semicircle of a dozen arm-chairs, which had evidently been arranged for the friends of the speaker, her sponsors and patrons. The hall was more and more full of premonitory sounds; people making a noise as they unfolded, on hinges, their seats, and itinerant boys, whose voices as they cried out "Photographs of Miss Tarrant — sketch of her life!" or "Portraits of the Speaker — story of her career!" sounded small and piping in the general immensity. Before Ransom was aware of it several of the arm-chairs, in the row behind the lecturer's desk, were occupied, with gaps, and in a moment he recognised, even across the interval, three of the persons who had appeared. The straight-featured woman with bands of glossy hair and eyebrows that told at a distance, could only be Mrs. Farrinder, just as the gentleman beside her, in a white overcoat, with an umbrella and a vague face, was probably her husband Amariah. At the opposite end of the row were another pair, whom Ransom, unacquainted with certain chapters of Verena's history, perceived without surprise to be Mrs. Burrage

and her insinuating son. Apparently their interest in Miss Tarrant was more than a momentary fad, since — like himself — they had made the journey from New York to hear her. There were other figures, unknown to our young man, here and there, in the semicircle; but several places were still empty (one of which was of course reserved for Olive), and it occurred to Ransom, even in his preoccupation, that one of them ought to remain so — ought to be left to symbolise the presence, in the spirit, of Miss Birdseye.

He bought one of the photographs of Verena, and thought it shockingly bad, and bought also the sketch of her life, which many people seemed to be reading, but crumpled it up in his pocket for future consideration. Verena was not in the least present to him in connection with this exhibition of enterprise and puffery; what he saw was Olive, struggling and yielding, making every sacrifice of state for the sake of the largest hearing, and conforming herself to a great popular system. Whether she had struggled or not, there was a catch-penny effect about the whole thing which added to the fever in his cheek and made him wish he had money to buy up the stock of the vociferous little boys. Suddenly the notes of the organ rolled out into the hall, and he became aware that the overture or prelude had begun. This, too, seemed to him a piece of claptrap, but he didn't wait to think of it; he instantly edged out of his place, which he had chosen near the end of a row, and reached one of the numerous doors. If he had had no definite plan he now had at least an irresistible impulse, and he felt the prick of shame at having faltered for a moment. It had been his tacit calculation that Verena, still enshrined in mystery by her companion, would not have reached the scene of her performance till within a few minutes of the time at which she was to come forth; so that he had lost nothing by waiting, up to this moment, before the platform. But now he must overtake his opportunity. Before passing out of the hall into the lobby he paused, and with his back to the stage, gave a look at the gathered auditory. It had become densely numerous, and, suffused with the evenly distributed gaslight, which fell from a great elevation, and the thick atmosphere that hangs for ever in such places, it appeared to pile itself high and to look dimly expectant and formidable. He had a throb of uneasiness at his private purpose of balking it of its entertainment, its victim — a glimpse of the ferocity that lurks in a disappointed mob. But the thought of that danger only made him pass more quickly through the ugly corridors; he felt that his plan was definite enough now, and he found that he had no need even of asking the way to a certain small door (one or more of them), which he meant to push open. In taking his place in the morning he had assured himself as to the side of the house on which

(with its approach to the platform), the withdrawing room of singers and speakers was situated; he had chosen his seat in that quarter, and he now had not far to go before he reached it. No one heeded or challenged him; Miss Tarrant's auditors were still pouring in (the occasion was evidently to have been an unprecedented success of curiosity), and had all the attention of the ushers. Ransom opened a door at the end of a passage, and it admitted him into a sort of vestibule, quite bare save that at a second door, opposite to him, stood a figure at the sight of which he paused for a moment in his advance.

The figure was simply that of a robust policeman, in his helmet and brass buttons — a policeman who was expecting him — Ransom could see that in a twinkling. He judged in the same space of time that Olive Chancellor had heard of his having arrived and had applied for the protection of this functionary, who was now simply guarding the ingress and was prepared to defend it against all comers. There was a slight element of surprise in this, as he had reasoned that his nervous kinswoman was absent from her house for the day — had been spending it all in Verena's retreat, wherever that was. The surprise was not great enough, however, to interrupt his course for more than an instant, and he crossed the room and stood before the belted sentinel. For a moment neither spoke; they looked at each other very hard in the eyes, and

Ransom heard the organ, beyond partitions, launching its waves of sound through the hall. They seemed to be very near it, and the whole place vibrated. The policeman was a tall, lean-faced, sallow man, with a stoop of the shoulders, a small, steady eye, and something in his mouth which made a protuberance in his cheek. Ransom could see that he was very strong, but he believed that he himself was not materially less so. However, he had not come there to show physical fight — a public tussle about Verena was not an attractive idea, except perhaps, after all, if he should get the worst of it, from the point of view of Olive's new system of advertising; and, moreover, it would not be in the least necessary. Still he said nothing, and still the policeman remained dumb, and there was something in the way the moments elapsed and in our young man's consciousness that Verena was separated from him only by a couple of thin planks, which made him feel that she too expected him, but in another sense; that she had nothing to do with this parade of resistance, that she would know in a moment, by quick intuition, that he was there, and that she was only praying to be rescued, to be saved. Face to face with Olive she hadn't the courage, but she would have it with her hand in his. It came to him that there was no one in the world less sure of her business just at that moment than Olive Chancellor; it was as if he could see, through the door, the terrible way her eyes were fixed on Verena while she held her watch in her hand and Verena looked away from her. Olive would have been so thankful that she should begin before the hour, but of course that was impossible. Ransom asked no questions — that seemed a waste of time; he only said, after a minute, to the policeman:

"I should like very much to see Miss Tarrant, if you will be so good as to take in my card."

The guardian of order, well planted just between him and the handle of the door, took from Ransom the morsel of pasteboard which he held out to him, read slowly the name inscribed on it, turned it over and looked at the back, then returned it to his interlocutor. "Well, I guess it ain't much use," he remarked.

"How can you know that? You have no business to decline my request."

"Well, I guess I have about as much business as you have to make it." Then he added, "You are just the very man she wants to keep out."

"I don't think Miss Tarrant wants to keep me out," Ransom returned.

"I don't know much about her, she hasn't hired the hall. It's the other one — Miss Chancellor; it's her that runs this lecture."

"And she has asked you to keep me out? How absurd!" exclaimed Ransom, ingeniously.

"She tells me you're none too fit to be round alone; you have got this thing on the brain. I guess you'd better be quiet," said the policeman.

"Quiet? It is possible to be more quiet than I am?"

"Well, I've seen crazy folks that were a good deal like you. If you want to see the speaker why don't you go and set round in the hall, with the rest of the public?" And the policeman waited, in an immovable, ruminating, reasonable manner, for an answer to this inquiry.

Ransom had one, on the instant, at his service. "Because I don't want simply to see her; I want also to speak to her — in private."

"Yes — it's always intensely private," said the policeman. "Now I wouldn't lose the lecture if I was you. I guess it will do you good."

"The lecture?" Ransom repeated, laughing. "It won't take place."

"Yes it will — as quick as the organ stops." Then the policeman added, as to himself, "Why the devil don't it?"

"Because Miss Tarrant has sent up to the organist to tell him to keep on."

"Who has she sent, do you s'pose?" And Ransom's new acquaintance entered into his humour. "I guess Miss Chancellor isn't her nigger."

"She has sent her father, or perhaps even her mother. They are in there too."

"How do you know that?" asked the policeman, consideringly.

"Oh, I know everything," Ransom answered, smiling.

"Well, I guess they didn't come here to listen to that organ. We'll hear something else before long, if he doesn't stop."

"You will hear a good deal, very soon," Ransom remarked.

The serenity of his self-confidence appeared at last to make an impression on his antagonist, who lowered his head a little, like some butting animal, and looked at the young man from beneath bushy eyebrows. "Well, I *have* heard a good deal, since I've ben in Boston."

"Oh, Boston's a great place," Ransom rejoined inattentively. He was not listening to the policeman or to the organ now, for the sound of voices had reached him from the other side of the door. The policeman took no further notice of it than to lean back against the panels, with folded arms; and there was another pause, between them, during which the playing of the organ ceased.

"I will just wait here, with your permission," said Ransom, "and presently I shall be called."

"Who do you s'pose will call you?"

"Well, Miss Tarrant, I hope."

"She'll have to square the other one first."

Ransom took out his watch, which he had adapted, on purpose, several hours before, to Boston time, and saw that the minutes had sped with increasing velocity during this interview, and that it now marked five minutes past eight. "Miss Chancellor will have to square the public," he said in a moment; and the words were far from being an empty profession of security, for the conviction already in possession of him, that a drama in which he, though cut off, was an actor, had been going on for some time in the apartment he was prevented from entering, that the situation was extraordinarily strained there, and that it could not come to an end without an appeal to him — this transcendental assumption acquired an infinitely greater force the instant he perceived that Verena was even now keeping her audience waiting. Why didn't she go on? Why, except that she knew he was there, and was gaining time?

"Well, I guess she has shown herself," said the door-keeper, whose discussion with Ransom now appeared to have passed, on his own part, and without the slightest prejudice to his firmness, into a sociable, gossiping phase.

"If she had shown herself, we should hear the reception, the applause."

"Well, there they air; they are going to give it to her," the policeman announced.

He had an odious appearance of being in the right, for there indeed they seemed to be — they were giving it to her. A general hubbub rose from the floor and the galleries of the hall — the sound of several thousand people stamping with their feet and rapping with their umbrellas and sticks. Ransom felt faint, and for a little while he stood with his gaze interlocked with that of the policeman. Then suddenly a wave of coolness seemed to break over him, and he exclaimed: "My dear fellow, that isn't applause — it's impatience. It isn't a reception, it's a call!"

The policeman neither assented to this proposition nor denied it; he only transferred the protuberance in his cheek to the other side, and observed:

"I guess she's sick."

"Oh, I hope not!" said Ransom, very gently. The stamping and rapping swelled and swelled for a minute, and then it subsided; but before it had done so Ransom's definition of it had plainly become the true one. The tone of the manifestation was good-humoured, but it was not gratulatory. He looked at his watch again, and saw that five minutes more had elapsed, and he remembered what the newspaper-man in Charles Street had said about Olive's guaranteeing Verena's punctuality. Oddly enough, at the moment the image of this gentleman recurred to him, the gentleman himself burst through the other door, in a state of the liveliest agitation.

"Why in the name of goodness don't she go on? If she wants to make them call her, they've done it about enough!" Mr. Pardon turned, pressingly, from Ransom to the policeman and back again, and in his preoccupation gave no sign of having met the Mississippian before.

"I guess she's sick," said the policeman.

"The public'll be sick!" cried the distressed reporter. "If she's sick, why doesn't she send for a doctor?

All Boston is packed into this house, and she has got to talk to it. I want to go in and see."

"You can't go in," said the policeman, drily.

"Why can't I go in, I should like to know? I want to go in for the 'Vesper'!"

"You can't go in for anything. I'm keeping this man out, too," the policeman added genially, as if to make Mr. Pardon's exclusion appear less invidious.

"Why, they'd ought to let *you* in," said Matthias, staring a moment at Ransom.

"May be they'd ought, but they won't," the policeman remarked.

"Gracious me!" panted Mr. Pardon; "I knew from the first Miss Chancellor would make a mess of it! Where's Mr. Filer?" he went on, eagerly, addressing himself apparently to either of the others, or to both.

"I guess he's at the door, counting the money," said the policeman.

"Well, he'll have to give it back if he don't look out!"

"Maybe he will. I'll let *him* in if he comes, but he's the only one. She is on now," the policeman added, without emotion.

His ear had caught the first faint murmur of another explosion of sound. This time, unmistakably, it was applause — the clapping of multitudinous hands, mingled with the noise of many throats. The demonstration, however, though considerable, was not what might have been expected, and it died away quickly. Mr. Pardon stood

listening, with an expression of some alarm. "Merciful fathers! can't they give her more than that?" he cried. "I'll just fly round and see!"

When he had hurried away again, Ransom said to the policeman — "Who is Mr. Filer?"

"Oh, he's an old friend of mine. He's the man that runs Miss Chancellor."

"That runs her?"

"Just the same as she runs Miss Tarrant. He runs the pair, as you might say. He's in the lecture-business."

"Then he had better talk to the public himself."

"Oh, *he* can't talk; he can only boss!"

The opposite door at this moment was pushed open again, and a large, heated-looking man, with a little stiff beard on the end of his chin and his overcoat flying behind him, strode forward with an imprecation. "What the h—— are they doing in the parlour? This sort of thing's about played out!"

"Ain't she up there now?" the policeman asked.

"It's not Miss Tarrant," Ransom said, as if he knew all about it. He perceived in a moment that this was Mr. Filer, Olive Chancellor's agent; an inference instantly followed by the reflection that such a personage would have been warned against him by his kinswoman and would doubtless attempt to hold him, or his influence, accountable for Verena's unexpected delay. Mr. Filer only glanced at him, however, and to Ransom's surprise appeared to have no theory of his identity; a fact implying that Miss Chancellor had considered that the greater discretion was (except to the policeman) to hold her tongue about him altogether.

"Up there? It's her jackass of a father that's up there!" cried Mr. Filer, with his hand on the latch of the door, which the policeman had allowed him to approach.

"Is he asking for a doctor?" the latter inquired, dispassionately.

"You're the sort of doctor he'll want, if he doesn't produce the girl! You don't mean to say they've locked themselves in? What the plague are they after?"

"They've got the key on that side," said the policeman, while Mr. Filer discharged at the door a volley of sharp knocks, at the same time violently shaking the handle.

"If the door was locked, what was the good of your standing before it?" Ransom inquired.

"So as you couldn't do that;" and the policeman nodded at Mr. Filer.

"You see your interference has done very little good."

"I dunno; she has got to come out yet."

Mr. Filer meanwhile had continued to thump and shake, demanding instant admission and inquiring if they were going to let the audience pull the house down. Another round of applause had broken out, directed perceptibly to some apology, some solemn circumlocution, of Selah Tarrant's; this covered the sound of the agent's voice, as well as that of a confused and divided response,

proceeding from the parlour. For a minute nothing definite was audible; the door remained closed, and Matthias Pardon reappeared in the vestibule.

"He says she's just a little faint — from nervousness. She'll be all ready in about three minutes." This announcement was Mr. Pardon's contribution to the crisis; and he added that the crowd was a lovely crowd, it was a real Boston crowd, it was perfectly good-humoured.

"There's a lovely crowd, and a real Boston one too, I guess, in here!" cried Mr. Filer, now banging very hard. "I've handled prima donnas, and I've handled natural curiosities, but I've never seen anything up to this. Mind what I say, ladies; if you don't let me in, I'll smash down the door!"

"Don't seem as if *you* could make it much worse, does it?" the policeman observed to Ransom, strolling aside a little, with the air of being superseded.

Chapter XLII

RANSOM made no reply; he was watching the door, which at that moment gave way from within. Verena stood there — it was she, evidently, who had opened it — and her eyes went straight to his. She was dressed in white, and her face was whiter than her garment; above it her hair seemed to shine like fire. She took a step forward;

The Bostonians

but before she could take another he had come down to her, on the threshold of the room. Her face was full of suffering, and he did not attempt — before all those eyes — to take her hand; he only said in a low tone, "I have been waiting for you — a long time!"

"I know it — I saw you in your seat — I want to speak to you."

"Well, Miss Tarrant, don't you think you'd better be on the platform?" cried Mr. Filer, making with both his arms a movement as if to sweep her before him, through the waiting-room, up into the presence of the public.

"In a moment I shall be ready. My father is making that all right." And, to Ransom's surprise, she smiled, with all her sweetness, at the irrepressible agent; appeared to wish genuinely to reassure him.

The three had moved together into the waiting-room, and there at the farther end of it, beyond the vulgar, perfunctory chairs and tables, under the flaring gas, he saw Mrs. Tarrant sitting upright on a sofa, with immense rigidity, and a large flushed visage, full of suppressed distortion, and beside her prostrate, fallen over, her head buried in the lap of Verena's mother, the tragic figure of Olive Chancellor. Ransom could scarcely know how much Olive's having flung herself upon Mrs. Tarrant's bosom testified to the convulsive scene that had just taken place behind the locked door. He closed it again, sharply, in the face of the reporter and the policeman, and at the same moment Selah Tarrant descended,

through the aperture leading to the platform, from his brief communion with the public. On seeing Ransom he stopped short, and, gathering his waterproof about him, measured the young man from head to foot.

"Well, sir, perhaps *you* would like to go and explain our hitch," he remarked, indulging in a smile so comprehensive that the corners of his mouth seemed almost to meet behind. "I presume that you, better than any one else, can give them an insight into our difficulties!"

"Father, be still; father, it will come out all right in a moment!" cried Verena, below her breath, panting like an emergent diver.

"There's one thing I want to know: are we going to spend half an hour talking over our domestic affairs?" Mr. Filer demanded, wiping his indignant countenance. "Is Miss Tarrant going to lecture, or ain't she going to lecture? If she ain't, she'll please to show cause why. Is she aware that every quarter of a second, at the present instant, is worth about five hundred dollars?"

"I know that — I know that, Mr. Filer; I will begin in a moment!" Verena went on. "I only want to speak to Mr. Ransom — just three words. They are perfectly quiet — don't you see how quiet they are? They trust me, they trust me, don't they, father? I only want to speak to Mr. Ransom."

"Who the devil is Mr. Ransom?" cried the exasperated, bewildered Filer.

739

Verena spoke to the others, but she looked at her lover, and the expression of her eyes was ineffably touching and beseeching. She trembled with nervous passion, there were sobs and supplications in her voice, and Ransom felt himself flushing with pure pity for her pain — her inevitable agony. But at the same moment he had another perception, which brushed aside remorse; he saw that he could do what he wanted, that she begged him, with all her being, to spare her, but that so long as he should protest she was submissive, helpless. What he wanted, in this light, flamed before him and challenged all his manhood, tossing his determination to a height from which not only Doctor Tarrant, and Mr. Filer, and Olive, over there, in her sightless, soundless shame, but the great expectant hall as well, and the mighty multitude, in suspense, keeping quiet from minute to minute and holding the breath of its anger — from which all these things looked small, surmountable, and of the moment only. He didn't quite understand, as yet, however; he saw that Verena had not refused, but temporised, that the spell upon her — thanks to which he should still be able to rescue her — had been the knowledge that he was near.

"Come away, come away," he murmured, quickly, putting out his two hands to her.

She took one of them, as if to plead, not to consent. "Oh, let me off, let me off — for *her*, for the

others! It's too terrible, it's impossible!"

"What I want to know is why Mr. Ransom isn't in the hands of the police!" wailed Mrs. Tarrant, from her sofa.

"I have been, madam, for the last quarter of an hour." Ransom felt more and more that he could manage it, if he only kept cool. He bent over Verena with a tenderness in which he was careless, now, of observation. "Dearest, I told you, I warned you. I left you alone for ten weeks; but could that make you doubt it was coming? Not for worlds, not for millions, shall you give yourself to that roaring crowd. Don't ask me to care for them, or for anyone! What do they care for you but to gape and grin and babble? You are mine, you are not theirs."

"What under the sun is the man talking about? With the most magnificent audience ever brought together! The city of Boston is under this roof!" Mr. Filer gaspingly interposed.

"The city of Boston be damned!" said Ransom.

"Mr. Ransom is very much interested in my daughter. He doesn't approve of our views," Selah Tarrant explained.

"It's the most horrible, wicked, immoral selfishness I ever heard in my life!" roared Mrs. Tarrant.

"Selfishness! Mrs. Tarrant, do you suppose I pretend not to be selfish?"

"Do you want us all murdered by the mob, then?"

"They can have their money — can't you give them back their money?" cried Verena, turning frantically round the circle.

"Verena Tarrant, you don't mean to say you are going to back down?" her mother shrieked.

"Good God! that I should make her suffer like this!" said Ransom to himself; and to put an end to the odious scene he would have seized Verena in his arms and broken away into the outer world, if Olive, who at Mrs. Tarrant's last loud challenge had sprung to her feet, had not at the same time thrown herself between them with a force which made the girl relinquish her grasp of Ransom's hand. To his astonishment, the eyes that looked at him out of her scared, haggard face were, like Verena's, eyes of tremendous entreaty. There was a moment during which she would have been ready to go down on her knees to him, in order that the lecture should go on.

"If you don't agree with her, take her up on the platform, and have it out there; the public would like that, first-rate!" Mr. Filer said to Ransom, as if he thought this suggestion practical.

"She had prepared a lovely address!" Selah remarked, mournfully, as if to the company in general.

No one appeared to heed the observation, but his wife broke out again. "Verena Tarrant, I should like to slap you! Do you call such a man as that a gentleman? I don't know where your father's spirit is, to let him stay!"

Olive, meanwhile, was literally praying to her kinsman. "Let her appear this once, just this once: not to ruin, not to shame! Haven't you any pity; do you want me to be hooted? It's only for an hour. Haven't you any soul?"

Her face and voice were terrible to Ransom; she had flung herself upon Verena and was holding her close, and he could see that her friend's suffering was faint in comparison to her own. "Why for an hour, when it's all false and damnable? An hour is as bad as ten years! She's mine or she isn't, and if she's mine, she's all mine!"

"Yours! Yours! Verena, think, think what you're doing!" Olive moaned, bending over her.

Mr. Filer was now pouring forth his nature in objurgations and oaths, and brandishing before the culprits — Verena and Ransom — the extreme penalty of the law. Mrs. Tarrant had burst into violent hysterics, while Selah revolved vaguely about the room and declared that it seemed as if the better day was going to be put off for quite a while. "Don't you see how good, how sweet they are — giving us all this time? Don't you think that when they behave like that — without a sound, for five minutes — they ought to be rewarded?" Verena asked, smiling divinely, at Ransom. Nothing could have been more tender, more exquisite, than the way she put her appeal upon the ground of simple charity, kindness to the great good-natured, childish public.

"Miss Chancellor may reward them in any way she likes. Give them back their money and a little present to each."

"Money and presents? I should like to shoot you, sir!" yelled Mr. Filer. The audience had really been very patient, and up to this point deserved Verena's praise; but it was now long past eight o'clock, and symptoms of irritation — cries and groans and hisses — began again to proceed from the hall. Mr. Filer launched himself into the passage leading to the stage, and Selah rushed after him. Mrs. Tarrant extended herself, sobbing, on the sofa, and Olive, quivering in the storm, inquired of Ransom what he wanted her to do, what humiliation, what degradation, what sacrifice he imposed.

"I'll do anything — I'll be abject — I'll be vile — I'll go down in the dust!"

"I ask nothing of you, and I have nothing to do with you," Ransom said. "That is, I ask, at the most, that you shouldn't expect that, wishing to make Verena my wife, I should say to her, 'Oh yes, you can take an hour or two out of it!' Verena," he went on "all this is out of it — dreadfully, odiously — and it's a great deal too much! Come, come as far away from here as possible, and we'll settle the rest!"

The combined effort of Mr. Filer and Selah Tarrant to pacify the public had not, apparently, the

success it deserved; the house continued in uproar and the volume of sound increased. "Leave us alone, leave us alone for a single minute!" cried Verena; "just let me speak to him, and it will be all right!" She rushed over to her mother, drew her, dragged her from the sofa, led her to the door of the room. Mrs. Tarrant, on the way, reunited herself with Olive (the horror of the situation had at least that compensation for her), and, clinging and staggering together, the distracted women, pushed by Verena, passed into the vestibule, now, as Ransom saw, deserted by the policeman and the reporter, who had rushed round to where the battle was thickest.

"Oh, why did you come — why, why?" And Verena, turning back, threw herself upon him with a protest which was all, and more than all, a surrender. She had never yet given herself to him so much as in that movement of reproach.

"Didn't you expect me, and weren't you sure?" he asked, smiling at her and standing there till she arrived.

"I didn't know — it was terrible — it's awful! I saw you in your place, in the house, when you came. As soon as we got here I went out to those steps that go up to the stage and I looked out, with my father — from behind him — and saw you in a minute. Then I felt too nervous to speak! I could never, never, if you were there! My father didn't know you, and I said nothing, but Olive guessed a soon as I came back. She rushed at me, and she looked at me — oh, how she looked! and she guessed. She didn't need to go out to see for herself, and when she saw how I was trembling she began to tremble herself, to believe, as I believed, we were lost. Listen to them, listen to them, in the house! Now I want you to go away — I will see you to-morrow, as long as you wish. That's all I want now; if you will only go away it's not too late, and everything will be all right!"

Preoccupied as Ransom was with the simple purpose of getting her bodily out of the place, he could yet notice her strange, touching tone, and her air of believing that she might really persuade him. She had evidently given up everything now — every pretense of a different conviction and of loyalty to her cause; all this had fallen from her as soon as she felt him near, and she asked him to go away just as any plighted maiden might have asked any favour of her lover. But it was the poor girl's misfortune that, whatever she did or said, or left unsaid, only had the effect of making her dearer to him and making the people who were clamouring for her seem more and more a raving rabble.

He indulged not in the smallest recognition of her request, and simply said, "Surely Olive must have believed, must have known, would come."

"She would have been sure if you hadn't become so unexpectedly quiet after I left Marmion. You seemed to concur, to be willing to wait."

"So I was, for a few weeks. But they ended yesterday. I was furious that morning, when I learned your flight, and during the week that followed I made two or three attempts to find you. Then I stopped — I thought it better. I saw you were very well hidden; I determined not even to write. I felt I *could* wait — with that last day at Marmion to think of. Besides, to leave you with her awhile, for the last, seemed more decent. Perhaps you'll tell me now where you were."

"I was with father and mother. She sent me to them that morning, with a letter. I don't know what was in it. Perhaps there was money," said Verena, who evidently now would tell him everything.

"And where did they take you?"

"I don't know — to places. I was in Boston once, for a day; but only in a carriage. They were as frightened as Olive; they were bound to save me!"

"They shouldn't have brought you here to-night then. How could you possibly doubt of my coming?"

"I don't know what I thought, and I didn't know, till I saw you, that all the strength I had hoped for would leave me in a flash, and that if I attempted to speak — with you sitting there — I should make the most shameful failure. We had a sickening scene here — I begged for delay, for time to recover. We waited and waited, and when I heard you at the door talking to the policeman, it seemed to me everything was gone. But it will still come back, if you will leave me. They are quiet again — father must be interesting them."

"I hope he is!" Ransom exclaimed. "If Miss Chancellor ordered the policeman, she must have expected me."

"That was only after she knew you were in the house. She flew out into the lobby with father, and they seized him and posted him there. She locked the door; she seemed to think they would break it down. I didn't wait for that, but from the moment I knew you were on the other side of it I couldn't go on — I was paralysed. It has made me feel better to talk to you — and now I could appear," Verena added.

"My darling child, haven't you a shawl or a mantle?" Ransom returned, for all answer, looking about him. He perceived, tossed upon a chair, a long, furred cloak, which he caught up, and, before she could resist, threw over her. She even let him arrange it and, standing there, draped from head to foot in it, contented herself with saying, after a moment:

"I don't understand — where shall we go? Where will you take me?"

"We shall catch the night-train for New York, and the first thing in the morning we shall be married."

Verena remained gazing at him, with swimming eyes. "And what will the people do? Listen, listen!"

"Your father is ceasing to interest them. They'll howl and thump, according to their nature."

"Ah, their nature's fine!" Verena pleaded.

"Dearest, that's one of the fallacies I shall have to woo you from. Hear them, the senseless brutes!" The storm was now raging in the hall, and it deepened to such a point that Verena turned to him in a supreme appeal.

"I could soothe them with a word!"

"Keep your soothing words for me — you will have need of them all, in our coming time," Ransom said, laughing. He pulled open the door again, which led into the lobby, but he was driven back, with Verena, by a furious onset from Mrs. Tarrant. Seeing her daughter fairly arrayed for departure, she hurled herself upon her, half in indignation, half in a blind impulse to cling, and with an outpouring of tears, reproaches, prayers, strange scraps of argument and iterations of farewell, closed her about with an embrace which was partly a supreme caress, partly the salutary castigation she had, three minutes before, expressed the wish to administer, and altogether for the moment a check upon her girl's flight.

"Mother, dearest, it's all for the best, I can't help it, I love you just the same; let me go, let me go!" Verena stammered, kissing her again, struggling to free herself, and holding out her hand to Ransom. He saw now that she only wanted to get away, to leave everything behind her. Olive was close at hand, on the threshold of the room, and as soon as Ransom looked at her he became aware that the weakness she had just shown had passed away. She had straightened herself again, and she was upright in her desolation. The expression of her face was a thing to remain with him for ever; it was impossible to imagine a more vivid presentment of blighted hope and wounded pride. Dry, desperate, rigid, she yet wavered and seemed uncertain; her pale, glittering eyes straining forward, as if they were looking for death. Ransom had a vision, even at that crowded moment, that if she could have met it there and then, bristling with steel or lurid with fire, she would have rushed on it without a tremor, like the heroine that she was. All this while the great agitation in the hall rose and fell, in waves and surges, as if Selah Tarrant and the agent were talking to the multitude, trying to calm them, succeeding for the moment, and then letting them loose again. Whirled down by one of the fitful gusts, a lady and a gentleman issued from the passage, and Ransom, glancing at them, recognised Mrs. Farrinder and her husband.

"Well, Miss Chancellor," said that more successful woman, with considerable asperity, "if this is the way you're going to reinstate our sex!" She passed rapidly through the room, followed by Amariah, who remarked in his transit that it seemed as if there had been a want of organisation, and the two retreated expeditiously, without the lady's having taken the smallest notice of Verena, whose conflict with her mother prolonged itself. Ransom, striving, with all needful consideration for Mrs. Tarrant, to separate these two, addressed not a word to Olive; it was the last of her, for him, and he neither saw how her livid face suddenly glowed, as if Mrs. Farrinder's words had been a lash, nor how, as if with a sudden inspiration, she rushed to the approach to the platform. If he had observed her, it might have seemed to him that she hoped to find the fierce expiation she sought for in exposure to the thousands she had disappointed and deceived, in offering herself to be trampled to death and torn to pieces. She might have suggested to him some feminine firebrand of Paris revolutions, erect on a barricade, or even the sacrificial figure of Hypatia, whirled through the furious mob of Alexandria. She was arrested an instant by the arrival of Mrs. Burrage and her son, who had quitted the stage on observing the withdrawal of the Farrinders, and who swept into the room in the manner of people seeking shelter from a thunder-storm. The mother's face expressed the well-bred surprise of a person who should have been asked out to dinner and seen the cloth pulled off the table; the young man, who supported her on his arm, instantly lost himself in the spectacle of Verena disengaging herself from Mrs. Tarrant, only to be again overwhelmed, and in the unexpected presence of the Mississippian. His handsome blue eyes turned from one to the other, and he looked infinitely annoyed and bewildered. It even seemed to occur to him that he might, perhaps, interpose with effect, and he evidently would have liked to say that, without really bragging, *he* would at least have kept the affair from turning into a row. But Verena, muffled and escaping, was deaf to him, and Ransom didn't look the right person to address such a remark as that to. Mrs. Burrage and Olive, as the latter shot past, exchanged a glance which represented quick irony on one side and indiscriminating defiance on the other.

"Oh, are *you* going to speak?" the lady from New York inquired, with a cursory laugh.

Olive had already disappeared; but Ransom heard her answer flung behind her into the room. "I am going to be hissed and hooted and insulted!"

"Olive, Olive!" Verena suddenly shrieked; and her piercing cry might have reached the front. But Ransom had already, by muscular force, wrenched her away, and was hurrying her out, leaving Mrs. Tarrant to heave herself into the arms of Mrs. Burrage, who, he was sure, would, within the minute, loom upon her attractively through her tears, and supply her with a reminiscence, destined to be valuable, of aristocratic support and clever composure. In the outer labyrinth hasty groups, a little scared, were leaving the hall, giving up the game. Ransom, as he went, thrust the hood of Verena's long cloak over her head, to conceal her face and her identity. It quite prevented recognition, and as they mingled in the issuing crowd he perceived the quick, complete, tremendous silence which, in the hall, had greeted Olive Chancellor's rush to the front. Every sound instantly dropped, the hush was respectful, the great public waited, and whatever she should say to them (and he thought she might indeed be rather embarrassed), it was not apparent that they were likely to hurl the benches at her. Ransom, palpitating with his victory, felt now a little sorry for her, and was relieved to know that, even when exasperated, a Boston audience is not ungenerous. "Ah, now I am glad!" said Verena, when they reached the street. But though she was glad, he presently discovered that, beneath her hood, she was in tears. It is to be feared that with the union, so far from brilliant, into which she was about to enter, these were not the last she was destined to shed.

"EUROPE"

I

"Our feeling is, you know, that Becky *should* go." That earnest little remark comes back to me, even after long years, as the first note of something that began, for my observation, the day I went with my sister-in-law to take leave of her good friends. It's a memory of the American time, which revives so at present — under some touch that doesn't signify — that it rounds itself off as an anecdote. That walk to say good-bye was the beginning; and the end, so far as I enjoyed a view of it, was not till long after; yet even the end also appears to me now as of the old days. I went, in those days, on occasion, to see my sister-in-law, in whose affairs, on my brother's death, I had had to take a helpful hand. I continued to go indeed after these little matters were straightened out, for the pleasure, periodically, of the impression — the change to the almost pastoral sweetness of the good Boston suburb from the loud longitudinal New York. It was another world, with other manners, a different tone, a different taste; a savour nowhere so mild, yet so distinct, as in the square white house — with the pair of elms, like gigantic wheat-sheaves, in front, the rustic orchard not far behind, the old-fashioned door-lights, the big blue-and-white jars in the porch, the straight bricked walk from the high gate — that enshrined the extraordinary merit of Mrs. Rimmle and her three daughters.

These ladies were so much of the place and the place so much of themselves that from the first of their being revealed to me I felt that nothing else at Brookbridge much mattered. They were what, for me, at any rate, Brookbridge had most to give: I mean in the way of what it was naturally strongest in, the thing we called in New York the New England expression, the air of Puritanism reclaimed and refined. The Rimmles had brought this down to a wonderful delicacy. They struck me even then — all four almost equally — as very ancient and very earnest, and I think theirs must have been the house in all the world in which "culture" first came to the aid of morning calls. The head of the family was the widow of a great public character — as public characters were understood at Brookbridge — whose speeches on anniversaries formed a part of the body of national eloquence spouted in the New England schools by little boys covetous of the most marked, though perhaps the easiest, distinction. He was reported to have been celebrated, and in such fine declamatory connexions that he seemed to gesticulate even from the tomb. He was understood to have made, in his wife's company, the tour of Europe at a date not immensely removed from that of the battle of Waterloo. What was the age then of the bland firm antique Mrs. Rimmle at the period of her being first revealed to me? That's a point I'm not in a position to determine — I remember mainly that I was young enough to regard her as having reached the limit. And yet the limit for Mrs. Rimmle must have been prodigiously extended; the scale of its extension is in fact the very moral of this reminiscence. She was old, and her daughters were old, but I was destined to know them all as older. It was only by comparison and habit that — however much I recede — Rebecca, Maria and Jane were the "young ladies."

I think it was felt that, though their mother's life, after thirty years of widowhood, had had a grand backward stretch, her blandness and firmness — and this in spite of her extreme physical frailty — would be proof against any surrender not overwhelmingly justified by time. It had appeared, years before, at a crisis of which the waves had not even yet quite subsided, a surrender not justified by anything nameable that she should go to Europe with her daughters and for her health. Her health was supposed to require constant support; but when it had at that period tried conclusions with the idea of Europe it was not the idea of Europe that had been insidious enough to prevail. She hadn't gone, and Becky, Maria and Jane hadn't gone, and this was long ago. They still merely floated in the air of the visit achieved, with such introductions and such acclamations, in the early part of the century; they still, with fond glances at the sunny parlour-walls, only referred, in conversation, to divers pictorial and other reminders of it. The Miss Rimmles had quite been brought up on it, but Becky, as the most literary, had most mastered the subject. There were framed letters — tributes to their eminent father — suspended among the mementoes, and of two or three of these, the most foreign and complimentary, Becky had executed translations that figured beside the text. She knew already, through this and other illumination, so much about Europe that it was hard to believe for her in that limit of adventure which consisted only of her having been twice to Philadelphia. The others hadn't been to Philadelphia, but there was a legend that Jane had been to Saratoga. Becky was a short stout fair person with round serious eyes, a high forehead, the sweetest neatest enunciation, and a miniature of her father — "done in Rome" — worn as a breastpin. She had written the life, she had edited the speeches, of the original of this ornament, and now at

748

last, beyond the seas, she was really to tread in his footsteps.

Fine old Mrs. Rimmle, in the sunny parlour and with a certain austerity of cap and chair — though with a gay new "front" that looked like rusty brown plush — had had so unusually good a winter that the question of her sparing two members of her family for an absence had been threshed as fine, I could feel, as even under that Puritan roof any case of conscience had ever been threshed. They were to make their dash while the coast, as it were, was clear, and each of the daughters had tried — heroically, angelically and for the sake of each of her sisters — not to be one of the two. What I encountered that first time was an opportunity to concur with enthusiasm in the general idea that Becky's wonderful preparation would be wasted if she were the one to stay with their mother. Their talk of Becky's preparation (they had a sly old-maidish humour that was as mild as milk) might have been of some mixture, for application somewhere, that she kept in a precious bottle. It had been settled at all events that, armed with this concoction and borne aloft by their introductions, she and Jane were to start. They were wonderful on their introductions, which proceeded naturally from their mother and were addressed to the charming families that in vague generations had so admired vague Mr. Rimmle. Jane, I found at Brookbridge, had to be

described, for want of other description, as the pretty one, but it wouldn't have served to identify her unless you had seen the others. *Her* preparation was only this figment of her prettiness — only, that is, unless one took into account something that, on the spot, I silently divined: the lifelong secret passionate ache of her little rebellious desire. They were all growing old in the yearning to go, but Jane's yearning was the sharpest. She struggled with it as people at Brookbridge mostly struggled with what they liked, but fate, by threatening to prevent what she *dis*liked and what was therefore duty — which was to stay at home instead of Maria — had bewildered her, I judged, not a little. It was she who, in the words I have quoted, mentioned to me Becky's case and Becky's affinity as the clearest of all. Her mother moreover had on the general subject still more to say.

"I positively desire, I really quite insist that they shall go," the old lady explained to us from her stiff chair. "We've talked about it so often, and they've had from me so clear an account — I've amused them again and again with it — of what's to be seen and enjoyed. If they've had hitherto too many duties to leave, the time seems to have come to recognise that there are also many duties to *seek*. Wherever we go we find them — I always remind the girls of that. There's a duty that calls them to those wonderful countries, just as it called, at the right time, their father and myself — if it be only that of laying-up for the years to come the same store of remarkable impressions, the same wealth of knowledge and food for conversation as, since my return, I've found myself so happy to possess." Mrs. Rimmle spoke of her return as of something of the year before last, but the future of her daughters was somehow, by a different law, to be on the scale of great vistas, of endless after-tastes. I think that, without my being quite ready to say it, even this first impression of her was somewhat upsetting; there was a large placid perversity, a grim secrecy of intention, in her estimate of the ages.

"Well, I'm so glad you don't delay it longer," I said to Miss Becky before we withdrew. "And whoever should go," I continued in the spirit of the sympathy with which the good sisters had already inspired me, "I quite feel, with your family, you know, that *you* should. But of course I hold that every one should." I suppose I wished to attenuate my solemnity; there was, however, something in it I couldn't help. It must have been a faint foreknowledge.

"Have you been a great deal yourself?" Miss Jane, I remembered, enquired.

"Not so much but that I hope to go a good deal more. So perhaps we shall meet," I encouragingly suggested.

I recall something — something in the nature of susceptibility to encouragement — that this brought into the more expressive brown eyes to which Miss Jane mainly owed it that she was the pretty one. "Where, do you think?"

I tried to think. "Well, on the Italian lakes — Como, Bellaggio, Lugano." I liked to say the names to them.

"'Sublime, but neither bleak nor bare — nor misty are the mountains there!'" Miss Jane softly breathed, while her sister looked at her as if her acquaintance with the poetry of the subject made her the most interesting feature of the scene she evoked.

But Miss Becky presently turned to me. "Do you know everything — ?"

"Everything?"

"In Europe."

"Oh yes," I laughed, "and one or two things even in America."

The sisters seemed to me furtively to look at each other. "Well, you'll have to be quick — to meet *us*," Miss Jane resumed.

"But surely when you're once there you'll stay on."

"Stay on?" — they murmured it simultaneously and with the oddest vibration of dread as well as of desire. It was as if they had been in presence of a danger and yet wished me, who "knew everything," to torment them with still more of it.

Well, I did my best. "I mean it will never do to cut it short."

"No, that's just what I keep saying," said brilliant Jane. "It would be better in that case not to go."

"Oh don't talk about not going

— at this time!" It was none of my business, but I felt shocked and impatient.

"No, not at *this* time!" broke in Miss Maria, who, very red in the face, had joined us. Poor Miss Maria was known as the flushed one; but she was not flushed — she only had an unfortunate surface. The third day after this was to see them embark.

Miss Becky, however, desired as little as any one to be in any way extravagant. "It's only the thought of our mother," she explained.

I looked a moment at the old lady, with whom my sister-in-law was engaged. "Well — your mother's magnificent."

"*Isn't* she magnificent?" — they eagerly took it up.

She *was* — I could reiterate it with sincerity, though I perhaps mentally drew the line when Miss Maria again risked, as a fresh ejaculation: "I think she's better than Europe!"

"Maria!" they both, at this, exclaimed with a strange emphasis: it was as if they feared she had suddenly turned cynical over the deep domestic drama of their casting of lots. The innocent laugh with which she answered them gave the measure of her cynicism.

We separated at last, and my eyes met Mrs. Rimmle's as I held for an instant her aged hand. It was doubtless only my fancy that her calm cold look quietly accused me of something. Of what *could* it accuse me? Only, I thought, of thinking.

II

I LEFT Brookbridge the next day, and for some time after that had no occasion to hear from my kinswoman; but when she finally wrote there was a passage in her letter that affected me more than all the rest. "Do you know the poor Rimmles never, after all, 'went'? The old lady, at the eleventh hour, broke down; everything broke down, and all of *them* on top of it, so that the dear things are with us still. Mrs. Rimmle, the night after our call, had, in the most unexpected manner, a turn for the worse — something in the nature (though they're rather mysterious about it) of a seizure; Becky and Jane felt it — dear devoted stupid angels that they are — heartless to leave her at such a moment, and Europe's indefinitely postponed. However, they think they're still going — or *think* they think it — when she's better. They also think — or think they think — that she *will* be better. I certainly pray she may." So did I — quite fervently. I was conscious of a real pang — I didn't know how much they had made me care.

Late that winter my sister-in-law spent a week in New York; when almost my first enquiry on meeting her was about the health of Mrs. Rimmle.

"Oh she's rather bad — she really is, you know. It's not surprising

that at her age she should be in-
firm."

"Then what the deuce *is* her
age?"

"I can't tell you to a year — but
she's immensely old."

"That of course I saw," I replied — "unless you literally mean
so old that the records have been
lost."

My sister-in-law thought. "Well,
I believe she wasn't positively
young when she married. She lost
three or four children before these
women were born."

We surveyed together a little, on
this, the "dark backward." "And
they were born, I gather, *after* the
famous tour? Well then, as the famous tour was in a manner to celebrate — wasn't it? — the restoration of the Bourbons — " I considered, I gasped. "My dear child,
what on earth do you make her
out?"

My relative, with her Brookbridge habit, transferred her share
of the question to the moral plane
— turned it forth to wander, by
implication at least, in the sandy
desert of responsibility. "Well, you
know, we all immensely admire
her."

"You can't admire her more than
I do. She's awful."

My converser looked at me with
a certain fear. "She's *really* ill."

"Too ill to get better?"

"Oh no — we hope not. Because
then they'll be able to go."

"And *will* they go if she should?"

"Oh the moment they should
be quite satisfied. I mean *really*,"
she added.

I'm afraid I laughed at her —
the Brookbridge "really" was a
thing so by itself. "But if she
shouldn't get better?" I went on.

"Oh don't speak of it! They want
so to go."

"It's a pity they're so infernally
good," I mused.

"No — don't say that. It's what
keeps them up."

"Yes, but isn't it what keeps *her*
up too?"

My visitor looked grave. "Would
you like them to kill her?"

I don't know that I was then
prepared to say I should — though
I believe I came very near it. But
later on I burst all bounds, for the
subject grew and grew. I went
again before the good sisters ever
did — I mean I went to Europe. I
think I went twice, with a brief
interval, before my fate again
brought round for me a couple of
days at Brookbridge. I had been
there repeatedly, in the previous
time, without making the acquaintance of the Rimmles; but now that
I had had the revelation I couldn't
have it too much, and the first request I preferred was to be taken
again to see them. I remember well
indeed the scruple I felt — the real
delicacy — about betraying that *I*
had, in the pride of my power,
since our other meeting, stood, as
their phrase went, among romantic scenes; but they were themselves the first to speak of it, and
what moreover came home to me
was that the coming and going of
their friends in general — Brookbridge itself having even at that
period one foot in Europe — was

such as to place constantly before them the pleasure that was only postponed. They were thrown back after all on what the situation, under a final analysis, had most to give — the sense that, as every one kindly said to them and they kindly said to every one, Europe would keep. Every one felt for them so deeply that their own kindness in alleviating every one's feelings was really what came out most. Mrs. Rimmle was still in her stiff chair and in the sunny parlour, but if *she* made no scruple of introducing the Italian lakes my heart sank to observe that she dealt with them, as a topic, not in the least in the leave-taking manner in which Falstaff babbled of green fields.

I'm not sure that after this my pretexts for a day or two with my sister-in-law weren't apt to be a mere cover for another glimpse of these particulars: I at any rate never went to Brookbridge without an irrepressible eagerness for our customary call. A long time seems to me thus to have passed, with glimpses and lapses, considerable impatience and still more pity. Our visits indeed grew shorter, for, as my companion said, they were more and more of a strain. It finally struck me that the good sisters even shrank from me a little as from one who penetrated their consciousness in spite of himself. It was as if they knew where I thought they ought to be, and were moved to deprecate at last, by a systematic silence on the subject of that hemisphere, the criminal-

ity I fain would fix on them. They were full instead — as with the instinct of throwing dust in my eyes — of little pathetic hypocrisies about Brookbridge interests and delights. I dare say that as time went on my deeper sense of their situation came practically to rest on my companion's report of it. I certainly think I recollect every word we ever exchanged about them, even if I've lost the thread of the special occasions. The impression they made on me after each interval always broke out with extravagance as I walked away with her.

"*She* may be as old as she likes — I don't care. It's the fearful age the 'girls' are reaching that constitutes the scandal. One shouldn't pry into such matters, I know; but the years and the chances are really going. They're all growing old together — it will presently be too late; and their mother meanwhile perches over them like a vulture — what shall I call it? — calculating. Is she waiting for them successively to drop off? She'll survive them each and all. There's something too remorseless in it."

"Yes, but what do you want her to do? If the poor thing *can't* die she can't. Do you want her to take poison or to open a blood-vessel? I dare say she'd prefer to go."

"I beg your pardon," I must have replied; "you daren't say anything of the sort. If she'd prefer to go she *would* go. She'd feel the propriety, the decency, the necessity of going. She just prefers *not* to go. She prefers to stay and keep up the tension, and her calling them "girls" and talking of the good time they'll still have is the mere conscious mischief of a subtle old witch. They won't have *any* time — there isn't any time to have! I mean there's, on her own part, no real loss of measure or of perspective in it. She *knows* she's a hundred and ten, and she takes a cruel pride in it."

My sister-in-law differed with me about this; she held that the old woman's attitude was an honest one and that her magnificent vitality, so great in spite of her infirmities, made it inevitable she should attribute youth to persons who had come into the world so much later. "Then suppose she should die?" — so my fellow student of the case always put it to me.

"Do you mean while her daughters are away? There's not the least fear of that — not even if at the very moment of their departure she should be *in extremis*. They'd find her all right on their return."

"But think how they'd feel not to have been with her!"

"That's only, I repeat, on the unsound assumption. If they'd only go to-morrow — literally make a good rush for it — they'll be with her when they come back. That will give them plenty of time." I'm afraid I even heartlessly added that if she *should,* against every probability, pass away in their absence they wouldn't have to come back at all — which would be just the compensation proper

to their long privation. And then Maria would come out to join the two others, and they would be — though but for the too scanty remnant of their career — as merry as the day is long.

I remained ready, somehow, pending the fulfilment of that vision, to sacrifice Maria; it was only over the urgency of the case for the others respectively that I found myself balancing. Sometimes it was for Becky I thought the tragedy deepest — sometimes, and in quite a different manner, I thought it most dire for Jane. It was Jane after all who had most sense of life. I seemed in fact dimly to descry in Jane a sense — as yet undescried by herself or by any one — of all sorts of queer things. Why didn't *she* go? I used desperately to ask; why didn't she make a bold personal dash for it, strike up a partnership with some one or other of the travelling spinsters in whom Brookbridge more and more abounded? Well, there came a flash for me at a particular point of the grey middle desert: my correspondent was able to let me know that poor Jane at last *had* sailed. She had gone of a sudden — I liked my sister-in-law's view of suddenness — with the kind Hathaways, who had made an irresistible grab at her and lifted her off her feet. They were going for the summer and for Mr. Hathaway's health, so that the opportunity was perfect and it was impossible not to be glad that something very like physical force had finally prevailed. This was the general feeling at Brookbridge, and I might imagine what Brookbridge had been brought to from the fact that, at the very moment she was hustled off, the doctor, called to her mother at the peep of dawn, had considered that *he* at least must stay. There had been real alarm — greater than ever before; it actually did seem as if this time the end had come. But it was Becky, strange to say, who, though fully recognising the nature of the crisis, had kept the situation in hand and insisted upon action. This, I remember, brought back to me a discomfort with which I had been familiar from the first. One of the two had sailed, and I was sorry it wasn't the other. But if it had been the other I should have been equally sorry.

I saw with my eyes that very autumn what a fool Jane would have been if she had again backed out. Her mother had of course survived the peril of which I had heard, profiting by it indeed as she had profited by every other; she was sufficiently better again to have come downstairs. It was there that, as usual, I found her, but with a difference of effect produced somehow by the absence of one of the girls. It was as if, for the others, though they hadn't gone to Europe, Europe had come to them: Jane's letters had been so frequent and so beyond even what could have been hoped. It was the first time, however, that I perceived on the old woman's part a certain failure of lucidity. Jane's flight was clearly the great fact

with her, but she spoke of it as if the fruit had now been plucked and the parenthesis closed. I don't know what sinking sense of still further physical duration I gathered, as a menace, from this first hint of her confusion of mind.

"My daughter has been; my daughter has been — " She kept saying it, but didn't say where; that seemed unnecessary, and she only repeated the words to her visitors with a face that was all puckers and yet now, save in so far as it expressed an ineffaceable complacency, all blankness. I think she rather wanted us to know how little she had stood in the way. It added to something — I scarce knew what — that I found myself desiring to extract privately from Becky. As our visit was to be of the shortest my opportunity — for one of the young ladies always came to the door with us — was at hand. Mrs. Rimmle, as we took leave, again sounded her phrase, but she added this time: "I'm so glad she's going to have always — "

I knew so well what she meant that, as she again dropped, looking at me queerly and becoming momentarily dim, I could help her out. "Going to have what *you* have?"

"Yes, yes — my privilege. Wonderful experience," she mumbled. She bowed to me a little as if I would understand. "She has things to tell."

I turned, slightly at a loss, to Becky. "She has then already arrived?"

Becky was at that moment looking a little strangely at her mother, who answered my question. "She reached New York this morning — she comes on to-day."

"Oh then —!" But I let the matter pass as I met Becky's eye — I saw there was a hitch somewhere. It was not she but Maria who came out with us; on which I cleared up the question of their sister's reappearance.

"Oh no, not to-night," Maria smiled; "that's only the way mother puts it. We shall see her about the end of November — the Hathaways are so indulgent. They kindly extend their tour."

"For *her* sake? How sweet of them!" my sister-in-law exclaimed.

I can see our friend's plain mild old face take on a deeper mildness, even though a higher colour, in the light of the open door. "Yes, it's for Jane they prolong it. And do you know what they write?" She gave us time, but it was too great a responsibility to guess. "Why that it has brought her out."

"Oh, I knew it *would!*" my companion sympathetically sighed.

Maria put it more strongly still. "They say we wouldn't know her."

This sounded a little awful, but it was after all what I had expected.

My correspondent in Brookbridge came to me that Christmas, with my niece, to spend a week; and the arrangement had of course been prefaced by an exchange of letters, the first of which from my sister-in-law scarce took space for acceptance of my invitation before going on to say: "The Hathaways are back — but without Miss Jane!" She presented in a few words the situation thus created at Brookbridge, but was not yet, I gathered, fully in possession of the other one — the situation created in "Europe" by the presence there of that lady. The two together, however that might be, demanded, I quickly felt, all my attention, and perhaps my impatience to receive my relative was a little sharpened by my desire for the whole story. I had it at last, by the Christmas fire, and I may say without reserve that it gave me all I could have hoped for. I listened eagerly, after which I produced the comment: "Then she simply refused —"

"To budge from Florence? Simply. She had it out there with the poor Hathaways, who felt responsible for her safety, pledged to restore her to her mother's, to her sisters' hands, and showed herself in a light, they mention under their breath, that made their dear old hair stand on end. Do you know what, when they first got back, they said of her — at least it was *his* phrase — to two or three people?"

I thought a moment. "That she had 'tasted blood'?"

My visitor fairly admired me. "How clever of you to guess! It's exactly what he did say. She appeared — she continues to appear; it seems — in a new character."

I wondered a little. "But that's exactly — don't you remember? — what Miss Maria reported to us from them; that we 'wouldn't know her.'"

My sister-in-law perfectly remembered. "Oh yes — she broke out from the first. But when they left her she was worse."

"Worse?"

"Well, different — different from anything she ever *had* been or — for that matter — had had a chance to be." My reporter hung fire a moment, but presently faced me. "Rather strange and free and obstreperous."

"Obstreperous?" I wondered again.

"Peculiarly so, I inferred, on the question of not coming away. She wouldn't hear of it and, when they spoke of her mother, said she had given her mother up. She had thought she should like Europe, but didn't know she should like it so much. They had been fools to bring her if they expected to take her away. She was going to see what she could — she hadn't yet seen half. The end of it at any rate was that they had to leave her alone."

I seemed to see it all — to see even the scared Hathaways. "So she *is* alone?"

"She told them, poor thing, it appears, and in a tone they'll never forget, that she was in any case quite old enough to be. She cried — she quite went on — over not having come sooner. That's why

the only way for her," my companion mused, "*is*, I suppose, to stay. They wanted to put her with some people or other — to find some American family. But she says she's on her own feet."

"And she's still in Florence?"

"No — I believe she was to travel. She's bent on the East."

I burst out laughing. "Magnificent Jane! It's most interesting. Only I feel that I distinctly *should* 'know' her. To my sense, always, I must tell you, she had it in her."

My relative was silent a little. "So it now appears Becky always felt."

"And yet pushed her off? Magnificent Becky!"

My companion met my eyes a moment. "You don't know the queerest part. I mean the way it has *most* brought her out."

I turned it over; I felt I should like to know — to that degree indeed that, oddly enough, I jocosely disguised my eagerness. "You don't mean she has taken to drink?"

My visitor had a dignity — and yet had to have a freedom. "She has taken to flirting."

I expressed disappointment. "Oh she took to *that* long ago. Yes," I declared at my kinswoman's stare, "she positively flirted — with *me!*"

The stare perhaps sharpened. "Then you flirted with *her?*"

"How else could I have been as sure as I wanted to be? But has she means?"

"Means to flirt?" — my friend looked an instant as if she spoke literally. "I don't understand about the means — though of course they have something. But I have my impression," she went on. "I think that Becky — " It seemed almost too grave to say.

But *I* had no doubts. "That Becky's backing her?"

She brought it out. "Financing her."

"Stupendous Becky! So that morally then — "

"Becky's quite in sympathy. But isn't it too odd?" my sister-in-law asked.

"Not in the least. Didn't we know, as regards Jane, that Europe was to bring her out? Well, it has also brought out Rebecca."

"It has indeed!" my companion indulgently sighed. "So what would it do if she were there?"

"I should like immensely to see. And we *shall* see."

"Do you believe then she'll still go?"

"Certainly. She *must*."

But my friend shook it off. "She won't."

"She shall!" I retorted with a laugh. But the next moment I said: "And what does the old woman say?"

"To Jane's behaviour? Not a word — never speaks of it. She talks now much less than she used — only seems to wait. But it's my belief she thinks."

"And — do you mean — knows?"

"Yes, knows she's abandoned. In her silence there she takes it in."

"It's her way of making Jane pay?" At this, somehow, I felt more

serious. "Oh dear, dear — she'll disinherit her!"

When in the following June I went on to return my sister-in-law's visit the first object that met my eyes in her little white parlour was a figure that, to my stupefaction, presented itself for the moment as that of Mrs. Rimmle. I had gone to my room after arriving and had come down when dressed; the apparition I speak of had arisen in the interval. Its ambiguous character lasted, however, but a second or two — I had taken Becky for her mother because I knew no one but her mother of that extreme age. Becky's age was quite startling; it had made a great stride, though, strangely enough, irrecoverably seated as she now was in it, she had a wizened brightness that I had scarcely yet seen in her. I remember indulging on this occasion in two silent observations: one on the article of my not having hitherto been conscious of her full resemblance to the old lady, and the other to the effect that, as I had said to my sister-in-law at Christmas, "Europe," even as reaching her only through Jane's sensibilities, had really at last brought her out. She was in fact "out" in a manner of which this encounter offered to my eyes a unique example: it was the single hour, often as I had been at Brookbridge, of my meeting her elsewhere than in her mother's drawing-room. I surmise that, besides being adjusted to her more marked time of life, the garments she wore abroad, and in particular her little plain bonnet, presented points of resemblance to the close sable sheath and the quaint old headgear that, in the white house behind the elms, I had from far back associated with the eternal image in the stiff chair. Of course I immediately spoke of Jane, showing an interest and asking for news; on which she answered me with a smile, but not at all as I had expected.

"*Those* are not really the things you want to know — where she is, whom she's with, how she manages and where she's going next — oh no!" And the admirable woman gave a laugh that was somehow both light and sad — sad, in particular, with a strange long weariness. "What you do want to know is when she's coming back."

I shook my head very kindly, but out of a wealth of experience that, I flattered myself, was equal to Miss Becky's. "I do know it. Never."

Miss Becky exchanged with me at this a long deep look. "Never."

We had, in silence, a little luminous talk about it, at the end of which she seemed to have told me the most interesting things. "And how's your mother?" I then enquired.

She hesitated, but finally spoke with the same serenity. "My mother's all right. You see she's not alive."

"Oh Becky!" my sister-in-law pleadingly interjected.

But Becky only addressed herself to me. "Come and see if she

is. *I* think she isn't — but Maria perhaps isn't so clear. Come at all events and judge and tell me."

It was a new note, and I was a little bewildered. "Ah but I'm not a doctor!"

"No, thank God — you're not. That's why I ask you." And now she said good-bye.

I kept her hand a moment. "*You're* more alive than ever!"

"I'm very tired." She took it with the same smile, but for Becky it was much to say.

IV

"NOT alive," the next day, was certainly what Mrs. Rimmle looked when, arriving in pursuit of my promise, I found her, with Miss Maria, in her usual place. Though wasted and shrunken she still occupied her high-backed chair with a visible theory of erectness, and her intensely aged face — combined with something dauntless that belonged to her very presence and that was effective even in this extremity — might have been that of some immemorial sovereign, of indistinguishable sex, brought forth to be shown to the people in disproof of the rumour of extinction. Mummified and open-eyed she looked at me, but I had no impression that she made me out. I had come this time without my sister-in-law, who had frankly pleaded to me — which also, for a daughter of Brookbridge, was saying much

— that the house had grown too painful. Poor Miss Maria excused Miss Becky on the score of her not being well — and that, it struck me, was saying most of all. The absence of the others gave the occasion a different note; but I talked with Miss Maria for five minutes and recognised that — save for her saying, of her own movement, anything about Jane — she now spoke as if her mother had lost hearing or sense, in fact both, alluding freely and distinctly, though indeed favourably, to her condition. "She has expected your visit and much enjoys it," my entertainer said, while the old woman, soundless and motionless, simply fixed me without expression. Of course there was little to keep me; but I became aware as I rose to go that there was more than I had supposed.

On my approaching her to take leave Mrs. Rimmle gave signs of consciousness. "Have you heard about Jane?"

I hesitated, feeling a responsibility, and appealed for direction to Maria's face. But Maria's face was troubled, was turned altogether to her mother's. "About her life in Europe?" I then rather helplessly asked.

The old lady fronted me on this in a manner that made me feel silly. "Her life?" — and her voice, with this second effort, came out stronger. "Her death, if you please."

"Her death?" I echoed, before I could stop myself, with the accent of deprecation.

Miss Maria uttered a vague sound of pain, and I felt her turn away, but the marvel of her mother's little unquenched spark still held me. "Jane's dead. We've heard," said Mrs. Rimmle. "We've heard from — where is it we've heard from?" She had quite revived — she appealed to her daughter.

The poor old girl, crimson, rallied to her duty. "From Europe."

Mrs. Rimmle made at us both a little grim inclination of the head. "From Europe." I responded, in silence, by a deflexion from every rigour, and, still holding me, she went on: "And now Rebecca's going."

She had gathered by this time such emphasis to say it that again, before I could help myself, I vibrated in reply. "To Europe — now?" It was as if for an instant she had made me believe it.

She only stared at me, however, from her wizened mask; then her eyes followed my companion. "Has she gone?"

"Not yet, mother." Maria tried to treat it as a joke, but her smile was embarrassed and dim.

"Then where is she?"

"She's lying down."

The old woman kept up her hard queer gaze, but directing it after a minute to me. "She's going."

"Oh some day!" I foolishly laughed; and on this I got to the door, where I separated from my younger hostess, who came no further.

Only, as I held the door open, she said to me under cover of it and very quietly: "It's poor mother's idea."

I saw — it was her idea. Mine was — for some time after this, even after I had returned to New York and to my usual occupations — that I should never again see Becky. I had seen her for the last time, I believed, under my sister-in-law's roof, and in the autumn it was given to me to hear from that fellow admirer that she had succumbed at last to the situation. The day of the call I have just described had been a date in the process of her slow shrinkage — it was literally the first time she had, as they said at Brookbridge, given up. She had been ill for years, but the other state of health in the contemplation of which she had spent so much of her life had left her till too late no margin for heeding it. The power of attention came at last simply in the form of the discovery that it *was* too late; on which, naturally, she had given up more and more. I had heard indeed, for weeks before, by letter, how Brookbridge had watched her do so; in consequence of which the end found me in a manner prepared. Yet in spite of my preparation there remained with me a soreness, and when I was next — it was some six months later — on the scene of her martyrdom I fear I replied with an almost rabid negative to the question put to me in due course by my kinswoman. "Call on them? Never again!"

I went none the less the very next day. Everything was the same in the sunny parlour — everything that most mattered, I mean: the centenarian mummy in the high chair and the tributes, in the little frames on the walls, to the celebrity of its late husband. Only Maria Rimmle was different: if Becky, on my last seeing her, had looked as old as her mother, Maria — save that she moved about — looked older. I remember she moved about, but I scarce remember what she said; and indeed what was there to say? When I risked a question, however, she found a reply.

"But *now* at least — ?" I tried to put it to her suggestively.

At first she was vague. " 'Now'?"

"Won't Miss Jane come back?"

Oh the headshake she gave me! "Never." It positively pictured to me, for the instant, a well-preserved woman, a rich ripe *seconde jeunesse* by the Arno.

"Then that's only to make more sure of your finally joining her."

Maria Rimmle repeated her headsake. "Never."

We stood so a moment bleakly face to face; I could think of no attenuation that would be particularly happy. But while I tried I heard a hoarse gasp that fortunately relieved me — a signal strange and at first formless from the occupant of the high-backed chair. "Mother wants to speak to you," Maria then said.

So it appeared from the drop of the old woman's jaw, the expression of her mouth opened as if for the emission of sound. It was somehow difficult to me to seem to sympathise without hypocrisy, but, so far as a step nearer could do that,

"Europe"

I invited communication. "Have you heard where Becky's gone?" the wonderful witch's white lips then extraordinarily asked.

It drew from Maria, as on my previous visits, an uncontrollable groan, and this in turn made me take time to consider. As I considered, however, I had an inspiration. "To Europe?"

I must have adorned it with a strange grimace, but my inspiration had been right. "To Europe," said Mrs. Rimmle.

JULIA BRIDE

SHE had walked with her friend to the top of the wide steps of the Museum, those that descend from the galleries of painting, and then, after the young man had left her, smiling, looking back, waving all gaily and expressively his hat and stick, had watched him, smiling too, but with a different intensity — had kept him in sight till he passed out of the great door. She might have been waiting to see if he would turn there for a last demonstration; which was exactly what he did, renewing his cordial gesture and with his look of glad devotion, the radiance of his young face, reaching her across the great space, as she felt, in undiminished truth. Yes, so she could feel, and she remained a minute even after he was gone; she gazed at the empty air as if he had filled it still, asking herself what more she wanted and what, if it didn't signify glad devotion, his whole air could have represented.

She was at present so anxious that she could wonder if he stepped and smiled like that for mere relief at separation; yet if he wanted in such a degree to break the spell and escape the danger why did he keep coming back to her, and why, for that matter, had she felt safe a moment before in letting him go? She felt safe, felt almost reckless — that was the proof — so long as he was with her; but the chill came as soon as he had gone, when she instantly took the measure of all she yet missed. She might now have been taking it afresh, by the testimony of her charming clouded eyes and of the rigour that had already replaced her beautiful play of expression. Her radiance, for the minute, had "carried" as far as his, travelling on the light wings of her brilliant prettiness — he on his side not being facially handsome, but only sensitive clean and eager. Then with its extinction the sustaining wings dropped and hung.

She wheeled about, however, full of a purpose; she passed back through the pictured rooms, for it pleased her, this idea of a talk with Mr. Pitman — as much, that is, as anything could please a young person so troubled. It had happened indeed that when she saw him rise at sight of her from the settee where he had told her five minutes before that she would find him, it was just with her nervousness that his presence seemed, as through an odd suggestion of help, to connect itself. Nothing truly would be quite so odd for her case as aid proceeding from

763

Julia Bride

Mr. Pitman; unless perhaps the oddity would be even greater for himself — the oddity of her having taken into her head an appeal to him.

She had had to feel alone with a vengeance — inwardly alone and miserably alarmed — to be ready to "meet," that way, at the first sign from him, the successor to her dim father in her dim father's lifetime, the second of her mother's two divorced husbands. It made a queer relation for her; a relation that struck her at this moment as less edifying, less natural and graceful, than it would have been even for her remarkable mother — and still in spite of this parent's third marriage, her union with Mr. Connery, from whom she was informally separated. It was at the back of Julia's head as she approached Mr. Pitman, or it was at least somewhere deep within her soul, that if this last of Mrs. Connery's withdrawals from the matrimonial yoke had received the sanction of the Court (Julia had always heard, from far back, so much about the "Court") she herself, as after a fashion, in that event, a party to it, wouldn't have had the cheek to make up — which was how she inwardly phrased what she was doing — to the long lean loose slightly cadaverous gentleman who was a memory, for her, of the period from her twelfth to her seventeenth year. She had got on with him, perversely, much better than her mother had, and the bulging misfit of his duck waistcoat, with his trick of swing-

ing his eye-glass, at the end of an extraordinarily long string, far over the scene, came back to her as positive features of the image of her remoter youth. Her present age — for her later time had seen so many things happen — gave her a perspective.

Fifty things came up as she stood there before him, some of them floating in from the past, others hovering with freshness: how she used to dodge the rotary movement made by his pince-nez while he always awkwardly, and kindly, and often funnily, talked — it had once hit her rather badly in the eye; how she used to pull down and straighten his waistcoat, making it set a little better, a thing of a sort her mother never did; how friendly and familiar she must have been with him for that, or else a forward little minx; how she felt almost capable of doing it again now, just to sound the right note, and how sure she was of the way he would take it if she did; how much nicer he had clearly been, all the while, poor dear man, than his wife and the Court had made it possible for him publicly to appear; how much younger too he now looked, in spite of his rather melancholy, his mildly-jaundiced, humorously-determined sallowness and his careless assumption, everywhere, from his forehead to his exposed and relaxed blue socks, almost sky-blue, as in past days, of creases and folds and furrows that would have been perhaps tragic if they hadn't seemed rather to show, like his whimsical

764

black eyebrows, the vague interrogative arch.

Of course he wasn't wretched if he wasn't more sure of his wretchedness than that! Julia Bride would have been sure — had she been through what she supposed *he* had! With his thick loose black hair, in any case, untouched by a thread of grey, and his kept gift of a certain big-boyish awkwardness — that of his taking their encounter, for instance, so amusedly, so crudely, though, as she was not unaware, so eagerly too — he could by no means have been so little his wife's junior as it had been that lady's habit, after the divorce, to represent him. Julia had remembered him as old, since she had so constantly thought of her mother as old; which Mrs. Connery was indeed now, for her daughter, with her dozen years of actual seniority to Mr. Pitman and her exquisite hair, the densest, the finest tangle of arranged silver tendrils that had ever enhanced the effect of a preserved complexion.

Something in the girl's vision of her quondam stepfather as still comparatively young — with the confusion, the immense element of rectification, not to say of rank disproof, that it introduced into Mrs. Connery's favourite picture of her own injured past — all this worked, even at the moment, to quicken once more the clearness and harshness of judgement, the retrospective disgust, as she might have called it, that had of late grown up in her, the sense of all the folly and vanity and vulgarity, the lies,

the perversities, the falsification of all life in the interest of who could say what wretched frivolity, what preposterous policy, amid which she had been condemned so ignorantly, so pitifully to sit, to walk, to grope, to flounder, from the very dawn of her consciousness. Didn't poor Mr. Pitman just touch the sensitive nerve of it when, taking her in with his facetious cautious eyes, he spoke to her, right out, of the old, old story, the everlasting little wonder of her beauty?

"Why, you know, you've grown up so lovely — you're the prettiest girl I've ever seen!" Of course she was the prettiest girl he had ever seen; she was the prettiest girl people much more privileged than he had ever seen; since when hadn't she been passing for the prettiest girl any one had ever seen? She had lived in that, from far back, from year to year, from day to day and from hour to hour — she had lived for it and literally *by* it, as who should say; but Mr. Pitman was somehow more illuminating than he knew, with the present lurid light that he cast upon old dates, old pleas, old values and old mysteries, not to call them old abysses: it had rolled over her in a swift wave, with the very sight of him, that her mother couldn't possibly have been right about him — as about what in the world had she ever been right? — so that in fact he was simply offered her there as one more of Mrs. Connery's lies. She might have thought she knew them all by this time; but he represented for her, coming in just as he did, a fresh discovery, and it was this contribution of freshness that made her somehow feel she liked him. It was she herself who, for so long, with her retained impression, had been right about him; and the rectification he represented had *all* shone out of him, ten minutes before, on his catching her eye while she moved through the room with Mr. French. She had never doubted of his probable faults — which her mother had vividly depicted as the basest of vices; since some of them, and the most obvious (not the vices, but the faults) were written on him as he stood there: notably, for instance, the exasperating "business slackness" of which Mrs. Connery had, before the tribunal, made so pathetically much. It might have been, for that matter, the very business slackness that affected Julia as presenting its friendly breast, in the form of a cool loose sociability, to her own actual tension; though it was also true for her, after they had exchanged fifty words, that he had as well his inward fever and that, if he was perhaps wondering what was so particularly the matter with her, she could make out not less that something was the matter with *him*. It had been vague, yet it had been intense, the mute reflexion, "Yes, I'm going to like him, and he's going somehow to help me!" that had directed her steps so straight to him. She was sure even then of this, that he wouldn't put to her a query about his former wife, that he took to-day no grain

of interest in Mrs. Connery; that his interest, such as it was — and he couldn't look *quite* like that, to Julia Bride's expert perception, without something in the nature of a new one — would be a thousand times different.

It was as a value of *disproof* that his worth meanwhile so rapidly grew: the good sight of him, the good sound and sense of him, such as they were, demolished at a stroke so blessedly much of the horrid inconvenience of the past that she thought of him, she clutched at him, for a *general* saving use, an application as sanative, as redemptive, as some universal healing wash, precious even to the point of perjury if perjury should be required. That was the terrible thing, that had been the inward pang with which she watched Basil French recede: perjury would have to come in somehow and somewhere — oh so quite certainly! — before the so strange, so rare young man, truly smitten though she believed him, could be made to rise to the occasion, before her measureless prize could be assured. It was present to her, it had been present a hundred times, that if there had only been some one to (as it were) "deny everything" the situation might yet be saved. She so needed some one to lie for her — ah she so needed some one to lie! Her mother's version of everything, her mother's version of anything, had been at the best, as they said, discounted; and she herself could but show of course for an interested party, however much she might claim to be none the less a decent girl — to whatever point, that is, after all that had both remotely and recently happened, presumptions of anything to be called decency could come in.

After what had recently happened — the two or three indirect but so worrying questions Mr. French had put to her — it would only be some thoroughly detached friend or witness who might effectively testify. An odd form of detachment certainly would reside, for Mr. Pitman's evidential character, in her mother's having so publicly and so brilliantly — though, thank the powers, all off in North Dakota! — severed their connexion with him; and yet mightn't it do *her* some good, even if the harm it might do her mother were so little ambiguous? The more her mother had got divorced — with her dreadful cheap-and-easy second performance in that line and her present extremity of alienation from Mr. Connery, which enfolded beyond doubt the germ of a third petition on one side or the other — the more her mother had distinguished herself in the field of folly the worse for her own prospect with the Frenches, whose minds she had guessed to be accessible, and with such an effect of dissimulated suddenness, to some insidious poison.

It was all unmistakeable, in other words, that the more dismissed and detached Mr. Pitman should have come to appear, the more as divorced, or at least as divorcing,

his before-time wife would by the same stroke figure — so that it was here poor Julia could but lose herself. The crazy divorces only, or the half-dozen successive and still crazier engagements only — gathered fruit, bitter fruit, of her own incredibly allowed, her own insanely fostered frivolity — either of these two groups of skeletons at the banquet might singly be dealt with; but the combination, the fact of each party's having been so mixed-up with whatever was least presentable for the other, the fact of their having so shockingly amused themselves together, made all present steering resemble the classic middle course between Scylla and Charybdis.

It was not, however, that she felt wholly a fool in having obeyed this impulse to pick up again her kind old friend. *She* at least had never divorced him, and her horrid little filial evidence in Court had been but the chatter of a parrakeet, of precocious plumage and croak, repeating words earnestly taught her and that she could scarce even pronounce. Therefore, as far as steering went, he *must* for the hour take a hand. She might actually have wished in fact that he shouldn't now have seemed so tremendously struck with her; since it was an extraordinary situation for a girl, this · crisis of her fortune, this positive wrong that the flagrancy, what she would have been ready to call the very vulgarity, of her good looks might do her at a moment when it was vital she should hang as straight as a picture on the wall. Had it ever yet befallen any young woman in the world to wish with secret intensity that she might have been, for her convenience, a shade less inordinately pretty? She had come to that, to this view of the bane, the primal curse, of their lavishly physical outfit, which had included everything and as to which she lumped herself resentfully with her mother. The only thing was that her mother was, thank goodness, still so much prettier, still so assertively, so publicly, so trashily, so ruinously pretty. Wonderful the small grimness with which Julia Bride put off on this parent the middle-aged maximum of their case and the responsibility of their defect. It cost her so little to recognise in Mrs. Connery at forty-seven, and in spite, or perhaps indeed just by reason, of the arranged silver tendrils which were so like some rare bird's-nest in a morning frost, a facile supremacy for the dazzling effect — it cost her so little that her view even rather exaggerated the lustre of the different maternal items. She would have put it *all* off if possible, all off on other shoulders and on other graces and other morals than her own, the burden of physical charm that had made so easy a ground, such a native favouring air, for the aberrations which, apparently inevitable and without far consequences at the time, had yet at this juncture so much better not have been.

She could have worked it out at her leisure, to the last link of the chain, the way their prettiness had set them trap after trap, all along — had foredoomed them to awful ineptitude. When you were as pretty as that you could, by the whole idiotic consensus, be nothing *but* pretty; and when you were nothing "but" pretty you could get into nothing but tight places, out of which you could then scramble by nothing but masses of fibs. And there was no one, all the while, who wasn't eager to egg you on, eager to make you pay to the last cent the price of your beauty. What creature would ever for a moment help you to behave as if something that dragged in its wake a bit less of a lumbering train would, on the whole, have been better for you? The consequences of being plain were only negative — you failed of this and that; but the consequences of being as *they* were, what were these but endless? though indeed, as far as failing went, your beauty too could let you in for enough of it. Who, at all events, would ever for a moment credit you, in the luxuriance of that beauty, with the study, on your own side, of such truths as these? Julia Bride could, at the point she had reached, positively ask herself this even while lucidly conscious of the inimitable, the triumphant and attested projection, all round her, of her exquisite image. It was only Basil French who had at last, in his doubtless dry but all distinguished way — the way, surely as it was borne in upon her, of all the blood of all the Frenches — stepped out of the vulgar rank. It was only he who, by the trouble she discerned in him, had made her see certain things. It was only for him — and not a bit ridiculously, but just beautifully, almost sublimely — that their being "nice," her mother and she between them, had *not* seemed to profit by their being so furiously handsome.

This had, ever so grossly and ever so tiresomely, satisfied every one else; since every one had thrust upon them, had imposed upon them as by a great cruel conspiracy, their silliest possibilities; fencing them in to these, and so not only shutting them out from others, but mounting guard at the fence, walking round and round outside it to see they didn't escape, and admiring them, talking to them, through the rails, in mere terms of chaff, terms of chucked cakes and apples — as if they had been antelopes or zebras, or even some superior sort of performing, of dancing, bear. It had been reserved for Basil French to strike her as willing to let go, so to speak, a pound or two of this fatal treasure if he might only have got in exchange for it an ounce or so more of their so much less obvious and less published personal history. Yes, it described him to say that, in addition to all the rest of him, and of *his* personal history, and of his family, and of theirs, in addition to their social posture, as that of a serried phalanx, and to their notoriously enormous wealth and crushing respectability, she might have been ever so much less

lovely for him if she had been only — well, a little prepared to answer questions. And it wasn't as if, quiet, cultivated, earnest, public-spirited, brought up in Germany, infinitely travelled, awfully like a high-caste Englishman, and all the other pleasant things, it wasn't as if he didn't love to be with her, to look at her, just as she was; for he loved it exactly as much, so far as that footing simply went, as any free and foolish youth who had ever made the last demonstration of it. It was that marriage was for him — and for them all, the serried Frenches — a great matter, a goal to which a man of intelligence, a real shy beautiful man of the world, didn't hop on one foot, didn't skip and jump, as if he were playing an urchins' game, but toward which he proceeded with a deep and anxious, a noble and highly just deliberation.

For it was one thing to stare at a girl till she was bored at it, it was one thing to take her to the Horse Show and the Opera, and to send her flowers by the stack, and chocolates by the ton, and "great" novels, the very latest and greatest, by the dozen; but something quite other to hold open for her, with eyes attached to eyes, the gate, moving on such stiff silver hinges, of the grand square forecourt of the palace of wedlock. The state of being "engaged" represented to him the introduction to this precinct of some young woman with whom his outside parley would have had the duration, distinctly, of his own convenience.

That might be cold-blooded if one choose to think so; but nothing of another sort would equal the high ceremony and dignity and decency, above all the grand gallantry and finality, of their then passing in. Poor Julia could have blushed red, before that view, with the memory of the way the forecourt, as she now imagined it, had been dishonoured by her younger romps. She had tumbled over the wall with this, that and the other raw playmate, and had played "tag" and leap-frog, and she might say, from corner to corner. That would be the "history" with which, in case of definite demand, she should be able to supply Mr. French: that she had already, again and again, any occasion offering, chattered and scuffled over ground provided, according to his idea, for walking the gravest of minutes. If that then had been all their *kind* of history, hers and her mother's, at least there was plenty of it: it was the superstructure raised on the other group of facts, those of the order of their having been always so perfectly pink and white, so perfectly possessed of clothes, so perfectly splendid, so perfectly idiotic. These things had been the "points" of antelope and zebra; putting Mrs. Connery for the zebra, as the more remarkably striped or spotted. Such were the data Basil French's enquiry would elicit: her own six engagements and her mother's three nullified marriages — nine nice distinct little horrors in all. What on earth was to be done about them?

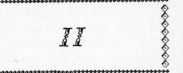

II

IT was notable, she was afterwards to recognise, that there had been nothing of the famous business slackness in the positive pounce with which Mr. Pitman put it to her that, as soon as he had made her out "for sure," identified her there as old Julia grown-up and gallivanting with a new admirer, a smarter young fellow than ever yet, he had had the inspiration of her being exactly the good girl to help him. She certainly found him strike the hour again with these vulgarities of tone — forms of speech that her mother had anciently described as by themselves, once he had opened the whole battery, sufficient ground for putting him away. Full, however, of the use she should have for him, she wasn't going to mind trifles. What she really gasped at was that, so oddly, he was ahead of her at the start. "Yes, I want something of you, Julia, and I want it right now: you can do me a turn, and I'm blest if my luck — which has once or twice been pretty good, you know — hasn't sent you to me." She knew the luck he meant — that of her mother's having so enabled him to get rid of her; but it was the nearest allusion of the merely invidious kind that he would make. It had thus come to our young woman on the spot and by divination: the service he desired of her matched

Julia Bride

with remarkable closeness what she had so promptly taken into her head to name to himself — to name in her own interest, though deterred as yet from having brought it right out. She had been prevented by his speaking, the first thing, in that way, as if he had known Mr. French — which surprised her till he explained that every one in New York knew by appearance a young man of his so quoted wealth ("What did she take them all in New York then *for?*") and of whose marked attention to her he had moreover, for himself, round at clubs and places, lately heard. This had accompanied the inevitable free question "Was she engaged to *him* now?" — which she had in fact almost welcomed as holding out to her the perch of opportunity. She was waiting to deal with it properly, but meanwhile he had gone on, and to such effect that it took them but three minutes to turn out, on either side, like a pair of pickpockets comparing, under shelter, their day's booty, the treasures of design concealed about their persons.

"I want you to tell the truth for me — as you only can. I want you to say that I was really all right — as right as you know; and that I simply acted like an angel in a story-book, gave myself away to have it over."

"Why my dear man," Julia cried, "you take the wind straight out of my sails! What I'm here to ask of *you* is that you'll confess to having been even a worse fiend

than you were shown up for; to having made it impossible mother should *not* take proceedings." There! — she had brought it out, and with the sense of their situation turning to high excitement for her in the teeth of his droll stare, his strange grin, his characteristic "Lordy, lordy! What good will that do you?" She was prepared with her clear statement of reasons for her appeal, and feared so he might have better ones for his own that all her story came in a flash. "Well, Mr. Pitman, I want to get married this time, by way of a change; but you see we've been such fools that, when something really good at last comes up, it's too dreadfully awkward. The fools we were capable of being — well, you know better than any one; unless perhaps not quite so well as Mr. Connery. It has got to be denied," said Julia ardently — "it has got to be denied flat. But I can't get hold of Mr. Connery — Mr. Connery has gone to China. Besides, if he were here," she had ruefully to confess, "he'd be no good — on the contrary. He wouldn't deny anything — he'd only tell more. So thank heaven he's away — there's *that* amount of good! I'm not engaged yet," she went on — but he had already taken her up.

"You're not engaged to Mr. French?" It was all, clearly, a wondrous show for him, but his immediate surprise, oddly, might have been greatest for that.

"No, not to any one — for the seventh time!" She spoke as with her head held well up both over

771

the shame and the pride. "Yes, the next time I'm engaged I want something to happen. But he's afraid; he's afraid of what may be told him. He's dying to find out, and yet he'd die if he did! He wants to be talked to, but he has got to be talked to right. You could talk to him right, Mr. Pitman — if you only *would!* He can't get over mother — that I feel: he loathes and scorns divorces, and we've had first and last too many. So if he could hear from you that you just made her life a hell — why," Julia concluded, "it would be too lovely. If she *had* to go in for another — after having already, when I was little, divorced father — it would 'sort of' make, don't you see? one less. You'd do the high-toned thing by her: you'd say what a wretch you then were, and that she had had to save her life. In that way he mayn't mind it. Don't you see, you sweet man?" poor Julia pleaded. "Oh," she wound up as if his fancy lagged or his scruple looked out, "of course I want you to *lie* for me!"

It did indeed sufficiently stagger him. "It's a lovely idea for the moment when I was just saying to myself — as soon as I saw you — that you'd speak the truth for *me!*"

"Ah what's the matter with 'you'?" Julia sighed with an impatience not sensibly less sharp for her having so quickly scented some lion in her path.

"Why, do you think there's no one in the world but you who has seen the cup of promised affec-tion, of something really to be depended on, only, at the last moment, by the horrid jostle of your elbow, spilled all over you? I want to provide for my future too as it happens; and my good friend who's to help me to that — the most charming of women this time — disapproves of divorce quite as much as Mr. French. Don't you see," Mr. Pitman candidly asked, "what that by itself must have done toward attaching me to her? *She* has got to be talked to — to be told how little I could help it."

"Oh lordy, lordy!" the girl emulously groaned. It was such a relieving cry. "Well, *I* won't talk to her!" she declared.

"You *won't*, Julia?" he pitifully echoed. "And yet you ask of *me —* !"

His pang, she felt, was sincere, and even more than she had guessed, for the previous quarter of an hour, he had been building up his hope, building it with her aid for a foundation. Yet was he going to see how their testimony, on each side, would, if offered, *have* to conflict? If he was to prove himself for her sake — or, more queerly still, for that of Basil French's high conservatism — a person whom there had been but that one way of handling, how could she prove him, in this other and so different interest, a mere gentle sacrifice to his wife's perversity? She had, before him there, on the instant, all acutely, a sense of rising sickness — a wan glimmer of foresight as to the end of the fond dream. Everything else was against

Julia Bride

her, everything in her dreadful past — just as if she had been a person represented by some "emotional actress," some desperate erring lady "hunted down" in a play; but was that going to be the case too with her own very decency, the fierce little residuum deep within her, for which she was counting, when she came to think, on so little glory or even credit? Was this also going to turn against her and trip her up — just to show she was really, under the touch and the test, as decent as any one; and with no one but herself the wiser for it meanwhile, and no proof to show but that, as a consequence, she should be unmarried to the end? She put it to Mr. Pitman quite with resentment: "Do you mean to say you're going to be married — ?"

"Oh my dear, I too must get engaged first!" — he spoke with his inimitable grin. "But that, you see, is where you come in. I've told her about you. She wants awfully to meet you. The way it happens is too lovely — that I find you just in this place. She's coming," said Mr. Pitman — and as in all the good faith of his eagerness now; "she's coming in about three minutes."

"Coming here?"

"Yes, Julia — right here. It's where we usually meet;" and he was wreathed again, this time as if for life, in his large slow smile. "She loves this place — she's awfully keen on art. Like *you*, Julia, if you haven't changed — I remember how you did love art." He looked at her quite tenderly, as to

keep her up to it. "You must still of course — from the way you're here. Just let her *feel* that," the poor man fantastically urged. And then with his kind eyes on her and his good ugly mouth stretched as for delicate emphasis from ear to ear: "Every little helps!"

He made her wonder for him, ask herself, and with a certain intensity, questions she yet hated the trouble of; as whether he were still as moneyless as in the other time — which was certain indeed, for any fortune he ever would have made. His slackness on that ground stuck out of him almost as much as if he had been of rusty or "seedy" aspect — which, luckily for him, he wasn't at all: he looked, in his way, like some pleasant eccentric ridiculous but real gentleman, whose taste might be of the queerest, but his credit with his tailor none the less of the best. She wouldn't have been the least ashamed, had their connexion lasted, of going about with him: so that what a fool, again, her mother had been — since Mr. Connery, sorry as one might be for him, was irrepressibly vulgar. Julia's quickness was, for the minute, charged with all this; but she had none the less her feeling of the right thing to say and the right way to say it. If he was after a future financially assured, even as she herself so frantically was, she wouldn't cast the stone. But if he had talked about her to strange women she couldn't be less than a little majestic. "Who then is the person in question for you — ?"

"Why such a dear thing, Julia —

Mrs. David E. Drack. Have you heard of her?" he almost fluted.

New York was vast, and she hadn't had that advantage. "She's a widow — ?"

"Oh yes: she's not — !" He caught himself up in time. "She's a real one." It was as near as he came. But it was as if he had been looking at her now so pathetically hard. "Julia, she has millions."

Hard, at any rate — whether pathetic or not — was the look she gave him back. "Well, so has — or so *will* have — Basil French. And more of them than Mrs. Drack, I guess," Julia quavered.

"Oh I know what *they've* got!" He took it from her — with the effect of a vague stir, in his long person, of unwelcome embarrassment. But was she going to give up because he was embarrassed? He should know at least what he was costing her. It came home to her own spirit more than ever; but meanwhile he had found his footing. "I don't see how your mother matters. It isn't a question of his marrying *her*."

"No; but, constantly together as we've always been, it's a question of there being so disgustingly much to get over. If we had, for people like them, but the one ugly spot and the one weak side; if we had made, between us, but the one vulgar *kind* of mistake: well, I don't say!" She reflected with a wistfulness of note that was in itself a touching eloquence. "To have our reward in this world we've had too sweet a time. We've had it all right down here!" said Julia Bride.

"I should have taken the precaution to have about a dozen fewer lovers."

"Ah my dear, 'lovers' — !" He ever so comically attenuated.

"Well they *were!*" She quite flared up. "When you've had a ring from each (three diamonds, two pearls and a rather bad sapphire: I've kept them all, and they tell my story!) what are you to call them?"

"Oh rings — !" Mr. Pitman didn't call rings anything. "I've given Mrs. Drack a ring."

Julia stared. "Then aren't you her lover?"

"That, dear child," he humorously wailed, "is what I want you to find out! But I'll handle your rings all right," he more lucidly added.

"You'll 'handle' them?"

"I'll fix your lovers. I'll lie about *them,* if that's all you want."

"Oh about 'them' — !" She turned away with a sombre drop, seeing so little in it. "That wouldn't count — from *you!*" She saw the great shining room, with its mockery of art and "style" and security, all the things she was vainly after, and its few scattered visitors who had left them, Mr. Pitman and herself, in their ample corner, so conveniently at ease. There was only a lady in one of the far doorways, of whom she took vague note and who seemed to be looking at them. "They'd have to lie for themselves!"

"Do you mean he's capable of putting it to them?"

Mr. Pitman's tone threw discredit on that possibility, but she

774

knew perfectly well what she meant. "Not of getting at them directly, not, as mother says, of nosing round himself; but of listening — and small blame to him! — to the horrible things other people say of me."

"But what other people?"

"Why Mrs. George Maule, to begin with — who intensely loathes us, and who talks to his sisters, so that they may talk to *him*: which they do, all the while, I'm morally sure (hating me as they also must). But it's she who's the real reason — I mean of his holding off. She poisons the air he breathes."

"Oh well," said Mr. Pitman with easy optimism, "if Mrs. George Maule's a cat — !"

"If she's a cat she has kittens — four little spotlessly white ones, among whom she'd give her head that Mr. French should make his pick. He could do it with his eyes shut — you can't tell them apart. But she has every name, every date, as you may say, for my dark 'record' — as of course they all call it: she'll be able to give him, if he brings himself to ask her, every fact in its order. And all the while, don't you see? there's no one to speak *for* me."

It would have touched a harder heart than her loose friend's to note the final flush of clairvoyance witnessing this assertion and under which her eyes shone as with the rush of quick tears. He stared at her, and what this did for the deep charm of her prettiness, as in almost witless admiration. "But can't you — lovely as you are, you beautiful thing! — speak for yourself?"

"Do you mean can't I tell the lies? No then, I can't — and I wouldn't if I could. I don't lie myself you know — as it happens; and it could represent to him then about the only thing, the only bad one, I don't do. I *did* — 'lovely as I am'! — have my regular time; I wasn't so hideous that I couldn't! Besides, do you imagine he'd come and ask me?"

"Gad, I wish he would, Julia!" said Mr. Pitman with his kind eyes on her.

"Well then I'd tell him!" And she held her head again high. "But he won't."

It fairly distressed her companion. "Doesn't he want then to know — ?"

"He wants *not* to know. He wants to be told without asking — told, I mean, that each of the stories, those that have come to him, is a fraud and a libel. *Qui s'excuse s'accuse*, don't they say? — so that do you see me breaking out to him, unprovoked, with four or five what-do-you-call-'ems, the things mother used to have to prove in Court, a set of neat little 'alibis' in a row? How can I get hold of so *many* precious gentlemen, to turn them on? How can *they* want everything fished up?"

She had paused for her climax, in the intensity of these considerations; which gave Mr. Pitman a chance to express his honest faith. "Why, my sweet child, they'd be just glad — !"

It determined in her loveliness

almost a sudden glare. "Glad to swear they never had anything to do with such a creature? Then I'd be glad to swear they had lots!"

His persuasive smile, though confessing to bewilderment, insisted. "Why, my love, they've got to swear either one thing or the other."

"They've got to keep out of the way — that's *their* view of it, I guess," said Julia. "Where *are* they, please — now that they *may* be wanted? If you'd like to hunt them up for me you're very welcome." With which, for the moment, over the difficult case, they faced each other helplessly enough. And she added to it now the sharpest ache of her despair. "He knows about Murray Brush. The others" — and her pretty white-gloved hands and charming pink shoulders gave them up — "may go hang!"

"Murray Brush — ?" It had opened Mr. Pitman's eyes.

"Yes — yes; I do mind *him*."

"Then what's the matter with his at least rallying — ?"

"The matter is that, being ashamed of himself, as he well might, he left the country as soon as he could and has stayed away. The matter is that he's in Paris or somewhere, and that if you expect him to come home for me — !" She had already dropped, however, as at Mr. Pitman's look.

"Why, you foolish thing, Murray Brush is in New York!" It had quite brightened him up.

"He has come back — ?"

"Why sure! I saw him — when

was it? Tuesday! — on the Jersey boat." Mr. Pitman rejoiced in his news. "*He's* your man!"

Julia too had been affected by it; it had brought in a rich wave her hot colour back. But she gave the strangest dim smile. "He *was!*"

"Then get hold of him, and — if he's a gentleman — he'll prove for you, to the hilt, that he wasn't."

It lighted her face, the kindled train of this particular sudden suggestion, a glow, a sharpness of interest, that had deepened the next moment, while she gave a slow and sad headshake, to a greater strangeness yet. "He isn't a gentleman."

"Ah lordy, lordy!" Mr. Pitman again sighed. He struggled out of it but only into the vague. "Oh then if he's a pig — !"

"You see there are only a few gentlemen — not enough to go round — and that makes them count so!" It had thrust the girl herself, for that matter, into depths; but whether most of memory or of roused purpose had had no time to judge — aware as he suddenly was of a shadow (since he mightn't perhaps too quickly call it a light) across the heaving surface of their question. It fell upon Julia's face, fell with the sound of the voice he so well knew, but which could only be odd to her for all it immediately assumed.

"There are indeed very few — and one mustn't try *them* too much!" Mrs. Drack, who had supervened while they talked, stood, in monstrous magnitude — at least to Julia's reimpressed eyes — between them: she was the lady our young woman had descried across the room, and she had drawn near while the interest of their issue so held them. We have seen the act of observation and that of reflexion alike swift in Julia — once her subject was within range — and she had now, with all her perceptions at the acutest, taken in, by a single stare, the strange presence to a happy connexion with which Mr. Pitman aspired and which had thus sailed, with placid majesty, into their troubled waters. She was clearly not shy, Mrs. David E. Drack, yet neither was she ominously bold; she was bland and "good," Julia made sure at a glance, and of a large complacency, as the good and the bland are apt to be — a large complacency, a large sentimentality, a large innocent elephantine archness: she fairly rioted in that dimension of size. Habited in an extraordinary quantity of stiff and lustrous black brocade, with enhancements, of every description, that twinkled and tinkled, that rustled and rumbled with her least movement, she presented a huge hideous pleasant face, a featureless desert in a remote quarter of which the disproportionately small eyes might have figured a pair of rash adventurers all but buried in the sand. They reduced themselves when she smiled to barely discernible points — a couple of mere tiny emergent heads — though the foreground of the scene, as if to make up for it, gaped with a vast be-

nevolence. In a word Julia saw — and as if she had needed nothing more; saw Mr. Pitman's opportunity, saw her own, saw the exact nature both of Mrs. Drack's circumspection and of Mrs. Drack's sensibility, saw even, glittering there in letters of gold and as a part of the whole metallic coruscation, the large figure of her income, largest of all her attributes, and (though perhaps a little more as a luminous blur beside all this) the mingled ecstasy and agony of Mr. Pitman's hope and Mr. Pitman's fear.

He was introducing them, with his pathetic belief in the virtue for every occasion, in the solvent for every trouble, of an extravagant genial professional humour; he was naming her to Mrs. Drack as the charming young friend he had told her so much about and who had been as an angel to him in a weary time; he was saying that the loveliest chance in the world, this accident of a meeting in those promiscuous halls, had placed within his reach the pleasure of bringing them together. It didn't indeed matter, Julia felt, what he was saying: he conveyed everything, as far as she was concerned, by a moral pressure as unmistakable as if, for a symbol of it, he had thrown himself on her neck. Above all, meanwhile, this high consciousness prevailed — that the good lady herself, however huge she loomed, had entered, by the end of a minute, into a condition as of suspended weight and arrested mass, stilled to artless awe by the ef-

fect of her vision. Julia had practised almost to lassitude the art of
tracing in the people who looked
at her the impression promptly sequent; but it was a singular fact
that if, in irritation, in depression,
she felt that the lighted eyes of
men, stupid at their clearest, had
given her pretty well all she should
ever care for, she could still gather
a freshness from the tribute of her
own sex, still care to see her reflexion in the faces of women.
Never, probably, never would that
sweet be tasteless — with such a
straight grim spoon was it mostly
administered, and so flavoured
and strengthened by the competence of their eyes. Women knew
so much best *how* a woman surpassed — how and where and why,
with no touch or torment of it lost
on them; so that as it produced
mainly and primarily the instinct
of aversion, the sense of extracting
the recognition, of gouging out the
homage, was on the whole the
highest crown one's felicity could
wear. Once in a way, however, the
grimness beautifully dropped, the
jealousy failed: the admiration was
all there and the poor plain sister
handsomely paid it. It had never
been so paid, she was presently
certain, as by this great generous
object of Mr. Pitman's flame, who
without optical aid, it well might
have seemed, nevertheless entirely
grasped her — might in fact, all benevolently, have been groping her
over as by some huge mild proboscis. She gave Mrs. Drack pleasure in short; and who could say of

what other pleasures the poor lady
hadn't been cheated?

It was somehow a muddled
world in which one of her conceivable joys, at this time of day,
would be to marry Mr. Pitman —
to say nothing of a state of things
in which this gentleman's own
fancy could invest such a union
with rapture. That, however, was
their own mystery, and Julia, with
each instant, was more and more
clear about hers: so remarkably
primed in fact, at the end of three
minutes, that though her friend,
and though *his* friend, were both
saying things, many things and
perhaps quite wonderful things,
she had no free attention for them
and was only rising and soaring.
She was rising to her value, she
was soaring *with* it — the value Mr.
Pitman almost convulsively imputed to her, the value that consisted
for her of being so unmistakeably
the most dazzling image Mrs.
Drack had ever beheld. These were
the uses, for Julia, in fine, of adversity; the range of Mrs. Drack's experience might have been as small
as the measure of her presence was
large: Julia was at any rate herself
in face of the occasion of her life,
and, after all her late repudiations
and reactions, had perhaps never
yet known the quality of this moment's success. She hadn't an idea
of what, on either side, had been
uttered — beyond Mr. Pitman's allusion to her having befriended
him of old: she simply held his
companion with her radiance and
knew she might be, for her effect,

as irrelevant as she chose. It was relevant to do what he wanted — it was relevant to dish herself. She did it now with a kind of passion, to say nothing of her knowing, with it, that every word of it added to her beauty. She gave him away in short, up to the hilt, for any use of her own, and should have nothing to clutch at now but the possibility of Murray Brush.

"He says I was good to him, Mrs. Drack; and I'm sure I hope I was, since I should be ashamed to be anything else. If I could be good to him now I should be glad — that's just what, a while ago, I rushed up to him here, after so long, to give myself the pleasure of saying. I saw him years ago very particularly, very miserably tried — and I saw the way he took it. I did see it, you dear man," she sublimely went on — "I saw it for all you may protest, for all you may hate me to talk about you! I saw you behave like a gentleman — since Mrs. Drack agrees with me so charmingly that there are not many to be met. I don't know whether you care, Mrs. Drack" — she abounded, she revelled in the name — "but I've always remembered it of him: that under the most extraordinary provocation he was decent and patient and brave. No appearance of anything different matters, for I speak of what I *know*. Of course I'm nothing and nobody; I'm only a poor frivolous girl, but I was very close to him at the time. That's all my little story — if it *should* interest you at all."

She measured every beat of her wing, she knew how high she was going and paused only when it was quite vertiginous. Here she hung a moment as in the glare of the upper blue; which was but the glare — what else could it be? — of the vast and magnificent attention of both her auditors, hushed, on their side, in the splendour she emitted. She had at last to steady herself, and she scarce knew afterwards at what rate or in what way she had still inimitably come down — her own eyes fixed all the while on the very figure of her achievement. She had sacrificed her mother on the altar — proclaimed her false and cruel; and if that didn't "fix" Mr. Pitman, as he would have said — well, it was all she could do. But the cost of her action already somehow came back to her with increase; the dear gaunt man fairly wavered, to her sight, in the glory of it, as if signalling at her, with wild gleeful arms, from some mount of safety, while the massive lady just spread and spread like a rich fluid a bit helplessly spilt. It was really the outflow of the poor woman's honest response, into which she seemed to melt, and Julia scarce distinguished the two apart even for her taking gracious leave of each. "Good-bye, Mrs. Drack; I'm awfully happy to have met you" — like as not it was for this she had grasped Mr. Pitman's hand. And then to him or to her, it didn't matter which, "Good-bye, dear good Mr. Pitman — hasn't it been nice after so long?"

III

JULIA floated even to her own sense swanlike away — she left in her wake their fairly stupefied submission: it was as if she had, by an exquisite authority, now *placed* them, each for each, and they would have nothing to do but be happy together. Never had she so exulted as on this ridiculous occasion in the noted items of her beauty. *Le compte y était*, as they used to say in Paris — every one of them, for her immediate employment, was there; and there was something in it after all. It didn't necessarily, this sum of thumping little figures, imply charm — especially for "refined" people: nobody knew better than Julia that inexpressible charm and quoteable "charms" (quoteable like prices, rates, shares, or whatever, the things they dealt in downtown) are two distinct categories; the safest thing for the latter being, on the whole, that it might include the former, and the great strength of the former being that it might perfectly dispense with the latter. Mrs. Drack wasn't refined, not the least little bit; but what would be the case with Murray Brush now — after his three years of Europe? He had done so what he liked with her — which had seemed so then just the meaning, hadn't it? of their being "engaged" — that he had made her not see, while the absurd-

ity lasted (the absurdity of their pretending to believe they could marry without a cent) how little he was of metal without alloy: this had come up for her, remarkably, but afterwards — come up for her as she looked back. Then she had drawn her conclusion, which was one of the many that Basil French had made her draw. It was a queer service Basil was going to have rendered her, this having made everything she had ever done impossible, if he wasn't going to give her a new chance. If he was it was doubtless right enough. On the other hand Murray might have improved, if such a quantity of alloy, as she called it, *were*, in any man, reducible, and if Paris were the place all happily to reduce it. She had her doubts — anxious and aching on the spot, and had expressed them to Mr. Pitman: certainly, of old, he had been more open to the quoteable than to the inexpressible, to charms than to charm. If she could try the quoteable, however, and with such a grand result, on Mrs. Drack, she couldn't now on Murray — in respect to whom everything had changed. So that if he hadn't a sense for the subtler appeal, the appeal appreciable by people *not* vulgar, on which alone she could depend, what on earth would become of her? She could but yearningly hope, at any rate, as she made up her mind to write to him immediately at his club. It was a question of the right sensibility in him. Perhaps he would have acquired it in Europe.

Two days later indeed — for he

780

Julia Bride

had promptly and charmingly replied, keeping with alacrity the
appointment she had judged best
to propose, a morning hour in a
sequestered alley of the Park — two
days later she was to be struck
well-nigh to alarm by everything
he had acquired: so much it
seemed to make that it threatened
somehow a complication, and her
plan, so far as she had arrived at
one, dwelt in the desire above all
to simplify. She wanted no grain
more of extravagance or excess in
anything — risking as she had done,
none the less, a recall of ancient
licence in proposing to Murray
such a place of meeting. She had
her reasons — she wished intensely
to discriminate: Basil French had
several times waited on her at her
mother's habitation, their horrible
flat which was so much too far up
and too near the East Side; he had
dined there and lunched there and
gone with her thence to other
places, notably to see pictures, and
had in particular adjourned with
her twice to the Metropolitan Museum, in which he took a great interest, in which she professed a
delight, and their second visit to
which had wound up in her encounter with Mr. Pitman, after her
companion had yielded, at her urgent instance, to an exceptional
need of keeping a business engagement. She mightn't in delicacy, in decency, entertain Murray Brush where she had entertained Mr. French — she was giv-
en over now to these exquisite perceptions and proprieties and bent
on devoutly observing them; and

Mr. French, by good luck, had
never been with her in the Park:
partly because he had never
pressed it, and partly because she
would have held off if he had, so
haunted were those devious paths
and favouring shades by the general echo of her untrammelled past.
If he had never suggested their
taking a turn there this was because, quite divineably, he held it
would commit him further than he
had yet gone; and if she on her
side had practised a like reserve it
was because the place reeked for
her, as she inwardly said, with old
associations. It reeked with nothing so much perhaps as with the
memories evoked by the young
man who now awaited her in the
nook she had been so competent
to indicate; but in what corner of
the town, should she look for them,
wouldn't those footsteps creak back
into muffled life, and to what expedient would she be reduced
should she attempt to avoid all
such tracks? The Museum was full
of tracks, tracks by the hundred —
the way really she had knocked
about! — but she had to see people
somewhere, and she couldn't pretend to dodge every ghost.

All she could do was not to make
confusion, make mixtures, of the
living; though she asked herself
enough what mixture she mightn't
find herself to have prepared if
Mr. French should, not so very im-
possibly for a restless roaming man
— her effect on him! — happen to
pass while she sat there with the
moustachioed personage round
whose name Mrs. Maule would

781

probably have caused detrimental anecdote most thickly to cluster. There existed, she was sure, a mass of luxuriant legend about the "lengths" her engagement with Murray Brush had gone; she could herself fairly feel them in the air, these streamers of evil, black flags flown as in warning, the vast redundancy of so cheap and so dingy social bunting, in fine, that flapped over the stations she had successively moved away from and which were empty now, for such an ado, even to grotesqueness. The vivacity of that conviction was what had at present determined her, while it was the way he listened after she had quickly broken ground, while it was the special character of the interested look in his handsome face, handsomer than ever yet, that represented for her the civilisation he had somehow taken on. Just so it was the quantity of that gain, in its turn, that had at the end of ten minutes begun to affect her as holding up a light to the wide reach of her step. "There was never anything the least serious between us, not a sign or a scrap, do you mind? of anything beyond the merest pleasant friendly acquaintance; and if you're not ready to go to the stake on it for me you may as well know in time what it is you'll probably cost me."

She had immediately plunged, measuring her effect and having thought it well over; and what corresponded to her question of his having become a better person to appeal to was the appearance of interest she had so easily created

in him. She felt on the spot the difference that made — it was indeed his form of being more civilised: it was the sense in which Europe in general and Paris in particular had made him develop. By every calculation — and her calculations, based on the intimacy of her knowledge, had been many and deep — he would help her the better the more intelligent he should have become; yet she was to recognise later on that the first chill of foreseen disaster had been caught by her as, at a given moment, this greater refinement of his attention seemed to exhale it. It was just what she had wanted — "if I can only get him interested —!" so that, this proving quite vividly possible, why did the light it lifted strike her as lurid? Was it partly by reason of his inordinate romantic good looks, those of a gallant genial conqueror, but which, involving so glossy a brownness of eye, so manly a crispness of curl, so red-lipped a radiance of smile, so natural a bravery of port, prescribed to any response he might facially, might expressively make a sort of florid disproportionate amplitude? The explanation, in any case, didn't matter; he was going to mean well — that she could feel, and also that he had meant better in the past, presumably, than he had managed to convince her of his doing at the time: the oddity she hadn't now reckoned with was this fact that from the moment he did advertise an interest it should show almost as what she would have called weird. It made a change in him that didn't go with the rest — as if he had broken his nose or put on spectacles, lost his handsome hair or sacrificed his splendid moustache: her conception, her necessity, as she saw, had been that something should be added to him for her use, but nothing for his own alteration.

He had affirmed himself, and his character, and his temper, and his health, and his appetite, and his ignorance, and his obstinacy, and his whole charming coarse heartless personality, during their engagement, by twenty forms of natural emphasis, but never by emphasis of interest. How in fact could you feel interest unless you should know, within you, some dim stir of imagination? There was nothing in the world of which Murray Brush was less capable than of such a dim stir, because you only began to imagine when you felt some approach to a need to understand. *He* had never felt it; for hadn't he been born, to his personal vision, with that perfect intuition of everything which reduces all the suggested preliminaries of judgement to the impertinence — when it's a question of your entering your house — of a dumpage of bricks at your door? He had had, in short, neither to imagine nor to perceive, because he had, from the first pulse of his intelligence, simply and supremely known: so that, at this hour, face to face with him, it came over her that she had in their old relation dispensed with any such convenience of comprehension on his part

even to a degree she had not measured at the time. What therefore must he not have seemed to her as a form of life, a form of avidity and activity, blatantly successful in its own conceit, that he could have dazzled her so against the interest of her very faculties and functions? Strangely and richly historic all that backward mystery, and only leaving for her mind the wonder of such a mixture of possession and detachment as they would clearly to-day both know. For each to be so little at last to the other when, during months together, the idea of all abundance, all quantity, had been, for each, drawn from the other and addressed to the other — what was it monstrously like but some fantastic act of getting rid of a person by going to lock yourself up in the *sanctum sanctorum* of that person's house, amid every evidence of that person's habits and nature? What was going to happen, at any rate, was that Murray would show himself as beautifully and consciously understanding — and it would be prodigious that Europe should have inoculated him with that delicacy. Yes, he wouldn't claim to know now till she had told him — an aid to performance he had surely never before waited for or been indebted to from any one; and then, so knowing, he would charmingly endeavour to "meet," to oblige and to gratify. He would find it, her case, ever so worthy of his benevolence, and would be literally inspired to reflect that he must hear about it first.

783

Julia Bride

She let him hear then everything, in spite of feeling herself slip, while she did so, to some doom as yet incalculable; she went on very much as she had done for Mr. Pitman and Mrs. Drack, with the rage of desperation and, as she was afterwards to call it to herself, the fascination of the abyss. She didn't know, couldn't have said at the time, *why* his projected benevolence should have had most so the virtue to scare her: he would patronise her, as an effect of her vividness, if not of her charm, and would do this with all high intention, finding her case, or rather *their* case, their funny old case, taking on of a sudden such refreshing and edifying life, to the last degree curious and even important; but there were gaps of connexion between this and the intensity of the perception here overtaking her that she shouldn't be able to move in *any* direction without dishing herself. That she couldn't afford it where she had got to — couldn't afford the deplorable vulgarity of having been so many times informally affianced and contracted (putting it only at that, as its being by the new lights and fashions so unpardonably vulgar): he took this from her without turning, as she might have said, a hair; except just to indicate, with his new superiority, that he felt the distinguished appeal and notably the pathos of it. He still took it from her that she hoped nothing, as it were, from any other *alibi* — the people to drag into court being too many and too scat-

tered; but that, as it was with him, Murray Brush, she had been *most* vulgar, most everything she had better not have been, so she depended on him for the innocence it was actually vital she should establish. He blushed or frowned or winced no more at that than he did when she once more fairly emptied her satchel and, quite as if they had been Nancy and the Artful Dodger, or some nefarious pair of that sort, talking things over in the manner of "Oliver Twist," revealed to him the fondness of her view that, could she but have produced a cleaner slate, she might by this time have pulled it off with Mr. French. Yes, he let her in that way sacrifice her honourable connexion with him — all the more honourable for being so completely at an end — to the crudity of her plan for not missing another connexion, so much more brilliant than what he offered, and for bringing another man, with whom she so invidiously and unflatteringly compared him, into her greedy life.

There was only a moment during which, by a particular lustrous look she had never had from him before, he just made her wonder which turn he was going to take; she felt, however, as safe as was consistent with her sense of having probably but added to her danger, when he brought out, the next instant: "Don't you seem to take the ground that we were guilty — that *you* were ever guilty — of something we shouldn't have been? What did we ever do that was secret, or underhand, or any way not to be acknowledged? What did we do but exchange our young vows with the best faith in the world — publicly, rejoicingly, with the full assent of every one connected with us? I mean of course," he said with his grave kind smile, "till we broke off so completely because we found that — practically, financially, on the hard worldly basis — we couldn't work it. What harm, in the sight of God or man, Julia," he asked in his fine rich way, "did we ever do?"

She gave him back his look, turning pale. "Am I talking of *that*? Am I talking of what *we* know? I'm talking of what others feel — of what they *have* to feel; of what it's just enough for them to know not to be able to get over it, once they do really know it. How do they know what *didn't* pass between us, with all the opportunities we had? That's none of their business — if we were idiots enough, on the top of everything! What you may or mayn't have done doesn't count, for *you;* but there are people for whom it's loathsome that a girl should have gone on like that from one person to another and still pretend to be — well, all that a nice girl is supposed to be. It's as if we had but just waked up, mother and I, to such a remarkable prejudice; and now we have it — when we could do so well without it! — staring us in the face. That mother should have insanely *let* me, should so vulgarly have taken it for my natural, my social career — *that's* the

disgusting humiliating thing: with the lovely account it gives of both of us! But mother's view of a delicacy in things!" she went on with scathing grimness; "mother's measure of anything, with her grand 'gained cases' (there'll be another yet, she finds them so easy!) of which she's so publicly proud! You see I've no margin," said Julia; letting him take it from her flushed face as much as he would that her mother hadn't left her an inch. It was that he should make use of the spade with her for the restoration of a bit of a margin just wide enough to perch on till the tide of peril should have ebbed a little, it was that he should give her *that* lift — !

Well, it was all there from him after these last words; it was before her that he really took hold. "Oh, my dear child, I can see! Of course there are . people — ideas change in our society so fast! — who are not in sympathy with the old American freedom and who read, I dare say, all sorts of uncanny things into it. Naturally you must take them as they are — from the moment," said Murray Brush, who had lighted, by her leave, a cigarette, "your life-path does, for weal or for woe, cross with theirs." He had every now and then an elegant phrase. "Awfully interesting, certainly, your case. It's enough for me that it *is* yours — I make it my own. I put myself absolutely in your place; you'll understand from me, without professions, won't you? that I do. Command me in every way! What I do like is the sympathy with which you've inspired *him*. I don't, I'm sorry to say, happen to know him personally" — he smoked away, looking off; "but of course one knows all about him generally, and I'm sure he's right for you, I'm sure it would be charming, if you yourself think so. Therefore trust me and even — what shall I say? — leave it to me a little, won't you?" He had been watching, as in his fumes, the fine growth of his possibilities; and with this he turned on her the large warmth of his charity. It was like a subscription of a half a million. "I'll take care of you."

She found herself for a moment looking up at him from as far below as the point from which the school-child, with round eyes raised to the wall, gazes at the particoloured map of the world. Yes, it was a warmth, it was a special benignity, that had never yet dropped on her from any one; and she wouldn't for the first few moments have known how to describe it or even quite what to do with it. Then as it still rested, his fine improved expression aiding, the sense of what had happened came over her with a rush. She was being, yes, patronised; and that was really as new to her — the freeborn American girl who might, if she had wished, have got engaged and disengaged not six times but sixty — as it would have been to be crowned or crucified. The Frenches themselves didn't do it — the Frenches themselves didn't dare it. It was as strange as one would:

she recognised it when it came, but anything might have come rather — and it was coming by (of all people in the world) Murray Brush! It overwhelmed her; still she could speak, with however faint a quaver and however sick a smile. "You'll lie for me like a gentleman?"

"As far as that goes till I'm black in the face!" And then while he glowed at her and she wondered if he would pointedly look his lies that way, and if, in fine, his florid gallant knowing, almost winking intelligence, *common* as she had never seen the common vivified, would represent his notion of "blackness": "See here, Julia; I'll do more."

" 'More' — ?"

"Everything. I'll take it right in hand. I'll fling over you — "

"Fling over me — ?" she continued to echo as he fascinatingly fixed her.

"Well, the biggest *kind* of rose-coloured mantle!" And this time, oh, he did wink: it *would* be the way he was going to wink (and in the grandest good faith in the world) when indignantly denying, under inquisition, that there had been "a sign or a scrap" between them. But there was more to come; he decided she should have it all. "Julia, you've got to know now." He hung fire but an instant more. "Julia, I'm going to be married." His "Julias" were somehow death to her; she could feel that even *through* all the rest. "Julia, I announce my engagement."

"Oh lordy, lordy!" she wailed: it

might have been addressed to Mr. Pitman.

The force of it had brought her to her feet, but he sat there smiling up as at the natural tribute of her interest. "I tell you before any one else; it's not to be 'out' for a day or two yet. But we want you to know; *she* said that as soon as I mentioned to her that I had heard from you. I mention to her everything, you see!" — and he almost simpered while, still in his seat, he held the end of his cigarette, all delicately and as for a form of gentle emphasis, with the tips of his fine fingers. "You've not met her, Mary Lindeck, I think: she tells me she hasn't the pleasure of knowing you, but she desires it so much — particularly longs for it. She'll take an interest too," he went on; "you must let me immediately bring her to you. She has heard so much about you and she really wants to see you."

"Oh mercy *me!*" poor Julia gasped again — so strangely did history repeat itself and so did this appear the echo, on Murray Brush's lips, and quite to drollery, of that sympathetic curiosity of Mrs. Drack's which Mr. Pitman, as they said, voiced. Well, there had played before her the vision of a ledge of safety in face of a rising tide; but this deepened quickly to a sense more forlorn, the cold swish of waters already up to her waist and that would soon be up to her chin. It came really but from the air of her friend, from the perfect benevolence and high unconsciousness with which he kept his pos-

ture — as if to show he could patronise her from below upward quite as well as from above down. And as she took it all in, as it spread to a flood, with the great lumps and masses of truth it was floating, she knew inevitable submission, not to say submersion, as she had never known it in her life; going down and down before it, not even putting out her hands to resist or cling by the way, only reading into the young man's very face an immense fatality and, for all his bright nobleness, his absence of rancour or of protesting pride, the great grey blankness of her doom. It was as if the earnest Miss Lindeck, tall and mild, high and lean, with eye-glasses and a big nose, but "marked" in a noticeable way, elegant and distinguished and refined, as you could see from a mile off, and as graceful, for common despair of imitation, as the curves of the "copy" set of old by one's writing-master — it was as if this stately wellwisher, whom indeed she had never exchanged a word with, but whom she had recognised and placed and winced at as soon as he spoke of her, figured there beside him now as also in portentous charge of her case.

He had ushered her into it in that way, as if his mere right word sufficed; and Julia could see them throned together, beautifully at one in all the interests they now shared, and regard her as an object of almost tender solicitude. It was positively as if they had become engaged for her good — in

Julia Bride

such a happy light as it shed. That was the way people you had known, known a bit intimately, looked at you as soon as they took on the high matrimonial propriety that sponged over the more or less wild past to which you belonged and of which, all of a sudden, they were aware only through some suggestion it made them for reminding you definitely that you still had a place. On her having had a day or two before to meet Mrs. Drack and to rise to her expectation she had seen and felt herself act, had above all admired herself, and had at any rate known what she said, even though losing, at her altitude, any distinctness in the others. She could have repeated afterwards the detail of her performance — if she hadn't preferred to keep it with her as a mere locked-up, a mere unhandled treasure. At present, however, as everything was for her at first deadened and vague, true to the general effect of sounds and motions in water, she couldn't have said afterwards what words she spoke, what face she showed, what impression she made — at least till she had pulled herself round to precautions. She only knew she had turned away, and that this movement must have sooner or later determined his rising to join her, his deciding to accept it, gracefully and condoningly — condoningly in respect to her natural emotion, her inevitable little pang — for an intimation that they would be better on their feet.

They trod then afresh their ancient paths; and though it pressed upon her hatefully that he must have taken her abruptness for a smothered shock, the flare-up of her old feeling at the breath of his news, she had still to see herself condemned to allow him this, condemned really to encourage him in the mistake of believing her suspicious of feminine spite and doubtful of Miss Lindeck's zeal. She was so far from doubtful that she was but too appalled at it and at the officious mass in which it loomed, and this instinct of dread, before their walk was over, before she had guided him round to one of the smaller gates, there to slip off again by herself, was positively to find on the bosom of her flood a plank under aid of which she kept in a manner and for the time afloat. She took ten minutes to pant, to blow gently, to paddle disguisedly, to accommodate herself, in a word, to the elements she had let loose; but as a reward of her effort at least she then saw how her determined vision accounted for everything. Beside her friend on the bench she had truly felt all his cables cut, truly swallowed down the fact that if he still perceived she was pretty — and *how* pretty! — it had ceased appreciably to matter to him. It had lighted the folly of her preliminary fear, the fear of his even yet, to some effect of confusion or other inconvenience for her, proving more alive to the quoteable in her, as she had called it, than to the inexpressible. She had reckoned with the awkwardness of that possible lapse of his measure of her charm, by which

788

his renewed apprehension of her grosser ornaments, those with which he had most affinity, might too much profit; but she need have concerned herself as little for his sensibility on one head as on the other. She had ceased personally, ceased materially — in respect, as who should say, to any optical or tactile advantage — to exist for him, and the whole office of his manner had been the more piously and gallantly to dress the dead presence with flowers. This was all to his credit and his honour, but what it clearly certified was that their case was at last not even one of spirit reaching out to spirit. *He* had plenty of spirit — had all the spirit required for his having engaged himself to Miss Lindeck; into which result, once she had got her head well up again, she read, as they proceeded, one sharp meaning after another. It was therefore toward the subtler essence of that mature young woman alone that he was occupied in stretching; what was definite to him about Julia Bride being merely, being entirely — which was indeed thereby quite enough — that she *might* end by scaling her worldly height. They would push, they would shove, they would "boost," they would arch both their straight backs as pedestals for her tiptoe; and at the same time, by some sweet prodigy of mechanics, she would pull them up and up with her.

Wondrous things hovered before her in the course of this walk; her consciousness had become, by an extraordinary turn, a music-box in which, its lid well down, the most remarkable tunes were sounding. It played for her ear alone, and the lid, as she might have figured, was her firm plan of holding out till she got home, of not betraying — to her companion at least — the extent to which she was demoralised. To see him think her demoralised by mistrust of the sincerity of the service to be meddlesomely rendered her by his future wife — she would have hurled herself publicly into the lake there at their side, would have splashed, in her beautiful clothes, among the frightened swans, rather than invite him to that ineptitude. Oh her sincerity, Mary Lindeck's — she would be drenched with her sincerity, and she would be drenched, yes, with *his;* so that, from inward convulsion to convulsion, she had, before they reached their gate, pulled up in the path. There was something her head had been full of these three or four minutes, the intensest little tune of the music-box, and it had made its way to her lips now; belonging — for all the good it could do her! — to the two or three sorts of solicitude she might properly express.

"I hope *she* has a fortune, if you don't mind my speaking of it: I mean some of the money we didn't in *our* time have — and that we missed, after all, in our poor way and for what we then wanted of it, so quite dreadfully."

She had been able to wreathe it in a grace quite equal to any he himself had employed; and it was to be said for him also that he kept up, on this, the standard. "Oh she's not, thank goodness, at all badly off, poor dear. We shall do very well. How sweet of you to have thought of it! May I tell her that too?" he splendidly glared. Yes, he glared — how couldn't he, with what his mind was really full of? But, all the same, he came just here, by her vision, nearer than at any other point to being a gentleman. He came quite within an ace of it — with his taking from her thus the prescription of humility of service, his consenting to act in the interest of her avidity, his letting her mount that way, on his bowed shoulders, to the success in which he could suppose she still believed. He couldn't know, he would never know, that she had then and there ceased to believe in it — that she saw as clear as the sun in the sky the exact manner in which, between them, before they had done, the Murray Brushes, all zeal and sincerity, all interest in her interesting case, would dish, would ruin, would utterly destroy her. He wouldn't have needed to go on, for the force and truth of this; but he did go on — he was as crashingly consistent as a motorcar without a brake. He was visibly in love with the idea of what they might do for her and of the rare "social" opportunity that they would, by the same stroke, embrace. How he had been offhand with it, how he had made it parenthetic, that he didn't happen "personally" to know Basil French — as if it would have been at all likely he *should* know him, even *imp*ersonally, and as if he could conceal from her the fact that, since she had made him her overture, this gentleman's name supremely baited her hook! Oh they would help Julia Bride if they could — they would do their remarkable best; but they would at any rate have made his acquaintance over it, and she might indeed leave the rest to their thoroughness. He would already have known, he would already have heard; her appeal, she was more and more sure, wouldn't have come to him as a revelation. He had already talked it over with *her,* with Miss Lindeck, to whom the Frenches, in their fortress, had never been accessible, and his whole attitude bristled, to Julia's eyes, with the betrayal of her hand, her voice, her pressure, her calculation. His tone in fact, as he talked, fairly thrust these things into her face. "But you must see her for yourself. You'll judge her. You'll love her. My dear child" — he brought it all out, and if he spoke of children he might, in his candour, have been himself infantine — "my dear child, she's the person to do it for you. Make it over to her; but," he laughed, "of course see her first! Couldn't you," he wound up — for they were now near their gate, where she was to leave him — "couldn't you just simply make us meet him, at tea, say, informally; just *us* alone, as pleasant old friends of whom you'd have so naturally and frankly spoken to him; and then see what we'd *make* of that?"

Julia Bride

It was all in his expression; he couldn't keep it undetected, and his shining good looks couldn't: ah he was so fatally much too handsome for her! So the gap showed just there, in his admirable mask and his admirable eagerness; the yawning little chasm showed where the gentleman fell short. But she took this in, she took everything in, she felt herself do it, she heard herself say, while they paused before separation, that she quite saw the point of the meeting, as he suggested, at her tea. She would propose it to Mr. French and would let them know; and he must assuredly bring Miss Lindeck, bring her "right away," bring her soon, bring *them,* his fiancée and her, together somehow, and as quickly as possible — so that they *should* be old friends before the tea. She would propose it to Mr. French, propose it to Mr. French: that hummed in her ears as she went — after she had really got away; hummed as if she were repeating it over, giving it out to the passers, to the pavement, to the sky, and all as in wild discord with the intense little concert of her music-box. The extraordinary thing too was that she quite believed she should do it, and fully meant to; desperately, fantastically passive — since she almost reeled with it as she proceeded — she was capable of proposing anything to any one: capable too of thinking it likely Mr. French would come, for he had never on her previous proposals declined anything. Yes, she would keep it up to the end, this pretence of owing them salvation, and might even live to take comfort in having done for them what they wanted. What they wanted *couldn't* but be to get at the Frenches, and what Miss Lindeck above all wanted, baffled of it otherwise, with so many others of the baffled, was to get at Mr. French — for all Mr. French would want of either of them! — still more than Murray did. It wasn't till after she had got home, got straight into her own room and flung herself on her face, that she yielded to the full taste of the bitterness of missing a connexion, missing the man himself, with power to create such a social appetite, such a grab at what might be ganied by them. He could make people, even people like these two and whom there were still other people to envy, he could make them push and snatch and scramble like that — and then remain as incapable of taking her from the hands of such patrons as of receiving her straight, say, from those of Mrs. Drack. It was a high note, too, of Julia's wonderful composition that, even in the long lonely moan of her conviction of her now certain ruin, all this grim lucidity, the perfect clearance of passion, but made her supremely proud of him.

THE JOLLY CORNER

i

"EVERY one asks me what I 'think' of everything," said Spencer Brydon; "and I make answer as I can — begging or dodging the question, putting them off with any nonsense. It wouldn't matter to any of them really," he went on, "for, even were it possible to meet in that stand-and-deliver way so silly a demand on so big a subject, my 'thoughts' would still be almost together about something that concerns only myself." He was talking to Miss Staverton, with whom for a couple of months now he had availed himself of every possible occasion to talk; this disposition and this resource, this comfort and support, as the situation in fact presented itself, having promptly enough taken the first place in the considerable array of rather unattenuated surprises attending his so strangely belated return to America. Everything was somehow a surprise; and that might be natural when one had so long and so consistently neglected everything, taken pains to give surprises so much margin for play. He had given them more than thirty years — thirty-three, to be exact; and they now seemed to him to have organ-ised their performance quite on the scale of that licence. He had been twenty-three on leaving New York — he was fifty-six to-day: unless indeed he were to reckon as he had sometimes, since his repatriation, found himself feeling; in which case he would have lived longer than is often allotted to man. It would have taken a century, he repeatedly said to himself, and said also to Alice Staverton, it would have taken a longer absence and a more averted mind than those even of which he had been guilty, to pile up the differences, the newnesses, the queernesses, above all the bignesses, for the better or the worse, that at present assaulted his vision wherever he looked.

The great fact all the while however had been the incalculability; since he *had* supposed himself, from decade to decade, to be allowing, and in the most liberal and intelligent manner, for brilliancy of change. He actually saw that he had allowed for nothing; he missed what he would have been sure of finding, he found what he would never have imagined. Proportions and values were upside-down; the ugly things he had expected, the ugly things of his far-away youth, when he had too promptly waked up to a sense of the ugly — these uncanny phenomena placed him rather, as it happened, under the charm; whereas the "swagger" things, the modern, the monstrous, the famous things, those he had more particularly, like thousands of ingenuous enquirers every year, come over to see, were exactly his sources of dismay. They were as so many set traps for displeasure, above all for reaction, of which his restless tread was constantly pressing the spring. It was interesting, doubtless, the whole show, but it would have been too disconcerting hadn't a certain finer truth saved the situation. He had distinctly not, in this steadier light, come over *all* for the monstrosities; he had come, not only in the last analysis but quite on the face of the act, under an impulse with which they had nothing to do. He had come — putting the thing pompously — to look at his "property," which he had thus for a third of a century not been within four thousand miles of; or, expressing it less sordidly, he had yielded to the humour of seeing again his house on the jolly corner, as he usually, and quite fondly, described it — the one in which he had first seen the light, in which various members of his family had lived and had died, in which the holidays of his overschooled boyhood had been passed and the few social flowers of his chilled adolescence gathered, and which, alienated then for so long a period, had, through the successive deaths of his two brothers and the termination of old arrangements, come wholly into his hands. He was the owner of another, not quite so "good" — the jolly corner having

been, from far back, superlatively extended and consecrated; and the value of the pair represented his main capital, with an income consisting, in these later years, of their respective rents which (thanks precisely to their original excellent type) had never been depressingly low. He could live in "Europe," as he had been in the habit of living, on the product of these flourishing New York leases, and all the better since, that of the second structure, the mere number in its long row, having within a twelvemonth fallen in, renovation at a high advance had proved beautifully possible.

These were items of property indeed, but he had found himself since his arrival distinguishing more than ever between them. The house within the street, two bristling blocks westward, was already in course of reconstruction as a tall mass of flats; he had acceded, some time before, to overtures for this conversion — in which, now that it was going forward, it had been not the least of his astonishments to find himself able, on the spot, and though without a previous ounce of such experience, to participate with a certain intelligence, almost with a certain authority. He had lived his life with his back so turned to such concerns and his face addressed to those of so different an order that he scarce knew what to make of this lively stir, in a compartment of his mind never yet penetrated, of a capacity for business and a sense for construction. These virtues, so common all round him now, had been dormant in his own organism — where it might be said of them perhaps that they had slept the sleep of the just. At present, in the splendid autumn weather — the autumn at least was a pure boon in the terrible place — he loafed about his "work" undeterred, secretly agitated; not in the least "minding" that the whole proposition, as they said, was vulgar and sordid, and ready to climb ladders, to walk the plank, to handle materials and look wise about them, to ask questions, in fine, and challenge explanations and really "go into" figures.

It amused, it verily quite charmed him; and, by the same stroke, it amused, and even more, Alice Staverton, though perhaps charming her perceptibly less. She wasn't however going to be better-off for it, as *he* was — and so astonishingly much: nothing was now likely, he knew, ever to make her better-off than she found herself, in the afternoon of life, as the delicately frugal possessor and tenant of the small house in Irving Place to which she had subtly managed to cling through her almost unbroken New York career. If he knew the way to it now better than to any other address among the dreadful multiplied numberings which seemed to him to reduce the whole place to some vast ledger-page, overgrown, fantastic, of ruled and criss-crossed lines and figures — if he had formed, for his consolation, that habit, it was really not a little because of the charm of his having encountered and recognised, in the vast wilderness of the wholesale, breaking through the mere gross generalisation of wealth and force and success, a small still scene where items and shades, all delicate things, kept the sharpness of the notes of a high voice perfectly trained, and where economy hung about like the scent of a garden. His old friend lived with one maid and herself dusted her relics and trimmed her lamps and polished her silver; she stood off, in the awful modern crush, when she could, but she sallied forth and did battle when the challenge was really to "spirit," the spirit she after all confessed to, proudly and a little shyly, as to that of the better time, that of *their* common, their quite far-away and antediluvian social period and order. She made use of the street-cars when need be, the terrible things that people scrambled for as the panic-stricken at sea scramble for the boats; she affronted, inscrutably, under stress, all the public concussions and ordeals; and yet, with that slim mystifying grace of her appearance, which defied you to say if she were a fair young woman who looked older through trouble, or a fine smooth older one who looked young through successful indifference; with her precious reference, above all, to memories and histories into which he could enter, she was as exquisite for him as some pale pressed flower (a rarity to begin with), and, failing other sweetnesses, she was a sufficient reward of his effort. They had communities of knowledge, "their" knowledge (this discriminating possessive was always on her lips) of presences of the other age, presences all overlaid, in his case, by the experience of a man and the freedom of a wanderer, overlaid by pleasure, by infidelity, by passages of life that were strange and dim to her, just by "Europe" in short, but still unobscured, still exposed and cherished, under that pious visitation of the spirit from which she had never been diverted.

She had come with him one day to see how his "apartment-house" was rising; he had helped her over gaps and explained to her plans, and while they were there had happened to have, before her, a brief but lively discussion with the man in charge, the representative of the building-firm that had undertaken his work. He had found himself quite "standing-up" to this personage over a failure on the latter's part to observe some detail of one of their noted conditions, and had so lucidly argued his case that, besides ever so prettily flushing, at the time, for sympathy in his triumph, she had afterwards said to him (though to a slightly greater effect of irony) that he had clearly for too many years neglected a real gift. If he had but stayed at home he would have anticipated the inventor of the sky-scraper. If he had but stayed at home he would have discovered his genius in time really to start some new variety of awful architectural hare and run it till it burrowed in a gold-mine. He was to remember these words, while the weeks elapsed, for the small silver ring they had sounded over the queerest and deepest of his own lately most disguised and most muffled vibrations.

It had begun to be present to him after the first fortnight, it had broken out with the oddest abruptness, this particular wanton wonderment: it met him there — and this was the image under which he himself judged the matter, or at least, not a little, thrilled and flushed with it — very much as he might have been met by some strange figure, some unexpected occupant, at a turn of one of the dim passages of an empty house. The quaint analogy quite hauntingly remained with him, when he didn't indeed rather improve it by a still intenser form: that of his opening a door behind which he would have made sure of finding nothing, a door into a room shuttered and void, and yet so coming, with a great suppressed start, on some quite erect confronting presence, something planted in the middle of the place and facing him through the dusk. After that visit to the house in construction he walked with his companion to see the other and always so much the better one, which in the eastward direction formed one of the corners, the "jolly" one precisely, of the street now so generally dishonoured and disfigured in its westward reaches, and of the comparatively conservative Avenue. The Avenue still had pretensions, as Miss Staverton said, to decency; the old people had mostly gone, the old names were unknown, and here and there an old association seemed to stray, all vaguely, like some very aged person, out too late, whom you might meet and feel the impulse to watch or follow, in kindness, for safe restoration to shelter.

They went in together, our friends; he admitted himself with his key, as he kept no one there, he explained, preferring, for his reasons, to leave the place empty, under a simple arrangement with a good woman living in the neighbourhood and who came for a daily hour to open windows and dust and sweep. Spencer Brydon had his reasons and was growingly aware of them; they seemed to him better each time he was there, though he didn't name them all to his companion, any more than he told her as yet how often, how quite absurdly often, he himself came. He only let her see for the present, while they walked through the great blank rooms, that absolute vacancy reigned and that, from top to bottom, there was nothing but Mrs. Muldoon's broomstick, in a corner, to tempt the burglar. Mrs. Muldoon was then on the premises, and she loquaciously attended the visitors, preceding them from room to room and pushing back shutters and throwing up sashes — all to show them, as she remarked, how little there was to see. There was little indeed to see in the great gaunt shell where the main dispositions and the general apportionment of space, the style of an age of ampler allowances, had nevertheless for its master their honest pleading message, affecting him as some good old servant's, some lifelong retainer's appeal for a character, or even for a retiring-pension; yet it was also a remark of Mrs. Muldoon's that, glad as she was to oblige him by her noonday round, there was a request she greatly hoped he would never make of her. If he should wish her for any reason to come in after dark she would just tell him, if he "plased," that he must ask it of somebody else.

The fact that there was nothing to see didn't militate for the worthy woman against what one *might* see, and she put it frankly to Miss Staverton that no lady could be expected to like, could she? "craping up to thim top storeys in the ayvil hours." The gas and the electric light were off the house, and she fairly evoked a gruesome vision of her march through the great grey rooms — so many of them as there were too! — with her glimmering taper. Miss Staverton met her honest glare with a smile and the profession that she herself certainly would recoil from such an adventure. Spencer Brydon meanwhile held his peace — for the moment; the question of the "evil" hours in his old home had already become too grave for him. He had begun some time since to "crape," and he knew just why a packet of candles addressed to that pursuit had been stowed by his own hand, three weeks before, at the back of a drawer of the fine old sideboard that occupied, as a "fixture," the deep recess in the dining-room. Just now he laughed at his companions — quickly however changing the subject; for the reason that, in the first place, his laugh struck him even at that moment as starting the odd echo, the conscious human resonance (he scarce knew how to qualify it) that sounds made while he was there alone sent back to his ear or his fancy; and that, in the second, he imagined Alice Staverton for the instant on the point of asking him, with a divination, if he ever so prowled. There were divinations he was unprepared for, and he had at all events averted enquiry by the time Mrs. Muldoon had left them, passing on to other parts.

There was happily enough to say, on so consecrated a spot, that could be said freely and fairly; so that a whole train of declarations was precipitated by his friend's having herself broken out, after a yearning look round: "But I hope you don't mean they want you to pull *this* to pieces!" His answer came, promptly, with his re-awakened wrath: it was of course exactly what they wanted, and what they were "at" him for, daily, with the iteration of people who couldn't for their life understand a man's liability to decent feelings. He had found the place, just as it stood and beyond what he could express, an interest and a joy. There were values other than the beastly rent-values, and in

short, in short — ! But it was thus Miss Staverton took him up. "In short you're to make so good a thing of your sky-scraper that, living in luxury on *those* ill-gotten gains, you can afford for a while to be sentimental here!" Her smile had for him, with the words, the particular mild irony with which he found half her talk suffused; an irony without bitterness and that came, exactly, from her having so much imagination — not, like the cheap sarcasms with which one heard most people, about the world of "society," bid for the reputation of cleverness, from nobody's really having any. It was agreeable to him at this very moment to be sure that when he had answered, after a brief demur, "Well yes: so, precisely, you may put it!" her imagination would still do him justice. He explained that even if never a dollar were to come to him from the other house he would nevertheless cherish this one; and he dwelt, further, while they lingered and wandered, on the fact of the stupefaction he was already exciting, the positive mystification he felt himself create.

He spoke of the value of all he read into it, into the mere sight of the walls, mere shapes of the rooms, mere sound of the floors, mere feel, in his hand, of the old silver-plated knobs of the several mahogany doors, which suggested the pressure of the palms of the dead; the seventy years of the past in fine that these things represented, the annals of nearly three generations, counting his grandfa-

797

The Jolly Corner

ther's, the one that had ended there, and the impalpable ashes of his long-extinct youth, afloat in the very air like microscopic motes. She listened to everything; she was a woman who answered intimately but who utterly didn't chatter. She scattered abroad therefore no cloud of words; she could assent, she could agree, above all she could encourage, without doing that. Only at the last she went a little further than he had done himself. "And then how do you know? You may still, after all, want to live here." It rather indeed pulled him up, for it wasn't what he had been thinking, at least in her sense of the words. "You mean I may decide to stay on for the sake of it?"

"Well, *with* such a home — !" But, quite beautifully, she had too much tact to dot so monstrous an *i*, and it was precisely an illustration of the way she didn't rattle. How could any one — of any wit — insist on any one else's "wanting" to live in New York?

"Oh," he said, "I *might* have lived here (since I had my opportunity early in life); I might have put in here all these years. Then everything would have been different enough — and, I dare say, 'funny' enough. But that's another matter. And then the beauty of it — I mean of my perversity, of my refusal to agree to a 'deal' — is just in the total absence of a reason. Don't you see that if I had a reason about the matter at all it would *have* to be the other way, and

would then be inevitably a reason of dollars? There are no reasons here *but* of dollars. Let us therefore have none whatever — not the ghost of one."

They were back in the hall then for departure, but from where they stood the vista was large, through an open door, into the great square main saloon, with its almost antique felicity of brave spaces between windows. Her eyes came back from that reach and met his own a moment. "Are you very sure the 'ghost' of one doesn't, much rather, serve — ?"

He had a positive sense of turning pale. But it was as near as they were then to come. For he made answer, he believed, between a glare and a grin: "Oh ghosts — of course the place must swarm with them! I should be ashamed of it if it didn't. Poor Mrs. Muldoon's right, and it's why I haven't asked her to do more than look in."

Miss Staverton's gaze again lost itself, and things she didn't utter, it was clear, came and went in her mind. She might even for the minute, off there in the fine room, have imagined some element dimly gathering. Simplified like the death-mask of a handsome face, it perhaps produced for her just then an effect akin to the stir of an expression in the "set" commemorative plaster. Yet whatever her impression may have been she produced instead a vague platitude. "Well, if it were only furnished and lived in — !"

She appeared to imply that in

The Jolly Corner

case of its being still furnished he might have been a little less opposed to the idea of a return. But she passed straight into the vestibule, as if to leave her words behind her, and the next moment he had opened the house-door and was standing with her on the steps. He closed the door and, while he re-pocketed his key, looking up and down, they took in the comparatively harsh actuality of the Avenue, which reminded him of the assault of the outer light of the Desert on the traveller emerging from an Egyptian tomb. But he risked before they stepped into the street his gathered answer to her speech. "For me it *is* lived in. For me it *is* furnished." At which it was easy for her to sigh "Ah yes — !" all vaguely and discreetly; since his parents and his favourite sister, to say nothing of other kin, in numbers, had run their course and met their end there. That represented, within the walls, ineffaceable life.

It was a few days after this that, during an hour passed with her again, he had expressed his impatience of the too flattering curiosity — among the people he met — about his appreciation of New York. He had arrived at none at all that was socially producible, and as for that matter of his "thinking" (thinking the better or the worse of anything there) he was wholly taken up with one subject of thought. It was mere vain egoism, and it was moreover, if she liked, a morbid obsession. He

found all things come back to the question of what he personally might have been, how he might have led his life and "turned out," if he had not so, at the outset, given it up. And confessing for the first time to the intensity within him of this absurd speculation — which but proved also, no doubt, the habit of too selfishly thinking — he affirmed the impotence there of any other source of interest, any other native appeal. "What would it have made of me, what would it have made of me? I keep for ever wondering, all idiotically; as if I could possibly know! I see what it has made of dozens of others, those I meet, and it positively aches within me, to the point of exasperation, that it would have made something of me as well. Only I can't make out *what,* and the worry of it, the small rage of curiosity never to be satisfied, brings back what I remember to have felt, once or twice, after judging best, for reasons, to burn some important letter unopened. I've been sorry, I've hated it — I've never known what was in the letter. You may of course say it's a trifle — !"

"I don't say it's a trifle," Miss Staverton gravely interrupted.

She was seated by her fire, and before her, on his feet and restless, he turned to and fro between this intensity of his idea and a fitful and unseeing inspection, through his single eye-glass, of the dear little old objects on her chimney-piece. Her interruption made him for an instant look at her harder. "I shouldn't care if you did!" he laughed, however; "and it's only a figure, at any rate, for the way I now feel. *Not* to have followed my perverse young course — and almost in the teeth of my father's curse, as I may say; not to have kept it up, so, 'over there,' from that day to this, without a doubt or a pang; not, above all, to have liked it, to have loved it, so much, loved it, no doubt, with such an abysmal conceit of my own preference: some variation from *that*, I say, must have produced some different effect for my life and for my 'form.' I should have stuck here — if it had been possible; and I was too young, at twenty-three, to judge, *pour deux sous,* whether it *were* possible. If I had waited I might have seen it was, and then I might have been, by staying here, something nearer to one of these types who have been hammered so hard and made so keen by their conditions. It isn't that I admire them so much — the question of any charm in them, or of any charm, beyond that of the rank money-passion, exerted by their conditions *for* them, has nothing to do with the matter: it's only a question of what fantastic, yet perfectly possible, development of my own nature I mayn't have missed. It comes over me that I had then a strange *alter ego* deep down somewhere within me, as the full-blown flower is in the small tight bud, and that I just took the course, I just transferred him to the climate, that blighted him for once and for ever."

"And you wonder about the flower," Miss Staverton said. "So do I, if you want to know; and so I've been wondering these several weeks. I believe in the flower," she continued, "I feel it would have been quite splendid, quite huge and monstrous."

"Monstrous above all!" her visitor echoed; "and I imagine, by the same stroke, quite hideous and offensive."

"You don't believe that," she returned; "if you did you wouldn't wonder. You'd know, and that would be enough for you. What you feel — and what I feel *for* you — is that you'd have had power."

"You'd have liked me that way?" he asked.

She barely hung fire. "How should I not have liked you?"

"I see. You'd have liked me, have preferred me, a billionaire!"

"How should I not have liked you?" she simply again asked.

He stood before her still — her question kept him motionless. He took it in, so much there was of it; and indeed his not otherwise meeting it testified to that. "I know at least what I am," he simply went on; "the other side of the medal's clear enough. I've not been edifying — I believe I'm thought in a hundred quarters to have been barely decent. I've followed strange paths and worshipped strange gods; it must have come to you again and again — in fact you've admitted to me as much — that I was leading, at any time these thirty years, a selfish frivolous scandalous life. And you see what it has made of me."

She just waited, smiling at him. "You see what it has made of *me*."

"Oh you're a person whom nothing can have altered. You were born to be what you are, anywhere, anyway: you've the perfection nothing else could have blighted. And don't you see how, without my exile, I shouldn't have been waiting till now — ?" But he pulled up for the strange pang.

"The great thing to see," she presently said, "seems to me to be that it has spoiled nothing. It hasn't spoiled your being here at last. It hasn't spoiled this. It hasn't spoiled your speaking — " She also however faltered.

He wondered at everything her controlled emotion might mean. "Do you believe then — too dreadfully! — that I *am* as good as I might ever have been?"

"Oh no! Far from it!" With which she got up from her chair and was nearer to him. "But I don't care," she smiled.

"You mean I'm good enough?"

She considered a little. "Will you believe it if I say so? I mean will you let that settle your question for you?" And then as if making out in his face that he drew back from this, that he had some idea which, however absurd, he couldn't yet bargain away: "Oh you don't care either — but very differently: you don't care for anything but yourself."

Spencer Brydon recognised it — it was in fact what he had absolutely professed. Yet he importantly qualified. "*He* isn't myself. He's the just so totally other person. But I do want to see him," he added. "And I can. And I shall."

Their eyes met for a minute while he guessed from something in hers that she divined his strange sense. But neither of them otherwise expressed it, and her apparent understanding, with no protesting shock, no easy derision, touched him more deeply than anything yet, constituting for his stifled perversity, on the spot, an element that was like breatheable air. What she said however was unexpected. "Well, *I've* seen him."

"You — ?"

"I've seen him in a dream."

"Oh a 'dream' — !" It let him down.

"But twice over," she continued. "I saw him as I see you now."

"You've dreamed the same dream — ?"

"Twice over," she repeated. "The very same."

This did somehow a little speak to him, as it also gratified him. "You dream about me at that rate?"

"Ah about *him!*" she smiled.

His eyes again sounded her. "Then you know all about him." And as she said nothing more: "What's the wretch like?"

She hesitated, and it was as if he were pressing her so hard that, resisting for reasons of her own, she had to turn away. "I'll tell you some other time!"

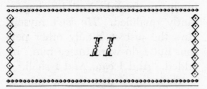

IT was after this that there was most of a virtue for him, most of a cultivated charm, most of a preposterous secret thrill, in the particular form of surrender to his obsession and of address to what he more and more believed to be his privilege. It was what in these weeks he was living for — since he really felt life to begin but after Mrs. Muldoon had retired from the scene and, visiting the ample house from attic to cellar, making sure he was alone, he knew himself in safe possession and, as he tacitly expressed it, let himself go. He sometimes came twice in the twenty-four hours; the moments he liked best were those of gathering dusk, of the short autumn twilight; this was the time of which, again and again, be found himself hoping most. Then he could, as seemed to him, most intimately wander and wait, linger and listen, feel his fine attention, never in his life before so fine, on the pulse of the great vague place: he preferred the lampless hour and only wished he might have prolonged each day the deep crepuscular spell. Later — rarely much before midnight, but then for a considerable vigil — he watched with his glimmering light; moving slowly, holding it high, playing it far, rejoicing above

all, as much as he might, in open vistas, reaches of communication between rooms and by passages; the long straight chance or show, as he would have called it, for the revelation he pretended to invite. It was a practice he found he could perfectly "work" without exciting remark; no one was in the least the wiser for it; even Alice Staverton, who was moreover a well of discretion, didn't quite fully imagine.

He let himself in and let himself out with the assurance of calm proprietorship; and accident so far favoured him that, if a fat Avenue "officer" had happened on occasion to see him entering at eleven-thirty, he had never yet, to the best of his belief, been noticed as emerging at two. He walked there on the crisp November nights, arrived regularly at the evening's end; it was as easy to do this after dining out as to take his way to a club or to his hotel. When he left his club, if he hadn't been dining out, it was ostensibly to go to his hotel; and when he left his hotel, if he had spent a part of the evening there, it was ostensibly to go to his club. Everything was easy in fine; everything conspired and promoted: there was truly even in the strain of his experience something that glossed over, something that salved and simplified, all the rest of consciousness. He circulated, talked, renewed, loosely and pleasantly, old relations — met indeed, so far as he could, new expectations and seemed to make out on the whole that in spite of the career, of such different contacts, which he had spoken of to Miss Staverton as ministering so little, for those who might have watched it, to edification, he was positively rather liked than not. He was a dim secondary social success — and all with people who had truly not an idea of him. It was all mere surface sound, this murmur of their welcome, this popping of their corks — just as his gestures of response were the extravagant shadows, emphatic in proportion as they meant little, of some game of *ombres chinoises*. He projected himself all day, in thought, straight over the bristling line of hard unconscious heads and into the other, the real, the waiting life; the life that, as soon as he had heard behind him the click of his great house-door, began for him, on the jolly corner, as beguilingly as the slow opening bars of some rich music follows the tap of the conductor's wand.

He always caught the first effect of the steel point of his stick on the old marble of the hall pavement, large black-and-white squares that he remembered as the admiration of his childhood and that had then made in him, as he now saw, for the growth of an early conception of style. This effect was the dim reverberating tinkle as of some far-off bell hung who should say where? — in the depths of the house, of the past, of that mystical other world that might have flourished for him had he not, for weal or woe, abandoned it. On this impression he did ever the same thing; he put his stick noiselessly away in a corner — feeling the place once more in the likeness of some great glass bowl, all precious concave crystal, set delicately humming by the play of a moist finger round its edge. The concave crystal held, as it were, this mystical other world, and the indescribably fine murmur of its rim was the sigh there, the scarce audible pathetic wail to his strained ear, of all the old baffled forsworn possibilities. What he did therefore by this appeal of his hushed presence was to wake them into such measure of ghostly life as they might still enjoy. They were shy, all but unappeasably shy, but they weren't really sinister; at least they weren't as he had hitherto felt them — before they had taken the Form he so yearned to make them take, the Form he at moments saw himself in the light of fairly hunting on tiptoe, the points of his evening-shoes, from room to room and from storey to storey.

That was the essence of his vision — which was all rank folly, if one would, while he was out of the house and otherwise occupied, but which took on the last verisimilitude as soon as he was placed and posted. He knew what he meant and what he wanted; it was as clear as the figure on a cheque presented in demand for cash. His *alter ego* "walked" — that was the note of his image of him, while his image of his motive for his own odd pastime was the desire to waylay him and meet him. He roamed, slowly, warily, but all restlessly, he himself did — Mrs. Muldoon had been right, absolutely, with her figure of their "craping"; and the presence he watched for would roam restlessly too. But it would be as cautious and as shifty; the conviction of its probable, in fact its already quite sensible, quite audible evasion of pursuit grew for him from night to night, laying on him finally a rigour to which nothing in his life had been comparable. It had been the theory of many superficially-judging persons, he knew, that he was wasting that life in a surrender to sensations, but he had tasted of no pleasure so fine as his actual tension, had been introduced to no sport that demanded at once the patience and the nerve of this stalking of a creature more subtle, yet at bay perhaps more formidable, than any beast of the forest. The terms, the comparisons, the very practices of the chase positively came again into play; there were even moments when passages of his occasional experience as a sportsman, stirred memories, from his younger time, of moor and mountain and desert, revived for him — and to the increase of his keenness — by the tremendous force of analogy. He found himself at moments — once he had placed his single light on some mantel-shelf or in some recess — stepping back into shelter or shade, effacing himself behind a door or in an embrasure, as he had sought of old the vantage of rock and tree; he found himself holding his breath and living in the joy of the instant, the supreme suspense created by big game alone.

He wasn't afraid (though putting himself the question as he believed gentlemen on Bengal tiger-shoots or in close quarters with the great bear of the Rockies had been known to confess to having put it); and this indeed — since here at least he might be frank! — because of the impression, so intimate and so strange, that he himself produced as yet a dread, produced certainly a strain, beyond the liveliest he was likely to feel. They fell for him into categories, they fairly became familiar, the signs, for his own perception, of the alarm his presence and his vigilance created; though leaving him always to remark, portentously, on his probably having formed a relation, his probably enjoying a consciousness, unique in the experience of man. People enough, first and last, had been in terror of apparitions, but who had ever before so turned the tables and become himself, in the apparitional world, an incalculable terror? He might have found this sublime had he quite dared to think of it; but he didn't too much insist, truly, on that side of his privilege. With habit and repetition he gained to an extraordinary degree the power to penetrate the dusk of distances and the darkness of corners, to resolve back into their innocence the treacheries of uncertain light, the evil-looking forms taken in the gloom by mere shadows, by accidents of the air, by shifting effects of perspective; putting down his dim luminary he could still wander on without it, pass into other rooms and, only knowing it was there behind him in case of need, see his way about, visually project for his purpose a comparative clearness. It made him feel, this acquired faculty, like some monstrous stealthy cat; he wondered if he would have glared at these moments with large shining yellow eyes, and what it mightn't verily be, for the poor hard-pressed *alter ego,* to be confronted with such a type.

He liked however the open shutters; he opened everywhere those Mrs. Muldoon had closed, closing them as carefully afterwards, so that she shouldn't notice: he liked — oh this he did like, and above all in the upper rooms! — the sense of the hard silver of the autumn stars through the window-panes, and scarcely less the flare of the street-lamps below, the white electric lustre which it would have taken curtains to keep out. This was human actual social; this was of the world he had lived in, and he was more at his ease certainly for the countenance, coldly general and impersonal, that all the while and in spite of his detachment it seemed to give him. He had support of course mostly in the rooms at the wide front and the prolonged side; it failed him considerably in the central shades and the parts at the back. But if he sometimes, on his rounds, was glad of his optical reach, so none the less often the rear of the house affected him as the very jungle of his prey. The place was there more subdivided; a large "extension" in particular, where small rooms for servants had been multiplied, abounded in nooks and corners, in closets and passages, in the ramifications especially of an ample back staircase over which he leaned, many a time, to look far down — not deterred from his gravity even while aware that he might, for a spectator, have figured some solemn simpleton playing at hide-and-seek. Outside in fact he might himself make that ironic *rapprochement;* but within the walls, and in spite of the clear windows, his consistency was proof against the cynical light of New York.

It had belonged to that idea of the exasperated consciousness of his victim to become a real test for him; since he had quite put it to himself from the first that, oh distinctly! he could "cultivate" his whole perception. He had felt it as above all open to cultivation — which indeed was but another name for his manner of spending his time. He was bringing it on, bringing it to perfection, by practice; in consequence of which it had grown so fine that he was now aware of impressions, attestations of his general postulate, that couldn't have broken upon him at once. This was the case more specifically with a phenomenon at last quite frequent for him in the upper rooms, the recognition — absolutely unmistakeable, and by a turn dating from a particular hour, his resumption of his campaign

The Jolly Corner

after a diplomatic drop, a calculated absence of three nights — of
his being definitely followed,
tracked at a distance carefully tak-
en and to the express end that he
should the less confidently, less ar-
rogantly, appear to himself merely
to pursue. It worried, it finally
quite broke him up, for it proved,
of all the conceivable impressions,
the one least suited to his book.
He was kept in sight while remaining himself — as regards the
essence of his position — sightless,
and his only recourse then was in
abrupt turns, rapid recoveries of
ground. He wheeled about, retracing his steps, as if he might so
catch in his face at least the stirred
air of some other quick revolution.
It was indeed true that his fully
dislocalised thought of these ma-
nœuvres recalled to him Panta-
loon, at the Christmas farce, buf-
feted and tricked from behind by
ubiquitous Harlequin; but it left
intact the influence of the conditions themselves each time he was
re-exposed to them, so that in fact
this association, had he suffered it
to become constant, would on a
certain side have but ministered
to his intenser gravity. He had
made, as I have said, to create on
the premises the baseless sense of
a reprieve, his three absences; and
the result of the third was to confirm the after-effect of the second.

On his return, that night — the
night succeeding his last intermission — he stood in the hall and
looked up the staircase with a certainty more intimate than any he
had yet known. "He's *there*, at the
top, and waiting — not, as in general, falling back for disappearance. He's holding his ground, and
it's the first time — which is a proof,
isn't it? that something has happened for him." So Brydon argued
with his hand on the banister and
his foot on the lowest stair; in
which position he felt as never before the air chilled by his logic. He
himself turned cold in it, for he
seemed of a sudden to know
what now was involved. "Harder
pressed? — yes, he takes it in, with
its thus making clear to him that
I've come, as they say, 'to stay.' He
finally doesn't like and can't bear
it, in the sense, I mean, that his
wrath, his menaced interest, now
balances with his dread. I've hunted him till he has 'turned': that, up
there, is what has happened — he's
the fanged or the antlered animal
brought at last to bay." There
came to him, as I say — but determined by an influence beyond my
notation! — the acuteness of this
certainty; under which however
the next moment he had broken
into a sweat that he would as little
have consented to attribute to fear
as he would have dared immediately to act upon it for enterprise.
It marked none the less a prodigious thrill, a thrill that represented sudden dismay, no doubt, but
also represented, and with the self-
same throb, the strangest, the most
joyous, possibly the next minute almost the proudest, duplication of
consciousness.

"He has been dodging, retreating, hiding, but now, worked up
to anger, he'll fight!" — this intense

impression made a single mouthful, as it were, of terror and applause. But what was wondrous was that the applause, for the felt fact, was so eager, since, if it was his other self he was running to earth, this ineffable identity was thus in the last resort not unworthy of him. It bristled there — somewhere near at hand, however unseen still — as the hunted thing, even as the trodden worm of the adage *must* at last bristle; and Brydon at this instant tasted probably of a sensation more complex than had ever before found itself consistent with sanity. It was as if it would have shamed him that a character so associated with his own should triumphantly succeed in just skulking, should to the end not risk the open; so that the drop of this danger was, on the spot, a great lift of the whole situation. Yet with another rare shift of the same subtlety he was already trying to measure by how much more he himself might now be in peril of fear; so rejoicing that he could, in another form, actively inspire that fear, and simultaneously quaking for the form in which he might passively know it.

The apprehension of knowing it must after a little have grown in him, and the strangest moment of his adventure perhaps, the most memorable or really most interesting, afterwards, of his crisis, was the lapse of certain instants of concentrated conscious *combat*, the sense of a need to hold on to something, even after the manner of a man slipping and slipping on some awful incline; the vivid impulse, above all, to move, to act, to charge, somehow and upon something — to show himself, in a word, that he wasn't afraid. The state of "holding-on" was thus the state to which he was momentarily reduced; if there had been anything, in the great vacancy, to seize, he would presently have been aware of having clutched it as he might under a shock at home have clutched the nearest chair-back. He had been surprised at any rate — of this he *was* aware — into something unprecedented since his original appropriation of the place; he had closed his eyes, held them tight, for a long minute, as with that instinct of dismay and that terror of vision. When he opened them the room, the other contiguous rooms, extraordinarily, seemed lighter — so light, almost, that at first he took the change for day. He stood firm, however that might be, just where he had paused; his resistance had helped him — it was as if there were something he had tided over. He knew after a little what this was — it had been in the imminent danger of flight. He had stiffened his will against going; without this he would have made for the stairs, and it seemed to him that, still with his eyes closed, he would have descended them, would have known how, straight and swiftly, to the bottom.

Well, as he had held out, here he was — still at the top, among the more intricate upper rooms and with the gauntlet of the others, of all the rest of the house, still to run when it should be his time to go. He would go at his time — only at his time: didn't he go every night very much at the same hour? He took out his watch — there was light for that: it was scarcely a quarter past one, and he had never withdrawn so soon. He reached his lodgings for the most part at two — with his walk of a quarter of an hour. He would wait for the last quarter — he wouldn't stir till then; and he kept his watch there with his eyes on it, reflecting while he held it that this deliberate wait, a wait with an effort, which he recognised, would serve perfectly for the attestation he desired to make. It would prove his courage — unless indeed the latter might most be proved by his budging at last from his place. What he mainly felt now was that, since he hadn't originally scuttled, he had his dignities — which had never in his life seemed so many — all to preserve and to carry aloft. This was before him in truth as a physical image, an image almost worthy of an age of greater romance. That remark indeed glimmered for him only to glow the next instant with a finer light; since what age of romance, after all, could have matched either the state of his mind or, "objectively," as they said, the wonder of his situation? The only difference would have been that, brandishing his dignities over his head as in a parchment scroll, he might then — that is in the heroic time — have proceeded downstairs with a drawn sword in his other grasp.

At present, really, the light he had set down on the mantel of the next room would have to figure his sword; which utensil, in the course of a minute, he had taken the requisite number of steps to possess himself of. The door between the rooms was open, and from the second another door opened to a third. These rooms, as he remembered, gave all three upon a common corridor as well, but there was a fourth, beyond them, without issue save through the preceding. To have moved, to have heard his step again, was appreciably a help; though even in recognising this he lingered once more a little by the chimney-piece on which his light had rested. When he next moved, just hesitating where to turn, he found himself considering a circumstance that, after his first and comparatively vague apprehension of it, produced in him the start that often attends some pang of recollection, the violent shock of having ceased happily to forget. He had come into sight of the door in which the brief chain of communication ended and which he now surveyed from the nearer threshold, the one not directly facing it. Placed at some distance to the left of this point, it would have admitted him to the last room of the four, the room without other approach or egress, had it not, to his intimate conviction, been closed *since* his former visitation, the matter probably of a quarter of an hour before. He stared with all his eyes at the wonder of the fact, arrested again where he stood and again holding his breath while he sounded its sense. Surely it had been *subsequently* closed — that is it had been on his previous passage indubitably open!

He took it full in the face that something had happened between — that he couldn't not have noticed before (by which he meant on his original tour of all the rooms that evening) that such a barrier had exceptionally presented itself. He had indeed since that moment undergone an agitation so extraordinary that it might have muddled for him any earlier view; and he tried to convince himself that he might perhaps then have gone into the room and, inadvertently, automatically, on coming out, have drawn the door after him. The difficulty was that this exactly was what he never did; it was against his whole policy, as he might have said, the essence of which was to keep vistas clear. He had them from the first, as he was well aware, quite on the brain: the strange apparition, at the far end of one of them, of his baffled "prey" (which had become by so sharp an irony so little the term now to apply!) was the form of success his imagination had most cherished, projecting into it always a refinement of beauty. He had known fifty times the start of perception that had afterwards dropped; had fifty times gasped to himself "There!" under some fond brief hallucination. The house, as the case stood, admirably lent itself; he might wonder at the taste, the native architecture of the par-

ticular time, which could rejoice so in the multiplication of doors — the opposite extreme to the modern, the actual almost complete proscription of them; but it had fairly contributed to provoke this obsession of the presence encountered telescopically, as he might say, focussed and studied in diminishing perspective and as by a rest for the elbow.

It was with these considerations that his present attention was charged — they perfectly availed to make what he saw portentous. He *couldn't*, by any lapse, have blocked that aperture; and if he hadn't, if it was unthinkable, why what else was clear but that there had been another agent? Another agent? — he had been catching, as he felt, a moment back, the very breath of him; but when had he been so close as in this simple, this logical, this completely personal act? It was so logical, that is, that one might have *taken* it for personal; yet for what did Brydon take it, he asked himself, while, softly panting, he felt his eyes almost leave their sockets. Ah this time at last they *were*, the two, the opposed projections of him, in presence; and this time, as much as one would, the question of danger loomed. With it rose, as not before, the question of courage — for what he knew the blank face of the door to say to him was "Show us how much you have!" It stared, it glared back at him with that challenge; it put to him the two alternatives: should he just push it open or not? Oh to have this consciousness was to *think* — and to think, Brydon knew, as he stood there, was, with the lapsing moments, not to have acted! Not to have acted — that was the misery and the pang — was even still not to act; was in fact *all* to feel the thing in another, in a new and terrible way. How long did he pause and how long did he debate? There was presently nothing to measure it; for his vibration had already changed — as just by the effect of its intensity. Shut up there, at bay, defiant, and with the prodigy of the thing palpably proveably *done*, thus giving notice like some stark signboard — under that accession of accent the situation itself had turned; and Brydon at last remarkably made up his mind on what it had turned to.

It had turned altogether to a different admonition; to a supreme hint, for him, of the value of Discretion! This slowly dawned, no doubt — for it could take its time; so perfectly, on his threshold, had he been stayed, so little as yet had he either advanced or retreated. It was the strangest of all things that now when, by his taking ten steps and applying his hand to a latch, or even his shoulder and his knee, if necessary, to a panel, all the hunger of his prime need might have been met, his high curiosity crowned, his unrest assuaged — it was amazing, but it was also exquisite and rare, that insistence should have, at a touch, quite dropped from him. Discretion — he jumped at that; and yet not,

verily, at such a pitch, because it saved his nerves or his skin, but because, much more valuably, it saved the situation. When I say he "jumped" at it I feel the consonance of this term with the fact that — at the end indeed of I know not how long — he did move again, he crossed straight to the door. He wouldn't touch it — it seemed now that he might *if* he would: he would only just wait there a little, to show, to prove, that he wouldn't. He had thus another station, close to the thin partition by which revelation was denied him; but with his eyes bent and his hands held off in a mere intensity of stillness. He listened as if there had been something to hear, but this attitude, while it lasted, was his own communication. "If you won't then — good: I spare you and I give up. You affect me as by the appeal positively for pity: you convince me that for reasons rigid and sublime — what do I know? — we both of us should have suffered. I respect them then, and, though moved and privileged as, I believe, it has never been given to man, I retire, I renounce — never, on my honour, to try again. So rest for ever — and let *me!*"

That, for Brydon was the deep sense of this last demonstration — solemn, measured, directed, as he felt it to be. He brought it to a close, he turned away; and now verily he knew how deeply he had been stirred. He retraced his steps, taking up his candle, burnt, he observed, well-nigh to the socket, and marking again, lighten it as

810

he would, the distinctness of his footfall; after which, in a moment, he knew himself at the other side of the house. He did here what he had not yet done at these hours — he opened half a casement, one of those in the front, and let in the air of the night; a thing he would have taken at any time previous for a sharp rupture of his spell. His spell was broken now, and it didn't matter — broken by his concession and his surrender, which made it idle henceforth that he should ever come back. The empty street — its other life so marked even by the great lamplit vacancy — was within call, within touch; he stayed there as to be in it again, high above it though he was still perched; he watched as for some comforting common fact, some vulgar human note, the passage of a scavenger or a thief, some nightbird however base. He would have blessed that sign of life; he would have welcomed positively the slow approach of his friend the policeman, whom he had hitherto only sought to avoid, and was not sure that if the patrol had come into sight he mightn't have felt the impulse to get into relation with it, to hail it, on some pretext, from his fourth floor.

The pretext that wouldn't have been too silly or too compromising, the explanation that would have saved his dignity and kept his name, in such a case, out of the papers, was not definite to him: he was so occupied with the thought of recording his Discretion — as an effect of the vow he had just uttered to his intimate adversary — that the importance of this loomed large and something had overtaken all ironically his sense of proportion. If there had been a ladder applied to the front of the house, even one of the vertiginous perpendiculars employed by painters and roofers and sometimes left standing overnight, he would have managed somehow, astride of the window-sill, to compass by outstretched leg and arm that mode of descent. If there had been some such uncanny thing as he had found in his room at hotels, a workable fire-escape in the form of notched cable or a canvas shoot, he would have availed himself of it as a proof — well, of his present delicacy. He nursed that sentiment, as the question stood, a little in vain, and even — at the end of he scarce knew, once more, how long — found it, as by the action on his mind of the failure of response of the outer world, sinking back to vague anguish. It seemed to him he had waited an age for some stir of the great grim hush; the life of the town was itself under a spell — so unnaturally, up and down the whole prospect of known and rather ugly objects, the blankness and the silence lasted. Had they ever, he asked himself, the hard-faced houses, which had begun to look livid in the dim dawn, had they ever spoken so little to any need of his spirit? Great builded voids, great crowded stillnesses put on, often, in the heart of cities, for the small hours, a sort of sinister mask, and it was of this large collective negation that Brydon presently became conscious — all the more that the break of day was, almost incredibly, now at hand, proving to him what a night he had made of it.

He looked again at his watch, saw what had become of his time-values (he had taken hours for minutes — not, as in other tense situations, minutes for hours) and the strange air of the streets was but the weak, the sullen flush of a dawn in which everything was still locked up. His choked appeal from his own open window had been the sole note of life, and he could but break off at last as for a worse despair. Yet while so deeply demoralised he was capable again of an impulse denoting — at least by his present measure — extraordinary resolution; of retracing his steps to the spot where he had turned cold with the extinction of his last pulse of doubt as to there being in the place another presence than his own. This required an effort strong enough to sicken him; but he had his reason, which overmastered for the moment everything else. There was the whole of the rest of the house to traverse, and how should he screw himself to that if the door he had seen closed were at present open? He could hold to the idea that the closing had practically been for him an act of mercy, a chance offered him to descend, depart, get off the ground and never again profane it. This conception held together, it worked; but what it meant for him depended now clearly on the amount of forbear-

ance his recent action, or rather his recent inaction, had engendered. The image of the "presence," whatever it was, waiting there for him to go — this image had not yet been so concrete for his nerves as when he stopped short of the point at which certainty would have come to him. For, with all his resolution, or more exactly with all his dread, he did stop short — he hung back from really seeing. The risk was too great and his fear too definite: it took at this moment an awful specific form.

He knew — yes, as he had never known anything — that, *should* he see the door open, it would all too abjectly be the end of him. It would mean that the agent of his shame — for his shame was the deep abjection — was once more at large and in general possession; and what glared him thus in the face was the act that this would determine for him. It would send him straight about to the window he had left open, and by that window, be long ladder and dangling rope as absent as they would, he saw himself uncontrollably insanely fatally take his way to the street. The hideous chance of this he at least could avert; but he could only avert it by recoiling in time from assurance. He had the whole house to deal with, this fact was still there; only he now knew that uncertainty alone could start him. He stole back from where he had checked himself — merely to do so was suddenly like safety — and, making blindly for the greater staircase, left gaping rooms and sounding passages behind. Here was the top of the stairs, with a fine large dim descent and three spacious landings to mark off. His instinct was all for mildness, but his feet were harsh on the floors, and, strangely, when he had in a couple of minutes become aware of this, it counted somehow for help. He couldn't have spoken, the tone of his voice would have scared him, and the common conceit or resource of "whistling in the dark" (whether literally or figuratively) have appeared basely vulgar; yet he liked none the less to hear himself go, and when he had reached his first landing — taking it all with no rush, but quite steadily — that stage of success drew from him a gasp of relief.

The house, withal, seemed immense, the scale of space again inordinate; the open rooms, to no one of which his eyes deflected, gloomed in their shuttered state like mouths of caverns; only the high skylight that formed the crown of the deep well created for him a medium in which he could advance, but which might have been, for queerness of colour, some watery under-world. He tried to think of something noble, as that his property was really grand, a splendid possession; but this nobleness took the form too of the clear delight with which he was finally to sacrifice it. They might come in now, the builders, the destroyers — they might come as soon as they would. At the end of two flights he had dropped to another zone, and from the middle of the third, with only one more left, he recognised the influence of the lower windows, of half-drawn blinds, of the occasional gleam of street-lamps, of the glazed spaces of the vestibule. This was the bottom of the sea, which showed an illumination of its own and which he even saw paved — when at a given moment he drew up to sink a long look over the banisters — with the marble squares of his childhood. By that time indubitably he felt, as he might have said in a commoner cause, better; it had allowed him to stop and draw breath, and the ease increased with the sight of the old black-and-white slabs. But what he most felt was that now surely, with the element of impunity pulling him as by hard firm hands, the case was settled for what he might have seen above had he dared that last look. The closed door, blessedly remote now, was still closed — and he had only in short to reach that of the house.

He came down further, he crossed the passage forming the access to the last flight; and if here again he stopped an instant it was almost for the sharpness of the thrill of assured escape. It made him shut his eyes — which opened again to the straight slope of the remainder of the stairs. Here was impunity still, but impunity almost excessive; inasmuch as the side-lights and the high fan-tracery of the entrance were glimmering straight into the hall; an appearance produced, he the next instant saw, by the fact that the vestibule gaped wide, that the hinged halves of the inner door had been thrown far back. Out of that again the *question* sprang at him, making his eyes, as he felt, half-start from his head, as they had done, at the top of the house, before the sign of the other door. If he had left that one open, hadn't he left this one closed, and wasn't he now in *most* immediate presence of some inconceivable occult activity? It was as sharp, the question, as a knife in his side, but the answer hung fire still and seemed to lose itself in the vague darkness to which the thin admitted dawn, glimmering archwise over the whole outer door, made a semicircular margin, a cold silvery nimbus that seemed to play a little as he looked — to shift and expand and contract.

It was as if there had been something within it, protected by indistinctness and corresponding in extent with the opaque surface behind, the painted panels of the last barrier to his escape, of which the key was in his pocket. The indistinctness mocked him even while he stared, affected him as somehow shrouding or challenging certitude, so that after faltering an instant on his step he let himself go with the sense that here *was* at last something to meet, to touch, to take, to know — something all unnatural and dreadful, but to advance upon which was the condition for him either of liberation or of supreme defeat. The penumbra, dense and dark, was the virtual screen of a figure which stood in it as still as some image erect in a niche or as some black-vizored sentinel guarding a treasure. Brydon was to know afterwards, was to recall and make out, the particular thing he had believed during the rest of his descent. He saw, in its great grey glimmering margin, the central vagueness diminish, and he felt it to be taking the very form toward which, for so many days, the passion of his curiosity had yearned. It gloomed, it loomed, it was something, it was somebody, the prodigy of a personal presence.

Rigid and conscious, spectral yet human, a man of his own substance and stature waited there to measure himself with his power to dismay. This only could it be — this only till he recognised, with his advance, that what made the face dim was the pair of raised hands that covered it and in which, so far from being offered in defiance, it was buried as for dark deprecation. So Brydon, before him, took him in; with every fact of him now, in the higher light, hard and acute — his planted stillness, his vivid truth, his grizzled bent head and white masking hands, his queer actuality of evening-dress, of dangling double eyeglass, of gleaming silk lappet and white linen, of pearl button and gold watch-guard and polished shoe. No portrait by a great modern master could have presented him with more intensity, thrust him out of his frame with more art, as if there had been "treatment," of the consummate sort, in his every shade and salience. The revulsion, for our friend, had become, before he knew it, immense — this drop, in the act of apprehension, to the sense of his adversary's inscrutable manœuvre. That meaning at least, while he gaped, it offered him; for he could but gape at his other self in this other anguish, gape as a proof that *he,* standing there for the achieved, the enjoyed, the triumphant life, couldn't be faced in his triumph. Wasn't the proof in the splendid covering hands, strong and completely spread? — so spread and so intentional that, in spite of a special verity that surpassed every other, the fact that one of these hands had lost two fingers, which were reduced to stumps, as if accidentally shot away, the face was effectually guarded and saved.

"Saved," though, *would* it be? — Brydon breathed his wonder till the very impunity of his attitude and the very insistence of his eyes produced, as he felt, a sudden stir which showed the next instant as a deeper portent, while the head raised itself, the betrayal of a braver purpose. The hands, as he looked, began to move, to open; then, as if deciding in a flash, dropped from the face and left it uncovered and presented. Horror, with the sight, had leaped into Brydon's throat, gasping there in a sound he couldn't utter; for the bared identity was too hideous as *his,* and his glare was the passion of his protest. The face, *that* face, Spencer Brydon's? — he searched it still, but looking away from it in dismay and denial, falling straight from his height of sublimity. It was

unknown, inconceivable, awful, disconnected from any possibility — ! He had been "sold," he inwardly moaned, stalking such game as this: the presence before him was a presence, the horror within him a horror, but the waste of his nights had been only grotesque and the success of his adventure an irony. Such an identity fitted his at *no* point, made its alternative monstrous. A thousand times yes, as it came upon him nearer now — the face was the face of a stranger. It came upon him nearer now, quite as one of those expanding fantastic images projected by the magic lantern of childhood; for the stranger, whoever he might be, evil, odious, blatant, vulgar, had advanced as for aggression, and he knew himself give ground. Then harder pressed still, sick with the force of his shock, and falling back as under the hot breath and the roused passion of a life larger than his own, a rage of personality before which his own collapsed, he felt the whole vision turn to darkness and his very feet give way. His head went round; he was going; he had gone.

III

WHAT had next brought him back, clearly — though after how long? — was Mrs. Muldoon's voice, coming to him from quite near, from so near that he seemed presently to see her as kneeling on the ground before him while he lay looking up at her; himself not wholly on the ground, but half-raised and upheld — conscious, yes, of tenderness of support and, more particularly, of a head pillowed in extraordinary softness and fainly refreshing fragrance. He considered, he wondered, his wit but half at his service; then another face intervened, bending more directly over him, and he finally knew that Alice Staverton had made her lap an ample and perfect cushion to him, and that she had to this end seated herself on the lowest degree of the staircase, the rest of his long person remaining stretched on his old black-and-white slabs. They were cold, these marble squares of his youth; but *he* somehow was not, in this rich return of consciousness — the most wonderful hour, little by little, that he had ever known, leaving him, as it did, so gratefully, so abysmally passive, and yet as with a treasure of intelligence waiting all round him for quiet appropriation; dissolved, he might call it, in the air of the place and producing the golden glow of a late autumn afternoon. He had come back, yes — come back from further away than any man but himself had ever travelled; but it was strange how with this sense what he had come back *to* seemed really the great thing, and as if his prodigious journey had been all for the sake of it. Slowly but surely his consciousness grew, his vision of his state thus completing itself: he had been

miraculously *carried* back — lifted and carefully borne as from where he had been picked up, the uttermost end of an interminable grey passage. Even with this he was suffered to rest, and what had now brought him to knowledge was the break in the long mild motion.

It had brought him to knowledge, to knowledge — yes, this was the beauty of his state; which came to resemble more and more that of a man who has gone to sleep on some news of a great inheritance, and then, after dreaming it away, after profaning it with matters strange to it, has waked up again to serenity of certitude and has only to lie and watch it grow. This was the drift of his patience — that he had only to let it shine on him. He must moreover, with intermissions, still have been lifted and borne; since why and how else should he have known himself, later on, with the afternoon glow intenser, no longer at the foot of his stairs — situated as these now seemed at that dark other end of his tunnel — but on a deep window-bench of his high saloon, over which had been spread, couch-fashion, a mantle of soft stuff lined with grey fur that was familiar to his eyes and that one of his hands kept fondly feeling as for its pledge of truth. Mrs. Muldoon's face had gone, but the other, the second he had recognised, hung over him in a way that showed how he was still propped and pillowed. He took it all in, and the more he took it the more it seemed to suffice: he was as much at peace as if he had

had food and drink. It was the two women who had found him, on Mrs. Muldoon's having plied, at her usual hour, her latch-key — and on her having above all arrived while Miss Staverton still lingered near the house. She had been turning away, all anxiety, from worrying the vain bell-handle — her calculation having been of the hour of the good woman's visit; but the latter, blessedly, had come up while she was still there, and they had entered together. He had then lain, beyond the vestibule, very much as he was lying now — quite, that is, as he appeared to have fallen, but all so wondrously without bruise or gash; only in a depth of stupor. What he most took in, however, at present, with the steadier clearance, was that Alice Staverton had for a long unspeakable moment not doubted he was dead.

"It must have been that I *was*." He made it out as she held him. "Yes — I can only have died. You brought me literally to life. Only," he wondered, his eyes rising to her, "only, in the name of all the benedictions, how?"

It took her but an instant to bend her face and kiss him, and something in the manner of it, and in the way her hands clasped and locked his head while he felt the cool charity and virtue of her lips, something in all this beatitude somehow answered everything. "And now I keep you," she said.

"Oh keep me, keep me!" he pleaded while her face still hung over him: in response to which it dropped again and stayed close, clingingly close. It was the seal of their situation — of which he tasted the impress for a long blissful moment in silence. But he came back. "Yet how did you know — ?"

"I was uneasy. You were to have come, you remember — and you had sent no word."

"Yes, I remember — I was to have gone to you at one to-day." It caught on to their "old" life and relation — which were so near and so far. "I was still out there in my strange darkness — where was it, what was it? I must have stayed there so long." He could but wonder at the depth and the duration of his swoon.

"Since last night?" she asked with a shade of fear for her possible indiscretion.

"Since this morning — it must have been: the cold dim dawn of to-day. Where have I been," he vaguely wailed, "where have I been?" He felt her hold him close, and it was as if this helped him now to make in all security his mild moan. "What a long dark day!"

All in her tenderness she had waited a moment. "In the cold dim dawn?" she quavered.

But he had already gone on piecing together the parts of the whole prodigy. "As I didn't turn up you came straight — ?"

She barely cast about. "I went first to your hotel — where they told me of your absence. You had dined out last evening and hadn't been back since. But they appeared to know you had been at your club."

The Jolly Corner

"So you had the idea of *this* — ?"

"Of what?" she asked in a moment.

"Well — of what has happened."

"I believed at least you'd have been here. I've known, all along," she said, "that you've been coming."

" 'Known' it — ?"

"Well, I've believed it. I said nothing to you after that talk we had a month ago — but I felt sure. I knew you *would*," she declared.

"That I'd persist, you mean?"

"That you'd seen him."

"Ah but I didn't!" cried Brydon with his long wail. "There's somebody — an awful beast; whom I brought, too horribly, to bay. But it's not me."

At this she bent over him again, and her eyes were in his eyes. "No — it's not you." And it was as if, while her face hovered, he might have made out in it, hadn't it been so near, some particular meaning blurred by a smile. "No, thank heaven," she repeated — "it's not you! Of course it wasn't to have been."

"Ah but it *was*," he gently insisted. And he stared before him now as he had been staring for so many weeks. "I was to have known myself."

"You couldn't!" she returned consolingly. And then reverting, and as if to account further for what she had herself done, "But it wasn't only *that*, that you hadn't been at home," she went on. "I waited till the hour at which we had found Mrs. Muldoon that day of my going with you; and she ar-

rived, as I've told you, while, failing to bring any one to the door, I lingered in my despair on the steps. After a little, if she hadn't come, by such a mercy, I should have found means to hunt her up. But it wasn't," said Alice Staverton, as if once more with her fine intention — "it wasn't only that."

His eyes, as he lay, turned back to her. "What more then?"

She met it, the wonder she had stirred. "In the cold dim dawn, you say? Well, in the cold dim dawn of this morning I too saw you."

"Saw *me* — ?"

"Saw *him*," said Alice Staverton. "It must have been at the same moment."

He lay an instant taking it in — as if he wished to be quite reasonable. "At the same moment?"

"Yes — in my dream again, the same one I've named to you. He came back to me. Then I knew it for a sign. He had come to you."

At this Brydon raised himself; he had to see her better. She helped him when she understood his movement, and he sat up, steadying himself beside her there on the window-bench and with his right hand grasping her left. "*He* didn't come to me."

"You came to yourself," she beautifully smiled.

"Ah I've come to myself now — thanks to you, dearest. But this brute, with his awful face — this brute's a black stranger. He's none of *me*, even as I *might* have been," Brydon sturdily declared.

But she kept the clearness that

was like the breath of infallibility. "Isn't the whole point that you'd have been different?"

He almost scowled for it. "As different as *that* — ?"

Her look again was more beautiful to him than the things of this world. "Haven't you exactly wanted to know *how* different? So this morning," she said, "you appeared to me."

"Like *him?*"

"A black stranger!"

"Then how did you know it was I?"

"Because, as I told you weeks ago, my mind, my imagination, had worked so over what you might, what you mightn't have been — to show you, you see, how I've thought of you. In the midst of that you came to me — that my wonder might be answered. So I knew," she went on; "and believed that, since the question held you too so fast, as you told me that day, you too would see for yourself. And when this morning I again saw I knew it would be because you had — and also then, from the first moment, because you somehow wanted me. *He* seemed to tell me of that. So why," she strangely smiled, "shouldn't I like him?"

It brought Spencer Brydon to his feet. "You 'like' that horror — ?"

"I *could* have liked him. And to me," she said, "he was no horror. I had accepted him."

"'Accepted' — ?" Brydon oddly sounded.

"Before, for the interest of his difference — yes. And as *I* didn't disown him, as *I* knew him — which you at last, confronted with him in his difference, so cruelly didn't, my dear — well, he must have been, you see, less dreadful to me. And it may have pleased him that I pitied him."

She was beside him on her feet, but still holding his hand — still with her arm supporting him. But though it all brought for him thus a dim light, "You 'pitied' him?" he grudgingly, resentfully asked.

"He has been unhappy, he has been ravaged," she said.

"And haven't I been unhappy? Am not I — you've only to look at me! — ravaged?"

"Ah I don't say I like him *better*," she granted after a thought. "But he's grim, he's worn — and things have happened to him. He doesn't make shift, for sight, with your charming monocle."

"No" — it struck Brydon: "I couldn't have sported mine 'downtown.' They'd have guyed me there."

"His great convex pince-nez — I saw it, I recognised the kind — is for his poor ruined sight. And his poor right hand — !"

"Ah!" Brydon winced — whether for his proved identity or for his lost fingers. Then, "He has a million a year," he lucidly added. "But he hasn't you."

"And he isn't — no, he isn't — *you!*" she murmured as he drew her to his breast.

819

CRAPY CORNELIA

THREE times within a quarter of an hour — shifting the while his posture on his chair of contemplation — had he looked at his watch as for its final sharp hint that he should decide, that he should get up. His seat was one of a group fairly sequestered, unoccupied save for his own presence, and from where he lingered he looked off at a stretch of lawn freshened by recent April showers and on which sundry small children were at play. The trees, the shrubs, the plants, every stem and twig just ruffled as by the first touch of the light finger of the relenting year, struck him as standing still in the blest hope of more of the same caress; the quarter about him held its breath after the fashion of the child who waits with the rigour of an open mouth and shut eyes for the promised sensible effect of his having been good. So, in the windless, sun-warmed air of the beautiful afternoon, the Park of the winter's end had struck White-Mason as waiting; even New York, under such an impression, was "good," good enough — for *him;* its very sounds were faint, were almost sweet, as they reached him from

so seemingly far beyond the wooded horizon that formed the remoter limit of his large shallow glade. The tones of the frolic infants ceased to be nondescript and harsh — were in fact almost as fresh and decent as the frilled and puckered and ribboned garb of the little girls, which had always a way, in those parts, of so portentously flaunting the daughters of the strange native — that is of the overwhelming alien — populace at him.

Not that these things in particular were his matter of meditation now; he had wanted, at the end of his walk, to sit apart a little and think — and had been doing that for twenty minutes, even though as yet to no break in the charm of procrastination. But he had looked without seeing and listened without hearing: all that had been positive for him was that he hadn't failed vaguely to feel. He had felt in the first place, and he continued to feel — yes, at forty-eight quite as much as at any point of the supposed reign of younger intensities — the great spirit of the air, the fine sense of the season, the supreme appeal of Nature, he might have said, to his time of life; quite as if she, easy, indulgent, indifferent, cynical Power, were offering him the last chance it would rest with his wit or his blood to embrace. Then with that he had been entertaining, to the point and with the prolonged consequence of accepted immobilization, the certitude that if he did call on Mrs. Worthingham and find her at home he couldn't in justice to himself not put to her the question that had lapsed the other time, the last time, through the irritating and persistent, even if accidental, presence of others. What friends she had — the people who so stupidly, so wantonly stuck! If they *should*, he and she, come to an understanding, that would presumably have to include certain members of her singularly ill-composed circle, in whom it was incredible to him that he should ever take an interest. This defeat, to do himself justice — he had bent rather predominantly on *that*, you see; ideal justice to *her*, with her possible conception of what it should consist of, being another and quite a different matter — he had had the fact of the Sunday afternoon to thank for; she didn't "keep" that day for him, since they hadn't, up to now, quite begun to cultivate the appointment or assignation founded on explicit sacrifices. He might at any rate look to find this pleasant practical Wednesday — should he indeed, at his actual rate, stay it before it ebbed — more liberally and intendingly given him.

The sound he at last most wittingly distinguished in his nook was the single deep note of half-past five borne to him from some high-perched public clock. He finally got up with the sense that the time from then on *ought* at least to be felt as sacred to him. At this juncture it was — while he stood there shaking his garments, settling his hat, his necktie, his shirt-cuffs, fixing the high polish of his fine shoes as if for some reflection in it of his straight and spare and grizzled, his refined and trimmed and dressed, his altogether distinguished person, that of a gentleman abundantly settled, but of a bachelor markedly nervous — at this crisis it was, doubtless, that he at once most measured and least resented his predicament. If he should go he would almost to a certainty find her, and if he should find her he would almost to a certainty come to the point. He wouldn't put it off again — there was that high consideration for him of justice at least to himself. He had never yet denied himself anything so apparently fraught with possibilities as the idea of proposing to Mrs. Worthingham — never yet, in other words, denied himself anything he had so distinctly wanted to do; and the results of that wisdom had remained for him precisely the precious parts of experience. Counting only the offers of his honourable hand, these had been on three remembered occasions at least the consequence of an impulse as sharp and a self-respect as reasoned; a self-respect that hadn't in the least suffered, moreover, from the failure of each appeal. He had been met in the three cases — the only ones he at all compared with his present case — by the frank confession that he didn't somehow, charming as he was, cause himself to be superstitiously believed in; and the lapse of life, afterward, had cleared up many doubts.

It *wouldn't* have done, he eventually, he lucidly saw, each time he had been refused; and the candour of his nature was such that he could live to think of these very passages as a proof of how right he had been — right, that is, to have put himself forward always, by the happiest instinct, only in impossible conditions. He had the happy consciousness of having exposed the important question to the crucial test, and of having escaped, by that persistent logic, a grave mistake. What better proof of his escape than the fact that he was now free to renew the all-interesting inquiry, and should be exactly, about to do so in different and better conditions? The conditions were better by as much more — as much more of his career and character, of his situation, his reputation he could even have called it, of his knowledge of life, of his somewhat extended means, of his possibly augmented charm, of his certainly improved mind and temper — as was involved in the actual impending settlement. Once he had got into motion, once he had crossed the Park and passed out of it, entering, with very little space to traverse, one of the short new streets that abutted on its east side, his step became that of a man young enough to find confidence, quite to find felicity, in the sense, in almost any sense, of action. He could still enjoy almost anything, absolutely an unpleasant thing, in default of a better, that might still remind him he wasn't so old. The standing newness of everything about him would, it was true, have weakened this cheer by too much presuming on it; Mrs. Worthingham's house, before which he stopped, had that gloss of new money, that glare of a piece fresh from the mint and ringing for the first time on any counter, which seems to claim for it, in any transaction, something more than the "face" value.

This could but be yet more the case for the impression of the observer introduced and committed. On our friend's part I mean, after his admission and while still in the hall, the sense of the general shining immediacy, of the still unhushed clamour of the shock, was perhaps stronger than he had ever known it. That broke out from every corner as the high pitch of interest, and with a candour that — no, certainly — he had never seen equalled; every particular expensive object shrieking at him in its artless pride that it had just "come home." He met the whole vision with something of the grimace produced on persons without goggles by the passage from a shelter to a blinding light; and if he had — by a perfectly possible chance — been "snap-shotted" on the spot, would have struck you as showing for his first tribute to the temple of Mrs. Worthingham's charming presence a scowl almost of anguish. He wasn't constitutionally, it may at once be explained for him, a goggled person; and he was condemned, in New York, to this frequent violence of transition — having to reckon with it whenever he went out, as who should say, from himself. The high pitch of interest, to his taste, was the pitch of history, the pitch of acquired and earned suggestion, the pitch of association, in a word; so that he lived by preference, incontestably, if not in a rich gloom, which would have been beyond his means and spirits, at least amid objects and images that confessed to the tone of time.

He had ever felt that an indispensable presence — with a need of it moreover that interfered at no point with his gentle habit, not to say his subtle art, of drawing out what was left him of his youth, of thinly and thriftily spreading the rest of that choicest jam-pot of the cupboard of consciousness over the remainder of a slice of life still possibly thick enough to bear it; or in other words of moving the melancholy limits, the significant signs, constantly a little further on, very much as property-marks or staked boundaries are sometimes stealthily shifted at night. He positively cherished in fact, as against the too inveterate gesture of distressfully guarding his eyeballs — so many New York aspects seemed to keep him at it — an ideal of adjusted appreciation, of courageous curiosity, of fairly letting the world about him, a world of constant breathless renewals and merciless substitutions, make its flaring assault on its own inordinate terms.

Newness *was* value in the piece — for the acquisitor, or at least sometimes might be, even though the act of "blowing" hard, the act marking a heated freshness of arrival, or other form of irruption, could never minister to the peace of those already and long on the field; and this if only because maturer tone was after all most appreciable and most consoling when one staggered back to it, wounded, bleeding, blinded, from the riot of the raw — or, to put the whole experience more prettily, no doubt, from excesses of light.

II

If he went in, however, with something of his more or less inevitable scowl, there were really, at the moment, two rather valid reasons for screened observation; the first of these being that the whole place seemed to reflect as never before the lustre of Mrs. Worthingham's own polished and prosperous little person — to smile, it struck him, with her smile, to twinkle not only with the gleam of her lovely teeth, but with that of all her rings and brooches and bangles and other gewgaws, to curl and spasmodically cluster as in emulation of her charming complicated yellow tresses, to surround the most animated of pink-and-white, of ruffled and ribboned, of frilled and festooned Dresden china shepherdesses with exactly the right system of rococo curves and convolutions and other flourishes, a perfect bower of painted and gilded and moulded conceits. The second ground of this immediate impression of scenic extravagance, almost as if the curtain rose for him to the first act of some small and expensively mounted comic opera, was that she hadn't, after all, awaited him in fond singleness, but had again just a trifle inconsiderately exposed him to the drawback of having to reckon, for whatever design he might amiably entertain, with the presence of a third and quite superfluous person, a small black insignificant but none the less oppressive stranger. It was odd how, on the instant, the little lady engaged with her did affect him as comparatively black — very much as if that had absolutely, in such a medium, to be the graceless appearance of any item not positively of some fresh shade of a light colour or of some pretty pretension to a charming twist. Any witness of their meeting, his hostess should surely have felt, would have been a false note in the whole rosy glow; but what note so false as that of the dingy little presence that she might actually, by a refinement of her perhaps always too visible study of effect, have provided as a positive contrast or foil? whose name and intervention, moreover, she appeared to be no more moved to mention and account for than she might have been to "present" — whether as stretched at her feet or erect upon disciplined haunches — some shaggy old domesticated terrier or poodle.

Extraordinarily, after he had been in the room five minutes — a space of time during which his fellow-visitor had neither budged nor uttered a sound — he had made Mrs. Worthingham out as all at once perfectly pleased to see him, completely aware of what he had most in mind, and singularly serene in face of his sense of their impediment. It was as if for all the world she didn't take it for one, the immobility, to say nothing of the seeming equanimity, of their tactless companion; at whom meanwhile indeed our friend himself, after his first ruffled perception, no more adventured a look than if advised by his constitutional kindness that to notice her in any degree would perforce be ungraciously to glower. He talked after a fashion with the woman as to whose power to please and amuse and serve him, as to whose really quite organised and indicated fitness for lighting up his autumn afternoon of life his conviction had lately strained itself so clear; but he was all the while carrying on an intenser exchange with his own spirit and trying to read into the charming creature's behaviour, as he could only call it, some confirmation of his theory that she also had her inward flutter and anxiously counted on him. He found support, happily for the conviction just named, in the idea, at no moment as yet really repugnant to him, the idea bound up in fact with the finer essence of her appeal, that she had her own vision too of her quality and her price, and that the last appearance she would have liked to bristle with was that of being forewarned and eager.

He had, if he came to think of it, scarce definitely warned her, and he probably wouldn't have taken to her so consciously in the first instance without an appreciative sense that, as she was a little person of twenty superficial graces, so she was also a little person with her secret pride. She might just have planted her mangy lion — not to say her muzzled house-dog — there in his path as a symbol that she wasn't cheap and easy; which would be a thing he couldn't possibly wish his future wife to have shown herself in advance, even if to him alone. That she could make him put himself such questions was precisely part of the attaching play of her iridescent surface, the shimmering interfusion of her various aspects; that of her youth with her independence — her pecuniary perhaps in particular, that of her vivacity with her beauty, that of her facility above all with her odd novelty; the high modernity, as people appeared to have come to call it, that made her so much more "knowing" in some directions than even he, man of the world as he certainly was, could pretend to be, though all on a basis of the most unconscious and instinctive and luxurious assumption. She was "up" to everything, aware of everything — if one counted from a short enough time back (from week before last, say, and as if quantities of history had burst upon the world within the fortnight); she was likewise surprised at nothing, and in that direction one might reckon as far ahead as the rest of her lifetime, or at any rate as the rest of his, which was all that would concern him: it was as if the suitability of the future to her personal and rather pampered tastes was what she most took for granted, so that he could see her, for all her Dresden-china shoes and her flutter of wondrous befrilled contemporary skirts, skip by the side of the coming age as over the floor of a ball-room, keeping step with its monstrous stride and prepared for every figure of the dance.

Her outlook took form to him suddenly as a great square sunny window that hung in assured fashion over the immensity of life. There rose toward it as from a vast swarming *plaza* a high tide of emotion and sound; yet it was at the same time as if even while he looked her light gemmed hand, flashing on him in addition to those other things the perfect polish of the prettiest pink finger-nails in the world, had touched a spring, the most ingenious of recent devices for instant ease, which dropped half across the scene a soft-coloured mechanical blind, a fluttered, fringed awning of charmingly toned silk, such as would make a bath of cool shade for the favoured friend leaning with her there — that is for the happy couple itself — on the balcony. The great view would be the prospect

825

and privilege of the very state he coveted — since didn't he covet it? — the state of being so securely at her side; while the wash of privacy, as one might count it, the broad fine brush dipped into clear umber and passed, full and wet, straight across the strong scheme of colour, would represent the security itself, all the uplifted inner elegance, the condition, so ïdeal, of being shut out from nothing and yet of having, so gaily and breezily aloft, none of the burden or worry of anything. Thus, as I say, for our friend, the place itself, while his vivid impression lasted, portentously opened and spread, and what was before him took, to his vision, though indeed at so other a crisis, the form of the "glimmering square" of the poet; yet, for a still more remarkable fact, with an incongruous object usurping at a given instant the privilege of the frame and seeming, even as he looked, to block the view.

The incongruous object was a woman's head, crowned with a little sparsely feathered black hat, an ornament quite unlike those the women mostly noticed by White-Mason were now "wearing," and that grew and grew, that came nearer and nearer, while it met his eyes, after the manner of images in the kinematograph. It had presently loomed so large that he saw nothing else — not only among the things at a considerable distance, the things Mrs. Worthingham would eventually, yet unmistakably, introduce him to, but among those of this lady's various attributes and appurtenances as to which he had been in the very act of cultivating his consciousness. It was in the course of another minute the most extraordinary thing in the world: everything had altered, dropped, darkened, disappeared; his imagination had spread its wings only to feel them flop all grotesquely at its sides as he recognised in his hostess's quiet companion, the oppressive alien who hadn't indeed interfered with his fanciful flight, though she had prevented his immediate declaration and brought about the thud, not to say the felt violent shock, of his fall to earth, the perfectly plain identity of Cornelia Rasch. It was she who had remained there at attention; it was she their companion hadn't introduced; it was she he had forborne to face with his fear of incivility. He stared at her — everything else went.

"Why it has been *you* all this time?"

Miss Rasch fairly turned pale. "I was waiting to see if you'd know me."

"Ah, my dear Cornelia" — he came straight out with it — "rather!"

"Well, it isn't," she returned with a quick change to red now, "from having taken much time to look at me!"

She smiled, she even laughed, but he could see how she had felt his unconsciousness, poor thing; the acquaintance, quite the friend of his youth, as she had been, the associate of his childhood, of his early manhood, of his middle age in fact, up to a few years back, not more than ten at the most; the associate too of so many of his associates and of almost all of his relations, those of the other time, those who had mainly gone for ever; the person in short whose noted disappearance, though it might have seemed final, had been only of recent seasons. She was present again now, all unexpectedly — he had heard of her having at last, left alone after successive deaths and with scant resources, sought economic salvation in Europe, the promised land of American thrift — she was present at this almost ancient and this oddly unassertive little rotund figure whom one seemed no more obliged to address than if she had been a black satin ottoman "treated" with buttons and gimp; a class of object as to which the policy of blindness was imperative. He felt the need of some explanatory plea, and before he could think had uttered one at Mrs. Worthingham's expense. "Why, you see we weren't introduced —— !"

"No — but I didn't suppose I should have to be named to you."

"Well, my dear woman, you haven't — do me that justice!" He could at least make this point. "I felt all the while — !" However, it would have taken him long to say what he had been feeling; and he was aware now of the pretty projected light of Mrs. Worthingham's wonder. She looked as if, out for a walk with her, he had put her to the inconvenience of his stopping to speak to a strange woman in the street.

"I never supposed you knew her!" — it was to him his hostess excused herself.

This made Miss Rasch spring up, distinctly flushed, distinctly strange to behold, but not vulgarly nettled — Cornelia was incapable of that; only rather funnily bridling and laughing, only showing that this was all she had waited for, only saying just the right thing, the thing she could make so clearly a jest. "Of course if you *had* you'd have presented him."

Mrs. Worthingham looked while answering at White-Mason. "I didn't want you to go — which you see you do as soon as he speaks to you. But I never dreamed —— !"

"That there was anything between us? Ah, there are no end of things!" He, on his side, though addressing the younger and prettier woman, looked at his fellow-guest; to whom he even continued: "When did you get back? May I come and see you the very first thing?"

Cornelia gasped and wriggled — she practically giggled; she had lost every atom of her little old, her little young, though always unaccountable prettiness, which used to peep so, on the bare chance of a shot, from behind indefensible features, that it almost made watching her a form of sport. He had heard vaguely of her, it came back to him (for there had been no letters; their later acquaintance, thank goodness, hadn't involved that) as experimenting, for economy, and then as settling, to the same rather dismal end, somewhere in England, at one of those intensely English places, St. Leonards, Cheltenham, Bognor, Dawlish — which, awfully, *was* it? — and she now affected him for all the world as some small squirming, exclaiming, genteelly conversing old maid of a type vaguely associated with the three-volume novels he used to feed on (besides his so often encountering it in "real life,") during a far-away stay of his own at Brighton. Odder than any element of his ex-gossip's identity itself, however, was the fact that she somehow, with it all, rejoiced his sight. Indeed the supreme oddity was that the manner of her reply to his request for leave to call should have absolutely charmed his attention. She didn't look at him; she only, from under her frumpy, crapy, curiously exotic hat, and with her good little near-sighted insinuating glare, expressed to Mrs. Worthingham, while she answered him, wonderful arch things, the overdone things of a shy woman. "Yes, you may call — but only when this dear lovely lady has done with you!" The moment after which she had gone.

III

FORTY minutes later he was taking his way back from the queer miscarriage of his adventure; taking it, with no conscious positive fe-

licity, through the very spaces that had witnessed shortly before the considerable serenity of his assurance. He had said to himself then, or had as good as said it, that, since he might do perfectly as he liked, it couldn't fail for him that he must soon retrace those steps, humming, to all intents, the first bars of a wedding-march; so beautifully had it cleared up that he was "going to like" letting Mrs. Worthingham accept him. He was to have hummed no wedding-march, as it seemed to be turning out — he had none, up to now, to hum; and yet, extraordinarily, it wasn't in the least because she had refused him. Why then hadn't he liked as much as he had intended to like it putting the pleasant act, the act of not refusing him, in her power? Could it all have come from the awkward minute of his failure to decide sharply, on Cornelia's departure, whether or no he would attend her to the door? He hadn't decided at all — what the deuce had been in him? — but had danced to and fro in the room, thinking better of each impulse and then thinking worse. He had hesitated like an ass erect on absurd hind legs between two bundles of hay; the upshot of which must have been his giving the falsest impression. In what way that was to be for an instant considered had their common past committed him to crapy Cornelia? He repudiated with a whack on the gravel any ghost of an obligation.

What he could get rid of with

scanter success, unfortunately, was the peculiar sharpness of his sense that, though mystified by his visible flurry — and yet not mystified enough for a sympathetic question either — his hostess had been, on the whole, even more frankly diverted: which was precisely an example of that newest, freshest, finest freedom in her, the air and the candour of assuming, not "heartlessly," not viciously, not even very consciously, but with a bright pampered confidence which would probably end by affecting one's nerves as the most impertinent stroke in the world, that every blest thing coming up for her in any connection was somehow matter for her general recreation. There she was again with the innocent egotism, the gilded and overflowing anarchism, really, of her doubtless quite unwitting but none the less rabid modern note. Her grace of ease was perfect, but it was all grace of ease, not a single shred of it grace of uncertainty or of difficulty — which meant, when you came to see, that, for its happy working, not a grain of provision was left by it to mere manners. This was clearly going to be the music of the future — that if people were but rich enough and furished enough and fed enough, exercised and sanitated and manicured and generally advised and advertised and made "knowing" enough, *avertis* enough, as the term appeared to be nowadays in Paris, all they had to do for civility was to take the amused ironic view of those who might be less initiated.

In *his* time, when he was young or even when he was only but a little less middle-aged, the best manners had been the best kindness, and the best kindness had mostly been some art of not insisting on one's luxurious differences, of concealing rather, for common humanity, if not for common decency, a part at least of the intensity or the ferocity with which one might be "in the know."

Oh, the "know" — Mrs. Worthingham was in it, all instinctively, inevitably, and as a matter of course, up to her eyes; which didn't, however, the least little bit prevent her being as ignorant as a fish of everything that really and intimately and fundamentally concerned *him*, poor dear old White-Mason. She didn't, in the first place, so much as know who he was — by which he meant know who and what it was to *be* a White-Mason, even a poor and a dear and old one, "anyway." That indeed — he did her perfect justice — was of the very essence of the newness and freshness and beautiful, brave, social irresponsibility by which she had originally dazzled him: just exactly that circumstance of her having no instinct for any old quality or quantity or identity, a single historic or social value, as he might say, of the New York of his already almost legendary past; and that additional one of his, on his side, having, so far as this went, cultivated blankness, cultivated positive prudence, as to her own personal background — the vagueness, at the best, with which all honest gentlefolk, the New Yorkers of his approved stock and conservative generation, were content, as for the most part they were indubitably wise, to surround the origins and antecedents and queer unimaginable early influences of persons swimming into their ken from those parts of the country that quite necessarily and naturally figured to their view as "God-forsaken" and generally impossible.

The few scattered surviving representatives of a society once "good" — *rari nantes in gurgite vasto* — were liable, at the pass things had come to, to meet, and even amid old shades once sacred, or what was left of such, every form of social impossibility, and, more irresistibly still, to find these apparitions often carry themselves (often at least in the case of the women) with a wondrous wild gallantry, equally imperturbable and inimitable, the sort of thing that reached its maximum in Mrs. Worthingham. Beyond that who ever wanted to look up their annals, to reconstruct their steps and stages, to dot their i's in fine, or to "go behind" anything that was theirs? One wouldn't do that for the world — a rudimentary discretion forbade it; and yet this check from elementary undiscussable taste quite consorted with a due respect for them, or at any rate with a due respect for oneself in connection with them; as was just exemplified in what would be his own, what would be poor dear old White-Mason's, insurmountable aversion to having, on any pretext, the doubtless very queer spectre of the late Mr. Worthingham presented to him. No question had he asked, or would he ever ask, should his life — that is should the success of his courtship — even intimately depend on it, either about that obscure agent of his mistress's actual affluence or about the happy headspring itself, and the apparently copious tributaries, of the golden stream.

From all which marked anomalies, at any rate, what was the moral to draw? He dropped into a Park chair again with that question, he lost himself in the wonder of why he had come away with his homage so very much unpaid. Yet it didn't seem at all, actually, as if he could say or conclude, as if he could do anything but keep on worrying — just in conformity with his being a person who, whether or no familiar with the need to make his conduct square with his conscience and his taste, was never wholly exempt from that of making his taste and his conscience square with his conduct. To this latter occupation he further abandoned himself, and it didn't release him from his second brooding session till the sweet spring sunset had begun to gather and he had more or less cleared up, in the deepening dusk, the effective relation between the various parts of his ridiculously agitating experience. There were vital facts he seemed thus to catch, to seize, with a nervous hand, and the twilight helping, by their vaguely whisked tails; unquiet truths that swarmed out after the fashion of creatures bold only at eventide, creatures that hovered and circled, that verily brushed his nose, in spite of their shyness. Yes, he had practically just sat on with his "mistress" — heaven save the mark! — as if *not* to come to the point; as if it had absolutely come up that there would be something rather vulgar and awful in doing so. The whole stretch of his stay after Cornelia's withdrawal had been consumed by his almost ostentatiously treating himself to the opportunity of which he was to make nothing. It was as if he had sat and watched himself — that came back to him: Shall I now or sha'n't I? Will I now or won't I? "Say within the next three minutes, say by a quarter past six, or by twenty minutes past, at the furthest — always if nothing more comes up to prevent."

What had already come up to prevent was, in the strangest and drollest, or at least in the most preposterous, way in the world, that not Cornelia's presence, but her very absence, with its distraction of his thoughts, the thoughts that lumbered after her, had made the difference; and without his being the least able to tell why and how. He put it to himself after a fashion by the image that, this distraction once created, his working round to his hostess again, his reverting to the matter of his errand, began suddenly to represent a return from so far. That was simply all — or rather a little less than all; for something else had contributed. "I never dreamed you knew her," and "I never dreamed *you* did," were inevitably what had been exchanged between them — supplemented by Mrs. Worthingham's mere scrap of an explanation: "Oh yes — to the small extent you see. Two years ago in Switzerland when I was at a high place for an 'aftercure,' during twenty days of incessant rain, she was the only person in an hotel full of roaring, gorging, smoking Germans with whom I could have a word of talk. She and I were the only speakers of English, and were thrown together like castaways on a desert island and in a raging storm. She was ill besides, and she had no maid, and mine looked after her, and she was very grateful — writing to me later on and saying she should certainly come to see me if she ever returned to New York. She *has* returned, you see — and there she was, poor little creature!" Such was Mrs. Worthingham's tribute — to which even his asking her if Miss Rasch had ever happened to speak of him caused her practically to add nothing. Visibly she had never thought again of any one Miss Rasch had spoken of or anything Miss Rasch had said; right as she was, naturally, about her being a little clever queer creature. This was perfectly true, and yet it was probably — by being *all* she could dream of about her — what had paralysed his proper gallantry. Its effect had been not in what it simply stated, but in what, under his secretly disintegrating criticism, it almost luridly symbolised.

He had quitted his seat in the Louis Quinze drawing-room without having, as he would have described it, done anything but give the lady of the scene a superior chance not to betray a defeated hope — not, that is, to fail of the famous "pride" mostly supposed to prop even the most infatuated women at such junctures; by which chance, to do her justice, she had thoroughly seemed to profit. But he finally rose from his later station with a feeling of better success. He had by a happy turn of his hand got hold of the most precious, the least obscure of the flitting, circling things that brushed his ears. What he wanted — as justifying for him a little further consideration — was there before him from the moment he could put it that Mrs. Worthingham had no data. He almost hugged that word — it suddenly came to mean so much to him. No data, he felt, for a conception of the sort of thing the New York of "his time" had been in his personal life — the New York so unexpectedly, so vividly and, as he might say, so perversely called back to all his senses by its identity with that of poor Cornelia's time: since even she had had a time, small show as it was likely to make now, and his time and hers had been the same. Cornelia figured to him while he walked away as, by contrast and opposition, a massive little bundle of data; his impatience to go to see her sharpened as he thought of this: so certainly should he find out that wherever he might touch her, with a gentle though firm pressure, he would, as the fond visitor of old houses taps and fingers a disfeatured, overpapered wall with the conviction of a wainscot-edge beneath, recognise some small extrusion of history.

IV

THERE would have been a wonder for us meanwhile in his continued use, as it were, of his happy formula — brought out to Cornelia Rasch within ten minutes, or perhaps only within twenty, of his having settled into the quite comfortable chair that, two days later, she indicated to him by her fireside. He had arrived at her address through the fortunate chance of his having noticed her card, as he went out, deposited, in the good old New York fashion, on one of the rococo tables of Mrs. Worthingham's hall. His eye had been caught by the pencilled indication that was to affect him, the next instant, as fairly placed there for his sake. This had really been his luck, for he shouldn't have liked to write to Mrs. Worthingham for guidance — that he felt, though too impatient just now to analyze the reluctance. There was nobody else he could have approached for a clue, and with this reflection he was already aware of how it testified to their rare little position, his and Cornelia's — position as conscious, ironic, pathetic survivors together of a dead and buried society — that there would have been, in all the town, under such stress, not a member of their old circle left to turn to. Mrs. Worthingham had practically, even if accidentally, helped him to knowledge; the last nail in the coffin of the poor dear extinct past had been planted for him by his having thus to reach his antique contemporary through perforation of the newest newness. The note of this particular recognition was in fact the more prescribed to him that the ground of Cornelia's return to a scene swept so bare of the associational charm was certainly inconspicuous. What had she then come back for? — he had asked himself that; with the effect of deciding that it probably would have been, a little, to "look after" her remnant of property. Perhaps she had come to save what little might still remain of that shrivelled interest; perhaps she had been, by those who took care of it for her, further dwindled and despoiled, so that she wished to get at the facts. Perhaps on the other hand — it was a more cheerful chance — her investments, decently administered, were making larger returns, so that the rigorous thrift of Bognor could be finally relaxed.

He had little to learn about the attraction of Europe, and rather expected that in the event of his union with Mrs. Worthingham he should find himself pleading for it with the competence of one more in the "know" about Paris and Rome, about Venice and Florence, than even she could be. He could have lived on in *his* New York, that is in the sentimental, the spiritual, the more or less romantic visitation of it; but had it been positive for him that he could live on in hers? — unless indeed the possibility of this had been just (like the famous *vertige de l'abîme,* like the solicitation of danger, or otherwise of the dreadful) the very hinge of his whole dream. However that might be, his curiosity was occupied rather with the conceivable hinge of poor Cornelia's: it was perhaps thinkable that even Mrs. Worthingham's New York, once it should have become possible again at all, might have put forth to this lone exile a plea that wouldn't be in the chords of Bognor. For himself, after all, too, the attraction had been much more of the Europe over which one might move at one's ease, and which therefore could but cost, and cost much, right and left, than of the Europe adapted to scrimping. He saw himself on the whole scrimping with more zest even in Mrs. Worthingham's New York than under the inspiration of Bognor. Apart from which it was yet again odd, not to say perceptibly pleasing to him, to note where the emphasis of his interest fell in this fumble of fancy over such felt oppositions as the new, the latest, the luridest power of money and the ancient reserves and moderations and mediocrities. These last struck him as showing by contrast the old brown surface and tone as of velvet rubbed and worn, shabby, and even a bit dingy, but all soft and subtle and still velvety — which meant still dignified; whereas the angular facts of current finance were as harsh and metallic and bewildering as some stacked "exhibit" of ugly patented inventions, things his mediæval mind forbade his taking in. He had for instance the sense of knowing the pleasant little old Rasch fortune — pleasant as far as it went; blurred memories and impressions of what it had been and what it hadn't, of how it had grown and how languished and how melted; they came back to him and put on such vividness that he could almost have figured himself testify for them before a bland and encouraging Board. The idea of taking the field in any manner on the subject of Mrs. Worthingham's resources would have affected him on the other hand as an odious ordeal, some glare of embarrassment and exposure in a circle of hard unhelpful attention, of converging, derisive, unsuggestive eyes.

In Cornelia's small and quite cynically modern flat — the house had a grotesque name, "The Gainsborough," but at least wasn't an awful boarding-house, as he had feared, and she could receive him quite honourably, which was so much to the good — he would have been ready to use at once to her the greatest freedom of friendly allusion: "Have you still your old 'family interest' in those two houses in Seventh Avenue? — one of which was next to a corner grocery, don't you know? and was occupied as to its lower part by a candy-shop where the proportion of the stock of suspectedly stale popcorn to that of rarer and stickier joys betrayed perhaps a modest capital on the part of your father's, your grandfather's, or whoever's tenant, but out of which I nevertheless remember once to have come as out of a bath of sweets, with my very garments, and even the separate hairs of my head, glued together. The other of the pair, a tobacconist's, further down, had before it a wonderful huge Indian who thrust out wooden cigars at an indifferent world — you could buy candy cigars too, at the popcorn shop, and I greatly preferred them to the wooden; I remember well how I used to gape in fascination at the Indian and wonder if the last of the Mohicans was like him; besides admiring so the resources of a family whose 'property' was in such forms. I haven't been round there lately — we must go round together; but don't tell me the forms have utterly perished!" It was after *that* fashion he might easily have been moved, and with almost no transition, to break out to Cornelia —

quite as if taking up some old talk, some old community of gossip, just where they had left it; even with the consciousness perhaps of over-doing a little, of putting at its max-imum, for the present harmony, re-covery, recapture (what should he call it?) the pitch and quan-tity of what the past had held for them.

He didn't in fact, no doubt, dart straight off to Seventh Avenue, there being too many other old things and much nearer and long subsequent; the point was only that for everything they spoke of after he had fairly begun to lean back and stretch his legs, and after she had let him, above all, light the first of a succession of cigar-ettes — for everything they spoke of he positively cultivated extrava-gance and excess, piling up the crackling twigs as on the very al-tar of memory; and that by the end of half an hour she had lent her-self, all gallantly, to their game. It was the game of feeding the beau-tiful iridescent flame, ruddy and green and gold, blue and pink and amber and silver, with anything they could pick up, anything that would burn and flicker. Thick-strown with such gleanings the occasion seemed indeed, in spite of the truth that they perhaps wouldn't have proved, under cross-examination, to have rubbed shoulders in the other life so very hard. Casual contacts, qualified communities enough, there had doubtless been, but not particular "passages," nothing that counted,

as he might think of it, for their "very own" together, for nobody's else at all. These shades of historic exactitude didn't signify; the more and the less that there had been made perfect terms — and just by his being there and by her rejoic-ing in it — with their present need to have *had* all their past could be made to appear to have given them. It was to this tune they pro-ceeded, the least little bit as if they knowingly pretended — he giving her the example and setting her the pace of it, and she, poor dear, after a first inevitable shyness, an uncertainty of wonder, a breath-lessness of courage, falling into step and going whatever length he would.

She showed herself ready for it, grasping gladly at the perception of what he must mean; and if she didn't immediately and completely fall in — not in the first half-hour, not even in the three or four oth-ers that his visit, even whenever he consulted his watch, still made nothing of — she yet understood enough as soon as she understood that, if their finer economy hadn't so beautifully served, he might have been conveying this, that, and the other incoherent and easy thing by the comparatively clumsy method of sound and statement. "No, I never made love to you; it would in fact have been absurd, and I don't care — though I al-most know, in the sense of almost remembering! — who did and who didn't; but you were always about, and so was I, and, little as you

Crapy Cornelia

may yourself care who *I* did it to, I dare say you remember (in the sense of having known of it!) any old appearances that told. But we can't afford at this time of day not to help each other to have had — well, everything there was, since there's no more of it now, nor any way of coming by it *except so;* and therefore let us make together, let us make over and recreate, our lost world; for which we have after all and at the worst such a lot of material. You were in particular my poor dear sisters' friend — they thought you the funniest little brown thing possible; so isn't that again to the good? You were mine only to the extent that you were so much in and out of the house — as how much, if we come to that, wasn't one in and out, south of Thirtieth Street and north of Washington Square, in those days, those spacious, sociable, Arcadian days, that we flattered ourselves we filled with the modern fever, but that were so different from any of these arrangements of pretended hourly Time that dash themselves forever to pieces as from the fiftieth floors of sky-scrapers."

This was the kind of thing that was in the air, whether he said it or not, and that could hang there even with such quite other things as more crudely came out; came in spite of its being perhaps calculated to strike us that these last would have been rather and most the unspoken and the indirect. They were Cornelia's contribution, and as soon as she had begun to talk of Mrs. Worthingham — *he* didn't

begin it! — they had taken their place bravely in the centre of the circle. There they made, the while, their considerable little figure, but all within the ring formed by fifty other allusions, fitful but really intenser irruptions that hovered and wavered and came and went, joining hands at moments and whirling round as in chorus, only then again to dash at the slightly huddled centre with a free twitch or peck or push or other taken liberty, after the fashion of irregular frolic motions in a country dance or a Christmas game.

"You're so in love with her and want to marry her!" — she said it all sympathetically and yearningly, poor crapy Cornelia; as if it were to be quite taken for granted that she knew all about it. And then when he had asked how she knew — why she took so informed a tone about it; all on the wonder of her seeming so much more "in" it just at that hour than he himself quite felt he could figure for: "Ah, how but from the dear lovely thing herself? Don't you suppose *she* knows it?"

"Oh, she absolutely 'knows' it, does she?" — he fairly heard himself ask that; and with the oddest sense at once of sharply wanting the certitude and yet of seeing the question, of hearing himself say the words, through several thicknesses of some wrong medium. He came back to it from a distance; as he would have had to come back (this was again vivid to him) should he have got round again to his ripe intention three days be-

836

Crapy Cornelia

fore — after his now present but then absent friend, that is, had left him planted before his now absent but then present one for the purpose. "Do you mean she — at all confidently! — expects?" he went on, not much minding if it couldn't but sound foolish; the time being given it for him meanwhile by the sigh, the wondering gasp, all charged with the unutterable, that the tone of his appeal set in motion. He saw his companion look at him, but it might have been with the eyes of thirty years ago; when — very likely! — he had put her some such question about some girl long since dead. Dimly at first, then more distinctly, didn't it surge back on him for the very strangeness that there had been some such passage as this between them — yes, about Mary Cardew! — in the autumn of '68?

"Why, don't you realise your situation?" Miss Rasch struck him as quite beautifully wailing — above all to such an effect of deep interest, that is, on her own part and in him.

"My situation?" — he echoed, he considered; but reminded afresh, by the note of the detached, the far-projected in it, of what he had last remembered of his sentient state on his once taking ether at the dentist's.

"Yours and hers — the situation of her adoring you. I suppose you at least know it," Cornelia smiled.

Yes, it was like the other time and yet it wasn't. *She* was like — poor Cornelia was — everything that used to be; that somehow was

most definite to him. Still he could quite reply "Do you call it — her adoring me — *my* situation?"

"Well, it's a part of yours, surely — if you're in love with her."

"Am I, ridiculous old person! in love with her?" White-Mason asked.

"I may be a ridiculous old person," Cornelia returned — "and, for that matter, of course I am! But she's young and lovely and rich and clever: so what could be more natural?"

"Oh, I was applying that opprobrious epithet — !" He didn't finish, though he meant he had applied it to himself. He had got up from his seat; he turned about and, taking in, as his eyes also roamed, several objects in the room, serene and sturdy, not a bit cheap-looking, little old New York objects of '68, he made, with an inner art, as if to recognise them — made so, that is, for himself; had quite the sense for the moment of asking them, of imploring them, to recognise *him*, to be for him things of his own past. Which they truly were, he could have the next instant cried out; for it meant that if three or four of them, small sallow carte-de-visite photographs, faithfully framed but spectrally faded, hadn't in every particular, frames and balloon skirts and false "property" balustrades of unimaginable terraces and all, the tone of time, the secret for warding and easing off the perpetual imminent ache of one's protective scowl, one would verily but have to let the scowl stiffen, or to take up seriously the

837

question of blue goggles, during what might remain of life.

WHAT he actually took up from a little old Twelfth-Street table that piously preserved the plain mahogany circle, with never a curl nor a crook nor a hint of a brazen flourish, what he paused there a moment for commerce with, his back presented to crapy Cornelia, who sat taking that view of him, during this opportunity, very protrusively and frankly and fondly, was one of the wasted mementos just mentioned, over which he both uttered and suppressed a small comprehensive cry. He stood there another minute to look at it, and when he turned about still kept it in his hand, only holding it now a little behind him. "You *must* have come back to stay — with all your beautiful things. What else does it mean?"

" 'Beautiful'?" his old friend commented with her brow all wrinkled and her lips thrust out in expressive dispraise. They might at that rate have been scarce more beautiful than she herself. "Oh, don't talk so — after Mrs. Worthingham's! *They're* wonderful, if you will: such things, such things! But one's own poor relics and odds and ends are one's own at least; and one *has* — yes — come back to them. They're all I have in the world to come back to. They were

stored, and what I was paying — !" Miss Rasch wofully added.

He had possession of the small old picture; he hovered there; he put his eyes again to it intently; then again held it a little behind him as if it might have been snatched away or the very feel of it, pressed against him, was good to his palm. "Mrs. Worthingham's things? You think them beautiful?"

Cornelia did now, if ever, show an odd face. "Why certainly prodigious, or whatever. Isn't that conceded?"

"No doubt every horror, at the pass we've come to, is conceded. That's just what I complain of."

"Do you *complain*?" — she drew it out as for surprise: she couldn't have imagined such a thing.

"To me her things are awful. They're the newest of the new."

"Ah, but the old forms!"

"Those are the most blatant. I mean the swaggering reproductions."

"Oh but," she pleaded, "we can't all be *really* old."

"No, we can't, Cornelia. But *you* can — !" said White-Mason with the frankest appreciation.

She looked up at him from where she sat as he could imagine her looking up at the curate at Bognor. "Thank you, sir! If that's all you want —— !"

"It *is*," he said, "all I want — or almost."

"Then no wonder such a creature as that," she lightly moralised, "won't suit you!"

He bent upon her, for all the weight of his question, his smoothest stare. "You hold she certainly won't suit me?"

"Why, what can I tell about it? Haven't you by this time found out?"

"No, but I think I'm finding." With which he began again to explore.

Miss Rasch immensely wondered. "You mean you don't expect to come to an understanding with her?" And then as even to this straight challenge he made at first no answer: "Do you mean you give it up?"

He waited some instants more, but not meeting her eyes — only looking again about the room. "What do you think of my chance?"

"Oh," his companion cried, "what has what I think to do with it? How can I think anything but that she must like you?"

"Yes — of course. But how much?"

"Then don't you really know?" Cornelia asked.

He kept up his walk, oddly preoccupied and still not looking at her. "Do you, my dear?"

She waited a little. "If you haven't really put it to her I don't suppose she knows."

This at last arrested him again. "My dear Cornelia, she doesn't know —— !"

He had paused as for the desperate tone, or at least the large emphasis of it, so that she took him up. "The more reason then to help her to find it out."

"I mean," he explained, "that she doesn't know anything."

"Anything?"

"Anything else, I mean — even if she does know *that*."

Cornelia considered of it. "But what else need she — in particular — know? Isn't that the principal thing?"

"Well" — and he resumed his circuit — "she doesn't know anything that *we* know. But nothing," he re-emphasised — "nothing whatever!"

"Well, can't she do without that?"

"Evidently she can — and evidently she does, beautifully. But the question is whether *I* can!"

He had paused once more with his point — but she glared, poor Cornelia, with her wonder. "Surely if you know for yourself —— !"

"Ah, it doesn't seem enough for me to know for myself! One wants a woman," he argued — but still, in his prolonged tour, quite without his scowl — "to know *for* one, to know *with* one. That's what you do now," he candidly put to her.

It made her again gape. "Do you mean you want to marry *me*?"

He was so full of what he did mean, however, that he failed even to notice it. "She doesn't in the least know, for instance, how old I am."

"That's because you're so young!"

"Ah, there you are!" — and he turned off afresh and as if almost in disgust. It left her visibly perplexed — though even the perplexed Cornelia was still the exceedingly pointed; but he had come to her aid after another turn.

839

"Remember, please, that I'm pretty well as old as you."

She had all her point at least, while she bridled and blinked, for this. "You're exactly a year and ten months older."

It checked him there for delight. "You remember my birthday?"

She twinkled indeed like some far-off light of home. "I remember every one's. It's a little way I've always had — and that I've never lost."

He looked at her accomplishment, across the room, as at some striking, some charming phenomenon. "Well, *that's* the sort of thing I want!" All the ripe candour of his eyes confirmed it.

What could she do therefore, she seemed to ask him, but repeat her question of a moment before? — which indeed presently she made up her mind to. "Do you want to marry *me*?"

It had this time better success — if the term may be felt in any degree to apply. All his candour, or more of it at least, was in his slow, mild, kind, considering head-shake. "No, Cornelia — not to *marry* you."

His discrimination was a wonder; but since she was clearly treating him now as if everything about him was, so she could as exquisitely meet it. "Not at least," she convulsively smiled, "until you've honourably tried Mrs. Worthingham. Don't you really *mean* to?" she gallantly insisted.

He waited again a little; then he brought out: "I'll tell you presently." He came back, and as by still another mere glance over the room, to what seemed to him so much nearer. "That table *was* old Twelfth-Street?"

"Everything here was."

"Oh, the pure blessings! With you, ah, with you, I haven't to wear a green shade." And he had retained meanwhile his small photograph, which he again showed himself. "Didn't we talk of Mary Cardew?"

"Why, do you remember it?" She marvelled to extravagance.

"You make me. You connect me with it. You connect it with *me*." He liked to display to her this excellent use she thus had, the service she rendered. "There are so many connections — there will *be* so many. I feel how, with you, they must all come up again for me: in fact you're bringing them out already, just while I look at you, as fast as ever you can. The fact that you knew every one — !" he went on; yet as if there were more in that too than he could quite trust himself about.

"Yes, I knew every one," said Cornelia Rasch; but this time with perfect simplicity. "I knew, I imagine, more than you do — or more than you did."

It kept him there, it made him wonder with his eyes on her. "Things about *them* — our people?"

"Our people. Ours only now."

Ah, such an interest as he felt in this — taking from her while, so far from scowling, he almost gaped, all it might mean! "Ours indeed — and it's awfully good they are; or that we're still here for them! Nobody else is — nobody but you: not a cat!"

"Well, I *am* a cat!" Cornelia grinned.

"Do you mean you can tell me things — ?" It was too beautiful to believe.

"About what really *was?*" she artfully considered, holding him immensely now. "Well, unless they've come to you with time; unless you've learned — or found out."

"Oh," he reassuringly cried — reassuringly, it most seemed, for himself — "nothing has come to me with time, everything has gone from me. How can I find out now! What creature has an idea —— ?"

She threw up her hands with the shrug of old days — the sharp little shrug his sisters used to imitate and that she hadn't had to go to Europe for. The only thing was that he blessed her for bringing it back. "Ah, the ideas of people now —— !"

"Yes, their ideas are certainly not about *us*." But he ruefully faced it. "We've none the less, however, to live with them."

"With their ideas — ?" Cornelia questioned.

"With *them* — these modern wonders; such as they are!" Then he went on: "It must have been to help me you've come back."

She said nothing for an instant about that, only nodding instead at his photograph. "What has become of yours? I mean of *her*."

This time it made him turn pale. "You remember I *have* one?"

She kept her eyes on him. "In

a 'pork-pie' hat, with her hair in a long net. That was so 'smart' then; especially with one's skirt looped up, over one's hooped magenta petticoat, in little festoons, and a row of very big onyx beads over one's braided velveteen sack — braided quite plain and very broad, don't you know?"

He smiled for her extraordinary possession of these things — she was as prompt as if she had had them before her. "Oh, rather — 'don't I know?' You wore brown velveteen, and, on those remarkably small hands, funny gauntlets — like mine."

"Oh, do *you* remember? But like yours?" she wondered.

"I mean like hers in my photograph." But he came back to the present picture. "This is better, however, for really showing her lovely head."

"Mary's head was a perfection!" Cornelia testified.

"Yes — it was better than her heart."

"Ah, don't say that!" she pleaded. "You weren't fair."

"Don't you think I was fair?" It interested him immensely — and the more that he indeed mightn't have been; which he seemed somehow almost to hope.

"She didn't think so — to the very end."

"She didn't?" — ah the right things Cornelia said to him! But before she could answer he was studying again closely the small faded face. "No, she doesn't, she doesn't. Oh, her charming sad eyes and the way they *say* that, across

841

the years, straight into mine! But I don't know, I don't know!" White-Mason quite comfortably sighed.

His companion appeared to appreciate this effect. "That's just the way you used to flirt with her, poor thing. Wouldn't you like to have it?" she asked.

"This — for my very own?" He looked up delighted. "I really may?"

"Well, if you'll give me yours. We'll exchange."

"That's a charming idea. We'll exchange. But you must come and get it at my rooms — where you'll see my things."

For a little she made no answer — as if for some feeling. Then she said: "You asked me just now why I've come back."

He stared as for the connection; after which with a smile: "Not to do *that* —— ?"

She waited briefly again, but with a queer little look. "I can do those things now; and — yes! — that's in a manner why. I came," she then said, "because I knew of a sudden one day — knew as never before — that I was old."

"I see. I see." He quite understood — she had notes that so struck him. "And how did you like it?"

She hesitated — she decided. "Well, if I liked it, it was on the principle perhaps on which some people like high game!"

"High game — that's good!" he laughed. "Ah, my dear, we're 'high'!"

She shook her head. "No, not

you — yet. I at any rate didn't want any more adventures," Cornelia said.

He showed their small relic again with assurance. "You wanted *us*. Then here we are. Oh how we can talk! — with all those things you know! You *are* an invention. And you'll see there are things *I* know. I shall turn up here — well, daily."

She took it in, but only after a moment answered. "There was something you said just now you'd tell me. Don't you mean to try —— ?"

"Mrs. Worthingham?" He drew from within his coat his pocketbook and carefully found a place in it for Mary Cardew's carte-de-visite, folding it together with deliberation over which he put it back. Finally he spoke. "No — I've decided. I can't — I don't want to."

Cornelia marvelled — or looked as if she did. "Not for all she has?"

"Yes — I know all she has. But I also know all she hasn't. And, as I told you, she herself doesn't — hasn't a glimmer of a suspicion of it; and never will have."

Cornelia magnanimously thought. "No — but she knows other things."

He shook his head as at the portentous heap of them. "Too many — too many. And other indeed — *so* other! Do you know," he went on, "that it's as if *you* — by turning up for me — had brought that home to me?"

"'For you,'" she candidly considered. "But what — since you can't marry me! — can you do with me?"

Well, he seemed to have it all. "Everything. I can live with you — just this way." To illustrate which he dropped into the other chair by her fire; where, leaning back, he gazed at the flame. "I can't give you up. It's very curious. It has come over me as it did over you when you renounced Bognor. That's it — I know it at last, and I see one can like it. I'm 'high.' You needn't deny it. That's my taste. I'm old." And in spite of the considerable glow there of her little household altar he said it without the scowl.

A ROUND OF VISITS

He had been out but once since his arrival, Mark Monteith; that was the next day after — he had disembarked by night on the previous; then everything had come at once, as he would have said, everything had changed. He had got in on Tuesday; he had spent Wednesday for the most part down town, looking into the dismal subject of his anxiety — the anxiety that, under a sudden decision, had brought him across the unfriendly sea at mid-winter, and it was through information reaching him on Wednesday evening that he had measured his loss, measured above all his pain. These were two distinct things, he felt, and, though both bad, one much worse than the other. It wasn't till the next three days had pretty well ebbed, in fact, that he knew himself for so badly wounded. He had waked up on Thursday morning, so far as he had slept at all, with the sense, together, of a blinding New York blizzard and of a deep sore inward ache. The great white savage storm would have kept him at the best within doors, but his stricken state was by itself quite reason enough.

He so felt the blow indeed, so gasped, before what had happened to him, at the ugliness, the bitterness, and, beyond these things, the sinister strangeness, that, the matter of his dismay little by little detaching and projecting itself, settling there face to face with him as something he must now live with always, he might have been in charge of some horrid alien thing, some violent, scared, unhappy creature whom there was small joy, of a truth, in remaining with, but whose behaviour wouldn't perhaps bring him under notice, nor otherwise compromise him, so long as he should stay to watch it. A young jibbering ape of one of the more formidable sorts, or an ominous infant panther, smuggled into the great gaudy hotel and whom it might yet be important he shouldn't advertise, couldn't have affected him as needing more domestic attention. The great gaudy hotel — The Pocahontas, but carried out largely on "Du Barry" lines — made all about him, beside, behind, below, above, in blocks and tiers and superpositions, a sufficient defensive hugeness; so that, between the massive labyrinth and the New York weather, life in a lighthouse during a gale would scarce have kept him more apart. Even when in the course of that worse Thursday it had occurred to him for vague relief that the odious certified facts couldn't be all his misery, and that, with his throat and a probable temperature, a brush of the epidemic, which was for ever brushing him, accounted for something, even then he couldn't resign himself to bed and broth and dimness, but only circled and prowled the more within his high cage, only watched the more from his tenth story the rage of the elements.

In the afternoon he had a doctor — the caravanserai, which supplied everything in quantities, had one for each group of so many rooms — just in order to be assured that he was *grippé* enough for anything. What his visitor, making light of his attack, perversely told him was that he was, much rather, "blue" enough, and from causes doubtless known to himself — which didn't come to the same thing; but he "gave him something," prescribed him warmth and quiet and broth and courage, and came back the next day as to readminister this last dose. He then pronounced him better, and on Saturday pronounced him well — all the more that the storm had abated and the snow had been dealt with as New York, at a push, knew how to deal with things. Oh, how New York knew how to deal — to deal, that is, with other accumulations lying passive to its hand — was exactly what Mark now ached with his impression of; so that, still threshing about in this consciousness, he had on the Saturday come near to breaking out

as to what was the matter with him. The Doctor brought in somehow the air of the hotel — which, cheerfully and conscientiously, by his simple philosophy, the good man wished to diffuse; breathing forth all the echoes of other woes and worries and pointing the honest moral that, especially with such a thermometer, there were enough of these to go round. Our sufferer, by that time, would have liked to tell some one; extracting, to the last acid strain of it, the full strength of his sorrow, taking it all in as he could only do by himself and with the conditions favourable at least to this, had been his natural first need. But now, he supposed, he *must* be better; there was something of his heart's heaviness he wanted so to give out.

He had rummaged forth on the Thursday night half a dozen old photographs stuck into a leather frame, a small show-case that formed part of his usual equipage of travel — he mostly set it up on a table when he stayed anywhere long enough; and in one of the neat gilt-edged squares of this convenient portable array, as familiar as his shaving-glass or the hairbrushes, of backs and monograms now so beautifully toned and wasted, long ago given him by his mother, Phil Bloodgood handsomely faced him. Not contemporaneous, and a little faded, but so saying what it said only the more dreadfully, the image seemed to sit there, at an immemorial window, like some long effective and only at last exposed "decoy" of fate. It was *because* he was so beautifully good-looking, because he was so charming and clever and frank — besides being one's third cousin, or whatever it was, one's early school-fellow and one's later college classmate — that one had abjectly trusted him. To live thus with his unremoved, undestroyed, engaging, treacherous face, had been, as our traveller desired, to live with all of the felt pang; had been to consume it in such a single hot, sore mouthful as would so far as possible dispose of it and leave but cold dregs. Thus, if the Doctor, casting about for pleasantness, had happened to notice him there, salient since he was, and possibly by the same stroke even to know him, as New York — and more or less to its cost now, mightn't one say? — so abundantly and agreeable had, the cup would have overflowed and Monteith, for all he could be sure of the contrary, would have relieved himself positively in tears.

"Oh *he's* what's the matter with me — that, looking after some of my poor dividends, as he for the ten years of my absence had served me by doing, he has simply jockeyed me out of the whole little collection, such as it was, and taken the opportunity of my return, inevitably at last bewildered and uneasy, to 'sail,' ten days ago, for parts unknown and as yet unguessable. It isn't the beastly values themselves, however; that's only awkward and I can still live, though I don't quite know how I shall turn round; it's the horror of *his* having done it, and done it to *me* — without a mitigation or, so to speak, a warning or an excuse." That, at a hint or a jog, is what he would have brought out — only to feel afterward, no doubt, that he had wasted his impulse and profaned even a little his sincerity. The Doctor didn't in the event so much as glance at his cluster of portraits — which fact quite put before our friend the essentially more vivid range of imagery that a pair of eyes transferred from room to room and from one queer case to another, in such a place as that, would mainly be adjusted to. It wasn't for *him* to relieve himself touchingly, strikingly or whatever, to such a man: such a man might much more pertinently — save for professional discretion — have emptied out there his own bag of wonders; prodigies of observation, flowers of oddity, flowers of misery, flowers of the monstrous, gathered in current hotel practice. Countless possibilities, making doctors perfunctory, Mark felt, swarmed and seethed at their doors; it showed for an incalculable world, and at last, on Sunday, he decided to leave his room.

EVERYTHING, as he passed through the place, went on — all the offices of life, the whole bustle of the market, and withal, surprisingly, scarce less that of the nursery and the playground; the whole sprawl in especial of the great gregarious fireside: it was a complete social scene in itself, on which types might figure and passions rage and plots thicken and dramas develop, without reference to any other sphere, or perhaps even to anything at all outside. The signs of this met him at every turn as he threaded the labyrinth, passing from one extraordinary masquerade of expensive objects, one portentous "period" of decoration, one violent phase of publicity, to another: the heavy heat, the luxuriance, the extravagance, the quantity, the colour, gave the impression of some wondrous tropical forest, where vociferous, bright-eyed, and feathered creatures, of every variety of size and hue, were half smothered between undergrowths of velvet and tapestry and ramifications of marble and bronze. The fauna and the flora startled him alike, and among them his bruised spirit drew in and folded its wings. But he roamed and rested, exploring and in a manner enjoying the vast rankness — in the depth of which he suddenly encountered Mrs. Folliott, whom he had last seen, six months before, in London, and who had spoken to him then, precisely, of Phil Bloodgood, for several years previous her confidential American agent and factotum too, as she might say, but at that time so little in her good books, for the extraordinary things he seemed to be doing, that she was just hurrying home, she had made no scruple of mention-

ing, to take everything out of his hands.

Mark remembered how uneasy she had made him — how that very talk with her had wound him up to fear, as so acute and intent a little person she affected him; though he had affirmed with all emphasis and flourish his own confidence and defended, to iteration, his old friend. This passage had remained with him for a certain pleasant heat of intimacy, his partner, of the charming appearance, being what she was; he liked to think how they had fraternised over their difference and called each other idiots, or almost, without offence. It was always a link to have scuffled, failing a real scratch, with such a character; and he had at present the flutter of feeling that something of this would abide. *He* hadn't been hurrying home, at the London time, in any case; he was doing nothing then, and had continued to do it; he would want, before showing suspicion — that had been his attitude — to have more, after all, to go upon. Mrs. Folliott also, and with a great actual profession of it, remembered and rejoiced; and, also staying in the house as she was, sat with him, under a spreading palm, in a wondrous rococo salon, surrounded by the pinkest, that is the fleshiest, imitation Boucher panels, and wanted to know if he *now* stood up for his swindler. She would herself have tumbled on a cloud, very passably, in a fleshy Boucher manner, hadn't she been over-dressed for such an exercise; but she was quite realistically aware of what had so naturally happened — she was prompt about Bloodgood's "flight."

She had acted with energy, on getting back — she had saved what she could; which hadn't, however, prevented her losing all disgustedly some ten thousand dollars. She was lovely, lively, friendly, interested, she connected Monteith perfectly with their discussion that day during the water-party on the Thames; but, sitting here with him half an hour, she talked only of her peculiar, her cruel sacrifice — since she should never get a penny back. He had felt himself, on their meeting, quite yearningly reach out to her — so decidedly, by the morning's end, and that of his scattered sombre stations, had he been sated with meaningless contacts, with the sense of people all about him intensely, though harmlessly, animated, yet at the same time raspingly indifferent. *They* would have, he and she at least, their common pang — through which fact, somehow, he should feel less stranded. It wasn't that he wanted to be pitied — he fairly didn't pity himself; he winced, rather, and even to vicarious anguish, as it rose again, for poor shamed Bloodgood's doom-ridden figure. But he wanted, as with a desperate charity, to give some easier turn to the mere ugliness of the main facts; to work off his obsession from them by mixing with it some other blame, some other pity, it scarce mattered what — if it might be some other experience; as an effect of which larger ventilation it would have, after a fashion and for a man of free sensibility, a diluted and less poisonous taste.

By the end of five minutes of Mrs. Folliott, however, he felt his dry lips seal themselves to a makeshift simper. She could *take* nothing — no better, no broader perception of anything than fitted her own small faculty; so that though she must have recalled or imagined that he had still, up to lately, had interests at stake, the rapid result of her egotistical little chatter was to make him wish he might rather have conversed with the French waiter dangling in the long vista that showed the oriental café as a climax, or with the policeman, outside, the top of whose helmet peeped above the ledge of a window. She bewailed her wretched money to excess — she who, he was sure, had quantities more; she pawed and tossed her bare bone, with her little extraordinarily gemmed and manicured hands, till it acted on his nerves; she rang all the changes on the story, the dire fatality, of her having wavered and muddled, thought of this and but done that, of her stupid failure to have pounced, when she had first meant to, in season. She abused the author of their wrongs — recognising thus too Monteith's right to loathe him — for the desperado he assuredly had proved, but with a vulgarity of analysis and an incapacity for the higher criticism, as her listener felt it to

848

be, which made him determine resentfully, almost grimly, that she shouldn't have the benefit of a grain of *his* vision or *his* version of what had befallen them, and of how, in particular, it had come; and should never dream thereby (though much would she suffer from that!) of how interesting he might have been. She had, in a finer sense, no manners, and to be concerned with her in any retrospect was — since their discourse was of losses — to feel the dignity of history incur the very gravest. It was true that such fantasies, or that any shade of inward irony, would be Greek to Mrs. Folliott.

It was also true, however, and not much more strange, when she had presently the comparatively happy thought of "Lunch with *us*, you poor dear!" and mentioned three or four of her "crowd" — a new crowd, rather, for her, all great Sunday lunches there and immense fun, who would in a moment be turning up — that this seemed to him as easy as anything else; so that after a little, deeper in the jungle and while, under the temperature as of high noon, with the crowd complete and "ordering," he wiped the perspiration from his brow, he felt he was letting himself go. He did that certainly to the extent of leaving far behind any question of Mrs. Folliott's manners. They didn't matter there — nobody's did; and if she ceased to lament her ten thousand it was only because, among higher voices, she couldn't make herself heard. Poor Bloodgood didn't have a show, as they might have said, didn't get through at any point; the crowd was so new that — there either having been no hue and cry for him, or having been too many others, for other absconders, in the intervals — they had never so much as heard of him and would have no more of Mrs. Folliott's true inwardness, on that subject at least, than she had lately cared to have of Monteith's.

There was nothing like a crowd, this unfortunate knew, for making one feel lonely, and he felt so increasingly during the meal; but he got thus at least in a measure away from the terrible little lady; after which, and before the end of the hour, he wanted still more to get away from every one else. He was in fact about to perform this manœuvre when he was checked by the jolly young woman he had been having on his left and who had more to say about the Hotels, up and down the town, than he had ever known a young woman to have to say on any subject at all; she expressed herself in hotel terms exclusively, the names of those establishments playing through her speech as the *leit-motif* might have recurrently flashed and romped through a piece of profane modern music. She wanted to present him to the pretty girl she had brought with her, and who had apparently signified to her that she must do so.

"I think you know my brother-in-law, Mr. Newton Winch," the

pretty girl had immediately said; she moved her head and shoulders together, as by a common spring, the effect of a stiff neck or of something loosened in her back hair; but becoming, queerly enough, all the prettier for doing so. He had seen in the papers, her brother-in-law, Mr. Monteith's arrival — Mr. Mark P. Monteith, wasn't it? — and where he was, and she had been with him, three days before, at the time; whereupon he had said "Hullo, what can have brought old Mark back?" He seemed to have believed — Newton had seemed — that that shirker, as he called him, never *would* come; and she guessed that if she had known she was going to meet such a former friend ("Which he claims you are, sir," said the pretty girl) he would have asked her to find out what the trouble could be. But the real satisfaction would just be, she went on, if his former friend would himself go and see him and tell him; he had appeared of late so down.

"Oh, I remember him" — Mark didn't repudiate the friendship, placing him easily; only then he wasn't married and the pretty girl's sister must have come in later: which showed, his not knowing such things, how they had lost touch. The pretty girl was sorry to have to say in return to this that her sister wasn't living — had died two years after marrying; so that Newton was up there in Fiftieth Street alone; where (in explanation of his being "down") he had been shut up for days with bad *grippe;* though now on the mend,

or she wouldn't have gone to him, not she, who had had it nineteen times and didn't want to have it again. But the horrid poison just seemed to have entered into poor Newton's soul.

"That's the way it *can* take you, don't you know?" And then as, with her single twist, she just charmingly hunched her eyes at our friend, "Don't you want to go to see him?"

Mark bethought himself: "Well, I'm going to see a lady —— "

She took the words from his mouth. "Of course you're going to see a lady — every man in New York is. But Newton isn't a lady, unfortunately for him, to-day; and Sunday afternoon in this place, in this weather, alone —— !"

"Yes, isn't it awful?" — he was quite drawn to her.

"Oh, *you've* got your lady!"

"Yes, I've got my lady, thank goodness!" The fervour of which was his sincere tribute to the note he had had on Friday morning from Mrs. Ash, the only thing that had a little tempered his gloom.

"Well then, feel for others. Fit him in. Tell him why!"

"Why I've come back? I'm glad I *have* — since it was to see *you!*" Monteith made brave enough answer, promising to do what he could. He liked the pretty girl, with her straight attack and her free awkwardness — also with her difference from the others through something of a sense and a distinction given her by so clearly having Newton on her mind. Yet it was odd to him, and it showed the lapse of the years, that Winch — as he had known him of old — could *be* to that degree on any one's mind.

III

OUTSIDE in the intensity of the cold — it was a jump from the Tropics to the Pole — he felt afresh the force of what he had just been saying; that if it weren't for the fact of Mrs. Ash's good letter of welcome, despatched, characteristically, as soon as she had, like the faithful sufferer in Fiftieth Street, observed his name, in a newspaper, on one of the hotel-lists, he should verily, for want of a connection and an abutment, have scarce dared to face the void and the chill together, but have sneaked back into the jungle and there tried to lose himself. He made, as it was, the opposite effort, resolute to walk, though hovering now and then at vague crossways, radiations of roads to nothing, or taking cold counsel of the long but still sketchy vista, as it struck him, of the northward Avenue, bright and bleak, fresh and harsh, rich and evident somehow, a perspective like a page of florid modern platitudes. He didn't quite know what he had expected for his return — not certainly serenades and deputations; but without Mrs. Ash his mail would have quite lacked geniality, and it was as if Phil Bloodgood had gone off not only with so large a slice of his small *peculium*, but with all the broken bits of the past, the loose ends of old relationships, that he had supposed he might pick up again. Well, perhaps he should still pick up a few — by the sweat of his brow; no motion of their own at least, he by this time judged, would send them fluttering into his hand.

Which reflections but quickened his forecast of this charm of the old Paris inveteracy renewed — the so-prized custom of nine years before, when he still believed in results from his fond frequentation of the Beaux Arts; that of walking over the river to the Rue de Marignan, precisely, every Sunday without exception, and sitting at her fireside, and often all offensively, no doubt, outstaying every one. How he had used to want those hours then, and how again, after a little, at present, the Rue de Marignan might have been before him! He had gone to her there at that time with his troubles, such as they were, and they had always worked for her amusement — which had been her happy, her clever way of taking them: she couldn't have done anything better for them in that phase, poor innocent things compared with what they might have been, than be amused by them. Perhaps that was what she would still be — with those of his present hour; now too they might inspire her with the touch she best applied and was most instinctive mistress of: this didn't at all events strike him as what he should most resent. It wasn't as if Mrs. Folliot, to make up for boring him with her own plaint, for example, had had so much as a gleam of conscious diversion over his.

"I'm *so* delighted to see you, I've such immensities to tell you!" — it began with the highest animation twenty minutes later, the very moment he stood there, the sense of the Rue de Marignan in the charming room and in the things about all reconstituted, regrouped, wonderfully preserved, down to the very sitting-places in the same relations, and down to the faint sweet mustiness of generations of cigarettes; but everything else different, and even vaguely alien, and by a measure still other than that of their own stretched interval and of the dear delightful woman's just a little pathetic alteration of face. He had allowed for the nine years, and so, it was to be hoped, had she; but the last thing, otherwise, that would have been touched, he immediately felt, was the quality, the intensity, of her care to see him. She cared, oh so visibly and touchingly and almost radiantly — save for her being, yes, distinctly, a little *more* battered than from even a good nine years' worth; nothing could in fact have perched with so crowning an impatience on the heap of what she had to "tell" as that special shade of revived consciousness of having him in particular to tell it to. It wasn't perhaps much to matter how soon she brought out and caused to ring, as it were, on the little recognised marqueterie table between them

(such an anciently envied treasure), the heaviest gold-piece of current history she was to pay him with for having just so felicitously come back: he knew already, without the telling, that intimate domestic tension must lately, within those walls, have reached a climax and that he could serve supremely — oh how he was going to serve! — as the most sympathetic of all pairs of ears.

The whole thing was upon him, in any case, with the minimum of delay: Bob had had it from her, definitely, the first of the week, and it was absolutely final now, that they must set up avowedly separate lives — without horrible "proceedings" of any sort, but with her own situation, her independence, secured to her once for all. She had been coming to it, taking her time, and she had gone through — well, so old a friend would guess enough what; but she was at the point, oh blessedly now, where she meant to stay, he'd see if she didn't; with which, in this wonderful way, he himself had arrived for the cream of it and she was just selfishly glad. Bob had gone to Washington — ostensibly on business, but really to recover breath; she had, speaking vulgarly, knocked the wind out of him and was allowing him time to turn round. Mrs. Folliott moreover, she was sure, would have gone — was certainly believed to have been seen there five days ago; and of course his first necessity, for public use, would be to patch up something with Mrs. Folliott. Mark knew about Mrs. Folliott? — who was only, for that matter, one of a regular "bevy." Not that it signified, however, if he didn't: she would tell him about *her* later.

He took occasion from the first fraction of a break not quite to know what he knew about Mrs. Folliott — though perhaps he could imagine a little; and it was probably at this minute that, having definitely settled to a position, and precisely in his very own tapestry *bergère*, the one with the delicious little spectral "subjects" on the back and seat, he partly exhaled, and yet managed partly to keep to himself, the deep resigned sigh of a general comprehension. He knew what he was "in" for, he heard her go on — she said it again and again, seemed constantly to be saying it while she smiled at him with her peculiar fine charm, her positive gaiety of sensibility, scarce dimmed: "I'm just selfishly glad, just selfishly glad!" Well, she was going to have reason to be; she was going to put the whole case to him, all her troubles and plans, and each act of the tragi-comedy of her recent existence, as to the dearest and safest sympathiser in all the world. There would be no chance for *his* case, though it was so much for his case he had come; yet there took place within him but a mild, dumb convulsion, the momentary strain of his substituting, by the turn of a hand, one prospect of interest for another.

Squaring himself in his old *bergère*, and with his lips, during the effort, compressed to the same passive grimace that had an hour or two before operated for the encouragement of Mrs. Folliott — just as it was to clear the stage completely for the present more prolonged performance — he shut straight down, as he even in the act called it to himself, on any personal claim for social consideration and rendered a perfect little agony of justice to the grounds of his friend's vividness. For it was all the justice that could be expected of him that, though, secretly, he wasn't going to be interested in her being interesting, she was yet going to be so, all the same, by the very force of her lovely material (Bob Ash *was* such a pure pearl of a donkey!) and he was going to keep on knowing she was — yes, to the very end. When after the lapse of an hour he rose to go, the rich fact that she *had* been was there between them, and with an effect of the frankly, fearlessly, harmlessly intimate fireside passage for it that went beyond even the best memories of the pleasant past. He hadn't "amused" her, no, in quite the same way as in the Rue de Marignan time — it had then been he who for the most part took frequent turns, emphatic, explosive, elocutionary, over that wonderful waxed parquet while she laughed as for the young perversity of him from the depths of the second, the matching *bergère*. To-day she herself held and swept the floor, putting him merely to the trouble of his perpetual "Brava!" But that was all through the change of basis — the amusement, another name only for the thrilled absorption, having been inevitably for *him;* as how could it have failed to be with such a regular "treat" to his curiosity? With the tea-hour now other callers were turning up, and he got away on the plea of his wanting so to think it all over. He hoped again he hadn't too queer a grin with his assurance to her, as if she would quite know what he meant, that he had been thrilled to the core. But she returned, quite radiantly, that he had carried *her* completely away; and her sincerity was proved by the final frankness of their temporary parting. "My pleasure of you is selfish, horribly, I admit; so that if *that* doesn't suit you — !" Her faded beauty flushed again as she said it.

IN the street again, as he resumed his walk, he saw how perfectly it would *have* to suit him and how he probably for a long time wouldn't be suited otherwise. Between them and that time, however, what mightn't, for him, poor devil, on his new basis, have happened? She wasn't at any rate within any calculable period going to care so much for anything as for the so quaintly droll terms in which her rearrangement with her husband — thanks to that gentleman's inimitable fatuity — would have to be made. This was what it

was to own, exactly, her special grace — the brightest gaiety in the finest sensibility; *such* a display of which combination, Mark felt as he went (if he could but have done it still more justice) she must have regaled him with! That exquisite last flush of her fadedness could only remain with him; yet while he presently stopped at a street-corner in a district redeemed from desolation but by the passage just then of a choked trolley-car that howled, as he paused for it, beneath the weight of its human accretions, he seemed to know the inward "sinking" that had been determined in a hungry man by some extravagant sight of the preparation of somebody else's dinner. Florence Ash was dining, so to speak, off the feast of appreciation, appreciation of what she had to "tell" him, that he had left her seated at; and she was welcome, assuredly—welcome, welcome, welcome, he musingly, he wistfully, and yet at the same time a trifle mechanically, repeated, stayed as he was a moment longer by the suffering shriek of another public vehicle and a sudden odd automatic return of his mind to the pretty girl, the flower of Mrs. Folliott's crowd, who had spoken to him of Newton Winch. It was extraordinarily as if, on the instant, she reminded him, from across the town, that *she* had offered him dinner: it was really quite strangely, while he stood there, as if she had told him where he could go and get it. With which, none the less, it was apparently where he wouldn't find her — and what was there, after all, of nutritive in the image of Newton Winch? He made up his mind in a moment that it owed that property, which the pretty girl had somehow made imputable, to the fact of its simply being just then the one image of anything known to him that the terrible place had to offer. Nothing, he a minute later reflected, could have been so "rum" as that, sick and sore, of a bleak New York eventide, he should have had nowhere to turn if not to the said Fiftieth Street.

That was the direction he accordingly took, for when he found the number given him by the same remarkable agent of fate also present to his memory he recognised the direct intervention of Providence and how it absolutely required a miracle to explain his so precipitately embracing this loosest of connections. The miracle indeed soon grew clearer: Providence had, on some obscure system, chosen this very ridiculous hour to save him from cultivation of the sin of selfishness, the obsession of egotism, and was breaking him to its will by constantly directing his attention to the claims of others. Who could say what at that critical moment mightn't have become of Mrs. Folliott (otherwise too then so sadly embroiled!) if she hadn't been enabled to air to him her grievance and her rage? — just as who could deny that it must have done Florence Ash a world of good to have put her thoughts about Bob in order by the aid of a person to whom the vision of Bob in the light of those thoughts (or in other words to whom *her* vision of Bob and nothing else) would mean so delightfully much? It was on the same general lines that poor Newton Winch, bereft, alone, ill, perhaps dying, and with the drawback of a not very sympathetic personality — as Mark remembered it at least — to contend against in almost any conceivable appeal to human furtherance, it was on these lines, very much, that the luckless case in Fiftieth Street was offered him as a source of salutary discipline. The moment for such a lesson might strike him as strange, in view of the quite special and independent opportunity for exercise that his spirit had during the last three days enjoyed there in his hotel bedroom; but evidently his languor of charity needed some admonition finer than any it might trust to chance for, and by the time he at last, Winch's residence recognised, was duly elevated to his level and had pressed the electric button at his door, he felt himself acting indeed as under stimulus of a sharp poke in the side.

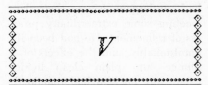

WITHIN the apartment to which he had been admitted, moreover, the fine intelligence we have imputed to him was in the course of three minutes confirmed; since it took him no longer than that to say to himself, facing his old acquaintance, that he had never seen any one so improved. The place, which had the semblance of a high studio light as well as a general air of other profusions and amplitudes, might have put him off a little by its several rather glaringly false accents, those of contemporary domestic "art" striking a little wild. The scene was smaller, but the rich confused complexion of the Pocahontas, showing through Du Barry paint and patches, might have set the example — which had been followed with the costliest candour — so that, clearly, Winch was in these days rich, as most people in New York seemed rich; as, in spite of Bob's depredations, Florence Ash was, as even Mrs. Folliott was in spite of Phil Bloodgood's, as even Phil Bloodgood himself must have been for reasons too obvious; as in fine every one had a secret for being, or for feeling, or for looking, every one at least but Mark Monteith.

These facts were as nothing, however, in presence of his quick and strong impression that his pale, nervous, smiling, clean-shaven host had undergone since their last meeting some extraordinary process of refinement. He had been ill, unmistakably, and the effects of a plunge into plain clean living, where any fineness had remained, were often startling, sometimes almost charming. But independently of this, and for a much longer time, some principle of intelli-

gence, some art of life, would discernibly have worked in him. Remembered from college years and from those two or three luckless and faithless ones of the Law School as constitutionally common, as consistently and thereby doubtless even rather powerfully coarse, clever only for uncouth and questionable things, he yet presented himself now as if he had suddenly and mysteriously been educated. There was a charm in his wide, "drawn," convalescent smile, in the way his fine fingers — had he anything like fine fingers of old? — played, and just fidgeted, over the prompt and perhaps a trifle incoherent offer of cigars, cordials, ash-trays, over the question of his visitor's hat, stick, fur coat, general best accommodation and ease; and how the deuce, accordingly, had charm, for coming out so on top, Mark wondered, "squared" the other old elements? For the short interval so to have dealt with him what force had it turned on, what patented process, of the portentous New York order in which there were so many, had it skilfully applied? Were these the things New York did when you just gave her *all* her head, and that he himself then had perhaps too complacently missed? Strange almost to the point of putting him positively off at first — quite as an exhibition of the uncanny — this sense of Newton's having all the while neither missed nor muffed anything, and having, as with an eye to the *coup de théâtre* to come, lowered one's expectations, at the start, to that abject pitch. It might have been taken verily for an act of bad faith — really for such a rare stroke of subtlety as could scarce have been achieved by a straight or natural aim.

So much as this at least came and went in Monteith's agitated mind; the oddest intensity of apprehension, admiration, mystification, which the high north-light of the March afternoon and the quite splendidly vulgar appeal of fifty overdone decorative effects somehow fostered and sharpened. Everything had already gone, however, the next moment, for wasn't the man he had come so much too intelligently himself to patronise absolutely bowling him over with the extraordinary speech: "See here, you know — you must be ill, or have had a bad shock, or some beastly upset: are you very sure you ought to have come out?" Yes, he after an instant believed his ears; coarse common Newton Winch, whom he had called on because he could, as a gentleman, after all afford to, coarse common Newton Winch, who had had troubles and been epidemically poisoned, lamentably sick, who bore in his face and in the very tension, quite exactly the "charm," of his manner, the traces of his late ordeal, and, for that matter, of scarce completed gallant emergence — this astonishing ex-comrade was simply writing himself at a stroke (into our friend's excited imagination at all events) the most distinguished of men. Oh, *he* was going to be interesting, if Florence Ash had been going to be; but Mark felt how, under the law of a lively present difference, that would be as an effect of one's having one's self thoroughly rallied. He knew within the minute that the tears stood in his eyes; he stared through them at his friend with a sharp "Why, how do you know? How *can* you?" To which he added before Winch could speak: "I met your charming sister-in-law a couple of hours since — at luncheon, at the Pocahontas; and heard from her that you were badly laid up and had spoken of me. So I came to minister to you."

The object of this design hovered there again, considerably restless, shifting from foot to foot, changing his place, beginning and giving up motions, striking matches for a fresh cigarette, offering them again, redundantly, to his guest and then not lighting himself — but all the while with the smile of another creature than the creature known to Mark; all the while with the history of something that had happened to him ever so handsomely shining out. Mark was conscious within himself from this time on of two quite distinct processes of notation — that of his practically instant surrender to the consequences of the act of perception in his host of which the two women trained supposably in the art of pleasing had been altogether incapable; and that of some other condition on Newton's part that left his own poor power of divination nothing less than shamed. This last was signally the case on the former's saying, ever so responsively, almost radiantly, in answer to his account of how he happened to come: "Oh then it's very interesting!" *That* was the astonishing note, after what he had been through: neither Mrs. Folliott nor Florence Ash had so much as hinted or breathed to him that *he* might have incurred that praise. No wonder therefore he was now taken — with this fresh party's instant suspicion and imputation of it; though it was indeed for some minutes next as if each tried to see which could accuse the other of the greater miracle of penetration. Mark was so struck, in a word, with the extraordinarily straight guess Winch had had there in reserve for him that, other quick impressions helping, there was nothing for him but to bring out, himself: "There must be, my dear man, something rather wonderful the matter with you!" The quite more intensely and more irresistibly drawn grin, the quite unmistakably deeper consciousness in the dark, wide eye, that accompanied the not quite immediate answer to which remark he was afterward to remember.

"How do you know that — or why do you think it?"

"Because there *must* be — for you to see! I shouldn't have expected it."

"Then you take me for a damned fool?" laughed wonderful Newton Winch.

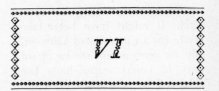

He could say nothing that, whether as to the sense of it or as to the way of it, didn't so enrich Mark's vision of him that our friend, after a little, as this effect proceeded, caught himself in the act of almost too curiously gaping. Everything, from moment to moment, fed his curiosity; such a question, for instance, as whether the quite ordinary peepers of the Newton Winch of their earlier youth could have looked, under any provocation, either dark or wide; such a question, above all, as how *this* incalculable apparition came by the whole startling power of play of its extravagantly sensitive labial connections — exposed, so to its advantage (he now jumped at one explanation) by the removal of what had probably been one of the vulgarest of moustaches. With this, at the same time, the oddity of that particular consequence was vivid to him; the glare of his curiosity fairly lasting while he remembered how he had once noted the very opposite turn of the experiment for Phil Bloodgood. He would have said in advance that poor Winch couldn't have afforded to risk showing his "real" mouth; just as he would have said that in spite of the fine ornament that so considerably muffled it Phil could only have gained by showing his. But to have seen Phil shorn — as he once had done

— was earnestly to pray that he might promptly again bristle; beneath Phil's moustache lurked nothing to "make up" for it in case of removal. While he thought of which things the line of grimace, as he could only have called it, the mobile, interesting, ironic line the great double curve of which connected, in the face before him, the strong nostril with the lower cheek, became the very key to his first idea of Newton's capture of refinement. He had shaved and was happily transfigured. Phil Bloodgood had shaved and been wellnigh lost; though why should he just now too precipitately drag the reminiscence in?

That question too, at the queer touch of association, played up for Mark even under so much proof that the state of his own soul was being with the lapse of every instant registered. Phil Bloodgood had brought about the state of his soul — there was accordingly that amount of connection; only it became further remarkable that from the moment his companion had sounded him, and sounded him, he knew, down to the last truth of things, his disposition, his necessity to talk, the desire that had in the morning broken the spell of his confinement, the impulse that had thrown him so defeatedly into Mrs. Folliott's arms and into Florence Ash's, these forces seemed to feel their impatience ebb and their discretion suddenly grow. His companion was talking again, but just then, incongruously, made his need to communicate lose itself. It was

as if his personal case had already been touched by some tender hand — and that, after all, was the modest limit of its greed. "I know now why you came back — did Lottie mention how I had wondered? But sit down, sit down — only let me, nervous beast as I am, take it standing! — and believe me when I tell you that I've now ceased to wonder. My dear chap, I *have* it! It can't but have been for poor Phil Bloodgood. He sticks out of you, the brute — as how, with what he has done to you, shouldn't he? There was a man to see me yesterday — Tim Slater, whom I don't think you know, but who's 'on' everything within about two minutes of its happening (I never saw such a fellow!) and who confirmed my supposition, all my own, however, mind you, at first, that you're one of the sufferers. So how the devil can you *not* feel knocked? Why *should* you look as if you were having the time of your life? What a hog to have played it on *you*, on *you*, of all his friends!" So Newton Winch continued, and so the air between the two men might have been, for a momentary watcher — which is indeed what I can but invite the reader to become — that of a nervously displayed, but all considerate, as well as most acute, curiosity on the one side, and that on the other, after a little, of an eventually fascinated acceptance of so much free and in especial of so much right attention. "Do you *mind* my asking you? Because if you do I won't press; but as a man whose own responsibilities, some of 'em at least, don't differ much, I gather, from some of his, one would like to know how he was ever allowed to get to the point — ! But I *do* plough you up?"

Mark sat back in his chair, moved but holding himself, his elbows squared on each arm, his hands a bit convulsively interlocked across him — very much in fact as he had appeared an hour ago in the old tapestry *bergère;* but as his rigour was all then that of the grinding effort to profess and to give, so it was considerably now for the fear of too hysterically gushing. Somehow too — since his wound was to that extent open — he winced at hearing the author of it branded. He hadn't so much minded the epithets Mrs. Folliott had applied, for they were to the appropriator of *her* securities. As the appropriator of his own he didn't so much want to brand him as — just more "amusingly" even, if one would! — to make out, perhaps, with intelligent help, how such a man, in such a relation, *could* come to tread such a path: which was exactly the interesting light that Winch's curiosity and sympathy were there to assist him to. He pleaded at any rate immediately his advertising no grievance. "I feel sore, I admit, and it's a horrid sort of thing to have had happen; but when you call him a brute and a hog I rather squirm, for brutes and hogs never live, I guess, in the sort of hell in which he now must be."

Newton Winch, before the fire-place, his hands deep in his pockets, where his guest could see his long fingers beat a tattoo on his thighs, Newton Winch dangled and swung himself, and threw back his head and laughed. "Well, I must say you take it amazingly! — all the more that to see you again this way is to feel that if, all along, there was a man whose delicacy and confidence and general attitude might have marked him for a particular consideration, you'd have been the man." And they were more directly face to face again; with Newton smiling and smiling *so* appreciatively; making our friend in fact almost ask himself when before a man had ever grinned from ear to ear to the effect of its so becoming him. What he replied, however, was that Newton described in those flattering terms a client temptingly fatuous; after which, and the exchange of another protest or two in the interest of justice and decency, and another plea or two in that of the still finer contention that even the basest misdeeds had always somewhere or other, could one get at it, their propitiatory side, our hero found himself on his feet again, under the influence of a sudden failure of everything but horror — a horror determined by some turn of their talk and indeed by the very fact of the freedom of it. It was as if a far-borne sound of the hue and cry, a vision of his old friend hunted and at bay, had suddenly broken in — this other friend's, this irresistibly intelligent other companion's, practically vivid projection of that making the worst ugliness real. "Oh, it's just making my wry face to somebody, and your letting me and caring and wanting to know: that," Mark said, "is what does me good; not any other hideous question. I mean I don't take any interest in *my* case — what one wonders about, you see, is what can be done for him. I mean, that is" — for he floundered a little, not knowing at last quite what he did mean, a great rush of mere memories, a great humming sound as of thick, thick echoes, rising now to an assault that he met with his face indeed contorted. If he didn't take care he should howl; so he more or less successfully took care — yet with his host vividly watching him while he shook the danger temporarily off. "I don't mind — though it's rather *that;* my having felt this morning, after three dismal dumb bad days, that one's friends perhaps would be thinking of one. All I'm conscious of now — I give you my word — is that I'd like to see him."

"You'd like to see him?"

"Oh, I don't say," Mark ruefully smiled, "that I should like him to see *me* ——— !"

Newton Winch, from where he stood — and they were together now, on the great hearth-rug that was a triumph of modern orientalism — put out one of the noted fine hands and, with an expressive headshake, laid it on his shoulder. "Don't wish him that, Monteith — don't wish him that!"

"Well, but," — and Mark raised his eyebrows still higher — "he'd see I bear up; pretty well!"

"God forbid he should see, my dear fellow!" Newton cried as for the pang of it.

Mark had for his idea, at any rate, the oddest sense of an exaltation that grew by this use of frankness. "I'd go to him. Hanged if I wouldn't — anywhere!"

His companion's hand still rested on him. "You'd go to him?"

Mark stood up to it — though trying to sink solemnity as pretentious. "I'd go like a shot." And then he added: "And it's probably what — when we've turned round — I *shall* do."

"When 'we' have turned round?"

"Well" — he was a trifle disconcerted at the tone — "I say that because you'll have helped me."

"Oh, I do nothing but want to help you!" Winch replied — which made it right again; especially as our friend still felt himself reassuringly and sustainingly grasped. But Winch went on: "You *would* go to him — in kindness?"

"Well — to understand."

"To understand how he could swindle you?"

"Well," Mark kept on, "to try and make out with him how, after such things — !" But he stopped; he couldn't name them.

It was as if his companion knew. "Such things as you've done for him of course — such services as you've rendered him."

"Ah, from far back. If I could tell you," our friend vainly wailed — "if I could tell you!"

Newton Winch patted his shoulder. "Tell me — tell me!"

"The sort of relation, I mean; ever so many things of a kind — !" Again, however, he pulled up; he felt the tremor of his voice.

"Tell me, tell me," Winch repeated with the same movement.

The tone in it now made their eyes meet again, and with this presentation of the altered face Mark measured as not before, for some reason, the extent of the recent ravage. "You must have been ill indeed."

"Pretty bad. But I'm better. And you do me good" — with which the light of convalescence came back. "I don't awfully bore you?"

Winch shook his head. "You keep me up — and you see how no one else comes near me."

Mark's eyes made out that he *was* better — though it wasn't yet that nothing was the matter with him. If there was ever a man with whom there was still something the matter — ! Yet one couldn't insist on that, and meanwhile he clearly did want company. "Then there we are. I myself had no one to go to."

"You save my life," Newton renewedly grinned.

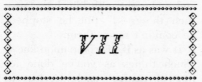

VII

"WELL, it's your own fault," Mark replied to that, "if you make me take advantage of you." Winch had withdrawn his hand, which was back, violently shaking keys or money, in his trousers pocket; and in this position he had abruptly a pause, a sensible, absence, that might have represented either some odd drop of attention, some turn-off to another thought, or just simply the sudden act of listening. His guest had indeed himself — under suggestion — the impression of a sound. "Mayn't you perhaps — if you hear something — have a call?"

Mark had said it so lightly, however, that he was the more struck with his host's appearing to turn just paler; and, with it, the latter now *was* listening. "You hear something?"

"I thought *you* did." Winch himself, on Mark's own pressure of the outside bell, had opened the door of the apartment — an indication then, it sufficiently appeared, that Sunday afternoons were servants', or attendants', or even trained nurses' holidays. It had also marked the stage of his convalescence, and to that extent — after his first flush of surprise — had but smoothed Monteith's way. At present he barely gave further attention; detaching himself as under some odd cross-impulse, he had quitted the spot and then taken, in the wide room, a restless turn — only, however, to revert in a moment to his friend's just-uttered deprecation of the danger of boring him. "If I make you take advantage of me — that is blessedly talk to me — it's exactly what I want to do. Talk to me — talk to me!" He positively waved it on; pulling up again, however, in his own talk, to say with a certain urgency: "Hadn't you better sit down?"

Mark, who stayed before the fire, couldn't but excuse himself. "Thanks — I'm very well so. I think of things and I fidget."

Winch stood a moment with his eyes on the ground. "Are you very sure?"

"Quite — I'm all right if you don't mind."

"Then as you like!" With which, shaking to extravagance again his long legs, Newton had swung off — only with a movement that, now his back was turned, affected his visitor as the most whimsical of all the forms of his rather unnatural manner. He was curiously different with his back turned, as Mark now for the first time saw it — dangling and somewhat wavering, as from an excess of uncertainty of gait; and this impression was so strange, it created in our friend, uneasily and on the spot, such a need of explanation, that his speech was stayed long enough to give Winch time to turn round again. The latter had indeed by this moment reached one of the limits of the place, the wide studio bay, where he paused, his back to the light and his face afresh presented, to let his just passingly depressed and quickened eyes take in as much as possible of the large floor, range over it with such brief freedom of search as the disposition of the furniture permitted. He was looking for something, though the betrayed reach of vision was but of an instant. Mark caught it,

however, and with his own sensibility all in vibration, found himself feeling at once that it meant something and that what it meant was connected with his entertainer's slightly marked appeal to him, the appeal of a moment before, not to remain standing. Winch knew by this time quite easily enough that he was hanging fire; which meant that they were suddenly facing each other across the wide space with a new consciousness.

Everything had changed — changed extraordinarily with the mere turning of that gentleman's back, the treacherous aspect of which its owner couldn't surely have suspected. If the question was of the pitch of their sensibility, at all events, it wouldn't be Mark's that should vibrate to least purpose. Visibly it had come to his host that something had within the few instants remarkably happened, but there glimmered on him an induction that still made him keep his own manner. Newton himself might now resort to any manner he liked. His eyes had raked the floor to recover the position of something dropped or misplaced, and something, above all, awkward or compromising; and he had wanted his companion not to command this scene from the hearth-rug, the hearth-rug where he had been just before holding him, hypnotising him to blindness, *because* the object in question would there be most exposed to sight. Mark embraced this with a further drop — while the apprehension penetrated — of his power to go on, and with an immense desire at the same time that his eyes should seem only to look at his friend; who broke out now, for that matter, with a fresh appeal. "Aren't you going to take advantage of me, man — aren't you going to *take* it?"

Everything had changed, we have noted, and nothing could more have proved it than the fact that, by the same turn, sincerity of desire had dropped out of Winch's chords, while irritation, sharp and almost imperious, had come in. "That's because he sees I see something!" Mark said to himself; but he had no need to add that it shouldn't prevent his seeing more — for the simple reason that, in a miraculous fashion, this was exactly what he did do in glaring out the harder. It was beyond explanation, but the very act of blinking thus in an attempt at showy steadiness became one and the same thing with an optical excursion lasting the millionth of a minute and making him aware that the edge of a rug, at the point where an arm-chair, pushed a little out of position, overstraddled it, happened just not wholly to have covered in something small and queer, neat and bright, crooked and compact, in spite of the strong toe-tip surreptitiously applied to giving it the right lift. Our gentleman, from where he hovered, and while looking straight at the master of the scene, yet saw, as by the tiny flash of a reflection from fine metal, *under* the chair. What he recognised, or at least guessed at, as sinister,

made him for a moment turn cold, and that chill was on him while Winch again addressed him — as differently as possible from any manner yet used. "I beg of you in God's name to talk to me — to *talk* to me!"

It had the ring of pure alarm and anguish, but was by this turn at least more human than the dazzling glitter of intelligence to which the poor man had up to now been treating him. "It's you, my good friend, who are in deep trouble," Mark was accordingly quick to reply, "and I ask your pardon for being so taken up with my own sorry business."

"Of course I'm in deep trouble" — with which Winch came nearer again; "but turning you on was exactly what I wanted."

Mark Monteith, at this, couldn't, for all his rising dismay, but laugh out; his sense of the ridiculous so swallowed up, for that brief convulsion, his sense of the sinister. Of such convenience in pain, it seemed, was the fact of another's pain, and of so much worth again disinterested sympathy! "Your interest was then —— ?"

"My interest was in your being interesting. For you *are!* And my nerves — !" said Newton Winch with a face from which the mystifying smile had vanished, yet in which distinction, as Mark so persistently appreciated it, still sat in the midst of ravage.

Mark wondered and wondered — he made strange things out. "Your nerves have needed company." He

864

could lay his hand on him now, even as shortly before he had felt Winch's own pressure of possession and detention. "As good for you yourself, that — or still better," he went on — "than I and my grievance were to have found you. Talk to *me*, talk to *me*, Newton Winch!" he added with an immense inspiration of charity.

"That's a different matter — that others but too much can do! But I'll say this. If you want to go to Phil Bloodgood —— !"

"Well?" said Mark as he stopped. He stopped, and Mark had now a hand on each of his shoulders and held him at arm's-length, held him with a fine idea that was not disconnected from the sight of the small neat weapon he had been fingering in the low luxurious morocco chair — it was of the finest orange colour — and then had laid beside him on the carpet; where, after he had admitted his visitor, his presence of mind coming back to it and suggesting that he couldn't pick it up without making it more conspicuous, he had thought, by some swing of the foot or other casual manœuvre, to dissimulate its visibility.

They were at close quarters now as not before and Winch perfectly passive, with eyes that somehow had no shadow of a secret left and with the betrayal to the sentient hands that grasped him of an intense, an extraordinary general tremor. To Mark's challenge he opposed afresh a brief silence, but the very quality of it, with his face

speaking, was that of a gaping wound. "Well, you needn't take *that* trouble. You see I'm such another."

"Such another as Phil — ?"

He didn't blink. "I don't know for sure, but I guess I'm worse."

"Do you mean you're guilty — ?"

"I mean I shall be wanted. Only I've stayed to take it."

Mark threw back his head, but only tightened his hands. He inexpressibly understood, and nothing in life had ever been so strange and dreadful to him as his thus helping himself by a longer and straighter stretch, as it were, to the monstrous sense of his friend's "education." It had been, in its immeasurable action, the education of business, of which the fruits were all around them. Yet prodigious was the interest, for prodigious truly — it seemed to loom before Mark — must have been the system. "To 'take' it?" he echoed; and then, though faltering a little, "To take what?"

He had scarce spoken when a long sharp sound shrilled in from the outer door, seeming of so high and peremptory a pitch that with the start it gave him his grasp of his host's shoulders relaxed an instant, though to the effect of no movement in *them* but what came from just a sensibly intenser vibration of the whole man. "For *that!*" said Newton Winch.

"Then you've known —— ?"

"I've expected. You've helped me to wait." And then as Mark gave an ironic wail: "You've tided me over. My condition has *wanted* somebody or something. Therefore, to complete this service, will you be so good as to open the door?"

Deep in the eyes Mark looked him, and still to the detection of no glimmer of the earlier man in the depths. The earlier man had been what he invidiously remembered — yet would *he* had been the whole simpler story! Then he moved his own eyes straight to the chair under which the revolver lay and which was but a couple of yards away. He felt his companion take this consciousness in, and it determined in them another long, mute exchange. "What do you mean to do?"

"Nothing."

"On your honour?"

"*My* 'honour'?" his host returned with an accent that he felt even as it sounded he should never forget. It brought to his own face a crimson flush — he dropped his guarding hands. Then as for a last look at him: "You're wonderful!"

"We *are* wonderful," said Newton Winch, while, simultaneously with the words, the pressed electric bell again and for a longer time pierced the warm cigaretted air.

Mark turned, threw up his arms, and it was only when he had passed through the vestibule and laid his hand on the door-knob that the horrible noise dropped. The next moment he was face to face with two visitors, a nondescript personage in a high hat and an astrakhan collar and cuffs, and a great belted constable, a splendid massive New York "officer" of the type he had had occasion to wonder at much again in the course of his walk, the type so by itself — his wide observation quite suggested — among those of the peacemakers of the earth. The pair stepped straight in — no word was said; but as he closed the door behind them Mark heard the infallible crack of a discharged pistol and, so nearly with it as to make all one violence, the sound of a great fall; things the effect of which was to lift him, as it were, with his company, across the threshold of the room in a shorter time than that taken by this record of the fact. But their rush availed little; Newton was stretched on his back before the fire; he had held the weapon horribly to his temple, and his upturned face was disfigured. The emissaries of the law, looking down at him, exhaled simultaneously a gruff imprecation, and then while the worthy in the high hat bent over the subject of their visit the one in the helmet raised a severe pair of eyes to Mark. "Don't you think, sir, you might have prevented it?"

Mark took a hundred things in, it seemed to him — things of the scene, of the moment, and of all the strange moments before; but one appearance more vividly even than the others stared out at him. "I really think I must practically have caused it."

THE IVORY TOWER

BOOK FIRST

It was but a question of leaving their own contracted "grounds," of crossing the Avenue and proceeding then to Mr. Betterman's gate, which even with the deliberate step of a truly massive young person she could reach in three or four minutes. So, making no other preparation than to open a vast pale-green parasol, a portable pavilion from which there fluttered fringes, frills and ribbons that made it resemble the roof of some Burmese palanquin or perhaps even pagoda, she took her way while these accessories fluttered in the August air, the morning freshness, and the soft sea-light. Her other draperies, white and voluminous, yielded to the mild breeze in the manner of those of a ship held back from speed yet with its canvas expanded; they conformed to their usual law of suggestion that the large loose ponderous girl, mistress as she might have been of the most expensive modern aids to the constitution of a "figure," lived, as they said about her, in wrappers and tea-gowns; so that, save for her enjoying obviously the rudest health, she might have been a convalescent creeping forth from the consciousness of stale bed-clothes. She turned in at the short drive, making the firm neat gravel creak under her tread, and at the end of fifty yards paused before the florid villa, a structure smothered in senseless architectural ornament, as if to put her question to its big fair foolish face. How Mr. Betterman might be this morning, and what sort of a night he might have had, was what she wanted to learn — an anxiety very real with her and which, should she be challenged, would nominally and decently have brought her; but her finer interest was in the possibility that Graham Fielder might have come.

The clean blank windows, however, merely gave her the impression of so many showy picture-frames awaiting their subjects; even those of them open to the charming Newport day seemed to tell her at the most that nothing had happened since the evening before and that the situation was still untouched by the change she dreamt of. A person essentially unobservant of forms, which her amplitude somehow never found of the right measure, so that she felt the misfit in many cases ridiculous, she now passed round the house instead of applying at the rather grandly gaping portal — which

867

might in all conscience have accommodated her — and, crossing a stretch of lawn to the quarter of the place turned to the sea, rested here again some minutes. She sought indeed after a moment the support of an elaborately rustic bench that ministered to ease and contemplation, whence she would rake much of the rest of the small sloping domain; the fair prospect, the great sea spaces, the line of low receding coast that bristled, either way she looked, with still more costly "places," and in particular the proprietor's wide and bedimmed verandah, this at present commonly occupied by her "prowling" father, as she now always thought of him, though if charged she would doubtless have admitted with the candour she was never able to fail of that she herself prowled during these days of tension quite as much as he.

He would already have come over, she was well aware — come over on grounds of his own, which were quite different from hers; yet she was scarce the less struck, off at her point of vantage, with the way he now sat unconscious of her, at the outer edge and where the light pointed his presence, in a low basket-chair which covered him in save for little more than his small sharp shrunken profile, detached against the bright further distance, and his small protrusive foot, crossed over a knee and agitated by incessant nervous motion whenever he was thus locked in thought. Seldom had he more produced for her the appearance from which she had during the last three years never known him to vary and which would have told his story, all his story, every inch of it and with the last intensity, she felt, to a spectator capable of being struck with him as one might after all happen to be struck. What she herself recognised at any rate, and really at this particular moment as she had never done, was how his having retired from active business, as they said, given up everything and entered upon the first leisure of his life, had in the oddest way the effect but of emphasising his absorption, denying his detachment and presenting him as steeped up to the chin. Most of all on such occasions did what his life had meant come home to her, and then most, frankly, did that meaning seem small; it was exactly as the contracted size of his little huddled figure in the basket-chair.

He was a person without an alternative, and if any had ever been open to him, at an odd hour or two, somewhere in his inner dimness, he had long since closed the gate against it and now revolved in the hard-rimmed circle from which he had not a single issue. You couldn't retire without something or somewhere to retire to, you must have planted a single tree at least for shade or be able to turn a key in some yielding door; but to say that her extraordinary parent was surrounded by the desert was almost to flatter the void into which he invited one to step. He conformed in short to his

The Ivory Tower

necessity of absolute interest — interest, that is, in his own private facts, which were facts of numerical calculation altogether: how could it not be so when he had dispossessed himself, if there had even been the slightest selection in the matter, of every faculty except the calculating? If he hadn't thought in figures how could he possibly have thought at all — and oh the intensity with which he was thinking at that hour! It was as if she literally watched him just then and there dry up in yet another degree to everything but his genius. His genius might at the same time have gathered in to a point of about the size of the end of a pin. Such at least was the image of these things, or a part of it, determined for her under the impression of the moment.

He had come over with the same promptitude every morning of the last fortnight and had stayed on nearly till luncheon, sitting about in different places as if they were equally his own, smoking, always smoking, the big portentously "special" cigars that were now the worst thing for him and lost in the thoughts she had in general long since ceased to wonder about, taking them now for granted with an indifference from which the apprehension we have noted was but the briefest of lapses. He had over and above that particular matter of her passing perception, he had as they all had, goodness knew, and as she herself must have done not least, the air of waiting for something he didn't speak of and in fact couldn't

gracefully mention; with which moreover the adopted practice, and the irrepressible need of it, that she had been having under her eye, brought out for her afresh, little as she invited or desired any renewal of their salience, the several most pointed parental signs — harmless oddities as she tried to content herself with calling them, but sharp little symbols of stubborn little facts as she would have felt them hadn't she forbidden herself to feel. She had forbidden herself to feel, but was none the less as undefended against one of the ugly truths that hovered there before her in the charming silver light as against another. That the terrible little man she watched at his meditations wanted nothing in the world so much in these hours as to know what was "going to be left" by the old associate of his operations and sharer of his spoils — this, as Mr. Gaw's sole interest in the protracted crisis, matched quite her certainty of his sense that, however their doomed friend should pan out, two-thirds of the show would represent the unholy profits of the great wrong he himself had originally suffered.

This she knew was what it meant — that her father should perch there like a ruffled hawk, motionless but for his single tremor, with his beak, which had pecked so many hearts out, visibly sharper than ever, yet only his talons nervous; not that he at last cared a straw, really, but that he was incapable of thought save in sublimities of arithmetic, and that the question of what old Frank would have done with the fruits of his swindle, on the occasion of the rupture that had kept them apart in hate and vituperation for so many years, was one of the things that could hold him brooding, day by day and week by week, after the fashion of a philosopher tangled in some maze of metaphysics. As the end, for the other participant in that history, appeared to draw near, she had with the firmest, wisest hand she could lay on it patched up the horrid difference; had artfully induced her father to take a house at Newport for the summer, and then, pleading, insisting, that they should in common decency, or, otherwise expressed, in view of the sick man's sore stricken state, meet again, had won the latter round, unable as he was even then to do more than shuffle downstairs and take an occasional drive, to some belief in the sincerity of her intervention. She had got at him — under stress of an idea with which her ostensible motive had nothing to do; she had obtained entrance, demanding as all from herself that he should see her, and had little by little, to the further illumination of her plan, felt that she made him wonder at her perhaps more than he had ever wondered at anything; so that after this everything else was a part of that impression.

Strange to say, she had presently found herself quite independently interested; more interested than by any transaction, any chapter of intercourse, in her whole specifically filial history. Not that it mattered indeed if, in all probability — and positively so far back as during the time of active hostilities — this friend and enemy of other days had been predominantly in the right: the case, at the best and for either party, showed so scantly for edifying that where was the light in which her success could have figured as a moral or a sentimental triumph? There had been no real beauty for her, at its apparent highest pitch, in that walk of the now more complacently valid of the two men across the Avenue, a walk taken as she and her companion had continued regularly to take it since, that he might hold out his so long clenched hand, under her earnest admonition, to the antagonist cut into afresh this year by sharper knives than any even in Gaw's armoury. They had consented alike to what she wished, and without knowing why she most wished it: old Frank, oddly enough, because he liked her, as she felt, for herself, once gave him the chance and took all the trouble; and her father because — well, that was an old story. For a long time now, three or four years at least, she had had, as she would have said, no difficulty with him; and she knew just when, she knew almost just how, the change had begun to show.

Signal and supreme proof had come to him one day that save for his big plain quiet daughter (quiet, that is, unless when she knocked over a light gilt chair or swept off a rash table-ornament in brushing

expansively by,) he was absolutely
alone on the human field, utterly
unattended by any betrayal whatever that a fellow-creature could
like him or, when the inevitable
day should come, could disinterestedly miss him. She knew how of
old her inexplicable, her almost ridiculous type had disconcerted and
disappointed him; but with this,
at a given moment, it had come to
him that she represented quantity
and mass, that there was a great
deal of her, so that she would have
pressed down even a balance appointed to weigh bullion; and as
there was nothing he was fonder
of than such attestations of value
he had really ended by drawing
closer to her, as who should say,
and by finding countenance in the
breadth of personal and social
shadow that she projected. This
was the sole similitude about him
of a living alternative, and it served
only as she herself provided it. He
had actually turned into a personal
relation with her as he might have
turned, out of the glare and the
noise and the harsh recognitions of
the market, into some large cool
dusky temple; a place where idols
other than those of *his* worship
vaguely loomed and gleamed, so
that the effect at moments might
be rather awful, but where at least
he could sit very still, could breathe
very softly, could look about
obliquely and discreetly, could in
fact wander a little on tiptoe and
treat the place, with a mixture of
pride and fear, almost as his
own.

   He had brooded and brooded,
even as he was brooding now; and
that habit she at least had in common with him, though their subjects of thought were so different.
Thus it was exactly that she began to make out at the time his
actual need to wonder at her, the
only fact outside his proper range
that had ever cost him a speculative impulse, still more a speculative failure; even as she was to
make it out later on in the case of
their Newport neighbour, and to
recognise above all that though a
certain savour of accepted discomfort had, in the connection, to pervade her father's consciousness, no
taste of resentment was needed, as
in the present case, to sweeten it.
Nothing had more interested our
intelligent young woman than to
note in each of these overstrained,
yet at the same time safely resting
accumulators — and to note it as a
thing unprecedented up to this latest season — an unexpressed, even
though to some extent invoked, relief under the sense, the confirmed
suspicion, of certain anomalies of
ignorance and indifference as to
what they themselves stood for,
anomalies they could scarcely have
begun, on the first glimmer, by so
much as taking for realities. It had
become verily, on the part of the
poor bandaged and bolstered and
heavily-breathing object of her
present solicitude, as she had found
it on that of his still comparatively
agile and intensely acute critic, the
queer mark of an inward relief to
meet, so far as they had arts or
terms for it, any intimation of what
she might have to tell them. From

871

her they would take things they never could have taken, and never had, from anyone else. There were some such intimations that her father, of old, had only either dodged with discernible art or directly set his little white face against; he hadn't wanted them, and had in fact been afraid of them — so that after all perhaps his caring so little what went on in any world not subject to his direct intelligence might have had the qualification that he guessed she could imagine, and that to see her, or at least to feel her, imagine was like the sense of an odd draught about him when doors and windows were closed.

Up in the sick man's room the case was quite other; she had been admitted there but three times, very briefly, and a week had elapsed since the last, yet she had created in him a positive want to communicate, or at any rate to receive communication. She shouldn't see him again — the pair of doctors and the trio of nurses had been at one about that; but he had caused her to be told that he liked to know of her coming and hoped she would make herself quite at home. This she took for an intended sign, a hint that what she had in spite of difficulties managed to say now kept him company in the great be-dimmed and disinfected room from which other society was banished. Her father in fine he ignored after that not particularly beautiful moment of bare recognition brought about by her at the bedside; her father was the last thing in the

world that actually concerned him. But his not ignoring herself could but have a positive meaning; which was that she had made the impression she sought. Only *would* Graham Fielder arrive in time? She was not in a position to ask for news of him, but was sure each morning that if there had been any gage of this Miss Mumby, the most sympathetic of the nurses and with whom she had established a working intelligence, would be sufficiently interested to come out and speak to her. After waiting a while, however, she recognised that there could be no Miss Mumby yet and went over to her father in the great porch.

"Don't you get tired," she put to him, "of just sitting round here?"

He turned to her his small neat finely-wrinkled face, of an extreme yellowish palor and which somehow suggested at this end of time an empty glass that had yet held for years so much strong wine that a faint golden tinge still lingered on from it. "I can't get any more tired than I am already." His tone was flat, weak and so little charged with petulance that it betrayed the long habit of an almost exasperating mildness. This effect, at the same time, so far from suggesting any positive tradition of civility was somehow that of a commonness instantly and peculiarly exposed. "It's a better place than ours," he added in a moment. "But I don't care." And then he went on: "I guess I'd be more tired in your position."

"Oh you know I'm never tired.

And now," said Rosanna, "I'm too interested."

"Well then, so am I. Only for me it ain't a position."

His daughter still hovered with her vague look about. "Well, if it's one for me I feel it's a good one. I mean it's the right one."

Mr. Gaw shook his little foot with renewed intensity, but his irony was not gay. "The right one isn't always a good one. But ain't the question what *his* is going to be?"

"Mr. Fielder's? Why, of course," said Rosanna quietly. "That's the whole interest."

"Well then, you've got to fix it."

"I consider that I *have* fixed it — I mean if we can hold out."

"Well" — and Mr. Gaw shook on — "I guess *I* can. It's pleasant here," he went on, "even if it *is* funny."

"Funny?" his daughter echoed — yet inattentively, for she had become aware of another person, a middle-aged woman, but with neatly-kept hair already grizzled and in a white dress covered with a large white apron, who stood at the nearest opening of the house. "Here we are, you see, Miss Mumby — but any news?" Miss Gaw was instantly eager.

"Why he's right there upstairs," smiled the lady of the apron, who was clearly well affected to the speaker.

This young woman flushed for pleasure. "Oh how splendid! But when did he come?"

"Early this morning — by the New York boat. I was up at five,

to change with Miss Ruddle, and there of a sudden were his wheels. He seems so nice!" Miss Mumby beamed.

Rosanna's interest visibly rose, though she was prompt to explain it. "Why it's *because* he's nice! And he has seen him?"

"He's seeing him now — alone. For five minutes. Not all at once." But Miss Mumby was visibly serene.

This made Miss Gaw rejoice. "I'm not afraid. It will do him good. It has *got* to!" she finely declared.

Miss Mumby was so much at ease that she could even sanction the joke. "More good than the strain of waiting. They're quite satisfied." Rosanna knew these judges for Doctor Root and Doctor Hatch, and felt the support of her friend's firm freshness. "So we can hope," this authority concluded.

"Well, let my daughter run it — !" Abel Gaw had got up as if this change in the situation qualified certain proprieties, but turned his small sharpness to Miss Mumby, who had at first produced in him no change of posture. "Well, if he couldn't stand *me* I suppose it was because he knows me — and doesn't know this other man. *May* Mr. Fielder prove acceptable!" he added, stepping off the verandah to the path. But as that left Rosanna's share in the interest still apparently unlimited he spoke again. "Is it going to make you settle over here?"

This mild irony determined her

at once joining him, and they took leave together of their friend. "Oh I feel it's right now!" She smiled back at Miss Mumby, whose agitation of a confirmatory hand before disappearing as she had come testified to the excellence of the understanding between the ladies, and presently was trailing her light vague draperies over the grass beside her father. They might have been taken to resemble as they moved together a big ship staying its course to allow its belittled tender to keep near, and the likeness grew when after a minute Mr. Gaw himself stopped to address his daughter a question. He had, it was again marked, so scant a range of intrinsic tone that he had to resort for emphasis or point to some other scheme of signs — this surely also of no great richness, but expressive of his possibilities when once you knew him. "Is there any reason for your not telling me why you're so worked up?"

His companion, as she paused for accommodation, showed him a large flat grave face in which the general intention of deference seemed somehow to confess that it was often at the mercy — and perhaps most in this particular relation — of such an inward habit of the far excursion as could but incorrigibly qualify for Rosanna Gaw certain of the forms of attention, certain of the necessities of manner. She was, sketchily speaking, so much higher-piled a person than her father that the filial attitude in her suffered at the best from the occasional air of her having to come down to him. You would have guessed that she was not a person to cultivate that air; and perhaps even if very acute would have guessed some other things bearing on the matter from the little man's careful way with her. This pair exhibited there in the great light of the summer Sunday morning more than one of the essential, or perhaps the rather finally constituted, conditions of their intercourse. Here was a parent who clearly appealed to nobody in the world but his child, and a child who condescended to nobody in the world but her parent; and this with the anomaly of a constant care not to be too humble on one side and an equal one not to be too proud on the other. Rosanna, her powerful exposed arm raised to her broad shoulder, slowly made her heavy parasol revolve, flinging with it a wide shadow that enclosed them together, for their question and answer, as in a great bestreamered tent. "Do I strike you as worked up? Why I've tried to keep as quiet about it as I possibly could — as one does when one wants a thing so tremendously much."

His eyes had been raised to her own, but after she had said this in her perfunctory way they sank as from a sense of shyness and might have rested for a little on one of their tent-pegs. "Well, daughter, that's just what I want to understand — your personal motive."

She gave a sigh for this, a

strange uninforming sigh. "Ah father, 'my personal motives' —— !"

With this she might have walked on, but when he barred the way it was as if she could have done so but by stepping on him. "I don't complain of your personal motives — I want you to have all you're entitled to and should like to know who's entitled to more. But couldn't you have a reason once in a while for letting me know what some of your reasons are?"

Her decent blandness dropped on him again, and she had clearly this time come further to meet him. "You've always wanted me to have things I don't care for — though really when you've made a great point of it I've often tried. But want me now to have this." And then as he watched her again to learn what "this," with the visibly rare importance she attached to it, might be: "To make up to a person for a wrong I once did him."

"You wronged the man who has come?"

"Oh dreadfully!" Rosanna said with great sweetness.

He evidently held that any notice taken of anyone, to whatever effect, by this great daughter of his was nothing less than an honour done, and probably overdone; so what preposterous "wrong" could count? The worst he could think of was still but a sign of her greatness. "You wouldn't have him round —— ?"

"Oh that would have been nothing!" she laughed; and this time she sailed on again.

II

ROSANNA found him again after luncheon shaking his little foot from the depths of a piazza chair, but now on their own scene and at a point where this particular feature of it, the cool spreading verandah, commanded the low green cliff and a part of the immediate approach to the house from the seaward side. She left him to the only range of thought of which he was at present capable — she was so perfectly able to follow it; and it had become for that matter an old story that as he never opened a book, nor sought a chance for talk, nor took a step of exercise, nor gave in any manner a sign of an unsatisfied want, the extent of his vacancy, a detachment in which there just breathed a hint of the dryly invidious, might thus remain unbroken for hours. She knew what he was waiting for, and that if she hadn't been there to see him he would take his way across to the other house again, where the plea of solicitude for his old friend's state put him at his ease and where, moreover, as she now felt, the possibility of a sight of Graham Fielder might reward him. It was disagreeable to her that he should have such a sight while she denied it to her own eyes; but the sense of their common want of application for their faculties was a thing that repeatedly checked in her the expression of judgments. Their idleness was as mean and bare on her own side, she too much felt, as on his; and heaven knew that if he could sit with screwed-up eyes for hours the case was as flagrant in her aimless driftings, her incurable restless revolutions, as a pretence of "interests" could consort with.

She revolved and drifted then, out of his sight and in another quarter of the place, till four o'clock had passed; when on returning to him she found his chair empty and was sure of what had become of him. There *was* nothing else in fact for his Sunday, as he on that day denied himself the resource of driving, or rather of being driven, from which the claim of the mechanical car had not, in the Newport connection, won him, and which, deep in his barouche, behind his own admirable horses, could maintain him in meditation for meditation's sake quite as well as a poised rocking-chair. Left thus to herself, though conscious she well might have visitors, she circled slowly and repeatedly round the gallery, only pausing at last on sight of a gentleman who had come into view by a path from the cliff. He presented himself in a minute as Davey Bradham, and on drawing nearer called across to her without other greeting: "Won't you walk back with me to tea? Gussy has sent me to bring you."

"Why yes, of course I will— that's nice of Gussy," she replied; adding moreover that she wanted a walk, and feeling in the prospect, though she didn't express this, a relief to her tension and a sanction for what she called to herself her tact. She might without the diversion not quite have trusted herself not to emulate, and even with the last crudity, her father's proceeding; which she knew she should afterwards be ashamed of. "Anyone that comes here," she said, "must come on to you — they'll know"; and when Davey had replied that there wasn't the least chance of anyone's not coming on she moved with him down the path, at the end of which they entered upon the charming cliff walk, a vast carpet of undivided lawns, kept in wondrous condition, with a meandering right-of-way for a seaward fringe and bristling wide-winged villas that spoke of a seated colony; many of these huge presences reducing to marginal meanness their strip of the carpet.

Davey was, like herself, richly and healthily replete, though with less of his substance in stature; a frankly fat gentleman, blooming still at eight-and-forty, with a large smooth shining face, void of a sign of moustache or whisker and crowned with dense dark hair cropped close to his head after the fashion of a French schoolboy or the inmate of a jail. But for his half-a-dozen fixed wrinkles, as marked as the great rivers of a continent on a map, and his thick and arched and active eyebrows, which left almost nothing over for his forehead, he would have scarce exhibited features — in spite of the absence of which, however, he could look in alternation the most portentous things and the most ridiculous. He would hang up a meaning in his large empty face as if he had swung an awful example on a gibbet, or would let loose there a great grin that you somehow couldn't catch in the fact but that pervaded his expanses of cheek as poured wine pervades water. He differed certainly from Rosanna in that he enjoyed, visibly, all he carnally possessed — whereas you could see in a moment that she, poor young woman, would have been content with, would have been glad of, a scantier allowance. "You'll find Cissy Foy, to begin with," he said as they went; "she arrived last night and told me to tell you she'd have walked over with me but that Gussy wants her for something. However, as you know, Gussy always wants her for something — she wants everyone for something so much more than something for everyone — and there are none of us that are not worked hard, even though we mayn't bloom on it like Cissy, who, by the way, is looking a perfect vision."

"Awfully lovely?" — Rosanna clearly saw as she asked.

"Prettier than at any time yet, and wanting tremendously to hear from you, you know, about your protégé — what's the fellow's name? Graham Fielder? — whose arrival we're all agog about."

Rosanna pulled up in the path; she somehow at once felt her possession of this interest clouded — shared as yet as it had been only with her father, whose share she could control. It then and there came to her in one of the waves of disproportionate despair in which she felt half the impressions of life break, that she wasn't going to be able to control at all the great participations. She had a moment of reaction against what she had done; she liked Gray to be called her protégé — forced upon her as endless numbers of such were, he would be the only one in the whole collection who hadn't himself pushed at her; but with the big bright picture of the villas, the palaces, the lawns and the luxuries in her eyes, and with something like the chink of money itself in the murmur of the breezy little waves at the foot of the cliff, she felt that, without her having thought of it enough in advance, she had handed him over to complications and relations. These things shimmered in the silver air of the wondrous perspective ahead, the region off there that awaited her present approach and where Gussy hovered like a bustling goddess in the enveloping cloud of her court. The man beside her was the massive Mercury of this urgent Juno; but — without mythological comparisons, which we make for her under no hint that she could herself have dreamed of one — she found herself glad just then that she liked Davey Bradham, and much less sorry than usual that she didn't respect him. An extraordinary thing happened, and all in the instant before she spoke again.

It was very strange, and it made him look at her as if he wondered that his words should have had so great an effect as even her still face showed. There was absolutely no one, roundabout and far and wide, whom she positively wanted Graham to know; no not one creature of them all — "all" figuring for her, while she stood, the great collection at the Bradhams'. She hadn't thought of this before in the least as it came to her now; yet no more had she time to be sure that even with the sharper consciousness she would, as her father was apt to say, have acted different. So much was true, yet while she still a moment longer hung fire Davey rounded himself there like something she could comparatively rest on. "How in the world," she put to him then, "do you know anything away off there —? He *has* come to his uncle, but so quietly that I haven't yet seen him."

"Why, my dear thing, is it new to you that we're up and doing — bright and lively? We're the most intelligent community on all this great coast, and when precious knowledge is in the air we're not to be kept from it. We knew at breakfast that the New York boat had brought him, and Gussy of course wants him up to dinner tonight. Only Cissy claims, you see, that she has rights in him first — rights beyond Gussy's, I mean," Davey went on; "I don't know that she claims them beyond yours."

She looked abroad again, his companion, to earth and sea and sky; she wondered and felt threat-ened, yet knowing herself at the same time a long way off from the point at which menace roused her to passion. She had always to suffer so much before that, and was for the present in the phase of feeling but weak and a little sick. But there was always Davey. She started their walk again before saying more, while he himself said things that she didn't heed. "I can't for the life of me imagine," she nevertheless at last declared, "what Cissy has to do with him. When and where has she ever seen him?"

Davey did as always his best to oblige. "Somewhere abroad, some time back, when she was with her mother at some baths or some cure-place. Though when I think of it," he added, "it wasn't with the man himself — it was with some relation: hasn't he an uncle, or perhaps a stepfather? Cissy seems to know all about him, and he takes a great interest in her."

It again all but stopped Rosanna. "Gray Fielder an interest in Cissy——?"

"Let me not," laughed Davey, "sow any seed of trouble or engage for more than I can stand to. She'll tell you all about it, she'll clothe it in every grace. Only I assure you I myself am as much interested as anyone," he added — "interested, I mean, in the question of whether the old man there has really brought him out at the last gasp this way to do some decent thing about him. An impression prevails," he further explained, "that you're in some wonderful way in the old wretch's confidence, and I therefore make no bones of telling you that your arrival on our scene there, since you're so good as to consent to come, has created an impatience beyond even what your appearances naturally everywhere create. I give you warning that there's no limit to what we want to know."

Rosanna took this in now as she so often took things — working it down in silence at first: it shared in the general weight of all direct contributions to her consciousness. It might then, when she spoke, have sunk deep. She looked about again, in her way, as if under her constant oppression, and seeing, a little off from their gravelled walk, a public bench to which a possible path branched down, she said, on a visibly grave decision: "Look here, I want to talk to *you* — you're one of the few people in all your crowd to whom I really can. So come and sit down."

Davey Bradham, arrested before her, had an air for his responsibilities that quite matched her own. "Then what becomes of them all there?"

"I don't care a hang what becomes of them. But if you want to know," Rosanna said, "I do care what becomes of Mr. Fielder, and I trust you enough, being as you are the only one of your lot I do trust, to help me perhaps a little to do something about it."

"Oh, my dear lady, I'm not a bit discreet, you know," Mr. Bradham amusedly protested; "I'm perfectly unprincipled and utterly indelicate. How can a fellow not be who likes as much as I do at all times to make the kettle boil and the plot thicken? I've only got my beautiful intelligence, though, as I say, I don't in the least *want* to embroil you. Therefore if I can really help you as the biggest babbler alive —— !"

She waited again a little, but this time with her eyes on his good worn worldly face, superficially so smooth, but with the sense of it lined and scratched and hacked across much in the manner of the hard ice of a large pond at the end of a long day's skating. The amount of obstreperous exercise that had been taken on that recording field! The difference between our pair, thus confronted, might have been felt as the greater by the very fact of their outward likeness as creatures so materially weighted; it would have been written all over Rosanna for the considering eye that every grain of her load, from innermost soul to outermost sense, was that of reality and sincerity; whereas it might by the same token have been felt of Davey that in the temperature of life as he knew it his personal identity had been, save for perhaps some small tough lurking residuum, long since puffed away in pleasant spirals of vapour. Our young woman was at this moment, however, less interested in quantities than in qualities of candour; she could get what passed for it by the bushel, by the ton, whenever, right or left, she chose to chink her pocket. Her requirement for actual use was such a glimmer from the candle of truth as a mere poor woman might have managed to kindle. What was left of precious in Davey might thus have figured but as a candle-end; yet for the lack of it she should perhaps move in darkness. And her brief intensity of watch was in a moment rewarded; her companion's candle-end was his not quite burnt-out value as a gentleman. This was enough for her, and she seemed to see her way. "If I don't trust you there's nobody else in all the wide world I can. So you've got to know, and you've got to be good to me."

"Then what awful thing *have* you done?" he was saying to her three minutes after they had taken their place temporarily on the bench.

"Well, I got at Mr. Betterman," she said, "in spite of all the difficulty. Father and he hadn't spoken for years — had had long ago the blackest, ugliest difference; believing apparently the horridest things of each other. Nevertheless it was as father's daughter that I went to him — though after a little, I think, it was simply for the worth itself of what I had to tell him that he listened to me."

"And what you had to tell him," Davey asked while she kept her eyes on the far horizon, "*was* then that you take this tender interest in Mr. Fielder?"

"You may make my interest as ridiculous as you like —— !"

"Ah, my dear thing," Davey pleadingly protested, "don't deprive me, please, of *anything* nice there is to know!"

"There was something that had happened years ago — a wrong I perhaps had done him, though in perfect good faith. I thought I saw my way to make up for it, and I seem to have succeeded beyond even what I hoped."

"Then what have you to worry about?" said Davey.

"Just my success," she answered simply. "Here he is and I've done it."

"Made his rich uncle want him — who hadn't wanted him before? Is that it?"

"Yes, interfered afresh in his behalf — as I had interfered long ago. When one has interfered one can't help wondering," she gravely explained.

"But dear lady, ever for his benefit of course," Davey extemporised.

"Yes — except for the uncertainty of what *is* for a person's benefit. It's hard enough to know," said Rosanna, "what's for one's own."

"Oh, as to that," Davey joked, "I don't think that where mine's concerned I've ever a doubt! But is the point that the old man had quarrelled with him and that you've brought about a reconciliation?"

She considered again with her far-wandering eyes; as if both moved by her impulse to confidence and weighted with the sense of how much of it there all was. "Well, in as few words as possible, it was like this. He's the son but of a half-sister, the daughter of Mr. Betterman's father by a second marriage which he in his youth hadn't at all liked, and who made her case worse with him, as time went on, by marrying a man, Graham's father, whom he had also some strong objection to. Yes," she summarized, "he seems to have been difficult to please, but he's making up for it now. His brother-in-law didn't live long to suffer from the objection, and the sister, Mrs. Fielder, left a widow badly provided for, went off with her boy, then very young, to Europe. There, later on, during a couple of years that I spent abroad with my mother, we met them and for the time saw much of them; she and my dear mother greatly took to each other, they formed the friendliest relation, and we had in common that my father's business association with Mr. Betterman still at that time subsisted, though the terrible man — as he then was — hadn't at all made it up with our friend. It was while we were with her in Dresden, however, that something happened which brought about, by correspondence, some renewal of intercourse. This was a matter on which we were in her confidence and in which we took the greatest interest, for we liked also the other person concerned in it. An opportunity had come up for her to marry again, she had practically decided to embrace it, and of this, though everything between them had broken off so short, her unforgiving brother had heard, indirectly, in New York."

Davey Bradham, lighting cigarettes, and having originally placed his case, in a manner promptly appreciated, at his companion's disposal, crowned this now adjusted relation with a pertinence of comment. "And only again of course to be as horrid as possible about it! He hated husbands in general."

"Well, he himself, it was to be said, had been but little of one. He had lost his own wife early and hadn't married again — though he was to lose early also the two children born to him. The second of these deaths was recent at the time I speak of, and had had to do, I imagine, with his sudden overture to his absent relations. He let his sister know that he had learnt her intention and thought very ill of it, but also that if she would get rid of her low foreigner and come back with the boy he would be happy to see what could be done for them."

"What a jolly situation!" — Davey exhaled fine puffs. "Her second choice then — at Dresden — was a German adventurer?"

"No, an English one, Mr. Northover; an adventurer only as a man in love is always one, I suppose, and who was there for us to see and extremely to approve. He had nothing to do with Dresden beyond having come on to join her; they had met elsewhere, in Switzerland or the Tyrol, and he had shown an interest in her, and had made his own impression, from the first. She answered her brother that his demand of her was excessive in the absence of anything she could recognise that she owed him. To this he replied that she might marry then whom she liked, but that if she would give up her boy and send him home, where he would take charge of him and bring him up to prospects she would be a fool not to appreciate, there need be no more talk and she could lead her life as she perversely preferred. This crisis came up during our winter with her — it was a very cruel one, and my mother, as I have said, was all in her confidence."

"Of course" — Davey Bradham abounded; "and you were all in your mother's!"

Rosanna leaned back on the bench, her cigarette between her strong and rounded fingers; she sat at her ease now, this chapter of history filling, under her view, the soft lap of space and the comfort of having it well out, and yet of keeping it, as her friend somehow helped her to do, well within her control, more and more operative. "Well, I was sixteen years old, and Gray at that time fourteen. I was huge and hideous and began then to enjoy the advantage — if advantage it was — of its seeming so ridiculous to treat the monster I had grown as negligible that I *had* to be treated as important. I wasn't a bit stupider than I am now — in fact I saw things much more sharply and simply and knew ever so much better what I wanted and didn't. Gray and I had become excellent friends — if you want to think of him as my 'first passion' you are welcome to, unless you want to think of him rather as my fifth! He was a charming little boy,

much nicer than any I had ever seen; he didn't come up higher than my shoulder, and, to tell you all, I remember how once, in some game with a party of English and American children whom my mother had got together for Christmas, I tried to be amusing by carrying half-a-dozen of them successively on my back — all in order to have the pleasure of carrying *him,* whom I felt, I remember, but as a feather-weight compared with most of the others. Such a romp was I — as you can of course see I must have been, and at the same time so horridly artful; which is doubtless now not so easy for you to believe of me. But the point," Rosanna developed, "is that I entered all the way into our friends' situation and that when I was with my mother alone we talked for the time of nothing else. The strange, or at least the certain, thing was that though we should have liked so to have them over here, we hated to see them hustled even by a rich relative: we were rich ourselves, though we rather hated that too, and there was no romance for us in being so stuffed up. We liked Mr. Northover, their so devoted friend, we saw how they cared for him, how even Graham did, and what an interest he took in the boy, for whom we felt that a happy association with him, each of them so open to it, would be a great thing; we threw ourselves in short, and I dare say to extravagance, into the idea of the success of Mr. Northover's suit. She was the charmingest little woman, very pretty, very lonely, very vague, but very sympathetic, and we perfectly understood that the pleasant Englishman, of great taste and thoroughly a gentleman, should have felt encouraged. We didn't in the least adore Mr. Betterman, between whom and my father the differences that afterwards became so bad were already threatening, and when I saw for myself how the life that might thus be opened to him where they were, with his mother's marriage and a further good influence crowning it, would compare with the awful game of grab, to express it mildly, for which I was sure his uncle proposed to train him, I took upon myself to get more roused and wound-up than I had doubtless any real right to, and to wonder what I might really do to promote the benefit that struck me as the greater and defeat the one against which my prejudice was strong."

She had drawn up a moment as if what was to come required her to gather herself, while her companion seemed to assure her by the backward set of his head, that of a man drinking at a cool spout, how little his attention had lapsed. "I see at once, you dear grand creature, that you were from that moment at the bottom of everything that was to happen; and without knowing yet what these things were I back you for it now up to the hilt."

"Well," she said, "I'm much obliged, and you're never for an instant, mind, to fail me; but I needed no backing then — I didn't even need my mother's: I took on myself so much from the moment my chance turned up."

"You just walked in and settled the whole question, of course." He quite flaunted the luxury of his interest. "Clearly what moved you *was* one of those crowning passions of infancy."

"Then why didn't I want, on the contrary, to have him, poor boy, where his presence would feed my flame?" Rosanna at once inquired. "Why didn't I obtain of my mother to say to his — for she would have said anything in the world I wanted: 'You just quietly get married, don't disappoint this delightful man; while we take Gray back to his uncle, which will be awfully good for him, and let him learn to make his fortune, the decent women that we are fondly befriending him and you and your husband coming over whenever you like, to see how beautifully it answers.' Why if I was so infatuated didn't I do *that?*" she repeated.

He kept her waiting not a moment. "Just because you *were* so infatuated. Just because when you're infatuated you're sublime." She had turned her eyes on him, facing his gorgeous hospitality, but facing it with a visible flush. "Rosanna Gaw" — he took undisguised advantage of her — "you're sublime now, just as sublime as you can be, and it's what you want to be. You liked your young man so much that you were really capable —— !"

He let it go at that, for even

with his drop she had not completed his sense. But the next thing, practically, she did so. "I've been capable ever since — that's the point: of feeling that I did act upon him, that, young and accessible as I found him, I gave a turn to his life."

"Well," Davey continued to comment, "he's not so young now, and no more, naturally, are you; but I guess, all the same, you'll give many another." And then, as facing him altogether more now, she seemed to ask how he could be so sure: "Why, if *I'm* so accessible, through my tough old hide, how is the exquisite creature formed to all the sensibilities for which you sought to provide going in the least to hold out? He owes you clearly everything he has become, and how can he decently not want you should know he feels it? All's well that ends well: that at least I foresee I shall want to say when I've had more of the beginning. You were going to tell me how it was in particular that you got your pull."

She puffed and puffed again, letting her eyes once more wander and rest; after which, through her smoke, she recovered the sense of the past. "One Sunday morning we went together to the great Gallery — it had been between us for weeks that he was some day to take me and show me the things he most admired: that wasn't at all what would have been my line with *him*. The extent to which he was 'cleverer' than I and knew about the things I didn't, and don't

know even now ——!" Greatly she made this point. "And yet the beauty was that I felt there were ways I could help him, all the same — I knew *that* even with all the things I didn't know, so that they remained ignorances of which I think I wasn't a bit ashamed: any more in fact than I am now, there being too many things else to be ashamed of. Never so much as that day, at any rate, had I felt ready for my part — yes, it came to me there as my part; for after he had called for me at our hotel and we had started together I knew something particular was the matter and that he of a sudden didn't care for what we were doing, though we had planned it as a great occasion much before; that in short his thoughts were elsewhere and that I could have made out the trouble in his face if I hadn't wished not to seem to look for it. I hated that he should have it, whatever it was — just how I hated it comes back to me as if from yesterday; and also how at the same time I pretended not to notice, and he attempted not to show *he* did, but to introduce me, in the rooms, to what we had come for instead — which gave us half-an-hour that I recover vividly, recover, I assure you, quite painfully still, as a conscious, solemn little farce. What put an end to it was that we at last wandered away from the great things, the famous Madonna, the Correggio, the Paul Veroneses, which he had quavered out the properest remarks about, and got off into a small room of little Dutch and other later masters, things that didn't matter and that we couldn't pretend to go into, but where the German sunshine of a bright winter day came down through some upper light and played on all the rich little old colour and old gilding after a fashion that of a sudden decided me. 'I don't care a hang for anything!' I stood before him and boldly spoke out: 'I haven't cared a hang since we came in, if you want to know — I care only for what you're worried about, and what must be pretty bad, since I can see, if you don't mind my saying it, that it has made you cry at home.' "

"He can hardly have thanked you for *that!*" Davey's competence threw off.

"No, he didn't pretend to, and I had known he wouldn't; he hadn't to tell me how a boy feels in taking such a charge from a girl. But there he was on a small divan, swinging his legs a little and with his head — he had taken his hat off — back against the top of the seat and the queerest look in his flushed face. For a moment he stared hard, and *then* at least, I said to myself, his tears were coming up. They didn't come, however — he only kept glaring as in fever; from which I presently saw that I had said not a bit the wrong thing, but exactly the very best. 'Oh if I were some good to you!' I went on — and with the sense the next moment, ever so happily, that that was really what I *was* being. 'She has put it upon me to choose

for myself — to think, to decide and to settle it that way for both of us. She has put it *all* upon me,' he said — 'and how *can* I choose, in such a difficulty,' he asked, 'when she tells me, and when I believe, that she'll do exactly as I say?' 'You mean your mother will marry Mr. Northover or give him up according as you prefer?' — but of course I knew what he meant. It was a joy to me to feel it clear up — with the good I had already done him, at a touch, by making him speak. I saw how this relieved him even when he practically spoke of his question as too frightful for his young intelligence, his young conscience — literally his young nerves. It was as if he had appealed to me to pronounce it positively cruel — while I had felt at the first word that I really but blessed it. It wasn't too much for *my* young nerves — extraordinary as it may seem to you," Rosanna pursued, "that I should but have wished to undertake at a jump such a very large order. I wonder now from where my lucidity came, but just as I stood there I saw some things in a light in which, even with still better opportunities, I've never so *much* seen them since. It was as if I took everything in — and what everything meant; and, flopped there on his seat and always staring up at me, he understood that I was somehow inspired for him."

"My dear child, you're inspired at this moment!" — Davey Bradham rendered the tribute. "It's too splendid to hear of amid our greedy wants, our timid ideas and our fishy passions. You ring out like Brünnhilde at the opera. How jolly to have pronounced his doom!"

"Yes," she gravely said, "and you see how jolly I now find it. I settled it. I was fate," Rosanna puffed. "He recognised fate — all the more that he really wanted to; and you see therefore," she went on, "how it was to be in every single thing that has happened since."

"You stuck him fast there" — Mr. Bradham filled in the picture. "Yet not so fast after all," he understandingly added, "but that you've been able to handle him again as you like. He does in other words whatever you prescribe."

"If he did it then I don't know what I should have done had he refused to do it now. For now everything's changed. Everyone's dead or dying. And I believe," she wound up, "that I was quite right then, that he has led his life and been happy."

"I see. If he hadn't been —— !" Her companion's free glance ranged.

"He would have had me to thank, yes. And at the best I should have cost him much!"

"Everything, you mean, that the old man had more or less from the first in mind?"

Davey had taken her up; but the next moment, without direct reply, she was on her feet. "At any rate you see!" she said to finish with it.

"Oh I see a lot! And if there's more in it than meets the eye I think I see that too," her friend declared. "I want to see it all at any rate — and just as you've started it. But what I want most naturally is to see your little darling himself."

"Well, if I had been afraid of you I wouldn't have spoken. You won't hurt him," Rosanna said as they got back to the cliff walk.

"Hurt him? Why I shall be his great warning light — or at least I shall be yours, which is better still." To this, however, always pondering, she answered nothing, but stood as if spent by her effort and half disposed in consequence to retrace her steps; against which possibility he at once protested. "You don't mean you're not coming on?"

She thought another instant; then her eyes overreached the long smooth interval beyond which the nondescript excrescences of Gussy's "cottage," vast and florid, and in a kindred company of hunches and gables and pinnacles confessed, even if in confused accents, to its monstrous identity. The sight itself seemed after all to give her resolution. "Yes, now for Cissy!" she said and braved the prospect.

III

HALF-AN-HOUR later, however, she still had this young lady before her in extended perspective and as a satisfaction, if not as an embarrassment, to come; thanks to the fact that Mrs. Bradham had forty persons, or something like it, though all casually turning up, at tea, and that she herself had perhaps never been so struck with the activity of the charming girl's response to the considerations familiar alike to all of them as Gussy's ideas about her. Gussy's ideas about her, as about everything in the world, could on occasion do more to fill the air of any scene over which Gussy presided than no matter what vociferation of any massed crowd surrounding that lady: exactly which truth might have been notable now to Rosanna in the light of Cissy's occasional clear smile at her, always as yet from a distance, during lapses of intervals and across shifting barriers of the more or less eminent and brilliant. Mrs. Bradham's great idea — notoriously the most disinterested Gussy had been known, through a career rich in announced intentions and glorious designs, to entertain with any coherence — was that by placing and keeping on exhibition, under her eye, the loveliest flower of girlhood a splendid and confident society could have wished to wear on its bosom she should at once signally enhance the dignity of the social part played by herself and steep the precious object in a medium in which the care of precious objects was supremely understood. "When she does so much for me what in the world mustn't I do for *her?*" Cecelia Foy had put that to Rosanna again and again with perfect lu-

cidity, making her sense of fair play shine out of it and her cultivation of that ideal form perhaps not the least of the complications under which our elder young woman, earnest in everything, endeavoured to stick to the just view of her. Cissy had from the first appealed to her with restrictions, but that was the way in which for poor brooding Rosanna every one appealed; only there was in the present case the difference that whereas in most cases the appeal, or rather her view of it, found itself somehow smothered in the attendant wrong possibilities, the interest of this bright victim of Mrs. Bradham's furtherance worked clearer, on the whole, with the closer, with the closest, relation, never starting the questions one might entertain about her except to dispose of them, even if when they had been disposed of she mostly started them again.

Not often had so big a one at all events been started for Rosanna as when she saw the girl earn her keep, as they had so often called it together, by multiplying herself for everyone else about the place instead of remaining as single and possessable as her anxious friend had come over to invite her to be. Present to this observer to the last point indeed, and yet as nothing new, was the impression of that insolence of ease on Gussy's part which was never so great as when her sense for any relation was least fine and least true. She was naturally never so the vulgar rich woman able to afford herself all luxuries as when she was most stupid about the right enjoyment of these and most brutally systematic, as Rosanna's inward voice phrased the matter, for some inferior and desecrating use of them. Mrs. Bradham would deeply have resented — as deeply as a woman might who had no depth — any imputation on her view of what would be fine and great for her young friend, but Rosanna's envy and admiration of possibilities, to say nothing of actualities, to which this view was quite blind, kept the girl before her at times as a sacrificed, truly an even prostituted creature; who yet also, it had to be added, could often alienate sympathy by strange, by perverse concurrences. However, Rosanna thought, Cissy wasn't in concurrence now, but was quite otherwise preoccupied than with what their hostess could either give her or take from her. She was happy — this our young woman perfectly perceived, to her own very great increase of interest; so happy that, as had been repeatedly noticeable before, she multiplied herself through the very agitation of it, appearing to be, for particular things they had to say to her, particular conversational grabs and snatches, all of the most violent, they kept attempting and mostly achieving, at the service of everyone at once, and thereby as obliging, as humane a beauty, after the fashion of the old term, as could have charmed the sight. What Rosanna most noted withal, and not for the first time either, every ob-

servation she had hitherto made seeming now but intensified, what she most noted was the huge general familiarity, the pitch of intimacy unmodulated, as if exactly the same tie, from person to person, bound the whole company together and nobody had anything to say to anyone that wasn't equally in question for all.

This, she knew, was the air and the sound, the common state, of intimacy, and again and again, in taking it in, she had remained unsure of whether it left her more hopelessly jealous or more rudely independent. She would have liked to be intimate — with someone or other, not indeed with every member of a crowd; but the faculty, as appeared, hadn't been given her (for with whom had she ever exercised it? not even with Cissy, she felt now,) and it was ground on which she knew alternate languor and relief. The fact, however, that so much as all this could be present to her while she encountered greetings, accepted tea, and failed of felicity before forms of address for the most part so hilarious, or at least so ingenious, as to remind her further that she might never expect to be funny either — that fact might have shown her as hugging a treasure of consciousness rather than as seeking a soil for its interment. What they all took for granted! — this again and again had been before her; and never so as when Gussy Bradham after a little became possessed of her to the extent of their sharing a settee in one of the great porch-es on the lawny margin of which, before sundry overarchings in other and quite contradictious architectural interests began to spread, a dozen dispersed couples and trios revolved and lingered in sight. How was *he*, the young man at the other house, going to like these enormous assumptions? — that of a sudden oddly came to her; so far indeed as it was odd that Gussy should suggest such questions. She suggested questions in her own way at all times; Rosanna indeed mostly saw her in a sort of immodest glare of such, the chief being doubtless the wonder, never assuaged, of how any circle of the supposed amenities could go on "putting up" with her. The present was as a fact perhaps the first time our young woman had seen her in the light of a danger to herself. If society, or what they called such, had to reckon with her and accepted the charge, that was society's own affair — it appeared on the whole to understand its interest; but why should she, Rosanna Gaw, recognise a complication she had done nothing ever to provoke? It was literally as if the reckoning sat there between them and all the terms they had ever made with felt differences, intensities of separation and opposition, had now been superseded by the need for fresh ones — forms of contact and exchange, forms of pretended intercourse, to be improvised in presence of new truths.

So it was at any rate that Rosanna's imagination worked while she asked herself if there mightn't be something in an idea she had more than once austerely harboured — the possibility that Mrs. Bradham could on occasion be afraid of her. If this lady's great note was that of an astounding assurance based on approved impunity, how, certainly, should a plain dull shy spinster, with an entire incapacity for boldness and a perfect horror, in general, of intermeddling, have broken the spell? — especially as there was no other person in the world, not one, whom she could have dreamed of wishing to put in fear. Deep was the discomfort for Miss Gaw of losing with her entertainer the commonest advantage she perhaps knew, that of her habit of escape from the relation of dislike, let alone of hostility, through some active denial for the time of any relation at all. What was there in Gussy that rendered impossible to Rosanna's sense this very vulgarest of luxuries? She gave her always the impression of looking at her with an exaggeration of ease, a guarded penetration, that consciously betrayed itself; though how could one know, after all, that this wasn't the horrid nature of her look for everyone? — which would have been publicly denounced if people hadn't been too much involved with her to be candid. With her wondrous bloom of life and health and her hard confidence that had nothing to do with sympathy, Gussy might have presented it as a matter of some pusillanimity, her present critic at the same time felt, that one should but detect the displeasing in such an exhibition of bright activity. The only way not to stand off from her, no doubt, was to be of her "bossed" party and crew, or in other words to be like everyone else; and perhaps one might on that condition have enjoyed as a work of nature or even of art, an example of all-efficient force, her braveries of aspect and attitude, resources of resistance to time and thought, things not of beauty, for some unyielding reason, and quite as little of dignity, but things of assertion and application in an extraordinary degree, things of a straight cold radiance and of an emphasis that was like the stamp of hard flat feet. Even if she was to be envied it would be across such gulfs; as it was indeed one couldn't so much as envy her the prodigy of her "figure," which had been at eighteen, as one had heard, that of a woman of forty and was now at forty, one saw that of a girl of eighteen: such a state of the person wasn't human, to the younger woman's sombre sense, but might have been that of some shining humming insect, a thing of the long-constricted waist, the minimised yet caparisoned head, the fixed disproportionate eye and tough transparent wing, gossamer guaranteed. With all of which, however, she had pushed through every partition and was in the centre of her guest's innermost preserve before she had been heard coming.

"It's too lovely that you should have got him to do what he ought

— that dreadful old man! But I don't know if you feel how interesting it's all going to be; in fact if you know yourself how wonderful it is that he has already — Mr. Fielder has, I mean — such a tremendous friend in Cissy."

Rosanna waited, facing her, noting her extraordinary perfections of neatness, of elegance, of arrangement, of which it couldn't be said whether they most handed over to you, as on some polished salver, the clear truth of her essential commonness or transposed it into an element that could please, that could even fascinate, as a supreme attestation of care. "Take her as an advertisement of all the latest knowledges of how to 'treat' every inch of the human surface and where to 'get' every scrap of the personal envelope, so far as she *is* enveloped, and she does achieve an effect sublime in itself and thereby absolute in a wavering world" — with so much even as that was Miss Gaw aware of helping to fill for her own use the interval before she spoke. "No," she said, "I know nothing of what any of you may suppose yourselves to know." After which, however, with a sudden inspiration, a quick shift of thought as though catching an alarm, "I haven't seen Mr. Fielder for a very long time, haven't seen him at all yet here," she added; "but though I hoped immensely he would come, and am awfully glad he has, what I want for him is to have the very best time he possibly can; a much better one than I shall myself at all know how to help him to."

"Why, aren't you helping him to the greatest time he can have *ever* had if you've waked up his uncle to a sense of decency?" Gussy demanded with her brightest promptness. "You needn't think, Rosanna," she proceeded with a well-nigh fantastic development of that ease, "you needn't think you're going to be able to dodge the least little consequence of your having been so wonderful. He's just going to owe you everything, and to follow that feeling up; so I don't see why you shouldn't want to let him — it would be so mean of him not to! — or be deprived of the credit of so good a turn. When I do things" — Gussy always had every account of herself ready — "I want to have them recognised; I like to make them pay, without the least shame, in the way of glory gained. However, it's between yourselves," her delicacy conceded, "and how can one judge — except just to envy you such a lovely relation? All I want is that you should feel that here we are if you do want help. He should have here the best there is, and should have it, don't you think? before he tumbles from ignorance into any mistake — mistakes have such a way of sticking. So don't be unselfish about him, don't sacrifice him to the fear of using your advantage: what are such advantages as you enjoy meant for — all of them, I mean — but to be used up to the limit? You'll see at any rate what Cissy says — she has great ideas about

him. I mean," said Mrs. Bradham with a qualification in which the expression of Rosanna's still gaze suddenly seemed reflected, "I mean that it's so interesting she should have all the clues."

Rosanna still gazed; she might even after a little have struck a watcher as held in spite of herself by some heavy spell. It was an old sense — she had already often had it: when once Gussy had got her head up, got away and away as Davey called it, she might appear to do what she would with her victim; appear, that is, to Gussy herself — the appearance never corresponded for Miss Gaw to an admission of her own. Behind the appearance, at all events, things on one side and the other piled themselves up, and Rosanna certainly knew what they were on her side. Nevertheless it was as a vocal note too faintly quavered through some loud orchestral sound that she heard herself echo: "The clues — ?"

"Why, it's so funny there should be such a lot — and all gathered about here!" To this attestation of how everything in the world, for that matter, was gathered right there Rosanna felt herself superficially yield; and even before she knew what was coming — for something clearly was — she was strangely conscious of a choice somehow involved in her attitude and dependent on her mind, and this too as at almost the acutest moment of her life. What it came to, with the presentiment of forces at play such as she had really never yet had to count with, was the

891

question, all for herself, of whether she should be patently lying in the profession of a readiness to hand the subject of her interest over unreservedly to all waiting, all so remarkably gathering contacts and chances, or whether the act wouldn't partake of the very finest strain of her past sincerity. She was to remember the moment later on as if she had really by her definition, by her selection, "behaved" — fairly feeling the breath of her young man's experience on her cheek before knowing with the least particularity what it would most be, and deciding then and there to swallow down every fear of any cost of anything to herself. She felt extraordinary in the presence of symptoms, symptoms of life, of death, of danger, of delight, of what did she know? But this it was exactly that cast derision, by contrast, on such poor obscurities as her feelings, and settled it for her that when she had professed a few minutes back that she hoped they would all, for his possible pleasure in it, catch him up and, so far as they might, make him theirs, she wasn't to have spoken with false frankness. Queer enough at the same time, and a wondrous sign of her state of sensibility, that she should see symptoms glimmer from so very far off. What was this one that was already in the air before Mrs. Bradham had so much as answered her question?

Well, the next moment at any rate she knew, and more extraordinary then than anything was the spread of her apprehension, off somehow to the incalculable, under Gussy's mention of a name. What did this show most of all, however, but how little the intensity of her private association with the name had even yet died out, or at least how vividly it could revive in a connection by which everything in her was quickened? "Haughty" Vint, just lately conversed with by Cissy in New York, it appeared, and now coming on to the Bradhams from one day to another, had fed the girl with information, it also, and more wonderfully, transpired — information about Gray's young past, all surprisingly founded on close contacts, the most interesting, between the pair, as well as the least suspected ever by Rosanna: to such an effect that the transmitted trickle of it had after a moment swelled from Gussy's lips into a stream by which our friend's consciousness was flooded. "Clues" these connections might well be called when every touch could now set up a vibration. It hummed away at once like a pressed button — if she had been really and in the least meanly afraid of complications she might now have sat staring at one that would do for oddity, for the oddity of that relation of her own with Cissy's source of anecdote which could so have come and gone and yet thrown no light for her on anything but itself; little enough, by what she had tried to make of it at the time, though that might have been. It had meanwhile scarce revived for her otherwise, even if reviving now, as we have said, to intensity, that Horton Vint's invitation to her some three years before to bestow her hand upon him in marriage had been attended by impressions as singular perhaps as had ever marked a like case in an equal absence of outward show. The connection with him remaining for her had simply been that no young man — in the clear American social air — had probably ever approached a young woman on such ground with so utter a lack of ostensible warrant and had yet at the same time so saved the situation for himself, or for what he might have called his dignity, and even hers; to the positive point of his having left her with the mystery, in all the world, that she could still most pull out from old dim confusions to wonder about, and wonder all in vain, when she had nothing better to do. Everything was over between them save the fact that they hadn't quarrelled, hadn't indeed so much as discussed; but here withal was association, association unquenched — from the moment a fresh breath, as just now, could blow upon it. He had had the appearance — it was unmistakeable — of absolutely believing she might accept him if he but put it to her lucidly enough and let her look at him straight enough; and the extraordinary thing was that, for all her sense of this at the hour, she hadn't imputed to him a real fatuity.

It had remained with her that, given certain other facts, no inci-dent of that order could well have had so little to confess by any of its aspects to the taint of vulgarity. She had seen it, she believed, as he meant it, meant it with entire conviction: he had intended a tribute, of a high order, to her intelligence, which he had counted on, or at least faced with the opportunity, to recognise him as a greater value, taken all round, appraised by the *whole* suitability, than she was likely ever again to find offered. He was of course to take or to leave, and she saw him stand there in that light as he had then stood, not pleading, not pressing, not pretending to anything but the wish and the capacity to serve, only holding out her chance, appealing to her judgment, inviting her inspection, meeting it without either a shade of ambiguity or, so far as she could see, any vanity beyond the facts. It had all been wonderful enough, and not least so that, although absolutely untouched and untempted, perfectly lucid on her own side and perfectly inaccessible, she had in a manner admired him, in a manner almost enjoyed him, in the act of denying him hope. Extraordinary in especial had it been that he was probably right, right about his value, right about his rectitude, of conscious intention at least, right even as to his general calculation of effect, an effect probably producible on most women; right finally in judging that should he strike at all this would be the one way. It was only less extraordinary that no faintest shade of regret, no lightest play of rueful imagination, no subordinate stir of pity or wonder, had attended her memory of having left him to the mere cold comfort of reflection. It was his truth that had fallen short, not his error; the soundness, as it were, of his claim — so far as his fine intelligence, matching her own, that is, could make it sound — had had nothing to do with its propriety. She had refused him, none the less, without disliking him, at the same time that she was at no moment afterwards conscious of having cared whether he had suffered. She had been too unaware of the question even to remark that she seemed indifferent; though with a vague impression — so far as that went — that suffering was not in his chords. His acceptance of his check she could but call inscrutably splendid — inscrutably perhaps because she couldn't quite feel that it had left nothing between them. Something there was, something there had to be, if only the marvel, so to say, of her present, her permanent, backward vision of the force with which they had touched and separated. It stuck to her somehow that they had touched still more than if they had loved, held each other still closer than if they had embraced: to such and so strange a tune had they been briefly intimate. Would any man ever look at her so for passion as Mr. Vint had looked for reason? and should her own eyes ever again so visit a man's depths and gaze about in them unashamed to a tune to match that adventure?

Literally what they had said was comparatively unimportant — once he had made his errand clear; whereby the rest might all have been but his silent exhibition of his personality, so to name it, his honour, his assumption, his situation, his life, and that failure on her own part to yield an inch which had but the more let him see how straight these things broke upon her. For all the straightness, it was true, the fact that might most have affected, not to say concerned, her had remained the least expressed. It wasn't for her now to know what difference it could have made that he was in relation with Gray Fielder; incontestably, however, *their* relation, or their missing of one, hers and Haughty's, flushed anew in the sudden light.

"Oh I'm so glad he has good friends here then — with such a clever one as Mr. Vint we can certainly be easy about him." So much Rosanna heard herself at last say, and it would doubtless have quite served for assent to Gussy's revelation without the further support given her by the simultaneous convergence upon them of various members of the party, who exactly struck our young woman as having guessed, by the sight of hostess and momentous guest withdrawn together, that the topic of the moment was there to be plucked from their hands. Rosanna was now on her feet — she couldn't sit longer and just take things; and she was to ask herself afterwards with what cold stare of denial she mightn't have appeared quite unprecedentedly to face the inquiring rout under the sense that now certainly, if she didn't take care, she should have nothing left of her own. It wasn't that they weren't, all laughter and shimmer, all senseless sound and expensive futility, the easiest people in the world to share with, and several the very prettiest and pleasantest, of the vaguest insistence after all, the most absurdly small awareness of what they were eager about; but that of the three or four things then taking place at once the brush across her heart of Gray's possible immediate question, "Have you brought me over then to live with *these*——?" had most in common with alarm. It positively helped her indeed withal that she found herself, the next thing, greeting with more sincerity of expression than she had, by her consciousness, yet used Mrs. Bradham's final leap to action in the form of "I want him to dinner of course right off!" She said it with the big brave laugh that represented her main mercy for the general public view of her native eagerness, an eagerness appraised, not to say proclaimed, by herself as a passion for the service of society, and in connection with which it was mostly agreed that she never so drove her flock before her as when paying this theoretic tribute to grace of manner. Before Rosanna could ejaculate, moved though she was to do so, the question had been taken up by the extremely pretty person who was

known to her friends, and known even to Rosanna, as Minnie Undle and who at once put in a plea for Mr. Fielder's presence that evening, her own having been secured for it. Before such a rate of procedure as this evocation implied even Gussy appeared to recoil, but with a prompt proviso in favour of the gentleman's figuring rather on the morrow, when Mrs. Undle, since she seemed so impatient, might again be of the party. Mrs. Undle agreed on the spot, though by this time Rosanna's challenge had ceased to hang fire. "But do you really consider that you *know* him so much as that?"—she let Gussy have it straight, even if at the disadvantage that there were now as ever plenty of people to react, to the last hilarity, at the idea that acquaintance enjoyed on either side was needfully imputable to these participations. "That's just why—if we don't know him!" Mrs. Undle further contributed; while Gussy declined recognition of the relevance of any word of Miss Gaw's. She declined it indeed in her own way, by a yet stiffer illustration of her general resilience; an "Of course I mean, dear, that I look to you to bring him!" expressing sufficiently her system.

"Then you really expect him when his uncle's dying——?" sprang in all honesty from Rosanna's lips; to be taken up on the instant, however, by a voice that was not Gussy's and that rang clear before Gussy could speak.

"There can't be the least question of it—even if we're dying

The Ivory Tower

ourselves, or even if I am at least!" was what Rosanna heard; with Cissy Foy, of a sudden supremely exhibited, giving the case at once all happy sense, all bright quick harmony with their general immediate interest. She pressed to Rosanna straight, as if nothing as yet had had time to pass between them — which very little in fact had; with the result for our young woman of feeling helped, by the lightest of turns, not to be awkward herself, or really, what came to the same thing, not to be anything herself. It was a fine perception she had had before — of how Cissy could on occasion "do" for one, and this, all extraordinarily and in a sort of double sense, by quenching one in her light at the very moment she offered it for guidance. She quenched Gussy, she was the single person who could, Gussy almost gruntingly consenting; she quenched Minnie Undle, she cheapened every other presence, scattering lovely looks, multiplying happy touches, grasping Rosanna for possession, yet at the same time, as with her free hand, waving away every other connection: so that a minute or two later — for it scarce seemed more — the pair were isolated, still on the verandah somewhere, but intensely confronted and talking at ease, or in a way that had to pass for ease, with its not mattering at all whether their companions, dazzled and wafted off, had dispersed and ceased to be, or whether they themselves had simply been floated to where they wished on the great surge of the girl's grace. The girl's grace was, after its manner, such a force that Miss Gaw had had repeatedly, on past occasions, to doubt even while she recognised — for *could* a young creature you weren't quite sure of use a weapon of such an edge only for good? The young creature seemed at any rate now as never yet to give out its play for a thing to be counted on and trusted; and with Gussy Bradham herself shown just there behind them as letting it take everything straight out of *her* hands, nobody else at all daring to touch, what were you to do but verily feel distinguished by its so wrapping you about? The only sharpness in what had happened was that with Cissy's act of presence Mrs. Bradham had exercised her great function of social appraiser by staring and then, as under conclusions drawn from it, giving way. One might have found it redeemingly soft in her that before this particular suggestion she *could* melt, or that in other words Cissy appeared the single fact in all the world about which she had anything to call imagination. She imagined her, she imagined her *now*, and as dealing somehow with their massive friend; which consciousness, on the latter's part, it must be said, played for the moment through everything else.

Not indeed that there wasn't plenty for the girl to fill the fancy with; since nothing could have been purer than the stream that she poured into Rosanna's as from an upturned crystal urn while she repeated over, holding her by the two hands, gazing at her in admiration: "I can *see* how you care for him — I can see, I can see!" And she felt indeed, our young woman, how the cover was by this light hand whisked off her secret — Cissy made it somehow a secret in the act of laying it bare; and that she blushed for the felt exposure as even Gussy had failed to make her. Seeing which her companion but tilted the further vessel of confidence. "It's too funny, it's too wonderful that I too should know something. But I do, and I'll tell you how — not now, for I haven't time, but as soon as ever I can; which will make you see. So what you must do for all you're worth," said Cissy, "is to care now more than ever. You must keep him from us, because we're not good enough and you *are;* you must act in the sense of what you feel, and must feel exactly as you've a right to — for, as I say, I know, I know!"

It was impossible, Rosanna seemed to see, that a generous young thing should shine out in more beauty; so that what in the world might one ever keep from her? Surpassingly strange the plea thus radiant on the very brow of the danger! "You mean you know Mr. Fielder's history? from your having met somebody —— ?"

"Oh that of course, yes; Gussy, whom I've told of my having met Mr. Northover, will have told you. That's curious and charming," Cissy went on, "and I want awfully we should talk of it. But it

isn't what I mean by what I know — and what you don't, my dear thing!"

Rosanna couldn't have told why, but she had begun to tremble, and also to try not to show it. "What I don't know — about Gray Fielder? Why, of course there's plenty!" she smiled.

Cissy still held her hands; but Cissy now was grave. "No, there isn't plenty — save so far as what I mean is enough. And I haven't told it to Gussy. It's too good for her," the girl added. "It's too good for anyone but you."

Rosanna just waited, feeling herself perhaps grimace. "What, Cissy, *are* you talking about?"

"About what I heard from Mr. Northover when we met him, when we saw so much of him, three years ago at Ragatz, where we had gone for Mamma and where we went through the cure with him. He and I struck up a friendship and he often spoke to me of his stepson — who wasn't there with him, was at that time off somewhere in the mountains or in Italy, I forget, but to whom I could see he was devoted. He and I hit it off beautifully together — he seemed to me awfully charming and to like to tell me things. So what I allude to is something he said to me."

"About me?" Rosanna gasped.

"Yes — I see now it was about you. But it's only to-day that I've guessed that. Otherwise, otherwise ——!" And as if under the weight of her great disclosure Cissy faltered.

But she had now indeed made

her friend desire it. "You mean that otherwise you'd have told me before?"

"Yes indeed — and it's such a miracle I didn't. It's such a miracle," said Cissy, "that the person should all this time have been you — or you have been the person. Of course I had no idea that all *this* — everything that has taken place now, by what I understand — was going so extraordinarily to happen. You see he never named Mr. Betterman, or in fact, I think," the girl explained, "told me anything about him. And he didn't name, either, Gray's friend — so that in spite of the impression made on me you've never till to-day been identified."

Immense, as she went, Rosanna felt, the number of things she gave her thus together to think about. What was coming she clearly needn't fear — might indeed, deep within, happily hold her breath for; but the very interest somehow made her rest an instant, as for refinement of suspense, on the minor surprises. "The impression then has been so great that you call him 'Gray'?"

The girl at this ceased holding hands; she folded her arms back together across her slim young person — the frequent habit of it in her was of the prettiest "quaint" effect; she laughed as if submitting to some just correction of a freedom. "Oh, but my dear, *he* did, the delightful man — and isn't it borne in upon me that you do? Of course the impression was great — and if Mr. Northover and I had

met younger I don't know," her laugh said, "what mightn't have happened. No, I never shall have had a greater, a more intelligent admirer! As it was we remained true, secretly true, for fond memory, to the end: at least I did, though ever so secretly — you see I speak of it only now — and I want to believe so in *his* impression. But how I torment you!" she suddenly said in another tone.

Rosanna, nursing her patience, had a sad slow headshake. "I don't understand."

"Of course you don't — and yet it's too beautiful. It was about Gray — once when we talked of him, as I've told you we repeatedly did. It was that he never would look at anyone else."

Our friend could but appear at least to cast about. "Anyone else than whom?"

"Why than you," Cissy smiled. "The girl he had loved in boyhood. The American girl who, years before, in Dresden, had done for him something he could never forget."

"And what had she done?" stared Rosanna.

"Oh he didn't tell me *that!* But if you don't take great care, as I say," Cissy went on, "perhaps *he* may — I mean Mr. Fielder himself may when we close round him in the way that, in your place, as I assure you, I would certainly do everything to prevent."

Rosanna looked about as with a sudden sense of weakness, the effect of overstrain; it was absurd, but these last minutes might almost, with their queer action, and as to the ground they covered, have been as many formidable days. A fine verandah settee again close at hand offered her support, and she dropped upon it, as for large retrieval of menaced ease, with a need she herself alone could measure. The need was to recover some sense of perspective, to be able to place her young friend's somehow portentous assault off in such conditions, if only of mere space and time, as would make for some greater convenience of relation with it. It did at once help her — and really even for the tone in which she smiled across: "So you're sure?"

Cissy hovered, shining, shifting, yet accepting the perspective as it were — when in the world had she to fear *any?* — and positively painted there in bright contradiction, her very grace again, after the odd fashion in which it sometimes worked, seeming to deny her sincerity, and her very candour seeming to deny her gravity. "Sure of what? Sure I'm right about you?"

Rosanna took a minute to say — so many things worked in her; yet when one of these came uppermost, pushing certain of the others back, she found for putting it forward a tone grateful to her own ear. This tone represented on her part too a substitute for sincerity, but that was exactly what she wanted. "I don't care a fig for any anecdote about myself — which moreover it would be very difficult for you to have right. What I ask you if you're certain of is your being really not fit for him. Are you

absolutely," said Miss Gaw, "as bad as that?"

The girl, placed before her, looked at her now, with raised hands folded together, as if she had been some seated idol, a great Buddha perched up on a shrine. "Oh Rosanna, Rosanna ——!" she admiringly, piously breathed.

But it was not such treatment that could keep Miss Gaw from completing her chosen sense. "I should be extremely sorry — so far as I claim any influence on him — to interfere against his getting over here whatever impressions he may; interfere by his taking you for more important, in any way, than seems really called for."

"Taking *me?*" Cissy smiled.

"Taking any of you — the people, in general and in particular, who haunt this house. We mustn't be afraid for him of his having the interest, or even the mere amusement, of learning all that's to be learnt about us."

"Oh Rosanna, Rosanna" — the girl kept it up — "how you adore him; and how you make me therefore, wretch that I am, fiendishly want to see him!"

But it might quite have glanced now from our friend's idol surface. "You're the best of us, no doubt — very much; and I immensely hope you'll like him, since you've been so extraordinarily prepared. It's to be supposed too that he'll have some sense of his own."

Cissy continued rapt. "Oh but you're deep — deep deep deep!"

It came out as another presence again, that of Davey Bradham, who had the air of rather restlessly looking for her, emerged from one of the long windows of the house, just at hand, to meet Rosanna's eyes. She found herself glad to have him back, as if further to inform him. Wasn't it after all rather he that was the best of them and by no means Cissy? Her face might at any rate have conveyed as much while she reported of that young lady. "She thinks me so deep."

It made the girl, who had not seen him, turn round; but with an immediate equal confidence. "And *she* thinks *me*, Davey, so good!"

Davey's eyes were only on Cissy, but Rosanna seemed to feel them on herself. "How you must have got mixed!" he exclaimed. "But your father has come for you," he then said to Rosanna, who had got up.

"Father has walked it?" — she was amazed.

"No, he's there in a hack to take you home — and too excited to come in."

Rosanna's surprise but grew. "Has anything happened——?"

"Wonders — I asked them. Mr. Betterman's sitting right up."

"Really improving——?" Then her mystification spread. "'Them,' you say?"

"Why his nurse, as I at least suppose her," said Davey, "is with him — apparently to give you the expert opinion."

"Of the fiend's recuperating?" Cissy cried with a wail. And then

before her friend's bewilderment, "How dreadfully horrid!" she added.

"Whose nurse, please?" Rosanna asked of Davey.

"Why, hasn't he got a nurse?" Davey himself, as always, but desired lucidity. "She's doing her duty by him all the same!"

On which Cissy's young wit at once apprehended. "It's one of Mr. Betterman's taking a joy-ride in honour of his recovery! Did you ever hear anything so cool?"

She had appealed to her friends alike, but Rosanna, under the force of her suggestion, was already in advance. "Then father himself must be ill!" Miss Gaw had declared, moving rapidly to the quarter in which he so incongruously waited and leaving Davey to point a rapid moral for Cissy's benefit while this couple followed.

"If he *is* so upset that he hasn't been trusted alone I'll be hanged if I don't just see it!"

But the marvel was the way in which after an instant Cissy saw it too. "You mean because he can't stand Mr. Betterman's perhaps not dying?"

"Yes, dear ingenuous child — he has wanted so to see him out."

"Well then; isn't it what we're all wanting?"

"Most undoubtedly, pure pearl of penetration!" Davey returned as they went. "His pick-up *will* be a sell," he ruefully added; "even though it mayn't quite kill anyone of us but Mr. Gaw!"

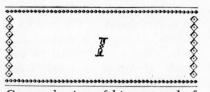

BOOK SECOND

GRAHAM'S view of his case and of all his proprieties, from the moment of his arrival, was that he should hold himself without reserve at his uncle's immediate disposition, and even such talk as seemed indicated, during the forenoon, with Doctor Hatch and Miss Mumby, the nurse then in charge, did little to lighten for him the immense prescription of delicacy. What he learnt was far from disconcerting; the patient, aware of his presence, had shown for soothed, not for agitated; the drop of the tension of waiting had had the benign effect; he had repeated over to his attendant that now "the boy" was there, all would be for the best, and had asked also with soft iteration if he were having everything he wanted. The happy assurance of this right turn of their affair, so far as they had got, he was now quietly to enjoy: he was to rest two or three hours, and if possible to sleep, while Graham, on his side, sought a like remedy — after the full indulgence in which their meeting would take place. The excellent fact for "the boy," who was two-and-thirty years of age and who now quite felt as if during the last few weeks he had lived through a dozen more, was thus that he was doing his uncle good and that somehow, to complete that harmony, he might feel the operation of an equal virtue. At his invitation, at his decision, the idea of some such wondrous matter as this had of course presided — for waiting and obliging good, which one was simply to open one's heart or one's hand to, had struck him ever as so little of the common stuff of life that now, at closer range, it could but figure as still more prodigious. At the same time there was nothing he dreaded, by his very nature, more than a fond fatuity, and he had imposed on himself from the first to proceed at every step as if without consideration he might well be made an ass of. It was true that even such a danger as this presented its interest — the process to which he should yield would be without precedent for him, and his imagination, thank heaven, had curiosity in a large measure for its principle; he wouldn't rush into peril, however, and flattered himself that after all he should not recognise its symptoms too late.

What he said to himself just now on the spot was, at any rate, that he should probably have been more excited if he hadn't been so amused. To be amused to a high pitch while his nearest kinsman, apparently nursing, as he had been told, a benevolence, lay dying a few rooms off — let this impute levity to our young man only till we

901

understand that his liability to recreation represented in him a function serious indeed. Everything played before him, everything his senses embraced; and since his landing in New York on the morning before this the play had been of a delightful violence. No slightest aspect or briefest moment of it but had held and, so to say, rewarded him: if he had come back at last for impressions, for emotions, for the sake of the rush upon him of the characteristic, these things he was getting in a measure beyond his dream. It was still beyond his dream that what everything merely seen from the window of his room meant to him during these first hours should move him first to a smile of such ecstasy, and then to such an inward consumption of his smile, as might have made of happiness a substance you could sweetly put under your tongue. He recognised — that was the secret, recognised wherever he looked — and knew that when, from far back, during his stretch of unbroken absence, he had still felt, and liked to feel, what air had originally breathed upon him, these piercing intensities of salience had really peopled the vision. He had much less remembered the actual than forecast the inevitable, and the huge involved necessity of its all showing as he found it seemed fairly to shout in his ear. He had brought with him a fine intention, one of the finest of which he was capable, and wasn't it, he put to himself, already working? Wasn't he

gathering in a perfect bloom of freshness the fruit of his design rather to welcome the impression to extravagance, if need be, than to undervalue it by the breadth of a hair? Inexpert he couldn't help being, but too estranged to melt again at whatever touch might make him, *that* he'd be hanged if he couldn't help, since what was the great thing again but to hold up one's face to *any* drizzle of light?

There it was, the light, in a mist of silver, even as he took in the testimony of his cool bedimmed room, where the air was toned by the closing of the great green shutters. It was ample and elegant, of an American elegance, which was so unlike any other, and so still more unlike any lapse of it, ever met by him, that some of its material terms and items held him as in rapt contemplation; what he had wanted, even to intensity, being that things should prove different, should positively glare with opposition — there would be no fun at all were they only imperfectly like, as that wouldn't in the least mean character. Their character might be if it would in their consistently having none — than which deficiency nothing was more possible; but he should have to decline to be charmed by unsuccessful attempts at sorts of expression he had elsewhere known more or less happily achieved. This particular disappointment indeed he was clearly not in for, since what could at once be more interesting than thus to note that the range and scale kept all their parts together, that each object or effect disowned connections, as he at least had all his life felt connections, and that his cherished hope of the fresh start and the broken link would have its measure filled to the brim. There was an American way for a room to be a room, a table a table, a chair a chair and a book a book — let alone a picture on a wall a picture, and a cold gush of water in a bath of a hot morning a promise of purification; and of this license all about him, in fine, he beheld the refreshing riot.

It cast on him for the time a spell; he moved about with soft steps and long pauses, staring out between the slats of the shutters, which he gently worked by their attachment, and then again living, with a subtlety of sense that it was a pleasure to exercise, into the conditions represented by whatever more nearly pressed. It was not only that the process of assimilation, unlike any other he had yet been engaged in, might stop short, to disaster, if he so much as breathed too hard; but that if he made the sufficient surrender he might absolutely himself be assimilated — and that was truly an experience he couldn't but want to have. The great thing he held on to withal was a decent delicacy, a dread of appearing even to himself to take big things for granted. This of itself was restrictive as to freedoms — it stayed familiarities, it kept uncertainty cool; for after all what had his uncle done but cause to be conveyed to him across the sea the bare wish that he should come? He had straightway come in consequence, but on no explanation and for no signified reward; he had come simply to avoid a possible ugliness in his not coming. Generally addicted to such avoidances, to which it indeed seemed to him that the quest of beauty was too often reduced, he had found his reason sufficient until the present hour, when it was as if all reasons, all of his own at least, had suddenly abandoned him, to the effect of his being surrounded only with those of others, of which he was up to now ignorant, but which somehow hung about the large still place, somehow stiffened the vague summer Sunday and twinkled in the universal cleanness, a real revelation to him of that possible immunity in things. He might have been sent for merely to be blown up for the relief of the old man's mind on the perversity and futility of his past. There was before him at all events no gage of anything else, no intimation other than his having been, materially speaking, preceded by preparations, to make him throw himself on a survey of prospects. What was before him at the least was a "big" experience — even to have come but to be cursed and dismissed would really be a bigger thing than yet had befallen him. Not the form but the fact of the experience accordingly mattered — so that wasn't it there to a fine intensity by his standing ever and anon at the closed door of his room and feeling that with his ear intent enough he could catch the pressure on the other side?

The pressure was at last unmistakeable, we note, in the form of Miss Mumby, who, having gently tapped, appeared there both to remark to him that he must surely at last want his luncheon and to affect him afresh and in the supreme degree as a vessel of the American want of correspondence. Miss Mumby was ample, genial, familiar and more radiantly clean than he had ever known any vessel, to whatever purpose destined; also the number of things *she* took for granted — if it was a question of that, or perhaps rather the number of things of which she didn't doubt and was incapable of doubting, surrounded her together with a kind of dazzling aura, a special radiance of disconnection. She wore a beautiful white dress, and he scarce knew what apparatus of spotless apron and cuffs and floating streamers to match; yet she could only again report to him of the impression that had most jumped at him from the moment of his arrival. He saw in a moment that any difficulty on his part of beginning with her at some point in social space, so to say, at which he had never begun before with any such person, would count for nothing in face of her own perfect power to begin. The faculty of beginning would be in truth Miss Mumby's very genius, and in the moment of his apprehension of this he felt too — he had in fact already felt it at their first meeting — how little his pale old postulates as to

persons being "such" might henceforth claim to serve him. What person met by him during his thirty hours in American air was "such" again as any other partaker of contact had appeared or proved, no matter where, before his entering it? What person had not at once so struck him in the light of violent repudiation of type, as he might save for his sensibility have imputed type, that nothing else in the case seemed predicable? He might have seen Miss Mumby, he was presently to recognise, in the light of a youngish mother perhaps, a sister, a cousin, a friend, even a possible bride, for these were aspects independent of type and boundlessly free of range; but a "trained nurse" was a trained nurse, and that was a category of the most evolved — in spite of which what category in all the world could have lifted its head in Miss Mumby's aura?

Still, she might have been a pleasant cousin, a first cousin, *the* very first a man had ever had and not in any degree "removed," while she thus proclaimed the cheerful ease of everything and everyone, her own above all, and made him yield on the spot to her lightest intimation. He couldn't possibly have held off from her in any way, and if ·this was in part because he always collapsed at a touch before nurses, it was at the same time not at all the nurse in her that now so affected him, but the incalculable other force, of which he had had no experience and which was apparently that of the familiar in tone and manner. He had known, of a truth, familiarity greater — much greater, but only with greater occasions and supports for it; whereas on Miss Mumby's part it seemed independent of any or of every motive. He could scarce have said in fine, as he followed her to their repast, at which he foresaw in an instant that they were both to sit down, whether it more alarmed or just more coolingly enveloped him; his slight first bewilderment at any rate had dropped — he had already forgotten the moment wasted two or three hours before in wondering, with his sense of having known Nurses who gloried in their title, how his dear second father, for instance, would in his final extremity have liked the ministrations of a Miss. By those he himself presently enjoyed in such different conditions, that is from across the table, bare and polished and ever so delicately charged, of the big dusky, yet just a little breezy dining-room, by those in short under which every association he had ever had with anything crashed down to pile itself as so much more tinklingly shivered glass at Miss Mumby's feet, that sort of question was left far behind — and doubtless would have been so even if the appeal of the particular refection served to them had alone had the case in hand. "I'm going to make you like our food, so you might as well begin at once," his companion had announced; and he felt it on the spot as scarce less than delicious that this element too

should play, and with such fineness, into that harmony of the amusingly exotic which was, under his benediction, working its will on him. "Oh yes," she rejoiced in answer to his exhibition of the degree in which what was before him did stir again to sweetness a chord of memory, "oh yes, food's a great tie, it's like language — you can always understand your own, whereas in Europe I had to learn about six others."

Miss Mumby had been to Europe, and he saw soon enough how there was nowhere one could say she hadn't gone and nothing one could say she hadn't done — one's perception could bear only on what she hadn't become; so that, as he thus perceived, though she might have affected Europe even as she was now affecting *him*, she was a pure negation of its having affected herself, unless perhaps by adding to her power to make him feel how little he could impose on her. She knew all about his references while he only missed hers, and that gave her a tremendous advantage — or would have done so hadn't she been too much his cousin to take it. He at any rate recognised in a moment that the so many things she had had to learn to understand over there were not forms of speech but alimentary systems — as to which view he quite agreed with her that the element of the native was equally rooted in both supports of life. This gave her of course her opportunity of remarking that she had indeed made for the assimilation of "his" cookery — whichever of the varieties his had most been — scarce less an effort than she must confess now to making for that of his terms of utterance; where she had at once again the triumph that he was nowhere, by his own reasoning, if he pretended to an affinity with the nice things they were now eating and yet stood off from the other ground. "Oh I *understand* you, which appears to be so much more than you do me!" he laughed; "but am I really committed to everything because I'm committed, in the degree you see me, oh yes, to waffles and maple syrup, followed, and on such a scale, by melons and ice-cream? You see in the one case I have but to take in, and in the other have to give out: so can't I have, in a quiet way the American palate without emitting the American sounds?" Thus was he on the straightest flattest level with Miss Mumby — it stretched, to his imagination, without a break, a rise or a fall, *à perte de vue;* and thus was it already attested that the Miss Mumbys (for it was evident there would be thousands of them) were in society, or were, at any rate, not out of it, society thereby becoming clearly colossal. What was it, moreover, but the best society — as who should say anywhere — when his companion made the bright point that if anything had to do with sounds the palate did? returning with it also to the one already made, her due warning that she wasn't going to have him not like everything. "But I do, I

do, I do," he declared, with his mouth full of a seasoned and sweetened, a soft, substantial coldness and richness that were at once the revelation of a world and the consecration of a fate; "I revel in everything, I already wallow, behold: I move as in a dream, I assure you, and I only fear to wake up."

"Well, I don't know as I want you to wallow, and I certainly don't want you to fear — though you'll wake up soon enough, I guess," his entertainer continued, "whatever you do. You'll wake up to some of our realities, and — well, we won't want anything better for you: will we, Doctor?" Miss Mumby freely proceeded on their being joined for a moment by the friendly physician who had greeted our young man, on his uncle's behalf, at his hour of arrival, and who, having been again for a while with their interesting host, had left the second nurse in charge and was about to be off to other cares. "I'm saying to Mr. Fielder that he's got to wake up to some pretty big things," she explained to Doctor Hatch, whom it struck Gray she addressed rather as he had heard doctors address nurses than nurses doctors; a fact contributing offhand to his awareness, already definite, that everyone addressed everyone as he had nowhere yet heard the address perpetrated, and that so, evidently, there were questions connected with it that must yet wait over. It was pertinently to be felt furthermore that Doctor Hatch's own freedom, which also had quite its own rare freshness of note, shared in the general property of the whole appeal to him, the appeal of the very form of the great sideboard, the very "school," though yet unrecognised by him, of the pictures hung about, the very look and dress, the apparently odd identity, of the selected and arrayed volumes in a bookcase charged with ornament and occupying the place of highest dignity in the room, to take his situation for guaranteed as it was surely not common for earthly situations to be. This he could feel, however, without knowing, to any great purpose, what it really meant; and he was afterwards even scarce to know what had further taken place, under Doctor Hatch's blessing, before he passed out of the house to the verandah and the grounds, as their limitations of reach didn't prevent their being called, and gave himself up to inquiries now permittedly direct.

Doctor Hatch's message or momentary act of quaint bright presence came to him thus, on the verandah, while shining expanses opened, as an invitation to some extraordinary confidence, some flight of optimism without a precedent, as a positive hint in fine that it depended on himself alone to step straight into the chariot of the sun, which on his mere nod would conveniently descend there to the edge of the piazza, and whirl away for increase of acquaintance with the time, as it was obviously going to be, of his life. This was but his reading indeed of the funny terms in which the delightful man put it to him that he seemed by his happy advent to have brought on for his uncle a prospect, a rise of pitch, not dissimilar from that sort of vision; by so high a tide of ease had the sick room above been flooded, and such a lot of good would clearly await the patient from seeing him after a little and at the perfect proper moment. It was to be that of Mr. Betterman's competent choice: he lay there as just for the foretaste of it, which was wholly tranquillising, and could be trusted — what else did doctor and nurse engage for? — to know the psychological hour on its striking and then, to complete felicity, have his visitor introduced. His present mere assurance of the visitor was in short so agreeable to him, and by the same token to Doctor Hatch himself — which was above all what the latter had conveyed — that the implication of the agreeable to Graham in return might fairly have been some imponderable yet ever so sensible tissue, voluminous interwoven gold and silver, flung as a mantle over his shoulders while he went. Gray had never felt around him any like envelope whatever; so that on his looking forth at all the candid clearness — which struck him too, ever so amusingly, as even more candid when occasionally and aggressively, that is residentially, obstructed than when not — what he inwardly and fantastically compared it to was some presented quarto page, vast and fair, ever so distinctly printed and ever so unexpectedly vignet-

The Ivory Tower

ted, of a volume of which the leaves would be turned for him one by one and with no more trouble on his own part than when a friendly service beside him at the piano, where he so often sat, relieved him, from sheet to sheet, of touching his score.

Wasn't he thus now again "playing," as it had been a lifelong resource to him to play in that other posture? — a question promoted by the way the composition suddenly broke into the vividest illustrational figure, that of a little man encountered on one of his turns of the verandah and who, affecting him at first as a small waiting and watching, an almost crouching gnome, the neat domestic goblin of some old Germanic, some harmonised, familiarised legend, sat and stared at him from the depths of an arrested rocking-chair after a fashion nothing up to then had led him to preconceive. This was a different note from any yet, a queer, sharp, hard particle in all the softness; and it was sensible too, oddly enough, that the small force of their concussion but grew with its coming over him the next moment that he simply had before him Rosanna Gaw's prodigious parent. *Of course* it was Mr. Gaw, whom he had never seen, and of whom Rosanna in the old time had so little talked; her mother alone had talked of him in those days, and to his own mother only — with whom Gray had indeed himself afterwards talked not a little; but the intensity of the certitude came not so much by any plain as by

quite the most roundabout presumption, the fact of his always having felt that she required some strange accounting for, and that here was the requirement met by just the ripest revelation. She had been involved in something, produced by something, intimately pressing upon her and yet as different as possible from herself; and here was the concentrated difference — which showed him too, with each lapsing second, its quality of pressure. Abel Gaw struck him in this light as very finely blanched, as somehow squeezed together by the operation of an inward energy or necessity, and as animated at the same time by the conviction that, should he sit there long enough and still enough, the young man from Europe, known to be on the premises, might finally reward his curiosity. Mr. Gaw was curiosity embodied — Gray was by the end of the minute entirely assured of that; it in fact quite seemed to him that he had never yet in all his life caught the prying passion so shamelessly in the act. Shamelessly, he was afterwards to remember having explained to himself, because his sense of the reach of the sharp eyes in the small white face, and of their not giving way for a moment before his own, suggested to him, even if he could scarce have said why to that extent, the act of listening at the door, at the very keyhole, of a room, combined with the attempt to make it good under sudden detection.

So it was, at any rate, that our

908

speculative friend, the impression of the next turn of the case aiding, figured the extension, without forms, without the shade of a form, of their unmitigated mutual glare. The initiation of this exchange by the little old gentleman in the chair, who gave for so long no sign of moving or speaking, couldn't but practically determine in Graham's own face some resistance to the purpose exhibited and for which it was clear no apology impended. By the time he had recognised that his presence was in question for Mr. Gaw with such an intensity as it had never otherwise, he felt, had the benefit of, however briefly, save under some offered gage or bribe, he had also made out that no "form" would survive for twenty seconds in any close relation with the personage, and that if ever he had himself known curiosity as to what might happen when manners were consistently enough ignored it was a point on which he should at once be enlightened. His fellow-visitor, of whose being there Doctor Hatch and Miss Mumby were presumably unaware, continued to ignore everything but the opportunity he enjoyed and the certainty that Graham would contribute to it — which certainty made in fact his profit. The profit, that is, couldn't possibly fail unless Gray should turn his back and walk off; which was of course possible, but would then saddle Gray himself with the repudiation of forms: so that — yes, infallibly — in proportion as the young man *had* to be commonly

civil would Mr. Gaw's perhaps unholy satisfaction of it be able to prevail. The young man had taken it home that he couldn't simply stare long enough for successful defence by the time that, presently moving nearer, he uttered his adversary's name with no intimation of a doubt. Mr. Gaw failed, Gray was afterwards to inform Rosanna, "to so much as take this up"; he was left with everything on his hands but the character of his identity, the indications of his face, the betrayals he should so much less succeed in suppressing than his adversary would succeed in reading them. The figure presented hadn't stirred from his posture otherwise than by a motion of eye just perceptible as Graham moved; it was drinking him in, our hero felt, and by this treatment of the full cup, continuously applied to the lips, stillness was of course imposed. It didn't again so much as recognise, by any sign given, Graham's remark that an acquaintance with Miss Gaw from of old involved naturally *their* acquaintance: there was no question of Miss Gaw, her friend found himself after another minute divining, as there was none of objects or appearances immediately there about them; the question was of something a thousand times more relevant and present, of something the interloper's silence, far more than breathed words could have done, represented the fond hope of mastering.

Graham thus held already, by the old man's conviction, a secret

909

of high value, yet which, with the occasion stretched a little, would practically be at his service — so much as that at least, with the passage of another moment, he had concluded to; and all the while, in the absurdest way, without his guessing, without his at all measuring, his secret himself. Mr. Gaw fairly made him want to — want, that is, as a preliminary or a stop-gap, to guess what it had best, most desirably and most effectively, become; for shouldn't he positively *like* to have something of the sort in order just to disoblige this gentleman? Strange enough how it came to him at once as a result of the father's refusal of attention to any connection he might have glanced at with the daughter, strange enough how it came to him, under the first flush of heat he had known since his arrival, that two could play at such a game and that if Rosanna's interests were to be so slighted her relative himself should miss even the minimum of application as one of them. "He must have wanted to know, he must have wanted to know ——!" this young woman was on a later day to have begun to explain; without going on, however, since by that time Gray had rather made out, the still greater rush of his impressions helping, the truth of Mr. Gaw's desire. It bore, that appetite, upon a single point and, daughter or no daughter, on nothing else in the world — the question of what Gray's "interest," in the light of his uncle's intentions, might size up to; those

intentions having, to the Gaw imagination, been of course apprehensible on the spot, and within the few hours that had lapsed, by a nephew even of but rudimentary mind. At the present hour meanwhile, short of the miracle which our friend's counter-scrutiny alone could have brought about, there worked for this young intelligence, and with no small sharpness, the fact itself of such a revealed relation to the ebb of their host's life — upon which was thrust the appearance of its being, watch in hand, all impatiently, or in other words all offensively, timed. The very air at this instant tasted to Gray, quite as if something under his tongue had suddenly turned from the sweet to the appreciably sour, of an assumption diffused through it in respect to the rudiments of mind. He was afterwards to date the breaking-in upon him of the general measure of the smallest vision of business a young man might self-respectingly confess to from Mr. Gaw's extraordinary tacit "Oh come, you can't fool *me:* don't I know you know what I want to know — don't I know what it must mean for you to have been here since six o'clock this morning with nothing whatever else to do than just to take it in?"

That was it — Gray was to have taken in the more or less definite value involved for him in his uncle's supposedly near extinction, and was to be capable, if not of expressing it on the spot in the only terms in which a value of any sort could exist for this worthy, yet still at least of liability to such a betrayal as would yield him something to conclude upon. It was only afterwards, once more, that our young man was to master the logic of the conclusive as it prevailed for Mr. Gaw; what concerned his curiosity was to settle whether or no they were in presence together of a really big fact — distinguishing as the Gaw mind did among such dimensions and addressed as it essentially was to a special question — a question as yet unrecognised by Gray. He was subsequently to have his friend's word to go upon — when, in the extraordinary light of Rosanna's explication, he read clear what he had been able on the verandah but half to glimmer out: the queer truth of Mr. Gaw's hunger to learn to what extent he had anciently, to what degree he had irremediably, ruined his whilom associate. He didn't know — so strange was it, at the time and since, that, thanks to the way Mr. Betterman had himself fixed things, he couldn't be sure; but what he wanted, and what he hung about so displeasingly to sniff up the least stray sign of, was a confirmation of his belief that Doctor Hatch's and Miss Mumby's patient had never really recovered from the wound of years before. They were nursing him now for another complaint altogether, this one admittedly such as must, with but the scantest further reprieve, dispose of him; whereas doubts were deep, as Mr. Gaw at least entertained them, as to whether the damage he supposed his own just resentment to have inflicted when propriety and opportunity combined to inspire him was amenable even to nursing the most expert or to medication the most subtle. These mysteries of calculation were of course impenetrable to Gray during the moments at which we see him so almost indescribably exposed at once and reinforced; but the effect of the sharper and sharper sense as of a spring pressed by his companion was that a *whole* consciousness suddenly welled up in him and that within a few more seconds he had become aware of a need absolutely adverse to any trap that might be laid for his candour. He could as little have then said why as he could vividly have phrased it under the knowledge to come, but that his mute interlocutor desired somehow their association in a judgment of what his uncle was "worth," a judgment from which a comparatively conceited nephew might receive an incidental lesson, played through him as a certitude and produced quite another inclination. That recognition of the pleasant on which he had been floating affirmed itself as in the very face of so embodied a pretension to affirm the direct opposite, to thrust up at him in fine a horrid contradiction — a contradiction which he next heard himself take, after the happiest fashion, the straightest way to rebut.

"I'm sure you'll be glad to know that I seem to be doing my uncle a tremendous lot of good. They tell me I'm really bringing him round" — and Graham smiled down at little blanched Mr. Gaw. "I don't despair at all of his getting much better."

It was on this that for the first time Mr. Gaw became articulate. "Better —— ?" he strangely quavered, and as if his very eyes questioned such conscious flippancy.

"Why yes — through cheering him up. He takes, I gather," Gray went on, "as much pleasure as I do —— !" His assurance, however, had within the minute dropped a little — the effect of it might really reach, he apprehended, beyond his idea. The old man had been odd enough, but now of a sudden he looked sick, and that one couldn't desire.

" 'Pleasure' —— ?" he was nevertheless able to echo; while it struck Gray that no sound so weak had ever been so sharp, or none so sharp ever so weak. "Pleasure in dying —— ?" Mr. Gaw asked in this flatness of doubt.

"But my dear sir," said Gray, his impulse to be jaunty still nevertheless holding out a little, "but, my dear sir, if, as it strikes me, he isn't dying —— ?"

"Oh twaddle!" snapped Mr. Gaw with the emphasis of his glare — shifted a moment, Gray next saw, to a new object in range. Gray felt himself even before turning for it rejoined by Miss Mumby, who, rounding the corner of the house, had paused as in presence of an odd conjunction; not made the less odd moreover by Mr. Gaw's in-

stant appeal to her. "You think he ain't then going to —— ?"

He had to leave it at that, but Miss Mumby supplied, with the loudest confidence, what appeared to be wanted. "He ain't going to get better? Oh we hope so!" she declared to Graham's delight.

It helped him to contribute in his own way. "Mr. Gaw's surprise seems for his holding out!"

"Oh I guess he'll hold out," Miss Mumby was pleased to say.

"Then if he ain't dying what's the fuss about?" Mr. Gaw wanted to know.

"Why there ain't any fuss — but what *you* seem to make," Miss Mumby could quite assure him.

"Oh well, if you answer for it —— !" He got up on this, though with an alertness that, to Gray's sense, didn't work quite truly, and stood an instant looking from one of his companions to the other, while our young man's eyes, for their part, put a question to Miss Mumby's — a question which, articulated, would have had the sense of "What on earth's the matter with him?" There seemed no knowing how Mr. Gaw would take things — as Miss Mumby, for that matter, appeared also at once to reflect.

"We're sure enough not to want to have *you* sick too," she declared indeed with more cheer than apprehension; to which she added, however, to cover all the ground, "You just leave Mr. Betterman to us and take care of yourself. We never say die and we won't have you say it—either about him or anyone else, Mr. Gaw."

This gentleman, so addressed, straightened and cleared himself in such a manner as to show that he saw, for the moment, Miss Mumby's point; which he then, a wondrous small concentration of studied blankness—studied, that is, his companions were afterwards both to show they had felt—commemorated his appreciation of in a tiny, yet triumphant, "Well, that's all right!"

"It ain't so right but what I'm going to see you home," Miss Mumby returned with authority; adding, however, for Graham's benefit, that she had come down to tell him his uncle was now ready. "You just go right up—you'll find Miss Goodenough there. And you'll see for yourself," she said, "how fresh he is!"

"Thanks—that will be beautiful!" Gray brightly responded; but with his eyes on Mr. Gaw, whom of a sudden, somehow, he didn't like to leave.

It at any rate determined on the little man's part a surprised inquiry. "Then you haven't seen him yet—with your grand account of him?"

"No—but the account," Gray smiled, "has an authority beyond mine. Besides," he kept on after this gallant reference, "I feel what I shall do for him."

"Oh they'll have great times!"—Miss Mumby, with an arm at the old man's service, bravely guaranteed it. But she also admonished Graham: "Don't keep him waiting, and mind what Miss Goodenough tells you! So now, Mr. Gaw—you're to mind *me!*" she concluded; while this subject of her more extemporised attention so far complied as slowly to face with her in the direction of the other house. Gray wondered about him, but immensely trusted Miss Mumby, and only watched till he saw them step off together to the lawn, Mr. Gaw independent of support, with something in his consciously stiffened even if not painfully assumed little air, as noted thus from behind, that quite warranted his protectress. Seen that way, yes, he was a tremendous little person; and Gray, excited, immensely readvised and turning accordingly to his own business, felt the assault of impressions fairly shake him as he went—shake him though it apparently seemed most capable of doing but to the effect of hilarity.

II

WHETHER or no by its so different appearance from that of Mr. Gaw, the figure propped on pillows in the vast cool room and lighted in such a way that the clear deepening west seemed to flush toward it, through a wide high window, in the interest of its full effect, impressed our young man as massive and expansive, as of a beautiful bland dignity indeed—though emulating Rosanna's relative, he was at first to gather, by a perfect readiness to stare rather than speak. Miss Goodenough had hovered a little, for full assurance, but then had thrown off with a *timbre* of voice never yet used for Gray's own ear in any sick room, "Well, I guess you won't come to blows!" and had left them face to face — besides leaving the air quickened by the freedom of her humour. They were face to face for the time across an interval which, to do her justice, she had not taken upon herself to deal with directly; this in spite of Gray's apprehension at the end of a minute that she might, by the touch of her hand or the pitch of her spirit, push him further forward than he had immediately judged decent to advance. He had stopped at a certain distance from the great grave bed, stopped really for consideration and deference, or through the instinct of submitting himself first of all to approval, or at least to encouragement; the space, not great enough for reluctance and not small enough for presumption, showed him ready to obey any sign his uncle should make. Mr. Betterman struck him, in this high quietude of contemplation, much less as formidable than as mildly and touchingly august; he had not supposed him, he became suddenly aware, so great a person — a presence like that of some weary veteran of affairs, one of the admittedly eminent whose last words would be expected to figure in history. The large fair face, rather square than heavy, was neither clouded nor ravaged, but finely serene; the silver-coloured hair seemed to bind the broad high brow as with a band of splendid silk, while the eyes rested on Gray with an air of acceptance beyond attestation by the mere play of cheer or the comparative gloom of relief.

"Ah le beau type, le beau type!" was during these instants the visitor's inward comment breaking into one of the strange tongues that experience had appointed him privately to use, in many a case, for the appropriation of aspects and appearances. It was not till afterwards that he happened to learn how his uncle had been capable, two or three hours before seeing him, of offering cheek and chin to the deft ministration of a barber, a fact highly illuminating, though by that time the gathered lights were thick. What the patient owed on the spot to the sacrifice, he easily made out, was that look as of the last refinement of preparation, that positive splendour of the immaculate, which was really, on one's taking it all in, but part of an earnest recognition of his guest's own dignity. The grave beauty of the personal presence, the vague anticipation as of something that might go on to be commemorated for its example, the great pure fragrant room, bathed in the tempered glow of the afternoon's end, the general lucidity and tranquility and security of the whole presented case, begot in fine, on our young friend's part, an extraordinary sense that as he himself was important enough to be on show, so these peculiar perfections that met him were but so many virtual honours rendered and signs of the high level to which he had mounted. On show, yes — that was it, and more wonderfully than could be said: Gray was sure after a little of how right he was to stand off as yet in any interest of his own significance that might be involved. There was clearly something his uncle so wanted him to be that he should run no possible danger of being it to excess, and that if he might only there and then grasp it he would ask but to proceed, for decency's sake, according to his lights: just as so short a time before a like force of suggestion had played upon him from Mr. Gaw — each of these appeals clothing him in its own way with such an oddity of pertinence, such a bristling set of attributes. This wait of the parties to the present one for articulate expression, on either side, of whatever it was that might most concern them together, promised also to last as the tension had lasted down on the verandah, and would perhaps indeed have drawn itself further out if Gray hadn't broken where he stood into a cry of admiration — since it could scarcely be called less — that blew to the winds every fear of overstepping.

"It's really worth one's coming so far, uncle, if you don't mind my saying so — it's really worth a great pilgrimage to see anything so splendid."

The old man heard, clearly, as by some process that was still deeply active; and then after a pause that represented, Gray was sure, no failure at all of perception, but only the wide embrace of a possibility of pleasure, sounded bravely back: "Does it come up to what you've seen?"

It was Gray rather who was for a moment mystified — though only to further spontaneity when he had caught the sense of the question. "Oh, you come up to everything — by which I mean, if I may, that nothing comes up to *you!* I mean, if I may," he smiled, "that you yourself, uncle, affect me as the biggest and most native American impression that I can possibly be exposed to."

"Well," said Mr. Betterman, and again as with a fond deliberation, "what I'm going to like, I see, is to listen to the way you talk. That," he added with his soft distinctness, a singleness of note somehow for the many things meant, "that, I guess, is about what I most wanted you to come for. Unless it be to look at you too. I like to look right *at* you."

"Well," Gray harmoniously laughed again, "if even *that* can give you pleasure —— !" He stood as for inspection, easily awkward, pleasantly loose, holding up his head as if to make the most of no great stature. "I've never been so sorry that there isn't more of me."

The fine old eyes on the pillow kept steadily taking him in; he could quite see that he happened to be, as he might have called it,

The Ivory Tower

right; and though he had never felt himself, within his years, extraordinarily or excitingly wrong, so that this felicity might have turned rather flat for him, there was still matter for emotion, for the immediate throb and thrill, in finding success so crown him. He had been spared, thank goodness, any positive shame, but had never known his brow brushed or so much as tickled by the laurel or the bay. "Does it mean," he might have murmured to himself, "the strangest shift of standards?" — but his uncle had meanwhile spoken. "Well, there's all of you I'm going to want. And there must be more of you than I see. Because you *are* different," Mr. Betterman considered.

"But different from what?" Truly was Gray interested to know.

It took Mr. Betterman a moment to say, but he seemed to convey that it might have been guessed. "From what you'd have been if you had come."

The young man was indeed drawn in. "If I had come years ago? Well, perhaps," he so far happily agreed — "for I've often thought of that myself. Only, you see," he laughed, "I'm different from *that* too. I mean from what I was when I didn't come."

Mr. Betterman looked at it quietly. "You're different in the sense that you're older — and you seem to me rather older than I supposed. All the better, all the better," he continued to make out. "You're the same person I didn't tempt, the same person I *couldn't* — that time

when I tried. I see you are, I see *what* you are."

"You see terribly much, sir, for the few minutes!" smiled Gray.

"Oh when I *want* to see ——!" the old man comfortably enough sighed. "I take you in, I take you in; though I grant that I don't quite see how you can understand. Still," he pursued, "there are things for you to tell me. You're different from *anything*, and if we had time for particulars I should like to know a little how you've kept so. I was afraid you wouldn't turn out perhaps so thoroughly the sort of thing I liked to think — for I hadn't much more to go upon than what *she* said, you know. However," Mr. Betterman wound up as with due comfort, "it's by what she says that I've gone — and I want her to know that I don't feel fooled."

If Gray's wonderment could have been said to rest anywhere, hour after hour, long enough to be detected in the act, the detaining question would have been more than any other perhaps that of whether Miss Gaw would "come up." Now that she did so however, in this quiet way, it had no strangeness that his being at once glad couldn't make but a mouthful of; and the recent interest of what she had lately written to him was as nothing to the interest of her becoming personally his uncle's theme. With which, at the same time, it was pleasanter to him than anything else to speak of her himself. "If you allude to Rosanna Gaw you'll no doubt understand

916

how tremendously I want to see her."

The sick man waited a little — but not, it quite seemed, from lack of understanding. "She wants tremendously to see you, Graham. You might know that of course from her going to work so." Then again he gathered his thoughts and again after a little went on. "She had a good idea, and I love her for it; but I'm afraid my own hasn't been so very much to give *her* the satisfaction. I've wanted it myself, and — well, here I am getting it from you. Yes," he kept up, his eyes never moving from his nephew, "you couldn't give me more if you had tried, from so far back, on purpose. But I can't tell you half!" He exhaled a long breath — he was a little spent. "You tell *me*. You tell *me*."

"I'm tiring you, sir," Gray said.

"Not by letting me see — you'd only tire me if you didn't." Then for the first time his eyes glanced about. "Haven't they put a place for you to sit? Perhaps they knew," he suggested, while Gray reached out for a chair, "perhaps they knew just how I'd want to see you. There seems nothing they don't know," he contentedly threw off again.

Gray had his chair before him, his hands on the back tilting it a little. "They're extraordinary. I've never seen anything like them. They help me tremendously," he cheerfully confessed.

Mr. Betterman, at this, seemed to wonder. "Why, have you difficulties?"

"Well," said Gray, still with his chair, "you say I'm different — if you mean it for my being alien from what I feel surrounding me. But if you knew how funny all *that* seems to me," he laughed, "you'd understand that I clutch at protection."

"'Funny'?" — his host was clearly interested, without offence, in the term.

"Well then terrific, sir!"

"So terrific that you need protection?"

"Well," Gray explained, gently shaking his chair-back, "when one simply sees that nothing of one's former experience serves, and that one doesn't know anything about anything —— !"

More than ever at this his uncle's look might have covered him. "Anything round here — no! That's it, that's it," the old man blandly repeated. "That's just the way — I mean the way I hoped. *She* knows you don't know — and doesn't want you to either. But put down your chair," he said; and then after, when Gray, instantly and delicately complying, had placed the precious article with every precaution back where it had stood: "Sit down here on the bed. There's margin."

"Yes," smiled Gray, doing with all consideration as he was told, "you don't seem anywhere very much à l'étroit."

"I presume," his uncle returned, "you know French thoroughly."

Gray confessed to the complication. "Of course when one has heard it almost from the cradle —— !"

"And the other tongues too?"

The Ivory Tower

He seemed to wonder if, for his advantage, he mightn't deny them. "Oh a couple of others. In the countries there they come easy."

"Well, they wouldn't have come easy here — and I guess nothing else would; I mean of the things *we* principally grow. And I won't have you tell me," Mr. Betterman said, "that if you had taken that old chance they might have done so. We don't know anything about it, and at any rate it would have spoiled you. I mean for what you *are*."

"Oh," returned Gray, on the bed, but pressing lightly, "oh what I 'am' —— !"

"My point isn't so much for what you are as for what you're not. So I won't have anything else; I mean I won't have you but as I want you," his host explained. "I want you just this way."

With which, while the young man kept his arms folded and his hands tucked away as for compression of his personal extent and weight, they exchanged, at their close range, the most lingering look yet. Extraordinary to him, in the gravity of this relation, his deeper impression of something beautiful and spreadingly clear — very much as if the wide window and the quiet clean sea and the finer sunset light had all had, for assistance and benediction, their word to say to it. They seemed to combine most to remark together "What an exquisite person is your uncle!" This is what he had for the minute the sense of taking from them, and the expression of his as-

sent to it was in the tone of his next rejoinder. "If I could only know what it is you'd most like — !"

"Never mind what I most like — only tell me, only tell me," his companion again said: "You can't say anything that won't absolutely suit me; in fact I defy you to, though you mayn't at all see why that's the case. I've got you — without a flaw. So!" Mr. Betterman triumphantly breathed. Gray's sense was by this time of his being examined and appraised as never in his life before — very much as in the exposed state of an important "piece," an object of value picked, for finer estimation, from under containing glass. There was nothing then but to face it, unless perhaps also to take a certain comfort in his being, as he might feel, practically clean and in condition. That such an hour had its meaning, and that the meaning might be great for him, this of course surged softly in, more and more, from every point of the circle that held him; but with the consciousness making also more at each moment for an uplifting, a fantastic freedom, a sort of sublime simplification, in which nothing seemed to depend on him or to have at any time so depended. He was *really* face to face thus with bright immensities, and the handsome old presence from which, after a further moment, a hand had reached forth a little to take his own, guaranteed by the quietest of gestures at once their truth and the irrelevance, as he could only feel it, of their scale. Cool and not weak, to

918

his responsive grasp, this retaining force, to which strength was added by what next came. "It's not for myself, it's not for myself — I mean your being as I say. What do I matter now except to have recognised it? No, Graham — it's in another connection." Was the connection then with Rosanna? Graham had time to wonder, and even to think what a big thing this might make of it, before his uncle brought out: "It's for the world."

"The world?" — Gray's vagueness again reigned.

"Well, our great public."

"Oh your great public —— !"

The exclamation, the cry of alarm, even if also of amusement in face of such a connection as that, quickened for an instant the good touch of the cool hand. "That's the way I like you to sound. It's the way she told me you *would* — I mean that would be natural to you. And it's precisely why — being the awful great public it is — we require the difference that you'll make. So you see you're for our people."

Poor Graham's eyes widened. "I shall make a difference for your people —— ?"

But his uncle serenely went on. "Don't think you know them yet, or what it's like over here at all. You may think so and feel you're prepared. But you don't know till you've had the whole thing up against you."

"May I ask, sir," Gray smiled, "what you're talking about?"

His host met his eyes on it, but let it drop. "You'll see soon enough for yourself. Don't mind what I say. That isn't the thing for you now — it's all done. Only be true," said Mr. Betterman. "You *are* and, as I've said, can't help yourself." With which he relapsed again to one of his good conclusions. "And after all don't mind the public either."

"Oh," returned Gray, "all great publics are awful."

"Ah no no — I won't have that. Perhaps they may be, but the trouble we're concerned with is about ours — and about some other things too." Gray felt in the hand's tenure a small emphasizing lift of the arm, while the head moved a little as off toward the world they spoke of — which amounted for our young man, however, but to a glance at all the outside harmony and prosperity, bathed as these now seemed in the colour of the flushed sky. Absurd altogether that he should be in any way enlisted against such things. His entertainer, all the same, continued to see the reference and to point it. "The enormous preponderance of money. Money is their life."

"But surely even here it isn't everyone who has it. Also," he freely laughed, "isn't it a good thing to have?"

"A very good thing indeed." Then his uncle waited as in the longest inspection yet. "But you don't know anything about it."

"Not about large sums," Gray cheerfully admitted.

"I mean it has never been near you. That sticks out of you — the way it hasn't. I knew it couldn't have been — and then she told me *she* knew. I see you're a blank — and nobody here's a blank, not a creature I've ever touched. That's what I've wanted," the old man went on — "a perfect clean blank. I don't mean there aren't heaps of them that are damned fools, just as there are heaps of others, bigger heaps probably, that are damned knaves; except that mostly the knave *is* the biggest fool. But those are not blanks; they're full of the poison — without a blest other idea. Now you're the blank I want, if you follow — and yet you're not the blatant ass."

"I'm not sure I quite follow," Gray laughed, "but I'm very much obliged."

"Have you ever done three cents' worth of business?" Mr. Betterman judicially asked.

It helped our young man to some ease of delay. "Well, I'm afraid I can't claim to have had much business to do. Also you're wrong, sir," he added, "about my not being a blatant ass. Oh please understand that I *am* a blatant ass. Let there be no mistake about that," Gray touchingly pleaded.

"Yes — but not on the subject of anything but business."

"Well — no doubt on the subject of business more than on any other."

Still the good eyes rested. "Tell me one thing, other than that, for which you haven't at least *some* intelligence."

"Oh sir, there are no end of things, and it's odd one should have to prove that — though it would take me long. But I allow there's nothing I understand so little and like so little as the mystery of the 'market' and the hustle of any sort."

"You utterly loathe and abhor the hustle! That's what I blissfully want of you," said Mr. Betterman.

"You ask of me the declaration —— ?" Gray considered. "But how can I *know*, don't you see? — when I *am* such a blank, when I've never had three cents' worth of business, as you say, to transact?"

"The people who don't loathe it are always finding it somehow to do, even if preposterously for the most part, and dishonestly. Your case," Mr. Betterman reasoned, "is that you haven't a grain of the imagination of any such interest. If you *had* had," he wound up, "it would have stirred in you that first time."

Gray followed, as his kinsman called it, enough to be able to turn his memory a moment on this. "Yes, I think my imagination, small scrap of a thing as it was, did work then somehow against you."

"Which was exactly against business" — the old man easily made the point. "I *was* business. I've *been* business and nothing else in the world. I'm business at this moment still — because I can't be anything else. I mean I've such a head for it. So don't think you can put it on me that I haven't thought out what I'm doing to good purpose. I do what I do but too abominably well." With which he weakened for the first time to a faint smile. "It's none of your affair."

The Ivory Tower

"Isn't it a little my affair," Gray as genially objected, "to be more touched than I can express by your attention to me — as well (if you'll let me say so) as rather astonished at it?" And then while his host took this without response, only engaged as to more entire repletion in the steady measure of him, he added further, even though aware in sounding it of the complacency or fatuity, of the particular absurdity, his question might have seemed to embody: "What in the world can I want but to meet you in every way?" His perception at last was full, the great strange sense of everything smote his eyes; so that without the force of his effort at the most general amenity possible his lids and his young lips might have convulsively closed. Even for his own ear "What indeed?" was thus the ironic implication — which he felt himself quite grimace to show he should have understood somebody else's temptation to make. Here, however, where his uncle's smile might pertinently have broadened, the graver blandness settled again, leaving him in face of it but the more awkwardly assured. He felt as if he couldn't say enough to abate the ugliness of that — and perhaps it even did come out to the fact of beauty that no profession of the decent could appear not to coincide with the very candour of the greedy. "I'm prepared for anything, yes — in the way of a huge inheritance": he didn't care if it *might* sound like that when he next went on, since what could he

do but just melt to the whole benignity? "If I only understood what it is I can best do for you."

"Do? The question isn't of your doing, but simply of your being."

Gray cast about. "But don't they come to the same thing?"

"Well, I guess that for you they'll have to."

"Yes, sir," Gray answered — "but suppose I should say 'Don't keep insisting so on me'?" Then he had a romantic flight which was at the same time, for that moment at least, a sincere one. "I don't know that I came out so very much for myself."

"Well, if you didn't it only shows the more what you are" — Mr. Betterman made the point promptly. "It shows you've got the kind of imagination that has nothing to do with the kind I so perfectly see you haven't. And if you don't do things for yourself," he went on, "you'll be doing them the more for just what I say." With which too, as Graham but pleadingly gaped: "You'll be doing them for everyone else — that is finding it impossible to do what *they* do. From the moment they notice that — well, it will be what I want. We know, we know," he remarked further and as if this quite settled it.

Any ambiguity in his "we" after an instant cleared up; he was to have alluded but ever so sparely, through all this scene, to Rosanna Gaw, but he alluded now, and again it had for Gray an amount of reference that was like a great sum of items in a bill imperfectly scanned. None the less it left him

921

desiring still more clearness. His whole soul centred at this point in the need not to have contributed by some confused accommodation to a strange theory of his future. Strange he could but feel this one to be, however simply, that is on however large and vague an assumption, it might suit others, amid their fathomless resources and their luxuries or perversities of waste, to see it. He wouldn't be smothered in the vague, whatever happened, and had now the gasp and upward shake of the head of a man in too deep water. "What I want to insist on," he broke out with it, "is that I mustn't consent to any exaggeration in the interest of your, or of any other, sublime view of me, view of my capacity of any sort. There's no sublime view of me to be taken that consorts in the least with any truth; and I should be a very poor creature if I didn't here and now assure you that no proof in the world exists, or has for a moment existed, of my being capable of anything whatever."

He might have supposed himself for a little to have produced something of the effect that would naturally attach to a due vividness in this truth — for didn't his uncle now look at him just a shade harder, before the fixed eyes closed, indeed, as under a pressure to which they had at last really to yield? They closed, and the old white face was for the couple of minutes so thoroughly still without them that a slight uneasiness quickened him, and it would have taken but another moment to make a slight sound, which he had to turn his head for the explanation of, reach him as the response to an appeal. The door of the room, opening gently, had closed again behind Miss Goodenough, who came forward softly, but with more gravity, Gray thought, than he had previously seen her show. Still in his place and conscious of the undiminished freshness of her invalid's manual emphasis, he looked at her for some opinion as to the latter's appearance, or to the move on his own part next indicated; during which time her judgment itself, considering Mr. Betterman, a trifle heavily waited. Gray's doubt, before the stillness which had followed so great even if so undiscourageable an effort, moved him to some play of disengagement; whereupon he knew himself again checked, and there, once more, the fine old eyes rested on him. "I'm afraid I've tired him out," he could but say to the nurse, who made the motion to feel her patient's pulse without the effect of his releasing his visitor. Gray's hand was retained still, but his kinsman's eyes and next words were directed to Miss Goodenough.

"It's all right — even more so than I told you it was going to be."

"Why of course it's all right — you look too sweet together!" she pronounced.

"But I mean I've got him; I mean I make him squirm" — which words had somehow the richest gravity of any yet; "but all it does for his resistance is that he squirms right *to* me."

The Ivory Tower

"Oh we won't have any resistance!" Miss Goodenough freely declared. "Though for all the fight you've got in you still —— !" she in fine altogether backed Mr. Betterman.

He covered his nephew again as for a final or crushing appraisement, then going on for Miss Goodenough's benefit: "He tried something a minute ago to settle me, but I wish you could just have heard how he expressed himself."

"It *is* a pleasure to hear him — when he's good!" She laughed with a shade of impatience.

"He's never so good as when he wants to be bad. So there you are, sir!" the old man said. "You're like the princess in the fairytale; you've only to open your mouth —— "

"And the pearls and diamonds pop out!" — Miss Goodenough, for her patient's relief, completed his meaning. "So don't try for toads and snakes!" she promptly went on to Gray. To which she added with still more point: "And now you must go."

"Not one little minute more?" His uncle still held him.

"Not one, sir!" Miss Goodenough decided.

"It isn't to talk," the old man explained. "I like just to look at him."

"So do I," said Miss Goodenough; "but we can't always do everything we like."

"No then, Graham — remember that. You'd like to have persuaded me that I don't know what I mean.

But you must understand you haven't."

His hand had loosened, and Gray got up, turning a face now flushed and a little disordered from one of them to the other. "I don't pretend to understand anything!"

It turned his uncle to their companion. "Isn't he fine?"

"Of course he's fine," said Miss Goodenough; "but you've quite worn him out."

"Have I quite worn you out?" Mr. Betterman calmly inquired.

As if indeed finished, each thumb now in a pocket of his trousers, the young man dimly smiled. "I think you must have — quite."

"Well, let Miss Mumby look after you. He'll find her there?" his uncle asked of her colleague. And then as the latter showed at this her first indecision, "Isn't she somewhere round?" he demanded.

Miss Goodenough had wavered, but as if it really mattered for the friend there present she responsibly concluded. "Well, no — just for a while." And she appealed to Gray's indulgence. "She's had to go to Mr. Gaw."

"Why, is Mr. Gaw sick?" Mr. Betterman asked with detachment.

"That's what we shall know when she comes back. She'll come back all right," she continued for Gray's encouragement.

He met it with proper interest. "I'm sure I hope so!"

"Well, don't be too sure!" his uncle judiciously said.

"Oh he has only borrowed her." Miss Goodenough smoothed it down even as she smoothed Mr.

Betterman's sheet, while with the same movement of her head she wafted Gray to the door.

"Mr. Gaw," her patient returned, "has borrowed from me before. Mr. Gaw, Graham —— !"

"Yes sir?" said Gray with the door ajar and his hand on the knob.

The fine old presence on the pillow had faltered before expression; then it appeared rather sighingly and finally to give the question up. "Well, Mr. Gaw's an abyss."

Gray found himself suddenly responsive. "*Isn't* he, the strange man?"

"The strange man — that's it." This summary description sufficed now to Mr. Betterman's achieved indifference. "But you've seen him?"

"Just for an instant."

"And that was enough?"

"Well, I don't know." Gray himself gave it up. "You're *all* so fiercely interesting!"

"I think Rosanna's lovely!" Miss Goodenough contributed, to all appearance as an attenuation, while she tucked their companion in.

"Oh Miss Gaw's quite another matter," our young man still paused long enough to reply.

"Well, I don't mean but what she's interesting in her way too," Miss Goodenough's conscience prompted.

"Oh he knows all about her. That's all right," Mr. Betterman remarked for his nurse's benefit.

"Why of course I know it," this lady candidly answered. "Miss Mumby and I have had to feel *that*. I guess he'll want to send her his love," she continued across to Gray.

"To Miss Mumby?" asked Gray, his general bewilderment having moments of aggravation.

"Why no — *she's* sure of his affection. To Miss Gaw. Don't you want," she inquired of her patient, "to send your love to that poor anxious girl?"

"Is she anxious?" Gray returned in advance of his uncle.

Miss Goodenough hung fire but a moment. "Well, I guess I'd be in her place. But you'll see."

"Then," said Gray to his host, "if Rosanna's in trouble I'll go to her at once."

The old man, at this, once more delivered himself. "She won't be in trouble — any more than I am. But tell her — tell her —— !"

"Yes, sir" — Gray had again to wait.

But Miss Goodenough now would have no more of it. "Tell her that *we're* about as fresh as we can live!" — the wave of her hand accompanying which Gray could take at last for his dismissal.

III

IT was nevertheless not at once that he sought out the way to find his old friend; other questions than that of at once seeing her hummed for the next half-hour about his ears — an interval spent by him in still further contemplative motion within his uncle's grounds. He strolled and stopped again and stared before him without seeing; he came and went and sat down on benches and low rocky ledges only to get up and pace afresh; he lighted cigarettes but to smoke them a quarter out and then chuck them away to light others. He said to himself that he was enormously agitated, agitated as never in his life before, but that, strangely enough, he disliked that condition far less than the menace of it would have made him suppose. He didn't, however, like it enough to say to himself "This is happiness!" — as could scarcely have failed if the kind of effect on his nerves had really consorted with the kind of advantage that he was to understand his interview with his uncle to have promised him; so far, that is, as he was yet to understand anything. His after-sense of the scene expanded rather than settled, became an impression of one of those great insistent bounties that are not of this troubled world; the anomaly expressing itself in such beauty and dignity, with all its elements conspiring together, as would have done honour to a great page of literary, of musical or pictorial art. The huge grace of the matter ought somehow to have left him simply captivated — so at least, all wondering, he hung about there to reflect; but excess of harmony might apparently work like excess of discord, might practically be a negation of the idea of the quiet life. Ignoble quiet he

had never asked for — this he could now with assurance remember; but something in the pitch of his uncle's guarantee of big things, whatever they were, which should at the same time be pleasant things, seemed to make him an accomplice in some boundless presumption. In what light had he ever seen himself that made it proper the pleasant should be so big for him or the big so pleasant? Suddenly, as he looked at his watch and saw how the time had passed — time already, didn't it seem, of his rather standing off and quaking? — it occurred to him that the last thing he had proposed to himself in the whole connection was to be either publicly or privately afraid; in the act of noting which he became aware again of Miss Mumby, who, having come out of the house apparently to approach him, was now at no great distance. She rose before him the next minute as in fuller possession than ever of his fate, and yet with no accretion of reserve in her own pleasure at this.

"What I want you to do is just to go over to Miss Gaw."

"It's just what *I* should like, thank you — and perhaps you'll be so good as to show me the way." He wasn't quite succeeding in not being afraid — that a moment later came to him; since if this extraordinary woman was in touch with his destiny what did such words on his own part represent but the impulse to cling to her and, as who should say, keep on her right side? His uncle had spoken to him of Rosanna as protective — and what better warrant for such a truth than that here was he thankful on the spot even for the countenance of a person speaking apparently in her name? All of which was queer enough, verily — since it came to the sense of his clutching for immediate light, through the now gathered dusk, at the surge of guiding petticoats, the charity of women more or less strange. Miss Mumby at once took charge of him, and he learnt more things still before they had proceeded far. One of these truths, though doubtless the most superficial, was that Miss Gaw proposed he should dine with her just as he was — he himself recognising that with her father suddenly and to all appearance gravely ill it was no time for vain forms. Wasn't the rather odd thing, none the less, that the crisis should have suggested her desiring company? — being as it was so acute that the doctor, Doctor Hatch himself, would even now have arrived with a nurse, both of which pair of ears Miss Mumby required for her report of those symptoms in their new patient that had appealed to her practised eye an hour before. Interesting enough withal was her explanation to Gray of what she had noted on Mr. Gaw's part as a consequence of her joining them at that moment under Mr. Betterman's roof; all the more that he himself had then wondered and surmised — struck as he was with the effect on the poor man's nerves of their visitor's announcement that her prime patient had

brightened. Mr. Gaw but too truly, our young man now learned, had taken that news ill — as, given the state of his heart, any strong shock might determine a bad aggravation. Such a shock Miss Mumby had, to her lively regret, administered, though she called Gray's attention to the prompt and intelligent action of her remorse. Feeling at once responsible she had taken their extraordinary little subject in charge — with every care indeed not to alarm him; to the point that, on his absolute refusal to let her go home with him and his arresting a hack, on the public road, which happened to come into view empty, the two had entered the vehicle and she had not lost sight of him till, his earnest call upon his daughter at Mrs. Bradham's achieved, he had been in effect restored to his own house. His daughter, who lived with her eyes on his liability to lapses, was now watching with him, and was well aware, Miss Mumby averred, of what the crisis might mean; as to whose own due presence of mind in the connection indeed how could there be better proof than this present lucidity of her appeal to Mr. Betterman's guest on such a matter as her prompt thought for sparing him delay?

"If she didn't want you to wait to dress, it can only be, I guess, to make sure of seeing you before anything happens," his guide was at no loss to remark; "and if she *can* mention dinner while the old gentleman is — well, *as* he is — it shows she's not too beside herself to feel that you'll at any rate want yours."

"Oh for mercy's sake don't talk of dinner!" Gray pulled up under the influence of these revelations quite impatiently to request. "That's not what I'm most thinking of, I beg you to believe, in the midst of such prodigies and portents." They had crossed the small stretch of road which separated Mr. Betterman's gate from that of the residence they were addressed to; and now, within the grounds of this latter, which loomed there, through vague boskages, with an effect of windows numerously and precipitately lighted, the forces of our young friend's consciousness were all in vibration at once. "My wondrous uncle, I don't mind telling you, since you're so kind to me, has given me more extraordinary things to think of than I see myself prepared in any way to do justice to; and if I'm further to understand you that we have between us, you and I, destroyed *this* valuable life, I leave you to judge whether what we may have to face in consequence finds me eager."

"How do you know it's such a valuable life?" Miss Mumby surprisingly rejoined; sinking that question, however, in a livelier interest, before his surprise could express itself. "If she has sent me for you it's because she knows what she's about, and because I also know what I am — so that, wanting you myself so much to come, I guess I'd have gone over for you

on my own responsibility. Why, Mr. Fielder, your place is right here *by* her at such a time as this, and if you don't already realise it I'm very glad I've helped you."

Such was the consecration under which, but a few minutes later, Gray found himself turning about in the lamp-lit saloon of the Gaws very much as he had a few hours before revolved at the other house. Miss Mumby had introduced him into this apartment straight from the terrace to which, in the warm air, a long window or two stood open, and then had left him with the assurance that matters upstairs would now be in shape for their friend to join him at once. It was perhaps because he had rather inevitably expected matters upstairs — and this in spite of his late companion's warning word — to assault him in some fulness with Miss Gaw's appearance at the door, that a certain failure of any such effect when she did appear had for him a force, even if it was hardly yet to be called a sense, beyond any air of her advancing on the tide of pain. He fairly took in, face to face with her, that what she first called for was no rattle of sound, however considerately pitched, about the question of her own fear; she had pulled no long face, she cared for no dismal deference: she but stood there, after she had closed the door with a backward push that took no account, in the hushed house, of some possible resonance, she but stood there smiling in her mild extravagance of majesty, smiling and smiling as he had seen women do as a preface to bursting into tears. He was to remember afterwards how he had felt for an instant that whatever he said or did would deprive her of resistance to an inward pressure which was growing as by the sight of him, but that she would thus break down much more under the crowned than under the menaced moment — thanks to which appearance what could be stranger than his inviting her to clap her hands? Still again was he later to recall that these hands had been the moment after held in his own while he knew himself smiling too and saying: "Well, well, well, what wonders and what splendours!" and seeing that though there was even more of her in presence than he had reckoned there was somehow less of her in time; as if she had at once grown and grown and grown, grown in all sorts of ways save the most natural one of growing visibly older. Such an oddity as that made her another person a good deal more than her show of not having left him behind by any break with their common youth could keep her the same.

These perceptions took of course but seconds, with yet another on their heels, to the effect that she had already seen him, and seen him to some fine sense of pleasure, as himself enormously different — arriving at that clearness before they had done more than thus waver between the "fun," all so natural, of their meeting as the frankest of friends and the quite other intelligence of their being parties to a crisis. It was to remain on record for him too, and however overscored, that their crisis, surging up for three or four minutes by its essential force, suffered them to stand there, with irrelevant words and motions, very much as if it were all theirs alone and nobody's else, nobody's more important, on either side, than they were, and so take a brush from the wing of personal romance. He let her hands go, and then, if he wasn't mistaken, held them afresh a moment in repeated celebration, he exchanged with her the commonest remarks and the flattest and the easiest, so long as it wasn't speaking but seeing, and seeing more and more, that mattered: they literally talked of his journey and his arrival and of whether he had had a good voyage and wasn't tired; they said "You sit here, won't you?" and "Shan't you be better there?" — they said "Oh I'm all right!" and "Fancy it's happening after all like this!" before there even faintly quavered the call of a deeper note. This was really because the deep one, from minute to minute, was that acute hush of her so clearly finding him not a bit what she might have built up. He had grown and grown just as she had, certainly; only here he was for her clothed in the right interest of it, not bare of that grace as he fancied her guessing herself in his eyes, and with the conviction sharply thrust upon him, beyond any humour he might have cultivated, that he was going to be so right for her and so predetermined, whatever he did and however he should react there under conditions incalculable, that this would perhaps more overload his consciousness than ease it. It could have been further taken for strange, had there been somebody so to note it, that even when their first vagueness dropped what she really at once made easiest for him was to tell her that *the* wonderful thing had come to pass, the thing she had whisked him over for — he put it to her that way; that it had taken place in conditions too exquisite to be believed, and that under the bewilderment produced by these she must regard him as still staggering.

"Then it's done, then it's done — as I knew it would be if he could but see you." Flushed, but with her large fan held up so that scarce more than her eyes, their lids drawn together in the same near-sighted way he remembered, presented themselves over it, she fairly hunched her high shoulders higher for emphasis of her success. The more it might have embarrassed her to consider him without reserve the more she had this relief, as he took it, of her natural, her helpful blinking; so that what it came to really for her general advantage was that the fine closing of the eyes, *the* fine thing in her big face, but expressed effective scrutiny. Below her in stature — as various other men, for that matter, couldn't but be — he hardly came higher than her ear; and

he for the shade of an instant struck himself as a small boy, literally not of man's estate, reporting, under some research, just to the amplest of mothers. He had reported to Mr. Betterman, so far as intent candour in him hadn't found itself distraught, and for the half hour had somehow affronted the immeasurable; but that didn't at all prevent his now quick sense of his never in his life having been so watched and waited upon by the uncharted infinite, or so subject to its operation — since infinities, at the rate he was sinking in, *could* apparently operate, and do it too without growing smaller for the purpose. He cast about, not at all upright on the small pink satin sofa to which he had unconsciously dropped; it was for *him* clearly to grow bigger, as everything about expressively smiled, smiled absolutely through the shadow cast by doctors and nurses again, in suggestion of; which, naturally, was what one would always want to do — but which any failure of, he after certain moments perfectly felt, wouldn't convert to the least difference for this friend. How could that have been more established than by her neglect of his having presently said, out of his particular need, that he would do anything in reason that was asked of him, but that he fairly ached with the desire to understand — ? She blinked upon his ache to her own sufficiency, no doubt; but no further balm dropped upon it for the moment than by her appearing to brood with still deeper assurance, in her place and her posture, on the beauty of the accomplished fact, the fact of her performed purpose and her freedom now but to take care — yes, herself take care — for what would come of it. She might understand that *he* didn't — all the way as yet; but nothing could be more in the line of the mild and mighty mother than her treating that as a trifle. It attenuated a little perhaps, it just let light into the dark warmth of her spreading possession of what she had done, that when he had said, as a thing already ten times on his lips and now quite having to come out, "I feel some big mistake about me somehow at work, and want to stop it in time!" she met this with the almost rude decision of "There's nothing you can stop now, Graham, for your fate, or our situation, has the gained momentum of a rush that began ever so far away and that has been growing and growing. It would be too late even if we wanted to — and you can judge for yourself how little that's my wish. So here we are, you see, to make the best of it."

"When you talk of my 'fate,'" he allowed himself almost the amusement of answering, "you freeze the current of my blood; but when you say 'our situation,' and that we're in it together, that's a little better, and I assure you that I shall not for a moment stay in anything, whatever it may be, in which you're not close beside me. So there *you* are at any rate — and I matter at least as much as this, whatever the mistake: that I

have hold of you as tight as ever you've been held in your life, and that, whatever and *whatever* the mistake, you've got to see me through."

"Well, I took my responsibility years ago, and things came of it" — so she made reply; "and the other day I took this other, and now *this* has come of it, and that was what I wanted, and wasn't afraid of, and am not afraid of now — like the fears that came to me after the Dresden time." No more direct than that was her answer to his protest, and what she subjoined still took as little account of it. "I rather lost them, those old fears — little by little; but one of the things I most wanted the other day was to see whether before you here they wouldn't wholly die down. They're over, they're over," she repeated; "I knew three minutes of you would do it — and not a ghost of them remains."

"I can't be anything but glad that you shouldn't have fears — and it's horrid to me to learn, I assure you," he said, "that I've ever been the occasion of any. But the extent to which," he then frankly laughed, "'three minutes' of me seems to be enough for people —— !"

He left it there, just throwing up his arms, passive again as he had accepted his having to be in the other place; but conscious more and more of the anomaly of her showing so markedly at such an hour a preoccupation, and of the very intensest, that should not have her father for its subject.

Nothing could have more represented this than her abruptly saying to him, without recognition of his point just made, so far as it might have been a point: "If your impression of your uncle, and of his looking so fine and being so able to talk to you, makes you think he has any power really to pick up or to last, I want you to know that you're wholly mistaken. It has kept him up," she went on, "and the effect may continue a day or two more — it *will*, in fact, till certain things are done. But then the flicker will have dropped — for he won't want it not to. He'll feel all right. The extraordinary inspiration, the borrowed force, will have spent itself — it will die down and go out, but with no pain. There has been at no time much of that," she said, "and now I'm positively assured there's none. It can't come back — nothing can but the weakness. It's too lovely," she remarkably added — "so there indeed and indeed we are."

To take in these words was to be, after a fashion he couldn't have expressed, on a basis of reality with her the very rarest and queerest; so that, bristling as it did with penetrative points, her speech left him scarce knowing for the instant which penetrated furthest. That she made no more of anything he himself said than if she had just sniffed it as a pale pink rose and then tossed it into the heap of his other sweet futilities, such another heap as had seemed to grow up for him in his uncle's room, this might have pressed sharpest hadn't something else, not wholly overscored by what followed, perhaps pricked his consciousness most. " 'It,' you say, has kept him up? May I ask you what 'it' then may so wonderfully have been?"

She had no more objection to say than she apparently had difficulty. "Why, his having let me get at him. *That* was to make the whole difference."

It was somehow as much in the note of their reality as anything could well be; which was perhaps why he could but respond with "Oh I see!" and remain lolling a little with a sense of flatness — a flatness moreover exclusively his own.

So without flatness of *her* own he didn't even mind his; something in her brushed quite above it while she observed next, as if it were the most important thing that now occurred to her: "That of course was my poor father's mistake." And then as Gray but stared: "I mean the idea that he *can* pick up."

"It's your father's mistake that *he* can —— ?"

She met it as if really a shade bewildered at his own misconception; she was literally so far off from any vision of her parent in himself, a philosopher might have said, that it took her an instant to do the question justice. "Oh no — I mean that your uncle can. It was your own report of that to him, with Miss Mumby backing you, that put things in the bad light to him."

"So bad a light that Mr. Gaw is

in danger by it?" This was catching on of a truth to realities — and most of all to the one he had most to face. "I've been then at the bottom of that?"

He was to wonder afterwards if she had very actually gone so far as to let slip a dim smile for the intensity of his candour on this point, or whether her so striking freedom from intensity in the general connection had but suggested to him one of the images that were most in opposition. Her answer at any rate couldn't have had more of the eminence of her plainness. "That you yourself, after your uncertainties, should have found Mr. Betterman surprising was perfectly natural — and how indeed could you have dreamed that father so wanted him to die?" And then as Gray, affected by the extreme salience of this link in the chain of her logic, threw up his head a little for the catching of his breath, her supreme lucidity, and which was lucidity all in his interest, further shone out. "Father is indeed ill. He has had these bad times before, but nothing quite of the present gravity. He has been in a critical state for months, but one thing has kept him alive — the wish to see your uncle so far on his way that there could be no doubt. It was the appearance of doubt so suddenly this afternoon that gave him the shock." She continued to explain the case without prejudice. "To take it there from you for possible that Mr. Betterman might revive and that he should have in his own so unsteady condition to

wait was simply what father couldn't stand."

"So that I just dealt the blow ——?"

But it was as if she cared too little even to try to make that right. "He doesn't *want*, you see, to live after."

"After having found he is mistaken?"

She had a faint impatience. "He isn't of course really — since what I told you of your uncle is true. And he knows that now, having my word for it."

Gray couldn't be clear enough about her clearness. "Your word for it that my uncle has revived but for the moment?"

"Absolutely. Wasn't my giving him that," Rosanna asked, "a charming filial touch?"

This was tremendously much again to take in, but Gray's capacity grew. "Promising him, you mean, for his benefit, that my uncle *shan't* last?"

The size of it on his lips might fairly, during the instant she looked at him, have been giving her pleasure. "Yes, making it a bribe to father's patience."

"Then why doesn't the bribe act?"

"Because it comes too late. It was amazing," she pursued, "that, feeling as he did, he could take that drive to the Bradhams' — and Miss Mumby was right in perfectly understanding that. The harm was already done — and there it is."

She had truly for the whole reference the most astounding tones.

"You literally mean then," said Gray, "that while you sit here with me he's dying — dying of my want of sense?"

"You've no want of sense" — she spoke as if this were the point really involved. "You've a sense the most exquisite — and surely you had best take in soon rather than late," she went on, "how you'll never be free not to have on every occasion of life to reckon with it and pay for it."

"Oh I say!" was all the wit with which he could at once meet this charge; but she had risen as she spoke and, with a remark about there being another matter, had moved off to a piece of furniture at a distance where she appeared to take something from a drawer unlocked with a sharp snap for the purpose. When she returned to him she had this object in her hand, and Gray recognised in it an oblong envelope, addressed, largely sealed in black, and seeming to contain a voluminous letter. She kept it while he noted that the seal was intact, and she then reverted not to the discomfiture she had last produced in him but to his rueful reference of a minute before that.

"He's not dying of anything you said or did, or of anyone's act or words. He's just dying of twenty millions."

"Twenty millions?" There was a kind of enormity in her very absence of pomp, and Gray felt as if he had dropped of a sudden, from his height of simplicity, far down into a familiar relation to quantities inconceivable — out of which

depths he fairly blew and splashed to emerge, the familiar relation, of all things in the world, being so strange a one. "That's what you mean here when you talk of money?"

"That's what we mean," said Rosanna, "when we talk of anything at all — for of what else but money do we ever talk? He's dying, at any rate," she explained, "of his having wished to have to do with it on that sort of scale. Having to do with it consists, you know, of the things you do for it — which are mostly very awful; and there are all kinds of consequences that they eventually have. You pay by these consequences for what you have done, and my father has been for a long time paying." Then she added as if of a sudden to summarise and dismiss the whole ugly truth: "The effect has been to dry up his life." Her eyes, with this, reached away for the first time as in search of something not at all before her, and it was on the perfunctory note that she had the next instant concluded. "There's nothing at last left for him to pay with."

For Gray at least, whatever initiations he had missed, she couldn't keep down the interest. "Mr. Gaw then will leave twenty millions —— ?"

"He has already left them — in the sense of having made his will; as your uncle, equally to my knowledge, has already made his." Something visibly had occurred to her, and in connection, it might seem, with the packet she had taken from her drawer. She looked about — there being within the scene, which was somehow at once blank and replete, sundry small scattered objects of an expensive negligibility; not one of which, till now, he could guess, had struck her as a thing of human application. Human application had sprung up, the idea of selection at once following, and she unmistakeably but wondered what would be best for her use while she completed the statement on which she had so strikingly embarked. "He has left me his whole fortune." Then holding up an article of which she had immediately afterwards, with decision, proceeded to possess herself, "Is *that* a thing you could at all bear?" she irrelevantly asked. She had caught sight, in her embarrassed way, of something apparently adapted to her unexplained end, and had left him afresh to assure herself of its identity, taking up from a table at first, however, a box in Japanese lacquer only to lay it down unsatisfied. She had circled thus at a distance for a time, allowing him now *his* free contemplation; she had tried in succession, holding them close to her eyes, several embossed or embroidered superfluities, a blotting-book covered with knobs of malachite, a silver box, flat, largely circular and finely fretted, a gold cigar case of absurd dimensions, of which she played for a moment the hinged lid. Such was the object on which she puzzlingly challenged him.

"I could bear it perhaps better if I ever used cigars."

"You don't smoke?" she almost wailed.

"Never cigars. Sometimes pipes — but mostly, thank goodness, cigarettes."

"Thank the powers then indeed!" — and, the golden case restored to the table, where she had also a moment before laid her prepared missive, she went straight to a corner of the mantel-shelf, hesitations dropping from her, and, opening there a plainer receptacle than any she had yet touched, turned the next instant with a brace of cigarettes picked out and an accent she had not yet used. "You *are* a blessing, Gray — I'm nowhere without one!" There were matches at hand, and she had struck a light and applied it, at his lips, to the cigarette passively received by him, afterwards touching her own with it, almost before he could wonder again at the oddity of their transition. Their light smoke curled while she went back to her table; it quickened for him with each puff the marvel of a domestic altar graced at such a moment by the play of that particular flame. Almost, to his fine vision, it made Rosanna different — for wasn't there at once a gained ease in the tone with which, her sealed letter still left lying on the table, she returned to that convenience for the pocket of the rich person of which she had clicked and re-clicked the cover? What strange things, Gray thought, rich persons had! — and what strange things they did, he might mentally even have added, when she devel-

The Ivory Tower

oped in a way that mystified him
but the more: "I don't mean for
your cigars, since you don't use
them; but I want you to have from
my hand something in which to
keep, with all due consideration, a
form of tribute that has been these
last forty-eight hours awaiting you
here, and which, it occurs to me,
would just slide into this preposterous piece of furniture and nestle
there till you may seem to feel you
want it." She proceeded to recover
the packet and slide it into the
case, the shape of which, on a
larger scale, just corresponded with
its own, and then, once more making the lid catch, shook container
and contents as sharply as she
might have shaken a bottle of
medicine. "So — there it is; I somehow don't want just to thrust at
you the letter itself."

"But may I be told what the letter itself *is?*" asked Gray, who had
followed these movements with
interest.

"Why of course — didn't I mention? Here are safely stowed," she
said, her gesture causing the
smooth protective surfaces to twinkle more brightly before him, "the
very last lines (and many there
appear to be of them!) that, if I
am not mistaken, my father's hand
will have traced. He wrote them,
in your interest, as he considers,
when he heard of your arrival in
New York, and, having sealed and
directed them, gave them to me
yesterday to take care of and deliver to you. I put them away for
the purpose, and an hour ago,
during our drive back from Mrs.

Bradham's, he reminded me of my
charge. Before asking Miss Mumby to tell you I should like to see
you I transferred the letter from
its place of safety in my room to
the cabinet from which, for your
benefit, I a moment ago took it. I
carefully comply, as you see, with
my father's request. I know nothing whatever of what he has written you, and only want you to have
his words. But I want also," she
pursued, "to make just this little
affair of them. I want" — and she
bent her eyes on the queer costli-
ness, rubbing it with her pocket-
handkerchief — "to do what the
Lord Mayor of London does,
doesn't he? when he offers the
Freedom of the City; present them
in a precious casket in which
they may always abide. I want
in short," she wound up, "to put
them, for your use, beautifully
away."

Gray went from wonder to wonder. "It isn't then a thing you
judge I should open at once?"

"I don't care whether you never
open it in your life. But you don't,
I can see, like *that* vulgar thing!"
With which having opened her
receptacle and drawn forth from
it the subject of her attention she
tossed back to its place on the
spread of brocade the former of
these trifles. The big black seal,
under this discrimination, seemed
to fix our young man with a sombre eye.

"Is there any objection to my
just looking at the letter now?"
And then when he had taken it
and yet was on the instant and as

935

by the mere feel and the nearer sight, rather less than more conscious of a free connection with it, "Is it going to be bad for me?" he said.

"Find out for yourself!"

"Break the seal?"

"Isn't it meant to break?" she asked with a shade of impatience.

He noted the impatience, sounding her nervousness, but saw at the same time that her interest in the communication, whatever it might be, was of the scantest, and that she suffered from having to defer to his own. "If I needn't answer to-night —— !"

"You needn't answer ever."

"Oh well then it can wait. But you're right — it mustn't just wait in my pocket."

This pleased her. "As I say, it must have a place of its own."

He considered of that. "You mean that when I *have* read it I may still want to treasure it?"

She had in hand again the great fan that hung by a long fine chain from her girdle, and, flaring it open, she rapidly closed it again, the motion seeming to relieve her. "I mean that my father has written you at this end of his days — and that that's all I know about it."

"You asked him no question —— ?"

"As to why he should write? I wouldn't," said Rosanna, "have asked him for the world. It's many a day since we've done that, either he or I — at least when a question could have a sense."

"Thank you then," Gray smiled, "for answering mine." He looked about him for whatever might still help them, and of a sudden had a light. "Why the ivory tower!" And while her eyes followed: "That beautiful old thing on the top of the secretary — happy thought if it *is* old!" He had seen at a glance that this object was what they wanted, and, a nearer view confirming the thought, had reached for it and taken it down. "There it was waiting for you. *Isn't* it an ivory tower, and doesn't living in an ivory tower just mean the most distinguished retirement? I don't want yet awhile to settle in one myself — though I've always thought it a thing I should like to come to; but till I do make acquaintance with what you have for me a retreat for the mystery is pleasant to think of." Such was the fancy he developed while he delicately placed his happy find on the closed and polished lid of the grand piano, where the rare surface reflected the pale rich ivory and his companion could have it well before her. The subject of this attention might indeed pass, by a fond conceit, on its very reduced scale, for a builded white-walled thing, very tall in proportion to the rest of its size and rearing its head from its rounded height as if a miniature flag might have flown there. It was a remarkable product of some eastern, probably some Indian, patience, and of some period as well when patience in such causes was at the greatest — thanks to which Gray, loving ancient artistry and having all his life seen much of it, had recognised at a glance the one piece in the room that presented an interest. It consisted really of a cabinet, of easily moveable size, seated in a circular socket of its own material and equipped with a bowed door, which dividing in the middle, after a minute gold key had been turned, showed a superposition of small drawers that went upwards diminishing in depth, so that the topmost was of least capacity. The high curiosity of the thing was in the fine work required for making and keeping it perfectly circular; an effect arrived at by the fitting together, apparently by tiny golden rivets, of numerous small curved plates of the rare substance, each of these, including those of the two wings of the exquisitely convex door, contributing to the artful, the total rotundity. The series of encased drawers worked to and fro of course with straight sides, but also with small bowed fronts, these made up of the same adjusted plates. The whole, its infinite neatness exhibited, proved a wonder of wasted ingenuity, and Rosanna, pronouncing herself stupid not to have anticipated him, rendered all justice, under her friend's admiring emphasis, to this choicest of her resources. Of how they had come by it, either she or her sparing parent, she couldn't at once bethink herself: on their taking the Newport house for the few weeks her direction had been general that an assortment of odds and ends from New York should disperse itself, for mitigation of bleak-

ness, in as many of the rooms as possible; and with quite different matters to occupy her since she had taken the desired effect for granted. Her father's condition had precluded temporary inmates, and with Gray's arrival also in mind she had been scarce aware of minor importances. "Of course you know — I knew you *would!*" were the words in which she assented to his preference for the ivory tower and which settled for him, while he made it beautifully slide, the fact that the shallowest of the drawers would exactly serve for his putting his document to sleep. So then he slipped it in, rejoicing in the tight fit of the drawer, carefully making the two divisions of the protective door meet, turning the little gold key in its lock and finally, with his friend's permission, attaching the key to a small silver ring carried in his pocket and serving for a cluster of others. With this question at rest it seemed at once, and as with an effect out of proportion to the cause, that a great space before them had been cleared: they looked at each other over it as if they had become more intimate, and as if now, in the free air, the enormities already named loomed up again. All of which was expressed in Gray's next words.

"May I ask you, in reference to something you just now said, whether my uncle took action for leaving me money before our meeting could be in question? Because if he did, you know, I understand less than ever. That he should want to see me if he was thinking of me, that of course I can conceive; but that he shouldn't wait till he had seen me is what I find extraordinary."

If she gave him the impression of keeping her answer back a little, it wasn't, he was next to see, that she was not fully sure of it. "He *had* seen you."

"You mean as a small boy?"

"No — at this distance of time that didn't count." She had another wait, but also another assurance. "He had seen you in the great fact about you."

"And what in the world do you call that?"

"Why, that you are more out of it all, out of the air he has breathed all his life and that in these last years has more and more sickened him, than anyone else in the least belonging to him, that he could possibly put his hand on."

He stood before her with his hands in his pockets — he could study her now quite as she had studied himself. "The extent, Rosanna, to which you must have answered for me!"

She met his scrutiny from between more narrowed lids. "I did put it all to him — I spoke for you as earnestly as one can ever speak for another. But you're not to gather from it," she thus a trifle awkwardly smiled, "that I have let you in for twenty millions, or for anything approaching. He will have left you, by my conviction, all he has; but he has nothing at all like that. That's all I'm sure of — of no details whatever. Even my father doesn't know," she added; "in spite of its having been for a long time the thing he has most wanted to, most sat here, these weeks, on some chance of his learning. The truth, I mean, of Mr. Betterman's affairs."

Gray felt a degree of relief at the restrictive note on his expectations which might fairly have been taken, by its signs, for a betrayed joy in their extent. The air had really, under Rosanna's touch, darkened itself with numbers; but what she had just admitted was a rift of light. In this light, which was at the same time that of her allusion to Mr. Gaw's unappeased appetite, his vision of that gentleman at the other house came back to him, and he said in a moment: "I see, I see. He tried to get some notion out of me."

"Poor father!" she answered to this — but without time for more questions, as at the moment she spoke the door of the room opened and Doctor Hatch appeared. He paused, softly portentous, where he stood, and so he met Rosanna's eyes. He held them a few seconds, and the effect was to press in her, to all appearance, the same spring our young man had just touched. "Poor, poor, poor father!" she repeated, but as if brought back to him from far away. She took in what had happened, but not at once nor without an effort what it called on her for; so that "Won't you come up?" her informant had next to ask.

To this, while Gray watched her, she rallied — "If you'll stay here."

With which, looking at neither of them again, as the Doctor kept the door open, she passed out, he then closing it on her and transferring his eyes to Gray — who hadn't to put a question, so sharply did the raised and dropped hands signify that all was over. The fact, in spite of everything, startled our young man, who had with his companion a moment's mute exchange.

"He has died while I've kept her here?"

Doctor Hatch just demurred. "You kept her through her having sent for you to talk to you."

"Yes, I know. But it's very extraordinary!"

"You seem to *make* people extraordinary. You've made your uncle, you know ——!"

"Yes indeed — but haven't I made *him* better?" Gray asked.

The Doctor again for a moment hesitated. "Yes — in the sense that he must be now at last really resting. But I go back to him."

"I'll go with you of course," said Gray, looking about for his hat. As he found it he oddly remembered. "Why she asked me to dinner!"

It all but amused the Doctor. "You inspire remarkable efforts."

"Well, I'm incapable of making them." It seemed now queer enough. "I can't stay to dinner."

"Then we'll go." With which however, Doctor Hatch was not too preoccupied to have had his attention, within the minute, otherwise taken. "What a splendid piece!" he exclaimed in presence of the ivory tower.

"It *is* splendid," said Gray, feeling its beauty again the brightest note in the strangeness; but with a pang of responsibility to it taking him too. "Miss Gaw has made me a present of it."

"Already? You do work them!" — and the good physician fairly grazed again the act of mirth. "So you'll take it away?"

Gray paused a moment before his acquisition, which seemed to have begun to guard, within the very minute, a secret of greater weight. Then "No, I'll come back to it," he said as they departed by the long window that opened to the grounds and through which Miss Mumby had brought him in.

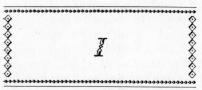

BOOK THIRD

"WHY I haven't so much as seen him yet," Cissy perforce confessed to her friend, Mrs. Bradham's friend, everybody's friend, even, already and so coincidentally, Graham Fielder's; this recipient of her avowal having motored that day from Boston, after detention there under a necessity of business and the stress of intolerable heat, but having reached Newport in time for tea, a bath, a quick "change" and a still quicker impression of blest refreshment from the fine air and from various other matters. He had come forth again, during the time left him between these performed rites and the more formal dressing-hour, in undisguised quest of our young lady, who had so disposed certain signs of her whereabouts that he was to waste but few steps in selection of a short path over the longest stretch of lawn and the mass of seaward rocks forming its limit. Arriving to spend with the Bradhams as many or as few days as the conditions to be recognised on the spot might enjoin, this hero, Horton Vint, had alighted at one of those hours of brilliant bustle which could show him as all in his element if he chose to appear so, or could otherwise appeal at once to his perfect apti-

tude for the artful escape and the undetected counterplot. But the pitch had by that moment dropped and the company dispersed, so far as the quarter before him was concerned: the tennis-ground was a velvet void, the afternoon breeze conveyed soft nothings — all of which made his occasion more spacious for Horton. Cissy, from below, her charmingly cool cove, had watchfully signalled up, and they met afresh, on the firm clear sand where the drowsy waves scarce even lapsed, with forms of intimacy that the sequestered spot happily favoured. The sense of waiting understood and crowned gave grace to her opened arms when the young man, as he was still called, erect, slim, active, brightly refreshed and, like herself, given the temperature, inconsiderably attired, first showed himself against the sky; it had cost him but a few more strides and steps, an easy descent, to spring to her welcome with the strongest answering emphasis. They met as on ground already so prepared that not an uncertainty, on either side, could make reunion less brave or confidence less fine; they had to effect no clearance, to stand off from no risk; and, observing them thus in their freedom, you might well have asked yourself by what infallible tact they had mastered for intercourse such perfect reciprocities of address. You would certainly have concluded to their entire confidence in these. "With a dozen people in the house it *is* luck," Horton had at once appreciatively said; but when their fellow-visitors had been handled between them for a minute or so only to collapse again like aproned puppets on removal of pressure from the squeak, he had jumped to the question of Gray Fielder and to frank interest in Cissy's news of him. This news, the death of Mr. Betterman that morning, quite sufficiently explained her inability to produce the more direct impression; that worthy's nephew and heir, in close and more and more quickened attendance on him during the previous days, had been seen as yet, to the best of her belief, by no one at all but dear Davey — not counting of course Rosanna Gaw, of the fact of whose own bereavement as well Horton was naturally in possession, and who had made it possible, she understood, for their friend to call on Graham.

"Oh Davey has called on Graham?" Horton was concerned to ask while they sat together on a rude worn slab. "What then, if he has told you, was his particular idea?"

"Won't his particular idea," Cissy returned, "be exactly the one he won't have told me? What he did speak to me of yesterday morning, and what I told him I thought would be beautiful of him, was his learning by inquiry, in case your friend could see him, whether there was any sort of thing he could do for him in his possible want of a

man to put a hand on. Because poor Rosanna, for all one thinks of her," said the girl, "isn't exactly a man."

Horton's attention was deeply engaged; his hands, a little behind him, rested, as props to his slight backward inclination, on the convenient stone; his legs, extended before him, enabled him to dig in his heels a little, while his eyes, attached to the stretch of sea commanded by their rocky retreat, betrayed a fixed and quickened vision. Rich in fine lines and proportions was his handsome face — with scarce less, moreover, to be said of his lean, light and long-drawn, though so much more pointed and rounded figure. His features, after a manner of their own, announced an energy and composed an array that his expression seemed to disavow, or at least to be indifferent to, and had the practical effect of toning down; as if he had been conscious that his nose, of the bravest, strongest curve and intrinsically a great success, was too bold and big for its social connections, that his mouth protested or at least asserted more than he cared to back it up to, that his chin and jaw were of too tactless an importance, and his fine eyes, above all, which suggested choice samples of the more or less precious stone called aquamarine, too disposed to darken with the force of a straight look — so that the right way to treat such an excess of resource had become for him quite the incongruous way, the cultivation of every sign and gage that liberties *might* be taken with him. He seemed to keep saying that he was not, temperamentally and socially, in his own exaggerated style, and that a bony structure, for instance, as different as possible from the one he unfortunately had to flaunt, would have been no less in harmony with his real nature than he sought occasion to show it was in harmony with his conduct. His hard mouth sported, to its visible relief and the admiration of most beholders, a beautiful mitigating moustache; his eyes wandered and adventured as for fear of their very own stare; his smile and his laugh went all lengths, you would almost have guessed, in order that nothing less pleasant should occupy the ground; his chin advanced upon you with a grace fairly tantamount to the plea, absurd as that might have seemed, that it was in the act of receding. Thus you gained the impression — or could do so if your fancy quickened to him — that he would perhaps rather have been as unwrought and unfinished as so many monstrous men, on the general peopled scene of those climes, appeared more and more to show themselves, than appointed to bristle with a group of accents that, for want of a sense behind them, could attach themselves but to a group of blanks. The sense behind the outward man in Horton Vint bore no relation, it incessantly signified, to his being *importantly* goodlooking; it was in itself as easily and freely human a sense, making as much for personal reassurance, as the appeal of opportunity in an enjoying world could ever have drawn forth and with the happy appearance of it confirmed by the whimsical, the quite ironic, turn given by the society in which he moved to the use of his name. It could never have been so pronounced and written Haughty if in spite of superficial accidents his charming clever humility and sociability hadn't thoroughly established themselves. He lived in the air of jokes, and yet an air in which bad ones fell flat; and there couldn't have been a worse one than to treat his designation as true.

It might have been, at the same time, scarce in the least as a joke that he presently said, in return for the remark on Cissy's part last reported: "Rosanna is surely enough of a man to be much more of one than Davey. However," he went on, "we agree, don't we? about the million of men it would have taken to handle Gussy. A Davey the more or the less, or with a shade more or less of the different sufficiency, would have made no difference in *that* question" — which had indeed no interest for them anyhow, he conveyed, compared with the fun apparently proposed by this advent of old Gray. That, frankly, was to him, Horton, as amusing a thing as could have happened — at a time when if it hadn't been for Cissy's herself happening to be for him, by exception, a comfort to think of, there wasn't a blest thing in his life of the smallest interest. "It hadn't struck me as probable at all, this revulsion of the old man's," he mentioned, "and though Fielder must be now an awfully nice chap, whom you'll like and find charming, I own I didn't imagine he would come so tremendously forward. Over there, simply with his tastes, his 'artistic interests,' or literary ones, or whatever — I mean his array of intellectual resources and lack of any others — he was well enough, by my last impression, and I liked him both for his decent life and ways and for his liking *me,* if you can believe it, so extraordinarily much as he seemed to. What the situation appears most to mean, however, is that of a sudden he pops into a real light, a great blazing light visible from afar — which is quite a different affair. It can't not mean at least all sorts of odd things — or one has a right to wonder if it *mayn't* mean them." And Horton might have been taken up for a minute of silence with his consideration of some of these glimmering possibilities; a moment during which Cissy Foy maintained their association by fairly, by quite visibly breathing with him in unison — after a fashion that testified more to her interest than any "cutting in" could have done. It would have been clear that they were far beyond any stage of association at which their capacity for interest in the contribution of either to what was between them should depend upon verbal proof. It depended in fact as little on any other sort, such for instance as searching eyes might invoke; she hadn't to look at her friend to follow him further —

she but looked off to those spaces where his own vision played, and it was by pressing him close *there* that she followed. Her companion's imagination, by the time he spoke again, might verily have travelled far.

"What comes to me is just the wonder of whether such a change of fortune may possibly not spoil him — he was so right and nice as he was. I remember he used really to exasperate me almost by seeming not to have wants, unless indeed it was by having only those that could be satisfied over there as a kind of matter of course and that were those I didn't myself have — in any degree at least that could make up for the non-satisfaction of my others. I suppose it amounted really," said Horton, "to the fact that, being each without anything to speak of in our pockets, or then any prospect of anything, he accepted that because he happened to like most the pleasures that were not expensive. I on my side raged at my inability to meet or to cultivate expense — which seemed to me good and happy, quite the thing most worth while, in itself: as for that matter it still seems. 'La lecture et la promenade,' which old Roulet, our pasteur at Neuchâtel used so to enjoin on us as the highest joys, really appealed to Gray, to all appearance, in the sense in which Roulet regarded, or pretended to regard, them — once he could have pictures and music and talk, which meant of course pleasant people, thrown in. He could go in for such things on his means — ready as he was to do all his travelling on foot (I wanted as much then to do all mine on horseback,) and to go to the opera or the play in the shilling seats when he couldn't go in the stalls. I loathed so everything *but* the stalls — the stalls everywhere in life — that if I couldn't have it that way I didn't care to have it at all. So when I think it strikes me I must have liked him very much not to have wanted to slay him — for I don't remember having given way at any particular moment to threats or other aggressions. That may have been because I felt he rather extravagantly liked me — as I shouldn't at all wonder at his still doing. At the same time if I had found him beyond a certain point objectionable his showing he took me for anything wonderful would have been, I think," the young man reflected, "but an aggravation the more. However that may be, I'm bound to say, I shan't in the least resent his taking me for whatever he likes now — if he can at all go on with it himself I shall be able to hold up my end. The dream of my life, if you must know all, dear — the dream of my life has been to be admired, *really* admired, admired for all he's worth, by some awfully rich man. Being admired by a rich woman even isn't so good — though I've tried for that too, as you know, and equally failed of it; I mean in the sense of their being ready to do it for all *they* are worth. I've only had it from the poor, haven't I? — and we've long since had to rec-

ognise, haven't we? how little that has done for either of us." So Horton continued — so, as if incited and agreeably, irresistibly inspired, he played, in the soft stillness and the protected nook, before the small salt tide that idled as if to listen, with old things and new, with actualities and possibilities, on top of the ancientries, that seemed to want but a bit of talking of in order to flush and multiply. "There's one thing at any rate I'll be hanged if I shall allow," he wound up; "I'll be hanged if what we may do for him shall — by any consent of mine at least — spoil him for the old relations without inspiring him for the new. He shan't become if I can help it as beastly vulgar as the rest of us."

The thing was said with a fine sincere ring, but it drew from Cissy a kind of quick wail of pain. "Oh, oh, oh — what a monstrous idea, Haughty, that he possibly *could*, ever!"

It had an immediate, even a remarkable effect; it made him turn at once to look at her, giving his lightest pleasantest laugh, than which no sound of that sort equally manful had less of mere male stridency. Then it made him, with a change of posture, shift his seat sufficiently nearer to her to put his arm round her altogether and hold her close, pressing his cheek a moment, with due precautions, against her hair. "That's awfully nice of you. We *will* pull something off. Is what you're thinking of what your friend out there *dans le temps*, the stepfather, Mr. Wendover, was it? told you about him in that grand manner?"

"Of course it is," said Cissy in lucid surrender and as if this truth were of a flatness almost to blush for. "Don't you know I fell so in love with Mr. Northover, whose name you mispronounce, that I've kept true to him forever, and haven't been really in love with you in the least, and shall never be with Gray himself, however much I may want to, or you perhaps may even try to make me? — any more than I shall ever be with anyone else. What's inconceivable," she explained, "is that anyone that dear delicious man thought good enough to talk of to me as he talked of his stepson should be capable of anything in the least disgusting in any way."

"I see, I see." It made Horton, for reasons, hold her but the closer — yet not withal as if prompted by her remarks to affectionate levity. It was a sign of the intercourse of this pair that, move each other though they might to further affection, and therewith on occasion to a congruous gaiety, they treated no cause and no effect of that sort as waste; they had somehow already so worked off, in their common interest, all possible mistakes and vain imaginings, all false starts and false pursuits, all failures of unanimity. "Why then if he's really so decent, not to say so superior," Haughty went on, "won't it be the best thing in the world and a great simplification for you to fall — that is for you to *be* — in love with him? That will be better for

me, you know, than if you're not; for it's the impression evidently made on you by the late Northover that keeps disturbing my peace of mind. I feel, though I can't quite tell you why," he explained, "that I'm never going to be in the least jealous of Gray, and probably not even so much as envious; so there's your chance — take advantage of it all the way. Like him at your ease, my dear, and God send he shall like you! Only be sure it's for himself you do it — and for your own self; as you make out your possibilities, de part et d'autre, on your getting nearer to them."

"So as to be sure, you mean," Cissy inquired, "of not liking him for his money?"

He waited a moment, and if she had not immediately after her words sighed "Oh dear, oh dear!" in quite another, that is a much more serious, key, the appearance would perhaps have been that for once in a blue moon she had put into his mind a thought he couldn't have. He couldn't have the thought that it was of the least importance she should guard herself in the way she mentioned; and it was in the air, the very next thing, that she couldn't so idiotically have strayed as to mean to impute it. He quickly enough made the point that what he preferred was her not founding her interest in Gray so very abjectly on another man's authority — given the uncanny fact of the other man's having cast upon her a charm which time and even his death had done so little to abate. Yes, the late Northover had clearly had something about him that it worried a fellow to have her perpetually rake up. *There* she was in peril of jealousy — his jealousy of the queer Northover ghost; unless indeed it was she herself who was queerest, ridden as her spirit seemed by sexagenarian charms! He could look after her with Gray — they were at one about Gray; what would truly alienate them, should she persist, would be his own exposure to comparison with the memory of a rococo Briton he had no arms to combat. Which extravagance of fancy had of course after a minute sufficiently testified to the clearance of their common air that invariably sprang from their feeling themselves again together and finding once more what this came to — all under sublime palpability of proof. The renewed consciousness did perhaps nothing for their difficulties as such, but it did everything for the interest, the amusement, the immediate inspiration of their facing them: there was in that such an element of their facing each other and knowing, each time as if they had not known it before, that this had absolute beauty. It had unmistakably never had more than now, even when their freedom in it had rapidly led them, under Cissy's wonderment, to a consideration of whether a happy

relation with their friend (he was already thus her friend too, without her ever having seen him!) mightn't have to count with some inevitable claim, some natural sentiment, asserted and enjoyed on Rosanna's part, not to speak of the effect on Graham himself of that young woman's at once taking such an interest in him and coming in for such a fortune.

"In addition to which who shall pretend to deny," the girl earnestly asked, "that Rosanna has in herself the most extraordinary charm?"

"Oh you think she has extraordinary charm?"

"Of course I do — and so do you: don't be absurd! She's simply superb," Cissy expounded, "in her own original way, which no other woman over here — except me a little perhaps! — has so much as a suspicion of anything to compare with; and which, for all we know, constitutes a luxury entirely at Graham's service." Cissy required but a single other look at it all to go on: "I shouldn't in the least wonder if they were already engaged."

"I don't think there's a chance of it," Haughty said, "and I hold that if any such fear is your only difficulty you may be quite at your ease. Not only do I so see it," he went on, "but I know *why* I do."

Cissy just waited. "You consider that because she refused Horton Vint she'll decline marriage altogether?"

"I think that throws a light," this gentleman smiled — "though it isn't *all* my ground. She turned me down, two years ago, as utterly as I shall ever have been turned in my life — and if I chose so to look at it the experience would do for me beautifully as that of an humiliation served up to a man in as good form as he need desire. That it was, that it still is when I live it through again; that it will probably remain, for my comfort — in the sense that I'm likely never to have a worse. I've had my dose," he figured, "of that particular black draught, and I've got the bottle there empty on the shelf."

"And yet you signify that you're all the same glad —— ?" Cissy didn't for the instant wholly follow.

"Well, it *all* came to me then; and that it did all come is what I have the advantage of now — I mean, you see, in being able to reassure you as I do. I had some wonderful minutes with her — it didn't take long," Haughty laughed. "We *saw* in those few minutes, being both so horribly intelligent; and what I recognised has remained with me. What she did is her own affair — and that she could so perfectly make it such, without leaving me a glimmer of doubt, is what I have, as I tell you, to blink at forever. I may ask myself if you like," he pursued, "why I should 'mind' so much if I saw even at the moment that she wasn't at any rate going to take someone else — and if you do I shall reply that I didn't need that to make it bad. It was bad enough just in itself. My point is, however," Horton concluded, "that I can give you at least the benefit of my feeling utterly sure that Gray will have no chance. She's in the dreadful position — and more than ever of course now — of not being able to believe she can be loved for herself."

"You mean because *you* couldn't make her believe it?" asked Cissy after taking this in.

"No — not that, for I didn't so much as try. I didn't — and it was awfully superior of me, you know — approach her at all on that basis. That," said Horton, "is where it cuts. The basis was that of my own capacity only — my capacity to serve her, in every particular, with every aptitude I possess in the world, and which I could see she *saw* I possess (it was given me somehow to send that home to her!) without a hair's breadth overlooked. I shouldn't have minded her taking me so for impossible, blackly impossible, if she had done it under an illusion; but she really believed in me as a general value, quite a first-rate value — *that* I stood there and didn't doubt. And yet she practically said 'You ass!' "

His encircling arm gained, for response to this, however, but the vibration of her headshake — without so much as any shudder at the pain he so vividly imaged. "She practically said that she was already *then* in love with Mr. Graham, and you wouldn't have had a better chance had a passion of your own stuck out of you. If I thought she didn't admire you," Cissy said, "I shouldn't be able to do with her at all — it would be too stupid of her; putting aside her not accepting you, I mean — for a woman can't accept *every* man she admires. I suppose you don't at present object," she continued, "to her admiring Mr. Graham enough to account for anything; especially as it accounts so for her having just acted on his behalf with such extraordinary success. Doesn't that make it out for him," she asked, "that he's admired by twenty millions *plus* the amount that her reconciliation of him with his uncle just in time to save it, without an hour to spare, will represent for his pocket? We don't know what that lucky amount may be —— "

"No, but we more or less *shall*" — Horton took her straight up. "Of course, without exaggeration, that will be interesting — even though it will be but a question, I'm quite certain, of comparatively small things. Old Betterman — there are people who practically know, and I've talked with them — isn't going to foot up to any faint likeness of what Gaw does. That, however, has nothing to do with it: all that *is* relevant — since I quite allow that, speculation for speculation, our association in this sort represents finer fun than it has yet succeeded in doing in other sorts — all that's relevant is that when you've seen Gray you mayn't be in such a hurry to figure him as a provoker of insatiable passions. Your insidious Northover has, as you say, worked you up, but wait a little to see if the reality corresponds."

"He showed me a photograph, my insidious Northover," Cissy promptly recalled; "he was *naïf* enough, poor dear, for that. In fact he made me a present of several, including one of himself; I owe him as well two or three other mementos, all of which I've cherished."

"What was he up to anyway, the old corrupter of your youth?" — Horton seemed really to wonder. "Unless it was that you simply reduced him to infatuated babble."

"Well, there are the photographs and things to show," she answered unembarrassed — "though I haven't them with me here; they're put away in New York. His portrait's extremely good-looking."

"Do you mean Mr. Northover's own?"

"Oh *his* is of course quite beautiful. But I mean Mr. Fielder's — at his then lovely age. I remember it," said Cissy, "as a nice, nice face."

Haughty on his side indulged in the act of memory, concluding after an instant to a headshake. "He isn't at all remarkable for looks; but putting his nice face at its best, granting that he *has* a high degree of that advantage, do you see Rosanna so carried away by it as to cast everything to the winds for him?"

Cissy weighed the question. "We've seen surely what she has been carried away enough to do."

"She has had other reasons — independent of headlong passion. And remember," he further argued — "if you impute to her a high degree of that sort of sensibility — how perfectly proof she was to *my* physical attractions, which I declare to you without scruple leave the very brightest you may discover in Gray completely in the shade."

Again his companion considered. "Of course you're dazzlingly handsome; but are you, my dear, after all — I mean in appearance — so very *interesting?*"

The inquiry was so sincere that it could be met but in the same spirit. "Didn't you then find me so from the first minute you ever looked at me?"

"We're not talking of me," she returned, "but of people who happen to have been subjects less predestined and victims less abject. "What," she then at once went on, "*is* Gray's appearance 'anyway'? Is he black, to begin with, or white, or betwixt and between? Is he little or big or neither one thing or t'other? Is he fat or thin or of 'medium weight'? There are always such lots to be told about people, and never a creature in all the wide world to tell. Even Mr. Northover, when I come to think of it, never mentioned his size."

"Well, you *wouldn't* mention it," Horton amiably argued. The appeal, he showed withal, stirred him to certain recoveries. "And I should call him black — black as to his straight thick hair, which I see rather distinctively 'slick' and soigné — the hair of a good little boy who never played at things that got it tumbled. No, he's only very middling tall; in fact so very mid-dling," Haughty made out, "that it probably comes to his being rather short. But he has neither a hump nor a limp, no marked physical deformity of any sort; has in fact a kind of futile fidgety quickness which suggests the little man, and the nervous and the active and the ready; the ready, I mean, for anything in the way of interest and talk — given that the matter isn't too big for him. The 'active,' I say, though at the same time," he noted, "I ask myself what the deuce the activity will have been *about.*"

The girl took in these impressions to the effect of desiring still more of them. "Doesn't he happen then to have eyes and things?"

"Oh yes" — Horton bethought himself — "lots and lots of eyes, though not perhaps so many of other things. Good eyes, fine eyes, in fact I think anything whatever you may require in the way of eyes."

"Then clearly they're not 'black': I never require black ones," she said, "in any conceivable connection: his eyes — blue-grey, or grey-blue, whichever you may call it, and far and away the most charming kind when one doesn't happen to be looking into your glorious green ones — his satisfactory eyes are what will more than anything else have done the business. They'll have done it so," she went on, "that if he isn't red in the face, which I defy him to be, his features don't particularly matter — though there's not the least reason either why he should have mean or common ones. In

The Ivory Tower

fact he hasn't them in the photograph, and what are photographs, the wretched things, but the very truth of life?"

"He's not red in the face," Haughty was able to state — "I think of him rather as of a pale, very pale, clean brown; and entirely unaddicted," he felt sure, "to flushing or blushing. What I do sort of remember in the feature way is that his teeth though good, fortunately, as they're shown a good deal, are rather too small and square; for a man's, that is, so that they make his smile a trifle ——"

"A trifle irresistible of course," Cissy broke in — "through their being, in their charming form, of the happy Latin model; extremely like my own, be so good as to notice for once in your life, and not like the usual Anglo-Saxon fangs. You're simply describing, you know," she added, "about as gorgeous a being as one could wish to see."

"It's not I who am describing him — it's you, love; and ever so delightfully." With which, in consistency with that, he himself put a question. "What does it come to, by the way, in the sense of a moustache? Does he, or doesn't he after all, wear one? It's odd I shouldn't remember, but what does the photograph say?"

"It seems odd indeed I shouldn't" — Cissy had a moment's brooding. She gave herself out as ashamed. "Fancy my not remembering if the photograph is moustache!"

"It can't be then very," Horton

contributed — the point was really so interesting.

"No," Cissy tried to settle, "the photograph can't be so very moustache."

"His moustaches, I mean, if he wears 'em, can't be so very prodigious; or one could scarcely have helped noticing, could one?"

"Certainly no one can ever have failed to notice yours — and therefore Gray's, if he has any, must indeed be very inferior. And yet he can't be shaved like a sneak-thief — or like all the world here," she developed; "for I won't have him with nothing at all any more than I'll have him with anything prodigious, as you say; which is worse than nothing. When I say I won't have him with nothing," she explained, "I mean I won't have him subject to the so universally and stupidly applied American law that every man's face without exception shall be scraped as clean, as glabre, as a fish's — which it makes so many of them so much resemble. I won't have him so," she said, "because I won't have him so idiotically gregarious and without that sense of differences in things, and of their relations and suitabilities, which such exhibitions make one so ache for. If he's gregarious to that sort of tune we must renounce our idea — that is you must drop yours — of my working myself up to snatch him from the arms of Rosanna. I must believe in him, for that, I must see him at least in my own way," she pursued; "believing in myself, or even believing in you, is a compar-

950

ative detail. I won't have him bristle with horrid demagogic notes. I shouldn't be able to act a scrap on that basis."

It was as if what she said had for him the interest at once of the most intimate and the most enlarged application; it was in fact as if she alone in all the world could touch him in such fine ways — could amuse him, could verily instruct him, to anything like such a tune. "It seems peculiarly a question of bristles if it all depends on his moustache. Our suspense as to that, however, needn't so much ravage us," Haughty aded, "when we remember that Davey, who, you tell me, will by this time have seen him, can settle the question for us as soon as we meet at dinner. It will by the same stroke then settle that of the witchcraft which has according to your theory so bedevilled poor dear Rosanna's sensibility — leading it such a dance, I mean, and giving such an empire to certain special items of our friend's 'personality,' that the connection was practically immediate with his brilliant status."

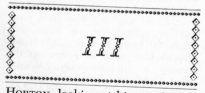

HORTON, looking at his watch, had got up as he spoke — which Cissy at once also did under this recall of the lapse of their precious minutes. There was a point, however, left for her to make; which she did with the remark that the item they had been discussing in particular couldn't have been by itself the force that had set their young woman originally in motion, inasmuch as Gray wouldn't have had a moustache when a small boy or whatever, and as since that young condition, she understood, Rosanna hadn't again seen him. A proposition to which Haughty's assent was to remain vague, merged as it suddenly became in the cry of "Hello, here he is!" and a prompt gay brandish of arms up at their host Bradham, arrayed for the evening, white-waistcoated and buttonholed, robustly erect on an overlooking ledge and explaining his presence, from the moment it was thus observed, by calling down that Gussy had sent him to see if she wasn't to expect them at dinner. It was practically a summons to Cissy, as the girl easily recognised, to leave herself at least ten minutes to dress decently — in spite of the importance of which she so challenged Davey on another score that, as a consequence, the good gorgeous man, who shone with every effect of the bath and every resource of the toilet, had within the pair of minutes picked out such easiest patent-leather steps as would enable him to convict the companions of a shameless dawdle. She had had time to articulate for Horton's benefit, with no more than due distinctness, that he must have seen them, and Horton had as quickly found the right note and the right wit for the simple reassurance "Oh Davey ⸺!" As occupants of a place of procrastination that they only were not such fools as to leave unhaunted they frankly received their visitor, any impulse in whom to sprinkle stale banter on their search for solitude would have been forestalled, even had it been supposable of so perfect a man of the world, by the instant action of his younger guest's strategic curiosity.

"Has he, please, just *has* he or no, got a moustache?" — she appealed as if the fate of empires depended on it.

"I've been telling her," Horton explained, "whatever I can remember of Gray Fielder, but she won't listen to anything if I can't first be sure as to *that*. So as I want her enormously to like him, we both hang, you see, on your lips; unless you call it, more correctly, on his."

Davey's evening bloom opened to them a dense but perfectly pathless garden of possibilities; out of which, while he faced them, he left them to pluck by their own act any bright flower they sufficiently desired to reach. Wonderful during the few instants, between these flagrant worldlings, the exchange of fine recognitions. It would have been hard perhaps to say of them whether it was most discernible that Haughty and Cissy trusted most his intelligence or his indifference, and whether he most applauded or ignored the high perfection of their assurance. What was testified to all round, at all events — [1]

[1] There is a gap here in the MS., with the following note by the author: "It is the security of the two others

"Ah then he *is* as 'odd' as I was sure — in spite of Haughty's perverse theory that we shall find him the flattest of the flat!"

It might have been at Haughty's perverse theory that Davey was most moved to stare — had he not quickly betrayed, instead of this, a marked attention to the girl herself. "Oh you little wonder and joy!"

"She *is* a little wonder and joy," Horton said — that at any rate came out clear.

"What you are, my boy, I'm not pretending to say," Davey returned in answer to this; "for I don't accept her account of your vision of Gray as throwing any light on it at all."

"On his judgment of Mr. Fielder, do you mean," Cissy earnestly asked, "or on your evidently awful opinion of his own dark nature?"

"Haughty knows that I lose myself in his dark nature, at my spare moments, and with wind enough on to whistle in that dark, very much as if I had the fine excite-

with him that is testified to; but I mustn't make any sort of spread about it or about anything else here now, and only put Davey on some noncommittal reply to the question addressed him, such as keeps up the mystery or ambiguity or suspense about Gray, his moustache and everything else, so as to connect properly with what follows. The real point is — *that* comes back to me, and it is in essence enough — that he pleads he doesn't remember, didn't notice, at all; and thereby oddly enough can't say. It will come to me right once I get into it. One sees that Davey plays with them."

ment of the Forêt de Bondy to deal with. He's well aware that I know no greater pleasure of the imagination than that sort of interest in him — when I happen also to have the time and the nerve. Let these things serve me now, however, only to hurry you up," Davey went on; "and to say that I of course had with our fortunate friend an impressive quarter of an hour — which everyone will want to know about, so that I must keep it till we sit down. But the great thing is after all for yourself, Haughty," he added — "and you had better know at once that he particularly wants to see you. He'll be glad of you at the very first moment —— "

But Horton had already taken him easily up. "Of course I know, my dear man, that he particularly wants to see me. He has written me nothing else from the moment he arrived."

"He has written you, you wretch," Cissy at once extravagantly echoed — "he has written you all sorts of things and you haven't so much as told me?"

"He hasn't written me all sorts of things" — Horton directed this answer to Davey alone — "but has written me in such straight confidence and friendship that I've been wondering if I mayn't go round to him this evening."

"Gussy will no doubt excuse you for that purpose with the utmost joy," Davey rejoined — "though I don't think I advise you to ask her leave if you don't want her at once to insist on going with you.

Go to him alone, very quietly — and with the happy confidence of doing him good."

It had been on Cissy that, for his part, Davey had, in speaking, rested his eyes; and it might by the same token have been for the benefit of universal nature, suspended to listen over the bosom of the deep, that Horton's lips phrased his frank reaction upon their entertainer's words. "Well then, ye powers, the amount of good that I shall undertake —— !"

Davey Bradham and Cissy Foy exchanged on the whole ground for a moment a considerable smile; his share in which, however, it might exactly have been that prompted the young woman's further expression of their intelligence. "It's too charming that he yearns so for Haughty — and too sweet that Haughty can now rush to him at once." To which she then appended in another tone: "One takes for granted of course that Rosanna was with him."

Davey at this but continued to bloom and beam; which gave Horton, even with a moment's delay, time to assist his better understanding. "She doesn't even yet embrace the fact, tremendously as I've driven it into her, that if Rosanna had been there he couldn't have breathed my name."

This made Davey, however, but throw up derisive hands; though as with an impatient turn now for their regaining the lawn. "My dear man, Rosanna breathes your name with all the force of her lungs!"

Horton, jerking back his head

The Ivory Tower

for the bright reassurance, laughed out with amusement. "What a jolly cue then for my breathing of hers! I'll roar it to all the echoes, and everything will be well. But what one's talking about," he said, "is the question of Gray's naming *me*." He looked from one of his friends to the other, and then, as gathering them into the interest of it: "I'll bet you a fiver that he doesn't at any rate speak to me of Miss Gaw."

"Well, what will that prove?" Davey asked, quite easy about it and leading the way up the rocks.

"In the first place how much he thinks of her," said Cissy, who followed close behind. "And in the second that it's ten to one Haughty will find her there."

"I don't care if I do — not a scrap!" Horton also took his way. "I don't care for anything now but the jolly fun, the jolly fun ——!" He had committed it all again, by the time they reached the cliff's edge, to the bland participating elements.

"Oh the treat the poor boy is evidently going to stand us *all!*" — well, was something that Davey, rather out of breath as they reached the lawn again and came in sight of the villa, had just yet no more than those light words for. He was more definite in remarking immediately after to Cissy that Rosanna would be as little at the other house that evening as she had been at the moment of his own visit, and that, since the nurses and other outsiders appeared to have dis-

persed, there would be no one to interfere with Gray's free welcome of his friend. The girl was so attentive for this that it made them pause again while she brought out in surprise: "There's nobody else there, you mean then, to watch with the dead —— ?"

It made Mr. Bradham for an instant wonder, Horton, a little apart from them now and with his back turned, seeming at the same moment, and whether or no her inquiry reached his ear, struck with something that had pulled him up as well and that made him stand and look down in thought. "Why, I suppose the nephew must be himself a sort of watcher," Davey found himself not other than decently vague to suggest.

But it scarce more contented Cissy than if the point had really concerned her. She appeared indeed to question the more, though her eyes were on Haughty's rather brooding back while she did so. "Then if he does stay in the room, when he comes out of it to see people —— ?"

Her very drop seemed to present the state of things to which the poor deceased was in that case left; for which, however, her good host declined to be responsible. "I don't suppose he comes out for so many."

"He came out at any rate for you." The sense of it all rather remarkably held her, and it might have been some communication of this that, overtaking Horton at his slight distance, determined in him the impulse to leave them, without more words, and walk by himself to the house. "We don't surround such occasions with any form or state of imagination — scarcely with any decency, do we?" Cissy adventured while observing Haughty's retreat. "I should like to think for him of a catafalque and great draped hangings — I should like to think for him of tall flambeaux in the darkened room, and of relays of watchers, sisters of charity or suchlike, surrounding the grand affair and counting their beads."

Davey's rich patience had a shrug. "The grand affair, my dear child, is *their* affair, over there, and not mine; though when you indulge in such fancies 'for him,' I can't but wonder who it is you mean."

"Who it is —— ?" She mightn't have understood his difficulty.

"Why the dead man or the living!"

They had gone on again; Horton had, with a quickened pace, disappeared; and she had before answering cast about over the fair face of the great house, paler now in the ebb of day, yet with dressing-time glimmers from upper windows flushing it here and there like touches of pink paint in an elegant evening complexion. "Oh I care for the dead man, I'm afraid, only because it's the living who appeals. I don't want *him* to like it."

"To like —— ?" Davey was again at a loss. "What on earth?"

"Why all that ugliness and bareness, that poverty of form."

He had nothing but derision for her here. "It didn't occur to me at all to associate him with the idea of poverty."

"The place must all the same be hideous," she said, "and the conditions mean — for him to prowl about in alone. It comes to me," she further risked, "that if Rosanna *isn't* there, as you say, she quite ought to be — and that in her place I should feel it no more than decent to go over and sit with him."

This appeared to strike Davey in a splendid number of lights — which, however, though collectively dazzling, allowed discriminations. "It perhaps bears a little on the point that she has herself just sustained a grave bereavement — with her offices to her own dead to think of first. That was present to me in your talk a moment since of Haughty's finding her."

"Very true" — it was Cissy's practice, once struck, ever amusedly to play with the missile: "it *is* of course extraordinary that those bloated old *richards*, at one time so associated, should have flickered out almost at the same hour. What it comes to then," she went on, "is that Mr. Gray might be, or perhaps even ought to be, condoling over at the other house with her. However, it's their own business, and all I really care for is that he should be so keen as you say about seeing Haughty. I just delight," she said, "in his being keen about Haughty."

"I'm glad it satisfies you then," Davey returned — "for I was on the point of suggesting that with the sense of his desolation you just expressed you might judge your own place to be at once at his side."

"That would have been helpful of you — but I'm content, dear Davey," she smiled. "We're all devoted to Haughty — but," she added after an instant, "there's just this. Did Mr. Graham while you were there say by chance a word about the likes of *me?*"

"Well, really, no — our short talk didn't take your direction. That would have been for me, I confess," Davey frankly made bold to add, "a trifle unexpected."

"I see" — Cissy did him the justice. "But that's a little, I think, because you don't know ——!" It was more, however, than with her sigh she could tell him.

"Don't know by this time, my dear, and after all I've been through," he nevertheless supplied, "what the American girl always so sublimely takes for granted?"

She looked at him on this with intensity — but that of compassion rather than of the conscious wound. "Dear old Davey, il n'y a que vous for not knowing, by this time, as you say, that I've notoriously nothing in common with the creature you mention. I loathe," she said with her purest gentleness, "the American girl."

He faced her an instant more as for a view of the whole incongruity; then he fetched, on his side, a sigh which might have signified, at her choice, either that he was wrong or that he was finally bored.

"Well, you do of course brilliantly misrepresent her. But we're all" — he hastened to patch it up — "unspeakably corrupt."

"That would be a fine lookout for Mr. Fielder if it were true," she judiciously threw off.

"But as you're a judge you know it isn't?"

"It's not as a judge I know it, but as a victim. I don't say we don't do our best," she added; "but we're still of an innocence, an innocence ——!"

"Then perhaps," Davey offered, "Mr. Fielder will help us; unless he proves, by your measure, worse than ourselves!"

"The worse he may be the better; for it's not possible, as I see him," she said, "that he doesn't know."

"Know, you mean," Davey blandly wondered, "how wrong we are — to be so right?"

"Know more on *every* subject than all of us put together!" she called back at him as she now hurried off to dress.

HORTON VINT, on being admitted that evening at the late Mr. Betterman's, walked about the room to which he had been directed and awaited there the friend of his younger time very much as we have seen that friend himself wait under stress of an extraordinary crisis. Horton's sense of a crisis might have been almost equally sharp; he was alone for some minutes during which he shifted his place and circled, indulged in wide vague movements and vacuous stares at·incongruous objects — the place being at once so spacious and so thickly provided — quite after the fashion in which Gray Fielder's nerves and imagination had on the same general scene sought and found relief at the hour of the finest suspense up to that moment possessing him. Haughty too, it would thus have appeared for the furtherance of our interest, had imagination and nerves — had in his way as much to reflect upon as we have allowed ourselves to impute to the dying Mr. Betterman's nephew. No one was dying now, all that was ended, or would be after the funeral, and the nephew himself was surely to be supposed alive, in face of great sequels, including preparations for those obsequies, with an intensity beyond all former experience. This in fact Horton had all the air of recognising under proof as soon as Gray advanced upon him with both hands out; he couldn't not have taken in the highly quickened state of the young black-clad figure so presented, even though soon and unmistakably invited to note that his own visit and his own presence had much to do with the quickening. Gray was in complete mourning, which had the effect of making his face show pale, as compared with old aspects of it remembered by his friend — who was, it may be mentioned, afterwards to describe

him to Cissy Foy as looking, in the conditions, these including the air of the big bedimmed palace room, for all the world like a sort of "happy Hamlet." For so happy indeed our young man at once proclaimed himself at sight of his visitor, for so much the most interesting thing that had befallen or been offered him within the week did he take, by his immediate testimony, his reunion with this character and every element of the latter's aspect and tone, that the pitch of his acclamation clearly *had*, with no small delay, to drop a little under some unavoidable reminder that they met almost in the nearest presence of death. Was the reminder Horton's own, some pull, for decorum, of a longer face, some expression of his having feared to act in undue haste on the message brought him by Davey? — which might have been, we may say, in view of the appearance after a little that it was Horton rather than Gray who began to suggest a shyness, momentary, without doubt, and determined by the very plenitude of his friend's welcome, yet so far incongruous as that it was not *his* adoption of a manner and betrayal of a cheer that ran the risk of seeming a trifle gross, but quite these indications on the part of the fortunate heir of the old person awaiting interment somewhere above. He could only have seen with the lapse of the moments that Gray was going to be simple — admirably, splendidly simple, one would probably have pronounced it, in estimating and comparing the various possible dangers; but the simplicity of subjects tremendously educated, tremendously "cultivated" and cosmopolitised, as Horton would have called it, especially when such persons were naturally rather extra-refined and ultra-perceptive, was a different affair from the crude candour of the common sort; the consequence of which apprehensions and reflections must have been, in fine, that he presently recognised in the product of "exceptional advantages" now already more and more revealed to him such a pliability of accent as would easily keep judgment, or at least observation, suspended. Gray wasn't going to be at a loss for any shade of decency that didn't depend, to its inconvenience, on some uncertainty about a guest's prejudice; so that once the air was cleared of awkwardness by that perception, exactly, in Horton's ready mind that he and his traditions, his susceptibilities, in fact (of all the queer things!) his own very simplicities and, practically, stupidities were being superfluously allowed for and deferred to, and that this, only this, was the matter, he should have been able to surrender without a reserve to the proposed measure of their common rejoicing. Beautiful might it have been to him to find his friend so considerately glad of him that the spirit of it could consort to the last point with any, with every, other felt weight in the consciousness so attested; in accordance with which we may remark that continued

embarrassment for our gallant caller would have implied on his own side, or in other words deep within his own spirit, some obscure source of confusion.

What distinguishably happened was thus that he first took Graham for exuberant and then for repentant, with the reflection accompanying this that he mustn't, to increase of subsequent shame, have been too open an accomplice in mere jubilation. Then the simple sense of his restored comrade's holding at his disposal a general confidence in which they might absolutely breathe together would have superseded everything else hadn't his individual self-consciousness been perhaps a trifle worried by the very pitch of so much openness. Open, not less generously so, was what he could himself have but wanted to be — in proof of which we may conceive him insist to the happy utmost, for promotion of his comfort, on those sides of their relation the working of which would cast no shadow. They had within five minutes got over much ground — all of which, however, must be said to have represented, and only in part, the extent of Gray's requisition of what he called just elementary human help. He was in a situation at which, as he assured his friend, he had found himself able, those several days, but blankly and inanely to stare. He didn't suppose it had been his uncle's definite design to make an idiot of him, but that seemed to threaten as the practical effect of the dear man's extraordinary course. "You see," he explained, bringing it almost pitifully out, "he appears to have left me a most monstrous fortune. I mean" — for under his appeal Haughty had still waited a little — "a really tremendous lot of money."

The effect of the tone of it was to determine in Haughty a peal of laughter quickly repressed — or reduced at least to the intention of decent cheer. "He 'appears,' my dear man? Do you mean there's an ambiguity about his will?"

Gray justified his claim of vagueness by having, with his animated eyes on his visitor's, to take an instant or two to grasp so technical an expression. "No — not an ambiguity. Mr. Crick tells me that he has never in all his experience seen such an amount of property disposed of in terms so few and simple and clear. It would seem a kind of masterpiece of a will."

"Then what's the matter with it?" Horton smiled. "Or at least what's the matter with *you*? — who are so remarkably intelligent and clever?"

"Oh no, I'm not the least little bit clever!" Gray in his earnestness quite excitedly protested. "I haven't a single ray of the intelligence that among you all here clearly passes for rudimentary. But the luxury of *you*, Haughty," he broke out on a still higher note, "the luxury, the pure luxury of you!"

Something of beauty in the very tone of which, some confounding force in the very clearness, might it have been that made Horton himself gape for a moment even as Gray had just described his own wit as gaping. They had first sat down, for hospitality offered and accepted — though with no production of the smokable or the drinkable to profane the general reference; but the agitation of all that was latent in this itself had presently broken through, and by the end of a few moments we might perhaps scarce have been able to say whether the host had more set the guest or the guest more the host in motion. Horton Vint had everywhere so the air of a prime social element that it took in any case, and above all in any case of the spacious provision or the sumptuous setting, a good deal of practically combative proof to reduce the implications of his presence to the minor right. He *might* inveterately have been master or, in quantitative terms, owner — so could he have been taken for the most part as offering you the enjoyment of anything fine that surrounded him: this in proportion to the scale of such matters and to any glimpse of that sense of them in you which was what came nearest to putting you on his level. All of which sprang doubtless but from the fact that his relation to things of expensive interest was so much at the mercy of his appearance; representing as it might be said to do a contradiction of the law under which it is mostly to be observed, in our modernest conditions, that the figure least congruous with scenic splendour is the figure awaiting the reference. More

The Ivory Tower

references than may here be detailed, at any rate, would Horton have seemed ready to gather up during the turns he had resumed his indulgence in after the original arrest and the measurements of the whole place practically determined for him by Gray's own so suggestive revolutions. It was positively now as if these last had all met, in their imperfect expression, what that young man's emotion was in the act of more sharply attaining to — the plain conveyance that if Horton had in his friendliness, not to say his fidelity, presumed to care to know, this disposition was as naught beside the knowledge apparently about to drench him. They were there, the companions, in their second brief arrest, with everything good in the world that he might have conceived or coveted just taking for him the radiant form of precious knowledges that he must be so obliging as to submit to. Let it be fairly inspiring to us to imagine the acuteness of his perception during these minutes of the possibilities of good involved; the refinement of pleasure in his seeing how the advantage thrust upon him would wear the dignity and grace of his consenting unselfishly to learn — inasmuch as, quite evidently, the more he learnt, and though it should be ostensibly and exclusively about Mr. Betterman's heir, the more vividly it all would stare at him as a marked course of his own. Wonderful thus the little space of his feeling the great wave set in motion by that quiet worthy

break upon him out of Gray's face, Gray's voice, Gray's contact of hands laid all appealingly and affirmingly on his shoulders, and then as it retreated, washing him warmly down, expose to him, off in the intenser light and the uncovered prospect, something like his entire personal future. Something extraordinarily like, yes, could he but keep steady to recognise it through a deepening consciousness, at the same time, of how he was more than matching the growth of his friend's need of him by growing there at once, and to rankness, under the friend's nose, all the values to which this need supplied a soil.

"Well, I won't pretend I'm not glad you don't adopt me as pure ornament — glad you see, I mean, a few connections in which one may perhaps be able, as well as certainly desirous, to be of service to you. Only one should honestly tell you," Horton went on, "that people wanting to help you will spring up round you like mushrooms, and that you'll be able to pick and choose as even a king on his throne can't. Therefore, my boy," Haughty said, "don't exaggerate my modest worth."

Gray, though releasing him, still looked at him hard — so hard perhaps that, having imagination, he might in an instant more have felt it go down too deep. It hadn't done that, however, when "What I want of you above all is exactly that *you* shall pick and choose" was merely what at first came of it. And the case was still all of the

rightest as Graham at once added:
"You see 'people' are exactly my
difficulty — I'm so mortally afraid
of them, and so equally sure that
it's the last thing you are. If I want
you for myself I want you still
more for others — by which you
may judge," said Gray, "that I've
cut you out work."

"That you're mortally afraid of
people is, I confess," Haughty answered, "news to me. I seem to remember you, on the contrary, as so
remarkably and — what was it we
used to call it? — so critico-analyti-
cally interested in 'em."

"That's just it — I *am* so beastly
interested! Don't you therefore
see," Gray asked, "how I may
dread the complication?"

"Dread it so that you seek to
work it off on another?" — and
Haughty looked about as if he
would after all have rather relished
a cigarette.

Clearly, none the less, this awkwardness was lost on his friend. "I
want to work off on you, Vinty,
every blest thing that you'll let
me; and when you've seen into my
case a little further my reasons will
so jump at your eyes that I'm convinced you'll have patience with
them."

"I'm not then, you think, too
beastly interested myself —— ? I've
got such a free mind, you mean,
and such a hard heart, and such a
record of failure to have been any
use at all to myself, that I *must* be
just the person, it strikes you, to
save you all the trouble and secure
you all the enjoyment?" That inquiry Horton presently made, but

with an addition ere Gray could
answer. "My difficulty for myself,
you see, has always been that I
also am by my nature too beastly
interested."

"Yes" — Gray promptly met it —
"but you like it, take that easily,
immensely enjoy it and are not a
bit afraid of it. You carry it off and
you don't pay for it."

"Don't you make anything,"
Horton simply went on, "of my
being for instance so uncannily interested in yourself?"

Gray's eyes again sounded him.
"*Are* you really and truly? — to the
extent of its not boring you?" But
with all he had even at the worst
to take for granted he waited for
no reassurance. "You'll be so sorry
for me that I shall wring your heart
and you'll assist me for common
pity."

"Well," Horton returned, a natural gaiety of response not wholly
kept under, "how can I absurdly
make believe that pitying you, if it
comes to that, won't be enough
against nature to have some fascination? Endowed with every advantage, personal, physical, material, moral, in other words, brilliantly clever, inordinately rich,
strikingly handsome and incredibly good, your state yet insists on
being such as to nip in the bud
the hardy flower of envy. What's
the matter with you to bring that
about would seem, I quite agree,
well worth one's looking into —
even if it proves, by its perversity
or its folly, something of a trial to
one's practical philosophy. When
I pressed you some minutes ago

for the reason of your not facing the future with a certain ease you gave as that reason your want of education and wit. But please understand," Horton added, "that I've no time to waste with you on sophistry that isn't so much as plausible." He stopped a moment, his hands in his pockets, his head thrown all but extravagantly back, so that his considering look might have seemed for the time to descend from a height designed a little to emphasise Gray's comparative want of stature. That young man's own eyes remained the while, none the less, unresentfully raised; to such an effect indeed that, after some duration of this exchange, the bigger man's fine irony quite visibly shaded into a still finer, and withal frankly kinder, curiosity. Poor Gray, with a strained face and an agitation but half controlled, breathed quick and hard, as from inward pressure, and then, renouncing choice — there were so many things to say — shook his head, slowly and repeatedly, after a fashion that discouraged levity. "My dear boy," said his friend under this sharper impression, "you do take it hard." Which made Graham turn away, move about in vagueness of impatience and, still panting and still hesitating for other expression, approach again, as from a blind impulse, the big chimney-piece, reach for a box that raised a presumption of cigarettes and, the next instant, thrust it out in silence at his visitor. The latter's

welcome of the motion, his prompt appropriation of relief, was also mute; with which he found matches in advance of Gray's own notice of them and had a light ready, of which our young man himself partook, before the box went back to its shelf. Odd again might have been for a protected witness of this scene — which of course is exactly what you are invited to be — the lapse of speech that marked it for the several minutes. Horton, truly touched now, and to the finer issue we have glanced at, waited unmistakably for the sign of something more important than his imagination, even at its best, could give him, and which, not less conceivably, would be the sort of thing he himself hadn't signs, either actual or possible, for. He waited while they did the place at last the inevitable small violence — this being long enough to make him finally say: "Do you mean, on your honour, that you don't *like* what has happened to you?"

This unloosed then for Gray the gate of possible expression. "Of course I like it — that is of course I try to. I've been trying here, day after day, as hard as ever a decent man can have tried for anything; and yet I remain, don't you see? a wretched little worm."

"Deary, deary me," stared Horton, "that you should have to bring up your appreciation of it from such depths! You go in for it as you would for the electric light or the telephone, and then find halfway that you can't stand the expense and want the next-door man somehow to combine with you?"

"That's exactly it, Vinty, and you're the next-door man!" — Gray embraced the analogy with glee. "I *can't* stand the expense, and yet I don't for a moment deny I should immensely enjoy the convenience. I *want*," he asseverated, "to like my luck. I want to go in for it, as you say, with every inch of any such capacity as I have. And I want to believe in my capacity; I want to work it up and develop it — I assure you on my honour I do. I've lashed myself up into feeling that if I don't I shall be a base creature, a worm of worms, as I say, and fit only to be utterly ashamed. But that's where you come in. You'll help me to develop. To develop my capacity I mean," he explained with a wondrous candour.

Horton was now, small marvel, all clear faith; even, the cigarettes helping, to the verge again of hilarity. "Your capacity — I see. Not so much your property itself."

"Well" — Gray considered of it — "what will my property be *except* my capacity?" He spoke really as for the pleasure of seeing very. finely and very far. "It won't if I don't like it, that is if I don't *understand* it, don't you see? enough to *make* it count. Yes, yes, don't revile me," he almost feverishly insisted: "I do want it to count for all it's worth, and to get everything out of it, to the very last drop of interest, pleasure, experience, whatever you may call it, that such

a possession can yield. And I'm going to keep myself up to it, to the top of the pitch, by every art and prop, by every helpful dodge, that I can put my hand on. You see if I don't. I breathe defiance," he continued, with his rare radiance, "at any suspicion or doubt. But I come back," he had to add, "to my point that it's you that I essentially most depend on."

Horton again looked at him long and frankly; this subject of appeal might indeed for the moment have been as embarrassed between the various requisitions of response as Gray had just before shown himself. But as the tide could surge for one of the pair so it could surge for the other, and the large truth of what Horton most grasped appeared as soon as he had spoken. "The name of your complaint, you poor dear delightful person, or the name at least of your necessity, your predicament and your solution, is marriage to a wife at short order. I mean of course to an amiable one. *There,* so obviously, is your aid and your prop, there are the sources of success for interest in your fortune, and for the whole experience and enjoyment of it, as you can't find them elsewhere. What are you but just 'fixed' to marry, and what is the sense of your remarks but a more or less intelligent clamour for it?"

Triumphant indeed, as we have said, for lucidity and ease, was this question, and yet it had filled the air, for its moment, but to drop at once by the practical puncture of

Gray's perfect recognition. "Oh of course I've thought of that — but it doesn't meet my case at all." Had he been capable of disappointment in his friend he might almost have been showing it now.

Horton had, however, no heat about it. "You mean you absolutely don't *want* a wife — in connection, so to speak, with your difficulties; or with the idea, that is, of their being resolved into blessings?"

"Well" — Gray was here at least all prompt and clear — "I keep down, in that matter, so much as I can any *a priori* or mere theoretic want. I see my possibly marrying as an effect, I mean — I somehow don't see it at all as a cause. A cause, that is" — he easily worked it out — "of my getting other things right. It may be, in conditions, the greatest rightness of all; but I want to be sure of the conditions."

"The first of which is, I understand then" — for this at least had been too logical for Haughty not to have to match it — "that you should fall so tremendously in love that you won't be able to help yourself."

Graham just debated; he was all intelligence here. "Falling tremendously in love — the way you *grands amoureux* talk of such things!"

"Where do you find, my boy," Horton asked, "that I'm a grand amoureux?"

Well, Gray had but to consult his memory of their young days together; there was the admission, under pressure, that he might have confused the appearances. "They were at any rate always up and at you — which seems to have left me with the impression that your life is full of them."

"Every man's life is full of them that has a door or a window they can come in by. But the question's of yourself," said Haughty, "and just exactly of the number of such that you'll have to keep open or shut in the immense façade you'll now present."

Our young man might well have struck him as before all else inconsequent. "I shall present an immense façade?" — Gray, from his tone of surprise, to call it nothing more, would have thought of this for the first time.

But Horton just hesitated. "You've great ideas if you see it yourself as a small one."

"I don't see it as *any*. I decline," Gray remarked, "to *have* a façade. And if I don't I shan't have the windows and doors."

"You've got 'em already, fifty in a row" — Haughty was remorseless — "and it isn't a question of 'having': you *are* a façade; stretching a mile right and left. How can you not be when I'm walking up and down in front of you?"

"Oh you walk up and down, you *make* the things you pass, and you can behave of course if you want like one of the giants in uniform, outside the big shops, who attend the ladies in and out. In fact," Gray went on, "I don't in the least judge that I *am*, or can be at all advertised as, one of the really big. You seem all here so hideously rich that I needn't fear to count as ex-

The Ivory Tower

traordinary; indeed I'm very competently assured I'm by all your standards a very moderate affair. And even if I were a much greater one" — he gathered force — "my appearance of it would depend only on myself. You can have means and not be blatant; you can take up, by the very fact itself, if you happen to be decent, no more room than may suit your taste. I'll be hanged if I consent to take up an inch more than suits mine. Even though not of the truly bloated I've at least means to be quiet. Every one among us — I mean among the moneyed — isn't a monster on exhibition." In proof of which he abounded. "I know people myself who aren't."

Horton considered him with amusement, as well apparently as the people that he knew! "Of course you may dig the biggest hole in the ground that ever was dug — spade-work comes high, but you'll have the means — and get down into it and sit at the very bottom. Only your hole will become then *the* feature of the scene, and we shall crowd a thousand deep all round the edge of it."

Gray stood for a moment looking down, then faced his guest as with a slight effort. "Do you know about Rosanna Gaw?" And then while Horton, for reasons of his own, failed at once to answer: "She has come in for millions ——"

"Twenty-two and a fraction," Haughty said at once. "Do you mean that she sits, like Truth, at the bottom of a well?" he asked still more divertedly.

Gray had a sharp gesture. "If there's a person in the world whom I don't call a façade —— !"

"You don't call *her* one?" — Haughty took it right up. And he added as for very compassion: "My poor man, my poor man — !"

"She loathes self-exhibition; she loathes being noticed; she loathes every form of publicity." Gray quite flushed for it.

Horton went to the mantel for another cigarette, and there was that in the calm way of it that made his friend, even though helping him this time to a light, wait in silence for his word. "She does more than that" — it was brought quite dryly out. "She loathes every separate dollar she possesses."

Gray's sense of the matter, strenuous though it was, could just stare at this extravagance of assent; seeing however, on second thoughts, what there might be in it. "Well then if what I have is a molehill beside her mountain, I can the more easily emulate her in standing back."

"What you have is a molehill?" Horton was concerned to inquire.

Gray showed a shade of guilt, but faced his judge. "Well — so I gather."

The judge at this lost patience. "Am I to understand that you positively *cultivate* vagueness and water it with your tears?"

"Yes" — the culprit was at least honest — "I should rather say I do. And I want you to let me. Do let me."

"It's apparently more then than Miss Gaw does!"

The Ivory Tower

"Yes" — Gray again considered; "she seems to know more or less what she's worth, and she tells me that I can't even begin to approach it."

"Very crushing of her!" his friend laughed. "You 'make the pair,' as they say, and you must help each other much. Her 'loathing' it exactly is — since we know all about it! — that gives her a frontage as wide as the Capitol at Washington. Therefore your comparison proves little — though I confess it would rather help us," Horton pursued, "if you could seem, as you say, to have asked one or two of the questions that I should suppose would have been open to you."

"Asked them of Mr. Crick, you mean?"

"Well, yes — if you've nobody else, and as you appear not to have been able to have cared to look at the will yourself."

Something like a light of hope, at this, kindled in Gray's face. "Would *you* care to look at it, Vinty?"

The inquiry gave Horton pause. "Look at it now, you mean?"

"Well — whenever you like. I think," said Gray, "it must be in the house."

"You're not sure even of *that?*" his companion wailed.

"Oh I know there are two" — our young man had coloured. "I don't mean different ones, but copies of the same," he explained; "one of which Mr. Crick must have."

"And the other of which" — Hor-ton pieced it together — "is the one you offer to show me?"

"Unless, unless —— !" and Gray, casting about, bethought himself. "Unless *that* one —— !" With his eyes on his friend's he still shamelessly wondered.

"Unless that one has happened to get lost," Horton tenderly suggested, "so that you can't after all produce it?"

"No, but it may be upstairs, upstairs —— " Gray continued to turn this over. "I think it *is*," he then recognised, "where I had perhaps better not just now disturb it."

His recognition was nothing, apparently, however, to the clear quickness of Horton's. "It's in your uncle's own room?"

"The room," Gray assented, "where he lies in death while we talk here." This, his tone suggested, sufficiently enjoined delay.

Horton's concurrence was immediately such that, once more turning off, he measured, for the intensity of it, half the room. "I can't advise you without the facts that you're unable to give," he said as he came back, "but I don't indeed invite you to go and rummage in that presence." He might have exhaled the faintest irony, save that verily by this time, between these friends — by which I mean of course as from one of them only, the more generally assured, to the other — irony would, to an at all exhaustive analysis, have been felt to flicker in their medium. Gray might in fact, on the evidence of his next words, have found it just distinguishable.

966

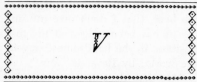

V

"WE do talk here while he lies in death" — they had in fine all serenity for it. "But the extraordinary thing is that my putting myself this way at my ease — and for that matter putting you at yours — is exactly what the dear man made to me the greatest point of. I haven't the shade of a sense, and don't think I ever shall have, of not doing what he wanted of me; for what he wanted of me," our particular friend continued, "is — well, so utterly unconventional. He would *like* my being the right sort of well-meaning idiot that you catch me in the very fact of. I warned him, I sincerely, passionately warned him, that I'm not fit, in the smallest degree, for the use, for the care, for even the most rudimentary comprehension, of a fortune; and that exactly it was which seemed most to settle him. He wanted me clear, to the last degree, not only of the financial brain, but of any sort of faint germ of the money-sense whatever — down to the very lack of power, if he might be so happy (or if *I* might!) to count up to ten on my fingers. Satisfied of the limits of my arithmetic he passed away in bliss."

To this, as fairly lucid, Horton had applied his understanding. "You can't count up to ten?"

"Not all the way. Still," our young man smiled, "the greater inspiration may now give me the lift."

His guest looked as if one might by that time almost have doubted. But it was indeed an extraordinary matter. "How comes it then that your want of arithmetic hasn't given you a want of order? — unless indeed I'm mistaken and you *were* perhaps at sixes and sevens?"

"Well, I think I was at sixes — though I never got up to sevens! I've never had the least rule or method; but that has been a sort of thing I could more or less cover up — from others, I mean, not from myself, who have always been helplessly ashamed of it. It hasn't been the disorder of extravagance," Gray explained, "but the much more ignoble kind, the wasteful thrift that doesn't really save, that simply misses, and that neither enjoys things themselves nor enjoys their horrid little equivalent of hoarded pence. I haven't needed to count far, the fingers of one hand serving for my four or five possessions; and also I've kept straight not by taking no liberties with my means, but by taking none with my understanding of them. From fear of counting wrong, and from loathing of the act of numerical calculation, and of the humiliation of having to give it up after so few steps from the start, I've never counted at all — and that, you see, is what has saved me. That has been *my* sort of disorder — which you'll agree is the most pitiful of all."

Horton once more turned away from him, but slowly this time, not in impatience, rather with something of the preoccupation of a cup-bearer whose bowl has been filled to the brim and who must carry it a distance with a steady hand. So for a minute or two might he have been taking this care; at the end of which, however, Gray saw him stop in apparent admiration before a tall inlaid and brassbound French *bahut;* with the effect, after a further moment, of a sharp break of their thread of talk. "You've got some things here at least to enjoy and that you ought to know how to keep hold of; though I don't so much mean," he explained, "this expensive piece of furniture as the object of interest perched on top."

"Oh the ivory tower! — yes, isn't that, Vinty, a prize piece and worthy of the lovely name?"

Vinty remained for the time all admiration, having, as you would easily have seen, lights enough to judge by. "It appears to have been your uncle's only treasure — as everything else about you here is of a newness! And it isn't so much too small, Gray," he laughed, "for you to get into it yourself, when you went to get rid of us, and draw the doors to. If it's a symbol of any retreat you really have an eye on I much congratulate you; I don't know what I wouldn't give myself for the 'run' of an ivory tower."

"Well, I can't ask you to share mine," Gray returned; "for the situation to have a sense, I take it, one must sit in one's tower alone. And I should properly say," he added after an hesitation, "that

mine is the one object, all round me here, that I don't owe my uncle: it has been placed at my disposition, in the handsomest way in the world, by Rosanna Gaw."

"Ah that does increase the interest — even if susceptible of seeming to mean, to one's bewilderment, that it's the sort of thing she would like to thrust you away into; which I hope, however, is far from the case. Does she then *keep* ivory towers, a choice assortment?" Horton quite gaily continued; "in the sense of having a row of them ready for occupation, and with tenants to match perchable in each and signalling along the line from summit to summit? Because" — and, facing about from his contemplation, he piled up his image even as the type of object represented by it might have risen in the air — "you give me exactly, you see, the formula of that young lady herself: perched aloft in an ivory tower is what *she* is, and I'll be hanged if this isn't a hint to you to mount, yourself, into just such another; under the same provocation, I fancy her pleading, as she has in her own case taken for sufficient." Thus it was that, suddenly more brilliant than ever yet, to Graham's apprehension, you might well have guessed, his friend stood nearer again — stood verily quite irradiating responsive ingenuity. Markedly would it have struck you that at such instants as this, most of all, the general hush that was so thick about them pushed upward and still further upward the fine flower of the inferential. Following the pair closely from the first, and beginning perhaps with your idea that this life of the intelligence had its greatest fineness in Gray Fielder, you would by now, I dare say, have been brought to a more or less apprehensive foretaste of its possibilities in our other odd agent. For how couldn't it have been to the full stretch of his elastic imagination that Haughty was drawn out by the time of his putting a certain matter beautifully to his companion? "Don't I, 'gad, take the thing straight over from you — all of it you've been trying to convey to me here! — when I see you, up in the blue, behind your parapet, just gracefully lean over and call down to where I mount guard at your door in the dust and comparative darkness? It's well to understand" — his thumbs now in his waistcoat-holes he measured his idea as if Gray's own face fairly reflected it: "you want me to take *all* the trouble for you simply, in order that you may have all the fun. And you want me at the same time, in order that things shall be for you at their ideal of the easiest, to make you believe, as a salve to your conscience, that the fun *isn't* so mixed with the trouble as that you can't have it, on the right arrangement made with me, quite by itself. This is most ingenious of you," Horton added, "but it doesn't in the least show me, don't you see? where *my* fun comes in."

"I wonder if I can do that," Gray returned, "without making you understand first something of the nature of mine — or for that matter without my first understanding myself perhaps what my queer kind of it is most likely to be."

His companion showed withal for more and more ready to risk amused recognitions. "You *are* 'rum' with your queer kinds, and might make my flesh creep, in these conditions, if it weren't for something in me of rude pluck." Gray, in speaking, had moved towards the great French *meuble* with some design upon it or upon the charge it carried; which Horton's eyes just wonderingly noted — and to the effect of an exaggeration of tone in his next remark. "However, there are assurances one doesn't keep repeating: it's so little in me, I feel, to refuse you any service I'm capable of, no matter how clumsily, that if you take me but confidently enough for the agent even of your unholiest pleasures, you'll find me still putting them through for you when you've broken down in horror yourself."

"Of course it's my idea that whatever I ask you shall be of interest to you, and of the liveliest, in itself — quite apart from any virtue of my connection with it. If it speaks to you that way so much the better," Gray went on, standing now before the big *bahut* with both hands raised and resting on the marble top. This lifted his face almost to the level of the base of his perched treasure — so that he stared at the ivory tower without as yet touching it. He only continued to talk, though with his thought, as he brought out the rest of it, almost superseded by the new preoccupation. "I shall absolutely decline any good of anything that isn't attended by some equivalent or — what do you call it? — proportionate good for you. I shall propose to you a percentage, if that's the right expression, on every blest benefit I get from you in the way of the sense of safety." Gray now moved his hands, laying them as in finer fondness to either smoothly-plated side of the tall repository, against which a finger or two caressingly rubbed. His back turned therefore to Horton, he was divided between the growth of his response to him and that of this more sensible beauty. "Don't I kind of insure my life, my moral consciousness, I mean, for your advantage? — or *with* you, as it were, taking you for the officeman or actuary, if I'm not muddling: to whom I pay a handsome premium for the certainty of there being to my credit, on my demise, a sufficient sum to clear off my debts and bury me."

"You propose to me a handsome premium? Catch me," Horton laughed, "not jumping at *that!*"

"Yes, and you'll of course fix the premium yourself." But Gray was now quite detached, occupied only in opening his ivory doors with light fingers and then playing these a little, whether for hesitation or for the intenser pointing of inquiry, up and down the row of drawers so exposed. Against the topmost they then rested a moment — drawing out this one, however, with scant further delay and enabling

themselves to feel within and so become possessed of an article contained. It was with this article in his hand that he presently faced about again, turning it over, resting his eyes on it and then raising them to his visitor, who perceived in it a heavy letter, duly addressed, to all appearance, but not stamped and as yet unopened. "The distinguished retreat, you see, *has* its tenant."

"Do you mean by its tenant the author of those evidently numerous pages? — unless you rather mean," Horton asked, "that you seal up in packets the love-letters addressed to you and find that charming receptacle a congruous place to keep them? Is there a packet in every drawer, and do you take them out this way to remind yourself fondly that you have them and that it mayn't be amiss to feel your conquests and their fine old fragrance dangled under my nose?"

Our young man, at these words, had but returned to the consideration of his odd property, attaching it first again to the superscription and then to the large firm seal. "I haven't the least idea what this is; and I'm divided in respect of it, I don't mind telling you, between curiosity and repulsion."

Horton then also eyed the ambiguity, but at his discreet distance and reaching out for it as little as his friend surrendered it. "Do you appeal to me by chance to help you to decide either way?"

Poor Gray, still wondering and fingering, had a long demur. "No

The Ivory Tower

— I don't think I want to decide." With which he again faced criticism. "The extent, Vinty, to which I think I must just *like* to drift — !"

Vinty seemed for a moment to give this indicated quantity the attention invited to it, but without more action for the case than was represented by his next saying: "Why then do you produce your question — apparently so much for my benefit?"

"Because in the first place you noticed the place it lurks in, and because in the second I like to tell you things."

This might have struck us as making the strained note in Vinty's smile more marked. "But that's exactly, confound you, what you *don't* do! Here have I been with you half an hour without your practically telling me anything!"

Graham, very serious, stood a minute looking at him hard; succeeding also quite it would seem in taking his words not in the least for a reproach but for a piece of information of the greatest relevance, and thus at once dismissing any minor importance. He turned back with his minor importance to his small open drawer, laid it within again and, pushing the drawer to, closed the doors of the cabinet. The act disposed of the letter, but had the air of introducing as definite a statement as Horton could have dreamt of. "It's a bequest from Mr. Gaw."

"A bequest" — Horton wondered — "of bank-notes?"   .

"No — it's a letter addressed to me just before his death, handed me by his daughter, to whom he intrusted it, and not likely, I think, to contain money. He was then sure, apparently, of my coming in for money; and even if he hadn't been would have had no ground on earth for leaving me anything."

Horton's visible interest was yet consonant with its waiting a little for expression. "He leaves you the great Rosanna."

Graham, at this, had a stare, followed by a flush as the largest possible sense of it came out. "You suppose it perhaps the expression of a wish —— ?" And then as Horton forbore at first as to what he supposed: "A wish that I may find confidence to apply to his daughter for her hand?"

"That hasn't occurred to you before?" Horton asked — "nor the measure of the confidence suggested been given you by the fact of your receiving the document from Rosanna herself? You do give me, you extraordinary person," he gaily proceeded, "as good opportunities as I could possibly desire to 'help' you!"

Graham, for all the felicity of this, needed but an instant to think. "I have it from Miss Gaw herself that she hasn't an idea of what the letter contains — any more than she has the least desire that I shall for the present open it."

"Well, mayn't that very attitude in her rather point to a suspicion?" was his guest's ingenious reply. "Nothing could be less like her certainly than to appear in such a case to want to force your hand. It

971

makes her position — with exquisite filial piety, you see — extraordinarily delicate."

Prompt as that might be, Gray appeared to show, no sportive sophistry, however charming, could work upon him. "Why should Mr. Gaw want me to marry his daughter?"

Horton again hung about a little. "Why should you be so afraid of ascertaining his idea that you don't so much as peep into what he writes on the subject?"

"Afraid? *Am* I afraid?" Gray fairly spoke with a shade of the hopeful, as if even that would be richer somehow than drifting.

"Well, you looked at your affair just now as you might at some small dangerous, some biting or scratching, animal whom you're not at all sure of."

"And yet you see I keep him about."

"Yes — you keep him in his cage, for which I suppose you have a key."

"I have indeed a key, a charming little golden key." With which Gray took another turn; once more facing criticism, however, to say with force: "He hated him most awfully!"

Horton appeared to wonder. "Your uncle hated old Gaw?"

"No — I don't think *he* cared. I speak of Mr. Gaw's own animus. He disliked so mortally his old associate, the man who lies dead upstairs — and in spite of my consideration for him I still preserve his record."

"How do you know about his hate," Horton asked, "or if your letter, since you haven't read it, *is* a record?"

"Well, I don't trust it — I mean not to be. I don't see what else he could have written me about. Besides," Gray added, "I've my personal impression."

"Of old Gaw? You have seen him then?"

"I saw him out there on this verandah, where he was hovering in the most extraordinary fashion, a few hours before his death. It was only for a few minutes," Gray said — "but they were minutes I shall never forget."

Horton's interest, though so deeply engaged, was not unattended with perplexity. "You mean he expressed to you such a feeling at such an hour?"

"He expressed to me in about three minutes, without speech, to which it seemed he couldn't trust himself, as much as it might have taken him, or taken anyone else, to express in three months at another time and on another subject. If you ever yourself saw him," Gray went on, "perhaps you'll understand."

"Oh I often saw him — and should indeed in your place perhaps have understood. I never heard him accused of not making people do so. But you hold," said Horton, "that he must have backed up for you further the mystic revelation?"

"He had written before he saw me — written on the chance of my being a person to be affected by it; and after seeing me he didn't destroy or keep back his message, but emphasised his wish for a punctual delivery."

"By which it is evident," Horton concluded, "that you struck him exactly *as* such a person."

"He saw me, by my idea, as giving my attention to what he had there ready for me." Gray clearly had talked himself into possession of his case. "That's the sort of person I succeeded in seeming to him — though I can assure you without my the least wanting to."

"What you feel is then that he thought he *might* attack with some sort of shock for you the character of your uncle?" Vinty's question had a special straightness.

"What I feel is that he has so attacked it, shock or no shock, and that that thing in my cabinet, which I haven't examined, can only be the proof."

It gave Horton much to turn over. "But your conviction has an extraordinary bearing. Do I understand that the thing was handed you by your friend with a knowledge of its contents?"

"Don't, please," Gray said at once, "understand anything either so hideous or so impossible. She but carried out a wish uttered on her father's deathbed, and hasn't so much as suggested that I break the portentous seal. I think in fact," he assured himself, "that she greatly prefers I shouldn't."

"Which fact," Horton observed, "but adds of course to your curiosity."

Gray's look at him betrayed on this a still finer interest in *his* interest. "You see the limits in me of that passion."

"Well, my dear chap, I've seen greater limits to many things than your having your little secret tucked away under your thumb. Do you mind my asking," Horton risked, "whether what deters you from action — and by action I mean opening your letter — is just a real apprehension of the effect designed by the good gentleman? Do you feel yourself exposed, by the nature of your mind or any presumption on Gaw's behalf, to give credit, vulgarly speaking, to whatever charge or charges he may bring?"

Gray weighed the question, his wide dark eyes would have told us, in his choicest silver scales. "Neither the nature of my mind, bless it, nor the utmost force of any presumption to the contrary, prevents my having found my uncle, in his wonderful latest development, the very most charming person that I've ever seen in my life. Why he impressed me as a model of every virtue."

"I confess I don't see," said Horton, "how a relative so behaving could have failed to endear himself. With such convictions why don't you risk looking?"

Gray was but for a moment at a loss — he quite undertook to know. "Because the whole thing would be so horrible. I mean the question itself is — and even our here and at such a time discussing it."

"Nothing is horrible — to the point of making one quake," Horton opined, "that falls to the ground with a smash from the mo-

The Ivory Tower

ment one drops it. The sense of your document is exactly what's to be appreciated. It would have no sense at all if you didn't believe."

Gray considered, but still differed. "Yes, to find it merely vindictive and base, and thereby to have to take it for false, that would still be an odious experience."

"Then why the devil don't you simply destroy the thing?" Horton at last quite impatiently inquired.

Gray showed perhaps he had scarce a reason, but had, to the very brightest effect, an answer. "That's just what I want you to help me to. To help me, that is," he explained, "after a little to decide for."

"After a little?" wondered Horton. "After how long?"

"Well, after long enough for me to feel sure I don't act in fear. I don't want," he went on as in fresh illustration of the pleasure taken by him, to the point, as it were, of luxury, in feeling no limit to his companion's comprehension, or to the patience involved in it either, amusedly as Horton might at moments attempt to belie that, adding thereby to the whole service something still more spacious — "I don't want to act in fear of anything or of anyone whatever; I said to myself at home three weeks ago, or whenever, that it wasn't for that I was going to come over; and I propose therefore, you see, to know so far as possible where I am and what I'm about: morally speaking at least, if not financially."

His friend but looked at him again on this in rather desperate diversion. "I don't see how you're to know where you are, I confess, if you take no means to find out."

"Well, my acquisition of property seems by itself to promise me information, and for the understanding of the lesson I shall have to take a certain time. What I want," Gray finely argued, "is to act but in the light of that."

"In the light of time? Then why do you begin by so oddly wasting it?"

"Because I think it may be the only way for me not to waste understanding. Don't be afraid," he went on, moving as by the effect of Horton's motion, which had brought that subject of appeal a few steps nearer the rare repository, "that I shall commit the extravagance of at all wasting *you*."

Horton, from where he had paused, looked up at the ivory tower; though as Gray was placed in the straight course of approach to it he had after a fashion to catch and meet his eyes by the way. "What you really want of me, it's clear, is to help you to fidget and fumble — or in other words to prolong the most absurd situation; and what I ought to do, if you'd believe it of me, is to take that stuff out of your hands and just deal with it myself."

"And what do you mean by dealing with it yourself?"

"Why destroying it unread by either of us — which," said Horton, looking about, "I'd do in a jiffy, on the spot, if there were only a fire in that grate. The place is clear, however, and we've match-

The Ivory Tower

es; let me chuck your letter in and enjoy the blaze with you."

"Ah, my dear man, don't! Don't!" Gray repeated, putting it rather as a plea for indulgence than as any ghost of a defiance, but instinctively stepping backward in defence of his treasure.

His companion, for a little, gazed at the cabinet, in speculation, it might really have seemed, as to an extraordinary reach of arm. "You positively prefer to hug the beastly thing?"

"Let me alone," Gray presently returned, "and you'll probably find I've hugged it to death."

Horton took, however, on his side, a moment for further reflection. "I thought what you wanted of me to be exactly *not* that I should let you alone, but that I should give you on the contrary my very best attention."

"Well," Gray found felicity to answer, "I feel that you'll see how your very best attention will sometimes consist in your not at all minding me."

So then for the minute Horton looked as if he took it. The great clock on the mantel appeared to have stopped with the stop of its late owner's life; so that he eyed his watch and startled at the hour to which they had talked. He put out his hand for good-night, and this returned grasp held them together in silence a minute. Something then in his sense of the situation determined his breaking out with an intensity not yet produced in him. "Yes — you're really prodigious. I mean for trust in a fellow.

For upon my honour you know nothing whatever about me."

"That's quite what I mean," said Gray — "that I suffer from my ignorance of so much that's important, and want naturally to correct it."

" 'Naturally'?" his visitor gloomed.

"Why, I do know *this* about you, that when we were together with old Roulet at Neuchâtel and, off on our *cours* that summer, had strayed into a high place, in the Oberland, where I was ass enough to have slid down to a scrap of a dizzy ledge, and so hung helpless over the void, unable to get back, in horror of staying and in greater horror of *not*, you got near enough to me, at the risk of your life, to lower to me the rope we so luckily had with us and that made an effort of my own possible by my managing to pass it under my arms. You helped that effort from a place of vantage above that nobody but you, in your capacity for playing up, would for a moment have taken for one, and you so hauled and steadied and supported me, in spite of your almost equal exposure, that little by little I climbed, I scrambled, my absolute confidence in you helping, for it amounted to inspiration, and got near to where you were."

"From which point," said Horton, whom this reminiscence had kept gravely attentive, "you in your turn rendered me such assistance, I remember, though I can't for the life of me imagine how you contrived, that the tables were quite turned and I shouldn't in the least have got out of my fix without you." He now pulled up short however; he stood a moment looking down. "It isn't pleasant to remember."

"It wouldn't," Gray judged, "be pleasant to forget. You gave proof of extraordinary coolness."

Horton still had his eyes on the ground. "We both kept our heads. I grant it's a decent note for us."

"If you mean we were associated in keeping our heads, you kept mine," Gray remarked, "much more than I kept yours. I should be without a head to-day if you hadn't seen so to my future, just as I should be without a heart, you must really let me remark, if I didn't look now to your past. I consider that to know that fact in it takes me of itself well-nigh far enough in appreciation of you for my curiosity, even at its most exasperated, to rest on a bed of roses. However, my imagination itself," Gray still more beautifully went on, "insists on making additions — since how can't it, for that matter, picture again the rate at which it made them then? I hadn't even at the time waited for you to save my life in order to think you a swell. If I thought you the biggest kind of one, and if in your presence now I see just as much as ever *why* I did, what does that amount to but that my mind *isn't* a blank about you?"

"Well, if mine had ever been one about you," said Horton, once more facing it, "our so interesting conversation here would have sufficed to cram it full. The least I can make of you, whether for your protection or my profit, is just that you're insanely romantic."

"Romantic — yes," Gray smiled; "but oh, but *oh*, so systematically!"

"It's your system that's exactly your madness. How can you take me, without a stroke of success, without a single fact of performance, to my credit, for anything but an abject failure? You're in possession of no faintest sign, kindly note, that I'm not a mere impudent ass."

Gray accepted this reminder, for all he showed to the contrary, in the admiring spirit in which he might have regarded a splendid somersault or an elegant trick with cards; indulging, that is, by his appearance, in the forward bend of attention to it, but then falling back to more serious ground. "It's my romance that's itself my reason; by which I mean that I'm never so reasonable, so deliberate, so lucid and so capable — to call myself capable at any hour! — as when I'm most romantic. I'm methodically and consistently so, and nothing could make and keep me, for any dealings with me, I hold, more conveniently safe and quiet. You see that you can lead me about by a string if you'll only tie it to my appropriate finger — which you'll find out, if you don't mind the trouble, by experience of the wrong ones, those where the attachment won't 'act.'" He drew breath to give his friend the benefit of this illustration, but another connection quickly caught him up. "How can you pretend to suggest

The Ivory Tower

that you're in these parts the faintest approach to an insignificant person? How can you pretend that you're not as clever as you can stick together, and with the cleverness of the right kind? For there are odious kinds, I know — the kind that redresses other people's stupidity instead of sitting upon it."

"I'll answer you those questions," Horton goodhumouredly said, "as soon as you tell me how you've come by your wonderful ground for them. Till you're able to do that I shall resent your torrent of abuse. The appalling creature you appear to wish to depict!"

"Well, you're simply a *figure* — what I call — in all the force of the term; one has only to look at you to see it, and I shall give up drawing conclusions from it only when I give up looking. You can make out that there's nothing in a prejudice," Gray developed, "for a prejudice may be, or must be, so to speak, single-handed; but you can't not count with a relation — I mean one you're a party to, because a relation is exactly a *fact* of reciprocity. Our reciprocity, which exists and which makes me a party to it by existing for my benefit, just as it makes you one by existing for yours, can't possibly result in your not 'figuring' to me, don't you see? with the most admirable intensity. And I simply decline," our young man wound up, "not to believe tremendous things of any subject of a relation of mine."

"'Any' subject?" Vinty echoed in a tone that showed how intelli-

gently he had followed. "That condition, I'm afraid," he smiled, "will cut down not a little your general possibilities of relation." And then as if this were cheap talk, but a point none the less remained: "In this country one's a figure (whatever you may mean by that!) on easy terms; and if I correspond to your idea of the phenomenon you'll have much to do — I won't say for my simple self, but for the comfort of your mind — to make your fond imagination fit the funny facts. You pronounce me an awful swell — which, like everything else over here, has less weight of sense in it for the saying than it could have anywhere else; but what barest evidence have you of any positive trust in me shown on any occasion or in any connection by one creature you can name?"

"Trust?" — Gray looked at the red tip of the cigarette between his fingers.

"Trust, trust, trust!"

Well, it didn't take long to say. "What do you call it but trust that such people as the Bradhams, and all the people here, as he tells me, receive you with open arms?"

"Such people as the Bradhams and as 'all the people here'!" — Horton beamed on him for the beauty of that. "Such authorities and such 'figures,' such allegations, such perfections and such proofs! Oh," he said, "I'm going to have great larks with you!"

"You give me then the evidence I want in the very act of challenging me for it. What better proof of your situation and your char-

977

acter than your possession exactly of such a field for whatever you like, of such a dish for serving me up? Mr. Bradham, as you know," Gray continued, "was this morning so good as to pay me a visit, and the form in which he put your glory to me — because we talked of you ever so pleasantly — was that, by his appreciation, you know your way about the place better than all the rest of the knowing put together."

Horton smiled, smoked, kept his hands in his pockets. "Dear deep old Davey!"

"Yes," said Gray consistently, "isn't he a wise old specimen? It's rather horrid for me having thus to mention, as if you had applied to me for a place, that I've picked up a good 'character' of you, but since you insist on it he assured me that I couldn't possibly have a better friend."

"Well, he's a most unscrupulous old person and ought really to be ashamed. What it comes to," Haughty added, "is that though I've repeatedly stayed with them they've to the best of his belief never missed one of the spoons. The fact is that even if they had poor Davey wouldn't know it."

"He doesn't take care of the spoons?" Gray asked in a tone that made his friend at once swing round and away. He appeared to note an unexpectedness in this, yet, "out" as he was for unexpectedness, it could grow, on the whole, clearly, but to the raising of his spirits. "Well, I shall take care of *my* loose valuables and, un-warned by the Bradhams and likely to have such things to all appearance in greater number than ever before, what can I do but persist in my notion of asking you to keep with me, at your convenience, some proper count of them?" After which as Horton's movement had carried him quite to the far end of the room, where the force of it even detained him a little, Gray had him again well in view for his return, and was prompted thereby to a larger form of pressure. "How can you pretend to palm off on me that women mustn't in prodigious numbers 'trust' you?"

Haughty made of his shoulders the most prodigious hunch. "What importance, under the sun, has the trust of women — in numbers however prodigious? It's never what's best in a man they trust — it's exactly what's worst, what's most irrelevant to anything or to any class but themselves. Their *kind* of confidence," he further elucidated, "is concerned only with the effect of their own operations or with those to which they are subject; it has no light either for a man's other friends or for his enemies: it proves nothing about him but in that particular and wholly detached relation. So neither hate me nor like me, please, for anything any woman may tell you."

Horton's hand had on this renewed and emphasised its proposal of good-night; to which his host acceded with the remark: "What superfluous precautions you take!"

"How can you call them superfluous," he asked in answer to this, "when you've been taking them at such a rate yourself? — in the interest, I mean, of trying to persuade me that you can't stand on your feet?"

"It hasn't been to show you that I'm silly about life — which is what you've just been talking of. It has only been to show you that I'm silly about affairs," Gray said as they went at last through the big bedimmed hall to the house doors, which stood open to the warm summer night under the protection of the sufficient outward reaches.

"Well, what are affairs but life?" Vinty, at the top of the steps, sought to know.

"You'll make me feel, no doubt, how much they are — which would be very good for me. Only life isn't affairs — that's *my* subtle distinction," Gray went on.

"I'm not sure, I'm not sure!" said Horton while he looked at the stars.

"Oh rot — I am!" Gray happily declared; to which he the next moment added: "What it makes you contend for, you see, is the fact of my silliness."

"Well, what is that but the most splendid fact about you, you jolly old sage?" — and his visitor, getting off, fairly sprang into the shade of the shrubberies.

BOOK FOURTH

AGAIN and again, during the fortnight that followed his uncle's death, were his present and his future to strike our young man as an extraordinary blank cheque signed by Mr. Betterman and which, from the moment he accepted it at all, he must fill out, according to his judgment, his courage and his faith, with figures, monstrous, fantastic, almost cabalistic, that it seemed to him he should never learn to believe in. It was not so much the wonder of there being in various New York institutions strange deposits of money, to amounts that, like familiar mountain masses, appeared to begin at the blue horizon and, sloping up and up toward him, grew bigger and bigger the nearer he or they got, till they fairly overhung him with their purple power to meet whatever drafts upon them he should make; it was not the tone, the climax of dryness, of that dryest of men Mr. Crick, whose answering remark as to any and every particular presumption of credit was "Well, I guess I've fixed it so as you'll find *something* there"; that sort of thing was of course fairy-tale enough in itself, was all the while and in a hundred connections a sweet assault on his credulity, but was at the same time a phase of experience comparatively vulgar and that tended to lose its edge with repetition. The real, the overwhelming sense of his adventure was much less in the fact that he could lisp in dollars, as it were, and see the dollars come, than in those vast vague quantities, those spreading tracts, of his own consciousness itself on which his kinsman's prodigious perversity had imposed, as for his exploration, the aspect of a boundless capital. This trust of the dead man in his having a nature that would show to advantage under a bigger strain than it had ever dreamed of meeting, and the corresponding desolate freedom on his own part to read back into the mystery such refinements either, or such crude candours, of meaning and motive as might seem best to fit it, *that* was the huge vague inscribable sum which ran up into the millions and for which the signature that lettered itself to the last neatness wherever his mind's eye rested was "good" enough to reduce any more casual sign in the scheme of nature or of art to the state of a negligible blur. Mr. Crick's want of colour, as Gray qualified this gentleman's idiosyncrasy from the moment he saw how it would be their one point of contact, became, by the extreme rarity and clarity with which it couldn't but affect him, the very most gorgeous gem, of the ruby or topaz order, that the smooth forehead of the actual was for the present to flash upon him.

The Ivory Tower

For dry did it appear inevitable to take the fact of a person's turning up, from New York, with no other retinue than an attendant scribe in a straw hat, a few hours before his uncle's last one, and being beholden to mere Miss Mumby for simple introduction to Gray as Mr. Betterman's lawyer. So had such sparenesses and barenesses of form to register themselves for a mind beset with the tradition that consequences were always somehow voluminous things; and yet the dryness was of a sort, Gray soon apprehended, that he might take up in handfuls, as if it had been the very sand of the Sahara, and thereby find in it, at the least exposure to light, the collective shimmer of myriads of fine particles. It was with the substance of the desert taken as monotonously sparkling under any motion to dig in it that the abyss of Mr. Crick's functional efficiency was filled. That efficiency, in respect to the things to be done, would clearly so answer to any demand upon it within the compass of our young man's subtlety, that the result for him could only be a couple of days of inexpressible hesitation as to the outward air he himself should be best advised to aim at wearing. He reminded himself at this crisis of the proprietor of a garden, newly acquired, who might walk about with his gardener and try to combine, in presence of abounding plants and the vast range of luxuriant nature, an ascertainment of names and properties and processes with a dissimulation, for decent appearance, of the positive side of his cockneyism. By no imagination of a state of mind so unfurnished would the gardener ever have been visited; such gaping seams in the garment of knowledge must affect him at the worst as mere proprietary languor, the offhandness of repletion; and no effective circumvention of traditional takings for granted could lateborn curiosity therefore achieve. Gray's hesitation ceased only when he had decided that he needn't care, comparatively speaking, for what Mr. Crick might think of him. He was going to care for what others might — this at least he seemed restlessly to apprehend; he was going to care tremendously, he felt himself make out, for what Rosanna Gaw might, for what Horton Vint might — even, it struck him, for what Davey Bradham might. But in presence of Mr. Crick, who insisted on having no more personal identity than the omnibus conductor stopping before you but just long enough to bite into a piece of pasteboard with a pair of small steel jaws, the question of his having a character either to keep or to lose declined all relevance — and for the reason in especial that whichever way it might turn for him would remain perhaps, so to speak, the most unexpressed thing that should ever have happened in the world.

The effect producible by him on the persons just named, and extending possibly to whole groups of which these were members, would be an effect because somehow expressed and encountered as expression: when had he in all his life, for example, so lived in the air of expression and so depended on the help of it, as in that 'so thrilling night-hour just spent with the mystifying and apparently mystified, yet also apparently attached and, with whatever else, attaching, Vinty? It wasn't that Mr. Crick, whose analogue he had met on every occasion of his paying his fare in the public conveyances — where the persons to whom he paid it, without perhaps in their particulars resembling each other, all managed nevertheless to be felt as gathered into this reference — wasn't in a high degree conversible; it was that the more he conversed the less Gray found out what he thought not only of Mr. Betterman's heir but of any other subject on which they touched. The gentleman who would, by Gray's imagination, have been acting for the executors of his uncle's will had not that precious document appeared to dispense with every superfluity, could state a fact, under any rash invitation, and endow it, as a fact, with the greatest conceivable amplitude — this too moreover not because he was garrulous or gossiping, but because those facts with which he was acquainted, the only ones on which you would have dreamed of appealing to him, seemed all perfect nests or bags of other facts, bristling or bulging thus with every intensity of the positive and leaving no room in their interstices for mere appreciation to so much

as turn round. They were themselves appreciation — they became so by the simple force of their existing for Mr. Crick's arid mention, and they so covered the ground of his consciousness to the remotest edge that no breath of the air either of his own mind or of anyone's else could have pretended to circulate about them. Gray made the reflection — tending as he now felt himself to waste rather more than less time in this idle trick — that the different matters of content in some misunderstandings have so glued themselves together that separation has quite broken down and one continuous block, suggestive of dimensional squareness, with mechanical perforations and other aids to use subsequently introduced, comes to represent the whole life of the subject. What it amounted to, he might have gathered, was that Mr. Crick was of such a common commonness as he had never up to now seen so efficiently embodied, so completely organised, so securely and protectedly active, in a word — not to say so garnished and adorned with strange refinements of its own: he had somehow been used to thinking of the extreme of that quality as a note of defeated application, just as the extreme of rarity would have to be. His domestic companion of these days again and again struck him as most touching the point at issue, and that point alone, when most proclaiming at every pore that there wasn't a difference, in all the world, between one thing and another. The refusal of his whole person to figure as a fact invidiously distinguishable, that of his aspect to have an identity, of his eyes to have a consciousness, of his hair to have a colour, of his nose to have a form, of his mouth to have a motion, of his voice to consent to any separation of sounds, made intercourse with him at once extremely easy and extraordinarily empty; it was deprived of the flicker of anything by the way and resembled the act of moving forward in a perfectly-rolling carriage with the blind of each window neatly drawn down.

Gray sometimes advanced to the edge of trying him, so to call it, as to the impression made on him by lack of recognitions assuredly without precedent in any experience, any, least of all, of the ways of beneficiaries; but under the necessity on each occasion of our young man's falling back from the vanity of supposing himself really presentable or apprehensible. For a grasp of him on such ground to take place he should have had first to show himself and to catch his image somehow reflected; simply walking up and down and shedding bland gratitude didn't convey or exhibit or express him in this case, as he was sure these things *had* on the other hand truly done where everyone else, where his uncle and Rosanna, where Mr. Gaw and even Miss Mumby, where splendid Vinty, whom he so looked to, and awfully nice Davey Bradham, whom he so took to, were concerned. It all

came back to the question of terms and to the perception, in varying degrees, on the part of these persons, of his own; for there were somehow none by which Mr. Crick was penetrable that would really tell anything about him, and he could wonder in freedom if he wasn't then to know too that last immunity from any tax on his fortune which would consist in his having never to wince. Against wincing in other relations than this one he was prepared, he only desired, to take his precautions — visionary precautions in those connections truly swarming upon him; but apparently he was during these first days of the mere grossness of his reality to learn something of the clear state of seeing every fond sacrifice to superstition that he could think of thrust back at him. If he could but have brought his visitor to say after twenty-four hours of him "Well, you're the damnedest little idiot I've ever had to pretend to hold commerce with!" *that* would on the spot have pressed the spring of his rich sacrificial "Oh I must be, I must be! — how can I not abjectly and gratefully be?" Something at least would so have been done to placate the jealous gods. But instead of that the grossness of his reality just flatly included this supremely useful friend's perhaps supposing him a vulgar voluptuary, or at least a mere gaping maw, cynically, which amounted to say frivolously, indifferent to everything but the general fact of his windfall. Strange that it should be impossible in any particular whatever to inform or to correct Mr. Crick, who sat unapproachable in the midst of the only knowledge that concerned him.

He couldn't help feeling it conveyed in the very breath of the summer airs that played about him, to his fancy, in a spirit of frolic still lighter and quicker than they had breathed in other climes, he couldn't help almost seeing it as the spray of sea-nymphs, or hearing it as the sounded horn of tritons, emerging, to cast their spell, from the foam-flecked tides around, that he was regarded as a creature rather unnaturally "quiet" there on his averted verandahs and in his darkened halls, even at moments when quite immense things, by his own measure, were happening to him. Everything, simply, seemed to be happening, and happening all at once — as he could say to himself, for instance, by the fact of such a mere matter as his pulling up at some turn of his now renewedly ceaseless pacing to take in he could scarce have said what huge though soft collective rumble, what thick though dispersed exhalation, of the equipped and appointed life, the life that phrased itself with sufficient assurance as the multitudinous throb of Newport, borne toward him from vague regions, from behind and beyond his temporary blest barriers, and representing for the first time in his experience an appeal directed at him from a source not somewhat shabbily single. An impression like that was in itself an event — so repeatedly in his other existence (it

was already his quite unconnectedly other) had the rumour of the world, the voice of society, the harmonies of possession, been charged, for his sensibility, with reminders which, so far from suggesting association, positively waved him off from it. Mr. Betterman's funeral, for all the rigour of simplicity imposed on it by his preliminary care, had enacted itself in a ponderous, numerous, in fact altogether swarming and resounding way; the old local cemetery on the seaward-looking hillside, as Gray seemed to identify it, had served for the final scene, and our young man's sense of the whole thing reached its finest point in an unanswered question as to whether the New York business world or the New York newspaper interest were the more copiously present. The business world broke upon him during the recent rites in large smooth tepid waves — he was conscious of a kind of generalised or, as they seemed to be calling it, standardised face, as of sharpness without edge, save when edge was unexpectedly improvised, bent upon him for a hint of what might have been better expressed could it but have been expressed humorously; while the newspaper interest only fed the more full, he felt even at the time, from the perfectly bare plate offered its flocking young emissaries by the most recognising eye at once and the most deprecating dumbness that he could command.

He had asked Vinty, on the morrow of Vinty's evening visit, to "act" for him in so far as this might be; upon which Vinty had said gaily — he was unexceptionally gay now — "Do you mean as your best man at your marriage to the bride who is so little like St. Francis's? much as you yourself strike me, you know, as resembling the man of Assisi." Vinty, at his great present ease, constantly put things in such wonderful ways; which were nothing, however, to the way he mostly did them during the days he was able to spare before going off again to other calls, other performances in other places, braver and breezier places on the bolder northern coast, it mostly seemed: his allusions to which excited absolutely the more curious interest in his friend, by an odd law, in proportion as he sketched them, under pressure, as probably altogether alien to the friend's sympathies. That was to be for the time, by every indication, his amusing "line" — his taking so confident and insistent a view of what it must be in Gray's nature and tradition to like or not to like that, as our young man for that matter himself assured him, he couldn't have invented a more successfully insidious way of creating an appetite than by passing under a fellow's nose every sort of whiff of the indigestible. One thing at least was clear, namely: that, let his presumption of a comrade's susceptibilities, his possible reactions, under general or particular exposure, approve itself or not, the extent to which this free interpreter was going personally to signify for the

savour of the whole stretched there as a bright assurance. Thus he was all the while acting indeed — acting so that fond formulations of it could only become in the promptest way mere redundancies of reference; he acted because his approach, his look, his touch made somehow, by their simply projecting themselves, a definite difference for any question, great or small, in the least subject to them; and this, after the most extraordinary fashion, not in the least through his pressing or interfering or even so much as intending, but just as a consequence of his having a sense and an intelligence of the given affair, such as it might be, to which, once he was present at it, he was truly ashamed not to conform. That concentrated passage between the two men while the author of their situation was still unburied would of course always hover to memory's eye like a votive object in the rich gloom of a chapel; but it was now disconnected, attached to its hook once for all, its whole meaning converted with such small delay into working, playing force and multiplied tasteable fruit.

Quiet as he passed for keeping himself, by the impression I have noted, how could Gray have felt more plunged in history, how could he by his own sense more have waked up to it each morning and gone to bed with it each night, sat down to it whenever he did sit down, which was never for long, whether at a meal, at a book, at a letter, or at the wasted endeavour to become, by way of a change, really aware of his consciousness, than through positively missing as he did the hint of anything in particular to do? — missing and missing it all the while and yet at no hour paying the least of the penalties that are supposed to attend the drop of responsibility and the substituted rule of fatuity. How couldn't it be agitation of a really sublime order to have it come over one that the personage in the world one must most resemble at such a pitch would be simply, at one's choice, the Kaiser or the Czar, potentates who only know their situation is carried on by attestation of the fact that push it wherever they will they never find it isn't? Thus they are referred to the existence of machinery, the working of which machinery is answered for, they may feel, whenever their eyes rest on one of those figures, ministerial or ceremonial, who may be, as it is called, in waiting. Mr. Crick was in waiting, Horton Vint was in waiting, Rosanna Gaw even, at this moment a hundred miles away, was in waiting, and so was Davey Bradham, though with but a single appearance at the palace as yet to his credit. Neither Horton nor Mr. Crick, it was true, were more materially, more recurrently present than a fellow's nerves, for the wonder of it all, could bear; but what was it but just *being* Czar or Kaiser to keep thrilling on one's own side before the fact that this made no difference? Vulgar reassurance was the greatest of vulgarities; monarchs could still be irresponsible, thanks to their ministers' not being, and Gray repeatedly asked himself how he should ever have felt as he generally did if it hadn't been so absolutely exciting that while the scattered moments of Horton's presence and the fitful snatches of telephonic talk with him lasted the gage of protection, perfectly certain patronising protection, added a still pleasanter light to his eye and ring to his voice, casual and trivial as he clearly might have liked to keep these things. Great monarchies might be "run," but great monarchs weren't — unless of course often by the favourite or the mistress; and one hadn't a mistress yet, goodness knew, and if one was threatened with a favourite it would be but with a favourite of the people too.

History and the great life surged in upon our hero through such images as these at their fullest tide, finding him out however he might have tried to hide from them, and shaking him perhaps even with no livelier question than when it occurred to him for the first time within the week, oddly enough, that the guest of the Bradhams never happened, while his own momentary guest, to meet Mr. Crick, in *his* counsels, by so much as an instant's overlapping, any more than it would chance on a single occasion that he should name his friend to that gentleman or otherwise hint at his existence, still less his importance. Was it just that the king was *usually* shy of mentioning the favourite to the head of the treasury and that various decencies attached, by tradition, to keeping public and private advisers separate? "Oh I absolutely decline to come in, at any point whatever, between you and *him;* as if there were any sort of help I can give you that he won't ever so much better!" — those words had embodied, on the morrow, Vinty's sole allusion to the main sense of their first talk, which he had gone on with in no direct fashion. He had thrown a ludicrous light on his committing himself to any such atrocity of taste while the empowered person and quite ideally right man was about; but points would come up more and more, did come up, in fact already had, that they doubtless might work out together happily enough; and it took Horton in fine the very fewest hours to give example after example of his familiar and immediate wit. Nothing could have better illustrated this than the interest thrown by him for Gray over a couple of subjects that, with many others indeed, beguiled three or four rides taken by the friends along the indented shores and other seaside stretches and reaches of their low-lying promontory in the freshness of the early morning and when the scene might figure for themselves alone. Gray, clinging as yet to his own premises very much even as a stripped swimmer might loiter to enjoy an air-bath before his dive, had yet mentioned that he missed exercise and had at once found Vinty full of resource for his taking it in that pleasantest way. Ev-

erything, by his assurance, was going to be delightful but the generality of the people; thus, accordingly, was the generality of the people not yet in evidence, thus at the sweet hour following the cool dawn could the world he had become possessed of spread about him unspoiled.

It was perhaps in Gray to wonder a little in these conditions what *was* then in evidence, with decks so invidiously cleared; this being, however, a remark he forebore to make, mystified as he had several times been, and somehow didn't like too much being, by having had to note that to differ at all from Vinty on occasions apparently offered was to provoke in him at once a positive excess of agreement. He always went further, as it were, and Gray himself, as he might say, didn't want to go *those* lengths, which were out of the range of practical politics altogether. Horton's habit, as it seemed to show itself, was to make out of saving sociability or wanton ingenuity or whatever, a distinction for which a companion might care, but for which he himself didn't with any sincerity, and then to give his own side of it away, from the moment doubt had been determined, with an almost desolating sweep of surrender. His own side of it was by that logic no better a side, in a beastly vulgar world, than any other, and if anyone wanted to mean that such a mundane basis was deficient why he himself had but meant it from the first and pretended something else only not to be too shocking. He was ready to mean the worst — was ready for anything, that is, in the interest of ceasing from humbug. And if Gray was prepared for *that* then il ne s'agissait que de s'entendre. What Gray was prepared for would really take, this young man frankly opined, some threshing out; but it wasn't at all in readiness for the worst that he had come to America — he had come on the contrary to indulge, by God's help, in appreciations, comparisons, observations, reflections and other luxuries, that were to minister, fond old prejudice aiding, to life at the high pitch, the pitch, as who should say, of immortality. If on occasion, under the dazzle of Horton's facility, he might ask himself how he tracked through it the silver thread of sincerity — consistency wasn't pretended to — something at once supervened that was better than any answer, some benefit of information that the circumstance required, of judgment that assisted or supported or even amused, by felicity of contradiction, and that above all pushed the question so much further, multiplying its relations and so giving it air and colour and the slap of the brush, that it straightway became a picture and, for the kind of attention Gray could best render, a conclusive settled matter. He hated somehow to detract from his friend, wanting so much more to keep adding to him; but it was after a little as if he had felt that his loyalty, or whatever he might call it, could yet not be mean in deciding that

Horton's generalisations, his opinions as distinguished from his perceptions and direct energies and images, signified little enough: if he would only go on bristling as he promised with instances and items, would only consent to consist at the same rate and in his very self of material for history, one might propose to gather from it all at one's own hours and without troubling him the occasional big inference.

How good he could be on the particular case appeared for example after Gray had expressed to him, just subsequently to their first encounter, a certain light and measured wonderment at Rosanna Gaw's appearing not to intend to absent herself long enough from her cares in the other State, immense though these conceivably were, to do what the rest of them were doing roundabout Mr. Betterman's grave. Our young man had half taken for granted that she would have liked, expressing it simply, to assist with him at the last attentions to a memory that had meant, in the current phrase, so much for them both — though of course he withal quite remembered that her interest in it had but rested on his own and that since his own, as promoted by her, had now taken such effect there was grossness perhaps in looking to her for further demonstrations: this at least in view of her being under her filial stress not unimaginably sated with ritual. He had caught himself at any rate in the act of dreaming that Rosanna's return for the funeral would be one of the inevitabilities of her sympathy with his fortune — every element of which (that was overwhelmingly certain) he owed to her; and even the due sense that, put her jubilation or whatever at its highest, it could scarce be expected to dance the same jig as his, didn't prevent his remarking to his friend that clearly Miss Gaw would come, since he himself was still in the stage of supposing that when you had the consciousness of a lot of money you sort of did violent things. He played with the idea that her arrival for the interment would partake of this element, proceeding as it might from the exhilaration of her monstrous advantages, her now assured state. "Look at the violent things *I'm* doing," he seemed to observe with this, "and see how natural I must feel it that any violence should meet me. Yours, for example" — Gray really went so far — "recognises how I want, or at least how I enjoy, a harmony; though at the same time, I assure you, I'm already prepared for any disgusted snub to the attitude of unlimited concern about me, gracious goodness, that I may seem to go about taking for granted." Unlimited concern about him on the part of the people who weren't up at the cool of dawn save in so far as they here and there hadn't yet gone to bed — this, in combination with something like it on the part of numberless others too, had indeed to be faced as the inveterate essence of Vinty's forecast, and formed

perhaps the hardest nut handed to Gray's vice of cogitation to crack; it was the thing that he just now most found himself, as they said, up against — involving as it did some conception of reasons other than ugly for so much patience with the boring side of him.

An interest founded on the mere beastly fact of his pecuniary luck, what was that but an ugly thing to see, from the moment his circle, since a circle he was apparently to have, shouldn't soon be moved to some decent reaction from it? How was he going himself to like breathing an air in which the reaction didn't break out, how was he going not to get sick of finding so large a part played, over the place, by the mere *constatation,* in a single voice, a huge monotone restlessly and untiringly directed, but otherwise without application, of the state of being worth dollars to inordinate amounts? Was he really going to want to live with many specimens of the sort of person who wouldn't presently rather loathe him than know him blindedly on such terms? would it be possible, for that matter, that he should feel people unashamed of not providing for their attention to him any better account of it than his uncle's form of it had happened to supply, without his by that token coming to regard them either as very "interested," according to the good old word, or as themselves much too foredoomed bores to merit tolerance? When it reached the pitch of his asking himself whether it could be possible Vinty wouldn't at once see what he meant by that reservation, he patched the question up but a bit provisionally perhaps by falling back on a remark about this confidant that was almost always equally in order. They weren't on the basis yet of any treatable reality, any that could be directly handled and measured, other than such as were, so to speak, the very children of accident, those the old man's still unexplained whim had with its own special shade of grimness let him in for. *Naturally* must it come to pass with time that the better of the set among whom this easy genius was the best would stop thinking money about him to the point that prevented their thinking anything else — so that he should only break off and not go in further after giving them a chance to show in a less flurried way to what their range of imagination might reach invited and encouraged. Should they markedly fail to take that chance it would be all up with them so far as any entertainment that *he* should care to offer them was concerned. How could it stick out *more* disconcertingly — so his appeal might have run — than that a fuss about him was as yet absolutely a fuss on a vulgar basis? having begun, by what he gathered, quite before the growth even of such independent rumours as Horton's testimony, once he was on the spot, or as Mr. Bradham's range of anecdote, consequent on Mr. Bradham's call, might give warrant for: it couldn't have behind it, he felt sure, so much as a word of Rosanna's, of the heralding or promising sort — he would so have staked his right hand on the last impossibility of the least rash overflow on that young woman's part.

There was this other young woman, of course, whom he heard of at these hours for the first time from Haughty and whom he remembered well enough to have heard praise of from his adopted father, three or four years previous, on his rejoining the dear man after a summer's separation. She would be, "Gussy's" charming friend, Haughty's charming friend, no end of other people's charming friend, as appeared, the heroine of the charming friendship his own admirable friend had formed, in a characteristically headlong manner (some exceptional cluster of graces, in her case, clearly much aiding) with a young American girl, the very nicest anyone had ever seen, met at the waters of Ragatz during one of several seasons there and afterwards described in such extravagant terms as were to make her remain, between himself and his elder, a subject of humorous reference and retort. It had had to do with Gray's liking his companion of those years always better and better that persons intrinsically distinguished inveterately took to him so naturally — even if the number of the admirers rallying was kept down a little by the rarity, of course, of intrinsic distinction. It wasn't, either, as if this blest associate had been by constitution an elderly flirt, or some such

The Ivory Tower

sorry type, addicted to vain philanderings with young persons he might have fathered: he liked young persons, small blame to him, but they had never, under Gray's observation, made a fool of him, and he was only as much of one about the young lady in question, Cecelia Foy, yes, of New York, as served to keep all later inquiry and pleasantry at the proper satiric pitch. She *would* have been a fine little creature, by our friend's beguiled conclusion, to have at once so quickened and so appreciated the accidental relation; for was anything truly quite so charming in a clever girl as the capacity for admiring *disinterestedly* a brave gentleman even to the point of willingness to take every trouble about him? — when the disinterestedness dwelt, that is, in the very pleasure she could seek and find, so much more creditable a matter to her than any she could give and be complimented for giving, involved as this could be with whatever vanity, vulgarity or other personal pretence.

Gray remembered even his not having missed by any measure of his own need or play of his own curiosity the gain of Miss Foy's acquaintance — so might the felicity of the quaint affair, given the actual parties, have been too sacred to be breathed on; he in fact recalled, and could still recall, every aspect of their so excellent time together reviving now in a thick rich light, how he had inwardly closed down the cover on his stepfather's accession of fortune — which the

pretty episode really seemed to amount to; extracting from it himself a particular relief of conscience. He could let him alone, by this showing, without black cruelty — so little had the day come for his ceasing to attract admirers, as they said, at public places or being handed over to the sense of desertion. That left Gray as little as possible haunted with the young Cecelia's image, so completely was his interest in her, in her photograph and in her letters, one of the incidents of his virtually filial solicitude; all the less in fact no doubt that she had written during the aftermonths frequently and very advertisedly, though perhaps, in spite of Mr. Northover's gay exhibition of it, not so very remarkably. She was apparently one of the bright persons who are not at their brightest with the pen — which question indeed would perhaps come to the proof for him, thanks to his having it ever so vividly, not to say derisively, from Horton that this observer didn't really know what had stayed her hand, for the past week, from an outpouring to the one person within her reach who would constitute a link with the delightful old hero of her European adventure. That so close a representative of the party to her romance was there in the flesh and but a mile or two off, was a fact so extraordinary as to have waked up the romance again in her and produced a state of fancy from which she couldn't rest — for some shred of the story that might be still

991

afloat. Gray therefore needn't be surprised to receive some sign of this commotion, and that he hadn't yet done so was to be explained, Haughty guessed, by the very intensity of the passions involved.

One of them, it thus appeared, burnt also in Gussy's breast; devoted as she was to Cissy, she had taken the fond anecdote that so occupied them as much under her protection as she had from far back taken the girl's every other interest, and what for the hour paralysed their action, that of the excited pair, must simply have been that Mrs. Bradham couldn't on the one hand listen to anything so horrid as that her young friend should make an advance unprepared and unaccompanied, and that the ardent girl, on the other, had for the occasion, as for all occasions, her ideal of independence. Gray was not himself impatient — he felt no jump in him at the chance to discuss so dear a memory in an air still incongruous; it depended on who might propose to him the delicate business, let alone its not making for a view of the great Gussy's fine tact that she should even possibly put herself forward as a proposer. However, he didn't mind thinking that if Cissy should prove all that was likely enough their having a subject in common couldn't but practically conduce; though the moral of it all amounted rather to a portent, the one that Haughty, by the same token, had done least to reassure him against, of the extent to which the native jungle harboured the female specimen and to which its ostensible cover, the vast level of mixed growths stirred wavingly in whatever breeze, was apt to be identifiable but as an agitation of the latest redundant thing in ladies' hats. It was true that when Rosanna had perfectly failed to rally, merely writing a kind short note to the effect that she should have to give herself wholly, for she didn't know how long, to the huge assault of her own questions, that might have seemed to him to make such a clearance as would count against any number of positively hovering shades. Horton had answered for her not turning up, and nothing perhaps had made him feel so right as this did for a faith in those general undertakings of assurance; only, when at the end of some days he saw that vessel of light obscured by its swing back to New York and other ranges of action, the sense of exposure — even as exposure to nothing worse than the lurking or pouncing ladies — became sharper through contrast with the late guarded interval; this to the extent positively of a particular hour at which it seemed to him he had better turn tail and simply flee, stepping from under the too vast orb of his fate.

He was alone with that quantity on the September morning after breakfast as he had not felt himself up to now; he had taken to pacing the great verandah that had become his own as he had paced it when it was still his uncle's, and it might truly have been a rush of nervous apprehension, a sudden determination of terror, that quickened and yet somehow refused to direct his steps. He had turned out there for the company of sea and sky and garden, less conscious than within doors, for some reason, that Horton was a lost luxury; but that impression was presently to pass with a return of a queer force in his view of Rosanna as above all somehow wanting, off and withdrawn verily to the pitch of her having played him some trick, merely let him in where she was to have seen him through, failed in fine of a sociability implied in all her preliminaries. He found his attention caught, in one of his revolutions, by the chair in which Abel Gaw had sat that first afternoon, pulling him up for their so unexpectedly intense mutual scrutiny, and when he turned away a moment after, quitting the spot almost as if the strange little man's death that very night had already made him apparitional, which was unpleasant, it was to drop upon the lawn and renew his motion there. He circled round the house altogether at last, looking at it more critically than had hitherto seemed relevant, taking the measure, disconcertedly, of its unabashed ugliness, and at the end coming to regard it very much as he might have eyed some monstrous modern machine, one of those his generation was going to be expected to master, to fly in, to fight in, to take the terrible women of the future out for airings in, and that mocked at *his* incompetence in such matters while he walked round and round it and gave it, as for dread of what it might do to him, the widest berth his enclosure allowed. In the midst of all of which, quite wonderfully, everything changed; he *wasn't* alone with his monster, he was in, by this reminder, for connections, nervous ass as he had just missed writing himself, and connections fairly glittered, swarming out at him, in the person of Mr. Bradham, who stood at the top of a flight of steps from the gallery, which he had been ushered through the house to reach, and there at once, by some odd felicity of friendliness, some pertinence of presence, of promise, appeared to make up for whatever was wrong and supply whatever was absent. It came over him with extraordinary quickness that the way not to fear the massed ambiguity was to trust it, and this florid, solid, smiling person, who waved a prodigious gold-coloured straw hat as if in sign of ancient amity, had come exactly at that moment to show him how.[1]

[1] This ends the first chapter of Book IV. The MS. breaks off with an unfinished sentence opening the next chapter: "Not the least pointed of the reflections Gray was to indulge in a fortnight later and as by a result of Davey Bradham's intervention in the very nick was that if he *had* turned tail that afternoon, at the very oddest of all his hours, if he had prematurely taken to his heels and missed the emissary from the wonderful place of his fresh domestication, the article on which he would most irretrievably have dished himself . . ."

A NOTE ON THE TYPE

The text of this book is set in Caledonia, a Linotype face designed by W. A. Dwiggins. Caledonia belongs to the family of printing types called "modern face" by printers — a term used to mark the change in style of type-letters that occurred about 1800. Caledonia borders on the general design of Scotch Modern, but is more freely drawn than that letter.

Mr. Dwiggins planned the typographic scheme and designed the binding. The book was composed, printed, and bound by The Plimpton Press, Norwood, Massachusetts.